John Bouvier

A Law Dictionary

Vol. I

John Bouvier

A Law Dictionary

Vol. I

Reprint of the original, first published in 1862.

1st Edition 2022 | ISBN: 978-3-37503-070-4

Verlag (Publisher): Salzwasser Verlag GmbH, Zeilweg 44, 60439 Frankfurt, Deutschland
Vertretungsberechtigt (Authorized to represent): E. Roepke, Zeilweg 44, 60439 Frankfurt, Deutschland
Druck (Print): Books on Demand GmbH, In de Tarpen 42, 22848 Norderstedt, Deutschland

A

LAW DICTIONARY,

ADAPTED TO THE

CONSTITUTION AND LAWS

OF THE

UNITED STATES OF AMERICA,

AND OF THE

Several States of the American Union:

WITH REFERENCES TO THE CIVIL AND OTHER SYSTEMS OF FOREIGN LAW.

TO WHICH IS ADDED

KELHAM'S DICTIONARY OF THE NORMAN AND OLD FRENCH LANGUAGE.

BY JOHN BOUVIER.

Ignoratis terminis ignoratur et ars.—Co. LITT. 2 a.

Je sais que chaque science et chaque art a ses termes propres, inconnu au commun des hommes.—FLEURY.

ELEVENTH EDITION, REVISED, IMPROVED, AND GREATLY ENLARGED.

VOL. I.

PHILADELPHIA

1862.

TO THE HONORABLE

JOSEPH STORY, LL. D.,

ONE OF THE JUDGES OF THE SUPREME COURT OF THE UNITED STATES,

THIS WORK

IS,

WITH HIS PERMISSION,

MOST RESPECTFULLY DEDICATED,

AS A TOKEN OF THE

GREAT REGARD ENTERTAINED FOR HIS TALENTS, LEARNING AND CHARACTER,

BY

THE AUTHOR.

ADVERTISEMENT

TO THE THIRD EDITION.

ENCOURAGED by the success of this work, the author has endeavored to render this edition as perfect as it was possible for him to make it. He has remodeled very many of the articles contained in the former editions, and added upwards of twelve hundred new ones.

To render the work as useful as possible, he has added a very copious index to the whole, which, at the same time that it will assist the inquirer, will exhibit the great number of subjects treated in these volumes.

PHILADELPHIA, November, 1848.

ADVERTISEMENT

TO THE FOURTH EDITION.

Since the publication of the last edition of this work, its author, sincerely devoted to the advancement of his profession, has given to the world his Institutes of American Law, in 4 vols. 8vo. Always endeavoring to render his Dictionary as perfect as possible, he was constantly revising it; and whenever he met with an article which he had omitted, he immediately prepared it for a new edition. After the completion of his Institutes, in September last, laboring too severely, he fell a victim to his zeal, and died on the 18th of November, 1851, at the age of sixty-four.

In preparing this edition, not only has the matter left by its author been made use of, but additional matter has been added, so that the present will contain nearly one-third more than the last edition. Under one head, that of Maxims, nearly thirteen hundred new articles have been added. The book has been very carefully examined, a great portion of it by two members of the bar, in order that it might be purged, as far as possible, from all errors of every description. The various changes in the constitutions of the states made since the last edition, have been noticed, so far as was compatible with this work; and every effort made to render it as perfect as a work of the kind would permit, in order that it might still sustain the reputation given to it by a Dublin barrister, "of being a work of a most elaborate character, as compared with English works of a similar nature, and one which should be in every library."

That it may still continue to receive the approbation of the Bench and Bar of the United States, is the sincere desire of the widow and daughter of its author.

PREFACE.

To the difficulties which the author experienced on his admission to the bar, the present publication is to be attributed. His endeavours to get forward in his profession were constantly obstructed, and his efforts for a long time frustrated, for want of that knowledge which his elder brethren of the bar seemed to possess. To find among the reports and the various treatises on the law the object of his inquiry, was a difficult task; he was in a labyrinth without a guide: and much of the time which was spent in finding his way out, might, with the friendly assistance of one who was acquainted with the construction of the edifice, have been saved, and more profitably employed. He applied to law dictionaries and digests within his reach, in the hope of being directed to the source whence they derived their learning, but he was too often disappointed; they seldom pointed out the authorities where the object of his inquiry might be found. It is true such works contain a great mass of information, but from the manner in which they have been compiled, they sometimes embarrassed him more than if he had not consulted them. They were written for another country, possessing laws different from our own, and it became a question how far they were or were not applicable here. Besides, most of the matter in the English law dictionaries will be found to have been written while the feudal law was in its full vigor, and not fitted to the present times, nor calculated for present use, even in England. And there is a great portion which, though useful to an

English lawyer, is almost useless to the American student. What, for example, have we to do with those laws of Great Britain which relate to the person of their king, their nobility, their clergy, their navy, their army; with their game laws; their local statutes, such as regulate their banks, their canals, their exchequer, their marriages, their births, their burials, their beer and ale houses, and a variety of similar subjects?

The most modern law dictionaries are compilations from the more ancient, with some modifications and alterations· and, in many instances, they are servile copies, without the slightest alteration. In the mean time the law has undergone a great change. Formerly the principal object of the law seemed to be to regulate real property, in all its various artificial modifications, while little or no attention was bestowed upon the rules which govern personal property and rights. The mercantile law has since arisen, like a bright pyramid, amid the gloom of the feudal law, and is now far more important in practice, than that which refers to real estate. The law of real property, too, has changed, particularly in this country.

The English law dictionaries would be very unsatisfactory guides, even in pointing out where the laws relating to the acquisition and transfer of real estate, or the laws of descent in the United States, are to be found. And the student who seeks to find in the Dictionaries of Cowel, Manly, Jacobs, Tomlins, Cunningham, Burn, Montefiore, Pott, Whishaw, Williams, the Termes de Ley, or any similar compilation, any satisfactory account in relation to international law, to trade and commerce, to maritime law, to medical jurisprudence, or to natural law, will probably not be fully gratified. He cannot, of course, expect to find in them anything in relation to our government, our constitutions, or our political or civil institutions.

It occurred to the author that a law dictionary, written entirely anew, and calculated to remedy those defects, would be useful to the profession. Probably overrating his strength, he resolved to undertake the task, and if he should not fully succeed, he will have the consolation to know, that his effort may induce some more gifted individual, and better qualified by his learning, to undertake such a task, and to render the American bar an important service. Upon an examination of the constitution and laws of the United States, and of the several states of the American Union, he perceived many technical expressions and much valuable information which he would be able to incorporate in his work. Many of these laws, although local in their nature, will be found useful to every lawyer, particularly those engaged in mercantile practice. As instances of such laws the reader is referred to the articles *Acknowledgment, Descent, Divorce, Letters of Administration,* and *Limitation.* It is within the plan of this work to explain such technical expressions as relate to the legislative, executive, or judicial departments of the government; the political and the civil rights and duties of the citizens; the rights and duties of persons, particularly such as are peculiar to our institutions, as, the rights of descent and administration; of the mode of acquiring and transferring property; to the criminal law, and its administration. It has also been an object with the author to embody in his work such decisions of the courts as appeared to him to be important, either because they differed from former judgments, or because they related to some point which was before either obscure or unsettled. He does not profess to have examined or even referred to all the American cases; it is a part of the plan, however, to refer to authorities generally, which will lead the student to nearly all the cases.

The author was induced to believe, that an occasional comparison of the civil, canon, and other systems of foreign law, with our own.

would be useful to the profession, and illustrate many articles which, without such aid, would not appear very clear; and also to introduce many terms from foreign laws, which may supply a deficiency in ours. The articles *Condonation, Extradition,* and *Novation,* are of this sort. He was induced to adopt this course because the civil law has been considered, perhaps not without justice, the best system of written reason, and as all laws are or ought to be founded in reason, it seemed peculiarly proper to have recourse to this fountain of wisdom: but another motive influenced this decision; one of the states of the Union derives most of its civil regulations from the civil law; and there seemed a peculiar propriety, therefore, in introducing it into an American law dictionary. He also had the example of a Story, a Kent, Mr. Angell, and others, who have ornamented their works from the same source. And he here takes the opportunity to acknowledge the benefits which he has derived from the learned labors of these gentlemen, and of those of Judge Sergeant, Judge Swift, Judge Gould, Mr. Rawle, and other writers on American law and jurisprudence.

In the execution of his plan, the author has, in the first place, defined and explained the various words and phrases, by giving their most enlarged meaning, and then all the shades of signification of which they are susceptible; secondly, he has divided the subject in the manner which to him appeared the most natural, and laid down such principles and rules as belong to it; in these cases he has generally been careful to give an illustration, by citing a case whenever the subject seemed to require it, and referring to others supporting the same point; thirdly, whenever the article admitted of it, he has compared it with the laws of other countries within his reach, and pointed out their concord or disagreement; and, fourthly, he has referred to the authorities, the abridgments, digests, and the ancient and modern treatises, where the subject is to be found, in order to facilitate the researches of the student. He desires not to be understood as professing to cite cases always exactly in point; on the contrary, in many instances the authorities will probably be found to be but distantly connected with the subject under examination, but still connected with it, and they have been added in order to lead the student to matter of which he may possibly be in pursuit.

To those who are aware of the difficulties of the task, the author deems it unnecessary to make any apology for the imperfections which may be found in the work. His object has been to be useful; if that has been accomplished in any degree, he will be amply rewarded for his labor; and he relies upon the generous liberality of the members of the profession to overlook the errors which may have been committed in his endeavors to serve them.

PHILADELPHIA, September, 1839.

A

LAW DICTIONARY.

A, the first letter of the English and most other alphabets, is frequently used as an abbreviation, (q. v.) and also in the marks of schedules or papers, as schedule A, B, C, &c. Among the Romans this letter was used in criminal trials. The judges were furnished with small tables covered with wax, and each one inscribed on it the initial letter of his vote; A, when he voted to absolve the party on trial; C, when he was for condemnation; and N L, (non liquet) when the matter did not appear clearly, and he desired a new argument.

A MENSA ET THORO, from bed and board. A divorce *a mensa et thoro,* is rather a separation of the parties by act of law, than a dissolution of the marriage. It may be granted for the causes of extreme cruelty or desertion of the wife by the husband. 2 Eccl. Rep. 208. This kind of divorce does not affect the legitimacy of children, nor authorize a second marriage. V. *A vinculo matrimonii; Cruelty; Divorce.*

A PRENDRE, French, to take, to seize, *in contracts,* as profits a prendre. Ham. N. P. 184; or a right to take something out of the soil. 5 Ad. & Ell. 764; 1 N. & P. 172; it differs from a right of way, which is simply an easement or interest which confers no interest in the land. 5 B. & C. 221.

A QUO, A Latin phrase, which signifies *from which;* example, in the computation of time, the day *à quo* is not to be counted, but the day *ad quem* is always included. 13 Toull. n. 52; 2 Duv. n. 22. A court *à quo,* the court from which an appeal has been taken; a judge *à quo* is a judge of a court below. 6 Mart. Lo. R. 520; 1 Har. Cond. L. R. 501. See *Ad quem.*

A RENDRE, French, to render, to yield, *in contracts. Profits a rendre;* under this term are comprehended rents and services. Ham N. P. 192.

A VINCULO MATRIMONII, from the bond of marriage. A marriage may be dissolved *a vinculo,* in many states, as in Pennsylvania, on the ground of canonical disabilities before marriage, as that one of the parties was legally married to a person who was then living; impotence, (q. v.,) and the like; adultery; cruelty; and malicious desertion for two years or more. In New York a sentence of imprisonment for life is also a ground for a divorce *a vinculo.* When the marriage is dissolved *a vinculo,* the parties may marry again; but when the cause is adultery, the guilty party cannot marry his or her paramour.

AB INITIO, from the beginning.

2.—When a man enters upon lands or into the house of another by authority of law, and afterwards abuses that authority, he becomes a trespasser *ab initio.* Bac. Ab. Trespass, B.; 8 Coke, 146; 2 Bl. Rep. 1218; Clayt. 44. And if an officer neglect to remove goods attached within a reasonable time and continue in possession, his entry becomes a trespass *ab initio.* 2 Bl. Rep. 1218. See also as to other cases, 2 Stra. 717; 1 H. Bl. 13; 11 East, 395; 2 Camp. 115; 2 Johns. 191; 10 Johns. 253; Ibid. 369.

3.—But in case of an authority *in fact,* to enter, an abuse of such authority will not, in general, subject the party to an action of trespass, Lane, 90; Bac. Ab. Trespass, B; 2 T. R. 166. See generally 1 Chit. Pl. 146. 169. 180.

AB INTESTAT. An heir, *ab intestat,* is one on whom the law casts the inheritance or estate of a person who dies intestate

AB IRATO, *civil law*. A Latin phrase, which signifies *by a man in anger*. It is applied to bequests or gifts, which a man makes adverse to the interest of his heir, in consequence of anger or hatred against him. Thus a devise made under these circumstances is called a testament *ab irato*. And the suit which the heirs institute to annul this will is called an *action ab irato*. Merlin, Rèpert. mots *Ab irato*.

ABANDONMENT, *contracts*. In the French law, the act by which a debtor surrenders his property for the benefit of his creditors. Merl. Rèp. mot Abandonment.

ABANDONMENT, *contracts*. In insurances the act by which the insured relinquishes to the assurer all the property to the thing insured.

2.—No particular form is required for an abandonment, nor need it be in writing; but it must be explicit and absolute, and must set forth the reasons upon which it is founded.

3.—It must also be made in reasonable time after the loss.

4.—It is not in every case of loss that the insured can abandon. In the following cases an abandonment may be made: when there is a total loss; when the voyage is lost or not worth pursuing, by reason of a peril insured against; or if the cargo be so damaged as to be of little or no value; or where the salvage is very high, and further expense be necessary, and the insurer will not engage to bear it; or if what is saved is of less value than the freight; or where the damage exceeds one half of the value of the goods insured; or where the property is captured, or even detained by an indefinite embargo; and in cases of a like nature.

5.—The abandonment, when legally made, transfers from the insured to the insurer the property in the thing insured, and obliges him to pay to the insured what he promised him by the contract of insurance. 3 Kent, Com. 265; 2 Marsh. Ins. 559; Pard. Dr. Com. n. 836 et seq.; Boulay Paty, Dr. Com. Maritime, tit. 11, tom. 4, p. 215.

ABANDONMENT. *In maritime contracts in the civil law*, principals are generally held indefinitely responsible for the obligations which their agents have contracted relative to the concern of their commission; but with regard to ship owners there is a remarkable peculiarity; they are bound by the contract of the master only to the amount of their interest in the ship, and can be discharged from their responsibility by abandoning the ship and freight. Poth. Chartes part. s. 2, art. 3, § 51; Ord. de la Mar. des proprietaires, art. 2; Code de Com. l. 2, t. 2, art. 216.

ABANDONMENT, *rights*. The relinquishment of a right; the giving up of something to which we are entitled.

2.—Legal rights, when once vested, must be divested according to law, but equitable rights may be abandoned. 2 Wash. R. 106. See 1 H. & M. 429; a mill site, once occupied, may be abandoned. 17 Mass. 297; an application for land, which is an inception of title, 5 S. & R. 215; 2 S. & R. 378; 1 Yeates, 193, 289; 2 Yeates, 81, 88, 318; an improvement, 1 Yeates, 515; 2 Yeates, 476; 5 Binn. 73; 3 S. & R. 319; Jones' Syllabus of Land Office Titles in Pennsylvania, chap. xx; and a trust fund, 3 Yerg. 258, may be abandoned.

3.—The abandonment must be made by the owner without being pressed by any duty, necessity or utility to himself, but simply because he wishes no longer to possess the thing; and further it must be made without any desire that any other person shall acquire the same; for if it were made for a consideration, it would be a sale or barter, and if without consideration, but with an intention that some other person should become the possessor, it would be a gift: and it would still be a gift though the owner might be indifferent as to whom the right should be transferred; for example, he threw money among a crowd with intent that some one should acquire the title to it.

ABANDONMENT *for torts*, a term used in the civil law. By the Roman law, when the master was sued for the tort of his slave, or the owner for a trespass committed by his animal, he might abandon them to the person injured, and thereby save himself from further responsibility.

2.—Similar provisions have been adopted in Louisiana. It is enacted by the civil code that the master shall be answerable for all the damages occasioned by an offence or quasi offence committed by his slave. He may, however, discharge himself from such responsibility by abandoning the slave to the person injured; in which case such person shall sell such slave at public auction in the usual form, to obtain payment of the damages and costs; and the balance, if any, shall be returned to the master of the slave, who shall be completely discharged, although the price of the slave should not be sufficient to pay the whole amount of the damages and costs; provided that the master shall make abandonment within three days after the judgment awarding such damages shall have been rendered; provided also that it shall not be proved that the crime or offence was committed by his order; for in such cases the master shall be answerable for all damages resulting therefrom, whatever be the amount, without being admitted to the benefit of abandonment.—Art. 180, 181.

3.—The owner of an animal is answerable for the damages he has caused; but if the animal had been lost, or had strayed more than a day, he may discharge himself from this responsibility, by abandoning him to the person who has sustained the injury, except where the master has turned loose a dangerous or noxious animal, for then he must pay for all the harm he has done, without being allowed to make the abandonment. Ib. art. 2301.

ABANDONMENT, *malicious*. The act of a husband or wife, who leaves his or her consort wilfully, and with an intention of causing perpetual separation.

2.—Such abandonment, when it has continued the length of time required by the local statutes, is sufficient cause for a divorce. Vide 1 Hoff. R. 47; *Divorce*.

ABATEMENT, *chancery practice*, is a suspension of all proceedings in a suit, from the want of proper parties capable of proceeding therein. It differs from an abatement at law in this, that in the latter the action is in general entirely dead, and cannot be revived, 3 Bl. Com. 168; but in the former, the right to proceed is merely suspended, and may be revived by a bill of revivor. Mitf. Eq. Pl. by Jeremy, 57; Story, Eq. Pl. § 354.

ABATEMENT, *contracts*, is a reduction made by the creditor, for the prompt payment of a debt due by the payor or debtor. Wesk. on Ins. 7.

ABATEMENT, *merc. law*. By this term is understood the deduction sometimes made at the custom-house from the duties chargeable upon goods when they are damaged. See Act of Congress, March 2, 1799, s. 52, 1 Story L. U. S. 617.

ABATEMENT, *pleading*, is the overthrow of an action in consequence of some error committed in bringing or conducting it, when the plaintiff is not forever barred from bringing another action. 1 Chit. Pl. 434. Abatement is by plea. There can be no demurrer in abatement. Willes' Rep. 479; Salk. 220.

2.—Pleas in abatement will be considered as relating, 1, to the jurisdiction of the court; 2, to the person of the plaintiff; 3, to that of the defendant; 4, to the writ; 5, to the qualities of such pleas; 6, to the form of such pleas; 7, to the affidavit of the truth of pleas in abatement.

3.—§ 1. As to pleas relating to the *jurisdiction* of the court, see article Jurisdiction, and Arch. Civ. Pl. 290; 1 Chit. Pl. Index. tit. Jurisdiction. There is only one case in which the jurisdiction of the court may be inquired of under the general issue, and that is where no court of the country has jurisdiction of the cause, for in that case no action can be maintained by the law of the land. 3 Mass. Rep. Rea *v.* Hayden, 1 Dougl. 450; 3 Johns. Rep. 113; 2 Penn. Law Journal 64, Meredith *v.* Pierie.

4.—§ 2. *Relating to the person of the plaintiff*. 1. The defendant may plead to the person of the plaintiff that there never was any such person in *rerum natura*. Bro. Brief, 25; 19 Johns. 308; Com. Dig. Abatement, E 16. And if one of several plaintiffs be a fictitious person, it abates the writ. Com. Dig. Abatement, E 16; 1 Chit. Pl. 435; Arch. Civ. Pl. 304. But a nominal plaintiff in ejectment may sustain an action. 5 Verm. 93; 19 John. 308. As to the rule in Pennsylvania, see 5 Watts, 423.

5.—2. The defendant may plead that the plaintiff is a feme covert. Co. Lit. 132, b.; or that she is his own wife. 1 Brown. Ent. 63; and see 3 T. R. 631; 6 T. R. 265; Com. Dig. Abatement, E 6; 1 Chit. Pl. 437; Arch. Civ. Pl. 302. Coverture occurring after suit brought is a plea in abatement which cannot be pleaded after a plea in bar, unless the matter arose after the plea in bar; but in that case the defendant must not suffer a continuance to intervene between the happening of this new matter, or its coming to his knowledge, and pleading it. 4 S & R. 238; Bac. Abr. Abatement, G; 4 Mass. 659; 4 S. & R. 238; 1 Bailey, 369; 4 Vern. 545; 2 Wheat. 111; 14 Mass. 295; 1 Blackf. 288; 2 Bailey, 349. See 10 S. & R. 208; 7 Verm. 508; 1 Yeates, 185; 2 Dall. 184; 3 Bibb, 246.

6.—3. That the plaintiff (unless he sue with others as executor) is an infant and has declared by attorney. 1 Chit. Pl. 436; Arch. Civ. Pl. 301: Arch. Pr. B. R. 142; 2 Saund. 212, a, n. 5; 1 Went. 58, 62; 7 John. R. 373; 3 N. H. Rep. 345; 8 Pick.

552; and see 7 Mass. 241; 4 Halst. 381; 2 N. H. Rep. 487.

7.—4. A suit brought by a lunatic under guardianship, shall abate. Brayt. 18.

8.—5. Death of plaintiff before the purchase of the original writ, may be pleaded in abatement. 1 Arch. Civ. Pl. 304, 5; Com. Dig. Abatement, E 17. Death of plaintiff pending the writ might have been pleaded since the last continuance, Com. Dig. Abatement, H 32; 4 Hen. & Munf. 410; 3 Mass. 296; Cam. & Nor. 72; 4 Hawks, 433; 2 Root, 57; 9 Mass. 422; 4 H. & M. 410; Gilmer, 145; 2 Rand. 454; 2 Greenl. 127. But in some states, as in Pennsylvania, the death of the plaintiff does not abate the writ: in such case the executor or administrator is substituted. The rule of the common law is, that whenever the death of any party happens, pending the writ, and yet the plea is in the same condition, as if such party were living, then such death makes no alteration; and on this rule all the diversities turn. Gilb. Com. Pleas, 242.

9.—6. Alienage, or that the plaintiff is an alien enemy. Bac. Abr. h. t.; 6 Binn. 241; 10 Johns. 183; 9 Mass. 363; Id. 377; 11 Mass. 119; 12 Mass. 8; 3 M. & S. 533; 2 John. Ch. R. 508; 15 East, 260; Com. Dig. Abatement, E 4; Id. Alien, C 5; 1 S. & R. 310; 1 Ch. Pl. 435; Arch. Civ. Pl. 3, 301.

10.—7. Misnomer of plaintiff may also be pleaded in abatement. Arch. Civ. Pl. 305; 1 Chitty's Pleading, Index, tit. Misnomer. Com. Dig. Abatement, E 19, E 20, E 21, E 22; 1 Mass. 75; Bac. Abr. h. t.

11.—8. If one of several joint tenants, sue in action ex contractu, Co. Lit. 180, b; Bac. Abr. Joint-tenants, K; 1 B. & P. 73; one of several joint contractors, Arch. Civ. Pl. 48—51, 53; one of several partners, Gow on Part. 150; one of several joint executors who have proved the will, or even if they have not proved the will, 1 Chit. Pl. 12, 13; one of several joint administrators, Ibid. 13; the defendant may plead the nonjoinder in abatement. Arch. Civ. Pl. 304; see Com. Dig. Abatement, E 9, E 12, E 13, E 14.

12.—9. If persons join as plaintiffs in an action who should not, the defendant may plead the misjoinder in abatement. Arch. Civ. Pl. 304; Com. Dig. Abatement, E 15.

13.—10. When the plaintiff is an alleged corporation, and it is intended to contest its existence, the defendant must plead in abatement. Wright, 12; 3 Pick. 236; 1 Mass 485; 1 Pet. 450; 4 Pet. 501; 5 Pet. 231. To a suit brought in the name of the "judges of the county court," after such court has been abolished, the defendant may plead in abatement that there are no such judges. Judges, &c. v. Phillips, 2 Bay, 519.

14.—§ 3. *Relating to the person of the defendant.* 1. In an action against two or more, one may plead in abatement that there never was such a person in *rerum natura* as A, who is named as defendant with him. Arch. Civ. Pl. 312.

15.—2. If the defendant be a married woman, she may in general plead her coverture in abatement, 8 T. R. 545; Com. Dig. Abatement, F 2. The exceptions to this rule arise when the coverture is suspended. Com. Dig. Abatement, F 2, § 3; Co. Lit. 132, b; 2 Bl. R. 1197; Co. B. L. 43.

16.—3. The death of the defendant abates the writ at common law, and in some cases it does still abate the action, see Com. Dig. Abatement, H 34; 1 Hayw. 500; 2 Binn. 1; 1 Gilm. 145; 1 Const. Rep. 83; 4 McCord, 160; 7 Wheat. 530; 1 Watts, 229; 4 Mass. 480; 8 Greenl. 128; In general where the cause of action dies with the person, the suit abates by the death of the defendant before judgment. Vide *Actio Personalis moritur cum personâ.*

17.—4. The misnomer of the defendant may be pleaded in abatement, but one defendant cannot plead the misnomer of another. Com. Dig. Abatement, F 18; Lutw. 36; 1 Chit. Pl. 440; Arch. Civ. Pl. 312. See form of a plea in abatement for a misnomer of the defendant in 3 Saund. 209, b., and see further, 1 Show. 394; Carth. 307; Comb. 188; 1 Lutw. 10; 5 T. R. 487.

18.—5. When one joint tenant, Com. Dig. Abatement, F 5, or one tenant in common, in cases where they ought to be joined, Ibid. F 6, is sued alone, he may plead in abatement. And in actions upon contracts if the plaintiff do not sue all the contractors, the defendant may plead the nonjoinder in abatement. Ibid. F 8, a; 1 Wash. 9; 18 Johns. 459; 2 Johns. Cas. 382; 3 Caines's Rep. 99; Arch. Civ. Pl. 309; 1 Chit. Pl. 441. When husband and wife should be sued jointly, and one is sued alone, the non-joinder may be pleaded in abatement. Arch. Civ. Pl. 309. The nonjoinder of all the executors, who have proved the will; and the non-joinder of all the administrators of the deceased, may be pleaded in abatement. Com. Dig. Abatement, F 10.

19.—6. In a real action if brought against several persons, they may plead several tenancy, that is that they hold in severalty and not jointly, Com. Dig. Abatement, F 12; or one of them may take the entire tenancy on himself, and pray judgment of the writ. Id. F 13. But misjoinder of defendant in a personal action is not the subject of a plea in abatement. Arch. Civ. Pl. 68, 310.

20.—7. In cases where the defendant may plead non-tenure, see Arch. Civ. Pl. 310; Cro. El. 559.

21.—8. Where he may plead a disclaimer, see Arch. Civ. Pl. 311; Com. Dig. Abatement, F 15.

22.—9. A defendant may plead his privilege of not being sued, in abatement. Bac. Ab. Abridgment C; see this Dict. tit. *Privilege.*

23.—§ 4. *Plea in abatement of the writ.* 1. Pleas in abatement of the writ or a bill are so termed rather from their effect, than from their being strictly such pleas, for as oyer of the writ can no longer be craved, no objection can be taken to matter which is merely contained in the writ, 3 B. & P. 399; 1 B. & P. 645—648; but if a mistake in the writ be carried into the declaration, or rather if the declaration, which is presumed to correspond with the writ or bill, be incorrect in respect of some extrinsic matter, it is then open to the defendant to plead in abatement to the writ or bill, 1 B. & P. 648; 10 Mod. 210; and there is no plea to the declaration alone but in bar; 10 Mod. 210; 2 Saund. 209, d.

24.—2. Pleas in abatement of the writ or bill and to the form or to the action. Com. Dig. Abatement, H 1, 17.

25.—3. Those of the first description were formerly either matter apparent on the face of the writ, Com. Dig. Abatement, H 1, or matters dehors. Id. H 17.

26.—4. Formerly very trifling errors were pleadable in abatement, 1 Lutw. 25; Lilly's Ent. 5; 2 Rich. C. P. 5, 8; 1 Stra. 556; Ld. Raym. 1541; 2 Inst. 668; 2 B. & P. 395. But as oyer of the writ can no longer be had, an omission in the defendant's declaration of the defendant's addition, which is not necessary to be stated in a declaration, can in no case be pleaded in abatement. 1 Saund. 318, n. 3; 3 B. & B. 395; 7 East, 382.

27.—5. Pleas in abatement to the form of the writ, are therefore now principally for matters dehors, Com. Dig. Abatement, H 17; Gilb. C. P. 51, existing at the time of suing out the writ, or arising afterwards, such as misnomer of the plaintiff or defendant in Christian or surname.

28.—6. Pleas in abatement to the action of the writ, and that the action is misconceived, as that it is in case where it ought to have been in trespass, Com. Dig. Abatement, G 5; or that it was prematurely brought, Ibid. Abatement, G 6, and tit. Action, E; but as these matters are grounds of demurrer or nonsuit, it is now very unusual to plead them in abatement. It may also be pleaded that there is another action pending. See tit. *Autre action pendant.* Com. Dig. Abatement, H 24; Bac. Ab. Abatement, M; 1 Chitty's Pl. 443.

29.—§ 5. *Qualities of pleas in abatement.* 1. A writ is divisible, and may be abated in part, and remain good for the residue; and the defendant may plead in abatement to part, and demur or plead in bar to the residue of the declaration. 1 Chit. Pl. 444; 2 Saund. 210, n. The general rule is, that whatever proves the writ false at the time of suing it out, shall abate the writ entirely, Gilb. C. P. 247; 1 Saund. Rep. 286, (n) 7; 2 do. 72, (i) *sub fin.*

30.—2. As these pleas delay the trial of the merits of the action, the greatest accuracy and precision are required in framing them; they should be certain to every intent, and be pleaded without any repugnancy. 3 T. R. 186; Willes, 42; 2 Bl. R. 1096; 2 Saund. 298, b, n. 1; Com. Dig. I, 11; Co. Lit. 392; Cro. Jac. 82; and must in general give the plaintiff a better writ. This is the true criterion to distinguish a plea in abatement from a plea in bar. 8 T. R. 515; Bromal. 139; 1 Saund. 274, n. 4; 284 n. 4; 2 B. & P. 125; 4 T. R. 227; 6 East, 600; Com. Dig. Abatement, J 1, 2; 1 Day, 28; 3 Mass. 24; 2 Mass. 362; 1 Hayw. 501; 2 Ld. Raym. 1178; 1 East, 634. Great accuracy is also necessary in the form of the plea as to the commencement and conclusion, which is said to make the plea. Latch. 178; 2 Saund. 209, c. d; 3 T. R. 186.

31.—§ 6. *Form of pleas in abatement.* 1. As to the form of pleas in abatement, see 1 Chit. Pl. 447; Com. Dig. Abatement, I 19; 2 Saund. 1, n. 2.

32.—§ 7. *Of the affidavit of truth.* 1.

All pleas in abatement must be sworn to be true, 4 Ann. c. 16, s. 11. The affidavit may be made by the defendant or a third person, Barnes, 344, and must be positive as to the truth of every fact contained in the plea, and should leave nothing to be collected by inference; Sayer's Rep. 293; it should be stated that the plea is true in substance and fact, and not merely that the plea is a true plea. 3 Str. 705; Litt. Ent. 1; 2 Chitt. Pl. 412, 417; 1 Browne's Rep. 77; see. 2 Dall. 184; 1 Yeates, 185.

See further on the subject of abatement of actions, Vin. Ab. tit. Abatement; Bac. Abr. tit. Abatement; Nelson's Abr. tit. Abatement; American Dig. tit. Abatement; Story's Pl. 1 to 70; 1 Chit. Pl. 425 to 458; Whart. Dig. tit. Pleading, F. (b.) Penna. Pract. Index, h. t.; Tidd's Pr. Index, h. t.; Arch. Civ. Pl. Index, h. t.; Arch. Pract. Index, h. t. *Death; Parties to Actions; Plaintiff; Puis darrein continuance.*

Abatement of a Freehold. The entry of a stranger after the death of the ancestor, and before the heir or devisee takes possession, by which the rightful possession of the heir or devisee is defeated. 3 Bl. Com. 167; Co. Lit. 277, a; Finch's Law, 195; Arch. Civ. Pl. 11.

2. By the ancient laws of Normandy, this term was used to signify the act of one who, having an apparent right of possession to an estate, took possession of it immediately after the death of the actual possessor, before the heir entered. Howard, Anciennes Lois des Français, tome 1, p. 539.

Abatement of Legacies, is the reduction of legacies for the purpose of paying the testator's debts.

2.—When the estate is short of paying the debts and legacies, and there are general legacies and specific legacies, the rule is that the general legatees must abate proportionably in order to pay the debts; a specific legacy is not abated unless the general legacies cannot pay all the debts; in that case what remains to be paid must be paid by the specific legatees, who must, where there are several, abate their legacies, proportionably. 2 Bl. Com. 513; 2 Ves. sen. 561 to 564; 1 P. Wms. 680; 2 P. Wms. 283. See 2 Bro. C. C. 19; Bac. Abr. Legacies, H; Rop. on Leg. 253, 284.

Abatement of Nuisances is the prostration or removal of a nuisance. 3 Bl. Com. 5.

2.—1. Who may abate a nuisance; 2, the manner of abating it.

§ 1. *Who may abate a nuisance.* 1. Any person may abate a public nuisance. 2 Salk. 458; 9 Co. 454.

3.—2. The injured party may abate a private nuisance, which is created by an act of *commission*, without notice to the person who has committed it; but there is no case which sanctions the abatement by an individual of nuisances from *omission*, except that of cutting branches of trees which overhang a public road, or the private property of the person who cuts them.

4.—§ 2. *The manner of abating it.* 1. A public nuisance may be abated without notice, 2 Salk. 458; and so may a private nuisance which arises by an act of commission. And, when the security of lives or property may require so speedy a remedy as not to allow time to call on the person on whose property the mischief has arisen to remedy it, an individual would be justified in abating a nuisance from omission without notice. 2 Barn. & Cres. 311; 3 Dowl. & R. 556.

5.—2. In the abatement of a public nuisance, the abator need not observe particular care in abating it, so as to prevent injury to the materials. And though a gate illegally fastened, might have been opened without cutting it down, yet the cutting would be lawful. However, it is a general rule that the abatement must be limited by its necessity, and no wanton or unnecessary injury must be committed. 2 Salk. 458.

6.—3. As to private nuisances, it has been held, that if a man in his own soil erect a thing which is a nuisance to another, as by stopping a rivulet, and so diminishing the water used by the latter for his cattle, the party injured may enter on the soil of the other, and abate the nuisance and justify the trespass; and this right of abatement is not confined merely to a house, mill, or land. 2 Smith's Rep. 9; 2 Roll. Abr. 565; 2 Leon. 202; Com. Dig. Pleader, 3 M. 42; 3 Lev. 92; 1 Brownl. 212; Vin. Ab. Nuisance; 12 Mass. 420; 9 Mass. 316; 4 Conn. 418; 5 Conn. 210; 1 Esp. 679; 3 Taunt. 99; 6 Bing. 379.

7.—4. The abator of a private nuisance cannot remove the materials further than is necessary, nor convert them to his own use. Dalt. c. 50. And so much only of the thing as causes the nuisance should be removed; as if a house be built too high, so much only as is too high should be pulled down. 9 Co. 53; God. 221; Str. 686.

8.—5. If the nuisance can be removed without destruction and delivered to a magistrate, it is advisable to do so; as in the case of a libellous print or paper affecting an individual, but still it may be destroyed. 5 Co. 125, b.; 2 Campb. 511. See as to cutting down trees, Roll. Rep. 394; 3 Buls. 198; Vin. Ab. tit. Trees, E, and Nuisance W.

ABATOR is, 1st, he who abates or prostrates a nuisance; 2, he who having no right of entry, gets possession of the freehold to the prejudice of an heir or devisee, after the time when the ancestor died, and before the heir or devisee enters. See article *Abatement*. Litt. § 397; Perk. § 383; 1 Inst. 271; 2 Prest. Abst. 296. 300. As to the consequence of an abator dying in possession, see Adams' Eject. 43.

ABATUDA, *obsolete*. Any thing diminished; as, moneta abatuda, which is money clipped or diminished in value. Cowell, h. t.

ABAVUS, *civil law*, is the great grandfather, or fourth male ascendant. Abavia, is the great grandmother, or fourth female ascendant.

ABBEY, *abbatia*, is a society of religious persons, having an abbot or abbess to preside over them. Formerly some of the most considerable abbots and priors in England had seats and votes in the house of lords. The prior of St. John's of Jerusalem, was styled the first baron of England, in respect to the lay barons, but he was the last of the spiritual barons.

ABBREVIATION, *practice*.—The omission of some words or letters in writing; as when fieri facias is written *fi. fa*.

2. In writing contracts it is the better practice to make no abbreviations; but in recognizances, and many other contracts, they are used; as John Doe tent to prosecute, &c. Richard Roe teni to appear, &c. When the recognizances are used, they are drawn out *in extenso*. See 4 Ca. & P. 51; S. C. 19 E. C. L. R. 268; 9 Co. 48.

ABBREVIATIONS *and abbreviated references*. The following list, though necessarily incomplete, may be useful to some readers.

A, a, the first letter of the alphabet, is sometimes used in the ancient law books to denote that the paging is the first of that number in the book. As an abbreviation, A is used for anonymous.

A. & A. on Corp. Angell & Ames on Corporations. Sometimes cited *Ang. on Corp.*

A. B. Anonymous Reports, printed at the end of Bendloe's Reports.

A. D. Anno Domini; in the year of our Lord.

A. & E. Adolphus and Ellis' Reports.

A. & E. N. S. Adolphus & Ellis' Queen's Bench Reports, New Series, commonly cited *Q. B.*

A. & F. on Fixt. Amos & Ferard on Fixtures.

A. K. Marsh. A. K. Marshall's (Kty.) Reports.

Ab. or *Abr.* Abridgment.

Abr. Ca Eq. Abridgment of cases in Equity.

Abs. Absolute.

Ab. Sh. Abbott on Shipping.

Acc. Accord or Agrees.

Act. Acton's Reports.

Act. Reg. Acta Regia.

Ad. Eject. Adams on Ejectment.

Ad. & Ell. Adolphus & Ellis' Reports

Ad. fin. Ad finem. At or near the end.

Ads. Ad sectum, vide *Ats.*

Addam's R. Addam's Ecclesiastical Reports. In E. Eccl. Rep.

Addis on Contr. Addison on the Law of Contracts and on Parties to actions ex contractu.

Addis. R. Addison's Reports.

Admr. Administrator.

Ady. C. M. Adye on Courts Martial.

Aik. R. Aiken's Reports.

Al. Aleyn's Cases.

Al. Alinea. *Al et.* Et alii, and others.

Al. & N. Alcock & Napier's Reports.

Ala. R. Alabama Reports.

Alc. Reg. Cas. Alcock's Registration Cases

Ald. & Van Hoes. Dig. A Digest of the Laws of Mississippi, by T. J. Fox Alden and J. A. Van Hoesen.

Aldr. Hist. Aldridge's History of the Courts of Law.

Alis. Prin. Alison's Principles of the Criminal Law of Scotland.

All. & Mor. Tr. Allen and Morris' Trial.

Alley L. D. of Mar. Alleyne's Legal Degrees of Marriage considered.

Alln. Part. Allnat on Partition.

Am. America, American, or Americana.

Amb. Ambler's Reports.

Am. & Fer. on. Fixt. Amos & Ferard on Fixtures.

Amer. America, American, or Americana.

Amer. Dig. American Digest.

Amer. Jur. American Jurist.

An. Anonymous.

And. Anderson's Reports.

Ander. Ch. War. Anderdon on Church Wardens

Andr. Andrew's Reports.

Ang. on Adv. Enj. Angell's Inquiry into the rule of law which creates a right to an incorporeal hereditament, by an adverse enjoyment of twenty years.

Ang. on Ass. Angell's Practical Summary of the Law of Assignments in trust for creditors.

Ang. on B. T. Angell on Bank Tax.

Ang. on Corp. Angell on the Law of Private Corporations

Ang. on Limit. Angell's Treatise on the Limitation of Actions at Law, and Suits in Equity.

Ang. on Tide Wat. Angell on the right of property in Tide Waters.

Ang. on Water Courses. Angell on the Common Law in relation to Water Courses.

Ann. Anne; as 1 Ann. c. 7.

Anna. Annaly's Reports. This book is usually cited Cas. Temp. Hardw.

Annesl. on Ins. Annesley on Insurance.

Anon. Anonymous.

Anstr. Anstruther's Reports.

Anth. N. P. C. Anthon's Nisi Prius Cases.

Anth. Shep. Anthon's edition of Sheppard's Touchstone.

Ap. Justin. Apud Justinianum, or Justinian's Institutes.

App. Apposition.

Appx. Appendix.

Arch Archbold. *Arch. Civ. Pl.* Archbold's Civil Pleadings. *Arch. Cr. Pl.* Archbold's Criminal Pleadings. *Arch. Pr.* Archbold's Practice. *Arch. B. L.* Archbold's Bankrupt Law. *Arch L. & T.* Archbold on the Law of Landlord and Tenant. *Arch. N. P* Archbold's Law of Nisi Prius.

Arg. Argumento, by an argument drawn from such a law. It also signifies *arguendo*.

Arg. Inst. Institution au Droit Français, par M. Argou.

Ark Rep. Arkansas Reports. See *Pike's Rep.*

Ark. Rev. Stat. Arkansas Revised Statutes.

Art. Article.

Ashm. R. Ashmead's Reports.

Aso & Man. Inst. Aso and Manuel's Institutes of the Laws of Spain.

Ass. or *Lib. Ass.* Liber Assissarium, or Pleas of the Crown.

Ast. Ent. Aston's Entries.

Atherl. on Mar. Atherley on the Law of Marriage and other Family Settlements.

Atk. Atkyn's Reports.

Atk. P. T. Atkyn's Parliamentary Tracts.

Atk. on Con. Atkinson on Conveyancing.

Atk. on Tit. Atkinson on Marketable Titles.

Ats. in practice, is an abbreviation for the words *at suit of*, and is used when the defendant files any pleadings; for example: when the defendant enters a plea he puts his name before that of the plaintiff, reversing the order in which they are on the record. C. D. (the defendant,) *ats.* A. B. (the plaintiff.)

Aust. on Jur. The Province of Jurisprudence determined, by John Austin

Auth. Authentica, in the Authentic; that is, the *Summary* of some of the Novels of the Civil Law inserted in the code under such a title.

Ayl. Ayliffe's Pandect.

Ayl. Parerg. Ayliffe's Parergon juris canonici Anglicani.

Azun. Mar. Law. Azuni's Maritime Law of Europe.

B, b, is used to point out that a number, used at the head of a page to denote the folio, is the second number of the same volume.

B. B. Bail Bond.

B. or *Bk.* Book.

B. & A. Barnewall & Alderson's Reports.

B. & B. Ball & Beatty's Reports.

B. C. R. Brown's Chancery Reports.

B. Eccl. L. Burn's Ecclesiastical Law.

B. Just. Burn's Justice.

B. N. C. Brooke's New Cases.

B. P. C or *Bro. Parl. Cas.* Brown's Parliamentary Cases.

B. & P. or *Bos. & Pull.* Bosanquet & Puller's Reports.

B. R or *K. B.* King's Bench.

B. Tr. Bishop's Trial

Bab. on Auct. Babington on the Law of Auctions.

Bab. Set off. Babington on Set off and mutual credit.

Bac. Abr. Bacon's Abridgment.

Bac. Comp. Arb. Bacon's (M.) Complete Arbitrator.

Bac. El. Bacon's Elements of the Common Law.

Bac. Gov. Bacon on Government.

Bac. Law Tr. Bacon's Law Tracts

Bac. Leas. Bacon (M.) on Leases and Terms of Years.

Bac. Lib. Reg. Bacon's (John) Liber Regis, vel Thesaurus Rerum Ecclesiasticarum.

Bac. Uses. Bacon's Reading on the Statute of Uses. This is printed in his Law Tracts.

Bach. Man. Bache's Manual of a Pennsylvania Justice of the Peace.

Bail. R. Bailey's Reports.

Bain. on M. & M. Bainbridge on Mines and Minerals.

Baldw. R. Baldwin's Circuit Court Reports.

Ball & Beat. Ball and Beatty's Reports.

Ballan. Lim. Ballantine on Limitations.

Banc. Sup. Upper Bench.

Barb. Eq. Dig. Barbour's Equity Digest.

Barb. Cr. Pl. Barbour's Criminal Pleadings.

Barb. Pract. in Ch. Barbour's Treatise on the Practice of the Court of Chancery.

Barb. R. Barbour's Chancery Roports.

Barb. Grot. Grotius on War and Peace, with notes by Barbeyrac.

Barb. Puff. Puffendorf's Law of Nature and Nations, with notes by M. Barbeyrac.

Barb. on Set off. Barbour on the Law of Set off, with an appendix of precedents.

Barn. C. Barnardiston's Chancery Reports.

Barn. Barnardiston's K. B. Reports.

Barn. & Ald. Barnewall & Alderson's Reports.

Barn. & Adolph. Barnewall & Adolphus' Reports.

Barn. & Cress. Barnewall & Cresswell's Reports.

Barn. Sher. Barnes' Sheriff.

Barnes. Barnes' Notes of Practice.

Barr. Obs. Stat. Barrington's Observations on the more ancient statutes.

Barr. Ten. Barry's Tenures.

Bart. El. Conv. Barton's Elements of Conveyancing. *Bart. Prec. Conv.* Barton's Precedents of Conveyancing. *Bart. S. Eq.* Barton's Suit in Equity.

Batty's R. Batty's Reports of Cases determined in the K. B. Ireland.

Bay's R. Bay's Reports.

Bayl. Bills. Bayley on Bills.

Bayl. Ch. Pr. Bayley's Chamber Practice.

Beam. Ne Exeat. Brief view of the writ of Ne Exeat Regno, as an equitable process, by J. Beams.

Beam. Eq. Beames on Equity Pleading.

Beam Ord. Chan. Beames' General Orders of the High Court of Chancery, from 1600 to 1815.

Beat. R. Beatty's Reports determined in the High Court of Chancery in Ireland.

Beav. R. Beavan's Chancery Reports.

Beawes. Beawes' Lex Mercatoria.

Beck's Med. Jur. Beck's Medical Jurisprudence.

Bee's R. Bee's Reports.

Bell's Com. Bell's Commentaries on the Laws of Scotland, and on the Principles of Mercantile Iurisprudence.

Bell. Del. U. L. Beller's Delineation of Universal Law.

Bell's Dict. Dictionary of the Law of Scotland. By Robert Bell.

Bell's Med. Jur. Bell's Medical Jurisprudence.

Bellew. Bellewe's Cases in the time of K. Richard II. Bellewe's Cases in the time of Henry VIII., Edw. VI., and Q. Mary, collected out of Brooke's Abridgment, and arranged under years, with a table, are cited as Brooke's New Cases.

Bellingh. Tr. Bellingham's Trial.

Belt's Sup. Belt's Supplement. Supplement to the Reports in Chancery of Francis Vesey, Senior, Esq., during the time of Lord Ch. J. Hardwicke.

Belt's Ves. sen. Belt's edition of Vesey senior's Reports.

Benl. Benloe & Dalison's Reports. See *New Benl.*

Ben. on Av. Benecke on Average.

Benn. Diss. Bennet's Short Dissertation on the nature and various proceedings in the Master's Office, in the Court of Chancery. Sometimes this book is called *Benn. Pract.*

Benn. Pract. See *Benn. Diss.*

Benth. Ev. Bentham's Treatise on Judicial Evidence.

Best on Pres. Best's Treatise on Presumptions of Law and Fact.

Bett's Adm. Pr. Bett's Admiralty Practice.

Bev. on Hom. Bevil on Homicide.

Bill. on Aw. Billing on the Law of Awards.

Bing. Bingham. *Bing. Inf.* Bingham on Infancy. *Bing on Judg.* Bingham on Judgments and Executions. *Bing L & T.* Bingham on the Law of Landlord and Tenant. *Bing. R.* Bingham's Reports. *Bing. N. C.* Bingham's New Cases.

Binn. Reports of Cases adjudged in the Supreme Cour. of Pennsylvania. By Horace Binney.

Bird on Conv. Bird on Conveyancing. *Bird L. & T.* Bird on the Laws respecting Landlords, Tenants and Lodgers. *Bird's Sol. Pr.* Bird's Solution of Precedents of Settlements.

Biret, De l'Abs. Traité de l'Absence et de ses effects, par M. Biret.

Biss. on Est. or *Biss. on Life Est.* Bissett on the Law of Estates for Life.

Biss. on Partn. Bissett on Partnership.

Bl. Blount's Law Dictionary and Glossary.

Bl. Comm. or *Comm.* Commentaries on the Laws of England, by Sir William Blackstone.

Bl. Rep. Sir William Blackstone's Reports.

Bl H. Henry Blackstone's Reports, sometimes cited *H. Bl.*

Black. L. T. Blackstone's Law Tracts.

Blackb. on Sales. Blackburn on the Effect of the Contract of Sales.

Blackb. on Sales. Blackburn on the Law of Sales.

Blackf. R. Blackford's Reports.

Blak. Ch. Pr. Blake's Practice of the Court of Chancery of the State of New York.

Blan. on Ann. Blaney on Life Annuities.

Bland's Ch. R. Bland's Chancery Reports.

Blansh. Lim. Blanshard on Limitations.

Bligh. R. Bligh's Reports of Cases decided in the House of Lords.

Blount. Blount's Law Dictionary and Glossary

Bo. R. Act. Booth on Real Actions.

Boh. Dec. Bohun's Declarations. *Boh. Eng. L.* Bohun's English Lawyer. *Boh. Priv. Lon.* Bohun's Privilegia Londini.

Boote. Boote's Ch. Pr. Boote's Chancery Practice. *Boote's S. L.* Boote's Suit at Law.

Booth's R. A. Booth on Real Actions.

Borth. L. L. Borthwick on the Law of Libels.

Bos. & Pull. Bosanquet and Puller's Reports. Vide *B. & P.*

Bosc. on Conv. Boscowen on Convictions.

Bott. Bott's Poor Laws.

Bouch. Inst. Dr. Mar. Boucher, Institution au Droit Maritime.

Boulay Paty, Dr. Com. Cours de Droit Commercial Maritime, par P. S. Boulay Paty.

Bousq. Dict. de Dr. Bousquet, Dictionnaire de Droit.

Bouv. L. D. Bouvier's Law Dictionary.

Bouv. Inst. Institutiones Theologicæ. Auctore J. Bouvier.

Bouv. Inst. Am. Law. Bouvier's Institutes of American Law.

Bowl. on Lib. Bowles on Libels.

Br. or *Brownl.* Brownlow's Reports.

Br. or *Br. Ab.* Brooke's Abridgment.

Bra. Brady's History of the Succession of the Crown of England, &c.

Brac. Bracton's Treatise on the Laws and Customs of England.

Bra. Princ. Branche's Principia Legis et Æquitatis.

Brack. L. Misc. Brackenridge's Law Miscellany.

Bradb. Bradby on Distresses.

Bradl. P. B. Bradley's Point Book.

Bran. Prin. or *Bran. Max.* Branch's Principia Legis Æquitatis, being an alphabetical collection of maxims, &c.

Brayt. R. Brayton's Reports.

Breese's R. Breese's Reports.

Brev. Sel. Brevia Selecta, or Choice Writs.

Brid. Bridgman's Reports. Reports from 12 to 19 K. James. By Sir John Bridgman.

Brid. Dig. Ind. Bridgman's Digested Index.

Brid. Leg. Bib. Bridgman's Legal Bibliography.

Brid. Conv. Bridgman's Precedents of Conveyancing. *Brid. Refl.* Bridgman's Reflections on the Study of the Law. *Brid. Synth.* Bridgman's Synthesis. *Brid. Thes. Jur.* Bridgman's Thesaurus Juridicus.

Bridg. O. Orlando Bridgman's Reports.

Bridg. The. Jur. Bridgman's Thesaurus Juridicus.

Britton. Treatise on the Ancient Pleas of the Crown.

Bro. or *Brownl.* Brownlow's Reports. Also, Reports by Richard Brownlow and John Goldesborough. Cited 1 Bro. 2 Bro.

Bro Ab. Brooke's Abridgment.

Bro. A. & C. L. Brown's Admiralty and Civil Law.

Bro. C. C. Brown's Chancery Cases.

Bro. Off. Not. A Treatise on the Office and Practice of a Notary in England, as connected with Mercantile Instruments, &c. By Richard Brooke.

Bro. P. C Brown's Parliamentary Cases.

Bro. Read. Brooke's Reading on the Statute of Limitations.

Bro. on Sales. Brown on Sales.
Bro. V. M. Brown's Vade Mecum.
Brock. R. Brockenbrough's Reports of Chief Justice Marshall's Decisions.
Brod. & Bing. Broderip & Bingham's Reports.
Broom on Part. Broom on Parties to Actions.
Brownl. Rediv. or *Brownl. Ent.* Brownlow Redivivus.
Bruce M. L. Bruce's Military Law.
Buck's Ca. Buck's Cases. Cases in Bankruptcy in 1817, 1818. By J. W. Buck.
Bull. or *Bull. N. P.* Buller's Nisi Prius.
Bulst. Bulstrode's Reports.
Bunb. Bunbury's Reports.
Burge Col. Law. Burge's Colonial Law.
Burge Confl. of Law. Burge on the Conflict of Laws.
Burge on Sur. Burge's Commentaries on the Law of Suretyship. &c.
Burge For. Law. Burge on Foreign Law.
Burlam. Burlamaqui's Natural and Political Law.
Burn's L. D. Burn's Law Dictionary.
Burn's Just. Burn's Justice of the Peace.
Burn's Eccl. Law or *Burn's E. L.* Burn's Ecclesiastical Law.
Burn. C. L. Burnett's Treatise on the Criminal Law of Scotland.
Burn. Com. Burnett's Commentaries on the Criminal Law of Scotland.
Burr. Burrow's Reports.
Burr. Pract. Burril's Practice.
Burr. Sett. Cas. Burrow's Settlement Cases.
Burr's Tr. Burr's Trial.
Burt. Man. Burton's Manual of the Law of Scotland. The work is in two parts, one relating to *public law,* and the other to the law of *private rights and obligations.* The former is cited *Burt. Man. P. L.;* the latter, *Burt Man. Pr.*
Burt. on Real Prop. Burton on Real Property.
Butl. Hor. Jur. Butler's Horæ Juridicæ Subsecivæ.
C. Codex, the Code of Justinian. *C.* Code. *C.* Chancellor.
C. & A. Cooke and Alcock's Reports.
C. B. Communi Banco, or Common Bench.
C. C. Circuit Court.
C. C. Cepi Corpus. *C. C.* and *B. B.* Cepi Corpus and Bail Bond.
C. C. or *Ch. Cas.* Cases in Chancery in three parts.
C. C. C. or *Cr. Cir. Com.* Crown Circuit Companion.
C. C. & C. Cepi corpus et committitur. See *Capias ad satisfaciendum,* in the body of the work.
C. C. E. or *Cain. Cas.* Caines' Cases in Error.
C. D or *Com Dig.* Comyn's Digest.
C. & D. C. C. Crawford and Dix's Criminal Cases.
C. & D. Ab. C. Crawford and Dix's Abridged Cases.
C. & F. Clark & Findley's Reports.
C. & F. Clarke & Finelly's Reports.
C. J. Chief Justice.
C. & J. Crompton & Jervis' Exchequer Reports.
C. J. C. P. Chief Justice of the Common Pleas.
C. J. K. B. Chief Justice of the King's Bench.
C. J. Q. B. Chief Justice of the Queen's Bench.
C. J. U. B. Chief Justice of the Upper Bench. During the time of the commonwealth, the English Court of the King's Bench was called the Upper Bench.
C. & K. Carrington & Kirwan's Reports.
C. & M. Crompton & Meeson's Reports.
C. & M. Carrington & Marshman's Reports.
C. M. & R. Crompton, Meeson & Roscoe's Exchequer Reports.
C. N. P. C. Campbell's Nisi Prius Cases.
C. P. Common Pleas.
C. P. Coop. C. P. Cooper's Reports.
C. & P. or *Car. & Payn.* Carrington & Payne's Reports.
C. & P. Craig & Phillips' Reports.
C. R. or *Ch. Rep.* Chancery Reports.
C. & R. Cockburn & Rowe's Reports.
C. W. Dudl. Eq. C. W. Dudley's Equity Reports.
C. Theod. Codice Theodosiano, in the Theodosian code.
Ca. Case or placitum.
Ca. T. K. Select Cases tempore King.
Ca. T. Talb. Cases tempore Talbot.
Ca. res. Capias ad respondendum.
Ca. sa., in practice, is the abbreviation of *capias ad satisfaciendum.*
Caines' R. Caines' Term Reports.
Caines' Cas Caines' Cases, in error.
Caines' Pr. Caines' Practice.
Cald. R. Caldecott's Reports.
Cald. S. C. Caldecott's Settlement Cases; sometimes cited *Cald. R.*
Caldw. Arbit. Caldwell on Arbitration.
Call on Sew. Callis on the Law relating to Sewers.
Call's R. Call's Reports.
Calth. R. Calthorp's Reports of Special Cases touching several customs and liberties of the City of London.
Calth. on Copyh. Calthorpe on Copyholds.
Calv. on Part. Calvert on Parties to Suits in Equity.
Cam & Norw. Cameron & Norwood's Reports.
Campb. Campbell's Reports.
Can. Canon.
Cap. Capitulo, chapter.
Car. Carolus: as 13 Car. 2, st. 2, c. 1.
Carr. Cr. L. Carrington's Criminal Law.
Carr. & Kirw. Carrington & Kirwan's Reports. See *C. & K.*
Carr. & Marsh. Carrington & Marshman's Reports.
Carr. & Oliv. R. and C. C. Carrow & Oliver's Railway and Canal Cases.
Cart. Carter's Reports. Reports in C. P. in 16, 17, 18 and 19, Charles II.
Carta de For. Carta de Foresta.
Carth. Carthew's Reports.
Cary. Cary's Reports.
Cary on Partn. Cary on the Law of Partnership.
Cas. of App. Cases of Appeals to the House of Lords.
Cas. L. Eq. Cases and Opinions in Law, Equity and Conveyancing.
Cas. of Pr. Cases of Practice in the Court of the King's Bench, from the reign of Eliz. to the 14 Geo. 3.
Cas. of Sett. Cases of Settlement.

Cas. Temp. Hardw. Cases during the time of Lord Hardwicke.

Cas. Temp. Talb. Cases during the time of Lord Talbot.

Ch. Chancellor.

Ch. Cas. Cases in Chancery.

Ch. Pr. Precedents in Chancery.

Ch. R. Reports in Chancery.

Ch. Rep. Vide Cb Cases.

Chamb. on Jur. of Chan. Chambers on the Jurisdiction of the High Court of Chancery, over the Persons and Property of Infants.

Chamb. L. & T. Chambers on the Law of Landlord and Tenant.

Char. Merc. Charta mercatoria. See Bac. Ab. Smuggling, C.

Charlt. Cbarlton. *T. U. P. Charl.* T. U. P. Cbarlton's Reports. *R. M. Charlt.* R. M. Charlton's Reports.

Chase's Tr. Chase's Trial.

Cher. Cas. Cherokee Case.

Chev. C. C. Cheves' Chancery Cases.

Chipm. R. Chipman's Reports. *D. Chipm.* D. Chipman's Reports

Chipm. Contr. Essay on the Law of Contracts for the payment of Specific Articles. By Daniel Chipman.

Ch. Contr. A Practical Treatise on the Law of Contracts. By Joseph Chitty, Jr.

Chitty. on App. Chitty's Practical Treatise on the Law relating to Apprentices and Journeymen.

Chit. on Bills. Chitty on Bills.

Chit. Jr. on Bills. Chitty, junior, on Bills.

Chit. Com. L. Chitty's Treatise on Commercial Law.

Chit. Cr. L. Chitty's Criminal Law.

Chit. on Des. Chitty on the Law of Descents.

Chit. F. Chitty's Forms and Practical Proceedings.

Chit. Med. Jur. Chitty on Medical Jurisprudence.

Chit. Rep. Chitty's Reports.

Chit. Pl. A Practical Treatise on Pleading, by Joseph Chitty.

Chit. Pr. Chitty's General Practice.

Chit. Prerog. Chitty on the Law of the Prerogatives of the Crown.

Chris. B. L. Christian's Bankrupt Laws.

Christ. Med. Jur. Christison's Treatise on Poisons, relating to Medical Jurisprudence, Physiology, and the Practice of Physic.

Civ. Civil.

Civ. Code Lo. Civil Code of Louisiana.

Cl. The Clementines.

Cl. Ass. Clerk's Assistant.

Clan. H. & W. Clancy on the Rights, Duties and Liabilities of Husband and Wife.

Clark on Leas. Clark's Enquiry into the Nature of Leases.

Clarke, R. Clarke's Reports.

Clark & Fin. Clark & Finelly's Reports.

Clark. Adm. Pr. Clarke's Practice in the Admiralty.

Clark. Prax. Clarke's Praxis, being the manner of proceeding in the Ecclesiastical Courts.

Clay. Clayton's Reports.

Cleir. Us et Coust Cleirac, Us et Coustumes de la Mer.

Clerke's Rud. Clerke's Rudiments of American Law and Practice.

Clift. Clift's Entries.

Co. A particle used before other words to imply that the person spoken of possesses the same character as other persons whose character is mentioned, as co-executor, an executor with others; co-heir, an heir with others; co-partner, a partner with others, etc.—*Co.* is also an abbreviation for *company*, as John Smith & Co. When so abbreviated it also represents *county*.

Co. Coke's Reports. Cited sometimes *Rep.*

Co. or *Co. Rep.* Coke's Reports.

Co. Ent. Coke's Entries.

Co. B. L. Cooke's Bankrupt Law.

Co. on Courts. Coke on Courts; 4th Institute. See *Inst.*

Co. Litt. Coke on Littleton. See *Inst.*

Co M. C. Coke's Magna Charta; 2d Institute. See *Inst.*

Co. P. C. Coke's Pleas of the Crown. See *Inst.*

Cock. & Rowe. Cockburn & Rowe's Reports.

Code Civ. Code Civil, or Civil Code of France. This work is usually cited by the article.

Code Nap. Code Napoleon. The same as Code Civil.

Code Com. Code de Commerce.

Code Pén. Code Pénal.

Code Pro. Code de Procedure.

Col. Column, in the first or second column of the book quoted.

Col. & Cai Cas. Coleman & Caines' Cases.

Cole on Inf. Cole on Criminal Informations, and Informations in the Nature of Quo Warranto.

Coll. on Pat. Collier on the Law of Patents.

Coll. on Idiots. Collinson on the Law concerning Idiots, &c.

Coll. Rep. Colle's Reports.

Coll. Collation

Colly. Rep. Collyer's Reports

Com. Communes, or Extravagantes Communes.

Com. or *Com. Rep.* Comyn's Reports.

Com. Contr. Comyn on Contract.

Com. on Us. Comyn on Usury.

Com. Dig. Comyn's Digest.

Com. L & T. Comyn on the Law of Landlord and Tenant.

Com. Law. Commercial Law.

Com. Law. Rep. Common Law Reports, edited by Sergeant and Lowber.

Comb. Comberbach's Reports.

Comm. Blackstone's Commentaries.

Con. & Law. Connor & Lawson's Reports.

Cond. Condensed.

Cond. Ch. R. Condensed Chancery Reports.

Cond. Ex. R Condensed Exchequer Reports

Conf. Chart. Confirmatio Chartorum.

Cong. Congress.

Conkl. Pr. Conkling's Practice of the Courts of the United States.

Conn. R. Connecticut Reports.

Conr. Cust. R. Conroy's Custodiam Reports.

Cons. del Mar Consolato del Mare.

Cons. Ct. R. Constitutional Court Reports.

Cont. Contra.

Cooke on Defam. Cooke on Defamation.

Coop. Eq. R. Cooper's Equity Reports.

Coop. Cas. Cases in the High Court of Chancery. By George Cooper.

Coop. on Lib. Cooper on the Law of Libels.

Coop. Eq. Pl. Cooper's Equity Pleading.

Coop. Just. Cooper's Justinian's Institutes.

Coop. Med. Jur. Cooper's Medical Jurisprudence.

Coop. t. Brough. Cooper's Cases in the time of Brougham.

Coop P. P. Cooper's Points of Practice.

Coote. Mortg. Coote on Mortgages.

Corb. & Dan. Corbet & Daniel's Election Cases

Corn. on Uses. Cornish on Uses.

Corn. on Rem. Cornish on Remainders.

Corp. Jur. Civ. Corpus Juris Civilis.

Corp. Jur. Can. Corpus Juris Canonicus.

Corvin. Corvinus. See Bac. Ab. Mortgage A, where this author is cited.

Cot. Abr. Cotton's Abridgment of Records.

Cov on Conv. Evi. Coventry on Conveyancers' Evidence.

Cow. Int. Cowel's Law Dictionary, or the Interpreter of words and terms, used either in the common or statute laws of Great Britain.

Cowp. Cowper's Reports.

Cow. R. Cowen's Reports, N. Y.

Cox's Cas. Cox's Cases.

Coxe's R. Coxe's Reports.

Crabb's C. L. Crabb's Common Law. A History of the English Law. By George Crabb.

Crabb, R. P. Crabb on the Law of Real Property.

Craig & Phil. Craig & Phillip's Reports.

Cranch, R. Cranch's Reports.

Cressw. R. Cresswell's Reports of Cases decided in the Court for the Relief of Insolvent Debtors.

Crim. Con. Criminal Conversation: adultery.

Cro. Croke's Reports. *Cro. Eliz.* Croke's Reports, during the time of Queen Elizabeth, also cited as 1 Cro. *Cro. Jac.* Croke's Reports during the time of King James I., also cited as 2 Cro. *Cro. Car.* Croke's Reports, during the time of Charles I., also cited as 3 Cro.

Crompt. Ex. Rep. Crompton's Exchequer Reports.

Crompt. J. C. Crompton's Jurisdiction of Courts.

Crompt. & Mees. Crompton & Meeson's Exchequer Reports.

Crompt. Mees. & Rosc. Crompton, Meeson and Roscoe's Exchequer Reports.

Cross on Liens. Cross' Treatise on the Law of Liens and Stoppage in Transitu.

Cru. Dig or *Cruise's Dig.* Cruise's Digest of the Law of Real Property.

Cul. culpabilis, guilty; *non cul.* not guilty; a plea entered in actions of trespass. *Cul. prit,* commonly written culprit; cul., as above mentioned, means culpabilis, or culpable; and prit, which is a corruption of prêt, signifies ready. 1 Chitty Cr. Law 416.

Cull. Bankr. L. Cullen's Principles of the Bankrupt Law.

Cun. Cunningham's Reports.

Cunn. Dicl. Cunningham's Dictionary.

Cur. adv. vult. Curia advisare vult. Vide *Ampliation.*

Cur. Scacc. Cursus Scaccarii, the Court of the Star Chamber.

Cur. Phil. Curia Philipica.

Curs. Can. Cursus Cancellariæ.

Curt. R. Curteis' Ecclesiastical Reports.

Curt. Am. Sea. Curtis on American Seamen.

Curt. on Copyr. Curtis on Copyrights.

Cush. Trust. Pr. Cushing on Trustee Process, or Foreign Attachment, of the Laws of Massachusetts and Maine.

Cust. de Norm. Custome de Normandie.

D. dialogue; as, Dr. and Stud. d. 2, c. 24, of Doctor and Student, dialogue 2, chapter 24.

D. dictum; *D.* Digest of Justinian.

D. The Digest or Pandects of the Civil Law, is sometimes cited thus, D. 6. 1. 5.

D. C District Court; District of Columbia.

D. C. L. Doctor of the Civil Law.

D. Chipm. R. D. Chipman's Reports.

D. S. B. Debit sans brève.

D. S. Deputy Sheriff.

D. & C. Dow & Clark's Reports.

D. & C. Deacon & Chitty's Reports.

D. & E. Durnford & East's Reports. This book is also cited as Term Reports, abbreviated T. R.

D. & L. Danson & Lloyd's Mercantile Cases.

D. & M. Davidson's & Merivale's Reports.

D. & R. Dowling and Ryland's Reports.

D. & R. N. P. C. Dowling and Ryland's Reports of Cases decided at Nisi Prius.

D. & S. Doctor and Student.

D. & W. Drury & Walsh's Reports.

D'Aguesseau, Œuvres. Œuvres complètes du Chancellier D'Aguesseau.

Dag. Cr L. Dagge's Criminal Law.

Dal. Dalison's Reports. See *Benl.*

Dall. Dallas' Reports.

Dall. Dallas' Laws of Pennsylvania.

Dalloz, Dict. Dictionaire General et raisonné de Legislation, de Doctrine, et de Jurisprudence, en matiere civile, commerciale, criminelle, administrative, et de Droit Public. Par Armand Dalloz, jeune.

Dalr Feud. Pr. Dalrymple's Essay, or History of Feudal Property in Great Britain. Sometimes cited *Dalr. F. L.*

Dalr. on Ent. Dalrymple on the Polity of Entails.

Dalr. F. L. Dalrymple's Feudal Law

Dalt. Just. Dalton's Justice.

Dalt. Sh. Dalton's Sheriff.

D'Anv. D'Anvers' Abridgment.

Dan. Ch. Pr. Daniell's Chancery Practice.

Dan. Ord. Danish Ordinances.

Dan. Rep. Daniell's Reports.

Dan. & Ll. Danson & Lloyd's Reports.

Dana's R. Dana's Reports.

Dane's Ab. Dane's Abridgment of American Law.

Dav. Davies' Reports.

Dav. on Pat. Davies' Collection of Cases respecting Patents.

Daw. Land. Pr. Dawe's Epitome of the Law of Landed Property.

Daw. Real Pr. Dawe's Introduction to the Knowledge of the Law on Real Estates.

Daw. on Arr. Dawe's Commentaries on the Law of Arrest in Civil Cases.

Daws. Or. Leg. Dawson's Origo Legum.

Deac. R. Deacon's Reports.

Deac. & Chit. Deacon & Chitty's Reports.

Deb. on Jud. Debates on the Judiciary.

Dec. temp. H. & M. Decisions in Admiralty during the time of Hay & Marriott.

Deft. Defendant.

De Gex & Sm. R. De Gex & Smale's Reports.

Den. Cr. Cas. Denison's Crown Cases.

Den. Rep. Denio's New York Reports.

Desaus. R. Desaussure's Chancery Reports.

Dev. R. Devereux's Reports.

Dev. Ch. R. Devereux's Chancery Reports.

Dev. & Bat. Devereux & Battle's Reports.
Di. or *Dy.* Dyer's Reports.
Dial. de Scac. Dialogus de Scaccario
Dick. Just. Dickinson's Justice.
Dick. Pr. Dickinson's Practice of the Quarter and other Sessions.
Dick. Dicken's Reports.
Dict. Dictionary.
Dict. Dr. Can. Dictionnaire de Droit Canonique.
Dict. de Jur. Dictionnaire de Jurisprudence.
Dig. Digest of writs. *Dig.* The Pandects or Digest of the Civil Law, cited Dig. 1, 2, 5, 6, for Digest, book 1, tit. 2, law 5, section 6.
Disn. on Gam. Disney's Law of Gaming.
Doct. & Stud. Doctor and Student.
Doct. Pl. Doctrina Placitandi
Doder. Eng. Law. Doderidge's English Lawyer.
Dods. R. Dodson's Reports.
Dom. Domat, Lois Civilles
Dom. Proc. Domo Procerum. In the House of Lords.
Domat. Lois Civilles dans leur ordre naturel. Par M. Domat.
Dougl. Douglas' Reports.
Doug. El. Cas. Douglas' Election Cases.
Dougl. (Mich.) R. Douglas' Michigan Reports.
Dow. or *Dow. P. C.* Dow's Parliamentary Cases.
Dow & Clarke. Dow and Clarke's Reports of Cases in the House of Lords.
Dowl. P. C. Dowling's Practical Cases.
Dow. & R. N. P. Dowling and Ryan's Nisi Prius Cases.
Dow. & Ry. M. C. Dowling & Ryan's Cases for Magistrates.
Dowl. & Ry. Dowling and Ryland's Reports.
Dr. & St. Doctor and Student.
Drew. on Inj. Drewry on Injunctions.
Dru. & Wal. Drury and Walsh's Reports.
Dru & War. Drury & Warren's Reports.
Dub. Dubitatur.
Dudl. R. Dudley's Law and Equity Reports.
Dug. S. or *Dugd. Sum.* Dugdale's Summons.
Dugd. Orig. Dugdale's Origines.
Dug. Sum. Dugdale's Summonses.
Duke. or *Duke's Ch. Uses.* Duke's Law of Charitable Uses.
Dunl. Pr. Dunlap's Practice.
Dunl. Admr. Pr. Dunlap's Admiralty Practice.
Duponc. on Jur. Duponceau on Jurisdictions.
Duponc. Const. Duponceau on the Constitution.
Dur. Dr. Fr. Duranton, Droit Français.
Durnf. & East. Durnford & East's Reports, also cited D. & E. or T. R.
Duv. Dr. Civ. Fr. Duvergier, Droit Civil Français. This is a continuation of Touiller's Droit Civil Français. The *first* volume of Duvergier is the *sixteenth* volume of the continuation. The work is sometimes cited 16 Toull. or 16 Toullier, instead of being cited 1 Duv. or 1 Duvergier, etc.
Dwar. on Stat. Dwarris on Statutes.
Dy. Dyer's Reports.
E. Easter Term.
E. Edward; as 9 E. 3, c. 9.
E. of Cov. Earl of Coventry's Case.
E. C. L. R. English Common Law Reports, sometimes cited Eng. Com Law Rep. (q. v.)
E. g., usually written *e. g.*, exempli gratia; for the sake of an instance or example.
E. P. C. or *East, P. C.* East's Pleas of the Crown.
East, P. C. East's Pleas of the Crown.
Eccl. Ecclesiastical.
Eccl. Law. Ecclesiastical Law.
Eccl. Rep. Ecclesiastical Reports. Vide *Eng Eccl. Rep.*
Ed. or *Edit.* Edition.
Ed. Edward; as, 3 Ed. 1, c. 9.
Ed. Inj. Eden on Injunction.
Ed. Eq. Reps. Eden's Equity Reports.
Ed. Prin. Pen. Law. Eden's Principles of Penal Law.
Edm. Exch. Pr. Edmund's Exchequer Practice.
Edw. Ad. Rep. Edward's Admiralty Reports.
Edw. Lead. Dec. Edward's Leading Decisions.
Edw. on Part. Edwards on Parties to Bills in Chancery.
Edw. on Rec. Edwards on Receivers in Chancery.
Eliz. Elizabeth; as, 13 Eliz. c. 15.
Ellis on D. and Cr. Ellis on the Law relating to Debtor and Creditor.
Elm. on Dil. Elmes on Ecclesiastical and Civil Dilapidations
Elsyn. on Parl. Elsynge on Parliaments.
Encycl. Encyclopædia, or Encyclopédie.
Eng. English.
Eng. Ch. R. English Chancery Reports. Vide *Cond. Ch. R.* (See App. A.)
Eng. Com. Law. Rep. English Common Law Reports.
Eng. Ecc. R. English Ecclesiastical Reports.
Eng. Plead. English Pleader.
Engl. Rep. English's Arkansas Reports.
Eod. Eodem, under the same title.
Eod. tit. In the same title.
Eq. Ca. Ab. Equity Cases Abridged.
Eq. Draft. Equity Draftsman.
Ersk. Inst. Erskine's Institute of the Law of Scotland. *Ersk. Prin. of Laws of Scotl.* Erskine's Principles of the Laws of Scotland
Esp. N. P. Espinasse's Nisi Prius.
Esp. N. P. R. Espinasse's Nisi Prius Reports
Esp. on Ev. Espinasse on Evidence.
Esp. on Pen. Ev. Espinasse on Penal Evidence.
Esq. Esquire.
Et. al. Et alii, and others.
Eunom. Eunomus.
Ev. Col. Stat. Evans' Collection of Statutes
Ev. on Pl. Evans on Pleading.
Ev. Tr. Evans' Trial.
Ex. or *Exor.* Executor. *Execx.* Executrix.
Exch. Rep. Exchequer Reports. Vide Cond. Exch. Rep.
Exec. Execution.
Exp. Expired.
Exton's Mar. Dicæo. Exton's Maritime Dicæologie.
Extrav. Extravagants.
F. Finalis, the last or latter part.
F. Fitzherbert's Abridgment.
F. & F. Falconer & Fitzherbert's Reports.
F. R. Forum Romanum.
F. & S. Fox & Smith's Reports.
F. N. B. Fitzherbert's Natura Brevium.
Fairf. R. Fairfield's Reports.
Fac. Coll. Faculty Collection; the name of a set of Scotch Reports.

Falc. & Fitzh. Falconer & Fitzherbert's Election Cases.

Far. Farresly, (7 Mod. Rep.) is sometimes so cited.

Farr's Med. Jur. Farr's Elements of Medical Jurisprudence.

Fearn. on Rem. Fearne on Remainders.

Fell. on Mer. Guar. Fell on Mercantile Guaranties.

Ferg. on M. & D. Fergusson on Marriage and Divorce.

Ferg Rep. Div. Fergusson's Reports in Actions of Divorce.

Ferg. R. Fergusson's Reports of the Consistorial Court of Scotland.

Ff. or *ff.* Pandects of Justinian: this is a careless way of writing the Greek π.

Ferr. Hist. Civ. L. Ferriere's History of the Civil Law.

Ferr. Mod. Ferrière Moderne, ou Nouveau Dictionnaire des Termes de Droit et de Pratique.

Fess. on Pat. Fessenden on Patents.

Fi. fa. Fieri Facias.

Field's Com. Law. Field on the Common Law of England.

Field. on Pen. Laws. Fielding on Penal Laws.

Finch. Finch's Law; or a Discourse thereof, in five books. *Finch's Pr.* Finch's Precedents in Chancery.

Finl. L. C. Finlayson's Leading Cases on Pleading.

Fish. Copyh. Fisher on Copyholds.

Fitz. C. Fitzgibbon's Cases.

Fitzh. Fitzherbert's Abridgment. *Fitzh. Nat. Bre.* Fitzherbert's Natura Brevium.

Fl. or *Fleta.* A Commentary on the English Law, written by an anonymous author, in the time of Edward I., while a prisoner in the Fleet.

Fletch. on Trusts. Fletcher on the Estates of Trustees.

Floy. Proct. Pr. Floyer's Proctor's Practice.

Fol. Foley's Poor Laws.

Fol. Folio.

Fonb. Fonblanque on Equity. *Fonb. Med. Jur.* Fonblanque on Medical Jurisprudence.

Forr. Forrester's Cases during the time of Lord Talbot, commonly cited Cas. Temp. Talb.

For. Pla. Brown's Formulæ Placitandi.

Forb. on Bills. Forbes' on Bills of Exchange.

Forb. Inst. Forbes' Institute of the Law of Scotland.

Forr. Exch. Rep. Forrest's Exchequer Reports.

Fors. on Comp. Forsyth on the Law relating to Composition with Creditors.

Fortesc. Fortescue, De Laudibus Legum Angliæ. *Fortesc. R.* Fortescue's Reports, temp. Wm. and Anne.

Fost. or *Fost. C. L.* Foster's Crown Law.

Fox. & Sm. Fox & Smith's Reports.

Fr. Fragmentum.

Fra. or *Fra. Max.* Francis' Maxims.

Fr. Ord. French Ordinance. Sometimes cited *Ord. de la Mar.*

Fras. Elect. Cas. Fraser's Election Cases.

Fred. Co. Frederician Code.

Freem. Freeman's Reports. *Freem. C. C.* Freeman's Cases in Chancery.

Freem. (Miss.) R. Freeman's Reports of Cases decided by the Superior Court of Chancery of Mississippi.

G. George; as, 13 G. 1, c. 29.

G. & J. Glyn & Jameson's Reports.

G. & J. Gill & Johnson's Reports.

G. M. Dudl. Rep. G. M. Dudley's Reports.

Gale & Dav. Gale & Davidson's Reports.

Gale's Stat. Gale's Statutes of Illinois.

Gall. or *Gall. Rep.* Gallison's Reports.

Garde on Ev. Garde's Practical Treatise on the General Principles and Elementary Rules of the Law of Evidence.

Geo. George; as, 13 Geo. 1, c. 29.

Geo. Dec. Georgia Decisions.

Geo. Lib. George on the Offence of Libel.

Gib. on D. & N. Gibbons on the Law of Dilapidations and Nuisances.

Gibs. Codex. Gibson's Codex Juris Civilis.

Gilb. R. Gilbert's Reports. *Gilb. Ev.* Gilbert's Evidence, by Lofft. *Gilb. U. & T.* Gilbert on Uses and Trusts. *Gilb. Ten.* Gilbert on Tenures. *Gilb. on Rents.* Gilbert on Rents. *Gilb. on Rep.* Gilbert on Replevin. *Gilb. Ex.* Gilbert on Executions. *Gilb. Exch.* Gilbert's Exchequer. *Gilb. For. Rom.* Gilbert's Forum Romanum. *Gilb. K. B* Gilbert's King's Bench. *Gilb. Rem* Gilbert on Remainders. *Gilb. on Dev.* Gilbert on Devises. *Gilb. Lex. Præt.* Gilbert's Lex Prætoria.

Gill & John. Gill & Johnson's Reports.

Gill's R. Gill's Reports.

Gilm. R. Gilmer's Reports.

Gilp. R. Gilpin's Circuit Court Reports.

Gl. Glossa, the Gloss.

Glanv. Glanville's Treatise of the Laws and Customs of England.

Glassf. Ev. Glassford on Evidence.

Glov. Mun. Corp. Glover on Municipal Corporations, or *Glov. on Corp.* Glover on the Law of Municipal Corporations.

Glyn & Jam. Glyn & Jameson's Reports of Cases in Bankruptcy.

Godb. Godbolt's Reports.

Godolph. Ad. Jur. Godolphin's View of the Admiralty Jurisdiction.

Godolph. Rep. Can. Godolphin's Repertorium Canonicum.

Godolph. Godolphin's Orphan's Legacy.

Gods. on Pat. Godson's Treatise on the Law of Patents.

Goldesb. Goldesborough's Reports.

Golds. Goldsborough's Reports.

Gord. Dig. Gordon's Digest of the Laws of the United States.

Gord. on Dec. Gordon on the Law of Decedente in Pennsylvania.

Gould on Pl. Gould on the Principles of Pleading in Civil Actions.

Gow on Part. Gow on Partnership.

Grah. Pr. Graham's Practice. *Grah. N. T.* Graham on New Trials.

Grand. Cout. Grand Coutumier de Normandie, (q. v.)

Grady on Fixt. Grady on the Law of Fixtures.

Grant on New. Tr. Grant on New Trials.

Grant's Ch. Pr. Grant's Chancery Practice.

Gratt. R. Grattan's Virginia Reports.

Green's B. L. Green's Bankrupt Laws.

Green's R. Green's Reports.

Greenl on Ev. Greenleaf's Treatise on the Law of Evidence.

Greenl. Ov. Cas. Greenleaf's Overruled Cases

Greenl. R. Greenleaf's Reports.

Greenw. on Courts. Greenwood on Courts.

Gres. Eq. Ev. Gresley's Equity Evidence.

Griff. Reg. Griffith's Law Register.
Grimk. on Ex. Grimkè on the Duty of Executors and Administrators.
Grisw. Rep. Griswold's Reports.
Grot. Grotius de Jure Belli.
Gude's Pr. Gude's Practice on the Crown side of King's Bench, &c.
Gwill. Gwillim's Tithe Cases
H. Henry; as, 19 H. 7, c. 15.
H. Hilary Term.
H. A. Hoc anno.
H. v. commonly written in small letters *h. v.* hoc verbo.
H. of L. House of Lords.
H. of R. House of Representatives.
H. & B. Hudson & Brooke's Reports.
H. & G. Harris & Gill's Reports.
H. & J. Harris & Johnson's Reports.
H. Bl. Henry Blackstone's Reports.
H. H. C. L. Hale's History of the Common Law.
H. & M. Henning & Munford's Reports.
H. & M'H. or *Harr. & M'Hen.* Harris & M'Henry's Reports.
Hab. fa. seis. Habere facias seisinam.
H. P. C. Hale's Pleas of the Crown.
H. t. usually put in small letters, *h. t.* hoc titulo.
Hab. Corp. Habeas Corpus.
Hab. fa. pos. Habere facias possessionem.
Hagg. Ad. R. Haggard's Admiralty Reports.
Hagg. Eccl. R. Haggard's Ecclesiastical Reports.
Hagg. C. R. Haggard's Reports in the Consistory Court of London.
Hale, P. C. Hale's Pleas of the Crown.
Hale's Sum. Hale's Summary of Pleas.
Hale's Jur. H. L. Hale's Jurisdiction of the House of Lords.
Hale's Hist. C. L. Hale's History of the Common Law.
Halif. Civ. Law. Halifax's Analysis of the Civil Law.
Hall's R. Hall's Reports of Cases decided in the Superior Court of the city of New York.
Halk. Dig. Halkerton's Digest of the Law of Scotland relating to Marriage.
Hall's Adm. Pr. Hall's Admiralty Practice.
Halst. R. Halstead's Reports.
Hamm. N. P. Hammond's Nisi Prius.
Ham. R. Hammond's (Ohio) Reports.
Hamm. on Part. Hammond on Parties to Actions.
Hamm. Pl. Hammond's Analysis of the Principles of Pleading.
Hamm. on F. I. Hammond on Fire Insurance.
Han. Hansard's Entries.
Hand's Ch. Pr. Hand's Chancery Practice.
Hand on Fines. Hand on Fines and Recoveries.
Hand's Cr. Pr. Hand's Crown Practice.
Hand on Pat. Hand on Patents.
Hans. Parl. Deb. Hansard's Parliamentary Debates.
Hard. Hardress' Reports.
Hardin's R. Hardin's Reports.
Hare R. Hare's Reports.
Hare & Wall. Sel. Dec. Hare & Wallace's Select Decisions of American Cases, with Notes.
Hare on Disc. Hare on the Discovery of Evidence by Bill and Answer in Equity.
Harg. Coll. Hargrave's Juridical Arguments and Collection.
Harg. St. Tr. Hargrave's State Trials.
Harg. Exer. Hargrave's Exercitations.
Harg. Law Tr. Hargrave's Law Tracts.
Harp. L. R. Harper's Law Reports.
Harp. Eq. R. Harper's Equity Reports.
Harr. Ch. Harrison's Chancery Practice.
Harr. Cond. Lo. R. Harrison's Condensed Reports of Cases in the Superior Court of the Territory of Orleans, and in the Supreme Court of Louisiana.
Harr. Dig. Harrison's Digest.
Harr. Ent. Harris' Entries.
Harr. (Mich.) R. Harrington's Reports of Cases in the Supreme Court of Michigan.
Harr. & Gill. Harris & Gill's Reports.
Harr. & John. Harris & Johnson's Reports.
Harr. & M'H. Harris & M'Henry's Reports.
Harringt. R. Harrington's Reports.
Hasl. Med. Jur. Haslam's Medical Jurisprudence.
Hawk. P. C. Hawkins' Pleas of the Crown.
Hawk's R. Hawk's Reports.
Hay on Est. An Elementary View of the Common Law of Uses, Devises, and Trusts, with reference to the Creation and Conveyance of Estates. By William Hayes.
Hay. on Lim. Hayes on Limitations.
Hay. Exch. R. Hayes' Exchequer Reports.
Hays on R. P. Hays on Real Property.
Heath's Max. Heath's Maxims.
Hein. Elem. Juris. Civ. Heineccii, Elementa juris Civilis, secundum ordinem Institutionum.
Hein. Elem. Juris. Nat. Heineccii, Elementa juris Naturæ et gentium.
Hen. on For. Law. Henry on Foreign Law.
Hen. J. P. Henning's Virginia Justice of the Peace.
Hen. & Munf. Henning & Munford's Reports.
Herne's Ch. Uses. Herne's Law of Charitable Uses.
Herne's Plead. Herne's Pleader
Het. Hetley's Reports.
Heyw. on El. Heywood on Elections.
Heyw. (N. C.) R. Heywood's North Carolina Reports.
Heyw. (Tenn.) R. Heywood's Tennessee Reports.
High. Highmore. *High on Bail.* Highmore on Bail. *High. on Lun.* Highmore on Lunacy.
High. on Mortm. Highmore on Mortmain.
Hill. Ab. Hilliard's Abridgment of the Law of Real Property.
Hill's R. Hill's Reports.
Hill's Ch. R. Hill's Chancery Reports.
Hill on Trust. A Practical Treatise on the Law relating to Trustees, &c.
Hind's Pr. Hind's Practice
Hob. Hobart's Reports.
Hodg. R. Hodge's Reports.
Hodges on Railw. Hodges on the Law of Railways.
Hoffm. Outl. Hoffman's Outlines of Legal Studies. *Hoffm. Leg. St.* Hoffman's Legal Studies.
Hoffm. Ch. Pr. Hoffman's Chancery Practice.
Hoffm. Mas. Ch. Hoffman's Master in Chancery.
Hoffm. R. Hoffman's Reports.
Hog. R. Hogan's Reports.
Hog. St. Tr. Hogan's State Trials.
Holt on Lib. Holt on the Law of Libels.
Holt on Nav. Holt on Navigation.
Holt. R. Holt's Reports.
Holt on Sh. Holt on the Law of Shipping.

Hopk. R. Hopkins' Chancery Reports.

Hopk. Adm. Dec. Hopkinson's Admiralty Decisions.

Houard's Ang. Sax. Laws. Houard's Anglo Saxon Laws and Ancient Laws of the French.

Houard's Dict. Houard's Dictionary of the Customs of Normandy.

Hough C. M. Hough on Courts Martial.

Hov. Fr. Hovenden on Frauds.

Hov. Supp. Hovenden's Supplement to Vesey Junior's Reports.

How. St. Tr. Howell's State Trials.

Howe's Pr. Howe's Practice in Civil Actions and Proceedings at Law in Massachusetts.

How. Pr. R. Howard's Practice Reports.

Hub. on Suc. Hubback on Successions.

Huds. & Bro. Hudson & Brooke's Reports.

Hugh. Ab. Hughes' Abridgment.

Hugh. Entr. Hughes' Entries.

Hugh. on Wills. Hughes on Wills.

Hugh. R. Hughes' Reports.

Hugh. Or. Writs. Hughes' Comments upon Original Writs.

Hugh. Ins. Hughes on Insurance.

Hugh. on Wills. Hughes' Practical Directions for Taking Instructions for Drawing Wills.

Hull. on Costs. Hullock on the Law of Costs.

Hult. on Conv. Hulton on Convictions.

Humph. R. Humphrey's Reports.

Hume's Com. Hume's Commentaries on the Criminal Law of Scotland.

Hut. Hutton's Reports.

I. The Institutes of Justinian (q. v.) are sometimes cited, l. 1, 3, 4.

I. Infra, beneath or below.

Ib. Ibidem.

Ictus. Jurisconsultus. This abbreviation is usually written with an *I*, though it would be more proper to write it with a J, the first letter of the word Jurisconsultus; *c* is the initial letter of the third syllable, and *tus* is the end of the word.

Id. Idem.

Il Cons. del Mar. Il Consolato del Mare. See *Consolato del Mare*, in the body of the work.

Imp. Pr. C. P. Impey's Practice in the Common Pleas. *Imp. Pr. K. B.* Impey's Practice in the King's Bench. *Imp. Pl.* Impey's Modern Pleader. *Imp. Sh.* Impey's Office of Sheriff.

In f. In fine, at the end of the title, law or paragraph quoted.

In pr. In principio, in the beginning and before the first paragraph of a law.

In princ. In principio. In the beginning.

In sum. In summa, in the summary.

Ind. Index.

Inf. Infra, beneath or below.

Ing. Dig. Ingersoll's Digest of the Laws of the United States.

Ing. Roc. Ingersoll's Roccus.

Ingr. on Insolv. Ingraham on Insolvency.

Inj. Injunction.

Ins. Insurance.

Inst. Coke on Littleton, is cited Co. Lit. or 1 Inst., for First Institute. Coke's Magna Charta, is cited Co. M. C. or 2 Inst., for Second Institute. Co. P. C. Coke's Pleas of the Crown, is cited 3 Inst., for Third Institute. Co. on Courts. Coke on Courts, is cited 4 Inst., for Fourth Institute.

Inst. Institutes. When the Institutes of Justinian are cited, the citation is made thus; Inst. 4, 2, 1; or Inst. lib. 4, tit. 2, l. 1; to signify Institutes, book 4, tit. 2, law 1. Coke's Institutes are cited, the first, either Co. Lit. or 1 Inst., and the others 2 Inst., 3 Inst. and 4 Inst.

Inst. Cl. or *Inst. Cler.* Instructor Clericalis.

Inst. Jur. Angl. Institutiones Juris Anglicani, by Doctor Cowell.

Introd. Introduction.

Ir. Eq. R. Irish Equity Reports.

Ir. T. R. Irish Term Reports. Sometimes cited *Ridg. Irish. T. R.* (q. v.)

J. Justice.

J. Institutes of Justinian.

J. C. Juris Consultus.

J. C. P. Justice of the Common Pleas.

J. Glo. Juncta Glossa, the Gloss joined to the text quoted.

JJ. Justices.

J. J. Marsh. J. J. Marshall's (Kentucky) Reports.

J. K. B. Justice of the King's Bench.

J. P. Justice of the Peace.

J. Q. B. Justice of the Queen's Bench.

J. U. B. Justice of the Upper Bench. During the Commonwealth the English Court of the King's Bench was called Upper Bench.

Jac. Jacobus, James; as, 4 Jac. 1, c. 1.

Jac. Introd. Jacob's Introduction to the Common, Civil, and Canon Law.

Jac. L. D. Jacob's Law Dictionary.

Jac. L. G. Jacob's Law Grammar.

Jac. Lex. Mer. Jacob's Lex Mercatoria, or the Merchant's Companion.

Jac. R. Jacob's Chancery Reports.

Jac. & Walk. Jacob & Walker's Chancery Reports.

Jack. Pl. Jackson on Pleading.

Jarm. on Wills. Jarman on the Law of Wills.

Jarm. Pow. Dev. Powell on Devises, with Notes by Jarman.

Jebb's Ir. Cr. Cas. Jebb's Irish Criminal Cases.

Jeff. Man. Jefferson's Manual.

Jeff. R. Thomas Jefferson's Reports.

Jenk. Jenkins' Eight Centuries of Reports; or Eight Hundred Cases solemnly adjudged in the Exchequer Chamber, or upon Writs of Error, from K. Henry III. to 21 K. James I.

Jer. Jeremy. *Jer. on Carr.* Jeremy's Law of Carriers. *Jer. Eq. Jur.* Jeremy on the Equity Jurisdiction of the High Court of Chancery.

Jer. on Cor. Jervis on Coroners.

John. Cas. Johnson's Cases.

John. R. Johnson's Reports.

John. Ch. R. Johnson's Chancery Reports.

John. Eccl. Law. Johnson's Ecclesiastical Law.

Johns. Civ. L. of Sp. Johnson's Civil Law of Spain.

Johns. on Bills. The Law of Bills of Exchange, Promissory Notes, Checks, &c. By Cuthbert W. Johnson.

Jon. Sir Wm. Jones' Reports.

Jon. & Car. Jones & Carey's Reports.

Jon. on Lib. Jones, De Libellis Famosis, or the Law of Libels.

Jon. Inst. Hind. L. Jones' Institutes of Hindoo Laws.

Jon. (1) Sir W. Jones' Reports.

Jon. (2) Sir T. Jones' Reports.

Jon. T. Thomas Jones' Reports.

Jon. on Bailm. Jones' Law of Bailments.

Jones' Intr. Jones' Introduction to Legal Science.

Joy on Ev. Acc. Joy on the Evidence of Accomplices.
Joy on Chal. Joy on Challenge to Jurors.
Joy Leg. Ed. Joy on Legal Education.
Jud. Chr. Judicial Chronicle.
Jud. Repos. Judicial Repository
Judg. Judgments.
Jur. Eccl. Jura Ecclesiastica, or a Treatise of the Ecclesiastical Law and Courts, interspersed with various cases of Law and Equity.
Jur. Mar. Molloy's Jure Maritimo. Sometimes cited *Molloy*.
Jus. Nav. Rhod. Jus Navale Rhodiorum.
Just. Inst. Justinian's Institutes.
K. B. King's Bench.
K. C. R. Reports in the time of Chancellor King.
K & O. Knapp & Omber's Election Cases.
Kames on Eq. Kames' Principles of Equity.
Kames' Ess. Kames' Essays.
Kames' Hist. L. T. Kames' Historical Law Tracts.
Keat. Fam. Settl. Keating on Family Settlements.
Keb. Keble's Reports.
Keb. Stat. Keble's English Statutes.
Keen's R. Keen's Reports.
Keil or *Keilw.* Keilway's Reports.
Kel. Sir John Kelyng's Reports. *Kel.* 1, 2, or *W. Kel.* William Kelyng's Reports, two parts.
Kelh. Norm L D. Kelham's Norman French Law Dictionary.
Kell. R. Kelly's Reports.
Ken. on Jur. Kennedy on Juries.
Kent, Com. Kent's Commentaries on American Law.
Keny. Kenyon's Reports of the Court of King's Bench.
Kit. or *Kitch.* Kitchen on Courts.
Kna. & Omb. Knapp & Omber's Election Cases.
Knapp's A. C. Knapp's Appeal Cases.
Knapp's R. Knapp's Privy Council Reports.
Kyd on Aw. Kyd on the Law of Awards.
Kyd on Bills. Kyd on the Law relating to Bills of Exchange.
Kyd on Corp. Kyd on the Law of Corporations.
L, in citation means *law*, as L. 1, 33. Furtum, ff de Furtis, i. e. law 1, section or paragraph beginning with the word Furtum; ff, signifies the Digest, and the words *de Furtis* denote the title. L. signifies also liber, book.
L. & G. Lloyd & Goold's Reports.
L. & W. Lloyd & Welsby's Mercantile Cases.
LL. Laws, as LL. Gul. 1, c. 42. Laws of William I. chapter 42; LL. of U. S., Laws of the United States.
L. S. Locus sigili.
L. R. Louisiana Reports.
La. Lane's Reports.
Lalaure, des Ser. Traité des Servitudes réelles, par M. Lalaure.
Lamb. Archai. Lambard's Archaionomia.
Lamb. Eiren. Lambard's Eirenarcha.
Lamb. on Dow. Lambert on Dower.
Lat. Latch's Reports.
Laus. on. Eq. Laussat's Essay on Equity Practice in Pennsylvania.
Law. on Chart. Part. Lawes on the Law of Charter Parties.
Law. Lib. Law Library.
Law Rep. Law Reporter.
Laws Eccl. Law. Laws' Ecclesiastical Law.
Law Intel. Law Intelligencer.
Law Fr. & Latin Dict. Law French and Latin Dictionary.
Law. Pl. Lawes' Elementary Treatise on Pleading in Civil Actions.
Law. Pl. in Ass. Lawes' Treatise on Pleading in Assumpsit.
Laws of Wom. Laws of Women.
Lawy. Mag. Lawyer's Magazine.
Le. Ley's Reports.
Leach. Leach's Cases in Crown Law.
Leç. Elm. Leçons Elèmentaire du Droit Civil Romain.
Lee Abst. Tit. Lee on the Evidence of Abstracts of Title to Real Property.
Lee on Capt. Lee's Treatise of Captures in War.
Lee's Dict. Lee's Dictionary of Practice.
Lee's Eccl. R. Lee's Ecclesiastical Reports.
Leg. Bibl. Legal Bibliography, by J. G. Marvin.
Leg. Legibus.
Leg. Obs. Legal Observer.
Leg. Oler. The Laws of Oleron.
Leg. on Outl. Legge on Outlawry.
Leg. Rhod. The Laws of Rhodes.
Leg. ult. The Last Law.
Leg. Wisb. Laws of Wisbury.
Leigh & Dal. on Conv. Leigh & Dalzell on Conversion of Property.
Leigh's R. Leigh's Reports.
Leigh's N. P. Leigh's Nisi Prius.
Leo. or *Leon.* Leonard's Reports.
Lev. Levinz's Reports.
Lev. Ent. Levinz's Entries
Lew. C. C. Lewin's Crown Cases.
Lew. Cr. Law. An Abridgment of the Criminal Law of the United States, by Ellis Lewis.
Lew. on Tr. Lewin on Trusts.
Lew. on Perp. Lewis on the Law of Perpetuities.
Lex Man. Lex Maneriorum.
Lex Mer. Lex Mercatoria. *Lex. Mer. Am.* Lex Mercatoria Americana.
Lex Parl. Lex Parliamentaria.
Ley. Ley's Reports.
Lib. Liber, book.
Libb. Ass. Liber Assisarum.
Lib. Ent. Old Book of Entries.
Lib. Feud. Liber Feudorum.
Lib. Intr. Liber Intrationum; or Old Book of Entries.
Lib. Nig. Liber Niger.
Lib. Pl. Liber Placitandi.
Lib. Reg. Register Books.
Lib. Rub. Liber Ruber.
Lib. Ten. Liberum Tenementum.
Lid. Jud. Adv. Liddel's Detail of the Duties of a Deputy Judge Advocate.
Lill. Entr. Lilly's Entries. *Lill. Reg.* Lilly's Register.
Lill. Rep. Lilly's Reports.
Lill. Conv. Lilly's Conveyancer.
Lind. Lindewoode's Provinciale; or Provincial Constitutions of England, with the Legantine Constitutions of Otho and Othobond.
Litt. s. Littleton, section.
Litt. R. Littell's Reports. *Litt. R.* Littleton's Reports.
Litt. Sel. Cas. Littell's Select Cases.

Litt. Ten. Littleton's Tenures.
Liv. Livre, book.
Liv. on Ag. Livermore on the Law of Principal and Agent.
Liv. Syst. Livingston's System of Penal Law for the State of Louisiana. This work is sometimes cited Livingston's Report on the Plan of a Penal Code.
Liverm. Diss. Livermore's Dissertations on the Contrariety of Laws.
Llo. & Go. Lloyd & Goold's Reports.
Llo. & Go. t. Sudg. Lloyd & Goold's Reports, during the time of Sugden.
Llo. & Go. t. Plunk. Lloyd & Goold during the time of Plunkett.
Llo. & Welsb. Lloyd & Welsby's Reports of Cases relating to Commerce, Manufactures, &c., determined in the Courts of Common Law.
Loc. cit. Loco citato, the place cited.
Log. Comp. Compendium of the Law of England, Scotland, and Ancient Rome. By James Logan.
Lofft. Lofft's Reports.
Lois des Batim. Lois des Batimens.
Lom. Dig. Lomax's Digest of the Law of Real Property in the United States.
Lom. Ex. Lomax on Executors.
Long. Quint. Year Book, part 10. Vide *Year Book.*
Louis. Code. Civil Code of Louisiana.
Louis. R. Louisiana Reports.
Lovel. on Wills. Lovelass on Wills.
Lown. Leg. Lowndes on the Law of Legacies.
Lubé, Pl. Eq. An Analysis of the Principles of Equity Pleading. By D. G. Lubé.
Luder's Elec Cas. Luder's Election Cases.
Luml. Ann. Lumley on Annuities.
Luml. Parl. Pr. Lumley's Parliamentary Practice.
Luml. on Settl. Lumley on Settlements and Removal.
Lut. Ent. Lutwyche's Entries.
Lutw. Lutwyche's Reports.
M. Michaelmas Term.
M. Maxim, or Maxims.
M. Mary; as 4 M. st. 3, c. 1.
M. & A. Montagu & Ayrton's Reports of Cases of Bankruptcy.
M. & B. Montagu and Bligh's Cases in Bankruptcy.
M. & C. Mylne & Craig's Reports.
M. & C. Montagu & Chitty's Reports.
M. & G Manning & Granger's Reports.
M. & G. Maddock & Geldart's Reports.
M. G. & S. Manning, Granger & Scott's Reports.
M. & K. Mylne & Keen's Chancery Reports.
M. & M. or Mo. & Malk. Rep. Moody & Malkin's Nisi Prius Reports.
M. P. Exch. Modern Practice Exchequer.
M. & P. Moore & Payne's Reports.
M. R. Master of the Rolls.
M. R. Martin's Reports of the Supreme Court of the State of Louisiana.
M. & R. Manning & Ryland's Reports.
M. & S. Moore & Scott's Reports.
M. & S. Maule & Selwyn's Reports.
M. & Y. or *Mart. & Yerg.* Martin & Yerger's Reports.
M. & W. Meeson & Welsby's Reports.
M. D. & G. Montagu, Deacon & Gex's Reports of Cases in Bankruptcy.
M'Arth. C. M. M'Arthur on Courts Martial.
M'Cl. & Yo. M'Clelland & Younge's Exchequer Reports.
M'Clel. E. R. M'Clelland's Exchequer Reports.
M'Cord's Ch. R. M'Cord's Chancery Reports.
M'Cord's R. M'Cord's Reports.
M'Kin. Phil. Ev. M'Kinnon's Philosophy of Evidence.
M'Naght. C. M. M'Naghton on Courts Martial.
McLean & Rob. McLean & Robinson's Reports.
M'Lean R. M'Lean's Reports.
Macn. on Null. Macnamara on Nullities and Irregularities in the Practice of the Law.
Macnal. Ev. Macnally's Rules of Evidence on Pleas of the Crown.
Macph. on Inf. Macpherson on Infants.
Macq. on H. & W. Macqueen on Husband and Wife.
Mad. Exch. Madox's History of the Exchequer.
Mad. Form. Madox's Formulare Anglicanum.
Madd. & Geld. Maddack & Geldart's Reports.
Madd., Madd. R. Maddock's Chancery Reports.
Madd. Pr. or *Madd. Ch.* Maddock's Chancery Practice.
Mag. Ins. Magens on Insurance.
Mal. Malyne's Lex Mercatoria.
Man. Manuscript.
Man. & Gra. Manning & Granger's Reports.
Man. Gr. & Sc. Manning, Granger & Scott's Reports.
Man. & Ry. Manning & Ryland's Reports.
Manb on Fines. Manby on Fines.
Mann. Comm. Manning's Commentaries of the Law of Nations.
Mann. Exch. Pr. Manning's Exchequer Practice.
Mans. on Dem. Mansel on Demurrers.
Mans. on Lim. Mansel on the Law of Limitations.
Manw. Manwood's Forest Laws.
Mar. Maritime.
Mar. N. C. March's New Cases. *Mar. R.* March's Reports.
Marg. Margin.
Marr. Adm. Dsc. Marriott's Admiralty Decisions.
Marr. Form. Inst. Marriott's Formulare Instrumentorum; or a Formulary of Authentic Instruments, Writs, and standing orders used in the Court of Admiralty of Great Britain, of Prize and Instance.
Marsh. Marshall's Reports in the Court of Common Pleas. *A. Marsh.* Marshall's (Kty.) Reports. *J. J Marsh.* J. J. Marshall's Reports.
Marsh. Ins. Marshall on the Law of Insurance.
Marsh. Decis. Brockenbrough's Reports of Chief Justice Marshall's Decisions.
Mart. Law Nat. Martin's Law of Nations.
Mart. (N. C.) R. Martin's North Carolina Reports.
Mart. (Lo.) R. Martin's Louisiana Reports.
Marv. Leg. Bibl. Marvin's Legal Bibliography.
Mart. & Yerg. Martin & Yerger's Reports.
Mart. N. S. Martin's Louisiana Reports, new series.

Mason R. Mason's Circuit Court Reports.
Mass. R. Massachusetts Reports.
Math. on Pres. Mathew on the Doctrine of Presumption and Presumptive Evidence.
Matth. on Port. Matthews on Portion.
Matth. on Ex. Matthews on Executors.
Maugh. Lit. Pr. Maughan on Literary Property.
Maule & Selw. Maule & Selwyn's Reports.
Max. Maxims.
Maxw. L. D. Maxwell's Dictionary of the Law of Bills of Exchange, &c.
Maxw. on Mar. L. Maxwell's Spirit of the Marine Laws.
Mayn. Maynard's Reports. See Year Books in the body of the work. The first part of the Y. B. is sometimes so cited.
Med. Jur. Medical Jurisprudence.
Mees. & Wels. Meeson & Welsby's Reports.
Meigs, R. Meigs' Tennessee Reports.
Mer. R. Merivale's Reports.
Merch. Dict. Merchant's Dictionary.
Merl. Quest. Merlin, Questions de Droit.
Merl. Répert. Merlin, Répertoire.
Merrif. Law of Att. Merrifield's Law of Attorneys.
Merrif. on Costs. Merrifield's Law of Costs.
Metc. R. Metcalf's Reports.
Metc. & Perk. Dig. Digest of the Decisions of the Courts of Common Law and Admiralty in the United States. By Theron Metcalf and Jonathan C. Perkins
Mich. Michaelmas.
Mich. Rev. St. Michigan Revised Statutes.
Miles' R. Miles' Reports.
Mill. Civ. Law. Miller's Civil Law.
Mill. Ins. Millar's Elements of the Law relating to Insurances. Sometimes this work is cited *Mill. El.*
Mill. on Eq. Mort. Miller on Equitable Mortgages.
Minor's Rep. Minor's Alabama Reports, sometimes cited *Ala. Rep.*
Mireh. on Adv. Mirehead on Advowsons.
Mirr. Mirroir des Justices.
Misso. R. Missouri Reports.
Mitf. Pl. Mitford's Pleadings in Equity. Also cited *Redesd. Pl.* Redesdale's Pleadings.
Mo. Sir Francis Moore's Reports in the reign of K. Henry VIII., Q. Elizabeth, and K. James.
Mo. & Malk. Moody & Malkin's Reports.
Mo. C. C. Moody's Crown Cases.
Mo. Cas. Moody's Nisi Prius and Crown Cases.
Mod. or *Mod. R.* Modern Reports.
Mod. Cas. Modern Cases.
Mod. C. L. & E. Modern Cases in Law and Equity. The 8 & 9 Modern Reports are sometimes so cited; the 8th cited as the 1st, and the 9th as the 2d.
Mod. Entr. Modern Entries.
Mod. Int. Modus Intrandi.
Mol. Molloy, De jure Maritimo.
Moll. R. Molloy's Chancery Reports.
Monr. R. Monroe's Reports.
Mont. & Ayrt. Montagu & Ayrton's Reports.
Mont. B. C. Montagu's Bankrupt Cases.
Mont. & Bligh. Montagu & Bligh's Cases in Bankruptcy.
Mont. & Chit. Montagu & Chitty's Reports.
Mont. on Comp. Montagu on the Law of Composition. *Mont. B. L.* Montagu on the Bankrupt Laws. *Mont. on Set-off.* Montagu on Set-off.
Mont. Deac. & Gex. Montagu, Deacon & Gex's Reports of Cases in Bankruptcy, argued and determined in the Court of Review, and on Appeals to the Lord Chancellor.
Mont. Dig. Montagu's Digest of Pleadings in Equity.
Mont. Eq. Pl. Montagu's Equity Pleading.
Mont. & Mac. Montagu & Macarthur's Reports.
Mont. Sp. of Laws. Montesquieu's Spirit of Laws.
Montesq. Montesquieu, Esprit des Lois.
Moo. & Malk. Moody & Malkin's Reports.
Moo. & Rob. Moody & Robinson's Reports.
Moore, R. J. B. Moore's Reports of Cases decided in the Court of Common Pleas.
Moore's A. C Moore's Appeal Cases.
Moore & Payne. Moore & Payne's Reports of Cases in C. P.
Moore & Scott. Moore & Scott's Reports of Cases in C P.
Mort. on Vend. Morton's Law of Vendors and Purchasers of Chattels Personal.
Mos. Mosely's Reports.
MSS. Manuscripts; as, Lord Colchester's MSS.
Much. D. & S. Muchall's Doctor and Student.
Mun. Municipal.
Munf. R. Munford's Reports.
Murph. R. Murphy's Reports.
My. & Keen. Mylne & Keen's Chancery Reports.
Myl. & Cr. Mylne & Craig's Reports.
N. Number. *N.* or *Nov.* Novellæ: the Novels.
N. A. Non allocatur.
N. B. Nulla bona.
N. Benl. New Benloe.
N. C. Cas. North Carolina Cases.
N. C. Law Rep. North Carolina Law Repository.
N. C. Term R. North Carolina Term Reports. This volume is sometimes cited 2 *Tayl.*
N. Chipm. R. N. Chipman's Reports.
N. E. I. Non est Inventus.
N. H. Rep. New Hampshire Reports.
N. H. & G. Nicholl, Hare & Garrow's Reports.
N. L. Nelson's edition of Lutwyche's Reports
N. L. Non liquet. Vide *Ampliation.*
N. & M. Neville & Manning's Reports.
N. & P. Neville & Perry's Reports.
N. P. Nisi Prius.
N. & M'C. Nott & M'Cord's Reports.
N. R. or *New R.* New Reports; the new series, or 4 & 5 Bos. & Pull. Reports, are usually cited N. R.
N. S. New Series of the Reports of the Supreme Court of Louisiana.
N Y. R. S. New York Revised Statutes.
Nar. Conv. Nares on Convictions.
Neal's F. & F. Neal's Feasts and Fasts; an Essay on the Rise, Progress and Present State of the Laws relating to Sundays and other Holidays, and other days of Fasting.
Nels. Ab. Nelson's Abridgment.
Nels. Lex Maner. Nelson's Lex Maneriorum.
Nels. R. Nelson's Reports.
Nem. con. Nemine contradicente, (q. v.)

Nem. dis. Nemine dissentiente.
Nev. & Mann. Neville & Manning's Reports.
Nev. & Per. Neville & Perry's Reports.
New Benl. Benloe's Reports. Reports in the Reign of Henry VIII., Edw. VI., Phil. and Mary, and Elizabeth, and other Cases in the times of Charles. By William Benloe. See *Benl.*
New Rep. New Reports. A continuation of Bosanquet & Puller's Reports. See B. & P.
Newf. Rep. Newfoundland Reports.
Newl. Contr. Newland's Treatise on Contracts.
Newl. Ch. Pr. Newland's Chancery Practice.
Newn. Conv. Newnam on Conveyancing.
Ni. Pri. Nisi Prius.
Nich. Adult. Bast. Nicholas on Adulterine Bastardy.
Nich. Har. & Gar. Nicholl, Hare & Garrow's Reports.
Nient cul. Nient culpable, old French, not guilty.
Nol. P. L. Nolan's Poor Laws.
Nol. R. Nolan's Reports of Cases relative to the Duty and Office of Justice of the Peace.
Non Cul. Non culpabilis, not guilty.
North. Northington's Reports.
Nott & M'Cord. Nott & M'Cord's Reports.
Nov. Novellæ, the Novels.
Nov. Rec. Novisimi Recopilacion de las Leyes de España.
Noy's Max. Noy's Maxims. *Noy's R.* Noy's Reports.
O. Benl. Old Benloe.
O. Bridg. Orlando Bridgman's Reports.
O. C. Old Code: so is denominated the Civil Code of Louisiana, 1808.
O. N. B. Old Natura Brevium. Vide *Vet. N. B.*, in the abbreviations, and *Old Natura Brevium*, in the body of the work.
O. Ni. These letters, which are an abbreviation for *oneratur nisi habent sufficientem exonerationem*, are, according to the practice of the English Exchequer, marked upon each head of a Sheriff's account for issues, amerciaments and mean profits. 4 Inst. 116.
Oblig. Obligations.
Observ. Observations.
Off. Office. *Off. Br.* Officina Brevium.
Off. Ex. Wentworth's Office of Executors.
Ohio R. Ohio Reports.
Oldn. Oldnall's Welsh Practice.
Onsl. N. P. Onslow's Nisi Prius.
Ord. Amst. Ordinance of Amsterdam.
Ord. Antw. Ordinance of Antwerp.
Ord. Bilb. Ordinance of Bilboa.
Ord. Ch. Orders in Chancery.
Ord. Cla. Lord Clarendon's Orders
Ord. Copenh. Ordinance of Copenhagen.
Ord. Cor. Orders of Court.
Ord. Flor. Ordinances of Florence.
Ord. Gen. Ordinance of Genoa.
Ord. Hamb. Ordinance of Hamburgh.
Ord. Konigs. Ordinance of Konigsburg.
Ord. Leg. Ordinances of Leghorn.
Ord. de la Mar. Ordonnance de la Marine, de Louis XIV.
Ord. Port. Ordinances of Portugal
Ord. Prus. Ordinances of Prussia.
Ord. Rott. Ordinances of Rotterdam.
Ord. Swed. Ordinances of Sweden.
Ord. on Us. Ord, on the Law of Usury.
Orfil. Med. Jur. Orfila's Medical Jurisprudence.
Orig. Original.
Ought. Oughton's Ordo Judiciorum.
Overt. R. Overton's Reports.
Ow. Owen's Reports.
Owen, Bankr. Owen on Bankruptcy.
P. Page or part. *Pp.* Pages.
P. Paschalis, Easter term.
P. C. Pleas of the Crown.
P. & D. Perry & Davison's Reports.
P. & K. Perry & Knapp's Election Cases.
P. & M. Philip and Mary; as, 1 & 2 P. & M c. 4.
P. N. P. Peake's Nisi Prius.
P. P. Propriâ personâ; in his own person.
Pa. R. Pennsylvania Reports.
P. R. or *P. R. C. P.* Practical Register in the Common Pleas.
P. Wms. Peere Williams' Reports.
Paige's R. Paige's Chancery Reports.
Paine's R. Paine's Reports.
Pal. Palmer's Reports.
Pal. Ag. Paley on the Law of Principal and Agent.
Pal. Conv. Paley on Convictions
Palm. Pr. Lords. Palmer's Practice in the House of Lords.
Pand. Pandects. Vide *Dig.*
Par. Paragraph; as, 29 Eliz. cap. 5, par. 21.
Par. & Fonb. M. J. Paris & Fonblanque on Medical Jurisprudence.
Pardess. Pardessus, Cours de Droit Commercial. In this work Pardessus is cited in several ways, namely: Pardes. Dr. Com. part 3, tit. 1, c. 2, s. 4, n. 286; or 2 Pardes. n. 286, which is the same reference.
Park on Dow. Park on Dower
Park, Ins. Park on Insurance.
Park. R. Sir Thomas Parker's Reports of Cases concerning the Revenue, in the Exchequer.
Park. on Ship. Parker on Shipping and Insurance.
Park. Pr. in Ch. Parker's Practice in Chancery.
Parl. Hist. Parliamentary History.
Patch. on Mortg. Patch's Treatise on the Law of Mortgages.
Paul's Par. Off. Paul's Parish Officer.
Pay. Mun. Rights. Payne's Municipal Rights.
Peak. Add. Cas. Peake's Additional Cases.
Peak. C. N. P. Peake's Cases determined at Nisi Prius, and in the K. B.
Peake, Ev. Peake on the Law of Evidence.
Peck. R. Peck's Reports.
Peck's Tr. Peck's Trial.
Peckw. E. C. Peckwell's Election Cases.
Penn. Bl. Pennsylvania Blackstone, by John Read, Esq.
Penn. Law Jo. Pennsylvania Law Journal.
Penn. R. Pennington's Reports. The Pennsylvania Reports are sometimes cited *Penn. R.*, but more properly, for the sake of distinction, *Penna. R.*
Penn. St. R. Pennsylvania State Reports.
Penna. Pr. Pennsylvania Practice; also cited Tro. & Hal. Pr., Troubat & Haly's Practice.
Penna. R. Pennsylvania Reports.
Pennsylv. Pennsylvania Reports.
Penr. Anal. Penruddocke's Analysis of the Criminal Law.
Penult. The last but one.
Per. & Dav. Perry & Davison's Reports.

Per. & Knapp. Perry & Knapp's Election Cases.
Perk. Perkins on Conveyancing.
Perk. Prof. B. Perkins' Profitable Book.
Perpig. on Pat. Perpigna on Patents. The full title of this work is, "The French Law and Practice of Patents for Inventions, Improvements, and Importations. By A. Perpigna, A. M. L B., Barrister in the Royal Court of Paris, Member of the Society for the Encouragement of Arts, &c." The work is well written in the English language. The author is a French lawyer, and has written another work on the same subject in French.
Pet. Ab. Petersdorff's Abridgment.
Pet. Adm. Dec. Peters' Admiralty Decisions.
Pet. on Bail, or *Petersd. on Bail.* Petersdorff on the Law of Bail.
Pet. R. Peters' Supreme Court Reports.
Pet. C. C. R. Peters' Circuit Court Reports.
Petting. on Jur. Pettingal on Juries.
Phil. Ev. Phillips' Evidence.
Phil. Ins. Phillips on Insurance.
Phil. St. Tr. Phillips' State Trials.
Phill. Civ. and Can. Laws. Phillimore on the Study of the Civil and Canon Law, considered in relation to the state, the church, and the universities, and in connexion with the college of advocates.
Phill. on Dom. Phillimore on the Law of Domicil.
Phillim. or *Phillim. E. R.* Phillimore's Ecclesiastical Reports.
Pick. R. Pickering's Reports.
Pig. Pigot on Recoveries.
Pike's Rep. Reports of Cases argued and determined in the Supreme Court of Law and Equity of the State of Arkansas. By Albert Pike. These Reports are cited *Ark. Rep.*
Pitm. Prin. and Sur. Pitman on Principal and Surety.
Pl. Placitum or plea. *Pl.* or *Plow.* or *Pl. Com.* Plowden's Commentaries, or Reports.
Plff. Plaintiff.
Platt on Cov. Platt on the Law of Covenants.
Platt on Lea. Platt on Leases.
Pol. Pollexfen's Reports.
Poph. Popham's Reports. The cases at the end of Popham's Reports are cited 2 Poph.
Port. R. Porter's Reports.
Poth. Pothier. The numerous works of Pothier are cited by abbreviating his name *Poth.* and then adding the name of the treatise; the figures generally refer to the number, as *Poth. Ob.* n. 100, which signifies Pothier's Treatise on the Law of Obligations, number 100. *Poth. du Mar.* Pothier du Mariage. *Poth. Vente.* Pothier Traité de Vente, &c. His Pandects, in 24 vols. are cited *Poth. Pand.* with the book, title, law, &c.
Pott's L. D. Pott's Law Dictionary.
Pow. Powell. *Pow. Contr.* Powell on Contracts. *Pow. Dev.* Powell on Devises. *Pow. Mortg.* Powell on Mortgages. *Pow. Powers.* Powell on Powers.
Poyn. on M. and D. Poynter on the Law of Marriage and Divorce.
Pr. Principio. *In pr.* In principio; in the beginning.
Pr. Ex. Rep. or *Price's E. R.* Price's Exchequer Reports.
Pr. Reg. Cha. Practical Register in Chancery.
Pr. St. Private Statute.
Pr. Stat. Private Statute.

Pract. Reg. C. P. Practical Register of the Common Pleas.
Pract. Reg. in Ch. Practical Register in Chancery.
Prat. on H. & W. Prater on the Law of Husband and Wife.
Pref. Preface.
Prel. Préliminaire.
Prest. Preston. *Prest. on Est.* Preston on Estates. *Prest. Abs. Tit.* Preston's Essay on Abstracts of Title. *Prest. on Conv.* Preston's Treatise on Conveyancing
Prest. on Leg. Preston on Legacies.
Pri. Price's Reports.
Price's Ex. Rep. Price's Exchequer Reports.
Price's Gen. Pr. Price's Gen. Practice.
Prin. Principium, the beginning of a title or law.
Prin. Dec. Printed Decisions.
Priv. Lond. Customs or Privileges of London.
Pro. L. Province Laws.
Pro quer. Pro querentem, for the plaintiff.
Proct. Pr. Proctor's Practice.
Puff. Puffendorff's Law of Nature.
Q. Quæstione, in such a Question.
Q. B. Queen's Bench.
Q. B. R. Queen's Bench Reports, by Adolphus & Ellis. New series.
Q. t. Qui tam.
Qu. Quere.
Q. Van Weyt. Q. Van Weytsen on Average.
Q. Warr. Quo Warranto; (q. v.) The letters (q. v.) *quod vide*, which see, refer to the article mentioned immediately before them.
Qu. Quæstione, in such a Question.
Qu. claus. freg. Quare clausum fregit. (q. v.)
Quæst. Quæstione, in such a Question.
Quest. Questions
Quinti Quinto. Year-book, 5 Henry V.
Quon. Attach. Quoniam Attachiamenta. See Dalr. F. L. 47.
R. Resolved, ruled, or repealed.
R. Richard; as, 2 R. 2, c. 1.
Rich. Rep. Richardson's (S. C.) Reports.
RC. Rescriptum.
R. & M. Russell and Mylne's Reports.
R. & M C. C. Ryan & Moody's Crown Cases.
R. & M. N. P. Ryan & Moody's Nisi Prius Cases.
R. & R. Russell & Ryan's Crown Cases.
R. M. Charlt. R M. Charlton's Reports.
RS. Responsum.
R. S. L. Reading on Statute Law.
Ram on Judgm. Ram on the Law relating to Legal Judgments.
Rand. Perp. Randall on the Law of Perpetuities
Rand. R. Randolph's Reports
Rast. Rastall's Entries.
Rawle's R. Rawle's Reports.
Rawle, Const. Rawle on the Constitution.
Ray's Med. Jur. Ray's Medical Jurisprudence of Insanity.
Raym. or, more usually, *Ld. Raym.* Lord Raymond's Reports. *T. Raym.* Sir Thomas Raymond's Reports.
Re. fa. lo. Recordari facias loquelam. Vide *Refalo* in the body of the work.
Rec. Recopilacion. *Rec.* Recorder; as, City Hall Rec.
Redd. on Mar. Com. Reddie's Historical View of the Law of Maritime Commerce.

Redesd. Pl. Redesdale's Equity Pleading. This work is also and most usually cited *Mitf. Pl.*

Reeves' H. E. L. Reeves' History of the English Law. *Reeves on Ship.* Reeves on the Law of Shipping and Navigation.

Reeves on Des. Reeves on Descents.

Reg. Regula, rule. *Reg.* Register.

Reg. Brev. Registrum Brevium, or Register of Writs.

Reg. Gen. Regulæ Generales.

Reg. Jud. Registrum Judiciale.

Reg. Mag. Regiam Magestatem.

Reg. Pl. Regula Placitandi.

Renouard, des Brev. d'Inv. Traitè des Brevets d'Invention, de Perfectionement, et d'Importation, par Augustin Charles Renouard.

Rep. The Reports of Lord Coke are frequently cited 1 Rep., 2 Rep., &c. and sometimes they are cited Co.

Rép. Répertoire.

Rep. Eq. Gilbert's Reports in Equity.

Rep. Q. A. Reports of Cases during the time of Queen Anne.

Rep. T. Finch. Reports tempore Finch.

Rep. T. Hard. Reports during the time of Lord Hardwicke.

Rep. T. Holt. Reports tempore Holt.

Rep. T. Talb. Reports of Cases decided during the time of Lord Talbot.

Res. Resolution. The cases reported in Coke's Reports, are divided into resolutions on the different points of the case, and are cited 1 Res. &c.

Ret. Brev. Retorna Brevium.

Rev. St. or *Rev. Stat.* Revised Statutes.

Rey, des Inst. de l'Anglet. Des Institutions Judiciaries de l'Angleterre comparées avec celles de la France. Par Joseph Rey.

Reyn. Inst. Institutions du Droit des Gens, &c. par Gerard de Reyneval.

Ric. Richard; as, 12 Ric. 2, c. 15.

Rice's Rep. Reports of Cases in Chancery argued and determined in the Court of Appeals and Court of Errors of South Carolina. By William Rice, State Reporter.

Rich. Pr. C. P. Richardson's Practice in the Common Pleas.

Rich. Pr. K. B. Richardson's Practice in the King's Bench.

Rich. Eq. R. Richardson's Equity Reports.

Rich. on Wills. Richardson on Wills.

Ridg. Irish. T. R. Ridgeway, Lapp & Schoales' Term Reports in the K. B., Dublin. Sometimes this is cited *Ridg. L. & S.*

Ridg. P. C. Ridgeway's Cases in Parliament.

Ridg. Rep. Ridgeway's Reports of Cases in K. B. and Chancery.

Ridg. St. Tr. Ridgeway's Reports of State Trials in Ireland

Ril. Ch. Cas. Riley's Chancery Cases.

Rob. Adm. Rep. Robinson's Admiralty Reports.

Rob. Cas. Robertson's Cases in Parliament, from Scotland.

Rob. Dig. Roberts' Digest of the English Statutes in force in Pennsylvania.

Rob. Entr. Robinson's Entries.

Rob. on Fr. Roberts on Frauds.

Rob. on Fraud. Conv. Roberts on Fraudulent Conveyances.

Rob. on Gavelk. Robinson on Gavelkind.

Rob. Lo. Rep. Robinson's Louisiana Reports.

Rob. Just. Robinson's Justice of the Peace.

Rob. Pr. Robinson's Practice in Suits at Law, in Virginia.

Rob. V. Rep. Robinson's (Virginia) Reports.

Rob. on Wills. Roberts' Treatise on the Law of Wills and Codicils.

Roc. Ins. Roccus on Insurance. Vide *Ing. Roc.*

Rog. Eccl. Law. Rogers' Ecclesiastical Law.

Rog. Rec. Rogers' City Hall Recorder.

Roll. Rolle's Abridgment. *Roll. R.* Rolle's Reports.

Rom. Cr. Law. Romilly's Observations on the Criminal Law of England, as it relates to capital punishments.

Rop. on H. & W. A Treatise on the Law of Property, arising from the relation between Husband and Wife. By R. S. Donnison Roper.

Rop. Leg. Roper on Legacies.

Rop. on Revoc. Roper on Revocations.

Rosc. Roscoe. *Rosc. on Act.* Roscoe on Actions relating to Real Property. *Rosc. Civ. Ev.* Roscoe's Digest of the Law of Evidence on the Trial of Actions at Nisi Prius. *Rosc. Cr. Ev.* Roscoe on Criminal Evidence. *Rosc. on Bills.* Roscoe's Treatise on the Law relating to Bills of Exchange, Promissory Notes, Bankers' Checks, &c.

Rose's R. Rose's Reports of Cases in Bankruptcy.

Ross on V. & P. Ross on the Law of Vendors and Purchasers.

Rot. Parl. Rotulæ Parliamentariæ.

Rowe's Sci. Jur. Rowe's Scintilla Juris.

Rub. or *Rubr.* Rubric, (q. v.)

Ruffh. Ruffhead's Statutes at Large.

Ruff. or *Ruffin's R.* Ruffin's Reports.

Runn. Ej. Runnington on Ejectments.

Runn. Stat. Runnington's Statutes at Large.

Rus. & Myl. Russell & Mylne's Chancery Reports.

Rush. Rushworth's Collections.

Russ. Cr. Russell on Crimes and Misdemeanors.

Russ. & Myl. Russell & Mylne's Reports of Cases in Chancery.

Russ. on Fact. Russell on the Laws relating to Factors and Brokers.

Russ. R. Russell's Reports of Cases in Chancery.

Russ. & Ry. Russell & Ryan's Crown Cases.

Rutherf. Inst. Rutherford's Institutes of Natural Law.

Ry. F. Rymer's Fœdera.

Ry. & Mo. Ryan & Moody's Nisi Prius Reports. *Ry. & Mo. C. C.* Ryan & Moody's Crown Cases.

Ry. Med. Jur. Ryan on Medical Jurisprudence.

S. §, section.

S. B. Upper Bench.

S. & B. Smith & Batty's Reports.

S. C. Same Case.

S. C. C. Select Cases in Chancery.

S. C. Rep. South Carolina Reports.

S. & L. Schoales & Lefroy's Reports.

S. & M. Shaw & Maclean's Reports.

S. & M. Ch. R. Smedes & Marshall's Reports of Cases decided by the Superior Court of Chancery of Mississippi.

S. & M. Err. & App. Smedes & Marshall's Reports of Cases in the High Court of Errors and Appeals of Mississippi.

S. P. Same Point.

S. & R. Sergeant & Rawle's Reports.

S. & S. Sausse & Scully's Reports.

S. & S. Simon & Stuart's Chancery Reports.
Sa. & Scul. Sausse & Scully's Reports.
Sandl. St. Pap Sandler's State Papers.
Salk. Salkeld's Reports.
Sandf. Rep. Reports of Cases argued and determined in the Court of Chancery of the State of New York, before the Hon. Lewis H. Sandford, Assistant Vice Chancellor of the First Circuit.
Sand. U. & T. Sanders on Uses and Trusts.
Sanf. on Ent. Sanford on Entails.
Sant. de Assec. Santerna, de Assecurationibus.
Saund. Saunders' Reports.
Saund. Pl. & Ev. Saunders' Treatise on the Law of Pleading and Evidence.
Sav. Saville's Reports.
Sav. Dr. Rom. Savigny, Droit Romain.
Sav. Dr. Rom. M. A. Savigny, Droit Romain au Moyen Age.
Sav. Hist. Rom. Law. Savigny's History of the Roman Law during the Middle Ages. Translated from the German of Carl Von Savigny, by E. Cathcart.
Say. Sayer's Reports. *Say. Costs.* Sayer's Law of Costs.
SC. Senatus consultum.
Scac. de Cam. Scaccia de Cambiis.
Scam. Rep. Scammon's Reports of Cases argued and determined in the Supreme Court of Illinois.
Scan. Mag. Scandalum Magnatum.
Sch. & Lef. Schoales & Lefroy's Reports.
Scheiff. Pr. Scheiffer's Practice.
Schul. Aq. R. Schultes on Aquatic Rights.
Sci. Fa. Scire Facias.
Sci. fa. ad. dis. deb. Scire facias ad disprobandum debitum, (q. v.)
Scil. Scilicet, i. e. scire licet, that is to say.
Sco. N. R. Scott's New Reports.
Scott's R. Scott's Reports.
Scriv. Copyh. Scriven's Copyholds.
Seat. F. Ch. Seaton's Forms in Chancery.
Sec. Section.
Sec. Leg. Secundum legem; according to law.
Sec. Reg. Secundum regulam; according to rule.
Sedgw on Dam. Sedgwick on Damages.
Sel. Ca. Chan. Select Cases in Chancery. Vide S. C. C.
Seld. Mar. Cla. Selden's Mare Clausum.
Self. Tr. Selfridge's Trial.
Sell. Pr. Sellon's Practice in K. B. and C. P.
Selw N. P. Selwyn's Nisi Prius. *Selw. R.* Selwyn's Reports. These Reports are usually cited M. & S. Maule & Selwyn's Reports.
Sem. or *Semb.* Semble, it seems.
Sen Senate.
Seq. Sequentia.
Serg. on Att. Sergeant on the Law of Attachment.
Serg. Const. Law. Sergeant on Constitutional Law.
Serg. on Land L. Sergeant on the Land Laws of Pennsylvania.
Serg. & Lowb. Sergeant & Lowber's edition of the English Common Law Reports; more usually cited *Eng. Com. Law Rep.*
Serg. & Rawle, or *S. R* Reports of Cases adjudged in the Supreme Court of Pennsylvania. By Thomas Sergeant and William Rawle, Jun.
Sess. Ca. Sessions Cases in K. B., chiefly touching Settlements.
Set. on Dec. Seton on Decrees.
Shaw & Macl. Shaw & Maclean's Reports.
Shelf. Lun. Shelford on Lunacy.
Shelf. on Mort. Shelford on the Law of Mortmain.
Shelf. on Railw. Shelford on Railways.
Shelf. on R. Pr. Shelford on Real Property.
Shep. To. Sheppard's Touchstone.
Shepl. R. Shepley's Reports.
Sher. Sheriff.
Show. P. C. Shower's Parliamentary Cases.
Show. R. Shower's Reports in the Court of King's Bench.
Shub. Jur. Lit. Shuback de Jure Littoris.
Sid. Siderfin's Reports.
Sim. Simon's Chancery Reports. In Con. C. R.
Sim. & Stu. Simon & Stuart's Chancery Reports.
Skene, Verb. Sign. Skene de Verborum Significatione; an explanation of terms, difficult words, &c.
Skin. Skinner's Reports.
Skirr. Und. Sher. Skirrow's Complete Practical Under Sheriff.
Slade's Rep. Slade's Reports. More usually cited Vermont Reports.
Smed. & Marsh. Ch. R. Smedes & Marshall's Reports of Cases decided by the Superior Court of Chancery of Mississippi.
Smed. & Marsh. Err. & App. Smedes & Marshall's Reports of Cases decided by the High Court of Errors and Appeals of Mississippi.
Smith & Batty. Smith & Batty's Reports.
Smith's Ch. Pr. Smith's Chancery Practice.
Smith's For. Med. Smith's Forensic Medicine.
Smith's Hints. Smith's Hints for the Examination of Medical Witnesses.
Smith on M. L. Smith on Mercantile Law.
Sm. on Pat. Smith on the Law of Patents.
Smith's R. Smith's Reports in K. B., together with Cases in the Court of Chancery.
Sol. Solutio, the answer to an objection.
South. Car. R. South Carolina Reports.
South. R. Southard's Reports.
Sp. of Laws. Spirit of Laws, by Montesquieu.
Spelm. Feuds. Spelman on Feuds.
Spel. Gl. Spelman's Glossary.
Spence on Eq. Jur. of Ch. Spence on the Equitable Jurisdiction of Chancery.
Spenc. R. Spencer's Reports.
Speers' Eq. Cas. Equity Cases argued and determined in the Court of Appeals of South Carolina. By R. H. Speers.
Speers' Rep. Speers' Reports.
Ss. usually put in small letters, *ss.* Scilicet, that is to say.
St. or *Stat.* Statute.
St. Armand, Hist. Ess. St. Armand's Historical Essay on the Legislative Power of England.
Stant. R. Stanton's Reports.
Stath. Ab. Statham's Abridgment.
Stath. Statham's Abridgment.
St. Cas. Stillingfleet's Cases.
St. Tr. State Trials.
Stair's Inst. Stair's Institutions of the Law of Scotland.
Stallm. on Elec. & Sat. Stallman on Election and Satisfaction.
Stark. Starkie's Ev. Starkie on the Law of Evidence. *Stark. Cr. Pl.* Starkie's Criminal Pleadings. *Stark. R.* Starkie's Reports. *Stark. on Sl.* Starkie on Slander and Libel.
Stat. Statutes.

Stat. Wes. Statute of Westminster.
Staunf. or *Staunf. P. C.* Staunford's Pleas of the Crown.
Stearn. on R. A. Stearne on Real Actions.
Steph. Comm. Stephen's New Commentaries on the Law of England.
Steph. Cr. Law. Stephen on Criminal Law. *Steph. Pl.* Stephen on Pleading. *Steph. Proc.* Stephen on Procurations.
Steph. on Slav. Stephens on Slavery.
Stev. on Av. Stevens on Average.
Stev. & B. on Av. Stevens & Beneke on Average.
Stew. Adm. Rep. Stewart's Reports of Cases argued and determined in the Court of Vice Admiralty at Halifax.
Stew. R. Stewart's Reports.
Stew. & Port. Stewart & Porter's Reports.
Story on Bail. Story's Commentaries on the Law of Bailments.
Story on Const. Story on the Constitution of the United States.
Story on Eq. Story's Commentaries on Equity Jurisprudence.
Story's L. U. S. Story's edition of the Laws of the United States, in 3 vols. The 4th and 5th volumes are a continuation of the same work by George Sharswood, Esq.
Story on Partn. Story on Partnership.
Story on Pl. Story on Pleading.
Story, R. Story's Reports.
Str. Strange's Reports.
Stracc. de Mer. Straccha de Mercatura, Navibus Assecurationibus.
Strah. Dom. Straham's Translation of Domat's Civil Law.
Strob. R. Strobhart's Reports.
Stroud's Dig. Stroud's Digest of the Laws of Pennsylvania.
Stuart's (L. C.) R. Reports of Cases in the Court of King's Bench in the Provincial Court of Appeals of Lower Canada, and Appeals from Lower Canada before the Lords of the Privy Council. By George O'Kill Stuart, Esq.
Sty. Style's Reports.
Sugd., Sugd. Pow. Sugden on Powers. *Sugd. Vend.* Sugden on Vendors. *Sugd. Lett.* Sugden's Letters.
Sull. Lect. Sullivan's Lectures on the Feudal Law, and the Constitution and Laws of England.
Sull. on Land Tit. Sullivan's History of Land Titles in Massachusetts.
Sum. Summa, the Summary of a law.
Sumn. R. Sumner's Circuit Court Reports.
Supers. Supersedeas.
Supp. Supplement. *Supp. to Ves. Jr.* Supplement to Vesey Junior's Reports.
Swan on Eccl. Cts. Swan on the Jurisdiction of Ecclesiastical Courts.
Swanst. Swanston's Reports.
Sweet on Wills. Sweet's Popular Treatise on Wills.
Swift's Ev. Swift's Evidence.
Swift's Sys. Swift's System of the Laws of Connecticut. *Swift's Dig.* Swift's Digest of the Laws of Connecticut.
Swinb. Swinburn on the Law of Wills and Testaments. This work is generally cited by reference to the part, book, chapter, &c.
Swinb. on Desc. Swinburne on the Law of Descents.
Swinb. on Mar. Swinburne on Marriage.
Swinb. on Spo. Swinburne on Spousals.
Sw. Swinburne on Wills.
Syst. Plead. System of Pleading.
T. Title.
T. & G. Tyrwhitt & Granger's Reports.
T. & P. Turner & Phillips' Reports.
T. Jo. Sir Thomas Jones' Reports.
T. L. Termes de la Ley, or Terms of the Law.
T. R. Term Reports. Ridgeway's Reports are sometimes cited *Irish Tr.*
T. R. Teste Rege.
T. & R. Turner & Russell's Chancery Reports
T. & R. Turner & Russell's Reports.
T. R. E. or *T. E. R.* Tempore Regis Edwardi. This abbreviation is frequently used in Domesday Book, and in the more ancient Law writers. See Tyrrel's Hist. Eng., Introd. viii. p. 49. See also Co. Inst. 86, a, where in a quotation from Domesday Book, this abbreviation is interpreted Terra Regis Edwardi; but in Cowell's Dict. verb. Reveland, it is said to be wrong.
T. Raym. Sir Thomas Raymond's Reports.
T. U. P. Charlt. T. U. P. Charlton's Reports.
Tait on Ev. Tait on Evidence.
Taml. on Ev. Tamlyn on Evidence, principally with reference to the Practice of the Court of Chancery, and in the Master's Office.
Taml. R. Tamlyn's Reports of Cases decided in Chancery.
Taml. T. Y. Tamlyn on Terms for Years.
Tapia. Jur. Mer. Tratade de Jurisprudentia Mercantil.
Taunt. Taunton's Reports.
Tayl. on Ev. Taylor on Evidence.
Tayl. Civ. L. Taylor's Civil Law.
Tayl. Law Glo. Taylor's Law Glossary.
Tayl. R. Taylor's Reports.
Tayl. L. & T Taylor's Treatise on the American Law of Landlord and Tenant.
Tech. Dict. Crabb's Technological Dictionary.
Thach. Crim. Cas. Thacher's Criminal Cases.
Th. Br. Thesaurus Brevium.
Th. Dig. Theloall's Digest.
Theo. of Pres. Pro. Theory of Presumptive Proof.
Theo. Pres. Pro. Theory of Presumptive Proof, or an Inquiry into the Nature of Circumstantial Evidence.
Tho. Co. Litt. Coke upon Littleton; newly arranged on the plan of Sir Matthew Hale's Analysis. By J. H. Thomas, Esq.
Thomp. on Bills. Thompson on Bills.
Tho. U. J. Thomas on Universal Jurisprudence.
Tidd's Pr. Tidd's Practice.
Tit. Title.
Toll. Ex. Toller's Executors.
Toml. L. D. Tomlin's Law Dictionary.
Toth. Tothill's Reports.
Touchs. Sheppard's Touchstone.
Toull. Le Droit Civil Français suivant l'ordre du Code; ouvrage dans lequel on a taché de reunir la théorie a la practique. Par M. C. B. M. Toullier. This work is sometimes cited Toull. Dr. Civ. Fr. liv. 3, t. 2, c. 1, n. 6; at other times, 3 Toull. n. 86, which latter signifies vol. 3 of Toullier's work, No. 86.
Tr. Eq. Treatise of Equity; the same as Fonblanque on Equity.
Traill, Med. Jur. Outlines of a Course of Lec-

ures on Medical Jurisprudence. By Thomas Stewart Traill, M. D.

Treb. Jur. de la Med. Jurisprudence de la Médecine, de la Chirurgie, et de la Pharmacie. Par Adolphe Trebuchet.

Trem. Tremaine's Pleas of the Crown.

Tri. of 7 Bish. Trial of the Seven Bishops.

Tri. per Pais. Trials per Pais.

Trin. Trinity Term.

Tuck. Bl. Com. Blackstone's Commentaries, edited by Judge Tucker.

Turn. R. Turner's Reports of Cases determined in Chancery.

Turn. & Russ. Turner & Russell's Chancery Reports.

Tuck. Com. Tucker's Commentaries.

Turn. & Phil. Turner & Phillips' Reports.

Tyl. R. Tyler's Reports.

Tyrw. Tyrwhitt's Exchequer Reports.

Tyrw. & Gra. Tyrwhitt & Granger's Reports.

Tyt. Mil. Law. Tytler's Essay on Military Law and the Practice of Military Courts Martial.

U. S. United States of America.

U. S. Dig. United States Digest. See *Metc. & Perk. Dig.*

Ult. Ultimo, ultima, the last, usually applied to the last title, paragraph or law.

Umfrev. Off. of Cor. Umfreville's Office of Coroner.

Under Sher. Under Sheriff, containing the office and duty of High Sheriff, Under Sheriffs and Bailiffs.

Ux. et. Et uxor, et uxorem, and wife.

V. Versus, against; as A B. v. C D.

V. Versiculo, in such a verse.

V. Vide, see.

V. or *v.* Voce; as Spelm. Gloss. v. Cancellarious.

V. & B. Vesey & Beames' Reports.

V. C. Vice Chancellor.

Voc. Voce, or Vocem.

V. & S. Vernon & Scriven's Reports.

Val. Com. Valin's Commentaries.

Van. Heyth. Mar. Ev. Van Heythuysen's Essay upon Marine Evidence, in Courts of Law and Equity.

Vand. Jud. Pr. Vanderlinden's Judicial Practice.

Vatt or *Vattel.* Vattel's Law of Nations.

Vaug. Vaughan's Reports.

Vend. Ex. Venditioni Exponas.

Ventr. Ventris' Reports.

Verm. R. Vermont Judges' Reports.

Vern. Vernon's Reports.

Vern. & Scriv. Vernon & Scriven's Reports of Cases in the King's Courts, Dublin.

Verpl. Contr. Verplanck on Contracts.

Verpl. Ev. Verplanck on Evidence.

Ves. Vesey Senior's Reports.

Ves. Jr. Vesey Junior's Reports.

Ves. & Bea. Vesey & Beames' Reports.

Vet. N. B. Old Natura Brevium.

Vid. Vidian's Entries.

Vin. Ab. Viner's Abridgment.

Vin. Supp. Supplement to Viner's Abridgment.

Vinn. Vinnius.

Viz. Videlicet, that is to say.

Vs. Versus.

W. 1, *W.* 2. Statutes of Westminster, 1 and 2.

W. C. C. R. Washington's Circuit Court Reports.

W. & C. Wilson & Courtenay's Reports.

W. Jo. Sir William Jones' Reports.

W. Kel. William Kelynge's Reports.

W. & M. William and Mary.

W. & M. Rep. Woodbury & Minot's Reports.

W. & S. Wilson & Shaw's Reports of Cases decided in the H. of L.

Wigr. on Disc. Wigram on Discovery.

Walf. on Part. Walford's Treatise on the Law respecting Parties to Actions.

Walk. Ch. Ca. Walker's Chancery Cases.

Walk. Am. R. or *Walk. Introd.* Walker's Introduction to American Law.

Walk. R. Walker's Reports.

Wall. R. Wallace's Circuit Court Reports.

Ward. on Leg. Ward on Legacies.

Ware's R. Reports of Cases argued and determined in the District Court of the United States, for the District of Maine.

Warr. L. S. Warren's Law Studies.

Wash. C. C. Washington's Circuit Court Reports.

Washb. R. Washburn's Vermont Reports.

Wat. Cop. Watkin's Copyhold.

Watk. Conv. Watkin's Principles of Conveyancing.

Wats. Cler. Law. Watson's Clergyman's Law.

Wats. on Arb. Watson on the Law of Arbitrations and Awards.

Wats. on Partn. Watson on the Law of Partnerships.

Wats. on Sher. Watson on the Law relating to the office and duty of Sheriff.

Watt's R. Watt's Reports.

Watts & Serg. Watts & Seargeant's Reports.

Welf. on Eq. Plead. Welford on Equity Pleading.

Wellw. Ab. Wellwood's Abridgment of Sea Laws.

Wend. R. Wendell's Reports.

Wentw. Wentworth. *Went. Off. Ex.* Wentworth's Office of Executor. *Wentw. Pl.* Wentworth's System of Pleading.

Wesk. Ins. Weskett on the Law of Insurance

West's Parl. Rep. West's Parliamentary Reports.

West's Rep. West's Reports of Lord Chancellor Hardwicke.

West's Symb. West's Symboliography, or a description of instruments and precedents, 2 parts.

Westm. Westminister; *Westm. I. Westminster primer.*

Weyt. on Av. Quintin Van Weytsen on Average.

Whart. Cr. Law. Wharton on the Criminal Law of the United States.

Whart. Dig. Wharton's Digest.

Whart. Law Lex. Wharton's Law Lexicon, or Dictionary of Jurisprudence.

Whart. R. Wharton's Reports.

Wheat Wheaton. *Wheat. R.* Wheaton's Reports. *Wheat. on Capt.* Wheaton's Digest of the Law of Maritime Captures and Prizes. *Wheat. Hist. of L. of N.* Wheaton's History of the Law of Nations in Europe and America.

Wheel. Ab. Wheeler's Abridgments.

Wheel. Cr. Cas. Wheeler's Criminal Cases.

Wheel. on Slav. Wheeler on Slavery.

Whish. L. D. Whishaw's Law Dictionary

Whit. on Liens. Whitaker on the Law of Liens.

Whit. on Trans. Whitaker on Stoppage in Transitu.

White's New Coll. A New Collection of the Laws, Charters, and Local Ordinances of the Governments of Great Britain, France, Spain, &c.

Whitm. B. L. Whitmarsh's Bankrupt Law.

Wicq. L'Ambassadeur et ses fonctions, par de Wicquefort.

Wightw. Wightwich's Reports in the Exchequer.

Wilc. on Mun. Cor. Wilcock on Municipal Corporations.

Wilc. R Wilcox's Reports.

Wilk. Leg. Ang. Sax. Wilkin's Leges Anglo-Saxonicæ.

Wilk. on Lim. Wilkinson on Limitations.

Wilk. on Pub. Funds. Wilkinson on the Law relating to the Public Funds, including the Practice of Distringas, &c.

Wilk. on Repl. Wilkinson on the Law of Replevin.

Will. Auct. Williams on the Law of Auctions.

Will. on Eq. Pl. Willis' Treatise on Equity Pleadings.

Will. on Inter. Willis on Interrogatories.

Will. L. D. Williams' Law Dictionary.

Will. Per. Pr. Williams' Principles of the Law of Personal Property.

Will. (P.) Rep. Peere Williams' Reports.

Willc. Off. of Const. Willcock on the Office of Constable.

Willes' R. Willes' Reports.

Wills on Cir. Ev. Wills on Circumstantial Evidence.

Wils. on Uses. Wilson on Springing Uses.

Wilm. on Mortg. Wilmot on Mortgages.

Wilm. Judg. Wilmot's Notes of Opinions and Judgments.

Wils. on Arb. Wilson on Arbitrations.

Wils. Ch. R. Wilson's Chancery Reports.

Wils. & Co. Wilson & Courtenay's Reports.

Wils. Ex. R. Wilson's Exchequer Reports.

Wils. & Sh. Wilson & Shaw's Reports decided by the House of Lords.

Wils. R. Wilson's Reports.

Win. Winch's Entries. *Win. R.* Winch's Reports.

Wing. Max. Wingate's Maxims.

Wms. Just. Williams' Justice.

Wms. R., more usually, *P. Wms.* Peere Williams' Reports.

Wolff. Inst. Wolffius Institutiones Juris Naturæ et gentium.

Wood's Inst., or *Wood's Inst. Com. L.* Wood's Institutes of the Common Law of England. *Wood's Inst. Civ. Law.* Wood's Institutes of the Civil Law.

Wood & Min. Rep. Woodbury and Minot's Reports.

Woodes. Wooddesson *Woodes. El Jur.* Wooddesson's Elements of Jurisprudence. *Woodes. Lect.* Wooddesson's Vinerian Lectures.

Woodf. L. and T. Woodfall on the Law of Landlord and Tenant.

Woodm. R. Woodman's Reports of Criminal Cases tried in the Municipal Court of the City of Boston.

Wool. Com. L. Woolrych's Commercial Law.

Wool. L. W. Woolrych's Law of Waters.

Woolr. on Com. Law. Woolrych's Treatise on the Commercial and Mercantile Law of England.

Wool. on Ways. Woolrych on Ways.

Worth. on Jur. Worthington's Inquiry into the Power of Juries to decide incidentally on Questions of Law.

Worth. Pre. Wills. Worthington's Genera Precedents for Wills, with practical notes.

Wright's R. Wright's Reports.

Wright, Fr. Soc. Wright on Friendly Societies.

Wright, Ten. Sir Martin Wright's Law of Tenores.

Wy. Pr. Reg. Wyatt's Practical Register.

X. The decretals of Gregory the Ninth are denoted by the letter X, thus, X̣.

Y. B. Year Books, (q. v.)

Y. & C. Younge & Collyer's Exchequer Reports.

Y. & C. N. C. Younge & Collyer's New Cases.

Y. & J. Younge & Jervis' Exchequer Reports.

Yeates, R. Yeates' Reports.

Yearb. Year Book.

Yelv. Yelverton's Reports.

Yerg. R. Yerger's Reports.

Yo. & Col. Younge & Collyer's Exchequer Reports.

Yo. & Col. N. C. Younge and Collyer's New Cases.

Yo. Rep. Younge's Reports.

Yo. & Jer. Younge & Jervis' Reports.

Zouch's Adm. Zouch's Jurisdiction of the Admiralty of England, asserted.

ABBREVIATORS, *eccl. law.* Officers whose duty it is to assist in drawing up the Pope's briefs, and reducing petitions into proper form, to be converted into Papal Bulls. Vide *Bulls.*

ABBROCHMENT, *obsolete.* The forestalling of a market or fair.

ABDICATION, *government.* 1. A simple renunciation of an office, generally understood of a supreme office. James II. of England; Charles V. of Germany; and Christiana, Queen of Sweden, are said to have abdicated. When James II. of England left the kingdom, the Commons voted that he had *abdicated* the government, and that thereby the throne had become vacant. The House of Lords preferred the word *deserted*, but the Commons thought it not comprehensive enough, for then, the king might have the liberty of returning. 2. When inferior magistrates decline or surrender their offices, they are said to make a resignation. (q. v.)

ABDUCTION, *crim. law.* The carrying away of any person by force or fraud. This is a misdemeanor punishable by indictment. 1 East, P. C. 458; 1 Russel. 569. The civil remedies are recaption, (q. v.) 3 Inst. 134; Hal. Anal. 46; 3 Bl. Com. 4; by writ of habeas corpus; and an action of trespass, Fitz. N. B. 89; 3 Bl. Com. 139, n. 27; Roscoe, Cr. Ev. 193.

ABEARANCE. Behaviour; as, a recognizance to be of good abearance, signifies to be of good behaviour. 4 Bl. Com. 251, 256.

ABEREMURDER, *obsolete.* An apparent, plain, or downright murder. It was used to distinguish a wilful murder, from chance-medley, or manslaughter. Spelman; Cowell; Blount.

TO ABET, *crim. law.* To encourage or set another on to commit a crime. This word is always taken in a bad sense. To abet another to commit a murder, is to command, procure, or counsel him to commit it. Old Nat. Brev. 21; Co. Litt. 475.

ABETTOR, *crim. law.* One who encourages or incites, persuades or sets another on to commit a crime. Such a person is either a principal or an accessory to the crime. When present, aiding, where a felony is committed, he is guilty as principal in the second degree; when absent, he is merely an accessory. 1 Russell, 21; 1 Leach, 66; Foster, 428.

ABEYANCE, *estates,* from the French *aboyer*, which in a figurative sense means *to expect, to look for, to desire.* When there is no person *in esse* in whom the freehold is vested, it is said to be in *abeyance*, that is, in expectation, remembrance and contemplation of law.

2. The law requires, however, that the freehold should never, if possible, be in *abeyance.* Where there is a tenant of the freehold, the remainder or reversion in fee may exist for a time without any particular owner, in which case it is said to be in abeyance. 9 Serg. & R. 367; 8 Plowd. 29 a. b 35 a.

3. Thus, if an estate be limited to A for life, remainder to the right heirs of B, the fee simple is in abeyance during the life of B, because it is a maxim of law, that *nemo est hæres viventis.* 2 Bl. Com. 107; 1 Cruise, 67—70; 1 Inst. 342; Merlin, Répertoire, mot Abeyance; 1 Com. Dig. 175; 1 Vin. Abr. 104.

4. Another example may be given in the case of a corporation. When a charter is given, and the charter grants franchises or property to a corporation which is to be brought into existence by some future acts of the corporators, such franchises or property are in abeyance until such acts shall be done, and when the corporation is thereby brought into life, the franchises instantaneously attach. 4 Wheat. 691. See, generally, 2 Mass. 500; 7 Mass. 445; 10 Mass. 93; 15 Mass. 464; 9 Cranch, 47. 293; 5 Mass. 555.

ABIDING BY PLEA. *English law.* A defendant who pleads a frivolous plea, or a plea merely for the purpose of delaying the suit; or who, for the same purpose, shall file a similar demurrrer, may be compelled by rule in term time, or by a Judge's order in vacation, either to abide by that plea, or by that demurrer, or to plead peremptorily on the morrow; or if near the end of the term, and in order to afford time for notice of trial, the motion may be made in court for rule to abide or plead instanter; that is, within twenty-four hours after rule served, Imp. B. R. 340, provided that the regular time for pleading be expired. If the defendant when ruled, do not abide, he can only plead the general issue; 1 T. R. 693; but he may add notice of set-off. Ib. 694, n. See 1 Chit. Rep. 565, n.

ABIGEAT, *civ. law.* A particular kind of larceny, which is committed not by taking and carrying away the property from one place to another, but by driving a living thing away with an intention of feloniously appropriating the same. Vide *Taking.*

ABIGEI, *civil law.* Stealers of cattle, who were punished with more severity than other thieves. Dig. 47, 14; 4 Bl. Com. 239.

ABJURATION. A renunciation of allegiance to a country by oath.

2.—1. The act of Congress of the 14th of April, 1802, 2 Story's Laws, U. S. 850, requires that when an alien shall apply to be admitted a citizen of the United States, he shall declare on oath or affirmation before the court where the application shall be made, inter alia, that he doth absolutely and entirely renounce and *abjure* all allegiance and fidelity which he owes to any foreign prince, &c., and particularly, by name, the prince, &c., whereof he was before a citizen or subject. Rawle on the Const. 98.

3.—2. In England *the oath of abjuration* is an oath by which an Englishman binds himself not to acknowledge any right in the Pretender to the throne of England.

4.—3. It signifies also, according to 25 Car. II., an oath abjuring to certain doctrines of the church of Rome.

5.—4. In the ancient English law it was a renunciation of one's country and taking an oath of perpetual banishment. A man who had committed a felony, and for safety fled to a sanctuary, might within forty days confess the fact, and take the oath of abjuration and perpetual banishment; he was then transported. This was abolished by Stat. 1 Jac. 1, c. 25. Ayl. Parerg. 14.

ABLEGATI, *diplomacy*. Papal ambassadors of the second rank, who are sent with a less extensive commission, to a court where there are no nuncios. This title is equivalent to *envoy*. (q. v.)

ABNEPOS, *civil law*. The grandson of a grandson or grand-daughter, or fourth descendant.—Abneptis, is the grand-daughter of a grandson or grand-daughter. These terms are used in making genealogical tables.

ABOLITION. An act by which a thing is extinguished, abrogated or annihilated. Merl. Répert, h. t., as the abolition of slavery is the destruction of slavery.

2. In the civil and French law abolition is used nearly synonymously with pardon, remission, grace. Dig. 39, 4, 3, 3. There is, however, this difference: *grace* is the generic term; *pardon*, according to those laws, is the clemency which the prince extends to a man who has participated in a crime, without being a principal or accomplice; *remission* is made in cases of involuntary homicides, and self-defence. *Abolition* is different: it is used when the crime cannot be remitted. The prince then may by letters of abolition remit the punishment, but the infamy remains, unless letters of abolition have been obtained before sentence. Encycl. de d'Alembert, h. t.

3. The term abolition is used in the German law in the same sense as in the French law. Encycl. Amer. h. t. The term abolition is derived from the civil law, in which it is sometimes used synonymously with absolution. Dig. 39, 4, 3, 3.

ABORTION, *med. jur.* and *criminal law*. The expulsion of the fœtus before the seventh month of utero-gestation, or before it is *viable*. (q. v.)

2. The causes of this accident are referable either to the mother, or to the fœtus and its dependencies. The causes in the mother may be: extreme nervous susceptibility, great debility, plethora, faulty conformation, and the like; and it is frequently induced immediately by intense mental emotion, violent exercise, &c. The causes seated in the fœtus are its death, rupture of the membranes, &c.

3. It most frequently occurs between the 8th and 12th weeks of gestation. When abortion is produced with a malicious design, it becomes a misdemeanor, at common law, 1 Russell, 553; and the party causing it may be indicted and punished.

4. The criminal means resorted to for the purpose of destroying the fœtus, may be divided into general and local. To the first belong venesection, emetics, cathartics, diuretics, emmenagogues, &c. The second embraces all kinds of violence directly applied.

5. When, in consequence of the mean used to produce abortion, the death of the woman ensues, the crime is murder.

6. By statute a distinction is made between a woman *quick with child*, (q. v.) and one who, though pregnant, is not so, 1 Bl. Com. 129. Physiologists, perhaps with reason, think that the child is a living being from the moment of conception. 1 Beck. Med. Jur. 291.

General references. 1 Beck, 288 to 331; and 429 to 435; where will be found an abstract of the laws of different countries, and some of the states, punishing criminal abortion; Roscoe, Cr. Ev. 190; 1 Russ. 553; Vilanova y Mañes, Materia Criminal Forense, Obs. 11, c. 7, n. 15—18. See also 1 Briand, Méd. Lég. 1ere partie, c. 4, where the question is considered, how far abortion is justifiable, and is neither a crime nor a misdemeanor. See Alis. Cr. L. of Scot. 628.

ABORTUS. The fruit of an abortion; the child born before its time, incapable of life. See *Abortion; Birth; Breath; Dead born; Gestation; Life.*

ABOVE. Literally *higher in place:* But in law this word is sometimes used to designate the superior court, or one which may revise proceedings of an inferior court on error, from such inferior jurisdiction. The court of error is called the court above; the court whose proceedings are to be examined is called the court below.

2. By bail above, is understood bail to the action entered with the prothonotary or clerk, which is an appearance. See *Bail above*. The bail given to the sheriff, in civil cases, when the defendant is arrested on bailable process, is called bail below; (q. v.) Vide *Below*.

TO ABRIDGE, *practice*. To make shorter in words, so as to retain the sense or substance. In law it signifies particularly the making a declaration or count shorter, by taking or severing away some of the substance from it. Brook, tit. Abridgment; Com. Dig. Abridgment; 1 Vin. Ab. 109.

2. Abridgment of the Plaint is allowed even after verdict and before judgment (Booth on R. A.) in all cases of real actions where the writ is *de lib. ten.* generally, as in assize, dower, &c.; because, after the abridgment the writ is still true, it being *liberum tenementum* still. But it is not allowed in a *præcipe quod reddat*, demanding a certain number of acres; for this would falsify the writ. See 2 Saund. 44, (n.) 4; Bro. Abr. Tit. Abr.; 12 Levin's Ent. 76; 2 Saund. 330; Gilb. C. P. 249—253; Thel. Dig. 76, c. 28, pl. 15, lib. 8.

AN ABRIDGMENT. An epitome or compendium of another and larger work, wherein the principal ideas of the larger work are summarily contained. When fairly made, it may justly be deemed, within the meaning of the law, a new work, the publication of which will not infringe the copyright of the work abridged. An injunction, however, will be granted against a mere colorable abridgment. 2 Atk. 143; 1 Bro. C. C. 451; 5 Ves. 709; Lofft's R. 775; Ambl. 403; 5 Ves. 709; 1 Story, R. 11. See *Quotation*.

2. Abridgments of the Law or Digests of Adjudged Cases, serve the very useful purpose of an index to the cases abridged, 5 Co. Rep. 25. Lord Coke says they are most profitable to those who make them. Co. Lit. in preface to the table at the end of the work. With few exceptions, they are not entitled to be considered authoritative. 2 Wils. R. 1, 2; 1 Burr. Rep. 364; 1 Bl. Rep. 101; 3 T. R. 64, 241. See North American Review, July, 1826, pp. 8, 13, for an account of the principal abridgments.

ABROGATION, *in the civil law, legislation.* The destruction or annulling of a former law, by an act of the legislative power, or by usage. A law may be abrogated or only derogated from; it is abrogated when it is totally annulled; it is derogated from when only a part is abrogated: *derogatur legi, cùm pars detrahitur; abrogatur legi, cùm prorsùs tollitur.* Dig. lib. 50, t. 17, 1, 102. Lex *rogatur* dum fertur; *abrogatur* dum tollitur; *derogatur* eidem dum quoddam ejus caput aboletur; *subrogatur* dum aliquid ei adjicitur; *abrogatur* denique, quoties aliquid in eâ mutatur. Dupin, Proleg. Juris, Art. iv.

2. Abrogation is express or implied; it is express when it is literally pronounced by the new law, either in general terms, as when a final clause abrogates or repeals all laws contrary to the provisions of the new one, or in particular terms, as when it abrogates certain preceding laws which are named.

3. Abrogation is implied when the new law contains provisions which are positively contrary to the former laws, without expressly abrogating such laws: for it is a maxim, *posteriora derogant prioribus.* 3 N. S. 190: 10 M. R. 172. 560. It is also implied when the order of things for which the law had been made no longer exists, and hence the motives which had caused its enactment have ceased to operate; *ratione legis omnino cessante cessat lex.* Toullier, Droit Civil Français, tit. prel. § 11, n. 151. Merlin, mot Abrogation.

ABSCOND. To go in a clandestine manner out of the jurisdiction of the courts, or to lie concealed in order to avoid their process.

ABSENTEE. One who is away from his domicil, or usual place of residence.

2. After an absence of seven years without being heard from, the presumption of death arises. 2 Campb. R. 113; Hardin's R. 479; 18 Johns. R. 141; 15 Mass R. 305; Peake's Ev. c. 14, s. 1; 2 Stark. Ev. 457, 8; 4 Barn. & A. 422; 1 Stark. C. 121; Park on Ins. 433; 1 Bl. R. 404, Burr *v.* Simm, 4 Wh. 150; Bradley *v.* Bradley, 4 Wh. 173.

3. In Louisiana, when a person possessed of either movable or immovable property within the state, leaves it, without having appointed somebody to take care of his estate; or when the person thus appointed dies, or is either unable or unwilling to continue to administer that estate, then and in that case, the judge of the place where the estate is situated, shall appoint a curator to administer the same. Civ. Code of Lo. art. 50. In the appointment of this curator the judge shall prefer the wife of the absentee to his presumptive heirs, the presumptive heirs to other relations; the relations to strangers, and creditors to those who are not otherwise interested; provided, however, that such persons be possessed of the necessary qualifications. Ib. art. 51. For the French law on this subject, vide Biret, de l'Absence; Code Civil, liv. 1, tit. 4; Fouss. lib. 1, tit. 4, n. 379–487; Merl. Rép. h. t.; and see also Ayl. Pand. 269; Dig. 50, 16, 198; Ib. 50, 16, 173; Ib. 3, 3 5; Code, 7 32 12.

ABSOLUTE. Without any condition or incumbrance, as an "absolute bond," *simplex obligatio*, in distinction from a conditional bond; an absolute estate, one that is free from all manner of condition or incumbrance. A rule is said to be absolute, when, on the hearing, it is confirmed. As to the effect of an absolute conveyance, see 1 Pow. Mortg. 125; in relation to absolute rights, 1 Chitty, Pl. 364; 1 Chitty, Pr. 32.

ABSOLUTION. A definite sentence whereby a man accused of any crime is acquitted.

ABSQUE HOC, *pleading*. When the pleadings were in Latin, these words were employed in a traverse. *Without this, that*, (q. v.) are now used for the same purpose.

ABSQUE IMPETITIONE VASTI. Without impeachment of waste. (q. v.) Without any right to prevent waste.

ABSQUE TALI CAUSA. This phrase is used in a traverse *de injuria*, by which the plaintiff affirms that *without the cause* in his plea alleged he did commit the said trespasses, &c. Gould on Pl. c. 7, part 2, § 9.

ABSTENTION, *French law*. This is the tacit renunciation by an heir of a succession. Merl. Rép. h. t.

ABSTRACT OF TITLE. A brief account of all the deeds upon which the title to an estate rests. See *Brief of Title*.

ABUSE. Every thing which is contrary to good order established by usage. Merl. Rép. h. t. Among the civilians, abuse has another signification; which is the destruction of the substance of a thing in using it. For example, the borrower of wine or grain, abuses the article lent by using it, because he cannot enjoy it without consuming it. Leç; El. Dr. Rom. § 414. 416.

ABUTTALS. The buttings and boundings of land, showing on what other lands, rivers, highways, or other places it does abut. More properly, it is said, the sides of land are *adjoining*, and the ends *abutting* to the thing contiguous. Vide *Boundaries*, and Cro. Jac. 184.

AC ETIAM, *Eng. law*. In order to give jurisdiction to a court, a cause of action over which the court has jurisdiction is alleged, *and also*, (ac etiam) another cause of action over which, without being joined with the first, the court would have no jurisdiction; for example, to the usual complaint of breaking the plaintiff's close, over which the court has jurisdiction, a clause is added containing the real cause of action. This juridical contrivance grew out of the Statute 13 Charles II. Stat. 2, c. 2. The clause was added by Lord North, Ch. J. of the C. P. to the *clausum fregit* writs of that court upon which writs of *capias* might issue. He balanced awhile whether he should not use the words *nec non* instead of *ac etiam*. The matter is fully explained in Burgess on Insolvency, 149. 155. 156. 157.

ACCEDAS AD CURIAM, *Eng. law*. That you go to court. An original writ, issuing out of chancery, now of course, returnable in K. B. or C. P. for the removal of a replevin sued by plaint in court of any lord, other than the county before the sheriff. See F. N. B. 18; Dyer, 169.

ACCEDAS AD VICECOMITEM, *Eng. law*. The name of a writ directed to the coroner, commanding him to deliver a writ to the sheriff, who having a *pone* delivered to him, suppresses it.

ACCEPTANCE, *contracts*. An agreement to receive something which has been offered.

2. To complete the contract, the acceptance must be absolute and past recall, 10 Pick. 326; 1 Pick. 278; and communicated to the party making the offer at the time and place appointed. 4 Wheat. R. 225; 6 Wend. 103.

3. In many cases acceptance of a thing waives the right which the party receiving before had; as, for example, the acceptance of rent after notice to quit, in general waives the notice. See Co. Litt. 211, b; Id. 215, a; and *Notice to quit*.

4. The acceptance may be express, as when it is openly declared by the party to be bound by it; or implied, as where the party acts as if he had accepted. The offer and acceptance must be in some medium understood by both parties; it may be language, symbolical, oral or written. For example, persons deaf and dumb may contract by symbolical or written language. At auction sales, the contract is generally symbolical; a nod, a wink, or some other sign by one party, imports that he makes an offer, and knocking down a hammer by the other, that he agrees to it. 3 D. & E. 148. This subject is further considered under the articles *Assent* and *Offer*, (q. v.)

5. *Acceptance of a bill of exchange* is the act by which the drawee or other person evinces his assent or intention to comply with, and be bound by, the request

contained in a bill of exchange to pay the same; or in other words, it is an engagement to pay the bill when due. 4 East, 72. It will be proper to consider, 1, by whom the acceptance ought to be made; 2, the time when it is to be made; 3, the form of the acceptance; 4, its extent or effect.

6.—1. The acceptance must be made by the drawee himself, or by one authorized by him. On the presentment of a bill, the holder has a right to insist upon such an acceptance by the drawee as will subject him at all events to the payment of the bill, according to its tenor; consequently such drawee must have capacity to contract, and to bind himself to pay the amount of the bill, or it may be treated as dishonored. Marius, 22. See 2 Ad. & Ell. N. S. 16, 17.

7.—2. As to the *time* when a bill ought to be accepted, it may be before the bill is drawn; in this case it must be in writing; 3 Mass. 1; or it may be after it is drawn; when the bill is presented, the drawee must accept the bill within twenty-four hours after presentment, or it should be treated as dishonored. Chit. Bills, 212. 217. On the refusal to accept, even within the twenty-four hours, it should be protested. Chit. Bills, 217. The acceptance may be made after the bill is drawn, and before it becomes due; or after the time appointed for payment; 1 H. Bl. 313; 2 Green, R. 339; and even after refusal to accept so as to bind the acceptor.

8. The acceptance may also be made *supra protest*, which is the acceptance of the bill, after protest for non-acceptance by the drawee, for the honor of the drawer, or a particular endorser. When a bill has been accepted supra protest for the honor of one party to the bill, it may be accepted *supra protest*, by another individual, for the honor of another. Beawes, tit. Bills of Exchange, pl. 52; 5 Campb. R. 447.

9.—3. As to the *form* of the acceptance, it is clearly established it may be in writing on the bill itself, or on another paper, 4 East, 91; or it may be verbal, 4 East, 67; 10 John. 207; 3 Mass. 1; or it may be expressed or implied.

10. An *express* acceptance is an agreement in direct and express terms to pay a bill of exchange, either by the party on whom it is drawn, or by some other person, for the honor of some of the parties. It is usually in the words *accepted* or *accepts*, but other express words showing an engagement to pay the bill will be equally binding.

11. An *implied* acceptance is an agreement to pay a bill, not by direct and express terms, but by any acts of the party from which an express agreement may be fairly inferred; for example, if the drawee writes "seen," "presented," or any other thing upon it, (as the day on which it becomes due,) this, unless explained by other circumstances, will constitute an acceptance.

12.—4. An acceptance in regard to its extent and effect, may be either absolute, conditional, or partial.

13. An *absolute* acceptance is a positive engagement to pay the bill according to its tenor, and is usually made by writing on the bill "accepted," and subscribing the drawee's name; or by merely writing his name either at the bottom or across the bill. Comb. 401; Vin. Ab. Bills of Exchange, L 4; Bayl. 77; Chit. Bills, 226 to 228. But in order to bind another than the drawee, it is requisite his name should appear. Bayl. 78.

14. A *conditional* acceptance is one which will subject the drawee or acceptor to the payment of the money on a contingency. Bayl. 83, 4, 5; Chit. Bills, 234; Holt's C. N. P. 182; 5 Taunt. 344; 1 Marsh. 186. The holder is not bound to receive such an acceptance, but if he do receive it he must observe its terms. 4 M. & S. 466; 2 W. C. C. R. 485; 1 Campb. 425.

15. A *partial* acceptance varies from the tenor of the bill; as where it is made to pay part of the sum for which the bill is drawn, 1 Stra. 214; 2 Wash. C. C. R. 485; or to pay at a different time, Molloy, b. 2, c. 10, s. 20; or place, 4 M. & S. 462.

ACCEPTILATION, *contracts*. In the civil law, is a release made by a creditor to his debtor of his debt, without receiving any consideration. Ayl. Pand. tit. 26, p. 570. It is a species of donation, but not subject to the forms of the latter, and is valid, unless in fraud of creditors. Merlin, Répert. de Jurisp. h. t. Acceptilation may be defined *verborum conceptio qua creditor debitori, quod debet, acceptum fert;* or, a certain arrangement of words by which on the question of the debtor, the creditor, wishing to dissolve the obligation, answers that he admits as received, what in fact, he has not received The acceptilation is an imaginary payment Dig. 46, 4, 1 and 19; Dig. 2, 14, 27, 9, Inst. 3, 30, 1.

ACCEPTOR, *contracts*. The person who agrees to pay a bill of exchange drawn upon him. There cannot be two separate acceptors of a bill of exchange, e. g. an acceptance by the drawee, and another for the honor of some party to the bill. Jackson *v.* Hudson, 2 Campb. N. P. C. 447.

2. The acceptor of a bill is the principal debtor, and the drawer the surety. He is bound, though he accepted without consideration, and for the sole accommodation of the drawer. By his acceptance he admits the drawer's handwriting, for, before acceptance it was incumbent upon him to inquire into the genuineness of the drawer's handwriting. 3 Burr. 1354; 1 Bla. Rep. 390, S. C.; 4 Dall. 234; 1 Binn. 27, S. C. When once made, the obligation of the acceptor is irrevocable. As to what amounts to an acceptance, see ante, *Acceptance;* Chitty on Bills, 242, et. seq.; 3 Kent, Com. 55, 6; Pothier, Traité du Contrat de Change, prêmiere part. n. 44.

3. The liability of the acceptor cannot in general be released or discharged, otherwise than by payment, or by express release or waiver, or by the act of limitations. Dougl. R. 247. What amounts to a waiver and discharge of the acceptor's liability, must depend on the circumstances of each particular case. Dougl. 236, 248; Bayl. on Bills, 90; Chitty on Bills, 249.

Acceptor supra protest, *in contracts,* is a third person, who, after protest for non-acceptance by the drawee, accepts the bill for the honor of the drawer, or of the particular endorser.

2. By this acceptance he subjects himself to the same obligations as if the bill had been directed to him. An acceptor supra protest has his remedy against the person for whose honor he accepted, and against all persons who stand prior to that person. If he takes up the bill for the honor of the endorser, he stands in the light of an endorsee paying full value for the bill, and has the same remedies to which an endorsee would be entitled against all prior parties, and he can, of course, sue the drawer and endorser. 1 Ld. Raym. 574; 1 Esp. N. P. Rep. 112; Bayley on Bills, 209; 3 Kent. Com. 57; Chitty on Bills, 312. The acceptor supra protest is required to give the same notice, in order to charge a party, which is necessary to be given by other holders. 8 Pick. 1. 79; 1 Pet. R. 262. Such acceptor is not liable, unless demand of payment is made on the drawee, and notice of his refusal given. 3 Wend. 491.

ACCESS, *persons.* Approach, or the means or power of approaching. Sometimes by access is understood sexual intercourse; at other times the opportunity of communicating together so that sexual intercourse may have taken place, is also called access. 1 Turn. & R. 141.

2. In this sense a man who can readily be in company with his wife, is said to have access to her; and in that case, her issue are presumed to be his issue. But this presumption may be rebutted by positive evidence that no sexual intercourse took place. Ib.

3. Parents are not allowed to prove non-access, for the purpose of bastardizing the issue of the wife; nor will their declarations be received after their deaths, to prove the want of access, with a like intent. 1 P. A. Bro. R. App. xlviii.; Rep. tem. Hard. 79; Bull. N. P. 113; Cowp. R. 592; 8 East, R. 203; 11 East, R. 133. 2 Munf. R. 242; 3 Munf. R. 599; 7 N. S. 553; 4 Hayw. R. 221; 3 Hawks, R. 623; 1 Ashm. R. 269; 6 Binn. R. 283; 3 Paige's R. 129; 7 N. S. 548. See Shelf. on Mar. & Div. 711; and *Paternity.*

ACCESSARY, *criminal law.* He who is not the chief actor in the perpetration of the offence, nor present at its performance, but is some way concerned therein, either before or after the fact committed.

2. *An accessary before the fact,* is one who being absent at the time of the crime committed, yet procures, counsels, or commands another to commit it. 1 Hale, P. C. 615. It is proper to observe that when the act is committed through the agency of a person who has no legal discretion nor a will, as in the case of a child or an insane person, the incitor, though absent when the crime was committed, will be considered, not an accessary, for none can be accessary to the acts of a madman, but a principal in the first degree. Fost. 340; 1 P. C. 118.

3. *An accessary after the fact,* is one who knowing a felony to have been committed, receives, relieves, comforts, or assists the felon. 4 Bl. Com. 37.

4. No one who is a principal (q. v.) can be an accessary.

5. In certain crimes, there can be no accessaries; all who are concerned are principals, whether they were present or absent at the time of their commission. These are treason, and all offences below the degree of felony. 1 Russ. 21, et seq.; 4 Bl. Com. 35 to 40; 1 Hale, P. C. 615; 1 Vin. Abr. 113; Hawk. P. C. b. 2, c. 29, s. 16; such is the English Law. But whether it is law

in the United States appears not to be determined as regards the cases of persons assisting traitors. Serg. Const. Law, 382; 4 Cranch, R. 472, 501; United States *v.* Fries, Pamphl. 199.

6. It is evident there can be no accessary when there is no principal; if a principal in a transaction be not liable under our laws, no one can be charged as a mere accessary to him. 1 W. & M. 221.

7. By the rules of the common law, accessaries cannot be tried, without their consent, before the principals. Foster, 360. The evils resulting from this rule, are stated at length in the 8th vol. of Todd's Spencer, pp. 329, 330.

ACCESSION, *property*. The ownership of a thing, whether it be real or personal, movable or immovable, carries with it the right to all that the thing produces, and to all that becomes united to it, either naturally or artificially; this is called the right of accession.

2.—1. The doctrine of property arising from accession, is grounded on the right of occupancy.

3.—2. The original owner of any thing which receives an accession by natural or artificial means, as by the growth of vegetables, the pregnancy of animals; Louis. Code, art. 491; the embroidering of cloth, or the conversion of wood or metal into vessels or utensils, is entitled to his right of possession to the property of it, under such its state of improvement; 5 H. 7, 15; 12 H. 8, 10; Bro. Ab. Propertie, 23; Moor, 20; Poph. 38. But the owner must be able to prove the identity of the original materials, for if wine, oil, or bread, be made out of another man's grapes, olives, or wheat, they belong to the new operator, who is bound to make satisfaction to the former proprietor for the materials which he has so converted. 2 Bl. Com. 404; 5 Johns. Rep. 348; Betts *v.* Lee, 6 Johns. Rep. 169; Curtiss *v.* Groat, 10 Johns. 288; Babcock *v.* Gill, 9 Johns. Rep. 363; Chandler *v.* Edson, 5 H. 7, 15; 12 H. 8, 10; Fits. Abr. Bar. 144; Bro. Abr. Property, 23; Doddridge Eng. Lawyer, 125, 126, 132, 134. See *Adjunction; Confusion of Goods*. See Generally, Louis. Code, tit. 2, c. 2 and 3.

ACCESSION, *international law*, is the absolute or conditional acceptance by one or several states, of a treaty already concluded between other sovereignties. Merl. Rép. mot Accession.

ACCESSORY, *property*. Everything which is joined to another thing, as an ornament, or to render it more perfect, is an accessory, and belongs to the principal thing. For example, the halter of a horse, the frame of a picture, the keys of a house, and the like; but a bequest of a house would not carry the furniture in it, as accessory to it. Domat, Lois Civ. Part. 2, liv. 4, tit. 2, s. 4, n. 1. *Accessorium non ducit, sed sequitur principale*. Co. Litt. 152, a. Co. Litt. 121, b. note (6). Vide *Accession; Adjunction; Appendant; Appurtenances; Appurtenant; Incident*.

ACCESSORY CONTRACT. One made for assuring the performance of a prior contract, either by the same parties or by others; such as suretyship, mortgages, and pledges.

2. It is a general rule, that payment of the debt due, or the performance of a thing required to be performed by the first or principal contract, is a full discharge of such accessory obligation. Poth. Ob. part. 1, c. 1, s. 1, art. 2, n. 14. Id. n. 182, 186. See 8 Mass. 551; 15 Mass. 233; 17 Mass 419; 4 Pick. 11; 8 Pick. 522.

3. An accessory agreement to guaranty an original contract, which is void, has no binding effect. 6 Hnmph. 261.

ACCIDENT. The happening of an event without the concurrence of the will of the person by whose agency it was caused: or the happening of an event without any human agency; the burning of a house in consequence of a fire being made for the ordinary purpose of cooking or warming the house, which is an accident of the first kind; the burning of the same house by lightning would have been an accident of the second kind. 1 Fonb. Eq. 374, 5, note.

2. It frequently happens that a lessee covenants to repair, in which case he is bound to do so, although the premises be burned down without his fault. 1 Hill. Ab. c. 15, s. 75. But if a penalty be annexed to the covenant, inevitable accident will excuse the former, though not the latter. 1 Dyer, 33, a. Neither the landlord nor the tenant is bound to rebuild a house burned down, unless it has been so expressly agreed. Amb. 619; 1 T. R. 708; 4 Paige, R. 355; 6 Mass. R. 67; 4 M'Cord, R. 431; 3 Kent, Com. 373.

3. In New Jersey, by statute, no action lies against any person on the ground that a fire began in a house or room occupied by

him, if accidental. But this does not affect any covenant. 1 N. J. Rev. C. 210.

ACCIDENT, *practice.* This term in chancery jurisprudence, signifies such unforeseen events, misfortunes, losses, acts or omissions, as are not the result of any negligence or misconduct in the party. Francis' Max. M. 120, p. 87; 1 Story on Eq. § 78.

Jeremy defines it as used in courts of equity, to be "an occurrence in relation to a contract, which was not anticipated by the parties, when the same was entered into, and which gives an undue advantage to one of them over the other in a court of law." Jer. on Eq. 358. This definition is objected to, because as accidents may arise in relation to other things besides contracts, it is inaccurate in confining accidents to contracts; besides, it does not exclude cases of unanticipated occurrences, resulting from the negligence or misconduct of the party seeking relief. 1 Story on Eq. § 78, note 1.

2. In general, courts of equity will relieve a party who cannot obtain justice in consequence of an accident, which will justify the interposition of a court of equity. The jurisdiction being concurrent, will be maintained only, first, when a court of law cannot grant suitable relief; and, secondly, when the party has a conscientious title to relief.

3. Many accidents are redressed in a court of law; as loss of deeds, mistakes in receipts and accounts, wrong payments, death, which makes it impossible to perform a condition literally, and a multitude of other contingencies; and many cannot be redressed even in a court of equity; as if by accident a recovery is ill suffered, a contingent remainder destroyed, or a power of leasing omitted in a family settlement. 3 Bl. Com. 431. Vide, generally, Com. Dig. Chancery, 3 F 8; 1 Fonb. Eq. B. 1, c. 3, s. 7; Coop. Eq. Pl. 129; 1 Chit. Pr. 408; Harr. Ch. Index, h. t.; Dane's Ab. h. t.; Wheat. Dig. 48; Mitf. Pl. Index, h. t.; 1 Madd. Ch. Pr. 23; 10 Mod. R. 1, 3; 3 Chit. Bl. Com. 426, n.

ACCOMENDA, *mar. law.* In Italy, is a contract which takes place when an individual entrusts personal property with the master of a vessel, to be sold for their joint account. In such case, two contracts take place; first, the contract called *mandatum,* by which the owner of the property gives the master power to dispose of it; and the contract of partnership, in virtue of which, the profits are to be divided between them. One party runs the risk of losing his capital, the other his labor. If the sale produces no more than first cost, the owner takes all the proceeds; it is only the profits which are to be divided. Emer. on Mar. Loans, s. 5.

ACCOMMODATION, *com. law.* That which is done by one merchant or other person for the convenience of some other, by accepting or endorsing his paper, or by lending him his notes or bills.

2. In general the parties who have drawn, endorsed or accepted bills or other commercial paper for the accommodation, of others, are, while in the hands of a holder who received them before they became due, other than the person for whom the accommodation was given, responsible as if they had received full value. Chit. Bills, 90, 91. See 4 Cranch, 141; 1 Ham. 413; 7 John. 361; 15 John. 355, 17 John. 176; 9 Wend. 170; 2 Whart. 344; 5 Wend. 566; 8 Wend. 437; 2 Hill, S. C. 362; 10 Conn. 308; 5 Munf. 381.

ACCOMMODATION, *contracts.* An amicable agreement or composition between two contending parties. It differs from *accord and satisfaction,* which may take place without any difference having existed between the parties.

ACCOMPLICE, *crim. law.* This term includes in its meaning, all persons who have been concerned in the commission of a crime, all *particepes criminis,* whether they are considered in strict legal propriety, as principals in the first or second degree, or merely as accessaries before or after the fact. Foster, 341; 1 Russell, 21; 4 Bl. Com. 331; 1 Phil. Ev. 28; Merlin, Répertoire, mot Complice. U. S. Dig. h. t.

2. But in another sense, by the word accomplice is meant, one who not being a principal, is yet in some way concerned in the commission of a crime. It has been questioned, whether one who was an accomplice to a suicide can be punished as such. A case occurred in Prussia where a soldier, at the request of his comrade, had cut the latter in pieces; for this he was tried capitally. In the year 1817, a young woman named Leruth received a recompense for aiding a man to kill himself. He put the point of a bistouri on his naked breast, and used the hand of the young woman to plunge it with greater force into his bosom; hearing some noise he ordered her away. The man receiving effectual aid was soon cured of the wound which had been inflicted

and she was tried and convicted of having inflicted the wound, and punished by ten years' imprisonment. Lepage, Science du Droit, ch. 2, art. 3, § 5. The case of Saul, the king of Israel, and his armor bearer, (1 Sam. xxxi. 4,) and of David and the Amelekite, (2 Sam. i. 2—16,) will doubtless occur to the reader.

ACCORD, *in contracts*. A satisfaction agreed upon between the party injuring and the party injured, which when performed is a bar to all actions upon this account. 3 Bl. Com. 15; Bac. Abr. Accord.

2. In order to make a good accord it is essential:—

1. That the accord be *legal*. An agreement to drop a criminal prosecution as a satisfaction for an assault and imprisonment, is void. 5 East, 294. See 2 Wils. 341; Cro. Eliz. 541.

3.—2. It must be *advantageous* to the contracting party; hence restoring to the plaintiff his chattels, or his land, of which the defendant has wrongfully dispossessed him, will not be any consideration to support a promise by the plaintiff not to sue him for those injuries. Bac. Abr. Accord, &c. A; Perk. s. 749; Dyer, 75; 5 East, R. 230; 1 Str. R. 426; 2 T. R. 24; 11 East, R. 390; 3 Hawks, R. 580; 2 Litt. R. 49; 1 Stew. R. 476; 5 Day, R. 360; 1 Root, R. 426; 3 Wend. R. 66; 1 Wend. R. 164; 14 Wend. R. 116; 3 J. J. Marsh. R. 497.

4.—3. It must be *certain;* hence an agreement that the defendant shall relinquish the possession of a house in satisfaction, &c., is not valid, unless it is also agreed at what time it shall be relinquished. Yelv. 125. See 4 Mod. 88; 2 Johns. 342; 3 Lev. 189.

5.—4. The defendant must be *privy* to the contract. If therefore the consideration for the promise not to sue proceeds from another, the defendant is a stranger to the agreement, and the circumstance that the promise has been made to him will be of no avail. Str. 592; 6 John. R. 37; 3 Monr. R. 302; but in such case equity will grant relief by injunction. 3 Monr. R. 302; 5 East, R. 294; 1 Smith's R. 515; Cro. Eliz. 541; 9 Co. 79, b; 3 Taunt. R. 117; 5 Co. 117, b.

6.—5 The accord must be *executed*. 5 Johns. R. 386; 3 Johns. Cas. 243; 16 Johns. R. 86; 2 Wash. C. C. R. 180; 6 Wend. R. 390; 5 N. H. Rep. 136; Com. Dig. Accord, B 4.

7. Accord with satisfaction when completed has two effects; it is a payment of the debt; and it is a species of sale of the thing given by the debtor to the creditor, in satisfaction; but it differs from it in this, that it is not valid until the delivery of the article, and there is no warranty of the thing thus sold, except perhaps the title; for in regard to this, it cannot be doubted, that if the debtor gave on an accord and satisfaction the goods of another, there would be no satisfaction. See *Dation en paiement*.

See in general Com. Dig. h. t.; Bac. Ab. h. t.; Com. Dig. Pleader, 2 V 8; 5 East, R. 230; 4 Mod. 88; 1 Taunt. R. 428; 7 East, R. 150; 1 J. B. Moore, 358, 460; 2 Wils. R. 86; 6 Co. 43, b; 3 Chit. Com. Law, 687 to 698; Harr. Dig. h. t.; 1 W. Bl. 388; 2 T. R. 24; 2 Taunt. 141; 3 Taunt. 117; 5 B. & A. 886; 2 Chit. R. 303, 324; 11 East, 390; 7 Price, 604; 2 Greenl. Ev. § 28; 1 Bouv. Inst. n. 805; 3 Bouv. Inst. n. 2478-79-80-81. Vide *Discharge of Obligations*.

ACCOUCHEMENT. The act of giving birth to a child. It is frequently important to prove the filiation of an individual; this may be done in several ways. The fact of the accouchement may be proved by the direct testimony of one who was present, as a physician, a midwife, or other person. 1 Bouv. Inst. n. 314.

ACCOUNT, *remedies*. This is the name of a writ or action more properly called *account render*.

2. It is applicable to the case of an unliquidated demand, against a person who is chargeable as bailiff or receiver. The use of it, is where the plaintiff wants an account and cannot give evidence of his right without it. 5 Taunt. 431. It is necessary where the receipt was directed to a merchandising which makes an uncertainty of the nett remain, till the account is finished; or where a man is charged as bailiff, whereupon the certainty of his receipt appears not till account. Hob. 209. See also 8 Cowen, R. 304; 9 Conn. R. 556; 2 Day, R. 28; Kirby, 164; 3 Gill & John. 388; 3 Verm. 485; 4 Watts, 420; 8 Cowen, 220. It is also the proper remedy by one partner against another. 15 S. & R. 153; 3 Binn. 317; 10 S. & R. 220; 2 Conn. 425, 4 Verm. 137; 1 Dall. 340; 2 Watts, 86.

3. The interlocutory judgment in this action is (*quod computet*) that the defendant render an account upon which judgment, auditors are assigned to him to hear and

report his account. (See 1 Lutwych, 47; 3 Leon. 149, for precedents.) As the principal object of the action is to compel a settlement of the account in the first instance, special bail cannot be demanded, (2 Roll. Rep. 53; 2 Keble, 404,) nor are damages awarded upon the first judgment, nor given, except *ratione interplacitationis*, (Cro. Eliz. 83; 5 Binn. 564; 24 Ed. 3. 16; 18 Ed. 3. 55; Reg. Brev. 136 b,) although it is usual to conclude the count with a demand of damages. (Lib. Int. fo. 16. fo. 20; 1 Lutw. 51. 58; 2 H. 7. 13.) The reason assigned for this rule, is, that it may be the defendant will not be found in arrear after he has accounted, and the court cannot know until the settlement of the account whether the plaintiff has been endamaged or not. 7 H. 6. 38.

4. This action combines the properties of a legal and equitable action. The proceedings up to the judgment *quod computet*, and subsequent to the account reported by the auditors are conducted upon the principles of the common law. But the account is to be adjusted upon the most liberal principles of equity and good faith. (Per Herle, Ch. J. 3 Ed. 3. 10.) The court it is said are judges of the action—the auditors of the account, Bro. Ab. Acc. 48, and both are judges of record, 4 H. 6. 17; Stat. West. 2. c. 11. This action has received a liberal extension in Pennsylvania. 1 Dall. 339, 340.

5. The first judgment (quod computet) is enforced by a *capias ad computandum* where defendant refuses to appear before the auditors, upon which he may be held to bail, or in default of bail be made to account in prison. The final judgment *quod recuperet* is enforced by *fi. fa.* or such other process as the law allows for the recovery of debts.

6. If the defendant charged as bailiff is found in surplusage, no judgment can be entered thereon to recover the amount so found in his favor against the plaintiff, but as the auditors are judges of record, he may bring an action of debt, or by some authorities a sci. fac. against the plaintiff, whereon he may have judgment and execution against the plaintiff. See Palm. 512; 2 Bulst. 277–8; 1 Leon. 219; 3 Keble Rep. 362; 1 Roll. Ab. 599, pl. 11; Bro. Ab. Acc. 62; 1 Roll. Rep. 87. See Bailiff, in *account render*.

7. In those states where they have courts of chancery, this action is nearly superseded, by the better remedy which is given by a bill in equity, by which the complainant can elicit a discovery of the facts from the defendant under his oath, instead of relying merely on the evidence he may be able to produce. 9 John. R. 470; 1 Paige, R. 41; 2 Caines' Cas. Err. 1, 38, 52; 1 J. J. Marsh. R. 82; Cooke, R. 420; 1 Yerg. R. 360; 2 John. Ch. R. 424; 10 John. R. 587; 2 Rand. R. 449; 1 Hen. & M. 9; 2 M'Cord's Ch. R. 469; 2 Leigh's R. 6.

8. Courts of equity have concurrent jurisdiction in matters of account with courts of law, and sometimes exclusive jurisdiction, at least in some respects: For example; if a plaintiff be entitled to an account, a court of equity will restrain the defendant from proceeding in a claim, the correctness of which cannot be ascertained until the account be taken; but not where the subject is matter of set-off. 1 Sch. & Lef. 309; Eden on Injunct. 23, 24.

9. When an account has voluntarily been stated between parties, an action of assumpsit may be maintained thereon. 3 Bl. Com. 162; 8 Com. Dig. 7; 1 Com. Dig. 180; 2 Ib. 468; 1 Vin. Ab. 135; Bac. Ab. h. t.; Doct. Pl. 26; Yelv. 202; 1 Supp. to Ves. Jr. 117; 2 Ib. 48, 136. Vide 1 Binn. R. 191; 4 Dall. R. 434; Whart. Dig. h. t.; 3 Wils. 73, 94; 3 D. & R. 596; Bull. N. P. 128; 5 Taunt. 431; U. S. Dig. h. t.; 2 Greenl. Ev. § 34—39.

Account, *practice*. A statement of the receipts and payments of an executor, administrator, or other trustee, of the estate confided to him.

2. Every one who administers the affairs of another is required at the end of his administration to render an account of his management of the same. Trustees of every description can, in general, be compelled by courts of chancery to settle accounts, or otherwise fully execute their trusts. Where there are no courts of chancery, the courts of common law are usually invested with power for the same purposes by acts of legislation. When a party has had the property of another as his agent, he may be compelled at common law to account by an action of account render.

3. An account is also the statement of two merchants or others who have dealt together, showing the debits and credits between them.

Account-Book. A book kept by a merchant, trader, mechanic, or other person, in which are entered from time to time the transactions of his trade or business. Vide *Books; Entry; Original entry*.

Account Current. A running or open account between two persons.

Account in Bank, *com. law*. 1. A fund which merchants, traders and others, have deposited into the common cash of some bank, to be drawn out by checks from time to time as the owner or depositor may require. 2. The statement of the amount deposited and drawn, which is kept in duplicate, one in the depositor's bank book, and the other in the books of the bank.

Account Stated. The settlement of an account between the parties, by which a balance is struck in favor of one of them, is called an account stated.

2. An acknowledgment of a single item of debt due from the defendant to the plaintiff, is sufficient to support a count on an account stated. 13 East, 249; 5 M. & S. 65.

3. It is proposed to consider, 1st, by whom an account may be stated; 2d, the manner of stating the account; 3d, the declaration upon such an account; 4th, the evidence.

4.—1. An account may be stated by a man and his wife of the one part, and a third person; and unless there is an express promise to pay by the husband, Foster *v.* Allanson, 2 T. R. 483, the action must be brought against husband and wife. Drue *v.* Thorne, Aleyn, 72. A plaintiff cannot recover against a defendant upon an account stated by him, partly as administrator and partly in his own private capacity. Herrenden *v.* Palmer, Hob. 88. Persons wanting a legal capacity to make a contract cannot, in general, state an account; as infants, Truman *v.* Hurst, 1 T. R. 40; and persons non compos mentis.

5. A plaintiff may recover on an account stated with the defendant, including debts due from the defendant alone, and from the defendant and a deceased partner jointly. Richards *v.* Heather, 1 B. & A. 29, and see Peake's Ev. 257. A settlement between partners, and striking a balance, will enable a plaintiff to maintain an action on such stated account for the balance due him, Ozeas *v.* Johnson, 4 Dall. 434; S. C. 1 Binn. 191; S. P. Andrews *v.* Allen, 9 S. & R. 241; and see Lamelere *v.* Caze, 1 W. C. C. R. 435.

6.—2. It is sufficient, although the account be stated of that which is due to the plaintiff only, without making any deduction for any counter-claim for the defendant, Styart *v.* Rowland, 1 Show. 215. It is not essential that there should be cross demands between the parties, or that the defendant's acknowledgment that a certain sum was due from him to the plaintiff, should relate to more than a single debt or transaction. 5 Maule & Selw. 65; Knowles et al. 13 East, 249. The acknowledgment by the defendant that a certain sum is due, creates an implied promise to pay the amount. Milward *v.* Ingraham, 2 Mod. 44; Foster *v.* Allanson, 2 T. R. 480.

7.—3. A count on an account stated is almost invariably inserted in declarations in assumpsit for the recovery of a pecuniary demand. See form, 1 Chit. Pl. 336. It is advisable, generally, to insert such a count, Milward *v.* Ingraham, 2 Mod. 44; Trueman *v.* Hurst, 1 T. R. 42; unless the action be against persons who are incapable in law to state an account. It is not necessary to set forth the subject-matter of the original debt, Milward *v.* Ingraham, 2 Mod. 44; nor is the sum alleged to be due material. Rolls *v.* Barnes, 1 Bla. Rep. 65; S. C. 1 Burr. 9.

8.—4. The count upon *an account stated*, is supported by evidence of an acknowledgment on the part of the defendant of money due to the plaintiff, upon an account between them. But the sum must have been stated between the parties; it is not sufficient that the balance may be deduced from partnership books. Andrews *v.* Allen, 9 S. &. R. 241. It is unnecessary to prove the items of which the account consists; it is sufficient to prove some existing antecedent debt or demand between the parties respecting which an account was stated, 5 Moore, 105; 4 B. & C. 235, 242; 6 D. & R. 306; and that a balance was struck and agreed upon; Bartlet *v.* Emery, 1 T. R. 42, n; for the stating of the account is the consideration of the promise. Bull. N. P. 129. An account stated does not alter the original debt, Aleyn, 72; and it seems not to be conclusive against the party admitting the balance against him. 1 T. R. 42. He would probably be allowed to show a gross error or mistake in the account, if he could adduce clear evidence to that effect. See 1 Esp. R. 159. And see generally tit. *Partners*; Chit. Contr. 197; Stark. Ev. 123; 1 Chit. Pl. 343.

9. In courts of equity when a bill for an account has been filed, it is a good defence that the parties have already in writing stated and adjusted the items of the account, and struck a balance; for then an action

lies at law, and there is no ground for the interference of a court of equity. 1 Atk. 1; 2 Freem. 62; 4 Cranch, 306; 11 Wheat. 237; 9 Ves. 265; 2 Bro. Ch. R. 310; 3 Bro. Ch. R. 266; 1 Cox, 435.

10. But if there has been any mistake, omission, fraud, or undue advantage, by which the account stated is in fact vitiated, and the balance incorrectly fixed, a court of equity will open it, and allow it to be re-examined; and where there has been gross fraud it will direct the whole account to be opened and examined *de novo*. Fonbl. Eq. b. 1, c. 1 § 3, note (f); 1 John. Ch. R. 550.

11. Sometimes the court will allow the account to stand, with liberty to the plaintiff to surcharge and falsify it; the effect of this is, to leave the account in full force and vigor, as a stated account, except so far as it can be impugned by the opposing party. 2 Ves. 565; 11 Wheat. 237. See *Falsification; Surcharge.*

ACCOUNT OF SALES. *comm. law.* An account delivered by one merchant or tradesman to another, or by a factor to his principal, of the disposal, charges, commissions and net proceeds of certain merchandise consigned to such merchant, tradesman or factor, to be sold.

ACCOUNTANT. This word has several significations: 1. One who is versed in accounts; 2. A person or officer appointed to keep the accounts of a public company; 3. He who renders to another or to a court a just and detailed statement of the administration of property which he holds as trustee, executor, administrator or guardian. Vide 16 Vin. Ab. 155.

ACCOUPLE. To accouple is to marry. See *Ne unques accouple.*

TO ACCREDIT, *international law.* The act by which a diplomatic agent is acknowledged by the government near which he is sent. This at once makes his public character known, and becomes his protection.

ACCRETION. The increase of land by the washing of the seas or rivers. Hale, De Jure Maris, 14. Vide *Alluvion; Avulsion.*

TO ACCRUE. Literally to grow to; as the interest accrues on the principal. *Accruing costs* are those which become due and are created after judgment; as the costs of an execution.

2. To accrue means also to arise, to happen, to come to pass; as the statute of limitations does not commence running until the cause of action has accrued. 1 Bouv. Inst. n. 861; 2 Rawle, 277; 10 Watts, 363; Bac. Abr. Limitation of Actions, D 3.

ACCUMULATIVE JUDGMENT. A second or additional judgment given against one who has been convicted, the execution or effect of which is to commence after the first has expired; as, where a man is sentenced to an imprisonment for six months on conviction of larceny, and, afterwards, he is convicted of burglary, he may be sentenced to undergo an imprisonment for the latter crime, to commence after the expiration of the first imprisonment; this is called an accumulative judgment.

ACCUSED. One who is charged with a crime or misdemeanor.

ACCUSATION, *crim. law.* A charge made to a competent officer against one who has committed a crime or misdemeanor, so that he may be brought to justice and punishment.

2. A neglect to accuse may in some cases be considered a misdemeanor, or misprision. (q. v.) 1 Bro. Civ. Law, 247; 2 Id. 389; Inst. lib. 4, tit. 18.

3. It is a rule that no man is bound to accuse himself, or to testify against himself in a criminal case. Accusare nemo se debet nisi coram Deo. Vide *Evidence; Interest; Witness.*

ACCUSER. One who makes an accusation.

ACHAT. This French word signifies a purchase. It is used in some of our law books, as well as *achetor*, a purchaser, which in some ancient statutes means purveyor. Stat. 36 Edw. III.

ACHERSET, *obsolete.* An ancient English measure of grain, supposed to be the same with their quarter or eight bushels.

ACKNOWLEDGMENT, *conveyancing.* The act of the grantor going before a competent officer, and declaring the instrument to be his act or deed, and desiring the same to be recorded as such. The certificate of the officer on the instrument, that such a declaration has been made to him, is also called an acknowledgment. The acknowledgment or due proof of the instrument by witnesses, must be made before it can be put upon record.

2. Below will be found the law of the several states relating to the officer before whom the acknowledgment must be made. Justice requires that credit should be here given for the valuable information which has been derived on this subject from Mr.

Hilliard's Abridgment of the American Law of Real Property, and from Griffith's Register. Much valuable information has also been received on this subject from the correspondents of the author.

3. *Alabama.* Before one of the judges of the superior court, or any one of the justices of the county court; Act of March 3, 1803; or before any one of the superior judges or justices of the quorum of the territory (state); Act of Dec. 12, 1812; or before the clerks of the circuit and county courts, within their respective counties; Act of Nov. 21, 1818; or any two justices of the peace; Act of Dec. 17, 1819; or clerks of the circuit courts, for deeds conveying lands anywhere in the state; Act of January 6, 1831; or before any notary public, Id. sec. 2; or before one justice of the peace; Act of January 5, 1836; or before the clerks of the county courts; Act of Feb. 1, 1839. See Aikin's Dig. 88, 89, 90, 91, 616; Meek's Suppl. 86.

4. When the acknowledgment is out of the state, in one of the United States or territories thereof, it may be made before the chief justice or any associate judge of the supreme court of the United States, or any judge or justice of the superior court of any state or territory in the Union. Aikin's Dig. 89.

5. When it is made out of the United States, it may be made before and certified by any court of law, mayor or other chief magistrate of any city, borough or corporation of the kingdom, state, nation, or colony, where it is made. Act of March 3, 1803.

6. When a feme covert is a grantor, the officer must certify that she was examined "separately and apart from her said husband, and that on such private examination, she acknowledged that she signed, sealed and delivered the deed as her voluntary act and deed, freely and without any threat, fear, or compulsion, of her said husband."

7. *Arkansas.* The proof or acknowledgment of every deed or instrument of writing for the conveyance of real estate, shall be taken by some one of the following courts or officers: 1. When acknowledged or proven within this state, before the supreme court, the circuit court, or either of the judges thereof, or of the clerk of either of the said courts, or before the county court, or the judge thereof, or before any justice of the peace or notary public.

8.—2. When acknowledged or proven without this state, and within the United States or their territories, before any court of the United States, or of any state or territory having a seal, or the clerk of any such court, or before the mayor of any city or town, or the chief officer of any city or town having a seal of office.

9.—3. When acknowledged or proven without the United States, before any court of any state, kingdom or empire having a seal, or any mayor or chief officer of any city or town having an official seal, or before any officer of any foreign country, who by the laws of such country, is authorized to take probate of the conveyance of real estate of his own country, if such officer has by law an official seal.

10. The conveyance of any real estate by any married woman, or the relinquishment of her dower in any of her husband's real estate, shall be authenticated, and the title passed, by such married woman voluntarily appearing before the proper court or officer, and, in the absence of her husband, declaring that she had of her own free will executed the deed or instrument in question, or that she had signed and sealed the relinquishment of dower for the purposes therein contained and set forth, without any compulsion or undue influence of her husband. Act of Nov. 30, 1837, s. 13, 21; Rev. Stat. 190, 191.

11. In cases of acknowledgment or proof of deeds or conveyances of real estate taken within the United States or territories thereof, when taken before a court or officer, having a seal of office, such deed or conveyance shall be attested under such seal of office; and if such officer have no seal of office, then under the official signature of such officer. Idem, s. 14; Rev. Stat. 190.

12. In all cases of deeds and conveyances proven or acknowledged without the United States or their territories, such acknowledgment or proof must be attested under the official seal of the court, or officer before whom such probate is had. Idem, s. 15.

13. Every court or officer that shall take the proof or acknowledgment of any deed or conveyance of real estate, or the relinquishment of dower of any married woman in any conveyance of the estate of her husband, shall grant a certificate thereof, and cause such certificate to be endorsed on the said deed, instrument, conveyance, or relinquishment of dower, which certificate shall be signed by the clerk of the court where the probate is taken in court, or by the offi-

cer before whom the same is taken and sealed, if he have a seal of office. Idem, s. 16.

14. *Connecticut.* In this state, deeds must be acknowledged before a judge of the supreme or district court of the United States, or the supreme or superior court, or court of common pleas or county court of this state, or a notary public.

15. When the acknowledgment is made in another state or territory of the United States, it must be before some officer or commissioner having power to take acknowledgments there.

16. When made out of the United States before a resident American consul, a justice of the peace, or notary public, no different form is used, and no different examination of a feme covert from others. See Act of 1828; Act of 1833; 1 Hill. Ab. c. 34, s. 82.

17. *Delaware.* Before the supreme court, or the court of common pleas of any county, or a judge of either court, or the chancellor, or two justices of the peace of the same county.

18. The certificate of an acknowledgment in court must be under the seal of the court.

19. A feme covert may also make her acknowledgment before the same officers, who are to examine her separately from her husband.

20. An acknowledgment out of the state, may be made before a judge of any court of the United States, the chancellor or judge of a court of record, of the said court itself, or the chief officer of a city or borough, the certificate to be under the official seal; if by a judge, the seal to be affixed to his certificate, or to that of the clerk or keeper of the seal. Commissioners appointed in other states may also take acknowledgments. 2 Hill. Ab. 441; Griff. Reg. h. t.

21. *Florida.* Deeds and mortgages must be acknowledged *within* the state before the officer authorized by law to record the same, or before some judicial officers of this state. *Out of the state*, but within some other state or territory of the United States, before a commissioner of Florida, appointed under the act passed January 24, 1831; and where there is no commissioner, or he is unable to attend, before the chief justice, judge, presiding judge, or president of any court of record of the United States or of any state or territory thereof having a seal and a clerk or prothonotary. The certificate must show, first, that the acknowledgment was taken within the territorial jurisdiction of the officer; secondly, the court of which he is such officer. And it must be accompanied by the certificate of the clerk or prothonotary of the court of which he is judge, justice or president, under the seal of said court that he is duly appointed and authorized as such. *Out of the United States.* If in Europe, or in North or South America, before any minister plenipotentiary, or minister extraordinary, or any chargé d'affaires, or consul of the United States, resident or accredited there. If in any part of Great Britain and Ireland, or the dominions thereunto belonging, before the consul of the United States, resident or accredited therein, or before the mayor or other chief magistrate of London, Bristol, Liverpool, Dublin or Edinburgh, the certificate to be under the hand and seal of the officer. In any other place out of the United States, where there is no public minister, consul or vice consul, commercial agent or vice commercial agent of the United States, before two subscribing witnesses and officers of such place, and the identity of such civil officer and credibility, shall be certified by a consul or vice consul of the United States, of the government of which such place is a part.

22. The certificate of acknowledgment of a married woman must state that she was examined apart from her husband, that she executed such deeds, &c., freely and without any fear or compulsion of her husband.

23. *Georgia.* Deeds of conveyance of land in the state must be executed in the presence of two witnesses, and proved before a justice of the peace, a justice of the inferior court, or one of the judges of the superior courts. If executed in the presence of one witness and a magistrate, no probate is required. Prince's Dig. 162; 1 Laws of Geo. 115.

24. When out of the state, but in the United States, they may be proved by affidavit of one or more of the witnesses thereto, before any governor, chief justice, mayor, or other justice, of either of the United States, and certified accordingly, and transmitted under the common or public seal of the state, court, city or place, where the same is taken. The affidavit must express the place of the affidant's abode. Idem.

25. There is no state law directing how the acknowledgment shall be made when it is made out of the United States.

26. By an act of the legislature passed in 1826, the widow is barred of her dower in all lands of her deceased husband, that he aliens or conveys away during the coverture, except such lands as he acquired by his intermarriage with his wife; so that no relinquishment of dower by the wife is necessary, unless the lands came to her husband by her. Prince's Dig. 249; 4 Laws of Geo. 217. The magistrate should certify that the wife did declare that freely, and without compulsion, she signed, sealed and delivered the instrument of writing between the parties, (naming them,) and that she did renounce all title or claim to dower, that she might claim or be entitled to after death of her husband, (naming him.) 1 Laws of Geo. 112; Prince's Dig. 160.

27. *Indiana.* Before the recorder of the county in which the lands may be situate, or one of the judges of the snpreme court of this state, or before one of the judges of the circuit court, or some justice of the peace of the county within which the estate may be situate, before notaries public, or before probate judges. Ind. Rev. Stat. c. 44, s. 7; Id. ch. 74; Act of Feb. 24, 1840.

28. All deeds and conveyances made and executed by any person without this state and brought within it to be recorded, the acknowledgment having been lawfully made before any judge or justice of the peace of the proper county in which such deed may have been made and executed, and certified under the seal of such county by the proper officer, shall be valid and effectual in law. Rev. Code, c. 44, s. 11; App. Jan. 24, 1831.

29. When acknowledged by a feme covert, it must be certified that she was examined separate and apart from her husband; that the full contents of the deed were made known to her; that she did then and there declare that she had, as her own voluntary act and deed, signed, sealed and executed the said deed of her own free will and accord, without any fear or compulsion from her said husband.

30. *Illinois.* Before a judge or justice of the supreme or district courts of the United States, a commissioner authorized to take acknowledgments, a judge or justice of the supreme, superior or district court of any of the United States or territories, a justice of the peace, the clerk of a court of record, mayor of a city, or notary public; the last three shall give a certificate under their official seal.

31. The certificate must state that the party is known to the officer, or that his identity has been proved by a credible witness, naming him. When the acknowledgment is taken by a justice of the peace of the state, residing in the county where the lands lie, no other certificate is required than his own; when he resides in another county, there shall be a certificate of the clerk of the county commissioners' court of the *proper county*, under seal, to his official capacity.

32. When the justice of the peace taking the acknowledgment resides out of the state, there shall be added to the deed a certificate of the *proper clerk*, that the person officiating is a justice of the peace.

33. The deed of a feme covert is acknowledged before the same officers. The certificate must state that she is known to the officer, or that her identity has been proved by a witness who must be named; that the officer informed her of the contents of the deed; that she was separately examined; that she acknowledged the execution and release to be made freely, voluntarily, and without the compulsion of her husband.

34. When the husband and wife reside in the state, and the latter is over eighteen years of age, she may convey her lands, with formalities substanially the same as those used in a release of dower; she acknowledges the instrument *to be her act and deed*, and that *she does not wish to retract*.

35. When she resides out of the state, if over eighteen, she may join her husband in any writing relating to lands in the state, in which case her acknowledgment is the same as if she were a feme sole. Ill. Rev. L. 135—8; 2 Hill. Ab. 455, 6.

36. *Kentucky.* Acknowledgments taken in the state must be before the clerk of a county court, clerk of the general court, or clerk of the court of appeals. 4 Litt. L. of K. 165; or before two justices of the peace, 1 Litt. L. of K. 152; or before the mayor of the city of Louisville. Acts of 1828, p. 219, s. 12.

37. When in another state or territory of the United States, before two justices of the peace, 1 Litt. L. of K. 152; or before any court of law, mayor, or other chief magistrate of any city, town or corporation of the county where the grantors dwell, Id. 567; or before any justice or judge of a

superior or inferior court of law. Acts of 1831, p. 128.

38. When made out of the United States, before a mayor of a city, or consul of the U. S. residing there, or before the chief magistrate of such state or country, to be authenticated in the usual manner such officers authenticate their official acts. Acts of 1831, p. 128, s. 5.

39. When a feme covert acknowledges the deed, the certificate must state that she was examined by the officer separate and apart from her husband, that she declared that she did freely and willingly seal and deliver the said writing, and wishes not to retract it, and acknowledged the said writing again shown and explained to her, to be her act and deed, and consents that the same may be recorded.

40. *Maine.* Before a justice of the peace in this state, or any justice of the peace, magistrate, or notary public, within the United States, or any commissioner appointed for that purpose by the governor of this state, or before any minister or consul of the United States, or notary public in any foreign country. Rev. St. t. 7, c. 91, § 7; 6 Pick. 86.

41. No peculiar form for the certificate of acknowledgment is prescribed; it is required that the husband join in the deed. "The joint deed of husband and wife shall be effectual to convey her real estate, but not to bind her to any covenant or estoppel therein." Rev. St. t. 7, c. 91, § 5.

42. *Maryland.* Before two justices of the peace of the county where the lands lie, or where the grantor lives, or before a judge of the county court of the former county, or the mayor of Annapolis for Anne Arundel county. When the acknowledgment is made in another county than that in which the lands are situated, and in which the party lives, the clerk of the court must certify under the court seal, the official capacity of the acting justices or judge.

43. When the grantor resides out of the state, a commission issues on application of the purchaser, and with the written consent of the grantor, from the clerk of the county court where the land lies, to two or more commissioners at the grantee's residence; any two of whom may take the acknowledgment, and shall certify it under seal, and return the commission to be recorded with the deed; or the grantor may empower an attorney in the state to acknowledge for him, the power to be incorporated in the deed, or annexed to it, and proved by a subscribing witness before the county court, or two justices of the peace where the land lies, or a district judge, or the governor or a mayor, notary public, court or judge thereof, of the place where it is executed; in each case the certificate to be under an official seal. By the acts of 1825, c. 58, and 1830, c. 164, the acknowledgment in another state may be before a judge of the U. S. or a judge of a court of record of the state and county where the grantor may be —the clerk to certify under seal, the official character of the magistrate.

44. By the act of 1837, c. 97, commissioners may be appointed by authority of the state, who shall reside in the other states or territories of the United States, who shall be authorized to take acknowledgment of deeds. The act of 1831, c. 205, requires that the officer shall certify his knowledge of the parties.

45. The acknowledgment of a feme covert must be made separate and apart from her husband. 2 Hill. Ab. 442; Griff. Reg. h. t. See also, 7 Gill & J. 480; 2 Gill. & J. 173; 6 Harr. & J. 336; 3 Harr. & J. 371; 1 Harr. & J. 178; 4 Harr. & M'H. 222.

46. *Massachusetts.* Before a justice of the peace or magistrate out of the state. It has been held that an American consul at a foreign port is a magistrate. 13 Pick. R. 523. An acknowledgment by one of two grantors has been held sufficient to authorize the registration of a deed; and a wife need not, therefore, acknowledge the conveyance when she joins with her husband. 2 Hill. Ab. c. 34, s. 45.

47. *Michigan.* Before a judge of a court of record, notary public, justice of the peace, or master in chancery; and in case of the death of the grantor, or his departure from the state, it may be proved by one of the subscribing witnesses before any court of record in the state. Rev. St. 208; Laws of 1840, p. 166.

48. When the deed is acknowledged out of the state of Michigan, but in the United States, or any of the territories of the U. S., it is to be acknowledged according to the laws of such state or territory, with a certificate of the proper county clerk, under his seal of office, that such deed is executed according to the laws of such state or territory, attached thereto.

49. When acknowledged in a foreign

country, it may be executed according to the laws of such foreign country, but it must in such case be acknowledged before a minister plenipotentiary, consul, or chargé d'affaires of the United States; and the acknowledgment must be certified by the officer before whom the same was taken. Laws of 1840, p. 166, sec. 2 and 3.

50. When the acknowledgment is made by a feme covert, the certificate must state that on a private examination of such feme covert, separate and apart from her husband, she acknowledged that she executed the deed without fear or compulsion from any one. Laws of 1840, p. 167, sec. 4.

51. *Mississippi.* When in the state, deeds may be acknowledged, or proved by one or more of the subscribing witnesses to them, before any judge of the high court of errors and appeals, or a judge of the circuit courts, or judge of probate, and certified by such judge; or before any notary public, or clerk of any court of record in this state, and certified by such notary or clerk under the seal of his office; How. & Hutch. c. 34, s. 99, p. 368, Law of 1833; or before any justice of that county, where the land, or any part thereof, is situated; Ib. p. 343, s. 1, Law of 1822; or before any member of the board of police, in his respective county. Ib. p. 445, c. 38, s. 50, Law of 1838.

52. When in another state or territory of the United States, such deeds must be acknowledged, or proved as aforesaid, before a judge of the supreme court or of the district courts of the United States, or before any judge of the supreme or superior court of any state or territory in the Union; How. & Hutch. 346, c. 34, s. 13, Law of 1832; or before and certified by any judge of any inferior or county court of record, or before any justice of the peace of the state or territory and county, wherein such person or witness or witnesses may then be or reside, and authenticated by the certificate of the clerk or register of the superior county or circuit court of such county, with a seal of his office thereto affixed; or if taken before or certified by a justice of the peace, shall be authenticated by the certificate of either the clerk of the said inferior or county court of record of such county, with the seal of his office thereto affixed. Laws of Mississippi, Jan. 27, 1841, p. 132.

53. When out of the United States, such acknowledgment, or proof as aforesaid, must be made before any court of law, or mayor, or other chief magistrate of any city, borough or corporation of such foreign kingdom, state, nation, or colony, in which the said parties or witnesses reside; certified by the court, mayor, or chief magistrate, in a manner such acts are usually authenticated by him. How. & Hutch, 346, c. 34, s. 14, Law of 1822.

54. When made by a feme covert, the certificate must state that she made previous acknowledgment, on a private examination, apart from her husband, before the proper officer, that she sealed and delivered the same as her act and deed, freely, without any fear, threat or compulsion of her husband. How. & Hutch. 347, c. 34, s. 19, Law 1822.

55. *Missouri.* In the state, before some court having a seal, or some judge, justice or clerk thereof, or a justice of the peace in the county where the land lies. Rev. Code, 1835, § 8, p. 120.

56. Out of the state, but in the United States, before any court of the United States, or of any state or territory, having a seal, or the clerk thereof. Id. cl. 2.

57. Out of the United States, before any court of any state, kingdom or empire having a seal, or the mayor of any city having an official seal.

58. Every court or officer taking the acknowledgment of such instrument or relinquishment of dower or the deed of the wife of the husband's land, shall endorse a certificate thereof upon the instrument; when made before a court, the certificate shall be under its seal; if by a clerk, under his hand and the seal of the court; when before an officer having an official seal, under his hand and seal; when by an officer having no seal, under his hand. The certificate must state that the party was personally known to the judge or other officer as the signer, or proved to be such by two credible witnesses. Misso. St. 120—122; 2 Hill. Ab. 453; Griff. h. t.

59. When the acknowledgment is made by a feme covert, releasing her dower, the certificate must state that she is personally known to a judge of the court, or the officer before whom the deed is acknowledged, or that her identity was proved by two credible witnesses; it must also state that she was informed of the contents of the deed; that it was acknowledged separate and apart from her husband; that she releases her dower freely without compulsion or nndue

influence of her husband. Ib. In the conveyance of her own lands, the acknowledgment may be made before any court authorized to take acknowledgments. It must be done as in the cases of release of dower, and have a similar certificate. Ib.

60. *New Hampshire.* Before a justice of the peace or a notary public; and the acknowledgment of a deed before a notary public in another state is good. 2 N. H. Rep. 420; 2 Hill. Ab. c. 34, s. 61.

61. *New Jersey.* In the state, before the chancellor, a justice of the supreme court of this state, a master in chancery, or a judge of any inferior court of common pleas, whether in the same or a different county; Rev. Laws, 458, Act of June 7, 1799; or before a commissioner for taking the acknowledgments or proofs of deeds, two of whom are appointed by the legislature in each township, who are authorized to take acknowledgments or proofs of deeds in any part of the state. Rev. Laws, 748, Act of June 5, 1820.

62. In another state or territory of the United States, before a judge of the supreme court of the United States, or a district judge of the United States, or any judge or justice of the supreme or superior court of any state in the Union; Rev. Laws, 459, Act of June 7, 1799; or before any mayor or other chief magistrate of any city in any other state or territory of the U. S., and duly certified under the seal of such city; or before a judge of any superior court, or court of common pleas of any state or territory; when taken before a judge of a court of common pleas, it must be accompanied by a certificate under the great seal of the state, or the seal of the county court in which it is made, that he is such officer; Rev. Laws, 747, Act of June 5, 1820; or before a commissioner appointed by the governor, who resides in such state; Harr. Comp. 158, Act of December 27, 1826; two of whom may be appointed for each of the States of New York and Pennsylvania. Elmer's Dig. Act of Nov. 3, 1836.

63. When made out of the United States, the acknowledgment may be before any court of law, or mayor, or other magistrate, of any city, borough or corporation of a foreign kingdom, state, nation or colony, in which the party or his witnesses reside, certified by the said court, mayor, or chief magistrate, in the manner in which such acts are usually authenticated by him. Rev. Laws, 459, Act of June 7, 1799. The certificate in all cases must state that the officer who makes it, first made known the contents of the deed to the person making the acknowledgment, and that he was satisfied such person was the grantor mentioned in the deed. Rev. Laws, 749, Act of June 5, 1820.

64. When the acknowledgment is made by a feme covert, the certificate must state that on a private examination, apart from her husband, before a proper officer, (ut supra,) she acknowledged that she signed, sealed, and delivered the deed, as her voluntary act and deed, freely, without any fear, threats or compulsion of her husband. Rev. Laws, 459, Act of June 7, 1799.

65. *New York.* Before the chancellor or justice of the supreme court, circuit judge, supreme court commissioner, judge of the county court, mayor or recorder of a city, or commissioner of deeds; a county judge or commissioner of deeds for a city or county, not to act out of the same.

66. When the party resides in another state, before a judge of the United States, or a judge or justice of the supreme, superior or circuit court of any state or territory of the United States, within his own jurisdiction. By a statute passed in 1840, chap. 290, the governor is authorized to appoint commissioners in other states, to take the acknowledgment and proof of deeds and other instruments.

67. When the party is in Europe or other parts of America, before a resident minister or chargé d'affaires of the United States; in France, before the United States' consul at Paris; in Russia, before the same officer at St. Petersburg; in the British dominions, before the Lord Mayor of London, the chief magistrate of Dublin, Edinburgh or Liverpool, or the United States' consul at London. The certificate to be under the hand and official seal of such officer. It may also be made before any person specially authorized by the court of chancery of this state.

68. The officer must in all cases be satisfied of the identity of the party, either from his own knowledge or from the oath or affirmation of a witness, who is to be named in the certificate.

69. A feme covert must be privately examined; but if out of the state this is unnecessary. 2 Hill. Ab. 434; Griff. Reg. h. t.

70. By the act passed April 7, 1848, it is provided, that:—

§ 1. The proof or acknowledgment of any deed or other written instrument required to be proved or acknowledged, in order to entitle the same to be recorded, or read in evidence, when made by any persou residing out of this state, and within any other state or territory of the United States, may be made before any officer of such state or territory, authorized by the laws thereof to take the proof and acknowledgment of deeds; and when so taken and certified as by the act is provided, shall be entitled to be recorded in any county in this state, and may be read in evidence in any court in this state, in the same manner and with like effect, as proofs and acknowledgments taken before any of the officers now authorized by law to take such proofs and acknowledgments: Provided that no such acknowledgment shall be valid unless the officer taking the same shall know or have satisfactory evidence that the person making such acknowledgment is the individnal described in, and who executed the said deed or instrument.

71.—§ 2. To entitle any conveyance or other written instrument acknowledged or proved under the preceding section, to be read in evidence or recorded in this state, there shall be subjoined to the certificate of proof or acknowledgment, signed by such officer, a certificate under the name and official seal of the clerk or register of the county in which such officer resides, specifying that such officer was at the time of taking such proof or acknowledgment, duly authorized to take the same, and that such clerk or register is well acquainted with the handwriting of such officer, and verily believes that the signature to said certificate of proof and acknowledgment, is genuine.

72. *North Carolina.* The acknowledgment or proof of deeds for the conveyance of lands, when taken or made in the state, must be "before one of the judges of the supreme court, or superior court, or in the court of the county where the land lieth." 1 Rev. Stat. c. 37, s. 1.

73. When in another state or territory of the United States, or the District of Columbia, the deed must be acknowledged, or proved, before some one of the judges of the superior courts of law, or circuit courts of law of superior jurisdiction, within the said state, &c., with a certificate of the governor of the said state or territory, or of the secretary of state of the United States, when in the District of Columbia, of the official character of the judge; or before a commissioner appointed by the governor of this state according to law. 1 Rev. Stat. c. 37, s. 5.

74. When out of the United States, the deeds must be acknowledged, or proved, before the chief magistrate of some city, town, or corporation of the countries where the said deeds were executed; or before some ambassador, publio minister, consul, or commercial agent, with proper certificates under their official seals; 1 Rev. Stat. c. 37 s. 6 and 7; or before a commissioner in such foreign country, under a commission from the county court where the land lieth. Sec. 8.

75. When acknowledged by a feme covert, the certificate must state that she was privily examined by the proper officer, that she acknowledged the due execution of the deed, and declared that she executed the same freely, voluntarily, and without the fear or compulsion of her husband, or any other person, and that she then assented thereto. When she is resident of another county, or so infirm that she cannot travel to the judge, or county court, the deed may be acknowledged by the husband, or proved by witnesses, and a commission in a prescribed form may be issued for taking the examination of the wife. 1 Rev. Stat. c. 37, s. 6, 8, 9, 10, 11, 13, and 14.

76. *Ohio.* In the state, deeds and other instruments affecting lands must be acknowledged before a judge of the supreme court, a judge of the court of common pleas, a justice of the peace, notary public, mayor, or other presiding officer of an incorporated town or city. Ohio Stat. vol. 29, p. 346, Act of February 22, 1831, which went in force June 1, 1831; Swan's Coll. L. 265, s. 1.

77. When made out of the state, whether in another state or territory, or out of the U. S., they must be acknowledged, or proved, according to the laws of the state, territory or country, where they are executed, or according to the laws of the state of Ohio. Swan's Coll. L. 265, s. 5.

78. When made by a feme covert, the certificate must state that she was examined by the officer, separate and apart from her husband, and the contents of the deed were fully made known to her; that she did declare, upon such separate examination, that she did voluntarily sign, seal, and acknowledge the same, and that she is still satisfied therewith.

79. *Pennsylvania.* Before a judge of the supreme court, or of the courts of common pleas, the district courts, or before any mayor or alderman, or justice of the peace of the commonwealth, or before the recorder of the city of Philadelphia.

80. When made out of the state, and within the United States, the acknowledgment may be before one of the judges of the supreme or district courts of the United States, or before any one of the judges or justices of the supreme or superior courts, or courts of common pleas of any state or territory within the United States; and so certified under the hand of the said judge, and the seal of the court. Commissioners appointed by the governor, residing in either of the United States or of the District of Columbia, are also authorized to take acknowledgment of deeds.

81. When made out of the United States, the acknowledgment may be made before any consul or vice-consul of the United States, duly appointed for and exercising consular functions in the state, kingdom, country or place where such an acknowledgment may be made, and certified under the public or official seal of such consul or vice-consul of the United States. Act of January 16, 1827. By the act May 27th, 1715, s. 4, deeds made out of the province [state] may be proved by the oath or solemn affirmation of one or more of the witnesses thereunto, before one or more of the justices of the peace of this province [state], or before any mayor or chief magistrate or officer of the cities, towns or places, where such deed or conveyances are so proved. The proof must be certified by the officer under the common or public seal of the cities, towns, or places where such conveyances are so proved. But by construction it is now established that a deed *acknowledged* before such officer is valid, although the act declares it shall be *proved.* 1 Pet. R. 433.

82. The certificate of the acknowledgment of a féme covert must state, 1, that she is of full age; 2, that the contents of the instrument have been made known to her; 3, that she has been examined separate and apart from her husband; and, 4, that she executed the deed of her own free will and accord, without any coercion or compulsion of her husband. It is the constant practice of making the certificate under seal, though if it be merely under the hand of the officer, it will be sufficient. Act of Feb. 19, 1835.

83. By the act of the 16th day of April, 1840, entitled "An act incorporating the Ebenezer Methodist Episcopal congregation for the borough of Reading, and for other purposes," Pamph. Laws, 357, 361, it is provided by § 15, "That any and every grant, bargain and sale, release, or other deed of conveyance or assurance of any lands, tenements, or hereditaments in this commonwealth, heretofore *bona fide* made, executed and delivered by husband and wife within any other of the United States, where the acknowledgment of the execution thereof has been taken, and certified by any officer or officers in any of the states where made and executed, who was, or were authorized by the laws of such state to take and certify the acknowledgment of deeds of conveyance of lands therein, shall be deemed and adjudged to be as good, valid and effectual in law for transferring, passing and conveying the estate, right, title and interest of such husband and wife of, in, and to the lands, tenements and hereditaments therein mentioned, and be in like manner entitled to be recorded, as if the acknowledgment of the execution of the same deed had been in the same and like way, manner and form taken and certified by any judge, alderman, or justice of the peace, of and within this commonwealth. § 16, That no grant, bargain and sale, feoffment, deed of conveyance, lease, release, assignment, or other assurance of any lands, tenements and hereditaments whatsoever, heretofore *bona fide* made and executed by husband and wife, and acknowledged by them before some judge, justice of the peace, alderman, or other officer authorized by law, within this state, or an officer in one of the United States, to take such acknowledgment, or which may be so made, executed and acknowledged as aforesaid, before the first day of January next, shall be deemed, held or adjudged, invalid or defective, or insufficient in law, or avoided or prejudiced, by reason of any informality or omission in setting forth the particulars of the acknowledgment made before such officer, as aforesaid, in the certificate thereof, but all and every such grant, bargain and sale, feoffment, deed of conveyance, lease, release, assignment or other assurance so made, executed and acknowledged as aforesaid, shall be as good, valid and effectual in law for transferring, passing and conveying the estate, right, title and interest of such husband and wife of, in, and to the lands, tenements and hereditaments mentioned in the same, as if all the requisites and par-

ticulars of such acknowledgment mentioned in the act, entitled an act for the better confirmation of the estates of persons holding or claiming under *feme coverts*, and for establishing a mode by which husband and wife may hereafter convey their estates, passed the twenty-fourth day of February, one thousand seven hundred and seventy, were particularly set forth in the certificate thereof, or appeared upon the face of the same."

84. By the act of the 3d day of April, 1840, Pamph. L. 233, it is enacted, "That where any deed, conveyance, or other instrument of writing has been or shall be made and executed, either within or out of this state, and the acknowledgment or proof thereof, duly certified, by any officer under seal, according to the existing laws of this commonwealth, for the purpose of being recorded therein, such certificate shall be deemed prima facie evidence of such execution and acknowledgment, or proof, without requiring proof of the said seal, as fully, to all intents and purposes, and with the same effect only, as if the same had been so acknowledged or proved before any judge, justice of the peace, or alderman within this commonwealth."

85. The act relating to executions and for other purposes, passed 16th April, 1840, Pamph. L. 412, enacts, § 7, "That the recorders of deeds shall have authority to take the acknowledgment and proof of the execution of any deed, mortgage, or other conveyance of any lands, tenements, or hereditaments lying or being in the county, for which they are respectively appointed as recorders of deeds, or within every city, district, or part thereof, or for any contract, letter of attorney, or any other writing, under seal, to be used or recorded within their respective counties; and such acknowledgment or proof, taken or made in the manner directed by the laws of this state, and certified by the said recorder, under his hand and seal of office; which certificate shall be endorsed or annexed to said deed or instrument aforesaid, shall have the same force and effect, and be as good and available in law, for all purposes, as if the same had been made or taken before any judge of the supreme court, or president or associate judge of any of the courts of common pleas within this commonwealth."

86. *Rhode Island.* Before any senator, judge, justice of the peace, or town clerk. When the acknowledgment is made in another state or country, it must be before a judge, justice, mayor or notary public therein, and certified under his hand and seal.

87. A wife releasing dower need not acknowledge the deed; but to a conveyance an acknowledgment and private examination are necessary. 2 Hill. Ab. c. 34, s. 94.

88. *South Carolina.* Before a judge of the supreme court. A feme covert may release her dower or convey her own estate, by joining with her husband in a deed, and being privately examined, in the latter case, seven days afterwards, before a judge of law or equity, or a justice of the quorum; she may also release dower by a separate deed.

89. The certificate of the officer is under seal and signed by the woman. Deeds may be proved upon the oath of one witness before a magistrate, and this is said to be the general practice.

90. When the deed is to be executed out of the state, the justices of the county where the land lies, or a judge of the court of common pleas, may by *dedimus* empower two or more justices of the county where the grantor resides, to take his acknowledgment upon the oath of two witnesses to the execution. 2 Hill. Ab. 448, 9; Griff. Reg. h. t.

91. *Tennessee.* A deed or power of attorney to convey land must be acknowledged or proved by two subscribing witnesses, in the court of the county, or the court of the district where the land lies.

92. The certificate of acknowledgment must be endorsed upon the deed by the clerk of the court.

93. The acknowledgment of a feme covert is made before a court of record in the state, or, if the parties live out of it, before a court of record in another state or territory; and if the wife is unable to attend court, the acknowledgment may be before commissioners empowered by the court of the county in which the husband acknowledges—the commission to be returned certified with the court seal, and recorded.

94. In all these cases the certificate must state that the wife has been privately examined. The seal of the court is to be annexed when the deed is to be used out of the state, when made in it, and *vice versa;* in which case there is to be a seal, and a certificate of the presiding judge or justice to the official station of the clerk, and the due formality of the attestation. By the statute of 1820, the acknowledgment in

other states may be conformable to the laws of the state, in which the grantor resides.

95. By the act of 1831, c. 90, s. 9, it is provided, that all deeds or conveyances for land made without the limits of this state, shall be proved as heretofore, or before a notary public under his seal of office. Caruthers & Nicholson's Compilation of the Stat. of Tenn. 593.

96. The officer must certify that he is acquainted with the grantor, and that he is an inhabitant of the state. There must also be a certificate of the governor or secretary, under the great seal, or a judge of the superior court that the acknowledgment is in due form Griff. Reg. h. t.; 2 Hill. Ab. 458.

97. By an act passed during the session of 1839—1840, chap. 26, it is enacted,—§ 1. "That deeds of every description may be proved by two subscribing witnesses, or acknowledged and recorded, and may then be read in evidence. 2. That deeds executed beyond the limits of the United States may be proved or acknowledged before a notary public, or before any consul, minister, or ambassador of the United States, or before a commissioner of the state. 3. That the governor may appoint commissioners in other states and in foreign countries for the proof, &c. of deeds. 4. Affidavits taken as above, as to pedigree or heirship, may be received as evidence, by executors or administrators, or in regard to the partition and distribution of property or estates." See 2 Yerg. 91, 108, 238, 400, 520; 3 Yerg. 81; Cooke, 431.

98. *Vermont*. 1. All deeds and other conveyances of lands, or any estate or interest therein, shall be signed and sealed by the party granting the same, and signed by two or more witnesses, and acknowledged by the grantor, before a justice of the peace. Rev. Stat. tit. 14, c. 6, s. 4.

99. Every deed by the husband and wife shall contain an acknowledgment by the wife, made apart from her husband, before a judge of the supreme court, a judge of the county court, or some justice of the peace, that she executed such conveyance freely, and without any fear or compulsion of her husband; a certificate of which acknowledgment, so taken, shall be endorsed on the deed by the authority taking the same. Id. s. 7.

100.—2. All deeds and other conveyances, and powers of attorney for the conveyance of lands, the acknowledgment or proof of which shall have been, or hereafter shall be taken without this state, if certified agreeably to the laws of the state, province or kingdom in which it was taken, shall be as valid as though the same were taken before some proper officer or court, within this state; and the proof of the same may be taken, and the same acknowledged with like effect, before any justice of the peace, magistrate, or notary public, within the United States, or in any foreign country, or before any commissioner appointed for that purpose by the governor of this state, or before any minister, chargé d'affaires, or consul of the United States in any foreign country; and the acknowledgment of a deed by a feme covert, in the form required by this chapter, may be taken by either of the said persons Id. 9.

101. *Virginia*. Before the general court, or the court of the district, county, city, or corporation where some part of the land lies; when the party lives out of the state or of the district or county where the land lies, the acknowledgment may be before any court of law, or the chief magistrate of any city, town, or corporation of the country where the party resides, and certified by him in the usual form.

102. When a married woman executes the deed, she appears in court and is examined privately by one of the judges, as to her freely signing the instrument, and continuing satisfied with it,—the deed being shown and explained to her. She acknowledges the deed before the court, or else before two justices of the county where she dwells, or the magistrate of a corporate town, if she lives within the United States; these officers being empowered by a commission from the clerk of the court where the deed is to be recorded, to examine her and to take her acknowledgment. If she is out of the United States, the commission authorizes two judges or justices of any court of law, or the chief magistrate of any city, town, or corporation, in her county, and is executed as by two justices in the United States.

103. The certificate is to be authenticated in the usual form. 2 Hill. Ab. 444, 5; Griff. Reg. h. t.; 2 Leigh's R. 186; 2 Call. R. 103; 1 Wash. R. 319.

ACQUETS, *estates in the civil law*. Property which has been acquired by purchase, gift, or otherwise than by succession. Merlin Rép. h. t., confines acquets to immovable property.

2. In Louisiana they embrace the profits of all the effects of which the husband has the administration and enjoyment, either of right or in fact, of the produce of the reciprocal industry and labor of both husband and wife, and of the estates which they may acquire during the marriage, either by donations, made jointly to them both, or by purchase, or in any other similar way, even although the purchase be only in the name of one of the two, and not of both, because in that case the period of time when the purchase is made is alone attended to, and not the person who made the purchase. Civ. Code, art. 2371.

3. This applies to all marriages contracted in that state, or out of it, when the parties afterward go there to live, as to acquets afterward made there. Ib. art. 2370.

4. The acquets are divided into two equal portions between the husband and wife, or between their heirs at the dissolution of their marriage. Ib. art. 2375.

5. The parties may, however, lawfully stipulate there shall be no community of profits or gains. Ib. art. 2369.

6. But the parties have no right to agree that they shall be governed by the laws of another country. 3 Martin's Rep. 581. Vide 17 Martin's Rep. 571; 2 Kent's Com. 153, note.

ACQUIESCENCE, *contracts*. The consent which is impliedly given by one or both parties, to a proposition, a clause, a condition, a judgment, or to any act whatever.

2. When a party is bound to elect between a paramount right and a testamentary disposition, his acquiescence in a state of things which indicates an election, when he was aware of his rights, will be *primâ facie* evidence of such election. Vide 2 Ves. Jr. 371; 12 Ves. 136; 1 Ves. Jr. 335; 3 P. Wms. 315; 2 Rop. Leg. 439.

3. The acts of acquiescence which constitute an implied election, must be decided rather by the circumstances of each case than by any general principle. 1 Swanst. R. 382, note, and the numerous cases there cited.

4. Acquiescence in the acts of an agent, or one who has assumed that character, will be equivalent to an express authority. 2 Bouv. Inst. n. 1309; Kent, Com. 478; Story on Eq. § 255; 4 W. C. C. R. 559; 6 Mass. R. 193; 1 John. Cas. 110; 2 John. Cas. 424; Liv. on Ag. 45; Paley on Ag. by Lloyd, 41; 3 Pet. R. 69, 81; 12 John R. 300; 3 Cowen's R. 281; 3 Pick. R. 495, 505; 4 Mason's R. 296. Acquiescence differs from assent. (q. v.)

ACQUIETANDIS PLEGIIS, *obsolete*. A writ of justices, lying for the surety against a creditor, who refuses to acquit him after the debt has been satisfied. Reg. of Writs, 158; Cowell; Blount.

TO ACQUIRE, *descents, contracts*. To make property one's own.

2. Title to property is acquired in two ways, by descent, (q. v.) and by purchase, (q. v.) Acquisition by purchase, is either by, 1. Escheat. 2. Occupancy. 3. Prescription. 4. Forfeiture. 5. Alienation, which is either by deed or by matter of record. Things which cannot be sold, cannot be acquired.

ACQUISITION, *property, contracts, descent*. The act by which the person procures the property of a thing.

2. An acquisition may be temporary or perpetual, and be procured either for a valuable consideration, for example, by buying the same; or without consideration, as by gift or descent.

3. Acquisition may be divided into original and derivative. Original acquisition is procured by occupancy, 1 Bouv. Inst. n. 490; 2 Kent. Com. 289; Menstr. Leç. du Dr. Civ. Rom. § 344; by accession, 1 Bouv. Inst. n. 499; 2 Kent. Com. 293; by intellectual labor, namely, for inventions, which are secured by patent rights, and for the authorship of books, maps, and charts, which is protected by copyrights. 1 Bouv. Inst. n. 508.

4. Derivative acquisitions are those which are procured from others, either by act of law, or by act of the parties. Goods and chattels may change owners by act of law in the cases of forfeiture, succession, marriage, judgment, insolvency, and intestacy. And by act of the parties, by gift or sale. Property may be acquired by a man himself, or by those who are in his power, for him; as by his children while minors; 1 N. Hamps. R. 28; 1 United States Law Journ. 513; by his apprentices or his slaves. Vide Ruth. Inst. ch. 6 & 7; Dig. 41, 1, 53; Inst. 2, 9; Ib. 2, 9, 3.

ACQUITTAL, *contracts*. A release or discharge from an obligation or engagement. According to Lord Coke there are three kinds of acquittal, namely; 1, By deed, when the party releases the obligation; 2, By prescription; 3, By tenure. Co. Lit. 100, a.

Acquittal, *crim. law practice.* The absolution of a party charged with a crime or misdemeanor.

2. Technically speaking, acquittal is the absolution of a party accused on a trial before a traverse jury. 1 N. & M. 36; 3 M'Cord, 461.

3. Acquittals are of two kinds, in fact and in law. The former takes place when the jury upon trial finds a verdict of not guilty; the latter when a man is charged merely as an accessary, and the principal has been acquitted. 2 Inst. 384. An acquittal is a bar to any future prosecution for the offence alleged in the first indictment.

ACQUITTANCE, *contracts.* An agreement in writing to discharge a party from an engagement to pay a sum of money; it is evidence of payment. It differs from a release in this, that the latter must be under seal, while an acquittance need not be under seal. Poth. Oblig. n. 781. In Pennsylvania, a receipt, (q. v.) though not under seal, has nearly the same effect as a release. 1 Rawle, R. 391. Vide 3 Salk. 298, pl. 2; Off. of Ex. 217; Co. Litt. 212 a, 273 a.

ACRE, *measures.* A quantity of land containing in length forty perches, and four in breadth, or one hundred and sixty square perches, of whatever shape may be the land. Serg. Land Laws of Penn. 185. See Cro. Eliz. 476, 665; 6 Co. 67; Poph. 55; Co. Litt. 5, b, and note 22.

ACREDULITARE, *obsolete.* To purge one's self of an offence by oath. It frequently happens that when a person has been arrested for a contempt, he comes into court and purges himself, on oath, of having intended any contempt. Blount, Leges. Inac. c. 36.

ACT, *civil law, contracts.* A writing which states in a legal form that a thing has been said, done, or agreed. In Latin, *Instrumentum.* Merl. Rép.

Act. In the legal sense, this word may be used to signify the result of a public deliberation, the decision of a prince, of a legislative body, of a council, court of justice, or a magistrate. Also, a decree, edict, law, judgment, resolve, award, determination. Also, an instrument in writing to verify facts, as act of assembly, act of congress, act of parliament, act and deed. See Webster's Dict. Acts are civil or criminal, lawful or unlawful, public or private.

2. *Public acts*, usually denominated *authentic*, are those which have a public authority, and which have been made before public officers, are authorized by a public seal, have been made public by the authority of a magistrate, or which have been extracted and been properly authenticated from public records.

3. *Acts under private signature* are those which have been made by private individuals, under their hands. An act of this kind does not acquire the force of an authentic act, by being registered in the office of a notary. 5 N. S. 693; 8 N. S. 568; 3 L. R. 419; 3 N. S. 396; 11 M. R. 243; unless it has been properly acknowledged before the officer by the parties to it. 5 N. S. 196.

4. *Private acts* are those made by private persons, as registers in relation to their receipts and expenditures, schedules, acquittances, and the like. Nov. 73, c. 2; Code, lib. 7, tit. 32, l. 6; lib. 4, t. 21; Dig. lib. 22, tit. 4; Civ. Code of Louis. art. 2231 to 2254; Toull. Dr. Civ. Français, tom. 8, p. 94.

Act, *evidence.* The act of one of several conspirators, performed in pursuance of the common design, is evidence against all of them. An overt act of treason must be proved by two witnesses. See *Overt.*

2. The term acts, includes written correspondence, and other papers relative to the design of the parties, but whether it includes unpublished writings upon abstract questions, though of a kindred nature, has been doubted. Foster's Rep. 198; 2 Stark. R. 116, 141.

3. In cases of partnership it is a rule that the act or declaration of either partner, in furtherance of the common object of the association, is the act of all. 1 Pet. R. 371; 5 B. & Ald. 267.

4. And the acts of an agent, in pursuance of his authority, will be binding on his principal. Greenl. Ev. § 113.

Act, *legislation.* A statute or law made by a legislative body; as an act of congress is a law by the congress of the United States; an act of assembly is a law made by a legislative assembly. If an act of assembly expire or be repealed while a proceeding under it is *in fieri* or pending, the proceeding becomes abortive; as a prosecution for an offence, 7 Wheat. 552; or a proceeding under insolvent laws. 1 Bl. R. 451; 3 Burr. 1456; 6 Cranch, 208; 9 Serg. & Rawle, 283.

2. Acts are *general* or *special; public* or *private.* A general or public act is a

universal rule which binds the whole community; of which the courts are bound to take notice *ex officio*.

3. Explanatory acts should not be enlarged by equity; Blood's case, Comb. 410; although such acts may be allowed to have a retrospective operation. Dupin, Notions de Droit, 145. 9.

4. Private or special acts are rather exceptions, than rules; being those which operate only upon particular persons and private concerns; of these the courts are not bound to take notice, unless they are pleaded. 1 Bl. Com. 85, 6; 1 Bouv. Inst. n. 105.

ACT IN PAIS. An act performed out of court, and not a matter of record. *Pais*, in law French, signifies country. A deed or an assurance transacted between two or more private persons in the country is matter *in pais*. 2 Bl. Com. 294.

ACT OF BANKRUPTCY. An act which subjects a person to be proceeded against as a bankrupt. The acts of bankruptcy enumerated in the late act of congress, of 19th Aug. 1841, s. 1, are the following:

1. Departure from the state, district, or territory of which a person, subject to the operation of the bankrupt laws, is an inhabitant, with intent to defraud his creditors. See, as to what will be considered a departure, 1 Campb. R. 279; Dea. & Chit. 451; 1 Rose, R. 387; 9 Moore, R. 217; 2 V. & B. 177; 5 T. R. 512; 1 C. & P. 77; 2 Bing. R. 99; 2 Taunt. 176; Holt, R. 175.

2. Concealment to avoid being arrested. 1 M. & S. 676; 2 Rose, R. 137; 15 Ves. 447; 6 Taunt. R. 540; 14 Ves. 86; 9 Taunt. 176; 1 Rose, R. 362; 5 T. R. 512; 1 Esp. 334.

3. Willingly or fraudulently procuring himself to be arrested, or his goods and chattels, lands, or tenements to be attached, distrained, sequestered, or taken in execution.

4. Removal of his goods, chattels and effects, or concealment of them to prevent their being levied upon, or taken in execution, or by other process.

5. Making any fraudulent conveyance, assignment, sale, gift, or other transfer of his lands, tenements, goods, or chattels, credits, or evidences of debt. 15 Wend. R. 588; 5 Cowen, R. 67; 1 Burr. 467, 471, 481; 4 C. & P. 315; 18 Wend. R. 375; 19 Wend. R. 414; 1 Dougl. 295; 7 East, R. 137; 16 Ves. 149; 17 Ves. 193; 1 Smith, R. 33; Rosé, R. 213.

ACT OF GOD, *in contracts*. This phrase denotes those accidents which arise from physical causes, and which cannot be prevented.

2. Where the law casts a *duty* on a party, the performance shall be excused, if it be rendered impossible by the act of God; but where the party, *by his own contract*, engages to do an act, it is deemed to be his own fault and folly that he did not thereby provide against contingencies, and exempt himself from responsibilities in certain events; and in such case, (that is, in the instance of an absolute general contract,) the performance is not excused by an inevitable accident, or other contingency, although not foreseen by, nor within the control of the party. Chitty on Contr. 272, 3; Aleyn, 27, cited by Lawrence, J. in 8 T. R. 267; Com. Dig. Action upon the Case upon Assumpsit, G; 6 T. R. 650; 8 T. R. 259; 3 M. & S. 267; 7 Mass. 325; 13 Mass. 94; Co. Litt. 206; Com. Dig. Condition, D 1, L 13; 2 Bl. Com. 340; 1 T. R. 33; Jones on Bailm. 104, 5; 1 Bouv. Inst. n. 1024.

3. Special bail are discharged when the defendant dies, Tidd, 243; *actus Dei nemini facit injuriam* being a maxim of law, applicable in such case; but if the defendant die after the return of the *ca. sa.*, and before it is filed, the bail are fixed. 6 T. R. 284; 5 Binn. 332, 338. It is, however, no ground for an exoneretur, that the defendant has become deranged since the suit was brought, and is confined in a hospital. 2 Wash. C. C. R. 464; 6 T. R. 133; 2 Bos. & Pull. 362; Tidd, 184. Vide 8 Mass. Rep. 264; 3 Yeates, 37; 2 Dall. 317; 16 Mass. Rep. 218; Stra. 128; 1 Leigh's N. P. 508; 11 Pick. R. 41; 2 Verm. R. 92; 2 Watt's Rep. 443.

See generally, *Fortuitous Event; Perils of the Sea.*

ACT OF GRACE, *Scotch law*. The name by which the statute which provides for the aliment of prisoners confined for civil debts, is usually known.

2. This statute provides that where a prisoner for debt declares upon oath, before the magistrate of the jurisdiction, that he has not wherewith to maintain himself, the magistrate may set him at liberty, if the creditor, in consequence of whose diligence he was imprisoned, does not aliment him within ten days after intimation for that purpose. 1695, c. 32; Ersk. Pr. L. Scot. 4, 3, 14. This is somewhat similar to a provision in the insolvent act of Pennsylvania

Act of law. An event which occurs in consequence of some principle of law. If, for example, land out of which a rent charge has been granted, be recovered by an elder title, and thereby the rent charge becomes avoided; yet the grantee shall have a writ of annuity, because the rent charge is made void by due course or act of law, it being a maxim *actus legis nemini est damnosus*. 2 Inst. 287.

Act of man. Every man of sound mind and discretion is bound by his own acts, and the law does not permit him to do any thing against it; and all acts are construed most strongly against him who does them. Plowd. 140.

2. A man is not only bound by his own acts, but by those of others who act or are presumed to act by his authority, and is responsible civilly in all such cases; and, in some cases, even when there is but a presumption of authority, he may be made responsible criminally; for example, a bookseller may be indicted for publishing a libel which has been sold in his store, by his regular salesmen, although he may possibly have had no knowledge of it.

ACTIO BONÆ FIDEI, *civil law*. An action of good faith.

ACTIO COMMODATI CONTRARIA. The name of an action in the civil law, by the borrower against the lender, to compel the execution of the contract. Poth. Prêt à Usage, n. 75.

ACTIO COMMODATI DIRECTA. In the civil law, is the name of an action, by a lender against a borrower, the principal object of which is to obtain restitution of the thing lent. Poth. Prêt. à Usage, n. 65, 68.

ACTIO CONDICTIO INDEBITI. The name of an action in the civil law, by which the plaintiff recovers the amount of a sum of money or other thing he paid by mistake. Poth. Promutuum, n. 140. See *Assumpsit*.

ACTIO EX CONDUCTIO, *civil law*. The name of an action which the bailor of a thing for hire may bring against the bailee, in order to compel him to re-deliver the thing hired. Poth. du Contr. de Louage, n. 59.

ACTIO DEPOSITI CONTRARIA. The name of an action in the civil law which the depositary has against the depositor to compel him to fulfil his engagement towards him. Poth. Du Dépot, n. 69.

ACTIO DEPOSITI DIRECTA. In the civil law, this is the name of an action which is brought by the depositor against the depositary, in order to get back the thing deposited. Poth. Du Dépot, n. 60.

ACTIO JUDICATI, *civil law*. Was an action instituted, after four months had elapsed after the rendition of judgment, in which the judge issued his warrant to seize, first, the movables, which were sold within eight days afterwards; and then the immovables, which were delivered in pledge to the creditors, or put under the care of a curator, and, if at the end of two months, the debt was not paid, the land was sold. Dig. 42, t. 1. Code, 8, 34.

ACTIO NON, *pleading*. After stating the appearance and defence, special pleas begin with this allegation, "that the said plaintiff ought not to have or maintain his aforesaid action thereof against him," *actio non habere debet*. This is technically termed the *actio non*. 1 Ch. Plead. 531; 2 Ch. Plead. 421; Steph. Plead. 394.

ACTIO NON ACCREVIT INFRA SEX ANNOS. The name of a plea to the statute of limitations, when the defendant insists that the plaintiff's action has not accrued within six years. It differs from *non assumpsit* in this: *non assumpsit* is the proper plea to an action on a simple contract, when the action accrues on the promise; but when it does not accrue on the promise but subsequently to it, the proper plea is *actio non accrevit*, &c. Lawes, Pl. in Ass. 733; 5 Binn. 200, 203; 2 Salk. 422; 1 Saund. Rep. 33, n. 2; 2 Saund. 63, b; 1 Sell. N. P. 121.

ACTIO PERSONALIS MORITUR CUM PERSONA. That a personal action dies with the person, is an ancient and uncontested maxim. But the term *personal action*, requires explanation. In a large sense all actions except those for the recovery of real property may be called *personal*. This definition would include contracts for the payment of money, which never were supposed to die with the person. See 1 Saund. Rep. 217, note 1.

2. The maxim must therefore be taken in a more restricted meaning. It extends to all wrongs attended with *actual force*, whether they affect the person or property; and to all injuries to the person only, though without actual force. Thus stood originally the common law, in which an alteration was made by the statute 4 Ed. III. c. 7, which gave an action to an executor for an injury done to the personal property of his testator in his lifetime, which was extended to

the executor of an executor, by statute of 25 Ed. III. c. 5. And by statute 31 Ed. III. c. 11, administrators have the same remedy as executors.

3. These statutes received a liberal construction from the judges, but they do not extend to injuries to the *person* of the deceased, nor to his *freehold*. So that no action lies by an executor or administrator for an assault and battery of the deceased, or trespass, *vi et armis* on his land, or for slander, because it is merely a personal injury. Neither do they extend to actions against executors or administrators for wrongs committed by the deceased. 13 S. & R. 184; Cowp. 376; 1 Saund. 216, 217, n. 1; Com. Dig. 241, B 13; 1 Salk. 252; 6 S. & R. 272; W. Jones, 215.

4. Assumpsit may be maintained by executors or administrators, in those cases where an injury has been done to the personal property of the deceased, and he might in his lifetime have waived the tort and sued in assumpsit. 1 Bay's R. 61; Cowp. 374; 3 Mass. 321; 4 Mass. 480; 13 Mass. 272; 1 Root, 216.

5. An action for a breach of a promise of marriage cannot be maintained by an executor, 2 M. & S. 408; nor against him, 13 S. & R. 183; 1 Picker. 71; unless, perhaps, where the plaintiff's testator sustained special damages. 13 S. & R. 185.

See further 12 S. & R. 76; 1 Day's Cas. 180; Bac. Abr. Ejectment, H; 11 Vin. Abr. 123; 1 Salk. 314; 2 Ld. Raym. 971; 1 Salk. 12; Id. 295; Cro. Eliz. 377, 8; 1 Str. 60; Went. Ex. 65; 1 Vent. 176; Id. 30; 7 Serg. & R. 183; 7 East, 134–6; 1 Saund. 216, a, n. 1; 6 Mass. 394; 2 Johns. 227; 1 Bos. & Pull. 330, n. a.; 1 Chit. Pl. 86; 3 Bouv. Inst. n. 2750; this Dictionary, tit. *Actions; Death; Parties to Actions; Survivor*.

ACTIO PRO SOCIO. In the civil law, is the name of an action by which either partner could compel his co-partners to perform their social contract. Poth. Contr. de Société, n. 134.

ACTION. Conduct, behaviour, something done. Nomen actionis latissime patere vulgo notum est ac comprehendere omnem omnino viventis operationem quæ passioni opponitur. Vinnius, Com. lib. 4, tit. 6. *De actionibus*.

2 Human actions have been divided into necessary actions, or those over which man has no control; and into free actions, or such as he can control at his pleasure. As man is responsible only when he exerts his will, it is clear he can be punished only for the latter.

3. Actions are also divided into positive and negative; the former is called an act of commission; the latter is the omission of something which ought to be done, and is called an act of omission. A man may be responsible as well for acts of omission, as for acts of commission.

4. Actions are voluntary and involuntary. The former are performed freely and without constraint—the latter are performed not by choice, against one's will or in a manner independent of the will. In general a man is not responsible for his involuntary actions. Yet it has been ruled that if a lunatic hurt a man, he shall be answerable in trespass, although, if he kill a man, it is not felony. See Hob. Rep. 134; Popham, 162; Ham. N. P. 68. See also *Duress; Will*.

ACTION, *French com. law*. Stock in a company, shares in a corporation.

ACTION, *in practice*. Actio nihil aliud est, quam jus persequendi in judicio quod sibi debetur. Just. Inst. Lib. 4, tit. 6; Vinnius, Com. Actions are divided into criminal and civil. Bac. Abr. Actions, A.

2.—§ 1. A criminal action is a prosecution in a court of justice, in the name of the government, against one or more individuals accused of a crime. See 1 Chitty's Cr. Law.

3.—§ 2. A civil action is a legal demand of one's right, or it is the form given by law for the recovery of that which is due. Co. Litt. 285; 3 Bl. Com. 116; 3 Bouv. Inst. n. 2639; Domat. Supp. des Lois Civiles, liv. 4, tit. 1, No. 1; Poth. Introd. generale aux Coutumes, 109; 1 Sell. Pr. Introd. s. 4, p. 73. Ersk. Princ. of Scot. Law, B. 4, t. 1, § 1. Till judgment the writ is properly called an action, but not after, and therefore, a release of all actions is regularly no bar of an execution. Co. Litt. 289 a; Roll. Ab. 291. They are real, personal and mixed. An action is real or personal, according as realty or personalty is recovered; not according to the nature of the defence. Willes' Rep. 134.

4.—1. Real actions are those brought for the specific recovery of lands, tenements, or hereditaments. Steph. Pl. 3. They are either *droitural*, when the demandant seeks to recover the *property*; or *possessory*, when he endeavors to obtain the *possession* Finch's Law, 257, 8. See Bac. Abr. Actions, A, contra. Real Actions are, 1st.

Writs of right; 2dly. Writs of entry, which lie in the *per*, the *per et cui*, or the *post*, upon *disseisin*, *intrusion*, or *alienation*. 3dly. Writs ancestral possessory, as *Mort d'ancester*, *aiel*, *besaiel*, *cosinage*, or *Nuper obiit*. Com. Dig. Actions, D 2. By these actions formerly all disputes concerning real estate, were decided; but now they are pretty generally laid aside in practice, upon account of the great nicety required in their management, and the inconvenient length of their process; a much more expeditious method of trying titles being since introduced by other actions, personal and mixed. 3 Bl. Com. 118. See Booth on Real Actions.

5.—2. Personal actions are those brought for the specific recovery of goods and chattels; or for damages or other redress for breach of contract, or other injuries, of whatever description; the specific recovery of lands, tenements, and hereditaments only excepted. Steph. Pl. 3; Com. Dig. Actions, D 3; 3 Bouv. Inst. n. 2641. Personal actions arise either upon contracts, or for wrongs independently of contracts. The former are account, assumpsit, covenant, debt, and detinue; see these words. In Connecticut and Vermont there is an action used which is peculiar to those states, called the action of *book debt*. 2 Swift's Syst. Ch. 15. The actions for wrongs, injuries, or torts, are trespass on the case, replevin, trespass, trover. See these words, and see *Actio personalis moritur cum persona.*

6.—3. Mixed actions are such as appertain, in some degree, to both the former classes, and, therefore, are properly reducible to neither of them, being brought for the specific recovery of lands, tenements, or hereditaments, and for damages for injury sustained in respect of such property. Steph. Pl. 3; Co. Litt. 284, b; Com. Dig. Actions, D 4. Every mixed action, properly so called, is also a real action. The action of ejectment is a personal action, and formerly, a count for an assault and battery might be joined with a count for the recovery of a term of years in land.

7. Actions are also divided into those which are *local* and such as are *transitory*.

1. A *local* action is one in which the venue must still be laid in the county, in which the cause of action actually arose. The locality of actions is founded in some cases, on common law principles, in others on the statute law.

8. Of those which continue local, by the common law, are, 1st, all actions in which the *subject* or *thing* to be recovered is in its nature local. Of this class are real actions, actions of waste, when brought on the statute of Gloucester, (6 Edw. I.) to recover with the damages, the *locus in quo* or place wasted; and actions of ejectment. Bac. Abr. Actions Local, &c., A, a; Com. Dig. Actions, N 1; 7 Co. 2 b; 2 Bl. Rep. 1070 All these are local, because they are brought to recover the seisin or possession of lands or tenements, which are local subjects.

9.—2dly. Various actions which do not seek the direct recovery of lands or tenements, are also local, by the common law; because they arise out of some local subject, or the violation of some local right or interest. For example, the action of *quare impedit* is local, inasmuch as the benefice, in the right of presentation to which the plaintiff complains of being obstructed, is so. 7 Co. 3 a; 1 Chit. Pl. 271; Com. Dig. Actions, N 4. Within this class of cases are also many actions in which only pecuniary damages are recoverable. Such are the common law action of *waste*, and trespass *quare clausum fregit;* as likewise trespass on the case for injuries affecting things real, as for nuisances to houses or lands; disturbance of rights of way or of common; obstruction or diversion of ancient water courses, &c. 1 Chit. Pl. 271; Gould on Pl. ch. 3, § 105, 106, 107. The action of replevin, also, though it lies for damages only, and does not arise out of the violation of any local right, is nevertheless local. 1 Saund. 347, n. 1. The reason of its locality appears to be the necessity of giving a local description of the taking complained of. Gould on Pl. ch. 3, § 111. A scire facias upon a record, (which is an action, 2 Term Rep. 46,) although to some intents, a continuation of the original suit, 1 Term Rep. 388, is also local.

10.—2. Personal actions which seek nothing more than the recovery of money or personal chattels, of any kind, are in most cases *transitory*, whether they sound in tort or in contract; Com. Dig. Actions, N 12; 1 Chit. Pl. 273; because actions of this class are, in most instances, founded on the violation of rights which, in contemplation of law, have no locality. 1 Saund. 241, b, note 6. And it will be found true, as a general position, that actions *ex delicto*, in which a mere personalty is recoverable, are, by the common law, transitory; except when founded upon, or arising out of some *local* subject. Gould on Pl. ch. 3, § 112. The venue in a transitory action may be laid in any county which the plaintiff may prefer. Bac. Abr. Actions Local, &c. A. (a.)

11. In the civil law, actions are divided into real, personal, and mixed.

A real action, according to the civil law, is that which he who is the owner of a thing, or has a right in it, has against him who is in possession of it, to compel him to give up such thing to the plaintiff, or to permit him to enjoy the right he has in it. It is a right which a person has in a thing, follows the thing, and may be instituted against him who possesses it; and this whether the thing be movable or immovable, and, in the sense of the common law, whether the thing be real or personal. See Domat, Supp. des Lois Civiles, Liv. 4, tit. 1, n. 5; Pothier, Introd. Générales aux Coutumes, 110; Ersk. Pr. Scot. Law, B. 4, t. 1, § 2.

12. A personal action is that which a creditor has against his debtor, to compel him to fulfil his engagement. Pothier, Ib. Personal actions are divided into civil actions and criminal actions. The former are those which are instituted to compel the payment or to do some other thing purely civil; the latter are those by which the plaintiff asks the reparation of a tort or injury which he or those who belong to him have sustained. Sometimes these two kinds of actions are united, when they assume the name of mixed personal actions. Domat, Supp. des Lois Civiles, Liv. 4, tit. 1, n. 4; 1 Brown's Civ. Law, 440.

13. Mixed actions participate both of personal and real actions. Such are the actions of partition, and to compel the parties to put down landmarks or boundaries. Domat, *ubi supra.*

ACTION AD EXHIBENDUM, *civil law.* This was an action instituted for the purpose of compelling the defendant to exhibit a thing or title, in his power. It was preparatory to another action, which was always a real action in the sense of the Roman law, that is, for the recovery of a *thing*, whether it was movable or immovable. Merl. Quest. de Dr. tome i. 84. This is not unlike a bill of discovery. (q. v.)

ACTION OF ADHERENCE, *Scotch law.* An action competent to a husband or wife to compel either party to adhere in case of desertion.

ACTION OF BOOK DEBT. The name of an action in Connecticut and Vermont, resorted to for the purpose of recovering payment for articles usually charged on book. 1 Day, 105; 4 Day, 105; 2 Verm. 366. See 1 Root, 59; 1 Conn. 75; Kirby, 289; 2 Root, 130; 11 Conn. 205.

ACTION REDHIBITORY, *civil law.* An action instituted to avoid a sale on account of some vice or defect in the thing sold, which renders it either absolutely useless, or its use so inconvenient and imperfect, that it must be supposed the buyer would not have purchased it, had he known of the vice. Civ. Code of Louis. art. 2496.

ACTION OF A WRIT. This phrase is used when one pleads some matter by which he shows that the plaintiff had no cause to have the writ which he brought, and yet he may have a writ or action for the same matter. Such a plea is called a plea to the action of the writ, whereas if it should appear by the plea that the plaintiff has no cause to have an action for the thing demanded, then it is called a plea to the action. Termes de la ley.

ACTIONS ORDINARY, *Scotch law.* By this term is understood all actions not rescissory. Ersk. Pr. L. Scot. 4, 1, 5.

ACTIONS RESCISSORY, *Scotch law.* Are divided into, 1, Actions of proper improbation; 2, Actions of reduction-improbation; 3, Actions of simple reduction. Ersk. Pr. L. Scot. 4, 1, 5.

2.—1. Proper improbation is an action brought for declaring writing false or forged.

3.—2. Reduction-improbation is an action whereby a person who may be hurt, or affected by a writing, insists for producing or exhibiting it in court, in order to have it set aside or its effects ascertained, under the certification, that the writing if not produced, shall be declared false and forged.

4.– 3. In an action of simple reduction, the certification is only temporary, declaring the writings called for, null, until they be produced; so that they recover their full force after their production. Ib. 4, 1, 8.

ACTIONARY. A commercial term used among foreigners, to signify stockholders.

ACTIONES NOMINATÆ. Formerly the English courts of chancery would make no writs when there was no precedent, and the cases for which there were precedents were called *actiones nominatæ*. The statute of Westm. 2, c. 24, gave chancery, authority to form new writs in consimili casu. Hence arose the action on the case. Bac. Ab Court of Chancery, A; 17 Serg. & R. 195.

ACTIVE. The opposite of *passive.*

We say active debts, or debts due to us; passive debts are those we owe.

ACTON BURNELL. Statute of, vide *de Mercatoribus*. Cruise, Dig. tit. 14, s. 6.

ACTOR, *practice*. 1. A plaintiff or complainant. 2. He on whom the burden of proof lies. In actions of replevin both parties are said to be actors. The proctor or advocate in the courts of the civil law, was called actor.

ACTS OF COURT. In courts of admiralty, by this phrase is understood legal memoranda of the nature of pleas. For example, the English court of admiralty disregards all tenders, except those formally made by acts of court. Abbott on Ship. pt. 3, c. 10, § 2, p. 403; 4 Rob. R. 103; 1 Hagg. R. 157; Dunl. Adm. Pr. 104, 5.

ACTS OF SEDERUNT. In the laws of Scotland, are ordinances for regulating the forms of proceeding, before the court of session, in the administration of justice, made by the judges, who have a delegated power from the legislature for that purpose. Ersk. Pr. L. Scot. B. 1, t. 1, s. 14.

ACTUAL. Real; actual.

2. *Actual notice.* One which has been expressly given, by which knowledge of a fact has been brought home to a party directly; it is opposed to constructive notice.

3. *Actual admissions.* Those which are expressly made; they are plenary or partial. 4 Bouv. Inst. n. 4405.

4. An *actual escape* takes place when a prisoner in fact gets out of prison, and unlawfully regains his liberty. Vide *Escape*.

ACTUARIUS. An ancient name or appellation of a notary.

ACTUARY. A clerk in some corporations vested with various powers. In the ecclesiastical law he is a clerk who registers the acts and constitutions of the convocation.

ACTUS. A foot way and horse way. Vide *Way*.

AD DAMNUM, *pleading*. To the damage. In all personal and mixed actions, with the exception of actions of debt *qui tam*, where the plaintiff has sustained no damages, the declaration concludes *ad damnum*. Archb. Civ. Pl. 169.

AD DIEM. At the day, as a plea of payment ad diem, on the day when the money became due. See *Solvit ad diem*, and Com. Dig. Pleader, 2 W. 29.

AD INQUIRENDUM, *practice*. A judicial writ, commanding inquiry to be made of any thing relating to a cause depending in court.

AD INTERIM. In the mean time. An officer is sometimes appointed *ad interim*, when the principal officer is absent, or for some cause incapable of acting for the time.

AD LARGUM. At large; as, title at large, assize at large. See Dane's Abr. ch. 144. a. 16, § 7.

AD QUEM. A Latin expression which signifies *to which*, in the computation of time or distance, as the day *ad quem*. The last day of the term, is always computed. See *A quo*.

AD QUOD DAMNUM, *Eng. law*. The name of a writ issuing out of and returnable into chancery, directed to the sheriff, commanding him to inquire by a jury what damage it will be to the king, or any other, to grant a liberty, fair, market, highway, or the like.

AD SECTAM. At the suit of, commonly abbreviated ads. It is usual in filing pleas, and other papers, for a defendant, instead of putting the name of the plaintiff first, as Peter *v.* Paul, to put his own first, and instead of *v.* to put ads., as Paul ads. Peter.

AD TERMINUM QUI PRETERIIT. The name of a writ of entry which lay for the lessor or his heirs, when a lease had been made of lands or tenements, for term of life or years, and, after the term had expired, the lands were withheld from the lessor by the tenant, or other person possessing the same. F. N. B. 201. The remedy now applied for holding over (q. v.) is by ejectment, or under local regulations, by summary proceedings.

AD TUNC ET IBIDEM. That part of an indictment, where it is stated that the subject-matter of the crime or offence "then and there being found," is technically so called. N. C. Term R. 93; Bac. Ab Indictment, G 4.

AD VITAM AUT CULPAM. An office to be so held as to determine only by the death or delinquency of the possessor; in other words it is held *quam diu se bene gesserit*.

AD VALOREM. According to the value. This Latin term is used in commerce in reference to certain duties, called *ad valorem* duties, which are levied on commodities at certain rates *per centum* on their value. See *Duties; Imposts;* Act of Cong. of March 2, 1799, s. 61; of March 1, 1823, s. 5.

ADDITION. Whatever is added to a man's name by way of title, as additions of estate, mystery, or place. 10 Went. Plead. 371; Salk. 5; 2 Lord Ray. 988; 1 Wils. 244, 5.

2. *Additions of an estate or quality* are

esquire, gentleman, and the like; these titles can however be claimed by none, and may be assumed by any one. In Nash *v.* Battersby (2 Lord Ray. 986; 6 Mod. 80,) the plaintiff declared with the addition of gentleman. The defendant pleaded in abatement that the plaintiff was no gentleman. The plaintiff demurred, and it was held ill; for, said the court, it amounts to a confession that the plaintiff is no gentleman, and then not the person named in the count. He should have replied that he is a gentleman.

3. *Additions of mystery* are such as scrivener, painter, printer, manufacturer, &c.

4. *Additions of places* are descriptions by the place of residence, as A. B. of Philadelphia and the like. See Bac. Ab. h. t.; Doct. Pl. 71; 2 Vin. Abr. 77; 1 Lilly's Reg. 39; 1 Metc. R. 151.

5. At common law there was no need of addition in any case, 2 Lord Ray. 988; it was required only by Stat. 1 H. 5, c. 5, in cases where process of outlawry lies. In all other cases it is only a description of the person, and common reputation is sufficient. 2 Lord Ray. 849. No addition is necessary in a Homine Replegiando. 2 Lord Ray. 987; Salk. 5; 1 Wils. 244, 5; 6 Rep. 67.

ADDITIONALES, *in contracts.* Additional terms or propositions to be added to a former agreement.

ADDRESS, *chan. plead.* That part of a bill which contains the appropriate and technical description of the court where the plaintiff seeks his remedy. Coop. Eq. Pl. 8; Bart. Suit in Eq. 26; Story, Eq. Pl. § 26; Van Hey. Eq. Draft. 2.

ADDRESS, *legislation.* In Pennsylvania it is a resolution of both branches of the legislature, two-thirds of each house concurring, requesting the governor to remove a judge from office. The constitution of that state, art. 5, s. 2, directs, that "for any reasonable cause, which shall not be sufficient ground for impeachment, the governor may remove any of them [the judges], on the address of two-thirds of each branch of the legislature." The mode of removal by address is unknown to the constitution of the United States, but it is recognized in several of the states. In some of the state constitutions the language is imperative; the governor when thus addressed *shall* remove; in others it is left to his discretion, he *may* remove. The relative proportion of each house that must join in the address, varies also in different states. In some a bare majority is sufficient; in others, two-thirds are requisite; and in others three-fourths. 1 Journ. of Law, 154.

ADEMPTION, *wills.* A taking away or revocation of a legacy by the testator.

2. It is either express or implied. It is the former when revoked in express terms by a codicil or later will; it is implied when by the acts of the testator it is manifestly his intention to revoke it; for example, when a specific legacy of a chattel is made, and afterwards the testator sells it; or if a father makes provision for a child by his will and afterwards gives to such child, if a daughter, a portion in marriage; or, if a son, a sum of money to establish him in life, provided such portion or sum of money be equal to or greater than the legacy. 2 Fonbl. 368 et seq.; Toll. Ex. 320; 1 Vern. R. by Raithby, 85 n. and the cases there cited. 1 Roper, Leg. 237, 256, for the distinction between specific and general legacies.

ADHERING. Cleaving to, or joining; as, adhering to the enemies of the United States.

2. The constitution of the United States, art. 3, s. 3, defines treason against the United States, to consist only in levying war against them or in *adhering* to their enemies, giving them aid and comfort.

3. The fact that a citizen is cruising in an enemy's ship, with a design to capture or destroy American ships, would be an adhering to the enemies of the United States. 4 State Tr. 328; Salk. 634; 2 Gilb. Ev. by Lofft, 798.

4. If war be actually levied, that is, a body of men be actually assembled for the purpose of effecting by force a treasonable enterprise, all those who perform any part, however minute, or however remote from the scene of action, and who are leagued in the general conspiracy, are to be considered as traitors. 4 Cranch. 126.

ADJOURNMENT. The dismissal by some court, legislative assembly, or properly authorized officer, of the business before them, either finally, which is called an adjournment *sine die*, without day; or, to meet again at another time appointed, which is called a temporary adjournment.

2. The constitution of the United States, art. 1, s. 5, 4, directs that "neither house, during the session of congress, shall, without the consent of the other, adjourn for more than three days, nor to any other

place, than that in which the two houses shall be sitting." Vide Com. Dig. h. t.; Vin. Ab. h. t.; Dict. de Jur. h. t.

ADJOURNMENT-DAY. In English practice, is a day so called from its being a further day appointed by the judges at the regular sittings, to try causes at nisi prius.

ADJOURNMENT-DAY IN ERROR. In the English courts, is a day appointed some days before the end of the term, at which matters left undone on the affirmance day are finished. 2 Tidd, 1224.

ADJUDICATION, *in practice*. The giving or pronouncing a judgment in a cause; a judgment.

ADJUDICATIONS, *Scotch law*. Certain proceedings against debtors, by way of actions, before the court of sessions; and are of two kinds, special and general.

2.—1. By statute 1672, c. 19, such part only of the debtor's lands is to be adjudged to the principal sum and interest of the debt, with the compositions due to the superior, and the expenses of infeoffment, and a fifth part more, in respect, the creditor is obliged to take lands for his money; but without penalties or sheriff fees. The debtor must deliver to the creditor a valid right to the lands to be adjudged, or transumpts thereof, renounce the possession in his favor, and ratify the decree of adjudication: and the law considers the rent of the lands as precisely commensurate to the interest of the debt. In this, which is called a special adjudication, the time allowed the debtor to redeem the lands adjudged, (called the legal reversion or the legal,) is declared to be five years.

3.—2. Where the debtor does not produce a sufficient right to the lands, or is not willing to renounce the possession and ratify the decree, the statute makes it lawful for the creditor to adjudge all right belonging to the debtor, in the same manner, and under the same reversion of ten years. In this kind, which is called a general adjudication, the creditor must limit his claim to the principal sum, interest and penalty, without demanding a fifth part more. See Act 26 Feb. 1684; Ersk. Pr. L. Scot. B. 2, t. 12, s. 15, 16. See *Diligences*.

ADJUNCTION, *in civil law*. Takes place when the thing belonging to one person is attached or united to that which belongs to another, whether this union is caused by *inclusion*, as if one man's diamond be enchased in another's ring; by *soldering*, as if one's guard be soldered on another's sword; by *sewing*, as by employing the silk of one to make the coat of another; by *construction*, as by building on another's land; by *writing*, as when one writes on another's parchment; or by *painting*, when one paints a picture on another's canvas.

2. In these cases, as a general rule, the accessory follows the principal; hence these things which are attached to the things of another become the property of the latter. The only exception which the civilians made was in the case of a picture, which although an accession, drew to itself the canvas, on account of the importance which was attached to it. Inst. lib. 2, t. 1, § 34; Dig. lib. 41, t. 1, l. 9, § 2. See *Accession*, and 2 Bl. Com. 404; Bro. Ab. Propertie; Com. Dig. Pleader, M. 28; Bac. Abr. Trespass, E 2. 1 Bouv. Inst. n. 499.

ADJUNCTS, *English law*. Additional judges appointed to determine causes in the High Court of Delegates, when the former judges cannot decide in consequence of disagreement, or because one of the law judges of the court was not one of the majority. Shelf. on Lun. 310.

ADJURATION. The act by which one person solemnly charges another to tell or swear to the truth. Wolff. Inst. § 374.

ADJUSTMENT, *maritime law*. The adjustment of a loss is the settling and ascertaining the amount of the indemnity which the insured after all proper allowances and deductions have been made, is entitled to receive, and the proportion of this, which each underwriter is liable to pay, under the policy; Marsh. Ins. B. 1, c. 14, p. 617; or it is a written admission of the amounts of the loss as settled between the parties to a policy of insurance. 3 Stark. Ev. 1167, 8.

2. In adjusting a loss, the first thing to be considered is, how the *quantity* of damages for which the underwriters are liable, shall be ascertained. When a loss is a total loss, and the insured decides to abandon, he must give notice of this to the underwriters in a reasonable time, otherwise he will waive his right to abandon, and must be content to claim only for a partial loss. Marsh. Ins. B. 1, c. 13, s. 2; 15 East, 559; 1 T. R. 608; 9 East, 283; 13 East, 304; 6 Taunt. 383. When the loss is admitted to be total, and the policy is a valued one, the insured is entitled to receive the whole sum insured, subject to

such deductions as may have been agreed by the policy to be made in case of loss.

3. The quantity of damages being known, the next point to be settled, is by what rule this shall be estimated. The price of a thing does not afford a just criterion to ascertain its true value. It may have been bought very dear or very cheap. The circumstances of time and place cause a continual variation in the price of things. For this reason, in cases of general average, the things saved contribute not according to prime cost, but according to the price for which they may be sold at the time of settling the average. Marsh. Ins. B. 1, c. 14, s. 2, p. 621; Laws of Wisbuy, art. 20; Laws of Oleron, art. 8; this Dict. tit. *Price*. And see 4 Dall. 430; 1 Caines' R. 80; 2 S. & R. 229; 2 S. & R. 257, 258.

4. An adjustment being endorsed on the policy, and signed by the underwriters, with the promise to pay in a given time, is *primâ facie* evidence against them, and amounts to an admission of all the facts necessary to be proved by the insured to entitle him to recover in an action on the policy. It is like a note of hand, and being proved, the insured has no occasion to go into proof of any other circumstances. Marsh. Ins. B. 1, c. 14, s. 3, p. 632; 3 Stark. Ev. 1167, 8; Park. ch. 4; Wesk. Ins. 8; Beaw. Lex. Mer. 310; Com. Dig. Merchant, E 9; Abbott on Shipp. 346 to 348. See *Damages*.

ADJUTANT. A military officer, attached to every battalion of a regiment. It is his duty to superintend, under his superiors, all matters relating to the ordinary routine of discipline in the regiment.

ADJUTANT-GENERAL. A staff officer; one of those next in rank to the commander-in-chief.

ADJUNCTUM ACCESSORIUM, *civil law*. Something which is an accessory and appurtenant to another thing. 1 Chit. Pr. 154.

ADMEASUREMENT OF DOWER, *remedies*. This remedy is now nearly obsolete, even in England; the following account of it is given by Chief Baron Gilbert. "The writ of admeasurement of dower lieth where the heir when he is within age, and endoweth the wife of more than she ought to have dower of; or if the guardian in chivalry, [for the guardian in socage cannot assign dower,] endoweth the wife of more than one-third part of the land of which she ought to have dower, then the heir, at full age, may sue out this writ against the wife; and thereby shall be admeasured, and the surplusage she hath in dower shall be restored to the heir; but in such case there shall not be assigned anew any lands to hold to dower, but to take from her so much of the lands as surpasseth the third part whereof she ought to be endowed; and he need not set forth of whose assignments she holds." Gilb. on Uses, 379; and see F. N. B. 148; Bac. Ab. Dower, K; F. N. B. 148; Co. Litt. 39 a; 2 Inst. 367; *Dower; Estate in Dower.*

ADMEASUREMENT OF PASTURE, *Eng. law*. The name of a writ which lies where many tenants have common appendant in another ground, and one overcharges the common with beasts. The other commoners, to obtain their just rights, may sue out this writ against him.

ADMINICLE. 1. A term, in the Scotch and French law, for any writing or deed referred to by a party, in an action at law, for proving his allegations. 2. An ancient term for aid or support. 3. A term in the civil law for imperfect proof. Tech. Dict h. t.; Merl. Répert. mot Adminicule.

ADMINICULAR EVIDENCE, *eccl. law* This term is used in the ecclesiastical law to signify evidence, which is brought to explain or complete other evidence. 2 Lee, Eccl. R. 595.

TO ADMINISTER, ADMINISTERING. The stat. 9 G. IV. c. 31, s. 11, enacts "that if any person unlawfully and maliciously shall *administer*, or attempt to administer to any person, or shall cause to be taken by any person any poison or other destructive things," &c. every such offender, &c. In a case which arose under this statute, it was decided that to constitute the act of administering the poison, it was not absolutely necessary there should have been a delivery to the party poisoned, but that if she took it from a place where it had been put for her by the defendant, and any part of it went into her stomach, it was an administering. 4 Carr. & Payne, 369; S. C. 19 E. C. L. R. 423; 1 Moody's C. C. 114; Carr. Crim. L. 237. Vide *Attempt; to Persuade.*

TO ADMINISTER, *trusts*. To do some act in relation to an estate, such as none but the owner, or some one authorized by him or by the law, in case of his decease, could legally do. 1 Harr. Cond. Lo. R. 666.

ADMINISTRATION, *trusts*. The management of the estate of an intestate, a minor, a lunatic, an habitual drunkard, or other person who is incapable of managing his own affairs, entrusted to an administrator or other trustee by authority of law. In a more confined sense, and in which it will be used in this article, administration is the management of an intestate's estate, or of the estate of a testator who, at the time administration was granted, had no executor.

2. Administration is granted by a public officer duly authorized to delegate the trust; he is sometimes called surrogate, judge of probate, register of wills and for granting letters of administration. It is to be granted to such persons as the statutory provisions of the several states direct. In general the right of administration belongs to him who has the right to the vendue of the personalty: as if A make his will, and appoint B his executor, who dies intestate, and C is the legatee of the residue of A's estate, C has the right of administration cum testamento annexo. 2 Strange, 956; 12 Mod. 437, 306; 1 Jones, 225; 1 Croke. 201; 2 Leo. 55; 1 Vent. 217.

3. There are several kinds of administrations, besides the usual kind which gives to the administrator the management of all the personal estate of the deceased for an unlimited time. Administration *durante minore ætate*, administration *durante absentia*, administration *pendente lite*, administration *de bonis non*, administration *cum testamento annexo*.

ADMINISTRATION, *government*. The management of the affairs of the government; this word is also applied to the persons entrusted with the management of the public affairs.

ADMINISTRATOR, *trusts*. An administrator is a person lawfully appointed, with his assent, by an officer having jurisdiction, to manage and settle the estate of a deceased person who has left no executor, or one who is for the time incompetent or unable to act.

2. It will be proper to consider, first, his rights; secondly, his duties; thirdly, the number of administrators, and their joint and several powers; fourthly, the several kinds of administrators.

3.—1. By the grant of the letters of administration, the administrator is vested with full and ample power, unless restrained to some special administration, to take possession of all the personal estate of the deceased and to sell it; to collect the debts due to him; and to represent him in all matters which relate to his chattels real or personal. He is authorized to pay the debts of the intestate in the order directed by law; and, in the United States, he is generally entitled to a just compensation, which is allowed him as commissions on the amount which passes through his hands.

4.—2. He is bound to use due diligenc in the management of the estate; and he is generally on his appointment required to give security that he will do so; he is responsible for any waste which may happen for his default. See *Devastavit*.

5. Administrators are authorized to bring and defend actions. They sue and are sued in their own names; as, A B, administrator of C D, *v.* E F; or E F *v.* A B, administrator of C D.

6.—3. As to the number of administrators. There may be one or more. When there are several they must, in general, act together in bringing suits, and they must all be sued; but, like executors, the acts of each, which relate to the delivery, gift, sale, payment, possession or release of the intestate's goods, are considered as of equal validity as the acts of all, for they have a joint power and authority over the whole. Bac. Ab. Executor, C 4; 11 Vin. Ab. 358, Com. Dig. Administration, B 12; 1 Dane's Ab. 383; 2 Litt. R. 315. On the death of one of several joint administrators, the whole authority is vested in the survivors.

7.—4. Administrators are general, or those who have right to administer the whole estate of the intestate; or special, that is, those who administer it in part, or for a limited time.

8.—1. General administrators are of two kinds, namely: first, when the grant of administration is unlimited, and the administrator is required to administer the whole estate under the intestate laws; secondly, when the grant is made with the annexation of the will, which is the guide to the administrator to administer and distribute the estate. This latter administration is granted when the deceased has made a will, and either he has not appointed an executor, or having appointed one he refuses to serve, or dies, or is incompetent to act; this last kind is called an administrator *cum testamento annexo*. 1 Will. on Wills, 309.

9.—2. Special administrators are of two

kinds; *first*, when the administration is limited to part of the estate, as for example, when the former administrator has died, leaving a part of the estate unadministered, an administrator is appointed to administer the remainder, and he is called an administrator *de bonis non*. He has all the powers of a common administrator. Bac. Ab. Executors, B 1; Sw. 396; Roll. Ab. 907; 6 Sm. & Marsh. 323. When an executor dies leaving a part of the estate unadministered, the administrator appointed to complete the execution of the will is called an administrator *de bonis non, cum testamento annexo*. Com. Dig. Administrator, B 1. *Secondly*, When the authority of the administrator is limited as to time. Administrators of this kind are, 1. An administrator *durante minore ætate*. This administrator is appointed to act as such during the minority of an infant executor, until the latter shall attain his lawful age to act. Godolph. 102; 5 Co. 29. His powers extend to administer the estate so far as to collect the same, sell a sufficiency of the personal property to pay the debts, sell *bona peritura*, and perform such other acts as require immediate attention. He may sue and be sued. Bac. Ab. Executor, B 1; Roll. Ab. 110; Cro. Eliz. 718. The powers of such an administrator cease, as soon as the infant executor attains the age at which the law authorizes him to act for himself, which, at common law, is seventeen years, but by statutory provision in several states twenty-one years.

10.—2. An administrator *durante absentiâ*, is one who is appointed to administer the estate during the absence of the executor, before he has proved the will. The powers of this administrator continue until the return of the executor, and then his powers cease upon the probate of the will by the executor. 4 Hagg. 360. In England it has been holden, that the death of the executor abroad does not determine the authority of the administrator *durante absentiâ*. 3 Bos. & Pull. 26.

11.—3. An administrator *pendente lite*. Administration *pendente lite* may be granted pending the controversy respecting an alleged will; and it has been granted pending a contest as to the right to administration. 2 P. Wms. 589; 2 Atk. 286; 2 Cas. temp. Lee, 258. The administrator *pendente lite* is merely an officer of the court, and holds the property only till the suit terminates. 1 Hagg. 313. He may maintain suits. 1 Ves sen. 325; 2 Ves. & B. 97; 1 Ball & B. 192; though his power does not extend to the distribution of the assets. 1 Ball & B. 192.

ADMINISTRATRIX. This term is applied to a woman to whom letters of administration have been granted. See *Administrator*.

ADMIRAL, *officer*. In some countries is the commander in chief of the naval forces. This office does not exist in the United States.

ADMIRALTY. The name of a jurisdiction which takes cognizance of suits or actions which arise in consequence of acts done upon or relating to the sea; or, in other words, of all transactions and proceedings relative to commerce and navigation, and to damages or injuries upon the sea. 2 Gall. R. 468. In the great maritime nations of Europe, the term "admiralty jurisdiction," is uniformly applied to courts exercising jurisdiction over maritime contracts and concerns. It is as familiarly known among the jurists of Scotland, France, Holland and Spain, as of England, and applied to their own courts, possessing substantially the same jurisdiction as the English Admiralty had in the reign of Edward III. Ibid., and the authorities there cited; and see, also, Bac. Ab. Court of Admiralty; Merl. Répert. h. t.; Encyclopédie, h. t.; 1 Dall. 323.

2. The Constitution of the United States has delegated to the courts of the national government cognizance "of all cases of admiralty and maritime jurisdiction;" and the act of September 24, 1789, ch. 20, s. 9, has given the district court "cognizance of all civil causes of admiralty and maritime jurisdiction," including all seizures under laws of imposts, navigation or trade of the United States, where the seizures are made on waters navigable from the sea, by vessels of ten or more tons burden, within their respective districts, as well as upon the high seas.

3. It is not within the plan of this work to enlarge upon this subject. The reader is referred to the article *Courts of the United States*, where he will find all which it has been thought necessary to say upon the subject. Vide, generally, Dunlap's Adm. Practice; Bett's Adm. Practice; 1 Kent's Com. 353 to 380; Serg. Const. Law, Index, h. t.; 2 Gall. R. 398 to 476; 2 Chit. P. 508; Bac. Ab. Courts of Admiralty; 6 Vin. Ab. 505; Dane's Ab. Index, h. t.; 2 Bro. Civ. and Adm. Law; Wheat. Dig. 1;

1 Story L. U. S. 56, 60; 2 Id. 905; 3 Id. 1564, 1696; 4 Sharsw. cont. of Story's L. U. S. 2262; Clerke's Praxis; Collectanea Maritima; 1 U. S. Dig. tit. Admiralty Courts, XIII.

ADMISSION, *in corporations or companies.* The act of the corporation or company by which an individual acquires the rights of a member of such corporation or company.

2. In trading and joint stock corporations no vote of admission is requisite; for any person who owns stock therein, either by original subscription or by conveyance, is in general entitled to, and cannot be refused, the rights and privileges of a member. 3 Mass. R. 364; Doug. 524; 1 Man. & Ry. 529.

3. All that can be required of the person demanding a transfer on the books, is to prove to the corporation his right to the property. See 8 Pick. 90.

4. In a Mutual Insurance Company, it has been held, that a person may become a member by insuring his property, paying the premium and deposit-money, and rendering himself liable to be assessed according to the rules of the corporation. 2 Mass. R. 315.

ADMISSIONS, *in evidence.* Concessions by a party of the existence of certain facts. The term admission is usually applied to civil transactions, and to matters of fact in criminal cases, where there is no criminal intent; the term confession, (q. v.) is generally considered as an admission of guilt.

2. An admission is the testimony which the party admitting, bears to the truth of a fact against himself. It is a voluntary act, by which he acknowledges as true the fact in dispute. [An admission and consent are, in fact, one and the same thing, unless indeed for more exactness we say, that consent is given to a present fact or agreement, and admission has reference to an agreement or a fact anterior; for properly speaking, it is not the admission which forms a contract, obligation or engagement, against the party admitting. The admission is, by its nature, only the proof of a pre-existing obligation, resulting from the agreement or the fact, the truth of which is acknowledged. There is still another remarkable difference between admission and consent: the first is always free in its origin; the latter, always morally forced. I may refuse to consent to a proposition made to me, abstain from a fact or an action which would subject me to an obligation; but once my consent given, or the action committed, I am no longer at liberty to deny or refuse either; I am constrained to admit, under the penalty of dishonor and infamy. But notwithstanding all these differences, admission is identified with consent, and they are both the manifestation of the will. These admissions are generally evidence of those facts, when the admissions themselves are proved.]

3. The admissibility and effect of evidence of this description will be considered generally, with respect to the nature and manner of the admission itself; and, secondly, with respect to the parties to be affected by it.

4. In the first place, as to the nature and manner of the admission; it is either made with a view to evidence; or, with a view to induce others to act upon the representation; or, it is an unconnected or casual representation.

5.—1. As an instance of admission made with a view to evidence may be mentionod the case where a party has solemnly admitted a fact under his hand and seal, in which case he is estopped, not only from disputing the deed itself, but every fact which it recites. B. N. P. 298; 1 Salk. 186; Com. Dig. Estoppel, B 5; Stark. Ev. pt. 4, p. 31.

6.—2. Instances of this second class of admissions which have induced others to act upon them, are those where a man has cohabited with a woman, and treated her in the face of the world as his wife, 2 Esp. 637; or where he has held himself out to the world in a particular character; Ib.; 1 Camp. 245; he cannot in the one case deny her to be his wife when sued by a creditor who has supplied her with goods as such, nor in the other can he divest himself of the character he has assumed.

7.—3. Where the admission or declaration is not direct to the question pending, although admissible, it is not in general conclusive evidence; and though a party may by falsifying his former declaration, show that he has acted illegally and immorally, yet if he is not guilty of any breach of good faith in the existing transaction, and has not induced others to act upon his admission or declaration, nor derived any benefit from it against his adversary, he is not bound by it. The evidence in such cases is merely presumptive, and liable to be rebutted.

8. Secondly, with respect to the parties to be affected by it. 1. By a party to a suit, 1 Phil. Ev. 74; 7 T. R. 563; 1 Dall. 65. The admissions of the party really interested, although he is no party to the suit, are evidence. 1 Wils. 257.

9.—2. The admissions of a partner during the existence of a partnership, are evidence against both. 1 Taunt. 104; Peake's C. 203; 1 Stark. C. 81. See 10 Johns. R. 66; Ib. 216; 1 M. & Selw. 249. As to admissions made *after* the dissolution of the partnership, see 3 Johns. R. 536; 15 Johns. R. 424; 1 Marsh. (Kentucky) R. 189. According to the English decisions, it seems, the admissions of one partner, after the dissolution, have been holden to bind the other partner; this rule has been partially changed by act of parliament. Colly. on Part. 282; Stat. 9 Geo. IV. c. 14, (May 9, 1828.) In the Supreme Court of the United States, a rule, the reverse of the English, has been adopted, mainly on the ground, that the admission is a new contract or promise, springing out of, and supported by the original consideration. 1 Pet. R. 351; 2 M'Lean, 87. The state courts have varied in their decisions; some have adopted the English rule; and in others it has been overruled. 2 Bouv. Inst. n. 1517; Story, Partn. § 324; 3 Kent, Com. Lect. 43, p. 49, 4th ed.; 17 S. & R. 126; 15 Johns. R. 409; 9 Cowen, R. 422; 4 Paige, R. 17; 11 Pick. R. 400; 7 Yerg. R. 534.

10.—3. By one of several persons who have a community of interest. Stark. Ev. pt. 4, p. 47; 3 Serg. & R. 9.

11.—4. By an agent, 1 Phil. Ev. 77–82; Paley Ag. 203–207.

12.—5. By an attorney, 4 Camp. 133; by wife, Paley, Ag. 139, n. 2; Whart. Dig. tit. Evidence, O; 7 T. R. 112; Nott & M'C. 374.

13. Admissions are express or implied. An express admission is one made in direct terms. An admission may be implied from the silence of the party, and may be presumed. As for instance, when the existence of the debt, or of the particular right, has been asserted in his presence, and he has not contradicted it. And an aquiescence and endurance, when acts are done by another, which, if wrongfully done, are encroachments, and call for resistance and opposition, are evidence, as a tacit admission that such acts could not be legally resisted. See 2 Stark. C. 471.

See, generally, Stark. Ev. part 4, tit. Admissions; 1 Phil. Ev. part 1, c. 5, s. 4; 1 Greenl. Ev. §§ 169—212; 2 Evans' Pothier, 319; 8 East, 549, n. 1; Com. Dig. Testemoigne, Addenda, vol. 7, p. 434; Vin. Abr. Evidence, A, b. 2, A, b. 23; Ib. Confessions; this Dict. tit. *Confessions, Examination;* Bac. Abr. Evidence, L.; Toulliér, Droit, Civil Français, tome 10, p. 375, 450; 3 Bouv. Inst. n. 3073.

ADMISSIONS, *of attorneys and counsellors.* To entitle counsellors and attorneys to practice in court, they must be admitted by the court to practice there. Different statutes and rules have been made to regulate their admission; they generally require a previous qualification by study under the direction of some practicing counsellor or attorney. See 1 Troub. & Haly's Pr. 18; 1 Arch. Pr. 16; Blake's Pr. 30.

ADMISSIONS, *in pleading.* Where one party means to take advantage of, or rely upon some matter alleged by his adversary, and to make it part of his case, he ought to admit such matter in his own pleadings; as if either party states the title under which his adversary claims, in which instances it is directly opposite in its nature to a protestation. See *Protestando.* But where the party wishes to prevent the application of his pleading to some matter contained in the pleading of his adversary, and therefore makes an express admission of such matter (which is sometimes the case,) in order to exclude it from the issue taken or the like, it is somewhat similar in operation and effect, to a protestation.

2. The usual mode of making an express admission in pleading, is, after saying that the plaintiff ought not to have or maintain his action, &c., to proceed thus, "*Because he says that although it be true that*," &c. repeating such of the allegations of the adverse party as are meant to be admitted. Express admissions are only matters of fact alleged in the pleadings; it never being necessary expressly to admit their legal sufficiency, which is always taken for granted, unless some objection be made to them. Lawes' Civ. Pl. 143, 144. See 1 Chit Pl. 600; Archb. Civ. Pl. 215.

3. In chancery pleadings, admissions are said to be plenary and partial. They are plenary by force of terms not only when the answer runs in this form, "the defendant admits it to be true," but also when he simply asserts, and generally speaking, when he says, that "he has been informed, and believes it to be true," without adding a qualification such as, "that he does not know it of his own knowledge to be so, and therefore does not admit the same." Partial admissions are those which are delivered in terms of uncertainty, mixed up as they frequently are, with explanatory or qualifying circumstances.

Admissions, *in practice*. It frequently occurs in practice, that in order to save expenses as to mere formal proofs, the attorneys on each side consent to admit, reciprocally, certain facts in the cause without calling for proof of them.

2. These are usually reduced to writing, and the attorneys shortly add to this effect, namely, "We agree that the above facts shall on the trial of this cause be admitted, and taken as proved on each side;" and signing two copies now called "admissions" in the cause, each attorney takes one. Gresl. Eq. Ev. c. 2, p. 38.

ADMITTANCE, *Eng. law*. The act of giving possession of a copyhold estate, as livery of seisin is of a freehold; it is of three kinds, namely upon a voluntary grant by the lord; upon a surrender by the former tenant; and upon descent.

ADMITTENDO IN SOCIUM, *Eng. law*. A writ associating certain persons to justices of assize.

ADMONITION. A reprimand from a judge to a person accused, on being discharged, warning him of the consequences of his conduct, and intimating to him, that should he be guilty of the same fault for which he has been admonished, he will be punished with greater severity. Merlin, Répert. h. t.

2. The admonition was authorized by the civil law, as a species of punishment for slight misdemeanors. Vide *Reprimand*.

ADNEPOS. A term employed by the Romans to designate male descendants in the fifth degree, in a direct line. This term is used in making genealogical tables.

ADOLESCENCE, *persons*. That age which follows puberty and precedes the age of majority; it commences for males at fourteen, and for females at twelve years completed, and continues till twenty-one years complete.

ADOPTION, *civil law*. The act by which a person chooses another from a strange family, to have all the rights of his own child. Merl. Répert. h. t.; Dig. 1, 7, 15, 1; and see *Arrogation*. By art. 232, of the civil code of Louisiana, it is abolished in that state. It never was in use in any other of the United States.

ADROGATION, *civil law*. The adoption of one who was *impubes*, that is, if a male, under fourteen years of age; if a female, under twelve. Dig. 1, 7, 17, 1.

ADULT, *in the civil law*. An infant who, if a boy, has attained his full age of fourteen years, and if a girl, her full age of twelve. Domat, Liv. Prel. t. 2, s. 2, n. 8. In the common law an adult is considered one of full age. 1 Swanst. R. 553.

ADULTERATION. This term denotes the act of mixing something impure with something pure, as, to mix an inferior liquor with wine; an inferior article with coffee, tea, and the like.

ADULTERINE. A term used in the civil law to denote the issue of an adulterous intercourse. See Nicholas on Adulterine Bastardy.

ADULTERIUM. In the old records this word does not signify the offence of adultery, but the fine imposed for its commission. Barr. on the Stat. 62, note.

ADULTERY, *criminal law*. From *ad* and *alter*, another person; a criminal conversation, between a man married to another woman, and a woman married to another man, or a married and unmarried person. The married person is guilty of adultery, the unmarried of fornication. (q. v.) 1 Yeates, 6; 2 Dall. 124; but see 2 Blackf. 318.

2. The elements of this crime are, 1st, that there shall be an unlawful carnal connexion; 2dly, that the guilty party shall at the time be married; 3dly, that he or she shall willingly commit the offence; for a woman who has been ravished against her will is not guilty of adultery. Domat, Supp. du Droit Public, liv. 3, t. 10, n. 13.

3. The punishment of adultery, in the United States, generally, is fine and imprisonment.

4. In England it is left to the feeble hands of the ecclesiastical courts to punish this offence.

5. Adultery in one of the married persons is good cause for obtaining a divorce by the innocent partner. See 1 Pick. 136; 8 Pick. 433; 9 Mass. 492: 14 Pick. 518; 7 Greenl. 57; 8 Greenl. 75; 7 Conn. 267; 10 Conn. 372; 6 Verm. 311; 2 Fairf. 391; 4 S. & R. 449; 5 Rand. 634; 6 Rand. 627; 8 S. & R. 159; 2 Yeates, 278, 466; 4 N. H. Rep. 501; 5 Day, 149; 2 N. & M. 167.

6. As to proof of adultery, see 2 Greenl. § 40, *Marriage*.

ADVANCEMENT. That which is given by a father to his child or presumptive heir, by anticipation of what he might inherit. 6 Watts, R. 87; 17 Mass. R. 358; 16 Mass. R. 200; 4 S. & R. 333; 11 John. R. 91; Wright, R. 339. See also Coop. Just. 515, 575; 1 Tho. Co. Lit. 835 &

3 Do. 345, 348; Toll. 301; 5 Vez. 721; 2 Rob. on Wills, 128; Wash. C. C. Rep. 225; 4 S. & R. 333; 1 S. & R. 312; 3 Conn. Rep. 31; and post *Collatio bonorum.*

2. To constitute an advancement by the law of England, the gift must be made by the father and not by another, not even by the mother. 2 P. Wms. 356. In Pennsylvania a gift of real or personal estate by the father or mother may be an advancement. 1 S. & R. 427; Act 19 April 1794, § 9; Act 8 April, 1833, § 16. There are in the statute laws of the several states provisions relative to real and personal estates, similar in most respects to those which exist in the English statute of distribution, concerning an advancement to a child. If any child of the intestate has been advanced by him by settlement, either out of the real or personal estate, or both, equal or superior to the amount in value of the share of such child which would be due from the real and personal estate, if no such advancement had been made, then such child and his descendants, are excluded from any share in the real or personal estate of the intestate.

3. But if the advancement be not equal, then such child, and in case of his death, his descendants, are entitled to receive, from the real and personal estate, sufficient to make up the deficiency, and no more.

4. The advancement is either express or implied. As to what is an implied advancement, see 2 Fonb. Eq. 121; 1 Supp. to Ves. Jr. 84; 2 Ib. 57; 1 Vern. by Raithby, 88, 108, 216; 5 Ves. 421; Bac. Ab. h. t.; 4 Kent, Com. 173.

5. A debt due by a child to his father differs from an advancement. In case of a debt, the money due may be recovered by action for the use of the estate, whether any other property be left by the deceased or not; whereas, an advancement merely bars the child's right to receive any part of his father's estate, unless he brings into hotch pot the property advanced. 17 Mass. R. 93, 359. See, generally, 17 Mass. R. 81, 356; 4 Pick. R. 21; 4 Mass. R. 680; 8 Mass. R. 143; 10 Mass. R. 437; 5 Pick. R. 527; 7 Conn. R. 1; 6 Conn. R. 355; 5 Paige's R. 318; 6 Watts' R. 86, 254, 309; 2 Yerg. R. 135; 3 Yerg. R. 95; Bac. Ab. Trusts, D; Math. on Pres. 59; 5 Hayw. 137; 11 John. 91; 1 Swanst. 13; 1 Ch. Cas. 58; 3 Conn. 31; 15 Ves. 43, 50; U. S. Dig. h. t.; 6 Whart. 370; 4 S. & R. 333; 4 Whart. 130, 540· 5 Watts, 9; 1 Watts & Serg. 390; 10 Watts, R. 158; 5 Rawle, 213; 5 Watts, 9, 80; 6 Watts & Serg. 203. The law of France in respect to advancements is stated at length in Morl. Rép. de Jurisp. *Rapport à succession.*

ADVANCES, *contracts.* Said to take place when a factor or agent pays to his principal, a sum of money on the credit of goods belonging to the principal, which are placed, or are to be placed, in the possession of the factor or agent, in order to reimburse himself out of the proceeds of the sale. In such case the factor or agent has a lien to the amount of his claim. Cowp. R. 251; 2 Burr. R. 931; Liverm. on Ag. 38; Journ. of Law, 146.

2. The agent or factor has a right not only to advances made to the owner of goods, but also for expenses and disbursements, made in the course of his agency, out of his own moneys, on account of, or for the benefit of his principal; such as incidental charges for warehouse-room, duties, freight, general average, salvage, repairs, journeys, and all other acts done to preserve the property of the principal, and to enable the agent to accomplish the objects of the principal, are to be paid fully by the latter. Story on Bailm. § 196, 197; Story on Ag. § 335.

3. The advances, expenses and disbursements of the agent must, however, have been made in good faith, without any default on his part. Liv. on Ag. 14—16; Smith on Merc. L. 56; Paley on Ag. by Lloyd, 109; 6 East, R. 392; 2 Bouv Inst. n. 1340.

4. When the advances and disbursements have been properly made, the agent is entitled not only to the return of the money so advanced, but to interest upon such advances and disbursements, whenever from the nature of the business, or the usage of trade, or the particular agreement of the parties, it may be fairly presumed to be stipulated for, or due to the agent. 7 Wend. R. 315; 3 Binn. R. 295; 3 Caines' R. 226; 1 H. Bl. 303; 3 Camp. R. 467; 15 East, R. 223; 2 Bouv. Inst. n. 1341. This just rule coincides with the civil law on this subject. Dig. 17, 1, 12, 9; Poth. Pand. lib. 17, t. 1, n. 74.

ADVENTITIOUS, *adventitius.* From advenio; what comes incidentally; as adventitia bona, goods that fall to a man otherwise than by inheritance; or adventitia dos, a dowry or portion given by some other friend beside the parent.

ADVENTURE, *bill of*. A writing signed by a merchant, to testify that the goods shipped on board a certain vessel are at the venture of another person, he himself being answerable only for the produce. Techn. Dict.

ADVENTURE, *crim. law*. See *Misadventure*.

ADVENTURE, *mer. law*. Goods sent abroad under the care of a supercargo, to be disposed of to the best advantage for the benefit of his employers, is called an adventure.

ADVERSARY. One who is a party in a writ or action opposed to the other party.

ADVERSE POSSESSION, *title to lands*. The enjoyment of land, or such estate as lies in grant, under such circumstances as indicate that such enjoyment has been commenced and continued, under an assertion or color of right on the part of the possessor. 3 East, R. 394; 1 Pick. Rep. 466; 1 Dall. R. 67; 2 Serg. & Rawle, 527; 10 Watts R. 289; 8 Conn. 440; 3 Penn. 132; 2 Aik. 364; 2 Watts, 23; 9 John. 174; 18 John. 40, 355; 5 Pet. 402; 4 Bibb, 550. Actual possession is a *pedis possessio* which can be only of ground enclosed, and only such possession can a wrongdoer have. He can have no constructive possession. 7 Serg. & R. 192; 3 Id. 517; 2 Wash. C. C. Rep. 478, 479.

2. When the possession or enjoyment has been adverse for twenty years, of which the jury are to judge from the circumstances, the law raises the presumption of a grant. Ang. on Wat. Courses, 85, et seq. But this presumption arises only when the use or occupation would otherwise have been unlawful. 3 Greenl. R. 120; 6 Binn. R. 416; 6 Cowen, R. 617, 677; 8 Cowen, R. 589; 4 S. & R. 456. See 2 Smith's Lead. Cas. 307-416.

3. There are four general rules by which it may be ascertained that possession is not adverse; these will be separately considered.

4.—1. When both parties claim under the same title; as, if a man seised of certain land in fee, have issue two sons and die seised, and one of the sons enter by abatement into the land, the statute of limitations will not operate against the other son; for when the abator entered into the land of his father, before entry made by his brother, the law intends that he entered claiming as heir to his father, by which title the other son also claims. Co Litt. s. 396.

5.—2. When the possession of the one party is consistent with the title of the other; as, where the rents of a trust estate were received by a *cestui que trust* for more than twenty years after the creation of the trust, without any interference of the trustee, such possession being consistent with and secured to the *cestui que trust* by the terms of the deed, the receipt was held not to be adverse to the title of the trustee. 8 East, 248.

6.—3. When, in contemplation of law, the claimant has never been out of possession; as, where Paul devised lands to John and his heirs, and died, and John died, and afterwards the heirs of John and a stranger entered, and took the profits for twenty years; upon ejectment brought by the devisee of the heir of John against the stranger, it was held that the perception of the rents and profits by the stranger was not adverse to the devisee's title; for when two men are in possession, the law adjudges it to be the possession of him who has the right. Lord Raym. 329.

7.—4. When the occupier has acknowledged the claimant's titles; as, if a lease be granted for a term, and, after paying the rent for the land during such term, the tenant hold for twenty years without paying rent, his possession will not be adverse. See Bos. & P. 542; 8 B. & Cr. 717; 2 Bouv. Inst. n. 2193-94, 2351.

ADVERTISEMENT. A notice published either in handbills or in a newspaper.

2. The law in many instances requires parties to advertise in order to give notice of acts which are to be done; in these cases, the advertisement is in general equivalent to notice.

3. When an advertisement contains the terms of sale, or description of the property to be sold, it will bind the seller; and if there be a material misrepresentation, it may avoid the contract, or at least entitle the purchaser to a compensation and reduction from the agreed price. Knapp's R. 344, 1 Chit. Pr. 295.

ADVICE, *com. law*. A letter containing information of any circumstances unknown to the person to whom it is written; when goods are forwarded by sea or land, the letter transmitted to inform the consignee of the fact, is termed advice of goods, or letter of advice. When one merchant draws upon another, he generally advises him of the fact. These letters are intended to give notice of the facts they contain.

Advice, *practice.* The opinion given by counsel to their clients; this should never be done but upon mature deliberation to the best of the counsel's ability; and without regard to the consideration whether it will affect the client favorably or unfavorably.

ADVISEMENT. Consideration, deliberation, consultation; as, the court holds the case under advisement.

ADVOCATE, *civil and ecclesiastical law.* 1. An officer who maintains or defends the rights of his client in the same manner as the counsellor does in the common law.

2. *Lord Advocate.* An officer of state in Scotland, appointed by the king, to advise about the making and executing the law, to prosecute capital crimes, &c.

3. *College* or *faculty of advocates.* A college consisting of 180 persons, appointed to plead in all actions before the lords of sessions.

4. *Church* or *ecclesiastical advocates.* Pleaders appointed by the church to maintain its rights.

5.—2. A patron who has the advowson or presentation to a church. Tech. Dict.; Ayl. Per. 53; Dane Ab. c. 31, § 20. See *Counsellor at law; Honorarium.*

ADVOCATIA, *civil law.* This sometimes signifies the quality, or functions, and at other times the privilege, or the territorial jurisdiction of an advocate. See Du Cange, voce *Advocatia, Advocatio.*

ADVOCATION, *Scotch law.* A writing drawn up in the form of a petition, called a *bill of advocation,* by which a party in an action applies to the supreme court to advocate its cause, and to call the action out of an inferior court to itself. *Letters of advocation,* are the decree or warrant of the supreme court or court of sessions, discharging the inferior tribunal from all further proceedings in the matter, and advocating the action to itself. This proceeding is similar to a certiorari (q. v.) issuing out of a superior court for the removal of a cause from an inferior.

ADVOCATUS. A pleader, a narrator. Bract. 412 a, 372 b.

ADVOWSON, *ecclesiastical law.* From advow or advocare, a right of presentation to a church or benefice. He who possesses this right is called the patron or advocate, (q. v.); when there is no patron, or he neglects to exercise his right within six months, it is called a *lapse,* i. e. a title is given to the ordinary to collate to a church; when a presentation is made by one who has no right it is called a *usurpation.*

2. Advowsons are of different kinds, as —*Advowson appendant,* when it depends upon a manor, &c.—*Advowson in gross,* when it belongs to a person and not to a manor.—*Advowson presentative,* where the patron presents to the bishop.—*Advowson donative,* where the king or patron puts the clerk into possession without presentation. —*Advowson of the moiety of the church,* where there are two several patrons and two incumbents in the same church.—*A moiety of advowson,* where two must join the presentation of one incumbent.—*Advowson of religious houses,* that which is vested in the person who founded such a house. Techn. Dict.; 2 Bl. Com. 21; Mirehouse on Advowsons; Com. Dig. Advowson, Quare Impedit; Bac. Ab. Simony; Burn's Eccl. Law, h. t.; Cruise's Dig. Index, h. t.

AFFECTION, *contracts.* The making over, pawning, or mortgaging a thing to assure the payment of a sum of money, or the discharge of some other duty or service. Techn. Dict.

AFFEERERS, *English law.* Those who upon oath settle and moderate fines in courts leet. Hawk. l. 2, c. 112.

TO AFFERE, *English law.* Signifies either "to affere an amercement," i. e. to mitigate the rigor of a fine; or "to affere an account," that is, to confirm it on oath in the exchequer.

AFFIANCE, *contracts.* From *affidare* or *dare fidem,* to give a pledge. A plighting of troth between a man and woman. Litt. s. 39. Pothier, Traité du Mariage, n. 24, defines it to be an agreement by which a man and a woman promise each other that they will marry together. This word is used by some authors as synonymous with marriage. Co. Litt. 34, a, note 2. See Dig 23, 1, 1; Code, 5, 1, 4; Extrav. 4, 1.

AFFIDARE. To plight one's faith, or give fealty, i. e. fidelity by making oath, &c. Cunn. Dict. h. t.

AFFIDATIO DOMINORUM, *Eng. law.* An oath taken by a lord in parliament.

AFFIDAVIT, *practice.* An oath or affirmation reduced to writing, sworn or affirmed to before some officer who has authority to administer it. It differs from a deposition in this, that in the latter the op posite party has had an opportunity to cross-examine the witness, whereas an affidavit is always taken *ex parte*. Gresl. Eq. Ev. 413. Vide Harr. Dig. h. t.

2. *Affidavit to hold to bail*, is in many cases required before the defendant can be arrested; such affidavit must be made by a person who is acquainted with the fact, and must state, 1st, an indebtedness from the defendant to the plaintiff; 2dly, show a distinct cause of action; 3dly, the whole must be clearly and certainly expressed. Sell. Pr. 104; 1 Chit. R. 165; S. C. 18 Com. Law, R. 59 note; Id. 99.

3. *An affidavit of defence*, is made by a defendant or a person knowing the facts, in which must be stated a positive ground of defence on the merits. 1 Ashm. R. 4, 19, n. It has been decided that when a writ of summons has been served upon three defendants, and only one appears, a judgment for want of an affidavit of defence may be rendered against all. 8 Watts, R. 367. Vide Bac. Ab. h. t.

AFFINITAS AFFINITATIS. That connexion between two persons which has neither consanguinity nor affinity; as, the connexion between the husband's brother and the wife's sister. This connexion is formed not between the parties themselves, nor between one of the spouses and the kinsmen of the other, but between the kinsmen of both. Ersk. Inst. B. 1, tit. 6, s. 8.

AFFINITY. A connexion formed by marriage, which places the husband in the same degree of nominal propinquity to the relations of the wife, as that in which she herself stands towards them, and gives to the wife the same reciprocal connexion with the relations of the husband. It is used in contradistinction to consanguinity. (q. v.) It is no real kindred.

2. Affinity or alliance is very different from kindred. Kindred are relations by blood; affinity is the tie which exists between one of the spouses with the kindred of the other; thus, the relations of my wife, her brothers, her sisters, her uncles, are allied to me by affinity, and my brothers, sisters, &c., are allied in the same way to my wife. But my brother and the sister of my wife are not allied by the ties of affinity. This will appear by the following paradigms

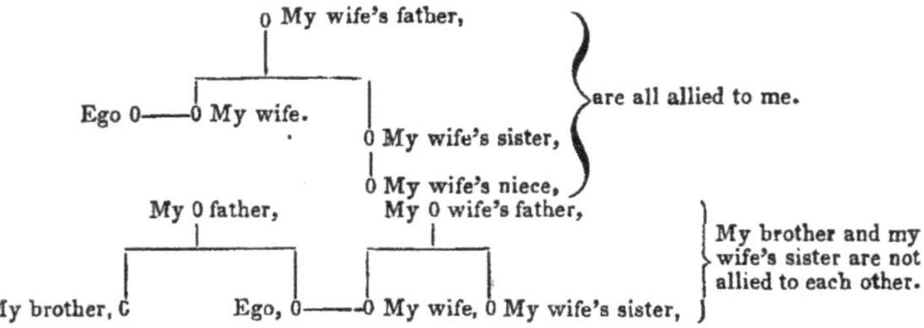

3. A person cannot, by legal succession, receive an inheritance from a relation by affinity; neither does it extend to the nearest relations of husband and wife, so as to create a mutual relation between them. The degrees of affinity are computed in the same way as those of consanguinity. See Pothier, Traité du Mariage, part 3, ch. 3, art. 2; and see 5 M. R. 296; Inst. 1, 10, 6; Dig. 38, 10, 4, 3; 1 Phillim. R. 210; S. C. 1 Eng. Eccl. R. 72; article *Marriage*.

TO AFFIRM, *practice*. 1. To ratify or confirm a former law or judgment; as when the supreme court affirms the judgment of the court of common pleas. 2. To make an affirmation, or to testify under an affirmation.

AFFIRMANCE. The confirmation of a voidable act; as, for example, when an infant enters into a contract, which is not binding upon him, if, after attaining his full age, he gives his affirmance to it, he will thereafter be bound, as if it had been made when of full age. 10 N. H. Rep. 194.

2. To be binding upon the infant, the affirmance must be made after arriving of age, with a full knowledge that it would be void without such confirmation. 11 S. & R. 305.

3. An affirmance may be express, that is, where the party declares his determination of fulfilling the contract; but a mere acknowledgment is not sufficient. Dudl. R. 203. Or it may be implied, as, for example, where an infant mortgaged his land, and, at full age, conveyed it subject to the mortgage. 15 Mass. 220. See 10 N. H. Rep. 561.

AFFIRMANCE-DAY, GENERAL. In the English Court of Exchequer, is a day appointed by the judges of the common pleas, and barons of the exchequer, to be held a few days after the beginning of every term for the general affirmance or reversal of judgments. 2 Tidd, 1091.

AFFIRMANT, *practice*. One who makes affirmation instead of making oath that the evidence which he is about to give shall be the truth, as if he had been sworn. He is liable to all the pains and penalty of perjury, if he shall be guilty of wilfully and maliciously violating his affirmation.

AFFIRMATION, *practice*. A solemn declaration and asseveration, which a witness makes before an officer competent to administer an oath in a like case, to tell the truth, as if he had been sworn.

2. In the United States, generally, all witnesses who declare themselves conscientiously scrupulous against taking a corporal oath, are permitted to make a solemn affirmation, and this in all cases, as well criminal as civil.

3. In England, laws have been enacted which partially relieve persons who have conscientious scruples against taking an oath, and authorize them to make affirmation. In France, the laws which allow freedom of religious opinion, have received the liberal construction that all persons are to be sworn or affirmed according to the dictates of their consciences; and a quaker's affirmation has been received and held of the same effect as an oath. Merl. Quest. de Droit, mot Serment, § 1.

4. The form is to this effect: "You, A B, do solemnly, sincerely, and truly declare and affirm," &c. For the violation of the truth in such case, the witness is subject to the punishment of perjury as if he had been sworn.

5. Affirmation also means confirming; as, an affirmative statute.

AFFIRMATIVE. Averring a fact to be true; that which is opposed to negative. (q. v.)

2. It is a general rule of evidence that the affirmative of the issue must be proved. Bull. N. P. 298; Peake, Ev. 2.

3. But when the law requires a person to do an act, and the neglect of it will render him guilty and punishable, the negative must be proved, because every man is presumed to do his duty, and in that case they who affirm he did not, must prove it. B. N. P. 298; 1 Roll, R. 83; Comb. 57; 3 B. & P. 307; 1 Mass. R. 56.

Affirmative pregnant, *pleading*. An affirmative allegation, implying some *negative*, in favor of the adverse party: for example, if to an action of assumpsit, which is barred by the act of limitations in *six* years, the defendant pleads that he did not undertake, &c. within *ten* years; a replication that he did undertake, &c. within ten years, would be an affirmative pregnant; since it would impliedly admit that the defendant had not promised within six years. As no proper issue could be tendered upon such plea, the plaintiff should, for that reason, demur to it. Gould, Pl. c. 6, § 29, 37; Steph. Pl. 381; Lawes, Civ. Pl. 113; Bac. Ab. Pleas, N 6.

AFFORCE, AFFORCEMENT OF THE ASSIZE, *Old English law, practice*. An ancient practice in trials by jury, which is explained by Bracton, (fo. 185, b. 292 a) and by the author of Fleta, lib. 4, cap. 9, § 2. It consisted in adding other jurors to the panel of jurors, after the cause had been committed to them, in case they could not agree in a verdict. The author of Fleta (ubi sup) thus describes it. The oath having been administered to the jury, the (prenotarius) prothonotary, addressed them thus "You will say upon the oath you have taken, whether such a one unjustly and without judgment disseized such a one of his freehold in such a ville within three years or not." The justices also repeat for the instruction of the jurors the plaint of the plaintiff, &c. The jurors then retire and confer together, &c. If the jurors differ among themselves and cannot agree in one (sententiam) finding, it will be in the discretion of the judges, &c. to *afforce the assize* by others, provided there remain of the jurors summoned as many as the major party of the dissenting jurors; or they may compel the same jurors to unanimity, *viz*. by directing the sheriff to keep them safely without meat or drink until they agree. The object of adding to the panel a number equal to the major party of the dissenting jurors, was to ensure a verdict by twelve of them, if the jurors thus added to the panel should concur with the minor party of the dissenting jurors. This practice of afforcing the assize, was in reality a second trial of the cause, and was abandoned, because the courts found it would save delay and trouble by insisting upon unanimity. The practice of confining jurors without meat and drink in order to enforce unanimity, has in more modern times also been abandoned, and the more rational practice adopted of discharging the jury and summoning a new one for the trial of the cause, in cases where they cannot agree. This expedient for enforcing unanimity was probably introduced from the canon law, as we find it was resorted to on the continent, in other cases where the unanimity of a consultative or deliberative body was deemed indispensable. See Barring. on Stats. 19, 20; 1 Fournel, Hist. des Avocats, 28, note.

TO AFFRANCHISE. To make free.

AFFRAY, *criminal law.* The fighting of two or more persons, in some public place, to the terror of the people.

2. To constitute this offence there must be, 1st, a fighting; 2d, the fighting must be between two or more persons; 3d, it must be in some public place; 4th, it must be to the terror of the people.

3. It differs from a riot, it not being premeditated; for if any persons meet together upon any lawful or innocent occasion, and happen on a sudden to engage in fighting, they are not guilty of a riot but an affray only; and in that case none are guilty except those actually engaged in it. Hawk. b. 1, c. 65, s. 3; 4 Bl. Com. 146; 1 Russell, 271.

AFFREIGHTMEET, *com. law.* The contract by which a vessel or the use of it, is let out to hire. See *Freight; General Ship.*

AFORESAID. Before mentioned; already spoken of. This is used for the purpose of identifying a person or thing; as where Peter, of the city of Philadelphia, has been mentioned; when it is necessary to speak of him, it is only requisite to say Peter aforesaid, and if the city of Philadelphia, it may be done as the city of Philadelphia, aforesaid.

AFORETHOUGHT, *crim. law.* Premeditated, prepense; the length of time during which the accused has entertained the thought of committing the offence is not very material, provided he has in fact entertained such thought; he is thereby rendered criminal in a greater degree than if he had committed the offence without premeditation. Vide *Malice; Aforethought; Premeditation;* 2 Chit. Cr. 785; 4 Bl. Com. 199; Fost. 132, 291, 292; Cro. Car. 131; Palm. 545; W. Jones, 198; 4 Dall. R. 146; 1 P. A. Bro. App. xviii.; Addis. R. 148; 1 Ashm. R. 289.

AFTERMATH. A right to have the last crop of grass or pasturage. 1 Chit. Pr 181.

AGAINST THE FORM OF THE STATUTE. When a statute prohibits a thing to be done, and an action is brought for the breach of the statute, the declaration or indictment must conclude against the form of the statute. See *Contra formam statuti.*

AGAINST THE WILL, *pleadings.* In indictments for robbery from the person, the words "feloniously and against the will," must be introduced; no other words or phrase will sufficiently charge the offence. 1 Chit. Cr. *244.

AGARD. An old word which signifies award. It is used in pleading, as *nul agard,* no award.

AGE. The time when the law allows persons to do acts which, for want of years, they were prohibited from doing before. See Coop. Justin. 446.

2. For *males,* before they arrive at fourteen years they are said not to be of discretion; at that age they may consent to marriage and choose a guardian. Twenty-one years is full age for all private purposes, and they may then exercise their rights as citizens by voting for public officers; and are eligible to all offices, unless otherwise provided for in the constitution. At 25, a man may be elected a representative in Congress; at 30, a senator; and at 35, he may be chosen president of the United States. He is liable to serve in the militia from 18 to 45 inclusive, unless exempted for some particular reason.

3. As to *females,* at 12, they arrive at years of discretion and may consent to marriage; at 14, they may choose a guardian; and 21, as in males, is full age, when they may exercise all the rights which belong to their sex.

4. In England no one can be chosen member of parliament till he has attained 21 years; nor be ordained a priest under the age of 24; nor made a bishop till he has completed his 30th year. The age of serving in the militia is from 16 to 45 years.

5. By the laws of France many provisions are made in respect to age, among which are the following. To be a member of the legislative body, the person must have attained 40 years; 25, to be a judge of a tribunal de première instance; 27, to be its president, or to be judge or clerk of a cour royale; 30, to be its president or procureur général; 25, to be a justice of the peace; 30, to be judge of a tribunal of commerce, and 35, to be its president; 25, to be a notary public; 21, to be a testamen-

tary witness; 30, to be a juror. At 16, a minor may devise one half of his property as if he were a major. A male cannot contract marriage till after the 18th year, nor a female before full 15 years. At 21, both males and females are capable to perform all the acts of civil life. Toull. Dr. Civ. Fr. Liv. 1, Intr. n. 188.

6. In the civil law, the age of a man was divided as follows: namely, the infancy of males extended to the full accomplishment of the 14th year; at 14, he entered the age of puberty, and was said to have acquired full puberty at 18 years accomplished, and was major on completing his 25th year. A female was an infant until 7 years; at 12, she entered puberty, and acquired full puberty at 14; she became of full age on completing her 25th year. Leçons Elem. du Dr. Civ. Rom. 22.

See Com. Dig. Baron and Feme, B 5, Dower, A 3, Enfant, C 9, 10, 11, D 3, Pleader, 2 G 3, 2 W 22, 2 Y 8; Bac. Ab. Infancy and Age; 2 Vin. Ab. 131; Constitution of the United States; Domat. Lois Civ. tome 1, p. 10; Merlin, Répert. de Jurisp. mot Age; Ayl. Pand. 62; 1 Coke Inst. 78; 1 Bl. Com. 463. See *Witness*.

AGE-PRAYER, AGE-PRIER, *ætatis precatio. English law, practice.* When an action is brought against an infant for lands which he hath by descent, he may show this to the court, and pray *quod loquela remaneat* until he shall become of age; which is called his age-prayer. Upon this being ascertained, the proceedings are stayed accordingly. When the lands did not descend, he is not allowed this privilege. 1 Lilly's Reg. 54.

AGED WITNESS. When a deposition is wanted to be taken on account of the age of a witness, he must be at least seventy years old to be considered an aged witness. Coop. Eq. Pl. 57; Amb. R. 65; 13 Ves. 56, 261.

AGENCY, *contracts.* An agreement, express or implied, by which one of the parties, called the principal, confides to the other, denominated the agent, the management of some business, to be transacted in his name, or on his account, and by which the agent assumes to do the business and to render an account of it. As a general rule, whatever a man may do by himself, except in virtue of a delegated authority, he may do by an agent. Combe's Case, 9 Co. 75. Hence the maxim *qui facit per alium facit per se.*

2. When the agency is express, it is created either by deed, or in writing not by deed, or verbally without writing. 3 Chit. Com. Law, 104; 9 Ves. 250; 11 Mass. Rep. 27; Ib. 97, 288; 1 Binn. R. 450. When the agency is not express, it may be inferred from the relation of the parties and the nature of the employment, without any proof of any express appointment. 1 Wash. R. 19; 15 East, R. 400; 5 Day's R. 556

3. The agency must be antecedently given, or subsequently adopted; and in the latter case there must be an act of recognition, or an acquiescence in the act of the agent, from which a recognition may be fairly implied. 9 Cranch, 153, 161; 26 Wend. 193, 226; 6 Man. & Gr. 236, 242; 1 Hare & Wall. Sel. Dec. 420; 2 Kent, Com. 478; Paley on Agency; Livermore on Agency.

4. An agency may be dissolved in two ways. 1, by the act of the principal or the agent; 2, by operation of law.

5.—1. The agency may be dissolved by the act of one of the parties. 1st. As a general rule, it may be laid down that the principal has a right to revoke the powers which he has given; but this is subject to some exceptions, of which the following are examples. When the principal has expressly stipulated that the authority shall be irrevocable, and the agent has an interest in its execution; it is to be observed, however, that although there may be an express agreement not to revoke, yet if the agent has no interest in its execution, and there is no consideration for the agreement, it will be considered a nude pact, and the authority may be revoked. But when an authority or power is coupled with an interest, or when it is given for a valuable consideration, or when it is a part of a security, then, unless there is an express stipulation that it shall be revocable, it cannot be revoked, whether it be expressed on the face of the instrument giving the authority, that it be so, or not. Story on Ag. 477; Smith on Merc. L. 71; 2 Liv. on Ag. 308; Paley on Ag. by Lloyd, 184; 3 Chit. Com. L. 223; 2 Mason's R. 244; Id. 342; 8 Wheat. R. 170; 1 Pet. R. 1; 2 Kent, Com. 643, 3d edit.; Story on Bailm. § 209; 2 Esp. R. 565; 3 Barnw. & Cressw. 842; 10 Barnw. & Cressw. 731; 2 Story, Eq. Jur. § 1041, 1042, 1043.

6.—2. The agency may be determined by the renunciation of the agent. If the renunciation be made after it has been partly executed, the agent by renouncing it, becomes liable for the damages which may thereby be sustained by his principal. Story on Ag. § 478; Story on Bailm. § 436; Jones on Bailm. 101; 4 John. R. 84.

7.—2. The agency is revoked by operation of law in the following cases: 1st. When the agency terminates by the expiration of the period, during which it was to exist, and to have effect; as, if an agency be created to endure a year, or till the happening of a contingency, it becomes extinct at the end of the year, or on the happening of the contingency.

8.—2. When a change of condition, or of state, produces an incapacity in either party; as, if the principal, being a woman, marry, this would be a revocation, because the power of creating an agent is founded on the right of the principal to do the business himself, and a married woman has no such power. For the same reason, when the principal becomes insane, the agency is *ipso facto* revoked. 8 Wheat. R. 174, 201 to 204; Story on Ag. § 481; Story on Bailm. § 206; 2 Liv. on Ag. 307. The incapacity of the agent also amounts to a revocation in law, as in case of insanity, and the like, which renders an agent altogether incompetent, but the rule does not reciprocally apply in its full extent. For instance, an infant or a married woman may in some cases be agents, although they cannot act for themselves. Co. Litt. 52 a.

9.—3. The death of either principal or agent revokes the agency, unless in cases where the agent has an interest in the thing actually vested in the agent. 8 Wheat. R. 174; Story on Ag. § 486 to 499; 2 Greenl. R. 14, 18; but see 4 W. & S. 282; 1 Hare & Wall. Sel. Dec. 415.

10.—4. The agency is revoked in law, by the extinction of the subject-matter of the agency, or of the principal's power over it, or by the complete execution of the trust. Story on Bailm. § 207. Vide generally, 1 Hare & Wall. Sel. Dec. 384–422; Pal. on Ag.; Story on Ag.; Liv. on Ag.; 2 Bouv. Inst. n. 1269–1382.

AGENT, *practice*. An agent is an attorney who transacts the business of another attorney.

2. The agent owes to his principal the unremitted exertions of his skill and ability, and that all his transactions in that character, shall be distinguished by punctuality, honor and integrity. Lee's Dict. of Practice.

AGENT, *international law*. One who is employed by a prince to manage his private affairs, or those of his subjects in his name, near a foreign government. Wolff, Inst. Nat. § 1237.

AGENT, *contracts*. One who undertakes to manage some affair to be transacted for another, by his authority, on account of the latter, who is called the *principal*, and to render an account of it.

2. There are various descriptions of agents, to whom different appellations are given according to the nature of their employments; as brokers, factors, supercargoes, attorneys, and the like; they are all included in this general term. The authority is created either by deed, by simple writing, by parol, or by mere employment, according to the capacity of the parties, or the nature of the act to be done. It is, therefore, *express* or *implied*. Vide *Authority*.

3. It is said to be *general* or *special* with reference to its object, i. e. according as it is confined to a single act, or is extended to all acts connected with a particular employment.

4. With reference to the manner of its execution, it is either *limited* or *unlimited*, i. e. the agent is bound by precise instructions, (q. v.) or left to pursue his own discretion. It is the duty of an agent, 1, To perform what he has undertaken in relation to his agency. 2, To use all necessary care. 3, To render an account. Pothier, Tr. du Contrat de Mandat, *passim;* Paley, Agency, 1 and 2; 1 Liverm. Agency, 2; 1 Suppl. to Ves. Jr. 67, 97, 409; 2 Id. 153, 165, 240; Bac. Abr. Master and Servant, I; 1 Ves. Jr. R. 317. Vide Smith on Merc. Law, ch. 3, p. 43, et seq., and the articles *Agency*, *Authority*, and *Principal*.

5. Agents are either joint or several. It is a general rule of the common law, that when an authority is given to two or more persons to do an act, and there is no several authority given, all the agents must concur in doing it, in order to bind the principal. 3 Pick. R. 232; 2 Pick. R. 345; 12 Mass. R. 185; Co. Litt. 49 b, 112 b, 113, and Harg. n. 2; Id. 181 b; 6 Pick. R. 198; 6 John. R. 39; 5 Barn. & Ald. 628.

6. This rule has been so construed that when the authority is given jointly and severally to three persons, two cannot properly execute it; it must be done by all or by one only. Co. Litt. 181 b; Com. Dig. Attorney, C 11; but if the authority is so

worded that it is apparent, the principal intended to give power to either of them, an execution by two will be valid. Co. Litt. 49 b; Dy. R. 62; 5 Barn. & Ald. 628. This rule applies to private agencies: for, in public agencies an authority executed by a majority would be sufficient. 1 Co. Litt. 181 b; Com. Dig. Attorney, C 15; Bac. Ab. Authority, C; 1 T. R. 592.

7. The rule in commercial transactions however, is very different; and generally when there are several agents each possesses the whole power. For example, on a consignment of goods for sale to two factors, (whether they are partners or not,) each of them is understood to possess the whole power over the goods for the purposes of the consignment. 3 Wils. R. 94, 114; Story on Ag. § 43.

8. As to the persons who are capable of becoming agents, it may be observed, that but few persons are excluded from acting as agents, or from exercising authority delegated to them by others. It is not, therefore, requisite that a person be *sui juris*, or capable of acting in his own right, in order to be qualified to act for others. Infants, femes covert, persons attainted or outlawed, aliens and other persons incompetent for many purposes, may act as agents for others. Co. Litt. 52; Bac. Ab. Authority, B; Com. Dig. Attorney, C 4; Id. Baron and Feme, P 3; 1 Hill, S. Car. R. 271; 4 Wend. 465; 3 Miss. R. 465; 10 John. R. 114; 3 Watts, 39; 2 S. & R. 197; 1 Pet. R. 170.

9. But in the case of a married woman, it is to be observed, that she cannot be an agent for another when her husband expressly dissents, particularly when he may be rendered liable for her acts. Persons who have clearly no understanding, as idiots and lunatics, cannot be agents for others. Story on Ag. § 7.

10. There is another class who, though possessing understanding, are incapable of acting as agents for others; these are persons whose duties and characters are incompatible with their obligations to the principal. For example, a person cannot act as agent in buying for another, goods belonging to himself. Paley on Ag. by Lloyd, 33 to 38; 2 Ves. Jr. 317.

11. An agent has rights which he can enforce, and is liable to obligations which he must perform. These will be briefly considered:

1. The *rights* to which agents are entitled, arise from obligations due to them by their principals, or by third persons.

12.—1. Their rights against their *principals* are, 1, to receive a just compensation for their services, when faithfully performed, in execution of a lawful agency, unless such services are entirely gratuitous, or the agreement between the parties repels such a claim; this compensation, usually called a commission, is regulated either by particular agreement, or by the usage of trade, or the presumed intention of the parties. 8 Bing. 65; 1 Caines, 349; 2 Caines, 357. 2. To be reimbursed all their just advances, expenses and disbursements made in the course of their agency, on account of, or for the benefit of their principal; 2 Liverm. on Ag. p. 11—23; Story on Ag. § 335; Story on Bailm. § 196; Smith on Mer. Law, 56; 6 East, 392; and also to be paid interest upon such advances, whenever, from the nature of the business, or the usage of trade, or the particular agreement of the parties, it may be fairly presumed to have been stipulated for, or due to the agent. 7 Wend. 315; 3 Binn. 295; 3 Caines, 226; 3 Camp. 467; 15 East, 223.

13. Besides the personal remedies which an agent has to enforce his claims against his principal for his commissions and advancements, he has a lien upon the property of the principal in his hand. See *Lien*, and Story on Ag. § 351 to 390.

14.—2. The rights of agents against *third persons* arise, either on contracts made between such third persons and them, or in consequence of torts committed by the latter. 1. The rights of agents against third persons on *contracts*, are, 1st, when the contract is in writing, and made expressly with the agent, and imports to be a contract personally with him, although he may be known to act as an agent; as, for example, when a promissory note is given to the agent as such, for the benefit of his principal, and the promise is to pay the money to the agent, *eo nomine*. Story on Ag. § 393, 394; 8 Mass. 103; see 6 S. & R. 420; 1 Lev. 235; 3 Camp. 320; 5 B. & A. 27. 2d. When the agent is the only known or ostensible principal, and, therefore, is, in contemplation of law, the real contracting party. Story on Ag. § 226, 270, 393. As, if an agent sell goods of his principal in his own name, as if he were the owner, he is entitled to sue the buyer in his own name; although his principal may also sue. 12 Wend. 413; 5 M. & S. 833. And, on the other hand, if he so buy, he may enforce the contract by action. 3d. When, by the usage of trade, the agent is authorized to act as owner, or as a principal contracting party, although his character as agent is known, he may enforce his contract by action. For example, an auctioneer, who sells the goods of another, may maintain an action for the price, because he has a possession coupled with an interest in the goods, and it is a general rule, that whenever an agent, though known as such, has a special property in the subject-matter of the contract, and not a bare custody, or when he has acquired an interest, or has a lien upon it, he may sue upon the contract. 2 Esp. R. 493; 1 H. Bl. 81, 84; 6 Wheat. 565; 3 Chit. Com. Law, 210; 3 B. & A. 276. But this right to bring an action by agents is subordinate to the rights of the principal, who may, unless in particular cases, where the agent has a lien, or some other vested right, bring a suit himself, and suspend or extinguish the right of the agent. 7 Taunt. 237, 243; 2 Wash. C. C. R. 283. 2. Agents are entitled to actions against third persons for *torts* committed against them in the course of their agency. 1st. They may maintain actions of trespass or trover against third persons for any torts or injuries affecting their possession of the goods which they hold as agents. Story on Ag. § 414; 13 East, 135; 9 B. & Cressw. 208; 1 Hen. Bl. 81. 2d. When an agent has been induced by the fraud of a third person to sell or buy goods for his principal, and he has sustained a loss, he may maintain an action against such third person for such wrongful act, deceit, or fraud. Story on Ag. § 415.

15.—§ 2. Agents are liable for their acts, 1, to their principals; and 2, to third persons.

16.—1. The liabilities of agents to their principals arise from a violation of their duties and obligations to the principal, by exceeding their authority, by misconduct, or by any negligence or omission, or act by which the principal sustains a loss. 1 B. & Adol. 415; 12 Pick. 328. Agents may become liable for damages and loss under a special contract, contrary to the general usages of trade. They may also become responsible when charging a *del credere* commission. Story on Ag. § 234.

17.—2. Agents become liable to *third persons*; 1st, on their *contracts;* 1, when the agent, undertaking to do an act for another, does not possess a sufficient authority from the principal, and that is unknown to the other party, he will be considered as having acted for himself as a principal. 3 B. & Adol. 114. 2. When the agent does not disclose his agency, he will be considered as a principal; 2 Esp. R. 567; 15 East, 62; 12 Ves. 352; 16 Martin's R. 530; and, in the case of agents or factors, acting for merchants residing in a foreign country, they will be considered liable whether they disclose their principal or not, this being the usage of trade; Paley on Ag. by Lloyd, 248, 373; 1 B. & P. 368; but this presumption may be rebutted by proof of a contrary agreement. 3. The agent will be liable when he expressly, or by implication, incurs a personal responsibility. Story on Ag. § 156—159. 4. When the agent makes a contract as such, and there is no other responsible as principal, to whom resort can be had; as, if a man sign a note as "guardian of A B," an infant; in that case neither the infant nor his property will be liable, and the agent alone will be responsible. 5 Mass. 299; 6 Mass. 58. 2d. Agents become liable to third persons in regard to *torts* or wrongs, done by them in the course of their agency. A distinction has been made, in relation to third persons, between acts of misfeasance and non-feasance: an agent is liable for the former, under certain circumstances, but not for the latter; he being responsible for his non-feasance only to his principal. Story on Ag. § 309, 310. An agent is liable for *misfeasance* as to third persons, when, intentionally or ignorantly, he commits a wrong, although authorized by his principal, because no one can lawfully authorize another to commit a wrong upon the rights or property of another. 1 Wils. R. 328; 1 B. & P. 410. 3d. An agent is liable to refund money, when payment to him is void *ab initio*, so that the money was never received for the use of his principal, and he is consequently not accountable to the latter for it, if he has not actually paid it over at the time he receives notice of the mistake. 2 Cowp. 565; 10 Mod. 23; 3 M. & S. 344. But unless "caught with the money in his possession," the agent is not responsible. 2 Moore, 5; 8 Taunt. 136; 9 Bing. 378; 7 B. & C. 111; 1 Cowp. 69; 4 Taunt. 198. This last rule is, however, subject to this qualification, that the money shall have been lawfully received by the agent; for if, in receiving it, the agent was a wrongdoer, he will not be exempted from liability by payment to his principal. 1 Campb. 396; 3 Bing. 424; 1 T. R. 62; 2 Campb. 122; 1 Selw. N. P. 90, n.; 12 M. & W. 588; 6 A. & Ell. N. S. 280; 1 Taunt. 359; 3 Esp. 153.

See *Diplomatic Agent*.

AGENT AND PATIENT. This phrase is used to indicate the state of a person who is required to do a thing, and is at the same time the person to whom it is done; as, when a man is indebted to another, and he appoints him his executor, the latter is required to pay the debt in his capacity of executor, and entitled to receive it in his own right, he is then *agent and patient*. Termes de la ley.

AGGRAVATION, *crimes, torts*. That which increases the enormity of a crime or the injury of a wrong. The opposite of extenuation.

2. When a crime or trespass has been committed under aggravating circumstances, it is punished with more severity; and, the damages given to vindicate the wrong are greater.

AGGRAVATION, *in pleading*. The introduction of matter into the declaration which tends to increase the amount of damages, but does not affect the right of action itself. Steph. Pl. 257; 12 Mod. 597. See 3 Am. Jur. 287–313. An example of this is found in the case where a plaintiff declares in trespass for entering his house, and breaking his close, and tossing his goods about; the entry of the house is the principal ground and foundation of the action, and the rest is only stated by way of aggravation; 3 Wils. R. 294; and this matter need not be proved by the plaintiff or answered by the defendant.

AGGREGATE. A collection of particular persons or items, formed into one body; as a corporation aggregate, which is one formed of a number of natural persons; the union of individual charges make an aggregate charge.

AGGRESSOR, *crim. law*. He who begins a quarrel or dispute, either by threatening or striking another. No man may strike another because he has threatened, or in consequence of the use of any words.

AGIO, *aggio*. This term is used to denote the difference of price between the value of bank notes and nominal money, and the coin of the country. *Encyc.*

AGIST, *in contracts*. The taking of other men's cattle on one's own ground at a certain rate. 2 Inst. 643; 4 Inst. 293.

AGISTER. One who takes horses or other animals to agist.

2. The agister is not, like an innkeeper, bound to take all horses offered to him, nor is he liable for any injury done to such animals in his care, unless he has been guilty of negligence, or from his ignorance, negligence may be inferred. Holt's R. 457.

AGISTMENT, *contracts*. The taking of another person's cattle into one's own ground to be fed, for a consideration to be paid by the owner. The person who receives the cattle is called an agister.

2. An agister is bound to ordinary diligence, and of course is responsible for losses by ordinary negligence; but he does not insure the safety of the cattle agisted. Jones, Bailm. 91; 1 Bell's Com. 458; Holt's N. P. Rep. 547; Story, Bail. § 443 Bac. Ab. Tythes, C 1.

AGNATES. In the sense of the Roman law, were those whose propinquity was connected by males only; in the relation of cognates, one or more females were interposed.

2. By the Scotch law, agnates are all those who are related by the father, even though females intervene; cognates are those who are related by the mother. Ersk. L. Scot. B. 1, t. 7, s. 4.

AGNATI, *in descents*. Relations on the father's side: they are different from the *cognati*, they being relations on the mother's side, *affines*, who are allied by marriage, and the *propinqui*, or relations in general. 2 Bl. Com. 235; Toull. Dr. Civ. Fr. tome 1, p. 139; Poth. Pand. tom. 22, p. 27. Calvini Lex.

AGNATION, *in descents*. The relation by blood which exists between such males as are descended from the same father; in distinction from cognation or consanguinity, which includes the descendants from females. This term is principally used in the civil law.

AGRARIAN LAW. Among the Romans, this name was given to a law, which had for its object, the division among the people of all the lands which had been conquered, and which belonged to the domain of the state.

AGREEMENT, *contract*. The consent of two or more persons concurring, respecting the transmission of some property, right or benefit, with a view of contracting an obligation. Bac. Ab. h. t.; Com. Dig. h. t.;

Vin. Ab. h. t.; Plowd. 17; 1 Com. Contr. 2; 5 East's R. 16. It will be proper to consider, 1, the requisites of an agreement; 2, the kinds of agreements; 3, how they are annulled.

2.—1. To render an agreement complete six things must concur; there must be, 1, a person able to contract; 2, a person able to be contracted with; 3, a thing to be contracted for; 4, a lawful consideration, or *quid pro quo;* 5, words to express the agreement; 6, the assent of the contracting parties. Plowd. 161; Co. Litt. 35, b.

3.—2. As to their form, agreements are of two kinds; 1, by parol, or in writing, as contradistinguished from specialties; 2, by specialty, or under seal. In relation to their performance, agreements are *executed* or *executory.* An agreement is said to be executed when two or more persons make over their respective rights in a thing to one another, and thereby change the property therein, either presently and at once, or at a future time, upon some event that shall give it full effect, without either party trusting to the other; as where things are bought, paid for and delivered. Executory agreements, in the ordinary acceptation of the term, are such contracts as rest on articles, memorandums, parol promises, or undertakings, and the like, to be performed in future, or which are entered into preparatory to more solemn and formal alienations of property. Powel on Cont. Agreements are also *conditional* and *unconditional.* They are conditional when some condition must be fulfilled before they can have full effect; they are unconditional when there is no condition attached.

4.—3. Agreements are annulled or rendered of no effect, first, by the acts of the parties, as, by payment; release; accord and satisfaction; rescission, which is express or implied; 1 Watts & Serg. 442; defeasance; by novation: secondly, by the acts of the law, as, confusion; merger; lapse of time; death, as when a man who has bound himself to teach an apprentice, dies; extinctinction of the thing which is the subject of the contract, as, when the agreement is to deliver a certain horse, and before the time of delivery he dies. See *Discharge of a Contract.*

5. The writing or instrument containing an agreement is also called an agreement, and sometimes articles of agreement. (q. v.)

6. It is proper to remark that there is much difference between an agreement and articles of agreement, which are only evidence of it. From the moment that the parties have given their consent, the agreement or contract is formed, and, whether it can be proved or not, it has not less the quality to bind both contracting parties. A want of proof does not make it null, because that proof may be supplied *aliunde,* and the moment it is obtained, the contract may be enforced.

7. Again, the agreement may be null as when it was obtained by fraud, duress, and the like; and the articles of agreement may be good, as far as the form is concerned. Vide *Contract: Deed; Guaranty; Parties to Contracts.*

AGRI. Arable land in the common fields. Cunn. Dict. h. t.

AGRICULTURE. The art of cultivating the earth in order to obtain from it the divers things it can produce; and particularly what is useful to man, as grain, fruits, cotton, flax, and other things. Domat, Dr. Pub. liv. tit. 14, s. 1, n. 1.

AID AND COMFORT. The constitution of the United States, art. 3, s. 3, declares, that adhering to the enemies of the United States, giving them aid and comfort, shall be treason. These words, as they are to be understood in the constitution, have not received a full judicial construction. They import, however, help, support, assistance, countenance, encouragement. The word *aid,* which occurs in the Stat. West. 1, c. 14, is explained by Lord Coke (2 Inst. 182) as comprehending all persons counselling, abetting, plotting, assenting, consenting, and encouraging to do the act, (and he adds, what is not applicable to the crime of treason,) who are not present when the act is done. See, also, 1 Burn's Justice, 5, 6; 4 Bl. Com. 37, 38.

AID PRAYER, *English law.* A petition to the court calling in help from another person who has an interest in the matter in dispute. For example, a tenant for life, by the courtesy or for years, being impleaded, may pray aid of him in reversion; that is, desire the court that he may be called by writ, to allege what he thinks proper for the maintenance of the right of the person calling him, and of his own. F. N. B. 50; Cowel.

AIDERS, *crim. law.* Those who assist, aid, or abet the principal, and who are principals in the second degree. 1 Russell, 21.

AIDS, *Engl. law.* Formerly they were certain sums of money granted by the tenant to his lord in times of difficulty and distress; but, as usual in such cases, what was received as a gratuity by the rich and powerful from the weak and poor, was soon claimed as a matter of right; and aids became a species of tax to be paid by the tenant to his lord, in these cases: 1. To ransom the lord's person, when taken prisoner; 2. To make the lord's eldest son a knight; 3. To marry the lord's eldest daughter, by giving her a suitable portion. The first of these remained uncertain; the other two were fixed by act of parliament at twenty shillings each, being the supposed twentieth part of a knight's fee. 2 Bl. Com. 64.

AILE or AYLE, *domestic relations*. This is a corruption of the French word *aïeul*, grandfather, *avus*. 3 Bl. Com. 186.

AIR. That fluid transparent substance which surrounds our globe.

2. No property can be had in the air; it belongs equally to all men, being indispensable to their existence. To poison or materially to change the air, to the annoyance of the public, is a nuisance. Cro. Car. 510; 2 Ld. Raym. 1163; 1 Burr. 333; 1 Str. 686; Hawk. B. 1, c. 75, s. 10; Dane's Ab. Index, h. t. But this must be understood with this qualification, that no one has a right to use the air over another man's land, in such a manner as to be injurious to him. See 4 Campb. 219; Bowy. Mod. Civ. Law, 62; 4 Bouv. Inst. n. 3601; Grot. Droit de la Guerre et de la Paix, liv. 2, c. 2, § 3, note 3 et 4.

3. It is the right of the proprietor of an estate to enjoy the light and air that will come to him, and, in general, no one has a right to deprive him of them; but sometimes in building, a man opens windows over his neighbor's ground, and the latter, desirous of building on his own ground, necessarily stops the windows already built, and deprives the first builder of light and air; this he has the right to do, unless the windows are ancient lights, (q. v.) or the proprietor has acquired a right by grant or prescription to have such windows open. See Crabb on R. P. § 444 to 479; and *Plan*. Vide *Nuisance*.

AJUTAGE. A conical tube, used in drawing water through an aperture, by the use of which the quantity of water drawn is much increased. When a privilege to draw water from a canal, through the forebay or tunnel, by means of an aperture, has been granted, it is not lawful to add an *ajutage*, unless such was the intention of the parties. 2 Whart. R. 477.

ALABAMA. The name of one of the new states of the United States of America. This state was admitted into the Union by the resolution of congress, approved December 14th, 1819, 3 Sto. L. U. S. 1804, by which it is resolved that the state of Alabama shall be one, and is hereby declared to be one of the United States of America, and admitted into the Union on an equal footing with the original states, in all respects whatever. The convention which framed the constitution in this state, assembled at the town of Huntsville, on Monday the fifth day of July, 1819, and continued in session by adjournment, until the second day of August, 1819, when the constitution was adopted.

2. The powers of the government are divided by the constitution into three distinct departments; and each of them confided to a separate body of magistracy, to wit: those which are legislative, to one; those which are executive, to another; and those which are judicial, to a third. Art. 2, s. 1.

3.—1. The *legislative* power of the state is vested in two distinct branches; the one styled the senate, the other the house of representatives, and both together, the general assembly of the state of Alabama. 1. The *senate* is never to be less than one-fourth, nor more than one-third of the whole number of representatives. Senators are chosen by the qualified electors for the term of three years, at the same time, in the same manner, and at the same place, where they vote for members of the house of representatives; one-third of the whole number of senators are elected every year. Art. 3, s. 12. 2. The *house of representatives* is to consist of not less than forty-four, nor more than sixty members, until the number of white inhabitants shall be one hundred thousand; and after that event, the whole number of representatives shall never be less than sixty, nor more than one hundred. Art. 3, s. 9. The members of the house of representatives are chosen by the qualified electors for the term of one year, from the commencement of the general election, and no longer.

4.—2. The supreme *executive* power is vested in a chief magistrate, styled the governor of the state of Alabama. He is elected by the qualified electors, at the time and places when they respectively vote for representatives; he holds his office for the term of two years from the time of his installation, and until a successor is duly qualified; and is not eligible more than four years in any term of six years. Art. 4. He is invested, among other things, with the veto power. Ib. s. 16. In cases of vacancies, the president of the senate acts as governor. Art. 4, s. 18.

5.—3. The *judicial* power is vested in one supreme court, circuit courts to be held in each county in the state, and such inferior courts of law and equity, to consist of not more than five members, as the general assembly may, from time to time direct, ordain, and establish. Art. 5, s. 1.

ALBA FIRMA, *Eng. law.* When quit rents were reserved payable in silver or white money, they were called *white rents*, or *blanch farms*, *reditus albi*. When they were reserved payable in work, grain, or the like, they were called *reditus nigri*, or *black mail*. 2 Inst. 19.

ALCADE, *Span. law.* The name of a judicial officer in Spain, and in those countries which have received the body of their laws from those of Spain.

ALDERMAN. An officer, generally appointed or elected in towns corporate, or cities, possessing various powers in different places.

2. The aldermen of the cities of Pennsylvania, possess all the powers and jurisdictions civil and criminal of justices of the peace. They are besides, in conjunction with the respective mayors or recorders, judges of the mayor's courts.

3. Among the Saxons there was an officer called the *ealderman*, *ealdorman*, or *alderman*, which appellation signified literally elderman. Like the Roman senator, he was so called, not on account of his age, but because of his wisdom and dignity, *non propter ætatem sed propter sapientiam et dignitatem*. He presided with the bishop at the scyregemote, and was, ex officio, a member of the witenagemote. At one time he was a military officer, but afterwards his office was purely judicial.

4. There were several kinds of aldermen, as king's aldermen, aldermen of all England, aldermen of the county, aldermen of the hundred, &c., to denote difference of rank and jurisdiction.

ALEA, *civil law.* The chance of gain or loss in a contract. This chance results either from the uncertainty of the thing sold, as the effects of a succession; or from the uncertainty of the price, as when a thing is sold for an annuity, which is to be greater or less on the happening of a future event; or it sometimes arises in consequence of the uncertainty of both. 2 Duv. Dr. Civ. Fr. n. 74.

ALEATORY CONTRACTS, *civil law.* A mutual agreement, of which the effects, with respect both to the advantages and losses, whether to all the parties, or to some of them, depend on an uncertain event. Civ. Code of Louis. art. 2951.

2. These contracts are of two kinds; namely, 1. When one of the parties exposes himself to lose something which will be a profit to the other, in consideration of a sum of money which the latter pays for the risk. Such is the contract of insurance; the insurer takes all the risk of the sea, and the assured pays a premium to the former for the risk which he runs.

3.—2. In the second kind, each runs a risk which is the consideration of the engagement of the other; for example, when a person buys an annuity, he runs the risk of losing the consideration, in case of his death soon after, but he may live so as to receive three times the amount of the price he paid for it. Merlin, Rép. mot Aléatoire.

ALER SANS JOUR, or *aller sans jour*, *in practice.* A French phrase, which means *go without day;* and is used to signify that the case has been finally dismissed the court, because there is no further day assigned for appearance. Kitch. 146.

ALFET, *obsolete.* A vessel in which hot water was put, for the purpose of dipping a criminal's arm in it up to the elbow.

ALIA ENORMIA, *pleading.* And other wrongs. In trespass, the declaration ought to conclude "and other wrongs to the said plaintiff then and there did, against the peace," &c.

2. Under this allegation of *alia enormia*, some matters may be given in evidence in aggravation of damages, though not specified in other parts of the declaration. Bull. N. P. 89; Holt, R. 699, 700. For example, a trespass for breaking and entering a house, the plaintiff may, in aggravation of damages, give in evidence the debauching of his daughter, or the beating of his servants, under the general allegation *alia enormia*, &c. 6 Mod. 127.

3. But under the *alia enormia* no evidence of the loss of service, or any other matter which would of itself sustain an action; for if it would, it should be stated specially

In trespass *quare clausum fregit*, therefore, the plaintiff would not, under the above general allegation, be permitted to give evidence of the defendant's taking away a horse, &c. Bull. N. P. 89; Holt, R. 700; 1 Sid. 225; 2 Salk. 643; 1 Str. 61; 1 Chit. Pl. 388; 2 Greenl. Ev. § 278.

ALIAS, *practice*. This word is prefixed to the name of a second writ of the same kind issued in the same cause; as, when a summons has been issued and it is returned by the sheriff, nihil, and *another* is issued, this is called an alias summons. The term is used to all kinds of writs, as alias fi. fa., alias vend. exp. and the like. *Alias dictus*, otherwise called; a description of the defendant by an addition to his real name of that by which he is bound in the writing; or when a man is indicted and his name is uncertain, he may be indicted as A B, alias dictus C D. See 4 John. 118; 1 John. Cas. 243; 2 Caines, R. 362; 3 Caines, R. 219.

ALIBI, *in evidence*. This is a Latin word, which signifies *elsewhere*.

2. When a person, charged with a crime, proves (*se eadem die fuisse alibi*,) that he was, at the time alleged, in a different place from that in which it was committed, he is said to prove an *alibi*, the effect of which is to lay a foundation for the necessary inference, that he could not have committed it. See Bract. fo. 140, lib. 3, cap. 20, De Corona.

3. This proof is usually made out by the testimony of witnesses, but it is presumed it might be made out by writings; as if the party could prove by a record, properly authenticated, that on the day or at the time in question, he was in another place.

4. It must be admitted that mere alibi evidence lies under a great and general prejudice, and ought to be heard with uncommon caution; but if it appears to be founded in truth, it is the best negative evidence that can be offered; it is really positive evidence, which in the nature of things necessarily implies a negative; and in many cases, it is the only evidence which an innocent man can offer.

ALIEN, *persons*. One born out of the jurisdiction of the United States, who has not since been naturalized under their constitution and laws. To this there are some exceptions, as the children of the ministers of the United States at foreign courts. See *Citizen*, *Inhabitant*.

2. Aliens are subject to *disabilities*, have *rights*, and are bound to perform *duties*, which will be briefly considered. 1. *Disabilities*. An alien cannot in general acquire title to real estate by the descent, or by other mere operation of law; and if he purchase land, he may be divested of the fee, upon an inquest of office found. To this general rule there are statutory exceptions in some of the states; in Pennsylvania, Ohio, Louisiana, New Jersey, Rev. Laws, 604, and Michigan, Rev. St. 266, s. 26, the disability has been removed; in North Carolina, (but see Mart. R. 48; 3 Dev. R. 138; 2 Hayw. 104, 108; 3 Murph. 194; 4 Dev. 247;) Vermont and Virginia, by constitutional provision; and in Alabama, 3 Stew. R. 60; Connecticut, act of 1824, Stat. tit. Foreigners, 251; Indiana, Rev. Code, c. 3, act of January 25, 1842; Illinois, Kentucky, 1 Litt. 399; 6 Monr. 266; Maine, Rev. St. tit. 7, c. 93, s. 5; Maryland, act of 1825, ch. 66; 2 Wheat. 259; and Missouri, Rev. Code, 1825, p. 66, by statutory provision it is partly so.

3. An alien, even after being naturalized, is ineligible to the office of president of the United States; and in some states, as in New York, to that of governor; he cannot be a member of congress, till the expiration of seven years after his naturalization. An alien can exercise no political rights whatever; he cannot therefore vote at any political election, fill any office, or serve as a juror. 6 John. R. 332.

4.—2. An alien has a *right* to acquire personal estate, make and enforce contracts in relation to the same; he is protected from injuries and wrongs, to his person and property, his relative rights and character; he may sue and be sued.

5.—3. He owes a temporary local allegiance, and his property is liable to taxation. Aliens are either alien friends or alien enemies. It is only alien friends who have the rights above enumerated; alien enemies are incapable during the existence of war to sue, and may be ordered out of the country. See generally 2 Kent, Com. 43 to 63; 1 Vin. Ab. 157; 13 Vin. Ab. 414; Bac. Ab. h. t.; 1 Saund. 8, n. 2; Wheat. Dig. h. t.; Bouv. Inst. Index, h. t.

ALIENAGE. The condition or state of an alien.

ALIENATE, *aliene*, *alien*. This is a generic term applicable to the various methods of transferring property from one person to another. Lord Coke says, (1 Inst. 118 b,) *alien* cometh of the verb *alienare*, that is, *alienum facere vel ex nostro dominio in alienum transferre sive rem aliquam in dominium alterius transferre.* These methods vary, according to the nature of the property to be conveyed and the particular objects the conveyance is designed to accomplish. It has been held, that under a prohibition to alienate, long leases are comprehended. 2 Dow's Rep. 210.

ALIENATION, *estates.* Alienation is an act whereby one man transfers the property and possession of lands, tenements or other things, to another. It is commonly applied to lands or tenements, as to alien (that is, to convey) land in fee, in mortmain. *Termes de la ley.* See Co. Litt. 118 b; Cruise Dig. tit. 32, c. 1, § 1–8.

2. Alienations may be made by deed; by matter of record; and by devise.

3. Alienations by *deed* may be made by *original* or *primary* conveyances, which are those by means of which the benefit or estate is created or first arises; by *derivative* or *secondary* conveyances, by which the benefit or estate originally created, is enlarged, restrained, transferred, or extinguished. These are conveyances by the common law. To these may be added some conveyances which derive their force and operation from the statute of uses. The *original* conveyances are the following: 1. Feoffment; 2. Gift; 3. Grant; 4. Lease; 5. Exchange; 6. Partition. The *derivative* are, 7. Release; 8. Confirmation; 9. Surrender; 10. Assignment; 11. Defeasance. Those deriving their force from the statute of uses, are, 12. Covenants to stand seised to uses; 13. Bargains and sale; 14. Lease and release; 15. Deeds to lead or declare the uses of other more direct conveyances; 16. Deeds of revocation of uses. 2 Bl. Com. ch. 20. Vide *Conveyance; Deed.* Alienations by *matter of record* may be, 1. By private acts of the legislature; 2. By Grants, as by patents of lands; 3. By fines; 4. By common recovery. Alienations may also be made by *devise.* (q. v.)

ALIENATION, *med. jur.* The term alienation or mental alienation is a generic expression, to express the different kinds of aberrations of the human understanding. Dict. des Science Med. h. t.; 1 Beck's Med. Jur. 535.

ALIENATION OFFICE, *English law.* An office to which all writs of covenants and entries are carried for the recovery of fines levied thereon. See *Alienate.*

TO ALIENE, *contracts.* See *Alienate.*

ALIENEE. One to whom an alienation is made.

ALIENI JURIS. Words applied to persons who are subject to the authority of another. An infant who is under the authority of his father or guardian, and a wife under the power of her husband, are said to be *alieni juris.* Vide *sui juris.*

ALIENOR. He who makes a grant or alienation.

ALIMENTS. In the Roman and French law this word signifies the food and other things necessary to the support of life, as clothing, and the like. The same name is given to the money allowed for aliments. Dig. 50, 16, 43.

2. By the common law, parents and children reciprocally owe each other aliments or maintenance. (q. v.) Vide 1 Bl. Com. 447; Merl. Rép. h. t.; Dig. 25, 3, 5. In the common law, the word alimony (q. v.) is used. Vide *Allowance to a Prisoner.*

ALIMONY. The maintenance or support which a husband is bound to give to his wife upon a separation from her; or the support which either father or mother is bound to give to his or her children, though this is more usually called maintenance.

2. The causes for granting alimony to the wife are, 1, desertion, (q. v.) or cruelty of the husband; (q. v.) 4 Desaus. R. 79; 1 M'Cord's Ch. R. 205; 4 Rand. R. 662; 2 J. J. Marsh. R. 324; 1 Edw. R. 62; and 2, divorce. 4 Litt. R. 252; 1 Edw. R. 382; 2 Paige, R. 62; 2 Binn. R. 202; 3 Yeates, R. 50; 3 S. & R. 248; 9 S. & R. 191; 3 John. Ch. R. 519; 6 John. Ch. R. 91.

3. In Louisiana by alimony is meant the nourishment, lodging and support of the person who claims it. It includes education, when the person to whom alimony is due is a minor. Civil Code of L. 246.

4. Alimony is granted in proportion to the wants of the person requiring it, and the circumstances of those who are to pay it. By the common law, parents and children owe each other alimony. 1 Bl. Com. 447; 2 Com. Dig. 498; 3 Ves. 358; 4 Vin. Ab. 175; Ayl. Parerg. 58; Dane's Ab. Index, h. t.; Dig. 34, 1. 6.

5. Alimony is allowed to the wife, *pendente lite,* almost as a matter of course whether she be plaintiff or defendant, for the obvious reason that she has generally no other means of living. 1 Clarke's R. 151. But there are special cases where it will not be allowed, as when the wife, pend-

ing the progress of the suit, went to her father's, who agreed with the husband to support her for services. 1 Clarke's R. 460. See Shelf. on Mar. and Div. 586; 2 Toull. n. 612.

ALITER, *otherwise*. This term is frequently used to point out a difference between two decisions; as, a point of law has been decided in a particular way, in such a case, *aliter* in another case.

ALIUNDE. From another place; evidence given *aliunde;* as, when a will contains an ambiguity, in some cases, in order to ascertain the meaning of the testator, evidence *aliunde* will be received.

ALL FOURS. This is a metaphorical expression, to signify that a case agrees in all its circumstances with another case; it goes as it were upon its four legs, as an animal does.

ALLEGATA. A word which the emperors formerly signed at the bottom of their rescripts and constitutions; under other instruments they usually wrote *signata* or *testata*. Ency. Lond.

ALLEGATA AND PROBATA. The allegations made by a party to a suit, and the proof adduced in their support. It is a general rule of evidence that the allegata and probata must correspond; that is, the proof must at least be sufficiently extensive to cover all the allegations of the party. Greenl. Ev. § 51; 3 N. S. 636.

ALLEGATION, *English ecclesiastical law*. According to the practice of the prerogative court, the facts intended to be relied on in support of the contested suit are set forth in the plea, which is termed an allegation; this is submitted to the inspection of the counsel of the adverse party, and, if it appear to them objectionable in form or substance, they oppose the admission of it. If the opposition goes to the substance of the allegation, and is held to be well founded, the court rejects it; by which mode of proceeding the suit is terminated without going into any proof of the facts. 1 Phil. 1, n.; 1 Eccl. Rep. 11, n. S. C. See 1 Brown's Civ. Law, 472, 3, n.

ALLEGATION, *common law*. The assertion, declaration or statement of a party of what he can prove.

ALLEGATION, *civil law*. The citation or reference to a voucher to support a proposition. Dict. de Jurisp.; Encyclopédie, mot Allegation; 1 Brown's Civ. Law, 473, n.

ALLEGATION OF FACULTIES. When a suit is instituted in the English ecclesiastical courts, in order to obtain alimony, before it is allowed, an allegation must be made on the part of the wife, stating the property of the husband. This allegation is called an *allegation of faculties*. Shelf. on Mar. and Div. 587.

ALLEGIANCE. The tie which binds the citizen to the government, in return for the protection which the government affords him.

2. It is natural, acquired, or local. Natural allegiance is such as is due from all men born within the United States; acquired allegiance is that which is due by a naturalized citizen. It has never been decided whether a citizen can, by expatriation, divest himself absolutely of that character. 2 Cranch, 64; 1 Peters' C. C. Rep. 159; 7 Wheat. R. 283; 9 Mass. R. 461. Infants cannot assume allegiance, (4 Bin. 49) although they enlist in the army of the United States. 5 Bin. 429.

3. It seems, however, that he cannot renounce his allegiance to the United States without the permission of the government, to be declared by law. But for commercial purposes he may acquire the rights of a citizen of another country, and the place of his domicil determines the character of a party as to trade. 1 Kent, Com. 71; Com. Rep. 677; 2 Kent, Com. 42.

4. Local allegiance is that which is due from an alien, while resident in the United States, for the protection which the government affords him. 1 Bl. Com. 366, 372, Com. Dig. h. t.; Dane's Ab. Index, h. t.; 1 East, P. C. 49 to 57.

ALLIANCE, *relationship*. The union or connexion of two persons or families by marriage, which is also called affinity. This word is derived from the Latin preposition *ad* and *ligare*, to bind. Vide Inst. 1, 10, 6; Dig. 38, 10, 4, 3; and *Affinity*.

ALLIANCE, *international law*. A contract, treaty, or league between two sovereigns or states, made to insure their safety and common defence.

2. Alliances made for warlike purposes are divided in general into defensive and offensive; in the former the nation only engages to defend her ally in case he be attacked; in the latter she unites with him for the purpose of making an attack, or jointly waging the war against another nation. Some alliances are both offensive and defensive; and there seldom is an offensive alliance which is not also a de-

fensive one. Vattel, B. 3, c. 6, § 79; 2 Dall. 15.

ALLISION, *maritime law.* The running of one vessel against another. It is distinguished from collision in this, that the latter means the running of two vessels against each other; this latter term is frequently used for allision.

ALLOCATION, *Eng. law.* An allowance upon account in the Exchequer; or rather, placing or adding to a thing. Ency. Lond.

ALLOCATIONE FACIENDA. *Eng. law.* A writ commanding that an allowance be made to an accountant, for such moneys as he has lawfully expended in his office. It is directed to the lord treasurer and barons of the exchequer.

ALLOCATUR, *practice.* The allowance of a writ; e. g. when a writ of *habeas corpus* is prayed for, the judge directs it to be done, by writing the word allowed, and signing his name; this is called the allocatur. In the English courts this word is used to indicate the master or prothonotary's allowance of a sum referred for his consideration, whether touching costs, damages, or matter of account. Lee's Dict. h. t.

ALLODIUM, *estates.* Signifies an absolute estate of inheritance, in contradistinction to a feud.

2. In this country the title to land is essentially allodial, and every tenant in fee simple has an absolute and perfect title, yet in technical language his estate is called an estate in fee simple, and the tenure free and common socage. 3 Kent, Com. 390; Cruise, Prel. Dis. c. 1, § 13; 2 Bl. Com. 45. For the etymology of this word, vide 3 Kent, Com. 398, note; 2 Bouv. Inst. n. 1692.

ALLONGE, *French law.* When a bill of exchange, or other paper, is too small to receive the endorsements which are to be made on it, another piece of paper is added to it, and bears the name of allonge. Pard. n. 343; Story on P. N. § 121, 151; Story on Bills, § 204. See *Rider.*

ALLOTMENT. Distribution by lot; partition. Merl. Rép. h. t.

TO ALLOW, *practice.* To approve; to grant; as to allow a writ of error, is to approve of it, to grant it. Vide *Allocatur.* To allow an amount is to admit or approve of it.

ALLOWANCE TO A PRISONER. By the laws of, it is believed, all the states, when a poor debtor is in arrest in a civil suit, the plaintiff is compelled to pay an allowance regulated by law, for his maintenance and support, and in default of such payment at the time required, the prisoner is discharged. Notice must be given to the plaintiff before the defendant can be discharged.

ALLOY, or ALLAY. An inferior metal, used with gold and silver in making coin or public money. Originally, it was one of the allowances known by the name of remedy for errors, in the weight and purity of coins. The practice of making such allowances continued in all the European mints after the reasons, upon which they were originally founded, had, in a great measure, ceased. In the imperfection of the art of coining, the mixture of the metals used, and the striking of the coins, could not be effected with perfect accuracy. There would be some variety in the mixture of metals made at different times, although intended to be in the same proportions, and in different pieces of coin, although struck by the same process and from the same die. But the art of coining metals has now so nearly attained perfection, that such allowances have become, if not altogether, in a great measure at least unnecessary. The laws of the United States make no allowance for deficiencies of weight. See Report of the Secretary of State of the United States, to the Senate of the U. S., Feb. 22, 1821, pp. 63, 64.

2. The act of Congress of 2d of April, 1792, sect. 12, directs that the standard for all gold coins of the United States, shall be eleven parts fine to one part of alloy; and sect. 13, that the standard for all silver coins of the United States, shall be one thousand four hundred and eighty-five parts fine, to one hundred and seventy-nine parts alloy. 1 Story's L. U. S. 230. By the act of Congress, 18th Feb. 1837, § 8, it is provided, that the standard for both gold and silver coins of the United States, shall be such, that of one thousand parts by weight, nine hundred shall be of pure metal, and one hundred of alloy; and the alloy of the silver coins shall be of copper, and the alloy of gold coins shall be of copper and silver, provided, that the silver do not exceed one-half of the whole alloy. See also, Smith's Wealth of Nations, vol. i., pp. 49, 50.

ALLUVION. The insensible increase of the earth on a shore or bank of a river by the force of the water, as by a current or by waves. It is a part of the definition that the addition should be so gradual that no one can judge how much is added at each moment of time. Just. Inst. lib. 2, tit. 1, § 20; 3 Barn. & Cress. 91; Code Civil Annoté, No. 556. The proprietor of the bank increased by alluvion is entitled to the addition. Alluvion differs from *avulsion* in this: that the latter is sudden and perceptible. See *Avulsion.* See 3 Mass. 352; Coop. Justin. 458; Lord Raym. 737; 2 Bl. Com. 262, and note by Chitty; 1 Swift's Dig. 111; Coop. Just. lib. 2, t. 1; Angell on Water Courses, 219; 3 Mass. R. 352; 1 Gill & Johns. R. 249; Schultes on Aq. Rights, 116; 2 Amer. Law Journ. 282, 293; Angell on Tide Waters, 213; Inst. 2, 1, 20; Dig. 41, 1, 7; Dig. 39, 2, 9; Dig. 6, 1, 23; Dig. 1, 41, 1, 5; 1 Bouv. Inst. pars 1, c. 1, art. 1, § 4, s. 4, p. 74.

ALLY, *international law.* A power which has entered into an alliance with another power. A citizen or subject of one of the powers in alliance, is sometimes called an ally; for example, the rule which renders it unlawful for a citizen of the United States to trade or carry on commerce with an enemy, also precludes an ally from similar intercourse. 4 Rob. Rep. 251; 6 Rob. Rep. 405; Dane's Ab. Index, h. t.; 2 Dall. 15.

ALMANAC. A table or calendar, in which are set down the revolutions of the seasons, the rising and setting of the sun, the phases of the moon, the most remarkable conjunctions, positions and phenomena of the heavenly bodies, the months of the year, the days of the month and week, and a variety of other matter.

2. The courts will take judicial notice of the almanac; for example, whether a certain day of the month was on a Sunday or not. Vin. Ab. h. t.; 6 Mod. 41; Cro. Eliz. 227, pl. 12; 12 Vin. Ab. Evidence (A, b, 4.) In dating instruments, some sects, the Quakers, for example, instead of writing January, February, March, &c., use the terms, First month, Second month, Third month, &c., and these are equally valid in such writings. Vide 1 Smith's Laws of Pennsylvania, 217.

ALLODARII, *Eng. law, Book of Domesday.* Such tenants who have as large an estate as a subject can have. 1 Inst. 1; Bac. Ab. Tenure, A.

ALMS. In its most extensive sense, this comprehends every species of relief bestowed upon the poor, and, therefore, including all charities. In a more limited sense, it signifies what is given by public authority for the relief of the poor. Shelford on Mortmain, 802, note (*x*); 1 Dougl. Election Cas. 370; 2 Id. 107; Heywood on Elections, 263.

ALTA PRODITIO, *Eng. law.* High treason.

ALTARAGE, *eccl. law.* Offerings made on the altar; all profits which accrue to the priest by means of the altar. Ayl. Par. 61; 2 Cro. 516.

TO ALTER. To change. Alterations are made either in the contract itself, or in the instrument which is evidence of it. The contract may at any time be altered with the consent of the parties, and the alteration may be either in writing or not in writing.

2. It is a general rule that the terms of a contract under seal, cannot be changed by a parol agreement. Cooke, 500; 3 Blackf. R. 353; 4 Bibb, 1. But it has been decided that an alteration of a contract by specialty, made by parol, makes it all parol. 2 Watts, 451; 1 Wash. R. 170; 4 Cowen, 564; 3 Harr. & John. 438; 9 Pick. 298; 1 East, R. 619; but see 3 S. & R. 579.

3. When the contract is in writing, but not under seal, it may be varied by parol, and the whole will make but one agreement. 9 Cowen, 115; 5 N. H. Rep. 99; 6 Harr. & John. 38; 18 John. 420; 1 John. Cas. 22; 5 Cowen, 506; Pet. C. C. R. 221; 1 Fairf. 414.

4. When the contract is evidenced by a specialty, and it is altered by parol, the whole will be considered as a parol agreement. 2 Watts, 451; 9 Pick. 298. For alteration of instruments, see *Erasure; Interlineation.* See, generally, 7 Greenl. 76, 121, 394; 15 John. 200; 2 Penna. R. 454.

ALTERATION. An act done upon an instrument in writing by a party entitled under it, without the consent of the other party, by which its meaning or language is changed; it imports some fraud or design on the part of him who made it. This differs from *spoliation*, which is the mutilation of the instrument by the act of a stranger.

2. When an alteration has a tendency to mislead by so changing the character of the instrument, it renders it void; but if the change has not such tendency, it will not be considered an alteration. 1 Greenl. Ev. § 566.

3. A spoliation, on the contrary, will not affect the legal character of the instrument, so long as the original writing remains legible; and, if it be a deed, any

trace of the seal remains. 1 Greenl. Ev. § 566. See *Spoliation*.

ALTERNAT. The name of a usage among diplomatists by which the rank and places of different powers, who have the same rights and pretensions to precedence, are changed from time to time, either in a certain regular order, or one determined by lot. In drawing up treaties and conventions, for example, it is the usage of certain powers to alternate, both in the preamble and the signatures, so that each power occupies, in the copy intended to be delivered to it, the first place. Wheat. Intern. Law, pt. 2, c. 3, § 4.

ALTERNATIVE. The one or the other of two things. In contracts a party has frequently the choice to perform one of several things, as, if he is bound to pay one hundred dollars, or to deliver a horse, he has the alternative. Vide *Election; Obligation; Alternative.*

ALTIUS NON TOLLENDI, *civil law.* The name of a servitude due by the owner of a house, by which he is restrained from building beyond a certain height. Dig. 8, 2, 4, and 1, 12, 17, 25.

ALTIUS TOLLENDI, *civil law.* The name of a servitude which consists in the right, to him who is entitled to it, to build his house as high as he may think proper. In general, however, every one enjoys this privilege, unless he is restrained by some contrary title.

ALTO ET BASSO. High and low. This phrase is applied to an agreement made between two contending parties to submit all matters in dispute, alto et basso, to arbitration. *Cowel.*

ALTUM MARE. The high sea. (q. v.)

ALUMNUS, *civil law.* A child which one has nursed; a foster child. Dig. 40, 2, 14.

AMALPHITAN CODE. The name given to a collection of sea-laws, compiled about the end of the eleventh century, by the people of Amalphi. It consists of the laws on maritime subjects which were or had been in force in countries bordering on the Mediterranean; and, on account of its being collected into one regular system, it was for a long time received as authority in those countries. 1 Azun. Mar. Law, 376.

AMANUENSIS. One who writes what another dictates. About the beginning of the sixth century, the tabellions (q. v.) were known by this name. 1 Sav. Dr. Rom. Moy. Age, n. 16.

AMBASSADOR, *international law.* A public minister sent abroad by some sovereign state or prince, with a legal commission and authority to transact business on behalf of his country with the government to which he is sent. He is a minister of the highest rank, and represents the person of his sovereign.

2. The United States have always been represented by ministers plenipotentiary, never having sent a person of the rank of an ambassador in the diplomatic sense. 1 Kent's Com. 39, n.

3. Ambassadors, when acknowledged as such, are exempted absolutely from all allegiance, and from all responsibility to the laws. If, however, they should be so regardless of their duty, and of the object of their privilege, as to insult or openly to attack the laws of the government, their functions may be suspended by a refusal to treat with them, or application can be made to their own sovereign for their recall, or they may be dismissed, and required to depart within a reasonable time. By fiction of law, an ambassador is considered as if he were out of the territory of the foreign power; and it is an implied agreement among nations, that the ambassador, while he resides in the foreign state, shall be considered as a member of his own country, and the government he represents has exclusive cognizance of his conduct, and control of his person. The attendants of the ambassador are attached to his person, and the effects in his use are under his protection and privilege, and, generally, equally exempt from foreign jurisdiction.

4. Ambassadors are ordinary or extraordinary. The former designation is exclusively applied to those sent on permanent missions; the latter, to those employed on particular or extraordinary occasions, or residing at a foreign court for an indeterminate period. Vattel, Droit des Gens, l. 4, c. 6, §§ 70—79.

5. The act of Congress of April 30th, 1790, s. 25, makes void any writ or process sued forth or prosecuted against any ambassador authorized and received by the president of the United States, or any domestic servant of such ambassador; and the 25th section of the same act, punishes any person who shall sue forth or prosecute such writ or process, and all attorneys and solicitors prosecuting or soliciting in such case, and all officers executing such writ or process, with an imprisonment not exceeding three

years, and a fine at the discretion of the court. The act provides that citizens or inhabitants of the United States who were indebted when they went into the service of an ambassador, shall not be protected as to such debt; and it requires also that the names of such servants shall be registered in the office of the secretary of state. The 16th section imposes the like punishment on any person offering violence to the person of an ambassador or other minister. Vide 1 Kent, Com. 14, 38, 182; Rutherf. Inst. b. 2, c. 9; Vatt. b. 4, c. 8, s. 113; 2 Wash. C. C. R. 435; Ayl. Pand. 245; 1 Bl. Com. 253; Bac. Ab. h. t.; 2 Vin. Ab. 286; Grot. lib. 2, c. 8, 1, 3; 1 Whart. Dig. 382; 2 Id. 314; Dig. l. 50, t. 7; Code, l. 10, t. 63, l. 4; Bouv. Inst. Index, h. t.

6. The British statute 7 Ann, cap. 12; is similar in its provisions; it extends to the family and servants of an ambassador, as well when they are the natives of the country in which the ambassador resides, as when they are foreigners whom he brings with him. (3 Burr. 1776-7.) To constitute a domestic servant within the meaning of the statute, it is not necessary that the servant should lodge at night in the house of the ambassador, but it is necessary to show the nature of the service he renders and the actual performance of it. 3 Burr. 1731; Cases Temp. Hardw. 5. He must, in fact, prove that he is *bona fide* the ambassador's servant. A land waiter at the custom house is not such, nor entitled to the privilege of the statute. 1 Burr. 401. A trader is not entitled to the protection of the statute. 3 Burr. 1731; Cases Temp. Hardw. 5. A person in debt cannot be taken into an ambassador's service in order to protect him. 3 Burr. 1677.

AMBIDEXTER. It is intended by this Latin word, to designate one who plays on both sides; in a legal sense it is taken for a juror or embraceor who takes money from the parties for giving his verdict. This is seldom or never done in the United States.

AMBIGUITY, *contracts, construction.* When an expression has been used in an instrument of writing which may be understood in more than one sense, it is said there is an ambiguity.

2. There are two sorts of ambiguities of words, *ambiguitas latens* and *ambiguitas patens*.

3. The first occurs when the deed or instrument is sufficiently certain and free from ambiguity, but the ambiguity is produced by something extrinsic, or some collateral matter out of the instrument; for example, if a man devise property to his cousin A B, and he has two cousins of that name, in such case parol evidence will be received to explain the ambiguity.

4. The second or patent ambiguity occurs when a clause in a deed, will, or other instrument, is so defectively expressed, that a court of law, which has to put a construction on the instrument, is unable to collect the intention of the party. In such case, evidence of the declaration of the party cannot be admitted to explain his intention, and the clause will be void for its uncertainty. In Pennsylvania, this rule is somewhat qualified. 3 Binn. 587; 4 Binn. 482. Vide generally, Bac. Max. Reg. 23; 1 Phil. Ev. 410 to 420; 3 Stark. Ev. 1021; 1 Com. Dig. 575; Sudg. Vend. 113. The civil law on this subject will be found in Dig. lib. 50, t. 17, l. 67; lib. 45, t. 1, l. 8; and lib. 22, t. 1, l. 4.

AMBULATORIA VOLUNTAS. A phrase used to designate that a man has the power to alter his will or testament as long as he lives. This form of phrase frequently occurs in writers on the civil law; as *ambulatoria res, ambulatoria actio, potestas, conditio*, &c. Calvini Lexic.

AMENABLE. Responsible; subject to answer in a court of justice; liable to punishment.

AMENDE HONORABLE, *English law.* A penalty imposed upon a person by way of disgrace or infamy, as a punishment for any offence, or for the purpose of making reparation for any injury done to another, as the walking into church in a white sheet, with a rope about the neck, and a torch in the hand, and begging the pardon of God, or the king, or any private individual, for some delinquency.

2. A punishment somewhat similar to this, and which bore the same name, was common in France; it was abolished by the law of the 25th of September, 1791. Merlin Rép. de Jur. h. t.

3. For the form of a sentence of amende honorable, see D'Aguesseau, Œuvres, 43e Plaidoyer, tom. 4, p. 246.

AMENDMENT, *legislation.* An alteration or change of something proposed in a bill.

2. Either house of the legislature has a right to make amendments; but, when so made, they must be sanctioned by the other house before they can become a law. The

senate has no power to originate any *money bills*, (q. v.) but may propose and make amendments to such as have passed the house of representatives. Vide *Congress; Senate*.

3. The constitution of the United States, art. 5, and the constitutions of some of the states, provide for their amendment. The provisions contained in the constitution of the United States, are as follows:—"Congress, whenever two-thirds of both houses shall deem it necessary, shall propose amendments to this constitution, or, on the application of the legislatures of two-thirds of the several states, shall call a convention for proposing amendments, which, in either case, shall be valid, to all intents and purposes, as part of this constitution, when ratified by the legislatures of three-fourths of the several states, or by conventions in three-fourths thereof, as the one or the other mode of ratification may be proposed by Congress: Provided, that no amendment, which may be made prior to the year one thousand eight hundred and eight, shall, in any manner, affect the first and fourth clauses in the ninth section of the first article; and that no state, without its consent, shall be deprived of its equal suffrage in the Senate."

Amendment, *practice*. The correction, by allowance of the court, of an error committed in the progress of a cause.

2. Amendments at common law, independently of any statutory provision on the subject, are in all cases in the discretion of the court, for the furtherance of justice; they may be made while the proceedings are in paper, that is, until judgment is signed, and during the term in which it is signed; for until the end of the term the proceedings are considered only in *fieri*, and consequently subject to the control of the court; 2 Burr. 756; 3 Bl. Com. 407; 1 Salk. 47; 2 Salk. 566; 3 Salk. 31; Co. Litt. 260; and even after judgment is signed, and up to the latest period of the action, amendment is, in most cases, allowable at the discretion of the court under certain statutes passed for allowing amendments of the record; and in later times the judges have been much more liberal than formerly, in the exercise of this discretion. 3 McLean, 379; 1 Branch, 437; 9 Ala. 547. They may, however, be made after the term, although formerly the rule was otherwise; Co. Litt. 260, a; 3 Bl. Com. 407; and even after error brought, where there has been a verdict in a civil or criminal case. 2 Serg. & R. 432, 3. A *remittitur damna* may be allowed after error; 2 Dall. 184; 1 Yeates, 186; Addis, 115, 116; and this, although error be brought on the ground of the excess of damages remitted. 2 Serg. & R. 221. But the application must be made for the remittitur in the court below, as the court of error must take the record as they find it. 1 Serg. & R. 49. So, the death of the defendant may be suggested after error *coram nobis*. 1 Bin. 486; 1 Johns. Cases, 29; Caines' Cases, 61. So by agreement of attorneys, the record may be amended after error. 1 Bin. 75; 2 Bin. 169.

3. Amendments are, however, always limited by due consideration of the rights of the opposite party; and, when by the amendment he would be prejudiced or exposed to unreasonable delay, it is not allowed. Vide Bac. Ab. h. t.; Com. Dig. h. t.; Viner's Ab. h. t.; 2 Arch. Pr. 230; Grah. Pr. 524; Steph. Pl. 97; 2 Sell. Pr. 453; 3 Bl. Com. 406; Bouv. Inst. Index, h. t.

AMENDS. A satisfaction, given by a wrong doer to the party injured, for a wrong committed. 1 Lilly's Reg. 81.

2. By statute 24 Geo. II. c. 44, in England, and by similar statutes in some of the United States, justices of the peace, upon being notified of an intended suit against them, may tender amends for the wrong alleged or done by them in their official character, and if found sufficient, the tender debars the action. See Act of Penn. 21 March, 1772, §§ 1 and 2; Willes' Rep. 671, 2; 6 Bin. 83; 5 Serg. & R. 517, 299; 3 Id. 295; 4 Bin. 20.

AMERCEMENT, *practice*. A pecuniary penalty imposed upon a person who is in misericordia; as, for example, when the demandant or plaintiff, tenant or defendant *se retraxit*, or *recessit in contemptum curiæ*. 8 Co. 58; Bar. Ab. Fines and Amercements. By the common law, none can be amerced in his absence, except for his default. Non licet aliquem in sua absentiâ amerciare nisi per ejus defaltas. Fleta, lib. 2, cap. 65, § 15.

2. Formerly, if the sheriff failed in obeying the writs, rules, or orders of the court, he might be amerced; that is, a penalty might be imposed upon him; but this practice has been superseded by attachment. In New Jersey and Ohio, the sheriff may, by statutory provision, be amerced for making a return contrary to the provision

of the statute. Coxe, 136, 169; 6 Halst. 334; 3 Halst. 270, 271; 5 Halst. 319; 1 Green, 159, 341; 2 Green, 350; 2 South. 433; 1 Ham. 275; 2 Ham. 503; 6 Ham. 452; Wright, 720.

AMERCIAMENT, AMERCEMENT, *English law.* A pecuniary punishment arbitrarily imposed by some lord or count, in distinction from a fine which is expressed according to the statute. Kitch. 78. *Amerciament royal,* when the amerciament is made by the sheriff, or any other officer of the king. 4 Bl. Com. 372.

AMI. A friend; or, as it is written in old works, amy. Vide *Prochein amy.*

AMICABLE ACTION, *Pennsylvania practice.* An action entered by agreement of parties on the dockets of the courts; when entered, such action is considered as if it had been adversely commenced, and the defendant had been regularly summoned. An amicable action may be entered by attorney, independently of the provisions of the act of 1806. 8 S. & R. 567.

AMICUS CURIÆ, *practice.* A friend of the court. One, who as a stander by, when a judge is doubtful or mistaken in a matter of law, may inform the court. 2 Inst. 178; 2 Vin. Abr. 475; and any one, as *amicus curiæ,* may make an application to the court in favor of an infant, though he be no relation. 1 Ves. Sen. 313.

AMITA. A paternal aunt; the sister of one's father. Inst. 3, 6, 3.

AMNESTY, *government.* An act of oblivion of past offences, granted by the government to those who have been guilty of any neglect or crime, usually upon condition that they return to their duty within a certain period.

2. An amnesty is either express or implied; it is express, when so declared in direct terms; and it is implied, when a treaty of peace is made between contending parties. Vide Vattel, liv. 4, c. 2, § 20, 21, 22; Encyclop. Amer. h. t.

3. Amnesty and pardon are very different. The former is an act of the sovereign power, the object of which is to efface and to cause to be forgotten, a crime or misdemeanor; the latter, is an act of the same authority, which exempts the individual on whom it is bestowed from the punishment the law inflicts for the crime he has committed. 7 Pet. 160. Amnesty is the abolition and forgetfulness of the offence; pardon is forgiveness. A pardon is given to one who is certainly guilty, or has been convicted; amnesty, to those who may have been so.

4. Their *effects* are also different. That of pardon, is the remission of the whole or a part of the punishment awarded by the law; the conviction remaining unaffected when only a partial pardon is granted: an amnesty, on the contrary, has the effect of destroying the criminal act, so that it is as if it had not been committed, as far as the public interests are concerned.

5. Their *application* also differs. Pardon is always given to individuals, and properly only after judgment or conviction: amnesty may be granted either before judgment or afterwards, and it is in general given to whole classes of criminals or supposed criminals, for the purpose of restoring tranquillity in the state. But sometimes amnesties are limited, and certain classes are excluded from their operation.

AMORTIZATION, *contracts, English law.* An alienation of lands or tenements in mortmain. 2 stat. Ed. I.

2. The reduction of the property of lands or tenements to mortmain.

AMORTISE, *contracts.* To alien lands in mortmain.

AMOTION. In corporations and companies, is the act of removing an officer from his office; it differs from disfranchisement, which is applicable to *members,* as such. Willc. on Corp. n. 708. The power of amotion is incident to a corporation. 2 Str. 819; 1 Burr. 539.

2. In Rex *v.* Richardson, Lord Mansfield specified three sorts of offences for which an officer might be discharged; first, such as have no immediate relation to the office, but are in themselves of so infamous a nature, as to render the offender unfit to execute any public franchise; secondly, such as are only against his oath, and the duty of his office as a corporator, and amount to breaches of the tacit condition annexed to his office; thirdly, the third offence is of a mixed nature; as being an offence not only against the duty of his office, but also a matter indictable at common law. 2 Binn. R. 448. And Lord Mansfield considered the law as settled, that though a corporation has express power of amotion, yet for the first sort of offences there must be a previous indictment and conviction; and that there was no authority since Bagg's Case, 11 Rep.

99, which says that the power of trial as well as of amotion, for the second offence, is not incident to every corporation. He also observed: "We think that from the reason of the thing, from the nature of the corporation, and for the sake of order and good government, this power is incident as much as the power of making by-laws." Doug. 149.

See generally, Wilcock on Mun. Corp. 268; 6 Conn. Rep. 532; 6 Mass. R. 462; Ang. & Am. on Corpor. 236.

AMOTION, *tort*. An amotion of possession from an estate, is an ouster which happens by a species of disseisin or turning out of the legal proprietor before his estate is determined. 3 Bl. Com. 198, 199. Amotion is also applied to personal chattels when they are taken unlawfully out of the possession of the owner, or of one who has a special property in them.

AMPLIATION, *civil law*. A deferring of judgment until the cause is further examined. In this case, the judges pronounced the word *amplius*, or by writing the letters N. L. for *non liquet*, signifying that the cause was not clear. In practice, it is usual in the courts, when time is taken to form a judgment, to enter a *curia advisare vult; cur. adv. vult*. (q. v.)

AMPLIATION, *French law*. Signifies the giving a duplicate of an acquittance or other instrument, in order that it may be produced in different places.

The copies which notaries make out of acts passed before them, and which are delivered to the parties, are also called *ampliations*. Dict. de Jur. h. t.

AMY or *ami*, a French word, signifying *friend*. *Prochein amy*, (q. v.) the next friend. *Alien amy*, a foreigner, the citizen or subject of some friendly power or prince.

AN, JOUR, ET WASTE. See *Year, day, and waste*.

ANALOGY, *construction*. The similitude of relations which exist between things compared.

2. To reason analogically, is to draw conclusions based on this similitude of relations, on the resemblance, or the connexion which is perceived between the objects compared. "It is this guide," says Toullier, "which leads the lawgiver, like other men, without his observing it. It is analogy which induces us, with reason, to suppose that, following the example of the Creator of the universe, the lawgiver has established general and uniform laws, which it is unnecessary to repeat in all analogous cases." Dr. Civ. Fr. liv. 3, t. 1, c. 1. Vide Ang. on Adv. Enjoym. 30, 31; Hale's Com. Law, 141.

3. Analogy has been declared to be an argument or guide in forming legal judgments, and is very commonly a ground of such judgments. 7 Barn. & Cres. 168; 3 Bing. R. 265; 8 Bing. R. 557, 563; 3 Atk. 313; 1 Eden's R. 212; 1 W. Bl. 151; 6 Ves. jr. 675, 676; 3 Swanst. R. 561; 1 Turn. & R. 103, 338; 1 R. & M. 352, 475, 477; 4 Burr. R. 1962, 2022, 2068; 4 T. R. 591; 4 Barn. & Cr. 855; 7 Dowl. & Ry. 251; Cas. t. Talb. 140; 3 P. Wms. 391; 3 Bro. C. C. 639, n.

ANARCHY. The absence of all political government; by extension, it signifies confusion in government.

ANATHEMA, *eccl. law*. A punishment by which a person is separated from the body of the church, and forbidden all intercourse with the faithful: it differs from excommunication, which simply forbids the person excommunicated, from going into the church and communicating with the faithful. Gal. 1. 8, 9.

ANATOCISM, *civil law*. Usury, which consists in taking interest on interest, or receiving compound interest. This is forbidden. Code, lib. 4, t. 32, 1, 30; 1 Postlethwaite's Dict.

2. Courts of equity have considered contracts for compounding interest illegal, and within the statute of usury. Cas. t. Talbot, 40; et vide Com. Rep. 349; Mass. 247; 1 Ch. Cas. 129; 2 Ch. Cas. 35. And contra, 1 Vern. 190. But when the interest has once accrued, and a balance has been settled between the parties, they may lawfully agree to turn such interest into principal, so as to carry interest *in futuro*. Com. on Usury, ch. 2, s. 14, p. 146 et seq.

ANCESTOR, *descents*. One who has preceded another in a direct line of descent; an ascendant. In the common law, the word is understood as well of the immediate parents, as of those that are higher; as may appear by the statute 25 Ed. III. *De natis ultra mare*, and so in the statute of 6 R. II. cap. 6, and by many others. But the civilians' relations in the ascending line, up to the great grandfather's *parents*, and those above them, they term majores, which common lawyers aptly expound antecessors or ancestors, for in the descendants of like degree they are called *posteriores*. Cary's Litt. 45. The term *ancestor* is applied to natural persons. The words predecessors and successors, are used in respect to the persons composing a body corporate. See 2 Bl. Com. 209; Bac. Abr. h. t.; Ayl. Pand. 58.

ANCESTRAL. What relates to or has been done by one's ancestors; as homage ancestral, and the like.

ANCHOR. A measure containing ten gallons. Lex Mercatoria.

ANCHORAGE, *mer. law.* A toll paid for every anchor cast from a ship into a river, and sometimes a toll bearing this name is paid, although there be no anchor cast. This toll is said to be incident to almost every port. 1 Wm. Bl. 413; 2 Chit. Com. Law, 16.

ANCIENT. Something old, which by age alone has acquired some force; as ancient lights, ancient writings.

Ancient demesne, *Eng. law.* Those lands which either were reserved to the crown at the original distribution of landed property, or such as came to it afterwards, by forfeiture or other means. 1 Salk. 57; Hob. 88; 4 Inst. 264; 1 Bl. Com. 286; Bac. Ab. h. t.; F. N. B. 14.

Ancient lights, *estates.* Windows which have been opened for twenty years or more, and enjoyed without molestation by the owner of the house. 5 Har. & John. 477; 12 Mass. R. 157, 220.

2. It is proposed to consider, 1, How the right of ancient light is gained. 2, What amounts to interruption of an ancient light. 3, The remedy for obstructing an ancient light.

3.—§ 1. How the right of opening or keeping a window open is gained. 1. By grant. 2. By lapse of time. Formerly it was holden that a party could not maintain an action for a nuisance to an ancient light, unless he had gained a right to the window by prescription. 1 Leon. 188; Cro. Eliz. 118. But the modern doctrine is, that upon proof of an adverse enjoyment of lights for twenty years or upwards, unexplained, a jury may be directed to presume a right by grant, or otherwise. 2 Saund. 175, a; 12 Mass. 159; 1 Esp. R. 148. See also 1 Bos. & Pull. 400; 3 East, 299; Phil. Ev. 126; 11 East, 372; Esp. Dig. 636. But if the window was opened during the seisin of a mere tenant for life, or a tenancy for years, and the owner in fee did not acquiesce in, or know of, the use of the light, he would not be bound. 11 East, 372; 3 Camp. 444; 4 Camp. 616. If the owner of a close builds a house upon one half of it, with a window lighted from the other half, he cannot obstruct lights on the premises granted by him; and in such case no lapse of time is necessary to confirm the grantee's right to enjoy them. 1 Vent. 237, 289; 1 Lev. 122; 1 Keb. 553; Sid. 167, 227; L. Raym. 87; 6 Mod. 116; 1 Price, 27; 12 Mass. 159, Rep. 24; 2 Saund. 114, n. 4; Hamm. N. P. 202; Selw. N. P. 1090; Com. Dig. Action on the Case for a Nuisance, A. Where a building has been used twenty years to one purpose, (as a malt house,) and it is converted to another, (as a dwelling-house,) it is entitled in its new state only to the same degree of light which was necessary in its former state. 1 Campb. 322; and see, 3 Campb. 80. It has been justly remarked, that the English doctrine as to ancient lights can hardly be regarded as applicable to narrow lots in the new and growing cities of this country; for the effect of the rule would be greatly to impair the value of vacant lots, or those having low buildings upon them, in the neighborhood of other buildings more than twenty years old. 3 Kent, Com. 446, n.

4.—§ 2. What amounts to an interruption of an ancient light. Where a window has been completely blocked up for twenty years, it loses its privilege. 3 Camp. 514. An abandonment of the right by express agreement, or by acts from which an abandonment may be inferred, will deprive the party having such ancient light of his right to it. The building of a blank wall where the lights formerly existed, would have that effect. 3 B. & Cr. 332. See Ad. & Ell. 325.

5.—§ 3. Of the remedy for interrupting an ancient light. 1. An action on the case will lie against a person who obstructs an ancient light. 9 Co. 58; 2 Rolle's Abr. 140, l. Nusans, G 10. And see Bac. Ab. Actions on the Case, D; Carth. 454; Comb. 481; 6 Mod. 116.

6.—2. Total deprivation of light is not necessary to sustain this action, and if the party cannot enjoy the light in so free and ample a manner as he did before, he may sustain the action; but there should be some sensible diminution of the light and air. 4. Esp. R. 69. The building a wall which merely obstructs the sight, is not actionable. 9 Co. 58, b; 1 Mod. 55.

7.—3. Nor is the opening windows and destroying the privacy of the adjoining property; but such new window may be immediately obstructed to prevent a right to it being acquired by twenty years' use. 3 Campb. 82.

8.—5. When the right is clearly established, courts of equity will grant an injunction to restrain a party from building so near the plaintiff's house as to darken his windows. 2 Vern. 646; 2 Bro. C. C. 65; 16 Ves. 338; Eden on Inj. 268, 9; 1 Story on Eq. § 926; 1 Smith's Chan. Pr. 593; 4 Simm. 559; 2 Russ. R. 121. See *Injunction, Plan.*

See generally on this subject, 1 Nels. Abr. 56, 7; 16 Vin. Abr. 26; 1 Leigh's N. P. C. 6, s. 8, p. 558; 12 E. C. L. R. 218; 24 Id. 401; 21 Id. 373; 1 Id. 161; 10 Id. 99; 28 Id. 143; 23 Am. Jur. 46 to 64; 3 Kent, Com. 446, 2d ed.; 7 Wheat. R. 109; 19 Wend. R. 309; Math. on Pres. 318 to 323; 2 Watts, 331; 9 Bing. 305; 1 Chit. Pr. 206, 208; 2 Bouv. Inst. n. 1619-23.

ANCIENT WRITINGS, *evidence.* Deeds, wills, and other writings more than thirty years old, are considered ancient writings. They may in general be read in evidence, without any other proof of their execution than that they have been in the possession of those claiming rights under them. Tr. per Pais, 370; 7 East, R. 279; 4 Esp. R. 1; 9 Ves. Jr. 5; 3 John. R. 292; 1 Esp. R. 275; 5 T. R. 259; 2 T. R. 466; 2 Day's R. 280. But in the case of deeds, possession must have accompanied them. Plowd. 6, 7. See Math. Pres. 271, n. (2.)

ANCIENTLY, *English law.* A term for eldership or seniority used in the statute of Ireland, 14 Hen. VIII.

ANCIENTS, *English law.* A term for gentlemen in the Inns of Courts who are of a certain standing. In the Middle Temple, all who have passed their readings are termed ancients. In Gray's Inn, the ancients are the oldest barristers; besides which the society consists of benchers, barristers and students. In the Inns of Chancery, it consists of ancients, and students or clerks.

ANCILLARY. That which is subordinate on, or is subordinate to, some other decision. Encyc. Lond.

ANDROLEPSY. The taking by one nation of the citizens or subjects of another, in order to compel the latter to do justice to the former. Wolff. § 1164; Molloy, de Jure Mar. 26.

ANGEL. An ancient English coin of the value of ten shillings sterling. Jac. L. D. h. t.

ANIENS. In some of our law books signifies void, of no force. F. N. B. 214.

ANIMAL, *property.* A name given to every animated being endowed with the power of voluntary motion. In law, it signifies all animals except those of the human species.

2. Animals are distinguished into such as are *domitæ*, and such as are *feræ naturæ.*

3. It is laid down, that in tame or domestic animals, such as horses, kine, sheep, poultry, and the like, a man may have an absolute property, because they continue perpetually in his possession and occupation, and will not stray from his house and person unless by accident or fraudulent enticement, in either of which cases the owner does not lose his property. 2 Bl. Com. 390; 2 Mod. 319.

4. But in animals *feræ naturæ*, a man can have no absolute property; they belong to him only while they continue in his keeping or actual possession; for if at any time they regain their natural liberty, his property instantly ceases, unless they have *animum revertendi*, which is only to be known by their usual habit of returning. 2 Bl. Com. 396; 3 Binn. 546; Bro. Ab. Propertie, 37; Com. Dig. Biens, F; 7 Co. 17 b; 1 Ch. Pr. 87; Inst. 2, 1, 15. See also 3 Caines' Rep. 175; Coop. Justin. 457, 458; 7 Johns. Rep. 16; Bro. Ab. Detinue, 44.

5. The owner of a mischievous animal, known to him to be so, is responsible, when he permits him to go at large, for the damages he may do. 2 Esp. Cas. 482; 4 Campb. 198; 1 Starkie's Cas. 285; 1 Holt, 617; 2 Str. 1264; Lord Raym. 110; B. N. P. 77; 1 B. & A. 620; 2 C. M. & R. 496; 5 C. & P. 1; S. C. 24 E. C. L. R. 187. This principle agrees with the civil law. Domat, Lois Civ. liv. 2, t. 8, s. 2. And any person may justify the killing of such ferocious animals. 9 Johns. 233; 10 Johns. 365; 13 Johns. 312. The owner of such an animal may be indicted for a common nuisance. 1 Russ. Ch. Cr. Law, 643; Burn's Just., Nuisance, 1.

6. In Louisiana, the owner of an animal is answerable for the damage he may cause; but if the animal be lost, or has strayed more than a day, he may discharge himself from this responsibility, by abandoning him to the person who has sustained the injury; except where the master turns loose a dangerous or noxious animal; for then he must pay all the harm done, without being allowed

to make the abandonment. Civ. Code, art. 2301. See Bouv. Inst. Index, h. t.

ANIMALS OF A BASE NATURE. Those which, though they may be reclaimed, are not such that at common law a larceny may be committed of them, by reason of the baseness of their nature. Some animals, which are now usually tamed, come within this class, as dogs and cats; and others which, though wild by nature, and oftener reclaimed by art and industry, clearly fall within the same rule; as, bears, foxes, apes, monkeys, ferrets, and the like. 3 Inst. 109; 1 Hale, P. C. 511, 512; 1 Hawk. P. C. 33, s. 36; 4 Bl. Com. 236; 2 East, P. C. 614. See 1 Saund. Rep. 84, note 2.

ANIMUS. The intent; the mind with which a thing is done, as animus cancellandi, the intention of cancelling; animus furandi, the intention of stealing; animus manendi, the intention of remaining; animus morandi, the intention or purpose of delaying.

2. Whether the act of a man, when in appearance criminal, be so or not, depends upon the intention with which it was done. Vide *Intention.*

ANIMUS CANCELLANDI. An intention to destroy or cancel. The least tearing of a will by a testator, *animus cancellandi*, renders it invalid. See *Cancellation.*

ANIMUS FURANDI, *crim. law.* The intention to steal. In order to constitute larceny, (q. v.) the thief must take the property *animo furandi*; but this is expressed in the definition of larceny by the word felonious. 3 Inst. 107; Hale, 503; 4 Bl. Com. 229. Vide 2 Russ. on Cr. 96; 2 Tyler's R. 272. When the taking of property is lawful, although it may afterwards be converted *animo furandi*, to the taker's use, it is not larceny. 3 Inst. 108; Bac. Ab. Felony, C; 14 Johns. R. 294; Ry. & Mood. C. C. 160; Id. 137; Prin. of Pen. Law, c. 22, § 3, p. 279, 281.

ANIMUS MANENDI. The intention of remaining. To acquire a domicil, the party must have his abode in one place, with the intention of remaining there; for without such intention no new domicil can be gained, and the old will not be lost. See *Domicil.*

ANIMUS RECIPIENDI. The intention of receiving. A man will acquire no title to a thing unless he possesses it with an intention of receiving it for himself; as, if a thing be bailed to a man, he acquires no title.

ANIMUS REVERTENDI. The intention of returning. A man retains his domicil, if he leaves it animo revertendi. 3 Rawle, R. 312; 1 Ashm. R. 126; Fost. 97; 4 Bl. Com. 225; 2 Russ. on Cr. 18; Pop 42, 52; 4 Co. 40.

ANIMUS TESTANDI. An intention to make a testament or will. This is required to make a valid will; for whatever form may have been adopted, if there was no *animus testandi*, there can be no will. An idiot, for example, can make no will, because he has no intention.

ANN, *Scotch law.* Half a year's stipend over and above what is owing for the incumbency due to a minister's relict, or child, or next of kin, after his decease. *Wishaw.* Also, an abbreviation of *annus*, year; also of *annates.* In the old law-French writers, *ann* or rather *an*, signifies a year. Com. Dig. *h. v.*

ANNATES, *eccl. law.* First fruits paid out of spiritual benefices to the pope, being the value of one year's profit.

ANNEXATION, *property.* The union of one thing to another.

2. In the law relating to fixtures, (q. v.) annexation is actual or constructive. By actual annexation is understood every movement by which a chattel can be joined or united to the freehold. By constructive annexation is understood the union of such things as have been holden parcel of the realty, but which are not actually annexed, fixed, or fastened to the freehold; for example, deeds, or chattels, which relate to the title of the "inheritance." Shep. Touch. 469. Vide Amos & Fer. on Fixtures, 2.

3. This term has been applied to the union of one country to another; as Texas was annexed to the United States by the joint resolution of Congress of March 1, 1845. See *Texas.*

ANNI NUBILES. The age at which a girl becomes by law fit for marriage, which is twelve years.

ANNIENTED. From the French *aneantir;* abrogated or made null. Litt. sect. 741.

ANNO DOMINI, *in the year of our Lord,* abreviated A. D. The computation of time from the incarnation of our Saviour, which is used as the date of all public deeds in the United States and Christian countries, on which account it is called the "vulgar æra."

ANNONÆ CIVILES, *civil law.* A

species of rent issuing out of certain lands, which were paid to some monasteries.

ANNOTATION, *civil law*. The designation of a place of deportation! Dig. 32, 1, 3! or the summoning of an absentee. Dig. lib. 5.

2. In another sense, annotations were the answers of the prince to questions put to him by private persons respecting some doubtful point of law. See *Rescript*.

ANNUAL PENSION, *Scotch law*. Annual rent. A yearly profit due to a creditor by way of interest for a given sum of money. *Right of annual rent*, the original right of burdening land with payment yearly for the payment of money.

ANNUITY, *contracts*. An annuity is a yearly sum of money granted by one party to another in fee for life or years, charging the person of the grantor only. Co. Litt. 144; 1 Lilly's Reg. 89; 2 Bl. Com. 40; 5 M. R. 312; Lumley on Annuities, p. 1; 2 Inst. 293; Davies' Rep. 14, 15.

2. In a less technical sense, however, when the money is chargeable on land and on the person, it is generally called an annuity. Doct. and Stud. Dial. 2, 230; Roll. Ab. 226. See 10 Watts, 127.

3. An annuity is different from a rent charge, with which it is frequently confounded, in this; a rent charge is a burden imposed upon and issuing out of *lands*, whereas an annuity is chargeable only upon the *person* of the grantee. Bac. Abr. Annuity, A. See, for many regulations in England relating to annuities, the Stat. 17 Geo. III. c. 26.

3. An annuity may be created by contract, or by will. To enforce the payment of an annuity, the common law gives a writ of annuity which may be brought by the grantee or his heirs, or their grantees, against the grantor and his heirs. The action of debt cannot be maintained at the common law, or by the Stat. of 8 Anne, c. 14, for the arrears of an annuity devised to A, payable out of lands during the life of B, to whom the lands are devised for life, B paying the annuity out of it, so long as the freehold estates continues. 4 M. & S. 113; 3 Brod. & Bing. 130; 6 Moore, 335. It has been ruled also, that if an action of annuity be brought, and the annuity determines pending the suit, the writ faileth forever, because no such action is maintainable for arrearages only, but for the annuity and the arrearages. Co. Litt. 285, a.

4. The first payment of an annuity is to be made at the time appointed in the instrument creating it. In cases where a testator directs the annuity to be paid at the end of the first quarter, or other period before the expiration of the first year after his death, it is then due: but in fact it is not payable by the executor till the end of the year. 3 Mad. Ch. R. 167. When the time is not appointed, as frequently happens in wills, the following distinction is presumed to exist. If the bequest be merely in the form of an annuity, as a gift to a man of "an annuity of one hundred dollars for life," the first payment will be due at the end of the year after the testator's death. But if the disposition be of a sum of money, and the interest to be given as an annuity to the same man for life, the first payment will not accrue before the expiration of the second year after the testator's death. This distinction, though stated from the bench, does not appear to have been sanctioned by express decision. 7 Ves. 96, 97.

5. The Civil Code of Louisiana makes the following provisions in relation to annuities, namely: The contract of annuity is that by which one party delivers to another a sum of money, and agrees not to reclaim it, so long as the receiver pays the rent agreed upon. Art. 2764.

6. This annuity may be perpetual or for life. Art. 2765.

7. The amount of the annuity for life can in no case exceed the double of the conventional interest. The amount of the perpetual annuity cannot exceed the double of the conventional interest. Art. 2766.

8. Constituted annuity is essentially redeemable. Art. 2767.

9. The debtor of a constituted annuity may be compelled to redeem the same: 1, If he ceases fulfilling his obligations during three years: 2, If he does not give the lender the securities promised by the contract. Art. 2768.

10. If the debtor should fail, or be in a state of insolvency, the capital of the constituted annuity becomes exigible, but only up to the amount at which it is rated, according to the order of contribution amongst the creditors. Art. 2769.

11. A similar rule to that contained in the last article has been adopted in England. See stat. 6 Geo. IV., c. 16, s. 54 and 108; note to Ex parte James, 5 Ves. 708; 1 Sup. to Ves. Jr. 431; note to Franks *v.* Cooper, 4 Ves. 763; 1 Supp. to Ves. Jr. 308. The debtor, continues the Code, may be com-

pelled by his security to redeem the annuity within the time which has been fixed in the contract, if any time has been fixed, or after ten years, if no mention be made of the time in the act. Art. 2770.

12. The interest of the sums lent, and the arrears of constituted and life annuity, cannot bear interest but from the day a judicial demand of the same has been made by the creditor, and when the interest is due for at least one whole year. The parties may only agree, that the same shall not be redeemed prior to a time which cannot exceed ten years, or without having warned the creditor a time before, which they shall limit. Art. 2771.

See generally, Vin. Abr. Annuity; Bac. Abr. Annuity and Rent; Com. Dig. Annuity; 8 Com. Dig. 909; Doct. Plac. 84; 1 Rop. on Leg. 588; Dict. de Jurisp. aux mots Rentes viageres, Tontine. 1 Harr. Dig. h. t.

ANNUM DIEM ET VASTUM, *English law.* The title which the king acquires in land, when a party, who held not of the king, is attainted of felony. He acquires the power not only to take the profits for a full year, but to waste and demolish houses, and to extirpate woods and trees.

2. This is but a chattel interest.

ANONYMOUS. Without name. This word is applied to such books, letters or papers, which are published without the author's name. No man is bound to publish his name in connexion with a book or paper he has published; but if the publication is libellous, he is equally responsible as if his name were published.

ANSWER, *pleading in equity.* A defence in writing made by a defendant, to the charges contained in a bill or information, filed by the plaintiff against him in a court of equity. The word answer involves a double sense; it is one thing when it simply replies to a question, another when it meets a charge; the answer in equity includes both senses, and may be divided into an examination and a defence. In that part which consists of an examination, a direct and full answer, or reply, must in general be given to every question asked. In that part which consists of a defence, the defendant must state his case distinctly; but is not required to give information respecting the proofs that are to maintain it. Gresl. Eq. Ev. 19.

2. As a defendant is called by a bill or information to make a discovery of the several charges it contains, he must do so, unless he is protected either by a demurrer, a plea or disclaimer. It may be laid down as an invariable rule, that whatever part of a bill or information is not covered by one of these, must be defended by answer. Redesd. Tr. Ch. Pl. 244.

3. In *form*, it usually begins, 1st, with its title, specifying which of the defendants it is the answer of, and the names of the plaintiffs in the cause in which it is filed as answer; 2d, it reserves to the defendant all the advantages which might be taken by exception to the bill; 3d, the substance of the answer, according to the defendant's knowledge, remembrance, information and belief, then follows, in which the matter of the bill, with the interrogatories founded thereon, are answered, one after the other, together with such additional matter as the defendant thinks necessary to bring forward in his defence, either for the purpose of qualifying, or adding to, the case made by the bill, or to state a new case on his own behalf; 4th, this is followed by a general traverse or denial of all unlawful combinations charged in the bill, and of all other matters therein contained; 5th, the answer is always upon oath or affirmation, except in the case of a corporation, in which case it is under the corporate seal.

4. In *substance*, the answer ought to contain, 1st, a statement of facts and not arguments; 2d, a confession and avoidance, or traverse and denial of the material parts of the bill; 3d, its language ought to be direct and without evasion. Vide generally as to answers, Redes. Tr. Ch. Pl. 244 to 254; Coop. Pl. Eq. 312 to 327; Beames Pl. Eq. 34 et seq.; Bouv. Inst. Index, h. t. For an historical account of this instrument, see 2 Bro. Civ. Law, 371, n. and Barton's Hist. Treatise of a Suit in Equity.

ANSWER, *practice.* The declaration of a fact by a witness after a question has been put asking for it.

2. If a witness unexpectedly state facts against the interest of the party calling him, other witnesses may be called by the same party, to disprove those facts. But the party calling a witness cannot discredit him, by calling witnesses to prove his bad character for truth and veracity, or by proving that he has made statements out of court contrary to what he has sworn on the trial; B. N. P.; for the production of the witness is virtually an assertion by the party producing him, that he is credible.

ANTECEDENT. Something that goes before. In the construction of laws, agreements, and the like, reference is always to be made to the last antecedent; *ad proximum antecedens fiat relatio.* But not only the antecedents but the subsequent clauses of the instrument must be considered : *Ex antecedentibus et consequentibus fit optima interpretatio.*

ANTE LITEM MOTAM. Before suit brought, before controversy moved.

ANTEDATE. To put a date to an instrument of a time before the time it was written. Vide *Date.*

ANTENATI. Born before. This term is applied to those who were born or resided within the United States before or at the time of the declaration of independence. These had all the rights of citizens. 2 Kent, Com. 51, et seq.

ANTE-NUPTIAL. What takes place before marriage; as, an ante-nuptial agreement, which is an agreement made between a man and a woman in contemplation of marriage. Vide *Settlement.*

ANTHETARIUS, *obsolete* See *Antithetarius.*

ANTI MANIFESTO. The declaration of the reasons which one of the belligerents publishes, to show that the war as to him is defensive. Wolff, § 1187. See *Manifesto.*

ANTICIPATION. The act of doing or taking a thing before its proper time.

2. In deeds of trust there is frequently a provision that the income of the estate shall be paid by the trustee as it shall accrue, and not by way of anticipation. A payment made contrary to such provision would not be considered as a discharge of the trustee.

ANTICHRESIS, *contracts.* A word used in the civil law to denote the contract by which a creditor acquires the right of reaping the fruit or other revenues of the immovables given to him in pledge, on condition of deducting, annually, their proceeds from the interest, if any is due to him, and afterwards from the principal of his debt. Louis. Code, art. 3143; Dict. de Juris. Antichrèse, Mortgage; Code Civ. 2085. Dig. 13, 7, 7; 4, 24, 1; Code, 8, 28, 1.

ANTINOMY. A term used in the civil law to signify the real or apparent contradiction between two laws or two decisions. Merl. Répert. h. t. Vide *Conflict of Laws.*

ANTIQUA CUSTOMA, *Eng. law.* A duty or imposition which was collected on wool, wool-felts, and leather, was so called. This custom was called *nova customa* until the 22 Edw. I., when the king, without parliament, set a new imposition of 40*s.* a sack, and then, for the first time, the *nova customa* went by the name of *antiqua customa.* Bac. Ab. Smuggling, &c. B.

ANTIQUA STATUTA. In England the statutes are divided into new and ancient statutes; since the time of memory; those from the time 1 R. I. to E. III., are called *antiqua statuta*—those made since, *nova statuta.*

ANTITHETARIUS, *old English law.* The name given to a man who endeavors to discharge himself of the crime of which he is accused, by retorting the charge on the accuser. He differs from an approver (q. v.) in this, that the latter does not charge the accuser, but others. Jacob's Law Dict.

APARTMENTS. A part of a house occupied by a person, while the rest is occupied by another, or others. 7 Mann. & Gr. 95; 6 Mod. 214; Woodf. L. & T. 178. See *House.*

APOSTACY, *Eng. law.* A total renunciation of the Christian religion, and differs from heresy. (q. v.) This offence is punished by the statute of 9 and 10 W. III. c. 32. Vide *Christianity.*

APOSTLES. In the British courts of admiralty, when a party appeals from a decision made against him, he prays *apostles* from the judge, which are brief letters of dismission, stating the case, and declaring that the record will be transmitted. 2 Brown's Civ. and Adm. Law, 438; Dig. 49. 6.

2. This term was used in the civil law. It is derived from *apostolos*, a Greek word, which signifies *one sent*, because the judge from whose sentence an appeal was made, sent to the superior judge these letters of dismission, or apostles. Merl. Rép. mot Apôtres.

APPARATOR or APPARITOR, *eccles. law.* An officer or messenger employed to serve the process of the spiritual courts in England.

APPARENT. That which is manifest; what is proved. It is required that all things upon which a court must pass, should be made to appear, if matter in pays, under oath; if matter of record, by the record. It is a rule that those things which do not appear, are to be considered as not existing: *de non apparentibus et non existentibus eadem est ratio.* Broom's Maxims, 20. What does not appear, does not exist: *quod non apparet, non est.*

APPARLEMENT. Resemblance. It is said to be derived from *pareillement*, French, in like manner. Cunn. Dict. h. t.

APPEAL, *English crim. law.* The accusation of a person, in a legal form, for a crime committed by him; or, it is the lawful declaration of another man's crime, before a competent judge, by one who sets his name to the declaration, and undertakes to prove it, upon the penalty which may ensue thereon. Vide Co. Litt. 123 b, 287 b; 5 Burr. R. 2643, 2793; 2 W. Bl. R. 713; 1 B. & A. 405. Appeals of murder, as well as of treason, felony, or other offences, together with wager of battle, are abolished by stat. 59 Geo. III. c. 46.

APPEAL, *practice.* The act by which a party submits to the decision of a superior court, a cause which has been tried in an inferior tribunal. 1 S. & R. 78; 1 Bin. 219; 3 Bin. 48.

2. The appeal generally annuls the judgment of the inferior court, so far that no action can be taken upon it until after the final decision of the cause. Its object is to review the whole case, and to secure a just judgment upon the merits.

3. An appeal differs from proceedings in error, under which the errors committed in the proceedings are examined, and if any have been committed the first judgment is reversed; because in the appeal the whole case is examined and tried as if it had not been tried before. Vide Dane's Ab. h. t.; Serg. Const. Law, Index, h. t.; and article *Courts of the United States.*

APPEARANCE, *practice.* Signifies the filing common or special bail to the action.

2. The appearance, with all other subsequent pleadings supposed to take place in court, should (in accordance with the ancient practice) purport to be in term time. It is to be observed, however, that though the proceedings are expressed as if occurring in term time, yet, in fact, much of the business is now done in periods of vacation.

3. The appearance of the parties is no longer (as formerly) by the actual presence in court, either by themselves or their attorneys; but, it must be remembered, an appearance of this kind is still supposed, and exists in contemplation of law. The appearance is effected on the part of the defendant (when he is not arrested) by making certain formal entries in the proper office of the court, expressing his appearance; 5 Watts & Serg. 215; 1 Scam. R. 250; 2 Scam. R. 462; 6 Port. R. 352; 9 Port. R. 272; 6 Miss. R. 50; 7 Miss. R. 411; 17 Verm. 531; 2 Pike, R. 26; 6 Ala. R. 784; 3 Watts & Serg. 501; 8 Port. R. 442; or, in case of arrest, it may be considered as effected by giving bail to the action. On the part of the plaintiff no formality expressive of appearance is observed.

4. In general, the appearance of either party may be in person or by attorney, and, when by attorney, there is always supposed to be a warrant of attorney executed to the attorney by his client, authorizing such appearance.

5. But to this general rule there are various exceptions; persons devoid of understanding, as idiots, and persons having understanding, if they are by law deprived of a capacity to appoint an attorney, as married women, must appear in person. The appearance of such persons must purport, and is so entered on the record, to be in person, whether in fact an attorney be employed or not. See Tidd's Pr. 68, 75; 1 Arch. Pract. 22; 2 John. 192; 8 John. 418; 14 John. 417; 5 Pick. 413; Bouv. Inst. Index, h. t.

6. There must be an appearance in person in the following cases:

1st. An idiot can appear only in person, and as a plaintiff he may sue in person or by his next friend.

2d. A married woman, when sued without her husband, should defend in person; 3 Wms. Saund. 209, b; and when the cause of action accrued before her marriage, and she is afterwards sued alone, she must plead her coverture in person, and not by attorney. Co. Litt. 125.

3d. When the party pleads to the jurisdiction, he must plead in person. Summ. on Pl. 51; Merrif. Law of Att. 58.

4th. A plea of misnomer must always be in person, unless it be by special warrant of attorney. 1 Chit. Pl. 398; Summ. on Pl. 50; 3 Wms. Saund. 209 b.

7. An infant cannot appoint an attorney; he must therefore prosecute or appear by guardian, or prochein ami.

8. A lunatic, if of full age, may appear by attorney; if under age, by guardian 2 Wms. Saund. 335; Id. 332 (*a*) n. (4.)

9. When an appearance is lawfully entered by the defendant, both parties are considered as being in court. Imp. Pr. 215. And if the defendant pleads to issue, defects of process are cured; but not, if he

demurs to the process, (1 Lord Raym. 21,) or, according to the practice of some courts, appears *de bene esse*, or otherwise conditionally.

10. In criminal cases, the personal presence of the accused is often necessary. It has been held, that if the record of a conviction of a misdemeanor be removed by certiorari, the personal presence of the defendant is necessary, in order to move in arrest of judgment: but, after a special verdict, it is not necessary that the defendant should be personally present at the argument of it. 2 Burr. 931; 1 Bl. Rep. 209, S. C.

So, the defendant must appear personally in court, when an order of bastardy is quashed; and the reason is, he must enter into a recognizance to abide the order of sessions below. 1 Bl. Rep. 198.

So, in a case, when two justices of the peace, having confessed an information for misbehaviour in the execution of their office, and a motion was made to dispense with their personal appearance, on their clerks undertaking in court to answer for their fines, the court declared the rule to be, that although such a motion was subject to the discretion of the court either to grant or refuse it, in cases where it is clear that the punishment would not be corporal, yet it ought to be denied in every case where it is either probable or possible that the punishment would be corporal; and therefore the motion was overruled in that case. And Wilmot and Ashton, Justices, thought, that even where the punishment would most probably be pecuniary only, yet in offences of a very gross and public nature, the persons convicted should appear in person, for the sake of example and prevention of the like offences being committed by other persons; as the notoriety of being called up to answer criminally for such offences, would very much conduce to deter others from venturing to commit the like. 3 Burr. 1786, 7.

APPEARANCE DAY. The day on which the parties are bound to appear in court. This is regulated in the different states by particular provisions.

APPELLANT, *practice*. He who makes an appeal from one jurisdiction to another.

APPELLATE JURISDICTION. The jurisdiction which a superior court has to hear appeals of causes which have been tried in inferior courts. It differs from original jurisdiction, which is the power to entertain suits instituted in the first instance. Vide *Jurisdiction; Original jurisdiction*.

APPELLEE, *practice*. The party in a cause against whom an appeal has been taken.

APPELLOR. A criminal who accuses his accomplices; one who challenges a jury.

APPENDANT. An incorporeal inheritance belonging to another inheritance.

2. By the word appendant in a deed, nothing can be conveyed which is itself substantial corporeal real property, and capable of passing by feoffment and livery of seisin: for one kind of corporeal real property cannot be appendant to another description of the like real property, it being a maxim that land cannot be appendant to land. Co. Litt. 121; 4 Coke, 86; 8 Barn. & Cr. 150; 6 Bing. 150. Only such things can be appendant as can consistently be so, as a right of way, and the like. This distinction is of importance, as will be seen by the following case. If a wharf with the appurtenances be demised, and the water adjoining the wharf were intended to pass, yet no distress for rent on the demised premises could be made on a barge on the water, because it is not a place which could pass as a part of the thing demised. 6 Bing. 150.

3. Appendant differs from appurtenant in this, that the former always arises from prescription, whereas an appurtenance may be created at any time. 1 Tho. Co. Litt. 206; Wood's Inst. 121; Dane's Abr. h. t.; 2 Vin. Ab. 594; Bac. Ab. Common, A 1. And things appendant must have belonged by prescription to another principal substantial thing, which is considered in law as more worthy. The principal thing and the appendant must be appropriate to each other in nature and quality, or such as may be properly used together. 1 Chit. Pr. 154.

APPENDITIA. From *appendo*, to hang at or on; the appendages or pertinances of an estate; the appurtenances to a dwelling, &c.; thus *pent-houses*, are the *appenditia domus*, &c.

APPLICATION. The act of making a request for something; the paper on which the request is written is also called an application; as an application to chancery fo leave to invest trust funds; an application to an insurance company for insurance. In the land law of Pennsylvania, an application is understood to be a request in writing to have a certain quantity of land at or near a certain place therein mentioned. 3 Binn. 21; 5 Id. 151; Jones on Land Office Titles, 24.

2. An application for insurance ought to state the facts truly as to the object to be insured, for if any false representation be made with a fraudulent intent, it will avoid the policy. 7 Wend. 72.

3. By application is also meant the use or disposition of a thing; as the application of purchase money.

4. In some cases a purchaser who buys trust property is required to see to the application of the purchase money, and if he neglects to do so, and it be misapplied, he will be considered as a trustee of the property he has so purchased. The subject will be examined by considering, 1, the kind of property to be sold; 2, the cases where the purchaser is bound to see to the application of the purchase money in consequence of the wording of the deed of trust.

5.—1. *Personal* property is liable, in the hands of the executor, for the payment of debts, and the purchaser is therefore exempted from seeing to the application of the purchase money, although it may have been bequeathed to be sold for the payment of debts. 1 Cox, R. 145; 2 Dick. 725; 7 John. Ch. Rep. 150, 160; 11 S. & R. 377, 385; 2 P. Wms. 148; 4 Bro. C. C. 136; White's L. C. in Eq. *54; 4 Bouv. Inst. n. 3946.

6. With regard to *real* estate, which is not a fund at law for the payment of debts, except where it is made so by act of assembly, or by direction in the will of the testator or deed of trust, the purchaser from an executor or trustee may be liable for the application of the purchase money. And it will now be proper to consider the cases where such liability exists.

7.—2. Upon the sale of real estate, a trustee in whom the legal title is vested, can at law give a valid discharge for the purchase money, because he is the owner at law. In equity, on the contrary, the persons among whom the produce of the sale is to be distributed are considered the owners; and a purchaser must obtain a discharge from them, unless the power of giving receipts is either expressly or by implication given to the trustees to give receipts for the purchase money. It is, for this reason, usual to provide in wills and trust deeds that the purchaser shall not be required to see to the application of the purchase money.

APPOINTEE. A person who is appointed or selected for a particular purpose, as the appointee under a power, is the person who is to receive the benefit of the trust or power.

APPOINTOR. One authorized by the *donor* under the statute of uses, to execute a power. 2 Bouv. Ins. n. 1923.

APPOINTMENT, *chancery practice.* The act of a person authorized by a will or other instrument to direct how trust property shall be disposed of, directing such disposition agreeably to the general directions of the trust.

2. The appointment must be made in such a manner as to come within the spirit of the power. And although at law the rule only requires that some allotment, however small, shall be given to each person, when the power is to appoint to and among several persons; the rule in equity differs, and requires a real and substantial portion to each, and a mere nominal allotment to one is deemed illusory and fraudulent. When the distribution is left to discretion, without any prescribed rule, as to *such* of the children as the trustee shall think proper, he may appoint to one only; 5 Ves. 857; but if the words be, *amongst* the children as he should think proper, each must have a share, and the doctrine of illusory appointment applies. 4 Ves. 771; Prec. Ch. 256; 2 Vern. 513. Vide, generally, 1 Supp. to Ves. Jr. 40, 95, 201, 235, 237; 2 Id. 127; 1 Vern. 67, n.; 1 Ves. Jr. 310, n.; 4 Kent, Com. 337; Sugd. on Pow. Index, h. t.; 2 Hill. Ab. Index, h. t.; 2 Bouv. Inst. n. 1921, et seq.

APPOINTMENT, *government, wills.* The act by which a person is selected and invested with an office; as the appointment of a judge, of which the making out of his commission is conclusive evidence. 1 Cranch, 137, 155; 10 Pet. 343. The appointment of an executor, which is done by nominating him as such in a will or testament.

2. By appointment is also understood a public employment, nearly synonymous with office. The distinction is this, that the term *appointment* is of a more extensive signification than office; for example, the act of authorizing a man to print the laws of the United States by authority, and the right conveyed by such an act, is an appointment, but the right thus conveyed is not an office. 17 S. & R. 219, 233. See 3 S. & R. 157; Coop. Just. 599, 604.

APPORTIONMENT, *contracts.* Lord

Coke defines it to be a division or partition of a rent, common, or the like, or the making it into parts. Co. Litt. 147. This definition seems incomplete. Apportionment frequently denotes, not division, but distribution; and in its ordinary technical sense, the distribution of one subject in proportion to another previously distributed. 1 Swanst. C. 37, n.

2. Apportionment will here be considered only in relation to contracts, by taking a view, 1, of such as are purely personal; and, 2, of such as relate to the realty.

3.—1. When a purely personal contract is entire and not divisible in its nature, it is manifest it cannot be apportioned; as when the subject of the contract is but one thing, and there is but one creditor and one debtor, neither can apportion the obligation without the consent of the other. In such case the creditor cannot force his debtor to pay him a part of his debt only, and leave the other part unpaid, nor can the debtor compel his creditor to receive a part only of what is due to him on account of his claim. Nor can the assignee of a part sustain an action for such part. 5 N. S. 192.

4. When there is a special contract between the parties, in general no compensation can be received unless the whole contract has been actually fulfilled. 4 Greenl. 454; 2 Pick. R. 267; 10 Pick. R. 209; 4 Pick. R. 103; 4 M'Cord, R. 26, 246; 6 Verm. R. 35. The subject of the contract being a complex event, constituted by the performance of various acts, the imperfect completion of the event, by the performance of only some of those acts, cannot, by virtue of that contract, of which it is not the subject, afford a title to the whole, or any part of the stipulated benefit. See 1 Swanst. C. 338, n. and the cases there cited; Story, Bailm. § 441; Chit. Contr. 168; 3 Watts, 331; 2 Mass. 147, 436; 3 Hen. & Munf. 407; 2 John. Cas. 17; 13 John. R. 365; 11 Wend. 257; 7 Cowen, 184; 8 Cowen, 84; 2 Pick. 332. See generally on the subject of the apportionment of personal obligations, 16 Vin. Ab. 138; 22 Vin. Ab. 13; Stark. Ev. part 4, p. 1622; Com. Dig. Chancery, 2 E and 4 N 5; 3 Chit. Com. Law, 129; Newl. Contr. 159; Long on Sales, 108. And for the doctrine of the civil law, see Dumoulin, de dividuo et individuo, part 2, n. 6, 7; Toull. Dr. Civ. Fr. liv. 3, tit 3, c. 4, n. 750, et seq.

5.—2. With regard to rents, the law is different. Rents may in general be apportioned, and this may take place in several ways; first, by the act of the landlord or reversioner alone, and secondly, by virtue of the statute of 11 Geo. II., c. 19, s. 15, or by statutes in the several states in which its principles have been embodied.

6.—1. When there is a subsisting obligation on the part of the tenant to pay a certain rent, the reversioner may sell his estate in different parts, to as many persons as he may deem proper, and the lessee or tenant will be bound to pay to each a proportion of the rent. 3 Watts, 404; 3 Kent, Com. 470, 3d. ed.; Co. Litt. 158 a; Gilb. on Rents, 173; 7 Car. 23; 13 Co. 57; Cro. Eliz. 637, 651; Archb. L. &. T. 172; 5 B. & A. 876; 6 Halst. 262. It is usual for the owners of the reversion to agree among themselves as to the amount which each is to receive; but when there is no agreement, the rent will be apportioned by the jury. 3 Kent, Com. 470; 1 Bouv. Inst. n. 697.

7.—2. Rent may be apportioned *as to time* by virtue of the stat. 11 Geo. II., c. 19, s. 15, by which it is provided that the rent due by a tenant for life, who dies during the currency of a quarter, of a year, or other division of time at which the rent was made payable, shall be apportioned to the day of his death. In Delaware, Missouri, New Jersey, and New York, it is provided by statutes, that if the tenant for life, lessor, die on the rent day, his executors may recover the whole rent; if before, a proportional part. In Delaware, Kentucky, Missouri, and New York, when one is entitled to rents, depending on the life of another, he may recover them notwithstanding the death of the latter. In Delaware, Kentucky, Missouri, and Virginia, it is specially provided, that the husband, after the death of his wife, may recover the rents of her lands. 1 Hill. Ab. c. 16, § 50. In Kentucky, the rent is to be apportioned when the lease is determined upon any contingency.

8. When the tenant is deprived of the land, as by eviction, by title paramount, or by quitting the premises with the landlord's consent, in the absence of any agreement to the contrary, his obligation to pay rent ceases, as regards the current quarter or half year, or other day of payment, as the case may be. But rent which is due may be recovered. Gilb. on Rents, 145; 3 Kent, Comm. 376; 4 Wend. 423; 8 Cowen, 727; 1 Har. &

Gill, 308; 11 Mass. 493. See 4 Cruise's Dig. 206; 3 Call's R. 268; 4 M'Cord 447; 1 Bailey's R. 469; 2 Bouv. Inst. n. 1675, et seq.

APPOSAL OF SHERIFFS, *English law.* The charging them with money received upon account of the Exchequer. 22 Car. II.

APPOSER, *Eng. law.* An officer of the Court of Exchequer, called the foreign apposer.

APPOSTILLE, *French law.* Postil. In general this means an addition or annotation made in the margin of an act, [contract in writing,] or of some writing. Mer. Rép.

APPRAISEMENT. A just valuation of property.

2. Appraisements are required to be made of the property of persons dying intestate, of insolvents and others; an inventory (q. v.) of the goods ought to be made, and a just valuation put upon them. When property real or personal is taken for public use, an appraisement of it is made, that the owner may be paid its value.

APPRAISER, *practice.* A person appointed by competent authority to appraise or value goods; as in case of the death of a person, an appraisement and inventory must be made of the goods of which he died possessed, or was entitled to. Appraisers are sometimes appointed to assess the damage done to property, by some public work, or to estimate its value when taken for public use.

APPREHENSION, *practice.* The capture or arrest of a person. The term apprehension is applied to criminal cases, and arrest to civil cases; as, one having authority may *arrest* on *civil* process, and *apprehend* on a *criminal* warrant.

APPRENTICE, *person, contracts.* A person bound in due form of law to a master, to learn from him his art, trade or business, and to serve him during the time of his apprenticeship. (q. v.) 1 Bl. Com. 426; 2 Kent, Com. 211; 3 Rawle, Rep. 307; Chit. on Ap. 4 T. R. 735; Bouv. Inst. Index, h. t.

2. Formerly the name of *apprentice en la ley* was given indiscriminately to all students of law. In the reign of Edward IV. they were sometimes called *apprentici ad barras.* And in some of the ancient law writers, the term apprentice and barrister are synonymous. 2 Inst. 214; Eunom. Dial, 2, § 53, p. 155.

APPRENTICESHIP, *contracts.* A contract entered into between a person who understands some art, trade or business, and called the master, and another person commonly a minor, during his or her minority, who is called the apprentice, with the consent of his or her parent or next friend; by which the former undertakes to teach such minor his art, trade or business, and to fulfil such other covenants as may be agreed upon; and the latter agrees to serve the master during a definite period of time, in such art, trade or business. In a common indenture of apprenticeship, the father is bound for the performance of the covenants by the son Doug. 500.

2. The term during which the apprentice is to serve is also called his apprenticeship. Pardessus, Dr. Com. n. 34.

3. This contract is generally entered into by indenture or deed, and is to continue no longer than the minority of the apprentice. The English statute law as to binding out minors as apprentices to learn some useful art, trade or business, has been generally adopted in the United States, with some variations which cannot be noticed here. 2 Kent, Com. 212.

4. The principal duties of the parties are as follows: 1st, *Duties of the master.* He is bound to instruct the apprentice by teaching him, bona fide, the knowledge of the art of which he has undertaken to teach him the elements. He ought to watch over the conduct of the apprentice, giving him prudent advice and showing him a good example, and fulfilling towards him the duties of a father, as in his character of master, he stands in loco parèntis. He is also required to fulfil all the covenants he has entered into by the indenture. He must not abuse his authority, either by bad treatment, or by employing his apprentice in menial employments, wholly unconnected with the business he has to learn. He cannot dismiss his apprentice except by application to a competent tribunal, upon whose decree the indenture may be cancelled. But an infant apprentice is not capable in law of consenting to his own discharge. 1 Burr. 501. Nor can the justices, according to some authorities, order money to be returned on the discharge of an apprentice. Strange, 69; Contra, Salk. 67, 68, 490; 11 Mod. 110; 12 Mod. 498, 553. After the apprenticeship is at an end, he cannot retain the apprentice on the ground that he has not fulfilled his contract, unless specially authorized by statute.

5.—2d. *Duties of the apprentice.* An apprentice is bound to obey his master in all his lawful commands, take care of his property, and promote his interest, endeavor to learn his trade or business, and perform all the covenants in his indenture not contrary to law. He must not leave his master's service during the term of the apprenticeship. The apprentice is entitled to payment for extraordinary services, when promised by the master; 1 Penn. Law Jour. 368. See 1 Whart. 113; and even when no express promise has been made, under peculiar circumstances. 2 Cranch, 240, 270; 3 Rob. Ad. Rep. 237; but see 1 Whart, 113. See generally, 2 Kent, Com. 211-214; Bac. Ab. Master and Servant; 1 Saund. R. 313, n. 1, 2, 3, and 4; 3 Rawle, R. 307; 3 Vin. Ab. 19; 1 Bouv. Inst. n. 396, et seq. The law of France on this subject is strikingly similar to our own. Pardessus, Droit Com. n. 518-522.

6. Apprenticeship is a relation which cannot be assigned at the common law; 5 Bin. 428; 4 T. R. 373; Doug. 70; 3 Keble, 519; 12 Mod. 554; although the apprentice may work with a second master by order and consent of the first, which is a service to the first under the indenture. 4 T. R. 373. But in Pennsylvania and some other states the assignment of indentures of apprenticeship is authorized by statute. 1 Serg. & R. 249; 3 Serg. & R. 161, 164, 166.

APPRIZING. A name for an action in the Scotch law, by which a creditor formerly carried off the estates of his debtor in payment of debts due to him; in lieu of which, adjudications are now resorted to.

APPROBATE AND REPROBATE. In Scotland this term is used to signify to approve and reject. It is a maxim *quod approbo non reprobo*. For example, if a testator give his property to A, and give A's property to B, A shall not be at liberty to approve of the will so far as the legacy is given to him, and reject it as to the bequest of his property to B; in other words, he cannot approve and reject the will. 1 Bligh. 21; 1 Bell's Com. 146.

APPROPRIATION, *contracts*. The application of the payment of a sum of money, made by a debtor to his creditor, to one of several debts.

2. When a voluntary payment is made, the law permits the debtor in the first place, or, if he make no choice, then it allows the creditor to make an appropriation of such payment to either of several debts which are due by the debtor to the creditor. And if neither make an appropriation, then the law makes the application of such payment. This rule does not apply to payments made under compulsory process of law. 10 Pick. 129. It will be proper to consider, 1, when the debtor may make the appropriation; 2, when the creditor may make it; 3, when it will be made by law.

3.—1. In general the appropriation may be made by the *debtor*, but this must be done by his express declaration, or by circumstances from which his intentions can be inferred. 2 C. M. & R. 723; 14 East, 239; 1 Tyrw. & Gr. 137; 15 Wend. 19; 5 Taunt. 596; 7 Wheat. 13; 2 Har. & Gill, 159; S. C. 4 Gill & Johns. 361; 1 Bibb, 334; 5 Watts, 544; 12 Pick. 463; 20 Pick. 441; 2 Bailey, 617; 4 Mass. 692; 17 Mass. 575. This appropriation, it seems, must be notified to the creditor at the time; for an entry made by the debtor in his own books, is not alone sufficient to determine the application of the payment. 2 Vern. 606; 4 B. & C. 715. In some cases, in consequence of the circumstances, the presumption will be that the payment was made on account of one debt, in preference to another. 3 Caines, 14; 2 Stark. R. 101. And in some cases the debtor has no right to make the appropriation, as, for example, to apply a partial payment to the liquidation of the principal, when interest is due. 1 Dall. 124; 1 H. & J. 754; 2 N. & M'C. 395; 1 Pick. 194; 17 Mass. 417.

4.—2. When the debtor has neglected to make an appropriation, the *creditor* may, in general, make it, but this is subject to some exceptions. If, for example, the debtor owes a debt as executor, and one in his own right, the creditor cannot appropriate a payment to the liquidation of the former, because that may depend on the question of assets. 2 Str. 1194. See 1 M. & Malk. 40; 9 Cowen, 409; 2 Stark. R. 74; 1 C. & Mees. 33.

5. Though it is not clearly settled in England whether a creditor is bound to make the appropriation immediately, or at a subsequent time; Ellis on D. and C. 406-408; yet in the United States, the right to make the application at any time has been recognized, and the creditor is not bound to make an immediate election. 4 Cranch, 317; 9 Cowen, 420, 436. See 12 S. & R. 301; 2 B. & C. 65; 2 Verm. 283; 10 Conn. 176.

6. When once made, the appropriation cannot be changed; and, rendering an account, or bringing suit and declaring in a particular way, is evidence of such appropriation. 1 Wash. 128; 3 Green. 314; 12

Shepl. 29; 2 N. H. Rep. 193; 2 Rawle, 316; 5 Watts, 544; 2 Wash. C. C. 47; 1 Gilp. 106; 12 S. & R. 305.

7.—3. When no application of the payment has been made by either party, the *law* will appropriate it, in such a way as to do justice and equity to both parties. 6 Cranch, 8, 28; 4 Mason, 333; 2 Sumn. 99, 112; 5 Mason, 82; 1 Nev. & Man. 746; 5 Bligh, N. S. 1; 11 Mass. 300; 1 H. & J. 754; 2 Vern. 24; 1 Bibb, 334; 2 Dea. & Chit. 534; 5 Mason, 11. See 6 Cranch, 253, 264; 7 Cranch, 575; 1 Mer. 572, 605; Burge on Sur. 126–138; 1 M. & M. 40. See 1 Bouv. Inst. n. 831-4.

8. In Louisiana, by statutory enactment, Civ. Code, art. 1159, et seq., it is provided that "the debtor of several debts has a right to declare, when he makes a payment, what debt he means to discharge. The debtor of a debt which bears interest or produces rents, cannot, without the consent of the creditor, impute to the reduction of the capital, any payment he may make, when there is interest or rent due. When the debtor of several debts has accepted a receipt, by which the creditor has imputed what he has received to one of the debts especially, the debtor can no longer require the imputation to be made to a different debt, unless there have been fraud or surprise on the part of the creditor. When the receipt bears no imputation, the payment must be imputed to the debt which the debtor had at the time most interest in discharging of those that are equally due, otherwise to the debt which has fallen due, though less burdensome than those which are not yet payable. If the debts be of a like nature, the imputation is made to the less burdensome; if all things are equal, it is made proportionally." This is a translation of the Code Napoleon, art. 1253–1256, slightly altered. See Poth. Obl. n. 528, translated by Evans, and the notes; Bac. Ab. Obligations, F; 6 Watts & Serg. 1; Amer. Law Mag. 31; 1 Hare & Wall. Sel. Dec. 123–158.

APPROPRIATION, *eccl. law.* The setting apart an ecclesiastical benefice, which is the general property of the church, to the perpetual and proper use of some religious house, bishop or college, dean and chapter, and the like. Ayl. Par. 86. See the form of an appropriation in Jacob's Introd. 411.

TO APPROVE, *approbare.* To increase the profits upon a thing; as to improve land by increasing the rent. 2 Inst. 784.

APPROVEMENT, *English crim. law.* The act by which a person indicted of treason or felony, and arraigned for the same, confesses the same before any plea pleaded, and accuses others, his accomplices, of the same crime, in order to obtain his pardon.

2 This practice is disused. 4 Bl. Com. 330; 1 Phil. Ev. 37. In modern practice, an accomplice is permitted to give evidence against his associates. 9 Cowen, R. 707; 2 Virg. Cas. 490; 4 Mass. R. 156; 12 Mass. R. 20; 4 Wash. C. C. R. 428; 1 Dev. R. 363; 1 City Hall Rec. 8. In Vermont, on a trial for adultery, it was held that a *particeps criminis* was not a competent witness, because no person can be allowed to testify his own guilt or turpitude to convict another. N. Chap. R. 9.

APPROVEMENT, *English law.* 1. The inclosing of common land within the lord's waste, so as to leave egress and regress to a tenant who is a commoner. 2. The augmentation of the profits of land. Stat. of Merton, 20 Hen. VIII.; F. N. B. 72; Crompt. Jus. 250; 1 Lilly's Reg. 110.

APPROVER, *Engl. crim. law.* One confessing himself guilty of felony, and approving others of the same crime to save himself. Crompt. Inst. 250; 3 Inst. 129.

APPURTENANCES. In common parlance and legal acceptation, is used to signify something belonging to another thing as principal, and which passes as incident to the principal thing. 10 Peters, R. 25; Angell, Wat. C. 43; 1 Serg. & Rawle, 169; 5 S. & R. 110; 5 S. & R. 107; Cro. Jac. 121; 3 Saund. 401, n. 2; Wood's Inst. 121; 4 Rawle, R. 342; 1 P. Wms. 603; Cro. Jac. 526; 2 Co. 32; Co. Litt. 5 b, 56 a, b; 1 Plowd. 171; 2 Saund. 401, n. 2; 1 Lev. 131; 1 Sid. 211; 1 Bos. & P. 371; 1 Cr. & M. 439; 4 Ad. & Ell. 761; 2 Nev. & M. 517; 5 Toull. n. 531.

2. The word appurtenances, at least in a deed, will not pass any corporeal real property, but only incorporeal easements, or rights and privileges. Co. Lit. 121; 8 B. & C. 150; 6 Bing. 150; 1 Chit. Pr. 153, 4. Vide *Appendant.*

APPURTENANT. Belonging to; pertaining to of right.

AQUA. Water. This word is used in composition, as aquæ ductus, &c.

2. It is a rule that water belongs to the land which it covers, when it is stationary: *aqua cedit solo.* But the owner of running

water, or of a water course, cannot stop it; the inferior inheritance having a right to the flow: *aqua currit et debet currere, ut currere solebat.*

AQUÆ DUCTUS, *civil law.* The name of a servitude which consists in the right to carry water by means of pipes or conduits over or through the estate of another. Dig. 8, 3, 1; Inst. 2, 3; Lalaure, Des Serv. c. 5, p. 23.

AQUÆ HAUSTUS, *civil law.* The name of a servitude which consists in the right to draw water from the fountain, pool, or spring of another. Inst. 2, 3, 2; Dig. 8, 3, 1, 1.

AQUÆ IMMITTENDÆ, *civil law.* The name of a servitude, which frequently occurs among neighbors. It is the right which the owner of a house, built in such a manner as to be surrounded with other buildings, so that it has no outlet for its waters, has, to cast water out of his windows on his neighbor's roof court or soil. Lalaure, Des. Serv. 23.

AQUAGIUM, i. e. aquæ agium. 1. A water course. 2. A toll for water.

AQUATIC RIGHTS. This is the name of those rights which individuals have in water, whether it be running, or otherwise.

ARBITER. One who decides without any control. A judge with the most extensive arbitrary powers; an arbitrator.

ARBITRAMENT. A term nearly synonymous with arbitration. (q. v.)

ARBITRAMENT AND AWARD. The name of a plea to an action brought for the same cause which had been submitted to arbitration, and on which an award had been made. Wats. on Arb. 256.

ARBITRARY. What depends on the will of the judge, not regulated or established by law. Bacon (Aphor. 8) says, Optima lex quæ minimum relinquit arbitrio judicis et (Aph. 46) optimus judex, qui minimum sibi.

2. In all well adjusted systems of law, every thing is regulated, and nothing arbitrary can be allowed; but there is a discretion which is sometimes allowed by law, which leaves the judge free to act as he pleases to a certain extent. See *Discretion.*

ARBITRARY PUNISHMENTS, *practice.* Those punishments which are left to the decision of the judge, in distinction from those which are defined by statute.

ARBITRATION, *practice.* A reference and submission of a matter in dispute concerning property, or of a personal wrong, to the decision of one or more persons as arbitrators.

2. They are voluntary or compulsory. The *voluntary* are, 1. Those made by mutual consent, in which the parties select the arbitrators, and bind themselves by bond to abide by their decision; these are made without any rule of court. 3 Bl. Com. 16.

3.—2. Those which are made in a cause depending in court, by a rule of court, before trial; these are arbitrators at common law, and the award is enforced by attachment. Kyd on Awards, 21.

4.—3. Those which are made by virtue of the statute, 9 & 10 Will. III., c. 15, by which it is agreed to refer a matter in dispute not then in court, to arbitrators, and agree that the submission be made a rule of court, which is enforced as if it had been made a rule of court; Kyd on Aw. 22; there are two other voluntary arbitrations which are peculiar to Pennsylvania.

5.—4. The first of these is the arbitration under the act of June 16, 1836 which provides that the parties to any suit may consent to a rule of court for referring all matters of fact in controversy to referees, reserving all matters of law for the decision of the court, and the report of the referees shall have the effect of a special verdict, which is to be proceeded upon by the court as a special verdict, and either party may have a writ of error to the judgment entered thereupon.

6.—5. Those by virtue of the act of 1806, which authorizes "any person or persons desirous of settling any dispute or controversy, by themselves, their agents or attorneys, to enter into an agreement in writing, or refer such dispute or controversy to certain persons to be by them mutually chosen; and it shall be the duty of the referees to make out an award and deliver it to the party in whose favor it shall be made, together with the written agreement entered into by the parties; and it shall be the duty of the prothonotary, on the affidavit of a subscribing witness to the agreement, that it was duly executed by the parties, to file the same in his office; and on the agreement being so filed as aforesaid, he shall enter the award on record, which shall be as available in law as an award made under a reference issued by the court, or entered on the docket by the parties."

7. *Compulsory* arbitrations are perhaps confined to Pennsylvania. Either party in a civil suit or action, or his attorney, may

enter at the prothonotary's office a rule of reference, wherein he shall declare his determination to have arbitrators chosen, on a day certain to be mentioned therein, not exceeding thirty days, for the trial of all matters in variance in the suit between the parties. A copy of this rule is served on the opposite party. On the day appointed they meet at the prothonotary's, and endeavor to agree upon arbitrators; if they cannot, the prothonotary makes out a list on which are inscribed the names of a number of citizens, and the parties alternately strike each one of them from the list, beginning with the plaintiff, until there are but the number agreed upon or fixed by the prothonotary left, who are to be the arbitrators; a time of meeting is then agreed upon—or appointed by the prothonotary, when the parties cannot agree,—at which time the arbitrators, after being sworn or affirmed justly and equitably to try all matters in variance submitted to them, proceed to hear and decide the case; their award is filed in the office of the prothonotary, and has the effect of a judgment, subject, however, to appeal, which may be entered at any time within twenty days after the filing of such award. Act of 16th June, 1836, Pamphl. p. 715.

8. This is somewhat similar to the arbitrations of the Romans; there the prætor selected from a list of citizens made for the purpose, one or more persons, who were authorized to decide all suits submitted to them, and which had been brought before him; the authority which the prætor gave them conferred on them a public character, and their judgments were without appeal. Toull. Dr. Civ. Fr. liv. 3, t. 3, ch. 4, n. 820. See generally, Kyd on Awards; Caldwell on Arbitrations; Bac. Ab. h. t.; 1 Salk. R. 69, 70–75; 2 Saund. R. 133, n 7; 2 Sell. Pr. 241; Doct. Pl. 96; 3 Vin. Ab. 40; 3 Bouv. Inst. n. 2482.

ARBITRATOR. A private extraordinary judge chosen by the parties who have a matter in dispute, invested with power to decide the same. Arbitrators are so called because they have generally an arbitrary power, there being in common no appeal from their sentences, which are called awards. Vide Caldw. on Arb. Index, h. t.; Kyd on Awards, Index, h. t.; 3 Bouv. Inst. n. 2491.

ARBOR CONSANGUINITATIS. A table, formed in the shape of a tree, in order to show the genealogy of a family. The progenitor is placed beneath, as if for the root or stem; the persons descended from him are represented by the branches, one for each descendant. For example: if it be desired to form the genealogical tree of Peter's family, Peter will be made the trunk of the tree; if he has two sons, John and James, their names will be written on the first two branches, which will themselves shoot as many twigs as John and James have children; these will produce others, till the whole family shall be represented on the tree.

ARCHAIONOMIA. The name of a collection of Saxon laws, published during the reign of the English Queen Elizabeth, in the Saxon language, with a Latin version, by Mr. Lambard. Dr. Wilkins enlarged this collection in his work, entitled Leges Anglo Saxonicæ, containing all the Saxon laws extant, together with those ascribed to Edward the Confessor, in Latin; those of William the Conqueror, in Norman and Latin; and of Henry I., Stephen, and Henry II., in Latin.

ARCHBISHOP, *eccl. law.* The chief of the clergy of a whole province. He has the inspection of the bishops of that province, as well as of the inferior clergy, and may deprive them on notorious cause. The archbishop has also his own diocese, in which he exercises episcopal jurisdiction, as in his province he exercises archiepiscopal authority. 1 Bl. Com. 380; L. Raym. 541; Code, 1, 2.

ARCHES' COURT. The name of one of the English ecclesiastical courts. Vide *Court of Arches.*

ARCHIVES. Ancient charters or titles, which concern a nation, state, or community, in their rights or privileges. The place where the archives are kept bears the same name. Jacob, L. D. h. t.; Merl. Rép. h. t.

ARCHIVIST. One to whose care the archives have been confided.

ARE. A French measure of surface. This is a square, the sides of which are of the length of ten mètres. The *are* is equal to 1076.441 square feet. Vide *Measure.*

AREA. An enclosed yard or opening in a house; an open place adjoining to a house. 1 Chit. Pr. 176.

AREOPAGITE. A senator, or a judge of the Areopagus. Solon first established the Areopagites; although some say, they were established in the time of Cecrops, (*Anno Mundi*, 2553,) the year that Aaron, the brother of Moses, died;—that Draco abolished the order, and Solon reëstablished it. Demosthenes, in his harangue against Aristocrates, before the Areopagus, speaks of the founders of that tribunal as unknown. See Acts of the Apostles, xviii. 34.

AREOPAGUS. A tribunal established in ancient Athens, bore this name. It is variously represented; some considered as having been a model of justice and perfection, while others look upon it as an aristocratic court, which had a very extended jurisdiction over all crimes and offences, and which exercised an absolute power. See Acts 17, 19 and 22.

ARGENTUM ALBUM. White money; silver coin. See *Alba Firma*,

ARGUMENT, *practice*. Cicero defines it a probable reason proposed in order to induce belief. Ratio probabilis et idonea ad faciendam fidem. The logicians define it more scientifically to be a means, which by its connexion between two extremes, establishes a relation between them. This subject belongs rather to rhetoric and logic than to law.

ARGUMENT LIST. A list of cases put down for the argument of some point of law.

ARGUMENTATIVENESS. What is used by way of reasoning in pleading is so called.

2. It is a rule that pleadings must not be argumentative. For example, when a defendant is sued for taking away the goods of the plaintiff, he must not plead that "the plaintiff never had any goods," because although this may be an infallible *argument* it is not a good plea. The plea should be not guilty. Com. Dig. Pleader R 3; Dougl. 60; Co. Litt. 126 a.

ARGUMENTUM AB INCONVENIENTI. An argument arising from the inconvenience which the construction of the law would create, is to have effect only in a case where the law is doubtful; where the law is certain, such an argument is of no force. Bac. Ab. Baron and Feme, H.

ARISTOCRACY. That form of government in which the sovereign power is exercised by a small number of persons to the exclusion of the remainder of the people.

ARISTODEMOCRACY. A form of government where the power is divided between the great men of the nation and the people.

ARKANSAS. The name of one of the new states of the United States. It was admitted into the Union by the act of congress of June 15th, 1836, 4 Sharsw. cont. of Story's L. U. S. 2444, by which it is declared that the state of Arkansas shall be one, and is hereby declared to be one of the United States of America, and admitted into the Union on an equal footing with the original states in all respects whatever.

2. A convention assembled at Little Rock, on Monday, the 4th day of January, 1836, for the purpose of forming a constitution, by which it is declared that "We, the people of the Territory of Arkansas, by our representatives in convention assembled," "in order to secure to ourselves and our posterity the enjoyments of all the rights of life, liberty and property, and the free pursuit of happiness do mutually agree with each other to form ourselves into a free and independent state, by the name and style of 'The State of Arkansas.'" The constitution was finally adopted on the 30th day of January, 1836.

3. The powers of the government are divided into three departments; each of them is confided to a separate body of magistry, to wit: those which are legislative, to one; those which are executive, to another; and those which are judicial, to a third.

4.—§ 1. The legislative authority of the state is vested in a general assembly, which consists of a senate and house of representatives.

Each house shall appoint its own officers, and shall judge of the qualifications, returns and elections of its own members. Two-thirds of each shall constitute a quorum to do business, but a smaller number may adjourn from day to day, and compel the attendance of absent members, in such manner, and under such penalties, as each house shall provide. Sect. 15. Each house may determine the rules of its own proceedings, punish its own members for disorderly behaviour, and with the concurrence of two-thirds of the members elected, expel a member; but no member shall be expelled a second time for the same offence. They shall each from time to time publish a journal of their proceedings, except such parts as, in their opinion, require secrecy; and the yeas and nays shall be entered on the journal, at the desire of any five members. Sect. 16.

5. The doors of each house while in session, or in a committee of the whole, shall be kept open, except in cases which may require secrecy; and each house may punish by fine and imprisonment, any person, not a member, who shall be guilty of disrespect to the house, by any disorderly or contemptuous behaviour in their pre-

sence, during their session; but such imprisonment shall not extend beyond the final adjournment of that session. Sect. 17.

6. Bills may originate in either house, and be amended or rejected in the other; and every bill shall be read on three different days in each house, unless two-thirds of the house where the same is pending shall dispense with the rules: and every bill having passed both houses shall be signed by the president of the senate, and the speaker of the house of representatives. Sect. 81.

7. Whenever an officer, civil or military, shall be appointed by the joint concurrent vote of both houses, or by the separate vote of either house of the general assembly, the vote shall be taken *viva voce*, and entered on the journal. Sect. 19.

8. The senators and representatives shall, in all cases except treason, felony, or breach of the peace, be privileged from arrest, during the session of the general assembly, and for fifteen days before the commencement and after the termination of each session; and for any speech or debate in either house, they shall not be questioned in any other place. Sect. 20.

9. The members of the general assembly shall severally receive, from the public treasury, compensation for their services, which may be increased or diminished; but no alteration of such compensation of members shall take effect during the session at which it is made. Sect. 21.

10.—1. The *senate* shall never consist of less than seventeen nor more than thirty-three members. Art. 4, Sect. 31. The members shall be chosen for four years, by the qualified electors of the several districts. Art. 4, Sect. 5. No person shall be a senator who shall not have attained the age of thirty years; who shall not be a free white male citizen of the United States; who shall not have been an inhabitant of this state for one year; and who shall not, at the time of his election, have an actual residence in the district he may be chosen to represent. Art. 4, Sect. 6.

11. All impeachments shall be tried by the senate; and when sitting for that purpose, the senators shall be on oath or affirmation to do justice according to law and evidence. When the governor shall be tried, the chief justice of the supreme court shall preside; and no person shall be convicted without the concurrence of two-thirds of the senators elected. Art. 4, Sect. 27.

12.—2. The *house of representatives* shall consist of not less than fifty-four, nor more than one hundred representatives, to be apportioned among the several counties in this state, according to the number of free white male inhabitants therein, taking five hundred as the ratio, until the number of representatives amounts to seventy-five; and when they amount to seventy-five, they shall not be further increased until the population of the state amounts to five hundred thousand souls. Provided that each county now organized shall, although its population may not give the existing ratio, always be entitled to one representative. The members are chosen every second year, by the qualified electors of the several counties. Art. 4, Sect. 2.

13. The qualification of an elector is as follows: he must 1, be a free, white male citizen of the United States; 2, have attained the age of twenty-one years; 3, have been a citizen of this state six months; 4, he must actually reside in the county, or district where he votes for an office made elective under this state or the United States. But no soldier, seaman, or marine, in the army of the United States, shall be entitled to vote at any election within this state. Art. 4, Sect. 2.

14. No person shall be a member of the house of representatives, who shall not have attained the age of twenty-five years; who shall not be a free, white male citizen of the United States; who shall not have been an inhabitant of this state one year; and who shall not, at the time of his election, have an actual residence in the county he may be chosen to represent. Art. 4, Sect. 4.

15. The house of representatives shall have the sole power of impeachment. Art. 4, Sect. 27.

16.—§ 2. The *supreme executive* power of this state is vested in a chief magistrate, who is styled "The Governor of the State of Arkansas." Art. 5, Sect. 1.

17.—1. He is elected by the electors of the representatives.

18.—2. He must be thirty years of age, a native born citizen of Arkansas, or a native born citizen of the United States, or a resident of Arkansas ten years previous to the adoption of this constitution, if not a native of the United States; and shall have been a resident of the same at least four years next before his election. Art. 4, s. 4.

19.—3. The governor holds his office for

the term of four years from the time of his installation, and until his successor shall be duly qualified; but he is not eligible for more than eight years in any term of twelve years. Art. 5, sect. 4.

20.—4. His principal duties are enumerated in the fifth article of the constitution, and are as follows: He shall be commander-in-chief of the army of this state, and of the militia thereof, except when they shall be called into the service of the United States; s. 6. He may require information, in writing, from the officers of the executive department, on any subject relating to the duties of their respective offices; s. 7. He may by proclamation, on extraordinary occasions, convene the general assembly, at the seat of government, or at a different place, if that shall have become, since their last adjournment, dangerous from an enemy, or from contagious diseases. In case of disagreement between the two houses, with respect to the time of adjournment, he may adjourn them to such time as he shall think proper, not beyond the day of the next meeting of the general assembly; s. 8. He shall, from time to time, give to the general assembly information of the state of the government, and recommend to their consideration such measures as he may deem expedient; s. 9. He shall take care that the laws be faithfully executed; s. 10. In all criminal and penal cases, except those of treason and impeachment, he shall have power to grant pardons, after conviction, and remit fines and forfeitures, under such rules and regulations as shall be prescribed by law. In cases of treason, he shall have power, by and with the advice and consent of the senate, to grant reprieves and pardons; and he may, in the recess of the senate, respite the sentence until the end of the next session of the general assembly; s. 11. He is the keeper of the seal of the state, which is to be used by him officially; s. 12. Every bill which shall have passed both houses, shall be presented to the governor. If he approve, he shall sign it; but if he shall not approve it, he shall return it, with his objections, to the house in which it shall have originated, who shall enter his objections at large upon their journals, and proceed to reconsider it. If, after such reconsideration, a majority of the whole number elected to that house shall agree to pass the bill, it shall be sent, with the objections, to the other house, by which, likewise, it shall be reconsidered; and if approved by a majority of the whole number elected to that house, it shall be a law; but in such cases, the votes of both houses shall be determined by yeas and nays; and the names of persons voting for or against the bill, shall be entered on the journals of each house respectively. If the bill shall not be returned by the governor within three days, Sundays excepted, after it shall have been presented to him, the same shall be a law, in like manner as if he had signed it, unless the general assembly, by their adjournment, prevent its return; in such case it shall not be a law; s. 16. 5. In case of the impeachment of the governor, his removal from office, death, refusal to qualify, or absence from the state, the president of the senate shall exercise all the authority appertaining to the office of governor, until another governor shall have been elected and qualified, or until the governor absent or impeached, shall return or be acquitted; s. 18. If, during the vacancy of the office of governor, the president of the senate shall be impeached, removed from office, refuse to qualify, resign, die, or be absent from the state, the speaker of the house of representatives shall, in like manner, administer the government; s. 19.

21.—§ 3. The *judicial* power of this state is vested by the sixth article of the constitution, as follows:

22.—1. The judicial power of this state shall be vested in one supreme court, in circuit courts, in county courts, and in justices of the peace. The general assembly may also vest such jurisdiction as may be deemed necessary, in corporation courts; and, when they deem it expedient, may establish courts of chancery.

23.—2. The supreme court shall be composed of three judges, one of whom shall be styled chief justice, any two of whom shall constitute a quorum; and the concurrence of any two of the said judges shall, in every case, be necessary to a decision. The supreme court, except in cases otherwise directed by this constitution, shall have appellate jurisdiction only, which shall be co-extensive with the state, under such rules and regulations as may, from time to time, be prescribed by law; it shall have a general superintending control over all inferior and other courts of law and equity; it shall have power to issue writs of error and supersedeas, certiorari and *habeas co pus*, *mandamus*, and *quo warranto*, and other remedial writs, and to hear and determine the same; said judges shall be conservators of the peace throughout the state, and shall severally have power to issue any of the aforesaid writs.

24.—3. The circuit court shall have jurisdiction over all criminal cases which shall not be otherwise provided for by law; and exclusive original jurisdiction of all crimes amounting to felony at common law; and original jurisdiction of all civil cases which shall not be cognizable before justices of the peace, until otherwise directed by the general assembly; and original jurisdiction in all matters of contract, when the sum in controversy is over one hundred dollars. It shall hold its terms at such place in each county, as may be by law directed.

25.—4. The state shall be divided into convenient circuits, each to consist of not less than five, nor more than seven counties contiguous to each other, for each of which a judge shall be elected, who, during his continuance in office, shall reside and be a conservator of the peace within the circuit for which he shall have been elected.

26.—5. The circuit courts shall exercise a superintending control over the county courts, and over justices of the peace, in each county in their respective circuits; and shall have power to issue all the necessary writs to carry into effect their general and specific powers.

27.—6. Until the general assembly shall deem it expedient to establish courts of chancery, the circuit courts shall have jurisdiction in matters of equity, subject to appeal to the supreme court, in such manner as may be prescribed by law.

28.—7. The general assembly shall, by joint vote of both houses, elect the judges of the supreme and circuit courts, a majority of the whole number in joint vote being necessary to a choice. The judges of the supreme court shall be at least thirty years of age; they shall hold their offices for eight years from the date of their commissions. The judges of the circuit courts shall be at least twenty-five years of age, and shall be elected for the term of four years from the date of their commissions.

29.—8. There shall be established in each county, a court to be holden by the justices of the peace, and called the county court, which shall have jurisdiction in all matters relating to county taxes, disbursements of money for county purposes, and in every other case that may be necessary to the internal improvement and local concerns of the respective counties.

30.—9. There shall be elected by the justices of the peace of the respective counties, a presiding judge of the county court, to be commissioned by the governor, and hold his office for the term of two years, and until his successor is elected or qualified. He shall, in addition to the duties that may be required of him by law, as presiding judge of the county court, be a judge of the court of probate, and have such jurisdiction in matters relative to the estates of deceased persons, executors, administrators, and guardians, as may be prescribed by law, until otherwise directed by the general assembly.

31.—10. No judge shall preside in the trial of any cause, in the event of which he may be interested, or where either of the parties shall be connected with him by affinity or consanguinity, within such degrees as may be prescribed by law, or in which he shall have been of counsel, or have presided in any inferior court, except by consent of all the parties.

32.—11. The qualified voters in each township shall elect the justices of the peace for their respective townships. For every fifty voters there may be elected one justice of the peace, provided, that each township, however small, shall have two justices of the peace. Justices of the peace shall be elected for two years, and shall be commissioned by the governor, and reside in the townships for which they shall have been elected, during their continuance in office. They shall have individually, or two or more of them jointly, exclusive original jurisdiction in all matters of contract, except in actions of covenant, where the sum in controversy is of one hundred dollars and under. Justices of the peace shall in no case have jurisdiction to try and determine any criminal case or penal offence against the state; but may sit as examining courts, and commit, discharge, or recognize to the court having jurisdiction, for further trial, offenders against the peace. For the foregoing purposes they shall have power to issue all necessary process; they shall also have power to bind to keep the peace, or for good behaviour.

ARM OF THE SEA. Lord Coke defines an arm of the sea to be where the sea or tide flows or reflows. Constable's Case, 5 Co. 107. This term includes bays, roads, creeks, coves, ports, and rivers where the water flows and reflows, whether it be salt or fresh. Ang. Tide Wat. 61. Vide *Creek; Haven; Navigable; Port; Reliction; River; Road.*

ARMISTICE. A cessation of hostilities between belligerent nations for a considerable time. It is either partial and local, or general. It differs from a mere suspension of arms which takes place to enable the two armies to bury their dead, their chiefs to hold conferences or pourparlers, and the like. Vattel, Droit des Gens, liv. 3, c. 16, § 233. The terms truce, (q. v.) and armistice, are sometimes used in the same sense. Vide *Truce.*

ARMS. Any thing that a man wears for his defence, or takes in his hands, or uses in his anger, to cast at, or strike at another. Co. Litt. 161 b, 162 a; Crompt. Just. P. 65; Cunn. Dict. h. t.

2. The Constitution of the United States, Amendm. art. 2, declares, that "a well regulated militia being necessary to the security of a free state, the right of the people to keep and bear arms shall not be infringed." In Kentucky, a statute "to prevent persons from wearing concealed arms," has been declared to be unconstitutional; 2 Litt. R. 90; while in Indiana a similar statute has been holden valid and constitutional. 3 Blackf. R. 229. Vide Story, Const. § 1889, 1890; Amer. Citizen, 176; 1 Tuck. Black. App. 300; Rawle on Const. 125.

ARMS, *in heraldry.* Signs of arms, or drawings, painted on shields, banners, and the like. The arms of the United States are described in the Resolution of Congress, of June 20, 1782. Vide *Seal of the United States.*

ARPENT. A quantity of land containing a French acre. 4 Hall's Law Journal, 518.

ARPENTATOR, from *arpent.* A measurer or surveyor of land.

ARRAIGNMENT, *crim. law practice.* Signifies the calling of the defendant to the bar of the court, to answer the accusation contained in the indictment. It consists of three parts.

2.—1. Calling the defendant to the bar by his name, and commanding him to hold up his hand; this is done for the purpose of completely identifying the prisoner as the person named in the indictment; the holding up his hand is not, however, indispensable, for if the prisoner should refuse to do so, he may be identified by any admission, that he is the person intended. 1 Bl. Rep. 3.

3.—2. The reading of the indictment to enable him fully to understand the charge to be produced against him. The mode in which it is read is, after saying, "A B, hold up your hand," to proceed, "you stand indicted by the name of A B, late of, &c., for that you, on, &c.," and then go through the whole of the indictment.

4.—3. After this is concluded, the clerk proceeds to the third part, by adding, "How say you, A B, are you guilty or not guilty?' Upon this, if the prisoner confesses the charge, the confession is recorded, and nothing further is done till judgment; if, on the contrary, he answers "not guilty," that plea is entered for him, and the clerk or attorney general, replies that he is guilty; when an issue is formed.

Vide generally, Dalt. J. h. t.; Burn's J. h. t.; Williams; J. h. t.; 4 Bl. Com. 322; Harg. St. Tr. 4 vol. 777, 661; 2 Hale, 219; Cro. C. C. 7; 1 Chit. Cr. Law, 414.

ARRAMEUR, *maritime law.* The name of an ancient officer of a port, whose business was to load and unload vessels.

2. In the Laws of Oleron, art 11, (published in English in the App. to 1 Pet. Adm. R. xxv.) some account of arrameurs will be found in these words: "There were formerly, in several ports of *Guyenne,* certain officers called *arrameurs,* or stowers, who were master-carpenters by profession, and were paid by the merchants, who loaded the ship. Their business was to dispose right, and stow closely, all goods in casks, bales, boxes, bundles or otherwise; to balance both sides, to fill up the vacant spaces, and manage every thing to the best advantage. It was not but that the greatest part of the ship's crew understood this as well as these stowers; but they would not meddle with it, nor undertake it, to avoid falling under the merchant's displeasure, or being accountable for any ill accident that might happen by that means. There were also *sacquiers,* who were very ancient officers, as may be seen in the 14th book of the Theodosian code, *Unica de Saccariis Portus Romæ,* lib. 14. Their business was to load and unload vessels loaded with salt, corn, or fish, to prevent the ship's crew defrauding the merchant by false tale, or cheating him of his merchandize otherwise." See *Sacquier; Stevedore.*

ARRAS, *Span. law.* The property contributed by the husband, ad sustinenda onera matrimonii, is called *arras.* The husband is under no obligation to give arras, but it is a donation purely voluntary. He is not permitted to give in *arras* more than a tenth of his property. The *arras* is the exclusive property of the wife, subject to the husband's usufruct during his life. Burge on the Confl. of Laws, 417.

2. By arras is also understood the donation which the husband makes to his wife, by reason or on account of marriage, and in consideration of the *dote*, or portion, which he receives from her. Aso & Man. Inst. B. 1, t. 7, c. 3.

ARRAY, *practice.* The whole body of jurors summoned to attend a court, as they are *arrayed* or arranged on the panel. Vide *Challenges*, and Dane's Ab. Index, h. t.; 1 Chit. Cr. Law, 536; Com. Dig. Challenge, B.

ARREARAGE. Money remaining unpaid after it becomes due; as rent unpaid; interest remaining due; Pow. Mortgages, Index, h. t.; a sum of money remaining in the hands of an accountant. Merl. Rép. h. t.; Dane's Ab. Index, h. t.

ARREST. To stop; to seize; to deprive one of his liberty by virtue of legal authority.

ARREST IN CIVIL CASES, *practice.* An arrest is the apprehension of a person by virtue of a lawful authority, to answer the demand against him in a civil action.

2. To constitute an arrest, no actual force or manual touching of the body is requisite; it is sufficient if the party be within the power of the officer, and submit to the arrest. 2 N. H. Rep. 318; 8 Dana, 190; 3 Harring. 416; 1 Baldw. 239; Harper, 453; 8 Greenl. 127; 1 Wend. 215; 2 Blackf. 294. Bare words, however, will not make an arrest, without laying hold of the person or otherwise confining him. 2 H. P. C. 129; 1 Burn's Just. 148; 1 Salk. 79. It is necessarily an assault, but not necessarily a battery. Cases Temp. Hardw. 300.

3. Arrests are made either on mesne or final process. 1. An arrest on mesne process is made in order that the defendant shall answer after judgment, to satisfy the claim of the plaintiff; on being arrested, the defendant is entitled to be liberated on giving sufficient bail, which the officer is bound to take. 2. When the arrest is on final process, as a ca. sa., the defendant cannot generally be discharged on bail; and his discharge is considered as an escape. Vide, generally, Yelv. 29, a, note; 3 Bl. Com. 288, n.; 1 Sup. to Ves. Jr. 374; Wats. on Sher. 87; 11 East, 440; 18 E. C. L. R. 169, note.

4. In all governments there are persons who are privileged from arrest in civil cases. In the United States this privilege continues generally while the defendant remains invested with a particular character. Members of congress and of the state legislatures are exempted while attending the respective assemblies to which they belong; parties and witnesses, while lawfully attending court; electors, while attending a public election; ambassadors and other foreign ministers; insolvent debtors, when they have been lawfully discharged; married women, when sued upon their contracts, are generally privileged; and executors and administrators, when sued in their representative characters, generally enjoy the same privilege. The privilege in favor of members of congress, or of the state legislatures, of electors, and of parties and witnesses in a cause, extend to the time of going to, remaining at, and returning from, the places to which they are thus legally called.

5. The code of civil practice of Louisiana enacts as follows, namely: Art. 210. The arrest is one of the means which the law gives the creditor to secure the person of his debtor while the suit is pending, or to compel him to give security for his appearance after judgment. Art. 211. Minors of both sexes, whether emancipated or not, interdicted persons, and women, married or single, cannot be arrested. Art. 212. Any creditor, whose debtor is about to leave the state, even for a limited time, without leaving in it sufficient property to satisfy the judgment which he expects to obtain in the suit he intends to bring against him, may have the person of such debtor arrested and confined until he shall give sufficient security that he shall not depart from the state without the leave of the court. Art. 213. Such arrest may be ordered in all demands brought for a debt, whether liquidated or not, when the term of payment has expired, and even for damages for any injury sustained by the plaintiff in either his person or property. Art. 214. Previous to obtaining an order of arrest against his debtor, to compel him to give sufficient security that he shall not depart from the state, the creditor must swear in the petition which he presents to that effect to any competent judge, that the debt, or the damages which he claims, and the amount of which he specifies, is really due to him, and that he verily believes that the defendant is about to remove from the state, without leaving in it

sufficient property to satisfy his demand; and lastly, that he does not take this oath with the intention of vexing the defendant, but only in order to secure his demand. Art. 215. The oath prescribed in the preceding article, may be taken either by the creditor himself, or in his absence, by his attorney in fact or his agent, provided either the one or the other can swear to the debt from his personal and direct knowledge of its being due, and not by what he may know or have learned from the creditor he represents. Art. 216. The oath which the creditor is required to take of the existence and nature of the debt of which he claims payment, in the cases provided in the two preceding articles, may be taken either before any judge or justice of the peace of the place where the court is held, before which he sues, or before the judge of any other place, provided the signature of such judge be proved or duly authenticated. Vide *Auter action pendant; Lis pendens: Privilege; Rights.*

ARREST, *in criminal cases.* The apprehending or detaining of the person, in order to be forthcoming to answer an alleged or suspected crime. The word *arrest* is more properly used in civil cases, and *apprehension* in criminal. A man is arrested under a *capias ad respondendum*, apprehended under a warrant charging him with a larceny.

2. It will be convenient to consider, 1, who may be arrested; 2, for what crimes; 3, at what time; 4, in what places; 5, by whom and by what authority.

3.—1. *Who may be arrested.* Generally all persons properly accused of a crime or misdemeanor, may be arrested; by the laws of the United States, ambassadors (q. v.) and other public ministers are exempt from arrest.

4.—2. *For what offences an arrest may be made.* It may be made for treason, felony, breach of the peace, or other misdemeanor.

5.—3. *At what time.* An arrest may be made in the night as well as in the day time; and for treasons, felonies, and breaches of the peace, on Sunday as well as on other days. It may be made before as well as after indictment found. Wallace's R. 23.

6.—4. *In what places.* No place affords protection to offenders against the criminal law; a man may therefore be arrested in his own house, (q. v.) which may be broken into for the purpose of making the arrest.

7.—5. *Who may arrest and by what authority.* An offender may be arrested either without a warrant or with a warrant. First, an arrest may be made without a warrant by a private individual or by a peace officer. *Private* individuals are enjoined by law to arrest an offender when present at the time a felony is committed, or a dangerous wound given. 11 Johns. R. 486; and vide Hawk. B. 1, c. 12, s. 1; c. 13, s. 7, 8; 4 Bl. Com. 292; 1 Hale, 587; Com. Dig. Imprisonment, H 4; Bac. Ab. Trespass, D 3. *Peace officers* may, a fortiori, make an arrest for a crime or misdemeanor committed in their view, without any warrant. 8 Serg. & R. 47. An arrest may therefore be made by a constable, (q. v.) a justice of the peace, (q. v.) sheriff, (q. v.) or coroner. (q. v.) Secondly, an arrest may be made by virtue of a warrant, (q. v.) which is the proper course when the circumstances of the case will permit it. Vide, generally, 1 Chit. Cr. Law, 11 to 71; Russ. on Cr. Index, h. t.

ARREST OF JUDGMENT. The act of a court by which the judges refuse to give judgment, because upon the face of the record, it appears that the plaintiff is not entitled to it. See *Judgment, arrest of.*

ARRESTANDIS *bonis ne dissipentur.* In the English law, a writ for him whose cattle or goods, being taken during a controversy, are likely to be wasted and consumed.

ARRESTEE, *law of Scotland.* He in whose hands a debt, or property in his possession, has been arrested by a regular arrestment. If, in contempt of the arrestment, he shall make payment of the sum, or deliver the goods arrested to the common debtor, he is not only liable criminally for breach of the arrestment, but he must pay the debt again to the arrester. Ersk. Pr. L. Scot. 3, 6, 6.

ARRESTER, *law of Scotland.* One who sues out and obtains an arrestment of his debtor's goods or movable obligations. Ersk. Pr. L. Scot. 3, 6, 1.

ARRESTMENT, *Scotch law.* By this term is sometimes meant the securing of a criminal's person till trial, or that of a debtor till he give security judicio sisti. Ersk. Pr. L. Scot. 1, 2, 12. It is also the order of a judge, by which he who is debtor in a movable obligation to the arrester's debtor, is prohibited to make payment or delivery till the debt due to the arrester be paid or secured. Ersk. Pr. L. Scot. 3, 6, 1. See *Attachment, foreign.* Where arrestment proceeds on a depending action, it may be loosed by the common debtor's giving security to the arrester for his debt, in the event it shall be found due. Id. 3, 6, 7.

ARRET, *French law.* An arrêt is a judgment, sentence, or decree of a court of competent jurisdiction. *Saisie-arrêt* is an attachment of property in the hands of a third person. Code of Pract. of Lo. art. 209.

ARRETTED, *arrectatus*, i. e. *ad rectum vocatus.* Convened before a judge and charged with a crime. *Ad rectum malefactorem*, is, according to Bracton, to have a malefactor forthcoming to be put on his trial. Sometimes it is used for imputed or laid to his charge; as, no folly may be *arretted* to any one under age. Bract. l. 3, tr. 2, c. 10; Cunn. Dict. h. t.

ARRHÆ, *contracts, in the civil law.* Money or other valuable things given by the buyer to the seller, for the purpose of evidencing the contract; earnest.

2. There are two kinds of arrhæ; one kind given when a contract has only been proposed; the other when a sale has actually taken place. Those which are given when a bargain has been merely proposed, before it has been concluded, form the matter of the contract, by which he who gives the arrhæ consents and agrees to lose them, and to transfer the title to them in the opposite party, in case he should refuse to complete the proposed bargain; and the receiver of arrhæ is obliged on his part to return double the amount to the giver of them in case he should fail to complete his part of the contract. Poth. Contr. de Vente, n. 498. After the contract of sale has been completed, the purchaser usually gives arrhæ as evidence that the contract has been perfected. Arrhæ are therefore defined quod ante pretium datur, et fidem fecit contractus, facti totiusque pecuniæ solvendæ. Id. n. 506; Code, 4, 45, 2.

TO ARRIVE. To come to a particular place; to reach a particular or certain place; as, the ship United States arrived in New York. See 1 Marsh. Dec. 411.

ARROGATION, *civil law.* Signifies nearly the same as adoption; the only difference between them is this, that adoption was of a person under full age; but as arrogation required the person arrogated, sui juris, no one could be arrogated till he was of full age. Dig. 1, 7, 5; Inst. 1, 11, 3; 1 Brown's Civ. Law, 119.

ARSER IN LE MAIN. Burning in the hand. This punishment was inflicted on those who received the benefit of clergy. Terms de la Ley.

ARSON, *criminal law.* At common law an offence of the degree of felony; and is defined by Lord Coke to be the malicious and voluntary burning of the house of another, by night or day. 3 Inst. 66.

2. In order to make this crime complete, there must be, 1st, a burning of the house, or some part of it; it is sufficient if any part be consumed, however small it may be. 9 C. & P. 45; 38 E. C. L. R. 29; 16 Mass. 105. 2d. The house burnt must belong to another; but if a man set fire to his own house with a view to burn his neighbor's, and does so, it is at least a great misdemeanor, if not a felony. 1 Hale, P. C. 568; 2 East, P. C. 1027; 2 Russ. 487. 3d. The burning must have been both malicious and willful.

3. The offence of arson at common law, does not extend further than the burning of the *house* of another. By statute this crime is greatly enlarged in some of the states, as in Pennsylvania, where it is extended to the burning of any barn or outhouse having hay or grain therein; any barrack, rick or stack of hay, grain, or bark; any public buildings, church or meeting-house, college, school or library. Act 23d April, 1829; 2 Russell on Crimes, 486; 1 Hawk. P. C. c. 39; 4 Bl. Com. 220; 2 East, P. C. c. 21, s. 1, p. 1015; 16 John. R. 203; 16 Mass. 105. As to the extension of the offence by the laws of the United States, see stat. 1825, c. 276, 3 Story's L. U. S. 1999.

ARSURA. The trial of money by fire after it was coined. This word is obsolete.

ART. The power of doing something not taught by nature or instinct. Johnson. Eunomus defines art to be a collection of certain rules for doing anything in a set form. Dial. 2, p. 74. The Dictionnaire des Sciences Médicales, h. v., defines it in nearly the same terms.

2. The arts are divided into mechanical and liberal arts. The mechanical arts are those which require more bodily than mental labor; they are usually called trades, and those who pursue them are called artisans or mechanics. The liberal are those which have for the sole or principal object, works of the mind, and those who are engaged in them are called artists. Pard. Dr. Com. n. 35.

3. The act of Congress of July 4, 1836, s. 6, in describing the subjects of patents,

uses the term *art*. The sense of this word in its usual acceptation is perhaps too comprehensive. The thing to be patented is not a mere elementary principle, or intellectual discovery, but a principle put in practice, and applied to some art, machine, manufacture, or composition of matter. 4 Mason, 1.

4. Copper-plate printing on the back of a bank note, is an art for which a patent may be granted. 4 Wash. C. C. R. 9.

Art and part, *Scotch law*. Where one is accessory to a crime committed by another; a person may be guilty, art and part, either by giving advice or counsel to commit the crime; or, 2, by giving warrant or mandate to commit it; or, 3, by actually assisting the criminal in the execution.

2. In the more atrocious crimes, it seems agreed, that the adviser is equally punishable with the criminal; and that in the slighter offences, the circumstances arising from the adviser's lesser age, the jocular or careless manner of giving the advice, &c., may be received as pleas for softening the punishment.

3. One who gives a mandate to commit a crime, as he is the first spring of the action, seems more guilty than the person employed as the instrument in executing it.

4. Assistance may be given to the committer of a crime, not only in the actual execution, but previous to it, by furnishing him, with a criminal intent, with poison, arms, or other means of perpetrating it. That sort of assistance which is not given till after the criminal act, and which is commonly called abetting, though it be itself criminal, does not infer art and part of the principal crime. Ersk. Pr. L. Scot. 4, 4, 4; Mack. Cr. Treat. tit. Art and Part.

ARTICLES. A division in some books. In agreements and other writings, for the sake of perspicuity, the subjects are divided into parts, paragraphs, or articles.

Articles, *chan. practice*. An instrument in writing, filed by a party to a proceeding in chancery, containing reasons why a witness in the cause should be discredited.

2. As to the matter which ought to be contained in these articles, Lord Eldon gave some general directions in the case of Carlos *v.* Brook, 10 Ves. 49. "The court," says he, "attending with great caution to an application to permit any witness to be examined after publication, has held, where the proposition was to examine a witness to credit, that the examination is either to be confined to general credit; that is, by producing witnesses to swear, that the person is not to be believed upon his oath; or, if you find him swearing to a matter, not to issue in the cause, (and therefore not thought material to the merits,) in that case, as the witness is not produced to vary the case in evidence by testimony that relates to matters in issue, but is to speak only to the truth or want of veracity, with which a witness had spoken to a fact not in issue, there is no danger in permitting him to state that such fact, not put in issue, is false; and, for the purpose of discrediting a witness, the court has not considered itself at liberty to sanction such a proceeding as an examination, to destroy the credit of another witness, who had deposed only to points put in issue. In Purcell *v.* M'Namara, it was agreed that after publication it was competent to examine any witness to the point, whether he would believe that man upon his oath. It is not competent, even at law, to ask the ground of that opinion; but the general question only is permitted. In Purcell *v.* M'Namara, the witness went into the history of his whole life; and as to his solvency, &c. It was not at all put at issue whether he had been insolvent, or had compounded with his creditors; but, having sworn the contrary, they proved by witnesses, that he, who had sworn to a matter not in issue, had sworn falsely to that fact; and that he had been insolvent, and had compounded with his creditors; and it would be lamentable, if the court could not find means of getting at it; for he could not be indicted for perjury, though swearing falsely, the fact not being material. The rule is, in general cases the cause is heard upon evidence given before publication; but that you may examine after publication, provided you examine to credit only, and do not go to matters in issue in the cause, or in contradiction of them, under pretence of examining to credit only. Those depositions," he continued, "appear to me material to what is in issue in the cause; and therefore must be suppressed." See a form of articles in Gresl. Eq. Ev. 140, 141; and also 8 Ves. 327; 9 Ves. 145; 1 S. & S. 469.

Articles, *eccl. law*. A complaint in the form of a libel, exhibited to an ecclesiastical court.

Articles of agreement, *contracts*. Relate either to real or personal estate, or to both. An article is a memorandum or minute of an agreement, reduced to writing to make some future disposition or modification of property; and such an instrument will create a trust or equitable estate, of which a specific performance will be decreed in chancery. Cruise on Real Pr. tit. 32, c. 1, s. 31. And see Id. tit. 12, c. 1.

2. This instrument should contain: 1, the name and character of the parties; 2, the subject-matter of the contracts; 3, the covenants which each of the parties bind themselves to perform; 4, the date; 5, the signatures of the parties.

3.—1. The parties should be named, and their addition should also be mentioned, in order to identify them. It should also be stated which persons are of the first, second, or other part. A confusion, in this respect, may occasion difficulties.

4.—2. The subject-matter of the contract ought to be set out in clear and explicit language, and the time and place of the performance of the agreement ought to be mentioned; and, when goods are to be delivered, it ought to be provided at whose expense they shall be removed, for there is a difference in the delivery of light and bulky articles. The seller of bulky articles is not in general bound to deliver them unless he agrees to do so. 5 S. & R. 19; 12 Mass. 300; 4 Shepl. 49.

5.—3. The covenants to be performed by each party should be specially and correctly stated, as a mistake in this respect leads to difficulties which might have been obviated had they been properly drawn.

6.—4. The instrument should be truly dated.

7.—5. It should be signed by the parties or their agents. When signed by an agent he should state his authority, and sign his principal's name, and then his own, as, A B, by his agent or attorney C D.

Articles of Confederation. The compact which was made by the original thirteen states of the United States of America, bore the name of the "Articles of Confederation and perpetual union between the states of New Hampshire, Massachusetts Bay, Rhode Island and Providence Plantations, Connecticut, New York, New Jersey, Pennsylvania, Delaware, Maryland, Virginia, North Carolina, South Carolina, and Georgia." It was adopted and went into force on the first day of March, 1781, and remained as the supreme law until the first Wednesday of March, 1789. 5 Wheat. R. 420. The following analysis of this celebrated instrument is copied from Judge Story's Commentaries on the Constitution of the United States, Book 2, c. 3.

2. "In pursuance of the design already announced, it is now proposed to give an analysis of the articles of confederation, or, as they are denominated in the instrument itself, the 'Articles of Confederation and Perpetual Union between the States,' as they were finally adopted by the thirteen states in 1781.

3. "The style of the confederacy was, by the first article, declared to be, 'The United States of America.' The second article declared, that each state retained its sovereignty, freedom, and independence, and every power, jurisdiction and right, which was not by this confederation *expressly* delegated to the United States, in congress assembled. The third article declared, that the states severally entered into a firm league of friendship with each other, for their common defence, the security of their liberties, and their mutual and general welfare; binding themselves to assist each other against all force offered to, or attacks made upon them, or any of them, on account of religion, sovereignty, trade, or any other pretence whatever. The fourth article declared, that the free inhabitants of each of the states, (vagabonds and fugitives from justice excepted,) should be entitled to all the privileges of free citizens in the several states; that the people of each state should have free ingress and regress to and from any other state, and should enjoy all the privileges of trade and commerce, subject to the same duties and restrictions, as the inhabitants; that fugitives from justice should, upon the demand of the executive of the state, from which they fled, be delivered up; and that full faith and credit should be given, in each of the states, to the records, acts, and judicial proceedings of the courts and magistrates of every other state.

4. "Having thus provided for the security and intercourse of the states, the next article (5th) provided for the organization of a general congress, declaring that delegates should be chosen in such manner, as the legislature of each state should direct; to meet in congress on the first Monday in every year, with a power, reserved to each state, to recall any or all of the delegates, and to send others in their stead. No state was to be represented in congress by less

than two, nor more than seven members. No delegate was eligible for more than three, in any term of six years; and no delegate was capable of holding any office of emolument under the United States. Each state was to maintain its own delegates; and, in determining questions in congress, was to have one vote. Freedom of speech and debate in congress was not to be impeached or questioned in any other place; and the members were to be protected from arrest and imprisonment, during the time of their going to and from, and attendance on congress, except for treason, felony, or breach of the peace.

5. "By subsequent articles, congress was invested with the sole and exclusive right and power of determining on peace and war, unless in case of an invasion of a state by enemies, or an imminent danger of an invasion by Indians; of sending and receiving ambassadors; entering into treaties and alliances, under certain limitations, as to treaties of commerce; of establishing rules for deciding all cases of capture on land and water, and for the division and appropriation of prizes taken by the land or naval forces, in the service of the United States; of granting letters of marque and reprisal in times of peace; of appointing courts for the trial of piracies and felonies committed on the high seas; and of establishing courts for receiving and finally determining appeals in all cases of captures.

6. "Congress was also invested with power to decide in the last resort, on appeal, all disputes and differences between two or more states concerning boundary, jurisdiction, or any other cause whatsoever; and the mode of exercising that authority was specially prescribed. And all controversies concerning the private right of soil, claimed under different grants of two or more states before the settlement of their jurisdiction, were to be finally determined in the same manner, upon the petition of either of the grantees. But no state was to be deprived of territory for the benefit of the United States.

7. "Congress was also invested with the sole and exclusive right and power of regulating the alloy and value of coin struck by their own authority, or that of the United States; of fixing the standard of weights and measures throughout the United States; of regulating the trade and managing all affairs with the Indians, not members of any of the states, provided, that the legislative right of any state within its own limits should not be infringed or violated; of establishing and regulating post-offices from one state to another, and exacting postage to defray the expenses; of appointing all officers of the land forces in the service of the United States, except regimental officers; of appointing all officers of the naval forces, and commissioning all officers whatsoever in the service of the United States; and of making rules for the government and regulation of the land and naval forces, and directing their operations.

8. "Congress was also invested with authority to appoint a committee of the states to sit in the recess of congress, and to consist of one delegate from each state, and other committees and civil officers, to manage the general affairs under their direction; to appoint one of their number to preside, but no person was to serve in the office of president more than one year in the term of three years; to ascertain the necessary sums for the public service, and to appropriate the same for defraying the public expenses; to borrow money and emit bills on credit of the United States; to build and equip a navy; to agree upon the number of land forces, and make requisitions upon each state for its quota, in proportion to the number of white inhabitants in such state. The legislatures of each state were to appoint the regimental officers, raise the men, and clothe, arm, and equip them at the expense of the United States.

9. "Congress was also invested with power to adjourn for any time not exceeding six months, and to any place within the United States; and provision was made for the publication of its journal, and for entering the yeas and nays thereon, when desired by any delegate.

10. "Such were the powers confided in congress. But even these were greatly restricted in their exercise; for it was expressly provided, that congress should never engage in a war; nor grant letters of marque or reprisal in time of peace; nor enter into any treaties or alliances; nor coin money or regulate the value thereof; nor ascertain the sums or expenses necessary for the defence and welfare of the United States; nor emit bills; nor borrow money on the credit of the United States; nor appropriate money; nor agree upon the number of vessels of war to be built, or purchased; or the number of land or sea forces to be raised; nor appoint a commander-in-

chief of the army or navy; unless nine states should assent to the same. And no question on any other point, except for adjourning from day to day, was to be determined, except by vote of the majority of the states.

11. "The committee of the states or any nine of them, were authorized in the recess of congress to exercise such powers, as congress, with the assent of nine states, should think it expedient to vest them with, except such powers for the exercise of which, by the articles of confederation, the assent of nine states was required, which could not be thus delegated.

12. "It was further provided, that all bills of credit, moneys borrowed, and debts contracted by or under the authority of congress before the confederation, should be a charge against the United States; that when land forces were raised by any state for the common defence, all officers of or under the rank of colonel should be appointed by the legislature of the state, or in such manner as the state should direct; and all vacancies should be filled up in the same manner; that all charges of war, and all other expenses for the common defence or general welfare, should be defrayed out of a common treasury, which should be supplied by the several states, in proportion to the value of the land within each state granted or surveyed, and the buildings and improvements thereon, to be estimated according to the mode prescribed by congress; and the taxes for that proportion were to be laid and levied by the legislatures of the states within the time agreed upon by congress.

13. "Certain prohibitions were laid upon the exercise of powers by the respective states. No state, without the consent of the United States, could send an embassy to, or receive an embassy from, or enter into, any treaty with any king, prince or state; nor could any person holding any office under the United States, or any of them, accept any present, emolument, office or title, from any foreign king, prince or state; nor could congress itself grant any title of nobility. No two states could enter into any treaty, confederation, or alliance with each other, without the consent of congress. No state could lay any imposts or duties, which might interfere with any proposed treaties. No vessels of war were to be kept up by any state in time of peace, except deemed necessary by congress for its defence, or trade; nor any body of forces, except such as should be deemed requisite by congress to garrison its forts, and necessary for its defence. But every state was required always to keep up a well regulated and disciplined militia, sufficiently armed and accoutred, and to be provided with suitable field-pieces, and tents, and arms, and amunition, and camp equipage. No state could engage in war without the consent of congress, unless actually invaded by enemies, or in danger of invasion by the Indians. Nor could any state grant commissions to any ships of war, nor letters of marque and reprisal, except after a declaration of war by congress, unless such state were infested by pirates, and then subject to the determination of congress. No state could prevent the removal of any property imported into any state to any other state, of which the owner was an inhabitant. And no imposition, duties, or restriction, could be laid by any state on the property of the United States or of either of them.

14. "There was also provision made for the admission of Canada into the Union, and of other colonies with the assent of nine states. And it was finally declared, that every state should abide by the determinations of congress on all questions submitted to it by the confederation; that the articles should be inviolably observed by every state; that *the union should be perpetual;* and that no alterations should be made in any of the articles, unless agreed to by congress, and confirmed by the legislatures of every state.

15. "Such is the substance of this celebrated instrument, under which the treaty of peace, acknowledging our independence, was negotiated, the war of the revolution concluded, and the union of the states maintained until the adoption of the present constitution."

ARTICLES OF IMPEACHMENT. An instrument which, in cases of impeachment, (q. v.) is used, and performs the same office which an indictment does in a common criminal case, is known by this name. These articles do not usually pursue the strict form and accuracy of an indictment. Wood. Lect. 40, p. 605; Foster, 389, 390; Com. Dig. Parliament, L 21. They are sometimes quite general in the form of the allegations, but always contain, or ought to contain, so much certainty, as to enable the party to put himself on the proper defence, and in case of an acquittal, to avail himself of it, as a bar to another impeachment. Additional articles may, perhaps, be exhibited at any stage of the prosecution. Story on the Const. § 806; Rawle on the Const. 216.

2. The answer to articles of impeachment is exempted from observing great strictness of form; and it may contain arguments as well as facts. It is usual to give a full and particular answer to each article of the accusation. Story, § 808.

ARTICLES OF PARTNERSHIP. The name given to an instrument of writing by which the parties enter into a partnership, upon the conditions therein mentioned. This instrument generally contains certain provisions which it is the object here to point out.

2. But before proceeding more particularly to the consideration of the subject, it will be proper to observe that sometimes preliminary agreements to enter into a partnership are formed, and that questions, not unfrequently, arise as to their effects. These are not partnerships, but agreements to enter into partnership at a future time. When such an agreement has been broken, the parties may apply for redress to a court of law, where damages will be given, as a compensation. Application is sometimes made to courts of equity for their more efficient aid to compel a specific performance. In general these courts will not entertain bills for specific performance of such preliminary contracts; but in order to suppress frauds, or manifestly mischievous consequences, they will compel such performance. 3 Atk. 383; Colly. Partn. B. 2, c. 2, § 2; Wats. Partn. 60; Gow, Partn. 109; Story, Eq. Jur. § 666, note; Story, Partn. § 189; 1 Swanst. R. 513, note. When, however, the partnership may be immediately dissolved, it seems the contract cannot be specifically enforced. 9 Ves. 360.

3. It is proper to premise that under each particular head, it is intended briefly to examine the decisions which have been made in relation to it.

4. The principal parts of articles of partnership are here enumerated.

1. The names of the contracting parties. These should all be severally set out.

5.—2. The agreement that the parties actually by the instrument enter into partnership; and care must be taken to distinguish this agreement from a covenant to enter into partnership at a future time.

6.—3. The commencement of the partnership. This ought always to be expressly provided for. When no other time is fixed by it, the commencement will take place from the date of the instrument. Colly Partn. 140; 5 Barn. & Cres. 108.

7.—4. The duration of the partnership. This may be for life, or for a specific period of time; partnerships may be conditional or indefinite in their duration, or for a single adventure or dealing; this period of duration is either express or implied, but it will not be presumed to be beyond life. 1 Swanst. R. 521. When a term is fixed, it is presumed to endure until that period has elapsed; and, when no term is fixed, for the life of the parties, unless sooner dissolved by the acts of one of them, by mutual consent, or operation of law. Story, Part. § 84.

8. A stipulation may lawfully be introduced for the continuance of the partnership after the death of one of the parties, either by his executors or administrators, or for the admission of one or more of his children into the concern. Colly. Partn. 147; 9 Ves. 500. Sometimes this clause provides that the interest of the partner shall go to such persons, as he shall by his last will name and appoint, and for want of appointment to such persons as are there named. In these cases it seems that the executors or administrators have an option to continue the partnership or not. Colly. Partn. 149; 1 McCl. & Yo. 569; Colles, Parl. Rep. 157.

9. When the duration of the partnership has been fixed by the articles, and the partnership expires by mere effluxion of time, and, after such determination it is carried on by the partners without any new agreement, in the absence of all circumstances which may lead as to the true intent of the partners, the partnership will not, in general, be deemed one for a definite period; 17 Ves. 298; but in other respects, the old articles of the expired partnership are to be deemed adopted by implication as the basis of the new partnership during its continuance. 5 Mason, R. 176, 185; 15 Ves. 218: 1 Molloy, R. 466.

10.—5. The business to be carried on, and the place where it is to be conducted. This clause ought to be very particularly written, as courts of equity will grant an injunction when one or more of the partners attempt, against the wishes of one or more of them, to extend such business beyond the provision contained in the articles. Story, Partn. § 193; Gow, Partn. 398.

11.—6. The name of the firm, as for example, John Doe and Company, ought to be ascertained. The members of the partnership are required to use the name thus agreed upon, and a departure from it will make them individually liable to third persons or to their partners, in particular cases. Colly. Partn. 141; 2 Jac. & Walk. 266: 9 Adol. & Ellis, 314; 11 Adol. & Ellis, 339; Story, Partn. § 102, 136, 142, 202.

12.—7. A provision is not unfrequently inserted that the business shall be managed and administered by a particular partner, or that one of its departments shall be under his special care. In this case, courts of equity will protect such partner in his rights. Story, Partn. § 172, 182, 193, 202, 204; Colly. Partn. 753. In Louisiana, this provision is incorporated in its civil code, art. 2838 to art. 2840. The French and civil law also agree as to this provision. Poth. de Societé, n. 71; Dig. 14, 1, 1, 13; Poth. Pand. 14, 1, 4.

13. Sometimes a provision is introduced that a majority of the partners shall have the management of the affairs of the partnership. This is requisite, particularly when the associates are numerous. As to the rights of the majority, see *Partners*.

14.—8. A provision should be inserted as to the manner of furnishing the capital or stock of the partnership. When a partner is required to furnish his proportion of the stock at stated periods, or pay by instalments, he will, where there are no stipulations to the contrary, be considered a debtor to the firm. Colly. Partn. 141; Story, Partn. § 203; 1 Swanst. R. 89. Sometimes a provision is inserted that real estate and fixtures belonging to the firm shall be considered, as between the partners, not as partnership but as several property. In cases of bankruptcy this property will be treated as the separate property of the partners. Colly. Partn. 141, 595, 600; 5 Ves. 189; 3 Madd. R. 63.

15.—9. A provision for the apportionment of the profits and losses among the partners should be introduced. In the absence of all proof, and controlling circumstances, the partners are to share in both equally, although one may have furnished all the capital, and the other only his skill. Wats. Partn. 59; Colly. Partn. 105; Story, Partn. § 24; 3 Kent, Com. 28; 4th ed.; 6 Wend. R. 263; but see 7 Bligh, R. 432; 5 Wils. & Shaw, 16.

16.—10. Sometimes a stipulation for an annual account of the property of the partnership whether in possession or in action, and of the debts due by partnership is inserted. These accounts when settled are at least *prima facie* evidence of the facts they contain. Colly. Partn. 146; Story, Partn. § 206; 7 Sim. R. 239.

17.—11. A provision is frequently introduced forbidding any one partner to carry on any other business. This should be provided for, though there is an implied provision in every partnership that no partner shall carry on any separate business inconsistent or contrary to the true interest of the partnership. Story, Partn. § 178, 179, 209.

18.—12. When the partners are numerous, a provision is often made for the expulsion of a partner for gross misconduct, for insolvency, bankruptcy, or other causes particularly enumerated. This provision will govern when the case occurs.

19.—13. This instrument should always contain a provision for winding up the business. This is generally provided for in one of three modes: first, by turning all the assets into cash, and, after paying all the liabilities of the partnership, dividing such money in proportion to the several interests of the parties; secondly, by providing that one or more of the partners shall be entitled to purchase the shares of the others at a valuation; thirdly, that all the property of partnership shall be appraised, and that after paying the partnership debts, it shall be divided in the proper proportions. The first of these modes is adopted by courts of equity in the absence of express stipulations. Colly. Partn. 145; Story, Partn. § 207; 8 Sim. R. 529.

20.—14. It is not unusual to insert in these articles, a provision that in case of disputes the matter shall be submitted to arbitration. This clause seems nugatory, for no action will lie for a breach of it, as that would deprive the courts of their jurisdiction, which the parties cannot do. Story, Partn. § 215; Gow, Partn. 72; Colly. Partn. 165; Wats. Partn. 383.

21.—15. The articles should be dated, and executed by the parties. It is not requisite that the instrument should be under seal.

Vide *Parties to contracts; Partners Partnership.*

ARTICLES OF THE PEACE, *Eng. practice.* An instrument which is presented to a court of competent jurisdiction, in which the exhibitant shows the grievances under which he labors, and prays the protection of the court. It is made on oath. See a form in 12 Adol. & Ellis, 599; 40 E. C. L. R. 125, 126; 1 Chit. Pr. 678.

2. The truth of the articles cannot be contradicted, either by affidavit or otherwise; but the defendant may either except to their sufficiency, or tender affidavits in reduction of the amounts of bail. 13 East, 171.

Articles of war. The name commonly given to a code made for the government of the army. The act of April 10, 1806, 2 Story's Laws U. S. 992, contains the rules and articles by which the armies of the United States shall be governed. The act of April 23, 1800, 1 Story's L. U. S. 761, contains the rules and regulations for the government of the navy of the United States.

ARTICULATE ADJUDICATION. A term used in Scotch law in cases where there is more than the debt due to the adjudging creditor, when it is usual to accumulate each debt by itself, so that any error that may arise in ascertaining one of the debts need not reach to all the rest.

ARTIFICERS. Persons whose employment or business consists chiefly of bodily labor. Those who are masters of their arts. Cunn. Dict. h. t. Vide *Art.*

ARTIFICIAL. What is the result of, or relates to, the arts; opposed to natural; thus we say a corporation is an artificial person, in opposition to a natural person. Artificial accession is the uniting one property to another by art, opposed to a simple natural union. 1 Bouv. Inst. n. 503.

Artificial person. In a figurative sense, a body of men or company are sometimes called an artificial person, because the law associates them as one, and gives them various powers possessed by natural persons. Corporations are such artificial persons. 1 Bouv. Inst. n. 177.

AS. A word purely Latin. It has two significations. First, it signifies *weight,* and in this sense, the Roman *as,* is the same thing as the Roman *pound,* which was composed of twelve ounces. It was divided also into many other parts (as may be seen in the law, *Servum de hæredibus,* Inst. Lib. xiii. *Pandect,*) *viz.* uncia, 1 ounce; sextans, 2 ounces; quodrans, 3 ounces; triens, 4 ounces; quincunx, 5 ounces; semis, 6 ounces; septunx, 7 ounces; bes, 8 ounces; dodrans, 9 ounces; dextans, 10 ounces; deunx, 11 ounces.

2. From this primitive and proper sense of the word another was derived: that *namely* of the totality of a thing, *Solidum quid.* Thus *as* signified the whole of an inheritance, so that an heir *ex asse,* was an heir of the whole inheritance. An heir *ex triente, ex semisse, ex besse,* or *ex deunce,* was an heir of *one-third, one-half, two-thirds,* or *eleven-twelfths.*

ASCENDANTS. Those from whom a person is descended, or from whom he derives his birth, however remote they may be.

2. Every one has two ascendants at the first degree, his father and mother; four at the second degree, his paternal grandfather and grandmother, and his maternal grandfather and grandmother; eight at the third. Thus in going up we ascend by various lines which fork at every generation. By this progress sixteen ascendants are found at the fourth degree; thirty-two, at the fifth; sixty-four, at the sixth; one hundred and twenty-eight at the seventh, and so on; by this progressive increase, a person has at the twenty-fifth generation, thirty-three millions five hundred and fifty-four thousand, four hundred and thirty-two ascendants. But as many of the ascendants of a person have descended from the same ancestor, the lines which were forked, reunite to the first common ancestor, from whom the other descends; and this multiplication thus frequently interrupted by the common ancestors, may be reduced to a few persons. Vide *Line.*

ASCRIPTITIUS, *civil law.* Among the Romans, ascriptitii were foreigners, who had been naturalized, and who had in general the same rights as natives. Nov. 22, ch. 17; Code 11, 47.

ASPHYXY, *med. jur.* A temporary suspension of the motion of the heart and arteries; swooning, fainting. This term includes persons who have been asphyxiated by submersion or drowning; by breathing mephitic gas; by the effect of lightning; by the effect of cold; by heat; by suspension or strangulation. In a legal point of view it is always proper to ascertain whether the person who has thus been deprived of his senses is the victim of another, whether the injury has been caused by accident, or whether it is the act of the sufferer himself.

2. In a medical point of view it is important to ascertain whether the person is merely asphyxiated, or whether he is dead. The following general remarks have been made as to the efforts which ought to be made to restore a person thus situated

1st. Persons asphyxiated are frequently in a state of only apparent death.

2d. Real from apparent death can be distinguished only by putrefaction.

3d. Till putrefaction commences, aid ought to be rendered to persons asphyxiated.

4th. Experience proves that remaining several hours under water does not always produce death.

5th. The red, violet, or black color of the face, the coldness of the body, the stiffness of the limbs, are not always signs of death.

6th. The assistance to persons thus situated, may be administered by any intelligent person; but to insure success, it must be done without discouragement for several hours together.

7th. All unnecessary persons should be sent away; five or six are in general sufficient.

8th. The place where the operation is performed should not be too warm.

9th. The assistance should be rendered with activity, but without precipitation.

ASPORTATION. The act of carrying a thing away; the removing a thing from one place to another. Vide *Carrying away; Taking*.

ASSASSIN, *crim. law*. An assassin is one who attacks another either traitorously, or with the advantage of arms or place, or of a number of persons who support him, and kills his victim. This being done with malice aforethought, is murder. The term assassin is but little used in the common law, it is borrowed from the civil law.

ASSASSINATION, *crim. law*. A murder committed by an assassin. By assassination is understood a murder committed for hire in money, without any provocation or cause of resentment given by the person against whom the crime is directed. Ersk. Inst. B. 4, t. 4, n. 45.

ASSAULT, *crim. law*. An assault is any unlawful attempt or offer with force or violence to do a corporal hurt to another, whether from malice or wantonness; for example, by striking at him or even holding up the fist at him in a threatening or insulting manner, or with other circumstances as denote at the time an intention, coupled with a present ability, of actual violence against his person, as by pointiug a weapon at him when he is within reach of it. 6 Rogers' Rec. 9. When the injury is actually inflicted, it amounts to a battery. (q. v.)

2. Assaults are either simple or aggravated. 1. A simple assault is one where there is no intention to do any other injury. This is punished at common law by fine and imprisonment. 2. An aggravated assault is one that has in addition to the bare intention to commit it, another object which is also criminal; for example, if a man should fire a pistol at another and miss him, the former would be guilty of an assault with intent to murder; so an assault with intent to rob a man, or with intent to spoil his clothes, and the like, are aggravated assaults, and they are more severely punished than simple assaults. General references, 1 East, P. C. 406; Bull. N P. 15; Hawk. P. B. b. 1, c. 62, s. 12; 1 Russ. Cr. 604; 2 Camp. Rep. 650; 1 Wheeler's Cr. C. 364; 6 Rogers' Rec. 9; 1 Serg & Rawle, 347; Bac. Ab. h. t.; Roscoe, Cr. Ev. 210.

ASSAY. A chemical examination of metals, by which the quantity of valuable or precious metal contained in any mineral or metallic mixture is ascertained.

2. By the acts of Congress of March 3, 1823, 3 Story's L. U. S. 1924; of June 25, 1834, 4 Shars. cont. Story's L. U. S. 2373; and of June 28, 1834, Id. 2377, it is made the duty of the secretary of the treasury to cause assays to be made at the mint of the United States, of certain coins made current by the said acts, and to make report of the result thereof to congress.

ASSEMBLY. The union of a number of persons in the same place. There are several kinds of assemblies.

2. *Political* assemblies, or those authorized by the constitution and laws; for example, the general assembly, which includes the senate and house of representatives; the meeting of the electors of the president and vice-president of the United States, may also be called an assembly.

3. *Popular* assemblies are those where the people meet to deliberate upon their rights; these are guaranteed by the constitution. Const. U. S. Amend. art. 1; Const. of Penn. art. 9, s. 20.

4. *Unlawful* assemblies. An unlawful assembly is the meeting of three or more persons to do an unlawful act, although they may not carry their purpose into execution. It differs from a riot or rout, (q. v.) because in each of the latter cases there is some act done besides the simple meeting.

ASSENT, *contracts*. An agreement to something that has been done before.

2. It is either express, where it is openly declared; or implied, where it is presumed by law. For instance, when a conveyance is made to a man, his assent to it is presumed, for the following reasons; 1. Because there is a strong intendment of law, that it is for a person's benefit to take, and no man can be supposed to be unwilling to do that which is for his advantage. 2. Because it would seem incongruous and absurd, that when a conveyance is completely executed on the part of the grantor, the estate should continue in him. 3. Because it is contrary to the policy of law to permit the freehold to remain in suspense and uncertainty. 2 Ventr. 201; 3 Mod. 296; 3 Lev. 284; Show. P. C. 150; 3 Barn. & Alders. 31; 1 Binn. R. 502; 2 Hayw. 234; 12 Mass. R. 461; 4 Day, 395; 5 S. & R. 523; 20 John. R. 184; 14 S. & R. 296; 15 Wend. R. 656; 4 Halst. R. 161; 6 Verm. R. 411.

3. When a devise draws after it no charge or risk of loss, and is, therefore, a mere bounty, the assent of the devisee to take it will be presumed. 17 Mass. 73, 4. A dissent properly expressed would prevent the title from passing from the grantor unto the grantee. 12 Mass. R. 461. See 3 Munf. R. 345; 4 Munf. R. 332, pl. 9; 5 Serg. & Rawle, 523; 8 Watts, R. 9, 11; 20 Johns. R. 184. The rule requiring an express dissent does not apply, however, when the grantee is bound to pay a consideration for the thing granted. 1 Wash. C. C. Rep. 70.

4. When an offer to do a thing has been made, it is not binding on the party making it, until the assent of the other party has been given; and such assent must be to the same subject-matter, in the same sense. 1 Summ. 218. When such assent is given, before the offer is withdrawn, the contract is complete. 6 Wend. 103. See 5 Wend. 523; 5 Greenl. R. 419; 3 Mass. 1; 8 S. & R. 243; 12 John. 190; 19 John. 205; 4 Call, R. 379; 1 Fairf. 185; and *Offer*.

5. In general, when an assignment is made to one for the benefit of creditors, the assent of the assignees will be presumed. 1 Binn. 502, 518; 6 W. & S. 339; 8 Leigh, R. 272, 281. But see 24 Wend. 280.

ASSERTORY COVENANT. One by which the covenantor affirms that a certain fact is in a particular way, as that the grantor of land is lawfully seised; that it is clear of incumbrances, and the like. If the assertion is false, these covenants are broken the moment that the instrument is signed. See 11 S. & R. 109, 112.

TO ASSESS. 1. To rate or to fix the proportion which every person has to pay of any particular tax. 2. To assess damages is to ascertain what damages are due to the plaintiff; in actions founded on writings, in many cases after interlocutory judgment the prothonotary is directed to assess the damages; in cases sounding in tort the damages are frequently assessed on a writ of inquiry by the sheriff and a jury.

2. In actions for damages, the jury are required to fix the amount or to assess the damages. In the exercise of this power or duty, the jury must be guided by a sound discretion, and, when the circumstances will warrant it, may give high damages. Const. Rep. 500. The jury must, in the assessment of damages, be guided by their own judgment, and not by a blind chance. They cannot lawfully, therefore, in making up their verdict, each one put down a sum, add the sums together, divide the aggregate by the number of jurors, and adopt the quotient for their verdict. 1 Cowen, 238.

ASSESSMENT. The making out a list of property, and fixing its valuation or appraisement; it is also applied to making out a list of persons, and appraising their several occupations, chiefly with a view of taxing the said persons and their property.

ASSESSMENT OF DAMAGES. After an interlocutory judgment has been obtained, the damages must be ascertained; the act of thus fixing the amount of damages is called the assessment of damages.

2. In cases sounding in damages, (q. v.) that is, when the object of the action is to recover damages only, and not brought for the specific recovery of lands, goods, or sums of money, the usual course is to issue a writ of inquiry, (q. v.) and, by virtue of such writ, the sheriff, aided by twelve lawful men, ascertains the amount of damages, and makes return to the court of the inquisition, which, unless set aside, fixes the damages, and a final judgment follows.

3. When, on the contrary, the action is founded on a promissory note, bond, or other contract in writing, by which the amount of money due may be easily computed, it is the practice, in some courts, to refer to the clerk or prothonotary the assessment of damages, and in such case no writ of inquiry is issued. 3 Bouv. Inst. n. 3300.

ASSESSORS, *civil law*. So called from

the word *adsidere*, which signifies to be seated with the judge. They were lawyers who were appointed to assist, by their advice, the Roman magistrates, who were generally ignorant of law, being mere military men. Dig. lib. 1, t. 22; Code, lib. 1, t. 51.

2. In our law an assessor is one who has been legally appointed to value and appraise property, generally with a view of laying a tax on it.

ASSETS. The property in the hands of an heir, executor, administrator or trustee, which is legally or equitably chargeable with the obligations, which such heir, executor, administrator or other trustee, is, as such, required to discharge, is called assets. The term is derived from the French word *assez*, enough; that is, the heir or trustee has enough property. But the property is still called assets, although there may not be enough to discharge *all* the obligations; and the heir, executor, &c., is chargeable in distribution as far as such property extends.

2. Assets are sometimes divided by all the old writers, into assets enter mains and assets per descent; considered as to their mode of distribution, they are legal or equitable; as to the property from which they arise, they are real or personal.

3. *Assets enter mains*, or assets in hand, is such property as at once comes to the executor or other trustee, for the purpose of satisfying claims against him as such. Termes de la Ley.

4. *Assets per descent*, is that portion of the ancestor's estate which descends to the heir, and which is sufficient to charge him, as far as it goes, with the specialty debts of his ancestor. 2 Williams on Ex. 1011.

5. *Legal assets*, are such as constitute the fund for the payment of debts according to their legal priority.

6. *Equitable assets*, are such as can be reached only by the aid of a court of equity, and are to be divided, *pari passu*, among all the creditors; as when a debtor has made his property subject to his debts generally, which, without his act would not have been so subject. 1 Madd. Ch. 586; 2 Fonbl. 401, et seq.; Willis on Trust, 118.

7. *Real assets*, are such as descend to the heir, as an estate in fee simple.

8. *Personal assets*, are such goods and chattels to which the executor or administrator is entitled.

9. In commerce, by assets is understood all the stock in trade, cash, and all available property belonging to a merchant or company.

Vide, generally, Williams on Exec. Index, h. t.; Toll. on Exec. Index, h. t.; 2 Bl. Com. 510, 511; 3 Vin. Ab. 141; 11 Vin. Ab. 239; 1 Vern. 94; 3 Ves. Jr. 117; Gordon's Law of Decedents, Index, h. t.; Ram on Assets.

ASSEVERATION. The proof which a man gives of the truth of what he says, by appealing to his conscience as a witness. It differs from an oath in this, that by the latter he appeals to God as a witness of the truth of what he says, and invokes him as the avenger of falsehood and perfidy, to punish him if he speak not the truth. Vide *Affirmation; Oath;* and Merl. Quest. de Droit, mot Serment.

TO ASSIGN, *contracts, practice*. 1. To make a right over to another; as to assign an estate, an annuity, a bond, &c., over to another. 5 John. Rep. 391. 2. To appoint; as, to appoint a deputy, &c. Justices are also said to be assigned to keep the peace. 3. To set forth or point out; as, to "assign errors," to show where the error is committed; or to assign false judgment, to show wherein it was unjust. F. N. B. 19.

ASSIGNATION, *Scotch law*. The ceding or yielding a thing to another of which intimation must be made.

ASSIGNEE. One to whom an assignment has been made.

2. Assignees are either assignees in fact or assignees in law. An assignee in fact is one to whom an assignment has been made in fact by the party having the right. An assignee in law is one in whom the law vests the right, as an executor or administrator. Co. Litt. 210 a, note 1; Hob. 9. Vide *Assigns*, and 1 Vern. 425; 1 Salk. 81; 7 East, 337; Bac. Ab. Covenant, E; 3 Saund. 182, note 1; Arch. Civ. Pl. 50, 58, 70; 1 Supp. to Ves. Jr. 72; 2 Phil. Ev. Index, h. t.

ASSIGNMENT, *contracts*. In common parlance this word signifies the transfer of all kinds of property, real, personal, and mixed, and whether the same be in possession or in action; as, a general assignment. In a more technical sense it is usually applied to the transfer of a term for years; but it is more properly used to signify a transfer of some particular estate or interest in lands.

2. The proper technical words of an assignment are, assign, transfer, and set

over; but the words grant, bargain, and sell, or any other words which will show the intent of the parties to make a complete transfer, will amount to an assignment.

3. A chose in action cannot be assigned at law, though it may be done in equity; but the assignee takes it subject to all the equity to which it was liable in the hands of the original party. 2 John. Ch. Rep. 443, and tho cases there cited. 2 Wash. Rep. 233.

4. The deed by which an assignment is made, is also called an assignment. Vide, generally, Com. Dig. h. t.; Bac. Ab. h. t.; Vin. Ab. h. t.; Nelson's Ab. h. t.; Civ. Code of Louis. art. 2612. In relation to general assignments, see Angell on Assignments, passim; 1 Hare & Wall. Sel. Dec. 78–85.

5. By an assignment of a right all the accessories which belong to it, will pass with it; as, if the assignor of a bond had collateral security, or a lien on property, the collateral security and the lien will pass with the assignment of the bond. 2 Penn. 361; 3 Bibb, 291; 4 B. Munroe, 529; 2 Drev. n. 218; 1 P. St. R. 454.

6. The assignment of a thing also carries with it all that belongs to it by right of accession; if, therefore, the thing produce interest or rent, the interest or the arrearages of the rent since the assignment, will belong to the assignee. 7 John. Cas. 90; 6 Pick. 360.

ASSIGNMENT OF DOWER. The act by which the rights of a widow, in her deceased husband's real estate, are ascertained and set apart for her benefit. 2 Bouv. Inst. 242.

ASSIGNMENT OF ERRORS. The act by which the plaintiff in error points out the errors in the record of which he complains.

2. The errors should be assigned in distinct terms, such as the defendant in error may plead to; and all the errors of which the plaintiff complains should be assigned. 9 Port. 186; 15 Conn. 83; 6 Dana, 242; 3 How. (Miss.) R. 77.

ASSIGNOR. One who makes an assignment; one who transfers property to another.

2. In general the assignor can limit the operation of his assignment, and impose whatever condition he may think proper; but when he makes a general assignment in trust for the use of his creditors, he can impose no condition whatever which will deprive them of any right; 14 Pick. 123; 15 John. 151; 7 Cowen, 735; 5 Cowen, 547; 20 John. 442; 2 Pick. 129; nor any condition forbidden by law; as giving preference when the law forbids it.

3. An assignor may legally choose his own trustees. 1 Binn. 514.

ASSIGNS, *contracts.* Those to whom rights have been transmitted by particular title, such as sale, gift, legacy, transfer, or cession. Vide Ham. Parties, 230; Lofft. 316. These words, and also the word *forever*, are commonly added to the word *heirs* in deeds conveying a fee simple—"heirs and assigns forever"—but they are in such cases inoperative. 2 Barton's Elem. Convey. 7 (n.) But see Fleta, lib. 3, cap. 14, § 6. The use of naming them, is explained in Spencer's Case, 5 Rep. 16; and Ham. Parties, 128. The word *heirs*, however, does not include or imply *assigns*. 1 Anderson's Rep. 299.

ASSISES OF JERUSALEM. The name of a code of feudal law, made at a general assembly of lords, after the conquest of Jerusalem. It was compiled principally from the laws and customs of France. They were reduced to form about the year 1290, by Jean d'Iblin, comte de Japhe et d'Ascalon. Fournel (Hist. des Avocats, vol. i. p. 49,) calls them the most precious monument of our (French) ancient law. He defines the word assises to signify the assemblies of the great men of the realm. See also, 2 Profession d'Avocat, par Dupin, 674 to 680; Steph. on Plead. App. p. xi.

ASSISORS, *Scotch law.* This term corresponds nearly to that of jurors.

ASSIZE, *Eng. law.* This was the name of an ancient court; it derived its name from *assideo*, to sit together. Litt. s. 234; Co. Litt. 153 b., 159 b. It was a kind of jury before which no evidence was adduced, their verdict being regarded as a statement of facts, which they knew of their own knowledge. Bract. iv. 1, 6.

2. The name of assize was also given to a remedy for the restitution of a freehold, of which the complainant had been disseised. Bac. Ab. h. t. Assizes were of four kinds Mort d'ancestor; Novel Disseisin; Darrien Presentment; and Utrum. Neale's F. & F. 84. This remedy has given way to others less perplexed and more expeditious. Bac. Ab. h. t.; Co. Litt. 153–155.

3. The final judgment for the plaintiff in an assize of Novel Disseisin, is, that he recover *per visum recognitorum*, and it is

sufficiently certain, if the recognitors can put the demandant in possession. Dyer, 84 b; 10 Wentw. Pl. 221, note. In this action, the plaintiff cannot be compelled to be nonsuited. Plowd. 11 b. See 17 Serg. & R. 187; 1 Rawle, Rep. 48, 9.

4. There is, however, in this class of actions, an interlocutory judgment, or award in the nature of a judgment, and which to divers intents and purposes, is a judgment; 11 Co. Rep. 40 b; like the judgment of quod computet, in account render; or quod partitio fiat, in partition; quod mensuratio fiat; ouster of aid; award of a writ of inquiry, in waste; of damages in trespass; upon these and the like judgments, a writ of error does not lie. 11 Co. Rep. 40 a; Metcalf's Case, 2 Inst. 344 a: 24 Ed. III., 29 B 19.

ASSIZE OF MORT D'ANCESTOR. The name of an ancient writ, now obsolete. It might have been sued out by one whose father, mother, brother, &c., died seised of lands and tenements, which they held in fee, and which, after their death, a stranger abated. Reg. Orig. 223. See *Mort d'Ancestor.*

ASSOCIATE. This term is applied to a judge who is not the president of a court; as associate judge.

ASSOCIATION. The act of a number of persons uniting together for some purpose; the persons so joined are also called an association. See *Company*.

ASSUMPSIT, *contracts*. An undertaking either express or implied, to perform a parol agreement. 1 Lilly's Reg. 132.

2. An express assumpsit is where one undertakes verbally or in writing, not under seal, or by matter of record, to perform an act, or to pay a sum of money to another.

3. An implied assumpsit is where one has not made any formal promise to do an act or to pay a sum of money to another, but who is presumed from his conduct to have assumed to do what is in point of law just and right; for, 1st, it is to be presumed that no one desires to enrich himself at the expense of another; 2d, it is a rule that he who desires the antecedent, must abide by the consequent; as, if I receive a loaf of bread or a newspaper daily sent to my house without orders, and I use it without objection, I am presumed to have accepted the terms upon which the person sending it had in contemplation, that I should pay a fair price for it; 3d, it is also a rule that every one is presumed to assent to what is useful to him. See *Assent*

ASSUMPSIT, *remedies, practice.* A form of action which may be defined to be an action for the recovery of damages for the non-performance of a parol or simple contract; or, in other words, a contract not under seal, nor of record; circumstances which distinguish this remedy from others. 7 T. R. 351; 3 Johns. Cas. 60. This action differs from the action of *debt;* for, in legal consideration, that is for the recovery of a debt *eo nomine*, and *in numero*, and may be upon a deed as well as upon any other contract. 1 H. Bl. 554; B. N. P. 167. It differs from *covenant*, which, though brought for the recovery of damages, can only be supported upon a contract under *seal*. See *Covenant*.

2. It will be proper to consider this subject with reference, 1, to the contract upon which this action may be sustained; 2, the declaration; 3, the plea; 4, the judgment.

3.—1. Assumpsit lies to recover damages for the breach of all parol or simple contracts, whether written or not written; express or implied; for the payment of money, or for the performance or omission of any other act. For example, to recover money lent, paid, or had and received, to the use of the plaintiff; and in some cases, where money has been received by the defendant, in consequence of some tortious act to the plaintiff's property, the plaintiff may waive the tort, and sue the defendant in assumpsit. 5 Pick. 285; 1 J. J. Marsh. 543; 3 Watts, R. 277; 4 Binn. 374; 3 Dana, R. 552; 1 N. H. Rep. 151; 12 Pick. 120; 4 Call. R. 451; 4 Pick. 452. It is the proper remedy for work and labor done, and services rendered; 1 Gill, 95; 8 S. & M. 397; 2 Gilman, 1; 3 Yeates, 250; 9 Ala. 788; but such work, labor, or services, must be rendered at the request, express or implied, of the defendant; 2 Rep. Cons. Ct 348; 1 M'Cord, 22; 20 John. 28; 11 Mass. 37; 14 Mass. 176; 5 Monr. 513; 1 Murph. 181; for goods sold and delivered, 6 J. J. Marsh. 441; 12 Pick. 120; 3 N. H. Rep. 384; 1 Mis. 430; for a breach of promise of marriage. 3 Mass. 73; 2 Overton, 233; 2 P. S. R. 80. Assumpsit lies to recover the purchase money for land sold, 14 Johns. R. 210; 14 Johns. R. 162; 20 Johns. R. 338; 3 M'Cord, R. 421; and it lies, specially, upon wagers; 2 Chit. Pl. 114; feigned issues; 2 Chit. Pl. 116; upon foreign judgments; 8 Mass. 273; Dougl. 1; 3 East, 221; 11 East, 124; 3 T. R. 493; 5 Johns.

R. 132. But it will not lie on a judgment obtained in a sister state. 1 Bibb, 361; 19 Johns. 162; 3 Fairf. 94; 2 Rawle, 431. Assumpsit is the proper remedy upon an account stated. Bac. Ab. Assumpsit, A. It will lie for a corporation, 2 Lev. 252; 1 Camp. 466. In England it does not lie against a corporation, unless by express authority of some legislative act; 1 Chit. Pl. 98; but in this country it lies against a corporation aggregate, on an express or implied promise, in the same manner as against an individual. 7 Cranch, 297; 9 Pet. 541; 3 S. & R. 117; 4 S. & R. 16; 12 Johns. 231; 14 Johns. 118; 2 Bay, 109; 1 Chipm. 371, 456; 1 Aik. 180; 10 Mass. 397. But see 3 Marsh. 1; 3 Dall. 496.

4.—2. The declaration must invariably disclose the consideration of the contract, the contract itself, and the breach of it; Bac. Ab. h. t. F; 5 Mass. 98; but in a declaration on a negotiable instrument under the statute of Anne, it is not requisite to allege any consideration; 2 Leigh, R. 198; and on a note expressed to have been given for value received, it is not necessary to aver a special consideration. 7 Johns. 321. See 5 Mass. 97. The gist of this action is the promise, and it must be averred. 2 Wash. 187; 2 N. H. Rep. 289; Hardin, 225. Damages should be laid in a sufficient amount to cover the real amount of the claim. See 4 Pick. 497; 2 Rep. Const. Ct. 339; 4 Munf. 95; 5 Munf. 23; 2 N. H. Rep. 289; 1 Breese, 286; 1 Hall, 201; 4 Johns. 280; 11 S. & R. 27; 5 S. & R. 519; 6 Conn. 176; 9 Conn. 508; 1 N. & M. 342; 6 Cowen, 151; 2 Bibb, 429; 3 Caines, 286.

5.—3. The usual plea is *non-assumpsit*, (q. v.) under which the defendant may give in evidence most matters of defence. Com. Dig. Pleader, 2 G 1. When there are several defendants they cannot plead the general issue severally; 6 Mass. 444; nor the same plea in bar, severally. 13 Mass. 152. The plea of *not guilty*, in an action of assumpsit, is cured by verdict. 8 S. & R. 541; 4 Call. 451. See 1 Marsh, 602; 17 Mass. 623; 2 Greenl. 362; Minor, 254; Bouv. Inst. Index, h. t.

6.—4. Judgment. Vide *Judgment in Assumpsit*.

Vide Bac. Ab. h. t.; Com. Dig. Action upon the Case upon Assumpsit; Dane's Ab. Index, h. t.; Viner's Ab. h. t.; 1 Chit. Pl. h. t.; Petersd. h. t.; Lawes' Pl. in Assumpsit; the various Digests, h. t. *Actions; Covenant; Debt; Indebitatus assumpsit, Pactum Constitutiæ pecuniæ.*

ASSURANCE, *com. law*. Insurance. (q. v.)

ASSURANCE, *conveyancing*. This is called a common assurance. But the term assurances includes, in an enlarged sense, all instruments which dispose of property, whether they be the grants of private persons, or not; such are fines and recoveries and private acts of the legislature. Eunom Dial. 2, s. 5.

ASSURED. A person who has been insured by some insurance company, or underwriter, against losses or perils mentioned in the policy of insurance. Vide *Insured*.

ASSURER. One who insures another against certain perils and dangers. The same as underwriter. (q. v.) Vide *Insurer*.

ASSYTHMENT, *Scotch law*. An indemnification which a criminal is bound to make to the party injured or his executors, though the crime itself should be extinguished by pardon. Ersk. Pr. L. Scot. 4, 3, 13.

ASYLUM. A place of refuge where debtors and criminals fled for safety.

2. At one time, in Europe, churches and other consecrated places served as asylums, to the disgrace of the law. These never protected criminals in the United States. It may be questioned whether the house of an ambassador (q. v.) would not afford protection temporarily, to a person who should take refuge there.

AT LAW. This phrase is used to point out that a thing is to be done according to the course of the common law; it is distinguished from a proceeding in equity.

2. In many cases when there is no remedy at law, one will be afforded in equity. See 3 Bouv. Inst. n. 2411.

ATAVUS. The male ascendant in the fifth degree, was so called among the Romans, and in tables of genealogy the term is still employed.

ATHEIST. One who denies the existence of God.

2. As atheists have not any religion that can bind their consciences to speak the truth, they are excluded from being witnesses. Bull. N. P. 292; 1 Atk. 40; Gilb. Ev. 129; 1 Phil. Ev. 19. See also, Co. Litt. 6 b.; 2 Inst. 606; 3 Inst. 165; Willes, R. 451; Hawk. B. 2, c. 46, s. 148; 2 Hale's P. C. 279.

TO ATTACH, *crim. law, practice*. To

take or apprehend by virtue of the order of a writ or precept, commonly called an attachment. It differs from an arrest in this, that he who arrests a man, takes him to a person of higher power to be disposed of; but he who attaches, keeps the party attached, according to the exigency of his writ, and brings him into court on the day assigned. Kitch. 279; Bract. lib. 4; Fleta, lib. 5, c. 24; 17 S. & R. 199.

ATTACHE'. Connected with, attached to. This word is used to signify those persons who are attached to a foreign legation. An attaché is a public minister within the meaning of the Act of April 30, 1790, s. 37, 1 Story's L. U. S. 89, which protects from violence "the person of an ambassador or other public minister." 1 Bald. 240. Vide 2 W. C. C. R. 205; 4 W. C. C. R. 531; 1 Dall. 117; 1 W. C. C. R. 232; 4 Dall. 321. Vide *Ambassador; Consul; Envoy; Minister.*

ATTACHMENT, *crim. law, practice.* A writ requiring a sheriff to apprehend a particular person, who has been guilty of a contempt of court, and to bring the offender before the court. Tidd's Pr. Index, h. t.; Grah. Pr. 555.

2. It may be awarded by the court upon a bare suggestion, though generally an oath stating what contempt has been committed is required, or on their own knowledge without indictment or information. An attachment may be issued against officers of the court for disobedience or contempt of their rules and orders, for disobedience of their process, and for disturbing them in their lawful proceedings. Bac. Ab. h. t. A. An attachment for contempt for the non-performance of an award is considered in the nature of a civil execution, and it was therefore held it could not be executed on Sunday; 1 T. R. 266; Cowper, 394; Willes, R. 292, note (b); yet, in one case, it was decided, that it was so far criminal, that it could not be granted in England on the affirmation of a Quaker. Stra. 441. See 5 Halst. 63; 1 Cowen, 121, note; Bac. Ab. h. t.

ATTACHMENT, *remedies.* A writ issued by a court of competent jurisdiction, commanding the sheriff or other proper officer to seize any property, credit, or right, belonging to the defendant, in whatever hands the same may be found, to satisfy the demand which the plaintiff has against him.

2. This writ always issues before judgment, and is intended to compel an appearance; in this respect it differs from an execution. In some of the states this process can be issued only against absconding debtors, or those who conceal themselves; in others it is issued in the first instance, so that the property attached may respond to the exigency of the writ, and satisfy the judgment.

3. There are two kinds of attachment in Pennsylvania, the foreign attachment, and the domestic attachment. 1. The *foreign* attachment is a mode of proceeding by a creditor against the property of his debtor, when the debtor is out of the jurisdiction of the state, and is not an inhabitant of the same. The object of this process is in the first instance to compel an appearance by the debtor, although his property may even eventually be made liable to the amount of the plaintiff's claim. It will be proper to consider, 1. by whom it be issued; 2. against what property; 3. mode of proceeding. 1. The plaintiff must be a creditor of the defendant; the claim of the plaintiff need not, however, be technically a debt, but it may be such on which an action of assumpsit would lie but an attachment will not lie for a demand which arises *ex delicto;* or when special bail would not be regularly required. Serg. on Att. 51. 2. The writ of attachment may be issued against the real and personal estate of any person not residing within the commonwealth, and not being within the county in which such writ may issue, at the time of the issuing thereof. And proceedings may be had against persons convicted of crime, and sentenced to imprisonment. 3. The writ of attachment is in general terms, not specifying in the body of it the name of the garnishee, or the property to be attached, but commanding the officer to attach the defendant, by all and singular his goods and chattels, in whose hands or possession soever the same may be found in his bailiwick, so that he be and appear before the court at a certain time to answer, &c. The foreign attachment is issued solely for the benefit of the plaintiff.

4.—2. The *domestic attachment* is issued by the court of common pleas of the county in which any debtor, being an inhabitant of the commonwealth, may reside; if such debtor shall have absconded from the place of his usual abode within the same, or shall have remained absent from the commonwealth, or shall have confined himself to his own house, or concealed himself elsewhere, with a design, in either case, to defraud his creditors. It is issued on an oath or affirmation, previously made by a creditor of such person, or by some one on his behalf, of the truth of his debt, and of the facts upon which the attachment may be founded. Any other creditor of such person, upon affidavit of his debt as aforesaid, may suggest his name upon the record, and thereupon such creditor may proceed to prosecute his said writ, if the person suing the same shall refuse or neglect to proceed thereon, or if he fail to establish his right to prosecute the same, as a creditor of the defendant. The property attached is vested in trustees to be appointed by the court, who are, after giving six months' public notice of their appointment, to distribute the assets attached among the creditors under certain regulations prescribed by the act of assembly. Perishable goods may be sold under an order of the court, both under a foreign and domestic attachment. Vide Serg. on Attachments; Whart. Dig. title Attachment.

5. By the code of practice of Louisiana, an attachment in the hands of third persons is declared to be a mandate which a creditor obtains from a competent officer, commanding the seizure of any property, credit or right, belonging to his debtor, in whatever hands they may be found, to satisfy the demand which he intends to bring against him. A creditor may obtain such attachment of the property of his debtor, in the following cases. 1. When such debtor is about permanently leaving the state, without there being a possibility, in the ordinary course of judicial proceedings, of obtaining or executing judgment against him previous to his departure; or when such debtor has already left the state never again to return. 2. When such debtor resides out of the state. 3. When he conceals himself to avoid being cited or forced to answer to the suit intended to be brought against him. Articles 239, 240.

6. By the local laws of some of the New England states, and particularly of the states of Massachusetts, New Hampshire and Maine, personal property and real estate may be attached upon mesne process to respond the exigency of the writ, and satisfy the judgment. In such cases it is the common practice for the officer to bail the goods attached, to some person, who is usually a friend of the debtor, upon an express or implied agreement on his part, to have them forthcoming on demand, or in time to respond the judgment, when the execution thereon shall be issued. Story on Bailm. § 124. As to the rights and duties of the officer or bailor in such cases, and as to the rights and duties of the bailee, who is commonly called the receiptor, see 2 Mass. 514; 9 Mass. 112; 11 Mass. 211; 6 Johns. R. 195; 9 Mass. 104, 265; 10 Mass. 125; 15 Mass. 310; 1 Pick. R. 232, 389. See Metc. & Perk. Dig. tit. Absent and Absconding Debtors.

ATTACHMENT OF PRIVILEGE, *Eng. law.* A process by which a man by virtue of his privilege, calls another to litigate in that court to which he himself belongs; and who has the privilege to answer there.

ATTAINDER, *English criminal law.* Attinctura, the stain or corruption of blood which arises from being condemned for any crime.

2. *Attainder by confession*, is either by pleading guilty at the bar before the judges, and not putting one's self on one's trial by a jury; or before the coroner in sanctuary, when in ancient times, the offender was obliged to abjure the realm.

3. *Attainder by verdict*, is when the prisoner at the bar pleads not guilty to the indictment, and is pronounced guilty by the verdict of the jury.

4. *Attainder by process* or *outlawry*, is when the party flies, and is subsequently outlawed. Co. Lit. 391.

5. *Bill of attainder*, is a bill brought into parliament for attainting persons condemned for high treason. By the constitution of the United States, art. 1, sect. 9, § 3, it is provided that no bill of attainder or ex post facto law shall be passed.

ATTAINT, *English law.* 1. *Attinctus*, attainted, stained, or blackened. 2. A writ which lies to inquire whether a jury of twelve men gave a false verdict. Bract. lib. 4, tr. 1, c. 134; Fleta, lib. 5, c. 22, § 8.

2. It was a trial by jury of twenty-four men empanelled to try the goodness of a former verdict. 3 Bl. Com. 351; 3 Gilb. Ev. by Lofft, 1146. See *Assize*.

ATTEMPT, *criminal law.* An attempt to commit a crime, is an endeavor to accomplish it, carried beyond mere preparation, but falling short of execution of the ultimate design, in any part of it.

2. Between preparations and attempts to commit a crime, the distinction is in many cases, very indeterminate. A man who buys poison for the purpose of committing a murder, and mixes it in the food intended for his victim, and places it on a table where he may take it, will or will not be guilty of an attempt to poison, from the

simple circumstance of his taking back the poisoned food before or after the victim has had an opportunity to take it; for if immediately on putting it down, he should take it up, and, awakened to a just consideration of the enormity of the crime, destroy it, this would amount only to preparations; and certainly if before he placed it on the table, or before he mixed the poison with the food, he had repented of his intention, there would have been no attempt to commit a crime; the law gives this as a *locus penitentiæ*. An attempt to commit a crime is a misdemeanor; and an attempt to commit a misdemeanor, is itself a misdemeanor. 1 Russ. on Cr. 44; 2 East, R. 8; 3 Pick. R. 26; 3 Benth. Ev. 69; 6 C. & P. 368.

ATTENDANT. One who owes a duty or service to another, or in some sort depends upon him. Termes de la Ley, h. t. As to attendant terms, see Powell on Mortg. Index, tit. Attendant terms; Park on Dower, c. 17.

ATTENTAT. In the language of the civil and canon laws, is anything whatsoever wrongfully innovated, or attempted, in the suit by the judge *a quo*, pending an appeal. 1 Addams, R. 22, n.; Ayl. Par. 100.

ATTERMINING. The granting a time or term for the payment of a debt. This word is not used. See *Delay*.

ATTESTATION, *contracts and evidence*. The act of witnessing an instrument of writing, at the request of the party making the same, and subscribing it as a witness. 3 P. Wms. 254; 2 Ves. 454; 1 Ves. & B. 362; 3 Marsh. 146; 3 Bibb. 494; 17 Pick. 373.

2. It will be proper to consider, 1. how it is to be made; 2. how it is proved; 3. its effects upon the witness; 4. its effect upon the parties.

3.—1. The attestation should be made in the case of wills, agreeably to the direction of the statute; Com. Dig. Estates, E 1; and in the case of deeds or other writings, at the request of the party executing the same. A person who sees an instrument executed, but is not desired by the parties to attest it, is not therefore an attesting witness, although he afterwards subscribes it as such. 3 Camp. 232. See, as to the form of attestation, 2 South. R. 449.

4.—2. The general rule is, that an attested instrument must be proved by the attesting witness. But to this rule there are various exceptions, namely: 1. If he reside out of the jurisdiction of the court; 22 Pick. R. 85; 2. or is dead; 3. or becomes insane; 3 Camp. 283; 4. or has an interest; 5 T. R. 371; 5. or has married the party who offers the instrument; 2 Esp. C. 698; 6. or refuses to testify; 4 M. & S. 353; 7. or where the witness swears he did not see the writing executed; 8. or becomes infamous; Str. 833; 9. or blind; 1 Ld. Raym. 734. From these numerous cases, and those to be found in the books, it would seem that, whenever from any cause the attesting witness cannot be had, secondary evidence may be given. But the inability to procure the witness must be absolute, and, therefore, when he is unable to attend from sickness only, his evidence cannot be dispensed with. 4 Taunt. 46. See 4 Halst. R. 322; Andr. 236; 2 Str. 1096; 10 Ves. 174; 4 M. & S. 353; 7 Taunt. 251; 6 Serg. & Rawle, 310; 1 Rep. Const. Co. So. Ca. 310; 5 Cranch, 13; Com. Dig. tit. Testmoigne, Evidence, Addenda; 5 Com. Dig. 441; 4 Yeates, 79.

5.—3. When the witness attests an instrument which conveys away, or disposes of his property or rights, he is estopped from denying the effects of such instrument; but in such case he must have been aware of its contents, and this must be proved. 1 Esp. C. 58.

6.—4. Proof of the attestation is evidence of the sealing and delivery. 6 Serg. & Rawle, 311; 2 East, R. 250; 1 Bos. & Pull. 360; 7 T. R. 266.

See, in general, Starkie's Ev. part 2, 332; 1 Phil. Ev. 419 to 421; 12 Wheat. 91; 2 Dall. 96; 3 Rawle's Rep. 312; 1 Ves. Jr. 12; 2 Eccl. Rep. 60, 214, 289, 367; 1 Bro. Civ. Law, 279, 286; Gresl. Eq. Ev. 119; Bouv. Inst. n. 3126.

ATTESTATION CLAUSE, *wills and contracts*. That clause wherein the witnesses certify that the instrument has been executed before them, and the manner of the execution of the same. The usual attestation clause to a will, is in the following formula, to wit: "Signed, sealed, published and declared by the above named A B, as and for his last will and testament, in the presence of us, who have hereunto subscribed our names as the witnesses thereto, in the presence of the said testator, and of each other." That of deeds is generally in these words: "Sealed and delivered in the presence of us."

2. When there is an attestation clause to a will, unsubscribed by witnesses, the presumption, though slight, is that the will is in an unfinished state; and it must be removed by some extrinsic circumstances. 2 Eccl. Rep. 60. This presumption is infinitely slighter, where the writer's intention to have it regularly attested, is to be collected only from the single word "witnesses." Id. 214. See 3 Phillim. R. 323; S. C. 1 Eng. Eccl. R. 407.

ATTESTING WITNESS. One who, upon being required by the parties to an instrument, signs his name to it to prove it, and for the purpose of identification.

2. The witness must be desired by the parties to attest it, for unless this be done, he will not be an attesting witness, although he may have seen the parties execute it. 3 Cambp. 232. See *Competent witness; Credible witness; Disinterested witness; Respectable witness; Subscribing witness;* and *Witness; Witness instrumentary;* 5 Watts, 399; 3 Bin. 194.

ATTORNEY. One who acts for another by virtue of an appointment by the latter. Attorneys are of various kinds.

2. *Attorney in fact.* A person to whom the authority of another, who is called the constituent, is by him lawfully delegated. This term is employed to designate persons who act under a special agency, or a special letter of attorney, so that they are appointed *in factum*, for the deed, or special act to be performed; but in a more extended sense it includes all other agents employed in any business, or to do any act or acts *in pais* for another. Bac. Ab. Attorney; Story, Ag. § 25.

3. All persons who are capable of acting for themselves, and even those who are disqualified from acting in their own capacity, if they have sufficient understanding, as infants of a proper age and femes coverts, may act as attorneys of others. Co. Litt. 52, a; 1 Esp. Cas. 142; 2 Esp. Cas. 511; 2 Stark. Cas. N. P. 204.

4. The form of his appointment is by letter of attorney. (q. v.)

5. The object of his appointment is the transaction of some business of the constituent by the attorney.

6. The attorney is bound to act with due diligence after having accepted the employment, and in the end, to render an account to his principal of the acts which he has performed for him. Vide *Agency; Agent; Authority;* and *Principal.*

7. *Attorney at law.* An officer in a court of justice, who is employed by a party in a cause to manage the same for him. Appearance by an attorney has been allowed in England, from the time of the earliest records of the courts of that country. They are mentioned in Glanville, Bracton, Fleta, and Britton; and a case turning upon the party's right to appear by attorney, is reported, Y. B. 17 Edw. III., p. 8, case 23. In France such appearances were first al lowed by letters patent of Philip le Bel, A. D. 1290. 1 Fournel, Hist. des Avocats, 42, 43, 92, 93; 2 Loisel Coutumes, 14, 15. It results from the nature of their functions, and of their duties, as well to the court as to the client, that no one can, even by consent, be the attorney of both the litigating parties, in the same controversy. Farresly, 47.

8. In some courts, as in the supreme court of the United States, advocates are divided into counsellors at law, (q. v.) and attorneys. The business of attorneys is to carry on the practical and formal parts of the suit. 1 Kent, Com. 307. See as to their powers, 2 Supp. to Ves. Jr. 241, 254; 3 Chit. Bl. 23, 338; Bac. Ab. h. t.; 3 Penna. R. 74; 3 Wils. 374; 16 S. & R. 368; 14 S. & R. 307; 7 Cranch, 452; 1 Penna. R. 264. In general, the agreement of an attorney at law, within the scope of his employment, binds his client; 1 Salk. 86; as to amend the record, 1 Binn. 75; to refer a cause; 1 Dall. Rep. 164; 6 Binn. 101; 7 Cranch, 436; 3 Taunt. 486; not to sue out a writ of error; 1 H. Bl. 21, 23; 2 Saund. 71, a, b; 1 Term Rep. 388; to strike off a *non pros;* 1 Bin. 469–70; to waive a judgment by default; 1 Arch. Pr. 26; and this is but just and reasonable. 2 Bin. 161. But the act must be within the scope of their authority. They cannot, for example, without special authority, purchase lands for the client at sheriff's sale. 2 S. & R. 21; 11 Johns. 464.

9. The name of attorney is given to those officers who practice in courts of common law; solicitors, in courts of equity and proctors, in courts of admiralty, and in the English ecclesiastical courts.

10. The principal duties of an attorney are, 1. To be true to the court and to his client; 2. To manage the business of his client with care, skill and integrity. 4 Burr 2061; 1 B. & A. 202; 2 Wils. 325; 1 Bing. R. 347; 3. To keep his client informed as to the state of his business; 4. To keep his

secrets confided to him as such. See *Client; Confidential Communication.*

11. For a violation of his duties, an action will in general lie; 2 Greenl. Ev. § 145, 146; and, in some cases, he may be punished by an attachment. His rights are, to be justly compensated for his services. Vide 1 Keen's R. 668; *Client; Counsellor at law.*

12. *Attorney-general of the United States*, is an officer appointed by the president. He should be learned in the law, and be sworn or affirmed to a faithful execution of his office.

13. His duties are to prosecute and conduct all suits in the supreme court, in which the United States shall be concerned; and give his advice upon questions of law, when required by the president, or when requested by the heads of any of the departments, touching matters that may concern their departments. Act of 24th Sept. 1789.

14. His salary is three thousand five hundred dollars per annum, and he is allowed one clerk, whose compensation shall not exceed one thousand dollars per annum. Act 20th Feb. 1819, 3 Story's Laws, 1720, and Act 20th April, 1818, s. 6, 3 Story's Laws, 1693. By the act of May 29, 1830, 4 Sharsw. cont. of Story, L. U. S. 2208, § 10, his salary is increased five hundred dollars per annum.

ATTORNMENT, *estates.* Was the agreement of the tenant to the grant of the seignory, or of a rent, or the agreement of the donee in tail, or tenant for life, or years, to a grant of a reversion or of a remainder made to another. Co. Litt. 309; Touchs. 253. Attornments are rendered unnecessary, even in England, by virtue of sundry statutes, and they are abolished in the United States. 4 Kent, Com. 479; 1 Hill. Ab. 128, 9. Vide 3 Vin. Ab. 317; 1 Vern. 330, n.; Saund. 234, n. 4; Roll. Ab. h. t.; Nelson's Ab. h. t.; Com. Dig. h. t.

AU BESOIN. This is a French phrase, used in commercial law. When the drawer of a foreign bill of exchange wishes as a matter of precaution, and to save expenses, he puts in the corner of the bill, "Au besoin chez Messieurs —— à ——," or, in other words, "In case of need, apply to Messrs. —— at ——." 1 Bouv. Inst. n. 1133; Pardess. Droit Com. 208.

AUBAINE, *French law.* When a foreigner died in France, the crown, by virtue of a right called *droit d'aubaine*, formerly claimed all the personal property such foreigner had in France at the time of his death. This barbarous law was swept away by the French revolution of 1789. Vide *Albinatus Jus.*; 1 Malleville's Analyse de la Discussion du Code Civil, pp. 26, 28; 1 Toullier, 236, n. 265.

AUCTION, *commerce, contract.* A public sale of property to the highest bidder. Among the Romans this kind of sale, was made by a crier under a spear (*sub hasta*) stuck in the ground.

2. Auctions are generally held by express authority, and the person who conducts them is licensed to do so under various regulations.

3. The manner of conducting an auction is immaterial; whether it be by public outcry or by any other manner. The essential part is the selection of a purchaser from a number of bidders. In a case where a woman continued silent during the whole time of the sale, but whenever any one bid she gave him a glass of brandy, and when the sale broke up, the person who received the last glass of brandy was taken into a private room, and he was declared to be the purchaser; this was adjudged to be an auction. 1 Dow. 115.

4. The law requires fairness in auction sales, and when a puffer is employed to raise the property offered for sale on bona fide bidders, or a combination is entered into between two or more persons not to overbid each other, the contract may in general be avoided. Vide *Puffer*, and 6 John. R. 194; 8 John. R. 444; 3 John. Cas. 29; Cowp. 395; 6 T. R. 642; Harr. Dig. Sale, IV.; and the article *Conditions of Sale.* Vide Harr. Dig. Sale, IV.; 13 Price, R. 76; M'Clel. R. 25; 6 East, R. 392; 5 B. & A. 257; S. C. 2 Stark. R. 295; 1 Esp. R. 340; 5 Esp. R. 103; 4 Taunt. R. 209; 1 H. Bl. R. 81; 2 Chit. R. 253; Cowp. R. 395; 1 Bouv. Inst. n. 976.

AUCTIONEER, *contracts, commerce.* A person authorized by law to sell the goods of others at public sale.

2. He is the agent of both parties, the seller and the buyer. 2 Taunt. 38, 209; 4 Greenl. R. 1; Chit. Contr. 208.

3. His rights are, 1. to charge a commission for his services; 2. he has an interest in the goods sold coupled with the possession; 3. he has a lien for his commissions; 4. he may sue the buyer for the purchase-money.

4. He is liable, 1. to the owner for a faithful discharge of his duties in the sale, and if he gives credit without authority, for the value of the goods; 2. he is responsible for the duties due to the government; 3. he is answerable to the purchaser when he does not disclose the name of the principal; 4. he may be sued when he sells the goods of a third person, after notice not to sell them. Peake's Rep. 120; 2 Kent, Com. 423, 4; 4 John. Ch. R. 659; 3 Burr. R. 1921; 2 Taunt. R. 38; 1 Jac. & Walk. R. 350; 3 V. & B. 57; 13 Ves. R. 472; 1 Y. & J. R. 389; 5 Barn. & Ald. 333; 1 H. Bl. 81; 7 East, R. 558; 4 B. & Adolph. R. 443; 7 Taunt. 209; 3 Chit. Com. L. 210; Story on Ag. § 27; 2 Liv. Ag. 335; Cowp. 395; 6 T. R. 642; 6 John. 194; Bouv. Inst. Index, h. t.

AUCTOR. Among the Romans the seller was called *auctor;* and public sales were made by fixing a spear in the forum, and a person who acted as crier stood by the spear; the catalogue of the goods to be sold was made in tables called *auctionariæ.*

AUDIENCE. A hearing. It is usual for the executive of a country to whom a minister has been sent, to give such minister an audience. And after a minister has been recalled, an *audience of leave* usually takes place.

AUDIENCE COURT, *Eng. eccl. law.* A court belonging to the archbishop of Canterbury, having the same authority with the court of arches. 4 Inst. 337.

AUDIENDO ET TERMINANDO, *oyer and terminer, English crim. law.* A writ, or rather a commission, directed to certain persons for the trial and punishment of such persons as have been concerned in a riotous assembly, insurrection or other heinous misdemeanor.

AUDITA QUERELA. A writ applicable to the case of a defendant against whom a judgment has been recovered, (and who is therefore in danger of execution or perhaps actually in execution,) grounded on some matter of discharge which happened after the judgment, and not upon any matter which might have been pleaded as a defence to the action. 13 Mass. 453; 12 Mass. 270; 6 Verm. 243; Bac. Ab. h. t.; 2 Saund. 148, n. 1; 2 Sell. Pr. 252.

2. It is a remedial process, which bears solely on the wrongful acts of the opposite party, and not upon the erroneous judgments or acts of the court. 10 Mass. 103; 17 Mass. 159; 1 Aik 363. It will not lie, therefore, where the cause of complaint is a proper subject for a writ of error. 1 Verm. 433, 491; Brayt. 27.

3. An audita querela is in the nature of an equitable suit, in which the equitable rights of the parties will be considered. 10 Mass. 101; 14 Mass. 448; 2 John. Cas. 227.

4. An *audita querela* is a regular suit, in which the parties may plead, take issue, &c. 17 John. 484. But the writ must be allowed in open court, and is not, of itself, a *supersedeas*, which may or may not be granted, in the discretion of the court, according to circumstances. 2 John. 227.

5. In modern practice, it is usual to grant the same relief, on motion, which might be obtained by *audita querela;* 4 John. 191; 11 S. & R. 274; and in Virginia, 5 Rand. 639, and South Carolina, 2 Hill, 298, the summary remedy, by motion, has superseded this ancient remedy. In Pennsylvania, this writ, it seems, may still be maintained, though relief is more generally obtained on motion. 11 S. & R. 274. Vide, generally, Pet. C. C. R. 269; Brayt. 27, 28; Walker, 66; 1 Chipm. 387; 3 Conn. 260; 10 Pick. 439; 1 Aik. 107; 1 Overt. 425; 2 John. Cas. 227; 1 Root, 151; 2 Root, 178; 9 John. 221; Bouv. Inst. Index, h. t.

AUDITOR. An officer whose duty is to examine the accounts of officers who have received and disbursed public moneys by lawful authority. See Acts of Congress, April 3, 1817, 3 Story's Laws U. S. 1630; and the Act of February 24, 1819, 3 Story's L. U. S. 1722.

AUDITORS, *practice.* Persons lawfully appointed to examine and digest accounts referred to them, take down the evidence in writing, which may be lawfully offered in relation to such accounts, and prepare materials on which a decree or judgment may be made; and to report the whole, together with their opinion, to the court in which such accounts originated. 6 Cranch, 8; 1 Aik. 145; 12 Mass. 412.

2. Their report is not, *per se*, binding and conclusive, but will become so, unless excepted to. 5 Rawle, R. 323. It may be set aside, either with or without exceptions to it being filed. In the first case, when errors are apparent on its face, it may be set aside or corrected. 2 Cranch, 124; 5 Cranch, 313. In the second case, it may be set aside for any fraud, corruption, gross misconduct, or error. 6 Cranch, 8; 4 Cranch, 308; 1 Aik. 145. The auditors

ought to be sworn, but this will be presumed. 8 Verm. 396.

3. Auditors are also persons appointed to examine the accounts subsisting between the parties in an action of account render, after a judgment *quod computet*. Bac. Ab. Accompt, F.

4. The auditors are required to state a special account, 4 Yeates, 514, and the whole is to be brought down to the time when they make an end of their account. 2 Burr. 1086. And auditors are to make proper charges and credits without regard to time, or the verdict. 2 S. & R. 317. When the facts or matters of law are disputed before them, they are to report them to the court, when the former will be decided by a jury, and the latter by the court, and the result sent to the auditors for their guidance. 5 Binn. 433.

AUGMENTATION, *old English law*. The name of a court erected by Henry VIII., which was invested with the power of determining suits and controversies relating to monasteries and abbey lands.

AULA REGIS. The name of an English court, so called because it was held in the great hall of the king's palace. Vide *Curia Regis*.

AUNT, *domestic relations*. The sister of one's father or mother; she is a relation in the third degree. Vide 2 Com. Dig. 474; Dane's Ab. c. 126, a. 3. § 4.

AUTER. Another. This word is frequently used in composition, as auter droit, auter vie, auter action, &c.

AUTRE ACTION PENDANT. A plea that another action is pending for the same cause.

2. It is evident that a plaintiff cannot have two actions at the same time, for the same cause, against the same defendant; and when a second action is so commenced, and this plea is filed, the first action must be discontinued, and the costs paid, and this ought to be done before the plaintiff replies *nul tiel record*. Grah. Pr. 98. See *Lis Pendens*.

3. But the suit must be for the same cause, in order to take advantage of it under these circumstances, for if it be for a different cause, as, if the action be for a lien, as, a proceeding *in rem* to enforce a mechanic's lien, it cannot be pleaded in abatement in an action for the labor and materials. 3 Scamm. 201. See 16 Verm. 234; 1 Richards, 438; 3 Watts & S. 395; 7 Metc. 570; 9 N. H. Rep. 545.

4. In general, the pending of another action must be pleaded in abatement; 3 Rawle, 320; 1 Mass. 495; 5 Mass. 174, 179; 2 N. H. Rep. 36; 7 Verm. 124; 3 Dana, 157; 1 Ashm. 4; 2 Browne, 175; 4 H. & M. 487; but in a penal action, at the suit of a common informer, the priority of a former suit for the same penalty in the name of a third person, may be pleaded in bar, because the party who first sued is entitled to the penalty. 1 Chit. Pl. 443.

5. Having once arrested a defendant, the plaintiff cannot, in general, arrest him again for the same cause of action. Tidd. 184. But under special circumstances, of which the court will judge, a defendant may be arrested a second time. 2 Miles, 99, 100, 141, 142. Vide Bac. Ab. Bail in civil cases, B 3; Grah. Pr. 98; Troub. & H. Pr. 44; 4 Yeates, 206; 1 John. Cas. 397; 7 Taunt. 151; 1 Marsh. 395; and *Lis Pendens*.

AUTER DROIT, or more properly, *Autre Droit*, another's right. A man may sue or be sued in another's right; this is the case with executors and administrators.

AUTHENTIC. This term signifies an original of which there is no doubt.

AUTHENTIC ACT, *civil law*, *contracts*, *evidence*. The authentic act is that which has been executed before a notary or other public officer authorized to execute such functions, or which is testified by a public seal, or has been rendered public by the authority of a competent magistrate, or which is certified as being a copy of a public register. Nov. 73, c. 2; Code, 7, 52, 6; Id. 4, 21; Dig. 22, 4.

2. In Louisiana, the authentic act, as it relates to contracts, is that which has been executed before a notary public or other officer authorized to execute such functions, in presence of two witnesses, free, male, and aged at least fourteen years; or of three witnesses, if the party be blind. If the party does not know how to sign, the notary must cause him to affix his mark to the instrument. Civil Code of Lo., art. 2231.

3. The authentic act is full proof of the agreement contained in it, against the contracting parties and their heirs or assigns, unless it be declared and proved to be a forgery. Id. art. 2233. Vide Merl. Rép. h. t.

AUTHENTICATION, *practice*. An attestation made by a proper officer, by which he certifies that a record is in due form of law, and that the person who certifies it is the officer appointed by law to do so.

2. The Constitution of the U. S., art. 4, s. 1, declares, "Full faith and credit shall be given in each state to the public acts, records and judicial proceedings of every other state. And congress may by general laws prescribe the manner in which such acts, records and proceedings shall be proved, and the effect thereof." The object of the authentication is to supply all other proof of the record. The laws of the United States have provided a mode of authentication of public records and office papers; these acts are here transcribed.

3. By the Act of May 26, 1790, it is provided, "That the act of the legislatures of the several states shall be authenticated by having the seal of their respective states affixed thereto: That the records and judicial proceedings of the courts of any state shall be proved or admitted, in any other court within the United States, by the attestation of the clerk, and the seal of the court annexed, if there be a seal, together with a certificate of the judge, chief justice or presiding magistrate, as the case may be, that the said attestation is in due form. And the said records and judicial proceedings, authenticated as aforesaid, shall have such faith and credit given to them, in every court within the United States, as they have, by law or usage, in the courts of the state from whence the said records are, or shall be taken."

4. The above act having provided only for one species of record, it was necessary to pass the Act of March 27, 1804, to provide for other cases. By this act it is enacted,

§ 1. "That, from and after the passage of this act, all records and exemplifications of office books, which are or may be kept in any public office of any state, not appertaining to a court, shall be proved or admitted in any other court or office in any other state, by the attestation of the keeper of the said records or books, and the seal of his office thereto annexed, if there be a seal, together with a certificate of the presiding justice of the court of the county or district, as the case may be, in which such office is or may be kept; or of the governor, the secretary of state, the chancellor or the keeper of the great seal of the state, that the said attestation is in due form, and by the proper officer; and the said certificate, if given by the presiding justice of a court, shall be further authenticated by the clerk or prothonotary of the said court, who shall certify, under his hand and the seal of his office, that the said presiding justice is duly commissioned and qualified; or if the said certificate be given by the governor, the secretary of state, the chancellor or keeper of the great seal, it shall be under the great seal of the state in which the said certificate is made. And the said records and exemplifications, authenticated as aforesaid, shall have such faith and credit given to them in every court and office within the United States, as they have by law or usage in the courts or offices of the state from whence the same are or shall be taken."

5.—§ 2. "That all the provisions of this act, and the act to which this is a supplement, shall apply, as well to the public acts, records, office books, judicial proceedings, courts, and offices of the respective territories of the United States, and countries subject to the jurisdiction of the United States, as to the public acts, records, office books, judicial proceedings, courts and offices of the several states."

6. The Act of May 8, 1792, s. 12, provides, "That all the records and proceedings of the court of appeals, heretofore appointed, previous to the adoption of the present constitution, shall be deposited in the office of the clerk of the supreme court of the United States, who is hereby authorized and directed to give copies of all such records and proceedings, to any person requiring and paying for the same, in like manner as copies of the records and other proceedings of the said court are by law directed to be given; which copies shall have like faith and credit as all other proceedings of the said court."

7. By authentication is also understood whatever act is done either by the party or some other person with a view of causing an instrument to be known and identified; as for example, the acknowledgment of a deed by the grantor; the attesting a deed by witnesses. 2 Benth. on Ev. 449.

AUTHENTICS, *civ. law.* This is the name given to a collection of the Novels of Justinian, made by an anonymous author. It is called authentic on account of its authority.

2. There is also another collection which bears the name of *authentics.* It is composed of extracts made from the Novels, by a lawyer named Irnier, and which he inserted in the code at such places as they refer; these extracts have the reputation of

not being correct. Merlin, Répertoire, mot Authentique.

AUTHORITIES, *practice*. By this word is understood the citations which are made of laws, acts of the legislature, and decided cases, and opinions of elementary writers. In its more confined sense, this word means, cases decided upon solemn argument which are said to be authorities for similar judgments in like cases. 1 Lilly's Reg. 219. These latter are sometimes called precedents. (q. v.) Merlin, Répertoire, mot Autorités.

2. It has been remarked, that when we find an opinion in a text writer upon any particular point, we must consider it not merely as the opinion of the author, but as the supposed result of the authorities to which he refers; 3 Bos. & Pull. 301; but this is not always the case, and frequently the opinion is advanced with the reasons which support it, and it must stand or fall as these are or are not well founded. A distinction has been made between writers who have, and those who have not holden a judicial station; the former are considered authority, and the latter are not so considered unless their works have been judicially approved as such. Ram. on Judgments, 93. But this distinction appears not to be well founded; some writers who have occupied a judicial station do not possess the talents or the learning of others who have not been so elevated, and the works or writings of the latter are much more deserving the character of an authority than those of the former. See 3 T. R. 64, 241.

AUTHORITY, *contracts*. The lawful delegation of power by one person to another.

2. We will consider, 1. The delegation. 2. The nature of the authority. 3. The manner it is to be executed. 4. The effects of the authority.

3.—1. The authority may be delegated by deed, or by parol. 1. It may be delegated by deed for any purpose whatever, for whenever an authority by parol would be sufficient, one by deed will be equally so. When the authority is to do something which must be performed through the medium of a deed, then the authority must also be by deed, and executed with all the forms necessary to render that instrument perfect; unless, indeed, the principal be present, and verbally or impliedly authorizes the agent to fix his name to the deed; 4 T. R. 313; W. Jones, R. 268; as, if a man be authorized to convey a tract of land, the letter of attorney must be by deed. Bac. Ab. h. t.; 7 T. R. 209; 2 Bos. & Pull, 338; 5 Binn. 613; 14 S. & R. 331; 6 S. & R. 90; 2 Pick. R. 345; 5 Mass. R. 11; 1 Wend. 424; 9 Wend. R. 54, 68; 12 Wend. R. 525; Story, Ag. § 49; 3 Kent, Com. 613, 3d edit.; 3 Chit. Com. Law, 195. But it does not require a written authority to sign an unsealed paper, or a contract in writing not under seal. Paley on Ag. by Lloyd, 161; Story, Ag. § 50.

4.—2. For many purposes, however, the authority may be by parol, either in writing not under seal, or verbally, or by the mere employment of the agent. Pal. on Agen. 2. The exigencies of commercial affairs render such an appointment indispensable; business would be greatly embarrassed, if a regular letter of attorney were required to sign or negotiate a promissory note or bill of exchange, or sell or buy goods, or write a letter, or procure a policy for another. This rule of the common law has been adopted and followed from the civil law. Story, Ag. § 47; Dig. 3, 3, 1, 1; Poth. Pand. 3, 3, 3; Domat, liv. 1, tit. 15, § 1, art. 5; see also 3 Chit. Com. Law, 5, 195; 7 T. R. 350.

5.—2. The authority given must have been possessed by the person who delegates it, or it will be void; and it must be of a thing lawful, or it will not justify the person to whom it is given. Dyer, 102; Kielw. 83. It is a maxim that *delegata potestas non potest delegari*, so that an agent who has a mere authority must execute it himself, and cannot delegate his authority to a sub-agent. See 5 Pet. 390; 3 Story, R. 411, 425; 11 Gill & John. 58; 26 Wend. 485; 15 Pick. 303, 307; 1 McMullan, 453; 4 Scamm. 127, 133; 2 Inst. 597. See *Delegation*.

6. Authorities are divided into general or special. A *general* authority is one which extends to all acts connected with a particular employment; a *special* authority is one confined to "an individual instance." 15 East, 408; Id. 38.

7. They are also divided into limited and unlimited. When the agent is bound by precise instructions, it is *limited;* and *unlimited* when he is left to pursue his own discretion. An authority is either express or implied.

8. An *express* authority may be by deed or by parol, that is, in writing not under seal, or verbally. The authority must have been actually given.

9. An *implied* authority is one which,

although no proof exists of its having been actually given, may be inferred from the conduct of the principal; for example, when a man leaves his wife without support, the law presumes he authorizes her to buy necessaries for her maintenance; or if a master, usually send his servant to buy goods for him upon credit, and the servant buy some things without the master's orders, yet the latter will be liable upon the implied authority. Show. 95; Pal. on Ag. 137 to 146.

10.—3. In considering in what manner the authority is to be executed, it will be necessary to examine, 1. By whom the authority must be executed. 2. In what manner. 3. In what time.

11.—1. A delegated authority can be executed only by the person to whom it is given, for the confidence being personal, cannot be assigned to a stranger. 1 Roll. Ab. 330; 2 Roll. Ab. 9; 9 Co. 77 b; 9 Ves. 236, 251; 3 Mer. R. 237; 2 M. & S. 299, 301.

12. An authority given to two cannot be executed by one. Co. Litt. 112 b, 181 b. And an authority given to three *jointly* and *separately*, is not, in general, well executed by two. Co. Litt. 181 b; sed vide 1 Roll. Abr. 329, l, 5; Com. Dig. Attorney, C 8; 3 Pick. R. 232; 2 Pick. R. 345; 12 Mass. R. 185; 6 Pick. R. 198; 6 John. R. 39; Story, Ag. § 42. These rules apply to an authority of a private nature, which must be executed by all to whom it is given; and not to a power of a public nature, which may be executed by a majority. 9 Watts, R. 466; 5 Bin. 484, 5; 9 S. & R. 99. 2. When the authority is particular, it must in general be strictly pursued, or it will be void, unless the variance be merely circumstantial. Co. Litt. 49 b, 303 b; 6 T. R. 591; 2 H. Bl. 623; Co. Lit. 181 b; 1 Tho. Co. Lit. 852.

13.—2. As to the form to be observed in the execution of an authority, it is a general rule that an act done under a power of attorney must be done in the name of the person who gives a power, and not in the attorney's name. 9 Co. 76, 77. It has been holden that the name of the attorney is not requisite. 1 W. & S. 328, 332; Moor, pl. 1106; Str. 705; 2 East, R. 142; Moor, 818; Paley on Ag. by Lloyd, 175; Story on Ag. § 146; 9 Ves. 236: 1 Y. & J. 387; 2 M. & S. 299; 4 Campb. R. 184; 2 Cox, R. 84; 9 Co. R. 75; 6 John. R. 94; 9 John. R. 334; 10 Wend. R. 87; 4 Mass. R. 595; 2 Kent, Com. 631, 3d ed. But it matters not in what words this is done, if it sufficiently appear to be in the name of the principal, as, for A B, (the principal,) C D, (the attorney,) which has been held to be sufficient. See 15 Serg. & R. 55; 11 Mass. R. 97; 22 Pick. R. 158; 12 Mass. R. 237; 9 Mass. 335; 16 Mass. R. 461; 1 Cowen, 513; 3 Wend. 94; Story, Ag. §§ 154, 275, 278, 395; Story on P. N. § 69; 2 East, R. 142; 7 Watt's R. 121; 6 John. R. 94 But see contra, Bac. Ab. Leases, J 10; 9 Co. 77; 1 Hare & Wall. Sel. Dec. 426.

14.—3. The execution must take place during the continuance of the authority, which is determined either by revocation, or performance of the commission.

15. In general, an authority is revocable, unless it be given as a security, or it be coupled with an interest. 3 Watts & Serg. 14; 4 Campb. N. P. 272; 7 Ver. 28; 2 Kent's Comm. 506; 8 Wheat. 203; 2 Cowen, 196; 2 Esp. N. P. Cases, 565; Bac. Abr. h. t. The revocation (q. v.) is either express or implied; when it is express and made known to the person authorized, the authority is at an end; the revocation is implied when the principal dies, or, if a female, marries; or the subject of the authority is destroyed, as if a man have authority to sell my house, and it is destroyed by fire; or to buy for me a horse, and before the execution of the authority, the horse dies.

16. When once the agent has exercised all the authority given to him, the authority is at an end.

17.—4. An authority is to be so construed as to include all necessary or usual means of executing it with effect; 2 H. Bl. 618; 1 Roll. R. 390; Palm. 394; 10 Ves. 441; 6 Serg. & R. 149; Com. Dig. Attorney, C 15; 4 Campb. R. 163; Story on Ag. § 58 to 142; 1 J. J. Marsh. R. 293; 5 Johns. R. 58; 1 Liv. on Ag. 103, 4; and when the agent acts, avowedly as such, within his authority, he is not personally responsible. Pal. on Ag. 4, 5.

Vide, generally, 3 Vin. Ab. 416; Bac. Ab. h. t.; 1 Salk. 95; Com. Dig. h. t., and the titles there referred to. 1 Roll. Ab. 330; 2 Roll. Ab. 9; Bouv. Inst. Index, h. t.; and the articles, *Attorney; Agency; Agent; Principal.*

AUTHORITY, *government*. The right and power which an officer has in the exercise of a public function to compel obedience to his lawful commands. A judge, for example, has authority to enforce obedience to his lawful orders. Domat, Dr. Pub. lib. 1, tit. 9, s. 1, n. 13.

AUTOCRACY. The name of a government where the monarch is unlimited by law. Such is the power of the emperor of Russia, who, following the example of his predecessors, calls himself the autocrat of all the Russias.

AUTRE VIE. Another's life. Vide, *Pur autre vie.*

AUTREFOIS. A French word, signifying formerly, at another time; and is usually applied to signify that something was done formerly, as autrefois acquit, autrefois convict, &c.

AUTREFOIS ACQUIT, *crim. law, pleading.* A plea made by a defendant, indicted for a crime or misdemeanor, that he has formerly been tried and acquitted of the same offence. See a form of this plea in Arch. Cr. Pl. 90.

2. To be a bar, the acquittal must have been by trial, and by the verdict of a jury on a valid indictment. Hawk. B. 2, c. 25, s. 1; 4 Bl. Com. 335. There must be an acquittal of the offence charged in law and in fact. Stark. Pl. 355; 2 Swift's Dig. 400; 1 Chit. Cr. Law, 452; 2 Russ. on Cr. 41.

3. The Constitution of the U. S., Amend. Art. 5, provides that no person shall be subject for the same offence to be put twice in jeopardy of life or limb. Vide, generally, 12 Serg. & Rawle, 389; Yelv. 205 a, note.

AUTREFOIS ATTAINT, *crim. law.* Formerly attainted.

2. This is a good plea in bar, where a second trial would be quite superfluous. Co. Litt. 390 b, note 2; 4 Bl. Com. 336. Where, therefore, any advantage either to public justice, or private individuals, would arise from a second prosecution, the plea will not prevent it; as where the criminal is indicted for treason after an attainder of felony, in which case the punishment will be more severe and more extensive. 3 Chit. Cr. Law, 464.

AUTREFOIS CONVICT, *crim. law, pleading.* A plea made by a defendant, indicted for a crime or misdemeanor, that he has formerly been tried and convicted of the same.

2. As a man once tried and acquitted of an offence is not again to be placed in jeopardy for the same cause, so, *a fortiori*, if he has suffered the penalty due to his offence, his conviction ought to be a bar to a second indictment for the same cause, least he should be punished twice for the same crime. 2 Hale, 251; 4 Co. 394; 2 Leon. 83.

3. The form of this plea is like that of autrefois acquit; (q. v.) it must set out the former record, and show the identity of the offence and of the person by proper averments. Hawk. B. 2, c. 36; Stark. Cr. Pl. 363; Arch. Cr. Pl. 92; 1 Chit. Cr. Law, 462; 4 Bl. Com. 335; 11 Verm. R. 516.

AVAIL. Profits of land; hence tenant paravail is one in actual possession, who makes avail or profits of the land. Ham. N. P. 393.

AVALUM. By this word is understood the written engagement of a third person to guaranty and to become security that a bill of exchange shall be paid when due.

AVERAGE. A term used in commerce to signify a contribution made by the owners of the ship, freight and goods, on board, in proportion to their respective interests, towards any particular loss or expense sustained for the general safety of the ship and cargo; to the end that the particular loser may not be a greater sufferer than the owner of the ship and the other owners of goods on board. Marsh. Ins. B. 1, c. 12, s. 7; Code de Com. art. 397; 2 Hov. Supp. to Ves. jr. 407; Poth. Aver. art. Prel.

2. Average is called general or gross average, because it falls generally upon the whole or gross amount of the ship, freight and cargo; and also to distinguish it from what is often though improperly termed particular average, but which in truth means a particular or partial, and not a general loss; or has no affinity to average properly so called. Besides these there are other small charges, called petty or accustomed averages; such as pilotage, towage, light-money, beaconage, anchorage, bridge toll, quarantine, river charges, signals, instructions, castle money, pier money, digging the ship out of the ice, and the like.

3. A contribution upon general average can only be claimed in cases where, upon as much deliberation and consultation between the captain and his officers as the occasion will admit of, it appears that the sacrifice at the time it was made, was absolutely and indispensably necessary for the preservation of the ship and cargo. To entitle the owner of the goods to an average contribution, the loss must evidently conduce to the preservation of the ship and the rest of the cargo; and it must appear that the ship and the rest of the cargo were in fact saved. Show. Ca. Parl. 20.

See generally Code de Com. tit. 11 and 12; Park, Ins. c. 6; Marsh. Ins. B. 1, c

12, s. 7; 4 Mass. 548; 6 Mass. 125; 8 Mass. 467; 1 Caines' R. 196; 4 Dall. 459; 2 Binn. 547; 4 Binn. 513; 2 Serg. & Rawle, 237, in note; 2 Serg. & Rawle, 229; 3 Johns. Cas. 178; 1 Caines' R. 43; 2 Caines' R. 263; Id. 274; 8 Johns. R. 237, 2d edit; 9 Johns. R. 9; 11 Johns. R. 315; 1 Caines' R. 573; 7 Johns. R. 412; Wesk. Ins. tit. Average; 2 Barn. & Cres. 811; 1 Rob. Adm. Rep. 293; 2 New Rep. 378; 18 Ves. 187; Lex. Mer. Amer. ch. 9; Bac. Abr. Merchant, F; Vin. Abr. Contribution and Average; Stev. on Av.; Ben. on Av.

AVERIA. Cattle. This word, in its most enlarged signification, is used to include horses of the plough, oxen and cattle. Cunn. Dict. h. t.

AVERIIS CAPTIS IN WITHERNAM, *Eng. law*. The name of a writ which lies in favor of a man whose cattle have been unlawfully taken by another, and driven out of the county where they were taken, so that they cannot be replevied.

2. This writ issues against the wrong doer to take his cattle to the plaintiff's use. Reg. of Writs, 82.

AVERMENT, *pleading*. Comes from the Latin *verificare*, or the French *averrer*, and signifies a positive statement of facts in opposition to argument or inference. Cowp. 683, 684.

2. Lord Coke says averments are two-fold, namely, general and particular. A *general* averment is that which is at the conclusion of an offer to make good or prove whole pleas containing new affirmative matter, (but this sort of averment only applies to pleas, replications, or subsequent pleadings; for counts and avowries which are in the nature of counts, need not be averred,) the form of such averment being *et hoc paratus est verificare*.

3. *Particular* averments are assertions of the truth of particular facts, as the life of tenant or of tenant in tail is averred: and, in these, says Lord Coke, *et hoc*, &c., are not used. Co Litt. 362 b. Again, in a particular averment the party merely protests and avows the truth of the fact or facts averred; but in general averments he makes an offer to prove and make good by evidence what he asserts.

4. Averments were formerly divided into *immaterial* and *impertinent*, but these terms are now treated as synonymous. 3 D. & R. 209. A better division may be made of *immaterial* or *impertinent* averments, which are those which need not be stated, and, if stated, need not be proved; and *unnecessary* averments, which consist of matters which need not be alleged, but if alleged, must be proved. For example, in an action of assumpsit, upon a warranty on the sale of goods, an allegation of deceit on the part of the seller is impertinent, and need not be proved. 2 East, 446; 17 John. 92. But if in an action by a lessor against his tenant, for negligently keeping his fire, a demise for seven years be alleged, and the proof be a lease at will only, it will be a fatal variance; for though an allegation of tenancy generally would have been sufficient, yet having unnecessarily qualified it, by stating the precise term, it must be proved as laid. Carth. 202.

5. Averments must contain not only matter, but form. General averments are always in the same form. The most common form of making particular averments is in express and direct words, for example: And the party *avers* or *in fact saith*, or *although*, or *because*, or *with this that*, or *being*, &c. But they need not be in these words, for any words which necessarily imply the matter intended to be averred are sufficient.

See, in general, 3 Vin. Abr. 357; Bac. Abr. Pleas, B 4; Com. Dig. Pleader, C 50, C 67, 68, 69, 70; 1 Saund. 235 a, n. 8; 3 Saund. 352, n. 3; 1 Chit. Pl. 308; Arch. Civ. Pl. 163; Doct. Pl. 120; 1 Lilly's Reg. 209; United States Dig. Pleading, II (c); 3 Bouv. Inst. n. 2835–40.

AVOIDANCE, *eccl. law*. It is when a benefice becomes vacant for want of an incumbent; and, in this sense, it is opposed to plenarty. Avoidances are in fact, as by the death of the incumbent; or in law.

AVOIDANCE, *pleading*. The introduction of new or special matter, which, admitting the premises of the opposite party, avoids or repels his conclusions. Gould on Pl. c. 1 § 24, 42.

AVOIR DU POIS, *comm. law*. The name of a peculiar weight. This kind of weight is so named in distinction from the Troy weight. One pound avoir du pois contains 7000 grains Troy; that is, fourteen ounces, eleven pennyweights and sixteen grains Troy; a pound avoir du pois contains sixteen ounces; and an ounce sixteen drachms. Thirty-two cubic feet of pure spring-water, at the temperature of fifty-six degrees of Fahrenheit's thermometer, make a ton of 2000 pounds avoir du pois, or two thousand two hundred and forty pounds net weight

Dane's Abr. c. 211, art. 12, § 6. The avoir du pois ounce is less than the Troy ounce in the proportion of 72 to 79; though the pound is greater. Encyc. Amer. art. Avoir du pois. For the derivation of this phrase, see Barr. on the Stat. 206. See the Report of Secretary of State of the United States to the Senate, February 22d, 1821, pp. 44, 72, 76, 79, 81, 87, for a learned exposition of the whole subject.

AVOUCHER. The call which the tenant makes on another who is bound to him by warranty to come into court, either to defend the right against the demandant, or to yield him other land in value. 2 Tho. Co. Lit. 304.

AVOW or ADVOW, *practice*. Signifies to justify or maintain an act formerly done. For example, when replevin is brought for a thing distrained, and the distrainer justifies the taking, he is said to avow. Termes de la Ley. This word also signifies to bring forth anything. Formerly when a stolen thing was found in the possession of any one, he was bound *advocare*, i. e. to produce the seller from whom he alleged he had bought it, to justify the sale, and so on till they found the thief. Afterwards the word was taken to mean anything which a man admitted to be his own or done by him, and in this sense it is mentioned in Fleta, lib. 1, c. 5, par 4. Cunn. Dict. h. t.

AVOWANT, *practice, pleading*. One who makes an avowry.

AVOWEE, *eccl. law*. An advocate of a church benefice.

AVOWRY, *pleading*. An avowry is where the defendant in an action of replevin, avows the taking of the distress in his own right, or in right of his wife, and sets forth the cause of it, as for arrears of rent, damage done, or the like. Lawes on Pl. 35; Hamm. N. P. 464; 4 Bouv. Inst. n. 3571.

2. An avowry is sometimes said to be in the nature of an action or of a declaration, and privity of estate is necessary. Co. Lit. 320 a; 1 Serg. & R. 170–1. There is no general issue upon an avowry and it cannot be traversed cumulatively. 5 Serg. & R. 377. Alienation cannot be replied to it without notice; for the tenure is deemed to exist for the purposes of an avowry till notice be given of the alienation. Ham. Parties, 131–2; Ham. N. P. 398, 426.

AVOWTERER, *Eng. law*. An adulterer with whom a married woman continues in adultery. T. L.

AVOWTRY, *Eng. law*. The crime of adultery.

AVULSION. Where, by the immediate and manifest power of a river or stream, the soil is taken suddenly from one man's estate and carried to another. In such case the property belongs to the first owner. An acquiescence on his part, however, will in time entitle the owner of the land to which it is attached to claim it as his own. Bract. 221; Harg. Tracts, De jure maris, &c.; Toull. Dr. Civ. Fr. tom. 3, p. 106; 2 Bl. Com. 262; Schultes on Aq. Rights, 115 to 138. Avulsion differs from alluvion (q. v.) in this, that in the latter case the change of the soil is gradual and imperceptible.

AVUS. Grandfather. This term is used in making genealogical tables.

AWAIT, *crim. law*. Seems to signify what is now understood by lying in wait, or way-laying.

AWARD. The judgment of an arbitrator or arbitrators on a matter submitted to him or them: *arbitrium est judicium*. The writing which contains such judgment is also called an award.

2. The qualifications requisite to the validity of an award are, that it be consonant to the submission; that it be certain; be of things possible to be performed, and not contrary to law or reason; and lastly, that it be final.

3.—1. It is manifest that the award must be confined within the powers given to the arbitrators, because, if their decisions extend beyond that authority, this is an assumption of power not delegated, which cannot legally affect the parties. Kyd on Aw. 140; 1 Binn. 109; 13 Johns. 187; Id. 271; 6 Johns. 13, 39; 11 Johns. 133; 2 Mass. 164; 8 Mass. 399; 10 Mass. 442; Caldw. on Arb. 98; 2 Harring. 347; 3 Harring. 22; 5 Sm. & Marsh. 172; 8 N. H. Rep. 82; 6 Shepl. 251; 12 Gill & John. 456; 22 Pick. 144. If the arbitrators, therefore, transcend their authority, their award *pro tanto* will be void; but if the void part affect not the merits of the submission, the residue will be valid. 1 Wend. 326; 13 John. 264; 1 Cowen, 117; 2 Cowen, 638; 1 Greenl. 300; 6 Greenl. 247; 8 Mass. 399; 13 Mass. 244; 14 Mass. 43; 6 Harr. & John. 10; Doddr. Eng. Lawyer, 168–176; Hardin, 326; 1 Yeates, R. 513.

4.—2. The award ought to be certain, and so expressed that no reasonable doubt can arise on the face of it, as to the arbitrator's meaning, or as to the nature and extent of the duties imposed by it on the parties. An example of such uncertainty may be found in the following cases: An award, directing one party to bind himself in an obligation for the quiet enjoyment of lands, without expressing in what sum the obligor should be bound. 5 Co. 77; Roll. Arbit. Q 4. Again, an award that one should give security to the other, for the payment of a sum of money, or the performance of any particular act, when the kind of security is not specified. Vin. Ab. Arbitr. Q 12; Com. Dig. Arbitrament, E 11; Kyd on Aw. 194; 3 S. & R. 340; 9 John. 43; 2 Halst. 90; 2 Caines, 235: 3 Harr. & John. 383; 3 Ham. 266; 1 Pike, 206; 7 Metc. 316; 5 Sm. & Marsh. 712; 13 Verm. 53; 5 Blackf. 128; 2 Hill, 75; 3 Harr. 442.

5.—3. It must be possible to be performed, be lawful and reasonable. An award that could not by any possibility be performed, as if it directed that the party should deliver a deed not in his possession, or pay a sum of money at a day past, it would of course be void. But the award that the party should pay a sum of money, although he might not then be able to do so, would be binding. The award must not direct anything to be done contrary to law, such as the performance of an act which would render the party a trespasser or a felon, or would subject him to an action. It must also be reasonable, for if it be of things nugatory in themselves, and offering no advantage to either of the parties, it cannot be enforced. Kirby, 253.

6.—4. The award must be final; that is, it must conclusively adjudicate all the matters submitted. 1 Dall. 173; 2 Yeates, 539; 4 Rawle, 304; 1 Caines, 304; 2 Harr. & Gill, 67; Charlt. 289; 3 Pike, 324; 3 Harr. 442; 1 P. S. R. 395; 4 Blackf. 253; 11 Wheat. 446. But if the award is as final as, under the circumstances of the case it might be expected, it will be considered as valid. Com. Dig. Arbitrament, E 15. As to the *form*, the award may be by parol or by deed, but in general it must be made in accordance with the provisions and requirements of the submission. (q. v.) Vide, generally, Kyd on Awards, Index, h. t.; Caldwell on Arbitrations, Index, h. t.; Dane's Ab. c. 13; Com. Dig. Arbitrament, E; Id. Chancery, 2 K 1, &c.; 3 Vin. Ab. 52, 372; 1 Vern. 158; 15 East, R. 215; 1 Ves. Jr. 364; 1 Saund. 326, notes 1, 2, and 3; Wats. on Arbitrations and Awards; 3 Bouv. Inst. n. 2402 to 2500.

AWM, or AUME. An ancient measure, used in measuring Rhenish wines; it contained forty gallons.

AYANT CAUSE, *French law.* This term, which is used in Louisiana, signifies one to whom a right has been assigned, either by will, gift, sale, exchange, or the like. An assignee. An *ayant cause* differs from an heir who acquires the right by inheritance. 8 Toull. n. 245.

AYUNTAMIENTO, *Spanish law.* A congress of persons; the municipal council of a city or town. 1 White's Coll. 416 12 Pet. 442, notes.

B.

BACHELOR. The first degree taken at the universities in the arts and sciences, as bachelor of arts, &c. It is called, in Latin, *Baccalaureus*, from *bacalus*, or *bacillus*, a staff, because a staff was given, by way of distinction, into the hands of those who had completed their studies. Some, however, have derived the word from *baccalaura*, others from *bas chevalier*, as designating young squires who aspire to the knighthood. (Dupin.) But the derivation of the word is uncertain.

BACK-BOND. A bond given by one to a surety, to indemnify such surety in case of loss. In Scotland, a back-bond is an instrument which, in conjunction with another which gives an absolute disposition, constitutes a trust. A declaration of trust.

BACK-WATER. That water in a stream which, in consequence of some obstruction below, is detained or checked in its course, or reflows.

2. Every riparian owner is entitled to the benefit of the water in its natural state. Whenever, therefore, the owner of land

dams or impedes the water in such a manner as to back it on his neighbor above, he is liable to an action; for no one has a right to alter the level of the water, either where it enters, or where it leaves his property. 9 Co. 59; 1 B. & Ald. 258; 1 Wils. R. 178; 6 East, R. 203; 1 S. & Stu. 190; 4 Day, R. 244; 7 Cowen, R. 266; 1 Rawle, R. 218; 5 N. H. Rep. 232; 9 Mass. R. 316; 7 Pick. R. 198; 4 Mason, R. 400; 1 Rawle, R. 27; 2 John. Ch. R. 162, 463; 1 Coxe's R. 460. Vide *Dam; Inundation; Water-course;* and 5 Ohio R. 322.

BACKING, *crim. law practice.* Backing a warrant occurs whenever it becomes necessary to execute it out of the jurisdiction of the magistrate who granted it; as when an offender escapes out of the county in which he committed the offence with which he is charged, into another county. In such a case, a magistrate of the county in which the offender may be found, endorses, or writes his name on the back of the warrant, and thereby gives authority to execute it within his jurisdiction. This is called *backing the warrant.* This may be repeated from county to county, if necessary.

BACKSIDE, *estates.* In England this term was formerly used in conveyances and even in pleadings, and is still adhered to with reference to ancient descriptions in deeds, in continuing the transfer of the same property. It imports a yard at the back part of, or behind a house, and belonging thereto: but although formerly used in pleadings, it is now unusual to adopt it, and the word yard is preferred. 1 Chitty's Pr. 177; 2 Ld. Raym. 1399.

BADGE. A mark or sign worn by some persons, or placed upon certain things for the purpose of designation. Some public officers, as watchmen, policemen, and the like, are required to wear badges that they may be readily known. It is used figuratively when we say, possession of personal property by the seller, is a badge of fraud.

BAGGAGE. Such articles as are carried by a traveller; luggage. Every thing which a passenger carries with him is not baggage. Large sums of money, for example, carried in a travelling trunk, will not be considered baggage, so as to render the carrier responsible. 9 Wend. R. 85. But a watch deposited in his trunk is a part of his baggage. 10 Ohio, R. 145. See, as to what is baggage, 6 Hill, R. 586; 5 Rawle, 188, 189; 1 Pick. 50.

2. In general a common carrier of passengers is responsible for baggage, if lost, though no distinct price be paid for transporting it, it being included in the passenger's fare. Id. The carrier's responsibility for the baggage begins as soon as it has been delivered to him, or to his servants, or to some other person authorized by him to receive it. Then the delivery is complete. The risk and responsibility of the carrier is at an end as soon as he has delivered the baggage to the owner or his agent; and if an offer to deliver it be made at a proper time, the carrier will be discharged from responsibility, as such; yet, if the baggage remain in his custody afterwards, he will hold as bailee, and be responsible for it according to the terms of such bailment. 3 Dana, R. 92. Vide *Common Carriers.*

3. By the act of congress of March 2, 1799, sect. 46, 1 Story's L. U. S. 612, it is declared that all wearing apparel and other personal baggage, &c., of persons who shall arrive in the United States, shall be free and exempted from duty.

BAIL, *practice, contracts.* By bail is understood sureties, given according to law, to insure the appearance of a party in court. The persons who become surety are called bail. Sometimes the term is applied, with a want of exactness, to the security given by a defendant, in order to obtain a stay of execution, after judgment, in civil cases. Bail is either civil or criminal.

2.—1. *Civil bail* is that which is entered in civil cases, and is common or special; bail below or bail above.

3. *Common bail* is a formal entry of fictitious sureties in the proper office of the court, which is called filing common bail to the action. It is in the same form as special bail, but differs from it in this, that the sureties are merely fictitious, as John Doe and Richard Roe: it has, consequently, none of the incidents of special bail. It is allowed to the defendant only when he has been discharged from arrest without bail, and it is necessary in such cases to perfect the appearance of the defendant. Steph. Pl. 56, 7; Grah. Pr. 155; Highm. on Bail 13.

4. *Special bail* is an undertaking by one or more persons for another, before some officer or court properly authorized for that purpose, that he shall appear at a certain time and place to answer a certain charge to be exhibited against him. The essential

qualifications to enable a person to become bail, are that he must be, 1. a freeholder or housekeeper; 2. liable to the ordinary process of the court; 3. capable of entering into a contract; and 4. able to pay the amount for which he becomes responsible. 1. He must be a freeholder or housekeeper. (q. v.) 2 Chit. R. 96; 5 Taunt. 174; Lofft, 148; 3 Petersd. Ab. 104. 2. He must be subject to the ordinary process of the court; and a person privileged from arrest, either permanently or temporarily, will not be taken. 4 Taunt. 249; 1 D. & R. 127; 2 Marsh. 232. 3. He must be competent to enter into a contract; a feme covert, an infant, or a person non compos mentis, cannot therefore become bail. 4. He must be able to pay the amount for which he becomes responsible. But it is immaterial whether his property consists of real or personal estate, provided it be his own, in his own right; 3 Peterd. Ab. 196; 2 Chit. Rep. 97; 11 Price, 158; and be liable to the ordinary process of the law; 4 Burr. 2526; though this rule is not invariably adhered to, for when part of the property consisted of a ship, shortly expected, bail was permitted to justify in respect of such property. 1 Chit. R. 286, n. As to the persons who cannot be received because they are not responsible, see 1 Chit. R. 9, 116; 2 Chit. R. 77, 8; Lofft, 72, 184; 3 Petersd. Ab. 112; 1 Chit. R. 309, n.

5. *Bail below.* This is bail given to the sheriff in civil cases, when the defendant is arrested on bailable process; which is done by giving him a bail bond; it is so called to distinguish it from *bail above.* (q. v.) The sheriff is bound to admit a man to bail, provided good and sufficient sureties be tendered, but not otherwise. Stat. 23 H. VI. c. 9, A. D. 1444; 4 Anne, c. 16, § 20; B. N. P. 224; 2 Term Rep. 560. The sheriff, is not, however, bound to demand bail, and may, at his risk, permit the defendant to be at liberty, provided he will appear, that is, enter bail above, or surrender himself in proper time. 1 Sell. Pr. 126, et seq. The undertaking of bail below is, that the defendant will appear or put in bail to the action on the return day of the writ.

6. *Bail above,* is putting in bail to the action, which is an appearance of the defendant. Bail above are bound either to satisfy the plaintiff his debt and costs, or to surrender the defendant into custody, provided judgment should be against him and he should fail to do so. Sell. Pr. 137.

7. It is a general rule that the defendant having been held to bail, in civil cases, cannot be held a second time for the same cause of action. Tidd's Pr. 184; Grah. Pr. 98; Troub. & Hal. 44; 1 Yeates, 206; 8 Ves. Jur. 594. See *Auter action Pendent; Lis pendens.*

8.—2. Bail in *criminal* cases is defined to be a delivery or bailment of a person to sureties, upon their giving, together with himself, sufficient security for his appearance, he being supposed to be in their friendly custody, instead of going to prison.

9. The Constitution of the United States directs that "excessive bail shall not be required." Amend. art. 8.

10. By the acts of congress of September, 24, 1789, s. 33, and March 2, 1793, s. 4, authority is given to take bail for any crime or offence against the United States, except where the punishment is death, to any justice or judge of the United States, or to any chancellor, judge of the supreme or superior court, or first judge of any court of common pleas, or mayor of any city of any state, or to any justice of the peace or other magistrate of any state, where the offender may be found; the recognizance taken by any of the persons authorized, is to be returned to the court having cognizance of the offence.

11. When the punishment by the laws of the United States is death, bail can be taken only by the supreme or circuit court, or by a judge of the district court of the United States. If the person committed by a justice of the supreme court, or by the judge of a district court, for an offence not punishable with death, shall, after commitment, offer bail, any judge of the supreme or superior court of law, of any state, (there being no judge of the United States in the district to take such bail,) may admit such person to bail.

12. Justices of the peace have in general power to take bail of persons accused; and, when they have such authority, they are required to take such bail. There are many cases, however, under the laws of the several states, as well as under the laws of the United States, as above mentioned, where justices of the peace cannot take bail, but must commit; and, if the accused offers bail, it must be taken by a judge or other officer lawfully authorized.

13. In Pennsylvania, for example, in

cases of murder, or when the defendant is charged with the stealing of any horse, mare, or gelding, on the direct testimony of one witness; or shall be taken having possession of such horse, mare, or gelding, a justice of the peace cannot admit the party to bail. 1 Smith's L. of Pa. 581.

14. In all cases where the party is admitted to bail, the recognizance is to be returned to the court having jurisdiction of the offence charged. Vide *Act of God; Arrest; Auter action pendent; Death; Lis pendens.*

BAIL BOND, *practice, contracts.* A specialty by which the defendant and other persons, usually not less than two, though the sheriff may take only one, become bound to the sheriff in a penalty equal to that for which bail is demanded, conditioned for the due appearance of such defendant to the legal process therein described, and by which the sheriff has been commanded to arrest him. It is only where the defendant is arrested or in the custody of the sheriff, under other than final process, that the sheriff can take such bond. On this bond being tendered to him, which he is compelled to take if the sureties are good, he must discharge the defendant. Stat. 23 H. VI. c. 9.

2. With some exceptions, as for example, where the defendant surrenders; 5 T. R. 754; 7 T. R. 123; 1 East, 387; 1 Bos. & Pull. 326; nothing can be a performance of the condition of the bail bond, but putting in bail to the action. 5 Burr. 2683.

3. The plaintiff has a right to demand from the sheriff an assignment of such bond, so that he may sue it for his own benefit. 4 Ann. c. 16, § 20; Wats. on Sheriff, 99; 1 Sell. Pr. 126, 174. For the general requisites of a bail bond, see 1 T. R. 422; 2 T. R. 569; 15 East, 320; 2 Wils. 69; 6 T. R. 702; 9 East, 55; 5 D. & R. 215; 4 M. & S. 338; 1 Moore, R. 514; 6 Moore, R. 264; 4 East, 568; Hurls. on Bonds, 56; U. S. Dig. Bail V.

BAIL PIECE A certificate given by a judge or the clerk of the court, or other person authorized to keep the record, in which it is certified that A B, the bail, became bail for C D, the defendant, in a certain sum, and in a particular case. It was the practice, formerly, to write these certificates upon small pieces of parchment, in the following form: (See 3 Bl. Com. Appendix.)

In the Court of ———, of the Term of ———, in the year of our Lord, ——.

City and County of ———, ss.

Theunis Thew is delivered to bail upon the taking of his body, to Jacobus Vanzant, of the city of ——, merchant, and to John Doe, of the same city, yeoman.

SMITH, JR. } At the suit of
Attor'y for Deft. } PHILIP CARSWELL.

Taken and acknowledged the — day of —, A. D. ——, before me. D. H.

2. As the bail is supposed to have the custody of the defendant, when he is armed with this process, he may arrest the latter, though he is out of the jurisdiction of the court in which he became bail, and even in a different state. 1 Baldw. 578; 3 Com. 84, 421; 2 Yeates, 263; 8 Pick. 138; 7 John. 145; 3 Day, 485. The bail may take him even while attending court as a suitor, or any time, even on Sunday. 4 Yeates, 123; 4 Conn. 170. He may break even an outer door to seize him; and command the assistance of the sheriff or other officers; 8 Pick. 138; and depute his power to others. 1 John. Cas. 413; 8 Pick. 140. See 1 Serg. & R. 311.

BAILABLE ACTION. One in which the defendant is entitled to be discharged from arrest, only upon giving bail to answer.

BAILABLE PROCESS. Is that process by which an officer is required to arrest a person, and afterwards to take bail for his appearance. A *capias ad respondendum* is bailable, but a *capias ad satisfaciendum* is not.

BAILEE, *contracts.* One to whom goods are bailed.

2. His duties are to act in good faith; he is bound to use extraordinary diligence in those contracts or bailments, where he alone receives the benefit, as in loans; he must observe ordinary diligence of those bailments, which are beneficial to both parties, as hiring; and he will be responsible for gross negligence in those bailments which are only for the benefit of the bailor, as deposit and mandate. Story's Bailm. § 17, 18, 19. He is bound to return the property as soon as the purpose for which it was bailed shall have been accomplished.

3. He has generally a right to retain and use the thing bailed, according to the contract, until the object of the bailment shall have been accomplished.

4. A bailee with a mere naked authority, having a right to remuneration for his trouble, but coupled with no other interest, may support trespass for any injury, amounting to a trespass, done while he was in the

actual possession of the thing. 4 Bouv. Inst. n. 3608.

BAILIFF, *account render*. A bailiff is a person who has, by delivery, the custody and administration of lands or goods for the benefit of the owner or bailor, and is liable to render an account thereof. Co. Lit. 271; 2 Leon. 245; 1 Mall. Ent. 65. The word is derived from the old French word *bailler*, to bail, that is, to deliver. Originally, the word implied the delivery of real estate, as of land, woods, a house, a part of the fish in a pond; Owen, 20; 2 Leon. 194; Keilw. 114 a, b; 37 Ed. III. 7; 10 H. VII. 7, 30; but was afterwards extended to goods and chattels. Every bailiff is a receiver, but every receiver is not a bailiff. Hence it is a good plea that the defendant never was receiver, but as bailiff. 18 Ed. III. 16. See Cro. Eliz. 82–3; 2 Anders. 62–3, 96–7; F. N. B. 134 F; 8 Co. 48 a, b.

2. From a bailiff is required administration, care, management, skill. He is, therefore, entitled to allowance for the expense of administration, and for all things done in his office, according to his own judgment, without the special direction of his principal, and also for casual things done in the common course of business; 1 Mall. Ent. 65, (4) 11; 1 Rolle, Ab. 125, 1, 7; Co. Lit. 89 a; Com. Dig. E 12; Bro. Ab. Acc. 18; Lucas, Rep. 23; but not for things foreign to his office. Bro. Ab. Acc. 26, 88; Plowd. 282 b, 14; Com. Dig. Acc. E 13; Co. Lit. 172; 1 Mall. Ent. 65, (4) 4. Whereas, a mere receiver, or a receiver who is not also a bailiff, is not entitled to allowance for any expenses. Bro. Ab. Acc. 18; 1 Mall. Ent. 66, (4) 10; 1 Roll. Ab. 118; Com. Dig. E 13; 1 Dall. 340.

3. A bailiff may appear and plead for his principal in an assize; "and his plea commences" thus, "J. S., bailiff of T. N., comes," &c., not "T. N., by his bailiff, J. S., comes," &c. 2 Inst. 415; Keilw. 117 b. As to what matters he may plead, see 2 Inst. 414.

BAILIFF, *office*. Magistrates who formerly administered justice in the parliaments or courts of France, answering to the English sheriffs as mentioned by Bracton. There are still bailiffs of particular towns in England; as the bailiff of Dover Castle, &c., otherwise bailiffs are now only officers or stewards, &c.; as *Bailiffs of liberties*, appointed by every lord within his liberty, to serve writs, &c. *Bailiff errent* or *itenerant*, appointed to go about the country for the same purpose. *Sheriff's bailiffs*, sheriff's officers to execute writs; these are also called *bound bailiffs*, because they are usually bound in a bond to the sheriff for the due execution of their office. *Bailiffs of court baron*, to summon the court, &c. *Bailiffs of husbandry*, appointed by private persons to collect their rents and manage their estates. *Water bailiffs*, officers in port towns for searching ships, gathering tolls, &c. Bac. Ab. h. t.

BAILMENT, *contracts*. This word is derived from the French, *bailler*, to deliver. 2 Bl. Com. 451; Jones' Bailm. 90; Story on Bailm. c. 1, § 2. It is a compendious expression, to signify a contract resulting from delivery. It has been defined to be a delivery of goods on a condition, express or implied, that they shall be restored by the bailee to the bailor, or according to his directions, as soon as the purpose for which they are bailed shall be answered. 1 Jones' Bailm. 1. Or it is a delivery of goods in trust, on a contract either expressed or implied, that the trust shall be duly executed, and the goods redelivered, as soon as the time or use for which they were bailed shall have elapsed or be performed. Jones' Bailm. 117.

2. Each of these definitions, says Judge Story, seems redundant and inaccurate if it be the proper office of a definition to include those things only which belong to the genus or class. Both these definitions suppose that the goods are to be restored or redelivered; but in a bailment for sale, as upon a consignment to a factor, no redelivery is contemplated between the parties. In some cases, no use is contemplated by the bailee; in others, it is of the essence of the contract: in some cases time is material to terminate the contract; in others, time is necessary to give a new accessorial right. Story on Bailm. c. 1, § 2.

3. Mr. Justice Blackstone has defined a bailment to be a delivery of goods in trust, upon a contract, either expressed or implied, that the trust shall be faithfully executed on the part of the bailee. 2 Bl. Com. 451. And in another place, as the delivery of goods to another person for a particular use. 2 Bl. Com. 395. Vide Kent's Comm. Lect. 40, 437.

4. Mr. Justice Story says, that a bailment is a delivery of a thing in trust for some special object or purpose, and upon a contract, express or implied, to conform to the object or purpose of the trust. Story on Bailm. c. 1, § 2. This corresponds very

nearly with the definition of Merlin. Vide Répertoire, mot Bail.

5. Bailments are divisible into three kinds: 1. Those in which the trust is for the benefit of the bailor, as deposits and mandates. 2. Those in which the trust is for the benefit of the bailee, as gratuitous loans for use. 3. Those in which the trust is for the benefit of both parties, as pledges or pawns, and hiring and letting to hire. See *Deposit; Hire; Loans; Mandates;* and *Pledges*.

6. Sir William Jones has divided bailments into five sorts, namely: 1. Depositum, or deposit. 2. Mandatum, or commission without recompense. 3. Commodatum, or loan for use, without pay. 4. Pignori acceptum, or pawn. 5. Locatum, or hiring, which is always with reward. This last is subdivided into, 1. Locatio rei, or hiring, by which the hirer gains a temporary use of the thing. 2. Locatio operis faciendi, when something is to be done to the thing delivered. 3. Locatio operis mercium vehendarum, when the thing is merely to be carried from one place to another. See these several words.

As to the obligations and duties of bailees in general, see *Diligence*, and Story on Bailm. c. 1; Chit. on Cont. 141; 3 John. R. 170; 17 Mass. R. 479; 5 Day, 415; 1 Conn. Rep. 487; 10 Johns. R. 1, 471; 12 Johns. R. 144, 232; 11 Johns. R. 107; 15 Johns. R. 39; 2 John. C. R. 100; 2 Caines' Cas. 189; 19 Johns. R. 44; 14 John. R. 175; 2 Halst. 108; 2 South. 738; 2 Harr. & M'Hen. 453; 1 Rand. 3; 2 Hawks, 145; 1 Murphy, 417; 1 Hayw. 14; 1 Rep. Con. Ct. 121, 186; 2 Rep. Con. Ct. 239; 1 Bay, 101; 2 Nott & M'Cord, 88, 489; 1 Browne, 43, 176; 2 Binn. 72; 4 Binn. 127; 5 Binn. 457; 6 Binn. 129; 6 Serg. & Rawle, 439; 8 Serg. & Rawle, 500, 533; 14 Serg. & R. 275; Bac. Ab. h. t.; 1 Bouv. Inst. n. 978–1099.

BAILOR, *contracts*. He who bails a thing to another.

2. The bailor must act with good faith towards the bailee; Story's Bailm. § 74, 76, 77; permit him to enjoy the thing bailed according to contract; and, in some bailments, as hiring, warrant the title and possession of the thing hired, and probably, to keep it in suitable order and repair for the purpose of the bailment. Id. § 388—392. Vide Inst. lib. 3, tit. 25.

BAILIWICK. The district over which a sheriff has jurisdiction; it signifies also the same as county, the sheriff's bailiwick extending over the county.

2. In England, it signifies generally that liberty which is exempted from the sheriff of the county over which the lord of the liberty appoints a bailiff. Vide Wood's Inst. 206.

BAIR-MAN, *Scottish law*. A poor insolvent debtor left bare.

BAIRN'S PART, *Scottish law*. Children's part; a third part of the defunct's free movables, debts deducted, if the wife survive, and a half if there be no relict.

BALANCE, *com. law*. The amount which remains due by one of two persons, who have been dealing together, to the other, after the settlement of their accounts.

2. In the case of mutual debts, the balance only can be recovered by the assignee of an insolvent, or the executor of a deceased person. But this mutuality must have existed at the time of the assignment by the insolvent, or at the death of the testator.

3. The term *general balance* is sometimes used to signify the difference which is due to a party claiming a lien on goods in his hands, for work or labor done, or money expended in relation to those and other goods of the debtor. 3 B. & P. 485; 3 Esp. R. 268.

BALANCE SHEET. A statement made by merchants and others to show the true state of a particular business. A balance sheet should exhibit all the balances of debits and credits, also the value of merchandize, and the result of the whole. Vide *Bilan*.

BALANCE OF TRADE, *com. law*. The difference between the exports and importations between two countries. The balance of trade is against that country which has imported more than it has exported, for which it is debtor to the other country.

BALIVA. A bailiwick or jurisdiction.

BALIVO AMOVENDO, *Eng. practice*. A writ to remove a bailiff out of his office.

BALLASTAGE, *mar. law*. A toll paid for the privilege of taking up ballast from the bottom of the port. This arises from the property in the soil. 2 Chit. Com. Law, 16.

BALLOT, *government*. A diminutive ball, i. e. a little ball used in giving votes; the act itself of giving votes. A little ball or ticket used in voting privately, and, for that purpose, put into a box, (commonly called a ballot-box,) or into some other contrivance.

BALNEARII, *civil law*. Stealers of

the clothes of persons who were washing in the public baths. Dig. 47, 17; 4 Bl. Com. 239; Calvini Lex. Jurid.

BAN. A proclamation, or public notice; any summons or edict by which a thing is forbidden or commanded. Vide *Bans of Matrimony; Proclamation;* Cowell's Interp.

BANC or BANK. The first of these is a French word signifying bench, pronounced improperly *bank*. 1. The seat of judgment, as *banc le roy*, the king's bench; *banc le common pleas*, the bench of common pleas. 2. The meeting of all the judges or such as may form a quorum, as, the court sit in *banc*. Cowell's Interp.

BANCO. A commercial term, adopted from the Italian, used to distinguish bank money from the common currency; as $1000, *banco*.

BANDIT. A man outlawed: one who is said to be under ban.

BANE. This word was formerly used to signify a malefactor. Bract. l. 2, t. 8, c. 1.

BANISHMENT, *crim. law*. A punishment inflicted upon criminals, by compelling them to quit a city, place, or country, for a specified period of time, or for life. Vide 4 Dall. 14. *Deportation; Relegation.*

BANK, *com. law*. 1. A place for the deposit of money. 2. An institution, generally incorporated, authorized to receive deposits of money, to lend money, and to issue promissory notes, usually known by the name of bank notes. 3. Banks are said to be of three kinds, viz: of *deposit*, of *discount*, and of *circulation;* they generally perform all these operations. Vide Metc. & Perk. Dig. Banks and Banking.

BANK BOOK, *commerce*. A book which persons dealing with a bank keep, in which the officers of the bank enter the amount of money deposited by them, and all notes or bills deposited by them, or discounted for their use.

BANK NOTE, *contracts*. A bank note resembles a common promissory note, (q. v.) issued by a bank or corporation authorized to act as a bank. It is in fact a promissory note, but such notes are not, for many purposes, to be considered as mere securities for money; but are treated as money, in the ordinary course and transactions of business, by the general consent of mankind; and, on payment of them, when a receipt is required, the receipts are always given as for money, not as for securities or notes. 1 Burr. R. 457; 12 John. R. 200; 1 John. Ch. R. 231; 9 John. R. 120; 19 John. 144; 1 Sch. & Lef. 318, 319; 11 Ves. 662; 1 Roper, Leg. 3; 1 Ham. R. 189, 524, 15 Pick. 177; 5 G. & John. 58; 3 Hawks, 328; 5 J. J. Marsh. 643.

2. Bank notes are assignable by delivery. Rep. Temp. Hard. 53; 9 East, R. 48; 4 East, R. 510; Dougl. 236. The holder of a bank note is *prima facie* entitled to prompt payment of it, and cannot be affected by the fraud of any former holder in obtaining it, unless evidence be given to bring it home to his privity. 1 Burr. 452; 4 Rawle, 185; 13 East, R. 135; Dane's Ab. Index, h. t.; Pow. on Mortg. Index, h. t.; U. S. Dig. h. t. Vide Bouv. Inst. Index, h. t.; *Note; Promissory note; Reissuable note.*

3. They cannot be taken in execution. Cunning. on Bills, 537; Hardw. Cases, 53; 1 Arch. Pr. 268; 1 Wils. Rep.; 9 Cro. Eliz. 746, pl. 25

BANK STOCK. The capital of a bank. It is usually divided in shares of a certain amount. This stock is generally transferable on the books of the bank, and considered as personal property. Vide *Stock*.

BANKER, *com. law*. A banker is one engaged in the business of receiving other persons' money on deposit, to be returned on demand;—discounting other persons' notes, and issuing his own for circulation. one who performs the business usually transacted by a bank. Private bankers are generally not permitted.

2. The business of bankers is generally performed through the medium of incorporated banks.

3. A banker may be declared a bankrupt by adverse proceedings against him. Act of Congress of 19th Aug. 1841. See 1 Atk. 218; 2 H. Bl. 235; 1 Mont. B. L. 12.

4. Among the ancient Romans there were bankers called *argentarii*, whose office was to keep registers of contracts between individuals, either to loan money, or in relation to sales and stipulations. These bankers frequently agreed with the creditor to pay him the debt due to him by the debtor. Calvini Lex. Jurid.

BANKERS' NOTE, *contracts*. In England a distinction is made between bank notes, (q. v.) and bankers' notes. The latter are promissory notes, and resemble bank notes in every respect, except that they are given by persons acting as private bankers. 6 Mod. 29; 3 Chit. Com. Law, 590; 1 Leigh's N. P. 338.

BANKRUPT. A person who has done, or suffered some act to be done, which is by law declared an act of bankruptcy; in such case he may be declared a bankrupt.

2. It is proper to notice that there is much difference between a bankrupt and an insolvent. A man may be a bankrupt, and yet be perfectly solvent; that is, eventually able to pay all his debts; or, he may be insolvent, and, in consequence of not having done, or suffered, an act of bankruptcy, he may not be a bankrupt. Again, the bankrupt laws are intended mainly to secure creditors from waste, extravagance, and mismanagement, by seizing the property out of the hands of the debtors, and placing it in the custody of the law; whereas the insolvent laws only relieve a man from imprisonment for debt after he has assigned his property for the benefit of his creditors. Both under bankrupt and insolvent laws the debtor is required to surrender his property for the benefit of his creditors. Bankrupt laws discharge the person from imprisonment, and his property, acquired after his discharge, from all liabilities for his debts; insolvent laws simply discharge the debtor from imprisonment, or liability to be imprisoned, but his after-acquired property may be taken in satisfaction of his former debts. 2 Bell, Com. B. 6, part 1, c. 1, p. 162; 3 Am. Jur. 218.

BANKRUPTCY. The state or condition of a bankrupt.

2. Bankrupt laws are an encroachment upon the common law. The first in England was the stat. 34 and 35 H. VIII., c. 4, although the word bankrupt appears only in the title, not in the body of the act. The stat. 13 Eliz. c. 7, is the first that defines the term bankrupt, and discriminates bankruptcy from mere insolvency. Out of a great number of bankrupt laws passed from time to time, the most considerable are the statutes 13 Eliz. c. 7; 1 James I., c. 19; 21 James I., c. 19; 5 Geo. II., c. 30. A careful consideration of these statutes is sufficient to give an adequate idea of the system of bankruptcy in England. See Burgess on Insolvency, 202–230.

3. The Constitution of the United States, art. 1, s. 8, authorizes congress "to establish an uniform rule of naturalization, and uniform laws on the subject of bankruptcies throughout the United States." With the exception of a short interval during which bankrupt laws existed in this country, this power lay dormant till the passage of the act of 1841, since repealed.

4. Any one of the states may pass a bankrupt law, but no state bankrupt or insolvent law can be permitted to impair the obligation of contracts; nor can the several states pass laws conflicting with an act of congress on this subject; 4 Wheat. 122; and the bankrupt laws of a state cannot affect the rights of citizens of another state. 12 Wheat. R. 213. Vide 3 Story on the Const. § 1100 to 1110; 2 Kent, Com. 321; Serg. on Const. Law, 322; Rawle on the Const. c. 9; 6 Pet. R. 348; Bouv. Inst. Index, h. t. Vide *Bankrupt*.

BANKS OF RIVERS, *estates*. By this term is understood what retains the river in its natural channel, when there is the greatest flow of water.

2. The owner of the bank of a stream, not navigable, has in general the right to the middle of the stream. Vide *Riparian Proprietor*.

3. When by imperceptible increase the banks on one side extend into the river, this addition is called alluvion. (q. v.) When the increase is caused by the sudden transfer of a mass of earth or soil from the opposite bank, it is called an increase by *avulsion*. (q. v.)

BANNITUS. One outlawed or banished. See *Calvini Lex*.

BANS OF MATRIMONY. The giving public notice or making proclamation of a matrimonial contract, and the intended celebration of the marriage of the parties in pursuance of such contract, to the end that persons objecting to the same, may have an opportunity to declare such objections before the marriage is solemnized. Poth. Du Mariage, partie 2, c. 2. Vide *Ban*.

BAR, *actions*. A perpetual destruction or temporary taking away of the action of the plaintiff. In ancient authors it is called *exceptio peremptoria*. Co. Litt. 303 b; Steph. Pl. Appx. xxviii. Loisel (Institutes Coutumieres, vol. ii. p. 204) says, "Exceptions (in pleas) have been called bars by our ancient practitioners, because, being opposed, they arrest the party who has sued out the process, as in war (*une barriere*) a barrier arrests an enemy; and as there have always been in our tribunals *bars* to separate the advocates from the judges, the place where the advocates stand (*pour parler*) when they speak, has been called for that reason (*barreau*) the bar."

2. When a person is bound in any action, real or personal, by judgment on demurrer, confession or verdict, he is barred, i. e. debarred, as to that or any other

action of the like nature or degree, for the same thing, forever; for *expedit reipublicæ ut sit finis litium.*

3. But there is a difference between real and personal actions.

4. In *personal actions*, as in debt or account, the bar is perpetual, inasmuch as the plaintiff cannot have an action of a higher nature, and therefore in such actions he has generally no remedy, but by bringing a writ of error. Doct. Plac. 65; 6 Co. 7, 8; 4 East, 507, 508.

5. But if the defendant be barred in a *real* action, by judgment on a verdict, demurrer or confession, &c., he may still have an action of a higher nature, and try the same right again. Lawes, Pl. 39, 40. See generally, Bac. Ab. Abatement, N; *Plea in bar*. Also the case of Outram *v.* Morewood, 3 East, Rep. 346–366; a leading case on this subject.

BAR, *practice*. A place in a court where the counsellors and advocates stand to make their addresses to the court and jury; it is so called because formerly it was closed with a bar. Figuratively the counsellors and attorneys at law are called the bar; the bar of Philadelphia, the New York bar.

2. A place in a court having criminal jurisdiction, to which prisoners are called to plead to the indictment, is also called the bar. Vide Merl. Rèpert. mot Barreau, and Dupin, Profession d'Avocat, tom. i. p. 451, for some eloquent advice to gentlemen of the bar.

BAR, *contracts*. An obstacle or opposition.

2. Some bars arise from circumstances, and others from persons. Kindred within the prohibited degree, for example, is a bar to a marriage between the persons related; but the fact that A is married, and cannot therefore marry B, is a circumstance which operates as a bar as long as it subsists; for without it the parties might marry.

BAR FEE, *Eng. law*. A fee taken time out of mind by the sheriff for every prisoner who is acquitted. Bac. Ab. Extortion.

BARBICAN. An ancient word to signify a watch-tower. Barbicanage was money given for the support of a barbican.

BARGAIN AND SALE, *conveyancing, contracts*. A contract in writing to convey lands to another person; or rather it is the sale of a use therein. In strictness it is not an absolute conveyance of the seizin, as a feoffment. Watk. Prin. Conv. by Preston, 190, 191. The consideration must be of money or money's worth. Id. 237.

2. In consequence of this conveyance a use arises to a bargainee, and the statute 27 Henry VIII. immediately transfers the legal estate and possession to him.

3. A bargain and sale may be in fee, for life, or for years.

4. The proper and technical words of this conveyance are *bargain and sale*, but any other words that would have been sufficient to raise a use, upon a valuable consideration, before the statute, are now sufficient to constitute a good bargain and sale. Proper words of limitation must, however, be inserted. Cruise Dig. tit. 32, c. 9; Bac. Ab. h. t.; Com. Dig. h. t.; and the cases there cited; Nels. Ab. h. t.; 2 Bl. Com. 338.

5. This is the most common mode of conveyance in the United States. 4 Kent, Com. 483; 3 Pick. R. 529; 3 N. H. Rep. 260; 6 Harr. & John. 465; 3 Wash. C. C. Rep. 376; 4 Mass. R. 66; 4 Yeates, R. 295; 1 Yeates, R. 328; 3 John. R. 388; 4 Cowen's R. 325; 10 John. R. 456, 505; 3 N. H. Rep. 261; 14 John. R. 126; 2 Harr. & John. 230; 2 Bouv. Inst. n. 2077-8.

BARGAINEE. A person to whom a bargain is made; one who receives the advantages of a bargain.

BARGAINOR. A person who makes a bargain, and who becomes bound to perform it.

BARGEMEN. Persons who own and keep a barge for the purpose of carrying the goods of all such other persons who may desire to employ them. They are liable as common carriers. Story, Bailm. § 496.

BARLEYCORN. A lineal measure, containing one-third of an inch. Dane's Ab. c. 211, a. 13, s. 9. The barleycorn was the first measure, with its division and multiples, of all our measures of length, superfices, and capacity. Id. c. 211, a. 12, s. 2.

BARN, *estates*. A building on a farm used to receive the crop, the stabling of animals, and other purposes.

2. The grant or demise of a barn, without words superadded to extend its meaning, would pass no more than the barn itself, and as much land as would be necessary for its complete enjoyment. 4 Serg. & Rawle, 342.

BARON. This word has but one signification in American law, namely, husband: we use baron and feme, for husband and wife. And in this sense it is going out of use.

2. In England, and perhaps some other countries, baron is a title of honor; it is the first degree of nobility below a viscount. Vide Com. Dig. Baron and Feme; Bac. Ab. Baron and Feme; and the articles *Husband; Marriage; Wife.*

3. In the laws of the middle ages, *baron* or *bers*, (baro) signifies a great vassal; lord of a fief and tenant immediately from the king: and the words *baronage*, *barnage* and *berner*, signify collectively the vassals composing the court of the king; as *Le roi et son barnage*, The king and his court. See Spelman's Glossary, verb. Baro.

BARONS OF EXCHEQUER, *Eng. law.* The name given to the five judges of the Exchequer; formerly these were barons of the realm, but now they are chosen from persons learned in the law.

BARRACK. By this term, as used in Pennsylvania, is understood an erection of upright posts supporting a sliding roof, usually of thatch. 5 Whart. R. 429.

BARRATOR, *crimes.* One who has been guilty of the offence of barratry.

BARRATRY, *crimes.* In old law French *barat*, *baraterie*, signifying robbery, deceit, fraud. In modern usage it may be defined the habitual moving, exciting, and maintaining suits and quarrels, either at law or otherwise. 1 Inst. 368; 1 Hawk. 243.

2. A man cannot be indicted as a common barrator in respect of any number of false and groundless actions brought in his own right, nor for a *single* act in right of another; for that would not make him a common barrator.

3. Barratry, in this sense, is different from maintenance (q. v.) and champerty. (q. v.)

4. An attorney cannot be indicted for this crime, merely for maintaining another in a groundless action. Vide 15 Mass. R. 229; 1 Bailey's R. 379; 11 Pick. R. 432; 13 Pick. R. 362; 9 Cowen, R. 587; Bac. Ab. h. t.; Hawk. P. C. B. 1, c. 21; Roll. Ab. 335; Co. Litt. 368; 3 Inst. 175.

BARRATRY, *maritime law, crimes.* A fraudulent act of the master or mariners, committed contrary to their duty as such, to the prejudice of the owners of the ship. Emer. tom. 1, p. 366; Merlin, Répert. h. t.; Roccus, h. t.; 2 Marsh. Insur. 515; 8 East, R. 138, 139. As to what will amount to barratry, see Abbott on Shipp. 167, n. 1; 2 Wash. C. C. R. 61; 9 East, R. 126; 1 Str. 581; 2 Ld. Raym. 1349; 1 Term R. 127; 6 Id. 379; 8 Id. 320; 2 Cain. R. 67, 222; 3 Cain. R. 1; 1 John. R. 229; 8 John. R. 209, n. 2d edit.; 5 Day. R. 1; 11 John. R. 40; 13 John. R. 451; 2 Binn. R. 274; 2 Dall. R. 137; 8 Cran. R. 39; 3 Wheat. R. 168; 4 Dall. R. 294; 1 Yeates, 114.

2. The act of Congress of April, 30, 1790, s. 8, 1 Story's Laws U. S. 84, punishes with death as piracy, "any captain or mariner of any ship or other vessel who shall piratically and feloniously run away with such ship or vessel, or any goods or merchandize to the value of fifty dollars; or yield up such ship or vessel to any pirate; or if any such seamen shall lay violent hands upon his commander, thereby to hinder or prevent his fighting in defence of his ship, or goods, committed to his trust, or shall make a revolt in the said ship."

BARREL. A measure of capacity, equal to thirty-six gallons.

BARREN MONEY, *civil law.* This term is used to denote money which bears no interest.

BARRENNESS. The incapacity to produce a child. This, when arising from impotence, is a cause for dissolving a marriage. 1 Foderé, Méd. Lèg. § 254.

BARRISTER, *English law.* A counsellor admitted to plead at the bar.

2. *Ouster barrister*, is one who pleads ouster or without the bar.

3. *Inner barrister*, a serjeant or king's counsel who pleads within the bar.

4. *Vacation barrister*, a counsellor newly called to the bar, who is to attend for several long vacations the exercise of the house.

5. Barristers are called *apprentices*, *apprentitii ad legem*, being looked upon as learners, and not qualified until they obtain the degree of serjeant. Edmund Plowden, the author of the Commentaries, a volume of elaborate reports in the reigns of Edward VI., Mary, Philip and Mary, and Elizabeth, describes himself as an apprentice of the common law.

BARTER. A contract by which the parties exchange goods for goods. To complete the contract the goods must be delivered, for without a delivery, the right of property is not changed.

2. This contract differs from a sale in this, that barter is always of goods for goods, whereas a sale is an exchange of goods for money. In the former there never is a price fixed, in the latter a price is indispensable. All the differences which may be pointed out between these two contracts,

are comprised in this; it is its necessary consequence. When the contract is an exchange of goods on one side, and on the other side the consideration is partly goods and partly money, the contract is not a barter, but a sale. See *Price; Sale.*

3. If an insurance be made upon returns from a country where trade is carried on by barter, the valuation of the goods in return shall be made on the cost of those given in barter, adding all charges. Wesk. on Ins. 42.

See 3 Camp. 351; Cowp. 818; 1 Dougl. 24, n.; 1 N. R. 151; Tropl. de l'Echange.

BARTON, *old English law.* The demesne land of a manor; a farm distinct from the mansion.

BASE. Something low; inferior. This word is frequently used in composition; as base court, base estate, base fee, &c.

BASE COURT. An inferior court, one not of record. Not used.

BASE ESTATE, *English law.* The estate which base tenants had in their lands. Base tenants were a degree above villeins, the latter being compelled to perform all the commands of their lords; the former did not hold their lands by the performance of such commands. See Kitch. 41.

BASE FEE, *English law.* A tenure in fee at the will of the lord. This was distinguished from socage free tenure. See Co. Litt. 1, 18.

BASILICA, *civil law.* This is derived from a Greek word, which signifies *imperial constitutions.* The emperor Basilius, finding the Corpus Juris Civilis of Justinian too long and obscure, resolved to abridge it, and under his auspices the work proceeded to the fortieth book, which, at his death, remained unfinished. His son and successor, Leo, the philosopher, continued the work, and published it in sixty books, about the year 880. Constantine Porphyro-genitus, younger brother of Leo, revised the work, re-arranged it, and republished it, Anno Domini, 910. From that time the laws of Justinian ceased to have any force in the eastern empire, and the Basilica were the foundation of the law observed there till Constantine XIII., the last of the Greek emperors, under whom, in 1453, Constantinople was taken by Mahomet the Turk, who put an end to the empire and its laws. Histoire de la Jurisprudence; Etienne, Intr. a l'étude du Droit Romain, § LIII. The Basilica were written in Greek. They were translated into Latin by J. Cujas (Cujacius) Professor of Law in the University of Bourges, and published at Lyons, 22d of January, 1566, in one vol. fo.

BASTARD. A word derived from *bas* or *bast*, signifying abject, low, base; and *aerd*, nature. Minshew, Co. Lit. 244, a. *Enfant de bas*, a child of low birth. Dupin. According to Blackstone, 1 Com. 454, a bastard, in the law sense of the word, is a person not only begotten, but born out of lawful matrimony. This definition does not appear to be complete, inasmuch as it does not embrace the case of a person who is the issue of an illicit connection, during the coverture of his mother. The common law, says the Mirror, only taketh him to be a son whom the marriage proveth to be so. Horne's Mirror, c. 2, § 7; see Glanv. lib. 8, cap. 13; Bract. 63, a. b.; 2 Salk. 427; 8 East, 204. A bastard may be perhaps defined to be one who is born of an illicit union, and before the lawful marriage of his parents.

2. A man is a bastard if born, *first*, *before* the marriage of his parents; but although he may have been begotten while his parents were single, yet if they afterwards marry, and he is born during the coverture, he is legitimate. 1 Bl. Com. 455, 6. *Secondly*, if born *during the coverture*, under circumstances which render it impossible that the husband of his mother can be his father. 6 Binn. 283; 1 Browne's R. Appx. xlvii.; 4 T. R. 356; Str. 940; Id. 51; 8 East, 193; Hardin's R. 479. It seems by the Gardner peerage case, reported by Dennis Le Marchant, esquire, that strong moral improbability that the husband is not the father, is sufficient to bastardize the issue. Bac. Ab. tit. Bastardy, A, last ed. *Thirdly*, if born beyond a competent time *after* the coverture has determined. Stark. Ev. part 4, p. 221, n. a; Co. Litt. 123, b, by Hargrave & Butler in the note. See *Gestation.*

3. The principal right which bastard children have, is that of maintenance from their parents. 1 Bl. Com. 458; Code Civ. of Lo. 254 to 262. To protect the public from their support, the law compels the putative father to maintain his bastard children. See *Bastardy; Putative father.*

4. Considered as nullius filius, a bastard has no inheritable blood in him, and therefore no estate can descend to him; but he may take by testament, if properly described, after he has obtained a name by reputation. 1 Rop. Leg. 76, 266; Com. Dig. Descent, C, 12; Id. Bastard, E; Co. Lit. 123, a; Id. 3, a; 1 T. R. 96; Doug.

548; 3 Dana, R. 233; 4 Pick. R. 93; 4 Desaus. 434. But this hard rule has been somewhat mitigated in some of the states, where, by statute, various inheritable qualities have been conferred upon bastards. See 5 Conn. 228; 1 Dev. Eq. R. 345; 2 Root, 280; 5 Wheat. 207; 3 H. & M. 229, n; 5 Call. 143; 3 Dana, 233.

5. Bastards can acquire the rights of legitimate children only by an act of the legislature. 1 Bl. Com. 460; 4 Inst. 36.

6. By the laws of Louisiana, a bastard is one who is born of an illicit union. Civ. Code of Lo. art. 27, 199. There are two sorts of illegitimate children; first, those who are born of two persons, who, at the moment such children were conceived, might have legally contracted marriage with each other; and, secondly, those who are born from persons, to whose marriage there existed at the time, some legal impediment. Id. art. 200. An adulterous bastard is one produced by an unlawful connexion between two persons, who, at the time he was conceived, were, either of them, or both, connected by marriage with some other person or persons. Id. art. 201. Incestuous bastards are those who are produced by the illegal connexion of two persons who are relations within the degrees prohibited by law. Id. art. 202.

7. Bastards, generally speaking, belong to no family, and have no relations; accordingly they are not subject to paternal authority, even when they have been acknowledged. See 11 East, 7, n. Nevertheless, fathers and mothers owe alimony to their children when they are in need. Id. art. 254, 256. Alimony is due to bastards, though they be adulterous or incestuous, by the mother and her ascendants. Id. art. 262.

8. Children born out of marriage, except those who are born from an incestuous or adulterous connexion, may be legitimated by the subsequent marriage of their father and mother, whenever the latter have legally acknowledged them for their children, either before the marriage or by the contract of marriage itself. Every other mode of legitimating children is abolished. Id. art. 217. Legitimation may even be extended to deceased children who have left issue, and in that ease, it enures to the benefit of that issue. Id. art. 218. Children legitimated by a subsequent marriage, have the same rights as if born during the marriage. Id. art. 219.

See, generally, Vin. Abr. Bastards; Bac. Abr. Bastard; Com. Dig. Bastard; Metc. & Perk. Dig. h. t.; the various other American Digests, h. t.; Harr. Dig. h. t.; 1 Bl. Com. 454 to 460; Co. Litt. 3, b.; Bouv. Inst. Index, h. t. And *Access, Bastardy; Gestation; Natural Children.*

Bastard eigne', *Eng. law.* Elder bastard. By the old English law, when a man had a bastard son, and he afterwards married the mother, and by her had a legitimate son, the first was called a bastard eigné, or, as it is now spelled, ainé, and the second son was called puisné, or since born, or sometimes he was called mulier puisné. See *Mulier;* Eigné, 2 Bl. Com. 248.

BASTARDY, *crim. law.* The offence of begetting a bastard child.

Bastardy, *persons.* The state or condition of a bastard. The law presumes every child legitimate, when born of a woman in a state of wedlock, and casts the *onus probandi* (q. v.) on the party who affirms the bastardy. Stark. Ev. h. t.

BASTON. An old French word, which signifies a staff, or club. In some old English statutes the servants or officers of the wardens of the Fleet are so called, because they attended the king's courts with a red staff. Vide *Tipstaff.*

BATTEL, in French *Bataille; Old English law.* An ancient and barbarous mode of trial, by single combat, called wager of battel, where, in appeals of felony, the appellee might fight with the appellant to prove his innocence. It was also used in affairs of chivalry or honor, and upon civil cases upon certain issues. Co. Litt. 294 Till lately it disgraced the English code This mode of trial was abolished in England by stat. 59 Geo. III. c. 46.

2. This mode of trial was not peculiar to England. The emperor Otho, A. D. 983, held a diet at Verona, at which several sovereigns and great lords of Italy, Germany and France were present. In order to put a stop to the frequent perjuries in judicial trials, this diet substituted in all cases, even in those which followed the course of the Roman law, proof by combat for proof by oath. Henrion de Pansey, Auth. Judic. Introd. c. 3; and for a detailed account of this mode of trial see Herb. Antiq. of the Inns of Court, 119—145.

BATTERY. It is proposed to consider, 1. What is a battery; 2. When a battery may be justified.

2.—§ 1. A battery is the unlawful touching the person of another by the aggressor himself, or any other substance put in motion by him. 1 Saund. 29, b. n. 1; Id. 13 & 14, n. 3. It must be either wilfully committed, or proceed from want of due care. Str. 596; Hob. 134; Plowd. 19; 3 Wend. 391. Hence an injury, be it never so small, done to the person of another, in an angry, spiteful, rude or insolent manner, as by spitting in his face, or any way touching him in anger, or violently jostling him, are batteries in the eye of the law. 1 Hawk. P. C. 263. See 1 Selw. N. P. 33, 4. And any thing attached to the person, partakes of its inviolability; if, therefore, A strikes a cane in the hands of B, it is a battery. 1 Dall. 114; 1 Ch. Pr. 37; 1 Penn. R. 380; 1 Hill's R. 46; 4 Wash. C. C. R. 534. 1 Baldw. R. 600.

3.—§ 2. A battery may be justified, 1. on the ground of the parental relation; 2. in the exercise of an office; 3. under process of a court of justice or other legal tribunal; 4. in aid of an authority in law; and lastly, as a necessary means of defence.

4. First. As a *salutary mode of correction*. For example: a parent may correct his child, a master his apprentice, a schoolmaster his scholar; 24 Edw. IV.; Easter, 17, p. 6; and a superior officer, one under his command. Keilw. pl. 120, p. 136; Bull. N. P. 19; Bee, 161; 1 Bay, 3; 14 John. R. 119; 15 Mass. 365; and vide Cowp. 173; 15 Mass. 347.

5.—2. As a means to *preserve the peace;* and therefore if the plaintiff assaults or is fighting with another, the defendant may lay hands upon him, and restrain him until his anger is cooled; but he cannot strike him in order to protect the party assailed, as he may in self-defence. 2 Roll. Abr. 359, E, pl. 3.

6.—3. Watchmen may arrest, and detain in prison for examination, persons walking in the streets by night, whom there is reasonable ground to suspect of felony, although there is no proof of a felony having been committed. 3 Taunt. 14.

7.—4. Any person has a right to arrest another to prevent a felony.

8.—5. Any one may arrest another upon suspicion of felony, provided a felony has actually been committed, and there is reasonable ground for suspecting the person arrested to be the criminal, and that the party making the arrest, himself entertained the suspicion.

9.—6. Any private individual may arrest a felon. Hale's P. C. 89.

10.—7. It is lawful for every man to lay hands on another to preserve public decorum; as to turn him out of church, and to prevent him from disturbing the congregation or a funeral ceremony. 1 Mod. 168: and see 1 Lev. 196; 2 Keb. 124. But a request to desist should be first made, unless the urgent necessity of the case dispenses with it.

11. Secondly. A battery may be justified in the exercise of an office. 1. A constable may freshly arrest one who, in his view, has committed a breach of the peace, and carry him before a magistrate. But if an offence has been committed out of the constable's sight, he cannot arrest, unless it amounts to a felony; 1 Brownl. 198; or a felony is likely to ensue. Cro. Eliz. 375.

12.—2. A justice of the peace may generally do all acts which a constable has authority to perform; hence he may freshly arrest one who, in his view has broken the peace; or he may order a constable at the moment to take him up. Kielw. 41.

13. Thirdly. A battery may be justified under the process of a court of justice, or of a magistrate having competent jurisdiction. See 16 Mass. 450; 13 Mass. 342.

14. Fourthly. A battery may be justified in aid of an authority in law. Every person is empowered to restrain breaches of the peace, by virtue of the authority vested in him by the law.

15. Lastly. A battery may be justified as a necessary means of defence. 1. Against the plaintiff's assaults in the following instances: In defence of himself, his wife, 3 Salk. 46, his child, and his servant. Ow. 150; sed vide 1 Salk. 407. So, likewise, the wife may justify a battery in defending her husband; Ld. Raym. 62; the child its parent; 3 Salk. 46; and the servant his master. In these situations, the party need not wait until a blow has been given, for then he might come too late, and be disabled from warding off a second stroke, or from protecting the person assailed. Care, however, must be taken, that the battery do not exceed the bounds of necessary defence and protection; for it is only permitted as a means to avert an impending evil, which might otherwise overwhelm the party, and not as a punishment or retaliation for the injurious attempt. Str. 953. The degree of force necessary to repel an assault,

will naturally depend upon, and be proportioned to, the violence of the assailant; but with this limitation any degree is justifiable. Ld. Raym. 177; 2 Salk. 642.

16.—2. A battery may likewise be justified in the necessary defence of one's property; if the plaintiff is in the act of entering peaceably upon the defendant's land, or having entered, is discovered, not committing violence, a request to depart is necessary in the first instance; 2 Salk. 641; and if the plaintiff refuses, the defendant may then, and not till then, gently lay hands upon the plaintiff to remove him from the close; and for this purpose may use, if necessary, any degree of force short of striking the plaintiff, as by thrusting him off. Skinn. 228. If the plaintiff resists, the defendant may oppose force to force. 8 T. R. 78. But if the plaintiff is in the act of forcibly entering upon the land, or having entered, is discovered subverting the soil, cutting down a tree or the like, 2 Salk. 641, a previous request is unnecessary, and the defendant may immediately lay hands upon the plaintiff. 8 T. R. 78. A man may justify a battery in defence of his *personal* property, without a previous request, if another forcibly attempt to take away such property. 2 Salk. 641. Vide *Rudeness; Wantonness.*

BATTURE. An elevation of the bed of a river *under* the surface of the water; but it is sometimes used to signify the same elevation when it has risen *above* the surface. 6 M. R. 19, 216. The term battures is applied, principally, to certain portions of the bed of the river Mississippi, which are left dry when the water is low, and are covered again, either in whole or in part, by the annual swells. The word *battures*, in French, signifies shoals or shallows, where there is not water enough for a ship to float. They are otherwise called *basses* or *brisans.* Neuman's Marine Pocket Dict.; Dict. de Trevoux.

BAWDY-HOUSE, *crim. law.* A house of ill-fame, (q. v.,) kept for the resort and unlawful commerce of lewd people of both sexes.

2. Such a house is a common nuisance, as it endangers the public peace by drawing together dissolute and debauched persons; and tends to corrupt both sexes by an open profession of lewdness. 1 Russ. on Cr. 299; Bac. Ab. Nuisances, A; Hawk. B. 1, c. 74, § 1-5.

3. The keeper of such a house may be indicted for the nuisance; and a married woman, because such houses are generally kept by the female sex, may be indicted with her husband for keeping such a house. 1 Salk. 383; vide Dane's Ab. Index, h. t. One who assists in establishing a bawdy-house is guilty of a misdemeanor. 2 B. Monroe, 417.

BAY. Is an enclosure to keep in the water for the supply of a mill or other contrivance, so that the water may be able to drive the wheels of such mill. Stat. 27 Eliz. c. 19.

2. A large open water or harbor where ships may ride, is also called a bay; as, the Chesapeake Bay, the Bay of New York.

BEACH. The sea shore. (q. v.)

BEACON. A signal erected as a sea mark for the use of mariners; also, to give warning of the approach of an enemy. 1 Com. Dig. 259; 5 Com. Dig. 173.

TO BEAR DATE. In the description of a paper in a declaration, to say it *bears date* such a day, is to aver that such date is upon it; and if, on being produced, it is dated at another day, the variance will be fatal. But if it be averred it was *made* on such a day, and upon its production it bears date on another day, it will not be a variance, because it might have been made one day and dated another. 3 Burr. 904.

BEADLE. *Eng. law.* A messenger or apparitor of a court, who cites persons to appear to what is alleged against them, is so called.

BEARER. One who bears or carries a thing.

2. If a bill or note be made payable to bearer, it will pass by delivery only, without endorsement; and whoever fairly acquires a right to it, may maintain an action against the drawer or acceptor.

3. It has been decided that the bearer of a bank note, payable to bearer, is not an assignee of a chose in action within the 11th section of the judiciary act of 1789, c. 20, limiting the jurisdiction of the circuit court. 3 Mason, R. 308.

4. Bills payable to bearer are contradistinguished from those payable to order, which can be transferred only by endorsement and delivery.

5. Bills payable to fictitious payees, are considered as bills payable to bearer.

BEARERS, *Eng. crim. law.* Such as bear down or oppress others; maintainers. In Ruffhead's Statutes it is employed to translate the French word *emparnours*, which signifies, according to Kelham, undertakers of suits. 4 Ed. III. c. 11. This word is no longer used in this sense.

BEARING DATE. These words are frequently used in conveyancing and in pleading; as, for example, a certain indenture bearing date the first day of January, 1851, which signifies not that the indenture was made on that day, but simply that such date has been put to it.

2. When in a declaration the plaintiff alleges that the defendant *made* his promissory note on such a day, he will not be considered as having alleged it *bore date* on that day, so as to cause a variance between the declaration and the note produced bearing a different date. 2 Greenl. Ev. § 160; 2 Dowl. & L. 759.

BEAU PLEADER, *Eng. law.* Fair pleading. See *Stultiloquuum.*

2. This is the name of a writ upon the statute of Marlbridge, 52 H. III. c. 11, which enacts, that neither in the circuit of justices, nor in counties, hundreds or courts-baron, any fines shall be taken for *fair pleading;* namely, for not pleading fairly or aptly to the purpose. Upon this statute this writ was ordained, directed to the sheriff, bailiff, or him who shall demand the fine; and it is a prohibition or command not to do it. New Nat. Br. 596; 2 Inst. 122; Termes de la Ley; 2 Reeves' Hist. Eng. Law, 70; Cowel; Crabb's Hist. of the Eng. Law, 150. The explanations given of this term are not very satisfactory.

BEDEL, *Eng. law.* A cryer or messenger of a court, who cites men to appear and answer. There are also inferior officers of a parish or liberty who bear this name.

BEE. The name of a well known insect.

2. Bees are considered *feræ naturæ* while unreclaimed; and they are not more subjects of property while in their natural state, than the birds which have their nests on the tree of an individual. 3 Binn. R. 546; 5 Sm. & Marsh. 333. This agrees with the Roman law. Inst. 2, 1, 14; Dig. 41, 1, 5, 2; 7 Johns. Rep. 16; 2 Bl. Com. 392; Bro. Ab. Propertie, 37; Coop. Justin. 458.

3. In New York it has been decided that bees in a tree belong to the owner of the soil, while unreclaimed. When they have been reclaimed, and the owner can identify them, they belong to him, and not to the owner of the soil 15 Wend. R. 550 See 1 Cowen, R. 243.

BEGGAR. One who obtains his livelihood by asking alms. The laws of several of the states punish begging as an offence.

BEHAVIOUR. In old English, *haviour* without the prefix *be.* It is the manner of *having*, holding, or keeping one's self; or the carriage of one's self with respect to propriety, morals, and the requirements of law. Surety to be of good behaviour is a larger requirement than surety to keep the peace. Dalton, c. 122; 4 Burn's J. 355.

BEHOOF. As a word of discourse, signifies need, (egestas, necessitas, indigentia.) It comes from *behoove*, (Sax. behoven,) to need or have need of. In a secondary sense, which is the law sense of the word, it signifies use, service, profit, advantage, (interesse, opus.) It occurs in conveyances of land in fee simple.

BELIEF. The conviction of the mind, arising from evidence received, or from information derived, not from actual perception by our senses, but from the relation or information of others who have had the means of acquiring actual knowledge of the facts, and in whose qualifications for acquiring that knowledge, and retaining it, and afterwards in communicating it, we can place confidence. "Without recurring to the books of metaphysicians," says Chief Justice Tilghman, 4 Serg. & Rawle, 137, "let any man of plain common sense, examine the operations of his own mind, he will assuredly find that on different subjects his belief is different. I have a firm belief that the moon revolves round the earth. I may believe, too, that there are mountains and valleys in the moon; but this belief is not so strong, because the evidence is weaker." Vide 1 Stark. Ev. 41; 2 Pow. Mortg. 555; 1 Ves. 95; 12 Ves. 80; 1 P. A. Browne's R. 258; 1 Stark. Ev. 127; Dyer, 53; 2 Hawk. c. 46, s. 167; 3 Wills. 427; 2 Bl. R. 881; Leach, 270; 8 Watts, R. 406; 1 Greenl. Ev. § 7–13, a.

BELOW. Lower in place, beneath, not so high as some other thing spoken of, or tacitly referred to.

2. The court below is an inferior court, whose proceedings may be examined on error by a superior court, which is called the court above.

3. Bail below is that given to the sheriff in bailable actions, which is so called to distinguish it from bail to the action, which is

called bail above. See *Above; Bail above; Bail below.*

BENCH. Latin *Bancus*, used for *tribunal*. In England there are two courts to which this word is applied. Bancus Regius, King's Bench; Bancus Communis, Common Bench or Pleas. The *jus banci*, says Spelman, properly belongs to the king's judges, who administer justice in the last resort. The judges of the inferior courts, as of the barons, are deemed to judge *plano pede*, and are such as are called in the civil law *pedanei judices*, or by the Greeks *Χαμαιδικαςται* that is, *humi judicantes*. The Greeks called the seats of their higher judges *Βυματα*, and of their inferior judges *Βαθρα*. The Romans used the word *sellae* and *tribunalia*, to designate the seats of their higher judges, and *subsellia*, to designate those of the lower. See Spelman's Gloss. (ad verb.) *Bancus;* also, 1 Reeves' Hist. Eng. Law, 40, 4to ed., and postea Curia Regis.

BENCH WARRANT, *crim. law.* The name of a process sometimes given to an attachment issued by order of a criminal court, against an individual for some contempt, or for the purpose of arresting a person accused; the latter is seldom granted unless when a true bill has been found.

BENCHER, *English law.* A bencher is a senior in the inns of court, entrusted with their government and direction.

BENEFICE, *eccles. law.* In its most extended sense, any ecclesiastical preferment or dignity; but in its more limited sense, it is applied only to rectories and vicarages.

BENEFICIA. In the early feudal times, grants were made to continue only during the pleasure of the grantor, which were called *munera*, (q. v.) but soon afterwards these grants were made for life, and then they assumed the name of *beneficia*. Dalr. Feud. Pr. 199. Pomponius Laetus, as cited by Hotoman, De Feudis, ca. 2, says, "That it was an ancient custom, revived by the emperor Constantine, to give lands and villas to those generals, prefects, and tribunes, who had grown old in enlarging the empire, to supply their necessities as long as they lived, which they called *parochial* parishes, &c. But, between (feuda) fiefs or feuds, and (*parochias*) parishes, there was this difference, that the latter were given to old men, veterans, &c., who, as they had deserved well of the republic, sustained the rest of their life (*publico beneficio*) by the public benefaction; or, if any war afterwards arose, they were called out, not so much as soldiers, as leaders, (*majistri militum.*) Feuds, (feuda,) on the other hand, were usually given to robust young men who could sustain the labors of war. In later times, the word *parochia* was appropriated exclusively to ecclesiastical persons, while the word beneficium (militare) continued to be used in reference to military fiefs or fees.

BENEFICIAL. Of advantage, profit or interest; as the wife has a beneficial interest in property held by a trustee for her. Vide *Cestui que trust.*

BENEFICIAL INTEREST. That right which a person has in a contract made with another; as if A makes a contract with B that he will pay C a certain sum of money, B has the legal interest in the contract, and C the beneficial interest. Hamm. on Part 6, 7, 25; 2 Bulst. 70.

BENEFICIARY. This term is frequently used as synonymous with the technical phrase *cestui que trust.* (q. v.)

BENEFICIO PRIMO ECCLESIASTICO HABENDO, *Eng. eccl. law.* A writ directed from the king to the chancellor, commanding him to bestow the benefice which shall first fall in the king's gift, above or under a certain value, upon a particular and certain person.

BENEFICIUM COMPETENTIÆ. The right which an insolvent debtor had, among the Romans, on making session of his property for the benefit of his creditors, to retain what was required for him to live honestly according to his condition. 7 Toull. n. 258.

BENEFIT. This word is used in the same sense as gain (q. v.) and profits. (q. v.) 20 Toull. n. 199.

BENEFIT OF CESSION, *civil law.* The release of a debtor from future imprisonment for his debts, which the law operates in his favor upon the surrender of his property for the benefit of his creditors, Poth. Procéd. Civ. 5eme part., c. 2, § 1. This was something like a discharge under the insolvent laws, which releases the person of the debtor, but not the goods he may acquire afterwards. See *Bankrupt; Cessio Bonorum; Insolvent.*

BENEFIT OF CLERGY, *English law.* An exemption of the punishment of death which the laws impose on the commission of certain crimes, on the culprit demanding it. By modern statutes, benefit of clergy was rather a substitution of a more mild punishment for the punishment of death.

2. It was lately granted, not only to the

clergy, as was formerly the case, but to all persons. The benefit of clergy seems never to have been extended to the crime of high treason, nor to have embraced misdemeanors inferior to felony. Vide 1 Chit. Cr. Law, 667 to 668; 4 Bl. Com. ch. 28. But this privilege improperly given to the clergy, because they had more learning than others, is now abolished by stat. 7 Geo. IV. c. 28, s. 6.

3. By the Act of Congress of April 30, 1790, it is provided, § 30, that the benefit of clergy shall not be used or allowed, upon conviction of any crime, for which, by any statute of the United States, the punishment is, or shall be declared to be, death.

BENEFIT OF DISCUSSION, *civil law.* The right which a surety has to cause the property of the principal debtor to be applied in satisfaction of the obligation in the first instance. See Civil Code of Lo. art. 3014 to 3020, and *Discussion.*

BENEFIT OF DIVISION. In the civil law, which, in this respect, has been adopted in Louisiana, although, when there are several sureties, each one is bound for the whole debt, yet when one of them is sued alone, he has a right to have the debt apportioned among all the solvent sureties on the same obligation, so that he shall be compelled to pay his own share only. This is called the *benefit of division.* Civil Code of Lo. art. 3014 to 3020. See 2 Bouv. Inst. n. 1414.

BENEFIT OF INVENTORY, *civil law.* The benefit of inventory is the privilege which the heir obtains of being liable for the charges and debts of the succession, only to the value of the effects of the succession, in causing an inventory of these effects within the time and manner prescribed by law. Civil Code of Louis. art. 1025. Vide Poth. Traité des Successions, c. 3, s. 3, a. 2.

BENEVOLENCE, *duty.* The doing a kind action to another, from mere good will, without any legal obligation. It is a moral duty only, and it cannot be enforced by law. A good man is benevolent to the poor, but no law can compel him to be so.

BENEVOLENCE, *English law.* An aid given by the subjects to the king under a pretended gratuity, but in realty it was an extortion and imposition.

TO BEQUEATH. To give personal property by will to another.

BEQUEST. A gift by last will or testament; a legacy. (q. v.) This word is sometimes, though improperly used, as synonymous with *devise.* There is, however, a distinction between them. A bequest is applied, more properly, to a gift by will of a legacy, that is, of personal property; devise is properly a gift by testament of real property. Vide *Devise.*

BESAILE or BESAYLE, *domestic relations.* The great-grandfather, *proavus.* 1 Bl. Com. 186. Vide *Aile.*

BEST EVIDENCE. Means the best evidence of which the nature of the case admits, not the highest or strongest evidence which the nature of the thing to be proved admits of: *e. g.* a copy of a deed is not the best evidence; the deed itself is better. Gilb. Ev. 15; 3 Campb. 236; 2 Starkey, 473; 2 Campb. 605; 1 Esp. 127.

2. The rule requiring the best evidence to be produced, is to be understood of the best *legal* evidence. 2 Serg. & R. 34; 3 Bl. Com. 368, note 10, by Christian. It is relaxed in some cases, as, *e. g.* where the words or the act of the opposite party avow the fact to be proved. A tavern keeper's sign avows his occupation; taking of tithes avows the clerical character; so, addressing one as "The Reverend T. S." 2 Serg. & R. 440; 1 Saund. on Plead. & Evid. 49.

BETROTHMENT. A contract between a man and a woman, by which they agree that at a future time they will marry together.

2. The requisites of this contract are 1. That it be reciprocal. 2. That the parties be able to contract.

3. The contract must be mutual; the promise of the one must be the consideration for the promise of the other. It must be obligatory on both parties at the same instant, so that each may have an action upon it, or it will bind neither. 1 Salk. 24; Carth. 467; 5 Mod. 411; 1 Freem. 95; 3 Keb. 148; Co. Lit. 79 a, b.

4. The parties must be able to contract. If either be married at the time of betrothment, the contract is void; but the married party cannot take advantage of his own wrong, and set up a marriage or previous engagement, as an answer to the action for the breach of the contract, because this disability proceeds from the defendant's own act. Raym. 387; 3 Inst. 89; 1 Sid. 112; 1 Bl. Com. 438.

5. The performance of this engagement or completion of the marriage, must be performed within a reasonable time. Either party may, therefore, call upon the other to fulfil the engagement, and in case of refusal

or neglect to do so, within a reasonable time after request made, may treat the betrothment as at an end, and bring action for the breach of the contract. 2 C. & P. 631.

6. For a breach of the betrothment, without a just cause, an action on the case may be maintained for the recovery of damages. See *Affiance; Promise of Marriage.*

BETTER EQUITY. In England this term has lately been adopted. In the case of Foster *v.* Blackston, the master of the rolls said, he could no where find in the authorities what in terms was a *better equity*, but on a reference to all the cases, he considered it might be thus defined: If a prior incumbrancer did not take a security which effectually protected him against any subsequent dealing to his prejudice, by the party who had the legal estate, a second incumbrancer, taking a security which in its nature afforded him that protection, had what might properly be called a *better equity*. 1 Ch. Pr. 470, note. Vide 4 Rawle, R. 144; 3 Bouv. Inst. n. 2462.

BETTERMENTS. Improvements made to an estate. It signifies such improvements as have been made to the estate which render it better than mere repairs. See 2 Fairf. 482; 9 Shepl. 110; 10 Shepl. 192; 13 Ohio, R. 308; 10 Yerg. 477; 13 Verm. 533; 17 Verm. 109.

BEYOND SEA. This phrase is used in the acts of limitations of several of the states, in imitation of the phraseology of the English statute of limitations. In Pennsylvania, the term has been construed to signify *out of the United States.* 9 S. & R. 288; 2 Dall. R. 217; 1 Yeates, R. 329. In Georgia, it is equivalent to *without the limits of the state;* 3 Wheat. R. 541; and the same construction prevails in Maryland; 1 Har. & John. 350; 1 Harr. & M'H. 89; in South Carolina; 2 McCord, Rep. 331; and in Massachusetts. 3 Mass. R. 271; 1 Pick. R. 263. Vide Kirby, R. 299; 3 Bibb. R. 510; 3 Litt. R. 48; 1 John. Cas. 76. Within the four seas, *infra quatuor maria*, and beyond the four seas, *extra quatuor maria*, in English law books signify within and without the kingdom of England, or the jurisdiction of the king of England. Co. Lit. 244 a; 1 Bl. Com. 457.

BIAS. A particular influential power which sways the judgment; the inclination or propensity of the mind towards a particular object.

2. Justice requires that the judge should have no bias for or against any individual; and that his mind should be perfectly free to act as the law requires.

3. There is, however, one kind of bias which the courts suffer to influence them in their judgments; it is a bias favorable to a class of cases, or persons, as distinguished from an individual case or person. A few examples will explain this. A bias is felt on account of convenience. 1 Ves. sen. 13, 14; 3 Atk. 524. It is also felt in favor of the heir at law, as when there is an heir on one side and a mere volunteer on the other. Willes, R. 570; 1 W. Bl. 256; Amb. R. 645; 1 Ball & B. 309; 1 Wils. R. 310; 3 Atk. 747; Id. 222. On the other hand, the court leans against double portions for children; M'Clell. R. 356; 13 Price, R. 599; against double provisions, and double satisfactions; 3 Atk. R. 421; and against forfeitures. 3 T. R. 172. Vide, generally, 1 Burr. 419; 1 Bos. & Pull. 614; 3 Bos. & Pull. 456; 2 Ves. jr. 648; Jacob, Rep. 115; 1 Turn. & R 350.

BID, *contracts.* A bid is an offer to pay a specified price for an article about to be sold at auction. The bidder has a right to withdraw his bid at any time before it is accepted, which acceptance is generally manifested by knocking down the hammer; 3 T. R. 148; Hardin's Rep. 181; Sugd. Vend. 29; Babington on Auct. 30, 42; or the bid may be withdrawn by implication. 6 Penn. St. R. 486; 8 Id. 408. Vide *Offer.*

BIDDER, *contracts.* One who makes an offer to pay a certain price for an article which is for sale.

2. The term is applied more particularly to a person who offers a price for goods or other property, while up for sale at an auction. The bidder is required to act in good faith, and any combination between him and others, to prevent a fair competition, would avoid the sale made to himself.

3. But there is nothing illegal in two or more persons agreeing together to purchase a property at sheriff's sale, fixing a certain price which they are willing to give, and appointing one of their number to be the bidder. 6 Watts & Serg. 122.

4. Till the bid is accepted, the bidder may retract it. Vide articles, *Auction* and *Bid;* 3 John. Cas. 29; 6 John. R. 194; 8 John. R. 444; 1 Fonbl. Eq. b. 1, c. 4, § 4, note (*x*).

BIENS. A French word, which signifies property. In law, it means property of every description, except estates of freehold and inheritance. Dane's Ab. c. 133, a, 3; Com. Dig. h. t.; Co. Litt. 118, b; Sugd. Vend. 495.

2. In the French law, this term includes all kinds of property, real and personal. Biens are divided into biens meubles, movable or personal property; and biens immeubles, immovable property or real estate. This distinction between movable and immovable property, is, however, recognized by them, and gives rise in the civil, as well as in the common law, to many important distinctions as to rights and remedies. Story, Confl. of Laws, § 13, note 1.

BIGAMUS, *Canon law*, Latin. One guilty of bigamy.

BIGAMY, *crim. law, domestic relations.* The wilful contracting of a second marriage when the contracting party knows that the first is still subsisting; or it is the state of a man who has two wives, or of a woman who has two husbands living at the same time. When the man has more than two wives, or the woman more than two husbands living at the same time, then the party is said to have committed polygamy, but the name of bigamy is more frequently given to this offence in legal proceedings. 1 Russ. on Cr. 187.

2. In England this crime is punishable by the stat. 1 Jac. 1, c. 11, which makes the offence felony; but it exempts from punishment the party whose husband or wife shall continue to remain absent for seven years before the second marriage, without being heard from, and persons who shall have been legally divorced. The statutory provisions in the U. S. against bigamy or polygamy, are in general similar to, and copied from the statute of 1 Jac. 1, c. 11, excepting as to the punishment. The several exceptions to this statute are also nearly the same in the American statutes, but the punishment of the offence is different in many of the states. 2 Kent, Com. 69; vide Bac. Ab. h. t.; Com. Dig. Justices, S 5; Merlin, Répert. mot Bigamie; Code, lib. 9, tit. 9, l. 18; and lib. 5, tit. 5, l. 2.

3. According to the canonists, bigamy is three-fold, viz.: (*vera, interpretativa*, et *similitudinaria*,) real, interpretative and similitudinary. The first consisted in marrying two wives successively, (virgins they may be,) or in once marrying a widow; the second consisted, not in a repeated marriage, but in marrying (v. g. meretricem vel ab alio corruptam) a harlot; the third arose from two marriages, indeed, but the one metaphorical or spiritual, the other carnal. This last was confined to persons initiated in sacred orders, or under the vow of continence. Deferriere's Tract, Juris Canon. tit. xxi. See also Bac. Abr. h. t.; 6 Decret, l. 12. Also *Marriage*.

BILAN. A book in which bankers, merchants and traders write a statement of all they owe and all that is due to them. This term is used in the French law, and in the state of Louisiana. 5 N. S. 158. A balance sheet. See 3 N. S. 446, 504.

BILATERAL CONTRACT, *civil law.* A contract in which both the contracting parties are bound to fulfil obligations reciprocally towards each other; Leç. Elem. § 781; as a contract of sale, where one becomes bound to deliver the thing sold, and the other to pay the price of it. Vide *Contract; Synallagmatic contract.*

BILINGUIS, *English law.* One who uses two tongues or languages. Formerly a jury, part Englishmen and part foreigners, to give a verdict between an Englishman and a foreigner. Vide *Medietas Linguæ*, Plowd. 2. It is abolished in Pennsylvania. Act April 14, 1834, § 149.

BILL, *legislation.* An instrument drawn or presented by a member or committee to a legislative body for its approbation and enactment. After it has gone through both houses and received the constitutional sanction of the chief magistrate, where such approbation is requisite, it becomes a law. See Meigs, R. 237.

BILL, *chancery practice.* A complaint in writing addressed to the chancellor, containing the names of the parties to the suit, both complainant and defendant, a statement of the facts on which the complainant relies, and the allegations which he makes, with an averment that the acts complained of are contrary to equity, and a prayer for relief and proper process. Its office in a chancery suit, is the same as a declaration in an action at law, a libel in a court of admiralty, or an allegation in the spiritual courts.

2. A bill usually consists of nine parts. 1. The address, which must be to the chancellor, court or judge acting as such. 2. The second part consists of the names of the plaintiffs and their descriptions; but the description of the parties in this part of the bill does not, it seems, constitute a sufficient averment, so as to put that fact in issue. 2. Ves. & Bea. 327. 3. The third

part is called the premises or stating part of the bill, and contains the plaintiff's case. 4. In the fourth place is a general charge of confederacy. 5. The fifth part consists of allegations of the defendant's pretences, and charges in evidence of them. 6. The sixth part contains the clause of jurisdiction, and an averment that the acts complained of are contrary to equity. 7. The seventh part consists of a prayer that the parties may answer the premises, which is usually termed the interrogatory part. 8. The prayer for relief sought forms the eighth part. And, 9. The ninth part is a prayer for process. 2 Mad. Ch. 166; Blake's Ch. P. 35; 1 Mitf. Pl. 41. The facts contained in the bill, as far as known to the complainant, must, in some cases, be sworn to be true; and such as are not known to him, he must swear he believes to be true; and it must be signed by counsel; 2 Madd. Ch. Pr. 167; Story, Eq. Pl. § 26 to 47; and for cases requiring an affidavit, see, 3 Brow. Chan. Cas. 12, 24, 463; Bunb. 35; 2 Brow. 11; 1 Fow. Proc. 256; Mitf. Pl. 51; 2 P. Wms. 451; 3 Id. 77; 1 Atk. 450; 3 Id. 17, 132; 3 Atk. 132; Preced. in Ch. 332; Barton's Equity, 48 n. 1, 53 n. 1, 56 n. 1; 2 Brow. Ch. Cas. 281, 319; 4 Id. 480.

3. Bills may be divided into three classes, namely: 1. Original bills. 2. Bills not original. 3. Bills in the nature of original bills.

4.—I. An *original* bill is one which prays the decree of the court, touching some right claimed by the person exhibiting the bill, in opposition to some right claimed by the person against whom the bill is exhibited. Hinde, 19; Coop. Eq. Pl. 43. Original bills always relate to some matter not before litigated in the court by the same persons, and standing in the same interests. Mitf. Eq. Pl. by Jeremy, 34; Story, Eq. Pl. § 16. They may be divided into those which pray relief, and those which do not pray relief.

5.—1st. Original bills *praying relief* are of three kinds. *First.* Bills praying the decree or order of the court, touching some right claimed by the party exhibiting the bill, in opposition to some right, real or supposed, claimed by the party against whom the bill is exhibited, or touching some wrong done in violation of the plaintiff's right. Mitf. Eq. Pl. 32.

6.—*Secondly.* A bill of *interpleader*, is one in which the person exhibiting it claims no right in opposition to the rights claimed by the person against whom the bill is exhibited, but prays the decree of the court touching the rights of those persons, for the safety of the person exhibiting the bill. Hinde, 20; Coop. Eq. Pl. 43; Mitf. Pl. 32. The Practical Register defines it to be a bill exhibited by a third person, who, not knowing to whom he ought of right to render a debt or duty, or pay his rent, fears he may be hurt by some of the claimants, and therefore prays he may interplead, so that the court may judge to whom the thing belongs, and he be thereby safe on the payment. Pr. Reg. 78; Harr. Ch. Pr. 45; Edw. Inj. 393; 2 Paige, 199; Id. 570; 6 John. Ch. R. 445.

7. The interpleader has been compared to the intervention (q. v.) of the civil law. Gilb. For. Rom. 47. But there is a striking difference between them. The *tertius* in our interpleader in equity, professes to have no interest in the subject, and calls upon the parties who allege they have, to come forward and discuss their claims: the *tertius* of the civil law, on the other hand, asserts a right himself in the subject, which two persons are at the time actually contesting, and insists upon his right to join in the discussion. A bill of interpleader may be filed, though the party has not been sued at law, or has been sued by one only of the conflicting claimants, or though the claim of one of the defendants is actionable at law, and the other in equity. 6 Johns. Chan. R. 445. The requisites of a bill of this kind are, 1. It must admit the want of interest in the plaintiff in the subject-matter of dispute. 2. The plaintiff must annex an affidavit that there is no collusion between him and either of the parties. 3. The bill must contain an offer to bring the money into court, when there is any due; the want of which is a ground of demurrer, unless the money has actually been paid into court. Mitf. Eq. Pl. 49; Coop. Eq. Pl. 49; Barton, Suit in Eq. 47, note 1. 4. The plaintiff should state his own rights, and thereby negative any interest in the thing in controversy; and also should state the several claims of the opposite parties; a neglect on this subject is good cause of demurrer. Mitf. Eq. Pl. by Jeremy, 142; 2 Story on Eq. § 821; Story, Eq. Pl. 292. 5. The bill should also show that there are persons in esse capable of interpleading, and setting up opposite claims. Coop. Eq. Pl. 46; 1 Mont. Eq. Pl. 234; Story, Eq. Pl. § 295; Story on Eq. § 821;

1 Ves. 248. 6. The bill should pray that the defendants set forth their several titles, and interplead, settle, and adjust their demands between themselves. The bill also generally prays an injunction to restrain the proceedings of the claimants, or either of them, at law; and, in this case, the bill should offer to bring the money into court; and the court will not in general act upon this part of the prayer, unless the money be actually brought into court. 4 Paige's R. 384; 6 John. Ch. R. 445.

8.—*Thirdly.* A bill of *certiorari*, is one praying the writ of *certiorari* to remove a cause from an inferior court of equity. Coop. Eq. 44. The requisites of this bill are that it state, 1st. the proceedings in the inferior court; 2d. the incompetency of such court, by suggesting that the cause is out of its jurisdiction; or that the witnesses live out of its jurisdiction; or are not able, by age or infirmity, or the distance of the place, to follow the suit there; or that, for some other cause, justice is not likely to be done; 3d. the bill must pray a writ of certiorari, to certify and remove the record and the cause to the superior court. Wyatt, Pr. Reg. 82; Harr. Ch. Pr. 49; Story, Eq. Pl. § 298. This bill is seldom used in the United States.

9.—2d. Original bills *not praying relief* are of two kinds. *First.* Bills to secure evidence, which are bills to perpetuate the testimony of witnesses; or bills to examine witnesses *de bene esse.* These will be separately considered.

10.—1. A bill to *perpetuate the testimony* of witnesses, is one which prays leave to examine them, and states that the witnesses are old, infirm, or sick, or going beyond the jurisdiction of the court, whereby the party is in danger of losing the benefit of their testimony. Hinde, 20. It does not pray for relief. Coop. Eq. Pl. 44.

11. In order to maintain such a bill, it is requisite to state on its face all the material facts to support the jurisdiction. It must state, 1. the subject-matter touching which the plaintiff is desirous of giving evidence. Rep. Temp. Finch, 391; 4 Madd. R. 8, 10. 2. It must show that the plaintiff has some interest in the subject-matter, which may be endangered if the testimony in support of it be lost; and a mere expectancy, however strong, is not sufficient. 6 Ves. 260; 1 Vern. 105; 15 Ves. 136; Mitf. Eq. Pl. by Jeremy, 51; Coop. Eq. Pl. 52. 3. It must state that the defendant has, or pretends to have, or that he claims an interest to contest the title of the plaintiff in the subject-matter of the proposed testimony. Coop. Pl. 56; Story, Eq. Pl. § 302. 4. It must exhibit some ground of necessity for perpetuating the evidence. Story, Eq. Pl. § 303; Mitf. Eq. Pl. by Jeremy, 52, 148 and note y; Coop. Eq. Pl. 53. 5. The right of which the bill is brought to perpetuate the evidence or testimony, should be described with reasonable certainty in the bill, so as to point the proper interrogations on both sides to the true merits of the controversy. 1 Vern. 312; Coop. Eq. Pl. 56. 6. It should pray leave to examine the witnesses touching the matter stated, to the end that their testimony may be preserved and perpetuated. Mitf. Pl. 52. A bill to perpetuate testimony differs from a bill to take testimony de bene esse, in this, that the latter is sustainable only when there is a suit already depending, while the former can be maintained only when no present suit can be brought at law by the party seeking the aid of a court to try his right. Story, Eq. Pl. § 307. The canonists had a similar rule. According to the canon law, witnesses could be examined before any action was commenced, for fear that their evidence might be lost. X, cap. 5; Boehmer, n. 5; 8 Toull. n. 23.

12.—2. Bill to *take testimony de bene esse.* This bill, the name of which is sufficiently descriptive of its object, is frequently confounded with a bill to perpetuate testimony; but although it bears a close analogy to it, it is very different. Bills to perpetuate testimony can be maintained only, when no present suit can be maintained at law by the party seeking the aid of the court to try his right; whereas bills to take testimony de bene esse, are sustainable only in aid of a suit already depending. 1 Sim. & Stu. 83. The latter may be brought by a person who is in possession, or out of possession; and whether he be plaintiff or defendant in the action at law. Story, Eq. Pl. § 307 and 303, note; Story on Eq. § 1813, note 3. In many respects the rules which regulate the framing of bills to perpetuate testimony, are applicable to bills to take testimony de bene esse.

13.—*Secondly.* A bill of *discovery*, emphatically so called, is one which prays for the discovery of facts resting within the knowledge of the person against whom the bill is exhibited, or of deeds, writings, or other things in his custody or power. Hinde, 20;

Blake's Ch. Pr. 37. Every bill, except the bill of certiorari, may in truth be considered a bill of discovery, for every bill seeks a disclosure of circumstances relative to the plaintiff's case; but that usually and emphatically distinguished by this appellation is a bill for the discovery of facts, resting in the knowledge of the defendant, or of deeds or writings, or other things in his custody or power, and seeking no relief in consequence of the discovery.

14. This bill is commonly used in aid of the jurisdiction of some other court; as to enable the plaintiff to prosecute or defend an action at law. Mitf. Pl. 52. The plaintiff, in this species of bill, must be entitled to the discovery he seeks, and shall only have a discovery of what is necessary for his own title, as of deeds he claims under, and not to pry into that of the defendant. 2 Ves. 445. See Blake's Ch. Pr. 45; Mitf. Pl. 52; Coop. Eq. Pl. 58; 1 Madd. Ch. Pr. 196; Hare on Disc. *passim;* Wagr. on Disc. *passim.*

15. The action *ad exhibendum,* in the Roman law, was not unlike a bill of discovery. Its object was to force the party against whom it was instituted, to exhibit a thing or a title in his power. It was always preparatory to another, which was always a real action in the sense of the word in the Roman law. See *Action ad exhibendum;* Merlin, Questions de Droit, tome i. 84.

16.—II. Bills *not original.* These are either in addition to, or a continuance of an original bill, or both. Mitf. c. 1, s. 2; Story, Eq. Pl. § 388; 4 Bouv. Inst. n. 4100.

17.—1st. Of the first class are, 1. A *supplemental* bill. This bill is occasioned by some defect in a suit already instituted, whereby the parties cannot obtain complete justice, to which otherwise the case by their bill would have entitled them. It is used for the purpose of supplying some irregularity discovered in the formation of the original bill, or some of the proceedings thereupon; or some defect in a suit, arising from events happening since the points in the original were at issue, which give an interest to persons not parties to the suit. Blake's Ch. Pr. 50. See 3 Johns. Ch. R. 423.

18. It is proper to consider more minutely, 1. in what cases such a bill may be filed; 2. its particular requisites.

19.—1. A supplemental bill may be filed, 1st. whenever the imperfection in the original bill arises from the omission of some material fact, which existed before the filing of the bill, but the time has passed in which it can be introduced into the bill by amendment; Mitf. Eq. Pl. 55, 61, 325; but leave of court must be obtained, before a bill which seeks to change the original structure of the bill, and to introduce a new and different case, can be filed. 2d. When a party necessary to the proceedings has been omitted, and cannot be admitted by an amendment. Mitf. Eq. Pl. 61; 6 Madd. R. 369; 4 John. Ch. R. 605. 3d. When, after the court has decided upon the suit as framed, it appears necessary to bring some other matter before the court to obtain the full effect of the decision; or before a decision has been obtained, but after the parties are at issue upon the points in the original bill, and witnesses have been examined, (in which case, an amendment is not in general permitted,) some other point appears necessary to be made, or some additional discovery is found requisite. Mitf. Eq. Pl. by Jeremy, 55; Coop. Eq. Pl. 73; 3 Atk. R. 110; 1 Paige, R. 200. 4th. When new events or new matters have occurred since the filing of the bill; Coop. Eq. Pl. 74; these events or matters, however, are confined to such as refer to and support the rights and interests already mentioned in the bill. Story, Eq. Pl. § 336.

20.—2. The supplemental bill must state the original bill, and the proceedings thereon; and when it is occasioned by an event which has occurred subsequently to the original bill, it must state that event, and the consequent alteration with regard to the parties. In general, the supplemental bill must pray that all defendants appear and answer the charges it contains. Mitf. Eq. Pl. by Jeremy, 75; Story, Eq. Pl. § 343.

21.—2. A bill of *revivor,* which is a continuance of the original bill, when by death some party to it has become incapable of prosecuting or defending a suit, or a female plaintiff has by marriage incapacitated herself from suing alone. Mitf. Pl. 33, 70; 2 Madd. Ch. Pr. 526. See 3 Johns. Ch. R. 60: Story, Eq. Pl. § 354, et. seq.

22.—3. A bill of *revivor and supplement.* This is a compound of a supplemental bill and bill of revivor, and not only continues the suit, which has abated by the death of the plaintiff, or the like, but supplies any defects in the original bill, arising from subsequent events, so as to entitle the party to relief on the whole merits of his case. 5 Johns. Ch R. 334; Mitf. Pl. 32, 74.

23.—2d. Among the second class may be placed, 1. A *cross* bill. This is one which is brought by a defendant in a suit against the plaintiff, respecting the matter in question in that bill. Coop. Eq. Pl. 85; Mitf. Pl. 75.

24. A bill of this kind is usually brought to obtain, either a necessary discovery, or full relief to all the parties. It frequently happens, and particularly if any questions arises between two defendants to a bill, that the court cannot make a complete decree without a cross bill, or cross bills to bring every matter in dispute completely before the court, litigated by the proper parties, and upon proper proofs. In this case it becomes necessary for some one of the defendants to the original bill to file a bill against the plaintiff and other defendants in that bill, or some of them, and bring the litigated point properly before the court.

25. A cross bill should state the original bill, and the proceedings thereon, and the rights of the party exhibiting the bill which are necessary to be made the subject of a cross litigation, or the grounds on which he resists the claims of the plaintiff in the original bill, if that is the object of the new bill.

26. A cross bill may be filed to answer the purpose of a plea *puis darrein continuance* at the common law. For example, where, pending a suit, and after replication and issue joined, the defendant having obtained a release and attempted to prove it *viva voce* at the hearing, it was determined that the release not being in issue in the cause, the court could not try the facts, or direct a trial at law for that purpose, and that a new bill must be filed to put the release in issue. Mitf. Pl. 75, 76; Coop. Eq. Pl. 85; 1 Harr. Ch. Pr. 135.

27. A cross bill must be brought before publication is passed on the first bill, 1 Johns. Ch. R. 62, and not after, except the plaintiff in the cross bill go to the hearing on the depositions already published; because of the danger of perjury and subornation, if the parties should, after publication of the former depositions, examine witnesses, *de novo*, to the same matter before examined into. 7 Johns. Ch. Rep. 250; Nels. Ch. R. 103.

28.—2. A bill of *review*. Bills of review are in the nature of writs of error. They are brought to have decrees of the court reviewed, altered, or reversed, and there are two sorts of these bills. The first is brought where the decree has been signed and enrolled; and the second, where the decree has not been signed and enrolled. 1 Ch. Cas. 54; 3 P. Wms. 371. The first of these is called, by way of preëminence, a bill of review; while the other is distinguished by the appellation of a bill in the nature of a bill of review, or a supplemental bill in the nature of a bill of review. Coop. Eq. Pl. 88; 2 Madd. Ch. Pr. 537.

29. A bill of review must be either for error in point of law; 2 Johns. C. R. 488; Coop. Eq. Pl. 89; or for some new matter of fact, relevant to the case, discovered since publication passed in the cause; and which could not, with reasonable diligence, have been discovered before. 2 Johns. C. R. 488; Coop. Eq. Pl. 94. See 3 Johns. R. 124.

30.—3. Bill to *impeach a decree* on the ground of fraud. When a decree has been obtained by fraud, it may be impeached by original bill, without leave of court. As the principal point in issue, is the fraud in obtaining it, it must be established before the propriety of the decree can be investigated, and the fraud must be distinctly stated in the bill. The prayer must necessarily be varied according to the nature of the fraud used, and the extent of its operation in obtaining an improper decision of the court. When the decree to set aside a fraudulent decree has been obtained, the court will restore the parties to their former situation, whatever their rights may be. Mitf. Eq. Pl. 84; Sto. Eq. Pl. § 426.

31.—4. Bill to *suspend* a decree. The operation of a decree may be suspended under special circumstances, or avoided by matter subsequent to the decree, upon a new bill for that purpose. See 1 Ch. Cas. 3, 61; 2 Ch. Cas. 8; Mitf. Eq. Pl. 85, 86.

32.—5. Bill to *carry a decree into execution*. This is one which is filed when, from the neglect of parties, or some other cause, it may become impossible to carry a decree into execution without the further decree of the court. Hinde, 68; 1 Harr. Ch. 148.

33.—6. Bills partaking of the qualities of some one or more of other bills. These are,

34. First. Bill *in the nature of a bill of revivor*. A bill in the nature of a bill of revivor, is one which is filed when the death of a party, whose interest is not determined by his death, is attended with such a transmission of his interest, that the

title to it, as well as the person entitled, may be litigated in the court of chancery, as in the case of a devise of real estate, the suit is not permitted to be continued by bill of revivor. 1 Ch. Cas. 123; Id. 174; 3 Ch. Rep. 39; Mosely, R. 44. In such cases an original bill, upon which the title may be litigated, must be filed, and this bill will have so far the effect of a bill of revivor, that if the title of the representative by the act of the deceased party is established, the same benefit may be had of the proceedings upon the former bill, as if the suit had been continued by bill of revivor. 1 Vern. 427; 2 Vern. 548; Id. 672; 2 Bro. P. C. 529; 1 Eq. Cas. Ab. 83; Mitf. Pl. 66, 67.

35. Secondly. Bill *in the nature of a supplemental bill*. An original bill in the nature of a supplemental bill, is one filed when the interest of the plaintiff or defendant, suing or defending, wholly determines, and the same property becomes vested in another person not claiming under him. Hinde, 71; Blake's Ch. Pr. 38. The principal difference between this and a supplemental bill, seems to be, that a supplemental bill is applicable to such cases only, where the same parties or the same interests remain before the court; whereas, an original bill in the nature of a supplemental bill, is properly applicable where new parties, with new interests, arising from events occurring since the institution of the suit, are brought before the court. Coop. Eq. Pl. 75; Story, Eq. Pl. § 345.

36. Thirdly. Bill *in the nature of a bill of review*. A bill in the nature of a bill of review, is one brought by a person not bound by a decree, praying that the same may be examined and reversed; as where a decree is made against a person who has no interest at all in the matter in dispute, or had not an interest sufficient to render the decree against him binding upon some person claiming after him. Relief may be obtained against error in the decree, by a bill in the nature of a bill of review. This bill in its frame resembles a bill of review, except that instead of praying that the former decree may be reviewed and reversed, it prays that the cause may be heard with respect to the new matter made the subject of the supplemental bill, at the same time that it is reheard upon the original bill; and that the plaintiff may have such relief as the nature of the case made by the supplemental bill may require. 1 Harr. Ch. P. 145.

37. There are also bills which derive their names from the object which the complainant has in view. These will be separately considered.

38.—1. Bill of *foreclosure*. A bill of foreclosure is one filed by a mortgagee against the mortgagor, for the purpose of having the estate sold, thereby to obtain the sum mortgaged on the premises, with interest and costs. 1 Madd. Ch. Pr. 528. As to the persons who are to be made parties to a bill of foreclosure, see Story, Eq. Pl. § 199–202.

39.—2. Bill of *information*. A bill of information is a bill instituted in behalf of the state, or those whose rights are the object of its care and protection. It is commenced by information exhibited in the name of the attorney-general, and differs from other bills little more than in name. If the suit immediately concerns the right of the state, the information is generally exhibited without a relator. If it does not immediately concern those rights, it is conducted at the instance and under the immediate direction of some person whose name is inserted in the information, and is termed the relator; the officers of the state, in such or the like cases, are not further concerned than as they are instructed and advised by those whose rights the state is called upon to protect and establish. Blake's Ch. Pl. 50; see Harr. Ch. Pr. 151.

40.—3. Bill to *marshal assets*. A bill to marshal assets is one filed in favor of simple contract creditors, and of legatees, devisees, and heirs, but not in favor of next of kin, to prevent specialty creditors from exhausting the personal estate. See *Marshaling of Assets*.

41.—4. Bill to *marshal securities*. A bill to marshal securities is one which is filed against a party who has two funds by which his debt is secured, by a person having an interest in only one of those funds. As if A has two mortgages and B has but one, B has a right to throw A upon the security which B cannot touch. 2 Atk. 446; see 8 Ves. 388, 395. This last case contains a luminous exposition in all its bearings. In Pennsylvania, and perhaps in some other states, the object of this bill is reached by subrogation, (q. v.) that is, by substituting the creditor, having but one fund to resort to, to the rights of the other creditor, in respect to the other fund.

42.—5. Bill *for a new trial*. This is a bill filed in a court of equity praying for an injunction after judgment at law, when there is any fact, which renders it against conscience to execute such judgment, and of which the injured party could not avail himself in a court of law; or, if he could, was prevented by fraud or accident, unmixed with any fault or negligence of himself or his agents. Mitf. Pl. by Jer. 131; 2 Story Eq. § 887. Of late years bills of this description are not countenanced. Id.; 1 John. Ch. R. 432; 6 John. Ch. R. 479.

43.—6. Bill *of peace*. A bill of peace is one which is filed when a person has a right which may be controverted by various persons, at different times, and by different actions. In such a case the court will prevent a multiplicity of suits, by directing an issue to determine the right, and ultimately grant an injunction. 1 Madd. Ch. Pr. 166; 1 Harr. Ch. Pr. 104; Blake's Ch. Pr. 48; 2 Story, Eq. Jur. § 852 to 860; Jeremy on Eq. Jurisd. 343; 2 John. Ch. R. 281; 8 Cranch, R. 426.

44. There is another class of cases in which a bill of peace is now ordinarily applied; namely, when the plaintiff, after repeated and satisfactory trials, has established his right at law, and is still in danger of new attempts to controvert it. In order to quiet the possession of the plaintiff, and to suppress future litigation, courts of equity, under such circumstances, will interfere, and grant a perpetual injunction. 3 John. R. 529; 8 Cranch, R. 462; Mit. Pl. by Jeremy, 143; 2 John. Ch. R. 281; Ed. on Inj. 356.

45.—7. Bill *quia timet*. A bill *quia timet*, is one which is filed when a person is entitled to property of a personal nature after another's death, and has reason to apprehend it may be destroyed by the present possessor; or when he is apprehensive of being subjected to a future inconvenience, probable or even possible to happen or be occasioned by the neglect, inadvertance, or culpability of another. Upon a proper case being made out, the court will, in one case, secure the property for the use of the party (which is the object of the bill) by compelling the person in possession of it, to give a proper security against any subsequent disposition or wilful destruction, and in the other case, they will quiet the party's apprehension of future inconvenience, by removing the causes which may lead to it. 1 Harr. Ch. Pr. 107; 1 Madd. Ch. Pr. 218: Blake's Ch. Pr. 37, 47; 2 Story, Eq. Jur. § 825 to 851. Vide, generally, Bouv. Inst. Index, h. t.

BILL, *merc. law*. An account containing the items of goods sold, or of work done by one person against another. It differs from an account stated (q. v.) in this, that the latter is a bill approved and sanctioned by the debtor, whereas a bill is made out by the creditor alone.

BILL OF ADVENTURE, *com. law, contracts*. A writing signed by a merchant, to testify that the goods shipped on board a certain vessel belong to another person who is to take the hazard, the subscriber signing only to oblige himself to account to him for the proceeds.

BILL OF ATTAINDER, *legislation, punishment*. An act of the legislature by which one or more persons are declared to be attainted, and their property confiscated.

2. The Constitution of the United States declares that no state shall pass any bill of attainder.

3. During the revolutionary war, bills of attainder, and ex post facto acts of confiscation, were passed to a wide extent. The evils resulting from them, in times of more cool reflection, were discovered to have far outweighed any imagined good. Story on Const. § 1367. Vide *Attainder; Bill of Pains and Penalties*.

BILL-BOOK, *commerce, accounts*. One in in which an account is kept of promissory notes, bills of exchange, and other bills payable or receivable: it ought to contain all that a man issues or receives. The book should show the date of the bill, the term it has to run before it becomes due, the names of all the parties to it, and the time of its becoming due, together with the amount for which it was given.

BILL OF CONFORMITY. The name of a bill filed by an executor or administrator, who finds the affairs of the deceased so much involved that he cannot safely administer the estate, except under the direction of a court of chancery. This bill is filed against the creditors generally, for the purpose of having all their claims adjusted, and procuring a final decree settling the order of payment of the assets. 1 Story, Eq. Jur. 440.

BILL OF COST, *practice*. A statement of the items which form the total amount of the costs of a suit or action. This is demandable as a matter of right before the payment of the costs.

BILL OF CREDIT. It is provided by the Constitution of the United States, art. 1, s. 10, that no state shall "emit bills of credit, or make anything but gold and silver coin a tender in payment or debts." Such bills of credit are declared to mean promissory notes or bills issued exclusively on the credit of the state, and for the payment of which the faith of the state only is pledged. The prohibition, therefore, does not apply to the notes of a state bank, drawn on the credit of a particular fund set apart for the purpose. 2 M'Cord's R. 12; 2 Pet. R. 318; 11 Pet. R. 257. Bills of credit may be defined to be paper issued and intended to circulate through the community for its ordinary purposes, as money redeemable at a future day. 4 Pet. U. S. R. 410; 1 Kent, Com. 407; 4 Dall. R. xxiii.; Story, Const. §§ 1362 to 1364; 1 Scam. R. 87, 526.

2. This phrase is used in another sense among merchants; it is a letter sent by an agent or other person to a merchant, desiring him to give credit to the bearer for goods or money. Com. Dig. Merchant, F 3; 5 Sm. & Marsh. 491; R. M. Charlt. 151; 4 Pike, R. 44; 3 Burr. Rep. 1667.

Bill of debt, bill obligatory, *contracts*. When a merchant by his writing acknowledges himself in debt to another, in a certain sum to be paid on a certain day, and subscribes it at a day and place certain. It may be under seal or not. Com. Dig. Merchant, F 2.

Bill of exception, *practice*. The statement in writing, of the objection made by a party in a cause, to the decision of the court on a point of law, which, in confirmation of its accuracy, is signed and sealed by the judge or court who made the decision. The object of the bill of exceptions is to put the question of law on record, for the information of the court of error having cognizance of such cause.

2. The bill of exception is authorized by the statute of Westminster 2, 13 Ed. I. c. 31, the principles of which have been adopted in all the states of the Union. It is thereby enacted, "when one impleaded before any of the justices, alleges an exception praying they will allow it, and if they will not, if he that alleges the exception writes the same, and requires that the justices will put their seals, the justices shall do so, and if one will not, another shall; and if, upon complaint made of the justice, the king cause the record to come before him, and the exception be not found in the roll, and the plaintiff show the written exception, with the seal of the justices thereto put, the justice shall be commanded to appear at a certain day, either to confess or deny his seal, and if he cannot deny his seal, they shall proceed to judgment according to the exception, as it ought to be allowed or disallowed." The statute extends to both plaintiff and defendant. Vide the form of confessing a bill of exceptions, 3 Burr. 1692. And for precedents see Bull. N. P. 317; Brownlow's Entries; Latine Redivio, 129; Trials per pais, 222, 3; 4 Yeates, 317, 18; 2 Yeates, 295, 6. 485, 6; 1 Morgan's Vade Mecum, 471—5. Bills of exception differ materially from special verdicts; 2 Bin. 92; and from the opinions of the court filed in the cause. 10 S. & R. 114, 15.

3. Here will be considered, 1 the cases in which a bill of exceptions may be had; 2. the time of making the exception; 3. the form of the bill; 4. the effect of the bill.

4.—1. In general a bill of exception can be had only in a *civil* case. When in the course of the trial of a cause, the judge, either in his charge to the jury, or in deciding an interlocutory question, mistakes the law, or is supposed by the counsel on either side, to have mistaken the law, the counsel against whom the decision is made may tender an exception to his opinion, and require him to seal a bill of exceptions. 3 Bl. Com. 372. See Salk. 284, pl. 16; 7 Serg. & Rawle, 178; 10 Id. 114, 115; Whart. Dig. Error, D, E; 1 Cowen, 622; 2 Caines, 168; 2 Cowen, 479; 5 Cowen, 243; 3 Cranch, 298; 4 Cranch, 62; 6 Cranch, 226; 17 Johns. R. 218; 3 Wend. 418; 9 Wend. 674. In *criminal* cases, the judges, it seems, are not required to seal a bill of exceptions. 1 Chit. Cr. Law, 622; 13 John R. 90; 1 Virg. Cas. 264; 2 Watts, R 285; 2 Sumn. R. 19. In New York, it is provided by statute, that on the trial of any indictment, exceptions to any decision of the court may be made by the defendant, in the same cases and manner provided by law in civil cases; and a bill thereof shall be settled, signed and sealed, and filed with the clerk of the court. But such bill of exception shall not stay or delay the rendering of judgment, except in some specified cases. Grah. Pr. 768, note. Statutory provisions have been made in several other states authorizing the taking of exceptions in criminal cases. 2 Virg. Cas. 60 and note; 14 Pick. R. 370; 4 Ham. R. 348; 6 Ham. R. 16; 7 Ham. R. 214; 1 Leigh, R. 598; 14 Wend. 546. See also 1 Halst. R. 405; 2 Penn. R. 637.

5.—2. The bill of exceptions must be tendered at the time the decision complained of is made; or if the exception be to the charge of the court, it must be made before the jury have given their verdict. 8 S. & R. 216; 4 Dall. 249; S. C. 1 Binn. 38; 6 John. 279; 1 John. 312; 5 Watts, R. 69; 10 John. R. 312; 5 Monr. R. 177; 7 Wend. R. 34; 7 S. & R. 219; 11 S. & R. 267; 4 Pet. R. 102; Ala. R. 66; 1 Monr. 215; 11 Pet. R. 185; 6 Cowen, R. 189. In practice, however, the point is merely noted, at the time, and the bill is afterwards settled. 8 S. & R. 216; 11 S. & R. 270; Trials per pais, 467; Salk. 288; Sir T. Ray. 405; Bull. N. P. 315-16; Jacob's Law Dict. They may be sealed by the judge after the record has been removed by a writ of error, and after the expiration of his office. Fitz. N. B. 21 N, note.

6.—3. The bill of exception must be signed by the judge who tried the cause; which is to be done upon notice of the time and place, when and where it is to be done. 3 Cowen, 32; 8 Cowen, 766; Bull. N. P. 316; 3 Bl. Com. 372. When the bill of exception is sealed, both parties are concluded by it. 3 Dall. 38; Bull. N. P. 316.

7.—4. The bill of exceptions, being part of the record, is evidence between the parties, as to the facts therein stated. 3 Burr. 1765. No notice can be taken of objections or exceptions not appearing on the bill. 8 East, 280; 3 Dall. 38, 422, n.; 2 Binn. 168. Vide, generally, Dunlap's Pr.; Grah. Pr.; Tidd's Pr.; Chit. Pr.; Penna. Pr.; Archibold's Pr.; Sellon's Pr.; in their several indexes, h. t.; Steph. Pl. 111; Bac. Ab. h. t.; 1 Phil. Ev. 214; 12 Vin. Ab. 262; Code of Pract. of Louisiana, art. 487, 8, 9; 6 Watts & Serg, 386, 397; 3 Bouv. Inst. n. 3228–32.

Bill of exchange, *contracts.* A bill of exchange is defined to be an open letter of request from, and order by, one person on another, to pay a sum of money therein mentioned to a third person, on demand, or at a future time therein specified. 2 Bl. Com. 466; Bayl. on Bills, 1; Chit. Bills, 1; 1 H. Bl. 586: 1 B. & P. 291, 654; Selw. N. P. 285. Leigh's N. P. 335; Byles on Bills, 1: 1 Bouv. Inst. n. 895.

2. The subject will be considered with reference, 1. to the parties to a bill; 2. the form; 3. their different kinds; 4. the indorsement and transfer; 5. the acceptance; 6. the protest.

3.—§ 1. The parties to a bill of exchange are the drawer, (q. v.) or he who makes the order; the drawee, (q. v.) or the person to whom it is addressed; the acceptor, (q. v.) or he who accepts the bill; the payee, (q. v.) or the party to whom, or in whose favor the bill is made. The indorser, (q. v.) is he who writes his name on the back of a bill; the indorsee, (q. v.) is one to whom a bill is transferred by indorsement; and the holder, (q. v.) is in general any one of the parties who is in possession of the bill, and entitled to receive the money therein mentioned.

4. Some of the parties are sometimes fictitious persons. When a bill is made payable to a fictitious person, and indorsed in the name of the fictitious payee, it is in effect a bill to bearer, and a bona fide holder, ignorant of that fact, may recover on it, against all prior parties, who were privy to the transaction. 2 H. Bl. 178, 288; 3 T. R. 174, 182, 481; 1 Camp. 130; 19 Ves. 311. In a case where the drawer and payee were fictitious persons, the acceptor was held liable to a bona fide holder. 10 B. & C. 468; S. C. 11 E. C. L. R. 116. Vide, as to parties to a bill, Chit. Bills, 15 to 76, (ed. of 1836.)

5.—§ 2. The form of the bill. 1. The general requisites of a bill of exchange, are, 1st. that it be in writing. R. T. Hardw. 2; 2 Stra. 955; 1 Pardess. 344–5.

6.—2d. That it be for the payment of money, and not for the payment of merchandise. 5 T. R. 485; 3 Wils. 213; 2 Bla. Rep. 782; 1 Burr. 325; 1 Dowl. & Ry. N. P. C. 33; 1 Bibb's R. 502; 3 Marsh. (Kty.) R. 184; 6 Cowen, 108; 1 Caines' R. 381; 4 Mass. 245; 10 S. & R. 64; 14 Pet. R. 293; 1 M'Cord, 115; 2 Nott & M'Cord, 519; 9 Watts, R. 102. But see 9 John. R. 120; and 19 John. R. 144, where it was held that a note payable in bank bills was a good negotiable note.

7.—3d. That the money be payable at all events, not depending on any contingency, either with regard to the fund out of which payment is to be made, or the parties by or to whom payment is to be made. 8 Mod. 363; 4 Vin. Ab. 240, pl. 16; 1 Burr. 323; 4 Dougl. 9; 4 Ves. 372; Russ. & Ry. C. C. 193; 4 Wend. R. 575; 2 Barn. & Ald. 417.

8.—2. The particular requisites of a bill of exchange. It is proper here to remark that no particular form or set of words is necessary to be adopted. An order "to deliver money," or a promise that "A B shall receive money," or a promise "to be accountable" or "responsible" for it, have been severally held to be sufficient for a bill or note. 2 Ld. Raym. 1396; 8 Mod. 364.

9. The several parts of a bill of exchange are, 1st. that it be properly dated as to place.

10.—2d. That it be properly dated as to the time of making. As the time a bill becomes due is generally regulated by the time when it was made, the date of the instrument ought to be clearly expressed. Beawes, pl. 3; 1 B. & C. 398; 2 Pardess. n. 333.

11.—3d. The superscription of the sum for which the bill is payable is not indispensable, but if it be not mentioned in the bill, the superscription will aid the omission. 2 East, P. C. 951.

12.—4th. The time of payment ought to be expressed in the bill; if no time be mentioned, it is considered as payable on demand. 7 T. R. 427; 2 Barn. & C. 157.

13.—5th. Although it is proper for the drawer to name the place of payment, either in the body or subscription of the bill, it is not essential; and it is the common practice for the drawer merely to write the address of the drawee, without pointing out any place of payment; in such case the bill is considered payable, and to be presented at the residence of the drawee, where the bill was made, or to him personally any where. 2 Pardess. n. 337; 10 B. & C. 4; Moody & M. 381; 4 Car. & Paine, 35. It is at the option of the drawer whether or not to prescribe a particular place of payment, and make the payment there part of the contract. Beawes, pl. 3. The drawee, unless restricted by the drawer, may also fix a place of payment by his acceptance. Chit. Bills, 172.

14.—6th. There must be an order or request to pay, and that must be a matter of right, and not of favor. Mood. & M. 171. But it seems that civility in the terms of request cannot alter the legal effect of the instrument; "il vous *plaira* de payer," is, in France, the proper language of a bill. Pailliet, Manuel de Droit Français, 841. The word *pay* is not indispensable, for the word *deliver* is equally operative. Ld. Raym. 1397.

15.—7th. Foreign bills of exchange consist, generally, of several parts; a party who has engaged to deliver a foreign bill, is bound to deliver as many parts as may be requested. 2 Pardess. n. 342. The several parts of a bill of exchange are called a set; each part should contain a condition that it shall be paid, provided the others remain unpaid. Id. The whole set make but one bill.

16.—8th. The bill ought to specify to whom it is to be paid. 2 Pardess. n. 338; 1 H. Bl. 608; Russ. & Ry. C. C. 195. When the name of the payee is in blank, and the bill has been negotiated by indorsement, the holder may fill the blank with his own name. 2 M. & S. 90; 4 Camp. 97. It may, however, be drawn payable to bearer, and then it is assignable by delivery. 3 Burr. 1526.

17.—9th. To make a bill negotiable, it must be made payable to order, or bearer, or there must be other operative and equivalent words of transfer. Beawes, pl. 3; Selw. N. P. 303, n. 16; Salk. 133. If, however, it is not intended to make the bill negotiable, these words need not be inserted, and the instrument will, nevertheless, be valid as a bill of exchange. 6 T. R. 123; 6 Taunt. 328; Russ. & Ry. C. C. 300; 3 Caines' R. 137; 9 John. R. 217. In France, a bill must be made payable to order. Code de Com. art. 110; 2 Pardess. n. 339.

18.—10th. The sum for which the bill is drawn, must be clearly expressed in the body of it, in writing at length. The sum must be fixed and certain, and not contingent. 2 Stark. R. 375. And it may be in the money of any country. Payment of part of the bill, the residue being unpaid, cannot be indorsed. The contract is indivisible, and the acceptor would thereby be compelled to make two payments instead of one. But when part of a bill has been paid the residue may be assigned, since then it becomes a contract for the residue only. 12 Mod. 213; 1 Salk. 65; Ld. Ray. 360.

19.—11th. It is usual to insert the words, *value received*, but it is implied that every bill and indorsement has been made for value received, as much as if it had been expressed *in totidem verbis*. 3 M. & S. 352; Bayl. 40, n. 83.

20—12th. It is usual, when the drawer of the bill is debtor to the drawee, to insert in the bill these words: "and put it to my account;" but when the drawee, or the person to whom it is directed, is debtor to the drawer, then he inserts these words: "and put it to *your* account;" and, sometimes, where a third person is debtor to the drawee, it may be expressed thus: "and put it to the account of A B;" Marius, 27; Com.

Dig. Merchant, F 5; R. T. Hardw. 1, 2, 3; but it is altogether unnecessary to insert any of these words. 1 B. & C. 398; S. C. 8 E. C. L. R. 108.

21.—13th. When the drawer is desirous to inform the drawee that he has drawn a bill, he inserts in it the words, "*as per advice;*" but when he wishes the bill paid without any advice from him, he writes, "*without further advice.*" In the former case the drawee is not authorized to pay the bill till he has received the advice; in the latter he may pay before he has received advice.

22.—14th. The drawee must either subscribe the bill, or, it seems, his name may be simply inserted in the body of the instrument. Beawes, pl. 3; Ld. Raym. 1376; 1 Stra. 609.

23.—15th. The bill being a letter of request from the maker to a third person, should be addressed to that person by the Christian name and surname, or by the full style of their firm. 2 Pardess. n. 335; Beawes, pl. 3; Chit. Bills, 186, 7.

24.—16th. The place of payment should be stated in the bill.

25.—17th. As a matter of precaution, the drawer of a foreign bill may, in order to prevent expenses, require the holder to apply to a third person, named in the bill for that purpose, when the drawee refuses to accept the bill. This requisition is usually in these words, placed in a corner, under the drawee's address: "*Au besoin chez* Messrs. —— at ——," in other words, "In case of need apply to Messrs. —— at ——."

26.—18th. The drawer may also add a request or direction, that in case the bill should not be honored by the drawee, it shall be returned without protest or without expense, by subscribing the words, "*retour sans protêt,*" or "*sans frais;*" in this case the omission of the holder to protest, having been induced by the drawer, he, and perhaps the indorsers, cannot resist the payment on that account, and thus the expense is avoided. Chit. Bills, 188.

27.—19th. The drawer may also limit the amount of damages, by making a memorandum on the bill, that they shall be a definite sum; as, for example: "*In case* of non-acceptance or non-payment, reëxchange and expenses not to exceed —— dollars." Id.

28.—§ 3. Bills of exchange are either foreign or inland. *Foreign,* when drawn by a person out of, on another in, the United States, or *vice versâ;* or by a person in a foreign country, on another person in another foreign country; or by a person in one state, on another in another of the United States. 2 Pet. R. 589; 10 Pet. R. 572; 12 Pick. 483; 15 Wend. 527; 3 Marsh. (Kty.) R. 488; 1 Rep. Const. Ct. 100; 4 Leigh's R. 37; 4 Wash. C. C. Rep. 148; 1 Whart. Dig. tit. Bills of Exchange, pl. 78. But see 5 John. R. 384, where it is said by Van Ness, Justice, that a bill drawn in the United States, upon any place within the United States, is an inland bill.

29. An *inland* bill is one drawn by a person in a state, on another in the same state. The principal difference between foreign and inland bills is, that the former must be protested, and the latter need not. 6 Mod. 29; 2 B. & A. 656; Chit Bills, (ed. of 1836,) p. 14. "The English rule requiring protest and notice of non-acceptance of foreign bills, has been adopted and followed as the true rule of mercantile law, in the states of Massachusetts, Connecticut, New York, Maryland, and South Carolina 3 Mass. Rep. 557; 1 Day's R. 11; 3 John Rep. 202; 4 John. R. 144; 1 Bay's Rep. 468; 1 Harr. & John. 187. But the supreme court of the United States, in Brown *v.* Berry, 3 Dall. R. 365, and in Clark *v.* Russel, cited in 6 Serg. & Rawle, 358, held, that in an action on a foreign bill of exchange, after a protest for non-payment, protest for non-acceptance, or notice of non-acceptance need not be shown, inasmuch as they were not required by the custom of merchants in this country; and those decisions have been followed in Pennsylvania. 6 Serg. & Rawle, 356. It becomes a little difficult, therefore, to know what is the true rule of the law-merchant in the United States, on this point, after such contrary decisions." 3 Kent's Com. 95. As to what will be considered a foreign or an inland bill, when part of the bill is made in one place and part in another, see 1 M. & S. 87; Gow. R. 56; S. C. 5 E. C. L. R. 460; 8 Taunt. 679; 4 E. C. L. R. 245; 5 Taunt. 529; 1 E. C. L. R. 179.

30.—§ 4. The indorsement. Vide articles *Indorsement; Indorser; Indorsee.*

31.—§ 5. The acceptance. Vide article *Acceptance.*

32.—§ 6. The protest. Vide article *Protest.*

Vide, generally, Chitty on Bills; Bayley

on Bills; Byles on Bills; Marius on Bills; Kyd on Bills; Cunningham on Bills; Pothier, h. t.; Pardess. Index, Lettre de Change; 4 Vin. Ab. 238; Bac. Ab. Merchant and Merchandise, M.; Com. Digest, Merchant; Dane's Ab. Index, h. t.; 1 Sup. to Ves. Jr. 86, 514; Smith on Mer. Law, Book 3, c. 1; Bouv. Inst. Index, h. t.

Bill of gross adventure. A phrase used in French maritime law; it comprehends every instrument of writing which contains a contract of bottomry, respondentia, and every species of maritime loan. We have no word of similar import. Hall on Mar. Loans, 182, n. See *Bottomry; Gross adventure; Respondentia.*

Bill of Health, *commercial law.* A certificate, properly authenticated, that a certain ship or vessel therein named, comes from a place where no contagious distempers prevail, and that none of the crew at the time of her departure were infected with any such distemper.

2. It is generally found on board of ships coming from the Levant, or from the coast of Barbary, where the plague so frequently prevails. 1 Marsh. on Ins. 408. The bill of health is necessary whenever a ship sails from a suspected port; or when it is required at the port of destination. Holt's R. 167; 1 Bell's Com. 553, 5th ed.

3. In Scotland the name of bill of health, has been given to an application made by an imprisoned debtor for relief under the Act of Sederunt. When the want of health of the prisoner requires it, the prisoner is indulged, under proper regulations, with such a degree of liberty as may be necessary to restore him. 2 Bell's Com. 549, 5th ed.

Bill of indictment. A written accusation of one or more persons, of a crime or misdemeanor, lawfully presented to a grand jury, convoked, to consider whether there is sufficient evidence of the charge contained therein to put the accused on trial. It is returned to the court with an indorsement of *true bill* (q. v.) when the grand jury are satisfied that the accused ought to be tried; or *ignoramus*, when they are ignorant of any just cause to put the accused upon his trial.

Bill, *contracts.* A bill or obligation, (which are the same thing, except that in English it is commonly called *bill*, but in Latin *obligatio*, obligation,) is a deed whereby the obligor acknowledges himself to owe unto the obligee a certain sum of money or some other thing, in which, besides the names of the parties, are to be considered the sum or thing due, the time, place, and manner of payment or delivery thereof. It may be indented or poll, and with or without a penalty. West's Symboleography s. 100, 101, and the various forms there given.

Bill of lading, *contracts* and *commercial law.* A memorandum or acknowledgment in writing, signed by the captain or master of a ship or other vessel, that he has received in good order, on board of his ship or vessel, therein named, at the place therein mentioned, certain goods therein specified, which he promises to deliver in like good order, (the dangers of the seas excepted,) at the place therein appointed for the delivery of the same, to the consignee therein named or to his assigns, he or they paying freight for the same. 1 T. R. 745; Bac. Abr. Merchant L; Com. Dig. Merchant E 8. b; Abbott on Ship. 216; 1 Marsh. on Ins. 407; Code de Com. art. 281. Or it is the written evidence of a contract for the carriage and delivery of goods sent by sea for a certain freight. Per Lord Loughborough, 1 H. Bl. 359

2. A bill of lading ought to contain the name of the consignor; the name of the consignee; the name of the master of the vessel; the name of the vessel; the place of departure and destination; the price of the freight; and in the margin, the marks and numbers of the things shipped. Code de Com. art. 281; Jacobsen's Sea Laws.

3. It is usually made in three originals, or parts. One of them is commonly sent to the consignee on board with the goods; another is sent to him by mail or some other conveyance; and the third is retained by the merchant or shipper. The master should also take care to have another part for his own use. Abbott on Ship. 217.

4. The bill of lading is assignable, and the assignee is entitled to the goods, subject, however, to the shipper's right, in some cases, of stoppage in transitu. See *In transitu; Stoppage in transitu.* Abbott on Shipping, 331; Bac. Ab. Merchant, L; 1 Bell's Com. 542, 5th ed.

Bills of mortality. Accounts of births and deaths which have occurred in a certain district, during a definite space of time.

Bill obligatory. An instrument in common use and too well known to be misunderstood. It is a bond without condition, sometimes called a single bill, and differs in nothing from a promissory note, but the seal which is affixed to it. 2 Serg. & Rawle, 115. See Read's Pleaders' Assistant, 256, for a declaration setting forth such a bill. Also West's Symboleography, s. 100, 101, for the forms both with and without a penalty.

Bill of pains and penalties. A special act of the legislature which inflicts a punishment, less than death, upon persons supposed to be guilty of high offences, such as treason and felony, without any conviction in the ordinary course of judicial proceedings. 2 Wood. Law Lect. 625. It differs from a bill of attainder in this, that the punishment inflicted by the latter is death.

2. The Constitution of the United States provides that "no bill of attainder shall be passed." It has been judicially said by the supreme court of the United States, that "a bill of attainder may affect the life of an individual, or may confiscate his property, or both." 6 Cranch, R. 138. In the sense of the constitution, then, it seems that bills of attainder include bills of pains and penalties. Story, Const. § 1338. Vide *Attainder; Bills of Attainder.*

Bill of parcels, *merc. law.* An account containing in detail the names of the items which compose a parcel or package of goods; it is usually transmitted with the goods to the purchaser, in order that if any mistake have been made, it may be corrected.

Bill of particulars, *practice.* A detailed informal statement of a plaintiff's cause of action, or of the defendants's set-off.

2. In all actions in which the plaintiff declares generally, without specifying his cause of action, a judge upon application will order him to give the defendant a bill of the particulars, and in the meantime stay proceedings. 3 John. R. 248. And when the defendant gives notice or pleads a set-off, he will be required to give a bill of the particulars of his set-off, on failure of which he will be precluded from giving any evidence in support of it at the trial. The object in both cases is to prevent surprise and procure a fair trial. 1 Phil. Ev. 152; 3 Stark Ev. 1055. The bill of particulars is an account of the items of the demand, and states in what manner they arose. Metc. & Perk. Dig. h. t. For forms, see Lee's Dict. of Pr., Particulars of demand.

Bill penal, *contracts.* A written obligation, by which a debtor acknowledges himself indebted in a certain sum, say one hundred dollars, and for the payment of the debt binds himself in a larger sum, say two hundred dollars. Bills penal do not frequently occur in modern practice; bonds, with conditions, have superseded them. Steph. on Pl. 265, note. See 2 Vent. 198. Bills penal are sometimes called bills obligatory. Cro. Car. 515; 2 Vent. 106. But a bill obligatory is not necessarily a bill penal. Com. Dig. Obligations, D.

Bill of privilege, *Eng. law.* A process issued out of the court against an attorney, who is privileged from arrest, instead of process demanding bail. 3 Bl. Com. 289.

Bill of proof. In the mayor's court, London, the claim made by a third person to the subject-matter in dispute between two others in a suit there, is called *bill of proof.* It is somewhat similar to an intervention. (q. v.) 3 Chit. Com. Law, 633; 2 Chit. Pr. 492; 1 Marsh, R. 233.

Bill of suffrance, *Eng. law.* The name of a license granted at the custom house to a merchant, authorizing him to trade from one English port to another without paying custom. Cunn. L. D.

Bill of rights. *English law.* A statute passed in the reign of William and Mary, so called, because it declared the true rights of British subjects. W. & M. stat. 2, c. 2.

Bill of sale, *contracts.* An agreement in writing, under seal, by which a man transfers the right or interest he has in goods and chattels, to another. As the law imports a consideration when an agreement is made by deed, a bill of sale alters the property. Yelv. 196; Cro. Jac. 270; 6 Co. 18.

2. The Act of Congress of January 14, 1793, 1 Story, L. U. S. 276, provides, that when any ship or vessel which shall have been registered pursuant to that act, or the act thereby partially repealed, shall in whole or in part be sold or transferred to a citizen of the United States, in every such sale or transfer, there shall be some instrument or writing in the nature of a bill of sale, which shall recite at length the certificate of registry; otherwise the said ship or vessel shall be incapable to be registered anew.

3. In England a distinction is made between a bill of sale for the transfer of a ship at sea, and one for the conveyance of a ship in the country; the former is called a *grand bill of sale,* the latter, simply, a bill of sale. In this country there does not appear to be such a distinction. 4 Mass. 661.

4. In general, the maritime law requires that the transfer of a ship should be evidenced by a bill of sale. 1 Mason, 306.

But a contract to sell, accompanied by delivery of possession, is sufficient. 8 Pick. 86; 16 Pick. 401; 16 Mass. 336; 7 John. 308. See 4 Mason, 515; 4 John. 54; 16 Pet. 215; 2 Hall, 1; 1 Wash. C. C. 226.

BILL OF SIGHT, *English commercial law.* When a merchant is ignorant of the real quantities or qualities of any goods consigned to him, so that he is unable to make a perfect entry of them, he is required to acquaint the collector or comptroller of the circumstances; and such officer is authorized, upon the importer or his agent making oath that he cannot, for want of full information, make a perfect entry, to receive an entry by *bill of sight*, for the packages, by the best description which can be given, and to grant a warrant that the same be landed and examined by the importer in presence of the officer; and within three days after the goods have been so landed, the importer is required to make a perfect entry. See stat. 3 & 4 Will. IV. c. 52, § 24.

BILL, SINGLE, *contracts.* A writing by which one person or more, promises to another or others, to pay him or them a sum of money at a time therein specified, without any condition. It is usually under seal; and when so, it is sometimes, if not commonly, called a bill obligatory. (q. v.) 2 S. & R. 115.

2. It differs from a promissory note in this, that the latter is always payable to order; and from a bond, because that instrument has always a condition attached to it, on the performance of which it is satisfied. 5 Com. Dig. 194; 7 Com. Dig. 357.

BILL OF STORE, *English commercial law.* A license granted by custom house officers to merchants, to carry such stores and provisions as are necessary for a voyage, free of duty. See stat. 3 and 4 Will. IV., c. 52.

BILL, TRUE. A true bill is an indictment approved of by a grand jury. Vide *Billa Vera; True Bill.*

BILLS PAYABLE, *commerce.* Engagements which a merchant has entered into in writing, and which he is to pay on their becoming due. Pard. n. 85.

BILLS RECEIVABLE, *commerce.* Promissory notes, bills of exchange, bonds, and other evidences or securities which a merchant or trader holds, and which are payable to him. Pard. n. 85.

BILLA VERA, *practice.* When the proceedings of the courts were recorded in Latin, and the grand jury found a bill of indictment to be supported by the evidence, they indorsed on it *billa vera;* now they indorse in plain English "a true bill."

TO BIND, BINDING, *contracts.* These words are applied to the contract entered into between a master and an apprentice; the latter is said to be bound.

2. In order to make a good binding, the consent of the apprentice must be had, together with that of his father, next friend, or some one standing in loco parentis. Bac. Ab. Master and Servant, A; 8 John. 328; 2 Pen. 977; 2 Yerg. 546; 1 Ashmead, 123; 10 Sergeant & Rawle, 416; 1 Massachusetts, 172; 1 Vermont, 69. Whether a father has, by the common law, a right to bind out his child, during his minority without his consent, seems not to be settled. 2 Dall. 199; 7 Mass. 147; 1 Mason, 78; 1 Ashm. 267. Vide *Apprentice; Father; Mother; Parent.*

3. The words to bind or binding, are also used to signify that a thing is subject to an obligation, engagement or liability; as, the judgment binds such an estate. Vide *Lien.*

TO BIND, OR TO BIND OVER, *crim law.* The act by which a magistrate or a court hold to bail a party, accused of a crime or misdemeanor.

2. A person accused may be bound over to appear at a court having jusisdiction of the offence charged, to answer; or he may be bound over to be of good behaviour, (q. v.) or to keep the peace. See *Surety of the Peace.*

3. On refusing to enter into the requisite recognizance, the accused may be committed to prison.

BIPARTITE. Of two parts. This term is used in conveyancing; as, this indenture bipartite, between A, of the one part, and B, of the other part. But when there are only two parties, it is not necessary to use this word.

BIRRETUM or BIRRETUS. A cap or coif used formerly in England, by judges and sergeants at law. Spelm. h. t.; Cunn. Dict. Vide *Coif.*

BIRTH. The act of being wholly brought into the world. The whole body must be detached from that of the mother, in order to make the birth complete. 5 C. & P. 329; S. C. 24 E. C. L. R. 344; 6 C. & P. 349; S. C. 25 E. C. L. R. 433.

2. But if a child be killed with design and maliciously after it has wholly come forth from the body of the mother, although still connected with her by means of the umbilical cord, it seems that such killing will be murder. 9 C. & P. 25; S. C. 38 E. C. L. R. 21; 7 C. & P. 814. Vide articles *Breath; Dead Born; Gestation; Life;* and 1 Beck's Med. Jur. 478, et seq.; 1 Chit. Med. Jur. 438; 7 C. & P. 814; 1 Carr. & Marsh. 650; S. C. 41 E. C. L. R. 352; 9 C. & P. 25.

3. It seems that unless the child be born alive, it is not properly a birth, but a miscarriage. 1 Chit. Pr. 35, note z. But see Russ. & Ry. C. C. 336.

BISAILE, *domestic relations.* A corruption of the French word *besaïeul*, the father of the grandfather or grandmother. In Latin he is called *proavus.* Inst. 3, 6, 3; Dig. 38, 10, 1, 5. Vide *Aile.*

BISHOP. An ecclesiastical officer, who is the chief of the clergy of his diocese, and is the archbishop's assistant. Happily for this country, these officers are not recognized by law. They derive all their authority from the churches over which they preside.

BISHOP'S COURT, *Eng. law.* An ecclesiastical court held in the cathedral of each diocese, the judge of which is the bishop's chancellor.

BISHOPRICK, *eccl. law.* The extent of country over which a bishop has jurisdiction; a see; a diocese. For their origin, see Francis Duarenus de sacris Eccles. Ministeriis ac beneficiis, lib. 1, cap. 7; Abbê Fleury, 2d Discourse on Ecclesiastical History, § v.

BISSEXTILE. The day which is added every fourth year to the month of February, in order to make the year agree with the course of the sun. It is called *bissextile*, because in the Roman calendar it was fixed on the *sixth* day before the calends of March, (which answers to the 24th day of February,) and this day was counted *twice;* the first was called *bissextus prior*, and the other *bissextus posterior*, but the latter was properly called bissextile or intercalary day. Although the name bissextile is still retained in its obsolete import, we intercalate the 29th of February every fourth year, which is called leap year; and for still greater accuracy, make only one leap year out of every four centenary years. The years 1700 and 1800 were not leap years, nor will the year A. D. 1900 be reckoned as one, but the year A. D. 2000 will be a leap year or bissextile. For a learned account of the Julian and Gregorian calendars, see Histoire du Calendrier Romain, by Mons. Blondel; also, Savigny Dr. Rom. § 192; and Brunacci's Tract on Navigation, 275, 6.

BLACK ACT, *English law.* An act of parliament made in the 9 Geo. II., which bears this name, to punish certain marauders who committed great outrages, in disguise, and with black faces. See Charlt. R. 166.

BLACK BOOK OF THE ADMIRALTY. An ancient book compiled in the reign of Edw. III. It has always been deemed of the highest authority in matters concerning the admiralty. It contains the laws of Oleron, at large; a view of the crimes and offences cognizable in the admiralty; ordinances and commentaries on matters of prize and maritime torts, injuries and contracts. 2 Gall. R. 404.

BLACK BOOK OF THE EXCHEQUER. The name of a book kept in the English exchequer, containing a collection of treaties, conventions, charters, &c.

BLACK MAIL. When rents were reserved payable in work, grain, and the like, they were called *reditus nigri*, or black mail, to distinguish them from *white rents* or *blanch farms*, or such as were paid in money. Vide *Alba firma.*

BLANCH FIRMES. The same as white rent. (q. v.)

BLANK. A space left in writing to be filled up with one or more words, in order to make sense. 1. In what cases the ambiguity occasioned by blanks not filled before execution of the writing may be explained; 2. in what cases it cannot be explained.

2.—1. When a blank is left in a written agreement which need not have been reduced to writing, and would have been equally binding whether written or unwritten, it is presumed, in an action for the non-performance of the contract, parol evidence might be admitted to explain the blank. And where a written instrument, which was made professedly to record a fact, is produced as evidence of that fact which it purports to record, and a blank appears in a material part, the omission may be supplied by other proof. 1 Phil. Ev. 475; 1 Wils. 215; 7 Verm. R. 522; 6 Verm. R. 411. Hence a blank left in an award for a name, was allowed to be supplied by parol proof. 2 Dall. 180. But where a creditor signs a deed of composition leaving the amount of his debt in blank, he binds himself to all existing debts. 1 B. & A. 101; S. C. 2 Stark. R. 195.

3.—2. If a blank is left in a policy of insurance for the name of the place of destination of a ship, it will avoid the policy. Molloy, b. 2, c. 7, s. 14; Park, Ins. 22; Wesk. Ins. 42. A paper signed and sealed in blank, with verbal authority to fill it up, which is afterwards done, is void, unless afterwards delivered or acknowledged and adopted. 1 Yerg. 69, 149; 1 Hill, 267; 2 N. & M. 125; 2 Brock. 64; 2 Dev. 379; 1 Ham. 368; 6 Gill & John. 250; but see *contra*, 17 S. & R. 438. Lines ought to be drawn wherever there are blanks, to prevent anything from being inserted afterwards. 2 Valin's Comm. 151.

4. When the filling up blanks after the execution of deeds and other writings will vitiate them or not, see 3 Vin. Abr. 268; Moore, 547; Cro. Eliz. 626; 1 Vent. 185; 2 Lev. 35; 2 Ch. R. 187; 1 Anst. 228; 5 Mass. 538; 4 Binn. 1; 9 Cranch, 28; Yelv. 96; 2 Show. 161; 1 Saund. Pl. & Ev. 77; 4 B. & A. 672; Com. Dig. Fait, F 1; 4 Bing. 123; 2 Hill. Ab. c. 25, § 80; n. 33, § 54 and 72; 1 Ohio, R. 368; 4 Binn. R. 1; 6 Cowen, 118; Wright, 176.

BLANK BAR, *pleading*. The same with that called a common bar, which, in an action of trespass, is put in to oblige the plaintiff to assign the certain place where the trespass was committed. Cro. Jac. 594, pl. 16.

BLANK INDORSEMENT, *contract*. An indorsement which does not mention the name of the person in whose favor it is made; it is usually made by writing the name of the indorser on the back of the bill. Chit. Bills, 170.

2. When a bill or note has been indorsed in blank, its negotiability cannot afterwards be restrained. 1 Esp. N. P. Cas. 180; 1 Bl. Rep. 295. As many persons as agree may join in suing on a bill when indorsed in blank; for although it was given to one alone, yet by allowing the others to join in the suit, he has made them sharers in his rights. 3 Camp. N. P. Cas. 239. Vide *Indorsement; Negotiable paper; Restrictive indorsement*.

BLASPHEMY, *crim. law*. To attribute to God that which is contrary to his nature, and does not belong to him, and to deny what does; or it is a false reflection uttered with a malicious design of reviling God Elym's Pref. to vol. 8, St. Tr.

2. This offence has been enlarged in Pennsylvania, and perhaps most of the states, by statutory provision. Vide *Christianity;* 11 Serg. & Rawle, 394. In England all blasphemies against God, the Christian religion, the Holy Scriptures, and malicious revilings of the established church, are punishable by indictment. 1 East, P. C 3; 1 Russ. on Cr. 217.

3. In France, before the 25th of September, 1791, it was a blasphemy also to speak against the holy virgin and the saints, to deny one's faith, to speak with impiety of holy things, and to swear by things sacred. Merl. Rép. h. t. The law relating to blasphemy in that country was totally repealed by the code of 25th of September, 1791, and its present penal code, art. 262, enacts, that any person who, by words or gestures, shall commit any outrage upon objects of public worship, in the places designed or actually employed for the performance of its rites, or shall assault or insult the ministers of such worship in the exercise of their functions, shall be fined from sixteen to five hundred francs, and be imprisoned for a period not less than fifteen days nor more than six months.

4. The civil law forbad the crime of blasphemy; such, for example, as to swear by the hair or the head of God; and it punished its violation with death. *Si enim contra homines* factæ blasphemiæ *impunitæ* non *relinquuntur; multo magis qui ipsum Deum blasphemant, digni sunt supplicia sustinere.* Nov. 77, ch. 1, § 1.

5. In Spain it is blasphemy not only to speak against God and his government, but to utter injuries against the Virgin Mary and the saints. Senen Villanova Y Mañes, Materia Criminal, forensé, Observ. 11, cap 3, n. 1.

BLIND. One who is deprived of the faculty of seeing.

2. Persons who are blind may enter into contracts and make wills like others. Carth. 53; Barn. 19, 23; 3 Leigh, R. 32. When an attesting witness becomes blind, his handwriting may be proved as if he were dead. 1 Stark. Ev. 341. But before proving his handwriting the witness must be produced, if within the jurisdiction of the court, and examined. Ld. Raym. 734; 1 M. & Rob. 258; 2 M. & Rob. 262.

BLOCKADE, *international law*. The actual investment of a port or place by a hostile force fully competent to cut off all communication therewith, so arranged or disposed as to be able to apply its force to every point of practicable access or approach to the port or place so invested.

2. It is proper here to consider, 1. by what authority a blockade can be established; 2. what force is sufficient to constitute a blockade; 3. the consequences of a violation of the blockade.

3.—1. Natural sovereignty confers the right of declaring war, and the right which nations at war have of destroying or capturing each other's citizens, subjects or goods, imposes on neutral nations the obligation not to interfere with the exercise of this right within the rules prescribed by the law of nations. A declaration of a siege or blockade is an act of sovereignty; 1 Rob. Rep. 146; but a direct declaration by the sovereign authority of the besieging belligerent is not always requisite; particularly when the blockade is on a distant station, for its officers may have power, either expressly or by implication, to institute such siege or blockade. 6 Rob. R. 367.

4.—2. To be sufficient, the blockade must be effective, and made known. By the convention of the Baltic powers of 1780, and again in 1801, and by the ordinance of congress of 1781, it is required there should be a number of vessels stationed near enough to the port to make the entry apparently dangerous. The government of the United States has uniformly insisted, that the blockade should be effective by the presence of a competent force, stationed and present, at or near the entrance of the port. 1 Kent, Com. 145, and the authorities by him cited; and see 1 Rob. R. 80; 4 Rob. R. 66; 1 Acton's R. 64, 5; and Lord Erskine's speech, 8th March, 1808, on the orders in council, 10 Cobbet's Parl. Debates, 949, 950. But "it is not an accidental absence of the blockading force, nor the circumstance of being blown off by wind, (if the suspension and the reason of the suspension are known,) that will be sufficient in law to remove a blockade." But negligence or remissness on the part of the cruizers stationed to maintain the blockade, may excuse persons, under circumstances, for violating the blockade. 3 Rob. R. 156; 1 Acton's R. 59. To involve a neutral in the consequences of violating a blockade, it is indispensable that he should have due notice of it: this information may be communicated to him in two ways; either actually, by a formal notice from the blockading power, or constructively by notice to his government, or by the notoriety of the fact. 6 Rob. R. 367; 2 Rob. R. 110; Id. 111, note; Id. 128; 1 Acton's R. 61.

4.—3. In considering the consequences of the violation of a blockade, it is proper to take a view of what will amount to such a violation, and, then, of its effects. As all criminal acts require an intention to commit them, the party must intend to violate the blockade, or his acts will be perfectly innocent; but this intention will be judged of by the circumstances. This violation may be, either, by going into the place blockaded, or by coming out of it with a cargo laden after the commencement of the blockade. Also placing himself so near a blockaded port as to be in a condition to slip in without observation, is a violation of the blockade, and raises the presumption of a criminal intent. 6 Rob. R. 30, 101, 182; 7 John. R. 47; 1 Edw. R. 202; 4 Cranch, 185. The sailing for a blockaded port, knowing it to be blockaded, is, it seems, such an act as may charge the party with a breach of the blockade. 5 Cranch, 335; 9 Cranch, 440, 446; 1 Kent, Com. 150. When the ship has contracted guilt by a breach of the blockade, she may be taken at any time before the end of her voyage, but the penalty travels no further than the end of her return voyage. 2 Rob. R. 128; 3 Rob. R. 147. When taken, the ship is confiscated; and the cargo is always, *prima facie*, implicated in the guilt of the owner or master of the ship; and the burden of rebutting the presumption that the vessel was going in for the benefit of the cargo, and with the direction of the owners, rests with them. 1 Rob. R. 67, 130; 3 Rob. R. 173; 4 Rob. R. 93; 1 Edw. R. 39. Vide, generally, 2 Bro. Civ. & Adm. Law, 314; Chit. Com. Law, Index, h. t.; Chit. Law of Nations, 128 to 147; 1 Kent's Com. 143 to 151; Marsh. Ins. Index, h. t., Dane's Ab. Index, h. t.; Mann. Com. B. 3, c. 9.

BLOOD, *kindred.* This word, in the law sense, is used to signify relationship, stock, or family; as, of the blood of the ancestor. 1 Roper on Leg. 103; 1 Supp. to Ves. jr. 365. In a more extended sense, it means kindred generally. Bac. Max. Reg. 18.

2. Brothers and sisters are said to be of the whole blood, (q. v.) if they have the

same father and mother—of the half blood, (q. v.) if they have only one parent in common. 5 Whart. Rep. 477.

BLOTTER, *mer. law.* A book among merchants, in which entries of sales, &c. are first made.

2. This book, containing the original entries, is received in evidence, when supported by the oaths or affirmations of those who keep it. See *Original entry.*

BOARD. This word is used to designate all the magistrates of a city or borough, or all the managers or directors of any institution; as, the board of aldermen; the board of directors of the Bank of North America. The majority of the board have in general the power to perform the acts of the whole board, but sometimes they are restrained by their charters, and it requires a greater number to perform certain acts.

BOARD OF CIVIL AUTHORITY. A term used in Vermont. This board is composed of the selectmen and justices of the peace of their respective towns. They are authorized to abate taxes, and the like.

BOCKLAND, *Eng. law.* The name of an ancient allodial tenure, which was exempt from feudal services. Bac. Ab. Gavelkind, A; Spelman's English Works, vol. 2, 233.

BODY. A person.

2. In practice, when the sheriff returns *cepi corpus* to a capias, the plaintiff may obtain a rule, before special bail has been entered, to bring in the body; and this must be done either by committing the defendant or entering special bail. See *Dead Body.*

BODY POLITIC, *government, corporations.* When applied to the government, this phrase signifies the *state.*

2. As to the persons who compose the body politic, they take collectively the name of *people*, or *nation;* and individually they are *citizens*, when considered in relation to their political rights, and *subjects* as being submitted to the laws of the state.

3. When it refers to corporations, the term *body politic* means that the members of such corporations shall be considered as an artificial person.

BOILARY. A term used to denote the water which arises from a salt well, belonging to one who has no right to the soil. Ejectment may be maintained for it. 2 Hill, Ab. c. 14, § 5; Co. Litt. 4 b.

BONA, *goods and chattels.* In the Roman law, it signifies every kind of property, real, personal, and mixed, but chiefly it was applied to *real estates;* chattels being chiefly distinguished by the words, *effects, movables,* &c. Bona were, however, divided into *bona mobilia*, and *bona immobilia.* It is taken in the civil law in nearly the sense of *biens* (q. v.) in the French law.

BONA FIDE. In or with good faith.

2. The law requires all persons in their transactions to act with good faith; and a contract where the parties have not acted *bona fide* is void at the pleasure of the innocent party. 8 John. R. 446; 12 John. R. 320; 2 John. Ch. R. 35. If a contract be made with good faith, subsequent fraudulent acts will not vitiate it; although such acts may raise a presumption of antecedent fraud, and thus become a means of proving the want of good faith in making the contract. 2 Miles' Rep. 229; and see also, Rob. Fraud. Conv. 33, 34; Inst. 2, 6; Dig. 41, 3, 10 and 44; Id. 41, 1, 48; Code, 7, 31; 9 Co. 11; Wingate's Maxims, max. 37; Lane, 47; Plowd. 473; 9 Pick. R. 265; 12 Pick. R. 545; 8 Conn. R. 336; 10 Conn. R. 30; 3 Watts, R. 25; 5 Wend. R. 20, 566. In the civil law these actions are called (actiones) bonæ fidei, in which the judge has a more unrestrained power (liberior potestas) of estimating how much one person ought to give to or do, for another; whereas, those actions are said to be stricti juris, in which the power of the judge is confined to the agreement of the parties. Examples of the former are the actions empti-venditi, locati-conducti, negitiorum gestorum, &c.; of the latter, the actions ex mutus, ex chirographo, ex stipilatu, ex indebito, actions præscriptis verbis, &c.

BONA GESTURA. Good behaviour.

BONA MOBILIA. Movable goods, personal property.

BONA NOTABILIA, *Engl. ecclesiastical law.* Notable goods. When a person dies having at the time of his death, goods in any other diocese, besides the goods in the diocese where he dies, amounting to the value of five pounds in the whole, he is said to have *bona notabilia;* in which case proof of his will, or granting letters of administration, belongs to the archbishop of the province. 1 Roll. Ab. 908; Toll. Ex. 51· Williams on Ex. Index, h. t.

BONA PERITURA. Perishable goods.

2. An executor, administrator, or trustee, is bound to use due diligence in disposing of perishable goods, such as fattened cattle, grain, fruit, or any other article which may be worse for keeping. Bac. Ab. Executors,

&c. D; 11 Vin. Ab. 102; 1 Roll. Ab. 910; 5 Co. 9; Cro. Eliz. 518; Godb. 104; 3 Munf. R. 288; 1 Beat. R. 5, 14; Dane's Ab. Index, h. t.

3. In Pennsylvania, when goods are attached, they may be sold by order of court, when they are of a perishable nature. Vide Wesk. on Ins. 390; Serg. on Attachm. Index.

BONA VACANTIA. Goods to which no one claims a property, as, shipwrecks, treasure trove, &c.; vacant goods.

BONA WAVIATA. Goods waived or thrown away by a thief, in his flight, for fear of being apprehended.

BOND, *contract*. An obligation or bond is a deed whereby the obligor, obliges himself, his heirs, executors and administrators, to pay a certain sum of money to another at a day appointed. But see 2 Shepl. 185. If this be all, the bond is called a single one, *simplex obligatio;* but there is generally a condition added, that if the obligor pays a smaller sum, or does, or omits to do some particular act, the obligation shall be void. 2 Bl. Com. 340. The word bond *ex vi termini* imports a sealed instrument. 2 S. & R. 502; 1 Bald. R. 129; 2 Porter, R. 19; 1 Blackf. R. 241; Harp. R. 434; 6 Verm. R. 40. See *Condition; Interest of money; Penalty*. It is proposed to conconsider: 1. The form of a bond, namely, the words by which it may be made, and the ceremonies required. 2. The condition. 3. The performance or discharge.

2.—I. 1. There must be parties to a bond, an obligor and obligee: for where a bond was made with condition that the obligor should pay twenty pounds to such person or persons; as E. H. should, by her last will and testament in writing, name and appoint the same to be paid, and E. H. did not appoint any person to whom the same should be paid, it was held that the money was not payable to the executors of E. H. Hob. 9. No particular form of words are essential to create an obligation, but any words which declare the intention of the parties, and denote that one is bound to the other, will be sufficient, provided the ceremonies mentioned below have been observed. Shep. Touch. 367–8; Bac. Abr. Obligations, B; Com. Dig. Obligations, B 1.

3.—2. It must be in writing, on paper or parchment, and if it be made on other materials it is void. Bac. Abr. Obligations, A.

4.—3. It must be sealed, though it is not necessary that it should be mentioned in the writing that it is sealed. As to what is a sufficient sealing, see the above case, and the word *Seal*.

5.—4. It must be delivered by the party whose bond it is, to the other. Bac. Abr. Obligations, C. But the delivery and acceptance may be by attorney. The date is not considered of the substance of a deed, and therefore a bond which either has no date or an impossible one is still good, provided the real day of its being dated or given, that is, delivered, can be proved. 2 Bl. Com. 304; Com. Dig. Fait, B 3; 3 Call, 309. See *Date*.

6.—II. The condition is either for the payment of money, or for the performance of something else. In the latter case, if the condition be against some rule of law merely, positively impossible at the time of making it, uncertain or insensible, the condition alone is void, and the bond shall stand single and unconditional; for it is the folly of the obligor to enter into such an obligation, from which he can never be released. If it be to do a thing *malum in se*, the obligation itself is void, the whole contract being unlawful. 2 Bl. Com. 340; Bac. Abr. Conditions, K, L; Com. Dig. Conditions, D 1, D 2, D 3, D 7, D 8.

7.—III. 1. When, by the condition of an obligation, the act to be done to the obligee is of its own nature transitory, as payment of money, delivery of charters, or the like, and no time is limited, it ought to be performed in convenient time. 6 Co. 31; Co. Lit. 208; Roll. Abr. 436.

8.—2. A payment before the day is good; Co. Lit. 212, a; or before action brought. 10 Mass. 419; 11 Mass. 217.

9.—3. If the condition be to do a thing within a certain time, it may be performed the last day of the time appointed. Bac. Abr. Conditions, P 3.

10.—4. If the condition be to do an act, without limiting any time, he who has the benefit may do it at what time he pleases. Com. Dig. Conditions, G 3.

11.—5. When the place where the act to be performed is agreed upon, the party who is to perform it, is not obliged to seek the opposite party elsewhere; nor is he to whom it is to be performed bound to accept of the performance in another place. Roll. 445, 446; Com. Dig. Conditions, G 9; Bac. Abr. Conditions, P 4. See *Performance*.

12.—6. For what amounts to a breach of a condition in a bond, see Bac. Abr.

Conditions, O; Com. Dig. Conditions, M; and this Dict. tit. *Breach.*

BOND TENANT, *Eng. law.* Copyholders and customary tenants are sometimes so called. Calth. on Copyh. 51, 54.

BONDAGE. Slavery.

BONIS NON AMOVENDIS. The name of a writ addressed to the sheriff, when a writ of error has been brought, commanding that the person against whom judgment has been obtained, be not suffered to remove his goods till the error be tried and determined. Reg. Orig. 131.

BONO ET MALO. The name of a special writ of jail delivery, which formerly issued of course for each particular prisoner. 4 Bl. Com. 270.

BONUS, *contracts.* A premium paid to a grantor or vendor; as, *e. g.* the bank paid a bonus to the state for its charter. A consideration given for what is received.

BOOK. A general name given to every literary composition which is printed; but appropriately to a printed composition bound in a volume.

2. The copyright, (q. v.) or exclusive right to print and publish a book, may be secured to the author and his assigns for the term of twenty-eight years; and, if the author be living, and a citizen of the United States, or resident therein, the same right shall be continued to him for the further term of fourteen years, by complying with the conditions of the act of Congress; one of which is, that he shall, within three months after publication, deliver, or cause to be delivered, a copy of the same to the clerk of the said district. Act of February 3, 1831. 4 Sharsw. cont. of Story's L. U. S. 2223.

BOOK-LAND, *English law.* Land, also called charter-land, which was held by deed under certain rents and fee services, and differed in nothing from free socage land. 2 Bl. Com. 90. See 2 Spelman's English Works, 233, tit. Of Ancient Deeds and Charters.

BOOKS, *commerce, accounts.* Merchants, traders, and other persons, who are desirous of understanding their affairs, and of explaining them when necessary, keep, 1. a day book; 2. a journal; 3. a ledger; 4. a letter book; 5. an invoice book; 6. a cash book; 7. a bill book; 8. a bank book; and 9. a check book. The reader is referred to these several articles. Commercial books are kept by single or by double entry.

BOOTY, *war.* The capture of personal property by a public enemy on land, in contradistinction to prize, which is a capture of such property, by such an enemy, on the sea.

2. After booty has been in complete possession of the enemy for twenty-four hours, it becomes absolutely his, without any right of postliminy in favor of the original owner, particularly when it has passed, *bona fide,* into the hands of a neutral. 1 Kent, Com. 110.

3. The right to the booty, Pothier says, belongs to the sovereign; but sometimes the right of the sovereign, or the public, is transferred to the soldiers, to encourage them. Tr. du Droit de Propriété, part 1, c. 2, art. 1, § 2; Burl. Nat. and Pol. Law, vol. ii. part 4, c. 7, n. 12.

BOROUGH. An incorporated town; so called in the charter. It is less than a city. 1 Mann. & Gran. 1; 39 E. C. L. R. 323.

BOROUGH ENGLISH, *English law.* This, as the name imports, relates exclusively to the English law.

2. It is a custom, in many ancient boroughs, by which the youngest son succeeds to the burgage tenement on the death of the father. 2 Bl. Com. 83.

3. In some parts of France, there was a custom by which the youngest son was entitled to an advantage over the other children in the estate of their father. Merl. Rép. mot Maineté.

BORROWER, *contracts.* He to whom a thing is lent at his request.

2. The contract of loan confers rights, and imposes duties on the borrower.

1. In general, he has the right to use the thing borrowed, during the time and for the purpose intended between the parties; the right of using the thing bailed, is strictly confined to the use, expressed or implied, in the particular transaction, and by any excess, the borrower will make himself responsible. Jones' Bailment, 58; 5 Mass. R. 104; Cro. Jac. 244; 2 Ld. Raym. 909; Ayl. Pand. B. 4, t. 16, p. 517; Domat, B. 1, t. 5, § 2, n. 10, 11, 12; Dig. 13, 6, 18; Poth. Prêt à Usage, c. 2, § 1, n. 22; 2 Bulst. 306; Ersk. Pr. Laws of Scotl. B. 3, t. 1, § 9; 1 Const. Rep. So. Car. 121; Bracton, Lib. 3, c. 2, § 1, p. 99. The loan is considered strictly personal, unless, from other circumstances, a different intention may be presumed. 1 Mod. Rep. 210; S. C. 3 Salk. 271.

3.—2. The borrower is bound to take extraordinary care of the thing borrowed; to use it according to the intention of the lender; to restore it in proper time; to restore it in a proper condition. Of these in their order.

4.—1. The loan being gratuitous, the borrower is bound to extraordinary diligence, and is responsible for slight neglect in relation to the thing loaned. 2 Ld. Raym. 909, 916; Jones on Bailm. 65; 1 Dane's Abr. c. 17, art. 12; Dig. 44, 7, 1, 4; Poth Prêt. à Usage, c. 2, § 2, art. 21, n. 48.

5.—2. The use is to be according to the condition of the loan; if there is any excess in the nature, time, manner, or quantity of the use, beyond what may be inferred to be within the intention of the parties, the borrower will be responsible, not only for any damages occasioned by the excess, but even for losses by accidents, which could not be foreseen or guarded against. 2 Ld. Raym. 909; Jones on Bailm. 68, 69.

6.—3. The borrower is bound to make a return of the thing loaned, at the time, in the place, and in the manner contemplated by the contract. Domat, Liv. 1, t. 5, § 1, n. 11; Dig. 13, 6, 5, 17. If the borrower does not return the thing at the proper time, he is deemed to be in default, and is geneally responsible for all injuries, even for accidents. Jones on Bailm. 70; Pothier, Prêt à Usage, ch. 2, § 3, art. 2, n. 60; Civil Code of Louis. art. 2870; Code Civil, art. 1881; Ersk. Inst. B. 3, t. 1, § 22; Ersk. Pr. Laws of Scotl. B. 3, t. 1, § 9.

7.—4. As to the condition in which the thing is to be restored. The borrower not being liable for any loss or deterioration of the thing, unless caused by his own neglect of duty, it follows, that it is sufficient if he returns it in the proper manner, and at the proper time, however much it may be deteriorated from accidental or other causes, not connected with any such neglect. Story on Bailm. ch. 4, § 268. See, generally, Story on Bailm. ch. 4; Poth. Prêt à Usage; 2 Kent, Com. 446–449; Vin. Abr. Bailment, B 6; Bac. Abr. Bailment; Civil Code of Louis. art. 2869–2876; 1 Bouv. Inst. n. 1078–1090. Vide *Lender*.

BOSCAGE, *Eng. law.* That food which wood and trees yield to cattle.

BOTE, *contracts* A recompense, satisfaction, amends, profit or advantage: hence came the word *man-bote*, denoting a compensation for a man slain; house-bote, cart-bote, plough-bote, signify that a tenant is privileged to cut wood for these uses. 2 Bl. Com. 35; Woodf. L. & T. 232.

BOTELESS, or bootless. Without recompense, reward or satisfaction made; unprofitable or without success.

BOTTOMRY, *maritime law.* A contract, in nature of a mortgage of a ship, on which the owner borrows money to enable him to fit out the ship, or to purchase a cargo, for a voyage proposed: and he pledges the keel or bottom of the ship, *pars pro toto*, as a security for the repayment; and it is stipulated that if the ship should be lost in the course of the voyage, by any of the perils enumerated in the contract, the lender also shall lose his money; but if the ship should arrive in safety, then he shall receive back his principal, and also the interest agreed upon, which is generally called marine interest, however this may exceed the legal rate of interest. Not only the ship and tackle, if they arrive safe, but also the person of the borrower, is liable for the money lent and the marine interest. See 2 Bl. Com. 458; Marsh. Ins. B. 2, c. 1; Ord. Louis XIV. B. 3, tit. 5; Laws of Wisbuy, art. 45; Code de Com. B. 2, tit. 9.

2. The contract of bottomry should specify the principal lent, and the rate of marine interest agreed upon; the subject on which the loan is effected; the names of the vessel and of the master; those of the lender and borrower; whether the loan be for an entire voyage; for what voyage; and for what space of time; and the period of repayment. Code de Com. art. 311; Marsh. Ins. B. 2.

3. Bottomry differs materially from a simple loan. In a loan, the money is at the risk of the borrower, and must be paid at all events. But in bottomry, the money is at the risk of the lender during the voyage. Upon a loan, only legal interest can be received; but upon bottomry, any interest may be legally reserved which the parties agree upon.

See, generally, Metc. & Perk. Dig. h. t.; Marsh. Inst. B. 2; Bac. Abr. Merchant, K; Com. Dig. Merchant. E 4; 3 Mass. 443; 8 Mass. 340; 4 Binn. 244; 4 Cranch, 328; 3 John. R. 352; 2 Johns. Cas. 250; 1 Binn. 405; 8 Cranch, 418; 1 Wheat. 96; 2 Dall. 194. See also this Dict. tit. *Respondentia;* Vin. Abr. Bottomry Bonds; 1 Bouv. Inst. n. 1246–57.

BOUGHT NOTE, *contracts.* An instrument in writing, given by a broker to the seller of merchandise, in which it is stated that the goods therein mentioned have been sold for him. There appears, however, some confusion in the books, on the subject of these notes; sometimes they are called *sold notes*. 2 B. & Ald. 144; Blackb. on Sales, 89.

2. This note is signed in the broker's name, as agent of the buyer and seller; and, if he has not exceeded his authority, the parties are thereby respectively bound. 1 Bell's Com. (5th ed.) 435; Holt's C. 170; Story on Agency, § 28; 9 B. & Cr. 78; 17 E. C. L. R. 335; 5 B. & Ad. 521; 1 N. R. 252; 1 Moo. & R. 368; Moo. & M. 43; 22 E. C. L. R. 243; 2 M. & W. 440; Moo. & M. 43; 6 A. & E. 486; 33 E. C. L. R. 122; 16 East, 62; Gow, R. 74; 1 Camp. R. 385; 4 Taunt. 209; 7 Ves. 265. Vide *Sold Note*.

BOUND BAILIFFS. Sheriff's officers, who serve writs and make arrests; they are so called because they are *bound* to the sheriff for the due execution of their office. 1 Bl. Com. 345.

BOUNDARY, *estates*. By this term is understood, in general, every separation, natural or artificial, which marks the confines or line of division of two contiguous estates. 3 Toull. n. 171.

2. Boundary also signifies stones or other materials inserted in the earth on the confines of two estates.

3. Boundaries are either natural or artificial. A river or other stream is a natural boundary, and in that case the centre of the stream is the line. 20 John. R. 91; 12 John. R. 252; 1 Rand. R. 417; 1 Halst. R. 1; 2 N. H. Rep. 369; 6 Cowen, R. 579; 4 Pick. 268; 3 Randolph's R. 33; 4 Mason's R. 349–397.

4. An artificial boundary is one made by man.

5. The description of land, in a deed, by specific boundaries, is conclusive as to the quantity; and if the quantity be expressed as a part of the description, it will be inoperative, and it is immaterial whether the quantity contained within the specific boundaries, be greater or less than that expressed; 5 Mass. 357; 1 Caines' R. 493; 2 John. R. 27; 15 John. 471; 17 John. R. 146; Id. 29; 6 Cranch, 237; 4 Hen. & Munf. 125; 2 Bay, R. 515; and the same rule is applicable, although neither the courses and distances, nor the estimated contents, correspond with such specific boundaries; 6 Mass. 131; 11 Mass. 193; 2 Mass. 380; 5 Mass. 497; but these rules do not apply in cases where adherence to them would be plainly absurd. 17 Mass. 207. Vide 17 S. & R. 104; 2 Mer. R. 507; 1 Swanst. 9; 4 Ves. 180; 1 Stark. Ev. 169; 1 Phil. Ev. Index, h. t.; Chit. Pr. Index, h. t.; 1 Supp. to Ves. jr. 276; 2 Hill. Ab. c. 24, § 209, and Index, h. t.

6. When a boundary, fixed and by mutual consent, has been permitted to stand for twenty-one years, it cannot afterwards be disturbed. In accordance with this rule, it has been decided, that where town lots have been occupied up to a line fence between them, for more than twenty-one years, each party gained an incontrovertible right to the line thus established, and this whether either party knew of the adverse claim or not; and whether either party has more or less ground than was originally in the lot he owns. 9 Watts, R. 565. See Hov. Fr. c. 8, p. 239 to 243; 3 Sum. R. 170; Poth. Contr. de Société, prém. app. n. 231.

7. Boundaries are frequently marked by partition fences, ditches, hedges, trees, &c. When such a fence is built by one of the owners of the land, on his own premises, it belongs to him exclusively; when built by both at joint expense, each is the owner of that part on his own land. 5 Taunt. 20. When the boundary is a hedge and a single ditch, it is presumed to belong to him on whose side the hedge is, because he who dug the ditch is presumed to have thrown the earth upon his own land, which was alone lawful to do, and that the hedge was planted, as is usual, on the top of the bank thus raised. 3 Taunt. 138. But if there is *a ditch on each side* of the hedge, or no ditch at all, the hedge is presumed to be the common property of both proprietors. Arch. N. P. 328; 2 Greenl. Ev. § 617. A tree growing in the boundary line is the joint property of both owners of the land. 12 N. H. Rep. 454.

8. Disputes arising from a confusion of boundaries may be generally settled by an action at law. But courts of equity will entertain a bill for the settlement of boundaries, when the rights of one of the parties may be established upon equitable grounds. 4 Bouv. Inst. n. 3923.

BOUNTY. A sum of money or other thing, given, generally by the government, to certain persons, for some service they have done or are about to do to the public. As bounty upon the culture of silk; the bounty given to an enlisted soldier; and the like. It differs from a reward, which is generally applied to particular cases; and from a payment, as there is no contract on the part of the receiver of the bounty.

BOVATA TERRÆ. As much land as one ox can plough.

BRANCH. This is a metaphorical expression, which designates, in the genealogy of a numerous family, a portion of that family which has sprung from the same root or stock; these latter expressions, like the first, are also metaphorical.

2. The whole of a genealogy is often called the *genealogical tree;* and sometimes it is made to take the form of a tree, which is in the first place divided into as many branches as there are children, afterwards into as many branches as there are grandchildren, then of great grandchildren, &c. If, for example, it be desired to form the genealogical tree of Peter's family, Peter will be made the trunk of the tree; if he has had two children, John and James, their names will be written on the first two branches; which will themselves shoot out as many smaller branches as John and James have children; from these others proceed, till the whole family is represented on the tree; thus the origin, the application, and the use of the word branch in genealogy will be at once perceived.

BRANCHES. Those solid parts of trees which grow above the trunk.

2. In general the owner of a tree is the owner of the branches; but when they grow beyond his line, and extend over the adjoining estate, the proprietor of the latter may cut them off as far as they grow over his land. Rolle's R. 394; 3 Bulst. 198. But as this nuisance is one of omission, and, as in the case of such nuisances, it is requisite to give notice before abating them, it would be more prudent, and perhaps necessary, to give notice to the owner of the tree to remove such nuisance. 1 Chit. Pr. 649, 650, 652. See *Root; Tree.*

TO BRAND. An ancient mode of punishment, which was to inflict a mark on an offender with a hot iron. This barbarous punishment has been generally disused.

BRANDY. A spirituous liquor made of wine by distillation. See stat. 22 Car. II. c. 4.

BREACH, *contract*, *torts*. The violation of an obligation, engagement or duty; as a breach of covenant is the non-performance or violation of a covenant; the breach of a promise is non-performance of a promise; the breach of a duty, is the refusal or neglect to execute an office or public trust, according to law.

2. Breaches of a contract are *single* or *continuing* breaches. The former are those which are committed at one single time. Skin. 367; Carth. 289. A continuing breach is one committed at different times, as, if a covenant to repair be broken at one time, and the same covenant be again broken, it is a continuing breach. Moore, 242; 1 Leon. 62; 1 Salk. 141; Holt, 178; Lord Raym. 1125. When a covenant running with the land is assigned after a single breach, the right of action for such breach does not pass to the assignee; but if it be assigned after the commencement of a continuing breach, the right of action then vests in such assignee. Cro. Eliz. 863; 8 Taunt. 227; 2 Moore, 164; 1 Leon. 62.

3. In general the remedy for breaches of contracts, or quasi contracts, is by a civil action.

BREACH OF THE PEACE. A violation of public order; the offence of disturbing the public peace. One guilty of this offence may be held to bail for his good behaviour. An act of public indecorum is also a breach of the peace. The remedy for this offence is by indictment. Vide *Peace.*

BREACH OF PRISON. An unlawful escape out of prison. This is of itself a misdemeanor. 1 Russ. Cr. 378; 4 Bl. Com. 129; 2 Hawk. P. C. c. 18, s. 1; 7 Conn. 752. The remedy for this offence is by indictment. See *Escape.*

BREACH OF TRUST. The wilful misappropriation, by a trustee, of a thing which had been lawfully delivered to him in confidence.

2. The distinction between larceny and a breach of trust is to be found chiefly in the terms or way in which the thing was taken originally into the party's possession; and the rule seems to be, that whenever the article is obtained upon a fair contract, not for a mere temporary purpose, or by one who is in the employment of the deliverer, then the subsequent misappropriation is to be considered as an act of breach of trust. This rule is, however, subject to many nice distinctions. 15 S. & R. 93, 97. It has been adjudged that when the owner of goods parts with the *possession* for a particular purpose, and the person who receives them avowedly for that purpose, has at the time a fraudulent intention to make use of the possession as the means of converting

the goods to his own use, and does so convert them, it is larceny; but if the owner part with the *property*, although fraudulent means have been used to obtain it, the act of conversion is not larceny. Id. Alis. Princ. c. 12, p. 354.

3. In the Year Book, 21 H. VII. 14, the distinction is thus stated: *Pigot.* If I deliver a jewel or money to my servant to keep, and he flees or goes from me with the jewel, is it felony? *Cutler* said, Yes: for so long as he is with me or in my house, that which I have delivered to him is adjudged to be in my possession; as my butler, who has my plate in keeping, if he flees with it, it is felony. Same law; if he who keeps my horse goes away with him: The reason is, they are always in my possession. But if I deliver a horse to my servant to ride to market or the fair, and he flee with him, it is no felony; for he comes lawfully to the possession of the horse by delivery. And so it is, if I give him a jewel to carry to London, or to pay one, or to buy a thing, and he flee with it, it is not felony: for it is out of my possession, and he comes lawfully to it. *Pigot.* It can well be: for the master in these cases has an action against him, viz., Detinue, or Account. See this point fully discussed in Stamf. P. C. lib. 1; Larceny, c. 15, p. 25. Also, 13 Ed. IV. fo. 9; 52 H. III. 7; 21 H. VII. 15.

BREACH, *pleading*. That part of the declaration in which the violation of the defendant's contract is stated.

2. It is usual in assumpsit to introduce the statement of the particular breach, with the allegation that the defendant, contriving and fraudulently intending craftily and subtilely to deceive and defraud the plaintiff, neglected and refused to perform, or performed the particular act, contrary to the previous stipulation.

3. In debt, the breach or cause of action complained of must proceed only for the non-payment of money previously alleged to be payable; and such breach is nearly similar, whether the action be in debt on simple contract, specialty, record or statute, and is usually of the following form: "Yet the said defendant, although often requested so to do, hath not as yet paid the said sum of —— dollars, above demanded, nor any part thereof, to the said plaintiff, but hath hitherto wholly neglected and refused so to do, to the damage of the said plaintiff —— dollars, and therefore he brings suit," &c.

4. The breach must obviously be governed by the nature of the stipulation; it ought to be assigned in the words of the contract, either negatively or affirmatively, or in words which are co-extensive with its import and effect. Com. Dig. Pleader, C 45 to 49; 2 Saund. 181, b, c; 6 Cranch, 127; and see 5 John. R. 168; 8 John. R. 111; 7 John. R. 376; 4 Dall. 436; 2 Hen. & Munf. 446.

5. When the contract is in the disjunctive, as, on a promise to deliver a horse by a particular day, or pay a sum of money, the breach ought to be assigned that the defendant did not do the one act nor the other. 1 Sid. 440; Hardr. 320; Com. Dig Pleader, C.

BREAKING. Parting or dividing by force and violence a solid substance, or piercing, penetrating, or bursting through the same.

2. In cases of burglary and house-breaking, the removal of any part of the house, or of the fastenings provided to secure it, with violence and a felonious intent, is called a breaking.

3. The breaking is actual, as in the above case; or constructive, as when the burglar or house-breaker gains an entry by fraud, conspiracy or threats. 2 Russ. on Cr. 2; 2 Chit. Cr. Law, 1092; 1 Hale, P. C. 553; Alis. Prin. 282, 291. In England it has been decided that if the sash of a window be partly open, but not sufficiently so to admit a person, the raising of it so as to admit a person is not a breaking of the house. 1 Moody, Cr. Cas. 178. No reasons are assigned. It is difficult to conceive, if this case be law, what further opening will amount to a breaking. But see 1 Moody, Cr. Cas. 327, 377; and *Burglary*.

BREAKING DOORS. The act of forcibly removing the fastenings of a house, so that a person may enter.

2. It is a maxim that every man's house is his castle, and it is protected from every unlawful invasion. An officer having a lawful process, of a criminal nature, authorizing him to do so, may break an outer door, if upon making a demand of admittance it is refused. The house may also be broken open for the purpose of executing a writ of habere facias possessionem. 5 Co. 93; Bac. Ab. Sheriff, N 3.

3. The house protects the owner from the service of all civil process in the first instance, but not, if once lawfully arrested,

he takes refuge in his own house; in that case the officer may pursue him, and break open any door for the purpose. Foster, 320; 1 Rolle's R. 138; Cro. Jac. 555. Vide *Door; House.*

BREATH, *med. juris.* The air expelled from the chest at each expiration.

2. Breathing, though a usual sign of life, is not conclusive that a child was *wholly* born alive, as breathing may take place before the whole delivery of the mother is complete. 5 Carr. & Payn, 329; S. C. 24 E. C. L. R. 344. Vide *Birth; Life; Infanticide.*

BREPHOTROPHI, *civil law.* Persons appointed to take care of houses destined to receive foundlings. Clef des Lois Rom. mot Administrateurs.

BREVE, *practice.* A writ in which the cause of action is *briefly* stated, hence its name. Fleta, lib. 2, c. 13, § 25; Co. Lit. 73 b.

2. Writs are distributed into several classes. Some are called *brevia formata,* others *brevia de cursu, brevia judicialia,* or *brevia magistralia.* There is a further distinction with respect to real actions into *brevia nominata* and *innominata.* The former, says Bacon, contain the time, place and demand very particularly; and therefore by such writ several lands by several titles cannot be demanded by the same writ. The latter contain only a general complaint, without expressing time, damages, &c., as in trespass *quare clausum fregit,* &c., and therefore several lands coming to the demandant by several titles may be demanded in such writ. F. N. B. 209; 8 Co. 87; Kielw. 105; Dy. 145; 2 Brownl. 274; Bac. Ab. Actions in General, C. See *Innominate contracts.*

Breve de recto. A writ of right. (q. v.)

Breve testatum, *feudal law.* A declaration by a superior lord to his vassal, made in the presence of the pares curiæ, by which he gave his consent to the grant of land, was so called. Ersk. Inst. B. 2, tit. 3, s. 17. This was made in writing, and had the operation of a deed. Dalr. Feud. Pr. 239.

BREVET. In France, a brevet is a warrant granted by the government to authorize an individual to do something for his own benefit, as a brevet d'invention, is a patent to secure a man a right as inventor.

2. In our army, it signifies a commission conferring on an officer a degree of rank immediately above the one which he holds in his particular regiment, without, however, conveying a right to receive a corresponding pay.

BREVIA, *writs.* They were called *brevia,* because of the brevity in which the cause of action was stated in them.

Brevia anticipantia. This name is given to a number of writs, which are also called writs of prevention. See *Quia Timet.*

Brevia formata, *Eng law.* The collection of writs found in the Registrum Brevium, was so called. The author of Fleta says, these writs were formed upon their cases. They were different from the writs *de cursu,* which were approved by the council of the whole realm, and could not be changed without the will of the same. Fleta, lib. 2, c. 13, § 2. See 17 S. & R. 194-5, and authorities there cited.

Brevia judicialia. Subsidiary process issued pending a suit, or process issued in execution of the judgment. They varied, says the author of Fleta, according to the variety of the pleadings of the parties and of their responses. Lib. 2. c. 13, § 3; Co. Lit. 73 b, 54 b. Many of them, however, long since became fixed in their forms, beyond the power of the courts to alter them, unless authorized to do so by the legislature. See 1 Rawle, Rep. 52; Act of Pennsylvania, June 16, 1836, §§ 3, 4, 5.

Brevia magistralia. These were writs formed by the masters in chancery, pursuant to the stat. West. 2, c. 24. They vary according to the diversity of cases and complaints, of which, says the author of Fleta, some are personal, some real, some mixed, according as actions are diverse or various, because so many will be the forms of writs as there are kinds of actions. Fleta, lib. 2, c. 13, § 4; Co. Lit. 73 b, 54 b.

BREVIARIUM. The name of a code of laws of Alaric II., king of the Visigoths.

BREVIBUS ET ROTULIS LIBERANDIS, *Eng. law.* A writ or mandate directed to a sheriff, commanding him to deliver to his successor the county and the appurtenances, with all the briefs, rolls, remembrances, and all other things belonging to his office.

BRIBE, *crim. law.* The gift or promise, which is accepted, of some advantage, as the inducement for some illegal act or omission; or of some illegal emolument, as a consideration, for preferring one person to another, in the performance of a legal act.

BRIBERY, *crim. law.* The receiving or offering any undue reward by or to any person whomsoever, whose ordinary profession or business relates to the administration of public justice, in order to influence his behaviour in office, and to incline him to act contrary to his duty and the known rules of honesty and integrity. 3 Inst. 149; 1 Hawk. P. C. 67, s. 2; 4 Bl. Com. 139; 1 Russ. Cr. 156.

2. The term bribery extends now further, and includes the offence of giving a bribe to many other officers. The offence of the giver and of the receiver of the bribe has the same name. For the sake of distinction, that of the former, viz: the briber, might be properly denominated active bribery; while that of the latter, viz: the person bribed, might be called passive bribery.

3. Bribery at elections for members of parliament, has always been a crime at common law, and punishable by indictment or information. It still remains so in England, notwithstanding the stat. 24 Geo. II. c. 14. 3 Burr. 1340, 1589. To constitute the offence, it is not necessary that the person bribed should, in fact, vote as solicited to do; 3 Burr. 1236; or even that he should have a right to vote at all; both are entirely immaterial. 3 Bur. 1590-1.

4. An attempt to bribe, though unsuccessful, has been holden to be criminal, and the offender may be indicted. 2 Dall. 384; 4 Burr. 2500; 3 Inst. 147; 2 Campb. R. 229; 2 Wash. 88; 1 Virg. Cas. 138; 2 Virg. Cas. 460.

BRIBOUR. One that pilfers other men's goods; a thief. See 28 E. II., c. 1.

BRIDGE. A building constructed over a river, creek, or other stream, or over a ditch or other place, in order to facilitate the passage over the same. 3 Harr. 108.

2. Bridges are of several kinds, public and private. *Public* bridges may be divided into, 1st. Those which belong to the public; as state, county, or township bridges, over which all the people have a right to pass, with or without paying toll; these are built by public authority at the public expense, either of the state itself, or a district or part of the state.

3.—2d. Those which have been built by companies, or at the expense of private individuals, and over which all the people have a right to pass, on the payment of a toll fixed by law. 3d. Those which have been built by private individuals, and which have been dedicated to public uses. 2 East, R. 356; 5 Burr. R. 2594; 2 Bl. R. 685; 1 Camp. R. 262, n.; 2 M. & S. 262.

4. A *private* bridge is one erected for the use of one or more private persons; such a bridge will not be considered a public bridge, although it may be occasionally used by the public. 12 East, R. 203-4. Vide 7 Pick. R. 344; 11 Pet. R. 539; 7 N. H. Rep. 59; 1 Pick. R. 432; 4 John. Ch. R. 150.

BRIEF, *eccl. law.* The name of a kind of papal rescript. Briefs are writings sealed with wax, and differ in this respect from *bulls*, (q. v.) which are sealed with lead. They are so called, because they usually are short compendious writings. Ayl. Parerg. 132. See *Breve.*

BRIEF, *practice.* An abridged statement of a party's case.

2. It should contain: 1st. A statement of the names of the parties, and of their residence and occupation, the character in which they sue and are sued, and wherefore they prosecute or resist the action. 2d. An abridgment of all the pleadings. 3d. A regular, chronological, and methodical statement of the facts in plain common language. 4th. A summary of the points or questions in issue, and of the proof which is to support such issues, mentioning specially the names of the witnesses by which the facts are to be proved, or if there be written evidence, an abstract of such evidence. 5th. The personal character of the witnesses should be mentioned; whether the moral character is good or bad, whether they are naturally timid or over-zealous, whether firm or wavering. 6th. If known, the evidence of the opposite party, and such facts as are adapted to oppose, confute, or repel it. Perspicuity and conciseness are the most desirable qualities of a brief, but when the facts are material they cannot be too numerous; when the argument is pertinent and weighty, it cannot be too extended.

3. Brief is also used in the sense of *breve.* (q. v.)

BRIEF OF TITLE, *practice, conveyancing.* An abridgment of all the patents, deeds, indentures, agreements, records, and papers relating to certain real estate.

2. In making a brief of title, the practitioner should be careful to place every deed and other paper in chronological order. The date of each deed; the names of the parties; the consideration; the description of the property; should be particularly

noticed, and all covenants should also be particularly inserted.

3. A vendor of an interest in realty ought to have his title investigated, abstracted, and evidence in proof of it ready to be produced and established before he sells; for if he sell with a confused title, or without being ready to produce deeds and vouchers, he must be at the expense of clearing it. 1 Chit. Pr. 304, 463.

BRINGING MONEY INTO COURT. The act of depositing money in the hands of the proper officer of the court, for the purpose of satisfying a debt or duty, or of an interpleader.

2. Whenever a tender of money is pleaded, and the debt is not discharged by the tender and refusal, money may be brought into court, without asking leave of the court; indeed, in such cases the money must be brought into court in order to have the benefit of the tender. In other cases, leave must be had, before the money can be brought into court.

3. In general, if the money brought into court is sufficient to satisfy the plaintiff's claim, he shall not recover costs. See Bac. Ab. Tender, &c.

BROCAGE, *contracts*. The wages or commissions of a broker; his occupation is also sometimes called brocage. This word is also spelled brokerage.

BROKERAGE, *contracts*. The trade or occupation of a broker; the commissions paid to a broker for his services.

BROKERS, *commerce*. Those who are engaged for others, in the negotiation of contracts, relative to property, with the custody of which they have no concern. Paley on Agency, 13; see Com. Dig. Merchant, C.

2. A broker is, for some purposes, treated as the agent of both parties; but in the first place, he is deemed the agent only of the person by whom he is originally employed; and does not become the agent of the other until the bargain or contract has been definitely settled, as to the terms, between the principals. Paley on Ag. by Lloyd, 171, note p; 1 Y. & J. 387.

3. There are several kinds of brokers, as, *Exchange Brokers*, such as negotiate in all matters of exchange with foreign countries.

4. *Ship Brokers*. Those who transact business between the owners of vessels, and the merchants who send cargoes.

5. *Insurance Brokers*. Those who manage the concerns both of the insurer and the insured.

6. *Pawn Brokers*. Those who lend money, upon goods, to necessitous people, at interest.

7. *Stock Brokers*. Those employed to buy and sell shares of stocks in corporations and companies. Vide Story on Ag. § 28 to 32; T. L. h. t.; Maly. Lex Mer. 143; 2 H. Bl. 555; 4 Burr, R. 2103; 4 Kent, Com. 622, note d, 3d ed.; Liv. on Ag. Index, h. t.; Chit. Com. L. Index, h. t.; and articles *Agency; Agent; Bought note; Factor; Sold note.*

BROTHELS, *crim. law*. Bawdy-houses, the common habitations of prostitutes; such places have always been deemed common nuisances in the United States, and the keepers of them may be fined and imprisoned.

2. Till the time of Henry VIII., they were licensed in England, when that lascivious prince suppressed them. Vide 2 Inst. 205, 6; for the history of these pernicious places, see Merl. Rép. mot Bordel Parent Duchatellet, De la Prostitution dans la ville de Paris, c. 5, § 1; Histoire de la Legislation sur les femmes publiques, &c., par M. Sabatier.

BROTHER, *domest. relat*. He who is born from the same father and mother with another, or from one of them only.

2. Brothers are of the whole blood, when they are born of the same father and mother, and of the half blood, when they are the issue of one of them only.

3. In the civil law, when they are the children of the same father and mother, they are called *brothers germain;* when they descend from the same father, but not the same mother, they are *consanguine brothers;* when they are the issue of the same mother, but not the same father, they are *uterine brothers*. A *half brother*, is one who is born of the same father or mother, but not of both. One born of the same parents before they were married, a *left-sided brother;* and a bastard born of the same father or mother, is called a *natural brother*. Vide *Blood; Half-blood; Line;* and Merl. Répert. mot Frère; Dict. de Jurisp. mot Frère; Code, 3, 28, 27; Nov. 84, præf; Dane's Ab. Index, h. t.

BROTHER-IN-LAW, *domestic relat*. The brother of a wife, or the husband of a sister. There is no *relationship*, in the former case, between the husband and the brother-in-law, nor in the latter, between the brother and the husband of the sister; there is only *affinity* between them. See Vaughan's Rep. 302, 329.

BRUISE, *med. jurisp.* An injury done with violence to the person, without breaking the skin; it is nearly synonymous with *contusion.* (q. v.) 1 Ch. Pr. 38; vide 4 Car. & P. 381, 487, 558, 565; Eng. C. L. Rep. 430, 526, 529. Vide *Wound.*

BUBBLE ACT, *Eng. law.* The name given to the statute 6 Geo. I., c. 18, which was passed in 1719, and was intended "for restraining several extravagant and unwarrantable practices therein mentioned." See 2 P. Wms. 219.

BUGGERY, *crim. law.* The detestable crime of having commerce contrary to the order of nature, by mankind with mankind, or with brute beasts, or by womankind with brute beasts. 3 Inst. 58: 12 Co. 36; Dane's Ab. Index, h. t.; Merl. Répert. mot Bestialité. This is a highly penal offence.

BUILDING, *estates.* An edifice erected by art, and fixed upon or over the soil, composed of stone, brick, marble, wood, or other proper substance, connected together, and designed for use in the position in which it is so fixed. Every building is an accessory to the soil, and is, therefore, real estate: it belongs to the owner of the soil. Cruise, tit. 1, s. 46. Vide 1 Chit. Pr. 148, 171; Salk. 459; Hob. 131; 1 Metc. 258; Broom's Max. 172.

BULK, *contracts.* Said to be merchandise which is neither counted, weighed, nor measured.

2. A sale by bulk, is a sale of a quantity of goods, such as they are, without measuring, counting, or weighing. Civ. Code of Louis. a. 3522, n. 6.

BULL, *eccles. law.* A letter from the pope of Rome, written on parchment, to which is attached a leaden seal, impressed with the images of Saint Peter and Saint Paul.

2. There are three kinds of apostolical rescripts, the *brief*, the *signature*, and the *bull*, which last is most commonly used in legal matters. Bulls may be compared to the edicts and letters-patent of secular princes: when the bull grants a favor, the seal is attached by means of silken strings; and when to direct execution to be performed, with flax cords. Bulls are written in Latin, in a round and Gothic hand. Ayl. Par. 132; Ayl. Pand. 21; Mer. Rép. h. t.

BULLETIN An official account of public transactions on matters of importance. In France, it is the registry of the laws.

BULLION. In its usual acceptation, is uncoined gold or silver, in bars, plates, or other masses. 1 East, P. C. 188.

2. In the acts of Congress, the term is also applied to copper properly manufactured for the purpose of being coined into money. For the acts of Congress, authorizing the coinage of bullion for private individuals, see Act of April 2, 1792, s. 14, 1 Story, 230; Act of May 19, 1828, 4 Sharsw. cont. of Story's Laws U. S. 2120; Act of June 28, 1834, Id. 2376; Act of January 18, 1837, Id. 2522 to 2529. See, for the English law on the subject of crimes against bullion, 1 Hawk. P. C. 32 to 41.

BUOY. A piece of wood, or an empty barrel, floating on the water, to show the place where it is shallow, to indicate the danger there is to navigation. The act of Congress, approved the 28th September, 1850, enacts, "that all buoys along the coast, in bays, harbors, sounds, or channels, shall be colored and numbered, so that passing up the coast or sound, or entering the bay, harbor or channel, red buoys, with even numbers, shall be passed on the starboard hand, black buoys, with uneven numbers, on the port hand, and buoys with red and black stripes on either hand. Buoys in channel ways to be colored with alternate white and black perpendicular stripes."

BURDEN OF PROOF. This phrase is employed to signify the duty of proving the facts in dispute on an issue raised between the parties in a cause.

2. The burden of proof always lies on the party who takes the affirmative in pleading. 1 Mass. 71, 335; 4 Mass. 593; 9 Pick. 39.

3. In criminal cases, as every man is presumed to be innocent until the contrary is proved, the burden of proof rests on the prosecutor, unless a different provision is expressly made by statute. 12 Wheat. 460. See *Onus probandi.*

BUREAU. A French word, which literally means a large writing table. It is used figuratively for the place where business is transacted; it has been borrowed by us, and used in nearly the same sense, as, the bureau of the secretary of state. Vide Merl. Répert. h. t.

BUREAUCRACY. The abuse of official influence in the affairs of government; corruption. This word has lately been adopted to signify that those persons who are employed in bureaus abuse their authority by intrigue to promote their own benefit, or that of friends, rather than the public good. The word is derived from the French.

BURGAGE, *English law.* A species of tenure in socage; it is where the king or other person is lord of an ancient borough, in which the tenements are held by a rent certain. 2 Bl. Com. 82.

BURGESS. A magistrate of a borough; generally, the chief officer of the corporation, who performs, within the borough, the same kind of duties which a mayor does in a city. In England, the word is sometimes applied to all the inhabitants of a borough, who are called burgesses; sometimes it signifies the representatives of a borough in parliament.

BURGH. A borough; (q. v.) a castle or town.

BURGLAR. One who commits a burglary. (q. v.)

BURGLARIOUSLY, *pleadings.* This is a technical word, which must be introduced into an indictment for burglary; no other word will answer the same purpose, nor will any circumlocution be sufficient. 4 Co. 39; 5 Co. 121; Cro. Eliz. 920; Bac. Ab. Indictment, G 1; Com. Dig. Indictment, G 6; 1 Chit. Cr. Law, *242.

BURGLARY, *crim. law.* The breaking and entering the house of another in the night time, with intent to commit a felony therein, whether the felony be actually committed or not. 3 Inst. 63; 1 Hale, 549; 1 Hawk. c. 38, s. 1; 4 Bl. Com. 224; 2 East, P. C. c. 15, s. 1, p. 484; 2 Russell on Cr. 2; Roscoe, Cr. Ev. 252; Coxe, R. 441; 7 Mass. Rep. 247.

2. The circumstances to be considered are, 1. in what place the offence can be committed; 2. at what time; 3. by what means; 4. with what intention.

3.—1. *In what place a burglary can be committed.* It must, in general, be committed in a mansion house, actually occupied as a dwelling; but if it be left by the owner *animo revertendi,* though no person resides in it in his absence, it is still his mansion. Fost. 77; 3 Rawle, 207. The principal question, at the present day, is what is to be deemed a dwelling-house. 1 Leach, 185; 2 Leach, 771; Id. 876; 3 Inst. 64; 1 Leach, 305; 1 Hale, 558; Hawk. c. 38, s. 18; 1 Russ. on Cr. 16; 3 Serg. & Rawle, 199 4 John. R. 424; 1 Nott & M'Cord, 583; 1 Hayw. 102, 242 Com. Dig. Justices, P 5; 2 East, P. C. 504.

4.—2. *At what time it must be committed.* The offence must be committed in the night, for in the day time there can be no burglary. 4 Bl. Com. 224. For this purpose, it is deemed night when by the light of the sun a person cannot clearly discern the face or countenance of another. 1 Hale, 550; 3 Inst. 63. This rule, it is evident, does not apply to moonlight. 4 Bl. Com. 224; 2 Russ. on Cr. 32. The breaking and entering need not be done the same night; 1 Russ. & Ry. 417; but it is necessary the breaking and entering should be in the night time, for if the breaking be in daylight and the entry in the night, or *vice versâ,* it will not be burglary. 1 Hale, 551; 2 Russ. on Cr. 32. Vide Com. Dig. Justices, P 2; 2 Chit. Cr. Law, 1092.

5.—3. *The means used.* There must be both a *breaking* and an *entry.* First, of the breaking, which may be actual or constructive. An *actual breaking* takes place when the burglar breaks or removes any part of the house, or the fastenings provided for it, with violence. Breaking a window, taking a pane of glass out, by breaking or bending the nails, or other fastenings, raising a latch where the door is not otherwise fastened; picking open a lock with a false key; putting back the lock of a door or the fastening of a window, with an instrument; turning the key when the door is locked in the inside, or unloosening any other fastening which the owner has provided, are several instances of actual breaking. According to the Scotch law, entering a house by means of the true key, while in the door, or when it had been stolen, is a breaking. Alis. Pr. Cr. Law, 284. *Constructive breakings* occur when the burglar gains an entry by fraud, conspiracy or threats. 2 Russ. on Cr. 2; 2 Chit. Cr. Law, 1093. The breaking of an inner door of the house will be sufficient to constitute a burglary. 1 Hale, 553. Any, the least, *entry,* with the whole or any part of the body, hand, or foot, or with any instrument or weapon, introduced for the purpose of committing a felony, will be sufficient to constitute the offence. 3 Inst. 64; 4 Bl. Com. 227; Bac. Ab. Burglary, B; Com. Dig. Justices, P 4. But the introduction of an instrument, in the act of breaking the house, will not be a sufficient entry, unless it be introduced for the purpose of committing a felony.

6.—4. *The intention.* The intent of the breaking and entry must be felonious; if a felony however be committed, the act will be *prima facie* evidence of an intent to commit it. If the breaking and entry be with an intention to commit a bare trespass, and nothing further is done, the offence will not be a burglary. 1 Hale, 560; East, P. C. 509, 514, 515; 2 Russ. on Cr. 33.

BURGOMASTER. In Germany this is the title by which an officer who performs the duties of a mayor is called.

BURIAL. The act of interring the dead.

2. No burial is lawful unless made in conformity with the local regulations; and when a dead body has been found, it cannot be lawfully buried until the coroner has holden an inquest over it. In England it is the practice for coroners to issue warrants to bury, after a view. 2 Umf. Lex. Coron. 497, 498.

BURNING. Vide *Accident; Arson; Fire, accidental.*

BURYING-GROUND. A place appropriated for depositing the dead; a cemetery. In Massachusetts, burying-grounds cannot be appropriated to roads without the consent of the owners. Massachusetts Revised St. 239.

BUSHEL, *measure.* The Winchester bushel, established by the 13 W. III. c. 5, A. D. 1701, was made the standard of grain; a cylindrical vessel, eighteen and a half inches in diameter, and eight inches deep inside, contains a bushel; the capacity is 2145.42 cubic inches. By law or usage it is established in most of the United States. The exceptions, as far as known, are Connecticut, where the bushel holds 2198 cubic inches; Kentucky, 2150$\frac{2}{3}$; Indiana, Ohio, Mississippi and Missouri, where it contains 2150$\frac{4}{10}$ cubic inches. Dane's Ab. c. 211, a. 12, s. 4. See the whole subject discussed in report of the Secretary of State of the United States to the Senate, Feb. 22, 1821.

BUSINESS HOURS. The time of the day during which business is transacted. In respect to the time of presentment and demand of bills and notes, business hours generally range through the whole day down to the hours of rest in the evening, except when the paper is payable at a bank or by a banker. 2 Hill, N. Y. R. 835. See 3 Shepl. 67; 5 Shepl. 230.

BUTT. A measure of capacity, equal to one hundred and eight gallons. See *Measure.*

BUTTS AND BOUNDS. This phrase is used to express the ends and boundaries of an estate. The word butt, being evidently derived from the French *bout*, the end; and bounds, from boundary.

TO BUY. To purchase. Vide *Sale.*

BUYER, *contracts.* A purchaser; (q. v.) a vendee.

BUYING OF TITLES. The purchase of the rights of a person to a piece of land when the seller is disseised.

2. When a deed is made by one who, though having a legal right to land, is at the time of the conveyance disseised, as a general rule of the common law, the sale is void; the law will not permit any person to sell a quarrel, or, as it is commonly termed, a pretended title. Such a conveyance is an offence at common law, and by a statute of Hen. VIII. This rule has been generally adopted in the United States, and is affirmed by express statute. In some of the states, it has been modified or abolished. It has been recognized in Massachusetts and Indiana. 1 Ind. R. 127. In Massachusetts, there is no statute on the subject, but the act has always been unlawful. 5 Pick. R. 356. In Connecticut the seller and the buyer forfeit, each one half the value of the land. 4 Conn. 575. In New York, a person disseised cannot convey, except by way of mortgage. But the statute does not apply to judicial sales. 6 Wend. 224; see 4 Wend. 474; 2 John. Cas. 58; 3 Cow. 89; 5 Wend. 532; 5 Cow. 74; 13 John. 466; 8 Wend. 629; 7 Wend. 53, 152; 11 Wend. 442; 13 John. 289. In North Carolina and South Carolina, a conveyance by a disseisee is illegal; the seller forfeits the land, and the buyer its value. In Kentucky such sale is void. 1 Dana, R. 566. But when the deeds were made since the passage of the statute of 1798, the grantee might, under that act, sue for land conveyed to him, which was adversely possessed by another, as the grantor might have done before. The statute rendered transfers valid to pass the title. 2 Litt. 393; 1 Wheat. 292; 2 Litt. 225; 3 Dana, 309. The statute of 1824, "to revive and amend the champerty and maintenance law," forbids the buying of titles where there is an adverse possession. See 3 J. J. Marsh. 549; 2 Dana, 374; 6 J. J. Marsh. 490, 584. In Ohio, the purchase of land from one against whom a suit is pending for it, is void, except against himself, if he prevails. Walk. Intr. 297, 351, 352. In Pennsylvania. 2 Watts, R. 272; Illinois, Ill. Rev. L. 130;

Missouri, Misso. St. 119, a deed is valid, though there be an adverse possession. 2 Hill, Ab. c. 33, § 42 to 52.

3. The Roman law forbade the sale of a right or thing in litigation. Code, 8. 37, 2.

BY ESTIMATION, *contracts*. In sales of land it not unfrequently occurs that the property is said to contain a certain number of acres, *by estimation*, or so many acres, *more or less*. When these expressions are used, if the land fall short by a small quantity, the purchaser will receive no relief. In one case of this kind, the land fell short two-fifths, and the purchaser received no relief. 2 Freem. 106. Vide 1 Finch, 109; 1 Call, R. 301; 6 Binn. Rep. 106; 1 Serg. & Rawle, R. 166; 1 Yeates, R. 322; 2 John. R. 37; 5 John. R. 508; 15 John. R. 471; 1 Caines, R. 493; 3 Mass. Rep. 380; 5 Mass. R. 355: 1 Root. R. 528; 4 Hen. & Munf. 184. The meaning of these words has never been precisely ascertained by judicial decision. See Sugd. Vend. 231 to 236; Wolff, Inst. § 658; and the cases cited under the articles *Constitution; More or less; Subdivision*.

BY-LAWS. Rules and ordinances made by a corporation for its own government.

2. The power to make by-laws is usually conferred by express terms of the charter creating the corporation, though, when not expressly granted, it is given by implication, and it is incident to the very existence of a corporation. When there is an express grant, limited to certain cases and for certain purposes, the corporate power of legislation is confined to the objects specified, all others being excluded by implication. 2 Kyd on Corp. 102; 2 P. Wms. 207; Ang. on Corp. 177. The power of making by-laws, is to be exercised by those persons in whom it is vested by the charter; but if that instrument is silent on that subject, it resides in the members of the corporation at large. Harris & Gill's R. 324; 4 Burr. 2515, 2521; 6 Bro. P. C. 519.

3. The constitution of the United States, and acts of congress made in conformity to it; the constitution of the state in which a corporation is located, and acts of the legislature, constitutionally made, together with the common law as there accepted, are of superior force to any by-law; and such by-law, when contrary to either of them, is therefore void, whether the charter authorizes the making of such by-law or not; because no legislature can grant power larger than they themselves possess. 7 Cowen's R. 585; Id. 604; 5 Cowen's R. 538. Vide, generally, Ang. on Corp. ch. 9; Willc. on Corp. ch. 2, s. 3; Bac. Ab. h. t.; 4 Vin. Ab. 301; Dane's Ab. Index, h. t.; Com. Dig. h. t.; and Id. vol. viii. h. t.

BY THE BYE, *Eng. law*. A declaration may be filed without a new process or writ, when the defendant is in court in another case, by the plaintiff in that case having filed common bail for him; the declaration thus filed is called a declaration by the bye. 1 Crompt. 96; Lee's Dict. of Pr. Declaration IV.

C.

CABALLERIA, *Spanish law*. A measure of land, which is different in different provinces. Diccionario por la Real Academia. In those parts of the United States, which formerly belonged to Spain, the caballeria is a lot of one hundred feet front and two hundred feet deep, and equal, in all respects, to five peonias. (q. v.) 2 White's Coll. 49; 12 Pet. 444. note. See *Fanegas*.

CABINET. Certain officers who taken collectively make a board; as, the president's cabinet, which is usually composed of the secretary of state, secretary of the treasury, the attorney general, and some others.

2. These officers are the advisers of the president.

CADASTRE. A term derived from the French, which has been adopted in Louisiana, and which signifies the official statement of the quantity and value of real property in any district, made for the purpose of justly apportioning the taxes payable on such property. 3 Am. St. Pap. 679; 12 Pet. 428, n.

CADET. A younger brother; one trained up for the army or navy.

CADI. The name of a civil magistrate among the Turks.

CALENDER. An almanac. Julius Cæsar ordained that the Roman year should consist of 365 days, except every fourth year, which should contain 366—the additional day to be reckoned by counting the twenty-fourth day of February (which was the 6th of the calends of March) twice. See *Bissextile*. This period of time exceeds the solar year by eleven minutes or thereabouts, which amounts to the error of a day in about 131 years. In 1582, the error amounted to eleven days or more, which was corrected by Pope Gregory. Out of this correction grew the distinction between Old and New Style. The Gregorian or New Style was introduced into England in 1752, the 2d day of September (O. S.) of that year being reckoned as the 14th day of September, (N. S.) See *Almanac*.

CALENDER, *crim. law*. A list of prisoners, containing their names, the time when they were committed, and by whom, and the cause of their commitments.

CALIFORNIA. The name of one of the states of the United States. It was admitted into the Union, by an Act of Congress, passed the 9th September, 1850, entitled "An act for the admission of the state of California into the Union."

§ 1. This section enacts and declares that the state of California shall be one of the United States, and admitted into the Union on an equal footing with the original states, in all respects whatever.

§ 2. Enacts that the state of California shall be entitled to two representatives, until the representatives in Congress shall be apportioned according to the actual enumeration of the inhabitants of the United States.

§ 3. By this section a condition is expressly imposed on the said state that the people thereof shall never interfere with the primary disposal of the public lands within its limits, nor pass any law, nor do any act, whereby the title of the United States to, and right to dispose of the same, shall be impaired or questioned. It also provides that they shall never lay any tax, or assessment of any description whatever, upon the public domain of the United States; and that in no case shall non-resident proprietors, who are citizens of the United States, be taxed higher than residents; that all navigable waters within the said state shall be common highways, forever free, as well to the inhabitants of said state, as to citizens of the United States, without any tax, impost or duty therefor; with this proviso, viz., that nothing contained in the act shall be construed as recognizing or rejecting the propositions tendered by the people of California, as articles of compact in the ordinance adopted by the convention which formed the constitution of that state.

2. The principal features of the constitution of California, are similar to those of most of the recently formed state constitutions. It establishes an elective judiciary, and confers on the executive a qualified veto. It prohibits the creation of a state debt exceeding $300,000. It provides for the protection of the homestead from execution, and secures the property of married females separate from that of their husbands. It makes a liberal provision for the support of schools, prohibits the legislature from granting divorces, authorizing lotteries, and creating corporations, except by general laws, and from establishing any banks of issue or circulation. It provides also that every stockholder of a corporation or joint-stock association, shall be individually and personally liable for his proportion of all its debts or liabilities. There is also a clause prohibiting slavery, which, it is said, was inserted by the unanimous vote of the delegates.

CALLING THE PLAINTIFF, *practice*. When a plaintiff perceives that he has not given evidence to maintain his issue, and intends to become nonsuited, he withdraws himself, when the cryer is ordered to call the plaintiff, and on his failing to appear, he becomes nonsuited. 3 Bl. Com. 376.

CALUMNIATORS, *civil law*. Persons who accuse others, whom they know to be innocent, of having committed crimes. Code 9, 46, 9.

CAMBIST. A person skilled in exchange; one who deals or trades in promissory notes or bills of exchange.

CAMERA STELLATA, *Eng. law*. The court of the Star Chamber, now abolished.

CAMPARTUM. A part or portion of a larger field or ground, which would otherwise be in gross or common. Vide *Champerty*.

CANAL. A trench dug for leading water in a particular direction, and confining it.

2. Public canals are generally protected by the law which authorizes their being made. Various points have arisen under numerous

laws authorizing the construction of canals, which have been decided in cases reported in 1 Yeates, 430; 1 Binn. 70; 1 Pennsyl. 462; 2 Pennsyl. 517; 7 Mass. 169; 1 Sumn. 46; 20 Johns. 103, 735; 2 Johns. 283; 7 John. Ch. 315; 1 Wend. 474; 5 Wend. 166; 8 Wend. 469; 4 Wend. 667; 6 Cowen, 698; 7 Cowen, 526; 4 Hamm. 253; 5 Hamm. 141, 391; 6 Hamm. 126; 1 N. H. Rep. 339; See *River*.

CANCELLARIA CURIA. The name formerly given to the court of chancery.

CANCELLATION. Its general acceptation, is the act of crossing a writing; it is used sometimes to signify the manual operation of tearing or destroying the instrument itself. Hyde *v.* Hyde, 1 Eq. Cas. Abr. 409; Rob. on Wills, 367, n.

2. Cancelling a will, *animo revocandi*, is a revocation of it, and it is unnecessary to show a complete destruction or obliteration. 2 B. & B. 650; 3 B. & A. 489; 2 Bl. R. 1043; 2 Nott & M'Cord, 272; Whart. Dig. Wills, c.; 4 Mass. 462. When a duplicate has been cancelled, *animo revocandi*, it is the cancellation of both parts. 2 Lee, Ecc. R. 532.

3. But the mere act of cancelling a will is nothing, unless it be done *animo revocandi*, and evidence is admissible to show, *quo animo*, the testator cancelled it. 7 Johns. 394; 2 Dall. 266; S. C. 2 Yeates, 170; 4 Serg. & Rawle, 297; cited 2 Dall. 267, n.; 3 Hen. & Munf. 502; Rob. on Wills, 365; Lovel, 178; Toll. on Ex'rs, Index, h. t.; 3 Stark. Ev. 1714; 1 Adams' Rep. 52; 9 Mass. 307; 5 Conn. 262; 4 Wend. 474; 4 Wend. 585; 1 Harr. & M'H. 162; 4 Conn. 550; 8 Verm. 373; 1 N. H. Rep. 1; 4 N. H. Rep. 191; 2 Eccl. Rep. 23.

4. As to the effect of cancelling a deed, which has not been recorded, see 1 Adams' Rep. 1; Palm. 403; Latch. 226; Gilb. Law, Ev. 109, 110; 2 H. Bl. 263; 2 Johns. 87; 1 Greenl. R. 78; 10 Mass. 403; 9 Pick. 105; 4 N. H. Rep. 191; Greenl. Ev. § 265; 5 Conn. 262; 4 Conn. 450; 5 Conn. 86; 2 John. R. 84; 4 Yerg. 375; 6 Mass. 24; 11 Mass. 337; 2 Curt. Ecc. R. 458.

5. As to when a court of equity will order an agreement or other instrument to be cancelled and delivered up, see 4 Bouv. Inst. n. 3917–22.

CANDIDATE. One who offers himself or is offered by others for an office.

CANON, *eccl. law.* This word is taken from the Greek, and signifies a rule or law. In ecclesiastical law, it is also used to designate an order of religious persons. Francis Duaren says, the reason why the ecclesiastics called the rules they established canons or rules, (canones id est regulas) and not *laws*, was modesty. They did not dare to call them (leges) laws, lest they should seem to arrogate to themselves the authority of princes and magistrates. De Sacris Ecclesiæ Ministeriis, p. 2, in pref. See *Law, Canon*.

CANONIST. One well versed in canon or ecclesiastical law.

CANNON SHOT, *war*. The distance which a cannon will throw a ball.

2. The whole space of the sea, within cannon shot of the coast, is considered as making a part of the territory; and for that reason, a vessel taken under the cannon of a neutral fortress, is not a lawful prize. Vatt. b. 1, c. 23, s. 289, in finem; Chitt. Law of Nat. 113; Mart. Law of Nat. b. 8, c. 6, s. 6; 3 Rob. Adm. Rep. 102, 336; 5 Id. 373; 3 Hagg. Adm. R. 257. This part of the sea being considered as part of the adjacent territory, (q. v.) it follows that magistrates can cause the orders of their governments to be executed there. Three miles is considered as the greatest distance that the force of gunpowder can carry a bomb or a ball. Azun. Mar. Law, part 2, c. 2, art. 2, § 15; Bouch. Inst. n. 1848. The anonymous author of the poem, Della Natura, lib. 5, expresses this idea in the following lines:

> Tanto s'avanza in mar questo dominio,
> Quant' esser può d'antemurale e guardia,
> Fin dove può da terra in mar vibrandosi
> Correr di cavo bronzo acceso fulmine.
>
> Far as the sovereign can defend his sway,
> Extends his empire o'er the watery way;
> The shot sent thundering to the liquid plain,
> Assigns the limits of his just domain.

Vide *League*.

CAPACITY. This word, in the law sense, denotes some ability, power, qualification, or competency of persons, natural, or artificial, for the performance of civil acts, depending on their state or condition, as defined or fixed by law; as, the capacity to devise, to bequeath, to grant or convey lands; to take; or to take and hold lands; to make a contract, and the like. 2 Com. Dig. 294; Dane's Abr. h. t.

2. The constitution requires that the president, senators, and representatives should have attained certain ages; and in the case of the senators and representatives, that

they should have local qualifications; without these they have no capacity to serve in these offices.

3. All laws which regulate the capacity of persons to contract, are considered personal laws; such are the laws which relate to minority and majority; to the powers of guardians or parents, or the disabilities of coverture. The law of the domicil generally governs in cases of this kind. Burge on Sureties, 89.

CAPAX DOLI. Capable of committing crime. This is said of one who has sufficient mind and understanding to be made responsible for his actions. See *Discretion*.

CAPE, *English law*. A judicial writ touching a plea of lands and tenements. The writs which bear this name are of two kinds, namely, cape magnum, or grand cape, and cape parvum, or petit cape. The petit cape is so called, not so much on account of the smallness of the writ, as of the letter. Fleta, lib. 6, c. 55, § 40. For the difference between the form and the use of these writs, see 2 Wms. Saund. Rep. 45, c, d; and Fleta, ubi sup.

CAPERS. Vessels of war owned by private persons, and different from ordinary privateers (q. v.) only in size, being smaller. Bea. Lex. Mer. 230.

CAPIAS, *practice*. This word, the signification of which is "that you take," is applicable to many heads of practice. Several writs and processes, commanding the sheriff to take the person of the defendant, are known by the name of capias. For example: there are writs of capias ad respondendum, writs of capias ad computandum, writs of capias ad satisfaciendum, &c., each especially adapted to the purposes indicated by the words used for its designation. See 3 Bl. Com. 281; 3 Bouv. Inst. n. 2794.

CAPIAS AD AUDIENDUM JUDICIUM, *practice*. A writ issued in a case of misdemeanor, after the defendant has appeared and is found guilty, and is not present when called. This writ is to bring him to judgment. 4 Bl. Com. 368.

CAPIAS AD COMPUTANDUM, *practice*. A writ issued in the action of account render, upon the judgment quod computet, when the defendant refuses to appear, in his proper person, before the auditors, and enter into his account. According to the ancient practice, the defendant, after arrest upon this process, might be delivered on mainprize, or in default of finding mainpernors, he was committed to the Fleet prison, where the auditors attended upon him to hear and receive his account. As the object of this process is to compel the defendant to render an account, it does not appear to be within the scope of acts abolishing imprisonment for debt. For precedents, see Thesaurus Brevium, 38, 39, 40; 3 Leon. 149; 1 Lutw. 47, 51; Co. Ent. 46, 47; Rast. Ent. 14, b, 15.

CAPIAS AD RESPONDENDUM, *practice*. A writ commanding the sheriff, or other proper officer, to "take the body of the defendant, and to keep the same to answer, *ad respondendum*, the plaintiff in a plea," &c. The amount of bail demanded ought to be indorsed on the writ.

2. A defendant arrested upon this writ must be committed to prison, unless he give a bail bond (q. v.) to the sheriff. In some states, (as, until lately, in Pennsylvania,) it is the practice, when the defendant is liable to this process, to indorse on the writ, "No bail required;" in which case he need only give the sheriff, in writing, an authority to the prothonotary to enter his appearance to the action, to be discharged from the arrest. If the writ has been served, and the defendant have not given bail, but remains in custody, it is returned C. C., *cepi corpus;* if he have given bail, it is returned C. C. B. B., *cepi corpus*, bail bond; if the defendant's appearance have been accepted, the return is, "C. C. and defendant's appearance accepted." According to the course of the practice at common law, the writ bears teste, in the name of the chief justice, or presiding judge of the court, on some day in term time, when the judge is supposed to be present, not being Sunday, and is made returnable on a regular return day. 1 Penna. Pr. 36; 1 Arch. Pr. 67.

CAPIAS AD SATISFACIENDUM, *practice*. A writ of execution issued upon a judgment in a personal action, for the recovery of money, directed to the sheriff or coroner, commanding him to take the defendant, and him safely keep, so that he may have his body in court on the return day, to satisfy, *ad satisfaciendum*, the plaintiff. This writ is tested on a general teste day, and returnable on a regular return day.

2. It lies after judgment in most instances in which the defendant was subject to a capias ad respondendum before, and plaintiffs are subject to it, when judgment has been given against them for costs. Members of congress and of the legislature,

(*eundo, morando, et redeundo,*) going to, remaining at, and returning from the places of sitting of congress, or of the legislature, are not liable to this process, on account of their public capacity; nor are ambassadors, (q. v.) and other public ministers, and their servants. Act of Congress of April 30, 1790, s. 25 and 26, Story's Laws United States, 88; 1 Dunl. Pr. 95, 96; Com. Dig. Ambassador, B; 4 Dall. 321. In Pennsylvania, women are not subject to this writ except in actions founded upon tort, or claims arising otherwise than *ex contractu.* 7 Reed's Laws of Pa. 150. In several of the United States, the use of this writ, as well as of the capias ad respondendum, has been prohibited in all actions instituted for the recovery of money due upon any contract, express or implied, or upon any judgment or decree, founded on any contract, or for the recovery of damages for the breach of any contract, with a few exceptions. See *Arrest.*

3. It is executed by arresting the body of the defendant, and keeping him in custody. Discharging him upon his giving security for the payment of the debt, or upon his promise to return into custody again before the return day, is an escape, although he do return; 13 Johns. R. 366; 8 Johns. R. 98; and the sheriff is liable for the debt. In England, a payment to the sheriff or other officer having the ca. sa., is no payment to the plaintiff. Freem. 842; Lutw. 587; 2 Lev. 203; 1 Arch. Pr. 278. The law is different in Pennsylvania. 3 Serg. & Rawle, 467. The return made by the officer is either C. C. & C., *cepi corpus et comittitur,* if the defendant have been arrested and held in custody; or N. E. I., *non est inventus,* if the officer has not been able to find him. This writ is, in common language, called a *ca. sa.*

Capias pro fine, *practice, crim. law.* The name of a writ which issues against a defendant who has been fined, and who does not discharge it according to the judgment. This writ commands the sheriff to arrest the defendant and commit him to prison, there to remain till he pay the fine, or be otherwise discharged according to law.

Capias utlagatum, *English practice.* A capias utlagatum is general or special; the former against the person only, the latter against the person, lands and goods.

2. This writ issues upon the judgment of outlawry being returned by the sheriff upon the *exigent,* and it takes its name from the words of the mandatory part of the writ, which states the defendant being outlawed *utlagatum,* which word comes from the Saxon *utlagh,* Latinized *utlagatus,* and signifies bannitus extra legem. Cowel.

3. The *general* writ of *capias utlagatum* commands the sheriff to take the defendant, so that he have him before the king on a general return day, wheresoever, &c., to do and receive what the court shall consider of him.

4. The *special capias utlagatum,* like the general writ, commands the sheriff to take the defendant. The defendant is discharged upon an attorney's undertaking, or upon giving bond to the sheriff, in the same manner as when the writ is general. But the special writ also commands the sheriff to inquire by a jury, of the defendant's goods and lands, to extend and appraise the same, and to take them in the king's hands and safely keep them, so that he may answer to the king for the value and issues of the same. 2 Arch. Pr. 161. See *Outlawry.*

Capias in withernam, *practice.* A writ issued after a return of *elongata* or *eloigned* has been made to a writ of *retorno habendo,* commanding the sheriff to take so many of the distrainer's goods by way of reprisal, as will equal the goods mentioned in the *retorno habendo.* 2 Inst. 140; F. N. B. 68; and see form in 2 Sell. Pr. 169.

CAPIATUR, *pro fine.* The name of a writ which was issued to levy a fine due to the king. Bac. Ab. Fines and Amercements, *in prin.* See *Judgment of Capiatur.*

CAPITA, or PER CAPITA. By heads. An expression of frequent occurrence in laws regulating the distribution of the estates of persons dying intestate. When all the persons entitled to shares in the distribution are of the same degree of kindred to the deceased person, (*e. g.* when all are grandchildren,) and claim directly from him in their own right and not through an intermediate relation, they take *per capita,* that is, equal shares, or share and share alike. But when they are of different degrees of kindred, (*e. g.* some the children, others the grandchildren or the great grandchildren of the deceased,) those more remote take *per stirpem* or *per stirpes,* that is, they take respectively the shares their parents (or other relation standing in the same degree with them of the surviving kindred entitled, who are in the nearest degree of kindred to the intestate,) would have taken had they respectively survived the intestate. Reeves' Law of Descent, Introd. xxvii.; also 1 Rop. on Leg. 126, 130. See *Per Capita; Per Stirpes; Stirpes.*

CAPITAL, *political economy, commerce.* In political economy, it is that portion of the produce of a country, which may be made directly available either to support the human species or to the facilitating of production.

2. In commerce, as applied to individuals, it is those objects, whether consisting of money or other property, which a merchant, trader, or other person adventures in an undertaking, or which he contributes to the common stock of a partnership. 2 Bouv. Inst. n. 1458.

3. It signifies money put out at interest.

4. The fund of a trading company or corporation is also called capital, but in this sense the word *stock* is generally added to it; thus we say the *capital stock* of the Bank of North America.

CAPITAL CRIME. One for the punishment of which death is inflicted, which punishment is called *capital punishment.* Dane's Ab. Index, h. t.

2. The subject of capital punishment has occupied the attention of enlightened men for a long time, particularly since the middle of the last century; and none deserves to be more carefully investigated. The right of punishing its members by society cannot be denied; but how far this right extends, by the laws of nature or of God, has been much disputed by theoretical writers, although it cannot be denied, that most nations, ancient and modern, have deemed capital punishment to be within the scope of the legitimate powers of government. Beccaria contends with zeal that the punishment of death ought not to be inflicted in times of peace, nor at other times, except in cases where the laws can be maintained in no other way. Bec. Chap. 28.

3. It is not within the plan of this work to examine the question, whether the punishment is allowed by the natural law. The principal arguments for and against it are here given.

4.—1. The arguments used in favor of the abolition of capital punishment, are,

5.—1st. That existence is a right which men hold from God, and which society in a body can, no more than a member of that society, deprive them of, because society is governed by the immutable laws of humanity.

6.—2d. That, even should the right be admitted, this is a restraint badly selected, which does not attain its end, death being less dreaded than either solitary confinement for life, or the performance of hard labor and disgrace for life.

7.—3d. That the infliction of the punishment does not prevent crimes, any more than other less severe but longer punishments.

8.—4th. That as a public example, this punishment is only a barbarous show, better calculated to accustom mankind to the contemplation of bloodshed, than to restrain them.

9.—5th. That the law by taking life, when it is unnecessary for the safety of society, must act by some other motive; this can be no other than revenge. To the extent the law punishes an individual beyond what is requisite for the preservation of society, and the restoration of the offender, is cruel and barbarous. The law, to prevent a barbarous act, commits one of the same kind; it kills one of the members of society, to convince the others that killing is unlawful.

10.—6th. That by depriving a man of life, society is deprived of the benefits which he is able to confer upon it; for, according to the vulgar phrase, a man hanged is good for nothing.

11.—7th. That experience has proved that offences which were formerly punished with death, have not increased since the punishment has been changed to a milder one.

12.—2. The arguments which have been urged on the other side, are,

13.—1st. That all that humanity commands to legislators is, that they should inflict only *necessary* and *useful* punishments; and that if they keep within these bounds, the law may permit an extreme remedy, even the punishment of death, when it is requisite for the safety of society.

14.—2d. That, whatever be said to the contrary, this punishment is more repulsive than any other, as life is esteemed above all things, and death is considered as the greatest of evils, particularly when it is accompanied by infamy.

15.—3d. That restrained, as this punishment ought to be, to the greatest crimes, it can never lose its efficacy as an example, nor harden the multitude by the frequency of executions.

16.—4th. That unless this punishment

be placed at the top of the scale of punishment, criminals will always kill, when they can, while committing an inferior crime, as the punishment will be increased only by a more protracted imprisonment, where they still will hope for a pardon or an escape.

17th.—5th. The essays which have been made by two countries at least; Russia, under the reign of Elizabeth, and Tuscany, under the reign of Leopold, where the punishment of death was abolished, have proved unsuccessful, as that punishment has been restored in both.

18. Arguments on theological grounds have also been advanced on both sides. See Caudlish's Contributions towards the Exposition of the Book of Genesis, pp.203—7.

Vide Beccaria on Crimes and Punishments; Voltaire, h. t.; Livingston's Report on a Plan of a Penal Code; Liv. Syst. Pen. Law, 22; Bentham on Legislation, part 3, c. 9; Report to the N. Y. Legislature; 18 Am. Jur. 334.

CAPITATION. A poll tax; an imposition which is yearly laid on each person according to his estate and ability.

2. The Constitution of the United States provides that "no capitation, or other direct tax, shall be laid, unless in proportion to the census, or enumeration, therein-before directed to be taken." Art. 1, s. 9, n. 4. See 3 Dall. 171; 5 Wheat. 317.

CAPITE, *descents*. By the head. Distribution or succession per capita, is said to take place when every one of the kindred in equal degree, and not *jure representationis*, receive an equal part of an estate.

CAPITULARIES. The Capitularia or Capitularies, was a code of laws promulgated by Childebert, Clotaire, Carloman, Pepin, Charlemagne, and other kings. It was so called from the small chapters or heads into which they were divided. The edition by Baluze, published in 1677, is said to be the best.

CAPITULATION, *war*. The treaty which determines the conditions under which a fortified place is abandoned to the commanding officer of the army which besieges it.

2. On surrender by capitulation, all the property of the inhabitants protected by the articles, is considered by the law of nations as neutral, and not subject to capture on the high seas, by the belligerent or its ally. 2 Dall.

CAPITULATION, *civ. law*. An agreement by which the prince and the people, or those who have the right of the people, regulate the manner in which the government is to be administered. Wolff, § 989.

CAPTAIN or SEA CAPTAIN, *mar. law*. The name given to the master or commander of a vessel. He is known in this country very generally by the name of master. (q. v.) He is also frequently denominated patron in foreign laws and books.

2. The captains in the navy of the United States, are officers appointed by government. Those who are employed in the mercantile service, have not strictly an official character. They are appointed or employed by the owners of the vessels they command.

3. It is proposed to consider the duty of the latter. Towards the owner of the vessel he is bound by his personal attention and care, to take all the necessary precautions for her safety; to proceed on the voyage in which such vessel may be engaged, and to obey faithfully his instructions; and by all means in his power to promote the interest of his owner. But he is not required to violate good faith, nor employ fraud even with an enemy. 3 Cranch, 242.

4. Towards others, it is the policy of the law to hold him responsible for all losses or damages that may happen to the goods committed to his charge; whether they arise from negligence, ignorance, or wilful misconduct of himself or his mariners, or any other person on board the ship. As soon, therefore, as goods are put on board, they are in the master's charge, and he is bound to deliver them again in the same state in which they were shipped, and he is answerable for all losses or damages they may sustain, unless it proceed from an inherent defect in the article, or from some accident or misfortune which could not be prevented.

5. It may be laid down as a general rule, that the captain is responsible when any loss occurs in consequence of his doing what he ought not to do, unless he was forced by the act of God, the enemies of the United States, or the perils of the sea. 1 Marsh. Ins. 241; Pard. n. 658.

6. The rights of the captain are, to choose his crew; as he is responsible for their acts, this seems but just, but a reasonable deference to the rights of the owner require that he should be consulted, as he, as well as the captain, is responsible for the acts of the crew. On board, the captain is

invested with almost arbitrary power over the crew, being responsible for the abuse of his authority. Ab. on Shipp. 162. He may repair the ship, and, if he is not in funds to pay the expenses of such repairs, he may borrow money, when abroad, on the credit of his owners or of the ship. Abb. on Sh. 127-8. In such cases, although contracting within the ordinary scope of his powers and duties, he is generally responsible as well as the owner. This is the established rule of the maritime law, introduced in favor of commerce; it has been recognized and adopted by the commercial nations of Europe, and is derived from the civil or Roman law. Abbott, Ship. 90; Story, Ag. § 116 to 123, § 294; Paley, Ag. by Lloyd, 244; 1 Liverm. Ag. 70; Poth. Ob. n. 82; Ersk. Inst. 3, 3, 43; Dig. 4, 9, 1; Poth. Pand. lib. 14, tit. 1; 3 Summ. R. 228. See Bell's Com. 505, 5th ed; Bouv. Inst. Index, h. t.

CAPTATION, *French law.* The act of one who succeeds in controlling the will of another, so as to become master of it. It is generally taken in a bad sense.

2. Captation takes place by those demonstrations of attachment and friendship, by those assiduous attentions, by those services and officious little presents which are usual among friends, and by all those means which ordinarily render us agreeable to others. When those attentions are unattended by deceit or fraud, they are perfectly fair, and the captation is lawful; but if, under the mask of friendship, fraud is the object, and means are used to deceive the person with whom you are connected, then the captation is fraudulent, and the acts procured by the captator are void. See *Influence.*

CAPTATOR, *French law.* The name which is sometimes given to him who by flattery and artifice endeavors to surprise testators, and induce them to give legacies or devices, or to make him some other gift. Dict. de Jur.

CAPTION, *practice.* That part of a legal instrument, as a commission, indictment, &c., which shows where, when, and by what authority it was *taken*, found or executed. As to the forms and requisites of captions, see 1 Murph. 281; 8 Yerg. 514; 4 Iredell, 113; 6 Miss. 469; 1 Scam. 456; 5 How. Mis. 20; 6 Blackf. 299; 1 Hawks, 354; 1 Brev. 169.

2. In the English practice, when an inferior court in obedience to the writ of certiorari, returns an indictment into the K. B., it is annexed to the caption, then called a schedule, and the caption concludes with stating, that "it is presented in manner and form as appears in a certain indictment thereto annexed," and the caption and indictment are returned on separate parchments. 1 Saund. 309, n. 2. Vide Dane's Ab. Index, h. t.

3. Caption is another name for arrest.

CAPTIVE. By this term is understood one who has been *taken;* it is usually applied to prisoners of war. (q. v.) Although he has lost his liberty, a captive does not by his captivity lose his civil rights.

CAPTOR, *war.* One who has taken property from an enemy; this term is also employed to designate one who has taken an enemy.

2. Formerly, goods taken in war were adjudged to belong to the captor; they are now considered to vest primarily, in the state or sovereign, and belong to the individual captors only to the extent that the municipal laws provide.

3. Captors are responsible to the owners of the property for all losses and damages, when the capture is tortious and without reasonable cause in the exercise of belligerent rights. But if the capture is originally justifiable, the captors will not be responsible, unless by subsequent misconduct they become trespassers *ab initio.* 1 Rob. R. 93, 96. See 2 Gall. 374; 1 Gall. 274; 1 Pet. Adm. Dec. 116; 1 Mason, R. 14.

CAPTURE, *war.* The taking of property by one belligerent from another.

2. To make a good capture of a ship, it must be subdued and taken by an enemy in open war, or by way of reprisals, or by a pirate, and with intent to deprive the owner of it.

3. Capture may be with intent to possess both ship and cargo, or only to seize the goods of the enemy, or contraband goods which are on board. The former is the capture of the ship in the proper sense of the word; the latter is only an arrest and detention, without any design to deprive the owner of it. Capture is deemed lawful, when made by a declared enemy, lawfully commissioned and according to the laws of war; and unlawful, when it is against the rules established by the law of nations. Marsh. Ins. B. 1, c. 12, s. 4.

See, generally, Lee on Captures, passim; 1 Chitty's Com. Law, 377 to 512; 2 Woddes. 435 to 457; 2 Caines' C. Err.

158; 7 Johns. R. 449; 3 Caines' R. 155; 11 Johns. R. 241; 13 Johns. R. 161; 14 Johns. R. 227; 3 Wheat. 183; 4 Cranch, 43; 6 Mass. 197; Bouv. Inst. Index, h. t.

CAPUT LUPINUM, *Eng. law.* Having the head of a wolf. An outlawed felon was said to have the head of a wolf, and might have been killed by any one legally. Now, such killing would be murder. 1 Hale, Pl. C. 497. The rules of the common law on this subject are much more severe in their consequences, than the doctrine of the civil law relating to civil death. See 1 Toull. Droit Civil, n. 280, and pp. 254–5, note 3.

CARAT, *weights.* A carat is a weight equal to three and one-sixth grains, in diamonds, and the like. Jac. L. Dict. See *Weight.*

CARCAN, *French law.* A French word, which is applied to an instrument of punishment somewhat resembling a pillory. It sometimes signifies the punishment itself. Biret Vocab.

CARDINAL, *eccl. law.* The title given to one of the highest dignitaries of the court of Rome. Cardinals are next to the pope in dignity; he is elected by them and out of their body. There are cardinal bishops, cardinal priests, and cardinal deacons. See Fleury, Hist. Eccles. liv. xxxv. n. 17, li. n. 19; Thomassin, part ii. liv. i. ch. 53, part iv. liv. i. c. 79, 80; Loiseau, Traité des Ordres, c. 3, n. 31; André, Droit Canon, *au mot.*

CARDS, *crim. law.* Small square pasteboards, generally of a fine quality, on which are painted figures of various colors, and used for playing different games. The playing of cards for amusement is not forbidden, but gaming for money is unlawful. Vide *Faro bank*, and *Gaming.*

CARGO, *mar. law.* The entire load of a ship or other vessel. Abb. on Sh. Index, h. t.; 1 Dall. 197; Merl. Rép. h. t.; 2 Gill & John. 136. This term is usually applied to *goods* only, and does not include human beings. 1 Phill. Ins. 185; 4 Pick. 429. But in a more extensive and less technical sense, it includes persons; thus we say a cargo of emigrants. See 7 Mann. & Gr. 729, 744.

CARNAL KNOWLEDGE, *crim. law.* This phrase is used to signify a sexual connexion; as, rape is the carnal knowledge of a woman, &c. See *Rape.*

CARNALLY KNEW, *pleadings.* This is a technical phrase, essential in an indictment to charge the defendant with the crime of rape; no other word or circumlocution will answer the same purpose as these words Vide *Ravished*, and Bac. Ab. Indictment, G 1; Com. Dig. Indictment, G 6; 1 Hale, 632; 3 Inst. 60; Co. Litt. 137; 1 Chit. Cr. Law, *243. It has been doubted whether these words were indispensable. 1 East, P. C. 448. But it would be unsafe to omit them.

CARRIERS, *contracts.* There are two kinds of carriers, namely, *common carriers*, (q. v.) who have been considered under another head; and private carriers. These latter are persons who, although they do not undertake to transport the goods of such as choose to employ them, yet agree to carry the goods of some particular person for hire, from one place to another.

2. In such case the carrier incurs no responsibility beyond that of any other ordinary bailee for hire, that is to say, the responsibility of ordinary diligence. 2 Bos. & Pull. 417; 4 Taunt. 787; Selw. N. P. 382 n.; 1 Wend. R. 272; 1 Hayw. R. 14; 2 Dana, R. 430; 6 Taunt. 577; Jones, Bailm. 121; Story on Bailm, § 495. But in Gordon *v.* Hutchinson, 1 Watts & Serg. 285, it was holden that a wagoner who carries goods for hire, contracts the responsibility of a common carrier, whether transportation be his principal and direct business, or only an occasional and incidental employment.

3. To bring a person within the description of a common carrier, he must exercise his business as a public employment; he must undertake to carry goods for persons generally; and he must hold himself out as ready to engage in the transportation of goods for hire, as a business; not as a casual occupation *pro hac vice.* 1 Salk. 249; 1 Bell's Com. 467; 1 Hayw. R. 14; 1 Wend. 272; 2 Dana, R. 430. See Bouv. Inst. Index, h. t.

CARRYING AWAY, *crim. law.* To complete the crime of larceny, the thief must not only feloniously take the thing stolen, but carry it away. The slightest carrying away will be sufficient; thus to snatch a diamond from a lady's ear, which is instantly dropped among the curls of her hair. 1 Leach, 320. To remove sheets from a bed and carry them into an adjoining room. 1 Leach, 222 n. To take plate from a trunk, and lay it on the floor with intent to carry it away. Ib. And to remove a package from one part of a wagon to another, with a view to steal it; 1 Leach, 236; have respectively been holden to be felonies. 2 Chit. Cr. Law, 919. Vide 3 Inst. 108, 109; 1 Hale, 507; Kel. 31; Ry. & Moody, 14; Bac. Ab. Felony, D; 4 Bl. Com. 231; Hawk. c. 32, s. 25. Where, however, there has not been a complete severance of the possession, it is not a complete carrying away. 2 East, P. C. 556; 1 Hale, 508; 2 Russ. on Cr. 96. Vide *Invito Domino; Larceny; Robbery; Taking.*

CART BOTE. An allowance to the tenant of wood, sufficient for carts and other instruments of husbandry.

CARTE BLANCHE. The signature of an individual or more, on a white paper, with a sufficient space left above it to write a note or other writing.

2. In the course of business, it not unfrequently occurs that for the sake of convenience, signatures in blank are given with authority to fill them up. These are binding upon the parties. But the blank must be filled up by the very person authorized. 6 Mart. L. R. 707. Vide Ch. on Bills, 70; 2 Penna. R. 200. Vide *Blank.*

CARTEL, *war.* An agreement between two belligerent powers for the delivery of prisoners or deserters, and also a written challenge to a duel.

2. *Cartel ship,* is a ship commissioned in time of war, to exchange prisoners, or to carry any proposals between hostile powers; she must carry no cargo, ammunitions, or implements of war, except a single gun for signals. The conduct of ships of this description cannot be too narrowly watched. The service on which they are sent is so highly important to the interests of humanity, that it is peculiarly incumbent on all parties to take care that it should be conducted in such a manner as not to become a subject of jealousy and distrust between the two nations. 4 Rob. R. 357. Vide Merl. Rép. h. t.; Dane's Ab. c. 40, a. 6, § 7; Pet. C. C. R. 106; 3 C. Rob. 141; 6 C. Rob. 336; 1 Dods. R. 60.

CARTMEN. Persons who carry goods and merchandise in carts, either for great or short distances, for hire.

2. Cartmen who undertake to carry goods for hire as a common employment, are common carriers. Story on Bailm. § 496; and see 2 Wend. 327; 2 N. & M. 88; 1 Murph. 417; 2 Bailey, 421; 2 Verm. 92; 1 M'Cord, 444; Bac. Ab. Carriers, A.

CASE, *practice.* A contested question before a court of justice; a suit or action; a cause. 9 Wheat. 738.

CASE, *remedies.* This is the name of an action in very general use, which lies where a party sues for damages for any wrong or cause of complaint to which covenant or trespass will not lie. Steph. Pl. 15; 3 Woodd. 167; Ham. N. P. 1. Vide *Writ of trespass on the case.* In its most comprehensive signification, *case* includes assumpsit as well as an action in form *ex delicto;* but when simply mentioned, it is usually understood to mean an action in form *ex delicto.* 7 T. R. 36. It is a liberal action; 2 Burr, 906, 1011; 1 Bl. Rep. 199; bailable at common law; 2 Burr, 927–8; founded on the justice and conscience of the plaintiff's case, and is in the nature of a bill in equity; 3 Burr, 1353, 1357; and the substance of a count in case is the damage assigned. 1 Bl. Rep. 200.

2. An action on the case lies to recover damages for torts not committed with force actual or implied, or having been occasioned by force, where the matter affected was not tangible, or where the injury was not immediate but consequential; 11 Mass. 59, 137; 1 Yeates, 586; 6 S. & R. 348; 12 S. & R. 210; 18 John. 257; 19 John. 381; 6 Call, 44; 2 Dana, 378; 1 Marsh. 194; 2 H. & M. 423; Harper, 113; Coxe, 339; or where the interest in the property was only in reversion. 8 Pick. 235; 7 Conn. 328; 2 Green, 8; 1 John. 511; 3 Hawks, 246; 2 Murph. 61; 2 N. H. Rep. 430. In these several cases trespass cannot be sustained. 4 T. R. 489; 7 T. R. 9. Case is also the proper remedy for a wrongful act done under legal process regularly issuing from a court of competent jurisdiction. 2 Conn. 700; 11 Mass. 500; 6 Greenl. 421; 1 Bailey, 441, 457; 9 Conn. 141; 2 Litt 234; 3 Conn. 537; 3 Gill & John. 377 Vide *Regular and irregular process.*

3. It will be proper to consider, 1. in what cases the action of trespass on the case lies; 2. the pleadings; 3. the evidence; 4. the judgment.

4.—§ 1. This action lies for injuries, 1. to the absolute rights of persons; 2. to the relative rights of persons; 3. to personal property; 4. to real property.

5.—1. When the injury has been done to the absolute rights of persons by an act not immediate but consequential, as in the case of special damages arising from a public nuisance; Willes, 71 to 74; or where an incumbrance had been placed in a public street, and the plaintiff passing there received an injury; or for a malicious prosecution. See *Malicious prosecution.*

6.—2. For injuries to the relative rights, as for enticing away an infaut child, *per quod servitium amisit*, 4 Litt. 25; for criminal conversation, seducing or harboring wives; debauching daughters,—but in this case the daughter must live with her father as his servant, see *Seduction;*—or enticing away or harboring apprentices or servants. 1 Chit. Pl. 137; 2 Chit. Plead. 313, 319. When the seduction takes place in the husband's or father's house, he may, at his election, have trespass or case; 6 Munf. 587; Gilmer, 33; but when the injury is done in the house of another, case is the proper remedy. 5 Greenl. 546.

7.—3. When the injury to personal property is without force and not immediate, but consequential, or when the plaintiff's right to it is in reversion, as, where property is injured by a third person while in the hands of a hirer; 3 Camp. 187; 2 Murph. 62; 3 Hawks, 246, case is the proper remedy. 3 East, 593; Ld. Raym. 1399; Str. 634; 1 Chit. Pl. 138.

8.—4. When the real property which has been injured is *corporeal*, and the injury is not immediate but consequential, as for example, putting a spout so near the plaintiff's land that the water runs upon it; 1 Chit. Pl. 126, 141; Str. 634; or where the plaintiff's property is only in reversion. When the injury has been done to *incorporeal* rights, as for obstructing a private way, or disturbing a party in the use of a pew, or for injury to a franchise, as a ferry, and the like, case is the proper remedy. 1 Chit. Pl. 143.

9.—§ 2. The declaration in case, technically so called, differs from a declaration in trespass, chiefly in this, that in case, it must not, in general, state the injury to have been committed *vi et armis;* 3 Conn. 64; see 2 Ham. 169; 11 Mass. 57; Coxe, 339; yet after verdict, the words "with force and arms" will be rejected as surplusage; Harp. 122; and it ought not to conclude *contra pacem*. Com. Dig. Action on the Case, C 3. The plea is usually the general issue, not guilty.

10.—§ 3. Any matter may, in general, be given in evidence, under the plea of not guilty, except the statute of limitations. In cases of slander and a few other instances, however, this cannot be done. 1 Saund. 130, n. 1; Willes, 20. When the plaintiff declares in case, with averments appropriate to that form of action, and the evidence shows that the injury was trespass; or when he declares in trespass, and the evidence proves an injury for which case will lie, and not trespass, the defendant should be acquitted by the jury, or the plaintiff should be nonsuited. 5 Mass. 560; 16 Mass. 451; Coxe, 339; 3 John. 468.

11.—§ 4. The judgment is, that the plaintiff recover a sum of money, ascertained by a jury, for his damages sustained by the committing of the grievances complained of in the declaration, and costs.

12. In the civil law, an action was given in all cases of nominate contracts, which was always of the same name. But in innominate contracts, which had always the same consideration, but not the same name, there could be no action of the same denomination, but an action which arose from the fact, *in factum*, or an action with a form which arose from the particular circumstance, *præscriptis verbis actio*. Leç. Elem. § 779. Vide, generally, Bouv. Inst. Index, h. t.

CASE STATED, *practice*. An agreement in writing, between a plaintiff and defendant, that the facts in dispute between them are as there agreed upon and mentioned. 3 Whart. 143.

2. The facts being thus ascertained, it is left for the court to decide for which party is the law. As no writ of error lies on a judgment rendered on a case stated, Dane's Ab. c. 137, art. 4, n. § 7, it is usual in the agreement to insert a clause that the case stated shall be considered in the nature of special verdict.

3. In that case, a writ of error lies on the judgment which may be rendered upon it. And a writ of error will also lie on a judgment on a case stated, when the parties have agreed to it. 8 Serg. & Rawle, 529.

4. In another sense, by a case stated is understood a statement of all the facts of a case, together with the names of the witnesses, and a detail of the documents which are to support them. In other words, it is a brief. (q. v.)

CASH, *commerce*. Money on hand, which a merchant, trader or other person has to do business with.

2. *Cash price*, in contracts, is the price of articles paid for in cash, in contradistinction to the credit price. Pard. n. 85; Chipm. Contr. 110. In common parlance, bank notes are considered as cash; but bills receivable are not.

CASH-BOOK, *commerce, accounts*. One in which a merchant or trader enters an account of all the money, or paper moneys he receives or pays. An entry of the same thing ought to be made under the proper dates, in the journal. The object of the cash-book is to afford a constant facility to ascertain the true state of a man's cash. Pard. n. 87.

CASHIER. An officer of a moneyed institution, who is entitled by virtue of his office to take care of the cash or money of such institution.

2. The cashier of a bank is usually entrusted with all the funds of the bank, its notes, bills, and other choses in action, to be used from time to time for the ordinary and extraordinary exigencies of the bank. He usually receives directly, or through subordinate officers, all moneys and notes of the bank; delivers up all discounted notes and other securities, when they have been paid; draws checks to withdraw the funds of the bank where they have been deposited; and, as the executive officer of the bank, transacts much of the business of the institution. In general, the bank is bound by the acts of the cashier within the scope of his authority, expressed or implied. 1 Pet. R. 46, 70; 8 Wheat. R. 300, 361; 5 Wheat. R. 326; 3 Mason's R. 505; 1 Breese, R. 45; 1 Monr. Rep. 179. But the bank is not bound by a declaration of the cashier, not within the scope of his authority; as when a note is about to be discounted by the bank, he tells a person that he will incur no risk nor responsibility by becoming an indorser upon such note. 6 Pet. R. 51; 8 Pet. R. 12. Vide 17 Mass. R. 1; Story on Ag. § 114, 115; 3 Halst. R. 1; 12 Wheat. R. 183; 1 Watts & Serg. 161.

To CASHIER, *punishment*. To break; to deprive a military man of his office. Example: every officer who shall be convicted, before a general court martial, of having signed a false certificate relating to the absence of either officer or private soldier, or relative to his daily pay, shall be cashiered. Articles of war, art. 14.

CASSATION, *French law*. A decision which emanates from the sovereign authority, and by which a sentence or judgment in the last resort is annulled. Merl. Rép. h. t. This jurisdiction is now given to the Cour de Cassation.

2. This court is composed of fifty-two judges, including four presidents, an attorney-general, and six substitutes, bearing the title of advocates general; a chief clerk, four subordinate clerks, and eight huissiers. Its jurisdiction extends to the examination and superintendence of the judgments and decrees of the inferior court, both in civil and criminal cases. It is divided into three sections, namely, the *section des requêtes*, the *section civile*, and the *section criminelle*. Merl. Rép. mots Cour de Cassation.

CASSETUR BREVE, *practice*. That the writ be quashed. This is the name of a judgment sometimes entered against a plaintiff when he cannot prosecute his writ with effect, in consequence of some allegation on the defendant's part. The plaintiff, in order to put an end to any further proceeding in the action, enters on the roll cassetur breve, the effect of which is to quash his own writ, which exonerates him from the liability to any future costs, and allows him to sue out new process. A cassetur billa may be entered with like effect. 3 Bl. Com. 340; and vide 5 T. R. 634; Gould's Plead. c. 5, § 139; 3 Bouv. Inst. n. 2913–14. Vide *To quash*.

CASTIGATORY, *punishments*. An engine used to punish women who have been convicted of being common scolds; it is sometimes called the trebucket, tumbrel, ducking stool, or cucking stool. This barbarous punishment has perhaps never been inflicted in the United States. 12 S. & R. 225. Vide *Common Scold*.

CASTING VOTE, *legislation*. The vote given by the president or speaker of a deliberate assembly; when the votes of the other members are equal on both sides, the casting vote then decides the question. Dane's Ab. h. t.

CASTRATION, *crim. law*. The act of gelding. When this act is maliciously performed upon a man, it is a mayhem, and punishable as such, although the sufferer consented to it.

2. By the ancient law of England this crime was punished by retaliation, *membrum pro membro*. 3 Inst. 118. It is punished in the United States generally by fine and imprisonment. The civil law punished it with death. Dig. 48, 8, 4, 2. For the French law, vide Code Pénal, art. 316.

3. The consequences of castration, when complete, are impotence and sterility. 1 Beck's Med. Jur. 72.

CASU PROVISO, *practice*. A writ of entry given by the statute of Gloucester, c. 7, when a tenant in dower aliens in fee or for life. It might have been brought by the reversioner against the alienee. This is perhaps an obsolete remedy, having yielded to the writ of ejectment. F. N. B. 205; Dane's Ab. Index, h. t.

CASUAL. What happens fortuitously; what is accidental; as, the casual revenues of the government, are those which are contingent or uncertain.

CASUAL EJECTOR, *practice, ejectment.* A person, supposed to come upon land casually, (although usually by previous agreement,) who turns out the lessee of the person claiming the possession against the actual tenant or occupier of the land. 3 Bl. Com. 201, 202.

2. Originally, in order to try the right by ejectment, several things were necessary to be made out before the court; first, a title to the land in question, upon which the owner was to make a formal entry; and being so in possession he executed a lease to some third person or lessee, leaving him in possession; then the prior tenant or some other person, called the casual ejector, either by accident or by agreement beforehand, came upon the land and turned him out, and for this ouster or turning out, the action was brought. But these formalities are now dispensed with, and the trial relates merely to the title, the defendant being bound to acknowledge the lease, entry, and ouster. 3 Bl. Com. 202; Dane's Ab. Index, h. t.

CASUS FŒDERIS. When two nations have formed a treaty of alliance, in anticipation of a war or other difficulty with another, and it is required to determine the case in which the parties must act in consequence of the alliance, this is called the *casus fœderis*, or case of alliance. Vattel, liv. 3, c. 6, § 88.

CASUS FORTUITUS. A fortuitous case; an uncontrollable accident; an act of God. See *Act of God; Cas fortuit; Fortuitous event.*

CASUS OMISSUS. An omitted case.

2. When a statute or an instrument of writing undertakes to foresee and to provide for certain contingencies, and through mistake, or some other cause, a case remains to be provided for, it is said to be a *casus omissus*. For example, when a statute provides for the descent of intestates' estates, and omits a case, the estate descends as it did before the statute, whenever that case occurs, although it appear to be within the general scope and intent of the statute. 2 Binn. R. 279.

3. When there has been a *casus omissus* in a statute, the subject is ruled by the common law: *casus omissus et oblivioni datus dispositioni juris communis relinquitur*. 5 Co. 38. Vide Dig. 38, 1, 44 and 55; Id. 38, 2, 10; Code, 6, 52, 21 and 30.

CATCHING BARGAIN, *contracts, fraud.* An agreement made with an heir expectant, for the purchase of his expectancy, at an inadequate price.

2. In such case, the heir is, in general, entitled to relief in equity, and may have the contract rescinded upon terms of redemption. 1 Vern. 167; 2 Cox, 80; 2 Ch Ca. 136; 2 Vern. 121; 2 Freem. 111; 2 Vent. 329; 2 Rep. in Ch. 396; 1 P. Wms. 312; 3 P. Wms. 290, 293, n.; 1 Cro. C. C. 7; 2 Atk. 133; 2 Swanst. 147, and the cases cited in the note; 1 Fonb. 140; 1 Supp. to Ves. Jr. 66; 2 Id. 361; 1 Vern 320, n. It has been said that all persons dealing for a reversionary interest are subject to this rule, but it may be doubted whether the course of decisions authorizes so extensive a conclusion; and whether, in order to constitute a title to relief, the reversioner must not combine the character of heir. 2 Swanst. 148, n. Vide 1 Ch. Pr 112, 113, n., 458, 826, 838, 839. A mere hard bargain is not sufficient ground for relief.

3. The French law is in unison with these principles. An agreement, which has for its object the succession of a man yet alive, is generally void. Merl. Rép. mots Succession Future. Vide also Dig. 14, 6 and *Lesion.*

CATCHPOLE, *officer.* A name formerly given to a sheriff's deputy, or to a constable, or other officer whose duty it is to arrest persons. He was a sort of serjeant. The word is not now in use as an official designation. Minshew ad verb.

CAUSA MATRIMONII PRÆLOCUTI, *Engl. law.* An obsolete writ, which lies when a woman gives land to a man in fee simple, or for a less estate, to the intent that he should marry her and he refuses upon request. New. Nat. Bre. 455.

CAUSE, *civ. law.* This word has two meanings. 1. It signifies the delivery of the thing, or the accomplishment of the act which is the object of a convention. *Datio vel factum, quibus ab unâ parte conventio, impleri cœpta est.* 6 Toull. n. 13, 166. 2. It is the consideration or motive for making a contract. An obligation without a cause, or with a false or unlawful cause, has no effect; but an engagement is not the less valid, though the cause be not expressed. The cause is illicit, when it is forbidden by law, when it is *contra bones mores*, or public order. Dig. 2, 14, 7, 4; Civ. Code of Lo. a. 1887–1894; Code Civil, liv. 3, c. 2, s. 4, art. 1131–1133; Toull. liv. 3, tit. 3, c. 2, s. 4.

CAUSE, *contr. torts, crim.* That which produces an effect.

2. In considering a contract, an injury, or a crime, the law for many purposes looks to the immediate, and not to any remote cause. Bac. Max. Reg. 1; Bac. Ab. Damages, E; Sid. 433; 2 Taunt. 314. If the cause be lawful, the party will be justified; if unlawful, he will be condemned. The following is an example in criminal law of an immediate and remote cause. If Peter, of malice prepense, should discharge a pistol at Paul, and miss him, and then cast away the pistol and fly; and, being pursued by Paul, he turn round, and kill him with a dagger, the law considers the first as the impulsive cause, and Peter would be guilty of murder. But if Peter, with his dagger drawn, had fallen down, and Paul in his haste had fallen upon it and killed himself, the cause of Paul's death would have been too remote to charge Peter as the murderer. Id.

3. In cases of insurance, the general rule is that the immediate and not the remote cause of the loss is to be considered; *causa proximo non remota spectatur*. This rule may, in some cases, apply to carriers. Story, Bailm. § 515.

4. For the breach of contracts, the contractor is liable for the immediate effects of such breach, but not for any remote cause, as the failure of a party who was to receive money, and did not receive it, in consequence of which he was compelled to stop payment. 1 Brock. Cir. C. Rep. 103. See *Remote;* and also Domat, liv. 3, t. 5, s. 2, n. 4; Toull. liv. 3, n. 286; 6 Bing. R. 716; 6 Ves. 496; Pal. Ag. by Lloyd, 10; Story, Ag. § 200; 3 Sumn. R. 38.

CAUSE, *pleading*. The reason; the motive.

2. In a replication *de injuria*, for example, the plaintiff alleges that the defendant of his own wrong, and *without the cause* by him in his plea alleged, did, &c. The word *cause* here means without the matter of excuse alleged, and though in the singular number, it puts in issue all the facts in the plea, which constitute but one cause. 8 Co. 67; 11 East, 451: 1 Chit. Pl. 585.

CAUSE, *practice*. A contested question before a court of justice; it is a suit or action. Causes are civil or criminal. Wood's Civ. Law, 302; Code, 2, 416.

CAUSE OF ACTION. By this phrase is understood the right to bring an action, which implies, that there is some person in existence who can assert, and also a person who can lawfully be sued; for example, where the payee of a bill was dead at the time when it fell due, it was held the cause of action did not accrue, and consequently the statute of limitations did not begin to run until letters of administration had been obtained by some one. 4 Bing. 686.

2. There is no cause of action till the claimant can legally sue, therefore the statute of limitations does not run from the making of a promise, if it were to perform something at a future time, but only from the expiration of that time, though, when the obligor promises to pay on demand, or generally, without specifying a day, he may be sued immediately, and then the cause of action has accrued. 5 Bar. & Cr. 360; 8 Dowl. & R. 346. When a wrong has been committed, or a breach of duty has occurred, the cause of action has accrued, though the claimant may be ignorant of it. 3 Barn. & Ald. 288, 626; 5 B. & C. 259; 4 C. & P. 127.

CAUTIO PRO EXPENSIS. Security for costs or expenses.

2. This term is used among the civilians, Nov. 112, c. 2, and generally on the continent of Europe. In nearly all the countries of Europe, a foreign plaintiff, whether resident there or not, is required to give caution *pro expensis;* that is, security for costs. In some states this requisition is modified, and, when such plaintiff has real estate, or a commercial or manufacturing establishment within the state, he is not required to give such caution. Fœlix, Droit. Intern. Privé, n. 106.

CAUTION. A term of the Roman civil law, which is used in various senses. It signifies, sometimes, *security*, or security promised. Generally every writing is called *cautio*, a caution by which any object is provided for. Vicat, ad verb. In the common law a distinction is made between a contract and the security. The contract may be good and the security void. The contract may be divisible, and the security entire and indivisible. 2 Burr, 1082. The securities or cautions judicially required of the defendant, are, *judicio sisti*, to attend and appear during the pendency of the suit; *de rato*, to confirm the acts of his attorney or proctor; *judicium solvi*, to pay the sum adjudged against him. Coop. Just. 647; Hall's Admiralty Practice, 12; 2 Brown, Civ. Law, 356.

CAUTION, JURATORY, *Scotch law*. Juratory caution is that which a suspender swears is the best he can offer in order to obtain a suspension. Where the suspender cannot, from his low or suspected circumstances, procure unquestionable security, juratory caution is admitted. Ersk. Pr. L. Scot. 4, 3, 6.

CAUTIONER, *Scotch law, contracts*. One who becomes bound as caution or surety for another, for the performance of any obligation or contract contained in a deed.

CAVEAT, *practice*. That he beware. Caveat is the name of a notice given by a party having an interest, to some officer, not to do an act, till the party giving the notice shall have been heard; as, a caveat to the register of wills, or judge of probate, not to permit a will to be proved, or not to grant letters of administration, until the party shall have been heard. A caveat is also frequently made to prevent a patent for inventions being issued. 1 Bouv. Inst. 71, 534; 1 Burn's Ecc. Law, 19, 263; Bac. Abr. Executors and Administrators, E 8; 3 Bl. Com. 246; Proctor's Pract. 68; 3 Bin. Rep. 314; 1 Siderf. 371; Poph. 133; Godolph. Orph. Leg. 258; 2 Brownl. 119; 2 Fonbl. Eq. book 4, pt. 2, c. 1, § 3; Ayl. Parer. 145; Nelson's Ab. h. t.; Dane's Ab. c. 223, a. 15, § 2, and a. 8, § 22. See 2 Chit. Pr. 502, note *b*, for a form.

CAVEAT EMPTOR. Let the purchaser take heed; that is, let him see to it, that the title he is buying is good. This is a rule of the common law, applicable to the sale and purchase of lands and other real estate. If the purchaser pay the consideration money, he cannot, as a general rule, recover it back after the deed has been executed; except in cases of fraud, or by force of some covenant in the deed which has been broken. The purchaser, if he fears a defect of title, has it in his power to protect himself by proper covenants, and if he fails to do so, the law provides for him no remedy. Cro. Jac. 197; 1 Salk. 211; Doug. 630, 654; 1 Serg. & R. 52, 53, 445. This rule is discussed with ability in Rawle on Covenants for Title, p. 458, et seq. c. 13, and the leading authorities collected. See also 2 Kent, Com. Lect. 39, p. 478; 2 Bl. Com. 451; 1 Story, Eq. § 212; 6 Ves. 678; 10 Ves. 505; 3 Cranch, 270; 2 Day, R. 128; Sugd. Vend. 221; 1 Bouv. Inst. n. 954–5.

2. This rule has been severely assailed, as being the instrument of falsehood and fraud; but it is too well established to be disregarded. Coop. Jnst. 611, n. See 8 Watts, 308, 309.

CAVIL. Sophism, subtlety. Cavil is a captious argument, by which a conclusion evidently false, is drawn from a principle evidently true: *Ea est natura cavillationis ut ab evidenter veris, per brevissimas mutationes disputatio, ad ea quæ evidentur falsa sunt perducatur*. Dig. 50, 16, 177 et 233; Id. 17, 65; Id. 33, 2, 88.

CÆSARIAN OPERATION, *med. juris*. An incision made through the parietes of the abdomen and uterus to extract the fœtus. It is said that Julius Cæsar was born in this manner. When the child is cut out after the death of the mother, his coming into being in this way confers on other persons none of the rights to which they would have been entitled if he had been born, in the usual course of nature, during her life. For example, his father would not be tenant by the curtesy; for to create that title, it ought to begin by the birth of issue alive, and be consummated by the death of the wife. 8 Co. Rep. 35; 2 Bl. Com. 128; Co. Litt. 29 b.; 1 Beck's Med. Jur. 264; Coop. Med. Jur. 7; 1 Foderé, Méd. Lég. § 334. The rule of the civil law on this subject will be found in Dig. lib. 50, t. 16, l. 132 et 141; lib. 5, t. 2, l. 6; lib. 28, t. 2, l. 12.

CÆTERORUM. The name of a kind of administration, which, after an administration has been granted for a limited purpose, is granted for the *rest* of the estate. 1 Will. on Ex. 357; 2 Hagg. 62; 4 Hagg. Eccl. R. 382, 386; 4 Mann. & Gr. 398. For example, where a wife had a right to devise or bequeath certain stock, and she made a will of the same, but there were accumulations that did not pass, the husband might take out letters of administration cæterorum. 4 Mann. & Grang. 398; 1 Curteis, 286.

TO CEDE, *civil law*. To assign; to transfer; as, France ceded Louisiana to the United States.

CEDENT, *civil law, Scotch law*. An assignor. The term is usually applied to the assignor of a chose in action. Kames on Eq. 43.

CELEBRATION, *contracts*. This word is usually applied, in law, to the celebration of marriage, which is the solemn act by which a man and woman take each other for husband and wife, conformably to the rules prescribed by law. Dict. de Juris. h. t.

CELL. A small room in a prison. See *Dungeon*.

CENOTAPH. An empty tomb. Dig. 11, 7, 42.

CENSUS. An enumeration of the inhabitants of a country.

2. For the purpose of keeping the representation of the several states in congress equal, the constitution provides, that "representatives and direct taxes shall be apportioned among the several states, which may be included in this Union, according to their respective numbers; which shall be determined by adding to the whole number of free persons, including those bound to service for a term of years, and excluding Indians not taxed, three-fifths of all other persons. The actual enumeration shall be made within three years after the first meeting of the congress of the United States, and within every subsequent term of ten years, in such a manner as they shall by law direct." Art. 1, s. 2; vide 1 Story, L. U. S., 73, 722, 751; 2 Id. 1134, 1139, 1169, 1194; 3 Id. 1776; 4 Sharsw. continuation, 2179.

CENT, *money*. A copper coin of the United States of the value of ten mills; ten of them are equal to a dime, and one hundred, to one dollar. Each cent is required to contain one hundred and sixty-eight grains. Act of January 18th, 1837, 4 Sharsw. cont. of Story's L. U. S. 2524.

CENTIME. The name of a French money; the one hundredth part of a franc.

CENTRAL. Relating to the centre, or placed in the centre; as, the central courts of the United States, are those located in the city of Washington, whose jurisdiction extends over the whole country. These are, first, the Senate of the United States, when organized to try impeachments; secondly, the Supreme Court of the United States.

2. The government of the United States is the central government.

CENTUMVIRI, *civil law*. The citizens of Rome were distributed into thirty-five tribes, and three persons out of each tribe were elected judges, who were called *centumviri*, although they were one hundred and five in number. They were distributed into four different tribunals, but in certain causes called *centumvirales causas*, the judgments of the four tribunals were necessary. Vicat, ad verb.; 3 Bl. Com. 315.

CENTURY, *civil law*. One hundred. The Roman people were divided into centuries. In England they were divided into hundreds. Vide *Hundred*. Century also means one hundred years.

CEPI. A Latin word signifying I have taken. *Cepi corpus*, I have taken the body; *cepi corpus and B. B.*, I have taken the body and discharged him on bail bond; *cepi corpus et est in custodia*, I have taken the body and it is in custody; *cepi corpus, et est languidus*, I have taken the body of, &c. and he is sick. These are some of the various returns made by the sheriff to a writ of capias.

CEPI CORPUS, *practice*. The return which the sheriff, or other proper officer, makes when he has arrested a defendant by virtue of a capias. 3 Bouv. Inst. n. 2804. See *Capias*. F. N. B. 26.

CEPIT. Took. This is a technical word, which cannot be supplied by any other in an indictment for larceny. The charge against the defendant must be that he *took* the thing stolen with a felonious design. Bac Ab. Indictment, G 1.

CEPIT ET ABDUXIT. He took and led away. These words are applied to cases of trespass or larceny, where the defendant took a living chattel, and led it away. It is used in contradistinction to took and carried away, *cepit et asportavit*. (q. v.)

CEPIT ET ASPORTAVIT. Took and carried away. (q. v.)

CEPIT IN ALIO LOCO, *pleadings*. He took in another place. This is a plea in replevin, by which the defendant alleges, that he took the thing replevied in another place than that mentioned in the plaintiff's declaration. 1 Chit. Pl. 490; 4 Bouv. Inst. n. 3569; 2 Chit. Pl. 558; Rast. 554, 555; Clift. 636; Willes, R. 475; Tidd's App. 686.

CERTAINTY, UNCERTAINTY, *contracts*. In matters of obligation, a thing is certain, when its essence, quality, and quantity, are described, distinctly set forth, &c. Dig. 12, 1, 6. It is uncertain, when the description is not that of one individual object, but designates only the kind. Louis. Code, art. 3522, No. 8; 5 Co. 121. Certainty is the mother of repose, and therefore the law aims at certainty. 1 Dick. 245.

2. If a contract be so vague in its terms, that its meaning cannot be certainly collected, and the statute of frauds preclude the admissibility of parol evidence to clear up the difficulty; 5 Barn. & Cr. 583; S. C. 12 Eng. Com. L. R. 327; or parol evidence cannot supply the defect, then neither at law, nor in equity, can effect be given to it. 1 Russ. & M. 116; 1 Ch. Pr. 123.

3. It is a maxim of law, that, that is certain which may be made certain; certum est quod certum reddi potest; Co. Litt. 43; for example, when a man sells the oil he has in his store at so much a gallon, although there is uncertainty as to the quantity of oil, yet inasmuch as it can be ascertained, the maxim applies, and the sale is good. Vide generally, Story, Eq. El. § 240 to 256; Mitf. Eq. Pl. by Jeremy, 41; Coop. Eq. Pl. 5; Wigr. on Disc. 77.

Certainty, *pleading*. By certainty is understood a clear and distinct statement of the facts which constitute the cause of action, or ground of defence, so that they may be understood by the party who is to answer them, by the jury who are to ascertain the truth of the allegations, and by the court who are to give the judgment. Cowp. 682; Co. Litt. 303; 2 Bos. & Pull. 267; 13 East, R. 107; Com. Dig. Pleader, C 17; Hob. 295. Certainty has been stated by Lord Coke, Co. Litt. 303, a, to be of three sorts; namely, 1. certainty to a common intent; 2. to a certain intent in general; and, 3. to a certain intent in every particular. In the case of Dovaston *v.* Paine, Buller, J. said he remembered to have heard Mr. Justice Ashton treat these distinctions as a jargon of words without meaning; 2 H. Bl. 530. They have, however, long been made, and ought not altogether to be departed from.

2.—1. Certainty to a common intent is simply a rule of construction. It occurs when words are used which will bear a natural sense, and also an artificial one, or one to be made out by argument or inference. Upon the ground of this rule the natural sense of words is adopted without addition. 2 H. Bl. 530.

3.—2. Certainty to a *certain intent in general*, is a greater degree of certainty than the last, and means what upon a fair and reasonable construction may be called certain, without recurring to possible facts which do not appear; 9 Johns. R. 317; and is what is required in declarations, replications, and indictments, in the charge or accusation, and in returns to writs of mandamus. See 1 Saund. 49, n. 1; 1 Dougl. 159; 2 Johns. Cas. 339; Cowp. 682; 2 Mass. R. 363; by some of which authorities, it would seem, certainty to a common intent is sufficient in a declaration.

4.—3. The third degree of certainty, is that which precludes all argument, inference, or presumption against the party pleading, and is that technical accuracy which is not liable to the most subtle and scrupulous objections, so that it is not merely a rule of construction, but of addition; for where this certainty is necessary, the party must not only state the facts of his case in the most precise way, but add to them such as show that they are not to be controverted, and, as it were, anticipate the case of his adversary. Lawes on Pl. 54, 55. See 1 Chitty on Pl. 235 to 241.

CERTIFICATE, *practice*. A writing made in any court, and properly authenticated, to give notice to another court of anything done therein; or it is a writing by which an officer or other person bears testimony that a fact has or has not taken place.

2. There are two kinds of certificates; those required by the law, and those which are merely voluntary. Of the first kind are certificates given to an insolvent of his discharge, and those given to aliens, that they have been naturalized. Voluntary certificates are those which are not required by law, but which are given of the mere motion of the party. The former are evidence of the facts therein mentioned, while the latter are not entitled to any credit, because the facts certified, may be proved in the usual way under the solemnity of an oath or affirmation. 2 Com. Dig. 306; Ayl Parerg. 157; Greenl. Ev. § 498.

Certificate, judge's, *English practice.* The judge who tries the cause is authorized by several statutes in certain cases to certify, so as to decide when the party or parties shall or shall not be entitled to costs. It is of great importance in many cases, that these certificates should be obtained at the time of trial. See 3 Camp. R. 316; 5 B. & A. 796; Tidd's Pr. 879; 3 Ch. Pr. 458, 486.

2. The Lord Chancellor often requires the opinion of the judges upon a question of law; to obtain this, a case is framed, containing the admissions on both sides, and upon these the legal question is stated; the case is then submitted to the judges, who, after hearing counsel, transmit to the chan-

cellor their opinion. This opinion, signed by the judges of the court, is called their *certificate*. See 3 Bl. Com. 453.

CERTIFICATE, ATTORNEY'S, *practice, English law.* By statute 37 Geo. III., c. 90, s. 26, 28, attorneys are required to deliver to the commissioners of stamp duties, a paper or note in writing, containing the name and usual place of residence of such person, and thereupon, on paying certain duties, such person is entitled to a certificate attesting the payment of such duties, which must be renewed yearly. And by the 30th section, an attorney is liable to the penalty of fifty pounds for practising without.

CERTIFICATION or CERTIFICATE OF ASSISE. A term used in the old English law, applicable to a writ granted for the reëxamination or re-trial of a matter passed by assise before justices. F. N. B. 181; 3 Bl. Com. 389. The summary motion for a new trial has entirely superseded the use of this writ, which was one of the means devised by the judges to prevent a resort to the remedy by attaint for a wrong verdict.

CERTIORARI, *practice.* To be certified of; to be informed of. This is the name of a writ issued from a superior court directed to one of inferior jurisdiction, commanding the latter to certify and return to the former, the record in the particular case. Bac. Ab. h. t.; 4 Vin. Ab. 330; Nels. Ab. h. t.; Dane's Ab. Index, h. t.; 3 Penna. R. 24. A certiorari differs from a writ of error. There is a distinction also between a hab. corp. and a certiorari. The certiorari removes the cause; the hab. corp. only supersedes the proceedings in the court below. 2 Lord Ray. 1102.

2. By the common law, a supreme court has power to review the proceedings of all inferior tribunals, and to pass upon their jurisdiction and decisions on questions of law. But in general, the determination of such inferior courts on questions of fact are conclusive, and cannot be reversed on certiorari, unless some statute confers the power on such supreme court. 6 Wend. 564; 10 Pick. 358; 4 Halst. 209. When any error has occurred in the proceedings of the court below, different from the course of the common law, in any stage of the cause, either civil or criminal cases, the writ of certiorari is the only remedy to correct such error, unless some other statutory remedy has been given. 5 Binn. 27; 1 Gill & John. 196; 2 Mass. R. 245; 11 Mass. R. 466; 2 Virg. Cas. 270; 3 Halst. 123; 3 Pick. 194; 4 Hayw. 100; 2 Greenl. 165; 8 Greenl. 293. A certiorari, for example, is the correct process to remove the proceedings of a court of sessions, or of county commissioners in laying out highways. 2 Binn. 250; 2 Mass. 249; 7 Mass. 158; 8 Pick. 440; 13 Pick. 195; 1 Overt. 131; 2 Overt. 109; 2 Pen. 1038; 8 Verm. 271; 3 Ham. 383; 2 Caines, 179.

3. Sometimes the writ of *certiorari* is used as auxiliary process, in order to obtain a full return to some other process. When, for example, the record of an inferior court is brought before a superior court by appeal, writ of error, or other lawful mode, and there is a manifest defect, or a suggestion of diminution, a *certiorari* is awarded requiring a perfect transcript and all papers. 3 Dall. R. 413; 3 John. R. 23; 7 Cranch, R. 288; 2 South. R. 270, 551; 1 Blackf. R. 32; 9 Wheat. R. 526; 7 Halst. R. 85; 3 Dev. R. 117; 1 Dev. & Bat. 382; 11 Mass. 414; 2 Munf. R. 229; 2 Cowen, R. 38. Vide Bouv. Inst. Index, h. t.

CESSET EXECUTIO. The staying of an execution.

2. When a judgment has been entered, there is sometimes, by the agreement of the parties, a *cesset executio* for a period of time fixed upon; and when the defendant enters security for the amount of the judgment, there is a *cesset executio* until the time allowed by law has expired.

CESSET PROCESSUS, *practice.* An entry made on the record that there be a *stay of the process or proceedings.*

2. This is made in cases where the plaintiff has become insolvent after action brought. 2 Dougl. 627.

CESSAVIT, *Eng. law.* An obsolete writ, which could formerly have been sued out when the defendant had for two years *ceased* or neglected to perform such service or to pay such rent as he was bound to do by his tenure, and had not upon his lands sufficient goods or chattels to be distrained. F. N. B. 208.

CESSIO BONORUM, *civil law.* The relinquishment which a debtor made of his property for the benefit of his creditors.

2. This exempted the debtor from imprisonment, not, however, without leaving an ignominious stain on his reputation. Dig. 2, 4, 25; Id. 48, 19, 1; Nov. 4, c. 3, and Nov. 135. By the latter Novel, an honest unfortunate debtor might be discharged, by

simply affirming that he was insolvent, without having recourse to the benefit of cession. By the cession the creditors acquired title to all the property of the insolvent debtor.

3. The cession discharged the debtor only to the extent of the property ceded, and he remained responsible for the difference. Dom. Lois Civ. liv. 4, tit. 5, s. 1, n. 2. Vide, for the law of Louisiana, Code, art. 2166, et seq. 2 M. R. 112; 2 L. R. 354; 11 L. R. 531; 5 N. S. 299; 2 L. R. 39; 2 N. S. 108; 3 M. R. 232; 4 Wheat. 122; and *Abandonment*.

CESSION, *contracts*. Yielding up; release.

2. France ceded Louisiana to the United States, by the treaty of Paris, of April 30, 1803; Spain made a cession of East and West Florida, by the treaty of February 22, 1819. Cessions have been severally made of a part of their territory, by New York, Virginia, Massachusetts, Connecticut, South Carolina, North Carolina, and Georgia. Vide Gord. Dig. art. 2236 to 2250.

CESSION, *civil law*. The act by which a party assigns or transfers property to another; an assignment.

CESSION, *eccl. law*. When an ecclesiastic is created bishop, or when a parson takes another benefice, without dispensation, the first benefice becomes void by a legal cession, or surrender. Cowel, h. t.

CESTUI. He. This word is frequently used in composition; as, cestui que trust, cestui que vie, &c.

CESTUI QUE TRUST. A barbarous phrase, to signify the beneficiary of an estate held in trust. He for whose benefit another person is enfeoffed or seised of land or tenements, or is possessed of personal property. The *cestui que trust* is entitled to receive the rents and profits of the land; he may direct such conveyances, consistent with the trust, deed or will, as he shall choose, and the trustee (q. v.) is bound to execute them: he may defend his title in the name of the trustee. 1 Cruise, Dig. tit. 12, c. 4, s. 4; vide Vin. Ab. Trust, U, W, X, and Y; 1 Vern. 14; Dane's Ab. Index, h. t.; 1 Story, Eq. Jur. § 321, note 1; Bouv. Inst. Index, h. t.

CESTUI QUE VIE. He for whose life land is holden by another person; the latter is called *tenant per auter vie*, or tenant for another's life. Vide Dane's Ab. Index, h. t.

CESTUI QUE USE. He to whose use land is granted to another person; the latter is called the terre-tenant, having in himself the legal property and possession; yet not to his own use, but to dispose of it according to the directions of the cestui que use, and to suffer him to take the profits. Vide Bac. Read. on Stat. of Uses, 303, 309, 310, 335, 349; 7 Com. Dig. 593.

CHAFEWAX, *Eng. law*. An officer in chancery who fits the wax for sealing, to the writs, commissions and other instruments then made to be issued out. He is probably so called because he warms (chaufe) the wax.

CHAFFERS. Anciently signified wares and merchandise; hence the word *chaffering*, which is yet used for buying and selling, or beating down the price of an article. The word is used in stat. 3 Ed. III. c. 4.

CHAIRMAN. The presiding officer of a committee; as, chairman of the committee of ways and means. The person selected to preside over a popular meeting, is also called a chairman or moderator.

CHALDRON. A measure of capacity, equal to fifty-eight and two-third cubic feet nearly. Vide *Measure*.

CHALLENGE. This word has several significations. 1. It is an exception or objection to a juror. 2. A call by one person upon another to a single combat, which is said to be a challenge to fight.

CHALLENGE, *criminal law*. A request by one person to another, to fight a duel.

2. It is a high offence at common law, and indictable, as tending to a breach of the peace. It may be in writing or verbally. Vide Hawk. P. C. b. 1, c. 63, s. 3; 6 East, R. 464; 3 East, R. 581; 1 Dana, R. 524; 1 South. R. 40; 3 Wheel. Cr. C. 245; 3 Rogers' Rec. 133; 2 M'Cord, R. 334; 1 Hawks. R. 487; 1 Const. R. 107. He who carries a challenge is also punishable by indictment. In most of the states, this barbarous practice is punishable by special laws.

3. In most of the civilized nations challenging another to fight, is a crime, as calculated to destroy the public peace; and those who partake in the offence are generally liable to punishment. In Spain, it is punished by loss of offices, rents, and honors received from the king, and the delinquent is incapable to hold them in future. Aso & Man. Inst. B. 2, t. 19, c. 2, § 6. See, generally, 6 J. J. Marsh. 120; 1 Munf. 468; 1 Russ. on Cr. 275; 6 J. J. Marsh. 119; Const. Rep. 107; Joy on Chal. *passim*.

CHALLENGE, *practice*. An exception made to jurors who are to pass on a trial; to a judge; or to a sheriff.

2. It will be proper here to consider, 1. the several kinds of challenges; 2. by whom they are to be made; 3. the time and manner of making them.

3.—§ 1. The several kinds of challenges may be divided into those which are peremptory, and those which are for cause.

1. Peremptory challenges are those which are made without assigning any reason, and which the court must allow. The number of these which the prisoner was allowed at common law, in all cases of felony, was thirty-five, or one under three full juries. This is regulated by the local statutes of the different states, and the number, except in capital cases, has been probably reduced.

4.—2. Challenges for cause are to the array or to the polls. 1. A challenge to the array is made on account of some defect in making the return to the venire, and is at once an objection to all the jurors in the panel. It is either a priucipal challenge, that is, one founded on some manifest partiality, or error committed in selecting, depositing, drawing or summoning the jurors, by not pursuing the directions of the acts of the legislature; or a challenge for favor.

5.—2. A challenge to the polls is an objection made separately to each juryman as he is about to be sworn. Challenges to the polls, like those to the array, are either principal or to the favor.

6. *First*, principal challenges may be made on various grounds: 1st. *propter defectum*, on account of some personal objection, as alienage, infancy, old age, or the want of those qualifications required by legislative enactment. 2d. *Propter affectum*, because of some presumed or actual partiality in the juryman who is made the subject of the objection; on this ground a juror may be objected to, if he is related to either within the ninth degree, or is so connected by affinity; this is supposed to bias the juror's mind, and is only a presumption of partiality. Coxe, 446; 6 Greenl. 307; 3 Day, 491. A juror who has conscientious scruples in finding a verdict in a capital case, may be challenged. 1 Bald. 78. Much stronger is the reason for this challenge, where the juryman has expressed his wishes as to the result of the trial, or his opinion of the guilt or innocence of the defendant. 4 Harg. St. Tr. 748; Hawk. b. 2, c. 43, s. 28; Bac. Ab. Juries, E 5. And the smallest degree of interest in the matter to be tried is a decisive objection against a juror. 1 Bay, 229; 8 S. & R. 444; 2 Tyler, 401. But see 5 Mass. 90. 3d. The third ground of principal challenge to the polls, is *propter delictum*, or the legal incompetency of the juror on the ground of infamy. The court, when satisfied from their own examination, decide as to the principal challenges to the polls, without any further investigation; and there is no occasion for the appointment of triers. Co. Litt. 157, b; Bac. Ab. Juries, E 12; 8 Watts. R. 304.

7.—*Secondly*. Challenges to the poll for favor may be made, when, although the juror is not so evidently partial that his supposed bias will be sufficient to authorize a principal challenge, yet there are reasonable grounds to suspect that he will act under some undue influence or prejudice. The causes for such challenge are manifestly very numerous, and depend on a variety of circumstances. The fact to be ascertained is, whether the juryman is altogether indifferent as he stands unsworn, because, even unconsciously to himself, he may be swayed to one side. The line which separates the causes for principal challenges, and for challenge to the favor, is not very distinctly marked. That the juror has acted as godfather to the child of the prosecutor or defendant, is cause for a principal challenge; Co. Litt. 157, a; while the fact that the party and the juryman are fellow servants, and that the latter has been entertained at the house of the former, is only cause for challenge to the favor. Co. Litt. 147; Bac. Ab. Juries, E 5. Challenges to the favor are not decided upon by the court, but are settled by triers. (q. v.)

8.—§ 2. The challenges may be made by the government, or those who represent it, or by the defendant, in criminal cases; or they may be made by either party in civil cases.

9.—§ 3. As to the time of making the challenge, it is to be observed that it is a general rule, that no challenge can be made either to the array or to the polls, until a full jury have made their appearance, because if that should be the case, the issue will remain pro defectu juratorum; and on this account, the party who intends to challenge the array, may, under such a contingency, pray a tales to complete the number, and then object to the panel. The proper time of challenging, is between the appearance and the swearing of the jurors. The order of making challenges is to the array first, and should not that be supported, then to the polls; challenging any one juror, waives the right of challenging the array. Co. Litt. 158, a; Bac. Ab. Jurics, E 11. The proper manner of making the challenge, is to state all the objections against the jurors at one time; and the party will not be allowed to make a second objection to the same juror, when the first has been overruled. But when a juror has been challenged on one side, and found indifferent, he may still be challenged on the other. When the juror has been challenged for cause, and been pronounced impartial, he may still be challenged peremptorily. 6 T. R. 531; 4 Bl. Com. 356; Hawk. b. 2, c. 46, s. 10.

10. As to the mode of making the challenge, the rule is, that a challenge to the array must be in writing; but when it is only to a single individual, the words "I challenge him" are sufficient in a civil case, or on the part of the defendant, in a criminal case; when the challenge is made for the prosecution, the attorney-general says, "We challenge him." 4 Harg. St. Tr. 740; Tr. per Pais, 172; and see Cro. C. 105; 2 Lil. Entr. 472; 10 Wentw. 474; 1 Chit. Cr. Law, 533 to 551.

11. Interest forms the only ground at common law for challenging a judge. It is no ground of challenge that he has given an opinion in the case before. 4 Bin. 349; 2 Bin. 454. By statute, there are in some states several other grounds of challenge. See Courts of the U. S., 63, 64.

12. The sheriff may be challenged for favor as well as affinity. Co. Litt. 158, a; 10 Serg. & R. 336-7. And the challenge need not be made to the court, but only to the prothonotary. Yet the sheriff cannot be passed by in the direction of process without cause, as he is the proper officer to execute writs, except in case of partiality. Yet if process be directed to the coroner without cause, it is not void. He cannot dispute the authority of the court, but must execute it at his peril, and the misdirection is aided by the statutes of amendment. 11 Serg. & R. 303.

CHAMBER. A room in a house.

2. It was formerly held that no freehold estate could be had in a chamber, but it was afterwards ruled otherwise. When a chamber belongs to one person, and the rest of the house with the land is owned by another the two estates are considered as two separate but adjoining dwelling houses. Co. Litt. 48, b; Bro. Ab. Demand, 20; 4 Mass. 575; 6 N. H. Rep. 555; 9 Pick. R. 297; vide 3 Leon. 210; 3 Watts. R. 243.

3. By chamber is also understood the place where an assembly is held; and, by the use of a figure, the assembly itself is called a chamber.

CHAMBER OF COMMERCE. A society of the principal merchants and traders of a city, who meet to promote the general trade and commerce of the place. Some of these are incorporated, as in Philadelphia.

CHAMBERS, *practice*. When a judge decides some interlocutory matter, which has arisen in the course of the cause, out of court, he is said to make such decision at his chambers. The most usual applications at chambers take place in relation to taking bail, and staying proceedings on process.

CHAMPART, *French law*. By this name was formerly understood the grant of a piece of land by the owner to another, on condition that the latter would deliver to him a portion of the crops. 18 Toull. n. 182.

CHAMPERTOR, *crim. law*. One who makes pleas or suits, or causes them to be moved, either directly or indirectly, and sues them at his proper costs, upon condition of having a part of the gain.

CHAMPERTY, *crimes*. A bargain with a plaintiff or defendant, *campum partire*, to divide the land or other matter sued for between them, if they prevail at law, the champertor undertaking to carry on the suit at his own expense. 1 Pick. 416; 1 Ham. 132; 5 Monr. 416; 4 Litt. 117; 5 John. Ch. R. 44; 7 Port. R. 488.

2. This offence differs from maintenance, in this, that in the latter the person assisting the suitor receives no benefit, while in the former he receives one half, or other portion, of the thing sued for. See *Punishment; Fine; Imprisonment;* 4 Bl. Com. 135.

3. This was an offence in the civil law. Poth. Pand. lib. 3, t. 1; App. n. 1, tom. 3, p. 104; 15 Ves. 139; 7 Bligh's R. 369; S. C. 20 E. C. L. R. 165; 5 Moore & P. 193; 6 Carr. & P. 749; S. C. 25 E. C. L. R. 631; 1 Russ. Cr. 179; Hawk. P. C. b. 1, c. 84, s. 5.

4. To maintain a defendant may be champerty. Hawk. P. C. b. 1, c. 84, s. 8 3 Ham. 541; 6 Monr. 392; 8 Yerg. 484; 8 John. 479; 1 John. Ch. R. 444; 7 Wend. 152; 3 Cowen, 624; 6 Cowen, 90.

CHAMPION. He who fights for another.

or takes his place in a quarrel; it also includes him who fights his own battles. Bract. lib. 4, t. 2, c. 12.

CHANCE, *accident*. As the law punishes a crime only when there is an intention to commit it, it follows that when those acts are done in a lawful business or pursuit by mere chance or accident, which would have been criminal if there had been an intention, express or implied, to commit them, there is no crime. For example, if workmen were employed in blasting rocks in a retired field, and a person not knowing of the circumstance should enter the field, and be killed by a piece of the rock, there would be no guilt in the workmen. 1 East, P. C. 262; Foster, 262; 1 Hale's P. C. 472; 4 Bl. Com. 192. Vide *Accident*.

CHANCE-MEDLEY, *criminal law*. A sudden affray. This word is sometimes applied to any kind of homicide by misadventure, but in strictness it is applicable to such killing only as happens *se defendendo*. (q. v.) 4 Bl. Com. 184.

CHANCELLOR. An officer appointed to preside over a court of chancery, invested with various powers in the several states.

2. The office of chancellor is of Roman origin. He appears, at first, to have been a chief scribe or secretary, but he was afterwards invested with judicial power, and had superintendence over the other officers of the empire. From the Romans, the title and office passed to the church, and therefore every bishop of the catholic church has, to this day, his chancellor, the principal judge of his consistory. When the modern kingdoms of Europe were established upon the ruins of the empire, almost every state preserved its chancellor, with different jurisdictions and dignities, according to their different constitutions. In all he seems to have had a supervision of all charters, letters, and such other public instruments of the crown, as were authenticated in the most solemn manner; and when seals came into use, he had the custody of the public seal.

3. An officer bearing this title is to be found in most countries of Europe, and is generally invested with extensive authority. The title and office of chancellor came to us from England. Many of our state constitutions provide for the appointment of this officer, who is by them, and by the laws of the several states, invested with power as they provide. Vide Encyclopédie, h. t.; Encycl. Amer. h. t.; Dict. de Jur. h. t.; Merl. Rép. h. t.; 4 Vin. Ab. 374; Blake's Ch. Index, h. t.; Woodes. Lect. 95.

CHANCERY. The name of a court exercising jurisdiction at law, but mainly in equity.

2. It is not easy to determine how courts of equity originally obtained the jurisdiction they now exercise. Their authority, and the extent of it, have been subjects of much question, but time has firmly established them; and the limits of their jurisdiction seem to be in a great degree fixed and ascertained. 1 Story on Eq. ch. 2; Mitf. Pl. Introd.; Coop. Eq. Pl. Introd. See also Butler's Reminiscences, 38, 40; 3 Bl. Com. 435; 2 Bin. 135; 4 Bin. 50; 6 Bin. 162; 2 Serg. & R. 356; 9 Serg. & R. 315; for the necessity, origin and use of courts of chancery.

3. The judge of the court of chancery, often called a court of equity, bears the title of chancellor. The equity jurisdiction, in England, is vested, principally, in the high court of chancery. This court is distinct from courts of law. "American courts of equity are, in some instances, distinct from those of law; in others, the same tribunals exercise the jurisdiction both of courts of law and equity, though their forms of proceeding are different in their two capacities. The supreme court of the United States, and the circuit courts, are invested with general equity powers, and act either as courts of law or equity, according to the form of the process and the subject of adjudication. In some of the states, as New York, Virginia, and South Carolina, the equity court is a distinct tribunal, having its appropriate judge, or chancellor, and officers. In most of the states, the two jurisdictions centre in the same judicial officers, as in the courts of the United States; and the extent of equity jurisdiction and proceedings is very various in the different states, being very ample in Connecticut, New York, New Jersey, Maryland, Virginia, and South Carolina, and more restricted in Maine, Massachusetts, Rhode Island, and Pennsylvania. But the salutary influence of these powers on the judicial administration generally, by the adaptation of chancery forms and modes of proceeding to many cases in which a court of law affords but an imperfect remedy, or no remedy at all, is producing a gradual extension of them in those states where they have been, heretofore, very limited."

4. The jurisdiction of a court of equity

differs essentially from that of a court of law. The remedies for wrongs, or for the enforcement of rights, may be distinguished into two classes; "those which are administered in courts of law, and those which are administered in courts of equity. The rights secured by the former are called *legal;* those secured by the latter are called *equitable.* The former are said to be rights and remedies at common law, because recognized and enforced in courts of common law. The latter are said to be rights and remedies in *equity*, because they are administered in courts of equity or chancery, or by proceedings in other courts analogous to those in courts of equity or chancery. Now, in England and America, courts of common law proceed by certain prescribed forms, and give a *general* judgment for or against the defendant. They entertain jurisdiction only in certain actions, and give remedies according to the particular exigency of such actions. But there are many cases in which a simple judgment for either party, without qualifications and conditions, and particular arrangements, will not do entire justice, *ex æquo et bono*, to either party. Some modification of the rights of both parties is required; some restraints on one side or the other; and some peculiar adjustments, either present or future, temporary or perpetual. Now, in all these cases, courts of common law have no methods of proceeding, which can accomplish such objects. Their forms of actions and judgment are not adapted to them. The proper remedy cannot be found, or cannot be administered to the full extent of the relative rights of all parties. Such prescribed forms of actions are not confined to our law. They were known in the civil law; and the party could apply them only to their original purposes. In other cases, he had a special remedy. In such cases, where the courts of common law cannot grant the proper remedy or relief, the law of England and of the United States (in those states where equity is administered) authorizes an application to the courts of equity or chancery, which are not confined or limited in their modes of relief by such narrow regulations, but which grant relief to all parties, in cases where they have rights, *ex æquo et bono*, and modify and fashion that relief according to circumstances. The most general description of a court of equity is, that it has jurisdiction in cases where a plain, adequate and complete remedy cannot be had at law; that is, in common law courts. The remedy must be *plain;* for, if it be doubtful and obscure at law, equity will assert a jurisdiction. So it must be *adequate* at law; for, if it fall short of what the party is entitled to, that founds a jurisdiction in equity. And it must be *complete;* that is, it must attain its full end at law; it must reach the whole mischief and secure the whole right of the party, now and for the future; otherwise equity will interpose, and give relief. The jurisdiction of a court of equity is sometimes concurrent with that of courts of law; and sometimes it is exclusive. It exercises concurrent jurisdiction in cases where the rights are purely of a *legal* nature, but where other and more efficient aid is required than a court of law can afford, to meet the difficulties of the case, and ensure full redress. In some of these cases courts of law formerly refused all redress; but now will grant it. But the jurisdiction having been once justly acquired at a time when there was no such redress at law, it is not now relinquished. The most common exercise of concurrent jurisdiction is in cases of account, accident, dower, fraud, mistake, partnership, and partition. The remedy is here often more complete and effectual than it can be at law. In many cases falling under these heads, and especially in some cases of fraud, mistake and accident, courts of law cannot and do not afford any redress; in others they do, but not always in so perfect a manner. A court of equity also is assistant to the jurisdiction of courts of law, in many cases, where the latter have no like authority. It will remove legal impediments to the fair decision of a question depending at law. It will prevent a party from improperly setting up, at a trial, some title or claim, which would be inequitable. It will compel him to discover, on his own oath, facts which he knows are material to the rights of the other party, but which a court of law cannot compel the party to discover. It will perpetuate the testimony of witnesses to rights and titles, which are in danger of being lost before the matter can be tried. It will provide for the safety of property in dispute pending litigation. It will counteract and control, or set aside, fraudulent judgments. It will exercise, in many cases, an *exclusive* jurisdiction This it does in all cases of merely *equitable rights*, that is, such rights as are not recognized in courts of law. Most cases of trust and confidence fall under this head. Its exclusive jurisdiction is also extensively exercised in granting special relief beyond the reach of the common law. It will grant injunctions to prevent waste, or irreparable injury, or to secure a settled right, or to prevent vexatious litigations, or to compel the restitution of title deeds; it will appoint receivers of property, where it is in danger of misapplication; it will compel the surrender of securities improperly obtained; it will prohibit a party from leaving the country in order to avoid a suit; it will restrain any undue exercise of a legal right, against conscience and equity; it will decree a specific performance of contracts respecting real estates; it will, in many cases, supply the imperfect execution of instruments, and reform and alter them according to the real intention of the parties; it will grant relief in cases of lost deeds or securities; and, in all cases in which its interference is asked, its general rule is, that he who asks equity must do equity. If a party, therefore, should ask to have a bond for a usurious debt given up, equity could not decree it, unless he could bring into court the money honestly due without usury. This is a very general and imperfect outline of the jurisdiction of a court of equity; in respect to which it has been justly remarked, that, in matters within its exclusive jurisdiction, where substantial justice entitles the party to relief, but the positive law is silent, it is impossible to define the boundaries of that jurisdiction, or to enumerate, with precision, its various principles." Ency. Am. art. Equity.

Vide Fonb. Eq.; Story on Eq.; Madd. Ch. Pr.; 10 Amer. Jur. 227; Coop. Eq. Pl.; Redesd. Pl.; Newl. Ch. Practice; Beame's Pl. Eq.; Jeremy on Eq.; Encycl. Amer. article Equity, Court.

CHANGE. The exchange of money for money. The giving, for example, dollars for eagles, dimes for dollars, cents for dimes. This is a contract which always takes place in the same place. By change is also understood small money. Poth. Contr. de Change, n. 1.

CHANGE TICKET. The name given in Arkansas to a species of promissory notes issued for the purpose of making change in small transactions. Ark. Rev. Stat. ch. 24.

CHAPLAIN. A clergyman appointed to say prayers and perform divine service. Each house of congress usually appoints its own chaplain.

CHAPMAN. One whose business is to buy and sell goods or other things. 2 Bl. Com. 476.

CHAPTER, *eccl. law.* A congregation of clergymen. Such an assembly is termed capitulum, which signifies a little head; it being a kind of head, not only to govern the diocese in the vacation of the bishopric, but also for other purposes. Co. Litt. 103.

CHARACTER, *evidence.* The opinion generally entertained of a person derived from the common report of the people who are acquainted with him. 3 Serg. & R 336; 3 Mass. 192; 3 Esp. C. 236.

2. There are three classes of cases on which the moral character and conduct of a person in society may be used in proof before a jury, each resting upon particular and distinct grounds. Such evidence is admissible, 1st. To afford a presumption that a particular party has not been guilty of a criminal act. 2d. To affect the damages in particular cases, where their amount depends on the character and conduct of any individual; and, 3d. To impeach or confirm the veracity of a witness.

3.—1. Where the guilt of an accused party is doubtful, and the character of the supposed agent is involved in the question, a presumption of innocence arises from his former conduct in society, as evidenced by his general character, since it is not probable that a person of known probity and humanity, would commit a dishonest or outrageous act in the particular instance. Such presumptions, however, are so remote from fact, and it is frequently so difficult to estimate a person's real character, that they are entitled to little weight, except in doubtful cases. Since the law considers a presumption of this nature to be admissible, it is in principle admissible whenever a reasonable presumption arises from it, as to the fact in question; in practice it is admitted whenever the character of the party is involved in the issue. See 2 St. Tr. 1038; 1 Coxe's Rep. 424; 5 Serg. & R. 352; 3 Bibb, R. 195; 2 Bibb, R. 286; 5 Day, R. 260; 5 Esp. C. 13; 3 Camp. C. 519; 1 Camp. C. 460; Str. R. 925. Tha. Cr. Cas. 230; 5 Port. 382.

4.—2. In some instances evidence in disparagement of character is admissible, not in order to prove or disprove the commission of a particular fact, but with a view to damages. In actions for criminal conversation with the plaintiff's wife, evidence may be given of the wife's general bad character, for want of chastity, and even of particular acts of adultery committed by her, previous to her intercourse with the defendant. B. N. P. 27, 296; 12 Mod. 232; 3 Esp. C. 236. See 5 Munf. 10. In actions for slander and libel, when the defendant has not justified, evidence of the plaintiff's bad character has also been admitted. 3 Camp. C. 251; 1 M. & S. 284; 2 Esp. C. 720; 2 Nott & M'Cord, 511; 1 Nott & M'Cord, 268; and see 11 Johns. R. 38; 1 Root, R. 449; 1 Johns. R. 46; 6 Penna. St. Rep. 170. The ground of admitting such evidence is, that a person of disparaged fame is not entitled to the same measure of damages with one whose character is unblemished. When, however, the defendant justifies the slander, it seems to be doubtful whether the evidence of reports as to the conduct and character of the plaintiff can be received. See 1 M. & S. 286, n (a); 3 Mass. R. 553; 1 Pick. R. 19. When evidence is admitted touching the general character of a party, it is manifest that it is to be confined to matters in reference to the nature of the charge against him. 2 Wend. 352.

5.—3. The party against whom a witness is called, may disprove the facts stated by him, or may examine other witnesses as to his general character; but they will not be allowed to speak of particular facts or parts of his conduct. B. N. P. 296. For example, evidence of the general character of a prosecutrix for a rape, may be given, as that she was a street walker; but evidence of specific acts of criminality cannot be admitted. 3 Carr. & P. 589. The regular mode is to inquire whether the witness under examination has the means of knowing the former witness' general character, and whether from such knowledge he would believe him on his oath. 4 St. Tr. 693; 4 Esp. C. 102. In answer to such evidence against character, the other party may cross-examine the witness as to his means of knowledge, and the grounds of his opinion; or he may attack such witness' general character, and by fresh evidence support the character of his own. 2 Stark. C. 151; Id. 241; St. Ev. pt. 4, 1753 to 1758; 1 Phil. Ev. 229. A party cannot give evidence to confirm the good character of a witness, unless his general character has been impugned by his antagonist. 9 Watts, R. 124.

See, in general, as to character, Phil. Ev. Index, tit. Character; Stark. Ev. pl. 4, 364; Swift's Ev 140 to 144; 5 Ohio R. 227; Greenl. Ev. § 54; 3 Hill, R. 178; Bouv Inst. Index, h. t.

CHARGE, *practice.* The opinion expressed by the court to the jury, on the law arising out of a case before them.

2. It should contain a clear and explicit exposition of the law, when the points of the law in dispute arise out of the facts proved on the trial of the cause; 10 Pet. 657; but the court ought at no time to undertake to decide the facts, for these are to be decided by the jury. 4 Rawle's R. 195; 2 Penna. R. 27; 4 Rawle's R. 356; Id. 100; 2 Serg. & Rawle, 464; 1 Serg. & Rawle, 515; 8 Serg. & Rawle, 150. See 3 Cranch, 298; 6 Pet. 622; 1 Gall. R. 53; 5 Cranch, 187; 2 Pet. 625; 9 Pet. 541.

CHARGE, *contracts.* An obligation entered into by the owner of an estate which makes the estate responsible for its performance. Vide 2 Ball & Beatty, 223; 8 Com. Dig. *306, Appendix, h. t. Any obligation binding upon him who enters into it, which may be removed or taken away by a discharge. T. de la Ley, h. t.

2. That particular kind of commission which one undertakes to perform for another, in keeping the custody of his goods, is called a charge.

CHARGE, *wills, devises.* An obligation which a testator imposes on his devisee; as, if the testator give Peter, Blackacre, and direct that he shall pay to John during his life an annuity of one hundred dollars, which shall be a charge on said land; or if a legacy be given and directed to be paid out of the real property. 1 Rop. Leg. 446. Vide 4 Vin. Ab. 449; 1 Supp. to Ves. jr. 309; 2 Id. 31; 1 Vern. 45, 411; 1 Swanst. 28; 4 East, R. 501; 4 Ves. jr. 815; Domat, Loix Civ. liv. 3, t. 1, s. 8, n. 2.

CHARGE' DES AFFAIRES or CHARGE' D'AFFAIRES, *international law.* These phrases, the first of which is used in the acts of congress, are synonymous.

2. The officer who bears this title is a diplomatic representative or minister of an inferior grade, to whose care are confided the affairs of his nation. He has not the title of minister, and is generally introduced and admitted through a verbal presentation of the minister, at his departure, or through letters of credence addressed to the minister of state of the court to which they are sent. He has the essential rights of a minister. Mart. Law of Nat. 206; 1 Kent, Com. 39, n.; 4 Dall. 321.

3. The president is authorized to allow

to any chargé des affaires a sum not greater than at the rate of four thousand five hundred dollars per annum, as a compensation for his personal services and expenses. Act of May 1, 1810, 2 Story's Laws U. S. 1171.

CHARGER, *Scotch law*. He in whose favor a decree suspended is pronounced; yet a decree may be suspended before a charge is given on it. Ersk. Pr. L. Scot. 4, 3, 7.

CHARGES. The term charges signifies the expenses which have been incurred in relation either to a transaction or to a suit; as the charges incurred for his benefit must be paid by a hirer; the defendant must pay the charges of a suit. The term charges, in relation to actions, includes something more than the costs, technically called.

CHARITY. In its widest sense it denotes all the good affections which men ought to bear towards each other; 1 Epistle to Cor. c. xiii.; in its most restricted and usual sense, it signifies relief to the poor. This species of charity is a mere moral duty, which cannot be enforced by the law. Kames on Eq. 17. But it is not employed in either of these senses in law; its signification is derived chiefly from the statute of 43 Eliz. c. 4. Those purposes are considered charitable which are enumerated in that act, or which by analogy are deemed within its spirit and intendment. 9 Ves. 405; 10 Ves, 541; 2 Vern. 387; Shelf. Mortm. 59. Lord Chancellor Camden describes a charity to be a gift to a general public use, which extends to the rich as well as to the poor. Ambl. 651; Boyle on Charities, 51; 2 Ves. sen. 52; Ambl. 713; 2 Ves. jr. 272; 6 Ves. 404; 3 Rawle, 170; 1 Penna. R. 49; 2 Dana, 170; 2 Pet. 584; 3 Pet. 99, 498; 9 Cow. 481; 1 Hawks, 96; 12 Mass. 537; 17 S. & R. 88; 7 Verm. 241; 5 Harr. & John. 392; 6 Harr. & John. 1; 9 Pet. 566; 6 Pet. 435; 9 Cranch, 331; 4 Wheat. 1; 9 Wend. 394; 2 N. H. Rep. 21, 510; 9 Cow. 437; 7 John. Ch. R. 292; 3 Leigh. 450; 1 Dev. Eq. Rep. 276, 4 Bouv. Inst. n. 3976, et seq.

CHARRE OF LEAD, *Eng. law, commerce*. A quantity of lead consisting of thirty pigs, each pig containing six stones wanting two pounds, and every stone being twelve pounds. Jacob.

CHARTA. An ancient word which signified not only a charter or deed in writing, but any signal or token by which an estate was held.

CHARTA CHYROGRAPHATA VEL COMMUNIS. Signifies an indenture. Shep. Touch. 50; Beames, Glanv. 197-8; Fleta, lib. 3, c. 14, § 3. It was so called, because each party had a part.

CHARTA DE UNA PARTE. A deed of one part; a deed poll.

2. Formerly this phrase was used to distinguish a *deed poll*, which is an agreement made by one party only, that is, only one of the parties does any act which is binding upon him, from a deed *inter partes*. Co. Litt. 229. Vide *Deed poll; Indenture; Inter partes*.

CHARTER. A grant made by the sovereign either to the whole people or to a portion of them, securing to them the enjoyment of certain rights. Of the former kind is the late charter of France, which extended to the whole country; the charters which were granted to the different American colonies by the British government were charters of the latter species. 1 Story, Const. L. § 161; 1 Bl. Com. 108; Encycl Amer. Charte Constitutionelle.

2. A charter differs from a constitution in this, that the former is granted by the sovereign, while the latter is established by the people themselves: both are the fundamental law of the land.

3. This term is susceptible of another signification. During the middle ages almost every document was called *carta, charta*, or *chartula*. In this sense the term is nearly synonymous with deed. Co. Litt. 6; 1 Co. 1; Moor. Cas. 687.

4. The act of the legislature creating a corporation, is called its charter. Vide 3 Bro. Civ. and Adm. Law, 188; Dane's Ab. h. t.

CHARTER, *mar. contr*. An agreement by which a vessel is hired by the owner to another; as A B chartered the ship Benjamin Franklin to C D.

CHARTER-LAND, *Eng. law*. Land formerly held by deed under certain rents and free services, and it differed in nothing from free socage land. It was also called bookland. 2 Bl. Com. 90.

CHARTER-PARTY, *contracts*. A contract of affreightment in writing, by which the owner of a ship or other vessel lets the whole, or a part of her, to a merchant or other person for the conveyance of goods, on a particular voyage, in consideration of the payment of freight. This term is derived from the fact, that the contract which bears this name, was formerly written on a card, and afterwards the card was cut into two parts from top to bottom, and one part was delivered to each of the parties, which was produced when required, and by this means counterfeits were prevented.

2. This instrument ought to contain, 1. the name and tonnage of the vessel; 2. the name of the captain; 3. the names of the letter to freight and the freighter; 4. the place and time agreed upon for the loading and discharge; 5. the price of the freight; 6. the demurrage or indemnity in case of delay; 7. such other conditions as the parties may agree upon. Abbott on Ship. pt. 3, c. 1, s. 1 to 6; Poth. h. t. n. 4; Pardessus, Dr. Com. pt. 4, t. 4, c. 1, n. 708.

3. When a ship is chartered, this instrument serves to authenticate many of the facts on which the proof of her neutrality must rest, and should therefore be always found on board chartered ships. 1 Marsh. Ins. 407. When the goods of several merchants unconnected with each other, are laden on board without any particular contract of affreightment with any individual for the entire ship, the vessel is called a *general ship*, (q. v.) because open to all merchants; but where one or more merchants contract for the ship exclusively, it is said to be a *chartered* ship. 3 Kent, Com. 158; Abbott, Ship. pt. 2, c. 2, s. 1; Harr. Dig. Ship. and Shipping, iv.

CHARTERED SHIP. When a ship is hired or freighted by one or more merchants for a particular voyage or on time, it is called a chartered ship. It is freighted by a special contract of affreightment, executed between the owners, ship's husband, or master on the one hand, and the merchants on the other. It differs from a *general ship*. (q. v.)

CHARTIS REDDENDIS, *Eng. law*. An ancient writ, now obsolete, which lays against one who had charters of feoffment entrusted to his keeping, and who refused to deliver them. Reg. Orig. 159.

CHASE, *Eng. law*. The liberty of keeping beasts of chase, or royal game, on another man's ground as well as on one's own ground, protected even from the owner of the land, with a power of hunting them thereon. It differs from a park, because it may be on another's ground, and because it is not enclosed. 2 Bl. Com. 38.

CHASE, *property*. The act of acquiring possession of animals *feræ naturæ* by force, cunning or address. The hunter acquires a right to such animals by occupancy, and they become his property. 4 Toull. n. 7. No man has a right to enter on the lands of another for the purpose of hunting, without his consent. Vide 14 East, R. 249; Poth. Tr. du Dr. de Propriété, part 1, c. 2, art. 2.

CHASTITY. That virtue which prevents the unlawful commerce of the sexes.

2. A woman may defend her chastity by killing her assailant. See *Self-defence*. And even the solicitation of her chastity is indictable in some of the states; 7 Conn. 267; though in England, and perhaps elsewhere, such act is not indictable. 2 Chit. Pr. 478. Words charging a woman with a violation of chastity are actionable in themselves. 2 Conn. 707.

CHATTELS, *property*. A term which includes all kinds of property, except the freehold or things which are parcel of it. It is a more extensive term than *goods* or *effects*. Debtors taken in execution, captives, apprentices, are accounted chattels. Godol. Orph. Leg. part 3, chap. 6, § 1.

2. Chattels are personal or real. *Personal*, are such as belong immediately to the person of a man; chattels *real*, are such as either appertain not immediately to the person, but to something by way of dependency, as a box with the title deeds of lands; or such as are issuing out of some real estate, as a lease of lands, or term of years, which pass like personalty to the executor of the owner. Co. Litt. 118; 1 Chit. Pr. 90; 8 Vin. Ab. 296; 11 Vin. Ab. 166; 14 Vin. Ab. 109; Bac. Ab. Baron, &c. C 2; 2 Kent, Com. 278; Dane's Ab. Index, h. t.; Com. Dig. Biens, A; Bouv. Inst. Index, h. t.

CHEAT, *criminal law, torts*. A cheat is a deceitful practice, of a public nature, in defrauding another of a known right, by some artful device, contrary to the plain rules of common honesty. 1 Hawk. 343.

2. To constitute a cheat, the offence must be, 1st. of a public nature; for every species of fraud and dishonesty in transactions between individuals is not the subject-matter of a criminal charge at common law; it must be such as is calculated to defraud numbers, and to deceive the people in general. 2 East, P. C. 816; 7 John. R. 201; 14 John. R. 371; 1 Greenl. R. 387; 6 Mass. R. 72; 9 Cowen, R. 588; 9 Wend. R. 187; 1 Yerg. R. 76; 1 Mass. 137. 2. The cheating must be done by false weights, false measures, false tokens, or the like, calculated to deceive numbers. 2 Burr,

1125; 1 W. Bl. R. 273; Holt, R. 354. 3. That the object of the defendant in defrauding the prosecutor was successful. If unsuccessful, it is a mere attempt. (q. v.) 2 Mass. 139. When two or more enter into an agreement to cheat, the offence is a conspiracy. (q. v.) To call a man a cheat is slanderous. Hetl. 167; 1 Roll's Ab. 53; 2 Lev. 62. Vide *Illiterate; Token.*

CHECK, *contracts.* A written order or request, addressed to a bank or persons carrying on the banking business, and drawn upon them by a party having money in their hands, requesting them to pay on presentment to a person therein named or to bearer, a named sum of money.

2. It is said that checks are uniformly payable to bearer: Chit. on Bills, 411; but that is not so in practice in the United States; they are generally payable to bearer, but sometimes they are payable to order.

3. Checks are negotiable instruments, as bills of exchange; though, strictly speaking, they are not due before payment has been demanded, in which respect they differ from promissory notes and bills of exchange payable on a particular day. 7 T. R. 430.

4. The differences between a common check and a bill of exchange, are, First, that a check may be taken after it is overdue, and still the holder is not subject to the equities which may exist between the drawer and the party from whom he receives it; in the case of bills of exchange, the holder is subject to such equity. 3 John. Cas. 5, 9; 9 B. & Cr. 388. Secondly, the drawer of a bill of exchange is liable only on the condition that it be presented in due time, and, if it be dishonored, that he has had notice; but such is not the case with a check, no delay will excuse the drawer of it, unless he has suffered some loss or injury on that account, and then only *pro tanto.* 3 Kent, Com. 104 n. 5th ed.; 3 John. Cas. 2; Story, Prom. Notes, § 492.

5. There is a kind of check known by the name of *memorandum* checks; these are given in general with an understanding that they are not to be presented at the bank on which they are drawn for payment; and, as between the parties, they have no other effect than an I O U, or common due bill; but third persons who become the holders of them, for a valuable consideration, without notice, have all the rights which the holders of ordinary checks can lawfully claim. Story, Prom. Notes, § 499.

6. Giving a creditor a check on a bank does not constitute payment of a debt. 1 Hall, 56, 78; 7 S. & R. 116; 2 Pick. 204; 4 John. 296. See 3 Rand. 481. But a tender was held good when made by a check contained in a letter, requesting a receipt in return, which the plaintiff sent back, demanding a larger sum, without objecting to the nature of the tender. 3 Bouv. Inst. n. 2436.

7. A check delivered by a testator in his lifetime to a person as a gift, and not presented till after his death, was considered as a part of his will, and allowed to be proved as such. 3 Curt. Ecc. R. 650. Vide, generally, 4 John. R. 304; 7 John. R. 26; 2 Ves. jr. 111; Yelv. 4, b, note; 7 Serg. & Rawle, 116; 3 John. Cas. 5, 259; 6 Wend. R. 445; 2 N. & M. 251; 1 Blackf. R. 104; 1 Litt. R. 194; 2 Litt. R. 299; 6 Cowen, R. 484; 4 Har. & J. 276; 13 Wend. R. 133; 10 Wend. R. 304; 7 Har. & J. 381; 1 Hall, R. 78; 15 Mass. R. 74; 4 Yerg. R. 210; 9 S. & R. 125; 2 Story, R. 502; 4 Whart. R. 252.

CHECK BOOK, *commerce.* One kept by persons who have accounts in bank, in which are printed blank forms of checks, or orders upon the bank to pay money.

CHEMISTRY, *med. jur.* The science which teaches the nature and property of all bodies by their analysis and combination. In considering cases of poison, the lawyer will find a knowledge of chemistry, even very limited in degree, to be greatly useful. 2 Chit. Pr. 42, n.

CHEVISANCE, *contracts, torts.* This is a French word, which signifies in that language, accord, agreement, compact. In the English statutes it is used to denote a bargain or contract in general. In a legal sense it is taken for an unlawful bargain or contract.

CHIEF, *principal.* One who is put above the rest; as, chief magistrate; chief justice: it also signifies the best of a number of things. It is frequently used in composition.

CHIEF CLERK IN THE DEPARTMENT OF STATE. This officer is appointed by the secretary of state; his duties are to attend to the business of the office under the superintendence of the secretary; and when the secretary shall be removed from office, by the president, or in any other case of vacancy, shall, during such vacancy, have the charge and custody of all records, books and papers appertaining to such department.

Act of the 27th of July, 1789, s. 2, 1 Story's Laws, 6. His compensation for his services shall not exceed two thousand dollars per annum. Gordon's Dig. art. 211.

CHIEF JUSTICE, *officer*. The president of a supreme court; as, the chief justice of the United States, the chief justice of Pennsylvania, and the like. Vide 15 Vin. Ab. 3.

CHIEF JUSTICIARY. An officer among the English, established soon after the conquest.

2. He had judicial power, and sat as a judge in the *Curia Regis*. (q. v.) In the absence of the king, he governed the kingdom. In the course of time, the power and distinction of this officer gradually diminished, until the reign of Henry III., when the office was abolished.

CHILD, CHILDREN, *domestic relations*. A child is the son or daughter in relation to the father or mother.

2. We will here consider the law, in general terms, as it relates to the condition, duties, and rights of children; and, afterwards, the extent which has been given to the word child or children by dispositions in wills and testaments.

3.—1. Children born in lawful wedlock, or within a competent time afterwards, are presumed to be the issue of the father, and follow his condition; those born out of lawful wedlock, follow the condition of the mother. The father is bound to maintain his children and to educate them, and to protect them from injuries. Children are, on their part, bound to maintain their fathers and mothers, when in need, and they are of ability so to do. Poth. Du Marriage, n. 384, 389. The father in general is entitled to the custody of minor children, but, under certain circumstances, the mother will be entitled to them, when the father and mother have separated. 5 Binn. 520. Children are liable to the reasonable correction of their parents. Vide *Correction*.

4.—2. The term children does not ordinarily and properly speaking comprehend grandchildren, or issue generally; yet sometimes that meaning is affixed to it, in cases of necessity; 6 Co. 16; and it has been held to signify the same as issue, in cases where the testator, by using the terms children and issue indiscriminately, showed his intention to use the former term in the sense of issue, so as to entitle grandchildren, &c., to take under it. 1 Ves. sen. 196; Ambl. 555; 3 Ves. 258; Ambl. 661; 3 Ves. & Bea. 69. When legally construed, the term children is confined to legitimate children. 7 Ves. 458. The civil code of Louisiana, art. 2522, n. 14, enacts, that "under the name of children are comprehended, not only children of the first degree, but the grandchildren, great-grandchildren, and all other descendants in the direct line."

5. Children are divided into legitimate children, or those born in lawful wedlock; and natural or illegitimate children, who are born bastards. (q. v.) Vide *Natural Children*. Illegitimate children are incestuous bastards, or those which are not incestuous.

6. Posthumous children are those who are born after the death of their fathers. Domat, Lois Civ. liv. prel. t. 2, s. 1, § 7; L. 3, § 1, ff de inj. rupt.

7. In Pennsylvania, the will of their fathers, in which no provision is made for them, is revoked, as far as regards them, by operation of law. 3 Binn. R. 498. See, as to the law of Virginia on this subject, 3 Munf. 20, and article *In ventre sa mere*.

Vide, generally, 8 Vin. Ab. 318; 8 Com. Dig. 470; Bouv. Inst. Index, h. t.; 2 Kent, Com. 172; 4 Kent, Com. 408, 9; 1 Rop. on Leg. 45 to 76; 1 Supp. to Ves. jr. 44; 2 Id. 158; *Natural children*.

CHILDISHNESS. Weakness of intellect, such as that of a child.

2. When the childishness is so great that a man has lost his memory, or is incapable to plan a proper disposition of his property, he is unable to make a will. Swinb. part. 11, § 1; 6 Co. 23. See 9 Conn. 102; 9 Phil. R. 57.

CHIMIN. This is a corruption of the French word *chemin*, a highway. It is used by old writers. Com. Dig. Chimin.

CHINESE INTEREST. Interest for money charged in China. In a case where a note was given in China, payable eighteen months after date, without any stipulation respecting interest, the court allowed the Chinese interest of one per cent. per month, from the expiration of the eighteen months. 2 Watts & Serg. 227, 264.

CHIROGRAPH, *conveyancing*. Signifies a deed of public instrument in writing. Chirographs were anciently attested by the subscription and crosses of witnesses; afterwards, to prevent frauds and concealments, deeds of mutual covenant were made in a *script* and *rescript*, or in a part and counterpart; and in the middle, between the two copies, they drew the capital letters of the alphabet, and then tallied, or cut asunder in an indented manner, the sheet or skin of parchment, one of which parts being delivered to each of the parties, were proved authentic by matching with and answering to one another. Deeds thus made were denominated *syngrapha*, by the canonists, because that word, instead of the letters of the alphabet, or the word *chirographum*, was used. 2 Bl. Com. 296. This method of preventing counterfeiting, or of detecting counterfeits, is now used by having some ornament or some word engraved or printed at one end of certificates of stocks, checks, and a variety of other instruments, which are bound up in a book, and after they are executed, are cut asunder through such ornament or word.

2. Chirograph is also the last part of a fine of land, commonly called the foot of the fine. It is an instrument of writing beginning with these words: "This is the final agreement," &c. It includes the whole matter, reciting the parties, day, year and place, and before whom the fine was acknowledged and levied. Cruise, Dig. tit. 35, c. 2, s. 52. Vide Chambers' Dict. h. t.; Encyclopædia Americana, Charter; Encyclopédie de D'Alembert, h. t.; Pothier, Pand. tom. xxii. p. 73.

CHIROGRAPHER. A word derived from the Greek, which signifies "a writing with a man's hand." A chirographer is an officer of the English court of C. P. who engrosses the fines, and delivers the indentures of them to the parties, &c.

CHIVALRY, *ancient Eng. law.* This word is derived from the French *chevelier*, a horseman. It is the name of a tenure of land by knight's service. Chivalry was of two kinds: the first, which was *regal*, or held only of the king; or *common*, which was held of a common person. Co. Litt. h. t.

CHOICE. Preference either of a person or thing, to one of several other persons or things. *Election.* (q. v.)

CHOSE, *property.* This is a French word, signifying *thing*. In law, it is applied to personal property; as *choses in possession*, are such personal things of which one has possession; *choses in action*, are such as the owner has not the possession, but merely a right of action for their possession. 2 Bl. Com. 389, 397; 1 Chit. Pract. 99; 1 Supp. to Ves. Jr. 26, 59. Chitty defines choses in actions to be rights to receive or recover a debt, or money, or damages for breach of contract, or for a tort connected with contract, but which cannot be enforced without action, and therefore termed choses, or things in action. Com. Dig. Biens; Harr. Dig. Chose in Action; Chitty's Eq. Dig. h. t. Vide 1 Ch. Pr. 140.

2. It is one of the qualities of a chose in action, that, at common law, it is not assignable. 2 John. 1; 15 Mass. 388; 1 Cranch, 367. But bills of exchange and promissory notes, though choses in action, may be assigned by indorsement, when payable to order, or by delivery when payable to bearer. See *Bills of Exchange.*

3. Bonds are assignable in Pennsylvania, and perhaps some other states, by virtue of statutory provisions. In equity, however, all choses in action are assignable, and the assignee has an equitable right to enforce the fulfilment of the obligation in the name of the assignor. 4 Mass. 511; 3 Day, 364; 1 Wheat. 236; 6 Pick. 316; 9 Cow. 34; 10 Mass. 316; 11 Mass. 157, n.; 9 S. & R. 244; 3 Yeates, 327; 1 Binn. 429; 5 Stew. & Port. 60; 4 Rand. 266; 7 Conn. 399; 2 Green, 510; Harp. 17; Vide, generally, Bouv. Inst. Index, h. t.

4. Rights arising ex delicto are not assignable either at law or in equity.

CHRISTIANITY. The religion established by Jesus Christ.

2. Christianity has been judicially declared to be a part of the common law of Pennsylvania; 11 Serg. & Rawle, 394; 5 Binn. R. 555; of New York, 8 Johns. R. 291; of Connecticut, 2 Swift's System, 321; of Massachusetts, Dane's Ab. vol. 7, c. 219, a. 2, 19. To write or speak contemptuously and maliciously against it, is an indictable offence. Vide Cooper on the Law of Libel, 59 and 114, et seq.; and generally, 1 Russ. on Cr. 217; 1 Hawk, c. 5; 1 Vent. 293; 3 Keb. 607; 1 Barn. & Cress. 26. S. C. 8 Eng. Com. Law R. 14; Barnard. 162; Fitzgib. 66; Roscoe, Cr. Ev. 524; 2 Str. 834; 3 Barn. & Ald. 161; S. C. 5 Eng. Com. Law R 249; Jeff. Rep. Appx. See 1 Cro. Jac 421; Vent. 293; 3 Keb. 607; Cooke on Def. 74; 2 How. S. C. Rep. 127, 197 to 201.

CHURCH. In a moral or spiritual sense this word signifies a society of persons who profess the Christian religion; and in a physical or material sense, the place where such persons assemble. The term church is *nomen collectivum;* it comprehends the chancel, aisles, and body of the church Ham. N. P. 204.

2. By the English law, the terms church or chapel, and church-yard, are expressly recognized as in themselves correct and technical descriptions of the building and place, even in criminal proceedings. 8 B. & C. 25; 1 Salk. 256; 11 Co. 25 b; 2 Esp. 5, 28.

3. It is not within the plan of this work to give an account of the different local regulations in the United States respecting churches. References are here given to enable the inquirer to ascertain what they are, where such regulations are known to exist. 2 Mass. 500; 3 Mass. 166; 8 Mass. 96; 9 Mass. 277; Id. 254; 10 Mass. 323; 15 Mass. 296; 16 Mass. 488; 6 Mass. 401; 10 Pick. 172; 4 Day, C. 361; 1 Root § 3, 440; Kirby, 45; 2 Caines' Cas. 336; 10 John. 217; 6 John. 85; 7 John. 112; 8 John. 464; 9 John. 147; 4 Desaus. 578; 5 Serg. & Rawle, 510; 11 Serg. & Rawle, 35; Metc. & Perk. Dig. h. t.; 4 Whart. 531.

CHURCH-WARDEN. An officer whose duties are, as the name implies, to take care of, or guard the church.

2. These officers are created in some ecclesiastical corporations by the charter, and their rights and duties are definitely explained. In England, it is said, their principal duties are to take care of, 1. the church or building; 2. the utensils and furniture; 3. the church-yard; 4. certain matters of good order concerning the church and church-yard; 5. the endowments of the church. Bac. Ab. h. t. By the common law, the capacity of church-wardens to hold property for the church, is limited to personal property. 9 Cranch, 43.

CINQUE PORTS, *Eng. law*. Literally, five ports. The name by which the five ports of Hastings, Ramenhale, Hetha or Hethe, Dover, and Sandwich, are known.

2. These ports have peculiar charges and services imposed upon them, and were entitled to certain privileges and liberties. See Harg. L. Tr. 106—113.

CIPHER. An arithmetical character, used for numerical notation. Vide *Figures*, and 13 Vin. Ab. 210; 18 Eng. C. L. R. 95; 1 Ch. Cr. Law, 176.

2. By cipher is also understood a mode of secret writing. Public ministers and other public agents frequently use ciphers in their correspondence, and it is sometimes very useful so to correspond in times of war. A key is given to each minister before his departure, namely, the cipher for writing ciphers, (*chiffre chiffrant*,) and the cipher for deciphering (*chiffre dechiffrant*.) Besides these, it is usual to give him a common cipher, (*chiffre banal*,) which is known to all the ministers of the same power, who occasionally use it in their correspondence with each other.

3. When it is suspected that a cipher becomes known to the cabinet where the minister is residing, recourse is had to a preconcerted *sign* in order to annul, entirely or in part, what has been written in cipher, or rather to indicate that the contents are to be understood in an inverted or contrary sense. A *cipher of reserve* is also employed in extraordinary cases.

CIRCUIT COURT. The name of a court of the United States, which has both civil and criminal jurisdiction. In several of the states there are courts which bear this name. Vide *Courts of the United States*.

CIRCUITY OF ACTION, *practice, remedies*. It is where a party, by bringing an action, gives an action to the defendant against him.

2. As, supposing the obligee of a bond covenanted that he would not sue on it; if he were to sue he would give an action against himself to the defendant for a breach of his covenant. The courts prevent such circuitous actions, for it is a maxim of law, so to judge of contracts as to prevent a multiplicity of actions; and in the case just put, they would hold that the covenant not to sue, operated as a release. 1 T. R. 441. It is a favorite object of courts of equity to prevent a multiplicity of actions. 4 Cowen, 682.

CIRCUITS. Certain divisions of the country, appointed for particular judges to visit for the trial of causes, or for the administration of justice. See 3 Bl. Com. 58; 3 Bouv. Inst. n. 2532.

CIRCULATING MEDIUM. By this term is understood whatever is used in making payments, as money, bank notes, or paper which passes from hand to hand in payment of goods, or debts.

CIRCUMDUCTION, *Scotch law*. A term applied to the time allowed for bringing proof of allegiance, which being elapsed, if either party sue for circumduction of the time of proving, it has the effect that no proof can afterwards be brought; and the cause must be determined as it stood when circumduction was obtained. Tech. Dict.

CIRCUMSTANCES, *evidence*. The particulars which accompany a fact.

2. The facts proved are either possible or impossible, ordinary and probable, or extraordinary and improbable, recent or ancient; they may have happened near us, or afar off; they are public or private, permanent or transitory, clear and simple, or complicated; they are always accompanied by circumstances which more or less influence the mind in forming a judgment. And in some instances these circumstances assume the character of irresistible evidence; where, for example, a woman was found dead in a room, with every mark of having met with a violent death, the presence of another person at the scene of action was made manifest by the bloody mark of a *left* hand visible on her *left* arm. 14 How. St. Tr. 1324. These points ought to be carefully examined, in order to form a correct opinion. The first question ought to be, is the fact possible? If so, are there any circumstances which render it impossible? If the facts are impossible, the witness ought not to be credited. If, for example, a man should swear that he saw the deceased shoot himself with his own pistol, and upon an examination of the ball which killed him, it should be found too large to enter into the pistol, the witness ought not to be credited. 1 Stark. Ev. 505; or if one should swear that another had been guilty of an impossible crime.

3. Toullier mentions a case, which, were it not for the ingenuity of the counsel, would require an apology for its introduction here, on account of its length. The case was this:—La Veuve Veron brought an action against M. de Morangiès on some notes, which the defendant alleged were fraudulently obtained, for the purpose of recovering 300,000 francs, and the question was, whether the defendant had received the money. Dujonquai, the grandson of the plaintiff, pretended he had himself, alone and on foot, carried this sum in gold to the defendant, at his hotel at the upper end of the rue Saint Jacques, in thirteen trips, between half-past seven and about one o'clock, that is, in about five hours and a half, or, at most, six hours. The fact was improbable; Linquet, the counsel of the defendant, proved it was impossible; and this is his argument:

4. Dujonquai said that he had divided the sum in thirteen bags, each containing six hundred louis d'ors, and in twenty-three other bags, each containing two hundred. There remained twenty-five louis to complete the whole sum, which, Dujonquai said, he received from the defendant as a gratuity. At each of these trips, he says, he put a bag, containing two hundred louis,—that is, about three pounds four ounces,—in each of his coat pockets, which, being made in the fashion of those times, hung about the thighs, and in walking must have incommoded him and obstructed his speed; he took, besides, a bag containing six hundred louis in his arms; by this means his movements were impeded by a weight of near ten pounds.

5. The measured distance between the house where Dujonquai took the bags to the foot of the stairs of the defendant, was five hundred and sixteen toises, which, multiplied by twenty-six, the thirteen trips going and returning, make thirteen thousand four hundred and sixteen toises, that is, more than five leagues and a half (near seventeen miles), of two thousand four hundred toises, which latter distance is considered sufficient for an hour's walk, of a good walker. Thus, if Dujonquai had been unimpeded by any obstacle, he would barely have had time to perform the task in five or six hours, even without taking any rest or refreshment. However strikingly improbable this may have been, it was not physically impossible. But

6.—1. Dujonquai, in going to the defendant's, had to descend sixty-three steps from his grandmother's, the plaintiff's chamber, and to ascend twenty-seven to that of the defendant, in the whole, ninety steps. In returning, the ascent and descent were changed, but the steps were the same; so that by multiplying by twenty-six, the number of trips going and returning, it would be seen there were two thousand three hundred and forty steps. Experience had proved that in ascending to the top of the tower of Notre Dame (a church in Paris), where there are three hundred and eighty nine steps, it occupied from eight to nine minutes of time. It must then have taken an hour out of the five or six which had been employed in making the thirteen trips.

7.—2. Dujonquai had to go up the rue Saint Jacques, which is very steep; its ascent would necessarily decrease the speed of a man burdened and encumbered with the bags which he carried in his pockets and in his arms.

8.—3. This street, which is very public, is usually, particularly in the morning, encumbered by a multitude of persons going in every direction, so that a person going along must make an infinite number of deviations from a direct line; each, by itself, is almost imperceptible, but at the end of five or six hours, they make a considerable sum, which may be estimated at a tenth part of the whole course in a straight line; this would make about half a league, to be added to the five and a half leagues, which is the distance in a direct line.

9.—4. On the morning that Dujonquai made these trips, the daily and usual incumbrances of this street were increased by sixty or eighty workmen, who were employed in removing, by hand and with machine, an enormous stone, intended for the church of Saint Geneviève, now the pantheon, and by the immense crowd which this attracted; this was a remarkable circumstance, which, supposing that Dujonquai had not yielded to the temptation of stopping a few moments to see what was doing, must necessarily have impeded his way, and made him lose seven or eight minutes each trip, which, multiplied by twenty-six, would make about two hours and a half.

10.—5. The witness was obliged to open and shut the doors at the defendant's house; it required time to take up the bags and place them in his pockets, to take them out and put them on the defendant's table, who, by an improbable supposition, counted the money in the intervals between the trips, and not in the presence of the witness. Dujonquai, too, must have taken receipts or acknowledgments at each trip, he must read them, and on arriving at home, deposited them in some place of safety; all these distractions would necessarily occasion the loss of a few minutes. By adding these with scrupulous nicety, and by further adding the time employed in taking and depositing the bags, the opening and shutting of the doors, the reception of the receipts, the time occupied in reading and putting them away, the time consumed in several conversations, which he admitted he had with persons in the street; all these joined to the obstacles above mentioned, made it evident that it was physically impossible that Dujonquai should have carried the 300,000 francs to the house of the defendant, as he affirmed he had done. Toull. tom. 9, n. 241, p. 384. Vide, generally, 1 Stark. Ev. 502; 1 Phil. Ev. 116. See some curious cases of circumstantial evidence in Alis. Pr. Cr. Law, 313, 314; and 2 Théorie des Lois Criminelles, 147, n.; 3 Benth. Jud. Ev. 94, 223; Harvey's Meditations on the Night, note 35; 1 Taylor's Med. Jur. 372; 14 How. St. Tr. 1324; Theory of Presumptive Proof, *passim;* Best on Pres. §§ 187, 188, 197. See *Death; Presumption; Sonnambulism.*

CIRCUMSTANDIBUS, *persons, practice.* Bystanders from whom jurors are to be selected when the panel has been exhausted. Vide *Tales de circumstandibus.*

CIRCUMVENTION, *torts, Scotch law.* Any act of fraud whereby a person is reduced to a deed by decreet. Tech. Dict. It has the same sense in the civil law. Dig. 50, 17, 49 et 155; Id. 12, 6, 6, 2; Id. 41, 2, 34. Vide *Parphrasis.*

CITATIO AD REASSUMENDAM CAUSAM, *civil law.* The name of a citation, which issued when a party died pending a suit, against the heir of the defendant, or when the plaintiff died, for the heir of the plaintiff. Our bill of revivor is probably borrowed from this proceeding.

CITATION, *practice.* A writ issued out of a court of competent jurisdiction, commanding a person therein named to appear and do something therein mentioned, or to show cause why he should not, on a day named. Proct. Pr. h. t. In the ecclesiastical law, the citation is the beginning and foundation of the whole cause; it is said to have six requisites, namely: the insertion of the name of the judge; of the promovert; of the impugnant; of the cause of suit; of the place; and of the time of appearance; to which may be added the affixing the seal of the court, and the name of the register or his deputy. 1 Bro. Civ. Law, 453–4; Ayl. Parer. xliii. 175; Hall's Adm. Pr. 5; Merl. Rép. h. t. By citation is also understood the act by which a person is summoned, or cited.

CITATION OF AUTHORITIES. The production or reference to the text of acts of legislatures and of treatises, and decided cases, in order to support what is advanced.

2. Works are sometimes surcharged with useless and misplaced citations; when they are judiciously made, they assist the reader in his researches. Citations ought not to be made to prove what is not doubted; but when a controverted point is mooted, it is highly proper to cite the laws and cases, or other authorities in support of the controverted proposition.

3. The mode of citing statutes varies in the United States; the laws of the United States are generally cited by their date. as

the act of Sept. 24, 1789, s. 35; or act of 1819, ch. 170, 3 Story's U. S. Laws, 1722. In Pennsylvania, acts of assembly are cited as follows: act of 14th of April, 1834; in Massachusetts, stat. of 1808, c. 92. Treatises and books of reports, are generally cited by the volume and page, as, 2 Powell on Mortg. 600; 3 Binn. R. 60. Judge Story and some others, following the examples of the civilians, have written their works and numbered the paragraphs; these are cited as follows: Story's Bailm. § 494; Gould on Pl. c. 5, § 30. For other citations the reader is referred to the article *Abbreviations*.

4. It is usual among the civilians on the continent of Europe, in imitation of those in the darker ages, in their references to the Institutes, the Code and the Pandects or Digest, to mention the number, not of the book, but of the law, and the first word of the title to which it belongs; and as there are more than a thousand of these, it is no easy task for one not thoroughly acquainted with those collections, to find the place to which reference is made. The American writers generally follow the natural mode of reference, by putting down the name of the collection, and then the number of the book, title, law, and section. For example, Inst. 4, 15, 2, signifies Institutes, book four, title fifteen, and section two; Dig. 41, 9, 1, 3, means Digest, book 41, title 9, law 1, section 3; Dig. pro dote, or *ff* pro dote, that is, section 3, law 1, of the book and title of the Digest or Pandects, entitled *pro dote*. It is proper to remark, that Dig. and *ff* are equivalent; the former signifies Digest, and the latter, which is a careless mode of writing the Greek letter *π*, the first letter of the word *πανδεχται*, Pandects, and the Digest and Pandects are different names for one and the same thing. The Code is cited in the same way. The Novels are cited by their number, with that of the chapter and paragraph; for example, Nov. 185, 2, 4; for Novella Justiniani 185, capite 2, paragrapho 4. Novels are also quoted by the Collation, the title, chapter, and paragraph, as follows: in Authentico, Collatione 1, titulo 1, cap. 281. The Authentics are quoted by their first words, after which is set down the title of the Code under which they are placed; for example, Authentica cum testator, Codice ad legem fascidiam. See Mackel. Man. Intro. § 65. Modus Legendi Abbreviaturas passim in jure tam civili quam pontificii occurrentes, 1577.

CITIZEN, *persons*. One who, under the constitution and laws of the United States, has a right to vote for representatives in congress, and other public officers, and who is qualified to fill offices in the gift of the people. In a more extended sense, under the word citizen, are included all white persons born in the United States, and naturalized persons born out of the same, who have not lost their right as such. This includes men, women, and children.

2. Citizens are either native born or naturalized. Native citizens may fill any office; naturalized citizens may be elected or appointed to any office under the constitution of the United States, except the office of president and vice-president. The constitution provides, that "the citizens of each state shall be entitled to all the privileges and immunities of citizens in the several states." Art. 4, s. 2.

3. All natives are not citizens of the United States; the descendants of the aborigines, and those of African origin, are not entitled to the rights of citizens. Anterior to the adoption of the constitution of the United States, each state had the right to make citizens of such persons as it pleased. That constitution does not authorize any but white persons to become citizens of the United States; and it must therefore be presumed that no one is a citizen who is not white. 1 Litt. R. 334; 10 Conn. R. 340; 1 Meigs, R. 331.

4. A citizen of the United States, residing in any state of the Union, is a citizen of that state. 6 Pet. 761; Paine, 594; 1 Brock. 391; 1 Paige, 183; Metc. & Perk. Dig. h. t.; vide 3 Story's Const. § 1687; Bouv. Inst. Index, h. t.; 2 Kent, Com. 258; 4 Johns. Ch. R. 430; Vatt. B. 1, c. 19, § 212; Poth. Des Personnes, tit. 2, s. 1. Vide *Body Politic; Inhabitant*.

CITY, *government*. A town incorporated by that name. Originally, this word did not signify a town, but a portion of mankind who lived under the same government: what the Romans called *civitas*, and the Greeks *polis;* whence the word *politeia, civitas seu reipublicæ status et administratio*. Toull. Dr. Civ. Fr. l. 1, t. 1, n. 202; Henrion de Pansey, Pouvoir Municipal, pp. 36, 37.

CIVIL. This word has various significations. 1. It is used in contradistinction to *barbarous* or *savage*, to indicate a state of society reduced to order and regular government; thus we speak of civil life, civil society, civil government, and civil liberty.

2. It is sometimes used in contradistinction to *criminal*, to indicate the private rights and remedies of men, as members of the community, in contrast to those which are public and relate to the government; thus we speak of civil process and criminal process, civil jurisdiction and criminal jurisdiction. 3. It is also used in contradistinction to *military* or *ecclesiastical*, to *natural* or *foreign;* thus we speak of a civil station, as opposed to a military or ecclesiastical station; a civil death as opposed to a natural death; a civil war as opposed to a foreign war. Story on the Const. § 789; 1 Bl. Com. 6, 125, 251; Montesq. Sp. of Laws, B. 1, c. 3; Ruth. Inst. B. 2, c. 2; Id. ch. 3; Id. ch. 8, p. 359; Hein. Elem. Jurisp. Nat. B. 2, ch. 6.

CIVIL ACTION. In New York, actions are divided only into two kinds, namely, criminal and civil. A criminal action is prosecuted by the state, as a party, against a person charged with a public offence, for the punishment thereof. Every other action is a civil action. Code of Procedure, s. 4, 5, 6; 3 Bouv. Inst. n. 2638. In common parlance, however, writs of mandamus, certiorari, habeas corpus, &c., are not comprised by the expression, civil actions. 6 Bin. Rep. 9.

CIVIL COMMOTION. Lord Mansfield defines a civil commotion to be "an insurrection of the people for general purposes, though it may not amount to rebellion where there is an usurped power." 2 Marsh. Insur. 793. In the printed proposals which are considered as making a part of the contract of insurance against fire, it is declared that the insurance company will not make good any loss happening by any civil commotion.

CIVIL DEATH, *persons*. The change of the state (q. v.) of a person who is declared civilly dead by judgment of a competent tribunal. In such case, the person against whom such sentence is pronounced is considered dead. 2 John. R. 248. See Gilb. Uses, 150; 2 Bulst. 188; Co. Lit. 132; Jenk. Cent. 250; 1 Keble, 398; Prest. on Convey. 140. Vide *Death, civil.*

CIVIL LAW. The municipal code of the Romans is so called. It is a rule of action, adopted by mankind in a state of society. It denotes also the municipal law of the land. 1 Bouv. Inst. n. 11. See *Law, civil.*

CIVIL LIST. The sum which is yearly paid by the state to its monarch, and the domains of which he is suffered to have the enjoyment.

CIVIL OBLIGATION, *civil law.* One which binds in law, *vinculum juris*, and which may be enforced in a court of justice. Poth Obl. 173, and 191. See *Obligation.*

CIVIL OFFICER. The constitution of the United States, art. 2, s. 4, provides, that the president, vice-president, and *civil officers* of the United States, shall be removed from office on impeachment for, and conviction of treason, bribery, or other high crimes and misdemeanors. By this term are included all officers of the United States who hold their appointments under the national government, whether their duties are executive or judicial, in the highest or the lowest departments of the government, with the exception of officers of the army and navy. Rawle on the Const. 213; 2 Story, Const. § 790; a senator of the United States, it was decided, was not a civil officer, within the meaning of this clause in the constitution. Senate Journals, 10th January, 1799; 4 Tuck. Bl. Com. Appx. 57, 58; Rawle, Const. 213; Serg. on Const. Law, 376; Story, Const. § 791.

CIVIL REMEDY, *practice.* This term is used in opposition to the remedy given by indictment in a criminal case, and signifies the remedy which the law gives to the party against the offender.

2. In cases of treason and felony, the law, for wise purposes, *suspends* this remedy in order to promote the public interest, until the wrongdoer shall have been prosecuted for the public wrong. 1 Miles, Rep. 316–17; 12 East, 409; R. T. H. 359; 1 Hale's P. C. 546; 2 T. R. 751, 756; 17 Ves. 329; 4 Bl. Com. 363; Bac. Ab. Trepass, E 2; and Trover, D. This principle has been adopted in New Hampshire; N. H. R. 239; but changed in New York by statutory provision; 2 Rev. Stat. 292, § 2; and by decisions in Massachusetts, except perhaps in felonies punishable with death; 15 Mass. R. 333; in Ohio; 4 Ohio R. 377; in North Carolina; 1 Tayl. R. 58. By the common law, in cases of homicide, the civil remedy is *merged* in the felony. 1 Chit. Pr. 10. Vide art. *Injuries; Merger.*

CIVIL STATE. The union of individual men in civil society under a system of laws and a magistracy, or magistracies, charged with the administration of the laws. It is a fundamental law of the civil state, that no member of it shall undertake to redress or avenge any violation of his rights, by another person, but appeal to the constituted authorities for that purpose, in all cases in which is is possible for him to do so. Hence the citizens are justly considered as being under the safeguard of the law. 1 Toull. n. 201. Vide *Self-defence*.

CIVILIAN. A doctor, professor or student of the civil law.

CIVILITER. Civilly; opposed to *criminaliter* or criminally.

2. When a person does an unlawful act injurious to another, whether with or without an intention to commit a tort, he is responsible *civiliter*. In order to make him liable *criminaliter*, he must have *intended* to do the wrong; for it is a maxim, *actus non facit reum nisi mens sit rea*. 2 East, 104.

CIVILITER MORTUUS. Civilly dead; one who is considered as if he were naturally dead, so far as his rights are concerned.

CLAIM. A claim is a challenge of the ownership of a thing which a man has not in possession, and is wrongfully withheld by another. Plowd. 359; see 1 Dall. 444; 12 S. & R. 179.

2. In Pennsylvania, the entry on record of the demand of a mechanic or materialman for work done or material furnished in the erection of a building, in those counties to which the lien laws extend, is called a claim.

3. A continual claim is a claim made in a particular way, to preserve the rights of a feoffee. See *Continual claim*.

4. Claim of conusance is defined to be an intervention by a third person, demanding jurisdiction of a cause against a plaintiff, who has chosen to commence his action out of the claimant's court. 2 Wils. 409; 1 Cit. Ph. 403; Vin. Ab. Conusance; Com. Dig. Courts, P; Bac. Ab. Courts, D 3; 3 Bl. Com. 298.

CLAIMANT. In the courts of admiralty, when the suit is *in rem*, the cause is entitled in the name of the libellant against the thing libelled, as A B *v.* Ten cases of calico; and it preserves that title through the whole progress of the suit. When a person is authorized and admitted to defend the libel, he is called the claimant. The United States *v.* 1960 bags of coffee; 8 Cranch, R. 398; United States *v.* The Mars; 8 Cranch, R. 417; 30 hhds. of sugar, (Brentzon, claimant,) *v.* Boyle. 9 Cranch, R. 191.

CLANDESTINE. That which is done in secret and contrary to law.

2. Generally a clandestine act in cases of the limitation of actions will prevent the act from running. A clandestine marriage is one which has been contracted without the form which the law has prescribed for this important contract. Alis. Princ. 543.

CLARENDON. The constitutions of Clarendon were certain statutes made in the reign of Henry II., of England, in a parliament holden at Clarendon, by which the king checked the power of the pope and his clergy. 4 Bl. Com. 415.

CLASS. The order according to which are arranged or distributed, or are supposed to be arranged or distributed, divers persons or things; thus we say, a class of legatees.

2. When a legacy is given to a class of individuals, all who answer the description at the time the will takes effect, are entitled; and though the expression be in the plural, yet if there be but one, he shall take the whole. 3 M'Cord, Ch. R. 440.

3. When a bond is given to a class of persons, it is good, and all composing that class are entitled to sue upon it; but if the obligor be a member of such class, the bond is void, because a man cannot be obligor and obligee at the same time; as, if a bond be given to the justices of the county court, and at the time the obligor is himself one of said justices. 3 Dev. 284, 287, 289; 4 Dev. 382.

4. When a charge is made against a class of society, a profession, an order or body of men, and cannot possibly import a personal application to private injury, no action lies; but if any one of the class have sustained special damages in consequence of such charge, he may maintain an action. 17 Wend. 52, 23, 186. See 12 John. 475. When the charge is against one of a class, without designating which, no action lies; as, where three persons had been examined as witnesses, and the defendant said in addressing himself to them, "one of you three is perjured." 1 Roll. Ab. 81; Cro. Jac. 107; 16 Pick. 132.

CLAUSE, *contracts*. A particular disposition which makes part of a treaty; of an act of the legislature; of a deed, written agreement, or other written contract or will. When a clause is obscurely written, it ought to be construed in such a way as to agree with what precedes and what follows, if possible. Vide Dig. 50, 17, 77; *Construction; Interpretation*.

CLAUSUM FREGIT, *torts, remedies*. He broke the close. These words are used in a writ for an action of trespass to real estate, the defendant being summoned to answer *quare clausum fregit*, that is, why he broke the close of the plaintiff. 3 Bl. Com. 209.

2. Trespass *quare clausum fregit* lies for

every unlawful intrusion into land, whether enclosed or not, though only grass may be trodden. 1 Dev. & Bat. 371. And to maintain this action there must be a possession in the plaintiff, and a right to that possession. 9 Cowen, 39; 4 Yeates, 418; 11 Conn. 60; 10 Conn. 225; 1 John. 511; 12 John. 183; 4 Watts, 377; 4 Bibb, 218; 15 Pick. 32; 6 Rand. 556; 2 Yeates, 210; 1 Har. & John. 295; 8 Mass. 411.

CLEARANCE, *com. law.* The name of a certificate given by the collector of a port, in which is stated the master or commander (naming him) of a ship or vessel named and described, bound for a port named, and having on board goods described, has entered and cleared his ship or vessel according to law.

2. The Act of Congress of 2d March, 1790, section 93, directs, that the master of any vessel bound to a foreign place, shall deliver to the collector of the district from which such vessel shall be about to depart, a manifest of all the cargo on board, and the value thereof, by him subscribed, and shall swear or affirm to the truth thereof; whereupon the collector shall grant a clearance for such vessel and her cargo; but without specifying the particulars thereof in such clearance, unless required by the master so to do. And if any vessel bound to any foreign place shall depart on her voyage to such foreign place, without delivering such a manifest and obtaining a clearance, the master shall forfeit and pay the sum of five hundred dollars for every such offence. Provided, anything to the contrary notwithstanding, the collectors and other officers of the customs shall pay due regard to the inspection laws of the states in which they respectively act, in such manner, that no vessel having on board goods liable to inspection, shall be cleared out, until the master or other person shall have produced such certificate, that all such goods have been duly inspected, as the laws of the respective states do or may require, to be produced to the collector or other officer of the customs. And provided, that receipts for the payment of all legal fees which shall have accrued on any vessel, shall, before any clearance is granted, be produced to the collector or other officer aforesaid.

3. According to Boulay-Paty, Dr. Com. tome 2, p. 19, the clearance is imperiously demanded for the safety of the vessel; for if a vessel should be found without it at sea, it may be legally taken and brought into some port for adjudication, on a charge of piracy. Vide *Ship's papers.*

CLEARING HOUSE, *com. law.* Among the English bankers, the clearing house is a place in Lombard street, in London, where the bankers of that city daily settle with each other the balances which they owe, or to which they are entitled. Desks are placed around the room, one of which is appropriated to each banking house, and they are occupied in alphabetical order. Each clerk has a box or drawer along side of him, and the name of the house he represents is inscribed over his head. A clerk of each house comes in about half-past three o'clock in the afternoon, and brings the drafts or checks on the other bankers, which have been paid by his house that day, and deposits them in their proper drawers. The clerk at the desk credits their accounts separately which they have against him, as found in the drawer. Balances are thus struck from all the accounts, and the claims transferred from one to another, until they are so wound up and cancelled, that each clerk has only to settle with two or three others, and the balances are immediately paid. When drafts are paid at so late an hour that they cannot be cleared that day, they are sent to the houses on which they are drawn, to be *marked,* that is, a memorandum is made on them, and they are to be cleared the next day. See Gilbert's Practical Treatise on Banking, pp. 16—20, Babbage on the Economy of Machines, n 173, 174; Kelly's Cambist; Byles on Bills, 106, 110; Pulling's Laws and Customs of London, 437.

CLEMENCY. The disposition to treat with leniency. See *Mercy; Pardon.*

CLEMENTINES, *eccl. law.* The name usually given to the collection of decretals or constitutions of Pope Clement V., which was made by order of John XXII. his successor, who published it in 1317. The death of Clement V., which happened in 1314, prevented him from publishing this collection, which is properly a compilation, as well of the epistles and constitutions of this pope, as of the decrees of the council of Vienna, over which he presided. The Clementines are divided in five books, in which the matter is distributed nearly upon the same plan as the Decretals of Gregory IX. Vide La Bibliothèque des auteurs ecclésiastiques, par Dupin.

CLERGY. All who are attached to the

ecclesiastical ministry are called the clergy; a clergyman is therefore an ecclesiastical minister.

2. Clergymen were exempted by the emperor Constantine from all civil burdens. Baronius ad ann. 319, § 30. Lord Coke says, 2 Inst. 3, ecclesiastical persons have more and greater liberties than other of the king's subjects, wherein to set down all, would take up a whole volume of itself.

3. In the United States the clergy is not established by law, but each congregation or church may choose its own clergyman.

CLERICAL ERROR. An error made by a clerk in transcribing or otherwise. This is always readily corrected by the court.

2. An error, for example, in the teste of a fi. fa.; 4 Yeates, 185, 205; or in the teste and return of a vend. exp.; 1 Dall. 197; or in writing Dowell for McDowell. 1 Serg. & R. 120; 8 Rep. 162 a; 9 Serg. & R. 284, 5. An error is amendable where there is something to amend by, and this even in a criminal case. 2 Bin. 516; 5 Burr. 2667; 1 Bin. 367—9; Dougl. 377; Cowp. 408. For the party ought not to be harmed by the omission of the clerk; 3 Bin. 102; even of his signature, if he affixes the seal. 1 Serg. & R. 97.

CLERK, *commerce, contract*. A person in the employ of a merchant, who attends only to a part of his business, while the merchant himself superintends the whole. He differs from a factor in this, that the latter wholly supplies the place of his principal in respect to the property consigned to him. Pard. Dr. Com. n. 38, 1 Chit. Pract. 80; 2 Bouv. Inst. n. 1287.

CLERK, *officer*. A person employed in an office, public or private, for keeping records or accounts. His business is to write or register, in proper form, the transactions of the tribunal or body to which he belongs. Some clerks, however, have little or no writing to do in their offices, as, the clerk of the market, whose duties are confined chiefly to superintending the markets. In the English law, clerk also signifies a clergyman.

CLERK, *eccl. law*. Every individual, who is attached to the ecclesiastical state, and who has submitted to the ceremony of the tonsure, is a clerk.

CLIENT, *practice*. One who employs and retains an attorney or counsellor to manage or defend a suit or action in which he is a party, or to advise him about some legal matters.

2. The duties of the client towards his counsel are, 1st. to give him a written authority, 1 Ch. Pr. 19; 2. to disclose his case with perfect candor; 3. to offer spontaneously, advances of money to his attorney; 2 Ch. Pr. 27; 4. he should, at the end of the suit, promptly pay his attorney his fees. Ib. His rights are, 1. to be diligently served in the management of his business, 2. to be informed of its progress; and, 3. that his counsel shall not disclose what has been professionally confided to him. See *Attorney at law; Confidential communication.*

CLOSE. Signifies the interest in the soil, and not merely a close or enclosure in the common acceptation of the term. Doct. & Stud. 30; 7 East, 207; 2 Stra. 1004; 6 East, 154; 1 Burr. 133; 1 Ch. R. 160.

2. In every case where one man has a right to exclude another from his land, the law encircles it, if not already enclosed, with an imaginary fence; and entitles him to a compensation in damages for the injury he sustains by the act of another passing through his boundary, denominating the injurious act a breach of the enclosure. Hamm. N. P. 151; Doct. & Stud. dial. 1, c. 8, p. 30; 2 Whart. 430.

3. An ejectment will not lie for a close. 11 Rep. 55; 1 Rolle's R. 55; Salk. 254; Cro. Eliz. 235; Adams on Eject. 24.

CLOSE ROLLS, or *close writs*, *Eng. law*. Writs containing grants from the crown, to particular persons, and for particular purposes, and, not being intended for public inspection, are closed up and sealed on the outside, and for that reason called close writs, in contradistinction to grants relating to the public in general, which are left open and not sealed up, and are called letters patent. (q. v.) 2 Bl. Com. 346.

CLOSED DOORS. Signifies that something is done privately. The senate sits with closed doors on executive business.

2. In general the legislative business of the country is transacted openly. And the constitution and laws require that courts of justice shall be open to the public.

CLUB. An association of persons. It differs from a partnership in this, that the members of a club have no authority to bind each other further than they are authorized, either expressly or by implication, as each other's agents in the particular transaction; whereas in trading associations, or common partnerships, one partner may bind his copartners, as each has a right of property in the whole. 2 Mees. & Welsb. 172; Colly, Partn. 31; Story, Partn. 144; Wordsworth on Joint Stock Companies, 154, et seq.; 6 W. & S. 67; 3 W. & S. 118.

CO. A prefix or particle in the nature of an inseparable proposition, signifying with or in conjunction. *Con* and the Latin *cum* are equivalent, as, co-executors, co-obligor. It is also used as an abbreviation for company; as, John Smith & Co.

COADJUTOR, *eccl. law.* A fellow helper or assistant; particularly applied to the assistant of a bishop.

COAL NOTE, *Eng. law.* A species of promissory note authorized by the st. 3 Geo. II., c. 26, §§ 7 and 8, which, having these words expressed therein, namely, "value received in coals," are to be protected and noted as inland bills of exchange.

COALITION, *French law.* By this word is understood an unlawful agreement among several persons, not to do a thing except on some conditions agreed upon.

2. The most usual coalitions are, 1st. those which take place among master workmen, to reduce, diminish or fix at a low rate the wages of journeymen and other workmen; 2d. those among workmen or journeymen, not to work except at a certain price. These offences are punished by fine and imprisonment. Dict. de Police, h. t. In our law this offence is known by the name of conspiracy. (q. v.)

CO-ADMINISTRATOR. One of several administrators. In general, they have, like executors, the power to act singly as to the personal estate of the intestate. Vide *Administrator*.

CO-ASSIGNEE. One who is assignee with another.

2. In general, the rights and duties of co-assignees are equal.

CO-EXECUTOR. One who is executor of a will in company with another. In general each co-executor has the full power over the personal estate of the testator, that all the executors have jointly. Vide *Joint Executors*. But one cannot bring suit without joining with the others.

COAST. The margin of a country bounded by the sea. This term includes the natural appendages of the territory which rise out of the water, although they are not of sufficient firmness to be inhabited or fortified. Shoals perpetually covered with water are not, however, comprehended under the name of coast. The small islands, situate at the mouth of the Mississippi, composed of earth and trees drifted down by the river, which are not of consistency enough to support the purposes of life, and are uninhabited, though resorted to for shooting birds, were held to form a part of the coast. 5 Rob. Adm. R. 385. (c).

COCKET, *commerce.* In England the office at the custom house, where the goods to be exported are entered, is so called; also the custom house seal, or the parchment sealed and delivered by the officers of customs to merchants, as a warrant that their goods are customed. Crabbe's Tech. Dict.

COCKETTUM, *commerce.* In the English law this word signifies, 1. the custom-house seal; 2. the office at the custom where cockets are to be procured. Crabbe's Tech. Dict.

CODE, *legislation.* Signifies in general a collection of laws. It is a name given by way of eminence to a collection of such laws made by the legislature. Among the most noted may be mentioned the following:

CODES, *Les Cinq Codes, French law.* The five codes.

2. These codes are, 1st. *Code Civil*, which is divided into three books; book 1, treats of persons, and of the enjoyment and privation of civil rights; book 2, of property and its different modifications; book 3, of the different ways of acquiring property One of the most perspicuous and able commentators on this code is Toullier, frequently cited in this work.

3.—2d. *Code de procédure civille*, which is divided into two parts. Part 1, is divided into five books; 1. of justices of the peace; 2. of inferior tribunals; 3. of royal courts; 4. of extraordinary means of proceeding; 5. of execution and judgment. Part 2, is divided into three books; 1. of tender and consignation; 2. of process in relation to the opening of a succession; 3. of arbitration.

4.—3d. *Code de Commerce*, in four books; 1. of commerce in general; 2. of maritime commerce; 3. of failures and bankruptcy; 4. of commercial jurisdiction. Pardessus is one of the ablest commentators on this code.

5.—4th. *Code d'Instructions Criminelle*, in two books; 1. of judiciary police, and its officers; 2. of the administration of justice

6.—5th. *Code Penal*, in four books; 1. of punishment in criminal and correctional cases, and their effects; 2. of the persons punishable, excusable or responsible, for their crimes or misdemeanors; 3. of crimes, misdemeanors, (délits,) and their punishment; 4. of contraventions of police, and their punishment. For the history of these codes, vide Merl. Rép. h. t.; Motifs, Rapports, Opinions et Discours sur les Codes; Encyclop. Amer. h. t. .

7. Henrion de Pansey, late a president of the Court of Cassation, remarks in reference to these codes:—"In the midst of the innovations of these later times, a system of uniformity has suddenly engrossed all minds, and we have had imposed upon us the same weights, the same measures, the same laws, civil, criminal, rural and commercial. These new codes, like everything which comes from the hand of man, have imperfections and obscurities. The administration of them is committed to nearly thirty sovereign courts and a multitude of petty tribunals, composed of only three judges, and yet are invested with the right of determining in the last resort, under many circumstances. Each tribunal, the natural interpreter of these laws, applies them according to its own view, and the new codes were scarcely in operation before this beautiful system of uniformity became nothing more than a vain theory. Authorité Judiciaire, c. 31, s. 10.

Code Henri. A digest of the laws of Hayti, enacted by Henri, king of Hayti. It is based upon the Code Napoléon, but not servilely copied. It is said to be judiciously adapted to the situation of Hayti. A collection of laws made by order of Henry III. of France, is also known by the name of *Code Henri*.

Code Justinian, *civil law*. A collection of the constitutions of the emperors, from Adrian to Justinian; the greater part of those from Adrian to Constantine are mere rescripts; those from Constantine to Justinian are edicts or laws, properly speaking.

2. The code is divided into twelve books, which are subdivided into titles, in which the constitutions are collected under proper heads. They are placed in chronological order, but often disjointed. At the head of each constitution is placed the name of the emperor who is the author, and that of the person to whom it is addressed. The date is at the end. Several of these constitutions, which were formerly in the code, were lost, it is supposed by the neglect of copyists. Some of them have been restored by modern authors, among whom may be mentioned Charondas, Cugas, and Contius, who translated them from Greek versions.

Code of Louisiana. In 1822, Peter Derbigny, Edward Livingston, and Moreau Lislet, were selected by the legislature to revise and amend the civil code, and to add to it such laws still in force as were not included therein. They were authorized to add a system of commercial law, and a code of practice. The code they prepared having been adopted, was promulgated in 1824, under the title of the "Civil Code of the State of Louisiana."

2. The code is based on the Code Napoléon, with proper and judicious modifications, suitable for the state of Louisiana. It is composed of three books: 1. the first treats of persons; 2. the second of things, and of the different modifications of property; 3. and the third of the different modes of acquiring the property of things. It contains 3522 articles, numbered from the beginning, for the convenience of reference.

3. This code, it is said, contains many inaccurate definitions. The legislature modified and changed many of the provisions relating to the positive legislation, but adopted the definitions and abstract doctrines of the code without material alterations. From this circumstance, as well as from the inherent difficulty of the subject, the positive provisions of the code are often at variance with the theoretical part, which was intended to elucidate them. 13 L. R. 237.

4. This code went into operation on the 20th day of May, 1825. 11 L. R. 60. It is in both the French and English languages; and in construing it, it is a rule that when the expressions used in the French text of the code are more comprehensive than those used in English, or *vice versâ*, the more enlarged sense will be taken, as thus full effect will be given to both clauses. 2 N. S. 582.

Code Napoleon. The *Code Civil* of France, enacted into law during the reign of Napoleon, bore his name until the restoration of the Bourbons, when it was deprived of that name, and is now cited Code Civil.

Code Papirian. The name of a collection of the Roman laws, promulgated by Romulus, Numa, and other kings who governed Rome till the time of Tarquin, the Proud. It was so called in honor of Sextus Paperius, the compiler. Dig. 1, 2, 2.

Code Prussian. Allgemeines Landrecht. This code is also known by the name of *Codex Fredericianus*, or Frederician code.

It was compiled by order of Frederic II., by the minister of justice, Samuel V. Cocceji, who completed a part of it before his death, in 1755. In 1780, the work was renewed under the superintendence of the minister Von Carmer, and prosecuted with unceasing activity, and was published from 1784 to 1788, in six parts. The opinions of those who understood the subject were requested, and prizes offered on the best commentaries on it; and the whole was completed in June, 1791, under the title "General Prussian Code."

CODE THEODOSIAN. This code, which originated in the eastern empire, was adopted in the western empire towards its decline. It is a collection of the legislation of the Christian emperors, from and including Constantine to Theodosius, the Younger; it is composed of sixteen books, the edicts, acts, rescripts, and ordinances of the two empires, that of the east and that of the west.

CO-DEFENDANT. One who is made defendant in an action with another person.

CODEX. Literally, a volume or roll. It is particularly applied to the volume of the civil law, collected by the emperor Justinian, from all pleas and answers of the ancient lawyers, which were in loose scrolls or sheets of parchment. These he compiled into a book which goes by the name of Codex.

CODICIL, *devises*. An addition or supplement to a will; it must be executed with the same solemnities. A codicil is a part of the will, the two instruments making but one will. 4 Bro. C. C. 55; 2 Ves. sen. 242; 4 Ves. 610; 2 Ridgw. Irish P. C. 11, 43.

2. There may be several codicils to one will, and the whole will be taken as one: the codicil does not, consequently, revoke the will further than it is in opposition to some of its particular dispositions, unless there be express words of revocation. 8 Cowen, Rep. 56.

3. Formerly, the difference between a will and a codicil consisted in this, that in the former an executor was named, while in the latter none was appointed. Swinb. part 1, s. 5, pl. 2; Godolph. Leg. part 1, c. 6, s. 2. This is the distinction of the civil law, and adopted by the canon law. Vide Williams on Wills, ch. 2; Rob. on Wills, 154, n. 388, 476; Lovelass on Wills, 185, 289; 4 Kent, Com. 516; 1 Ves. jr. 407, 497; 3 Ves. jr. 110; 4 Ves. jr. 610; 1 Supp. to Ves. jr. 116, 140.

4. Codicils were chiefly intended to mitigate the strictness of the ancient Roman law, which required that a will should be attested by seven Roman citizens, *omni exceptione majores*. A legacy could be bequeathed, but the heir could not be appointed by codicil, though he might be made heir indirectly by way of fidei commissum.

5. Codicils owe their origin to the following circumstances. Lucius Lentulus dying in Africa, left codicils, confirmed by anticipation in a will of former date, and in those codicils requested the emperor Augustus, by way of fidei commissum, or trust, to do something therein expressed. The emperor carried this will into effect, and the daughter of Lentulus paid legacies which she would not otherwise have been legally bound to pay. Other persons made similar fidei commissa, and then the emperor, by the advice of learned men whom he consulted, sanctioned the making of codicils, and thus they became clothed with legal authority. Inst. 2, 25; Bowy. Com. 155, 156.

6. The *form* of devising by codicil is abolished in Louisiana; Code, 1563; and whether the disposition of the property be made by testament, under this title, or under that of institution of heir, of legacy, codicil, donation mortis causa, or under any other name indicating the last will, provided it be clothed with the forms required for the validity of a testament, it is, as far as form is concerned, to be considered a testament. Ib. Vide 1 Brown's Civil Law, 292; Domat, Lois Civ. liv. 4, t. 1, s. 1; Leçons Elément, du Dr. Civ. Rom. tit. 25.

COERCION, *criminal law, contracts*. Constraint; compulsion; force.

2. It is positive or presumed. 1. Positive or direct coercion takes place when a man is by physical force compelled to do an act contrary to his will; for example, when a man falls into the hands of the enemies of his country, and they compel him, by a just fear of death, to fight against it.

3.—2. It is presumed where a person is legally under subjection to another, and is induced, in consequence of such subjection, to do an act contrary to his will. A married woman, for example, is legally under the subjection of her husband, and if in his company she commit a crime or offence, not *malum in se*, (except the offence of keeping a bawdy-house, in which case she is considered by the policy of the law as a principal,) she is presumed to act under this coercion.

4. As will (q. v.) is necessary to the commission of a crime, or the making of a contract, a person coerced into either, has no will on the subject, and is not responsible. Vide Roscoe's Cr. Ev. 785, and the cases there cited; 2 Stark. Ev. 705, as to what will amount to coercion in criminal cases.

CO-EXECUTOR. One who is executor with another.

2. In general, the rights and duties of co-executors are equal.

COGNATION, *civil law*. Signifies generally the kindred which exists between two persons who are united by ties of blood or family, or both.

2. Cognation is of three kinds: natural, civil, or mixed. Natural cognation is that which is alone formed by ties of blood; such is the kindred of those who owe their origin to an illicit connexion, either in relation to their ascendants or collaterals.

3. Civil cognation is that which proceeds alone from the ties of families, as the kindred between the adopted father and the adopted child.

4. Mixed cognation is that which unites at the same time the ties of blood and family, as that which exists between brothers, the issue of the same lawful marriage. Inst. 3, 6; Dig. 38, 10.

COGNATI, *cognates*. This term occurs frequently in the Roman civil law, and denotes collateral heirs through females. It is not used in the civil law as it now prevails in France. In the common law it has no technical sense, but as a word of discourse in English it signifies, generally, allied by blood, related in origin, of the same family. See Vicat, ad verb.; also, Biret's Vocabulaire.

COGNISANCE, *pleading*. Where the defendant in an action of replevin (not being entitled to the distress or goods which are the subject of the replevin) acknowledges the taking of the distress, and insists that such taking was legal, not because he himself had a right to distrain on his own account, but because he made the distress by the command of another, who had a right to distrain on the goods which are the subject of the suit. Lawes on Pl. 35, 36; 4 Bouv. Inst. n. 3571.

COGNISANCE, *practice*. Sometimes signifies jurisdiction and judicial power, and sometimes the hearing of a matter judicially. It is a term used in the acknowledgment of a fine. See Vaughan's Rep. 207.

COGNISANCE OF PLEAS, *Eng. law*. A privilege granted by the king to a city or town, to hold pleas within the same; and when any one is impleaded in the courts at Westminster, the owner of the franchise may demand cognisance of the plea. T. de la Ley.

COGNISEE. He to whom a fine of lands, &c. is acknowledged. See *Cognisor*.

COGNISOR, *English law*. One who passes or acknowledges a fine of lands or tenements to another, in distinction from the *cognisee*, to whom the fine of the lands, &c. is acknowledged.

COGNITIONIBUS ADMITTENDIS, *English law, practice*. A writ to a justice or other person, who has power to take a fine, and having taken the acknowledgment of a fine, delays to certify it in the court of common pleas, requiring him to do it. Crabbe's Tech. Dict.

COGNOMEN. A Latin word, which signifies a family name. The *prænomen* among the Romans distinguished the person,—the *nomen*, the gens, or all the kindred descended from a remote common stock through males,—while the *cognomen* denoted the particular family. The *agnomen* was added on account of some particular event, as a further distinction. Thus, in the designation Publius Cornelius Scipio Africanus, Publius is the prænomen, Cornelius is the nomen, Scipio the cognomen, and Africanus the agnomen. Vicat. These several terms occur frequently in the Roman laws. See Cas. temp. Hardw. 286; 1 Tayl. 148. See *Name; Surname*.

COGNOVIT, *contr., pleading*. A written confession of an action by a defendant, subscribed but not sealed, and authorizing the plaintiff to sign judgment and issue execution, usually for a sum named.

2. It is given after the action is brought to save expense.

3. It differs from a warrant of attorney, which is given before the commencement of any action, and is under seal. A *cognovit actionem* is an acknowledgment and confession of the plaintiff's cause of action against the defendant to be just and true. Vide 3 Ch. Pr. 664; 3 Bouv. Inst. n. 3299.

COHABITATION. Living together.

2. The law presumes that husband and wife cohabit, even after a voluntary separation has taken place between them: but where there has been a divorce *a mensa et thoro*, or a sentence of separation, the presumption then arises that they have obeyed

the sentence or decree, and do not live together.

3. A criminal cohabitation will not be presumed by the proof of a single act of criminal intercourse between a man and woman not married. 10 Mass. R. 153.

4. When a woman is proved to cohabit with a man and to assume his name with his consent, he will generally be responsible for her debts as if she had been his wife; 2 Esp. R. 637; 1 Campb. R. 245; this being presumptive evidence of marriage; B. N. P. 114; but this liability will continue only while they live together, unless she is actually his wife. 4 Campb. R. 215.

5. In civil actions for criminal conversation with the plaintiff's wife, after the husband and wife have separated, the plaintiff will not in general be entitled to recover. 1 Esp. R. 16; S. C. 5 T. R. 357; Peake's Cas. 7, 39; sed vide 6 East, 248; 4 Esp. 39.

CO-HEIR. One of several men among whom an inheritance is to be divided.

CO-HEIRESS. A woman who inherits an estate in common with other women. A joint heiress.

COIF. A head-dress. In England there are certain serjeants at law, who are called serjeants of the coif, from the lawn coif they wear on their heads under their thin caps when they are admitted to that order.

COIN, *commerce, contracts.* A piece of gold, silver or other metal stamped by authority of the government, in order to determine its value, commonly called money. Co. Litt. 207; Rutherf. Inst. 123. For the different kinds of coins of the United States, see article *Money*. As to the value of foreign coins, see article *Foreign Coins.*

COLLATERAL, *collateralis.* From *latus*, a side; that which is sideways, and not direct.

COLLATERAL ASSURANCE, *contracts.* That which is made over and above the deed itself.

COLLATERAL FACTS, *evidence.* Facts unconnected with the issue or matter in dispute.

2. As no fair and reasonable inference can be drawn from such facts, they are inadmissible in evidence, for at best they are useless, and may be mischievous, because they tend to distract the attention of the jury, and to mislead them. Stark. Ev. h. t.; 2 Bl. Rep. 1169; 1 Stark. Ev. 40; 3 Bouv. Inst. n. 3087.

3. It is frequently difficult to ascertain *a priori*, whether a particular fact offered in evidence, will, or will not clearly appear to be material in the progress of the cause, and in such cases it is usual in practice for the court to give credit to the assertion of the counsel who tenders such evidence, that the facts will turn out to be material; but this is always within the sound discretion of the court. It is the duty of the counsel, however, to offer evidence, if possible, in such order that each part of it will appear to be pertinent and proper at the time it is offered; and it is expedient to do so, as this method tends to the success of a good cause.

4. When a witness is cross-examined as to collateral facts, the party cross-examining will be bound by the answer, and he cannot, in general, contradict him by another witness. Rosc. Ev. 139.

COLLATERAL ISSUE, *practice, pleading.* Where a criminal convict pleads any matter, allowed by law, in bar of execution; as pregnancy, a pardon, and the like.

COLLATERAL KINSMEN, *descent, distribution.* Those who descend from one and the same common ancestor, but not from one another; thus brothers and sisters are collateral to each other; the uncle and the nephew are collateral kinsmen, and cousins are the same. The term collateral is used in opposition to the phrase *lineal kinsmen.* (q. v.)

COLLATERAL SECURITY, *contracts.* A separate obligation attached to another contract, to guaranty its performance. By this term is also meant the transfer of property or of other contracts to insure the performance of a principal engagement. The property or securities thus conveyed are also called collateral securities. 1 Pow. Mortg. 393; 2 Id. 666, n. 871; 3 Id. 944, 1001.

COLLATERAL WARRANTY, *contracts, descent.* Where the heir's title to the land neither was, nor could have been, derived from the warranting ancestor; and yet barred the heir from ever claiming the land, and also imposed upon him the same obligation of giving the warrantee other lands, in case of eviction, as if the warranty were lineal, provided the heir had assets. 4 Cruise, Real Prop. 436.

2. The doctrine of collateral warranty, is, according to Justice Story, one of the most unjust, oppressive and indefensible, in the whole range of the common law. 1 Sumn. R. 262.

3. By the statute of 4 & 5 Anne, c. 16,

§ 21, all collateral warranties of any land to be made after a certain day, by any ancestor who has no estate of inheritance in possession in the same, were made void against the heir. This statute has been reënacted in New York; 4 Kent, Com. 460, 3d ed.; and in New Jersey. 3 Halst. R. 106. It has been adopted and is in force in Rhode Island; 1 Sumn. R. 235; and in Delaware. Harring. R. 50. In Kentucky and Virginia, it seems that collateral warranty binds the heir to the extent of assets descended. 1 Dana, R. 59. In Pennsylvania, collateral warranty of the ancestor, with sufficient real assets descending to the heirs, bars them from recovering the lands warranted. 4 Dall. R. 168; 2 Yeates, R. 509; 9 S. & R. 275. See 1 Sumn. 262; 3 Halst. 106; Harring. 50; 3 Rand. 549; 9 S. & R. 275; 4 Dall. 168; 2 Yeates, 509; 1 Dana, 50.

COLLATIO BONORUM, *descent, distribution.* Where a portion or money advanced to a son or daughter, is brought into hotchpot, in order to have an equal distributive share of the ancestor's personal estate. The same rule obtains in the civil law. Civil Code of Louis. 1305; Dict. de Jur. mot Collation; Merlin Rép. mot Collation.

COLLATION, *descents.* A term used in the laws of Louisiana. Collation of goods is the supposed or real return to the mass of the succession, which an heir makes of the property he received in advance of his share or otherwise, in order that such property may be divided, together with the other effects of the succession. Civil Code of Lo. art. 1305.

2. As the object of collation is to equalize the heirs, it follows that those things are excluded from collation, which the heir acquired by an onerous title from the ancestor; that is, where he gave a valuable consideration for them. And upon the same principle, if a co-heir claims no share of the estate, he is not bound to collate. *Qui non vult hereditatem, non cogitur ad collationem.* See Id. art. 1305 to 1367; and *Hotchpot.*

COLLATION, *eccl. law.* The act by which the bishop, who has the bestowing of a benefice, gives it to an incumbent. T. L.

COLLATION, *practice.* The comparison of a copy with its original, in order to ascertain its correctness and conformity; the report of the officer who made the comparison, is also called a collation.

COLLATION OF SEALS. Where, on the same label, one seal was set on the back or reverse of the other, this was said to be a collation of seals. Jacob. L. D. h. t.

COLLECTOR, *officer.* One appointed to receive taxes or other impositions; as collector of taxes; collector of militia fines, &c. A collector is also a person appointed by a private person to collect the credits due him. Metc. & Perk. Dig. h. t.

COLLECTORS OF THE CUSTOMS. Officers of the United States, appointed for the term of four years, but removable at the pleasure of the president. Act of May 15, 1820, sect. 1, 3 Story's U. S. Laws, 1790.

2. The duties of a collector of customs are described in general terms, as follows: "He shall receive all reports, manifests and documents, to be made or exhibited on the entry of any ship or vessel, according to the regulations of this act; shall record in books to be kept for the purpose, all manifests; shall receive the entries of all ships or vessels, and of the goods, wares and merchandise imported in them; shall, together with the naval officer, where there is one, or alone, where there is none, estimate the amount of duties payable thereupon, endorsing the said amounts upon the respective entries; shall receive all moneys paid for duties, and shall take bonds for securing the payment thereof; shall grant all permits for the unlading and delivery of goods; shall, with the approbation of the principal officer of the treasury department, employ proper persons as weighers, gaugers, measurers and inspectors, at the several ports within his district; and also, with the like approbation, provide, at the public expense, storehouses for the safe keeping of goods, and such scales, weights and measures, as may be necessary." Act of March 2, 1799, s. 21, 1 Story, U. S. Laws, 590. Vide, for other duties of collectors, 1 Story, U. S. Laws, 592, 612, 620, 632, 659, and vol. 3, 1650, 1697, 1759, 1761, 1791, 1811, 1848, 1854; 10 Wheat. 246.

COLLEGE. A civil corporation, society or company, authorized by law, having in general a literary object. In some countries by college is understood the union of certain voters in one body; such bodies are called electoral colleges; as, the college of electors or their deputies to the diet of Ratisbon; the college of cardinals. The term is used in the United States; as, the college of electors of president and vice-president of the United States. Act of Congress of January 23, 1845.

COLLISION, *maritime law.* It takes

place when two ships or other vessels run foul of each other, or when one runs foul of the other. In such cases there is almost always a damage incurred.

2. There are four possibilities under which an accident of this sort may occur. 1. It may happen without blame being imputable to either party, as when the loss is occasioned by a storm, or any other *vis major;* in that case the loss must be borne by the party on whom it happens to light, the other not being responsible to him in any degree.

3.—2. Both parties may be to blame, as when there has been a want of due diligence or of skill on both sides; in such cases, the loss must be apportioned between them, as having been occasioned by the fault of both of them. 6 Whart. R. 311.

4.—3. The suffering party may have been the cause of the injury, then he must bear the loss.

5.—4. It may have been the fault of the ship which ran down the other; in this case the injured party would be entitled to an entire compensation from the other. 2 Dodson's Rep. 83, 85; 3 Hagg. Adm. R. 320; 1 How. S. C. R. 89. The same rule is applied to steamers. Id. 414.

6.—5. Another case has been put, namely, when there has been some fault or neglect, but on which side the blame lies is uncertain. In this case, it does not appear to be settled whether the loss shall be apportioned or borne by the suffering party; opinions on this subject are divided.

7. A collision between two ships on the high seas, whether it be the result of accident or negligence, is, in all cases, to be deemed a peril of the seas within the meaning of a policy of insurance. 2 Story, R. 176; 3 Sumn. R. 389.

Vide, generally, Story, Bailm. § 607 to 612; Marsh. Ins. B. 1, c. 12, s. 2; Wesk. Ins. art. Running Foul; Jacobsen's Sea Laws, B. 4, c. 1; 4 Taunt. 126; 2 Chit. Pr. 513, 535; Code de Com. art. 407; Boulay-Paty, Cours de Dr. Commercial, tit. 12, s. 6; Pard. n. 652 to 654; Pothier, Avaries, n. 155; 1 Emerig. Assur. ch. 12, § 14.

COLLISTRIGIUM. The pillory.

COLLOCATION, *French law.* The act by which the creditors of an estate are arranged in the order in which they are to be paid according to law. The order in which the creditors are placed, is also called collocation. Merl. Rép. h. t. Vide *Marshalling Assets.*

COLLOQUIUM, *pleading.* A discourse; a conversation or conference.

2. In actions of slander, it is generally true that an action does not lie for words, on account of their being merely disgraceful to a person in his office, profession or trade; unless it be averred, that at the time of publishing the words, there was a colloquium concerning the office, profession or trade of the plaintiff.

3. In its technical sense, the term colloquium signifies an averment in a declaration that there was a conversation or discourse on the part of the defendant, which connects the slander with the office, profession or trade of the plaintiff; and this colloquium must extend to the whole of the prefatory matter to render the words actionable. 3 Bulst. 83. Vide Bac. Ab. Slander, S, n. 3; Dane's Ab. Index, h. t.; Com. Dig. Action upon the case for Defamation, G 7, 8, &c.; Stark. on Sland. 290, et seq.

COLLUSION, *fraud.* An agreement between two or more persons, to defraud a person of his rights by the forms of law, or to obtain an object forbidden by law; as, for example, where the husband and wife collude to obtain a divorce for a cause not authorized by law. It is nearly synonymous with *covin.* (q. v.)

2. Collusion and fraud of every kind vitiate all acts which are infected with them, and render them void. Vide Shelf. on Mar. & Div. 415, 450; 3 Hagg. Eccl. R. 130, 133; 2 Greenl. Ev. § 51; Bousq. Dict. de Dr. mot Abordage.

COLONEL. An officer in the army, next below a brigadier general, bears this title.

COLONY. A union of citizens or subjects who have left their country to people another, and remain subject to the mother country. 3 W. C. C. R. 287. The country occupied by the colonists is also called a colony. A colony differs from a possession, or a dependency. (q. v.) For a history of the American colonies, the reader is referred to Story on the Constitution, book I.; 1 Kent, Com. 77 to 80; 1 Dane's Ab. Index, h. t.

COLOR, *pleading.* It is of two kinds, namely, express color, and implied color.

2. *Express color.* This is defined to be a feigned matter, pleaded by the defendant, in an action of trespass, from which the plaintiff seems to have a good cause of action, whereas he has in truth only an appearance or color of cause. The practice

of giving express color in pleas, obtained in the mixed actions of assize, the writ of entry in the nature of assize, as well as in the personal action of trespass. Steph. on Plead. 230; Bac. Ab. Trespass, I 4.

3. It is a general rule in pleading that no man shall be allowed to plead specially such plea as amounts to the general issue, or a total denial of the charges contained in the declaration, and must in such cases plead the general issue in terms, by which the whole question is referred to the jury; yet, if the defendant in an action of trespass, be desirous to refer the validity of his title to the court, rather than to the jury, he may in his plea state his title specially, by expressly giving color of title to the plaintiff, or supposing him to have an appearance of title, bad indeed in point of law, but of which the jury are not competent judges. 3 Bl. Com. 309. Suppose, for example, that the plaintiff was in wrongful possession of the close, without any further appearance of title than the possession itself, at the time of the trespass alleged, and that the defendants entered upon him in assertion of their title; but being unable to set forth this title in the pleading, in consequence of the objection that would arise for want of color, are driven to plead the general issue of not guilty. By this plea an issue is produced whether the defendants are guilty or not of the trespass; but upon the trial of the issue, it will be found that the question turns entirely upon a construction of law. The defendants say they are not guilty of the trespasses, because they are not guilty of breaking the *close of the plaintiff*, as alleged in the declaration; and that they are not guilty of breaking the close of the plaintiff, because they themselves had the property in that close; and their title is this, that the father of one of the defendants being seised of the close in fee, gave it in tail to his eldest son, remainder in tail to one of the defendants; the eldest son was disseised, but made continual claim till the death of the disseisor; after whose death, the descent being cast upon the heir, the disseisee entered upon the heir, and afterwards died, when the remainder took effect in the said defendant who demised to the other defendant. Now, this title involves a legal question; namely, whether continual claim will not preserve the right of entry in the disseisee, notwithstanding a descent cast on the heir of the disseisor. (See as to this point, *Continual Claim.*) The issue however is merely not guilty, and this is triable by jury; and the effect, therefore, would be, that a jury would have to decide this question of law, subject to the direction upon it, which they would receive from the court. But, let it be supposed that the defendants, in a view to the more satisfactory decision of the question, wish to bring it under the consideration of the court in bank, rather than have it referred to a jury. If they have any means of setting forth their title specially in the plea, the object will be attained; for then the plaintiff, if disposed to question the sufficiency of the title, may demur to the plea, and thus refer the question to the decision of the judges. But such plea if pleaded simply, according to the state of the fact, would be informal for want of color; and hence arises a difficulty.

4. The pleaders of former days, contrived to overcome this difficulty in the following singular manner. In such case as that supposed, the plea wanting *implied* color, they gave in lieu of it an *express* one, by inserting a fictitious allegation of some colorable title in the plaintiff, which they, at the same time *avoided* by the preferable title of the defendant. See Steph. Pl. 225; Brown's Entr. 343, for a form of the plea. Plowd. Rep. 22, b.

5. Formerly various suggestions of apparent right, might be adopted according to the fancy of the pleader; and though the same latitude is, perhaps, still available, yet, in practice, it is unusual to resort to any except certain known fictions, which long usage has applied to the particular case; for example, in trespass to land, the color universally given is that of a defective charter of the demise.

See, in general, 2 Saund. 410; 10 Co. 88; Cro. Eliz. 76; 1 East, 215; Doct. Pl 17; Doct. & Stud. lib. 2, c. 53; Bac. Abr. Pleas, I 8; Trespass, I 4; 1 Chit. Pl. 500; Steph. on Pl. 220.

6. *Implied color.* That in pleading which admits, by implication, an apparent right in the opposite party, and avoids it by pleading some new matter by which that apparent right is defeated. Steph. Pl. 225.

7. It is a rule that every pleading by way of confession and avoidance, must give color; that is, it must admit an apparent right in the opposite party, and rely, therefore, on some new matter by which that apparent right is defeated. For example, where the defendant pleads a release to an action for breach of covenant, the tendency

of the plea is to admit an apparent right in the plaintiff, namely, that the defendant did, as alleged in the declaration, execute the deed, and break the covenant therein contained, and would therefore, prima facie, be liable on that ground; but shows new matter not before disclosed, by which that apparent right is done away, namely, that the plaintiff executed to him a release. Again, if the plaintiff reply that such release was obtained by duress, in his replication, he impliedly admits that the defendant has, prima facie, a good defence, namely, that such release was executed as alleged in the plea; and that the defendant therefore would be discharged; but relies on new matter by which the plea is avoided, namely, that the release was obtained by duress. The plea, in this case, therefore, gives color to the declaration, and the replication, to the plea. But let it be supposed that the plaintiff has replied, that the release was executed by him, but to another person, and not to the defendant; this would be an informal replication *wanting color;* because, if the release were not to the defendant, there would not exist even an apparent defence, requiring the allegation of new matter to avoid it, and the plea might be sufficiently answered by a traverse, denying that the deed stated in the plea, is the deed of the plaintiff. See Steph. Pl. 220; 1 Chit. Pl. 498; Lawes, Civ. Pl. 126; Arch. Pl. 211; Doct. Pl. 17; 4 Vin. Abr. 552; Bac. Abr. Pleas, &c. I 8; Com. Dig. Pleader, 3 M 40, 3 M 41. See an example of giving color in pleading in the Roman law, Inst. lib. 4, tit. 14, De replicationibus.

COLOR OF OFFICE, *criminal law.* A wrong committed by an officer under the pretended authority of his office; in some cases the act amounts to a misdemeanor, and the party may then be indicted. In other cases, the remedy to redress the wrong is by an action.

COLT. An animal of the horse species, whether male or female, not more than four years old. Russ. & Ry. 416.

COMBAT, *Eng. law.* The form of a forcible encounter between two or more persons or bodies of men; an engagement or battle. A duel.

COMBINATION. A union of different things. A patent may be taken out for a new combination of existing machinery, or machines. See 2 Mason, 112; and *Composition of matter.*

2. By combination is understood, in a bad sense, a union of men for the purpose of violating the law.

COMBUSTIO DOMORUM. Burning of houses; *arson.* Vide 4 Bl. Com. 372.

COMES, *pleading.* In a plea, the defendant says, "And the said C D, by E F, his attorney, *comes,* and defends, &c. The word comes, *venit,* expresses the appearance of the defendant in court. It is taken from the style of the entry of the proceedings on the record, and formed no part of the *viva voce* pleading. It is, accordingly, not considered as, in strictness, constituting a part of the plea. 1 Chit. Pl. 411; Steph. Pl. 432.

COMES, *offices.* A Count. An officer during the middle ages, who possessed civil and military authority. Sav. Dr. Rom. Moy. age, n. 80.

2. *Vice-comes,* the Latin name for sheriff, was originally the lieutenant of the *comes.*

COMITATUS. A county. Most of the states are divided into counties; some, as Louisiana, are divided into parishes.

COMITES. Persons who are attached to a public minister, are so called. As to their privileges, see 1 Dall. 117; Baldw. 240; and *Ambassador.*

COMITY. Courtesy; a disposition to accomodate.

2. Courts of justice in one state will, out of comity, enforce the laws of another state, when by such enforcement they will not violate their laws or inflict an injury on some one of their own citizens; as, for example, the discharge of a debtor under the insolvent laws of one state, will be respected in another state, where there is a reciprocity in this respect.

3. It is a general rule that the municipal laws of a country do not extend beyond its limits, and cannot be enforced in another, except on the principle of comity. But when those laws clash and interfere with the rights of citizens, or the laws of the countries where the parties to the contract seek to enforce it, as one or the other must give way, those prevailing where the relief is sought must have the preference. 2 Mart. Lo. Rep. N. S. 93; S. C. 2 Harr. Cond. Lo. Rep. 606, 609; 2 B. & C. 448, 471; 6 Binn. 353; 5 Cranch, 299; 2 Mass. 84; 6 Mass. 358; 7 Mart. Lo. R. 318. See *Conflict of Laws; Lex loci contractus.*

COMMAND. This word has several meanings. 1. It signifies an order; an apprentice is bound to obey the lawful command of his master; a constable may command rioters to keep the peace. 2. He who commands another to do an unlawful act, is accessary to it. 3 Inst. 51, 57; 2 Inst. 182; 1 Hayw. 4. 3. Command is also equivalent to deputation or voluntary substitution; as, when a master employs one to do a thing, he is said to have commanded him to do it; and he is responsible accordingly. Story, Ag. § 454, note.

COMMENCEMENT OF A SUIT OR ACTION. The suit is considered as commenced from the issuing of the writ; 3 Bl. Com. 273, 285; 7 T. R. 4; 1 Wils. 147; 18 John. 14; Dunl. Pr. 120; 2 Phil. Ev. 95; 7 Verm. R. 426; 6 Monr. R. 560; Peck's R. 276; 1 Pick. R. 202; Id. 227; 2 N. H. Rep. 36; 4 Cowen, R. 158; 8 Cowen, 203; 3 John. Cas. 133; 2 John. R. 342; 3 John. R. 42; 15 John. R. 42; 17 John. R. 65; 11 John. R. 473; and if the teste or date of the writ be fictitious, the true time of its issuing may be averred and proved, whenever the purposes of justice require it; as in cases of a plea of tender or of the statute of limitations. Bac. Ab. Tender D; 1 Stra. 638; Peake's Ev. 259; 2 Saund. 1, n. 1. In Connecticut, the service of the writ is the commencement of the action. 1 Root, R. 487; 4 Conn. 149; 6 Conn. R. 30; 9 Conn. R. 530; 7 Conn. R. 558; 21 Pick. R. 241; 2 C. & M. 408, 492; 1 Sim. R. 393. Vide *Lis Pendens.*

COMMENDAM, *eccles. law.* When a benefice or church living is void or vacant, it is *commended* to the care of some sufficient clerk to be supplied, until it can be supplied with a pastor. He to whom the church is thus commended is said to hold *in commendam*, and he is entitled to the profits of the living. Hob. 144; Latch, 236.

2. In Louisiana, there is a species of limited partnership called a partnership *in commendam.* It is formed by a contract, by which one person or partnership agrees to furnish another person or partnership a certain amount, either in property or money, to be employed by the person or partnership to whom it is furnished, in his or their own name or firm, on condition of receiving a share in the profits, in the proportion determined by the contract, and of being liable to losses and expenses, to the amount furnished, and no more. Civ. Code of Lo. 2810. A similar partnership exists in France. Code de Comm. 26, 33; Sirey, tom. 12, part 2, p. 25. He who makes this contract is called, in respect to those to whom he makes the advance of capital, a partner *in commendam.* Civ. Code of Lo. art. 2811.

COMMENDATARY. A person who holds a church living or presentment *in commendam.*

COMMENDATION. The act of recommending, praising. A merchant who merely commends goods he offers for sale, does not by that act warrant them, unless there is some fraud: *simplex commendatio non obligat.*

COMMENDATORS, *eccl. law.* Secular persons upon whom ecclesiastical benefices are bestowed, because they were commended and instructed to their oversight: they are merely trustees.

COMMERCE, *trade, contracts.* The exchange of commodities for commodities; considered in a legal point of view, it consists in the various agreements which have for their object to facilitate the exchange of the products of the earth or industry of man, with an intent to realize a profit. Pard. Dr. Com. n. 1. In a narrower sense, commerce signifies any reciprocal agreements between two persons, by which one delivers to the other a thing, which the latter accepts, and for which he pays a consideration; if the consideration be money, it is called a sale; if any other thing than money, it is called exchange or barter. Domat, Dr. Pub. liv. 1, tit. 7, s. 1, n. 2.

2. Congress have power by the constitution to regulate commerce with foreign nations and among the several states, and with the Indian tribes. 1 Kent. 431; Story on Const. § 1052, et seq. The sense in which the word commerce is used in the constitution seems not only to include traffic, but intercourse and navigation. Story, § 1057; 9 Wheat. 190, 191, 215, 229; 1 Tuck. Bl. App. 249 to 252. Vide 17 John. R. 488; 4 John. Ch. R. 150; 5 John. Ch. R. 300; 1 Halst. R. 285; Id. 236; 3 Cowen, R. 713; 12 Wheat. R. 419; 1 Brock. R. 423; 11 Pet. R. 102; 6 Cowen, R. 169; 3 Dana, R. 274; 6 Pet. R. 515; 13 S. & R. 205.

COMMISSARIATE. The whole body of officers who act in the department of the commissary, are called the commissariate.

COMMISSARY. An officer whose principal duties are to supply the army with provisions.

2. The Act of April 14, 1818, s. 6, requires that the president, by and with the consent of the senate, shall appoint a com-

missary general with the rank, pay, and emoluments of colonel of ordnance, and as many assistants, to be taken from the subalterns of the line, as the service may require. The commissary general and his assistants shall perform such duties, in the purchasing and issuing of rations to the armies of the United States, as the president may direct. The duties of these officers are further detailed in the subsequent sections of this act, and in the Act of March 2, 1821.

COMMISSION, *contracts, civ. law.* When one undertakes, without reward, to do something for another in respect to a thing bailed. This term is frequently used synonymously with mandate. (q. v.) Ruth. Inst. 105; Halifax, Analysis of the Civil Law, 70. If the service the party undertakes to perform for another is the custody of his goods, this particular sort of commission is called a *charge.*

2. In a commission, the obligation on his part who undertakes it, is to transact the business without wages, or any other reward, and to use the same care and diligence in it, as if it were his own.

3. By commission is also understood an act performed, opposed to omission, which is the want of performance of such an act; as, when a nuisance is created by an act of *commission*, it may be abated without notice; but when it arises from *omission*, notice to remove it must be given before it is abated. 1 Chit. Pr. 711. Vide *Abatement of Nuisances; Branches; Trees.*

COMMISSION, *office.* Persons authorized to act in a certain matter; as, such a matter was submitted to the commission; there were several meetings before the commission. 4 B. & Cr. 850; 10 E. C. L. R. 459.

COMMISSION, *crim. law.* The act of perpetrating an offence. There are crimes of commission and crimes of omission.

COMMISSION, *government.* Letters-patent granted by the government, under the public seal, to a person appointed to an office, giving him authority to perform the duties of his office. The commission is not the appointment, but only evidence of it; and as soon as it is signed and sealed, vests the office in the appointee. 1 Cranch, 137; 2 N. & M. 357; 1 M'Cord, 233, 238. See Pet. C. C. R. 194; 2 Summ. 299; 8 Conn. 109; 1 Penn. 297; 2 Const. Rep. 696; 2 Tyler, 235.

COMMISSION, *practice.* An instrument issued by a court of justice, or other competent tribunal, to authorize a person to take depositions, or do any other act by authority of such court, or tribunal, is called a commission. For a form of a commission to take depositions, see Gresley, Eq. Ev. 72.

COMMISSION OF LUNACY. A writ issued out of chancery, or such court as may have jurisdiction of the case, directed to a proper officer, to inquire whether a person named therein is a lunatic or not. 1 Bouv. Inst. n. 382, et seq.

COMMISSION MERCHANT. One employed to sell goods for another on commission; a factor. He is sometimes called a consignee, (q. v.) and the goods he receives are a consignment. 1 Bouv. Inst. n. 1013.

COMMISSION OF REBELLION, *chan. prac.* The name of a writ issuing out of chancery, generally directed to four special commissioners, named by the plaintiff, commanding them to attach the defendant wheresoever he may be found within the state, as a rebel and contemner of the law, so as to have him in chancery on a certain day therein named. This writ may be issued after an attachment with proclamation, and a return of *non est inventus.* Blake's Ch. Pr. 102; Newl. Ch. Pr. 14.

COMMISSIONER, *officer.* One who has a lawful commission to execute a public office. In a more restricted sense it is one who is authorized to execute a particular duty, as, commissioner of the revenue, canal commissioner. The term when used in this latter sense is not applied, for example, to a judge. There are commissioners, too, who have no regular commissions, and derive their authority from the elections held by the people. County commissioners, in Pennsylvania, are officers of the latter kind.

COMMISSIONER OF PATENTS. The name of an officer of the United States, whose duties are detailed in the act to promote the useful arts, &c., which will be found under the article *Patent.*

COMMISSIONERS OF BAIL, *practice.* Officers appointed by some courts to take recognizances of bail in civil cases.

COMMISSIONERS OF SEWERS, *Eng. law.* Officers whose duty it is to repair sea banks and walls, survey rivers, public streams, ditches, &c.

COMMISSIONS, *contracts, practice.* An allowance of compensation to an agent, factor, executor, trustee or other person who manages the affairs of others, for his services in performing the same.

2. The right of agents, factors or other contractors to commissions, may either be the subject of a special contract, or rest upon the *quantum meruit*. 9 C. & P. 559; 38 E. C. L. R. 227; 3 Smith's R. 440; 7 C. & P. 584; 32 E. C. L. R. 641; Sugd. Vend. Index, tit. Auctioneer

3. This compensation is usually the allowance of a certain per centage upon the actual amount or value of the business done. When there is a usage of trade at the particular place, or in the particular business in which the agent is engaged, the amount of commissions allowed to auctioneers, brokers and factors, is regulated by such usage. 3 Chit. Com. Law, 221; Smith on Merc. Law, 54; Story, Ag. § 326; 3 Camp. R. 412; 4 Camp. R. 96; 2 Stark. R. 225, 294.

4. The commission of an agent is either ordinary or *del credere*. (q. v.) The latter is an increase of the ordinary commission, in consideration of the responsibility which the agent undertakes, by making himself answerable for the solvency of those with whom he contracts. Liverm. Agency, 3, et seq.; Paley, Agency, 88, et seq.

5. In Pennsylvania, the amount of commissions allowed to executors and trustees is generally fixed at five per centum on the sum received and paid out, but this is varied according to circumstances. 9 S. & R. 209, 223; 4 Whart. 98; 1 Serg. & Rawle, 241. In England, no commissions are allowed to executors or trustees. 1 Vern. R. 316, n. and the cases there cited. 4 Ves. 72, n.

TO COMMIT. To send a person to prison by virtue of a warrant or other lawful writ, for the commission of a crime, offence or misdemeanor, or for a contempt, or non-payment of a debt.

COMMITMENT, *criminal law, practice*. The warrant or order by which a court or magistrate directs a ministerial officer to take a person to prison. The commitment is either for further hearing, (q. v.) or it is final.

2. The formal requisites of the commitment are, 1st. that it be in writing, under hand and seal, and show the authority of the magistrate, and the time and place of making it. 3 Har. & McHen. 113; Charl. 280; 3 Cranch, R. 448; see Harp. R. 313. In this case it is said a seal is not indispensable.

3.—2d. It must be made in the name of the United States, or of the commonwealth, or people, as required by the constitution of the United States or of the several states.

4.—3d. It should be directed to the keeper of the prison, and not generally to carry the party to prison. 2 Str. 934; 1 Ld. Raym. 424.

5.—4th. The prisoner should be described by his name and surname, or the name he gives as his.

6.—5th. The commitment ought to state that the party has been charged on oath. 3 Cranch, R. 448. But see 2 Virg. Cas. 504; 2 Bail. R. 290.

7.—6th. The particular crime charged against the prisoner should be mentioned with convenient certainty. 3 Cranch, R. 448; 11 St. Tr. 304. 318; Hawk. B. 2, c. 16, s. 16; 1 Chit. Cr. Law, 110.

8.—7th. The commitment should point out the place of imprisonment, and not merely direct that the party be taken to prison. 2 Str. 934; 1 Ld. Ray. 424.

9.—8th. In a final commitment, the command to the keeper of the prison should be to keep the prisoner "until he shall be discharged by due course of law," when the offence is not bailable; when it is bailable the gaoler should be directed to keep the prisoner in his "said custody for want of sureties, or until he shall be discharged by due course of law." When the commitment is not final, it is usual to commit the prisoner "for further hearing." The commitment is also called a mittimus. (q. v.)

10. The act of sending a person to prison charged with the commission of a crime by virtue of such a warrant is also called a commitment. Vide, generally, 4 Vin. Ab. 576; Bac. Ab. h. t.; 4 Cranch, R. 129; 4 Dall. R. 412; 1 Ashm. R. 248; 1 Cowen, R. 144; 3 Conn. R. 502; Wright, R. 691; 2 Virg. Cas. 276; Hardin, R. 249; 4 Mass. R. 497; 14 John. R. 371; 2 Virg. Cas. 594; 1 Tyler, R. 444; U. S. Dig. h. t.

COMMITTEE, *practice*. When a person has been found non compos, the law requires that a guardian should be appointed to take care of his person and estate; this guardian is called the committee.

2. It is usual to select the committee from the next of kin; Shelf. on Lun. 137; and in case of the lunacy of the husband or wife, the one who is of sound mind is entitled, unless under very special circumstances, to be the committee of the other. Id. 140. This is the committee of the person. For committee of the estate, the

heir at law is most favored. Relations are preferred to strangers, but the latter may be appointed. Id. 144.

3. It is the duty of the committee of the person to take care of the lunatic; and the committee of the estate is bound to administer the estate faithfully, and to account for his administration. He cannot in general make contracts in relation to the estate of the lunatic, or bind it, without a special order of the court or authority that appointed him. Id. 179; 1 Bouv. Inst. n. 389–91.

COMMITTEE, *legislation.* One or more members of a legislative body to whom is specially referred some matter before that body, in order that they may investigate and examine into it and report to those who delegated this authority to them.

COMMITTITUR PIECE, *Eng. law.* An instrument in writing, on paper or parchment, which charges a person already in prison, in execution at the suit of the person who arrested him.

COMMIXTION, *civil law.* This term is used to signify the act by which goods are mixed together.

2. The matters which are mixed are dry or liquid. In the commixtion of the former, the matter retains its substance and individuality; in the latter, the substances no longer remain distinct. The commixtion of liquids is called *confusion,* (q. v.) and that of solids, a mixture. Leç. Elem. du Dr. Rom. § 370, 371; Story, Bailm. § 40; 1 Bouv. Inst. n. 506.

COMMODATE, *contracts.* A term used in the Scotch law, which is synonymous to the Latin commodatum, or loan for use. Ersk. Inst. B. 3, t. 1, § 20; 1 Bell's Com. 225; Ersk. Pr. Laws of Scotl. B. 3, t. 1, § 9.

2. Judge Story regrets this term has not been adopted and naturalized, as mandate has been from mandatum. Story, Com. § 221. Ayliffe, in his Pandects, has gone further, and terms the bailor the *commodant,* and the bailee the *commodatory,* thus avoiding those circumlocutions, which, in the common phraseology of our law, have become almost indispensable. Ayl. Pand. B. 4, t. 16, p. 517. Browne, in his Civil Law, vol. 1, 352, calls the property loaned "*commodated* property." See *Borrower; Loan for use; Lender.*

COMMODATUM. A contract, by which one of the parties binds himself to return to the other certain personal chattels which the latter delivers to him, to be used by him, without reward; loan for use. Vide *Loan for use.*

COMMON, *or right of common, English law.* An incorporeal hereditament, which consists in a profit which a man has in the lands of another. 12 S. & R. 32; 10 Wend. R. 647; 11 John. R. 498; 2 Bouv. Inst. n. 1640, et seq.

2. Common is of four sorts; of pasture, piscary, turbary and estovers. Finch's Law, 157; Co. Litt. 122; 2 Inst. 86; 2 Bl. Com. 32.

3.—1. Common of pasture is a right of feeding one's beasts on another's land, and is either appendant, appurtenant, or in gross.

4. Common appendant is of common right, and it may be claimed in pleading as appendant, without laying a prescription. Hargr. note to 2 Inst. 122, a note.

5. Rights of common appurtenant to the claimant's land are altogether independent of the tenure, and do not arise from any absolute necessity; but may be annexed to lands in other lordships, or extended to other beasts, besides such as are generally commonable.

6. Common in gross, or at large, is such as is neither appendant nor appurtenant to land, but is annexed to a man's person. All these species of pasturable common, may be and usually are limited as to number and time; but there are also commons without stint, which last all the year. 2 Bl. Com. 34.

7.—2. Common of piscary is the liberty of fishing in another man's water. Ib. See *Fishery.*

8.—3. Common of turbary is the liberty of digging turf in another man's ground. Ib.

9.—4. Common of estovers is the liberty of taking necessary wood for the use or furniture of a house or farm from another man's estate. Ib.; 10 Wend. R. 639. See *Estovers.*

10. The right of common is little known in the United States, yet there are some regulations to be found in relation to this subject. The constitution of Illinois provides for the continuance of certain commons in that state. Const. art. 8, s. 8.

11. All unappropriated lands on the Chesapeake Bay, on the shore of the sea, or of any river or creek, and the bed of any river or creek, in the eastern parts of the commonwealth, ungranted and used as com-

mon, it is declared by statute in Virginia, shall remain so, and not be subject to grant. 1 Virg. Rev. C. 142.

12. In most of the cities and towns in the United States, there are considerable tracts of land appropriated to public use. These commons were generally laid out with the cities or towns where they are found, either by the original proprietors or by the early inhabitants. Vide 2 Pick. Rep. 475; 12 S. & R. 32; 2 Dane's. Ab. 610; 14 Mass. R. 440; 6 Verm. 355.

See, in general, Vin. Abr. Common; Bac. Abr. Common; Com. Dig. Common; Stark. Ev. part 4, p. 383; Cruise on Real Property, h. t.; Metc. & Perk. Dig. Common, and Common lands and General fields.

COMMON APPENDANT, *Eng. law.* A right attached to arable land, and is an incident of tenure, and supposed to have originated by grant of the lord or owner of a manor or waste, in consideration of certain rents or services, or other value, to a freeholder or copyholder of plough land, and at the same time either expressly or by implication, and as of commmon right and necessity common appendant over his other wastes and commons. Co. Litt. 122 a; Willis, 222.

COMMON APPURTENANT, *Eng. law.* A right granted by deed, by the owner of waste or other land, to another person, owner of other land, to have his cattle, or a particular description of cattle, levant and couchant upon the land, at certain seasons of the year, or at all times of the year. An uninterrupted usage for twenty years, is evidence of a grant. 15 East, 116.

COMMON ASSURANCES. Title by deeds are so called, because, it is said, every man's estate is assured to him; these deeds or instruments operate either as conveyances or as charges.

2.—1. Deeds of *conveyance* are, first, at common law, and include feoffments, gifts, grants, leases, exchanges, partitions, releases, confirmations, surrenders, assignments, and defeasances; *secondly*, deeds of conveyance under the statute of uses, as covenants to stand seised to uses, bargains and sale, lease and release, deeds to lead or declare uses, and deeds of appointment and revocation.

3.—2. Deeds which do not convey, but only *charge* or *discharge* lands, are obligations, recognizances, and defeasances. Vide *Assurance; Deed.*

COMMON BAIL. The formal entry of fictitious sureties in the proper office of the court, which is called filing common bail to the action. See *Bail.*

COMMON BAR, *pleading.* A plea to compel the plaintiff to assign the particular place where the trespass has been committed. Steph. Pl. 256. It is sometimes called a blank bar. (q. v.)

COMMON BENCH, *bancus communis.* The court of *common pleas* was anciently called *common bench*, because the pleas and controversies there determined were between common persons. See *Bench.*

COMMON CARRIER, *contracts.* One who undertakes for hire or reward to transport the goods of any who may choose to employ him, from place to place. 1 Pick. 50, 53; 1 Salk. 249, 250; Story, Bailm. § 495; 1 Bouv. Inst. n. 1020.

2. Common carriers are generally of two descriptions, namely, carriers by land and carriers by water. Of the former description are the proprietors of stage coaches, stage wagons or expresses, which ply between different places, and carry goods for hire; and truckmen, teamsters, cartmen, and porters, who undertake to carry goods for hire, as a common employment, from one part of a town or city to another, are also considered as common carriers. Carriers by water are the masters and owners of ships and steamboats engaged in the transportation of goods for persons generally, for hire; and lightermen, hoymen, barge-owners, ferrymen, canal boatmen, and others employed in like manner, are so considered.

3. By the common law, a common carrier is generally liable for all losses which may occur to property entrusted to his charge in the course of business, unless he can prove the loss happened in consequence of the act of God, or of the enemies of the United States, or by the act of the owner of the property. 8 S. & R. 533; 6 John. R. 160; 11 John. R. 107; 4 N. H. Rep. 304; Harp. R. 469; Peck. R. 270; 7 Yerg. R. 340; 3 Munf. R. 239; 1 Conn. R. 487; 1 Dev. & Bat. 273; 2 Bail. Rep. 157.

4. It was attempted to relax the rigor of the common law in relation to carriers by water, in 6 Cowen, 266; but that case seems to be at variance with other decisions. 2 Kent, Com. 471, 472; 10 Johns. 1; 11 Johns. 107.

5. In respect to carriers by land, the rule of the common law seems every where

admitted in its full rigor in the states governed by the jurisprudence of the common law. Louisiana follows the doctrine of the civil law in her code. Proprietors of stage coaches or wagons, whose employment is solely to carry passengers, as hackney coachmen, are not deemed common carriers; but if the proprietors of such vehicles for passengers, also carry goods for hire, they are, in respect of such goods, to be deemed common carriers. Bac. Ab. Carriers, A; 2 Show. Rep. 128; 1 Salk. 282; Com. Rep. 25; 1 Pick. 50; 5 Rawle, 179. The like reasoning applies to packet ships and steam-boats, which ply between different ports, and are accustomed to carry merchandise as well as passengers. 2 Watts. R. 443; 5 Day's Rep. 415; 1 Conn. R. 54; 4 Greenl. R. 411; 5 Yerg. R. 427; 4 Har. & J. 291; 2 Verm. R. 92; 2 Binn. Rep. 74; 1 Bay, Rep. 99; 10 John. R. 1; 11 Pick. R. 41; 3 Stew. and Port. 135; 4 Stew. & Port. 382; 3 Misso. R. 264; 2 Nott. & M. 88. But see 6 Cowen, R. 266. The rule which makes a common carrier responsible for the loss of goods, does not extend to the carriage of persons; a carrier of slaves is, therefore, answerable only for want of care and skill. 2 Pet. S. C. R. 150; 4 M'Cord, R. 223; 4 Port. R. 238.

6. A common carrier of goods is in all cases entitled to demand the price of carriage before he receives the goods, and, if not paid, he may refuse to take charge of them; if, however, he take charge of them without the hire being paid, he may afterwards recover it. The compensation which becomes due for the carriage of goods by sea, is commonly called *freight* (q. v.); and see also, Abb. on Sh. part 3, c. 7. The carrier is also entitled to a lien on the goods for his hire, which, however, he may waive; but if once waived, the right cannot be resumed. 2 Kent, Com. 497. The consignor or shipper is commonly bound to the carrier for the hire or freight of goods. 1 T. R. 659. But whenever the consignee engages to pay it, he also becomes responsible. It is usual in bills of lading to state, that the goods are to be delivered to the consignee or to his assigns, he or they paying freight, in which case the consignee and his assigns, by accepting the goods, impliedly become bound to pay the freight, and the fact that the consignor is also liable to pay it, will not, in such case, make any difference. Abbott on Sh. part 3, c. 7, § 4.

7. What is said above, relates to common carriers of goods. The duties, liabilities, and rights of carriers of passengers, are now to be considered. These are divided into carriers of passengers on land, and carriers of passengers on water.

8. First, of carriers of passengers on land. The *duties* of such carriers are, 1st. those which arise on the commencement of the journey. 1. To carry passengers whenever they offer themselves and are ready to pay for their transportation. They have no more right to refuse a passenger, if they have sufficient room and accommodation, than an innkeeper has to refuse a guest. 3 Brod. & Bing. 54; 9 Price's R. 408; 6 Moore, R. 141; 2 Chit. R. 1; 4 Esp. R. 460; 1 Bell's Com. 462; Story, Bailm. § 591.

9.—2. To provide coaches reasonably strong and sufficient for the journey, with suitable horses, trappings and equipments.

10.—3. To provide careful drivers of reasonable skill and good habits for the journey; and to employ horses which are steady and not vicious, or likely to endanger the safety of the passengers.

11.—4. Not to overload the coach either with passengers or luggage.

12.—5. To receive and take care of the usual luggage allowed to every passenger on the journey. 6 Hill, N. Y. Rep. 586.

13.—2d. Their duties on the progress of the journey. 1. To stop at the usual places, and allow the usual intervals for the refreshment of the passengers. 5 Petersd. Ab. Carriers, p. 48, note.

14.—2. To use all the ordinary precautions for the safety of passengers on the road.

15.—3d. Their duties on the termination of the journey. 1. To carry the passengers to the end of the journey.

16.—2. To put them down at the usual place of stopping, unless there has been a special contract to the contrary, and then to put them down at the place agreed upon. 1 Esp. R. 27.

17. The *liabilities* of such carriers. They are bound to use extraordinary care and diligence to carry safely those whom they take in their coaches. 2 Esp. R. 533; 2 Camp. R. 79; Peake's R. 80. But, not being insurers, they are not responsible for accidents, when all reasonable skill and diligence have been used.

18. The *rights* of such carriers. 1. To demand and receive their fare at the time

the passenger takes his seat. 2. They have a lien on the baggage of the passenger for his fare or passage money, but not on the person of the passenger, nor the clothes he has on. Abb. on Sh. part 3, c. 3, § 11; 2 Campb. R. 631.

19. Second, carriers of passengers by water. By the act of Congress of 2d March, 1819, 3 Story's Laws U. S. 1722, it is enacted, 1. that no master of a vessel bound to or from the United States shall take more than two passengers for every five tons of the ship's custom-house measurement. 2. That the quantity of water and provisions, which shall be taken on board and secured under deck, by every ship bound from the United States to any port on the continent of Europe, shall be sixty gallons of water, one hundred pounds of salted provisions, one gallon of vinegar, and one hundred pounds of wholesome ship bread for each passenger, besides the stores of the crew. The tonnage here mentioned, is the measurement of the custom-house; and in estimating the number of passengers in a vessel, no deduction is to be made for children or persons not paying, but the crew is not to be included. Gilp. R. 334.

20. The act of Congress of February 22, 1847, section 1, provides: "That if the master of any vessel, owned in whole or in part by a citizen of the United States of America, or by a citizen of any foreign country, shall take on board such vessel, at any foreign port or place, a greater number of passengers than in the following proportion to the space occupied by them and appropriated for their use, and unoccupied by stores or other goods, not being the personal luggage of such passengers, that is to say, on the lower deck or platform one passenger for every fourteen clear superficial feet of deck, if such vessel is not to pass within the tropics during such voyage; but if such vessel is to pass within the tropics during such voyage, then one passenger for every twenty such clear superficial feet of deck, and on the orlop deck (if any) one passenger for every thirty such superficial feet in all cases, with intent to bring such passengers to the United States of America, and shall leave such port or place with the same, and bring the same, or any number thereof, within the jurisdiction of the United States aforesaid, or if any such master of a vessel shall take on board of his vessel at any port or place within the jurisdiction of the United States aforesaid, any greater number of passengers than the proportions aforesaid admit, with intent to carry the same to any foreign port or place, every such master shall be deemed guilty of a misdemeanor, and, upon conviction thereof before any circuit or district court of the United States aforesaid, shall, for each passenger taken on board beyond the above proportions, be fined in the sum of fifty dollars, and may also be imprisoned for any term not exceeding one year: *Provided*, That this act shall not be construed to permit any ship or vessel to carry more than two passengers to five tons of such ship or vessel."

21. Children under one year of age not to be computed in counting the passengers, and those over one year and under eight, are to be counted as two children for one passenger. Sect. 4. But this section is repealed so far as authorizes shippers to estimate two children of eight years of age and under as one passenger by the act of March 2, 1847, s. 2.

22. In New York, statutory regulations have been made in relation to their canal navigation. Vide 6 Cowen's R. 698. As to the conduct of carrier vessels on the ocean, vide Story, Bailm. § 607 et seq.; Marsh. Ins. B. 1, c. 12, s. 2. And see, generally, 1 Vin. Ab. 219; Bac. Ab. h. t.; 1 Com. Dig. 423; Petersd. Ab. h. t.; Dane's Ab. Index, h. t.; 2 Kent, Com. 464; 16 East, 247, note; Bouv. Inst. Index, h. t.

23. In Louisiana carriers and watermen are subject, with respect to the safe-keeping and preservation of the things entrusted to them, to the same obligations and duties, as are imposed on tavern keepers; Civ. Code, art. 2722; that is, they are responsible for the effects which are brought, though they were not delivered into their personal care; provided, however, they were delivered to a servant or person in their employment; art. 2937. They are responsible if any of the effects be stolen or damaged, either by their servants or agents, or even by strangers; art. 2938; but they are not responsible for what is stolen by force of arms or with exterior breaking open of doors, or by any other extraordinary violence; art. 2939.

For the authorities on the subject of common carriers in the civil law, the reader is referred to Dig. 4, 9, 1 to 7; Poth. Pand. lib. 4, t. 9; Domat, liv. 1, t. 16, s. 1 and 2; Pard. art. 537 to 555; Code Civil, art. 1782, 1786, 1952; Moreau & Carlton, Partidas 5, t. 8, l. 26; Ersk. Inst. B. 2, t. 1

§ 28; 1 Bell's Com. 465; Abb. on Sh. part 3, c. 3, § 3, note (1); 1 Voet, ad Pand. lib. 4, t. 9; Merl. Rép. mots Voiture, Voiturier; Dict. de Police, Voiture.

COMMON COUNCIL. In many cities the charter provides for their government, in imitation of the national and state governments. There are two branches of the legislative assembly; the less numerous, called the select, the other, the common council.

2. In English law, the common council of the whole realm means the parliament. Fleta, lib. 2, cap. 13.

COMMON COUNTS. Certain general counts, not founded on any special contract, which are introduced in a declaration, for the purpose of preventing a defeat of a just right by the accidental variance of the evidence. These are in an action of assumpsit; counts founded on express or implied promises to pay money in consideration of a precedent debt, and are of four descriptions: 1. The indebitatus assumpsit; 2. The quantum meruit; 3. The quantum valebant; and, 4. The account stated.

COMMON FISHERY. A fishery to which all persons have a right, such as the cod fisheries off Newfoundland. A common fishery is different from a *common of fishery*, which is the right to fish in another's pond, pool, or river. See *Fishery*.

COMMON HIGHWAY. By this term is meant a road to be used by the community at large for any purpose of transit or traffic. Hamm. N. P. 239. See *Highway*.

COMMON INFORMER. One who, without being specially required by law, or by virtue of his office, gives information of crimes, offences or misdemeanors, which have been committed, in order to prosecute the offenders; a prosecutor. Vide *Informer; Prosecutor*.

COMMON INTENT, *construction*. The natural sense given to words.

2. It is a rule that when words are used which will bear a natural sense and an artificial one, or one to be made out by argument and inference, the natural sense shall prevail; it is simply a rule of construction and not of addition; common intent cannot add to a sentence words which have been omitted. 2 H. Black. 530. In pleading, certainty is required, but certainty to a common intent is sufficient; that is, what upon a reasonable construction may be called certain, without recurring to *possible* facts. Co. Litt. 203, a; Dougl. 163. See *Certainty*.

COMMON LAW. That which derives its force and authority from the universal consent and immemorial practice of the people. See *Law, common*.

COMMON NUISANCE. One which affects the public in general, and not merely some particular person. 1 Hawk. P. C. 197. See *Nuisance*.

COMMON PLEAS. The name of a court having jurisdiction generally of civil actions. For a historical account of the origin of this court in England, see Boote's Suit at Law, 1 to 10. Vide *Common Bench* and *Bench*.

2. By common pleas, is also understood, such pleas or actions as are brought by private persons against private persons; or by the government, when the cause of action is of a civil nature. In England, whence we derived this phrase, common pleas are so called to distinguish them from *pleas of the crown*. (q. v.)

COMMON RECOVERY. A judgment recovered in a fictitious suit, brought against the tenant of the freehold, in consequence of a default made by the person who is last vouched to warranty in the suit. A common recovery is a kind of conveyance. 2 Bouv. Inst. n. 2088, 2092–3. Vide *Recovery*.

COMMON SCOLD, *crim. law, communis rixatrix*. A woman, who, in consequence of her boisterous, disorderly and quarrelsome tongue, is a public nuisance to the neighborhood.

2. Such a woman may be indicted, and on conviction, punished. At common law, the punishment was by being placed in a certain engine of correction called the trebucket or cucking stool.

3. This punishment has been abolished in Pennsylvania, where the offence may be punished by fine and imprisonment. 12 Serg. & Rawle, 220; vide 1 Russ. on Cr. 302; Hawk. B. 2, c. 25, s. 59; 1 T. R. 756; 4 Rogers' Rec. 90; Roscoe on Cr. Ev. 665.

COMMON SEAL. A seal used by a corporation. See *Corporation*.

COMMON SENSE, *med. jur.* When a person possesses those perceptions, associations and judgments, in relation to persons and things, which agree with those of the generality of mankind, he is said to possess common sense. On the contrary, when a particular individual differs from the generality of persons in these respects, he is said not to have common sense, or not to be in his senses. 1 Chit. Med. Jur. 334.

COMMON, TENANTS IN. Tenants in common are such as hold an estate, real or personal, by several distinct titles, but by a unity of possession. Vide *Tenant in common; Estate in common.*

COMMON TRAVERSE. This kind of traverse differs from those called technical traverses principally in this, that it is preceded by no inducement general or special; it is taken without an *absque hoc*, or any similar words, and is simply a direct denial of the adverse allegations, in common language, and always concludes to the country. It can be used properly only when an inducement is not requisite; that is, when the party traversing has no need to allege any new matter. 1 Saund. 103 b. n. 1.

2. This traverse derives its name, it is presumed, from the fact that common language is used, and that it is more informal than other traverses.

COMMON VOUCHEE. In common recoveries, the person who vouched to warranty. In this fictitious proceeding, the crier of the court usually performs the office of a common vouchee. 2 Bl. Com. 358; 2 Bouv. Inst. n. 2093.

COMMONALTY, *Eng. law.* This word signifies, 1st. the common people of England, as contradistinguished from the king and the nobles; 2d. the body of a society, as the masters, wardens, and *commonalty* of such a society.

COMMONER. One who is entitled with others to the use of a common.

COMMONS, *Eng. law.* Those subjects of the English nation who are not noblemen. They are represented in parliament in the house of commons.

COMMONWEALTH, *government.* A commonwealth is properly a free state, or republic, having a popular or representative government. The term has been applied to the government of Great Britain. It is not applicable to absolute governments. The states composing the United States are, properly, so many commonwealths.

2. It is a settled principle, that no sovereign power is amenable to answer suits, either in its own courts or in those of a foreign country, unless by its own consent. 4 Yeates, 494.

COMMORANCY, *persons.* An abiding dwelling, or continuing as an inhabitant in any place. It consists, properly, in sleeping usually in one place.

COMMORANT. One residing or inhabiting a particular place. Barnes, 162.

COMMORIENTES. This Latin word signifies those who die at the same time, as, for example, by shipwreck.

2. When several persons die by the same accident, and there is no evidence as to who survived, the presumption of law is, they all died at the same time. 2 Phillim. R. 261; Fearne on Rem. iv.; 5 B. & Adol. 91; Cro. Eliz. 503; Bac. Ab. Execution, D; 1 Mer. R. 308. See *Death; Survivor.*

COMMUNICATION, *contracts.* Information; consultation; conference.

2. In order to make a contract, it is essential there should be an agreement; a bare communication or conference will not, therefore, amount to a contract; nor can evidence of such communication be received in order to take from, contradict, or alter a written agreement. 1 Dall. 426; 4 Dall. 340; 3 Serg. & Rawle, 609. Vide *Pourparler;* Wharton's Dig. Evid. R.

COMMUNINGS, *Scotch law.* This term is used to express the negotiations which have taken place before making a contract, in relation thereto. See *Pourparler.*

2. It is a general rule, that such communings or conversations, and the propositions then made, are no part of the contract; for no parol evidence will be allowed to be given to contradict, alter, or vary a written instrument. 1 Serg. & R. 464; Id. 27; Add. R. 361; 2 Dall. R. 172; 1 Binn. 616; 1 Yeates, R. 140; 12 John. R. 77; 20 John. R. 49; 3 Conn. R. 9; 11 Mass. R. 30; 13 Mass. R. 443; 1 Bibb's R. 271; 4 Bibb's R. 473; 3 Marsh. (Kty.) R. 333; Bunb. 175; 1 M. & S. 21; 1 Esp. C. 53; 3 Campb. R. 57.

COMMUNIO BONORUM, *civil law.* Common goods.

2. When a person has the management of common property, owned by himself and others, not as partners, he is bound to account for the profits, and is entitled to be reimbursed for the expenses which he has sustained by virtue of the quasi-contract which is created by his act, called *communio bonorum.* Vicat; 1 Bouv. Inst. n. 907, note.

COMMUNITY. This word has several meanings; when used in common parlance it signifies the body of the people.

2. In the civil law, by community is understood corporations, or bodies politic. Dig. 3, 4.

3. In the French law, which has been adopted in this respect in Louisiana, Civ. Code, art. 2371, community is a species of

partnership which a man and woman contract when they are lawfully married to each other. It consists of the profits of all the effects of which the husband has the administration and enjoyment, either of right or in fact; of the produce of the reciprocal industry and labor of both husband and wife, and of the estates which they may acquire during the marriage, either by donations made jointly to them, or by purchase, or in any other similar way, even although the purchase be made in the name of one of the two, and not of both; because in that case the period of time when the purchase is made is alone attended to, and not the person who made the purchase. 10 L. R. 146; Id. 172, 181; 1 N. S. 325; 4 N. S. 212. The debts contracted during the marriage enter into the community, and must be acquitted out of the common fund; but not the debts contracted before the marriage.

4. The community is either, first, conventional, or that which is formed by an express agreement in the contract of marriage itself; by this contract the legal community may be modified, as to the proportions which each shall take, or as to the things which shall compose it; Civ. Code of L. art. 2393; second, legal, which takes place when the parties make no agreement on this subject in the contract of marriage; when it is regulated by the law of the domicil they had, at the time of marriage.

5. The effects which compose the community of gains, are divided into two equal portions between the heirs, at the dissolution of the marriage. Civ. Code of L. art. 2375. See Poth. h. t.; Toull. h. t.; Civ. Code of Lo. tit. 6, c. 2, s. 4.

6. In another sense, community is the right which all men have, according to the laws of nature, to use all things. Wolff, Inst. § 186.

COMMUTATION, *punishments*. The change of a punishment to which a person has been condemned into a less severe one. This can be granted only by the executive authority in which the pardoning power resides.

COMMUTATIVE CONTRACT, *civil law*. One in which each of the contracting parties gives and receives an equivalent. The contract of sale is of this kind. The seller gives the thing sold, and receives the price, which is the equivalent. The buyer gives the price and receives the thing sold, which is the equivalent.

2. These contracts are usually distributed into four classes, namely; Do ut des; Facio ut facias; Facio ut des; Do ut facias. Poth. Obl. n. 13. See Civ. Code of Lo. art. 1761.

COMMUTATIVE JUSTICE. That virtue whose object is, to render to every one what belongs to him, as nearly as may be, or that which governs contracts.

2. The word commutative is derived from *commutare*, which signifies to exchange. Lepage, El. du Dr. ch. 1, art. 3, § 3. See *Justice*.

TO COMMUTE. To substitute one punishment in the place of another. For example, if a man be sentenced to be hung, the executive may, in some states, commute his punishment to that of imprisonment.

COMPACT, *contracts*. In its more general sense, it signifies an agreement. In its strict sense, it imports a contract between parties, which creates obligations and rights capable of being enforced, and contemplated as such between the parties, in their distinct and independent characters. Story, Const. B. 3, c. 3; Rutherf. Inst. B. 2, c. 6, § 1.

2. The constitution of the United States declares that "no state shall, without the consent of congress, enter into agreement or compact with another state, or with a foreign power." See 11 Pet. 1; 8 Wheat. 1; Bald. R. 60; 11 Pet. 185.

COMPANION, *dom. rel.* By 25 Edw. III., st. 5, c. 2, § 1, it is declared to be high treason in any one who "doth compass or imagine the death of our lord the king, or our lady his *companion*," &c. See 2 Inst. 8, 9; 1 H. H. P. C. 124.

COMPANIONS, *French law*. This is a general term, comprehending all persons who compose the crew of a ship or vessel. Poth. Mar. Contr. n. 163.

COMPANY. An association of a number of individuals for the purpose of carrying on some legitimate business.

2. This term is not synonymous with partnership, though every such unincorporated company is a partnership.

3. Usage has reserved this term to associations whose members are in greater number, their capital more considerable, and their enterprizes greater, either on account of their risk or importance.

4. When these companies are authorized by the government, they are known by the name of corporations. (q. v.)

5. Sometimes the word is used to represent those members of a partnership whose names do not appear in the name of the

firm; as, A B & Company. Vide 12 Toull. n. 97; Mortimer on Commerce, 128. Vide *Club, Corporation; Firm; Parties to actions; Partnership.*

COMPARISON OF HANDWRITING, *evidence.* It is a general rule that comparison of hands is not admissible; but to this there are some exceptions. In some instances, when the antiquity of the writing makes it impossible for any living witness to swear that he ever saw the party write, comparison of handwriting, with documents known to be in his handwriting, has been admitted. For the general principle, see Skin. 579, 639; 6 Mod. 167; 1 Lord Ray. 39, 40; Holt. 291; 4 T. R. 497; 1 Esp. N. P. C. 14, 351; Peake's Evid. 69; 7 East, R. 282; B. N. P. 236; Anthon's N. P. 98, n.; 8 Price, 653; 11 Mass. R. 309; 2 Greenl. R. 33; 2 Johns. Cas. 211; 1 Esp. 351; 1 Root, 307; Swift's Ev. 29; 1 Whart. Dig 245; 5 Binn. R. 349; Addison's R. 33; 2 M'Cord, 518; 1 Tyler, R. 4; 6 Whart. R. 284; 3 Bouv. Inst. n. 3129–30. Vide *Diploma.*

TO COMPASS. To imagine; to contrive.

2. In England, to compass the death of the king is high treason. Bract. l. 3, c. 2; Britt. c. 8; Mirror, c. 1, s. 4.

COMPATIBILITY. In speaking of public offices, it is meant by this term to convey the idea that two of them may be held by the same person at the same time. It is the opposite of *incompatibility.* (q. v.)

COMPENSATIO CRIMINIS. The compensation or set-off of one crime against another; for example, in questions of divorce, where one party claims the divorce on the ground of adultery of his or her companion, the latter may show that the complainant has been guilty of the same offence, and having himself violated the contract, he cannot complain of its violation on the other side. This principle is incorporated in the codes of most civilized nations. 1 Ought. Ord. per tit. 214; 1 Hagg. Consist. R. 144; 1 Hagg. Eccl. R. 714; 2 Paige, 108; 2 Dev. & Batt. 64. See *Condonation.*

COMPENSATION, *chancery practice.* The performance of that which a court of chancery orders to be done on relieving a party who has broken a condition, which is to place the opposite party in no worse situation than if the condition had not been broken.

2. Courts of equity will not relieve from the consequences of a broken condition, unless compensation can be made to the opposite party. Fonb. c. 6, s. 5, n. (k), Newl. Contr. 251, et seq.

3. When a simple mistake, not a fraud, affects a contract, but does not change its essence, a court of equity will enforce it, upon making compensation for the error. "The principle upon which courts of equity act," says Lord Chancellor Eldon, "is by all the authorities brought to the true standard, that though the party had not a title at law, because he had not strictly complied with the terms so as to entitle him to an action, (as to time for instance,) yet if the time, though introduced, as some time must be fixed, where something is to be done on one side, as a consideration for something to be done on the other, is not the essence of the contract; a material object, to which they looked in the first conception of it, even though the lapse of time has not arisen from accident, a court of equity will compel the execution of the contract upon this ground, that one party is ready to perform, and that the other may have a performance in substance if he will permit it." 13 Ves. 287. See 10 Ves. 505; 13 Ves. 73, 81, 426; 6 Ves. 675; 1 Cox, 59.

COMPENSATION, *contracts.* A reward for services rendered.

COMPENSATION, *contracts, civil law.* When two persons are equally indebted to each other, there takes place a compensation between them, which extinguishes both debts. Compensation is, therefore, a reciprocal liberation between two persons who are creditors and debtors to each other, which liberation takes place instead of payment, and prevents a circuity. Or it may be more briefly defined as follows: *compensatio est debiti et crediti inter se contributio.*

2. Compensation takes places, of course, by the mere operation of law, even unknown to the debtors; the two debts are reciprocally extinguished, as soon as they exist simultaneously, to the amount of their respective sums. Compensation takes place only between two debts, having equally for their object a sum of money, or a certain quantity of consumable things of one and the same kind, and which are equally liquidated and demandable. Compensation takes place, whatever be the cause of either of the debts, except in case, 1st. of a demand of restitution of a thing of which the owner has been unjustly deprived; 2d. of a demand of restitution of a deposit and a

loan for use; 3d. of a debt which has for its cause, aliments declared not liable to seizure. Civil Code of Louis. 2203 to 2208. Compensation is of three kinds: 1. legal or by operation of law; 2. compensation by way of exception; and, 3. by reconvention. 8 L. R. 158; Dig. lib. 16, t. 2; Code, lib. 4, t. 31; Inst. lib. 4, t. 6, s. 30; Poth. Obl. partie 3eme, ch. 4eme, n. 623; Burge on Sur., Book 2, c. 6, p. 181.

3. Compensation very nearly resembles the set-off (q. v.) of the common law. The principal difference is this, that a set-off, to have any effect, must be pleaded; whereas compensation is effectual without any such plea, only the balance is a debt. 2 Bouv. Inst. n. 1407.

Compensation, *crim. law; eccl. law.* Compensatio criminum, or recrimination. (q. v.)

2. In cases of suits for divorce on the ground of adultery, a compensation of the crime hinders its being granted; that is, if the defendant proves that the party has also committed adultery, the defendant is absolved as to the matters charged in the libel of the plaintiff. Ought. tit. 214, pl. 1; Clarke's Prax. tit. 115; Shelf. on Mar. & Div. 439; 1 Hagg. Cons. R. 148. See *Condonation; Divorce.*

Compensation, *remedies.* The damages recovered for an injury, or the violation of a contract. See *Damages.*

COMPERUIT AD DIEM, *pleading.* He appeared at the day. This is the name of a plea in bar to an action of debt on a bail-bond. The usual replication to this plea is *nul tiel record:* that there is not any such record of appearance of the said ——. For forms of this plea, vide 5 Wentw. 470; Lil. Entr. 114; 2 Chit. Pl. 527.

2. When the issue is joined on this plea, the trial is by the record. Vide 1 Taunt. 23; Tidd, 239. And see, generally, Com. Dig. Pleader, 2 W. 31; 7 B. & C. 478.

COMPETENCY, *evidence.* The legal fitness or ability of a witness to be heard on the trial of a cause. This term is also applied to written or other evidence which may be legally given on such trial, as, depositions, letters, account-books, and the like.

2. Prima facie every person offered is a competent witness, and must be received, unless his incompetency (q. v.) appears. 9 State Tr. 652.

3. There is a difference between competency and credibility. A witness may be competent, and, on examination, his story may be so contradictory and improbable that he may not be believed; on the contrary he may be incompetent, and yet be perfectly credible if he were examined.

4. The court are the sole judges of the competency of a witness, and may, for the purpose of deciding whether the witness is or is not competent, ascertain all the facts necessary to form a judgment. Vide 8 Watts, R. 227; and articles *Credibility; Incompetency; Interest; Witness.*

5. In the French law, by competency is understood the right in a court to exercise jurisdiction in a particular case; as, where the law gives jurisdiction to the court when a thousand francs shall be in dispute, the court is competent if the sum demanded is a thousand francs or upwards, although the plaintiff may ultimately recover less.

COMPETENT WITNESS. One who is legally qualified to be heard to testify in a cause. In Kentucky, Michigan, and Missouri, a will must be attested, for the purpose of passing lands, by competent witnesses; but if wholly written by the testator, in Kentucky, it need not be so attested. See *Attesting witness; Credible witness; Disinterested witness; Respectable witness;* and *Witness.*

COMPETITORS, *French law.* Persons who compete or aspire to the same office, rank or employment. As an English word in common use, it has a much wider application. Ferrière, Dict. de Dr. h. t.

COMPILATION. A literary production, composed of the works of others, and arranged in some methodical manner.

2. When a compilation requires in its execution taste, learning, discrimination and intellectual labor, it is an object of copyright; as, for example, Bacon's Abridgment. Curt. on Copyr. 186.

COMPLAINANT. One who makes a complaint. A plaintiff in a suit in chancery is so called.

COMPLAINT, *crim. law.* The allegation made to a proper officer, that some person, whether known or unknown, has been guilty of a designated offence, with an offer to prove the fact, and a request that the offender may be punished.

2. To have a legal effect, the complaint must be supported by such evidence as shows that an offence has been committed, and renders it certain or probable that it was committed by the person named or described in the complaint.

COMPOS MENTIS. Of sound mind. See *non compos mentis*.

COMPOSITION, *contracts*. An agreement, made upon a sufficient consideration, between a debtor and creditor, by which the creditor accepts part of the debt due to him in satisfaction of the whole. Montagu on Compos. 1; 3 Co. 118; Co. Litt. 212, b; 4 Mod. 88; 1 Str. 426; 2 T. R. 24, 26; 2 Chit. R. 541, 564; 5 D. & R. 56; 3 B. & C. 242; 1 R. & M. 138; 1 B. & A. 103, 440; 3 Moore's R. 11; 6 T. R. 263; 1 D. & R. 493; 2 Campb. R. 283; 2 M. & S. 120; 1 N. R. 124; Harr. Dig. Deed VIII.

2. In England, compositions were formerly allowed for crimes and misdemeanors, even for murder. But these compositions are no longer allowed, and even a *qui tam* action cannot be lawfully compounded. Bac. Ab. Actions *qui tam*, G. See 2 John. 405; 9 John. 251; 10 John. 118; 11 John. 474; 6 N. H. Rep. 200.

Composition of matter. In describing the subjects of patents, the Act of Congress of July 4, 1836, sect. 6, uses the words "*composition of matter;*" these words are usually applied to mixtures and chemical compositions, and in these cases it is enough that the compound is new. Both the composition and the mode of compounding may be considered as included in the invention, when the compound is new.

COMPOUND INTEREST. Interest allowed upon interest; for example, when a sum of money due for interest, is added to the principal, and then bears interest. This is not, in general, allowed. See *Interest for money*.

COMPOUNDER, *in Louisiana*. He who makes a composition. An amicable compounder is one who has undertaken by the agreement of the parties to compound or settle differences between them. Code of Pract. of Lo. art. 444.

COMPOUNDING A FELONY, *crimes*. The act of a party immediately aggrieved, who agrees with a thief or other felon that he will not prosecute him, on condition that he return to him the goods stolen, or who takes a reward not to prosecute. This is an offence punishable by fine and imprisonment. The mere retaking by the owner of stolen goods is no offence, unless the offender is not to be prosecuted. Hale, P. C. 546; 1 Chit. Cr. Law, 4.

COMPROMISE, *contracts*. An agreement between two or more persons, who, to avoid a lawsuit, amicably settle their differences, on such terms as they can agree upon. Vide Com. Dig. App. tit. Compromise.

2. It will be proper to consider, 1. by whom the compromise must be made; 2. its form; 3. the subject of the compromise; 4. its effects.

3. It must be made by a person having a right and capacity to enter into the contract, and carry out his part of it, or by one having lawful authority from such person.

4. The compromise may be by parol or in writing, and the writing may be under seal or not: though as a general rule a partner cannot bind his copartner by deed, unless expressly authorized, yet it would seem that a compromise with the principal is an act which a partner may do in behalf of his copartners, and that, though under seal, it would conclude the firm. 2 Swanst. 539.

5. The compromise may relate to a *civil* claim, either as a matter of contract, or for a tort, but it must be of something uncertain; for if the debt be certain and undisputed, a payment of a part will not, of itself, discharge the whole. A claim connected with a *criminal* charge cannot be compromised. 1 Chit. Pr. 17. See Nev. & Man. 275.

6. The compromise puts an end to the suit, if it be proceeding, and bars any suit which may afterwards be instituted. It has the effect of *res judicata*. 1 Bouv. Inst. n. 798-9.

7. In the civil law, a compromise is an agreement between two or more persons, who, wishing to settle their disputes, refer the matter in controversy to arbitrators, who are so called because those who choose them give them full powers to arbitrate and decide what shall appear just and reasonable, to put an end to the differences of which they are made the judges. 1 Domat, Lois Civ. liv. 1, t. 14. Vide *Submission*; Ch. Pr. Index, h. t.

COMPROMISSARIUS, *civil law*. A name sometimes given to an arbitrator; because the parties to the submission usually agree to fulfil his award as a compromise.

COMPTROLLERS. There are officers who bear this name, in the treasury depart ment of the United States.

2. There are two comptrollers. It is the duty of the *first* to examine all accounts settled by the first and fifth auditors, and certify the balances arising thereon to the

register; to countersign all warrants drawn by the secretary of the treasury, other than those drawn on the requisitions of the secretaries of the war and navy departments, which shall be warranted by law; to report to the secretary the official forms to be issued in the different offices for collecting the public revenues, and the manner and form of stating the accounts of the several persons employed therein; and to superintend the preservation of the public accounts, subject to his revision; and to provide for the payment of all moneys which may be collected. Act of March 3, 1817, sect. 8; Act of Sept. 2, 1789, s. 2; Act of March 7, 1822.

3. To superintend the recovery of all debts due to the United States; to direct suits and legal proceedings, and to take such measures as may be authorized by the laws, to enforce prompt payment of all such debts; Act of March 3, 1817, sect. 10; Act of Sept. 2, 1789, s. 2; to lay before congress annually, during the first week of their session, a list of such officers as shall have failed in that year to make the settlement required by law; and a statement of the accounts in the treasury, war, and navy departments, which may have remained more than three years unsettled, or on which balances appear to have been due more than three years prior to the thirteenth day of September, then last past; together with a statement of the causes which have prevented a settlement of the accounts, or the recovery of the balances due to the United States. Act of March 3, 1809, sect. 2.

4. Besides these, this officer is required to perform minor duties, which the plan of this work forbids to be enumerated here.

5. His salary is three thousand five hundred dollars per annum. Act of Feb. 20, 1804, s. 1.

6. The duties of the *second* comptroller are to examine all accounts settled by the second, third and fourth auditors, and certify the balances arising thereon to the secretary of the department in which the expenditure has been incurred; to countersign all the warrants drawn by the secretary of the treasury upon the requisition of the secretaries of the war and navy departments, which shall be warranted by law; to report to the said secretaries the official forms to be issued in the different offices for disbursing public money in those departments, and the manner and form of keeping and stating the accounts of the persons employed therein, and to superintend the preservation of public accounts subject to his revision. His salary is three thousand dollars per annum. Act of March 3, 1817, s. 9 and 15; Act of May 7, 1822.

7. A similar officer exists in several of the states, whose official title is comptroller of the public accounts, auditor general, or other title descriptive of the duties of the office.

COMPULSION. The forcible inducement to an act.

2. Compulsion may be lawful or unlawful. 1. When a man is compelled by lawful authority to do that which he ought to do, that compulsion does not affect the validity of the act; as for example, when a court of competent jurisdiction compels a party to execute a deed, under the pain of attachment for contempt, the grantor cannot object to it on the ground of compulsion. 2. But if the court compelled a party to do an act forbidden by law, or not having jurisdiction over the parties or the subject-matter, the act done by such compulsion would be void. Bowy. Mod. C. L. 305.

3. Compulsion is never presumed. *Coercion.* (q. v.)

COMPURGATOR. Formerly, when a person was accused of a crime, or sued in a civil action, he might purge himself upon oath of the accusation made against him, whenever the proof was not the most clear and positive; and if upon his oath he declared himself innocent, he was absolved.

2. This usage, so eminently calculated to encourage perjury by impunity, was soon found to be dangerous to the public safety. To remove this evil the laws were changed, by requiring that the oath should be administered with the greatest solemnity; but the form was soon disregarded, for the mind became easily familiarized to those ceremonies which at first imposed on the imagination, and those who cared not to violate the truth did not hesitate to treat the form with contempt. In order to give a greater weight to the oath of the accused, the law was again altered so as to require that the accused should appear before the judge with a certain number of his neighbors, relations or friends, who should swear that they believed the accused had sworn truly. This new species of witnesses were called compurgators.

3. The number of compurgators varied according to the nature of the charge and other circumstances. Encyclopédie, h. t

Vide Du Cange, Gloss. voc. Juramentum; Spelman's Gloss. voc. Assarth; Merl. Rép. mot Conjurateurs.

4. By the English law, when a party was sued in debt or simple contract, detinue, and perhaps some other forms of action, the defendant might wage his law, by producing eleven compurgators who would swear they believed him on his oath, by which he discharged himself from the action in certain cases. Vide 3 Bl. Com. 341—348; Barr. on the Stat. 344; 2 Inst. 25; Terms de la Ley; Mansel on Demurrer, 130, 131; *Wager of Law.*

COMPUTATION, *counting, calculation.* It is a reckoning or ascertaining the number of any thing.

2. It is sometimes used in the common law for the true reckoning or account of time. Time is computed in two ways; first, naturally, counting years, days and hours; and secondly, civilly, that is, that when the last part of the time has once commenced, it is considered as accomplished. Savig. Dr. Rom. § 182. See *Infant; Fraction.* For the computation of a year, see Com. Dig. Ann; of a month, Com. Dig. Temps. A; 1 John. Cas. 100; 15 John. R. 120; 2 Mass. 170, n.; 4 Mass. 460; 4 Dall. 144; 3 S. & R. 169; of a day, vide *Day;* and 3 Burr. 1434; 11 Mass. 204; 2 Browne, 18; Dig. 3, 4, 5; Salk. 625; 3 Wils. 274.

3. It is a general rule that when an act is to be done within a certain time, one day is to be taken inclusively, and one exclusively. Vide Lofft, 276; Dougl. 463; 2 Chit. Pr. 69; 3 Id. 108, 9; 3 T. R. 623; 2 Campb. R. 294; 4 Man. and Ryl. 300, n. (*b*); 5 Bingh. R. 339; S. C. 15, E. C. L. R. 462; 3 East, R. 407; Hob. 139; 4 Moore, R. 465; Har. Dig. Time, computation of; 3 T. R. 623; 5 T. R. 283; 2 Marsh. R. 41; 22 E. C. L. R. 270; 13 E. C. L. R. 238; 24 E. C. L. R. 53; 4 Wash. C. C. R. 232; 1 Mason, 176; 1 Pet. 60; 4 Pet. 349; 9 Cranch, 104; 9 Wheat. 581. Vide *Day; Hour; Month; Year.*

CONCEALMENT, *contracts.* The unlawful suppression of any fact or circumstance, by one of the parties to a contract, from the other, which in justice ought to be made known. 1 Bro. Ch. R. 420; 1 Fonbl. Eq. B. 1, c. 3, § 4, note (*n*); 1 Story, Eq. Jur. § 207.

2. Fraud occurs when one person substantially misrepresents or conceals a material fact peculiarly within his own knowledge, in consequence of which a delusion exists; or uses a device naturally calculated to lull the suspicions of a careful man, and induce him to forego inquiry into a matter upon which the other party has information, although such information be not exclusively within his reach. 2 Bl. Com. 451; 3 Id. 166; Sugd. Vend. 1 to 10; 1 Com. Contr. 38; 3 B. & C. 623; 5 D. & R. 490; 2 Wheat. 183; 11 Id. 59; 1 Pet. Sup. C. R. 15, 16. The party is not bound, however, to disclose *patent* defects. Sugd. Vend. 2.

3. A distinction has been made between the concealment of latent defects in real and personal property. For example, the concealment by an agent that a nuisance existed in connexion with a house the owner had to hire, did not render the lease void. 6 W. & M. 358; 1 Smith, 400. The rule with regard to personalty is different. 3 Camp. 508; 3 T. R. 759.

4. In insurances, where fairness is so essential to the contract, a concealment which is only the effect of accident, negligence, inadvertence, or mistake, if material, is equally fatal to the contract as if it were intentional and fraudulent. 1 Bl. R. 594; 3 Burr. 1909. The insured is required to disclose all the circumstances within his own knowledge only, which increase the risk. He is not, however, bound to disclose general circumstances which apply to all policies of a particular description, notwithstanding they may greatly increase the risk. Under this rule, it has been decided that a policy is void, which was obtained by the concealment by the assured of the fact that he had heard that a vessel like his was taken. 2 P. Wms. 170. And in a case where the assured had information of "a violent storm," about eleven hours after his vessel had sailed, and had stated only that "there had been blowing weather and severe storms on the coast after the vessel had sailed," but without any reference to the particular storm, it was decided that this was a concealment which vitiated the policy. 2 Caines, R. 57. Vide 1 Marsh. Ins. 468; Park, Ins. 276; 14 East, R. 494; 1 John. R. 522; 2 Cowen, 56; 1 Caines, 276; 3 Wash. C. C. Rep. 138; 2 Gallis. 353; 12 John. 128.

5. Fraudulent concealment avoids the contract. See, generally, Verpl. on Contr., passim; Bouv. Inst. Index, h. t.; Marsh Ins. B. 1, c. 9; 1 Bell's Com. B. 2, pt. 3, c. 1, s. 3, § 1; 1 M. & S. 517; 2 Marsh. R. 336.

CONCESSI, *conveyancing.* This is a

Latin word, signifying, I have granted. It was frequently used when deeds and other conveyances were written in Latin. It is a word of general extent, and is said to amount to a grant, feoffment, lease, release, and the like. 2 Saund. 96; Co. Litt. 301, 302; Dane's Ab. Index, h. t.; 5 Whart. R. 278.

2. It has been held that this word in a feoffment or fine implies no warranty. Co. Lit. 384; Noke's Case, 4 Rep. 80; Vaughan's Argument in Hayes *v.* Bickersteth, Vaughan, 126; Butler's Note, Co. Lit. 384. But see 1 Freem. 339, 414.

CONCESSION. A grant. This word is frequently used in this sense when applied to grants made by the French and Spanish governments in Louisiana.

CONCESSIMUS. A Latin word, which signifies, *we have granted.* This word creates a covenant in law, for the breach of which the grantors may be jointly sued. It imports no warranty of a freehold, but as in case of a lease for years. Spencer's Case, 5 Co. Rep. 16; Brown *v.* Heywood, 3 Keble, Rep. 617; Bac. Ab. Covenant, B. See Bac. Ab. officers, &c. E.

CONCESSOR. A grantor; one who makes a concession to another.

CONCILIUM. A day allowed to a defendant to make his defence; an imparlance. 4 Bl. Com. 356, n.; 3 T. R. 530.

CONCILIUM REGIS. The name of a tribunal which existed in England during the times of Edward I. and Edward II., composed of the judges and sages of the law. To them were referred cases of great difficulty. Co. Litt. 304.

CONCLAVE. An assembly of cardinals for the purpose of electing a pope; the place where the assembly is held is also called a conclave. It derives this name from the fact that all the windows and doors are locked, with the exception of a single panel, which admits a gloomy light.

CONCLUSION, *practice.* Making the last argument or address to the court or jury. The party on whom the *onus probandi* is cast, in general has the conclusion.

CONCLUSION, *remedies.* An estoppel; a bar; the act of a man by which he has confessed a matter or thing which he can no longer deny; as, for example, the sheriff is concluded by his return to a writ, and therefore, if upon a capias he return *cepi corpus,* he cannot afterwards show that he did not arrest the defendant, but is concluded by his return. Vide Plowd. 276, b; 3 Tho Co. Litt. 600.

CONCLUSION TO THE COUNTRY, *pleading.* The tender of an issue to be tried by a jury is called the *conclusion to the country.*

2. This conclusion is in the following words, when the issue is tendered by the defendant: "And of this the said C D puts himself upon the country." When it is tendered by the plaintiff, the formula is as follows: "And this the said A B prays may be inquired of by the country." It is held, however, that there is no material difference between these two modes of expression, and that, if *ponit se,* be substituted for *petit quod inquiratur,* or *vice versa,* the mistake is unimportant. 10 Mod. 166.

3. When there is an affirmative on one side, and a negative on the other, or *vice versa,* the conclusion should be to the country. T. Raym. 98; Carth. 87; 2 Saund. 189; 2 Burr. 1022. So it is, though the affirmative and negative be not in express words, but only tantamount thereto. Co. Litt. 126, a; Yelv. 137; 1 Saund. 103; 1 Chit. Pl. 592; Com. Dig. Pleader, E 32.

CONCLUSIVE. What puts an end to a thing. A conclusive presumption of law, is one which cannot be contradicted even by direct and positive proof. Take, for example, the presumption that an infant is incapable of judging whether it is or is not against his interest; when infancy is pleaded and proved, the plaintiff cannot show that the defendant was within one day of being of age when the contract was made, and perfectly competent to make a contract. 3 Bouv. Inst. n. 3061.

CONCLUSIVE EVIDENCE. That which cannot be contradicted by any other evidence; for example, a record, unless impeached for fraud, is conclusive evidence between the parties. 3 Bouv. Inst. n. 3061-62.

CONCLUSUM, *intern. law.* The form of an acceptance or conclusion of a treaty; as, the treaty was ratified purely and simply by a *conclusum.* It is the name of a decree of the Germanic diet, or of the aulic council.

CONCORD, *estates, conveyances, practice.* An agreement or supposed agreement between the parties in levying a fine of lands, in which the deforciant (or he who keeps the other out of possession,) acknowledges that the lands in question, are the right of the complainant; and from the acknowledgment or recognition of right thus made, the party who levies the fine is called the cognisor, and the person to whem it is levied, the cognisee. 2 Bl. Com. 350; Cruise, Dig. tit. 35, c. 2, s. 33; Com. Dig. Fine, E 9.

CONCORDATE. A convention; a pact; an agreement. The term is generally confined to the agreements made between independent governments; and, most usually applied to those between the pope and some prince.

CONCUBINAGE. This term has two different significations; sometimes it means a species of marriage which took place among the ancients, and which is yet in use in some countries. In this country it means the act or practice of cohabiting as man and woman, in sexual commerce, without the authority of law, or a legal marriage. Vide 1 Bro. Civ. Law, 80; Merl. Rép. h. t.; Dig. 32, 49, 4; Id. 7, 1, 1; Code, 5, 27, 12.

CONCUBINE. A woman who cohabits with a man as his wife, without being married.

TO CONCUR. In Louisiana, to concur, signifies, to claim a part of the estate of an insolvent along with other claimants; 6 N. S. 460; as "the wife concurs with her husband's creditors, and claims a privilege over them."

CONCURRENCE, *French law.* The equality of rights, or privilege which several persons have over the same thing; as, for example, the right which two judgment creditors, whose judgments were rendered at the same time, have to be paid out of the proceeds of real estate bound by them. Dict. de Jur. h. t.

CONCURRENT. Running together; having the same authority; thus we say a concurrent consideration occurs in the case of mutual promises; such and such a court have concurrent jurisdiction; that is, each has the same jurisdiction.

CONCUSSION, *civ. law.* The unlawful forcing of another by threats of violence to give something of value. It differs from robbery in this, that in robbery the thing is taken by force, while in concussion it is obtained by threatened violence. Hein. Leç. El. § 1071.

CONDEDIT, *eccl. law.* The name of a plea, entered by a party to a libel filed in the ecclesiastical court, in which it is pleaded that the deceased made the will which is the subject of the suit, and that he was of sound mind. 2 Eng. Eccl. Rep. 438; 6 Eng. Eccl. Rep. 431.

CONDELEGATES. Advocates who have been appointed judges of the high court of delegates are so called. Shelf. on Lun. 310.

CONDEMNATION, *mar. law.* The sentence or judgment of a court of competent jurisdiction that a ship or vessel taken as a prize on the high seas, was liable to capture, and was properly and legally captured.

2. By the general practice of the law of nations, a sentence of condemnation is, at present, generally deemed necessary in order to divest the title of a vessel taken as a prize. Until this has been done the original owner may regain his property, although the ship may have been in possession of the enemy twenty-four hours, or carried infra præsidia. 1 Rob. Rep. 134; 3 Rob. Rep 97, n.; Carth. 423; Chit. Law of Nat. 99, 100; 10 Mod. 79; Abb. on Sh. 14; Wesk. on Ins. h. t.; Marsh. on Ins. 402. A sentence of condemnation is generally binding everywhere. Marsh. on Ins. 402.

3. The term condemnation is also applied to the sentence which declares a ship to be unfit for service; this sentence and the grounds of it may, however, be reëxamined and litigated by parties interested in disputing it. 5 Esp. N. P. C. 65; Abb. on Shipp. 4.

CONDEMNATION, *civil law.* A sentence of judgment which condemns some one to do, to give, or to pay something; or which declares that his claim or pretensions are unfounded. This word is also used by common lawyers, though it is more usual to say conviction, both in civil and criminal cases. It is a maxim that no man ought to be condemned unheard, and without the opportunity of being heard.

CONDICTIO INDEBITI, *civil law.* When the plaintiff has paid to the defendant by mistake what he was not bound to pay either in fact or in law, he may recover it back by an action called *condictio indebiti.* This action does not lie, 1. if the sum was due *ex æquitate*, or by a natural obligation; 2. if he who made the payment knew that nothing was due, for *qui consulto dat, quod non debetat, præsumitur donare.* Vide *Quasi contract.*

CONDICTION, Lat. *condictio.* This term is used in the civil law in the same sense as action. *Condictio certi*, is an action for the recovery of a certain thing, as our action of replevin; *condictio incerti*, is an action given for the recovery of an uncertain thing. Dig. 12, 1.

CONDITION, *contracts, wills.* In its most extended signification, a condition is a clause in a contract or agreement which has for its object to suspend, to rescind, or to modify the principal obligation; or in case of a will, to suspend, revoke, or modify the devise or bequest. 1 Bouv. Inst. n. 730. It is in fact by itself, in many cases, an agreement; and a sufficient foundation *as* an agreement in writing, for a bill in equity, praying for a specific performance. 2 Burr. 826. In pleading, according to the course of the common law, the bond and its condition are to some intents and purposes, regarded as distinct things. 1 Saund. Rep. by Wms. 9 b. Domat has given a definition of a condition, quoted by Hargrave, in these words: "A condition is any portion or agreement which regulates what the parties have a mind should be done, if a case they foresee should come to pass." Co. Litt. 201 a.

2. Conditions sometimes suspend the obligation; as, when it is to have no effect until they are fulfilled; as, if I bind myself to pay you one thousand dollars on condition that the ship Thomas Jefferson shall arrive in the United States from Havre; the contract is suspended until the arrival of the ship.

3. The condition sometimes rescinds the contract; as, when I sell you my horse, on condition that he shall be alive on the first day of January, and he dies before that time.

4. A condition may modify the contract; as, if I sell you two thousand bushels of corn, upon condition that my crop shall produce that much, and it produces only fifteen hundred bushels.

5. In a less extended acceptation, but in a true sense, a condition is a future and uncertain event, on the existence or nonexistence of which is made to depend, either the accomplishment, the modification, or the rescission of an obligation or testamentary disposition.

6. There is a marked difference between a condition and a limitation. When a thing is given generally, but the gift may be defeated upon the happening of an uncertain event, the latter is called a condition; but when it is given to be enjoyed until the event arrives, it is a limitation. See *Limitation; Estates.* It is not easy to say when a condition will be considered a covenant and when not, or when it will be holden to be both. Platt on Cov. 71.

7. Events foreseen by conditions are of three kinds. Some depend on the acts of the persons who deal together, as, if the agreement should provide that a partner should not join another partnership. Others are independent of the will of the parties, as, if I sell you one thousand bushels of corn, on condition that my crop shall not be destroyed by a fortuitous event, or act of God. Some depend in part on the contracting parties and partly on the act of God, as, if it be provided that such merchandise shall arrive by a certain day.

8. A condition may be created by inserting the very word *condition*, or on *condition*, in the deed or agreement; there are, however, other words that will do so as effectually, as *proviso*, *if*, &c. Bac. Ab. Conditions, A.

9. Conditions are of various kinds; 1. as to their *form*, they are express or implied. This division is of feudal origin. 2 Woodes. Lect. 138. 2. As to their *object*, they are lawful or unlawful; 3. as to the *time when they are to take effect*, they are precedent or subsequent; 4. as to their *nature*, they are possible or impossible; 5. as to their *operation*, they are positive or negative; 6. as to their *divisibility*, they are copulative or disjunctive; 7. as to their *agreement with the contract*, they are consistent or repugnant; 8. as to their *effect*, they are resolutory or suspensive. These will be severally considered.

10. An *express* condition is one created by express words; as for instance, a condition in a lease that if the tenant shall not pay the rent at the day, the lessor may reënter. Litt. 328. Vide *Reëntry.*

11. An *implied* condition is one created by law, and not by express words; for example, at common law, the tenant for life holds upon the implied condition not to commit waste. Co. Litt. 233, b.

12. A *lawful* or *legal* condition is one made in consonance with the law. This must be understood of the law as existing at the time of making the condition, for no change of the law can change the force of the condition. For example, a conveyance was made to the grantee, on condition that he should not aliene until he reached the age of twenty-five years. Before he acquired this age he aliened, and made a second conveyance after he obtained it; the first deed was declared void, and the last valid. When the condition was imposed, twenty-five was the age of majority in the state; it was afterwards changed to twenty-one. Under these circumstances the condition was held to be binding. 3 Miss. R. 40.

13. An *unlawful* or *illegal* condition is one forbidden by law. Unlawful conditions have for their object, 1st. to do something *malum in se*, or *malum prohibitum;* 2d. to omit the performance of some duty required by law; 3d. to encourage such act or omission. 1 P. Wms. 189. When the law prohibits, in express terms, the transaction in respect to which the condition is made, and declares it void, such condition is then void; 3 Binn. R. 533; but when it is prohibited, without being declared void, although unlawful, it is not void. 12 S. & R. 237. Conditions in restraint of marriage are odious, and are therefore held to the utmost rigor and strictness. They are contrary to sound policy, and by the Roman law were all void. 4 Burr. Rep. 2055; 10 Barr. 75, 350; 3 Whart. 575.

14. A condition *precedent* is one which must be performed before the estate will vest, or before the obligation is to be performed. 2 Dall. R. 317. Whether a condition shall be considered as precedent or subsequent, depends not on the form or arrangement of the words, but on the manifest intention of the parties, on the fair construction of the contract. 2 Fairf. R. 318; 5 Wend. R. 496; 3 Pet. R. 374; 2 John. R. 148; 2 Caines, R. 352; 12 Mod. 464; 6 Cowen, R. 627; 9 Wheat. R. 350; 2 Virg. Cas. 138; 14 Mass. R. 453; 1 J. J. Marsh. R. 591; 6 J. J. Marsh. R. 161; 2 Bibb, R. 547; 6 Litt. R. 151; 4 Rand. R. 352; 2 Burr. 900.

15. A *subsequent* condition is one which enlarges or defeats an estate or right, already created. A conveyance in fee, reserving a life estate in a part of the land, and made upon condition that the grantee shall pay certain sums of money at divers times to several persons, passes the fee upon condition subsequent. 6 Greenl. R. 106. See 1 Burr. 39, 43; 4 Burr. 1940. Sometimes it becomes of great importance to ascertain whether the condition is precedent or subsequent. When a precedent condition becomes impossible by the act of God, no estate or right vests; but if the condition is subsequent, the estate or right becomes absolute. Co. Litt. 206, 208; 1 Salk. 170.

16. A *possible* condition is one which may be performed, and there is nothing in the laws of nature to prevent its performance.

17. An *impossible* condition is one which cannot be accomplished according to the laws of nature; as, to go from the United States to Europe in one day; such a condition is void. 1 Swift's Dig. 93; 5 Toull. n. 242—247. When a condition becomes impossible by the act of God, it either vests the estate, or does not, as it is precedent or subsequent: when it is the former, no estate vests; when the latter, it becomes absolute. Co. Litt. 206, a, 218, a; 3 Pet. R. 374; 1 Hill. Ab. 249. When the performance of the condition becomes impossible by the act of the party who imposed it, the estate is rendered absolute. 5 Rep. 22; 3 Bro. Parl. Cas. 359. Vide 1 Paine's R. 652; Bac. Ab. Conditions, M; Roll. Ab. 420; Co. Litt. 206; 1 Rop. Leg. 505; Swinb. pt. 4, s. 6; Inst. 2, 4, 10; Dig. 28, 7, 1; Id. 44, 7, 31; Code 6, 25, 1; 6 Toull. n. 486, 686; and the article *Impossibility*.

18. A *positive* condition requires that the event contemplated shall happen; as, *If I marry*. Poth. Ob. part 2, c. 3, art. 1, § 1.

19. A *negative* condition requires that the event contemplated shall not happen; as, *If I do not marry*. Poth. Ob. n. 200.

20. A *copulative* condition, is one of several distinct matters, the whole of which are made precedent to the vesting of an estate or right. In this case the entire condition must be performed, or the estate or right can never arise or take place. 2 Freem. 186. Such a condition differs from a disjunctive condition, which gives to the party the right to perform the one or the other; for, in this case, if one becomes impossible by the act of God, the whole will, in general, be excused. This rule, however, is not without exception. 1 B. & P. 242; Cro. Eliz. 780; 5 Co. 21; 1 Lord Raym. 279. Vide *Conjunctive; Disjunctive*.

21. A *disjunctive* condition is one which gives the party to be affected by it, the right to perform one or the other of two alternatives.

22. A *consistent* condition is one which agrees with other parts of the contract.

23. A *repugnant* condition is one which is contrary to the contract; as, if I grant to you a house and lot in fee, upon condition that you shall not aliene, the condition is repugnant and void, as being inconsistent with the estate granted. Bac. Ab. Conditions, L; 9 Wheat. 325; 2 Ves. jr. 324.

24. A *resolutory* condition in the civil law is one which has for its object, when accomplished, the revocation of the principal obligation. This condition does not suspend either the existence or the execution of the obligation, it merely obliges the creditor to return what he has received.

25. A *suspensive* condition is one which suspends the fulfilment of the obligation until it has been performed; as, if a man bind himself to pay one hundred dollars, upon condition that the ship Thomas Jefferson shall arrive from Europe. The obligation, in this case, is suspended until the arrival of the ship, when the condition having been performed, the obligation becomes absolute, and it is no longer conditional. A suspensive condition is in fact a condition precedent.

26. Pothier further divides conditions into potestative, casual and mixed.

27. A *potestative* condition is that which is in the power of the person in whose favor it is contracted; as, if I engage to give my neighbor a sum of money, in case he cuts down a tree which obstructs my prospect. Poth. Obl. Pt. 2, c. 3, art. 1, § 1.

28. A *casual* condition is one which depends altogether upon chance, and not in the power of the creditor, as the following: if I have children; if I have no children; if such a vessel arrives in the United States, &c. Poth. Ob. n. 201.

29. A *mixed* condition is one which depends on the will of the creditor and of a third person; as, if you marry my cousin. Poth. Ob. n. 201. Vide, generally, Bouv. Inst. Index, h. t.

CONDITION, *persons*. The situation in civil society which creates certain relations between the individual, to whom it is applied, and one or more others, from which mutual rights and obligations arise. Thus the situation arising from marriage gives rise to the conditions of husband and wife; that of paternity to the conditions of father and child. Domat, tom. 2, liv. 1, tit. 9, s. 1, n. 8.

2. In contracts every one is presumed to know the condition of the person with whom he deals. A man making a contract with an infant cannot recover against him for a breach of the contract, on the ground that he was not aware of his condition.

CONDITIONAL OBLIGATION. One which is superseded by a condition under which it was created and which is not yet accomplished. Poth. Obl. n. 176, 198.

CONDITIONS OF SALE, *contracts*. The terms upon which the vendor of property by auction proposes to sell it; the instrument containing these terms, when reduced to writing or printing is also called the conditions of sale.

2. It is always prudent and advisable that the conditions of sale should be printed and exposed in the auction room; when so done, they are binding on both parties, and nothing that is *said* at the time of sale, to add to or vary such printed conditions, will be of any avail. 1 H. Bl. 289; 12 East, 6; 6 Ves. 330; 15 Ves. 521; 2 Munf. Rep. 119; 1 Desauss. Ch. Rep. 573; 2 Desauss. Ch. R. 320; 11 John. Rep. 555; 3 Camp. 285. Vide forms of conditions of sale in Babington on Auctions, 233 to 243; Sugd. Vend. Appx. No. 4. Vide *Auction; Auctioneer; Puffer*.

CONDONATION. A term used in the canon law. It is a forgiveness by the husband of his wife, or by a wife of her husband, of adultery committed, with an implied condition that the injury shall not be repeated, and that the other party shall be treated with conjugal kindness. 1 Hagg. R. 773; 3 Eccl. Rep. 310. See 5 Mass. 320; 5 Mass. 69; 1 Johns. Ch. R. 488.

2. It may be express or implied, as, if a husband, knowing of his wife's infidelity, cohabit with her. 1 Hagg. Rep. 789; 3 Eccl. R. 338.

3. Condonation is not, for many reasons, held so strictly against a wife as against a husband. 3 Eccl. R. 330; Id. 341, n.; 2 Edw. R. 207. As all condonations, by operation of law, are expressly or impliedly conditional, it follows that the effect is taken off by the repetition of misconduct; 3 Eccl. R. 329; 3 Phillim. Rep. 6; 1 Eccl. R. 35; and cruelty revives condoned adultery. Worsley *v.* Worsley, cited in Durant *v.* Durant, 1 Hagg. Rep. 733; 3 Eccl. Rep. 311.

4. In New York, an act of cruelty alone, on the part of the husband, does not revive condoned adultery, to entitle the wife to a divorce. 4 Paige's R. 460. See 3 Edw. R. 207.

5. Where the parties have separate beds, there must, in order to found condonation, be something of matrimonial intercourse presumed; it does not rest merely on the wife's not withdrawing herself. 3 Eccl. R. 341, n.; 2 Paige, R. 108.

6. Condonation is a bar to a sentence of divorce. 1 Eccl. Rep. 284; 2 Paige, R. 108.

7. In Pennsylvania, by the Act of the 13th of March, 1815, § 7, 6 Reed's Laws of Penna. 288, it is enacted that "in any suit or action for divorce for cause of adultery, if the defendant shall allege and prove that the plaintiff has admitted the defendant

into conjugal society or embraces, after he or she knew of the criminal fact, or that the plaintiff (if the husband) allowed of his wife's prostitutions, or received hire for them, or exposed his wife to lewd company, whereby she became ensnared to the crime aforesaid, it shall be a good defence, and perpetual bar against the same." The same rule may be found, perhaps, in the codes of most civilized countries. Villanova Y Mañes, Materia Criminal Forense, Obs. 11, c. 20, n. 4. Vide, generally, 2 Edw. 207; Dev. Eq. R. 352; 4 Paige, 432; 1 Edw. R. 14; Shelf. on M. & D. 445; 1 John. Ch. R. 488; 4 N. Hamp. R. 462; 5 Mass. 320.

CONDUCT, *law of nations.* This term is used in the phrase *safe conduct*, to signify the security given, by authority of the government, under the great seal, to a stranger, for his quietly coming into and passing out of the territories over which it has jurisdiction. A safe conduct differs from a passport; the former is given to enemies, the latter to friends or citizens.

CONDUCT MONEY. The money advanced to a witness who has been subpœnaed to enable him to attend a trial, is so called.

CONDUCTOR OPERARUM, *civil law.* One who undertakes, for a reward, to perform a job or piece of work for another. See *Locator Operis.*

CONFEDERACY, *intern. law.* An agreement between two or more states or nations, by which they unite for their mutual protection and good. This term is applied to such agreement between two independent nations, but it is used to signify the union of different states of the same nation, as the confederacy of the states.

2. The original thirteen states, in 1781, adopted for their federal government the "Articles of confederation and perpetual union between the States," which continued in force until the present constitution of the United States went into full operation, on the 30th day of April, 1789, when president Washington was sworn into office. Vide 1 Story on the Const. B. 2, c. 3 and 4.

CONFEDERACY, *crim. law.* An agreement between two or more persons to do an unlawful act, or an act, which though not unlawful in itself, becomes so by the confederacy. The technical term usually employed to signify this offence, is *conspiracy.* (q. v.)

CONFEDERACY, *equity pleading.* The fourth part of a bill in chancery usually charges a confederacy; this is either general or special.

2. The first is by alleging a general charge of confederacy between the defendants and other persons to injure or defraud the plaintiff. The common form of the charge is, that the defendants, combining and confederating together, to and with divers other persons as yet to the plaintiff unknown, but whose names, when discovered, he prays may be inserted in the bill, and they be made parties thereto, with proper and apt words to charge them with the premises, in order to injure and oppress the plaintiff in the premises, do absolutely refuse, &c. Mitf. Eq. Pl. by Jeremy, 40; Coop. Eq. Pl. 9; Story, Eq. Pl. § 29; 1 Mont. Eq. Pl. 77; Barton, Suit in Eq. 33; Van Heyth. Eq. Drafts, 4.

3. When it is intended to rely on a confederacy or combination as a ground of equitable jurisdiction, the confederacy must be specially charged to justify an assumption of jurisdiction. Mitf. Eq. Pl. by Jeremy, 41; Story, Eq. Pl. § 30.

4. A general allegation of confederacy is now considered as mere form. Story, Eq. Pl. § 29; 4 Bouv. Inst. n. 4169.

CONFEDERATION, *government.* The name given to that form of government which the American colonies, on shaking off the British yoke, devised for their mutual safety and government.

2. The articles of confederation, (q. v.) were finally adopted on the 15th of November, 1777, and with the exception of Maryland, which, however, afterwards also agreed to them, were speedily adopted by the United States, and by which they were formed into a federal body, and went into force on the first day of March, 1781; 1 Story Const. § 225; and so remained until the adoption of the present constitution, which acquired the force of the supreme law of the land on the first Wednesday of March, 1789. 5 Wheat. R. 420. Vide *Articles of Confederation.*

CONFERENCE, *practice, legislation.* In practice, it is the meeting of the parties or their attorneys in a cause, for the purpose of endeavoring to settle the same.

2. In legislation, when the senate and house of representatives cannot agree on a bill or resolution which it is desirable should be passed, committees are appointed by the two bodies respectively, who are called com-

mittees of conference, and whose duty it is, if possible, to reconcile the differences between them.

3. In the French law, this term is used to signify the similarity and comparison between two laws, or two systems of law; as the Roman and the common law. Encyclopédie, h. t.

4. In diplomacy, conferences are verbal explanations between ministers of two nations at least, for the purpose of accelerating various difficulties and delays, necessarily attending written communications.

CONFESSION, *crim. law, evidence.* The voluntary declaration made by a person who has committed a crime or misdemeanor, to another, of the agency or participation which he had in the same.

2. When made without bias or improper influence, confessions are admissible in evidence, as the highest and most satisfactory proof; because it is fairly presumed that no man would make such a confession against himself, if the facts confessed were not true; but they are excluded, if liable to the imputation of having been unfairly obtained.

3. Confessions should be received with great caution, as they are liable to many objections. There is danger of error from the misapprehension of witnesses, the misuse of words, the failure of a party to express his own meaning, the prisoner being oppressed by his unfortunate situation, and influenced by hope, fear, and sometimes a worse motive, to make an untrue confession. See the case of the two Booms in Greenl. Ev. § 214, note 1; North American Review, vol. 10, p. 418; 6 Carr. & P. 451; Joy on Confess. s. 14, p. 100; and see 1 Chit. Cr. Law, 85.

4. A confession must be made voluntarily, by the party himself, to another person. 1. *It must be voluntary.* A confession, forced from the mind by the flattery of hope, or the torture of fear, comes in so questionable a shape, when it is to be considered as evidence of guilt, that no credit ought to be given to it. 1 Leach, 263. This is the principle, but what amounts to a promise or a threat, is not so easily defined. Vide 2 East, P. C. 659; 2 Russ. on Cr. 644; 4 Carr. & Payne, 387; S. C. 19 Eng. Com. L. Rep. 434; 1 Southard, R. 231; 1 Wend. R. 625; 6 Wend. R. 268; 5 Halst. R. 163; Miña's Trial, 10; 5 Rogers' Rec. 177; 2 Overton, R. 86; 1 Hayw. (N. C.) R, 482; 1 Carr. & Marsh. 584. But it must be observed that a confession will be considered as voluntarily made, although it was made after a promise of favor or threat of punishment, by a person *not in authority,* over the prisoner. If, however, a person having such authority over him be present at the time, and he express no dissent, evidence of such confession cannot be given. 8 Car. & Payne, 733.

5.—2. *The confession must be made by the party to be affected by it.* It is evidence only against him. In case of a conspiracy, the acts of one conspirator are the acts of all, while active in the progress of the conspiracy, but after it is over, the confession of one as to the part he and others took in the crime, is not evidence against any but himself. Phil. Ev. 76, 77; 2 Russ. on Cr. 653.

6.—3. *The confession must be to another person.* It may be made to a private individual, or under examination before a magistrate. The whole of the confession must be taken, together with whatever conversation took place at the time of the confession. Roscoe's Ev. N. P. 36; 1 Dall. R. 240; Id. 392; 3 Halst. 275; 2 Penna. R. 27; 1 Rogers' Rec. 66; 3 Wheeler's C. C. 533; 2 Bailey's R. 569; 5 Rand. R. 701.

7. *Confession,* in another sense, is where a prisoner being arraigned for an offence, confesses or admits the crime with which he is charged, whereupon the plea of guilty is entered. Com. Dig. Indictment, K; Id. Justices, W 3; Arch. Cr. Pl. 121; Harr. Dig. h. t.; 20 Am. Jur. 68; Joy on Confession.

8. Confessions are classed into judicial and extra judicial. *Judicial* confessions are those made before a magistrate, or in court, in the due course of legal proceedings; when made freely by the party, and with a full and perfect knowledge of their nature and consequences, they are sufficient to found a conviction. These confessions are such as are authorized by a statute, as to take a preliminary examination in writing; or they are by putting in the plea of guilty to an indictment. Extra judicial confessions are those which are made by the party elsewhere than before a magistrate or in open court. 1 Greenl. Ev. § 216. See, generally, 3 Bouv. Inst. n. 3081-2.

CONFESSIONS AND AVOIDANCE, *pleadings.* Pleas in confession and avoidance are those which admit the averments in the plaintiff's declaration to be true, and allege new facts which obviate and repel their legal effects.

2. These pleas are to be considered, first, with respect to their *division*. Of pleas in confession and avoidance, some are distinguished (in reference to their subject-atter) as pleas in justification or excuse, thers as pleas in discharge. Com. Dig. Pleader, 3 M 12. The pleas of the former class, show some justification or excuse of the matter charged in the declaration; those of the latter, some discharge or release of that matter. The effect of the former, therefore, is to show that the plaintiff never had any right of action, because the act charged was lawful; the effect of the latter, to show that though he had once a right of action, it is discharged or released by some matter subsequent. Of those in justification or excuse, the plea of son assault demesne is an example; of those in discharge, a release. This division applies to *pleas* only; for replications and other subsequent pleadings in confession and avoidance, are not subject to such classification.

3. Secondly, they are to be considered in respect to their form. As to their form, the reader is referred to Stephens on Pleading, 72, 79, where forms are given. In common with all pleadings whatever, which do not tender issue, they always conclude with a verification and prayer of judgment.

4. Thirdly, with respect to the quality of these pleadings, it is a rule that every pleading by way of confession and avoidance must give color. (q. v.) And see, generally, 1 Chit. Pl. 599; 2 Chit. Pl. 644; Co. Litt. 282, b; Arch. Civ. Pl. 215; Dane's Ab. Index, h. t.; 3 Bouv. Inst. n. 2921, 2931.

CONFESSOR, *evid.* A priest of some Christian sect, who receives an account of the sins of his people, and undertakes to give them absolution of their sins.

2. The general rule on the subject of giving evidence of confidential communications is, that the privilege is confined to counsel, solicitors, and attorneys, and the interpreter between the counsel and the client. Vide *Confidential Communications*. Contrary to this general rule, it has been decided in New York, that a priest of the Roman Catholic denomination could not be compelled to divulge secrets which he had received in auricular confession. 2 City Hall Rec. 80, n.; Joy on Conf. § 4, p. 49. See Bouv. Inst. n. 3174 and note.

CONFIDENTIAL COMMUNICATIONS, *evidence*. Whatever is communicated professedly by a client to his counsel, solicitor, or attorney, is considered as a confidential communication.

2. This the latter is not permitted to divulge, for this is the privilege of the client and not of the attorney.

3. The rule is, in general, strictly confined to counsel, solicitors or attorneys, except, indeed, the case of an interpreter between the counsel and client, when the privilege rests upon the same grounds of necessity. 3 Wend. R. 339. In New York, contrary to this general rule, under the statute of that state, it has been decided that information disclosed to a physician while attending upon the defendant in his professional character, which information was necessary to enable the witness to prescribe for his patient, was a confidential communication which the witness need not have testified about; and in a case where such evidence had been received by the master, it was rejected. 4 Paige, R. 460.

4. As to the matter communicated, it extends to all cases where the party applies for professional assistance. 6 Mad. R. 47; 14 Pick. R. 416. But the privilege does not extend to extraneous or impertinent communications; 3 John. Cas. 198; nor to information imparted to a counsellor in the character of a friend, and not as counsel. 1 Caines' R. 157.

5. The cases in which communications to counsel have been holden not to be privileged may be classed under the following heads: 1. When the communication was made before the attorney was employed as such; 1 Vent. 197; 2 Atk. 524; 2. after the attorney's employment has ceased; 4 T. R. 431; 3. when the attorney was consulted because he was an attorney, yet he refused to act as such, and was therefore only applied to as a friend; 4 T. R. 753; 4. where a fact merely took place in the presence of the attorney, Cowp. 846; 2 Ves. 189; 2 Curt. Eccl. R. 866; but see Str. 1122; 5. when the matter communicated was not in its nature private, and could in no sense be termed the subject of a confidential communication; 7 East, R. 357; 2 B. & B. 176; 3 John. Cas. 198; 6. when the things disclosed had no reference to professional employment, though disclosed while the relation of attorney and client subsisted; Peake's R. 77; 7. when the attorney made himself a subscribing witness; 10 Mod. 40; 2 Curt. Eccl. R. 866; 3 Burr. 1687; 8. when he was directed to plead the facts to

which he is called to testify. 7 N. S. 179. See a well written article on this subject in the American Jurist, vol. xvii. p. 304. Vide, generally, Stark. Ev. h. t.; 1 Greenl. Ev. §§ 236–247; 1 Peters' R. 356; 1 Root, 383; Whart. Dig. 275; Cary's R. 88, 126, 143; Toth. R. 177; Peake's Cas. 77; 2 Stark. Cas. 274; 4 Wash. C. C. R. 718; 11 Wheat. 280; 3 Yeates, R. 4; 4 Munf. R. 273; 1 Porter, R. 433; Wright, R. 136; 13 John. R. 492. As to a confession made to a catholic priest, see 2 N. Y. City Hall Rec. 77. Vide 2 Ch. Pr. 18–21; *Confessor*.

CONFIRMATIO CHARTORUM. The name given to a statute passed during the reign of the English king Edward I. 25 Ed. I., c. 6. See Bac. Ab. Smuggling, B.

CONFIRMATION, *contracts*, *conveyancing*. 1. A contract by which that which was voidable, is made firm and unavoidable. 2. A species of conveyance.

2.—1. When a contract has been entered into by a stranger without authority, he in whose name it has been made may, by his own act, confirm it; or if the contract be made by the party himself in an informal and voidable manner, he may in a more formal manner confirm and render it valid; and in that event it will take effect, as between the parties, from the original making. To make a valid confirmation, the party must be apprised of his rights, and where there has been a fraud in the transaction, he must be aware of it, and intend to confirm his contract. Vide 1 Ball & Beatty, 353; 2 Scho. & Lef. 486; 12 Ves. 373; 1 Ves. Jr. 215; Newl. Contr. 496; 1 Atk. 301; 8 Watts. R. 280.

3.—2. Lord Coke defines a confirmation of an estate, to be "a conveyance of an estate or right *in esse*, whereby a voidable estate is made sure and unavoidable; or where a particular estate is increased."

4. The first part of this definition may be illustrated by the following case, put by Littleton, § 516; where a person lets land to another for the term of his life, who lets the same to another for forty years, by force of which he is in possession; if the lessor for life confirms the estate of the tenant for years by deed, and afterwards the tenant for life dies, during the term; this deed will operate as a confirmation of the term for years. As to the latter branch of the definition; whenever a confirmation operates by way of increasing the estate, it is similar in every respect to a release that operates by way of enlargement, for there must be privity of estate, and proper words of limitation. The proper technical words of a confirmation are, ratify and confirm; although it is usual and prudent to insert also the words *given and granted*. Watk. Prin. Convey. chap. vii.

5. A confirmation does not strengthen a void estate. *Confirmatio est nulla, ubi donum precedens est invalidum, et ubi donatio nulla est nec valebit confirmatio*. For confirmation may make a voidable or defeasible estate good, but cannot operate on an estate void in law. Co. Litt. 295. The canon law agrees with this rule, and hence the maxim, *qui confirmat nihil dat*. Toull. Dr. Civ. Fr. liv. 3, t. 3, c. 6, n. 476. Vide Vin. Ab. h. t.; Com. Dig. h. t.; Ayliffe's Pand. *386; 1 Chit. Pr. 315; 3 Gill & John. 290; 3 Yerg. R. 405; Co. Litt. 295; Gilbert on Ten. 75; 1 Breese's R. 236; 9 Co. 142, a; 2 Bouv. Inst. n. 2067–9.

6. An infant is said to confirm his acts performed during infancy, when, after coming to full age, he expressly approves of them, or does acts from which such confirmation may be implied. See *Ratification*.

CONFIRMEE. He to whom a confirmation is made.

CONFIRMOR. He who makes a confirmation to another.

CONFISCATION. The act by which the estate, goods or chattels of a person who has been guilty of some crime, or who is a public enemy, is declared to be forfeited for the benefit of the public treasury. Domat, Droit Public, liv. 1, tit. 6, s. 2, n. 1. When property is forfeited as a punishment for the commission of crime, it is usually called a forfeiture. 1 Bl. Com. 299.

2. It is a general rule that the property of the subjects of an enemy found in the country may be appropriated by the government, without notice, unless there be a treaty to the contrary. 1 Gallis. R. 563; 3 Dall. R. 199; N. Car. Cas. 79. It has been frequently provided by treaty that foreign subjects should be permitted to remain and continue their business, notwithstanding a rupture between the governments, so long as they conducted themselves innocently; and when there was no such treaty, such a liberal permission has been announced in the very declaration of war. Vattel, liv. 3, c. 4, § 63. Sir Michael Foster, (Discourses on High Treason, p. 185, 6,) mentions several instances of such declarations by the king of Great Britain; and he says

that aliens were thereby enabled to acquire personal chattels and to maintain actions for the recovery of their personal rights, in as full a manner as alien friends. 1 Kent, Com. 57.

3. In the United States, the broad principle has been assumed "that war gives to the sovereign full right to take the persons and confiscate the property of the enemy, wherever found. The mitigations of this rigid rule, which the policy of modern times has introduced into practice, will more or less affect the exercise of this right, but cannot impair the right itself." 8 Cranch, 122–3. Commercial nations have always considerable property in the possession of their neighbors; and when war breaks out, the question, what shall be done with enemies property found in the country, is one rather of policy than of law, and is properly addressed to the consideration of the legislature, and not to courts of law. The strict right of confiscation exists in congress; and without a legislative act authorizing the confiscation of enemies' property, it cannot be condemned. 8 Cranch, 128, 129.

See Chit. Law of Nations, c. 3; Marten's Law of Nat. lib. 8, c. 3, s. 9; Burlamaqui, Princ. of Pol. Law, part 4, c. 7; Vattel, liv. 3, c. 4, § 63.

4. The claim of a right to confiscate debts, contracted by individuals in time of peace, and which remain due to subjects of the enemy in time of war, rests very much upon the same principles as that concerning the enemy's tangible property, found in the country at the commencement of the war. But it is the universal practice to forbear to seize and confiscate debts and credits. 1 Kent, Com. 64, 5; vide 4 Cranch, R. 415; Charlt. 140; 2 Harr. & John. 101, 112, 471; 6 Cranch, R. 286; 7 Conn. R. 428; 2 Tayl. R. 115; 1 Day, R. 4; Kirby, R. 228, 291; C. & N. 77, 492.

CONFLICT. The opposition or difference between two judicial jurisdictions, when they both claim the right to decide a cause, or where they both declare their incompetency. The first is called a *positive* conflict, and the latter a *negative* conflict.

CONFLICT OF JURISDICTION. The contest between two officers, who each claim to have cognizance of a particular case.

CONFLICT OF LAWS. This phrase is used to signify that the laws of different countries, on the subject-matter to be decided, are in opposition to each other; or that certain laws of the same country are contradictory.

2. When this happens to be the case, it becomes necessary to decide which law is to be obeyed. This subject has occupied the attention and talents of some of the most learned jurists, and their labors are comprised in many volumes. A few general rules have been adopted on this subject, which will here be noticed.

3.—1. Every nation possesses an exclusive sovereignty and jurisdiction within its own territory. The laws of every state, therefore, affect and bind directly all property, whether real or personal, within its territory; and all persons who are resident within it, whether citizens or aliens, natives or foreigners; and also all contracts made, and acts done within it. Vide *Lex Loci contractus;* Henry, For. Law, part 1, c. 1, § 1; Cowp. R. 208; 2 Hagg. C. R. 383. It is proper, however, to observe, that ambassadors and other public ministers, while in the territory of the state to which they are delegates, are exempt from the local jurisdiction. Vide *Ambassador.* And the persons composing a foreign army, or fleet, marching through, or stationed in the territory of another state, with whom the foreign nation is in amity, are also exempt from the civil and criminal jurisdiction of the place. Wheat. Intern. Law, part 2, c. 2, § 10; Casaregis, Disc. 136–174; vide 7 Cranch, R. 116.

4. Possessing exclusive authority, with the above qualification, a state may regulate the manner and circumstances, under which property, whether real or personal, in possession or in action, within it shall be held, transmitted or transferred, by sale, barter, or bequest, or recovered or enforced; the condition, capacity, and state of all persons within it; the validity of contracts and other acts done there; the resulting rights and duties growing out of these contracts and acts; and the remedies, and modes of administering justice in all cases. Story, Confl. of Laws, § 18; Vattel, B. 2, c. 7, § 84, 85; Wheat. Intern. Law, part 1, c. 2, § 5.

5.—2. A state or nation cannot, by its laws, directly affect or bind property out of its own territory, or persons not resident therein, whether they are natural born or naturalized citizens or subjects, or others. This result flows from the principle that each sovereignty is perfectly independent. 13 Mass. R. 4. To this general rule there appears to be an exception, which is this, that a nation has a right to bind its own citizens or subjects by its own laws in every place; but this exception is not to be adopted without some qualification. Story, Confl. of Laws, § 21; Wheat. Intern. Law, part 2, c. 2, § 7.

6.—3. Whatever force and obligation the laws of one country have in another, depends upon the laws and municipal regulations of the latter; that is to say, upon its own proper jurisprudence and polity, and upon its own express or tacit consent. Huberus, lib. 1, t. 3, § 2. When a statute, or the unwritten or common law of the country forbids the recognition of the foreign law, the latter is of no force whatever. When both are silent, then the question arises, which of the conflicting laws is to have effect. Whether the one or the other shall be the rule of decision must necessarily depend on a variety of circumstances, which cannot be reduced to any certain rule. No nation will suffer the laws of another to interfere with her own, to the injury of her own citizens; and whether they do or not, must depend on the condition of the country in which the law is sought to be enforced, the particular state of her legislation, her policy, and the character of her institutions. 2 Mart. Lo. Rep. N. S. 606. In the conflict of laws, it must often be a matter of doubt which should prevail; and, whenever a doubt does exist, the court which decides, will prefer the law of its own country to that of the stranger. 17 Mart. Lo. R. 569, 595, 596.

Vide, generally, Story, Confl. of Laws; Burge, Confl. of Laws; Liverm. on Contr. of Laws; Fœlix, Droit Intern.; Huberus, De Conflictu Legum; Hertius, de Collisione Legum; Boullenois, Traité de la personnalité et de la réalité de lois, coutumes et statuts, par forme d'observations; Boullenois, Dissertations sur des questions qui naissent de la contrarieté des lois et des coutumes.

CONFRONTATION, *crim. law, practice.* The act by which a witness is brought in the presence of the accused, so that the latter may object to him, if he can, and the former may know and identify the accused, and maintain the truth in his presence. No man can be a witness unless confronted with the accused, except by consent.

CONFUSION. The concurrence of two qualities in the same subject, which mutually destroy each other. Poth. Ob. P. 3, c. 5; 3 Bl. Com. 405; Story Bailm. § 40.

CONFUSION OF GOODS. This takes place where the goods of two or more persons become mixed together so that they cannot be separated. There is a difference between *confusion* and *commixtion;* in the former it is impossible, while in the latter it is possible, to make a separation. Bowy. Comm. 88.

2. When the confusion takes place by the mutual consent of the owners, they have an interest in the mixture in proportion to their respective shares. 2 Bl. Com. 405; 6 Hill, N. Y. Rep. 425. But if one wilfully mixes his money, corn or hay, with that of another man, without his approbation or knowledge, the law, to guard against fraud, gives the entire property without any account, to him whose original dominion is invaded and endeavored to be rendered uncertain, without his consent. Ib.; and see 2 Johns. Ch. R. 62; 2 Kent's Comm. 297.

3. There may be a case neither of consent nor of wilfulness, in the confusion of goods; as where a bailee by negligence or unskilfulness, or inadvertence, mixes up his own goods of the same sort with those bailed; and there may be a confusion arising from accident and unavoidable casualty. Now, in the latter case of accidental intermixture, the rule, following the civil law, which deemed the property to be held in common, might be adopted; and it would make no difference whether the mixture produced a thing of the same sort or not; as, if the wine of two persons were mixed by accident. See Dane's Abr. ch. 76, art. 5, § 19.

4. But in cases of mixture by unskilfulness, negligence, or inadvertence, the true principle seems to be, that if a man having undertaken to keep the property of another distinct from, mixes it with his own, the whole must, both at law and in equity, be taken to be the property of the other, until the former puts the subject under such circumstances, that it may be distinguished as satisfactorily as it might have been before the unauthorized mixture on his part. 15 Ves. 432, 436, 439, 440; 2 John. Ch. R. 62; Story on Bailm. c. 1, § 40. And see 7 Mass. R. 123; Dane's Abr. c. 76, art. 3, § 15; Com. Dig. Pleader, 3 M 28; Bac. Ab. Trespass, E 2; 2 Campb. 576; 2 Roll. 566, l. 15; 2 Bul. 323; 2 Cro. 366, 2 Roll. 393; 5 East, 7; 21 Pick. R. 298.

CONFUSION OF RIGHTS, *contracts.* When the qualities of debtor and creditor are united in the same person, there arises a confusion of rights, which extinguishes the two credits; for instance, when a woman obligee marries the obligor, the debt is extinguished. 1 Salk. 306; Cro. Car. 551; 1 Ld. Raym. 515; Ca. Ch. 21, 117. There is, however, an excepted case in relation to a bond given by the husband to the wife; when it is given to the intended wife for a provision to take effect after his death. 1 Ld. Raym. 515; 5 T. R. 381; Hut. 17; Hob. 216; Cro. Car. 376; 1 Salk. 326; Palm. 99; Carth. 512; Com. Dig. Baron & Feme, D. A further exception is the case of a divorce. If one be bound in an obligation to a feme sole and then marry her, and afterwards they are divorced, she may sue her former husband on the obligation, notwithstanding her action was in suspense during the marriage. 26 H. VIII. 1.

2. Where a person possessed of an estate, becomes in a different right entitled to a charge upon the estate; the charge is in general merged in the estate, and does not revive in favor of the personal representative against the heir; there are particular exceptions, as where the person in whom the interests unite is a minor, and can therefore dispose of the personalty, but not of the estate; but in the case of a lunatic the merger and confusion was ruled to have taken place. 2 Ves. jun. 261. See Louis. Code, art. 801 to 808; 2 Ld. R. 527; 3 L. R. 552; 4 L. R. 399, 488. Burge on Sur. Book 2, c. 11, p. 253.

CONGE'. A French word which signifies permission, and is understood in that sense in law. Cunn. Dict. h. t. In the French maritime law, it is a species of passport or permission to navigate, delivered by public authority. It is also in the nature of a clearance. (q. v.) Bouch. Inst. n. 812; Répert. de la Jurisp. du Notoriat, by Rolland de Villargues. *Congé*.

CONGEABLE, *Eng. law.* This word is nearly obsolete. It is derived from the French *congé*, permission, leave; it signifies that a thing is lawful or lawfully done, or done with permission; as entry congeable, and the like. Litt. s. 279.

CONGREGATION. A society of a number of persons who compose an ecclesiastical body. In the ecclesiastical law this term is used to designate certain bureaux at Rome, where ecclesiastical matters are attended to. In the United States, by congregation is meant the members of a particular church, who meet in one place to worship. See 2 Russ. 120.

CONGRESS. This word has several significations. 1. An assembly of the deputies convened from different governments, to treat of peace or of other political affairs, is called a congress.

2.—2. Congress is the name of the legislative body of the United States, composed of the senate and house of representatives. Const. U. S. art. 1, s. 1.

3. Congress is composed of two independent houses. 1. The senate; and, 2. The house of representatives.

4.—1. The senate is composed of two senators from each state, chosen by the legislature thereof for six years, and each senator has one vote. They represent the states rather than the people, as each state has its equal voice and equal weight in the senate, without any regard to the disparity of population, wealth or dimensions. The senate have been, from the first formation of the government, divided into three classes; and the rotation of the classes was originally determined by lots, and the seats of one class are vacated at the end of the second year, and one-third of the senate is chosen every second year. Const. U. S. art 1, s. 3. This provision was borrowed from a similar one in some of the state constitutions, of which Virginia gave the first example.

5. The qualifications which the constitution requires of a senator, are, that he should be thirty years of age, have been nine years a citizen of the United States, and, when elected, be an inhabitant of that state for which he shall be chosen. Art. 1, s. 3.

6.—2. The house of representatives is composed of members chosen every second year by the people of the several states, who are qualified electors of the most numerous branch of the legislature of the state to which they belong.

7. No person can be a representative until he has attained the age of twenty-five years, and has been seven years a citizen of the United States, and is, at the time of his election, an inhabitant of the state in which he is chosen. Const. U. S. art. 1, § 2.

8. The constitution requires that the representatives and direct taxes shall be apportioned among the several states, which may be included within this Union, according to their respective numbers, which shall be determined by adding to the whole number of free persons, including those bound to service for a term of years, and excluding

Indians not taxed, three-fifths of all other persons. Art. 1, s. 1.

9. The number of representatives shall not exceed one for every thirty thousand, but each state shall have at least one representative. Ib.

10. Having shown how congress is constituted, it is proposed here to consider the privileges and powers of the two houses, both aggregately and separately.

11. Each house is made the judge of the election, returns, and qualifications of its own members. Art. 1, s. 5. As each house acts in these cases in a judicial character, its decisions, like the decisions of any other court of justice, ought to be regulated by known principles of law, and strictly adhered to, for the sake of uniformity and certainty. A majority of each house shall constitute a quorum to do business; but a smaller number may adjourn from day to day, and may be authorized to compel the attendance of absent members, in such manner, and under such penalties, as each may provide. Each house may determine the rules of its proceedings; punish its members for disorderly behaviour; and, with the concurrence of two-thirds, expel a member. Each house is bound to keep a journal of its proceedings, and from time to time, publish the same, excepting such parts as may, in their judgment, require secrecy; and to enter the yeas and nays on the journal, on any question, at the desire of one-fifth of the members present. Art. 1, s. 5.

12. The members of both houses are in all cases, except treason, felony, and breach of the peace, privileged from arrest during their attendance at the session of their respective houses, and in going to, and returning from the same. Art. 1, s. 6.

13. These privileges of the two houses are obviously necessary for their preservation and character; and, what is still more important to the freedom of deliberation, no member can be questioned in any other place for any speech or debate in either house. Ib.

14. There is no express power given to either house to punish for contempts, except when committed by their own members, but they have such an implied power. 6 Wheat. R. 204. This power, however, extends no further than imprisonment, and that will continue no further than the duration of the power that imprisons. The imprisonment will therefore terminate with the adjournment or dissolution of congress.

15. The house of representatives has the exclusive right of originating bills for raising revenue, and this is the only privilege that house enjoys in its legislative character, which is not shared equally with the other; and even those bills are amendable by the senate, in its discretion. Art. 1, s. 7.

16. The two houses are an entire and perfect check upon each other, in all business appertaining to legislation; and one of them cannot even adjourn, during the session of congress, for more than three days, without the consent of the other; nor to any other place than that in which the two houses shall be sitting. Art. 1, s. 5.

17. The powers of congress extend generally to all subjects of a national nature. Congress are authorized to provide for the common defence and general welfare; and for that purpose, among other express grants, they have the power to lay and collect taxes, duties, imposts and excises; to borrow money on the credit of the United States; to regulate commerce with foreign nations, and among the several states, and with the Indians; 1 McLean, R. 257; to establish an uniform rule of naturalization, and uniform laws of bankruptcy throughout the United States; to establish post offices and post roads; to promote the progress of science and the useful arts, by securing for a limited time to authors and inventors, the exclusive right to their respective writings and discoveries; to constitute tribunals inferior to the supreme court; to define and punish piracies on the high seas, and offences against the laws of nations; to declare war; to raise and support armies; to provide and maintain a navy; to provide for the calling forth of the militia; to exercise exclusive legislation over the District of Columbia; and to give full efficacy to the powers contained in the constitution.

18. The rules of proceeding in each house are substantially the same; the house of representatives choose their own speaker; the vice-president of the United States is, ex officio, president of the senate, and gives the casting vote when the members are equally divided. The proceedings and discussions in the two houses are generally in public.

19. The ordinary mode of passing laws is briefly this; one day's notice of a motion for leave to bring in a bill, in cases of a general nature, is required; every bill must have three readings before it is passed, and these

readings must be on different days; and no bill can be committed and amended until it has been twice read. In the house of representatives, bills, after being twice read, are committed to a committee of the whole house, when a chairman is appointed by the speaker to preside over the committee, when the speaker leaves the chair, and takes a part in the debate as an ordinary member.

20. When a bill has passed one house, it is transmitted to the other, and goes through a similar form, though in the senate there is less formality, and bills are often committed to a select committee, chosen by ballot. If a bill be altered or amended in the house to which it is transmitted, it is then returned to the house in which it originated, and if the two houses cannot agree, they appoint a committee to confer on the subject See *Conference.*

21. When a bill is engrossed, and has received the sanction of both houses, it is sent to the president for his approbation. If he approves of the bill, he signs it. If he does not, it is returned, with his objections, to the house in which it originated, and that house enters the objections at large on their journal, and proceeds to re-consider it. If, after such re-consideration, two-thirds of the house agree to pass the bill, it is sent, together with the objections, to the other house, by which it is likewise re-considered, and if approved by two-thirds of that house, it becomes a law. But in all such cases, the votes of both houses are determined by yeas and nays; and the names of the persons voting for and against the bill, are to be entered on the journal of each house respectively.

22. If any bill shall not be returned by the president within ten days (Sundays excepted) after it shall have been presented to him, the same shall be a law, in like manner as if he had signed it, unless the congress, by their adjournment, prevent its return; in which case it shall not be a law. Art. 1, s. 7. See *House of Representatives; President; Senate; Veto;* Kent, Com. Lecture xi.; Rawle on the Const. ch. ix.

CONGRESS, *med. juris.* This name was anciently given in France, England, and other countries, to the indecent intercourse between married persons, in the presence of witnesses appointed by the courts, in cases when the husband or wife was charged by the other with impotence. Trebuchet, Jurisp. de Med. 101; Dictionnaire des Sciences Medicales, art. *Congrès*, by Marc.

CONJECTURE. Conjectures are ideas or notions founded on probabilities without any demonstration of their truth. Mascardus has defined conjecture "rationabile vestigium latentis veritatis, unde nascitur opinio sapientis;" or a slight degree of credence arising from evidence too weak or too remote to produce belief. De Prob. vol. i. quæst. 14, n. 14. See Dict. de Trévoux, h. v.; Denisart, h. v.

CONJOINTS. Persons married to each other. Story, Confl. of L. § 71; Wolff. Dr. de la Nat. § 858.

CONJUGAL. Matrimonial; belonging to marriage; as, conjugal rights, or the rights which belong to the husband or wife as such.

CONJUNCTIVE, *contracts, wills, instruments.* A term in grammar used to designate particles which connect one word to another, or one proposition to another proposition.

2. There are many cases in law, where the conjunctive *and* is used for the disjunctive *or*, and *vice versa.*

3. An obligation is conjunctive when it contains several things united by a conjunction to indicate that they are all equally the object of the matter or contract; for example, if I promise for a lawful consideration, to deliver to you my copy of the Life of Washington, my Encyclopædia, and my copy of the History of the United States, I am then bound to deliver all of them and cannot be discharged by delivering one only. There are, according to Toullier, tom. vi. n. 686, as many separate obligations as there are things to be delivered, and the obligor may discharge himself pro tanto by delivering either of them, or in case of refusal the tender will be valid. It is presumed, however, that only one action could be maintained for the whole. But if the articles in the agreement had not been enumerated, I could not, according to Toullier, deliver one in discharge of my contract, without the consent of the creditor; as if, instead of enumerating the books above mentioned, I had bound myself to deliver all my books, the very books in question. Vide *Disjunctive, Item,* and the cases there cited; and also, Bac. Ab. Conditions, P; 1 Bos. & Pull. 242; 4 Bing. N. C. 463; S. C. 33 E. C. L. R. 413; 1 Bouv. Inst. n. 687-8.

CONJURATION. A swearing together. It signifies a plot, bargain, or compact made by a number of persons under oath, to dc some public harm. In times of ignorance, this word was used to signify the personal conference which some persons were supposed to have had with the devil, or some evil spirit, to know any secret, or effect any purpose.

CONNECTICUT. The name of one of the original states of the United States of America. It was not until the year 1665 that the territory now known as the state of Connecticut was united under one government. The charter was granted by Charles II. in April, 1662, but as it included the whole colony of New Haven, it was not till 1665 that the latter ceased its resistance, when both the colony of Connecticut and that of New Haven agreed, and then they were indissolubly united, and have so remained. This charter, with the exception of a temporary suspension, continued in force till the American revolution, and afterwards continued as a fundamental law of the state till the year 1818, when the present constitution was adopted. 1 Story on the Const. § 86—88.

2. The constitution was adopted on the fifteenth day of September, 1818. The powers of the government are divided into three distinct departments, and each of them confided to a separate magistracy, to wit: those which are legislative, to one; those which are executive to another; and those which are judicial to a third. Art. 2.

3.—1st. The legislative power is vested in two distinct houses or branches, the one styled the senate, and the other the house of representatives, and both together the general assembly. 1. The senate consists of twelve members, chosen annually by the electors. 2. The house of representatives consists of electors residing in towns from which they are elected. The number of representatives is to be the same as at present practised and allowed; towns which may be hereafter incorporated are to be entitled to one representative only.

4.—2d. The executive power is vested in a governor and lieutenant-governor. 1. The supreme executive power of the state is vested in a governor, chosen by the electors of the state; he is to hold his office for one year from the first Wednesday of May, next succeeding his election, and until his successor be duly qualified. Art. 4, s. 1. The governor possesses the veto power, art. 4, s. 12. 2. The lieutenant-governor is elected immediately after the election of governor, in the same manner as is provided for the election of governor, who continues in office the same time, and is to possess the same qualifications as the governor. Art. 4, s. 3. The lieutenant-governor, by virtue of his office, is president of the senate; and in case of the death, resignation, refusal to serve, or removal from office of the governor, or of his impeachment or absence from the state, the lieutenant-governor exercises all the powers and authority appertaining to the office of governor, until another be chosen, at the next periodical election for governor, and be duly qualified; or until the governor, impeached or absent, shall be acquitted or return. Art. 4, s. 14.

5.—3d. The judicial power of the state is vested in a supreme court of errors, a superior court, and such inferior courts as the general assembly may, from time to time, ordain and establish; the powers of which courts shall be defined. A sufficient number of justices of the peace, with such jurisdiction, civil and criminal, as the general assembly may prescribe, are to be appointed in each county. Art. 5.

CONNIVANCE. An agreement or consent, indirectly given, that something unlawful shall be done by another.

2. The connivance of the husband to his wife's prostitution deprives him of the right of obtaining a divorce; or of recovering damages from the seducer. 4 T. R. 657. It may be satisfactorily proved by implication.

3. Connivance differs from condonation, (q. v.) though either may have the same legal consequences. Connivance necessarily involves criminality on the part of the individual who connives; condonation may take place without imputing the slightest blame to the party who forgives the injury.

4. Connivance must be the act of the mind before the offence has been committed; condonation is the result of a determination to forgive an injury which was not known until after it was inflicted. 3 Hagg. Eccl. R. 350.

5. Connivance differs, also, from collusion (q. v.); the former is generally collusion for a particular purpose, while the latter may exist without connivance. 3 Hagg, Eccl. R. 130. Vide Shelf. on Mar. & Div. 449; 3 Hagg. R. 82: 2 Hagg. R 376; Id. 278; 3 Hagg. R. 58, 107, 119, 131, 312; 3 Pick. R. 299; 2 Caines, 219; Anth. N. P. 196.

CONQUEST, *feudal law*. This term

was used by the feudists to signify *purchase.*

CONQUEST, *international law.* The acquisition of the sovereignty of a country by force of arms, exercised by an independent power which reduces the vanquished to the submission of its empire.

2. It is a general rule, that where conquered countries have laws of their own, these laws remain in force after the conquest, until they are abrogated, unless they are contrary to our religion, or enact any *malum in se.* In all such cases the laws of the conquering country prevail; for it is not to be presumed that laws opposed to religion or sound morals could be sanctioned. 1 Story, Const. § 150, and the cases there cited.

3. The conquest and military occupation of a part of the territory of the United States by a public enemy, renders such conquered territory, during such occupation, a foreign country with respect to the revenue laws of the United States. 4 Wheat. R. 246; 2 Gallis. R. 486. The people of a conquered territory change their allegiance; but, by the modern practice, their relations to each other, and their rights of property, remain the same. 7 Pet. R. 86.

4. Conquest does not, *per se,* give the conqueror *plenum dominium et utile,* but a temporary right of possession and government. 2 Gallis. R. 486; 3 Wash. C. C. R. 101. See 8 Wheat. R. 591; 2 Bay, R. 229; 2 Dall. R. 1; 12 Pet. 410.

5. The right which the English government claimed over the territory now composing the United States, was not founded on conquest, but discovery. Id. § 152, et seq.

CONQUETS, *French law.* The name given to every acquisition which the husband and wife, jointly or severally, make during the conjugal community. Thus, whatever is acquired by the husband and wife, either by his or her industry or good fortune, enures to the extent of one-half for the benefit of the other. Merl. Rép. mot Conquêt; Merl. Quest. mot Conquêt. In Louisiana, these gains are called *aquets.* (q. v.) Civ. Code of Lo. art. 2369.

CONSANGUINITY. The relation subsisting among all the different persons descending from the same stock, or common ancestor. Vaughan, 322, 329; 2 Bl. Com. 202; Toull. Dr. Civ. Fr. liv. 3, t. 1, ch. n. 115; 2 Bouv. Inst. n. 1955, et seq.

2. Some portion of the blood of the common ancestor flows through the veins of all his descendants, and though mixed with the blood flowing from many other families, yet it constitutes the kindred or alliance by blood between any two of the individuals. This relation by blood is of two kinds, lineal and collateral.

3. Lineal consanguinity is that relation which exists among persons, where one is descended from the other, as between the son and the father, or the grandfather, and so upwards in a direct ascending line; and between the father and the son, or the grandson, and so downwards in a direct descending line. Every generation in this direct course makes a degree, computing either in the ascending or descending line. This being the natural mode of computing the degrees of lineal consanguinity, it has been adopted by the civil, the canon, and the common law.

4. Collateral consanguinity is the relation subsisting among persons who descend from the same common ancestor, but not from each other. It is essential to constitute this relation, that they spring from the same common root or stock, but in different branches. The mode of computing the degrees is to discover the common ancestor, to begin with him to reckon downwards, and the degree the two persons, or the more remote of them, is distant from the ancestor, is the degree of kindred subsisting between them. For instance, two brothers are related to each other in the first degree, because from the father to each of them is one degree. An uncle and a nephew are related to each other in the second degree, because the nephew is two degrees distant from the common ancestor, and the rule of computation is extended to the remotest degrees of collateral relationship. This is the mode of computation by the common and canon law The method of computing by the civil law, is to begin at either of the persons in question, and count up to the common ancestor, and then downwards to the other person, calling it a degree for each person, both ascending and descending, and the degrees they stand from each other is the degree in which they stand related. Thus, from a nephew to his father, is one degree; to the grandfather, two degrees; and then to the uncle, three; which points out the relationship.

5. The following table, in which the Roman numeral letters express the degrees by the civil law, and those in Arabic figures at the bottom, those by the common law, will fully illustrate the subject.

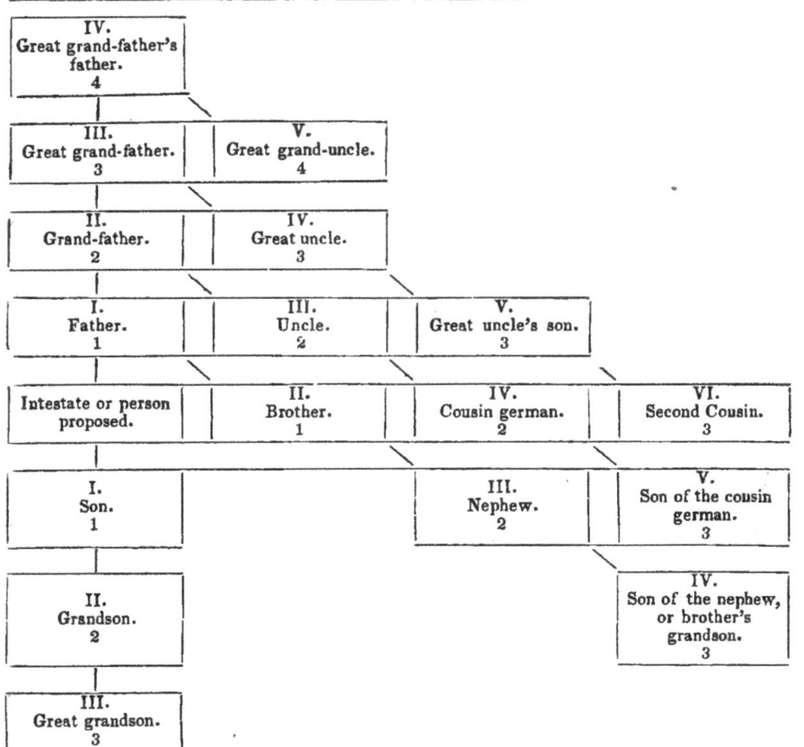

6. The mode o the civil law is preferable, for it points out the actual degree of kindred in all cases; by the mode adopted by the common law, different relations may stand in the same degree. The uncle and nephew stand related in the second degree by the common law, and so are two first cousins, or two sons of two brothers; but by the civil law the uncle and nephew are in the third degree, and the cousins are in the fourth. The mode of computation, however, is immaterial, for both will establish the same person to be the heir. 2 Bl. Com. 202; 1 Swift's Dig. 113; Toull. Civ. Fr. liv. 3, t. 1, c. 3, n. 115. Vide *Branch; Degree; Line.*

CONSCIENCE. The moral sense, or that capacity of our mental constitution, by which we irresistibly feel the difference between right and wrong.

2. The constitution of the United States wisely provides that "no religious test shall ever be required." No man, then, or body of men, have a right to control a man's belief or opinion in religious matters, or to forbid the most perfect freedom of inquiry in relation to them, by force or threats, or by any other motives than arguments or persuasion. Vide Story, Const. § 1841-1843.

CONSENSUAL, *civil law.* This word is applied to designate one species of contract known in the civil laws; these contracts derive their name from the consent of the parties which is required in their formation, as they cannot exist without such consent.

2. The contract of sale, among the civilians, is an example of a consensual contract, because the moment there is an agreement between the seller and the buyer as to the thing and the price, the vendor and the purchaser have reciprocal actions On the contrary, on a loan, there is no action by the lender or borrower, although there may have been consent, until the thing is delivered or the money counted. This is a

real contract in the sense of the civil law. Leç. El. Dr. Rom. § 895; Poth. Ob. pt. 1, c. 1, s. 1, art. 2; 1 Bell's Com. (5th ed.) 435. Vide *Contract*.

CONSENT. An agreement to something proposed, and differs from assent. (q. v.) Wolff, Ins. Nat. part 1, §§ 27-30; Pard. Dr. Com. part 2, tit. 1, n. 1, 38 to 178. Consent supposes, 1. a physical power to act; 2. a moral power of acting; 3. a serious, determined, and free use of these powers. Fonb. Eq. B. 1, c. 2, s. 1; Grot. de Jure Belli et Pacis, lib. 2, c. 11, s. 5.

2. Consent is either express or implied. Express, when it is given viva voce, or in writing; implied, when it is manifested by signs, actions, or facts, or by inaction or silence, which raise a presumption that the consent has been given.

3.—1. When a legacy is given with a condition annexed to the bequest, requiring the consent of executors to the marriage of the legatee, and under such consent being given, a mutual attachment has been suffered to grow up, it would be rather late to state terms and conditions on which a marriage between the parties should take place; 2 Ves. & Beames, 234; Ambl. 264; 2 Freem. 201; unless such consent was obtained by deceit or fraud. 1 Eden, 6; 1 Phillim. 200; 12 Ves. 19.

4.—2. Such a condition does not apply to a *second* marriage. 3 Bro. C. C. 145; 3 Ves. 239.

5.—3. If the consent has been substantially given, though not *modo et forma*, the legatee will be held duly entitled to the legacy. 1 Sim. & Stu. 172; 1 Meriv. 187; 2 Atk. 265.

6.—4. When trustees under a marriage settlement are empowered to sell "with the consent of the husband and wife," a sale made by the trustees without the distinct consent of the wife, cannot be a due execution of their power. 10 Ves. 378.

7.—5. Where a power of sale requires that the sale should be with the consent of certain specified individuals, the fact of such consent having been given, ought to be evinced in the manner pointed out by the creator of the power, or such power will not be considered as properly executed. 10 Ves. 308. Vide, generally, 2 Supp. to Ves. jr. 161, 165, 169; Ayliffe's Pand. 117; 1 Rob. Leg. 345, 539.

8.—6. Courts of equity have established the rule, that when the true owner of property stands by, and knowingly suffers a stranger to sell the same as his own, without objection, this will be such implied consent as to render the sale valid against the true owner. Story on Ag. § 91; Story on Eq. Jur. § 385 to 390. And courts of law, unless restrained by technical formalities, act upon the principles of justice; as, for example, when a man permitted, without objection, the sale of his goods under an execution against another person. 6 Adolph. & Ell. 469; 9 Barn. & Cr. 586; 3 Barn. & Adolph. 318, note.

9. The consent which is implied in every agreement is excluded, 1. By error in the essentials of the contract; as, if Paul, in the city of Philadelphia, buy the horse of Peter, which is in Boston, and promise to pay one hundred dollars for him, the horse at the time of the sale, unknown to either party, being dead. This decision is founded on the rule that he who consents through error does not consent at all; *non consentiunt qui errant*. Dig. 2, 1, 15; Dig. lib. 1, tit ult. l. 116, § 2. 2. Consent is excluded by duress of the party making the agreement 3. Consent is never given so as to bind the parties, when it is obtained by fraud. 4. It cannot be given by a person who has no understanding, as an idiot, nor by one who, though possessed of understanding, is not in law capable of making a contract, as a feme covert. See Bouv. Inst. Index, h. t.

CONSENT RULE. In the English practice, still adhered to in some of the states of the American Union, the defendant in ejectment is required to enter on record that he confesses the lease, entry, and ouster of the plaintiff; this is called the consent rule.

2. The consent rule contains the following particulars, namely: 1. The person appearing consents to be made defendant instead of the casual ejector; 2. To appear at the suit of the plaintiff; and, if the proceedings are by bill, to file common bail; 3. To receive a declaration in ejectment, and plead not guilty; 4. At the trial of the case to confess lease, entry, and ouster, and insist upon his title only; 5. That if at the trial, the party appearing shall not confess lease, entry, and ouster, whereby the plaintiff shall not be able to prosecute his suit, such party shall pay to the plaintiff the costs of the *non pros*, and suffer judgment to be entered against the casual ejector; 6. That if a verdict shall be given for the defendant, or the plaintiff shall not prosecute his suit for any other cause than the non-confession

of lease, entry, and ouster, the lessor of the plaintiff shall pay costs to the defendant; 7. When the landlord appears alone, that the plaintiff shall be at liberty to sign judgment immediately against the casual ejector, but that execution shall be stayed until the court shall further order. Adams, Ej. 233, 234; and for a form see Ad. Ej. Appx. No. 25.

Vide 2 Cowen, 442; 4 John. R. 311; Caines' Cas. 102; 12 Wend. 105; 3 Cowen, 356; 6 Cowen, 587; 1 Cowen, 166; and *Casual Ejector; Ejectment.*

CONSEQUENTIAL DAMAGES, *torts.* Those damages or those losses which arise not from the immediate act of the party, but in consequence of such act; as if a man throw a log into the public streets, and another fall upon it and become injured by the fall; or if a man should erect a dam over his own ground, and by that means overflow his neighbor's, to his injury.

2. The form of action to be instituted for consequential damages caused without force, is by action on the case. 3 East, 602; 1 Stran. 636; 5 T. R. 649; 5 Vin. Ab. 403; 1 Chit. Pl. 127; Kames on Eq. 71; 3 Bouv. Inst. n. 3484, et seq. Vide *Immediate.*

CONSERVATOR. A preserver, a protector.

2. Before the institution of the office of justices of the peace in England, the public order was maintained by officers who bore the name of conservators of the peace. All judges, justices, sheriffs and constables, are conservators of the peace, and are bound, ex officio, to be aiding and assisting in preserving order.

3. In Connecticut, this term is applied to designate a guardian who has the care of the estate of an idiot. 5 Conn. R. 280.

CONSIDERATIO CURIÆ, *practice.* The judgment of the court. In pleadings where matters are determined by the court, it is said, therefore it is considered and adjudged by the court, *ideo consideratum est per curiam.*

CONSIDERATION, *contracts.* A compensation which is paid, or an inconvenience suffered by the party from whom it proceeds. Or it is the reason which moves the contracting party to enter into the contract. 2 Bl. Com. 443. Viner defines it to be a cause or occasion meritorious, requiring a mutual recompense in deed or in law. Abr. tit. Consideration, A.

2. A consideration of some sort or other, is so absolutely necessary to the forming a good contract, that a *nudum pactum,* or an agreement to do or to pay any thing on one side, without any compensation to the other, is totally void in law, and a man cannot be compelled to perform it. Dr. & Stud. d. 2, c. 24; 3 Call, R. 439; 7 Conn. 57; 1 Stew. R. 51; 5 Mass. 301; 4 John. R. 235; 6 Yerg. 418; Cooke, R. 467; 6 Halst. R. 174; 4 Munf. R. 95. But contracts under seal are valid without a consideration; or, perhaps, more properly speaking, every bond imports in itself a sufficient consideration, though none be mentioned. 11 Serg. & R. 107. Negotiable instruments, as bills of exchange and promissory notes, carry with them prima facie evidence of consideration. 2 Bl. Com. 445.

3. The consideration must be some benefit to the party by whom the promise is made, or to a third person at his instance; or some detriment sustained at the instance of the party promising, by the party in whose favor the promise is made. 4 East, 455; 1 Taunt. 523; Chitty on Contr. 7; Dr. & Stu. 179; 1 Selw. N. P. 39, 40; 2 Pet. 182; 1 Litt. 123; 3 John. 100; 6 Mass. 58; 2 Bibb. 30; 2 J. J. Marsh. 222; 5 Cranch, 142, 150; 2 N. H. Rep. 97; Wright, R. 660; 14 John. R. 466; 13 S & R. 29; 3 M. Gr. & Sc. 321.

4. Considerations are good, as when they are for natural love and affection; or valuable, when some benefit arises to the party to whom they are made, or inconvenience to the party making them. Vin. Abr. Consideration, B; 5 How. U. S. 278; 4 Barr, 364; 3 McLean, 330; 17 Conn. 511; 1 Branch, 301; 8 Ala. 949.

5. They are legal, which are sufficient to support the contract; or illegal, which render it void. As to illegal considerations, see 1 Hov. Supp. to Ves. jr. 295; 2 Hov. Supp. to Ves. jr. 448; 2 Burr. 924; 1 Bl. Rep. 204. If the performance be utterly impossible, in fact or in law, the consideration is void. 2 Lev. 161; Yelv. 197, and note; 3 Bos. & Pull. 296, n.: 14 Johns. R. 381.

6. A mere *moral* obligation to pay a debt or perform a duty, is a sufficient consideration for an express promise, although no legal liability existed at the time of making such promise. Cowp. 290; 2 Bl. Com. 445; 3 Bos. & Pull. 249, note; 2 East, 506; 3 Taunt. 311; 5 Taunt. 36; 13 Johns. R. 259; Yelv. 41, b, note; 3 Pick. 207. But it is to be observed, that

in such cases there must have been a good or valuable consideration; for example, every one is under a moral obligation to relieve a person in distress, a promise to do so, however, is not binding in law. One is bound to pay a debt which he owes, although he has been released; a promise to pay such a debt is obligatory in law on the debtor, and can therefore be enforced by action. 12 S. & R. 177; 19 John. R. 147; 4 W. C. C. R. 86, 148; 7 John. R. 36; 14 John. R. 178; 1 Cowen, R. 249; 8 Mass. R. 127. See 7 Conn. R. 57; 1 Verm. R. 420; 5 Verm. R. 173; 5 Ham. R. 58; 3 Penna. R. 172; 5 Binn. R. 33.

7. In respect of time, a consideration is either, 1st. Executed, or something done before the making of the obligor's promise. Yelv. 41, a. n. In general, an *executed* consideration is insufficient to support a contract; 7 John. R. 87; 2 Conn. R. 404; 7 Cowen, R. 358; but an executed consideration *on request;* 7 John. R. 87; 1 Caines R. 584; or by some previous duty, or if the debt be continuing at the time, or it is barred by some rule of law, or some provision of a statute, as the act of limitation, it is sufficient to maintain an action. 4 W. C. C. R. 148; 14 John. R. 378; 17 S. & R. 126. 2d. Executory, or something to be done after such promise. 3d. Concurrent, as in the case of mutual promises; and, 4th. A continuing consideration. Chitty on Contr. 16.

8. As to cases where the contract has been set aside on the ground of a total failure of the consideration, see 11 Johns. R. 50; 7 Mass. 14; 3 Johns. R. 458; 8 Mass. 46; 6 Cranch, 53; 2 Caines' Rep. 246; and 1 Camp. 40, n. When the consideration turns out to be false and fails, there is no contract; as, for example, if my father by his will gives me all his estate, charged with the payment of a thousand dollars, and I promise to give you my house instead of the legacy to you, and you agree to buy it with the legacy, and before the contract is completed, and I make you a deed for the house, I discover that my father made a codicil to his will and by it he revoked the gift to you, I am not bound to complete the contract by making you a deed for my house. Poth. on Oblig. part 1, c. 1, art. 3, § 6.

See, in general, *Obligation; New Promise;* Bouv. Inst. Index. h. t.; Evans' Poth. vol. ii. p. 19; 1 Fonb. Eq. 335; Newl. Contr. 65; 1 Com. Contr. 26; Fell on Guarrant. 337; 3 Chit. Com. Law, 63 to 99; 3 Bos. & Pull. 249, n; 1 Fonb. Eq. 122, note z; Id. 370, note g; 5 East, 20, n.; 2 Saund. 211, note 2; Lawes Pl. Ass. 49; 1 Com. Dig. Action upon the case upon Assumpsit, B; Vin. Abr. Actions of Assumpsit, Q; Id. tit. Consideration.

CONSIDERATUM EST *per curiam.* It is considered by the court. This formula is used in giving judgments. A judgment is the decision or sentence of the law, given by a court of justice, as the result of proceedings instituted therein, for the redress of an injury. The language of the judgment is not, therefore, that "it is decreed," or "resolved," by the court; but that "it is considered by the court," *consideratum est per curiam*, that the plaintiff recover his debt, &c. 3 Bouv. Inst. n. 3298.

CONSIGNATION, *contracts.* In the civil law, it is a deposit which a debtor makes of the thing that he owes, into the hands of a third person, and under the authority of a court of justice. Poth. Oblig. P. 3, c. 1, art. 8.

2. Generally the consignation is made with a public officer; it is very similar to our practice of paying money into court.

3. The term to consign, or consignation, is derived from the Latin *consignare,* which signifies to seal, for it was formerly the practice to seal up the money thus received in a bag or box. Aso & Man. Inst. B. 2, t. 11, c. 1, § 5. See Burge on Sur. 138.

CONSIGNEE, *contracts.* One to whom a consignment is made.

2. When the goods consigned to him are his own, and they have been ordered to be sent, they are at his risk the moment the consignment is made according to his direction; and the persons employed in the transmission of the goods are his agents. 1 Liverm. on Ag. 9. When the goods are not his own, if he accept the consignment, he is bound to pursue the instructions of the consignor; as if the goods be consigned upon condition that the consignee will accept the consignor's bills, he is bound to accept them; Id. 139; or if he is directed to insure, he must do so. Id. 325.

3. It is usual in bills of lading to state that the goods are to be delivered to the consignee or his assigns, he or they paying freight; in such case the consignee or his assigns, by accepting the goods, by implication, become bound to pay the freight. Abbott on Sh. p. 3, c. 7, § 4; 3 Bing. R. 383.

4. When a person acts, publicly as a consignee, there is an implied engagement on his part that he will be vigilant in receiving goods consigned to his care, so as to make him responsible for any loss which the owner may sustain in consequence of his neglect. 9 Watts & Serg. 62.

CONSIGNMENT. The goods or property sent by a common carrier from one or more persons called the consignors, from one place, to one or more persons, called the consignees, who are in another. By this term is also understood the goods sent by one person to another, to be sold or disposed of by the latter for and on account of the former.

CONSIGNOR, *contracts.* One who makes a consignment to another.

2. When goods are consigned to be sold on commission, and the property remains in the consignor; or when goods have been consigned upon a credit, and the consignee has become a bankrupt or failed, the consignor has a right to stop them *in transitu.* (q. v.) Abbott on Sh. p. 3, c. 9, s. 1.

3. The consignor is generally liable for the freight or the hire for the carriage of goods. 1 T. R. 659.

CONSILIUM, or *dies consilii, practice.* A time allowed for the accused to make his defence, and now more commonly used for a day appointed to argue a demurrer. In civil cases, it is a special day appointed for the purpose of hearing an argument. Jer. Eq. Jur. 296; 4 Bouv. Inst. n. 3753.

CONSIMILI CASU. These words occur in the Stat. West. 2, c. 24, 13 Ed. I. which gave authority to the clerks in chancery to form new writs in consimili casu simili remedio indigente sicut prius fit breve. In execution of the powers granted by this statute, many new writs were formed by the clerks in chancery, especially in real actions—as writs of quod permittat prosternere, against the alienee of land after the erection of a nuisance thereon, according to the analogy of the assize of nuisance, writs of juris utrum, &c. &c. In respect to personal actions, it has long been the practice to issue writs in *consimili casu,* in the most general form, *e. g.* in trespass on the case upon promises, leaving it to the plaintiff to state fully, and at large, his case in the declaration; the sufficiency of which in point of law is always a question for the court to consider upon the pleadings and evidence. See Willes, Rep. 580; 2 Lord Ray. 957; 2 Durnf. & East, 51; 2 Wils. 146; 17 Serg. & R. 195; 3 Bl. Com. 51; 7 Co. 4; F. N. B. 206; 3 Bouv. Inst. n. 3482.

CONSISTENT. That which agrees with something else; as a consistent condition, which is one which agrees with all other parts of a contract, or which can be reconciled with every other part. 1 Bouv. Inst. n. 752.

CONSISTORY, *ecclesiastical law.* An assembly of cardinals convoked by the pope. The consistory is public or secret. It is *public,* when the pope receives princes or gives audience to ambassadors; *secret,* when he fills vacant sees, proceeds to the canonization of saints, or judges and settles certain contestations submitted to him.

2. A court which was formerly held among protestants, in which the bishop presided, assisted by some of his clergy, also bears this name. It is now held in England, by the bishop's chancellor or commissary, and some other ecclesiastical officers, either in the cathedral, church, or other place in his diocese, for the determination of ecclesiastical cases arising in that diocese. Merl. Rép. h. t.; Burns' Dict. h. t.

CONSOLATO DEL MARE, (IL). The name of a code of sea laws compiled by order of the ancient kings of Arragon. Its date is not very certain, but it was adopted on the continent of Europe, as the code of maritime law, in the course of the eleventh, twelfth, and thirteenth centuries. It comprised the ancient ordinances of the Greek and Roman emperors, and of the kings of France and Spain; and the laws of the Mediterranean islands, and of Venice and Genoa. It was originally written in the dialect of Catalonia, as its title plainly indicates, and it has been translated into every language of Europe. This code has been reprinted in the second volume of the "Collection de Lois Maritimes Anterieures au XVIII[e]. Siecle, par J. M. Pardessus, (Paris, 1831)." A collection of sea laws, which is very complete.

CONSOLIDATION, *civil law.* The union of the usufruct with the estate out of which it issues, in the same person; which happens when the usufructuary acquires the estate, or vice versa. In either case the usufruct is extinct. In the common law this is called a merger. Leç. El. Dr. Rom. 424. U. S. Dig. tit. Actions, V.

2. Consolidation may take place in two ways: first, by the usufructuary surrender-

ing his right to the proprietor, which in the common law is called a surrender; secondly, by the release of the proprietor of his rights to the usufructuary, which in our law is called a release.

CONSOLIDATION RULE, *practice, com. law.* When a number of actions are brought on the same policy, it is the constant practice, for the purpose of saving costs, to consolidate them by a rule of court or judge's order, which restrains the plaintiff from proceeding to trial in more than one, and binds the defendants in all the others to abide the event of that one; but this is done upon condition that the defendant shall not file any bill in equity, or bring any writ of error for delay. 2 Marsh. Ins. 701. For the history of this rule, vide Parke on Ins. xlix.; Marsh. Ins. B. 1, c. 16, s. 4. And see 1 John. Cas. 29; 19 Wend. 23; 13 Wend. 644; 5 Cowen, 282; 4 Cowen, 78; Id. 85; 1 John. 29; 9 John. 262.

2. The term consolidation seems to be rather misapplied in those cases, for in point of fact there is a mere stay of proceedings in all those cases but one. 3 Chit. Pr. 644. The rule is now extended to other cases: when several actions are brought on the same bond against several obligors, an order for a stay of proceedings in all but one will be made. 3 Chit. Pr. 645; 3 Carr. & P. 58. See 4 Yeates, R. 128; 3 S. & R. 262; Coleman, 62; 3 Rand. 481; 1 N. & M. 417, n.; 1 Cowen, 89; 3 Wend. 441; 9 Wend. 451; 2 N. & M. 438, 440, n.; 5 Cowen, 282; 4 Halst. 335; 1 Dall. 145; 1 Browne, Appx. lxvii.; 1 Ala. R. 77; 4 Hill, R. 46; 19 Wend. 23; 5 Yerg. 297; 7 Miss. 477; 2 Tayl. 200.

3. The plaintiff may elect to join in the same suit several causes of action, in many cases, consistently with the rules of pleading, but having done so, his election is determined. He cannot ask the court to consolidate them; 3 Serg. & R. 266; but the court will sometimes, at the instance of the defendant, order it against the plaintiff. 1 Dall. Rep. 147, 355; 1 Yeates, 5; 4 Yeates, 128; 2 Arch. Pr. 180; 3 Serg. & R. 264.

CONSOLS, *Eng. law.* This is an abbreviation for consolidated annuities. Formerly when a loan was made, authorized by government, a particular part of the revenue was appropriated for the payment of the interest and of the principal. This was called the fund, and every loan had its fund. In this manner the Aggregate fund originated in 1715; the South Sea fund, in 1717; the General fund, 1617; and the Sinking fund, into which the surplus of these three funds flowed, which, although destined for the diminution of the national debt, was applied to the necessities of the government. These four funds were consolidated into one in the year 1787, under the name of consolidated fund.

2. The income arises from the receipts on account of excise, customs, stamps, and other perpetual taxes. The charges on it are the interest on and the redemption of the public debt; the civil list; the salaries of the judges and officers of state, and the like.

3. The annual grants on account of the army and navy, and every part of the revenue which is considered temporary, are excluded from this fund.

4. Those persons who lent the money to the government, or their assigns, are entitled to an annuity of three per cent. on the amount lent, which, however, is not to be returned, except at the option of the government; so that the holders of consols are simply annuitants.

CONSORT. A man or woman married. The man is the consort of his wife, the woman is the consort of her husband.

CONSPIRACY, *crim. law, torts.* An agreement between two or more persons to do an unlawful act, or an act which may become by the combination injurious to others. Formerly this offence was much more circumscribed in its meaning than it is now. Lord Coke describes it as "a consultation or agreement between two or more to appeal or indict an innocent person falsely and maliciously, whom accordingly they cause to be indicted or appealed; and afterwards the party is acquitted by the verdict of twelve men."

2. The crime of conspiracy, according to its modern interpretation, may be of two kinds, namely, conspiracies against the public, or such as endanger the public health, violate public morals, insult public justice, destroy the public peace, or affect public trade or business. See 3 Burr. 1321.

3. To remedy these evils the guilty persons may be indicted in the name of the commonwealth. Conspiracies against individuals are such as have a tendency to injure them in their persons, reputation, or property. The remedy in these cases is either by indictment or by a civil action.

4. In order to render the offence complete, there is no occasion that any act

should be done in pursuance of the unlawful agreement entered into between the parties, or that any one should have been defrauded or injured by it. The conspiracy is the gist of the crime. 2 Mass. R. 337; Id. 538; 6 Mass. R. 74; 3 S. & R. 220; 4 Wend. R. 259; Halst. R. 293; 2 Stew. Rep. 360; 5 Harr. & John. 317; 8 S. & R. 420. But see 10 Verm. 353.

5. By the laws of the United States, st. 1825, c. 76, § 23, 3 Story's L. U. S., 2006, a wilful and corrupt conspiracy to cast away, burn or otherwise destroy any ship or vessel. with intent to injure any underwriter thereon, or the goods on board thereof, or any lender of money on such vessel, on bottomry or respondentia, is, by the laws of the United States, made felony, and the offender punishable by fine not exceeding ten thousand dollars, and by imprisonment and confinement at hard labor, not exceeding ten years.

6. By the Revised Statutes of New York, vol. 2, p. 691, 692, it is enacted, that if any two or more persons shall conspire, either, 1. To commit any offence; or, 2. Falsely and maliciously to indict another for any offence; or, 3. Falsely to move or maintain any suit; or, 4. To cheat and defraud any person of any property, by any means which are in themselves criminal; or, 5. To cheat and defraud any person of any property, by means which, if executed, would amount to a cheat, or to obtaining property by false pretences; or, 6. To commit any act injurious to the public health, to public morals, or to trade and commerce, or for the perversion or obstruction of justice, or the due administration of the laws; they shall be deemed guilty of a misdemeanor. No other conspiracies are there punishable criminally. And no agreement, except to commit a felony upon the person of another, or to commit arson or burglary, shall be deemed a conspiracy, unless some act besides such agreement be done to effect the object thereof, by one or more of the parties to such agreement.

7. When a felony has been committed in pursuance of a conspiracy, the latter, which is only a misdemeanor, is merged in the former; but when a misdemeanor only has been committed in pursuance of such conspiracy, the two crimes being of equal degree, there can be no legal technical merger. 4 Wend. R. 265. Vide 1 Hawk. 444 to 454; 3 Chit. Cr. Law, 1138 to 1193; 3 Inst. 143; Com. Dig. Justices of the Peace, B 107; Burn's Justice, Conspiracy; Williams' Justice, Conspiracy; 4 Chit. Blacks. 92; Dick. Justice Conspiracy, Bac. Ab. Actions on the Case, G; 2 Russ. on Cr. 553 to 574; 2 Mass. 329; Id. 536; 5 Mass. 106; 2 Day, R. 205; Whart. Dig. Conspiracy; 3 Serg. & Rawle, 220; 7 Serg. & Rawle, 469; 4 Halst. R. 293; 5 Harr. & Johns. 317; 4 Wend. 229; 2 Stew. R. 360; 1 Saund. 230, n. 4. For the French law, see Merl. Rep. mot Conspiration; Code Penal, art. 89.

CONSPIRATORS. Persons guilty of a conspiracy. See 3 Bl. Com. 126–7; 1 Wils. Rép. 210–11. See *Conspiracy*.

CONSTABLE. An officer, who is generally elected by the people.

2. He possess power, virture officii, as a conservator of the peace at common law, and by virtue of various legislative enactments; he may therefore apprehend a supposed offender without a warrant, as treason, felony, breach of the peace, and for some misdemeanors less than felony, when committed in his view. 1 Hale, 587; 1 East, P. C. 303; 8 Serg. & Rawle, 47. He may also arrest a supposed offender upon the information of others; but he does so at his peril, unless he can show that a felony has been committed by some person, as well as the reasonableness of the suspicion that the party arrested is guilty. 1 Chit. Cr. L. 27; 6 Binn. R. 316; 2 Hale, 91, 92; 1 East, P. C. 301. He has power to call others to his assistance; or he may appoint a deputy to do ministerial acts. 3 Burr. Rep. 1262.

3. A constable is also a ministerial officer, bound to obey the warrants and precepts of justices, coroners and sheriffs. Constables are also in some states bound to execute the warrants and process of justices of the peace in civil cases.

4. In England, they have many officers, with more or less power, who bear the name of constables; as, lord high constable of England, high constable; 3 Burr. 1262; head constables, petty constables, constables of castles, constables of the tower, constables of the fees, constable of the exchequer, constable of the staple, &c.

5. In some of the cities of the United States, there are officers who are called high constables, who are the principal police officers where they reside. Vide the various Digests of American Law, h. t.; 1 Chit. Cr. L. 20; 5 Vin. Ab. 427; 2 Phil. Ev. 253; 2 Sell. Pr. 70; Bac. Ab. h. t.; Com. Dig

Justices of the Peace, B 79; Id. D 7; Id. Officer, E 2; Willo. Off. Const.

CONSTABLEWICK. In England, by this word is meant the territorial jurisdiction of a constable. 5 Nev. & M. 261.

CONSTAT, *English law.* The name of a certificate, which the clerk of the pipe and uditors of the exchequer make at the request of any person who intends to plead or move in the court for the discharge of anything; and the effect of it is, the certifying what *constat* (appears) upon record touching the matter in question.

2. A *constat* is held to be superior to an ordinary certificate, because it contains nothing but what is on record. An exemplification under the great seal, of the enrolment of any letters-patent, is called a *constat.* Co. Litt. 225. Vide *Exemplification; Inspeximus.*

3. Whenever an officer gives a certificate that such a thing *appears* of record, it is called a *constat;* because the officer does not say that the fact is so, but it appears to be as he certifies. A certificate that *it appears* to the officer that a judgment has been entered, &c., is insufficient. 1 Hayw. 410.

CONSTITUENT. He who gives authority to another to act for him. 1 Bouv. Inst. n. 893.

2. The constituent is bound with whatever his attorney does by virtue of his authority. The electors of a member of the legislature are his constituents, to whom he is responsible for his legislative acts.

CONSTITUIMUS. A Latin word, which signifies *we constitute.* Whenever the king of England is vested with the right of creating a new office, he must use proper words to do so; for example, *erigimus, constituimus,* &c. Bac. Ab. Offices, &c. E.

TO CONSTITUTE, *contr.* To empower, to authorize. In the common form of letters of attorney, these words occur, "I nominate, constitute and appoint."

CONSTITUTED AUTHORITIES. Those powers which the constitution of each people has established to govern them, to cause their rights to be respected, and to maintain those of each of its members.

2. They are called *constituted,* to distinguish them from the *constituting* authority which has created or organized them, or has delegated to an authority, which it has itself created, the right of establishing or regulating their movements. The officers appointed under the constitution are also collectively called the constituted authorities. Dall. Dict. mots Contrainte par corps, n. 526.

CONSTITUTION, *government.* The fundamental law of the state, containing the principles upon which the government is founded, and regulating the divisions of the sovereign powers, directing to what persons each of these powers is to be confided, and the manner it is to be exercised; as, the Constitution of the United States. See Story on the Constitution; Rawle on the Const.

2. The words constitution and government (q. v.) are sometimes employed to express the same idea, the manner in which sovereignty is exercised in each state. Constitution is also the name of the instrument containing the fundamental laws of the state.

3. By constitution, the civilians, and, from them, the common law writers, mean some particular law; as the constitutions of the emperors contained in the Code.

CONSTITUTION, *contracts.* The constitution of a contract, is the making of the contract; as, the written constitution of a debt. 1 Bell's Com. 332, 5th ed.

CONSTITUTION OF THE UNITED STATES OF AMERICA. The fundamental law of the United States.

2. It was framed by a convention of the representatives of the people, who met at Philadelphia, and finally adopted it on the 17th day of September, 1787. It became the law of the land on the first Wednesday in March, 1789. 5 Wheat. 420.

3. A short analysis of this instrument, so replete with salutary provisions for insuring liberty and private rights, and public peace and prosperity, will here be given.

4. The preamble declares that the people of the United States, in order to form a more perfect union, establish justice, insure public tranquillity, provide for the common defence, promote the general welfare, and secure the blessings of liberty to themselves and their posterity, do ordain and establish this constitution for the United States of America.

5.—1. The first article is divided into ten sections. By the *first* the legislative power is vested in congress. The *second* regulates the formation of the house of representatives, and declares who shall be electors. The *third* provides for the organization of the senate, and bestows on it the power to try impeachments. The *fourth* directs the times and places of holding elections; and the time of meeting of congress. The *fifth* determines the power of the respective houses. The *sixth* provides for a compensation to members of congress, and for their safety from arrests; and disqualifies them from holding certain offices. The *seventh* directs the manner of passing bills. The *eighth* defines the powers vested in congress. The *ninth* contains the following provisions: 1st. That the migration or importation of persons shall not be prohibited prior to the year 1808. 2d. That the writ of habeas corpus shall not be suspended, except in particular cases. 3d. That no bill of attainder, or ex post facto law, shall be passed. 4th. The manner of laying taxes. 5th. The manner of drawing money out of the treasury. 6th. That no title of nobility shall be granted. 7th. That no officer shall receive a present from a foreign government. The *tenth* forbids the respective states to exercise certain powers there enumerated.

6.—2. The second article is divided into four sections. The *first* vests the executive power in the president of the United States of America, and provides for his election, and that of the vice-president. The *second* section confers various powers on the president. The *third* defines his duties. The *fourth* provides for the impeachment of the president, vice-president, and all civil officers of the United States.

7.—3. The third article contains three sections. The *first* vests the judicial power in sundry courts, provides for the tenure of office by the judges, and for their compensation. The *second* provides for the extent of the judicial power, vests in the supreme court original jurisdiction in certain cases, and directs the manner of trying crimes. The *third* defines treason, and vests in congress the power to declare its punishment.

8.—4. The fourth article is composed of four sections. The *first* relates to the faith which state records, &c., shall have in other states. The *second* secures the rights of citizens in the several states—for the delivery of fugitives from justice or from labor. The *third* for the admission of new states, and the government of the territories. The *fourth* guaranties to every state in the Union the republican form of government, and protection from invasion or domestic violence.

9.—5. The fifth article provides for amendments to the constitution.

10.—6. The sixth article declares that the debts due under the confederation shall be valid against the United States; that the constitution and treaties made under its powers shall be the supreme law of the land; that public officers shall be required by oath or affirmation to support the Constitution of the United States; that no religious test shall be required as a qualification for office.

11.—7. The seventh article directs what shall be a sufficient ratification of this constitution by the states.

12. In pursuance of the fifth article of the constitution, articles in addition to, and amendment of, the constitution, were proposed by congress, and ratified by the legislatures of the several states. These additional articles are to the following import:

13.—1. Relates to religious freedom; the liberty of the press; the right of the people to assemble and petition.

14.—2. Secures to the people the right to bear arms.

15.—3. Provides for the quartering of soldiers.

16.—4. Regulates the right of search, and of arrest on criminal charges.

17.—5. Directs the manner of being held to answer for crimes, and provides for the security of the life, liberty and property of the citizens.

18.—6. Secures to the accused the right to a fair trial by jury.

19.—7. Provides for a trial by jury in civil cases.

20.—8. Directs that excessive bail shall not be required; nor excessive fines imposed; nor cruel and unusual punishments inflicted

21.—9. Secures to the people the rights retained by them.

22.—10. Secures the rights to the states, or to the people the rights they have not granted.

23.—11. Limits the powers of the courts as to suits against one of the United States.

24.—12. Points out the manner of electing the president and vice-president.

CONSTITUTIONAL. That which is consonant to, and agrees with the constitution.

2. When laws are made in violation of the constitution, they are null and void: but the courts will not declare such a law void unless there appears to be a clear and unequivocal breach of the constitution. 4 Dall. R. 14; 3 Dall. R. 399; 1 Cranch, R. 137; 1 Binn. R. 415; 6 Cranch, R. 87,

136; 2 Hall's Law Journ. 96, 255, 262; 3 Hall's Law Journ. 267; Wheat. Dig. tit. Constitutional Law; 2 Pet. R. 522; 2 Dall. 309; 12 Wheat. R. 270; Charlt. R. 175, 235; 1 Breese, R. 70, 209; 1 Blackf. R. 206; 2 Porter, R. 303; 5 Binn. 355; 3 S. & R. 169; 2 Penn. R. 184; 19 John. R. 58; 1 Cowen, R. 550; 1 Marsh. R. 290; Pr. Dec. 64, 89; 2 Litt. R. 90; 4 Munr. R. 43; 1 South. R. 192; 7 Pick. R. 466; 13 Pick. R. 60; 11 Mass. R. 396; 9 Greenl. R. 60; 5 Hayw. R. 271; 1 Harr. & J. 236; 1 Gill & J. 473; 7 Gill & J. 7; 9 Yerg. 490; 1 Rep. Const. Ct. 267; 3 Desaus. R. 476; 6 Rand. 245; 1 Chip. R. 237, 257; 1 Aik. R. 314; 3 N. H. Rep. 473; 4 N. H. Rep. 16; 7 N. H. Rep. 65; 1 Murph. R. 58. See 3 Law Intell. 65, for a list of decisions made by the supreme court of the United States, declaring laws to be unconstitutional.

CONSTITUTOR, *civil law.* He who promised by a simple pact to pay the debt of another; and this is always a principal obligation. Inst. 4, 6, 9.

CONSTRAINT. In the civil and Scottish law, by this term is understood what, in the common law, is known by the name of *duress.*

2. It is a general rule, that when one is compelled into a contract, there is no effectual consent, though, ostensibly, there is the form of it. In such case the contract will be declared void.

3. The constraint requisite thus to annul a contract, must be a *vis aut metus qui cadet in constantem virum,* such as would shake a man of firmness and resolution. 3 Ersk. 1, § 16; and 4, 1, § 26; 1 Bell's Com. B. 3, part 1, c. 1, s. 1, art. 1, page 295.

CONSTRUCTION, *practice.* It is defined by Mr. Powell to be "the drawing an inference by the act of reason, as to the intent of an instrument, from given circumstances, upon principles deduced from men's general motives, conduct and action." This definition may, perhaps, not be sufficiently complete, inasmuch as the term *instrument* generally implies something reduced into writing, whereas construction is equally necessary to ascertain the meaning of engagements merely verbal. In other respects it appears to be perfectly accurate. The Treatise of Equity, defines interpretation to be the collection of the meaning out of signs the most probable. 1 Powell on Con. 370.

2. There are two kinds of constructions; the first, is literal or strict; this is uniformly the construction given to penal statutes. 1 Bl. Com. 88; 6 Watts & Serg. 276; 3 Taunt. 377. 2d. The other is liberal, and applied, usually, to remedial laws, in order to enforce them according to their spirit.

3. In the supreme court of the United States, the rule which has been uniformly observed "in construing statutes, is to adopt the construction made by the courts of the country by whose legislature the statute was enacted. This rule may be susceptible of some modification when applied to British statutes which are adopted in any of these states. By adopting them, they become our own, as entirely as if they had been enacted by the legislature of the state.

4. The received construction, in England, at the time they are admitted to operate in this country—indeed, to the time of our separation from the British empire—may very properly be considered as accompanying the statutes themselves, and forming an integral part of them. But, however we may respect the subsequent decisions, (and certainly they are entitled to great respect,) we do not admit their absolute authority. If the English courts vary their construction of a statute, which is common to the two countries, we do not hold ourselves bound to fluctuate with them. 5 Pet. R. 280.

5. The great object which the law has, in all cases, in contemplation, as furnishing the leading principle of the rules to be observed in the construction of contracts, is, that justice is to be done between the parties, by enforcing the performance of their agreement, according to the sense in which it was mutually understood and relied upon at the time of making it.

6. When the contract is in writing, the difficulty lies only in the construction of the words; when it is to be made out by parol testimony, that difficulty is augmented by the possible mistakes of the witnesses as to the words used by the parties; but still, when the evidence is received, it must be assumed as correct, when a construction is to be put upon it. The following are the principal rules to be observed in the construction of contracts.

7.—1. When the words used are of precise and unambiguous meaning, leading to no absurdity, that meaning is to be taken as conveying the intention of the parties. But should there be manifest absurdity in the application of such meaning, to the particular occasion, this will let in construction to discover the true intention of the parties: for example; 1st. When words are manifestly inconsistent with the declared purpose and object of the contract, they will be rejected; as if, in a contract of sale, the price of the thing sold should be acknowledged as received, while the obligation of the seller was *not* to deliver the commodity. 2 Atk. R. 32. 2d. When words are omitted so as to defeat the effect of the contract, they will be supplied by the obvious sense and inference from the context; as, if the contract stated that the seller, for the consideration of one hundred dollars, sold a horse, and the buyer promised to pay him for the said horse one hundred, the word *dollars* would be supplied. 3d. When the words, taken in one sense, go to defeat the contract, while they are susceptible of another construction which will give effect to the design of the parties, and not destroy it, the latter will be preferred. Cowp. 714.

8.—2. The plain, ordinary, and popular sense of the words, is to be preferred to the more unusual, etymological, and recondite meaning; or even to the literal, and strictly grammatical construction of the words, where these last would lead to any inefficacy or inconsistency.

9.—3. When a peculiar meaning has been stamped upon the words by the usage of a particular trade or place in which the contract occurs, such technical or peculiar meaning will prevail. 4 East, R. 135. It is as if the parties in framing their contract had made use of a foreign language, which the court is not bound to understand, but which on evidence of its import, must be applied. 7 Taunt. R. 272; 1 Stark. R. 504. But the expression so made technical and appropriate, and the usage by which it has become so, must be so clear that the court cannot entertain a doubt upon the subject. 2 Bos. & P. 164; 3 Stark. Ev. 1036; 6 T. R. 320. Technical words are to be taken according to their approved and known use in the trade in which the contract is entered into, or to which it relates, unless they have manifestly been understood in another sense by the parties. Vide 16 Serg. & R. 126.

10.—4. The place where a contract has been made, is a most material consideration in its construction. Generally its validity is to be decided by the law of the place where it is made; if valid there, it is considered valid every where. 2 Mass. R. 88; 1 Pet. R. 317; Story, Confl. of Laws, § 242; 4 Cowen's R. 410, note; 2 Kent, Com. p. 39, 457, in the notes; 3 Conn. R. 253, 472; 4 Conn. R. 517. Its construction is to be according to the laws of the place where it is made; for example, where a note was given in China, payable eighteen months after date, without any stipulation as to the amount of interest, the court allowed the Chinese interest of one per centum per month from the expiration of the eighteen months. 1 Wash. C. C. R. 253; see 12 Mass. R. 4, and the article *Interest for money.*

11.—5. Previous conversations, and all that passes in the course of correspondence or negotiation leading to the contract, are entirely superseded by the written agreement. The parties having agreed to reduce the terms of their contract to writing, the document is constituted as the only true and final exposition of their admissions and intentions; and nothing which does not appear in the written agreement will be considered as a part of the contract. 5 Co. R. 26; 2 B. & C. 634; 4 Taunt. R. 779. But this rule admits of some exceptions; as, where a declaration is made before a deed is executed, showing the design with which it was to be executed, in cases of frauds; 1 S. & R. 464; 10 S. & R. 292; and trusts, though no trust was declared in the writing. 1 Dall. R. 426; 7 S. & R. 114.

12.—6. All contracts made in general terms, in the ordinary course of trade, are presumed to incorporate the usage and custom of the trade to which they relate. The parties are presumed to know such usages, and not to intend to exclude them. But when there is a special stipulation in opposition to, or inconsistent with the custom, that will of course prevail. Holt's R. 95.

13.—7. When there is an ambiguity which impedes the execution of the contract, it is first, if possible, to be resolved, on a view of the whole contract or instrument, aided by the admitted views of the parties, and, if indispensable, parol evidence may be admitted to clear it, consistently with the words. 1 Dall. R. 426; 4 Dall. R. 340; 3 S. & R. 609.

14.—8. When the words cannot be reconciled with any practicable or consistent interpretation, they are to be considered as not made use of "perinde sunt ac si scripta non essent."

15. It is the duty of the court to give a construction to all written instruments; 3

Binn. R. 337; 7 S. & R. 372; 15 S. & R. 100; 4 S. & R. 279; 8 S. & R. 381; 1 Watts. R. 425; 10 Mass. R. 384; 3 Cranch, R. 180; 3 Rand. R. 586; to written evidence; 2 Watts, R. 347; and to foreign laws. 1 Penna. R. 388.

For general rules respecting the construction of contracts, see 2 Bl. Com. 379; 1 Bouv. Inst. n. 658, 669; 2 Com. on Cont. 23 to 28; 3 Chit. Com. Law, 106 to 118; Poth. Oblig. P. 1, c. 1, art. 7; 2 Evans' Poth. Ob. 35; Long on Sales, 106; 1 Fonb. Eq. 145, n. b; Id. 440, n. 1; Whart. Dig. Contract, F; 1 Powell on Contr. 370; Shepp. Touchst. c. 5; Louis. Code, art. 1940 to 1957; Com. Dig. Merchant, (E 2,) n. j.; 8 Com. Dig. tit. Contract, iv.; Lilly's Reg. 794; 18 Vin. Abr. 272, tit. Reference to Words; 16 Vin. Abr. 199, tit. Parols; Hall's Dig. 33, 339; 1 Ves. Jun. 210, n.; Vattel, B. 2, c. 17; Chit. Contr. 19 to 22; 4 Kent. Com. 419; Story's Const. § 397—456; Ayl. Pand. B. 1, t. 4; Rutherf. Inst. B. 2, c. 7, § 4—11; 20 Pick. 150; 1 Bell's Com. 5th ed. 431; and the articles, *Communings; Evidence; Interpretation; Parol; Pourparler.*

As to the construction of wills, see 1 Supp. to Ves. Jr. 21, 39, 56, 63, 228, 260, 273, 275, 364, 399; 1 United States Law Journ. 583; 2 Fonb. Eq. 309; Com. Dig. Estates by Devise. N 1; 6 Cruise's Dig. 171; Whart. Dig. Wills, D.

As to the construction of Laws, see Louis. Code, art. 13 to 21; Bac. Ab. Statutes, J; 1 Bouv. Inst. n. 86—90; 3 Bin. 358; 4 Bin. 169, 172; 2 S. & R. 195; 2 Bin. 347; Rob. Digest, Brit. Stat. 370; 7 Term. Rep. 8; 2 Inst. 11, 136; 3 Bin. 284-5; 3 S. & R. 129; 1 Peere Wms. 207; 3 Burr. Rep. 1755-6; 3 Yeates, 108; 11 Co. 56, b; 1 Jones 26; 3 Yeates, 113; 117, 118, 120; Dwarris on Statutes.

16. The following words and phrases have received judicial construction in the cases referred to. The references may be useful to the student and convenient to the practitioner.

A and his associates. 2 Nott & M'Cord, 400.

A B, agent. 1 Breese's R. 172.

A B, (seal) *agent for C D.* 1 Blackf. R. 242.

A case. 9 Wheat. 738.

A piece of land. Moor. 702; S. C. Owen, 18.

A place called the vestry. 3 Lev. R. 96; 2 Ld. Raym. 1471.

A slave set at liberty. 3 Conn. R. 467.

A true bill. I Meigs, 109.

A two penny bleeder. 3 Whart. R. 138.

Abbreviations. 4 C. & P. 51; S. C. 19 Engl. C. L. R. 268.

Abide. 6 N. H. Rep. 162.

About. 2 Barn. & Adol. 106; 22 E. C. L. R. 36; 5 Greenl. R. 482. See 4 Greenl. 286. *About —— dollars.* 5 Serg. & Rawle, 402. *About* $150. 9 Shep. 121.

Absolute disposal. 2 Eden, 87; 1 Bro. P. C. 476; 2 Johns. R. 391; 12 Johns. R. 389.

Absolutely. 2 Pa. St. R. 133.

Accept. 4 Gill & Johns. 5, 129

Acceptance. There is your bill, it is all right. 1 Esp. 17. If you will send it to the counting-house again, I will give directions for its being accepted. 3 Camp. 179. What, not accepted? We have had the money, and they ought to have been paid; but I do not interfere; you should see my partner. 3 Bing. R. 625; S. C. 13 Eng. C. L. R. 78. The bill shall be duly honored, and placed to the drawer's credit. 1 Atk. 611. Vide Leigh's N. P. 420.

Accepted. 2 Hill, R. 582.

According to the bill delivered by the plaintiff to the defendant. 3 T. R. 575.

According to their discretion. 5 Co. 100; 8 How. St. Tr. 55 n.

Account. 5 Cowen, 587, 593. Account closed. 8 Pick. 191. Account stated. 8 Pick. 193. Account dealings. 5 Mann. & Gr 392, 398.

Account and risk. 4 East, R. 211; Holt on Sh. 376.

Accounts. 2 Conn. R. 433.

Across. 1 Fairf. 391.

Across a country. 3 Mann. & Gr. 759.

Act of God. 1 Cranch, 345; 22 E. C. L. R. 36; 12 Johns. R. 44; 4 Add. Eccl. R. 490.

Acts. Platt on Cov. 334.

Actual cost. 2 Mason, R. 48, 393; 2 Story's C. C. R. 422.

Actual damages. 1 Gall. R. 429.

Adhere. 4 Mod. 153.

Adjacent. Cooke, 128.

Adjoining. 1 Turn. R. 21.

Administer. 1 Litt. R. 93, 100.

Ad tunc et ibidem. 1 Ld. Raym. 576

Advantage, priority or preference. 4 W. C. C. R. 447.

Adverse possession. 3 Watts, 70, 77, 205, 345; 3 Penna. R. 134; 2 Rawle's R. 305; 17 Serg. & Rawle, 104; 2 Penna. R. 183; 3 Wend. 337, 357; 4 Wend. 507; 7 Wend. 62; 8 Wend. 440; 9 Wend. 523; 15 Wend. 597; 4 Paige, 178; 2 Gill & John. 173; 6 Pet. R. 61, 291; 11 Pet. R. 41; 4 Verm. 155; 14 Pick. 461.

Advice. As per advice. Chit. Bills, 185.

Affecting. 9 Wheat. 855.

Aforesaid. Ld. Raym. 256; Id. 405.

After paying debts. 1 Ves. jr. 440; 3 Ves. 738; 2 Johns. Ch. R. 614; 1 Bro. C. C. 34; 2 Sch. & Lef. 188.

Afterwards to wit. 1 Chit. Cr. Laws, 174.

Against all risks. 1 John. Cas. 337.

Aged, impotent, and poor people. Preamble to stat. 43 Eliz. c. 4; 17 Ves. 373, in notes; Amb. 595; 7 Ves. 423; Scho. & Lef. 111; 1 P. Wms. 674; S. C. Eq. Cas. Ab. 192, pl. 9; 4 Vin. Ab. 485; 7 Ves. 98, note; 16 Ves. 206; Duke's Ch. Uses, by Bridgman, 361; 17 Ves. 371; Boyle on Charities, 31.

Agreed. 1 Roll's Ab. 518.

Agreement. 7 E. C. L. R. 331; 3 B. & B. 14;

Fell on Guar. 262. Of a good quality and moderate price. 1 Mo. & Malk. 483; S. C. 22 E. C. L. R. 363.

Aiding and abetting. Act of Congress of 1818, c. 86, § 3; 12 Wheat. 460.

Aliments. Dig. 34, 1, 1.

All. 1 Vern. 3; 3 P. Wms. 56; 1 Vern. 341; Dane's Ab. Index, h. t. All debts due to me. 1 Meriv. 541, n.; 3 Meriv. 434. All I am worth. 1 Bro. C. C. 437, 8 Ves. 604. All I am possessed of. 5 Ves. 816. All my clothes and linen whatsoever. 3 Bro. C. C. 311. All my household goods and furniture, except my plate and watch. 2 Munf. 234. All my estate. Cowp 299; 9 Ves. 604. All my real property. 18 Ves. 193. All my freehold lands. 6 Ves. 642. All and every other my lands, tenements, and hereditaments. 8 Ves. 256; 2 Mass. 56; 2 Caines' R. 345; 4 Johns. R. 388. All the inhabitants. 2 Conn. R. 20. All sorts of. 1 Holt's N. P. R. 69. All business. 8 Wendell. 498; 23 E. C. L. R. 398; 1 Taunt. R. 349; 7 B & Cr. 278, 283, 284. All claims and demands whatsoever. 1 Edw. Ch. R. 34. All baggage is at the owner's risk. 13 Wend. R. 611; 5 Rawle's R. 179; 1 Pick. R. 53; 3 Fairf. R. 422; 4 Har. & John. 317. All civil suits. 4 S. & R. 76. All demands. 2 Caines' R. 320, 327; 15 John R. 197; 1 Ld. Raym. 114. All lots I own in the town of F. 4 Bibb, R. 288. All the buildings thereon. 4 Mass. R. 110; 7 John. R. 217. All my rents. Cro. Jac. 104. All I am worth. 1 Bro. C. C. 437. All and every other my lands, tenements, and hereditaments. 8 Ves. 246; 2 Mass. 56; 2 Caines' R. 345; 4 John. Ch. 388.

All other articles perishable in their own nature. 7 Cowen, 202.

All and every. Ward on Leg. 105; Cox, R. 213.

All minerals, or magnesia of any kind. 5 Watts, 34.

All my notes. 2 Dev. Eq. R. 488.

All that I possess, in doors and out of doors. 3 Hawks, R. 74.

All timber trees and other trees, but not the annual fruit thereof. 8 D. & R. 657; S. C. 5 B. & C. R. 842.

All two lots. 7 Gill & Johns. 227.

All actions. 5 Binn. 457.

Also. 4 Rawle, R. 69; 2 Hayw. 161

Amongst. 9 Ves. 445; 9 Wheat. R. 164; 6 Munf. 352.

And, construed *or.* 3 Ves. 450; 7 Ves. 454; 1 Supp. to Ves. jr. 435; 2 Supp. to Ves. jr. 9, 43, 114; 1 Yeates, 41, 319; 1 Serg. & Rawle, 141. Vide *Disjunction, Or.*

And all the buildings thereon. 4 Mass. R. 110; 7 John R. 217.

And also. 1 Hayw. 161.

And so on, from year to year, until the tenancy hereby created shall be determined as hereinafter mentioned. 1 P. & D. 454; and see 2 Campb. R. 573; 3 Campb. 510; 1 T. R. 378.

And the plaintiff doth the like. 1 Breese's R. 125.

Annual interest. 16 Verm. 44.

Annually, or in any way she may wish. 2 M'Cord's Ch. R. 281.

Any person or persons. 11 Wheat. R. 392; 3 Wheat. R. 631.

Any court of record. 6 Co. 19.

Any goods. 3 Campb. 321.

Any creditor. 5 B. & A. 869.

Any other fund. 1 Colly. R. 693.

Any other matter or thing from the beginning of the world. 4 Mason, 227.

Apartment. 10 Pick. 293.

Apparel. Goods and wearing apparel, in a will 3 Atk. 61.

Apparatus. 9 Law Rep. 207.

Appeals. 1 Breese's R. 261.

Appear. 2 Bailey's R. 513.

Appellate. 1 Breese's R. 261.

Appropriation. 1 Scam. R. 314.

Approved paper. 4 Serg. & Rawle, 1; 20 Wend. R. 431; 2 Campb. 532.

Appurtenances. 1 Serg. & Rawle, 169; 8 Johns. R. 47, 2d edit.; Com. Dig. Grant, E 9; 5 Serg. & Rawle, 110; Holt on Shipp. 404; 9 Pick. 293; 7 Mass. 6; 12 Pick. 436.

Are. 2 B. & B. 223.

Arrears. Ward on Leg. 219; 2 Ves. 430.

Arrive. 17 Mass. 188.

Articles perishable in their own nature. 7 Cowen, 202.

As appears by the bond or by the books. 1 Wils. 339, 279, 121; 2 Str. 1157, 1209, 1219.

As appears by the master's allocatur. 2 T. R. 55.

As executors are bound in law to do. 2 Ohio R. 346.

As follows. 1 Chit. Cr. Law, 233.

As this deponent believes. 2 M. & S. 563.

Ass. 2 Moody, C. C. 3.

Asses—Cattle. 1 R. & M. C. C. 3; 2 Russ. Cr & M. 498.

Assent to. 4 Gill & Johns. 5, 129.

Assignment, actual or potential. 5 M. & S. 228.

Assigns. 5 Co. 77 b.

At. 2 Caines' Err. 158.

At and from. 1 Marsh. Ins. 358, 261, a; 1 Caines' R. 75, 79; 1 New Rep. 23; 4 East, R. 130.

At any port or places. 1 Marsh. Ins. 191.

At his will. Roll's Ab. 845; Bac. Ab. Estate for life and occupancy, A.

At least. 8 W. & S. 470.

At such time and manner. 19 Ves. 387.

At twenty-one. Payable at twenty-one. 6 Ves. 245; 7 Ves. 421; 9 Ves. 225; 1 Bro. C. C. 91.

At the trial of the cause. 9 E. C. L. R. 202, 186.

At the wholesale factory prices. 2 Conn. R. 69.

Attention, shall meet. 3 E. C. L. R. 407; 13 Id. 329.

Attest. 9 Mees. & W. 404.

Authority—Jurisdiction. 2 Bl. R. 1141.

Baggage. 6 Hill, N. Y. 586.

Baggage of passengers at the risk of the owners. 19 Wend 234, 251; 21 Wend. 153; 26 Wend. 591; 10 Ohio R. 145.

Balance. 2 J. & W. 248.

Balance due on general account. 3 Pet. R. 430.

Bank bills—Bank notes. 2 Scamm. R. 301; 17 Verm. 151.

Bank money. 5 Humph. R. 140.

Bank notes. 5 Mason's R. 549; 6 Wend. 346, 354.

Bankruptcy. 6 T. R. 684.

Bar-keeper. 3 S. & R. 351.

Bargain and sell. 4 Monr. R. 463.

Barley. 4 C. & P. 548.

Barrels. 7 Cowen, R. 681.

Beans. Bac. Ab. Merchant, &c. I. 1 Mood. C. C. 323.

Bearing Interest. 1 Stark. R. 452; 2 E. C. L R. 466.

Beast. 1 Russ. C. & M. 568; 1 Russ. on Cr. 568; Bac. Ab. Sodomy.
Beef. 6 W. & S. 279.
Before the next term. 1 Binn. 76; 4 Yeates, 511.
Before the first day of the term after the action has been commenced. 4 Dall. 433.
Before the sitting of the court. 5 Mass. R. 197.
Beginning to keep house. 6 Bing. R. 363; 19 Ves. 543.
Begotten. To be begotten. Co. Litt. 20 b, and n. 3; 3 Leon. 5.
Belongs—Belonging. 3 Conn. R. 467; 2 Bing. 76; Chit. Pr. 475 n.; 11 Conn. R. 240; 1 Coxe's R. 255.
Believe. 2 Wend. 298.
Belong. 3 Conn. R. 467.
Benefits of my real estate, construed, 4 Yates, 23.
Benevolent purposes. 3 Mer. 17; Amb. 585, n. (Blunt's edit.)
Best of his knowledge and belief. 1 Paige, 404; 3 Id. 107, 212.
Between. 2 Saund. 158 b. n. 6; 1 Shipl. R. 201; 1 Mass. 91.
Between them. 2 Mer. R. 70.
Beyond sea. 3 Wheat. R. 541; 3 Cranch, R. 177; 14 Pet. C. 141; 1 Harr. & McHen. 89; 1 Har. & J. 350; 2 McCord, R. 331; 3 Mass. R. 271; 1 Pick. R. 263; 9 Serg. & Rawle, 288; 2 Dall. 217; 1 Yeates, 329. Vide *Beyond sea*, in the body of the work.
Beyond seas. 3 Wheat. 343; 9 S. & R. 291.
Bien. 2 Ves. 163.
Big. 2 Dev R. 115.
Blubber. 1 Story, R. 603.
Board, boarding. 2 Miles, R. 323.
Bag. Cro. Car. 511.
Boiler. Wright, 143.
Book 2 Campb. 25, 28, n.; 11 East, 244.
Book debt—Book entries. 2 Miles, R. 101, 102; 3 Ired. R. 77, 443; 4 Ired. 110.
Bona fide. 1 Leigh. N. P. 326.
Boons. Sugd. Pow. 633, 571.
Bound by surety. 5 Serg. & Rawle, 329. Bound *with* surety, 6 Binn. 53.
Bounded on the margin. 6 Cowen, 526.
Bounded on the road. 13 Mass. 259.
Breach of good behaviour. 2 Mart. N. S. 683.
Brick factory. 21 Pick. R. 25.
Building. 16 John. R. 14; 13 John. R. 346; 9 Bing. 305; 5 Mann. & Gr. 9, 33.
Business. 1 M. & Selw. 95.
Butcher. 1 Barn. & A. 617; 6 Watts & Serg. 269, 277.
By act and operation of law. 3 Caines' R. 64. By surety. 5 Serg. & Rawle, 329. By a certain time. Penna. R. 48. By any other means. 2 Co. 46. By virtue of his office. 3 E. C. L. R. 425.
By a stream. 3 Sumn. R. 170.
By next November. 3 Pa. 48.
By the year. 2 Miles, R. 302.

Cabinet of curiosities. 1 Cox, R. 77; 1 Bro. C. C. 467.
Came by descent, gift, or devise. 2 Pet. 58.
Cargo. 4 Pick. 433; 2 Gill & John. 134, 162.
Case—suit. 2 Murph. 320.
Catchings. 1 Story, R. 603.
Cattle. 1 R. & M. C. C. 3; 2 Russ. C. & M. 498; R. & R. C. C. 77; 2 East, P. C. 1074; 1 Leach, C. C. 72; 2 W. Black. 721; 2 Moody, C. C. 3.

Cause. 1 Supp. to Ves. jr. 510. Cause of action. Wilk. on Lim. [49].
Cease. Coop. Ch. R. 145.
Cede. 1 Har. (N. J.) 181.
Certificate of deposit. 6 Watts & Serg. 227.
Chamber or room. 3 Leon. 210.
Chambres. 5 Watts, R. 243.
Charged in execution. 4 T. R. 367.
Charges, costs, and expenses, 2 Wils. 267; 13 Serg. & Rawle, 79.
Charitable uses. Boyle on Charities, 281; 7 Ves. 79; 1 Mer. 86, 92, 93; 1 Sim. & Stu. 69; 1 Myl & Craig, 286; 4 Wheat. App. p. 6.
Charity. 9 Ves. 399.
Chest. 2 Hale's Hist. P. C. 183: Bac. Ab. Indictment, G 3.
Chiefest and discreetest. 13 Ves. 13.
Child, grandchild, issue, son; see *Legatee;* 1 Ves. 290; Id. 335; Ambl. 397; Id. 701; 5 Burr. 2703; Cowp. 314; 3 Anstr. 684; Lofft, 19; 7 T. R. 322; 1 East, 120; 2 Eden, 194; 2 Bro. C. C. 33: 2 Ves. jr. 673; 3 Ves. 232; Id. 421; 4 Ves. 437; Id. 692; 5 Ves. 530; 6 Ves. 43, Id. 345; 7 Ves. 522; 10 Ves. 166, Id. 176; Id. 195; 13 Ves. 340; 1 Cox, 248; Id. 327; 2 Cox, 184; 1 Ves. & Bea. 422, 462, 469; 2 Ves. & Bea. 213; 3 Ves. & Bea. 59, 67, 69, 113; 1 Meriv. 654; 2 Meriv. 382; Dick. 344; 1 Eden, 64; 1 Bro. C. C. 530; 2 Bro. C. C. 68, 230, 658; 3 Bro. C. C. 148, 347, 352, 434: 1 Bro. C. C. 55; 19 Ves. 125; 1 Ball & B. 486; Com. Dig. App., Devise of real property, x. 5, 6, 7, 8, 9; Id. Devise of personal property, viii. 13.
Child's part. 2 Roll. R. 104; Poph. 148; 1 Roll. R. 193; Cro. Jac. 417.
Children. 3 Paige, 10; 5 Ves. 530; 1 Ves. & Bea. 434; 4 Eng. Ch. R. 565; 5 Conn. R. 228. To such child or children, if more than one, as A may happen to be enceinte by me. 17 Ves. 528. To the children which I may have by A, living at my decease. 1 Ves. & Bea. 422.
Chromate of iron. 5 Watts, 34.
Civil action. 6 Binn. 5; 1 Binn. 197.
Civil suit. 4 S. & R. 76.
Chuck-a-luck. 3 J. J. Marsh. 133.
Claim. 16 Pet. 538, 575, 576, 604, 615.
Clear. Ambl. 273; 2 Ves. 500. Ward on Leg. 222; 2 Atk. 376.
Clear of all charges and assessments whatever 4 Yeates, 386.
Clear deed. 3 W. & S. 563, 565.
Closing an account. 7 Serg. & Rawle, 128; 8 Pick. 187.
Clothes. All my clothes and linen whatsoever. 3 Bro. C. C. 311.
Coal mine. Cro. Jac. 150; Noy, 121; Gilb. Ej. 61, 2d ed.; Rosc. R. Act. 486.
Coasting trade. 3 Cowen, R. 713.
Coffer. 2 Hale's Hist. P. C. 183; Bac. Ab. Indictment, G 3.
Cohabitation. 1 Add. R. 476; 3 Add. R. 277; 2 Tyrw. 76; 2 Cr. & J. 66; Rogers' Eccl. Law, tit. Marriage.
Collateral. Sugd. Pow. 76.
Collectable. 8 Watts, R. 361.
Come to. 1 Serg. & Rawle, 224; 2 Pet. R. 69, 94.
Commenced. 14 East, 539.
Commerce—Navigation. 9 Wheat. 1.
Commission and guaranty. 3 Whart. 288.
Commit. 3 Man. Gr & Scott, 465, 477.

Commit suicide. 8 Man. Gr. & Scott, 477.
Commodities. 12 Mass 256.
Common low. 3 Pet. 447; 1 Gall. R. 19.
Complete Steam engine. 2 Hall, 328.
Concealed. 12 Wheat. 493; 12 Wheat. R. 486.
Conclusive. 5 Binn. 387; 6 Binn. 128; 4 Yeates, 351.
Conditions performed. 1 Call. 567.
Confidence. Boyle on Char. 319; 2 Pa. St. R. 133.
Consent—Submission. 9 C. & P. 722.
Consentable lines. 10 Serg. & Rawle, 114.
Construction. 3 Monr. 166.
Containing. 1 Murph. 348.
Contents unknown. 3 Taunt. R. 303.
Contrary to law. 1 Blackf. R. 318.
Convenient speed, or as soon as convenient. 19 Ves. 336, 390, notes; 1 Ves. jr. 366.
Convey. 3 A. K. Marsh. 618.
Conveyance. 2 Serg. & Rawle, 498; 3 Mass. 487.
Convicted. 1 Wheat. 461; 15 East, R. 570; 7 Mann. & Gr. 481, 508.
Copper-fastened. 24 E. C. L. R. 415.
Coppered ship. 8 Pet. 557.
Corrupt. 1 Benth. Ev. 351.
Correcting—revising. 2 Shepl. 205.
Cost. 2 Wash. C. C. R. 498.
Costs. Wright, 121. Pay his own costs. 1 Hayw. 485.
Cotton in bales. 2 C. & P. 525.
County aforesaid. 2 Bl. R. 847.
Court of record. 5 Ohio R. 546. Vide 3 Wend. 267.
Cousins. 2 Brn. R. 125; Ward on Leg. 121.
Covenants. Provided always, and it is agreed that the lessor shall find great timber, Bac. Ab Covenant, A. I oblige myself to pay so much money. Hard. 178. I am content to give A ten pounds at Michaelmas, and ten pounds at Lady-day. 3 Leon. 119. With usual covenants. 15 Ves. 528; 3 Anstr. 700.
Covenants performed absque hoc. 6 Penn. St. Rep. 398.
Credible. Com. R. 91; S. C. 1 Freem. 510.
Credible witness. 5 Mass. 219; 12 Mass. 358; 17 Pick. 134; 2 Bailey, R. 24; 8 Conn. 254.
Credit. Mutual credit. 1 Atk. 228; 7 T. R. 378; Montag. on Set-off, 48; 8 Taunt. 22; S. C. 4 Eng. Com. Law Rep. 4; 1 Marsh. R. 190; S. C. 4 Eng. C. L. 335.
Creditors and subsequent purchasers. 5 Cranch, 165.
Criminal proceeding. 2 Q. B. 1.
Cross. 5 Pick. 163.
Cruise of three months. 2 Gallis. 526.
Cultivation. 2 N. H. Rep. 56.
Curby hock. Oliph. on Horses, 40.
Currency. 1 Ohio R. 119.
Current money. 1 Dall. 126, 176.
Current rate of exchange to be added. 2 Miles, R. 442, 443.
Current lawful money. 1 Dall 175.
Current bank notes. 1 Hamm. R. 178. See also 1 Hamm. R. 531; 1 Breese, R. 152; 3 Litt. R. 245; 19 John. R. 146; 1 Dall. 126, 176; 1 Ohio R. 119
Current bank money. 5 Humph. R. 140.
Curricle. Anthon, 114.
Cutting. Russ. & Ry. Cr. Cas. 104.

Damages. 5 Cowen, 161.
Damna. Bac. Ab. Costs, (L.)
Dangerous weapon. 1 Baldw. 78.
Dangers of the navigation. 9 Watts, R. 87.
Date. Co. Litt. 46, b, note (8); Bulstr. n. 177 Stiles, 382; Com. Dig. Estates, G 8; Id. Bargain and Sale, B 8; Id. Temps, A; Vin. Ab. Estates, Z a; Id. Time, A.
Day. (fraction of,) 1 Cowen, 594; 6 Cowen, 611; 1 Nott & McC. 405; 3 Penna. R. 245.
Day of the date. Co. Litt. 46 b, note, (8); Powell on Powers, 498, et seq. to 533. Vide *Date*, above.
Day time. 9 Mass. 154.
Days. Running days. Working days. 1 Bell's Com. 577, 5th ed.
Dealings. M. & M. 137; 3 C. & P. 85; S. C. 14 E. C. L. R. 219.
Death. Swanst. 161.
Debt, contracted. 2 B. & C. 762; 9 E. C. L. R. 236.
Debts due to me at my decease. 9 Sim. 16.
Debts now due. 3 Leigh, R. 389. See 4 Rawle, R. 307.
Declare. 3 Co. 82, b; Co. Litt. 76, a, 290, b; 3 T. R. 546.
Deed. A good and sufficient deed. Wright's R. 644. A good and sufficient warranty deed. 15 Pick. R. 546.
Default. Platt on Cov. 335
Definitive. 1 Watts, 257.
Delivered. 7 D. & R. 131; 16 E. C. L. R. 277.
Demands in full. 9 S. & R. 123.
Demise. 2 Caines' R. 188; 8 Cowen's R. 36; 4 Taunt. 329; 8 Mass. R. 201; 8 Cowen, 36.
To depart. 3 M. & S. 461.
Depending. 5 Co. 47, 48; 7 Co. 30; 9 B. & C. 755; 4 Bing. 561; 8 B. & C. 635.
Deponent believes. 2 Str. 1209, 1226; 2 Burr. 655; 1 Wils. 231.
Descendants. 3 Bro. C. C. 367.
Descent. 2 Pet. R. 94; 1 S. & R. 224; 11 S. & R. 232.
Desire. 1 Caines' R. 84; 1 Bro. C. C. 489.
Deviation. 3 Ch. Com. L. 471.
Devise. All messuages, lands. 17 Ves. 64.
Devolve. 1 M. & K. 647.
Die by his own hands. 5 Mann. & Gr. 639.
Diligent inquiry. 1 Meigs, R. 70.
Discharge. Her receipt to be a sufficient discharge. 3 Bro. C. C. 362.
Discharge of all demands. Ward on Leg. 222; 2 Vern. 114, by Raithb.
Discount—Discounted. 15 Johns. 168; 8 Wheat. 338; 4 Yeates, 223; 2 Cowen, 376; 19 Johns. 332.
Discounting. 5 Mann. & Gr. 590.
Disfiguring. Cheves, 157.
Disparagement. 1 Ired. Eq. R. 232.
Dispose of. 1 Watts, 386; 3 Atk. 287; Rob. on Wills, 3, Appx. note 3; 14 Pet. R. 529.
Disposing mind and memory. 2 South. 454.
Distiller. Pet. C. C. R. 180; 2 Wheat. 248.
Distribute. 11 S. & R. 232.
Divide. Boyle on Charities, 291.
Division. 4 T. R. 224, 459.
Do the needful. 4 Esp. 65; 4 Esp. R. 66.
Doctor. 2 Camph. 441.
Domus. 4 Leon. 16.
Doth bargain and sell. 4 Monr. R 463.
Down the said creek with the several meanders thereof. 2 Ohio R. 309.
Due. 3 Leigh, 389; 4 Rawle, 307.
Due A B. 2 Penn. R. 67.
Due A B $94 on demand. 5 Day, R. 337; and see 2 Cowen, R. 536.

Due course of law. 3 Cranch, 300; 5 Cranch, 363; 1 Wheat. 447.

Due security. Sax. Ch R. 259.

Duly honored. 7 Taunt. 167; 2 E. C. L. R. 63; 7 Taunt R. 164.

Dunce. Cro. Car. 382; 1 Roll. Ab. 55; Bac. Ab. Slander, I.

Dying without children. 5 Day, 517.

Dying by his own hands. 5 Mann. & Gr. 639.

Dying without issue. 12 East, 253; 3 East, 303, 491; 1 Ves. Jr. 562; 10 Ves. 562; 17 Ves. 482.

Dying without lawful issue. 10 Johns. R. 12; 5 Day, 20; 2 Bro. C. C. 553.

Each. 1 B. & C. 682; 8 C. & R. 184; 4 Watts, 51; 10 Serg. & R. 33.

Eadem. Co. Litt. 20 b.

Effects. 13 Ves. 39; 15 Ves. 326, 507; Cowp. 299; 1 Hill, S. C. 155. Estates and effects. 1 Ves. & Beam. 406; 1 East. R. 53; 11 East, 290; Russ. & Ry. Cr. Cas. 66.

Emigrant laborers. 2 Man. & Gr. 574, 589; 40 E. C. L. R. 520, 528.

Ended. 10 S. & R. 391.

Engagement. 15 John. 385, 390.

Entreat. 2 Madd. 458; 2 Ves. & Bea. 378.

Equally. Cowp. 657; 3 Ves. 260; Dougl. 760; 9 East, 276.

Equally to be divided, this phrase construed. 1 Rop. Leg. 266; 1 Atk. 494; 3 Bro. C. C 25; 5 Ves. 510; Addis. 310; 3 S. & R. 135; 1 Wils. R. 341; 1 Desaus. 329.

Erect. 8 Ves. 191; 3 Mad. R. 306; 2 Ves. 181; 2 Ves. 247; 1 Bro. C. C. 444; Amb. 751.

Erection. 9 Car. & P. 233.

Erections and improvements. 2 Man. & Gr. 756, 757; 40 E. C. L. R. 612.

Errors excepted. Gow on Partn. 136; 3 Bro. C. C. 266.

Establishing. 3 Madd R. 306; Boyle on Char. 93; 2 Cox, 387; S. C. 4 Bro. C C. 326.

Estate. 3 Cranch, 97; 3 Yeates, 187; 6 Binn. 97; 2 Binn. 20; 6 Johns. R. 185; 1 Wash. R. 96; 1 Call, 127; 3 Call, 306; 2 Nott & M'Cord, 380; 1 Dall. 226; 12 Serg. & Rawle, 54; 1 Yeates, 250, 380; 1 Salk. 236; 6 T. R. 610, 11 East, 246; 2 Ves. & Bea 222; 2 Atk. 38; 3 Atk. 486; Ambl. 155, 216; 12 Mod 592; 1 T. R. 659, n.; 8 Ves. 604; 9 Ves. 137; 1 Cox, 362; 2 Ves. & Bea. 225; 19 Ves. 195; 3 Ves. & Bea. 160. Estates and effects. 1 Ves. & Bea. 406. Temporal estate. 8 Ves. 617. All the residue of my estate of every name and kind. 4 Law Rep. 256.

Every of them. 12 S. & R. 158.

Evidence. Conclusive evidence. 1 Leigh's N. P. 307.

Except what shall be mentioned hereafter. Monr. 399.

Excepting. Perk. s. 439; Crabb on R. P. § 157.

Execute. 2 Green's R 350.

Exclusive of costs. 1 Edw. R. 483.

Expectation. Boyle on Char. 319.

Expenses. 15 Serg. & Rawle, 55.

Extend. 1 Paine's R. 385.

Fac similes. 7 Mann. & Gr. 399

Factory prices. 2 Conn. R. 69; 2 Mason, 89, 90.

Factum. 1 Leon. 310.

Faithful. 12 Pick. 303.

Falsely. 2 M. & Selw. 379; Noy. 35; Owen, 51.

Farcy. Oliph. on Horses, 42.

Family. Cooper's R. 117; 8 Ves. 604.

Farm. 6 T. R. 345.

Father, on the part of the. 1 Serg. & Rawle, 224.

Feeder. 13 Pick. 50.

Fifty pounds, (50l.) Sid. 151.

Filled. 1 Breese's R. 70.

Final. Final and conclusive. 5 Binn. 387; 6 Binn. 128. Final judgment. 2 Pet. R. 264, 464 Final decree. 8 Wend. 242. Final settlement and decree. 4 Am. Dig. 283; 1 Halst. 195; 17 Serg. & Rawle, 59, 340; 14 Serg. & Rawle, 396; 1 Penn. R. 282; 2 Pet. R. 464.

Final process. 16 Pet. 313.

Fine. 5 M. & W. 535.

Firmly. 4 S. & R. 135; 1 Browne, R. 258.

First born son. 1 Ves. 290.

First cousin or cousins german. 4 M. & C. 56.

First had and obtained. 1 Serg. & Rawle, 89.

First or sterling cost. 1 Stuart's (L. C.) R. 215.

Fixed furniture. 6 C. & P. 653.

Flats. 8 W. & S. 442.

Flock. Inst. 4, 3, 1.

Flock of sheep. Inst. 2, 20, 18.

Fold course. Touchs. 93; Co. Litt. 6

For. Dougl. 688; 1 Saund. 320, n. 4; Willes, 157.

For and in consideration of dollars. 7 Verm. 522; 6 Verm. 411.

For such times as we think fit. 1 Chit. Com. Law. 495.

For value received. 18 John. 60; 8 D. & R. 163; S. C. 5 B. & C. 501.

For which he has not accounted. 4 Burr. 2126; 1 T. R. 716.

For whom it may concern. 1 Pet. R. 151.

Foreign bills. 19 John. R. 146.

Foreign part, place. 2 Gall. R. 4; 19 John. 375. Foreign voyage. 1 Gall. R. 55, 142. Foreign part. 19 Johns. 375; 4 Am. Law Journ. 101.

Foreign state. 5 Pet. 1.

Foreign vessel. 1 Gall. R. 58.

Foreigner. 1 Pet. R. 349.

Forever. 6 Cruise, 281; 4 Dane's Ab. c. 129, art. 2, § 14.

Forthwith. 1 Mo. & Malk. 300; S. C. 22 E. C. L. R. 313; 9 C. & P. 706; S. C. 38 E. C. L. R. 299, 301; 12 Ad. & Ell. 672; S. C. 40 E. C. L. R. 158, 160, 161, 162; 7 Mann. & Gr. 493.

Forwards and backwards. 2 New Rep. 434.

Four mills. 1 Mod. 90.

Fourth part of house in N. Cro. Eliz. 286; 1 Str. 695.

Fowl. 1 Russ. C. & M. 568.

Frame house filled with bricks. 7 Wend. 270.

Fraudulently. Willes, 584; 1 Chit. Pl. 376.

Free. 1 Wh. 335; 2 Salk. 637.

Free of average. 16 East, R. 214.

Free of particular average. 16 East, R. 14; 15 East, R. 559; Code de Commerce, art. 409.

Free on board a foreign ship. 3 Campb. R. 270.

Freely to be enjoyed. Cowp. 352; 3 Burr. 1895; 11 East, R. 229.

Freight. 1 Mason, R. 11, 12.

From. 1 Marsh. Ins. 261, a; 2 Cowen, 605, 606, n. 518; 15 Mass. 193; 1 S. & R. 411; 3 S. & R. 496; 5 T. R. 283; 2 Saund. 158, b, n. 6; 5 Com. Dig. 335; 4 Cruise, 72; Greenl. Cas. 9; 6 W. & S. 328. From and after. 9 Cranch, 104; 2 Cowen, 606 n.; 4 T. R. 659. From the day of the date. Cowper, 717, 725. From the date, 15 S. & R. 135.

From 1000 to 3000 bushels of potatoes. 4 Greenl 497.

From thenceforth. 2 Mer. R. 431.
From and after the passing of the act. 4 T. R. 660.
Front to the river. 6 M. R. 19, 228, 229 ; 8 N. S. 576 ; 9 M. R. 656.
Full and free. 1 Wh. 335.
Full cargo. 7 Taunt. 272.
Fully. Pow. on Mortg. 83, 858.
Fur. 7 Cowen, 202.
Furniture. Amb. 605 ; 3 Ves. 311 ; 1 John. Ch. R. 329. Furniture at —— —— 3 Madd. 276.
Future. 7 W. & S. 305; 2 Pa. St. R. 146.
Future increase. 3 Yerg. 546. See 2 Bibb, 76 ; 4 Hen. & Munf. 283.
Future conveyances. 2 P. St. R. 146.

Gamble. 2 Yerger, 472.
Geldings, cattle. 1 Leach, C. C. 73, n.
Gentlemen. 2 Y. & C. 683 ; 21 Jurist, 152.
Gift. I give this note to A. 4 Ves. 565. I return to A his bond. 3 Ves. 231.
Gelding—horse. 3 Humph. 323.
Give. 2 Caines' Rep. 188 ; 7 John. R. 258 ; 11 John. R. 122 ; 5 Greenl. R. 227.
Give and grant. 1 Hayw. R. 251.
Given. 1 Harr. (N. J.) R. 286.
Giving testimony in a suit. 3 Harr. Cond. Lo. R. 157.
Giving way. 10 (Eng.) Jur. 1065.
Glass with care, this side up. 11 Pick. R. 41.
Glass eye. Oliph. on Horses, 44.
Good. 5 M. & W. 535.
Good and lawful men. 1 Blackf. R. 396.
Good note. 7 Verm. 67.
Good custom cowhide. Brayt. 77.
Good and sufficient deed. Wright, 644. Good and sufficient warranty deed. 15 Pick. 546 ; 20 John. 130 ; 4 Paige R. 628.
Good merchantable goods. 3 Campb. R. 462.
Good work. Wright, R. 471.
Goods. 2 Ves. Jr. 163 ; 3 Atk. 63 ; 1 P. Wms. 267 ; 2 P. Wms. 302 ; 1 Atk. 171, 177, 180, 182 ; 1 Ves. Jr. 237 ; 1 Bro. C. C. 127 ; 11 Ves. 666 ; 1 Marsh. Ins. 319 ; 7 Taunt. 191 ; 2 B. & A. 327 ; 4 B. & A. 206 ; 9 East, 215 ; 5 Mason's R. 544.
Goods and chattels. 2 B. & A. 335 ; 1 Leigh's N. P. 244 ; 1 Yeates, 101 ; 2 Watts, 61 ; 8 Co. 33 ; 2 East, P. C. C. 16, s. 37 ; 2 B. & A. 259, 327 ; 6 Bing. 363 ; 4 Mo. & P. 36 ; 1 Ves. sen. 363 ; 1 Atk. 165.
Goods and movables. 1 Yeates, R. 101.
Government security. 3 Younge & C. 397.
Government or other securities. 9 Sim. 104.
Grange. Co. Litt. 5 ; Plowd. 197 ; Touch. 93.
Grant, bargain, sell, alien, and confirm. 2 Caines' R. 188 ; 7 Johns. R. 258 ; Com. Dig. Guaranty, A.
Grant, bargain, sell. 4 Dall. 441 ; 2 Binn. 99 ; 1 Rawle, 377 ; 1 Serg. & R. 50, 438 ; 4 Kent's Com. 460.
Grant and demise. 4 Wend. 502 ; 8 Cowen, 36 ; 9 Ves. 330.
Grantee. 1 Cowen, 509.
Ground. 1 Supp. to Ves. jr. 510.
Ground-rents. 1 Meriv. 26 ; 2 Str. 1020 ; 1 Bro. C. C. 76.
Growing. 4 Leon. 36.
Gutta serena. Oliph. on Horses, 44.

Habitable repair. 2 Mo. & Rob. 186
Half mile. 9 B. & C. 774.
Has bargained and sold. 4 Cowen, 225.
Have. 2 Bendl. 34.
Having. 2 Ves. 427 ; 11 Ad. & El. 273 ; 39 E. C. L. R. 80.
Having children. 7 T. R. 322 ; 7 Ves. 453.
He has removed land-marks. 10 S. & R. 18. See Minor, 138.
He is perjured. 1 Caines, 347. 2 Caines, 91.
He is forsworn. 1 Caines, 347.
He is a corrupt old tory. 2 Port. 212.
He keeps false books, and I can prove it. 17 John. 217 ; 5 John. 476.
He paying thereout. Dick. 444 ; 3 East, 590.
He shall be well satisfied. 2 John. Rep. 395.
He swore a lie before the church session, and I can prove it. 1 Penna. 12.
He swore a false oath, and I can prove it. 2 Binn. 60 ; 4 Bibb, 99 ; 2 Dall. 58.
Heir male. 4 Ves. 794 ; Id. 326.
Heirs. 1 Car. Law Rep. 484.
Heirs at law. 4 Rand. R. 95.
Heirs of the body. 2 Bligh, 49. Vide 4 T. R. 300 ; Id. 88 ; 3 T. R. 378 ; 3 Ves. jr. 257 ; 13 Ves. jr. 340.
Heirs female. Co. Litt. 24 b, n. 3 ; 5 Bro. Parl. Rep. 93 ; Goodtitle *v.* Burtenshaw, Fearne, Rem. Appx. No. 1.
Heirs of the wife. 6 Yerg. R. 96.
Henceforth. 8 Serg. & Rawle, 183.
Her. 1 Desaus R. 353.
Her increase. 1 Iredell, 460.
Her part aforesaid. 4 Dowl. & R. 387.
Hereinafter—Hereinbefore. 1 Sim. Rep. 173.
Hereditament. 1 Salk. 238, Mos. 242 ; 3 T. R. 358 ; 7 T. R. 558 ; 8 N. R. 505 ; 2 B. & P. 247, 251 ; 6 Nev. & M. 441 ; 4 Ad. & Ell. 805.
Head of a family. 2 How. S. C. Rep. 581, 590.
Hides. 7 Cowen, 202.
High seas. Russ. & Ry. 243 ; 2 Leach, 109 ; 3 Mason's R. 290.
Him or His. 2 Ves. 213.
Hiring. 6 T. R. 452.
Holiday. 4 Clark & Fin. 234.
Homestead—Homestead farm. 7 N. H. Rep. 241 ; 15 John. R. 471.
Hope. Boyle on Char. 319.
Horse. 1 Scam. R. 304.
Horse—Gelding. 3 Humph. 323.
Horse, Mares and Colts—Cattle. 2 East, P. C. 1074 ; 1 Leach, C. C. 72.
Hotel keeper. 1 Carr. & Marsh. 458.
House. 7 Mann. & Gr. 66, 122.
House I live in and garden to B. 2 T. R. 298.
Household goods. 3 Ves. jr. 310 ; 1 John. Ch. R. 329 ; 3 P. Wms. 335.
Household furniture. 2 Hall, R. 490.

I guaranty the payment of the within note at the insolvency of the drawers. 5 Humph. 476.
I return A his bond. 3 Ves. 231.
I warrant this note good. 14 Wend. 231.
If. Touchs 123 ; Co Lit. 204 ; Id. 214 b
Immediate. 2 Lev. 77 ; 7 Mann. & Gr. 493.
Immediately. 4 Younge & Col. 511.
Immovables. Ward on Leg. 210.
Impedimentum. Bac. Tr. 211.
Impetitio. Bac. Tr. 211.
Implements. 9 Law Reporter, 207.
Improvement. 4 Pick. 204.
In all the month of May. 3 W. C. C. R. 140.
In actual military service. 3 Curt. R. 522 ; 7 Eng. Eccl. R. 496.

In current bank notes. 1 Ham. R. 178. See also 1 Ham. R. 531; 1 Breese, R. 152, Litt. R. 245; 1 Ohio R. 119; 1 Dall. R. 126, 176; 19 John. R. 146.
In default of such issue. 7 East, R. 521; 3 T. R. 484.
In fullest confidence. T. & R. 143.
In like manner. Ward on Leg. 246; 4 Ves. 732; 1 Sim. & St. 517.
In manner aforesaid. Ward on Leg. 246; 5 Ves. 465.
In the fullest confidence. Turn. & Russ. 157.
In money or negroes. 4 Bibb, R. 97.
In the occupation of. 2 Bing. R. 456. 1 B. & C. 350.
In case of the death. Swanst. 162.
Income. 9 Mass. R. 372; 1 Metc. 75.
Inde. Co. Litt. 82 b.
Indebted. 15 Serg. & Rawle, 142; 3 Caines' R. 323; 17 S. & R 285.
Indefeasible title. 3 Bibb, R. 317.
Indirect. 2 Gill & John. 382.
Indorse. 7 Pick. 117.
Infamous crime. 1 Moody, Cr. Cas. 34, 38.
Inferior tradesmen. 1 Lord Raym. 149; Com. Rep. 26; 5 Mod. 307; Bac. Ab. Costs, B.
Inhabitants of a neighborhood. 10 Pick. R. 367.
Insolvent circumstances. 2 Harr. Dig. 202; Chit. on Bills, 120; McClel. & Yo. 407.
Instantly. 3 Perr. & Dav. 52; 8 Dowl. 157.
Intended to be recorded. 2 Rawle, 14.
Intent to defraud—Intent to deceive. Rob. Fr. Conv. 30; and see 8 John. R. 446; 12 John. 320; 2 John. Ch. R. 35; 4 Wheat. R. 466.
Intents and purposes. To all intents and purposes. 11 Ves. 530.
Investment. 15 Johns. 384, 392
Irregularity. 1 Cowen, 735, b.
Irreparable. 3 Mart. N. S. 25.
Is indebted to the plaintiff in trover. 1 H. Bl. 218.
Is indebted to the plaintiff upon promises. 2 Dougl. 467; and see Say, R. 109.
Issue. 3 Ves. & Bea. 67; 13 Ves. 340; 3 Ves. 421; 7 Ves. 522; 1 Dall. 47; 1 Yeates, 332; 3 Ves. 257; 1 Cox, 38. Failure of issue. 1 B. & B. 1. Die without issue. 17 Ves. 482.
Issuably. 3 Chit. Pr. 705.
It shall and may be lawful. 1 Edw. R. 84.
It shall be lawful. 8 N. S. 538.
It shall be lawful for the court. 1 John. Ch. R. 491.
Ita quod. Ld. Raym. 760.

Jewels. Ward on Leg. 221; Mos. 112.
Jewelry. 14 Pick 370 Vide infra *Trinkets.*
Jockey. 8 Scott, N. S 584.
Joint and equal proportions. Jointly. Ambl. 656; 1 Bro. C. C. 118; 2 Rop. Leg. 267. Joint and several. 2 Day, 442; 1 Caines' Cas. 122; 1 Consts. R. 486; 1 Cox, 200; 4 Desaus. 148; 7 Serg. & Rawle, 356.
Judicial proceedings. 5 Ohio, 547; 3 M. R. 248; 4 M. R. 451; 6 M. R. 668; 7 M. R. 325; 9 M. R. 204, 325; 10 M. R. 1; L. R. 438; 3 N. S. 551; 5 N. S. 519.
Junior. 8 John. 549; 8 Conn. R. 293.
Just debts. 1 Binn. 209; 9 Mass. 62.
Justifiable cause. 1 Sumn. 194.

Kept. 4 Scamm. 168.
Kin. Next of kin. 15 Ves. 109; Id. 583; 3 Bro. C. C. 355. Next of kin or heir at law. 4 Ves. 469. Next of kin, in equal degree. 12 Ves. 433.
King's enemies. 1 Leigh's N. P. 509.
Knowing and being privy to. Platt on Cov. 338.

Laborer. 1 Lo. Rep. 268.
Lamb—Mutton. 1 Moody, Cr. Cas. 242; and see Russ. & Ry. 497.
Lampooner. 3 Lev. 248.
Last past—August last past. 3 Cowen, 70.
Last sickness. 20 John. 502.
Last will. 7 T. R. 138.
Law charges. 3 Mart. Lo. R. 282.
Law of the land. 2 Yerg. 554; 6 Penna. St. Rep. 87, 91; 4 Dev. 1.
Lawful. Lawful heir. 2 T. R. 720. Lawful deed of conveyance. 2 Serg. & R. 498. Lawful money. 1 Yeates, 349; 1 Dall. 126, 176. Shall be lawful. 2 D. & R. 172; 4 B. & A. 271; 1 B. & C. 35, 8. Lawful title. 1 Blackf. 380; 2 Greenl. R. 22; 10 John. R. 266. Lawful deed. 2 S. & R. 498; Coxe, 106. Lawful current money of Pennsylvania. 1 Dall. 124.
Lawfully demanded. 2 M. & S. 525.
Leaving children. 7 T. R. 332, and see 7 Ves. 453; 9 Ves. 204; 6 T. R 307. Vide *Having Children.*
Leasehold ground rents. Ward on Leg. 222; 1 Bro. 76.
Legal representatives. 3 Ves. 486; 3 Bro. C. C. 224; 1 Yeates, 213; 2 Yeates, 585; 2 Dall. 205; 6 Serg. & Rawle, 83; 1 Anstr. 128.
Lend. 1 Hill's Ch. 37.
Lent. Bac. Ab. Assumpsit F; 2 Wils. 141.
Let. 5 Whart. R. 278.
Level. 5 Ad. & El. 302; 4 Nev. & Man. 602.
Life estate. £500 to the sole use of N, or of her children, forever. 1 Cox, 341; vide 12 Ves. 295; 1 Rose, 200; 13 Ves. 486; 13 Ves. 445; 2 Eden, 323; Amb. 499; 4 Bro. C. C. 542; 1 Bay, 447.
Limit and appoint. 5 D. & E. 124.
Linen. 3 Bro. C. C. 311.
Literary composition. Eden, Inj. 324.
Live and dead stock. Ward on Leg. 220; 3 Ves. 311.
Livelihood. 3 Atk. 399.
Living together. 1 Add. R. 476; 3 Add. R. 277; 2 Tyrw. 76; 2 Cr. & J. 66; Rogers' Eccl. Law, tit. Marriages.
Loaded arm. 1 Carr. & Kirw. 530; S. C. 47 Eng. C. L. R. 530.
Lost or not lost. 1 Marsh. Ins. 332; Park, Ins. 25; 5 Burr. 2803; Wesk. 345.
Loaf sugar. 1 Sumn. R. 159.
Lot No. 54. 1 Verm. R. 336; 18 John. R. 107, 5 N. R. Rep. 58.
Lots. 4 Ohio, 5.
Lying at the wharf. 2 McCord, 105.

Made. 1 Cranch, 239.
Made his note to the plaintiff for $760. 1 Breese's R. 122.
Magistrate. 13 Pick. 523.
Make over and grant. 18 John. 60; 3 John. R. 484.
Maintenance. 4 Conn. R. 558; 2 Conn. R. 155, 2 Sandf. Ch. R. 91. See *Support.*
Mange. Oliph. on Horses, 46.
Mankind. Fortescue. 91.
Mare. 1 Leach, 72; 2 W. Bl. 721; 2 East, P. C. 1074.

Mariner or Seaman. 2 Curt. Eccl. R. 336.

Mark. Trade mark. See 19 Pick. 214.

Married. Dying unmarried; without being married, and having children. 1 Rop. Leg. 412; 3 Ves. 450, 454; 7 Ves. 454.

Matter in controversy. 2 Yeates, 276; 1 Serg. & Rawle, 269; 5 Binn. 522; 3 Dall. 404; 2 Dall. 260, n.

Matter in dispute. 3 Cranch, 159.

Matters in difference. 5 Mass. 334.

May. 1 Saund. 58, n. 1; 5 Johns. Ch. R. 101; 5 Cowen, 195; 14 Serg. & Rawle, 429; 1 E. C. L. R. 46; 1 Pet. R. 46. May assign. May suggest. Ib.; St. 8 and 9 W. 3, c. 11, s. 8.

Meadows. 5 Cowen's R. 216; Co. Litt. 4, b.

Means. Platt. on Cov. 334–5.

Medals. Ward. on Leg. 221; 3 Atk. 201.

Merchandise. 8 Pet. 277.

Merchantable. 3 Campb. R. 462.

Merchantable quality. 20 Wend. R. 61.

Merits. 3 Watts & Serg. 273.

Mess. 2 Russ. C. & M. 360.

Mess Pork of Scott & Co. 2 Bing. N. C. 668.

Messuage and house. Cro. Eliz. 89; 2 Ch. Cas. 27; 2 T. R. 498; 1 Boss. & Pull. 53.

Mill. 5 Serg. & Rawle, 107.

Mill privilege. 4 Shepl. R. 63.

Mill saw. 1 Fairf. R. 135.

Mill site. 15 Pick. 57; 6 Cowen, R. 677; 11 John. R. 191.

Minerals. 5 Watts, 34.

Misapply. 12 Ad. & Ell. 140; 40 E. C. L. R. 140.

Misnomer. 16 East, 110; 2 Stark. N. P. C. 29; Dunl. Pr. 238; 3 Camp. 29; 2 Caines' R. 362; 13 John. 486.

Mobilier. 3 Harr. Cond. R. 430.

Molest. Mo. 402; S. C. Cro. Eliz. 421.

Money. 15 Ves. 319; 3 Meriv. 691; 1 John. Ch. R. 231. Money only. 7 T. R. 539, 549.

Money—Moneys. 14 John. R. 12.

Money deposited in court. 2 Gall. R. 146.

Money in the funds. 5 Price, R. 217.

Moneys. 1 John. Ch. R. 231.

More or less. 2 Pow. Mortg. 445, a, note; 2 Hen. & Munf. 164; 1 Ves. & B. 376; 2 Barn. & Adol. 106; S. C. 22 E. C. L. R. 36; 1 Yeates, 309; 6 Binn. 102; 4 Serg. & Rawle, 493; 1 Serg. & Rawle, 166; 5 Serg. & Rawle, 260; 1 Munf. 336; 2 Saund. 305, b, n.; 4 Mason's R. 418; Sudg. Vend. 231–2; Ow. 133; 1 Campb. 337.

Mountain. 1 Str. 71; 1 Burr. 629.

Movables. Ward. on Leg. 210; Off. Ex. 252; Sir W. Jo. 225.

Mr. 3 C. & P 59; S. C. 1 M. & M. 118.

Mrs. 3 C. & P. 59; S. C. 1 M. & M. 118.

Mutual credit. 8 Taunt. 499; 4 Burr. 2222; Cooke's Bankr. Laws, 536; 4 T. R. 211; 2 Smith's Lead. Cas. 178, and the cases there cited.

My fishing place. 1 Whart. R. 137.

My half part. 11 East, R. 163.

My inheritance. Hob. 2; 7 East, R. 97.

My seven children, naming only *six.* 2 Coxe, R. 184.

My property. 17 John. R. 281.

My house, and all that shall be in it at my death. 1 Bro. C. C. 129, n.; 11 Ves. 662.

My right heirs on the part of my mother. 4 Ves. 766.

Name and blood. 15 Ves. 92.

Navicular disease. Oliph. on Horses, 47.

Navigable river. 6 Cowen, 528; 21 Pick. R 344.

Necessary. 4 Wheat. 413, 418; 7 Cowen, 606, 2 A. K. Marsh. R. 84.

Necessary charges. 3 Greenl. 191.

Necessary implication. 1 Ves. & B. 466.

Necessary tools of a tradesman. 2 Whart. 26.

Needful. 4 Esp. R. 66.

Nerving. Oliph. on Law of Horses, 47; R. & M. 290.

Neurotomy. Oliph. on Horses, 47; R. & M. 290.

Never. 2 Atk. 32; Bayl. Bills, 4; Chit. Bills, 54; 3 Q. B. 239, 242.

New manufacture. 4 Mann. & Gr. 580.

Next. Stra. 394; Cro. Jac. 646, 677: Bac. Ab. Conditions, P. 3; 2 John. 190; 9 Cowen. 255.

Next of kin. 15 Ves. 109; 15 Ves. 536; 3 Bro. C. C. 355; Id. 64; 14 Ves. 372.

Next of kin, or heir at law. 4 Ves. 469.

Next of kin, equal in degree. 12 Ves. 433.

Non-arrival. 2 B. & C. 564.

Non-resident. 4 L. R. 11.

Northerly. 1 John. 156. See 3 Caines, 293.

Northward. 3 Caines' R. 293; 1 John. R. 158.

Not liable for any damage to or from her sheathing. 20 Pick. 389.

Note or Notes. 7 Serg. & Rawle, 465.

Notes current in the city of New York. 19 John. R. 146.

Notice of action. 1 Holt's N. P. R. 27.

Now. 3 Penna. R. 288, 9; 4 Mann. & Gr. 99, 100.

Occupation. 7 W. & S. 330.

Occupied. 1 Breese's R. 70.

Of. 2 T. R. 431.

Of and concerning. 4 M. & Selw. 169; 3 Caines' R. 329; 5 Johns. R. 211; 7 Johns. R. 264; Id. 359; 3 Binn. 517; 1 Binn. 537. 5 Binn. 218.

Offence. 9 Car. & P. 525; S. C. 38 E. C. L. R. 222.

Office, or public trust. 2 Cowen, 29 n.; 20 Johns. 492; 1 Munf. 468.

Office of trust. 6 Blackf. 529.

On. 2 T. R. 431.

On arrival. 2 Campb. R. 532; Id. 327.

On condition. 4 Watts & Serg. 302.

On shore. 1 Bos. & Pull. 187.

On a stream. 3 Sumn. R. 170.

On the trial. 2 Whart. 159.

On payment of costs. 6 Cowen, R. 582; 5 J. J. Marsh. 243.

One day after date. 2 P. S. R. 496.

One pair of boots. 3 Harring. 559.

One whole year. 12 Mass. 262.

Once a week. 4 Peters' R. 361; 2 Miles, R. 150, 151.

One thousand dollars to the children of ——. 9 Verm. R. 41.

Openly. 2 Inst. 57; Bac. Ab. Merchant, &c.

Or, construed *and.* 2 Rop. Leg. 290; 1 P. Wms. 483; 2 Cox. 213; 2 P. Wms. 383; 2 Atk. 643; 6 Ves. 341; 2 Ves. Sen. 67; 2 Str. 1175, Cro. Eliz. 525; Pollexf. 645; 1 Bing. 500; 3 T. R. 470; 1 Ves. Sen. 409; 3 Atk. 83, 85; 1 Supp. to Ves. Jr. 485; 2 Id. 9, 43, 114; 1 Yeates, 41, 319; 1 Serg. & Rawle, 141; 1 Wend. 396; 6 Toull. n. 703 and 704. Vide *Disjunctive.* Or any other person. 15 Wend. 147. Or by any other person. 3 Marsh. 720. Or elsewhere. 2 Gall. R.

477. Or otherwise. 1 Chit. R. 265, 6; Hawk. c. 25, s. 4.
Orchard. Cro. Eliz. 854.
Ordained minister. 4 Conn. 134.
Order, in chancery pleading. 7 Sim. R. 17.
Original. 6 Wheat. 396; 5 Serg. & Rawle, 549. Vide *Courts of the United States*.
Orphan. 3 Mer. 48; 2 Sim. & Stu. 93.
Other. 1 Brock. R. 187.
Other offices. 1 B. & C. 237. See 5 T. R. 375, 379; 5 B. & C. 640; 8 D. & R. 393.
Other writing. 1 Rawle, 231.
Otherwise. 1 Gall. R. 39.
Out of the State. 1 Johns. Cas. 76.
Out of the country. 3 Bibb, 510.
Out of their joint funds, according to the articles of association. 4 S. & R. 356.
Outfits. 1 Story, R. 603.
Out-house. 5 Day, 151; 4 Conn. 446.
Over the sea. Kirby, 299.
Overseers. 7 Mann. & Gr. 481.
Own use. 4 Rawle, R. 68.
Owned by them. 5 Cowen, 509.
Owner. 6 Nev. & M. 340.
Oxgang. Touchs. 93; Co. Litt. 5.
Oyster spat. 12 Ad. & Ell. 13; S. C. 40 E. C. L. R. 15.

Passage room. 2 Ld. Raym. 1470.
Passing through the town. 6 Ohio, R. 142.
Payable. 14 Ves. 470; 16 Ves. 172; 2 Supp. to Ves. jr. 296; 13 Ves. 113; 3 Ves. 13; 2 Bro. C. C. 365.
Paying. Roll. Ab. 411; Bac. Ab. Conditions, A; Lane, 56, 78.
Paying thereout. Dick. 444.
Paying yearly and every year. 3 Lom. Dig. 187.
Pearls. Dig. 34, 2, 18.
Peas. Bac. Ab. Merchant, &c. I.
Pencil writing. 1 Eccl. R. 406, 7; 5 B. & C. 234; 7 Dowl. & R. 653; 1 Stark. R. 267; 1 Phillim. R. 52, 53; 2 Phillim. R. 173.
Per annum. Bac. Ab. Covenant, F
Percussit. 2 Virg. Car. 111.
Perishable articles. 7 Cowen, 202.
Permitting and suffering. 6 Barn. & Cres. 295; Platt on Cov. 338.
Perpetual. 2 Bro. & B. 27; S. C. 6 B. Moo. 159.
Person liable. Eden's Bankr. Law, 146.
Personal estate. 1 Ves. & Bea. 415; 4 Ves. 76; 1 M'Cord, 349; 1 Dall. 403; 2 Rawle, 162; 5 Mason, 544.
Personal ornaments. 1 Beav. R. 189.
Personal representatives. 1 Anst. 128.
Persons of color. 3 Iredell, 455.
Pigs.—Cattle. Russ. & Ry. Cr. Cas. 76.
Pilfering. 4 Blackf. 499.
Piratical. 2 How. S. C. 210.
Place.—Office. 1 Munf. 468.
Places. 5 T. R. 375, 379; 5 B. & C. 640; 8 D. & R. 393. See 1 B. & B. C. 237.
Placitum. Skin. 550, 554.
Plant. 1 Mo. & Malk. 341; S. C. 22 E. C. L. R. 330.
Plantation. 2 Humph. 315.
Planting. 7 Conn. 186.
Pleasure. At her pleasure. Boyle on Char. 307.
Pleasure carriage. 9 Conn. 371; 11 Conn. 185; 18 John. 128; 19 John. 442.
Plow land. Co. Litt. 5; Plowd. 167; Touchs. 93.
Plundered. 16 Pick. 1.
Poll-evil. Oliph. on Law of Horses, 49.
Poor. Poor kindred. Boyle on Char. 31; 17 Ves. 371; 1 Caines' R. 59.
Poor inhabitants. Ambl. 422.
Port. 2 B. & Ad. 43; S. C. 22 E. C. L. R. 23.
Port of destination.—Port of discharge. 5 Mason, 404.
Possess. 1 Dev. & Bat. 452.
Possession. Coming into possession. 3 Br. C C. 180.
Postea. 1 Saund. 287.
Power coupled with an interest. 8 Wheat. 203; 2 Cowen, 196.
Power of attorney. 8 Pick. 490.
Prædict. Co. Litt. 20 b.
Preference. 1 Paine, 630.
Premises. All the premises. 17 Ves. 75; 1 East R. 456.
Presented. 2 Hill, R. 582.
Price. A price clear of all expenses. 2 V. & B. 341.
Prime cost. 2 Mason, 53, 55.
Prior in date. 3 Day, 66.
Prison charges. 4 Greenl. 82.
Private charity. Turn. & Russ. 260.
Privileges and appurtenances. 14 Mass. 49; 1 Mass. 443.
Pro A B, C D. 11 Mass. R. 97.
Proceed to sea. 9 Serg. & Rawle, 154; 2 Pet. Adm. Dec. 97, 98.
Proceeding. 2 East, R. 213; 3 Com. Dig. 48, note; 1 Hall, 166; 8 Wend. 167.
Proceedings thereupon. 16 Pet. 303, 313.
Proceeds. 4 Mason, 529.
Procreatis—Procreandis. 1 M. & S. 124.
Procure. 1 Car. & Marsh. 458.
Procurement. Platt. on Cov. 337.
Produce of a farm. 6 Watts & Serg. 269, 280.
Professions. 7 W. & S. 330.
Promise. "I don't consider the land as yours; prove your right to it, and I'll pay you for it." 9 Dow. & R. 480; S. C. 22 E. C. L. R. 394. "I promise *never* to pay." 2 Atk. 32; Bayl. Bills, 4; Chit. Bills, 54.
Promise to pay out of the proceeds of the next crop. 2 L. R. 258.
Promissory note. Due A B three hundred and twenty-five dollars, payable on demand. 10 Wend. 675. To pay P D, or plaintiffs, or his or their order. 2 B. & A. 417. "I, B C, promise to pay E F the sum of £51 or his order," signed, "B C or else H B." 4 B. & A. 679; 6 E. C. L. R. 563.
Proper county. 2 Yeates, 152; 7 Watts, 245.
Property. 6 Serg. & Rawle, 452; 17 Johns. R. 281; 6 Binn. 94; 18 Ves. 193; 14 East, R. 370; 2 N. R. 214.
Property, personal and real. 1 Speers, Eq. Cas. 51, 56.
Property on board. 2 Metc. 1.
Proportion. Charge on estates in equal proportions. 3 Br. C. C. 286. In just and equal proportion. 7 Serg. & Rawle, 514.
Proprietor. 6 Nev. & M. 340; Wordsw. Jo. St. Co. 338.
Prosecute with effect. 12 Mod. 380; 2 Selw. N. P. 1013, note.
Proviso. Com. Dig. Condition, A 2; Lit. s. 329; Id. 203, b; 2 Co. 71, b; 1 Roll. Ab. 410, l. 30

Public house. 4 Leigh, 680.
Public policy. 9 E. C. L. R. 452. Public sale. 4 Watts, R. 258. Public trust. 20 Johns. 492; 2 Cowen, 29, n.
Public trade. 3 Q. B. 39.
Publish. 2 Dev. 115.
Published. 3 M. & W. 461; 9 Bing. 605; 5 B. & Adol. 518; 6 M. & W. 473; 8 D. P. C. 392.
Purchasing. 6 Ves. 404.

Quamdiu. Orl. Bridg. 202.
Quantity and boundary. 2 Caines' Rep. 146.
Quit. 2 N. H. Rep. 402.
Quotation. Eden. Inj. 327, 328.

Race-field. 9 Leigh, 648.
Raffle. 2 Rep. Const. Conn. 128.
Raise. 1 Atk. 421; 2 Vern. 153.
Rascal. 2 Rep. Const. Ct. 235.
Real action. 10 Pick. 473; and see 16 Mass. 448; 7 Mass. 476; 4 Pick. 169; 8 Greenl. 106, 138.
Real cost. 2 Mason, 53, 55.
Realm. 1 Taunt. 270; 4 Campb. 289; Rose, 387.
Reasonable notice. 1 Penn. R. 466. Vide *Reasonable time*, in the body of this work.
Rebuild. 3 Rawle, 482.
Receipts. 2 Gill & Johns. 511.
Received for record. 3 Conn. 544; 1 Root, R. 500; 2 Root, R. 298; Kirb. 72.
Received note in payment. 2 Gill & John. 511.
Recollect. 1 Dana, R. 56.
Recommendation. 2 Ves. jun. 333, 529; 3 Ves. 150; 9 Ves. 546; Jacob's R. 317; 1 Sim. & Stu. 387.
Record and Docket. 1 Watts, 395.
Recovered in a suit. 5 Wend. R. 620.
Recovery. 2 Caines' R. 214; 1 Paine, 230, 238.
Rectifier of spirits. 1 Pet C. C. R. 180.
Refine. 1 Pet. C. C. R. 113.
Refuse. Renounce. 3 Rawle, 398. Refuse to execute. 10 E. C. L. R. 65; 1 Har. Dig. 442.
Relations, see *Legatee.* 2 Ch. Rep. 146, 394; Pr. Ch. 401; Cas. Temp. Talb. 215; 1 P. Wms. 327; 2 Ves. jr. 527; Ambl. 70, 507, 595, 636; Dick. 50, 380; 1 Bro. C. C. 31; 3 Bro. C. C. 64, 234; 2 Vern. 381; 3 Ves. 231; 19 Ves. 323; 1 Taunt. 163; 3 Meriv. 689; 5 Ves. 529; 16 Ves. 206; Coop. R. 275; Com. Dig. App. Devise of personal property, viii. 30, 31, 32; 9 Ves. 323; 3 Mer. 689. Next relations, as sisters, nephews and nieces. 1 Cox, 234. Poor relations. Dick. 380.
Release and forever quit claim. 10 Johns. R. 456.
Remaining untried. 5 Binn. 390.
Rents. 2 Penn. St. R. 165.
Rents and profits. 2 Ves. & Bea. 67; 6 Johns. Ch. R 73; 1 Sand. Uses and Trusts, 318; 1 Ves. 171; 2 Atk. 358.
Repairs. 1 M'Cord, 517.
Reprises. 1 Yeates, 477; 3 Penna. 477
Request. 2 Bro. C. C. 38; 3 Ves. & Bea. 198; 5 Madd. 118; 18 Ves. 41; 1 Moody, Cr. Cas. 300.
Resident. 20 John. R. 211; 2 Pet. Adm. R. 450; 2 Scam. R. 377; 20 John. 208; 7 Mann. & Gr. 9.
Residence. 8 Wend. 45.
Residuary. 11 Ves. 92.
Residue, surplus, &c. 2 Atk. 168; 11 Ves. 330; 14 Ves. 364; 15 Ves. 406; 18 Ves. 466; Dick. 477; 1 Bro. C. C. 589; 4 Bro. C. C. 207; 1 Ves. jr. 63; 1 Wash. 45, 202; 3 Cal. 507; 3 Munf 76; 2 Des. Ch. R. 573; Prec. Ch. 264; 2 Vern 690; Boyle on Char. 399; 8 Ves. 25-6.
Respective, Respectively. 2 Atk. 121; 3 Bro. C C. 404; 1 Meriv. 358; 2 East, 41; Cowd. 34.
Rest. Alleyn, 28; 3 P. Wms. 63, n.
Rest and Residue. 2 Lee's Eccl. R. 270; 6 Eng. Eccl. Rep. 122; 11 East, R. 164.
Retained. 5 D. & E. 143.
Reversion. If the reversion should never fall to the testator. 10 Ves. 453.
Revising—correcting. 2 Shepl. 205.
Revoked. 1 Cowen, R. 335; 16 John. R. 205.
Rice. 5 B. & P. 213.
Right. 2 Caines' R. 345.
Right and title in the deed. 2 Ham 221.
Right, title, and interest. 4 Pick. 179.
Ringbone. Oliph. on Law of Horses, 48, 50.
River-feeder. 13 Pick. 50.
Rolling-mill. 2 Watts & Serg. 390.
Roots. 7 John. R. 385.
Running days. 1 Bell's Com. 577, 5th ed.

Said—saith. 3 Dowl. P. C. 455; 5 Tyr. 391; 1 Gale, 47.
Said. 1 Chit. Cr. Law, *174; 2 Car. Law Rep. 75.
To sail. 3 M. & S. 461.
Sail from. 3 B. & C. 501.
Same. Cro. Eliz. 838.
Sand crack. Oliph. on Law of Horses, 53.
Sanguini suo. Bac. Ab. Legacies and Devises, C 1.
Sans recours. Chit. Bills, 266; 1 Leigh's N. P. 405.
Sarsaparilla. 7 John. R. 385.
Satisfied. 1 M'Cord, Ch. 53; 2 John. 395.
Satisfactory proof. 10 John. R. 167.
Saving. 2 Roll. Ab. 449.
School. 1 M. & S. 95; Vin. Ab. h. t.
Schools of learning. Wilm. Opin. & Judgm. 14; 2 Vern. 387; 14 Ves. 7; 1 Sim. 109; Jac. 474.
Sea stores. 1 Baldw. R. 504.
Sealed. Harp. R. 1.
Security. 13 John. 481; 3 Blackf. 431.
Secured to be paid. 1 Paine's R. 518; 12 Wheat. 487.
See him paid. Fell on Guar. 36-7; 1 Ld. Raym. 224; Cowp. 227; 2 T. R. 86.
Seised. Bac. Ab. Uses and Trusts, part 1, D.
Sell. To sell. Boyle on Char. 307; 9 Greenl. 128.
Sell and convey. 3 Fairf. 460. See also 2 Greenl. 22.
Sell for at the pit's mouth. 7 T. R. 676; S. C. 1 B. & P. 524; 5 T. R. 564.
Seen. 2 Hill, R. 582.
Semini suo. Bac. Ab. Legacies and Devises, C 1.
Servant. 5 Lo. Rep. 15.
Served. 6 S. & R. 281.
Settled. 2 Leach, 910.
Setting fire. 2 East, P. C. 1020.
Seventh child. 3 Bro. C. C. 148; S. C. 2 Cox, 258.
Seventy acres, being and lying in the southwest corner of —— section. 2 Ham. 327; see 4 Monr. 63
Shall. 1 Vern. 153. Shall be lawful. 2 D. & R. 172; 4 B. & A. 271; 1 B. & C. 35; 2 T. R. 172; 1 B. & C. 85; 4 B. & A. 271; 3 N. S. 532 Shall and may. 1 E. C. L. R. 46; 5 John. Ch. R

101; 5 Cowen, 193; 1 Cr. & Mees. 355; 3 Tyrrw. 272.

Shall sell at the pit's mouth. 7 T. R. 676.

Share. 3 Mer. 348.

Share and share alike. 3 Desaus. 143.

Ship damage. Abbott on Shipm. 204; Bac. Ab. Merchant, &c. H.

Shop. 5 Day. 131; 4 Conn. 446.

Shovel plough. 3 Brev. 5.

Should be secured. 5 Binn. 496.

Signing. I, A B, do make this my will. 18 Ves. 183.

Silks. 1 Carr. & Marsh. 45.

Silver dollars—Goods, wares, and merchandise. 2 Mason, R. 407.

Sitfasts. Oliph. on Law of Horses, 53; 9 M. & W. 670.

Six handkerchief. 1 Moody, Cr. Cas. 25.

Sixty pounds in specie, or tobacco at specie price. Mart. S. C. R 20.

Skins. 7 John. R. 385; 7 Cowen, R. 202.

So long as wood grows or water runs. 1 Verm. 303.

Sold. 3 Wend. R. 112.

Sold and conveyed. 2 Serg. & Rawle, 473.

Sole. 1 Madd. R. 207; 1 Supp. to Ves. jr. 410; 4 Rawle, 66; 10 Serg. & Rawle, 209; 4 W. C. C. R. 241; 3 Penna. R. 64, 201.

Solvent. 10 Ves. 100; Gow on Partn. 409.

Soon as convenient. 1 Ves. jr. 366; 19 Ves. 387.

Southwest corner of —— section. 2 Ham. 327.

Spawn. 12 Add. & Ell. 13; S. C. 40 E. C. L. R. 15.

Specially. 1 Dall. 208; 1 Binn. 254.

Specifically. 16 Ves. 451.

Splint. Oliph. on Law of Horses, 55; 1 M. & Sco. 622.

Stab, stick and thrust. 2 Virg. Cas. 111.

Stable. 1 Lev. R. 58; 3 M. & R. 475.

Stage. Stage coach. 8 Adol. & Ell. 386; 35 E. C. L. R. 409; 9 Con. 371; 11 Conn. 385.

Steam boiler. Wright, R. 143.

Sterling. 1 Carr. & P. 286.

Stock in the funds. 5 Price, R. 217.

Stock in trade. Bunb. 28.

Store. 10 Mass. 153. See 4 John. 424; 1 N. & M. 583; 2 N. H. Rep. 9.

Straw. 4 C. & P. 245; S. C. 19 Eng. Com. Law Rep. 367; 1 Moody, C. C. 239.

Stretching along the bay. 2 John. R. 357; Harg. Law Tracts, 12.

Strict settlement. 4 Bing. N. C. 1.

Stringhalt. Oliph. on Law of Horses, 56.

Subject to the payment of rent. 5 Penn. St. Reps. 204.

Subject to incumbrances 2 P. Wms. 385; 1 Atk. 487; 2 P. Wms. 659, note by Cox.

Submission—consent. 9 C. & P. 722; S. C. 38 E. C. L. R. 306.

Subscriber. 6 B. & Cr. 341.

Subscription list. 2 Watts, 112.

Substantial inhabitants. 2 M. & R. 98; S. C. 8 B. & Cr. 62.

Such. 2 Atk. 292.

Suit at law. 23 Pick. 10

Sum in controversy. 9 Serg. & Rawle, 301.

Summit of a mountain. 3 Watts & Serg. 379.

Superfine flour. 9 Watts, R. 121.

Supersede. 1 Pick. R. 261.

Superstitious use. 1 Watts, 224.

Support. A decent and comfortable *support* and maintenance out of my estate, in sickness and in health during my natural life. 2 Sandf. Ch. R. 91.

Surety. 1 Scam. R. 35.

Surplus. 18 Ves. 466; 3 Bac. Ab. 67; 2 Pa. St. R. 129.

Survivors. 17 Ves. 482; 5 Ves. 465.

Survivor and survivors. 3 Burr. 1881; 8 B. & Cr. 231.

Swine. 15 Mass. 205.

Take. 2 Pet. R. 538.

Take and fill shares. 1 Fairf. 478.

Taken out of the state. 1 Hill, 150.

Tapering. 2 Stark. N. P. C. 249.

Taxes and other public dues. 2 Leigh, R. 178.

Tea kettle and appurtenances. Ward on Leg. 222; Mos. 47; 1 Eq. Ab. 201.

Ten acres of pease. 1 Brownl. 149.

Terra. Cro. Jac. 573; Palm. 102; 4 Mod. 98; Cowp. 349.

Testamentary estate. 2 H. Bl. 444. Vide 6 B. & Moo. 268; S. C. 3 Bro. & B. 85.

That is to say. 1 Serg. & Rawle, 141.

The county aforesaid. 2 Bl. R. 847.

The dangers of the river excepted. 1 Miss. R. 81; 2 Bailey's R. 157.

The said defendant. 2 Marsh. R. 101; S. C. 6 Taunt. R. 122, 406.

The said E. R. 9 C. & P. 215; S. C. 38 E. C. L. R. 87.

The said N. 2 Car. Law Repos. 75.

The said property. 3 Mann & Gr. 356.

The parties shall abide by the award of arbitrators, 6 N. H. Rep. 162.

The said plaintiff. 2 Marsh. R. 101; S. C. 6 Taunt. R. 122, 406.

The same rents and covenants. 1 Bro. P. C. 522; 3 Atk. 83; Cowp. 819; 2 Bro. Ch. R. 639, note.

Them. 9 Watts, R. 346; Orl. Bridg. 214.

Them or any of them. 3 Serg. & Rawle, 393.

Then. Then and there. 2 Atk. 310; 4 Ves. 698; 1 P. Wms. 594; 1 Brown's C. C. 190; Ld. Raym. 577; Id. 123.

Then next. 9 Cowen, 255.

Thereabouts. Moll. 232.

Thereafter. 13 L. R. 556.

Thereafter built. 2 Leigh, 721.

Thereinbefore mentioned. Ward. on Leg. 105, 344; 7 Ves. 391.

Thereafterwards continuing his said assault. 2 Mass. 50.

Therefore the defendant is indebted. 1 T. R 716; 2 B. & P. 48.

Thing patented. 1 How. U. S. 202.

Thereunto belonging. 22 E. C. L. R. 171.

This indenture. 2 Wash. 58.

Things. 11 Ves. 666.

Third parties. 1 N. S. 384.

This demise. 2 Bl. R. 973.

Thrush. Oliph. on Law of Horses, 59.

Thousand. 3 B. & Ad. 728.

Through. 7 Pick. R. 274.

To be kept by the secretary. 1 Scott's N. R. 215.

Timber. 7 Johns. R. 234; 1 Madd. Ch. 140, n.

Time. Till she arrives.—From her beginning to load.—On the ship's arrival.—And is there moored twenty-four hours in good safety. 3 Chit. Com. Law, 462. Within four days. 15 Serg. & Rawle, 43. Time being. Ang. Corp. 281.

Title. An indefeasable title in fee simple, such as the state makes. 3 Bibb, R. 317; 4 Shepl. R. 164.

To a stream. 3 Sumn. R. 170

To be begotten. 1 M. & S. 124.

To be by her freely possessed and enjoyed. 12 S. & R. 56; Cowp. 352.

To be signed and published by her, in the presence of, and to be attested by two or more credible witnesses. Curt. Eccl. R. 1.

To be paid when in funds. Minor's R. 173; 7 Greenl. R. 126.

To them. 9 Watts, 351, 352.

To do the needful. 4 Esp. R. 66.

To, from or by. 1 Shepley's R. 198.

To settle. 2 Miles, R. 1.

To his knowledge and belief. 1 H. Bl. 245.

To the best of his knowledge and belief. 8 T. R. 418; 1 Wils. 232.

To the legatees above named. 17 S. & R. 61.

To the order. 1 Watts & Serg. 418.

To render a fair and perfect account, in writing, of all sums received. 1 Dougl. R. 382

To sue. 3 B. & C. 178, 183.

To wait awhile. 1 Penns. R. 385.

Toll. 2 Show. 34.

Took the oath in such case required by the act of congress. 5 Leigh's R. 743.

Tools. 2 Whart. 26.

Touch and stay. 1 Marsh. Ins. 188; 1 Esp. N. R. 610; Wesk. Ins. 548.

Transact all business. 22 E. C L. R. 397; 1 Taunt. R. 349; 5 B. & Ald. 204, 210, 211; 1 Yo. & Col. 394.

Transaction. 7 Mann. & Gr. 538.

Treasonable practices. 1 Stuart's L. C. R. 4.

Tree. 2 Dev. 162.

Trees, woods, coppice—wood grounds, of what kind or growth soever. 4 Taunt. 316.

True value. 17 Wheat. R. 419; 1 Stuart's L. C. R. 419.

Trifling. 1 W. & S. 328; 14 S. & R. 349.

Trinkets. 1 Carr. & Marsh. 45.

Truly. 2 Brock. R 484, 5.

Tune. 5 Mann. & Gr. 696.

Turnpike Road. 20 Johns. R. 742.

Two years after demand. 8 D. & R. 347.

Unavoidable accident. 1 Brock. R. 187.

Understood. 2 Cox's Ch. R. 16.

Underwood. 2 Rolle's R. 485.

Unexecuted writ. 1 Harr. N. J. Rep. 154.

Unless. Boyle on Char. 291; 1 Mer. 102; 3 Id. 65, 79; 3 Burr. 1550.

Unmarried. 2 Supp. to Ves. jr. 43; 2 Barn. & Ald. 452. Without being married. 7 Ves. 458.

Until. Cowp. 571; 5 East, 250; Cas. t. Hard. 116. Until she hath moored at anchor twenty-four hours in good safety. Park, Ins. 35; 1 Marsh. Ins. 262; 2 Str. 1248; 1 Esp. Rep. 412.

Unto and amongst. 9 Ves. 445.

Up the creek. 1 Wilc. R. 508.

Used. 1 Chit. Pr. 214.

Use till paid. Kirb. 145.

Useful invention. 1 Mason, R. 302; 4 Wash. C. C. R. 9.

Usque. 2 Mod. 280.

Usual clauses. 2 Chit. Com. Law, 227; 1 Mer. R. 459.

Usual covenants. Platt on Cov. 430.

Usual terms. 8 Mod. 308; Barnes, 330; 3 Chit. Pr. 705.

Usurped power. 2 Marsh. Ins. 700; 2 Wils. 363.

Usury. Vide 2 Pick. (2d ed.) 152, n. 1; 5 Mass. R. 53; 7 Mass. R. 36; 10 Mass. R. 121; 13 Mass. R. 443; 4 Day, R 37; 2 Com. R. 341; 7 Johns. R. 402; S. C. 8 Johns. R. 218; 4 Dall. R. 216; 2 Dall. R. 92; 6 Munf. R. 430, 433; 3 Ohio R. 18; 1 Blackford's R 336; 1 Fairfield, R. 315; 2 Chit. Cr. Law, *549; 3 Ld. Raym. 36; Trem. P. C. 269; Co. Entr. 394, 435; Rast. Entr. 689; Cro. C. C. 743; Com. Dig. Usury, C; 4 Bl. Com. 158; Hard. 420.

Vacancies. 2 Wend. 273.

Vacancy. 1 Breese's R. 70.

Valuable things. 1 Cox, 77; 1 Bro. C. C. 467.

Value received. 3 M. & S. 351; 5 M. & S. 65; 5 B. & C. 360; S. C. 11 Engl. C. L. R. 252; 3 Kent, Com. 50; Maxw. L. Dict. h. t.; 1 Hall, 201; 1 Blackf. R. 41; 2 M'Lean, R. 213. True value. 11 Wheat. 419.

Vegetable production. 1 Mo. & Mal. 341.

Victual. 3 Inst. 195; Hale's P. C. 152; Cro. Car. 231; Bac. Ab. Forestalling, B; 1 East, R. 169.

Victualler. 9 E. & E. 406; 6 Watts & Serg. 278.

Videlicet. 3 Ves. 194.

Village or town. Co. Litt. 5; Plowd. 168; Touchst. 92.

Voluntary assignment. 3 Sumn. R. 345.

Wantonness. 1 Wheel. Cr. Cas. 365; 4 W. C. C. R. 534; 1 Hill, 46, 363.

Warbles. Oliph. on Law of Horses, 53; 9 M. & W. 670.

Warehouse. Cro. Car. 554; Gilb. Ej. 57; 2 Rosc. R. Act. 484; 8 Mass. 490.

Waste. 1 Ves. 461; 2 Ves. 71.

Watch. Ward on Leg. 221; Mos. 112.

Water lots. 14 Pet. R. 302.

Way. In, through, and along. 1 T. R. 560.

Well and truly executes the duties of his office. 1 Pet. R. 69. Well and truly to administer. 9 Mass. 114, 119, 370; 13 John. 441; 1 Bay, 328.

Well and truly to administer according to law. 1 Litt. R. 93, 100.

What I may die possessed of. 8 Ves. 604; 3 Call, 225.

What remains. 11 Ves. 330.

Wharf. 6 Mass. 332.

Wheat. An unthrashed parcel of wheat. 1 Leach, 484; 2 East, P. C. 1018; 2 T. R 255.

Wheezing. Oliph. on Law of Horses, 61.

When. 6 Ves. 239; 11 Ves. 489; 3 Bro. C. C. 471. When able. 3 Esp. 159; 3 E. C L. R. 264, note; 4 Esp 36. When received. 13 Ves. 325. When the same shall be recovered. Ib.

When or if. 1 Hare, R. 10.

When paid. 15 S. & R. 114.

Wherefore he prays judgment, &c. 2 John. Cas. 312.

Whereupon. 6 T. R. 573.

Whilst. 7 East, 116.

Wholesale factory prices. 2 Conn. R. 69.

Widows and Orphans. 2 Sim. & Stu. 93.

Wife. 3 Ves. 570.

Wilful. 1 Benth. Ev. 351.

Wilful and corrupt. 1 Benth. Rat. Jud. Ev. 351.

Wilfully. 8 Law Rep. 78.

Will. He will change. 2 B. & B. 223.

With. 2 Vern. 466; Prec. Ch. 200; 1 Atk. 469; 2 Sch. & Lef. 189; 3 Mer. 437; 2 B. & Ald. 710; 2 B. & P. 443.

With all faults. 5 B. & A. 240; 7 E. C. L. R

82; 3 E. C. L. R. 475. With surety. 6 Binn. 53; 12 Serg. & Rawle, 312. With the prothonotary. 5 Binn. 461.

With all usual and reasonable covenants. 12 Ves. 179, 186; 3 Bro. C. C. 632; 15 Ves. 528; 3 Anstr. 700.

With sureties. 2 Bos. & Pull. 443.

With effect. 2 Watts & Serg. 33.

With liberty. 8 Gill & John. 190.

Within four days. 15 Serg. & Rawle, 43. Within — days after. 3 Serg. & Rawle, 395.

Without fraud, deceit or oppression. 6 Wend. 454.

Without prejudice. 2 Chit. Pr. 24, note (x); 3 Mann. & Gr. 903.

Without recourse. 1 Cowen, 538; 3 Cranch, 193; 7 Cranch, 159; 12 Mass. 172; 14 Serg. & Rawle, 325; 8 W. & S. 353; 2 Penn. St. R. 200. Vide article *Sans Recours*, in the body of this work.

Without reserve. 5 Mass. R. 34.

Wm. William. 1 Scam. R. 451.

Wood. Cro. Jac. 166.

Wood-land. 1 Serg. & Rawle, 169.

Woods. 4 Mass. 268.

Working days. 1 Bell's Com. 577, 5th ed.

Worldly labor. 4 Bing. 84; S. C. 13 E. C. L. R. 351.

Worth and value. 3 B. & C. 516.

Writing. 14 John. 484; 8 Ves. 504; 2 M. & S. 286; 17 Ves. 459.

Writing in pencil. 1 Eng. Eccl. Rep. 406.

Yard lane. Touchs. 93; Co. Litt. 5.

Yearly meeting of Quakers. 6 Conn. 393.

Yearly meeting. 6 Conn. 292.

You. 2 Dowl. R. 145; S. C. 6 Leg. Obs. 138.

CONSTRUCTIVE. That which is interpreted.

2. *Constructive presence.* The commission of crimes, is, when a party is not actually present, an eye-witness to its commission; but, acting with others, watching while another commits the crime. 1 Russ. Cr. 22.

3. *Constructive larceny.* One where the taking was not apparently felonious, but by construction of the prisoner's acts it is just to presume he intended at the time of taking to appropriate the property feloniously to his own use; 2 East, P. C. 685; 1 Leach, 212; as when he obtained the delivery of the goods *animo furandi.* 2 N. & M. 90. See 15 S. & R. 93; 4 Mass. 580; 1 Bay, 242.

4. *Constructive breaking into a house.* In order to commit a burglary, there must be a breaking of the house; this may be actual or constructive. A constructive breaking is when the burglar gains an entry into the house by fraud, conspiracy, or threat. See *Burglary.* A familiar instance of constructive breaking is the case of a burglar who coming to the house under pretence of business, gains admittance, and after being admitted, commits such acts, as, if there had been an actual breaking, would have amounted to a burglary. Bac. Ab. Burglary, A. See 1 Moody, Cr. Cas. 87, 250.

5. *Constructive notice.* Such a notice, that although it be not actual, is sufficient in law; an example of this is the recording of a deed, which is notice to all the world, and so is the pendency of a suit a general notice of an equity. 4 Bouv. Inst. n. 3874. See *Lis pendens.*

6. *Constructive annexation.* The annexation to the inheritance by the law, of certain things which are not actually attached to it; for example, the keys of a house; and heir looms are constructively annexed. Shep. Touch. 90; Poth. Traité des Choses, § 1.

7. *Constructive fraud.* A contract or act, which, not originating in evil design and contrivance to perpetuate a positive fraud or injury upon other persons, yet, by its necessary tendency to deceive or mislead them, or to violate a public or private confidence, or to impair or injure public interest, is deemed equally reprehensible with positive fraud, and therefore is prohibited by law, as within the same reason and mischief as contracts and acts done *malo animo.* 1 Story, Eq. § 258 to 440.

CONSUETUDINES FEUDORUM. The name of an institute of the feudal system and usages, compiled about the year 1170, by authority of the emperor Frederic, surnamed Barbarossa. Ersk. Inst. B. 2, t. 3, n. 5.

CONSUL, *government, commerce.* Consuls are commercial agents appointed by a government to reside in the seaports of a foreign country, and commissioned to watch over the commercial rights and privileges of the nation deputing them. A vice-consul is one acting in the place of a consul.

2. Consuls have been greatly multiplied. Their duties and privileges are now generally limited, defined and secured by commercial treaties, or by the laws of the countries they represent. As a general rule, it may be laid down that they represent the subjects or citizens of their own nation, not otherwise represented. Bee, R. 209; 3 Wheat. R. 435; 6 Wheat. R. 152; 10 Wheat. 66; 1 Mason's R. 14.

3. This subject will be considered by a view, first, of the appointment, duties, powers, rights, and liabilities of American consuls; and secondly, of the recognition, duties, rights, and liabilities of foreign consuls.

4.—1. *Of American consuls. First.* The president is authorized by the Constitution of the United States, art. 2, s. 2, cl. 3, to nominate, and, by and with the advice and consent of the senate, appoint consuls.

5.—*Secondly.* Each consul and vice-consul is required, before he enters on the execution of his office, to give bond, with such sureties as shall be approved by the secretary of state, in a sum not less than two thousand nor more than ten thousand dollars, conditioned for the true and faithful discharge of the duties of his office, and also for truly accounting for all moneys, goods and effects which may come into his possession by virtue of the act of 14th April, 1792, which bond is to be lodged in the office of the secretary of state. Act of April 14, 1792, sect. 6.

6.—*Thirdly.* They have the power and are required to perform many duties in relation to the commerce of the United States and towards masters of ships, mariners, and other citizens of the United States; among these are the authority to receive protests or declarations which captains, masters, crews, passengers, merchants, and others make relating to American commerce; they are required to administer on the estate of American citizens, dying within their consulate, and leaving no legal representatives, when the laws of the country permit it; [see 2 Curt. Ecc. R. 241;] to take charge and secure the effects of stranded American vessels in the absence of the master, owner or consignee; to settle disputes between masters of vessels and the mariners; to provide for destitute seamen within their consulate, and send them to the United States, at the public expense. See Act of 14th April, 1792; Act of 28th February, 1803, ch. 62; Act of 20th July, 1840, ch. 23. The consuls are also authorized to make certificates of certain facts in certain cases, which receive faith and credit in the courts of the United States. But those consular certificates are not to be received in evidence, unless they are given in the performance of a consular function; 2 Cranch, R. 187; Paine, R. 594; 2 Wash. C. C. R. 478; 1 Litt. R. 71; nor are they evidence, between persons not parties or privies to the transaction, of any fact, unless, either expressly or impliedly, made so by statute. 2 Sumn. R. 355.

7.—*Fourthly.* Their rights are to be protected agreeably to the laws of nations, and of the treaties made between the nation to which they are sent, and the United States. They are entitled, by the act of 14th April, 1792, s. 4, to receive certain fees, which are there enumerated. And the consuls in certain places, as London, Paris, and the Barbary states, receive, besides, a salary.

8.—*Fifthly.* A consul is liable for negligence or omission to perform, seasonably, the duties imposed upon him, or for any malversation or abuse of power, to any injured person, for all damages occasioned thereby; and for all malversation and corrupt conduct in office, a consul is liable to indictment, and, on conviction by any court of competent jurisdiction, shall be fined not less than one, nor more than ten thousand dollars; and be imprisoned not less than one nor more than five years. Act of July 20, 1840, ch. 23, cl. 18. The act of February 28, 1803, ss. 7 and 8, imposes heavy penalties for falsely and knowingly certifying that property belonging to foreigners is the property of citizens of the United States; or for granting a passport, or other paper, certifying that any alien, knowing him or her to be such, is a citizen of the United States.

9. The duties of consuls residing on the Barbary coast are prescribed by a particular statute. Act of May 1, 1810, s. 4.

10.—2. *Of foreign consuls. First.* Before a consul can perform any duties in the United States, he must be recognized by the president of the United States, and have received his exequatur. (q. v.)

11.—*Secondly.* A consul is clothed only with authority for commercial purposes, and he has a right to interpose claims for the restitution of property belonging to the citizens or subjects of the country he represents; 10 Wheat. R. 66; 1 Mason, R. 14; Bee, R. 209; 6 Wheat. R. 152; but he is not to be considered as a minister or diplomatic agent, entrusted by virtue of his office to represent his sovereign in negotiations with foreign states. 3 Wheat. R. 435.

12.—*Thirdly.* Consuls are generally invested with special privileges by local laws and usages, or by international compacts· but by the laws of nations they are not entitled to the peculiar immunities of ambassadors. In civil and criminal cases, they are subject to the local laws, in the sam manner with other foreign residents owing a temporary allegiance to the state. Wicquefort, De l'Ambassadeur, liv. 1, § 5; Bynk cap. 10; Martens, Droit des Gens, liv. 4, c. 3, § 148. In the United States, the act of September 24th, 1789, s. 13, gives to the supreme court original, but not exclusive jurisdiction of all suits in which a consul or vice-consul shall be a party. The act last cited, section 9, gives to the district courts of the United States, jurisdiction exclusively of the courts of the several states, of all suits against consuls or vice-consuls, except for offences where whipping exceeding thirty stripes, a fine exceeding one hundred dollars, or a term of imprisonment exceeding six months, is inflicted. For offences punishable beyond these penalties, the circuit has jurisdiction in the case of consuls. 5 S. & R. 545. See 1 Binn. 143; 2 Dall. 299; 2 N. & M. 217; 3 Pick. R. 80; 1 Green, R. 107; 17 Johns. 10; 6 Pet. R. 41; 7 Pet. R. 276; 6 Wend. 327.

13.—*Fourthly.* His functions may be suspended at any time by the government to which he is sent, and his *exequatur* revoked. In general, a consul is not liable, personally, on a contract made in his official capacity on account of his government. 3 Dall. 384.

14. During the middle ages, the term consul was sometimes applied to ordinary judges; and, in the Levant, maritime judges are yet called *consuls.* 1 Boul. Paty, Dr. Mar. Tit. Prél. s. 2, p. 57.

15. Among the Romans, consuls were chief magistrates who were annually elected by the people, and were invested with powers and functions similar to those of kings.

See, generally, Abbott on Ship. 210; 2 Bro. Civ. Law, 503; Merl. Répert. h. t.; Ayl. Pand. 160; Warden on Consuls; Marten on Consuls; Borel, de l'Origine et des Fonctions des Consuls; Rawle on the Const. 222, 223; Story on the Const. § 1654; Serg. Const. Law, 225; Azuni, Mar. Law, part 1, c. 4, art. 8, § 7.

CONSULTATION, *practice.* A conference between the counsel or attorneys engaged on the same side of a cause, for the purpose of examining their case, arranging their proofs, and removing any difficulties there may be in their way.

2. This should be had sufficiently early to enable the counsel to obtain an amendment of the pleadings, or further evidence. At these consultations, the exact course to be taken by the plaintiff in exhibiting his proofs should be adopted, in consultation, by the plaintiff's counsel. In a consultation on a defendant's case, it is important to ascertain the statement of the defence, and the evidence which may be depended upon to support it; to arrange the exact course of defence, and to determine on the cross-examination of the plaintiff's witnesses; and, above all, whether or not evidence shall be given on the part of the defendant, or withheld, so as to avoid a reply on the part of the plaintiff. The wishes of the client should, in all cases, be consulted. 3 Chit. Pr. 864.

CONSULTATION, *Eng. law.* The name of a writ whereby a cause, being formerly removed by prohibition out of an inferior court into some of the king's courts in Westminster, is returned thither again; for if the judges of the superior court, comparing the proceedings with the suggestion of the party, find the suggestion false or not proved, and that therefore the cause was wrongfully called from the inferior court, then, upon consultation and deliberation, they decree it to be returned, whereupon this writ issues. T. de la Ley.

CONSULTATION, *French law.* The opinion of counsel, on a point of law submitted to them. Dict. de Jur. h. t.

CONSUMMATE. What is completed. A right is said to be *initiate*, when it is not complete; and when it is perfected, it is consummated.

CONSUMMATION. The completion of a thing; as the consummation of marriage; (q. v.) the consummation of a contract, and the like.

2. A contract is said to be consummated, when everything to be done in relation to it, has been accomplished. It is frequently of great importance to know when a contract has been consummated, in order to ascertain the rights of the parties, particularly in the contract of sale. Vide *Delivery*, where the subject is more fully examined. It is also sometimes of consequence to ascertain where the consummation of the contract took place, in order to decide by what law it is to be governed.

3. It has been established as a rule, that when a contract is made by persons absent from each other, it is considered as consummated in, and is governed by the law of, the country where the final assent is given. If, therefore, Paul in New Orleans, order goods from Peter in London, the contract is governed by the laws of the latter place. 8 M. R. 135; Plowd. 343. Vide *Conflict of Laws; Inception; Lex Loci Contractus; Lex Fori; Offer.*

CONSUMMATION OF MARRIAGE. The first time that the husband and wife cohabit together, after the ceremony of marriage has been performed, is thus called.

2. The marriage, when otherwise legal, is complete without this; for it is a maxim of law, borrowed from the civil law, that *consensus, non concubitus, facit nuptias*. Co. Litt. 33; Dig. 50, 17, 30; 1 Black. Com. 434.

CONTAGIOUS DISORDERS, *police, crim. law*. Diseases which are capable of being transmitted by mediate or immediate contact.

2. Unlawfully and injuriously to expose persons infected with the small-pox or other contagious disease in the public streets where persons are passing, or near the habitations of others, to their great danger, is indictable at common law. 1 Russ. Cr. 114. Lord Hale seems to doubt whether if a person infected with the plague, should go abroad with intent to infect another, and another should be infected and die, it would not be murder; and he thinks it clear that though there should be no such intent, yet if another should be infected, it would be a great misdemeanor. 1 Pl. Cor. 422. Vide 4 M. & S. 73, 272; Dane's Ab. h. t.

CONTEMPORANEOUS EXPOSITION. The construction of a law, made shortly after its enactment, when the reasons for its passage were then fresh in the minds of the judges, is considered as of great weight: *contemporanea expositio est optima et fortissima in lege*. 1 Cranch, 299.

CONTEMPT, *crim. law*. A wilful disregard or disobedience of a public authority.

2. By the Constitution of the United States, each house of congress may determine the rules of its proceedings, punish its members for disorderly behaviour, and, with the concurrence of two-thirds, expel a member. The same provision is substantially contained in the constitutions of the several states.

3. The power to make rules carries that of enforcing them, and to attach persons who violate them, and punish them for contempts. This power of punishing for contempts, is confined to punishment during the session of the legislature, and cannot extend beyond it; 6 Wheat. R. 204, 230, 231; and, it seems this power cannot be exerted beyond imprisonment.

4. Courts of justice have an inherent power to punish all persons for contempt of their rules and orders, for disobedience of their process, and for disturbing them in their proceedings. Bac. Ab. Courts and their jurisdiction in general, E; Rolle's Ab. 219; 8 Co. 38 b; 11 Co. 43 b.; 8 Shepl. 550; 5 Ired. R. 199.

5. In some states, as in Pennsylvania, the power to punish for contempts is restricted to offences committed by the officers of the court, or in its presence, or in disobedience of its mandates, orders, or rules; but no one is guilty of a contempt for any publication made or act done out of court, which is not in violation of such lawful rules or orders, or disobedience of its process. Similar provisions, limiting the power of the courts of the United States to punish for contempts, are incorporated in the Act March 2, 1831. 4 Sharsw. cont. of Stor. L. U. S. 2256. See Oswald's Case, 4 Lloyd's Debates, 141, et seq.

6. When a person is in prison for a contempt, it has been decided in New York that he cannot be discharged by another judge, when brought before him on a *habeas corpus;* and, according to Chancellor Kent, 3 Com. 27, it belongs exclusively to the court offended to judge of contempts, and what amounts to them; and no other court or judge can, or ought to undertake, in a collateral way, to question or review an adjudication of a contempt made by another competent jurisdiction.

This may be considered as the established doctrine equally in England as in this country. 3 Wils. 188; 14 East, R. 1; 2 Bay, R. 182; 6 Wheat. R. 204; 7 Wheat. R. 38; 1 Breese, R. 266; 1 J. J. Marsh. 575; Charlt. R. 136; 1 Blackf. 166; 9 Johns. 395; 6 John. 337.

CONTENTIOUS JURISDICTION, *eccl. law*. In those cases where there is an action or judicial process, and it consists in hearing and determining the matter between party and party, it is said there is contentious jurisdiction, in contradistinction to *voluntary* jurisdiction, which is exercised in matters that require no judicial proceeding, as in taking probate of wills, granting letters of administration, and the like. 3 Bl. Com. 66.

CONTESTATIO LITIS, *civil law*. The joinder of issue in a cause. Code of Pr. of Lo. art. 357.

CONTESTATION. The act by which two parties to an action claim the same right, or when one claims a right to a thing which the other denies; a controversy. Wolff, Dr. de la Nat. § 762.

CONTEXT. The general series or composition of a law, contract, covenant, or agreement.

2. When there is any obscurity in the words of an agreement or law, the context must be considered in its construction, for it must be performed according to the intention of its framers. 2 Cowen, 781; 3 Miss. 447; 1 Harringt. 154; 6 John. 43; 5 Gill & John. 239; 3 B. & P. 565; 8 East, 80; 1 Dall. 426; 4 Dall. 340; 3 S. & R. 609. See *Construction; Interpretation.*

CONTINGENT. What may or may not happen; what depends upon a doubtful event; as, a contingent debt, which is a debt depending upon some uncertain event. 9 Ves. R. 110; Co. Bankr. Laws, 245; 7 Ves. R. 301; 1 Ves. & Bea. 176; 8 Ves. R. 334; 1 Rose, R. 523; 3 T. R. 539; 4 T. R. 570. A contingent legacy is one which is not vested. Will. on Executors, h. t. See *Contingent Remainder; Contingent Use.*

CONTINGENT DAMAGES. Those given where the issues upon counts to which no demurrer has been filed, are tried, before demurrer to one or more counts in the same declaration has been decided. 1 Str. 431.

CONTINGENT ESTATE. A contingent estate depends for its effect upon an event which may or may not happen: as an estate limited to a person not *in esse* or not yet born. Crabb on Real Property, b. 3, c. 1, sect. 2. § 946.

CONTINGENT REMAINDER, *estates.* An estate in remainder which is limited to take effect, either to a dubious and uncertain *person*, or upon a dubious and uncertain *event*, by which no present or particular interest passes to the remainder-man, so that the particular estate may chance to be determined and the remainder never take effect. 2 Bouv. Inst. n. 1832. Vide *Remainder.*

CONTINGENT USE, *estates.* A use limited in a deed or conveyance of land which may or may not happen to vest, according to the contingency expressed in the limitation of such use. A contingent use is such as by possibility may happen in possession, reversion or remainder. 1 Rep. 121; Com. Dig. Uses, K. 6.

CONTINUAL CLAIM, *English law.* When the feoffee of land is prevented from taking possession by fear of menaces or bodily harm, he may make a claim to the land in the presence of the *pares*, and if this claim is regularly made once every year and a day, which is then called a continual claim, it preserves to the feoffee his rights, and is equal to a legal entry. 3 Bl. Com. 175; 2 Bl. Com. 320; 1 Chit. Pr. 278 (a) in note; Crabbe's Hist. E. L. 403.

CONTINUANCE, *practice.* The adjournment of a cause from one day to another is called a continuance, an entry of which is made upon the record.

2. If these continuances are omitted, the cause is thereby discontinued, and the defendant is discharged *sine die*, (q. v.) without a day, for this term. By his appearance he has obeyed the command of the writ, and, unless he be adjourned over to a certain day, he is no longer bound to attend upon that summons. 3 Bl. Com. 316.

3. Continuances may, however, be entered at any time, and if not entered, the want of them is aided or cured by the appearance of the parties; and as a discontinuance can never be objected to *pendente placito*, so after the judgment it is cured by the statute of jeofails. Tidd's Pr. 628, 835.

4. Before the declaration the continuance is by *dies datus prece partium;* after the declaration and before issue joined, by imparlance; after issue joined and before verdict, by *vicecomes non misit breve;* and after verdict or demurrer, by *curia advisare vult.* 1 Chit. Pl. 421, n. (p); see Vin. Abr. 454; Bac. Abr. Pleas, &c. P; Bac. Abr. Trial, H; Com. Dig. Pleader, V. See, as to the origin of continuances, Steph. Pl 31; 1 Ch. Pr. 778, 779.

CONTINUANDO, *plead.* The name of an averment sometimes contained in a declaration in trespass, that the injury or trespass has been *continued.* For example, if Paul turns up the ground of Peter and tramples upon his grass, for three days together, and Peter desires to recover damages, as well for the subsequent acts of treading down the grass and subverting the soil, as for the first, he must complain of such subsequent trespasses in his actions brought to compensate the former. This he may do by averring that Paul, on such a day, trampled upon the herbage and turned up the ground, "*continuing* the said trespasses for three days following." This averment seems to impart a continuation of the same identical act of trespass, it has, however, received, by continued usage, another interpretation, and is taken, also, to denote a repetition of the same kind of injury. When the trespass is not of the same kind, it cannot be averred in a *continuando;* for example, when the injury consists in killing and carrying away an animal, there remains nothing to which a similar injury may again be offered. 1 Wms. Saund. 24, n. 1.

2. There is a difference between the *continuando* and the averment *diversis diebus et temporibus*, on divers days and times. In the former, the injuries complained of have been committed upon one and the same occasion; in the latter, the acts complained of, though of the same kind, are distinct and unconnected. See Gould, Pl. ch. 3, § 86, et seq.; Ham. N. P. 90, 91; Bac. A. Trespass, I 2, n. 2.

CONTINUING CONSIDERATION. A continuing consideration is one which in point of time remains good and binding, although it may have served before to support a contract. 1 Bouv. Inst. n. 628; 1 Saund. 320 e, note (5.)

CONTINUING DAMAGES. Those which are continued at different times, or which endure from one time to another. If a person goes upon successive days and tramples the grass of the plaintiff, he commits continuing damages; or if one commit a trespass to the possession, and it is in fact injurious to him who has the reversion or remainder, this will be continuing damages. In this last case the person in possession may have an action of trespass against the wrong doer to his possession, and the reversioner has an action against him for an injury to the reversion. 1 Chit. Pr. 266, 268, 385; 4 Burr. 2141, 3 Car. & P. 817.

CONTRA. Over; against; opposite to anything: as, such a case lays down a certain principle; such other case, *contra.*

CONTRA BONOS MORES. Against good morals.

2. All contracts contra bonos mores, are illegal. These are reducible to several classes, namely, those which are, 1. *Incentive to crime.* A claim cannot be sustained, therefore, on a bond for compounding a crime; as, for example, a prosecution for perjury; 2 Wils. R. 341, 447; or for procuring a pardon. A distinction has been made between a contract made as a reparation for an injury to the honor of a female, and one which is to be the reward of future illicit cohabitation; the former is good and valid, and the latter is illegal. 3 Burr. 1568; 1 Bligh's R. 269.

3.—2. *Indecent or mischievous consideration.* An obligation or engagement prejudicial to the feelings of a third party; or offensive to decency or morality; or which has a tendency to mischievous or pernicious consequences, is void. Cowp. 729; 4 Campb. R. 152; Rawle's R. 42; 1 B. & A. 683; 4 Esp. Cas. 97; 16 East, R. 150. Vide *Wagers.*

4.—3. *Gaming.* The statutes against gaming render all contracts made for the purpose of gaming, void. Vide *Gaming; Unlawful; Void.*

CONTRA FORMAM STATUTI. Contrary to the form of the statute.

2.—1. When one statute prohibits a thing and another gives the penalty, in an action for the penalty, the declaration should conclude *contra formam statutorum.* Plowd. 206; 2 East, R. 333; Esp. on Pen. Act. 111; 1 Gallis. R. 268. The same rule applies to informations and indictments. 2 Hale, P. C. 172; 2 Hawk. c. 25, § 117; Owen, 135.

3.—2. But where a statute refers to a former one, and adopts and continues the provisions of it, the declaration or indictment should conclude *contra formam statuti.* Hale, P. C. 172; 1 Lutw. 212.

4.—3. Where a thing is prohibited by several statutes, if one only gives the action, and the others are explanatory and restrictive, the conclusion should be *contra formam statuti.* Yelv. 116; Cro. Jac. 187; Noy, 125, S. C.; Rep. temp. Hard. 409; Andr. 115, S. C.; 2 Saund. 377.

5.—4. When the act prohibited was not an offence or ground of action at common law, it is necessary both in criminal and civil cases to conclude against the form of the statute or statutes. 1 Saund. 135, c.; 2 East, 333; 1 Chit. Pl. 358; 1 Saund. 249; 7 East, 516; 2 Mass. 116; 7 Mass. 9; 11 Mass. 280; 10 Mass. 36; 1 M'Cord, 121; 1 Gallis. 30.

6.—5. But if the act prohibited by the statute is an offence or ground of action at common law, the indictment or action may be in the common law form, and the statute need not be noticed, even though it prescribe a form of prosecution or of action—the statute remedy being merely cumulative. 2 Inst. 200; 2 Burr. 803; 4 Burr. 2351; 3 Burr. 1418; 2 Wils. 146; 3 Mass. 515.

7.—6. When a statute only inflicts a punishment on that which was an offence at common law, the offence prescribed may be inflicted, though the statute is not noticed in the indictment. 2 Binn. 332.

8.—7. If an indictment for an offence at

common law only, conclude "against the form of the statute in such case made and provided;" or "the form of the statute" generally, the conclusion will be rejected as surplusage, and the indictment maintained as at common law. 1 Saund. 135, n. 3.

9.—8. But it will be otherwise if it conclude against the form of "the statute aforesaid," when a statute has been previously recited. 1 Chit. Cr. Law, 266, 289. See further, Com. Dig. Pleader, C 76; 5 Vin. Abr. 552, 556; 1 Gallis. 26, 257; 9 Pick. 162; 5 Pick. 128; 2 Yerg. 390; 1 Hawks. 192; 3 Conn. 1; 11 Mass. 280; 5 Greenl. 79.

CONTRA PACEM, *pleadings*. Against the peace.

2. In actions of trespass, the words *contra pacem* should uniformly accompany the allegation of the injury; in some cases they are material to the foundation of the action. Trespass to lands in a foreign country cannot be sustained. 4 T. R. 503; 2 Bl. Rep. 1058.

3. The conclusion of the declaration, in trespass or ejectment, should be contra pacem, though these are now mere words of form, and not traversable, and the omission of that allegation will be aided, if not specially demurred to. 1 Chit. Pl. 375, 6; vide Arch. Civ. Pl. 169; 5 Vin. Ab. 557; Com. Dig. Action upon the case, C 4; Pleader, 3, M 8; Prohibition, F 7.

CONTRABAND, *mar. law*. Its most extensive sense, means all commerce which is carried on contrary to the laws of the state. This term is also used to designate all kinds of merchandise which are used, or transported, against the interdictions published by a ban or solemn cry.

2. The term is usually applied to that unlawful commerce which is so carried on in time of war. Merlin, Rèpert. h. t. Commodities particularly useful in war are contraband, as arms, ammunition, horses, timber for ship building, and every kind of naval stores. When articles come into use as implements of war, which were before innocent, they may be declared to be contraband. The greatest difficulty to decide what is contraband seems to have occurred in the instance of provisions, which have not been held to be universally contraband, though Vattel admits that they become so on certain occasions, when there is an expectation of reducing an enemy by famine.

3. In modern times, one of the principal criteria adopted by the courts for the decision of the question, whether any particular cargo of provisions be confiscable as contraband, is to examine whether those provisions be in a rude or manufactured state; for all articles, in such examinations, are treated with greater indulgence in their natural condition than when wrought up for the convenience of the enemy's immediate use. Iron, unwrought, is therefore treated with indulgence, though anchors, and other instruments fabricated out of it, are directly contraband. 1 Rob. Rep. 189. See Vattel, b. 3, c. 7; Chitty's L. of Nat. 120; Marsh. Ins. 78; 2 Bro. Civ. Law, 311; 1 Kent. Com. 135; 3 Id. 215.

4. Contraband of war, is the act by which, in times of war, a neutral vessel introduces, or attempts to introduce into the territory of one of the belligerent parties, arms, ammunition, or other effects intended for, or which may serve, hostile operations. Merlin, Rèpert. h. t.; 1 Kent, Com. 135; Mann. Comm. B. 3, c. 7; 6 Mass. 102; 1 Wheat. 382; 1 Cowen, 56; 2 John. Cas. 77, 120.

CONTRACT. This term, in its more extensive sense, includes every description of agreement or obligation, whereby one party becomes bound to another to pay a sum of money, or to do or omit to do a certain act; or, a contract is an act which contains a perfect obligation. In its more confined sense, it is an agreement between two or more persons, concerning something to be done, whereby both parties are bound to each other, or one is bound to the other. 1 Pow. Contr. 6; Civ. Code of Lo. art. 1754; Code Civ. 1101; Poth. Oblig. pt. i. c. 1, s. 1, § 1; Blackstone, (2 Comm. 442,) defines it to be an agreement, upon a sufficient consideration, to do or not to do a particular thing. A contract has also been defined to be a compact between two or more persons. 6 Cranch, R. 136.

2. Contracts are divided into express or implied. An express contract is one where the terms of the agreement are openly uttered and avowed at the time of making, as to pay a stated price for certain goods. 2 Bl. Com. 443.

3. Express contracts are of three sorts; 1. By parol, or in writing, as contradistinguished from specialties. 2. By specialty or under seal. 3. Of record.

4.—1. A parol contract is defined to be a bargain or voluntary agreement made, either orally or in writing not under seal, upon a good consideration, between two or more persons capable of contracting, to do a lawful act, or to omit to do something, the performance whereof is not enjoined by law. 1 Com. Contr. 2; Chit. Contr. 2.

5. From this definition it appears, that to constitute a sufficient parol agreement, there must be, 1st. The reciprocal or mutnal assent of two or more persons competent to contract. Every agreement ought to be so certain and complete, that each party may have an action upon it; and the agreement would be incomplete if either party withheld his assent to any of its terms. Peake's R. 227; 3 T. R. 653; 1 B. & A. 681; 1 Pick. R. 278. The agreement must, in general, be obligatory on both parties, or it binds neither. To this rule there are, however, some exceptions, as in the case of an infant's contract. He may always sue, though he cannot be sued, on his contract. Stra. 937. See other instances; 6 East, 307; 3 Taunt. 169; 5 Taunt. 788; 3 B. & C. 232.

6. –2d. There must be a good and valid consideration, motive or inducement to make the promise, upon which a party is charged, for this is of the very essence of a contract under seal, and must exist, although the contract be reduced to writing. 7 T. R. 350, note (a); 2 Bl. Com. 444. See this Dict. *Consideration;* Fonb. Tr. Eq. 335, n. (a); Chit. Bills. 68.

7.—3d. There must be a thing to be done, which is not forbidden; or a thing to be omitted, the performance of which is not enjoined by law. A fraudulent or immoral contract, or one contrary to public policy is void; Chit. Contr. 215, 217, 222; and it is also void if contrary to a statute. Id. 228 to 250; 1 Binn. 118; 4 Dall. 298; 4 Yeates, 24, 84; 6 Binn. 321; 4 Serg. & Rawle, 159; 4 Dall. 269; 1 Binn. 110; 2 Browne's R. 48. As to contracts which are void for want of a compliance with the statutes of frauds, see *Frauds, Statute of.*

8.—2. The second kind of express contracts are specialties, or those which are made under seal, as deeds, bonds, and the like; they are not merely written, but delivered over by the party bound. The solemnity and deliberation with which, on account of the ceremonies to be observed, a deed or bond is presumed to be entered into, attach to it an importance and character which do not belong to a simple contract. In the case of a specialty, no consideration is necessary to give it validity, even in a court of equity. Plowd. 308, 7 T. R. 477; 4 B. & A. 652; 3 T. R. 438; 3 Bingh. 111, 112; 1 Fonb. Eq. 342, note. When a contract by specialty has been changed by a parol agreement, the whole of it becomes a parol contract. 2 Watts, 451; 9 Pick. 298; see 13 Wend. 71.

9.—3. The highest kind of express contracts are those of record, such as judgments, recognizances of bail, and in England, statutes merchant and staple, and other securities of the same nature, entered into with the intervention of some public authority. 2 Bl. Com. 465. See *Authentic Facts.*

10. Implied contracts are such as reason and justice dictates, and which, therefore, the law presumes every man undertakes to perform; as if a man employs another to do any business for him, or perform any work, the law implies that the former contracted or undertook to pay the latter as much as his labor is worth; see *Quantum meruit;* or if one takes up goods from a tradesman, without any agreement of price, the law concludes that he contracts to pay their value. 2 Bl. Com. 443. See *Quantum valebant; Assumpsit.* Com. Dig. Action upon the case upon assumpsit, A 1; Id. Agreement.

11. By the laws of Louisiana, when considered as to the obligation of the parties, contracts are either unilateral or reciprocal. When the party to whom the engagement is made, makes no express agreement on his part, the contract is called unilateral, even in cases where the law attaches certain obligations to his acceptance. Civ. Code of Lo. art. 1758. A loan for use, and a loan of money, are of this kind. Poth. Ob. P. 1, c. 1, s. 1, art. 2. A reciprocal contract is where the parties expressly enter into mutual engagements, such as sale, hire, and the like. Id.

12. Contracts, considered in relation to their substance, are either commutative or independent, principal or accessory.

13. Commutative contracts, are those in which what is done, given or promised by one party, is considered as equivalent to, or in consideration of what is done, given or promised by the other. Civ. Code of Lo. art. 1761.

14. Independent contracts are those in which the mutual acts or promises have no relation to each other, either as equivalents or as considerations. Id. art. 1762.

15. A principal contract is one entered

into by both parties, on their accounts, or in the several qualities they assume.

16. An accessory contract is made for assuring the performance of a prior contract, either by the same parties or by others, such as suretyship, mortgage, and pledges. Id. art. 1764. Poth. Obl. p. 1, c. 1, s. 1, art. 2, n. 14.

17. Contracts, considered in relation to the motive for making them, are either gratuitous or onerous. To be gratuitous, the object of a contract must be to benefit the person with whom it is made, without any profit or advantage, received or promised, as a consideration for it. It is not, however, the less gratuitous, if it proceed either from gratitude for a benefit before received, or from the hope of receiving one hereafter, although such benefits be of a pecuniary nature. Id. art. 1766. Any thing given or promised, as a consideration for the engagement or gift; any service, interest, or condition, imposed on what is given or promised, although unequal to it in value, makes a contract onerous in its nature. Id. art. 1767.

18. Considered in relation to their effects, contracts are either certain or hazardous. A contract is certain, when the thing to be done is supposed to depend on the will of the party, or when, in the usual course of events, it must happen in the manner stipulated. It is hazardous, when the performance of that which is one of its objects, depends on an uncertain event. Id. art. 1769.

19. Pothier, in his excellent treatise on Obligations, p. 1, c. 1, s. 1, art. 2, divides contracts under the five following heads:

20.—1. Into reciprocal and unilateral.

21.—2. Into consensual, or those which are formed by the mere consent of the parties, such as sale, hiring and mandate; and those in which it is necessary there should be something more than mere consent, such as loan of money, deposite or pledge, which from their nature require a delivery of the thing, (rei); whence they are called real contracts. See *Real Contracts.*

22.—3. Into—first, contracts of mutual interest, which are such as are entered into for the reciprocal interest and utility of each of the parties, as sales, exchange, partnership, and the like.

23.—2d. Contracts of beneficence, which are those by which only one of the contracting parties is benefited, as loans, deposit and mandate. 3d. Mixed contracts, which are those by which one of the parties confers a benefit on the other, receiving something of inferior value in return, such as a donation subject to a charge.

24.—4. Into principal and accessory.

25.—5. Into those which are subjected by the civil law to certain rules and forms, and those which are regulated by mere natural justice.

See, generally, as to contracts, Bouv. Inst. Index, h. t.; Chitty on Contracts; Comyn on Contracts; Newland on Contracts; Com. Dig. titles Abatement, E 12, F 8; Admiralty, E 10, 11; Action upon the Case upon Assumpsit; Agreement; Bargain and Sale; Baron and Feme, Q; Condition; Dett, A 8, 9; Enfant, B 5; Idiot, D 1; Merchant, E 1; Pleader, 2 W, 11, 43; Trade D 3; War, B 2; Bac. Abr. tit. Agreement; Id. Assumpsit; Condition; Obligation; Vin. Abr. Condition; Contracts and Agreements; Covenants; Vendor, Vendee; Supp. to Ves. jr. vol. 2, p. 260, 295, 376, 441; Yelv. 47; 4 Ves. jr. 497, 671; Archb. Civ. Pl. 22; Code Civ. L. 3, tit. 3 to 18; Pothier's Tr. of Obligations; Sugden on Vendors and Purchasers; Story's excellent treatise on Bailments; Jones on Bailments; Toullier, Droit Civil Français, tomes 6 et 7; Ham. Parties to Actions, Ch. 1; Chit. Pr. Index, h. t.; and the articles *Agreement; Apportionment; Appropriation; Assent; Assignment; Assumpsit; Attestation; Bailment; Bargain and sale; Bidder; Bilateral contract; Bill of Exchange; Buyer; Commodate; Condition; Consensual contract; Conjunctive; Consummation; Construction; Contract of benevolence; Covenant; Cumulative contracts; Debt; Deed; Delegation; Delivery; Discharge of a contract; Disjunctive; Equity of a redemption; Exchange; Guaranty; Impairing the obligation of contracts; Insurance; Interested contracts; Item; Misrepresentation; Mortgage; Mixed contract; Negociorum gestor; Novation; Obligation; Pactum constitutæ pecuniæ; Partners; Partnership; Pledge; Promise; Purchaser; Quasi contract; Representation; Sale; Seller; Settlement; Simple contract; Synallagmatic contract; Subrogation; Title; Unilateral contract.*

CONTRACT OF BENEVOLENCE, *civil law.* One which is made for the benefit of only one of the contracting parties; such as loan for use, deposit, and mandate. Poth. Obl. n. 12. See *Contracts.*

CONTRACTION. An abbreviation; a mode of writing or printing by which some of the letters of a word are omitted. See *Abbreviations.*

CONTRACTOR. One who enters into a contract; this term is usually applied to persons who undertake to do public work, or the work for a company or corporation on a large scale, at a certain fixed price, or to furnish goods to another at a fixed or ascertained price. 2 Pardess. n. 300. Vide 5 Whart. 366.

CONTRADICTION. The incompatibility, contrariety, and evident opposition of two ideas, which are the subject of one and the same proposition.

2. In general, when a party accused of a crime contradicts himself, it is presumed he does so because he is guilty; for truth does not contradict itself, and is always consistent, whereas falsehood is in general inconsistent; and the truth of some known facts will contradict the falsehood of those which are falsely alleged to be true. But there must still be much caution used by the judge, as there may be sometimes apparent contradictions which arise either from the timidity, the ignorance, or the inability of the party to explain himself, when in fact he tells the truth.

3. When a witness contradicts himself as to something which is important in the case, his testimony will be much weakened, or it may be entirely discredited; and when he relates a story of facts which he alleges passed only in his presence, and he is contradicted as to other facts which are known to others, his credit will be much impaired.

4. When two witnesses, or other persons, state things directly opposed to each other, it is the duty of the judge or jury to reconcile these apparent contradictions; but when this cannot be done, the more improbable statement must be rejected; or, if both are entitled to the same credit, then the matter is as if no proof had been given. See *Circumstances.*

CONTRAFACTION, *crim. law.* Counterfeiting, imitating. In the French law contrafaction (contrefaçon) is the illegal reprinting of a book for which the author or his assignee has a copyright, to the prejudice of the latter. Merl. Répert. mot Contrefaçon.

CONTRAVENTION, *French law.* An act which violates the law, a treaty or an agreement which the party has made. The Penal Code, art. 1, denominates a contravention, that infraction of the law punished by a fine, which does not exceed fifteen francs, and an imprisonment not exceeding three days.

CONTRECTATION. The ability to be removed. In order to commit a larceny, the property must have been removed. When, from its nature, it is incapable of contrectation, as real estate, there can be no larceny. Bowy. Mod. Civ. Law, 268. See *Larceny Furtum est contrectatio rei fraudulosa.* Dig. 47, 2. See *Taking.*

CONTREFACON, *French law.* Counterfeit. This is a bookseller's term, which signifies the offence of those who print or cause to be printed, without lawful authority, a book of which the author or his assigns have a copyright. Merl. Rép. h. t.

CONTRIBUTION, *civil law.* A partition by which the creditors of an insolvent debtor divide among themselves the proceeds of his property, proportionably to the amount of their respective credits. Civ. Code of Lo. art. 2522, n. 10. It is a division pro rata. Merl. Rép. h. t.

CONTRIBUTION, *contracts.* When two or more persons jointly owe a debt, and one is compelled to pay the whole of it, the others are bound to indemnify him for the payment of their shares; this indemnity is called a contribution. 1 Bibb. R. 562; 4 John. Ch. R. 545; 4 Bouv. Inst. n. 3935-6.

2. The subject will be considered by taking a view, 1. Of right of the creditors where there are several debtors. 2. Of the right of the debtor who pays the whole debt. 3. Of the liabilities of the debtors who are liable to contribution. 4. Of the liability of land owned by several owners, when it is subject to a charge. 5. Of the liability of owners of goods in a vessel, when part is thrown overboard to save the rest.

3.—1. The creditor of several debtors, jointly bound to him, has a right to compel the payment by any he may choose; but he cannot sue them severally, unless they are severally bound.

4.—2. When one of several debtors pays a debt, the creditor is bound in conscience, if not by contract, to give to the party paying the debt all his remedies against the other debtors. 1 Cox, R. 318; S. C. 2 B. & P. 270; 2 Swanst. R. 189, 192; 3 Bligh, 59; 14 Ves. 160; 14 Ves. 31; 12 Wheat. 596; 1 Hill, Ch. R. 344, 351; 1 Tenn. St. R. 512, 517; 1 Ala. R. 23, 28; 11 Ohio R. 444, 449; 8 Misso. R. 169, 175.

5.—3. A debtor liable to contribution is not responsible upon a contract, but is so in equity. But courts of common law, in modern times, have assumed a jurisdiction to compel contribution among sureties, in the absence of any positive contract, on the ground of an implied assumpsit, and each of the sureties may be sued for his respective quota or proportion. White's L. C. in Eq. 66. The remedy in equity is, however, much more effective. For example, a surety who pays an entire debt, can, in equity, compel the solvent sureties to contribute towards the payment of the entire debt. 1 Chan. R. 34; 1 Chan. Cas. 246; Finch, R. 15, 203. But at law he can recover no more than an aliquot part of the whole, regard being had to the number of co-sureties. 2 B. & P. 268; 6 B. & C. 697.

6.—4. When land is charged with the payment of a legacy, or an estate with the portion of a posthumous child, every part is bound to make contribution. 3 Munf. R. 29; 1 John. Ch. R. 425; 2 Bouv. Inst. n. 1301.

7.—5. Contribution takes place in another case; namely, when in order to save a ship or cargo, a part of the goods are cast overboard, the ship and cargo are liable to contribution in order to indemnify the owner of the goods lost, except his just proportion. No contribution can be claimed between joint wrong doers. Bac. Ab. Assumpsit A; Vide 3 Com. Dig. 143; 8 Com. Dig. 373; 5 Vin. Ab. 561; 2 Supp. to Ves. jr. 159, 343; 3 Ves. jr. 64; Wesk. Ins. 130; 10 S. & R. 75; 5 B. & Ad. 936; S. C. 3 N. & M. 258; Rast. Entr. 161; 2 Ventr. 348; 2 Vern. 592; 2 B. & P. 268; 3 B. & P. 235; 5 East, 225; 1 J. P. Smith, 411; 5 Esp. 194; 3 Campb. 480; Gow. N. P. C. 13; 2 A. & E. 57; 4 N. & M. 64; 6 N. & M. 494.

CONTRIBUTIONS, *public law*. Taxes or money contributed to the support of the government.

2. Contributions are of three kinds, namely: first, those which arise from persons on account of their property, real or personal, or which are imposed upon their industry—those which are laid on and paid by real estate without regard to its owner; and—those to which personal property is subject, in its transmission from hand to hand, without regard to the owner. See Domat, Dr. Publ. l. 1, t. 5, s. 2, n. 2.

3. This is a generic term which includes all kinds of impositions for the public benefit. See *Duties; Imports; Taxes.*

4. By contributions is also meant a forced levy of money or property by a belligerent in a hostile country which he occupies, by which means the country is made to contribute to the support of the army of occupation. These contributions are usually taken instead of pillage. Vatt. Dr. des Gens, liv. 3, 9, § 165; Id. liv. 4, c. 3, § 29.

CONTROLLERS. Officers who are appointed to examine the accounts of other officers. More usually written *comptrollers.* (q. v.)

CONTROVER, *obsolete*. One who invents false news. 2 Inst. 227.

CONTROVERSY. A dispute arising between two or more persons. It differs from case, which includes all suits criminal as well as civil; whereas controversy is a civil and not a criminal proceeding. 2 Dall. R. 419, 431, 432; 1 Tuck. Bl. Com. App. 420, 421; Story, Const. § 1668.

2. By the constitution of the United States the judicial power shall extend to controversies to which the United States shall be a party. Art. 2, 1. The meaning to be attached to the word controversy in the constitution, is that above given.

CONTUBERNIUM, *civ. law*. As among the Romans, slaves had no civil state, their marriages, although valid according to natural law, when contracted with the consent of their masters, and when there was no legal bar to them, yet were without civil effects; they having none except what arose from natural law; a marriage of this kind was called *contubernium*. It was so called whether both or only one of the parties was a slave. Poth. Contr. de Mariage, part 1, c. 2, § 4. Vicat, ad verb.

CONTUMACY, *civil law*. The refusal or neglect of a party accused to appear and answer to a charge preferred against him in a court of justice. This word is derived from the Latin *contumacia*, disobedience. 1 Bro. Civ. Law, 455; Ayl. Parer. 196; Dig. 50, 17, 52; Code Nap. art. 22.

2. Contumacy is of two kinds, actual and presumed: actual contumacy is when the party before the court refuses to obey some order of the court; presumed contumacy is the act of refusing or declining to appear upon being cited. 3 Curt. Ecc. R. 1.

CONTUMAX, *civ. law*. One accused of a crime who refuses to appear and answer to the charge. An outlaw.

CONTUSION, *med. jurisp*. An injury or lesion, arising from the shock of a body with a large surface, which presents no loss of substance, and no apparent wound. If the skin be divided, the injury takes the name of a contused wound. Vide 1 Ch. Pr. 38; 4 Carr. & P. 381, 487, 558, 565; 6 Carr. & P. 684; 2 Beck's Med. Jur. 178.

CONUSANCE, CLAIM OF, *English law*. This is defined to be an intervention by a third person, demanding judicature in the cause against the plaintiff, who has chosen to commence his action out of claimant's court. 2 Wilson's R. 409.

2. It is a question of jurisdiction between the two courts; Fortesc. R. 157; 5 Vin. Abr. 588; and not between the plaintiff and defendant, as in the case of plea to the jurisdiction, and therefore it must be demanded by the party entitled to conusance, or by his representative, and not by the defendant or his attorney. Id. ibid. A plea to the jurisdiction must be pleaded in person, but a claim of conusance may be made by attorney. 1 Chit. Pl. 403.

3. There are three sorts of conusance. 1. *Tenere placita*, which does not oust another court of its jurisdiction, but only creates a concurrent one. 2. *Cognitio placitorum*, when the plea is commenced in one court, of which conusance belongs to another. 3. A conusance of exclusive jurisdiction; as that no other court shall hold plea, &c. Hard. 509; Bac. Ab. Courts, D.

CONUSANT. One who knows; as if a party knowing of an agreement in which he has an interest, makes no objection to it, he is said to be conusant. Co. Litt. 157.

CONUSOR. The same as cognizor; one who passes or acknowledges a fine of lands or tenements to another. See *Consignor*.

CONVENE, *civil law*. This is a technical term, signifying to bring an action.

CONVENTIO, *canon law*. The act of convening or calling together the parties, by summoning the defendant. Vide *Reconvention*. When the defendant was brought to answer, he was said to be convened, which the canonists called *conventio*, because the plaintiff and defendant met to contest. Sto. Eq. Pl. § 402; 4 Bouv. Inst. n. 4117.

CONVENTION, *contracts, civil law*. A general term which comprehends all kinds of contracts, treaties, pacts, or agreements. It is defined to be the consent of two or more persons to form with each other an engagement, or to dissolve or change one which they had previously formed. Domat, Lois Civ. l. 1, t. 1, s. 1; Dig. lib. 2, t. 14, l. 1; Lib. 1, t. 1, l. 1, 4 and 5; 1 Bouv. Inst. n. 100.

CONVENTION, *legislation*. This term is applied to a meeting of the delegates elected by the people for other purposes than usual legislation. It is mostly used to denote an assembly to make or amend the constitution of a state, but it sometimes indicates an assembly of the delegates of the people to nominate officers to be supported at an election.

CONVERSANT. One who is in the habit of being in a particular place, is said to be conversant there. Barnes, 162.

CONVERSION, *torts*. The unlawful turning or applying the personal goods of another to the use of the taker, or of some other person than the owner; or the unlawful destroying or altering their nature Bull. N. P. 44; 6 Mass. 20; 14 Pick 356; 3 Brod. & Bing. 2; Cro. Eliz. 219; 12 Mod. 519; 5 Mass. 104; 6 Shepl. 382; Story, Bailm. § 188, 269, 306; 6 Mass. 422; 2 B. & P. 438; 3 B. & Ald. 702, 11 M. & W. 363; 8 Taunt. 237; 4 Taunt. 24.

2. When a party takes away or wrongfully assumes the right to goods which belong to another, it will in general be sufficient evidence of a conversion; but when the original taking was lawful, as when the party found the goods, and the detention only is illegal, it is absolutely necessary to make a demand of the goods, and there must be a refusal to deliver them before the conversion will be complete. 1 Ch. Pr. 566; 2 Saund. 47 e, note; 1 Ch. Pl. 179; Bac. Ab. Trover, B; 1 Com. Dig. 439; 3 Com. Dig. 142; 1 Vin. Ab. 236; Yelv. 174, n.; 2 East, R. 405; 6 East, R. 540; 4 Taunt. 799; 5 Barn. & Cr. 146; S. C. 11 Eng. C. L. Rep. 185; 3 Bl. Com. 152; 3 Bouv. Inst. n. 3522, et seq. The refusal by a servant to deliver the goods entrusted to him by his master, is not evidence of a conversion by his master. 5 Hill, 455.

3. The tortious taking of property is, of itself, a conversion; 15 John. R. 431, and any intermeddling with it, or any exercise of dominion over it, subversive of the dominion of the owner, or the nature of the bailment, if it be bailed, is evidence of a conversion. 1 Nott & McCord, R. 592; 2 Mass. R. 398; 1 Har. & John. 519; 7 John. R. 254; 10 John. R. 172; 14 John. R. 128; Cro. Eliz. 219; 2 John. Cas. 411. Vide *Trover*.

CONVERSION, *in equity*. The considering of one thing as changed into another; for example, land will be considered as converted into money, and treated as such by a court of equity, when the owner has contracted to sell his estate; in which case, if he die before the conveyance, his executors and not his heirs will be entitled to the money. 2 Vern. 52; S. C. 3 Chan. R. 217; 1 Bl. Rep. 129. On the other hand, money is converted into land in a variety of ways; as for example, when a man agrees to buy land, and dies before he has received the conveyance, the money he was to pay for it will be considered as converted into lands, and descend to the heir. 1 P. Wms. 176; 2 Vern. 227; 10 Pet. 563; Bouv. Inst. Index, h. t.

CONVEYANCE, *contracts*. The transfer of the title to land by one or more persons to another or others. By the term persons is here understood not only natural persons but corporations. The instrument which conveys the property is also called a conveyance. For the several kinds of conveyances see *Deed*. Vide, generally, Roberts on Fraud. Conv. *passim;* 16 Vin. Ab. 138; Com. Dig. Chancery, 2 T 1; 3 M 2; 4 S 2; Id. Discontinuance, C 3, 4, 5; Id. Guaranty, D; Id. Pleader, C 37; Id. Poiar, C 5; Bouv. Inst. Index, h. t. The whole of a conveyance, when it consists of different parts or instruments, must be taken together, and the several parts of it relate back to the principal part; 4 Burr. Rep. 1962; as a fine; 2 Burr. R. 704; or a recovery; 2 Burr. Rep. 135.

2. When there is no express agreement to the contrary, the expense of the conveyance falls upon the purchaser; 2 Ves. Jr. 155, note; who must prepare and tender the conveyance; but see contra, 2 Rand. 20. The expense of the execution of the conveyance is, on the contrary, always borne by the vendor. Sugd. Vend. 296; *contra*, 2 Rand. 20; 2 McLean, 495. Vide 5 Mass. R. 472; 3 Mass. 487; Euuom. Dial. 2, § 12; *Voluntary Conveyance*.

CONVEYANCE OF VESSELS. The act of congress, approved the 29th July, 1850, entitled an act to provide for recording the conveyances of vessels and for other purposes, enacts that no bill of sale, mortgage, hypothecation or conveyance of any vessel, or part of any vessel of the United States, shall be valid against any person, other than the grantor or mortgagor, his heirs and devisees, and persons having actual notice thereof, unless such bill of sale, mortgage, hypothecation or conveyance be recorded in the office of the collector of the customs, where such vessel is registered or enrolled. Provided, that the lien by bottomry on any vessel, created during her voyage, by a loan of money or materials necessary to repair or enable such vessel to prosecute a voyage, shall not lose its priority or be in any way affected by the provisions of the act.

Sec. 2 enacts, that the collectors of the customs shall record all such bills of sale, mortgages, hypothecations or conveyances, and also all certificates for discharging and cancelling any such conveyances, in a book or books to be kept for that purpose, in the order of their reception; noting in said book or books, and also on the bill of sale, mortgage, hypothecation or conveyance, the time when the same was received; and shall certify on the bill of sale, mortgage, hypothecation or conveyance, or certificate of discharge or cancellation, the number of the book and page where recorded; and shall receive, for so recording such instrument of conveyance or certificate of discharge, fifty cents.

Sec. 3 enacts, that the collectors of the customs shall keep an index of such records, inserting alphabetically the names of the vendor or mortgagor, and of the vendee or mortgagee, and shall permit said index and books of records to be inspected during office hours, under such reasonable regulations as they may establish; and shall, when required, furnish to any person a certificate setting forth the names of the owners of any vessel registered or enrolled, the parts or proportions owned by each, if inserted in the register or enrollment, and also the material facts of any existing bill of sale, mortgage, hypothecation, or other incumbrance upon such vessel, recorded since the issuing of the last register or enrollment; viz. the date, amount of such incumbrance, and from and to whom or in whose favor made. The collector shall receive for each such certificate one dollar.

Sec. 4. By this section it is enacted, that the collectors of the customs shall furnish certified copies of such records, on the receipt of fifty cents for each bill of sale, mortgage, or other conveyance.

Sect. 5. This section provides that the owner or agent of the owner of any vessel of the United States, applying to a collector of the customs for a register or enrollment of a vessel, shall, in addition to the oath now prescribed by law, set forth, in the oath of ownership, the part or proportion of such vessel belonging to each owner, and the same shall be inserted in the register of enrollment; and that all bills of sale of vessels registered or enrolled shall set forth the part of the vessel owned by each person selling, and the part conveyed to each person purchasing.

CONVEYANCER. One who makes it his business to draw deeds of conveyance of lands for others. 3 Bouv. Inst. n. 2422.

2. It is usual also for conveyancers to act as brokers for the seller. In these cases the conveyancer should examine with scrupulous exactness into the title of the lands which are conveyed by his agency, and, if this be good, to be very cautious that the estate be not encumbered. In cases of doubt he should invariably propose to his employer to take the advice of his counsel.

3. Conveyancers also act as brokers for the loan of money on real estate, secured by mortgage. The same care should be observed in these cases.

CONVICIUM, *civil law*. The name of a species of slander, or, in the meaning of the civil law, injury, uttered in public, and which charged some one with some act *contra bonos mores*. Vicat, ad verb; Bac. Ab. Slander.

CONVICT. One who has been condemned by a competent court. This term is more commonly applied to one who has been convicted of a crime or misdemeanor. There are various local acts which punish the importation of convicts.

CONVICTION, *practice*. A condemnation. In its most extensive sense this word signifies the giving judgment against a defendant, whether criminal or civil. In a more limited sense, it means the judgment given against the criminal. And in its most restricted sense it is a record of the summary proceedings upon any penal statute before one or more justices of the peace, or other persons duly authorized, in a case where the offender has been convicted and sentenced: this last is usually termed a summary conviction.

2. As summary convictions have been introduced in derogation of the common law, and operate to the exclusion of trial by jury, the courts have required that the strict letter of the statute should be observed; 1 Burr. Rep. 613; and that the magistrates should have been guided by rules similar to those adopted by the common law, in criminal prosecution, and founded in natural justice; unless when the statute dispenses with the form of stating them.

3. The general rules in relation to convictions are, first, it must be under the hand and seal of the magistrate before whom it is taken; secondly, it must be in the present tense, but this, perhaps, ought to extend only to the judgment; thirdly, it must be certain; fourthly, although it is well to lay the offence to be contra pacem, this is not indispensable; fifthly, a conviction cannot be good in part and bad in part.

4. A conviction usually consists of six parts; first, the information; which should contain, 1. The day when it was taken. 2. The place where it was taken. 3. The name of the informer. 4. The name and style of the justice or justices to whom it was given. 5. The name of the offender. 6. The time of committing the offence. 7. The place where the offence was committed. 8. An exact decription of the offence.

5. Secondly, the summons.

6. Thirdly, the appearance or non-appearance of the defendant.

7. Fourthly, his defence or confessions.

8. Fifthly, the evidence. Dougl. 469; 2 Burr. 1163; 4 Burr. 2064.

9. Sixthly, the judgment or adjudication, which should state, 1. That the defendant is convicted. 2. The forfeiture or penalty. Vide Bosc. on Conviction; Espinasse on Penal Actions; 4 Dall. 266; 3 Yeates, 475; 1 Yeates, 471. As to the effect of a conviction as evidence in a civil case, see 1 Phil. Ev. 259; 3 Bouv. Inst. n. 3183.

CONVOCATION, *eccles. law*. This word literally signifies *called together*. The assembly of the representatives of the clergy. As to the powers of convocations, see Shelf. on M. & D. 23. See *Court of Convocation*.

CONVOY, *mar. law*. A naval force under the command of an officer appointed by government, for the protection of merchant ships and others, during the whole voyage, or such part of it as is known to require such protection. Marsh. Ins. B. 1, c. 9, s. 5; Park. Ins. 388.

2. Warranties are sometimes inserted in policies of insurance that the ship shall sail with convoy. To comply with this warranty, five things are essential; first, the ship must sail with the regular convoy appointed by the government; secondly, she must sail from the place of rendezvous appointed by government; thirdly, the

convoy must be for the voyage; fourthly, the ship insured must have sailing instructions; fifthly, she must depart and continue with the convoy till the end of the voyage, unless separated by necessity. Marsh. Ins. B. 1, c. 9, s. 5.

CO-OBLIGOR, *contracts*. One who is bound together with one or more others to fulfil an obligation. As to what will constitute a joint obligation, see 5 Bin. 199; Windham's Case, 5 Co. 7; 2 Ev. Poth. 63; Ham. Parties, 29, 20, 24; 1 Saund. 155; Saunders, Arguendo and note 2; 5 Co. 18 b, 19 a, Slingsly's Case. He may be jointly or severally bound.

2. When obligors are jointly and not severally bound to pay a joint debt, they must be sued jointly during their joint lives, and after the death of some of them, the survivors alone can be sued; each is bound to pay the whole debt, having recourse to the others for contribution. See 1 Saund. 291, n. 4; Hardress, 198; 2 Ev. Poth. 63, 64, 66. Yet an infant co-obligor need not be joined, for his infancy may be replied to a plea of non-joinder in abatement. 3 Esp. 76; 5 Esp. 47; also, see 5 Bac. Abr. 163-4; 2 Vern. 99; 2 Moss. Rep. 577; 1 Saund. 291 b, n. 2; 6 Serg. & R. 265, 266; 1 Caines' Cases in Err. 122.

3. When co-obligors are severally bound, each may be sued separately; and in case of the death of any one of them, his executors or administrators may be sued.

4. On payment of the obligation by any one of them, when it was for a joint debt, the payer is entitled to contribution from the other co-obligors.

COOL BLOOD. A phrase sometimes used to signify tranquillity, or calmness; that is, the condition of one who has the calm and undisturbed use of his reason. In cases of homicide, it frequently becomes necessary to ascertain whether the act of the person killing was done in cool blood or not, in order to ascertain the degree of his guilt. Bac. Ab. Murder, B; Kiel. 56; Sid. 177; Lev. 180. Vide *Intention; Murder; Manslaughter; Will.*

CO-OPTATION. A concurring choice. Sometimes applied to the act of the members of a corporation, in choosing a person to supply a vacancy in their body.

COPARCENERS, *estates*. Persons on whom lands of inheritance descend from their ancestor. According to the English law, there must be no males; that is not the rule in this country. Vide *Estates in coparcenary*, and 4 Kent. Com. 262; 2 Bouv. Inst. n. 1871-'.

COPARTNER. One who is a partner with one or more other persons; a member of a partnership.

COPARTNERSHIP. This word is frequently used in the sense of partnership. (q. v.)

CO-PLAINTIFF. One who is plaintiff in an action with another.

COPULATIVE TERM. One which is placed between two or more others to join them together: the word *and* is frequently used for this purpose. For example, a man promises to pay another a certain sum of money, *and* to give his note for another sum: in this case he must perform both.

2. But the copulative may sometimes be construed into a disjunctive, (q. v.) as, when things are copulated which cannot possibly be so; for example, "to die testate and intestate." For examples of construction of disjunctive terms, see the cases cited at the word *Disjunctive*, and Ayl. Pand. 55; 5 Com. Dig. 338; Bac. Ab. Conditions, P 5; Owen, 52; Leon. 74; Golds. 71; Roll. Ab. 444; Cro. Jac. 594.

COPY. A copy is a true transcript of an original writing.

2. Copies cannot be given in evidence, unless proof is made that the originals, from which they are taken, are lost, or in the power of the opposite party; and in the latter case, that notice has been given him to produce the original. See 12 Vin. Abr. 97; Phil. Ev. Index, h. t.; Poth. Obl. Pt. 4, c. 1, art. 3; 3 Bouv. Inst. n. 3055.

3. To prove a copy of a record, the witness must be able to swear that he has examined it, line for line, with the original, or has examined the copy, while another person read the original. 1 Campb. R. 469. It is not requisite that the persons examining should exchange papers, and read them alternately. 2 Taunt. R. 470. Vide, generally, 3 Bouv. Inst. n. 3106-10; 1 Stark. R. 183; 2 E. C. L. Rep. 183; 4 Campb. 372; 2 Burr. 1179; B. N. P. 129; 1 Carr. & P. 578. An examined copy of the books of unincorporated banks are not, *per se*, evidence. 12 S. & R. 256. See 13 S. & R. 135, 334; 2 N. & McC. 299.

COPYRIGHT. The property which has been secured to the author of a book, map, chart, or musical composition, print, cut or engraving, for a limited time, by the constitution and laws of the United States. Lord Mansfield defines copy, or as it is now termed copyright, as follows: "I use the word copy in the technical sense in which that name or term has been used for ages, to signify an incorporeal right to the sole printing and publishing of something intellectual, communicated by letters. 4 Burr. 3296; Merl. Rèpert. mot Contrefaçon.

2. This subject will be considered by taking a view of, 1. The legislation of the United States. 2. Of the persons entitled to a copyright. 3. For what it is granted. 4. Nature of the right. 5. Its duration. 6. Proceedings to obtain such right. 7. Requisites after the grant. 8. Remedies. 9. Former grants.

3.—§ 1. *The legislation of the United States.* The Constitution of the United States, art. 1, s. 8, gives power to congress "to promote the progress of science, and the useful arts, by securing, for limited times, to authors and inventors, the exclusive right to their respective writings and discoveries." In pursuance of this constitutional authority, congress passed the act of May 31, 1790; 1 Story's L. U. S. 94, and the act of April 29, 1802, 2 Story's L. U. S. 866, but now repealed by the act of February 3, 1831, 4 Shars. Cont. of Story, 2221, saving, always, such rights as may have been obtained in conformity to their provision. By this last mentioned act, entitled "An act to amend the several acts respecting copyrights," the subject is now regulated.

4.—§ 2. *Of the persons entitled to a copyright.* Any person or persons, being a citizen or citizens of the United States, or resident therein, who is the author or authors of any book or books, map, chart, or musical composition, or who has designed, etched, engraved, worked, or caused to be engraved, etched or worked from his own design, any print or engraving, and the executors, administrators, or legal representatives of such person or persons. Sect. 1, and sect. 8.

5.—§ 3. *For what work the copyright is granted.* The copyright is granted for any book or books, map, chart, or musical composition, which may be now, (February 3, 1831, the date of the act,) made or composed, and not printed or published, or shall hereafter be made or composed, or any print or engraving, which the author has invented, designed, etched, engraved or worked, or caused to be engraved, etched or worked from his own design. Sect. 1.

6.—§ 4. *Nature of the right.* The person or persons to whom a copyright has been lawfully granted, have the sole right and liberty of printing, reprinting, publishing and vending such book or books, map, chart, musical composition, print, cut or engraving, in whole or in part. Sect. 1.

7.—§ 5. *Duration of the copyright.* The right extends for the term of twenty-eight years from the time of recording the title of the book, &c., in the office of the clerk of the court, as directed by law. Sect. 1.

8. But this time may be extended by the following provisions of the act.

9. Sect. 2. If, at the expiration of the aforesaid term of years, such author, inventor, designer, engraver, or any of them, where the work had been originally composed and made by more than one person, be still living, and a citizen or citizens of the United States, or resident therein, or being dead, shall have left a widow, or child, or children, either or all then living, the same exclusive right shall be continued to such author, designer, or engraver, or if dead, then to such widow and child, or children, for the further term of fourteen years: *Provided*, That the title of the work so secured shall be a second time recorded, and all such other regulations as are herein required in regard to original copyrights, be complied with in respect to such renewed copyright, and that within six months before the expiration of the first term.

10. Sect. 3. In all cases of renewal of copyright under this act, such author or proprietor shall, within two months from the date of said renewal, cause a copy of the record thereof to be published in one or more of the newspapers printed in the United States, for the space of four weeks.

11.—Sect. 16. Whenever a copyright has been heretofore obtained by an author or authors, inventor, designer, or engraver, of any book, map, chart, print, cut, or engraving, or by a proprietor of the same; if such author or authors, or either of them, such inventor, designer, or engraver, be living at the passage of this act, then, such author or authors, or the survivor of them, such inventor, engraver, or designer, shall continue to have the same exclusive right to his book, chart, map, print, cut or engraving, with the benefit of each and all the provisions of this act, for the security thereof, for such additional period of time as will, together with the time which shall have elapsed from the first entry of such copyright, make up the term of twenty-eight years, with the same right to his widow, child, or children, to renew the copyright, at the expiration thereof, as is provided in relation to copyrights originally secured under this act. And if such author or authors, inventor, designer, or engraver, shall not be living at the passage of this act, then, his or their heirs, executors and administrators, shall be entitled to the like exclusive enjoyment of said copyright, with the benefit of each and all the provisions of this act for the security thereof, for the period of twenty-eight years from the first entry of said copyright; with the like privilege of renewal to the widow, child, or children, of author or authors, designer, inventor, or engraver, as is provided in relation to copyrights originally secured under this act.

12.—§ 6. *Proceedings to obtain a copyright.* No person shall be entitled to the benefit of this act, unless he shall, before publication, deposit a printed copy of the title of such book, or books, map, chart, musical composition, print, cut, or engraving, in the clerk's office of the district court of the district wherein the author or proprietor shall reside, and the clerk of such court is hereby directed and required to record the same therein forthwith, in a book to be kept for that purpose, in the words following (giving a copy of the title under the seal of the court, to the said author or proprietor, whenever he shall require the same:) "District of —— to wit: Be it remembered, that on the —— day of —— Anno Domini, ——A. B. of the said district, hath deposited in this office the title of a book, (map, chart, or otherwise, as the case may be,) the title of which is in the words following, to wit; (here insert the title;) the right whereof he claims as author (or proprietor, as the case may be;) in conformity with an act of congress, entitled 'An act to amend the several acts respecting copyrights.' C. D. clerk of the district." For which record, the clerk shall be entitled to receive, from the person claiming such right as aforesaid, fifty cents; and the like sum for every copy, under seal, actually given to such person or his assigns. The act to establish the Smithsonian Institution, for the increase and diffusion of knowledge among men, enacts, section 10, that the author or proprietor of any book, map, chart, musical composition, print, cut, or engraving, for which a copyright shall be secured under the existing acts of congress, or those which shall hereafter be enacted respecting copyrights, shall, within three months from the publication of said book, etc., deliver or cause to be delivered, one copy of the same to the librarian of the Smithsonian Institution, and one copy to the librarian of Congress Library, for the use of the said libraries.

13.—§ 7. *Requisites after the grant.* No person shall be entitled to the benefit of this act, unless he shall give information of copyright being secured, by causing to be inserted, in the several copies of each and every edition published during the term secured, on the title page, or the page immediately following, if it be a book, or, if a map, chart, musical composition, print, cut, or engraving, by causing to be impressed on the face thereof, or if a volume of maps, charts, music or engravings, upon the title or frontispiece thereof, the following words, viz: "Entered according to act of congress, in the year —— by A. B., in the clerk's office of the district court of ——" (as the case may be.)

14. The author or proprietor of any such book, map, chart, musical composition, print, cut, or engraving, shall, within three months from the publication of said book, map, chart, musical composition, print, cut, or engraving, deliver or cause to be delivered a copy of the same to the clerk of said district. And it shall be the duty of the clerk of each district court, at least once in every year, to transmit a certified list of all such records of copyright, including the titles so recorded, and the date of record. and also all the several copies of books or other works deposited in his office, according to this act, to the secretary of state, to be preserved in his office.

15.—§ 8. *The remedies* may be considered with regard, 1. To the penalties which may be incurred. 2. The issue in actions under this act. 3. The costs. 4. The limitation.

16.—1. The *penalties* imposed by this act relate, first, to the violation of the copyright of books; secondly, the violation of the copyright of prints, cuts or engravings, maps, charts, or musical compositions; thirdly, the printing or publishing of any manuscripts without the consent of the author or legal proprietor; fourthly, for inserting in any book, &c., that the copyright has been secured contrary to truth

17.—*First.* If any other person or persons, from and after recording the title of any book or books, according to this act, shall, within the term or terms herein limited, print, publish, or import, or cause to be printed, published, or imported, any copy of such book or books, without the consent of the person legally entitled to the copyright thereof, first had and obtained in writing, signed in presence of two or more credible witnesses, or shall, knowing the same to be so printed or imported, publish, sell, or expose to sale, or cause to be published, sold, or exposed to sale, any copy of such book, without such consent in writing, then such offender shall forfeit every copy of such book to the person legally, at the time, entitled to the copyright thereof; and shall also forfeit and pay fifty cents for every such sheet which may be found in his possession, either printed or printing, published, imported, or exposed to sale, contrary to the intent of this act; the one moiety thereof to such legal owner of the copyright as aforesaid, and the other to the use of the United States; to be recovered by action of debt in any court having competent jurisdiction thereof.

18.—*Secondly.* If any person or persons, after the recording the title of any print, cut or engraving, map, chart, or musical composition, according to the provisions of this act, shall, within the term or terms limited by this act, engrave, etch, or work, sell, or copy, or cause to be engraved, etched, worked, or sold, or copied, either on the whole, or by varying, adding to, or diminishing the main design, with intent to evade the law, or shall print or import for sale, or cause to be printed or imported for sale, any such map, chart, musical composition, print, cut, or engraving, or any parts thereof, without the consent of the proprietor or proprietors of the copyright thereof, first obtained in writing, signed in the presence of two credible witnesses; or, knowing the same to be so printed or imported, without such consent, shall publish, sell, or expose to sale, or in any manner dispose of any such map, chart, musical composition, engraving, cut, or print, without such consent, as aforesaid; then such offender or offenders shall forfeit the plate or plates on which such map, chart, musical composition, engraving, cut, or print, shall be copied, and also all and every sheet thereof so copied or printed, as aforesaid, to the proprietor or proprietors of the copyright thereof; and shall further forfeit one dollar for every sheet of such map, chart, musical composition, print, cut, or engraving, which may be found in his or their possession, printed or published, or exposed to sale, contrary to the true intent and meaning of this act; the one moiety thereof to the proprietor or proprietors, and the other moiety to the use of the United States, to be recovered in any court having competent jurisdiction thereof.

19. Nothing in this act shall be construed to extend to prohibit the importation or vending, printing or publishing, of any map, chart, book, musical composition, print, or engraving, written, composed, or made by any person not being a citizen of the United States, nor resident within the jurisdiction thereof.

20.—*Thirdly.* Any person or persons, who shall print or publish any manuscript whatever, without the consent of the author or legal proprietor first obtained as aforesaid, (if such author or proprietor be a citizen of the United States, or resident therein,) shall be liable to suffer and pay to the author or proprietor all damages occasioned by such injury, to be recovered by a special action on the case founded upon this act, in any court having cognizance thereof; and the several courts of the United States empowered to grant injunctions to prevent the violation of the rights of authors and inventors, are hereby empowered to grant injunctions, in like manner, according to the principles of equity, to restrain such publication of any manuscript, as aforesaid.

21.—*Fourthly.* If any person or persons, from and after the passing of this act, shall print or publish any book, map, chart, musical composition, print, cut, or engraving, not having legally acquired the copyright thereof, and shall insert or impress that the same hath been entered according to act of congress, or words purporting the same, every person so offending shall forfeit and pay one hundred dollars; one moiety thereof to the person who shall sue for the same, and the other to the use of the United States, to be recovered by action of debt, in any court of record having cognizance thereof.

22.—2. The *issue.* If any person or persons shall be sued or prosecuted, for any matter, act or thing done under or by virtue of this act, he or they may plead the general issue, and give the special matter in evidence.

23.—3. The *costs.* In all recoveries under this act, either for damages, forfeitures, or penalties, full costs shall be allowed thereon, anything in any former act to the contrary notwithstanding.

24.—4. The *limitation* of actions is regulated as follows. No action or prosecution shall be maintained in any case of forfeiture or penalty under this act, unless the same shall have been commenced within two years after the cause of action shall have arisen.

25.—§ 9. *Former grants.* All and several the provisions of this act, intended for the protection and security of copyrights, and providing remedies, penalties, and forfeitures in case of violation thereof, shall be held and construed to extend to the benefit of the legal proprietor or proprietors of each and every copyright heretofore obtained, according to law, during the term thereof, in the same manner as if such copyright had been entered and secured according to the directions of this act. And by the 16th section it is provided that this act shall not extend to any copyright heretofore secured, the term of which has already expired.

26. Copyrights are secured in most countries of Europe.

In Great Britain, an author has a copyright in his work absolutely for twenty-eight years, and if he be living at the end of that period, for the residne of his life.

In France, the copyright of an author extends to twenty years after his death.

In most, if not in all the German states, it is perpetual; it extends only over the state in which it is granted.

In Russia, the right of an author or translator continues during his life, and his heirs enjoy the privilege twenty-five years afterwards. No manuscript or printed work of an author can be sold for his debts. 2 Am. Jur. 253, 4. Vide, generally, 2 Am. Jur. 248; 10 Am. Jur. 62; 1 Law Intell. 66; and the articles *Literary property; Manuscript.*

COPYHOLD, *estate in the English law.* A copyhold estate is a parcel of a manor, held at the will of the lord, according to the custom of the manor, by a grant from the lord, and admittance of the tenant, entered on the rolls of the manor court. Cruise, Dig. t. 10, c. 1, s. 3. Vide Ch. Pr. Index, h. t.

CORAM. In the presence of; before. *Coram nobis*, before us; *coram vobis*, before you; *coram non judice*, is said of those acts of a court which has no jurisdiction, either over the person, the cause, or the process. 1 Con. 40. Such acts have no validity. Where a thing is required to be done before a particular person, it would not be considered as done before him, if he were asleep or non compos. Vide Dig. 4, 8, 27, 5; Dane's Ab. Index, h. t.; 5 Harr. & John. 42; 8 Cranch, 9; Paine's R. 55; Bouv. Inst. Index, h. t.

CORD, *measures.* A cord of wood must, when the wood is piled close, measure eight feet by four, and the wood must be four feet long. There are various local regulations in our principal cities as to the manner in which wood shall be measured and sold.

CORN. In its most comprehensive sense, this term signifies every sort of grain, as well as peas and beans; this is its meaning in the memorandum usually contained in policies of insurance. But it does not include rice. Park. Ins. 112; Marsh. Ins. 223, note; Stev. on Av. part 4, art. 2; Ben. on Av. ch. 10; 1 Marsh. Ins. 223; Park on Ins. 112; Wesk. Ins. 145. Vide Com. Dig. Biens, G 1.

CORNAGE. The name of a species of tenure in England. The tenant by cornage was bound to blow a horn for the sake of alarming the country on the approach of an enemy. Bac. Ab. Tenure, N.

CORNET. A commissioned officer in a regiment of cavalry.

CORODY, *incorporeal hereditaments.* An allowance of meat, drink, money, clothing, lodging, and such like necessaries for sustenance. 1 Bl. Com. 282; 1 Ch. Pr. 225.

CORONER. An officer whose principal duty it is to hold an inquisition, with the assistance of a jury, over the body of any person who may have come to a violent death, or who has died in prison. It is his duty also, in case of the death of the sheriff, or when a vacancy happens in that office, to serve all the writs and process which the sheriff is usually bound to serve. The chief justice of the King's Bench is the sovereign or chief coroner of all England, although it is not to be understood that he performs the active duties of that office in any one county. 4 Rep. 57, b. Vide Bac. Ab. h. t.; 6 Vin. Ab. 242; 3 Com. Dig. 242; 5 Com. Dig. 212; and the articles *Death; Inquisition.*

2. The duties of the coroner are of the greatest consequence to society, both for the purpose of bringing to punishment murderers and other offenders against the lives of the citizens, and of protecting innocent persons from criminal accusations. His office, it is to be regretted, is regarded with too much indifference. This officer should be properly acquainted with the medical and legal knowledge so absolutely indispensable in the faithful discharge of his

office. It not unfrequently happens that the public mind is deeply impressed with the guilt of the accused, and when probably he is guilty, and yet the imperfections of the early examinations leave no alternative to the jury but to acquit. It is proper in most cases to procure the examination to be made by a physician, and in some cases, it is his duty. 4 Car. & P. 571.

CORPORAL. An epithet for anything belonging to the body, as, corporal punishment, for punishment inflicted on the person of the criminal; corporal oath, which is an oath by the party who takes it being obliged to lay his hand on the Bible.

CORPORAL, *in the army*. A non-commissioned officer in a battalion of infantry.

CORPORAL TOUCH. It was once decided that before a seller of personal property could be said to have stopped it in transitu, so as to regain the possession of it, it was necessary that it should come to his corporal touch. 3 T. R. 466; 5 East, 184. But the contrary is now settled. These words were used merely as a figurative expression. 3 T. R. 464; 5 East, 184.

CORPORATION. An aggregate corporation is an ideal body, created by law, composed of individuals united under a common name, the members of which succeed each other, so that the body continues the same, notwithstanding the changes of the individuals who compose it, and which for certain purposes is considered as a natural person. Browne's Civ. Law, 99; Civ. Code of Lo. art. 418; 2 Kent's Com. 215. Mr. Kyd, (Corpor. vol. 1, p. 13,) defines a corporation as follows: "A corporation, or body politic, or body incorporate, is a collection of many individuals united in one body, under a special denomination, having perpetual succession under an artificial form, and vested by the policy of the law, with a capacity of acting in several respects as an individual, particularly of taking and granting property, contracting obligations, and of suing and being sued; of enjoying privileges and immunities in common, and of exercising a variety of political rights, more or less extensive, according to the design of its institution, or the powers conferred upon it, either at the time of its creation, or at any subsequent period of its existence." In the case of Dartmouth College against Woodward, 4 Wheat. Rep. 626, Chief Justice Marshall describes a corporation to be "an artificial being, invisible, intangible, and existing only in contemplation of law. Being the mere creature of law," continues the judge, "it possesses only those properties which the charter of its creation confers upon it, either expressly or as incidental to its very existence. These are such as are supposed best calculated to effect the object for which it was created. Among the most important are immortality, and if the expression may be allowed, individuality; properties by which a perpetual succession of many persons are considered as the same, and may act as the single individual. They enable a corporation to manage its own affairs, and to hold property without the perplexing intricacies, the hazardous and endless necessity of perpetual conveyance for the purpose of transmitting it from hand to hand. It is chiefly for the purpose of clothing bodies of men, in succession, with these qualities and capacities, that corporations were invented, and are in use." See 2 Bl. Com. 37.

2. The words corporation and incorporation are frequently confounded, particularly in the old books. The distinction between them is, however, obvious; the one is the institution itself, the other the act by which the institution is created.

3. Corporations are divided into public and private.

4. Public corporations, which are also called political, and sometimes municipal corporations, are those which have for their object the government of a portion of the state; Civil Code of Lo. art. 420; and although in such case it involves some private interests, yet, as it is endowed with a portion of political power, the term public has been deemed appropriate.

5. Another class of public corporations are those which are founded for public, though not for political or municipal purposes, and the whole interest in which belongs to the government. The Bank of Philadelphia, for example, if the whole stock belonged exclusively to the government, would be a public corporation; but inasmuch as there are other owners of the stock, it is a private corporation. Domat's Civil Law, 452; 4 Wheat. R. 668; 9 Wheat. R. 907; 3 M'Cord's R. 377; 1 Hawk's R. 36; 2 Kent's Com. 222.

6. Nations or states, are denominated by publicists, bodies politic, and are said to have their affairs and interests, and to deliberate and resolve, in common. They thus become as moral persons, having an understanding and will peculiar to them-

selves, and are susceptible of obligations and laws. Vattel, 49. In this extensive sense the United States may be termed a corporation; and so may each state singly. Per Iredell, J. 3 Dall. 447.

7. Private corporations. In the popular meaning of the term, nearly every corporation is public, inasmuch as they are created for the public benefit; but if the whole interest does not belong to the government, or if the corporation is not created for the administration of political or municipal power, the corporation is private. A bank, for instance, may be created by the government for its own uses; but if the stock is owned by private persons, it is a private corporation, although it is created by the government, and its operations partake of a private nature. 9 Wheat. R. 907. The rule is the same in the case of canal, bridge, turnpike, insurance companies, and the like. Charitable or literary corporations, founded by private benefaction, are in point of law private corporations, though dedicated to public charity, or for the general promotion of learning. Ang. & Ames on Corp. 22.

8. Private corporations are divided into ecclesiastical and lay.

9. Ecclesiastical corporations, in the United States, are commonly called religious corporations; they are created to enable religious societies to manage with more facility and advantage, the temporalities belonging to the church or congregation.

10. Lay corporations are divided into civil and eleemosynary. *Civil* corporations are created for an infinite variety of temporal purposes, such as affording facilities for obtaining loans of money; the making of canals, turnpike roads, and the like. And also such as are established for the advancement of learning. 1 Bl. Com. 471.

11. *Eleemosynary* corporations are such as are instituted upon a principle of charity, their object being the perpetual distribution of the bounty of the founder of them, to such persons as he has directed. Of this kind are hospitals for the relief of the impotent, indigent and sick, or deaf and dumb. 1 Kyd on Corp. 26; 4 Conn. R. 272; Angell & A. on Corp. 26.

12. Corporations, considered in another point of view, are either sole or aggregate.

13. A sole corporation, as its name implies, consists of only one person, to whom and his successors belongs that legal perpetuity, the enjoyment of which is denied to all natural persons. 1 Black. Com. 469. Those corporations are not common in the United States. In those states, however, where the religious establishment of the church of England was adopted, when they were colonies, together with the common law on that subject, the minister of the parish was seised of the freehold, as persona ecclesiæ, in the same manner as in England; and the right of his successors to the freehold being thus established was not destroyed by the abolition of the regal government, nor can it be divested even by an act of the state legislature. 9 Cranch, 328.

14. A sole corporation cannot take personal property in succession; its corporate capacity of taking property is confined altogether to real estate. 9 Cranch, 43.

15. An aggregate corporation consists of several persons, who are united in one society, which is continued by a succession of members. Of this kind are the mayor or commonalty of a city; the heads and fellows of a college; the members of trading companies, and the like. 1 Kyd on Corp. 76; 2 Kent's Com. 221; Ang. & A. on Corp. 20. See, generally, Bouv. Inst. Index, h. t.

CORPORATOR. One who is a member of a corporation.

2. In general, a corporator is entitled to enjoy all the benefits and rights which belong to any other member of the corporation as such. But in some corporations, where the rights are of a pecuniary nature, each corporator is entitled to those rights in proportion to his interest; he will therefore be entitled to vote only in proportion to the amount of his stock, and be entitled to dividends in the same proportion.

3. A corporator is not in general liable personally for any act of the corporation, unless he has been made so by the charter creating the corporation.

CORPOREAL PROPERTY, *civil law*. That which consists of such subjects as are palpable. In the common law, the term to signify the same thing is *property in possession*. It differs from *incorporeal property*, (q. v.) which consists of choses in action and easements, as a right of way, and the like.

CORPSE. The *dead body* (q. v.) of a human being. Russ. & Ry. 366, n.; 2 T. R. 733; 1 Leach, 497; 16 Eng. Com. L. Rep. 413; 8 Pick. 370, Dig. 47, 12, 3, 7; Id. 11, 7, 38; Code, 3, 44, 1.

2. As a corpse is considered as *nullius bonis*, or the property of no one, it follows that stealing it, is not, at common law, a larceny. 3 Inst. 203.

CORPUS. A Latin word, which signifies body; as, *corpus delicti*, the body of the offence, the essence of the crime; *corpus juris canonis*, the body of the canon law; *corpus juris civilis*, the body of the civil law.

CORPUS COMITATUS. The body of the county; the inhabitants or citizens of a whole county, used in contradistinction to a part of a county, or a part of its citizens. See 5 Mason, R. 290.

CORPUS JURIS CIVILIS. The body of the civil law. This is the name given to a collection of the civil law, consisting of Justinian's Institutes, the Pandects or Digest, the Code, and the Novels.

CORPUS CUM CAUSA, *practice*. The writ of *habeas corpus cum causa* (q. v.) is a writ commanding the person to whom it is directed, *to have the body*, together *with the cause* for which he is committed, before the court or judge issuing the same.

CORPUS DELICTI. The body of the offence; the essence of the crime.

2. It is a general rule not to convict unless the *corpus delicti* can be established, that is, until the dead body has been found. Best on Pres. § 201; 1 Stark. Ev. 575. See 6 C. & P. 176; 2 Hale, P. C. 290. Instances have occurred of a person being convicted of having killed another, who, after the supposed criminal has been put to death for the supposed offence, has made his appearance alive. The wisdom of the rule is apparent; but it has been questioned whether, in extreme cases, it may not be competent to prove the basis of the *corpus delicti* by presumptive evidence. 3 Benth. Jud. Ev. 234; Wills on Circum. Ev. 105; Best on Pres. § 204. See *Death*.

CORPUS JURIS CANONICI. The body of the canon law. A compilation of the canon law bears this name. See *Law, canon*.

CORRECTION, *punishment*. Chastisement by one having authority, of a person who has committed some offence, for the purpose of bringing him to legal subjection.

2. It is chiefly exercised in a parental manner, by parents, or those who are placed in loco parentis. A parent may therefore justify the correction of the child either corporally or by confinement; and a schoolmaster, under whose care and instruction a parent has placed his child, may equally justify similar correction; but the correction in both cases must be moderate, and in a proper manner. Com. Dig. Pleader, 3 M 19; Hawk. c. 60, s. 23, and c. 62, s. 2; c. 29, s. 5.

3. The master of an apprentice, for disobedience, may correct him moderately; 1 Barn. & Cres. 469; Cro. Car. 179; 2 Show. 289; 10 Mart. Lo. R. 38; but he cannot delegate the authority to another. 9 Co. 96.

4. A master has no right to correct his servants who are not apprentices.

5. Soldiers are liable to moderate correction from their superiors. For the sake of maintaining their discipline on board of the navy, the captain of a vessel, either belonging to the United States, or to private individuals, may inflict moderate correction on a sailor for disobedience or disorderly conduct. Abbott on Shipp. 160; 1 Ch. Pr. 73; 14 John. R. 119; 15 Mass. 365; 1 Bay, 3; Bee, 161; 1 Pet. Adm. Dec. 168; Molloy, 209; 1 Ware's R. 83. Such has been the general rule. But by a proviso to an act of congress, approved the 28th of September, 1850, flogging in the navy and on board vessels of commerce was abolished.

6. Any excess of correction by the parent, master, officer, or captain, may render the party guilty of an assault and battery, and liable to all its consequences. In some prisons, the keepers have the right to correct the prisoners.

CORREGIDOR, *Spanish law*. A magistrate who took cognizance of various misdemeanors, and of civil matters. 2 White's Coll. 53.

CORRELATIVE. This term is used to designate those things, one of which cannot exist without another; for example, father and child; mountain and valley, &c. Law, obligation, right, and duty, are therefore correlative to each other.

CORRESPONDENCE. The letters written by one to another, and the answers thereto, make what is called the correspondence of the parties.

2. In general, the correspondence of the parties contains the best evidence of the facts to which it relates. See *Letter, contracts; Proposal*.

3. When an offer to contract is made by letter, it must be accepted unconditionally; for if the precise terms are changed, even in the slightest degree, there is no contract. 1 Bouv. Inst. n. 904. See, as to the power

of revoking an offer made by letter, 1 Bouv. Inst. n. 933.

CORRUPTION. An act done with an intent to give some advantage inconsistent with official duty and the rights of others. It includes bribery, but is more comprehensive; because an act may be corruptly done, though the advantage to be derived from it be not offered by another. Merl. Rép. h. t.

2. By corruption, sometimes, is understood something against law; as, a contract by which the borrower agreed to pay the lender usurious interest. It is said, in such case, that it was corruptly agreed, &c.

CORRUPTION OF BLOOD, *English crim. law.* The incapacity to inherit, or pass an inheritance, in consequence of an attainder to which the party has been subject.

2. When this consequence flows from an attainder, the party is stripped of all honors and dignities he possessed, and becomes ignoble.

3. The Constitution of the United States, Amendm. art. 5, provides, that "no person shall be held to answer for a capital, or otherwise infamous crime, unless on a presentment or indictment of a grand jury, except in cases arising in the land or naval forces, or in the militia, when in actual service in time of war or public danger;" and by art. 3, s. 3, n. 2, it is declared that "no attainder of treason shall work corruption of blood, or forfeiture, except during the life of the person attainted."

4. The Constitution of Pennsylvania, art. 9, s. 19, directs that "no attainder shall work corruption of blood." 3 Cruise, 240, 378 to 381, 473; 1 Cruise, 52; 1 Chit. Cr. Law, 740; 4 Bl. Com. 388.

CORSNED, *ancient Eng. law.* This was a piece of accursed bread, which a person accused of a crime swallowed to test his innocence. It was supposed that, if he was guilty, it would choke him.

CORTES. The name of the legislative assemblies of Spain and Portugal.

COSENAGE, *torts.* Deceit, fraud: that kind of circumvention and wrong, which has no other specific name. Vide Ayl. Pand. 103; Dane's Ab. Index, h. t.

COSMOPOLITE. A citizen of the world; one who has no fixed residence. Vide *Citizen.*

COSTS, *practice.* The expenses of a suit or action which may be recovered by law from the losing party.

2. At common law, neither the plaintiff nor the defendant could recover costs *eo nomine;* but in all actions in which damages were recoverable, the plaintiff, in effect, recovered his costs when he obtained a verdict, for the jury always computed them in the damages. When the defendant obtained a verdict, or the plaintiff became non-suit, the former was wholly without remedy for any expenses he had incurred. It is true, the plaintiff was amerced *pro falso clamore suo*, but the amercement was given to the king. Hull on Costs, 2; 2 Arch. Pr. 281.

3. This defect was afterwards corrected by the statute of Gloucester, 6 Ed. I, c. 1, by which it is enacted that "the demandant in assise of novel disseisin, in writs of *mort d'ancestor, cosinage, aiel and besail,* shall have damages. And the demandant shall have the costs of the writ purchased, together with damages, and this act shall hold place in *all cases where the party recovers damages,* and every person shall render damages where land is recovered against him upon his own intrusion, or his own act." About forty-six years after the passing of this statute, costs were for the first time allowed in France, by an ordinance of Charles le Bel, (January, 1324.) See Hardw. Cas. 356; 2 Inst. 283, 288; 2 Loisel, Coutumes, 328-9.

4. The statute of Gloucester has been adopted, substantially, in all the United States. Though it speaks of the costs of the writ only, it has, by construction, been extended to the costs of the suit generally. The costs which are recovered under it are such as shall be allowed by the master or prothonotary upon taxation, and not those expenses which the plaintiff may have incurred for himself, or the extraordinary fees he may have paid counsel, or for the loss of his time. 2 Sell. Pr. 429.

5. Costs are single, when the party receives the same amount he has expended, to be ascertained by taxation; double, vide *Double costs;* and treble, vide *Treble costs.*

Vide, generally, Bouv. Inst. Index, h. t.; Hullock on Costs; Sayer's Law of Costs, Tidd's Pr. c. 40; 2 Sell. Pr. c. 19; Archb. Pr. Index, h. t.; Bac. Ab. h. t.; Com. Dig. h. t.; 6 Vin. Ab. 321; Grah. Pr. c. 23; Chit. Pr. h. t.; 1 Salk. 207; 1 Supp. to Ves. jr. 109; Amer. Dig. h. t.; Dane's Ab. h. t.; Harr. Dig. h. t. As to the liability of executors and administrators for costs, see 1 Chit. R. 628, note; 18 E. C. L. R. 185· 2 Bay's R. 166, 399; 1 Wash. R. 138; 2

Hen. & Munf. 361, 369; 4 John. R. 190; 8 John. R. 389; 2 John. Ca. 209. As to costs in actions *qui tam*, see Esp. on Pen. Act. 154 to 165.

COTTAGE, *estates*. A small dwelling-house. See 1 Tho. Co. Litt. 216; Sheph. Touchst. 94; 2 Bouv. Inst. n. 1571, note.

2. The grant of a cottage, it is said, passes a small dwelling-house, which has no land belonging to it. Shep. To. 94.

COUCHANT. Lying down. Animals are said to have been *levant* and *couchant*, when they have been upon another person's land, damage feasant, one night at least. 3 Bl. Com. 9.

COUNCIL, *legislation*. This word signifies an assembly.

2. It was used among the Romans to express the meeting of only a part of the people, and that the most respectable, in opposition to the assemblies of the whole people.

3. It is now usually applied to the legislative bodies of cities and boroughs.

4. In some states, as in Massachusetts, a body of men called the council, are elected, whose duties are to advise the governor in the executive part of the government. Const. of Mass. part 2, c. 2, s. 3, art. 1 and 2. See 14 Mass. 470; 3 Pick. 517; 4 Pick. 25; 19 John. R. 58. In England, the king's council are the king's judges of his courts of justice. 3 Inst. 125; 1 Bl. Com. 229.

COUNSEL. Advice given to another as to what he ought to do or not to do.

2. To counsel another to do an unlawful act, is to become accessory to it, if it be a felony, or principal, if it be treason, or a misdemeanor. By the term counsel is also understood counsellor at law. Vide *To open; Opening*.

COUNSEL, *an officer of court*. One who undertakes to conduct suits and actions in court. The same as counsellor.

COUNSEL, *practice, crim. law*. In the oath of the grand jurors, there is a provision requiring them to keep secret "the commonwealth's counsel, their fellows, and their own." In this sense, this word is synonymous with knowledge; therefore, all the knowledge acquired by grand jurors, in consequence of their office, either from the officers of the commonwealth, from their fellow-jurors, or which they have obtained in any manner, in relation to cases which come officially before them, must be kept secret. See *Grand Jury*.

COUNSELLOR, *government*. A counsellor is a member of a council. In some of the states the executive power is vested in a governor, or a governor and lieutenant governor, and council. The members of such council are called counsellors. See the names of the several states.

COUNSELLOR AT LAW, *offices*. An officer in the supreme court of the United States, and in some other courts, who is employed by a party in a cause, to conduct the same on its trial on his behalf. He differs from an attorney at law. (q. v.)

2. In the supreme court of the United States, the two degrees of attorney and counsel are kept separate, and no person is permitted to practise both. It is the duty of the counsel to draft or review and correct the special pleadings, to manage the cause on trial, and, during the whole course of the suit, to apply established principles of law to the exigencies of the case. 1 Kent, Com. 307.

3. Generally in the other courts of the United States, as well as in the courts of Pennsylvania, the same person performs the duty of counsellor and attorney at law.

4. In giving their advice to their clients, counsel and others, professional men have duties to perform to their clients, to the public, and to themselves. In such cases they have thrown upon them something which they owe to the fair administration of justice, as well as to the private interests of their employers. The interests propounded for them ought, in their own apprehension, to be just, or at least fairly disputable; and when such interests are propounded, they ought not to be pursued *per fas et nefas*. 1 Hagg. R. 222.

5. A counsellor is not a hired person, but a mandatory; he does not render his services for a price, but an honorarium, which may in some degree recompense his care, is his reward. Doubtless, he is not indifferent to this remuneration, but nobler motives influence his conduct. Follow him in his study when he examines his cause, and in court on the trial; see him identify himself with the idea of his client, and observe the excitement he feels on his account; proud when he is conqueror, discouraged, sorrowful, if vanquished; see his whole soul devoted to the cause he has undertaken, and which he believes to be just, then you perceive the elevated man, ennobled by the spirit of his profession, full of sympathy for his cause and his client.

He may receive a reward for his services, but such things cannot be paid for with money. No treasures can purchase the sympathy and devotedness of a noble mind to benefit humanity; these things are given, not sold. See *Honorarium*.

6. Ridley says, that the law has appointed no stipend to philosophers and lawyers, not because they are not reverend services and worthy of reward or stipend, but because either of them are most honorable professions, whose worthiness is not to be valued or dishonored by money. Yet, in these cases, many things are honestly taken, which are not honestly asked, and the judge may, according to the quality of the cause, and the skill of the advocate, and the custom of the court, and the worth of the matter that is in hand, appoint them a fee answerable to their place. View of the Civil and Eccles. Law, 38, 39.

COUNT, *pleading*. This word, derived from the French *conte*, a narrative, is in our old law books used synonymously with declaration; but practice has introduced the following distinction: when the plaintiff's complaint embraces only a single cause of action, and he makes only one statement of it, that statement is called, indifferently, a declaration or count; though the former is the more usual term.

2. But when the suit embraces two or more causes of action, (each of which of course requires a different statement;) or when the plaintiff makes two or more different statements of one and the same cause of action, each several statement is called a count, and all of them, collectively, constitute the declaration.

3. In all cases, however, in which there are two or more counts, whether there is actually but one cause of action or several, each count purports, upon the face of it, to disclose a distinct right of action, unconnected with that stated in any of the other counts.

4. One object proposed, in inserting two or more counts in one declaration, when there is in fact but one cause of action, is, in some cases, to guard against the danger of an insufficient statement of the cause, where a doubt exists as to the legal sufficiency of one or another of two different modes of declaring; but the more usual end proposed in inserting more than one count in such case, is to accommodate the statement to the cause, as far as may be, to the possible state of the proof to be exhibited on trial; or to guard, if possible, against the hazard of the proofs varying materially from the statement of the cause of action; so that if one or more of several counts be not adapted to the evidence, some other of them may be so. Gould on Pl. c. 4, s. 2, 3, 4; Steph. Pl. 279; Doct. Pl. 178; 3 Com. Dig. 291; Dane's Ab. Index, h. t.; Bouv. Inst. Index, h. t. In real actions, the declaration is most usually called a count. Steph. Pl. 36. See *Common count; Money count*.

COUNTER, *Eng. law*. The name of an ancient prison in the city of London, which has now been demolished.

COUNTER AFFIDAVIT. An affidavit made in opposition to one already made; this is allowed in the preliminary examination of some cases.

COUNTER SECURITY. Security given to one who has become security for another, the condition of which is, that if the one who first became surety shall be damnified, the one who gives the counter security will indemnify him.

TO COUNTERFEIT, *criminal law*. To make something false, in the semblance of that which is true; it always implies a fraudulent intent. Vide Vin. Ab. h. t.; *Forgery*.

COUNTERMAND. This word signifies a change or recall of orders previously given.

2. It may be express or implied. Express, when contrary orders are given and a revocation of the former order is made. Implied, when a new order is given which is inconsistent with the former order: as, if a man should order a merchant to ship him in a particular vessel certain goods which belonged to him, and then, before the goods were shipped, he directed him to ship them in another vessel; this would be a countermand of the first order.

3. While the first command is unrecalled, the person who gave it would be liable to all the consequences in case he should be obeyed; but if, for example, a man should command another to commit a crime, and, before its perpetration, he should repent and countermand it, he would not be liable for the consequences if the crime should afterwards be committed.

4. When a command or order has been given, and property delivered, by which a right vests in a third person, the party giving the order cannot countermand it; for example, if a debtor should deliver to A a sum of money to be paid to B, his creditor,

B has a vested right in the money, and unless he abandon that right, and refuse to take the money, the debtor cannot recover it from A. 1 Roll. Ab. 32, pl. 13; Yelv. 164; Sty. 296. See 3 Co. 26 b.; 2 Vent. 298; 10 Mod. 432; Vin. Ab. Countermand, A 1; Vin. Ab. Bailment, D; 9 East, 49; Roll. Ab. 606; Bac. Ab. Bailment, D; Com. Dig. Attorney, B 9, c. 8; Dane's Ab. h. t.; and *Command.*

COUNTERPART, *contracts.* Formerly each party to an indenture executed a separate deed; that part which was executed by the grantor was called the original, and the rest the counterparts. It is now usual for all the parties to execute every part, and this makes them all originals. 2 Bl. Com. 296.

2. In granting lots subject to a ground-rent reserved to the grantor, both parties execute the deeds, of which there are two copies; although both are original, one of them is sometimes called the counterpart. Vide 12 Vin. Ab. 104; Dane's Ab. Index, h. t.; 7 Com. Dig. 443; Merl. Répert. mots Double Ecrit.

COUNTERPLEA, *pleading.* When a tenant in any real action, tenant by the curtesy, or tenant in dower, in his answer and plea, vouches any one to warrant his title, or prays in aid another who has a larger estate, as of the remainder-man or reversioner; or when a stranger to the action comes and prays to be received to save his estate; then that which the defendant alleges against it, why it should not be admitted, is called a counterplea. T. de la Ley; Doct. Placit. 300; Com. Dig. h. t.; Dane's Ab. Index, h. t.

COUNTERS, *English law.* Formerly there were in London two prisons belonging to the sheriff's courts, which bore this name. They are now demolished. 4 Inst. 248.

COUNTERSIGN. To countersign is to sign on the opposite side of an instrument already signed by some other person or officer, in order to secure its character of a genuine paper; as, a bank note is signed by the president and countersigned by the cashier.

COUNTRY. By country is meant the state of which one is a member.

2. Every man's country is in general the state in which he happens to have been born, though there are some exceptions. See *Domicil; Inhabitant.* But a man has the natural right to expatriate himself, i. e. to abandon his country, or his right of citizenship acquired by means of naturalization in any country in which he may have taken up his residence. See *Allegiance; Citizen; Expatriation.* In another sense, country is the same as païs. (q. v.)

COUNTY. A district into which a state is divided.

2. The United States are generally divided into counties; counties are divided into townships or towns.

3. In Pennsylvania the division of the province into three counties, *viz.* Philadelphia, Bucks and Chester, was one of the earliest acts of William Penn, the original proprietary. There is no printed record of this division, or of the original boundaries of these counties. Proud says it was made about the year 1682. Proud's Hist. vol. 1, p. 234; vol. 2, p. 258.

4. In some states, as Illinois; 1 Breese, R. 115; a county is considered as a corporation; in others it is only a quasi corporation. 16 Mass. R. 87; 2 Mass. R. 544; 7 Mass. R. 461; 1 Greenl. R. 125; 3 Greenl. R. 131; 9 Greenl. R. 88; 8 John. R. 385; 3 Munf. R. 102. Frequent difficulties arise on the division of a county. On this subject, see 16 Mass. R. 86; 6 J. J. Marsh. 147; 4 Halst. R. 357; 5 Watts R. 87; 1 Cowen, R. 550; 6 Cowen, R. 642; 9 Cowen, R. 640; 4 Yeates, R. 399; 10 Mass. Rep. 290; 11 Mass. Rep. 339.

5. In the English law this word signifies the same as *shire,* county being derived from the French and shire from the Saxon. Both these words signify a circuit or portion of the realm, into which the whole land is divided, for the better government thereof, and the more easy administration of justice. There is no part of England that is not within some county, and the shire-reve, (sheriff) originally a yearly officer, was the governor of the county. Four of the counties of England, *viz.* Lancaster, Chester, Durham and Ely, were called counties Palatine, which were jurisdictions of a peculiar nature, and held by especial charter from the king. See stat. 27 H. VIII. c. 25.

COUNTY COMMISSIONERS. Certain officers generally entrusted with the superintendence of the collection of the county taxes, and the disbursements made for the county. They are administrative officers, invested by the local laws with various powers.

2. In Pennsylvania the office of county commissioner originated in the act of 1717, which was modified by the act of 1721, and afterwards enlarged by the act of 1724.

Before the office of county commissioner was established, assessors were elected who performed similar duties. See Act of 1700, 4 Votes of Assembly, 205, 209.

COUPONS. Those parts of a commercial instrument which are to be *cut*, and which are evidence of something connected with the contract mentioned in the instrument. They are generally attached to certificates of loan, where the interest is payable at particular periods, and, when the interest is paid, they are cut off and delivered to the payor.

COURIER. One who is sent on some public occasion as an express, to bear despatches, letters, and other papers.

2. Couriers sent by an ambassador or other public minister, are protected from arrest or molestation. Vattel, liv. 4, c. 9, § 123.

COURSE. The direction in which a line runs in surveying.

2. When there are no monuments, (q. v.) the land must be bounded by the courses and distances mentioned in the patent or deed. 4 Wheat. 444; 3 Pet. 96; 3 Murph. 82; 2 Har. & John. 267; 5 Har. & John. 254. When the lines are actually marked, they must be adhered to, though they vary from the course mentioned in the deeds. 2 Overt. 304; 7 Wheat. 7. See 3 Call, 239; 7 Monr. 333. Vide *Boundary; Line.*

COURSE OF TRADE. What is usually done in the management of trade or business.

2. Men are presumed to act for their own interest, and to pursue the way usually adopted by men generally; hence it is presumed in law, that men in their actions will pursue the usual course of trade. For this reason it is presumed that a bank note was signed before it was issued, though the signature be torn off. 2 Rob. Lo. R. 112. That one having possession of a bill of exchange upon him, has paid it; that one who pays an order or draft upon him, pays out of the funds of the drawer in his hands. But the case is different where the order is for the delivery of goods, they being presumed to have been sold by the drawee to the drawer. 9 Wend. 323; 1 Greenl. Ev. § 38.

COURSE OF THE VOYAGE. By this term is understood the regular and customary track, if such there be, which a ship takes in going from one port to another, and the shortest way. Marsh. on Ins. 185.

COURT, *practice*. A court is an incorporeal political being, which requires for its existence, the presence of the judges, or a competent number of them, and a clerk or prothonotary, at the time during which, and at the place where it is by law authorized to be held; and the performance of some public act, indicative of a design to perform the functions of a court.

2. In another sense, the judges, clerk, or prothonotary, counsellors and ministerial officers, are said to constitute the court.

3. According to Lord Coke, a court is a place where justice is judicially administered. Co. Litt. 58, a.

4. The judges, when duly convened, are also called the court. Vide 6 Vin. Ab. 484; Wheat. Dig. 127; Merl. Rép. h. t.; 3 Com. Dig. 300; 8 Id. 386; Dane's Ab. Index, h. t.; Bouv. Inst. Index, h. t.

5. It sometimes happens that the judges composing a court are equally divided on questions discussed before them. It has been decided, that when such is the case on an appeal or writ of error, the judgment or decree is affirmed. 10 Wheat. 66; 11 Id. 59. If it occurs on a motion in arrest of judgment, a judgment is to be entered on the verdict. 2 Dall. Rep. 388. If on a motion for a new trial, the motion is rejected. 6 Wheat. 542. If on a motion to enter judgment on a verdict, the judgment is entered. 6 Binn. 100. In England, if the house of lords be equally divided on a writ of error, the judgment of the court below is affirmed. 1 Arch. Pr. 235. So in Cam. Scacc. 1 Arch. Pr. 240. But in error coram nobis, no judgment can be given if the judges are equally divided, except by consent. 1 Arch. Pr. 246. When the judges are equally divided on the admission of testimony, it cannot be received. But see 3 Yeates, 171. Also, 2 Bin. 173; 3 Bin. 113; 4 Bin. 157; 1 Johns. Rep. 118; 4 Wash. C. C. Rep. 332, 3. See *Division of Opinion.*

6. Courts are of various kinds. When considered as to their powers, they are of record and not of record; Bac. Ab. Courts, D; when compared to each other, they are supreme, superior, and inferior, Id.; when examined as to their original jurisdiction, they are civil or criminal; when viewed as to their territorial jurisdiction, they are central or local; when divided as to their object, they are courts of law, courts of equity, courts martial, admiralty courts, and ecclesiastical courts. They are also courts of original jurisdiction, courts of

error, and courts of appeal. Vide *Open Court*.

7. Courts of record cannot be deprived of their jurisdiction except by express negative words. 9 Serg. & R. 298; 3 Yeates, 479; 2 Burr. 1042; 1 Wm. Bl. Rep. 285. And such a court is the court of common pleas in Pennsylvania. 6 Serg. & R. 246.

8. Courts of equity are not, in general, courts of record. Their decrees touch the person, not lands or goods. 3 Caines, 36. Yet, as to personalty, their decrees are equal to a judgment; 2 Madd. Chan. 355; 2 Salk. 507; 1 Ver. 214; 3 Caines, 35; and have preference according to priority. 3 P. Wms. 401 n.; Cas. Temp. Talb. 217; 4 Bro. P. C. 287; 4 Johns. Chan. Cas. 638. They are also conclusive between the parties. 6 Wheat. 109. Assumpsit will lie on a decree of a foreign court of chancery for a sum certain; 1 Campb. Rep. 253, per Lord Kenyon; but not for a sum not ascertained. 3 Caines, 37, (n.) In Pennsylvania, an action at law will lie on a decree of a court of chancery, but the pleas *nil debet* and nul tiel record cannot be pleaded in such an action. 9 Serg. & R. 258.

COURT CHRISTIAN. An ecclesiastical judicature, known in England, so called from its handling matters of an ecclesiastical or religious nature. 2 Inst. 488. Formerly the jurisdiction of these courts was not thus limited. The emperor Theodosius promulgated a law that all suits (lites) and forensic controversies should be remitted to the judgment of the church, if *either* of the litigating parties should require it. Fr. Duaren De Sac. Minist. Eccl. lib. 1, c. 2. This law was renewed and confirmed by Charlemagne.

COURT OF ARCHES, *eccl. law*. The most ancient consistory court belonging to the archbishop of Canterbury for the trial of spiritual causes. It is so called, because it was anciently held in the church of *Saint Mary le bow;* which church had that appellation from its steeple, which was raised at the top with stone pillars, in the manner of an arch or bow. Termes de la Ley.

COURT OF ADMIRALTY. A court having jurisdiction of all maritime causes. Vide *Admiralty; Courts of the United States; Instance Courts; Prize Court;* 2 Chit. Pr. 508 to 538.

COURT OF AUDIENCE, *Eng. eccl. law*. The name of a court kept by the archbishop in his palace, in which are transacted matters of form only; as confirmation of bishops, elections, consecrations, and the like.

COURT OF COMMON PLEAS. The name of an English court which was established on the breaking up of the *aula regis*, for the determination of pleas merely civil. It was at first ambulatory, but was afterwards located. This jurisdiction is founded on original writs issuing out of chancery, in the cases of common persons. But when an attorney or person belonging to the court, is plaintiff, he sues by writs of privilege, and is sued by bill, which is in the nature of a petition; both which originate in the common pleas. See *Bench; Banc.*

2. There are courts in most of the states of the United States which bear the name of common pleas; they have various powers and jurisdictions.

COURT OF CONSCIENCE, *Eng. law*. The name of a court in London. It has equity jurisdiction in certain cases. The reader is referred to Bac. Ab. Courts in London, 2.

COURT OF CONVOCATION, *eccles. law.* The name of an English ecclesiastical court. It is composed of every bishop, dean, and archdeacon, a proctor for the chapter, and two proctors for the clergy of each diocese in the province of Canterbury; for the province of York, there are two proctors for each archdeaconry.

2. This assembly meets at the time appointed in the king's writ, and constitute an ecclesiastical parliament. The archbishop and his suffragans, as his peers, are sitting together, and composing one house, called the upper house of convocation; the deans, archdeacons, and a proctor for the chapter, and two proctors for the clergy, the lower house. In this house a prolocutor, performing the duty of a president, is elected.

3. The jurisdiction of this tribunal extends to matters of heresy, schisms, and other mere spiritual or ecclesiastical causes. Bac. Ab. Ecclesiastical Courts, A 1.

COURT OF EXCHEQUER, *Eng. law.* A court of record anciently established for the trial of all matters relating to the revenue of the crown. Bac. Ab. h. t.

COURT OF FACULTIES, *Eng. eccl. law.* The name of a court which belongs to the archbishop, in which his officer, called *magister ad facultates*, grants dispensations to marry, to eat flesh on days prohibited, or to ordain a deacon under age, and the like. 4 Inst. 337.

COURT, INSTANCE. One of the branches

of the English admiralty is called an instance court. Vide *Instance Court.*

COURT OF INQUIRY. A court constituted by authority of the articles of war, invested with the power to examine into the nature of any transaction, accusation, or imputation against any officer or soldier; the said court shall consist of one or more officers, not exceeding three, and a judge advocate, or other suitable person, as a recorder, to reduce the proceedings and evidence to writing, all of whom shall be sworn to the performance of their duty. Art. 91. Gord. Dig. Laws U. S., art. 3558 to 3560.

COURT OF KING'S BENCH. The name of the supreme court of law in England. Vide *King's Bench.*

COURT MARTIAL. A court authorized by the articles of war, for the trial of all offenders in the army or navy, for military offences. Article 64, directs that general courts martial may consist of any number of commissioned officers, from five to thirteen, inclusively; but they shall not consist of less than thirteen, where the number can be convened, without manifest injury to the service.

2. The decision of the commanding officer who appoints the court, as to the number that can be convened without injury to the service, is conclusive. 12 Wheat. R. 19. Such a court has not jurisdiction over a citizen of the United States not employed in military service 12 John. R. 257. It has merely a limited jurisdiction, and to render its jurisdiction valid, it must appear to have acted within such jurisdiction. 3 S. & R. 590; 11 Pick. R. 442; 19 John. R. 7; 1 Rawle, R. 143.

3. A court martial must have jurisdiction over the subject-matter of inquiry, and over the person; for a want of these will render its judgment null, and the members of the court and the officers who execute its sentence, trespassers. 3 Cranch, 331. See 5 Wheat. 1; 12 Wheat. 19; 1 Brock. 324. Vide Gord. Dig. Laws U. S., art. 3331 to 3357; 2 Story, L. U. S. 1000; and also the Treatises of Adye, Delafon, Hough, J. Kennedy, M. V. Kennedy, McArthur, McNaghten, Simmons and Tyler on Courts Martial; and 19 John. R. 7; 12 John. R. 257; 20 John. R. 343; 5 Wheat. R. 1; 1 U. S. Dig. tit. Courts, V.

COURT OF PECULIARS, *Eng. eccl. law.* The name of a court, which is a branch of, and annexed to, the court of arches.

2. It has jurisdiction over all those parishes dispersed through the province of Canterbury, in the midst of other dioceses. In the other peculiars, the jurisdiction is exercised by commissaries. 1 Phill. R. 202, n.

3. There are three sorts of peculiars: 1. Royal peculiars. 3 Phill. R. 245. 2. The second sort are those in which the bishop has no concurrent jurisdiction, and are exempt from his visitation. 3. The third are subject to the bishop's visitation, and liable to his superintendence and jurisdiction. 3 Phill. R. 245; Skinn. R. 589.

COURT PREROGATIVE. Vide *Prerogative Court.*

COURT, PRIZE. One of the branches of the English admiralty, is called a prize court. Vide *Prize Court.*

COURT OF RECORD. At common law, any jurisdiction which has the power to fine and imprison, is a court of record. Salk. 200; Bac. Ab. Fines and Amercements, A. And courts which do not possess this power are not courts of record. See *Court.*

2. The act of congress, to establish an uniform rule of naturalization, &c., approved April 14, 1802, enacts, that for the purpose of admitting aliens to become citizens, that every court of record in any individual state, having common law jurisdiction and a seal, and a clerk or prothonotary, shall be considered as a district court within the meaning of this act.

COURT, SUPREME. Supreme court is the name of a court having jurisdiction over all other courts. Vide *Courts of the United States.*

COURTS OF THE UNITED STATES. The judiciary of the United States is established by virtue of the following provisions, contained in the third article of the constitution, namely:

2.—"§ 1. The judicial power of the United States shall be vested in one supreme court, and in such inferior courts as congress may, from time to time, ordain and establish. The judges, both of the supreme and inferior courts, shall hold their offices during good behaviour, and shall, at stated times, receive for their services a compensation, which shall not be diminished during their continuance in office.

3.—"§ 2. (1.) The judicial power shall exend to all cases in law and equity arising under this constitution, the laws of the United States, and treaties made, or which shall be made, under their authority; to all cases affecting ambassadors, other public ministers and consuls; to all cases of admiralty and maritime jurisdiction; to controversies to which the United States shall be a party; to controversies between two or more states, between a state and a citizen of another state, between citizens of different states, between citizens of the same state claiming lands under grants of different states, and between a state, or the citizens thereof, and foreign states, citizens or subjects.

4.—"(2.) In all cases affecting ambassadors, other public ministers and consuls, and those in which a state shall be party, the supreme court shall have original jurisdiction. In all the other cases before mentioned, the supreme court shall have appellate jurisdiction, both as to law and fact, with such exceptions, and under such regulations, as congress shall make.

5.—"(3.) The trial of all crimes, except in cases of impeachment, shall be by jury; and such trial shall be held in the state where the said crime shall have been committed; but when not committed within any state, the trial shall be at such place or places as congress may by law have directed."

6. By the amendments to the constitution, the following alteration has been made: "Art. 11. The judicial power of the United States shall not be construed to extend to any suit in law or equity, commenced or prosecuted against one of the United States by citizens of another state, or by citizens or subjects of any foreign state."

7. This subject will be considered by taking a view of, 1. The central courts; and 2. The local courts.

Art. 1 *The Central Courts of the United States.*

8. The central courts of the United States are, the senate, for the trial of impeachments, and the supreme court. The territorial jurisdiction of these courts extends over the whole country.

1. *Of the Senate of the United States.*

9.—1. The constitution of the United States, art. 1, § 3, provides that the senate shall have the sole power to try all impeachments. When sitting for that purpose, the senate shall be on oath or affirmation. When the president of the United States is tried, the chief justice shall preside; and no person shall be convicted without the concurrence of two-thirds of the members present.

10. It will be proper here to consider, 1. The organization of this extraordinary court; and, 2. Its jurisdiction.

11.—§ 1. Its *organization* differs according as it has or has not the president of the United States to try. For the trial of an impeachment of the president, the presence of the chief justice is required. There must also be a sufficient number of senators present to form a quorum. For the trial of all other impeachments, it is sufficient if a quorum be present.

12.—§ 2. The *jurisdiction* of the senate, as a court for the trial of impeachments, extends to the following officers, namely: the president, vice-president, and all civil officers of the United States, art. 2, § 4, when they shall have been guilty of treason, bribery, and other high crimes and misdemeanors. Id. The constitution defines treason, art. 3, § 3, but recourse must be had to the common law for a definition of bribery. Not having particularly mentioned what is to be understood by "other high crimes and misdemeanors," resort, it is presumed, must be had to parliamentary practice and the common law, in order to ascertain what they are. Story, Const. § 795.

2. *Of the Supreme Court.*

13. The constitution of the United States directs that the judicial power of the United States shall be vested in one supreme court; and in such inferior courts as congress may, from time to time, ordain and establish. It will be proper to consider, 1st. Its organization; 2dly. Its jurisdiction.

14.—§ 1. *Of the organization of the supreme court.* Under this head will be considered, 1. The appoinment of the judges. 2. The number necessary to form a quorum. 3. The time and place of holding the court.

15.—1. The judges of the supreme court are appointed by the president, by and with the consent of the senate. Const. art. 2, § 2. They hold their office during good behaviour, and receive for their services a compensation, which shall not be diminished during their continuance in office. Const. art. 3, § 1. They consist of a chief justice and eight associate justices. Act of March 3, 1837, § 1.

16.—2. Five judges are required to make a quorum, Act of March 3, 1837, § 1; but by the act of the 21st of January, 1829, the judges attending on the day appointed for holding a session of the court, although fewer than a quorum, at that time, four have authority to adjourn the court from day to day, for twenty days, after the time appointed for the commencement of said session, unless a quorum shall sooner attend:

and the business shall not be continued over till the next session of the court, until the expiration of the said twenty days. By the same act, if, after the judges shall have assembled, on any day less than a quorum shall assemble, the judge or judges so assembling shall have authority to adjourn the said court, from day to day, until a quorum shall attend, and, when expedient and proper, may adjourn the same without day.

17—3. The supreme court is holden at the city of Washington. Act of April 29, 1802. The session commences on the second Monday of January, in each and every year. Act of May, 4, 1826. The first Monday of August in each year is appointed as a return day. Act of April 29, 1802. In case of a contagious sickness, the chief justice or his senior associate may direct in what other place the court shall be held, and the court shall accordingly be adjourned to such place. Act of February 25, 1799, § 7. The officers of the court are a clerk, who is appointed by the court, a marshal, appointed by the president, by and with the advice and the consent of the senate, crier, and other inferior officers.

18.—§ 2. *Of the jurisdiction of the supreme court*. The jurisdiction of the supreme court is either civil or criminal.

19.—1. The *civil* jurisdiction is either original or appellate.

20.—(1.) The provisions of the constitution that relate to the *original* jurisdiction of the supreme court, are contained in the articles of the constitution already cited.

21. By the act of September 24th, 1789, § 13, the supreme court shall have exclusive jurisdiction of all controversies of a civil nature where a state is a party, except between a state and its citizens; and except also, between a state and citizens of other states or aliens, in which latter case it shall have original, but not exclusive jurisdiction. And shall have, exclusively, all such jurisdiction of suits or proceedings *against* ambassadors or other public ministers, or their domestics or domestic servants, as a court of law can have or exercise consistently with the law of nations. And original, but not exclusive jurisdiction of all suits brought *by* ambassadors or other public ministers, or in which a consul or vice-consul shall be a party. And the trial of issues in fact, in the supreme court, in all actions at law, against citizens of the United States, shall be by jury.

22. In consequence of the decision of the case of Chisholm *v.* Georgia, where it was held that assumpsit might be maintained against a state by a citizen of a different state, the 11th article of the amendments of the constitution above quoted, was adopted.

23. In those cases in which original jurisdiction is given to the supreme court, the judicial power of the United States cannot be exercised in its appellate form. With the exception of those cases in which original jurisdiction is given to this court, there is none to which the judicial power extends, from which the original jurisdiction of the inferior courts is excluded by the constitution.

24. The constitution establishes the supreme court and defines its jurisdiction. It enumerates the cases in which its jurisdiction is original and exclusive, and defines that which is appellate. See 11 Wheat. 467.

25. Congress cannot vest in the supreme court original jurisdiction in a case in which the constitution has clearly not given that court original jurisdiction; and affirmative words in the constitution, declaring in what cases the supreme court shall have original jurisdiction, must be construed negatively as to all other cases, or else the clause would be inoperative and useless. 1 Cranch, 137. See 5 Pet. 1; 5 Pet. 284; 12 Pet. 657; 9 Wheat. 738; 6 Wheat. 264.

26.—2. The supreme court exercises *appellate* jurisdiction in the following different modes:

(1.) By writ of error from the final judgments of the circuit courts; of the district courts, exercising the powers of circuit courts; and of the superior courts of the territories, exercising the powers of circuit courts, in certain cases. A writ of error does not lie to the supreme court to reverse the judgment of a circuit court, in a civil action by writ of error carried from the district court to the circuit court. The United States *v.* Goodwin, 7 Cranch, 108. But now, by the act of July 4, 1840, c. 20, § 3, it is enacted that writs of error shall lie to the supreme court from all judgments of a circuit court, in cases brought there by writs of error from the district court, in like manner and under the same regulations, as are provided by law for writs of error for judgments rendered upon suits originally brought in the circuit court.

27.—(2.) The supreme court has jurisdiction by appeals from the final decrees of the circuit courts; of the district courts exercising the powers of circuit courts; and of the superior courts of territories, exercising the powers of circuit courts in certain cases. See 8 Cranch, 251; 6 Wheat. 448.

28.—(3.) The supreme court has also jurisdiction by writ of error from the final judgments and decrees of the highest courts of law or equity in a state, in the cases provided for by the twenty-fifth section of the act of September 24th, 1789, which enacts that a final judgment or decree, in any suit in the highest court of law or equity of a state, in which a decision in the suit could be had, where is drawn in question the validity of a treaty, or statute of, or an authority exercised under, the United States, and the decision is against their validity; or where is drawn in question the validity of a statute of, or an authority exercised under any state, on the ground of their being repugnant to the constitution, treaties, or laws of the United States, and the decision is in favor of such their validity; or where is drawn in question the construction of any clause of the constitution, or of a treaty or statute of, or commission held under the United States, and the decision is against the title, right, privilege, or exemption specially set up or claimed by either party, under such clause of the said constitution, treaty, statute, or commission, may be re-examined, and reversed or affirmed in the supreme court of the United States, upon a writ of error, the citation being signed by the chief-justice or judge, or chancellor of the court rendering or passing the judgment or decree complained of, or by a justice of the supreme court of the United States, in the same manner, and under the same regulations, and the writ shall have the same effect as if the judgment or decree complained of had been rendered or passed in a circuit court; and the proceeding upon the reversal shall also be the same, except that the supreme court, instead of remanding the cause for a final decision as before provided, may, at their discretion, if the cause shall have been once remanded before, proceed to a final decision of the same, and award execution. But no other error shall be assigned or regarded as a ground of reversal, in any such case as aforesaid, than such as appears on the face of the record, and immediately respects the before mentioned questions of validity, or construction of the said constitution, treaties, statutes, commissions, or authorities in dispute. See 5 How. S. C. R. 20, 55.

29. The appellate jurisdiction of the supreme court extends to all cases pending in the state courts; and the twenty-fifth section of the judiciary act, which authorizes the exercise of this jurisdiction in the specified cases by writ of error, is supported by the letter and spirit of the constitution. 1 Wheat. 304.

30. When the construction or validity of a treaty of the United States is drawn in question in the state courts, and the decision is against its validity, or the title specially set up by either party under the treaty, the supreme court has jurisdiction to ascertain that title, and to determine its legal meaning. 1 Wheat. 358; 5 Cranch, 344; 9 Wheat. 738; 1 Pet. 94; 9 Pet. 224; 10 Pet. 368; 6 Pet. 515.

31. The supreme court has jurisdiction although one of the parties is a state, and the other a citizen of that state. 6 Wheat. 264.

32. Under the twenty-fifth section of the judiciary act, when any clause of the constitution or any statute of the United States is drawn in question, the decision must be against the title or right set up by the party under such clause or statute; otherwise the supreme court has no appellate jurisdiction of the case. 12 Wheat. 117, 129; 6 Wheat. 598; 3 Cranch, 268; 4 Wheat. 311; 7 Wheat. 164; 2 Peters, 449; 2 Pet. 241; 11 Pet. 167; 1 Pet. 655; 6 Pet. 41; 5 Pet. 248.

33. When the judgment of the highest court of law of a state, decides in favor of the validity of a statute of a state drawn in question, on the ground of its being repugnant to the constitution of the United States, it is not a final judgment within the twenty-fifth section of the judiciary act; if the suit has been remanded to the inferior court, where it originated, for further proceedings, not inconsistent with the judgment of the highest court. 12 Wheat. 135.

34. The words "matters in dispute" in the act of congress, which is to regulate the jurisdiction of the supreme court, seem appropriated to civil causes. 3 Cranch, 159. As to the manner of ascertaining the matter in dispute, see 4 Cranch, 216; 4 Dall. 22; 3 Pet. 33; 3 Dall. 365; 2 Pet. 243; 7 Pet. 634; 5 Cranch, 13; 4 Cranch, 316.

35.—(4.) The supreme court has jurisdiction by certificate from the circuit court, that the opinions of the judges are opposed on points stated, as provided for by the sixth section of the act of April 29th, 1802.

The provisions of the act extend to criminal as well as to civil cases. See 2 Cranch, 33, 10 Wheat. 20; 2 Dall. 385; 4 Hall's Law Journ. 462; 5 Wheat. 434; 6 Wheat. 542; 12 Wheat. 212; 7 Cranch, 279.

36.—(5.) It has also jurisdiction by mandamus, prohibition, habeas corpus, certiorari, and procedendo.

37.—2. The *criminal* jurisdiction of the supreme court is derived from the constitution and the act of September 24th, 1789, s. 13, which gives the supreme court exclusively, all such jurisdiction of suits or proceedings against ambassadors, or other public ministers, or their domestics, as a court of law can have or exercise consistently with the law of nations. But it must be remembered that the act of April 30th, 1790, sections 25 and 26, declares void any writ or process whereby the person of any ambassador, or other public minister, their domestics or domestic servants, may be arrested or imprisoned.

Art. 2. *The local courts.*

38. The local courts of the United States are, circuit courts, district courts, and territorial courts.

1. *The circuit courts.*

39. In treating of circuit courts, it will be convenient to consider, 1st. Their organization; and, 2d. Their jurisdiction.

40.—§ 1. *Of the organization of the circuit courts.* The circuit courts are the principal inferior courts established by congress. There are nine circuit courts, composed of the districts which follow, to wit:

41.—1. The *first* circuit consists of the districts of New Hampshire, Massachusetts, Rhode Island, and Maine. It consists of a judge of the supreme court and the district judge of the district where such court is holden. See Acts April 29, 1802; March 26, 1812; and March 30, 1820.

42.—2. The *second* circuit is composed of the districts of Vermont, Connecticut and New York. Act of March 3, 1837.

43.—3. The *third* circuit consists of the districts of New Jersey, and eastern and western Pennsylvania. Act of March 3, 1837.

44.—4. The *fourth* circuit is composed of Maryland, Delaware, and Virginia. Act of Aug. 16, 1842.

45.—5. The *fifth* circuit is composed of Alabama and Louisiana. Act of August 16, 1842.

46.—6. The *sixth* circuit consist of the districts of North Carolina, South Carolina, and Georgia. Act of Aug. 16, 1842.

47.—7. The *seventh* circuit is composed of Ohio, Indiana, Illinois, and Michigan. Act of March 3, 1837, § 1.

48.—8. The *eighth* circuit includes Kentucky, East and West Tennessee, and Missouri. Act of March 3, 1837, § 1. By the Act of April 14, 1842, ch. 20, § 1, it is enacted that the district court of the United States at Jackson, in the district of West Tennessee, shall in future be attached to, and form a part of the eighth judicial district of the United States, with all the power and jurisdiction of the circuit court held at Nashville, in the middle district of Tennessee.

49.—9. The *ninth* circuit is composed of the districts of Alabama, the eastern district of Louisiana, the district of Mississippi, and the district of Arkansas. Act of March 3, 1837, § 1.

50. In several districts of the United States, owing to their remoteness from any justice of the supreme court, there are no circuit courts held. But in these, the district court there is authorized to act as a circuit court, except so far as relates to writs of error or appeals from judgments or decrees in such district court.

51. The Act of March 3, 1837, provides, "That so much of any act or acts of congress as vests in the district courts of the United States for the districts of Indiana, Illinois, Missouri, Arkansas, the eastern district of Louisiana, the district of Mississippi, the northern district of New York, the western district of Virginia, and the western district of Pennsylvania, and the district of Alabama, or either of them, the power and jurisdiction of circuit courts, be, and the same is hereby, repealed; and there shall hereafter be circuit courts held for said districts by the chief or associate justices of the supreme court, assigned or allotted to the circuit to which such districts may respectively belong, and the district judges of such districts, severally and respectively, either of whom shall constitute a quorum; which circuit courts, and the judges thereof, shall have like powers, and exercise like jurisdiction as other circuit courts and the judges thereof; and the said district courts, and the judges thereof, shall have like powers, and exercise like jurisdiction, as the district courts, and the judges thereof in the other circuits. From all judgments and decrees, rend/red in the

district courts of the United States for the western district of Louisiana, writs of error and appeals shall lie to the circuit court in the other district in said state, in the same manner as from decrees and judgments rendered in the districts within which a circuit court is provided by this act."

52. In all cases where the day of meeting of the circuit court is fixed for a particular day of the month, if that day happen on Sunday, then, by the Act of 29th April, 1802, and other acts, the court shall be held the next day.

53. The Act of April 29, 1802, § 5, further provides, that on every appointment which shall be hereafter made, of a chief justice, or associate justice, the chief justice and associate justices shall allot among themselves the aforesaid circuits, as they shall think fit, and shall enter such allotment on record.

54. The Act of March 3, 1837, § 4, directs that the allotment of the chief justice and the associate justices of the said supreme court to the several circuits shall be made as heretofore.

55. And by the Act of August 16, 1842, the justices of the supreme court of the United States, or a majority of them, are required to allot the several districts among the justices of the said court.

56. And in case no such allotment shall be made by them, at their sessions next succeeding such appointment, and also, after the appointment of any judge as aforesaid, and before any other allotment shall have been made, it shall and may be lawful for the president of the United States, to make such allotment as he shall deem proper—which allotment, in either case, shall be binding until another allotment shall be made. And the circuit courts constituted by this act shall have all the power, authority and jurisdiction, within the several districts of their respective circuits, that before the 13th February, 1801, belonged to the circuit courts of the United States.

57. The justices of the supreme court of the United States, and the district judge of the district where the circuit is holden, compose the judges of the circuit court. The district judge may alone hold a circuit court, though no judge of the supreme court may be allotted to that circuit. Pollard *v.* Dwight, 4 Cranch, 421.

58. The Act of September 24th, 1789, § 6, provides, that a circuit court may be adjourned from day to day, by one of its judges, or if none are present, by the marshal of the district, until a quorum be convened. By the Act of May 19, 1794, a circuit court in any district, when it shall happen that no judge of the supreme court attends within four days after the time appointed by law, for the commencement of the sessions, may be adjourned to the next stated term, by the judge of the district, or, in case of his absence also, by the marshal of the district. But by the 4th section of the Act of April 29, 1802, where only one of the judges thereby directed to hold the circuit courts shall attend, such circuit court may be held by the judge so attending.

59. By the Act of March 2, 1809, certain duties are imposed on the justices of the supreme court, in case of the disability of a district judge within their respective circuits to hold a district court. Sect. 2, enacts, that in case of the disability of the district judge of either of the district courts of the United States, to hold a district court, and to perform the duties of his office, and satisfactory evidence thereof being shown to the justice of the supreme court allotted to that circuit, in which such district court ought, by law to be holden, and on application of the district attorney, or marshal of such district, in writing, the said justice of the supreme court shall, thereupon, issue his order in the nature of a certiorari, directed to the clerk of such district court, requiring him forthwith to certify unto the next circuit court, to be holden in said district, all actions, suits, causes, pleas, or processes, civil or criminal, of what nature or kind soever, that may be depending in such district court, and undetermined, with all the proceedings thereon, and all files, and papers relating thereto, which said order shall be immediately published in one or more newspapers, printed in said district, and at least thirty days before the session of such circuit court, and shall be deemed a sufficient notification to all concerned. And the said circuit court shall, thereupon, have the same cognizance of all such actions, suits, causes, pleas, or processes, civil or criminal, of what nature or kind soever, and in the like manner, as the district court of said district by law might have, or the circuit court, had the same been originally commenced therein, and shall proceed to hear and determine the same accordingly; and the said justice of the supreme court, during

the continuance of such disability, shall, moreover, be invested with, and exercise all and singular the powers and authority, vested by law in the judge of the district court in said district. And all bonds and recognizances taken for, or returnable to, such district court, shall be construed and taken to be the circuit court to be holden thereafter, in pursuance of this act, and shall have the same force and effect in such court as they would have had in the district court to which they were taken. *Provided*, that nothing in this act contained shall be so construed, as to require of the judge of the supreme court, within whose circuit such district may lie, to hold any special court, or court of admiralty, at any other time than the legal time for holding the circuit court of the United States in and for such district.

60. Sect. 2, provides, that the clerk of such district shall, during the continuance of the disability of the district judge, continue to certify, as aforesaid, all suits or actions, of what nature or kind soever, which may thereafter be brought to such district court, and the same transmit to the circuit court next thereafter to be holden in the same district. And the said circuit court shall have cognizance of the same, in like manner as is hereinbefore provided in this act, and shall proceed to hear and determine the same. *Provided*, nevertheless, that when the disability of the district judge shall cease, or be removed, all suits or actions then pending and undetermined in the circuit court, in which, by law, the district courts have an exclusive original cognizance, shall be remanded, and the clerk of the said circuit court shall transmit the same, pursuant to the order of the said court, with all matters and things relating thereto, to the district court next thereafter to be holden in said district, and the same proceedings shall be had therein, as would have been, had the same originated, or been continued, in the said district court.

61. Sect. 3, enacts, that in case of the district judge in any district being unable to discharge his duties as aforesaid, the district clerk of such district shall be authorized and empowered, by leave or order of the circuit judge of the circuit in which such district is included, to take, during such disability of the district judge, all examinations, and depositions of witnesses, and to make all necessary rules and orders, preparatory to the final hearing of all causes of admiralty and maritime jurisdiction. See 1 Gall. 337; 1 Cranch, 309; note to Hayburn's case, 3 Dall. 410.

62. If the disability of the district judge terminate in his death, the circuit court must remand the certified causes to the district court. Ex parte United States, 1 Gall. 337.

63. By the first section of the Act of March 3, 1821, in all suits and actions in any district court of the United States, in which it shall appear that the judge of such court is any ways concerned in interest, or has been of counsel for either party, or is so related to, or connected with, either party, as to render it improper for him, in his opinion, to sit on the trial of such suit or action, it shall be the duty of such judge, on application of either party, to cause the fact to be entered on the records of the court, and also an order that an authenticated copy thereof, with all the proceedings in such suit or action, shall be forthwith certified to the next circuit court of the district, and if there be no circuit court in such district, to the next circuit court in the state, and if there be no circuit court in such state, to the most convenient circuit court in an adjacent state; which circuit court shall, upon such record being filed with the clerk thereof, take cognizance thereof, in like manner as if such suit or action had been originally commenced in that court, and shall proceed to hear and determine the same accordingly, and the jurisdiction of such circuit court shall extend to all such cases to be removed, as were cognizable in the district court from which the same was removed.

64. And the Act of February 28, 1839, § 8, enacts, "That in all suits and actions, in any circuit court of the United States, in which it shall appear that both the judges thereof, or the judge thereof, who is solely competent by law to try the same, shall be any ways concerned in interest therein, or shall have been of counsel for either party, or is, or are so related to, or connected with, either party as to render it improper for him or them, in his or their opinion, to sit in the trial of such suit or action, it shall be the duty of such judge, or judges, on application of either party, to cause the fact to be entered on the records of the court; and, also, to make an order that an authenticated copy thereof, with all the proceedings in such suit or action, shall be

certified to the most convenient circuit court in the next adjacent state, or in the next adjacent circuit; which circuit court shall, upon such record and order being filed with the clerk thereof, take cognizance thereof in the same manner as if such suit or action had been rightfully and originally commenced therein, and shall proceed to hear and determine the same accordingly; and the proper process for the due execution of the judgment or decree rendered therein, shall run into, and may be executed in, the district where such judgment or decree was rendered; and, also, into the district from which such suit or action was removed."

65. The judges of the supreme court are not appointed as circuit court judges, or, in other words, have no distinct commission for that purpose: but practice and acquiescence under it, for many years, were held to afford an irresistible argument against this objection to their authority to act, when made in the year 1803, and to have fixed the construction of the judicial system. The court deemed the contemporary exposition to be of the most forcible nature, and considered the question at rest, and not to be disturbed then. Stuart *v.* Laird, 1 Cranch, 308. If a vacancy exist by the death of the justice of the supreme court to whom the district was allotted, the district judge may, under the act of congress, discharge the official duties, (Pollard *v.* Dwight, 4 Cranch, 428. See the fifth section of the Act of April 29, 1802,) except that he cannot sit upon a writ of error from a decision in the district court. United States *v.* Lancaster, 5 Wheat. 434.

66. It is enacted, by the Act of February 28, 1839, § 2, that all the circuit courts of the United States shall have the appointment of their own clerks; and in case of disagreement between the judges, the appointment shall be made by the presiding judge of the court.

67. The marshal of the district is an officer of the court, and the clerk of the district court is also clerk of the circuit court in such district. Act of September 24, 1789, § 7.

68. In the District of Columbia, there is a circuit court established by particular acts of congress, composed of a chief justice and two associates. See Act of February 27, 1801; 12 Pet. 524; 7 Pet. 203; 7 Wheat. R. 534; 3 Cranch, 159; 8 Cranch, 251 · 6 Cranch, 233.

§ 2. *Of the Jurisdiction of the Circuit Courts.*

69. The jurisdiction of the circuit courts is either civil or criminal.

(1.) *Civil Jurisdiction.*

The civil jurisdiction is either at law or in equity.

Their civil jurisdiction *at law* is, 1st. Original. 2d. By removal of actions from the state courts. 3d. By writ of mandamus. 4th. By appeal.

70.—1st. The *original* jurisdiction of the circuit courts at law, may be considered, first, as to the matter in controversy; second, with regard to the parties litigant.

(1.) *The Matter in Dispute.*

71. By the Act of September 24, 1789, § 11, to give jurisdiction to the circuit court, the matter in dispute must exceed $500. In actions to recover damages for torts, the sum laid in the declaration is the criterion as to the matter in dispute. 3 Dall. 358. In an action of covenant on an instrument under seal, containing a penalty less than $500, the court has jurisdiction if the declaration demand more than $500. 1 Wash. C. C. R. 1. In ejectment, the value of the land should appear in the declaration; 4 Wash. C. C. R. 624; 8 Cranch, 220; 1 Pet. 73; but though the jury do not find the value of the land in dispute, yet if evidence be given on the trial, that the value exceeds $500, it is sufficient to fix the jurisdiction; or the court may ascertain its value by affidavits. Pet. C. C. R. 73.

72. If the matter in dispute arise out of a local injury, for which a local action must be brought, in order to give the circuit court jurisdiction, it must be brought in the district where the lands lie. 4 Hall's Law Journal, 78.

73. By various acts of congress, jurisdiction is given to the circuit courts in cases where actions are brought to recover damages for the violation of patent and copyrights, without fixing any amount as the limit. See Acts of April 17, 1800, § 4; Feb. 15, 1819; 7 Johns. 144; 9 Johns. 507.

74. The circuit courts have jurisdiction in cases arising under the patent laws. By the Act of July 4, 1836, § 17, it is enacted, "That all actions, suits, controversies, and cases arising under any law of the United States, granting or confirming to inventors the exclusive right to their inventions or discoveries, shall be originally cognizable,

as well in equity as at law, by the circuit courts of the United States, or any district court having the powers and jurisdiction of a circuit court; which courts shall have power, upon bill in equity filed by any party aggrieved, in any such case, to grant injunctions, according to the course and principles of courts of equity, to prevent the violation of the rights of any inventor, as secured to him by any law of the United States, on such terms and conditions as said courts may deem reasonable. *Provided, however*, That from all judgments and decrees, from any such court rendered in the premises, a writ of error or appeal, as the case may require, shall lie to the supreme court of the United States, in the same manner and under the same circumstances as is now provided by law in other judgments and decrees of circuit courts, and in all other cases in which the court shall deem it reasonable to allow the same."

75. In general, the circuit court has no original jurisdiction of suits for penalties and forfeitures arising under the laws of the United States, nor in admiralty cases. 2 Dall. 365; 4 Dall. 342; Bee, 19.

(2.) *The character of the parties.*

76. Under this head will be considered, 1. The United States. 2. Citizens of different states. 3. Suits where an alien is a party. 4. When an assignee is plaintiff. 5. Defendant must be an inhabitant of the circuit.

(i.) *The United States.*

77. The United States may sue on all contracts in the circuit courts where the sum in controversy exceeds, besides costs, the sum of $500; but, in cases of penalties, the action must be commenced in the district court, unless the law gives express jurisdiction to the circuit courts. 4 Dall. 342. Under the Act of March 3, 1815, § 4, the circuit court has jurisdiction concurrently with the district court of all suits at common law where any officer of the United States sues under the authority of an act of congress; as where the post-master general sues under an act of congress for debts or balances due to the general post-office. 12 Wheat. 136. See 2 Pet. 447; 1 Pet. 318.

78. The circuit court has jurisdiction on a bill in equity filed by the United States against the debtor of their debtor, they claiming priority under the statute of March 2, 1798, c. 28, § 65, though the law of the state where the suit is brought permits a creditor to proceed against the debtor of his debtor by a peculiar process at law. 4 Wheat. 108.

(ii.) *Suits between citizens of different states.*

79. The Act of September 24, 1789, § 11, gives jurisdiction to the circuit court in suits of civil nature when the matter in dispute is of a certain amount, between a citizen of the state where the suit is brought, and a citizen of another state; one of the parties must therefore be a citizen of the state where the suit is brought. See 4 Wash. C. C. R. 84; Pet. C. C. R. 431; 1 Sumn. 581; 1 Mason, 520; 5 Cranch, 288; 3 Mason, 185; 8 Wheat. 699; 2 Mason, 472; 5 Cranch, 57; Id. 51; 6 Wheat. 450; 1 Pet. 238; 4 Wash. C. C. R. 482, n.; Id. 595.

80. Under this section the division of a state into two or more districts does not affect the jurisdiction of the circuit court, on account of citizenship. The residence of a party in a different district of a state from that in which the suit is brought, does not exempt him from the jurisdiction of the court; if he is found in the district where he is sued he is not within the prohibition of this section. 11 Pet. 25. A territory is not a state for the purpose of giving jurisdiction, and, therefore, a citizen of a territory cannot sue the citizen of a state in the circuit court. 1 Wheat. 91.

(iii.) *Suits where an alien is a party.*

81. The Act of September 24, 1780, § 11, gives the circuit court cognizance of all suits of a civil nature where an alien is a party; but these general words must be restricted by the provision in the constitution which gives jurisdiction in controversies between a state, or the citizens of a state, and foreign states, citizens or subjects; and the statute cannot extend the jurisdiction beyond the limits of the constitution. 4 Dall. 11; 5 Cranch, 303. When both parties are aliens, the circuit court has no jurisdiction. 4 Cranch, 46; 4 Dall. 11. An alien who holds lands under a special law of the state in which he is resident, may maintain an action in relation to those lands, in the circuit court. 1 Baldw. 216.

(iv.) *When an assignee is the plaintiff.*

82. The court has no jurisdiction unless a suit might have been prosecuted in such court to recover on the contract assigned, if no assignment had been made, except in cases of bills of exchange. Act of September 24, 1789, § 11; see 2 Pet. 319; 1 Mason, 243; 6 Wheat. 146; 11 Pet. 83;

9 Wheat. 537; 6 Cranch, 332; 4 Wash. C. C. R. 349; 4 Mason, 435; 12 Pet. 164; 2 Mason, 252. It is said that this section of the act of congress has no application to the conveyance of lands from a citizen of one state to a citizen of another. The grantee in such case may maintain his action in the circuit court, when otherwise properly qualified, to try the title to such lands. 2 Sumn. 252.

(v.) *The defendant must be an inhabitant of, or found in the circuit.*

83. The circuit court has no jurisdiction of an action against a defendant unless he be an inhabitant of the district in which such court is located, or found therein, at the time of serving the writ. 3 Wash. C. C. R. 456. A citizen of one state may be sued in another, it the process be served upon him in the latter; but in such cases, the plaintiff must be a citizen of the latter state, or an alien. 1 Pet. C. C. R. 431.

2d. *Removal of actions from the state courts.*

84. The Act of September 24, 1789, gives, in certain cases, the right of removing a suit instituted in a state court to the circuit court of the district. It is enacted by that law, that if a suit be commenced in any state court against an alien, or by a citizen of the state in which the suit is brought, against a citizen of another state, and the matter in dispute exceeds the aforesaid sum or value of five hundred dollars, exclusive of costs, to be made to appear to the satisfaction of the court, and the defendant shall, at the time of entering his appearance in such state court, file a petition for the removal of the cause for trial, into the next circuit court, to be held in the district where the suit is pending, and offer good and sufficient security for his entering in such court, on the first day of its session, copies of the said process against him, and also for his then appearing and entering special bail in the cause, if special bail was originally required therein, it shall then be the duty of the state court to accept the surety, and proceed no further in the cause. And any bail that may have been originally taken shall be discharged. And the said copies being entered as aforesaid in such court of the United States, the cause shall there proceed in the same manner as if it had been brought there by original process. And any attachment of the goods or estate of the defendant, by the original process, shall hold the goods or estate so attached, to answer the final judgment, in the same manner as by the laws of such state they would have been holden to answer final judgment, had it been rendered by the circuit court in which the suit commenced. Vide Act of September 24, 1789, § 12; 4 Dall. 11; 5 Cranch, 303; 4 Johns. R. 493; 1 Pet. R. 220; 2 Yeates, R. 275; 4 W. C. C. R. 286, 344.

85. By the Constitution, art. 3, § 2, 1, the judicial power shall extend to controversies between citizens of the same state, claiming lands under grants of different states.

86. By a clause of the 12th section of the Act of September 24th, 1789, it is enacted, that, if in any action commenced in a state court, the title of land be concerned, and the parties are citizens of the same state, and the matter in dispute exceeds the sum or value of five hundred dollars, exclusive of costs, the sum or value being made to appear to the satisfaction of the court, either party, before the trial, shall state to the court, and make affidavit, if it require it, that he claims, and shall rely upon a right or title to the land, under grant from a state, other than that in which the suit is pending, and produce the original grant, or an exemplification of it, except where the loss of records shall put it out of his power, and shall move that the adverse party inform the court, whether he claims a right of title to the land under a grant from the state in which the suit is pending; the said adverse party shall give such information, otherwise not be allowed to plead such grant, or give it in evidence upon the trial; and if he informs that he does claim under any such grant, the party claiming under the grant first mentioned, may then, on motion, remove the cause for trial, to the next circuit court to be holden in such district. But if he is the defendant, he shall do it under the same regulations as in the before mentioned case of the removal of a cause into such court by an alien. And neither party removing the cause shall be allowed to plead, or give evidence of, any other title than that by him stated as aforesaid, as the ground of his claim. See 9 Cranch, 292; 2 Wheat. R. 378.

87. Application for removal must be made during the term at which the defendant enters his appearance. 1 J. J. Marsh. 232. If a state court agree to consider a petition to remove the cause as filed of the preceding term, yet if the circuit court see by the record, that it was not filed till a

subsequent term, they will not permit the cause to be docketed. Pet. C. C. R. 44; Paine, 410; but see 2 Penning. 625.

88. In chancery, when the defendant wishes to remove the suit, he must file his petition when he enters his appearance; 4 Johns. Ch. 94; and in an action in a court of law, at the time of putting in special bail. 12 Johns. 153. And if an alien file his petition when he filed special bail, he is in time, though the bail be excepted to. 1 Caines, 248; Coleman, 58. A defendant in ejectment may file his petition when he is let in to defend. 4 Johns. 493. See Pet. C. C. R. 220; 2 Wash. C. C. R. 463; 2 Yeates, 275, 352; 3 Dall. 467; 4 Wash. C. C. R. 286; 2 Root 444; 5 John. Ch. R. 300; 3 Ham. 48; 4 Wash. C. C. R. 84.

3d. Remedy by Mandamus.

89. The power of the circuit court to issue a mandamus, is confined, exclusively, to cases in which it may be necessary for the exercise of a jurisdiction already existing; as, for instance, if the court below refuse to proceed to judgment, then a mandamus in the nature of a procedendo may issue. 7 Cranch, 504; 6 Wheat. R. 598. After the state court had refused to permit the removal of a cause on petition, the circuit court issued a mandamus to transfer the cause.

4th. Appellate Jurisdiction.

90. The appellate jurisdiction is exercised by means of, 1. Writs of error. 2 Appeals from the district courts in admiralty and maritime jurisdiction. 3. Certiorari. 4. Procedendo.

91.—[1.] This court has jurisdiction to issue writs of error to the district court, on judgments of that court in civil cases at common law.

92. The 11th section of the Act of September 24, 1789, provides, that the circuit courts shall also have appellate jurisdiction from the district courts, under the regulations and restrictions thereinafter provided.

93. By the 22d section, final decrees and judgments in civil actions in a district court, where the matter in dispute exceeds the sum or value of fifty dollars, exclusive of costs, may be reëxamined, and reversed or affirmed in a circuit court holden in the same district, upon a writ of error, whereto shall be annexed and returned therewith at the day and place therein mentioned, an authenticated transcript of the record and assignment of errors, and prayer for reversal, with a citation to the adverse party, signed by the judge of such district court, or a justice of the supreme court, the adverse party having at least twenty days' notice. But there shall be no reversal on such writ of error, for error in ruling any plea in abatement, other than a plea to the jurisdiction of the court, or for any error in fact. And writs of error shall not be brought but within five years after rendering or passing the judgment or decree complained of; or, in case the person entitled to such writ of error be an infant, *non compos mentis*, or imprisoned, then within five years, as aforesaid, exclusive of the time of such disability. And every justice or judge signing a citation or any writ of error as aforesaid, shall take good and sufficient security, that the plaintiff in error shall prosecute his writ to effect, and answer all damages and costs, if he fail to make his plea good.

94. The district judge cannot sit in the circuit court on a writ of error to the district court. 5 Wheat. R. 434.

95. It is observed above, that writs of error may be issued to the district court in civil cases at common law, but a writ of error does not lie from a circuit to a district court in an admiralty or maritime cause. 1 Gall. R. 5.

96.—[2.] Appeals from the district to the circuit court take place generally in civil causes of admiralty or maritime jurisdiction.

97. By the Act of March 3, 1803, § 2, it is enacted, that from all final judgments or decrees in any of the district courts of the United States, an appeal where the matter in dispute, exclusive of costs, shall exceed the sum or value of fifty dollars, shall be allowed to the district court next to be holden in the district where such final judgment or judgments, decree or decrees shall be rendered: and the circuit courts are thereby authorized and required, to hear and determine such appeals.

98.—[3.] Although no act of congress authorizes the circuit court to issue a certiorari to the district court for the removal of a cause, yet if the cause be so removed, and instead of taking advantage of the irregularity in proper time and in a proper manner, the defendant makes the defence and pleads to issue, he thereby waives the objection, and the suit will be considered as an original one in the circuit court, made so by consent of parties. 2 Wheat. R. 221.

99.—[4.] The circuit court may issue a writ of procedendo to the district court.

2. *Equity Jurisdiction of the Circuit Courts.*

100. Circuit courts are vested with equity jurisdiction in certain cases. The Act of September, 1789, § 11, gives original cognizance, concurrent with the courts of the several states, of all suits of a civil nature at common law or in *equity*, where the matter in dispute exceeds, exclusive of costs, the sum or value of five hundred dollars, and the United States are plaintiffs or petitioners, or an alien is a party, or the suit is between a citizen of the state where the suit is brought and a citizen of another state.

101. The Act of April 15, 1819, § 1, provides, "That the circuit court of the United States shall have original cognizance, as well in equity as at law, of all actions, suits, controversies, and cases arising under any law of the United States, granting or comfirming to authors or inventors, the exclusive right to their respective writings, inventions, and discoveries; and upon any bill in equity filed by any party aggrieved, in such cases, shall have authority to grant injunctions according to the course and principles of courts of equity, to prevent the violation of the rights of any authors or inventors, secured to them by any laws of the United States, on such terms and conditions as the said courts may deem fit and reasonable: *provided, however*, that from all judgments and decrees of any circuit courts rendered in the premises, a writ of error or appeal, as the case may require, shall lie to the supreme court of the United States, in the same manner and under the same circumstances, as is now provided by law, in other judgments and decrees of such circuit court."

102. By the Act of August 23, 1842, it is enacted, § 5, "That the district courts, as courts of admiralty, and the circuit courts, as courts of equity, shall be deemed always open for the purpose of filing libels, bills, petitions, answers, pleas, and other pleadings, for issuing and returning mesne and final process and commissions, and for making and directing all interlocutory motions, orders, rules, and other proceedings whatever, preparatory to the hearing of all causes pending therein upon their merits. And it shall be competent for any judge of the court, upon reasonable notice to the parties, in the clerk's office or at chambers, and in vacation as well as in term, to make and direct, and award all such process, commissions, and interlocutory orders, rules, and other proceedings, whenever the same are not grantable of course according to the rules and practice of the court."

(2.) *Criminal Jurisdiction of the Circuit Courts.*

103. The often cited 11th section of the Act of the 24th of September, 1789, gives the circuit courts exclusive cognizance of all crimes and offences cognizable under the authority of the United States, except where that act otherwise provides, or the laws of the United States shall otherwise direct, and concurrent jurisdiction with the district courts of the crimes and offences cognizable therein. The jurisdiction of the circuit courts in criminal cases is confined to offences committed within the district for which those courts respectively sit when they are committed on land. Serg. Const. Law, 129; 1 Gallis. 488.

2. *Of the District Courts.*

104. In treating of *district courts*, the same division which was made, in considering circuit courts, will here be adopted, by taking a view, 1. Of their organization; and, 2. Of their jurisdiction.

§ 1. *Of the Organization of the District Courts.*

105. The United States are divided into districts, in each of which is a court called a district court, which is to consist of one judge, who is to reside in the district for which he is appointed, and to hold annually four sessions. Act of September 24, 1789. By subsequent acts of congress, the number of annual sessions in particular districts, is sometimes more and sometimes less; and they are to be held at various places in the district. There is also a district court in the District of Columbia, held by the chief justice of the circuit court of that district.

§ 2. *Jurisdiction of the District Courts.*

106. Their jurisdiction is either civil or criminal.

107.—(1.) Their *civil* jurisdiction extends, 1. To admiralty and maritime causes: the admiralty and maritime jurisdiction, is either the ordinary jurisdiction, which comprehends prize suits; cases of salvage; actions for torts; and actions on contracts, such as seamen's wages, pilotage, bottomry, ransom, materials, and the like; or the extraordinary or expressly vested jurisdiction, which includes cases of seizures under the revenue laws, &c.; and captures within the jurisdiction of the United States.

108.—2. To cases of seizure on land

under the laws of the United States, and in suits for penalties and forfeitures, incurred under the laws of the United States.

109.—3. To cases in which an alien sues for a tort, in violation of the laws of nations, or a treaty of the United States.

110.—4. To suits instituted by the United States.

111.—5. To actions by and against consuls.

112.—6. To certain cases in equity.

113.—1. The admiralty and maritime jurisdiction of the district court is ordinary or extraordinary.

114.—1st. The *ordinary* jurisdiction is granted by the Act of September 24th, 1789, § 9. It is there enacted, that the district court shall have exclusive original cognizance of all civil causes of admiralty and maritime jurisdiction. This jurisdiction is exclusive. Bee, 19; 3 Dall. 16; Paine, 111; 4 Mason, 139.

115. This ordinary jurisdiction is exercised in,

116.—(1.) *Prize suits.* The Act of September 24, 1789, § 9, vests in the district courts as full jurisdiction of all prize causes as the admiralty of England; and this jurisdiction is an ordinary inherent branch of the powers of the court of admiralty, whether considered as *prize* courts or *instance* courts. 3 Dall. 16; Paine, 111.

117. The act of congress marks out not only the general jurisdiction of the district courts, but also that of the several courts in relation to each other, in cases of seizure on the waters of the United States, navigable, &c. When the seizure is made within the waters of one district, the court of that district has exclusive jurisdiction, though the offence may have been committed out of the district. When the seizure is made on the high seas, the jurisdiction is in the court of the district where the property may be brought. 9 Wheat. 402; 6 Cranch, 281; 1 Mason, 360; Paine, 40.

118. When the seizure has been made within the waters of a foreign nation, the district court has jurisdiction, when the property has been brought into the district, and a prosecution has been instituted there. 9 Wheat. 402; 9 Cranch. 102.

119. The district court has jurisdiction of seizures, and of the question who is entitled to their proceeds, as informers or otherwise; and the principal jurisdiction is exclusive; the question, as to who is the informer, is also exclusive. 4 Mason, 139.

120.—(2.) *Cases of salvage.* Under the constitution and laws of the United States, this court has exclusive original cognizance in cases of salvage; and, as a consequence, it has the power to determine to whom the residue of the property belongs, after deducting the salvage. 3 Dall. 183.

121.—(3.) *Actions arising out of torts and injuries.* The district court has jurisdiction over all torts and injuries committed on the high seas, and in ports or harbors within the ebb and flow of the tide. Vide 1 Wheat. R. 304; 2 Gall. R. 389; 1 Mason, 96; 3 Mason, 242; 4 Mason, 380; 18 Johns. R. 257.

122. A court of admiralty has jurisdiction to redress personal wrongs committed on a passenger, on the high seas, by the master of a vessel, whether those wrongs be by direct force or consequential injuries. 3 Mason, 242.

123. The admiralty may decree damages for an unlawful capture of an American vessel by a French privateer, and may proceed by attachment *in rem.* Bee, 60.

124. It has jurisdiction in cases of maritime torts, *in personam* as well as *in rem.* 10 Wheat. 473.

125. This court has also jurisdiction of petitory suits to reinstate owners of vessels who have been displaced from their possession. 5 Mason, 465. It exercises jurisdiction of all torts and injuries committed on the high seas, and in ports or harbors within the flow or ebb of the tide. 2 Gallis. 398; Bee, 51.

126. A father, whose minor son has been tortiously abducted and seduced on a voyage on the high seas, may sue, in the admiralty, in the nature of an action *per quod*, &c., also for wages earned by such son in maritime service. 4 Mason, 380.

127.—(4.) *Suits on contracts.* As a court of admiralty, the district court has a jurisdiction, concurrent with the courts of common law, over all maritime contracts, wheresoever the same may be made or executed, or whatsoever be the form of the contract. 2 Gallis. 398. It may enforce the performance of charter-parties for foreign voyages, and by proceeding *in rem*, a lien for freight under them. 1 Sumn. 551; 2 Sumn. 589. It has jurisdiction over contracts for the hire of seamen, when the service is substantially performed on the sea, or on waters within the flow and reflow of the tide 10 Wheat. 428; 7 Pet. 324; Bee, 199; Gilp. 529. But unless the services are essentially maritime, the jurisdiction does not attach. 10 Wheat. 428; Gilp. 529.

128. The master of a vessel may sue in the admiralty, for his wages; and the mate, who on his death succeeds him, has the same right. 1 Sumn. 157; 9 Mason, 161; 4 Mason, 196. But when the services for which he sues have not been performed by him as master, they cannot be sued for in admiralty. 3 Mason, 161.

129. The jurisdiction of the admiralty attaches when the services are performed on a ship in port where the tide ebbs and flows. 7 Pet. 324; Gilp. 529.

130. Seamen, employed on board of steamboats and lighters engaged in trade or commerce on tide-water, are within the admiralty jurisdiction. But those in ferry-boats are not so. Gilp. 532; Gilp. 203.

131. Wages may be recovered in the admiralty by the pilot, deck-hands, engineer, and firemen, on board of a steamboat. Gilp. 505.

132. But unless the service of those employed contribute in navigating the vessel, or to its preservation, they cannot sue for their wages in the admiralty; musicians on board of a vessel, who are hired and employed as such, cannot therefore enforce a payment of their wages by a suit *in rem* in the admiralty. Gilp. 516.

133.—2d. The *extraordinary* jurisdiction of the district court, as a court of admiralty, or that which is vested by various acts of congress, consists of—

(1.) Seizures under the laws of imposts, navigation, or trade of the United States. It is enacted, by the Act of September 24, 1789, § 9, that the district court shall have exclusive original cognizance of all civil causes of admiralty and maritime jurisdiction, including all seizures under laws of impost, navigation, or trade of the United States, when the seizures are made on waters which are navigable from the sea, by vessels of ten or more tons burden, within their respective districts, as well as upon the high seas; saving to suitors, in all cases, the right of a common law remedy, when the common law is competent to give it.

134. Causes of this kind are to be tried by the district court, and not by a jury. 4 Cranch, 438; 5 Cranch, 281; 1 Wheat. 9, 20; 7 Cranch, 112; 3 Dall. 297.

135. It is the place of seizure, and not the committing of the offence, that, under the Act of September 24, 1789, gives jurisdiction to the court; 4 Cranch, 443; 5 Cranch, 304; for until there has been a seizure, the forum cannot be ascertained. 9 Cranch, 289.

136. When the seizure has been voluntarily abandoned, it loses its validity, and no jurisdiction attaches to any court, unless there be a new seizure. 10 Wheat. 325; 1 Mason, 361.

137.—(2.) The admiralty jurisdiction, expressly vested in the district court, embraces, also, captures made within the jurisdictional limits of the United States. By the Act of April 20, 1818, § 7, the district court shall take cognizance of complaints, by whomsoever instituted, in cases of captures made within the waters of the United States, or within a marine league of the coasts and shores thereof.

138.—2. The civil jurisdiction of the district court extends to cases of seizure on land, under the laws of the United States, and in suits for penalties and forfeitures incurred under the laws of the United States.

139. The Act of September 24, 1789, § 9, gives to the district court exclusive original cognizance of all seizures made on land, and other waters than as aforesaid, (that is, those which are navigable by vessels of ten or more tons burden, within their respective districts, or on the high seas,) and of all suits for penalties and forfeitures incurred under the laws of the United States.

140. In all cases of seizure on land, the district court sits as a court of common law, and its jurisdiction is entirely distinct from that exercised in case of seizure on waters navigable by vessels of ten tons burden and upwards. 8 Wheat. 395.

141. Seizures of this kind are triable by jury; they are not cases of admiralty and maritime jurisdiction. 4 Cranch, 443.

142.—3. The civil jurisdiction of the district court extends also to cases in which an alien sues for a tort, in violation of the law of nations, or a treaty of the United States.

143. The Act of September 24, 1789, § 9, directs that the district court shall have cognizance, concurrent with the courts of the several states, or the circuit courts, as the case may be, of all causes where an alien sues for a tort only, in violation of the law of nations, or of a treaty of the United States.

144.—4. The civil jurisdiction of this

court extends further to suits instituted by the United States. By the 9th section of the Act of September 24, 1789, the district court shall also have cognizance, concurrent as last mentioned, of all suits at common law, where the United States sue, and the matter in dispute amounts, exclusive of costs, to the sum or value of one hundred dollars. And by the Act of March 3, 1815, § 4, it has cognizance, concurrent with the courts and magistrates of the several states, and the circuit courts of the United States, of all suits at common law where the United States, or any officer thereof, under the authority of any act of congress sue, although the debt, claim, or other matter in dispute, shall not amount to one hundred dollars.

145. These last words do not confine the jurisdiction given by this act to one hundred dollars, but prevent it from stopping at that sum: and consequently, suits for sums over one hundred dollars are cognizable in the district, circuit, and state courts, and before magistrates, in the cases here mentioned. By virtue of this act, these tribunals have jurisdiction over suits brought by the postmaster-general, for debts and balances due the general post office. 12 Wheat. 147; 2 Pet. 447; 1 Pet. 318.

146.—5. This court has jurisdiction of actions by and against consuls or vice-consuls, exclusively of the courts of the several states, except for offences where other punishment than whipping not exceeding thirty stripes, a fine not exceeding one hundred dollars, or a term of imprisonment not exceeding six months, is inflicted.

147. For offences above this description formerly the circuit court only had jurisdiction in cases of consuls. 5 S. & R. 545; 2 Dall. 299. But by the Act of August 23, 1842, the district courts shall have concurrent jurisdiction with the circuit courts of all crimes and offences against the United States, the punishment of which is not capital. And by the Act of February 28, 1839, § 5, the punishment of whipping is abolished. See also the Act of 28th Sept. 1850, making appropriations for the naval service, &c.

148.—6. The jurisdiction of the district court under the bankrupt laws will be found under the title *Bankrupt*.

149.—7. The district courts have equitable jurisdiction in certain cases.

150. By the first section of the Act of February 13, 1807, the judges of the district courts of the United States shall have as full power to grant writs of injunctions, to operate within their respective districts, as is now exercised by any of the judges of the supreme court of the United States, under the same rules, regulations, and restrictions, as are prescribed by the several acts of congress establishing the judiciary of the United States, any law to the contrary notwithstanding. *Provided*, that the same shall not, unless so ordered by the circuit court, continue longer than to the circuit then next ensuing; nor shall an injunction be issued by a district judge in any case, where the party has had a reasonable time to apply to the circuit court for the writ.

151. An injunction may be issued by the district judge under the Act of March 3, 1820, §§ 4, 5, where proceedings have taken place by warrant and distress against a debtor to the United States or his sureties, subject by § 6, to appeal to the circuit court from the decision of such district judge in refusing or dissolving the injunction, if such appeal be allowed by a justice of the supreme court. On which, with an exception as to the necessity of an answer on the part of the United States, the proceedings are to be as in other cases.

152. The Act of September 24, 1789, § 14, vests in the judges of the district courts, power to grant writs of habeas corpus, for the purpose of an inquiry into the cause of commitment.

153. Other acts give them power to issue writs, make rules, take depositions, &c. The acts of congress already treated of relating to the privilege of not being sued out of the district of which the defendant is an inhabitant, or in which he is found, restricting suits by assignees, and various others, apply to the district court as well as to the circuit court.

154. By the 9th section of the Act of September 24, 1789, the trial of issues in fact in the district courts, in all causes except civil causes of admiralty and maritime jurisdiction, shall be by jury. Serg. Const. Law, 226, 227.

(2.) *The criminal jurisdiction of the district court.*

155. By the Act of August 23, 1842, § 3, it is enacted that the district courts of the United States shall have concurrent jurisdiction with the circuit courts, of all crimes and offences against the United States, the punishment of which is not capital.

156. There is a class of district courts of a peculiar description. These exercise the power of a circuit court, under the same regulations as they were formerly exercised by the district court of Kentucky, which was the first of the kind.

157. The Act of September 24, 1789, § 10, gives the district court of the Kentucky district, besides the usual jurisdiction of a district court, the jurisdiction of all causes, except of appeals and writs of error, thereinafter made cognizable in a circuit court, and writs of error and appeals were to lie from decisions therein to the supreme court, and under the same regulations. By the 12th section, authority was given to remove cases from a state court to such court, in the same manner as to a circuit court.

3. *The territorial courts.*

158. The act to establish the territorial government of Oregon, approved August 14, 1848, establishes the judicial power of the said territory as follows:

§ 9. The judicial power of said territory shall be vested in a supreme court, district courts, probate courts, and in justices of the peace. The supreme court shall consist of a chief justice and two associate justices, any two of whom shall constitute a quorum, and who shall hold a term at the seat of government of said territory annually; and they shall hold their offices during the period of four years, and until their successors shall be appointed and qualified. The said territory shall be divided into three judicial districts, and a district court shall be held in each of said districts by one of the justices of the supreme court, at such times and places as may be prescribed by law; and the said judges shall after their appointments, respectively, reside in the districts which shall be assigned them. The jurisdiction of the several courts herein provided for, both appellate and original, and that of the probate courts and of justices of the peace, shall be as limited by law: *Provided*, That justices of the peace shall not have jurisdiction of any case in which the title to land shall in anywise come in question, or where the debt or damages claimed shall exceed one hundred dollars; and the said supreme and district courts, respectively, shall possess chancery, as well as common law, jurisdiction. Each district court, or the judge thereof, shall appoint its clerk, who shall also be the register in chancery, and shall keep his office at the place where the court may be held. Writs of error, bills of exception, and appeals, shall be allowed in all cases from the final decisions of said district courts to the supreme court, under such regulations as may be prescribed by law; but in no case removed to the supreme court shall trial by jury be allowed in said court. The supreme court, or the justices thereof, shall appoint its own clerk, and every clerk shall hold his office at the pleasure of the court for which he shall have been appointed. Writs of error and appeals from the final decisions of the said supreme court shall be allowed, and may be taken to the supreme court of the United States, in the same manner, and under the same regulations, as from the circuit courts of the United States, where the value of the property, or the amount in controversy, to be ascertained by the oath or affirmation of either party, or other competent witness, shall exceed two thousand dollars; and in all cases where the constitution of the United States, or acts of congress, or a treaty of the United States, is brought in question; and each of the said district courts shall have and exercise the same jurisdiction in all cases arising under the constitution of the United States, and the laws of said territory, as is vested in the circuit and district courts of the United States; writs of error and appeal in all such cases shall be made to the supreme court of said territory, the same as in other cases. Writs of error and appeals from the final decisions of said supreme court shall be allowed, and may be taken to the supreme court of the United States, in the same manner as from the circuit courts of the United States, where the value of the property, or the amount in controversy, shall exceed two thousand dollars; and each of said district courts shall have and exercise the same jurisdiction in all cases arising under the constitution and laws of the United States, as is vested in the circuit and district courts of the United States, and also of all cases arising under the laws of the said territory, and otherwise. The said clerk shall receive, in all such cases, the same fees which the clerks of the district courts of the late Wisconsin Territory received for similar services

159.—§ 10. There shall be appointed an attorney for said territory, who shall continue in office for four years, and until his successor shall be appointed and qualified, unless sooner removed by the president, and who shall receive the same fees and salary as were provided by law for the attorney of the United States for the late territory of Wisconsin. There shall also be a marshal for the territory appointed, who shall hold his office for four years, and until his successor shall be appointed and qualified, unless sooner removed by the president, and who shall execute all processes issuing from the said courts, when exercising their jurisdiction as circuit and district courts of the United States; he shall perform the duties, be subject to the same regulation and penalties, and be entitled to the same fees, as were provided by law for the marshal of the district court of the United States, for the present [late] territory of Wisconsin; and shall, in addition, be paid two hundred dollars annually as a compensation for extra services.

160. The act to establish a territorial government for Utah, approved September 9, 1850, contains the following provisions relative to this subject. They are the same in most respects with the preceding.

Section 9 of this act provides, "That the judicial power of said territory shall be vested in a supreme court, district courts, probate courts, and in justices of the peace. The supreme court shall consist of a chief justice and two associate justices, any two of whom shall constitute a quorum, and who shall hold a term at the seat of government of said territory annually, and they shall hold their offices during the period of four years. The said territory shall be divided into three judicial districts, and a district court shall be held in each of said districts by one of the justices of the supreme court, at such time and place as may be prescribed by law; and the said judges shall, after their appointments, respectively, reside in the districts which shall be assigned them. The jurisdiction of the several courts herein provided for, both appellate and original, and that of the probate courts and of justices of the peace, shall be as limited by law: *Provided*, That justices of the peace shall not have jurisdiction of any *matter* in controversy when the title or boundaries of land may be in dispute, or where the debt or sum claimed shall exceed one hundred dollars; and the said supreme and district courts, respectively, shall possess chancery as well as common law jurisdiction. Each district court, or the judge thereof, shall appoint its clerk, who shall also be the register in chancery, and shall keep his office at the place where the court may be held. Writs of error, bills of exception, and appeals shall be allowed in all cases from the final decisions of said district courts to the supreme court, under such regulations as may be prescribed by law; but in no case removed to the supreme court shall trial by jury be allowed in said court. The supreme court, or the justices thereof, shall appoint its own clerk, and every clerk shall hold his office at the pleasure of the court for which he shall have been appointed. Writs of error, and appeals from the final decisions of said supreme court, shall be allowed, and may be taken to the supreme court of the United States, in the same manner and under the same regulations as from the circuit courts of the United States, where the value of the property or the amount in controversy, to be ascertained by the oath or affirmation of either party, or other competent witness, shall exceed two thousand dollars, except only that, in all cases involving title to slaves, the said writs of error or appeals shall be allowed and decided by the said supreme court, without regard to the value of the matter, property, or title in controversy; and except, also, that a writ of error or appeal shall also be allowed to the supreme court of the United States, from the decisions of the said supreme court created by this act, or of any judge thereof, or of the district courts created by this act, or of any judge thereof, upon any writ of habeas corpus involving the question of personal freedom: and each of the said district courts shall have and exercise the same jurisdiction in all cases arising under the constitution and laws of the United States as is vested in the circuit and district courts of the United States; and the said supreme and district courts of the said territory, and the respective judges thereof, shall and may grant writs of habeas corpus in all cases in which the same are granted by the judges of the United States in the District of Columbia; and the first six days of every term of said courts, or so much thereof as shall be necessary, shall be appropriated to the trial of causes arising under the said constitution and laws; and writs of error and appeal, in all such cases, shall be made to the supreme court of said territory, the same as in other cases. The said clerk shall receive in all such cases the same fees which the clerks of the district courts of Oregon territory now receive for similar services.

161. "There shall be appointed an attorney for said territory, who shall continue

in office for four years, unless sooner removed by the president, and who shall receive the same fees and salary as the attorney of the United States for the present territory of Oregon. There shall also be a marshal for the territory appointed, who shall hold his office for four years, unless sooner removed by the president, and who shall execute all processes issuing from the said courts, when exercising their jurisdiction as circuit and district courts of the United States: he shall perform the duties, be subject to the same regulation and penalties, and be entitled to the same fees as the marshal of the district court of the United States for the present territory of Oregon; and shall, in addition, be paid two hundred dollars annually as a compensation for extra services."

COURTESY, OR CURTESY, *Scotch law*. A right which vests in the husband, and is in the nature of a life-rent. It is a counterpart of the terce. Courtesy requires, 1st. That there shall have been a living child born of the marriage, who is heir of the wife, or who, if surviving, would have been entitled to succeed. 2d. That the wife shall have succeeded to the subjects in question as heir either of line, or of talzie, or of provision. 1 Bell's Com. 61; 2 Ersk. 9, § 53. See *Curtesy*.

COURTESY OF ENGLAND. See Estates by the Courtesy.

COUSIN, *domest. rel*. Cousins are kindred who are the issue of two brothers or two sisters, or of a brother and a sister. Those who descend from the brother or sister of the father of the person spoken of are called paternal cousins; maternal cousins are those who are descended from the brothers or sisters of the mother. Vide 2 Bro. C. C. 125; 1 Sim. & Stu. 301; 3 Russ. C. C. 140; 9 Sim. R. 386, 457.

COVENANT, *remedies*. The name of an action instituted for the recovery of damages for the breach of a covenant or promise *under seal*. 2 Ld. Raym. 1536; F. N. B. 145; Com. Dig. Pleader, 2 V 2; Id. Covenant, A 1; Bouv. Inst. Index, h. t.

2. The subject will be considered with reference, 1. To the kind of claim or obligation on which this action may be maintained. 2. The form of the declaration. 3. The plea. 4. The judgment.

3.—1. To support this action, there must be a breach of a promise under seal. 6 Port. R. 201; 5 Pike, 263; 4 Dana, 381; 6 Miss. R. 29. Such promise may be contained in a deed-poll, or indenture, or be express or implied by law from the terms of the deed; or for the performance of something *in futuro*, or that something has been done; or in some cases, though it relate to something *in presenti*, as that the covenantor has a good title. 2 Saund. 181, b Though, in general, it is said that covenan. will not lie on a contract *in presenti*, as on a covenant to stand seized, or that a certain horse shall henceforth be the property of another. Plowd. 308; Com. Dig. Covenant, A 1; 1 Chit. Pl. 110. The action of covenant is the peculiar remedy for the non-performance of a promise under seal, where the damages are *unliquidated*, and depend in amount on the opinion of a jury, in which case neither debt nor assumpsit can be supported; but covenant as well as the action of debt, may be maintained upon a single bill for a sum certain. When the breach of the covenant amounts to misfeasance, the covenantee has an election to proceed by action of covenant, or by action on the case for a tort, as against a lessee, either during his term or afterwards, for waste; 2 Bl. R. 1111; 2 Bl. R. 848; but this has been questioned. When the contract under seal has been enlarged by parol, the substituted agreement will be considered, together with the original agreement, as a simple contract. 2 Watt's R. 451; 1 Chit. Pl. 96; 3 T. R. 590.

4.—2. The declaration must state that the contract was under seal; and it should make profert of it, or show some excuse for the omission. 3 T. R. 151. It is not, in general, requisite to state the consideration of the defendant's promise, because a contract under seal usually imports a consideration; but when the performance of the consideration constitutes a condition precedent, such performance must be averred. So much only of the deed and covenant should be set forth as is essential to the cause of action: although it is usual to declare in the words of the deed, each covenant may be stated as to its legal effect. The breach may be in the negative of the covenant generally; 4 Dall. R. 436; or, according to the legal effect, and sometimes in the alternative; and several breaches may be assigned at common law. Damages being the object of the suit, should be laid sufficient to cover the real amount. Vide 3 Serg. & Rawle, 364; 4 Dall. R. 436; 2 Yeates' R. 470; 3 Serg. & Rawle, 564, 567; 9 Serg. & Rawle, 45.

5.—3. It is said that strictly there is no general issue in this action, though the plea of *non est factum* has been said by an intelligent writer to be the general issue. Steph. Pl. 174. But this plea only puts in issue the fact of sealing the deed. 1 Chit. Pl. 116. *Non infregit conventionem*, and *nil debet*, have both been held to be insufficient. Com. Dig. Pleader, 2 V 4. In Pennsylvania, by a practice peculiar to that state, the defendant may plead *covenants performed*, and under this plea, upon notice of the special matter, in writing, to the plaintiff, without form, he may give anything in evidence which he might have pleaded. 4 Dall. 439; 2 Yeates, 107; 15 Serg. & Rawle, 105. And this evidence, it seems, may be given in the circuit courts of the United States in that state without notice, unless called for. 2 W. C. C. R. 456.

6.—4. The judgment is that the plaintiff recover a named sum for his damages, which he has sustained by reason of the breach or breaches of covenant, together with costs.

COVENANT, *contracts.* A covenant, *conventio*, in its most general signification, means any kind of promise or contract, whether it be made in writing or by parol. Hawk. P. C. b. 1, c. 27, § 7, s. 4. In a more technical sense, and the one in which it is here considered, a covenant is an agreement between two or more persons, entered into in writing and under seal, whereby either party stipulates for the truth of certain facts, or promises to perform or give something to the other, or to abstain from the performance of certain things. 2 Bl. Com. 303–4; Bac. Ab. Covenant, *in pr.;* 4 Cruise, 446; Sheppard, Touchs. 160; 1 Harring. 151, 233; 1 Bibb, 379; 2 Bibb, 614; 3 John. 44; 20 John. 85; 4 Day, 321.

2. It differs from an express assumpsit in this, that the former may be verbal, or in writing not under seal, while the latter must always be by deed. In an assumpsit, a consideration must be shown; in a covenant no consideration is necessary to give it validity, even in a court of equity. Plowd. 308; 7 T. R. 447; 4 Barn. & Ald. 652; 3 Bingh. 111.

3. It is proposed to consider, first, the general requisites of a covenant; and secondly, the several kinds of covenants.

4.—§ 1. The general requisites are, 1st. Proper parties. 2d. Words of agreement. 3d A legal purpose. 4th. A proper form.

5.—1st. The parties must be such as by law can enter into a contract. If either for want of understanding, as in the case of an idiot or lunatic; or in the case of an infant, where the contract is not for his benefit; or where there is understanding, but owing to certain causes, as coverture, in the case of a married woman, or duress, in every case, the parties are not competent, they cannot bind themselves. See *Parties to Actions.*

6.—2d. There must be an agreement. The assent or consent must be mutual; for the agreement would be incomplete if either party withheld his assent to any of its terms. The assent of the parties to a contract necessarily supposes a free, fair, serious exercise of the reasoning faculty. Now, if from any cause, this free assent be not given, the contract is not binding. See *Consent.*

7.—3d. A covenant against any positive law, or public policy, is, generally speaking, void. See *Nullity;* Shep. Touchs. 163. As an example of the first, is a covenant by one man that he will rob another; and of the last, a covenant by a merchant or tradesman that he will not follow his occupation or calling. This, if it be unlimited, is absolutely void; but, if the covenant be that he shall not pursue his business in a particular place, as, that he will not trade in the city of Philadelphia, the covenant is no longer against public policy. See Shep. Touchs. 164. A covenant to do an impossible thing is also void. Ib.

8.—4th. To make a covenant, it must, according to the definition above given, be by deed, or under seal. No particular form of words is necessary to make a covenant, but any words which manifest the intention of the parties, in respect to the subject matter of the contract, are sufficient. See numerous examples in Bac. Abr. Covenant, A; Selw. N. P. 469; Com. Dig. Covenant, A 2; 3 Johns. R. 44; 5 Munf. 483.

9. In Pennsylvania, Delaware, and Missouri, it is declared by statute that the words *grant, bargain,* and *sell,* shall amount to a covenant that the grantor was seised of an estate in fee, free from all incumbrances done or suffered by him, and for quiet enjoyment against his acts. But it has been adjudged that those words in the Pennsylvania statute of 1715, (and the decision will equally apply to the statutory language in the other two states,) did not amount to a general warranty, but merely to a covenant that the grantor had not done any act, nor created any incumbrance

whereby the estate might be defeated. 2 Bin. 95; 11 S. & R. 111, 112; 4 Kent, Com. 460.

10.—§ 2. The several kinds of covenants. They are,

1. Express or implied. 1. An *express* covenant, or a covenant in fact, is one expressly agreed between the parties and inserted in the deed. The law does not require any particular form to create an express covenant. The formal word "covenant" is therefore not indispensably requisite. 2 Mod. 268; 3 Keb. 848; 1 Leon, 324; 1 Bing. 433; 8 J. B. Moore, 546; 1 Ch. Cas. 294; 16 East, 352; 12 East, 182, n.; 1 Bibb, 379; 2 Bibb, 614; 3 John. 44; 5 Cowen, 170; 4 Day, 321; 4 Conn. 508; 1 Harring. 233. The words "I oblige;" "agree," 1 Ves. 516; 2 Mod. 266; or, "I bind myself to pay so much such a day, and so much such another day;" Hardr. 178; 3 Leon. 119, pl. 199; are held to be covenants; and so are the words of a bond. 1 Ch. Cas. 194. But words importing merely an order or direction that other persons should pay a sum of money, are not a covenant. 6 J. B. Moore, 202, n. (a.)

11.—1. An *implied* covenant is one which the law intends and implies, though it be not expressed in words. 1 Common Bench Rep. 402; Co. Lit. 139, b; Vaughan's Rep. 118; Rawle on Covenants, 364. There are some words which of themselves do not import an express covenant, yet being made use of in certain contracts, have a similar operation and are called covenants in law. They are as effectually binding on the parties as if expressed in the most unequivocal terms. Bac. Ab. Covenant, B. A few examples will fully explain this. If a lessor demise and grant to his lessee a house or lands for a certain term, the law will imply a covenant on the part of the lessor, that the lessee shall during the term quietly enjoy the same against all incumbrances. Co. Litt. 384. When in a lease the words "grant," 1 Mod. 113; Freem. 367; Cro. Eliz. 214; 4 Taunt. 609; "grant and demise," 4 Wend. 502; "demise," 10 Mod. 162; 4 Co. 80; Hob. 12; or "demiserunt," 1 Show. 79; 1 Salk. 137, are used, they are so many instances of implied covenants. And the words "yielding and paying" in a lease, imply a covenant, on the part of lessee, that he will pay the rent. 9 Verm. 151; 3 Penn. 461, 464.

12.—2. Real and personal.

1st. A *real* covenant is one which has for its object something annexed to, or inherent in, or connected with land or other real property. Co Litt. 334; Jenk. 241; Cruise, Dig. tit. 32, c. 25, s. 22; Platt. on Cov. 60, 61; 2 Bl. Com. 304. A covenant real, which necessarily runs with the land, as to pay rent, not to cut timber, and the like, is said to be an *inherent covenant*. Shep. To. 161. A covenant real runs with the land and descends to the heir; it is also transferred to a purchaser. Such covenants are said to run with the land, so that he who has the one is subject to the other. Bac. Ab. Covenants, E 2. See 2 Penn. 507; 10 Wend 180; 12 Mass. 306; 17 Mass. 586; 5 Cowen, 137; 5 Ham. 156; 5 Conn. 497; 1 Wash. C. C. 375; 8 Cowen, 206; 1 Dall. 210; 11 Shep. 283; 6 Met. 139; 3 Metc. 81; 3 Harring. 338; 17 Wend. 136.

13.—2. As commonly reckoned, there are five covenants for title, viz: 1. Covenant for seisin. 2. That the grantor has a perfect right to convey. 3. That the grantee shall quietly possess and enjoy the premises without interruption, called a covenant for quiet enjoyment. 4. The covenant against incumbrances. 5. The covenant for further assurance. 6. Besides these covenants, there is another frequently resorted to in the United States, which is relied on more, perhaps, than any other, called the covenant of warranty. See Rawle on Covenants for Title, where the import and effect of these covenants are elaborately and luminously discussed.

14.—3. A *personal* covenant relates only to matters personal, as distinguished from real, and is binding on the covenantor during life, and on his personal representatives after his decease, in respect of his assets. According to Sir William Blackstone, a personal convenant may be transformed into a real, by the mere circumstance of the heirs being named therein, and having assets by descent from the covenantor. 2 Bl. Com. 304. A covenant is personal in another sense, where the covenantor is bound to fulfil the covenant himself; as, to teach an apprentice. F. N. B. 340, A.

15. Personal covenants are also said to be transitive and intransitive; the former, when the duty of performing them passes to the covenantor's representatives; the latter, when it is limited to himself; as, in the case of teaching an apprentice. Bac. Ab. h. t.

16. As they affect each other in the same deed, covenants may be divided into three classes.

1st. *Dependent* covenants are those in which the performance of one depends on the performance of the other; there may be conditions which must be performed before the other party is liable to an action on his covenant. 8 S. & R. 268; 4 Conn. 3; 1 Blackf. 175; 2 John. 209; 2 Stew. & Port. 60; 6 Cowen, 296; 3 Ala. R. 330; 3 Pike, 581; 2 W. & S. 227; 5 Shep. 232; 11 Verm. 549; 4 W. C. C. 714; Platt on Cov. 71; 2 Dougl. 689; Lofft, 191; 2 Selw. N. P. 443, 444. To ascertain whether covenants are dependent or not, the intention of the parties is to be sought for and regarded rather than the order or time in which the acts are to be done, or the structure of the instrument, or the arrangements of the covenant. 4 Wash. C. C. 714; 1 Root, 170; 4 Rand. 352; 4 Rawle, 26; 5 Wend. 496; 2 John. 145; 13 Mass. 410; 2 W. & S. 227; 4 W. & S. 527: Willis, 157; 7 T. R. 130; 8 T. R. 366; 5 B. & P. 223; 1 Saund. 320 n.

17.—2d. Some covenants are mutual conditions to be performed at the same time; these are *concurrent* covenants. When, in these cases, one party is ready and offers to perform his part, and the other refuses or neglects to perform his, he who is ready and offers, has fulfilled his engagement, and may maintain an action for the default of the other, though it is not certain that either is obliged to do the first act. 4 Wash. C. C. 714; Dougl. 698; 2 Selw. N. P. 443; Platt. on Cov. 71.

18.— 3d. Covenants are *independent* or mutual, when either party may recover damages from the other for the injury he may have received by a breach of the covenants in his favor, and when it is no excuse for the defendant to allege a breach of the covenants on the part of the plaintiff. 2 Wash. C. C. R. 456; 5 Shepl. 372; 4 Leigh, 21; 3 Watts & S. 300; 13 Mass. 410; 2 Pick. 300; 2 John. 145; 10 John. 203; Minor, 21; 2 Bibb, 15; 3 Stew. 361; 1 Fairf. 49; 6 Binn. 166; 2 Marsh. 429; 7 John. 249; 5 Wend. 496; 3 Miss. 329; 2 Har. & J. 467; 4 Har. & J. 285; 2 Marsh. 429; 4 Conn. 3.

19. Covenants are affirmative and negative.

1st. An *affirmative* covenant is one by which the covenantor binds himself that something has already been done or shall be performed hereafter. Such a covenant will not deprive a man of a right lawfully enjoyed by him independently of the covenant; as, if the lessor agreed with the lessee that he shall have thorns for hedges growing upon the land, by assignment of the lessor's bailiff; here no restraint is imposed upon the exercise of that liberty which the law allows to the lessee, and therefore he may take hedge-bote without assignment. Dy. 19 b, pl. 115; 1 Leon, 251.

20.—2d. A *negative* covenant is one where the party binds himself that he has not performed and will not perform a certain act; as, that he will not encumber. Such a covenant cannot be said to be performed until it becomes impossible to break it. On this ground the courts are unwilling to construe a covenant of this kind to be a condition precedent. Therefore, where a tailor assigned his trade to the defendant, and covenanted thenceforth to desist from carrying on the said business with any of the customers, and the defendant, in consideration of the performance thereof, covenanted to pay him a life annuity of £190, it was held that if the words *in consideration of the performance thereof*, should be deemed to amount to a condition precedent, the plaintiff would never obtain his annuity; because as at any time during his life he might exercise his former trade, until his death it could never be ascertained whether he had performed the covenant or not. 2 Saund. 156; 1 Sid. 464; 1 Mod. 64; 2 Keb. 674. The defendant, however, on a breach by plaintiff, might have his remedy by a cross-action of covenant. There is also a difference between a negative covenant, which is only in affirmance of an affirmative covenant precedent, and a negative covenant which is additional to the affirmative covenant. 1 Sid. 87; 1 Keb. 334, 372. To a covenant of the former class a plea of performance generally is good, but not to the latter; the defendant in that case must plead specially. Id.

21. Covenants, considered with regard to the parties who are to perform them, are joint or several.

1st. A *joint* covenant is one by which several parties agree to perform or do a thing together. In this case although there are several covenantors there is but one contract, and if the covenant be broken, all the covenantors living must be sued; as there is not a separate obligation of each, they cannot be sued separately.

22.—2d. A *several* covenant is one entered into by one person only. It frequently happens that a number of persons enter into the same contract, and that each binds himself to perform the whole of it; in such case, when the contract is under seal, the covenantors are severally bound for the performance of it. The terms usually employed to make a several covenant are "severally," or "each of us." In practice, it is common for the parties to bind themselves jointly and severally, and then the covenant is both joint and several. Vide Hamm. on Parties, 19; Cruise, Dig. tit. 32, c. 25, s. 18; Bac. Ab. Covenant D.

23. Covenants are executed or executory.

1st. An *executed* covenant is one which relates to an act already performed. Shep. To. 161.

24.—2d. An *executory* covenant is one to be performed at a future time. Shep. To. 161.

25. Covenants are obligatory or declaratory.

1st. An *obligatory* covenant is one which is binding on the party himself, and shall never be construed to raise a use. 1 Sid. 27; 1 Keb. 334.

26.—2d. A *declaratory* covenant is one which serves to limit and direct uses. 1 Sid. 27; 1 Heb. 334.

27. Covenants are principal and auxiliary.

1st. A *principal* covenant is one which relates directly to the principal matter of the contract entered into between the parties; as, if A covenants to serve B for one year.

28.—2d. An *auxiliary* covenant is one, which, not relating directly to the principal matter of the contract between the parties, yet relates to something connected with it; as, if A covenants with B, that C will perform his covenant to serve him for one year. In this case, if the principal covenant is void, the auxiliary is discharged. Anstr. 256.

29. Covenants are legal or illegal.

1st. A *legal* covenant is one not forbidden by law. Covenants of this kind are always binding on the parties.

30.—2d. An *illegal* covenant is one forbidden by law, either expressly or by implication. A covenant entered into in violation of the express provision of a statute is absolutely void. 5 Har. & J. 193; 5 N. H. Rep. 96; 6 N. H. Rep. 225; 4 Dall. 298; 6 Binn. 321; 4 S. & R. 159; 1 Binn. 118; 4 Halst. 252. A covenant is also void, if it be of immoral nature; as, a covenant for future illicit intercourse and cohabitation; 3 Monr. 35; 3 Burr. 1568; S. C. 1 Bl. Rep. 517; 1 Esp. 13; 1 B. & P. 340; or against public policy; 5 Mass. 385; 7 Greenl. 113; 4 Mass. 370; 5 Halst. 87; 4 Wash. C. C. 297; 11 Wheat. 258; 3 Day, 145; 2 McLean, 464; 7 Watts, 152; 5 Watts & S. 315; 5 How. Miss. 769; Geo. Decis. part 1, 39; in restraint of trade, when the restraint is general; 21 Wend. 166, 19 Pick. 51; 6 Pick. 206; 7 Cowen, 307; or fraudulent between the parties; 5 Mass. 16; 4 S. & R. 483; 4 Dall. 250; 7 W. & S. 111; or third persons. 3 Day, 450; 14 S. & R. 214; 3 Caines, 213; 15 Pick. 49; 2 John. 286; 12 John. 306.

31. Covenants, in the *disjunctive* or *alternative*, are those which give the covenantor the choice of doing, or the covenantee the choice of having performed one of two or more things at his election; as, a covenant to make a lease to Titus, or pay him one hundred dollars on the fourth day of July, as the covenantor, or the covenantee, as the case may be, shall prefer. Platt on Cov. 21.

32. *Collateral* covenants are such as concern some collateral thing, which does not at all, or not so immediately relate to the thing granted; as, to pay a sum of money in gross, that the lessor shall distrain for rent, on some other land than that which is demised, or the like. Touchs. 161; 4 Burr. 2446; 2 Wils. R. 27; 1 Ves. R. 56. These covenants are also termed covenants in gross. Vide 5 Barn. & Ald. 7, 8; Platt on Cov. 69, 70.

COVENANT NOT TO SUE. This is a covenant entered into by a party who had a cause of action at the time of making it, and by which he agrees not to sue the party liable to such action.

2. Covenants of this nature, are either covenants perpetual not to sue, or covenants not to sue for a limited time; for example, seven years.

3.—§ 1. Covenants perpetual not to sue. These will be considered with regard to their effect as relates, 1. To the covenantee, 2. To his partners or co-debtors.

4.—1. A covenant not to sue the covenantee at all, has the effect of a release to him, and may be pleaded as such to avoid a circuity of action. Cro. Eliz. 623; 1 T. R. 446; 8 T. R. 486; 1 Ld. Raym. 688; S. C. Holt, 178; 2 Salk. 575; 3 Salk. 298; 12 Mod. 415, 548; 7 Mass. 153, 265; 16 Mass. 24; 17 Mass. 623. And see 11 Serg. & Rawle, 149.

5.—2. Where the covenantee is jointly and *severally* bound with another to the covenantor, a covenant not to sue him will be no protection to the other who may be sued on his several obligation, and such a covenant does not amount to a release to him. 2 Salk. 575; S. C. 12 Mod. 551; 8 T. R. 168; 6 Munf. 6; 1 Com. 139; 4 Greenl. 421; 2 Dana, 107; 17 Mass. 623, 628; 16 Mass. 24; 8 Mass. 480. A covenant not to sue, entered into by only one of several partners, cannot be set up as a release in an action by all the partners. 3 P. & D. 149.

6.—§ 2. Covenant not to sue for a limited time. Such a covenant does not operate as a release, nor can it be pleaded as such, but is a covenant only for a breach of which the obligor may bring his action. Carth. 63; 1 Show. 46; Comb. 123, 4; 2 Salk. 573: 6 Wend. 471.

COVENANT FOR QUIET ENJOYMENT. A covenant usually contained in a lease, by which the lessor covenants or agrees that the tenant shall quietly enjoy the premises leased. 11 East, 641.

2. Such a covenant is express or implied; express, when it is so mentioned in the deed; it is implied, either from the words used, or from the conduct of the lessor. The words "grant" or "demise" are held to amount to an implied covenant for quiet enjoyment, unless afterwards restrained by a qualified express covenant. 1 Chit. Pr. 344.

COVENANT TO STAND SEISED TO USES. A species of conveyance which derives its effect from the statute of uses, and operates without transmutation of possession.

2. By this conveyance, a person seised of lands, covenants that he will stand seised of them to the use of another. On executing the covenant, the other party becomes seised of the use of the land, according to the terms of the use; and the statute immediately annexes the possession to the use. This conveyance has the same force and effect as a common deed of bargain and sale; the great distinction between them is, that the former can only be made use of among near domestic relations, for it must be founded on the consideration of blood or marriage. 2 Bl. Com. 338; 2 Bouv. Inst. n. 2080; 4 Kent, Com. 480; Lilly's Reg. h. t.; 1 Vern. by Raithby, 40, n.; Cruise, Dig. tit. 32, c. 10; 11 John. R. 337; 1 John. Cas. 91; 7 Pick. R. 111; 1 Hayw. R. 251, 259, 271, note; 1 Conn. R. 354; 20 John. R. 85; 4 Mass. R. 135; 4 Hayw. R. 229; 1 Cowen, R. 622; 3 N. H. Rep. 234; 16 John. R. 515; 9 Wend. R. 641; 7 Mass. R. 384.

COVENANT FOR TITLE. An assurance to the purchaser that the grantor has the very estate in quantity and quality which he purports to convey. 11 East, 642. See 4 Dall. Rep. 439.

COVENANTEE. One in whose favor a covenant is made.

COVENANTOR. One who becomes bound to perform a covenant.

2. To become a covenantor a person must be *sui juris*, and intend, at the time of becoming bound, to covenant to perform some act mentioned in the covenant. He can be discharged from his covenant by performance, or by the act of the covenantee, as the non-performance of a condition precedent, a release, or a rescission of the contract.

COVENANTS PERFORMED, *pleading*. In Pennsylvania, the defendant may plead covenants performed to an action of covenant, and upon this plea, upon informal notice to the plaintiff, he may give anything in evidence which he might have pleaded. 4 Dall. 439; 2 Yeates, 107; 15 S. & R. 105. And this evidence, it seems, may be given in the circuit court without notice, unless called for. 2 Wash. C. C. R. 456.

COVENTRY ACT, *criminal law*. The common name for the statute 22 and 23 Car. II. c. 1; it having been enacted in consequence of an assault on Sir John Coventry in the street, and slitting his nose, in revenge, as was supposed, for some obnoxious words uttered by him in parliament.

2. By this statute it is enacted, that if any person shall, of malice aforethought, and by laying in wait, unlawfully cut or disable the tongue, put out an eye, slit the nose, cut off the nose or lip, or cut off or disable any limb, or member of any other person, with intent to maim or disfigure him, such person, his counsellors, aiders and abettors, shall be guilty of felony, without benefit of clergy. 4 Bl. Com. 207. This statute is copied by the act of the legislature of Pennsylvania, of April 22,

1794, s. 6, 3 Smith's Laws of Pa. 188; and the offence is punished by fine and imprisonment. For the act of Connecticut, see 2 Swift's Dig. 293.

COVERT, BARON. A wife; so called, from her being under the cover or protection of her husband, baron or lord.

COVERTURE. The state or condition of a married woman.

2. During coverture, the being of the wife is civilly merged, for many purposes, into that of her husband; she can, therefore, in general, make no contracts without his consent, express or implied. Com. Dig. Baron and Feme, W; Pleader, 2 A 1; 1 Ch. Pl. 19, 45; Litt. s. 28; Chit. Contr. 39: 1 Bouv. Inst. n. 276.

3. To this rule there are some exceptions; she may contract, when it is for her benefit, as to save her from starvation. Chit. Contr. 40.

4. In some cases, when coercion has been used by the husband to induce her to commit crime, she is exempted from punishment. 1 Hale, P. C. 516; 1 Russ. Cr. 16.

COVIN, *fraud*. A secret contrivance between two or more persons to defraud and prejudice another of his rights. Co. Litt. 357, b; Com. Dig. Covin, A; 1 Vin. Abr. 473. Vide *Collusion; Fraud.*

COW. In a penal statute which mentions both cows and heifers, it was held that by the term cow, must be understood one that had had a calf. 2 East, P. C. 616; 1 Leach, 105.

COWARDICE. Pusillanimity; fear.

2. By the act for the better government of the navy of the United States, passed April 21, 1800, 1 Story, L. U. S. 761, it is enacted, art. 5, "every officer or private who shall not properly observe the orders of his commanding officer, or shall not use his utmost exertions to carry them into execution, when ordered to prepare for, join in, or when actually engaged in battle; or shall, at such time, basely desert his duty or station, either then, or while in sight of an enemy, or shall induce others to do so, every person so offending, shall, on conviction thereof by a general court martial, suffer death, or such other punishment as the said court shall adjudge.

3.—Art. 6. "Every officer or private who shall, through cowardice, negligence, or disaffection, in the time of action, withdraw from, or keep out of battle, or shall not do his utmost to take or destroy every vessel which it is his duty to encounter, or shall not do his utmost endeavor to afford relief to ships belonging to the United States, every such offender shall, on conviction thereof by a general court martial, suffer death, or such other punishment as the said court shall adjudge."

4. By the act for establishing rules and articles for the government of the armies of the United States, passed April 10, 1806, it is enacted, art. 52, "any officer or soldier, who shall misbehave himself before the enemy, run away, or shamefully abandon any fort, post, or guard, which he or they may be commanded to defend, or speak words inducing others to do the like, or shall cast away his arms and ammunition, or who shall quit his post or colors to plunder and pillage, every such offender, being duly convicted thereof, shall suffer death, or such other punishment as shall be ordered by the sentence of a general court martial."

CRANAGE. A toll paid for drawing merchandise out of vessels to the wharf, so called, because the instrument used for the purpose is called a crane. 8 Co. 46.

TO CRAVE. To ask; to demand.

2. This word is frequently used in pleading; as, to crave oyer of a bond on which the suit is brought; and in the settlement of accounts, the accountant general craves a credit or an allowance. 1 Chit. Pr. 520. See *Oyer*.

CRAVEN. A word of obloquy, which in trials by battel, was pronounced by the vanquished; upon which judgment was rendered against him.

CREANCE. This is a French word, which, in its extensive sense, signifies claim; in a narrower sense it means a debt. 1 Bouv. Inst. n. 1040, note.

CREDENTIALS, *international law*. The instruments which authorize and establish a public minister in his character with the state or prince to whom they are addressed. If the state or prince receive the minister, he can be received only in the quality attributed to him in his credentials. They are, as it were, his letter of attorney, his mandate patent, mandatum manifestum. Vattel, liv. 4, c. 6, § 76.

CREDIBILITY. Worthiness of belief. To entitle a witness to credibility, he must be competent. Vide *Competency*.

2. Human testimony can seldom acquire the certainty of demonstration. Witnesses not unfrequently are mistaken or wish to deceive; the most that can be expected is that moral certainty which arises

from analogy. The credibility which is attached to such testimony, arises from the double presumption that the witnesses have good sense and intelligence, and that they are not mistaken nor deceived; they are further presumed to have probity, and that they do not wish to deceive.

3. To gain credibility, we must be assured, first, that the witness has not been mistaken nor deceived. To be assured as far as possible on this subject, it is proper to consider the nature and quality of the facts proved; the quality and person of the witness; the testimony in itself; and to compare it with the depositions of other witnesses on the subject, and with known facts. Secondly, we must be satisfied that he does not wish to deceive: there are strong assurances of this, when the witness is under oath, is a man of integrity, and disinterested. Vide Arch. Civ. Pl. 444; 5 Com. Dig. 449; 8 Watts, R. 227; *Competency*.

CREDIBLE WITNESS. A credible witness is one who is competent to give evidence, and is worthy of belief. 5 Mass. 219; 17 Pick. 134; 2 Curt. Ecc. R. 336. In deciding upon the credibility of a witness, it is always pertinent to consider whether he is capable of knowing the thing thoroughly about which he testifies. 2. Whether he was actually present at the transaction. 3. Whether he paid sufficient attention to qualify himself to be a reporter of it; and 4. Whether he honestly relates the affair fully as he knows it, without any purpose or desire to deceive, or suppress or add to the truth.

2. In some of the states, as Delaware, Illinois, Maine, Maryland, Rhode Island, Vermont, and Virginia, wills must be attested by credible witnesses. See *Attesting Witness; Competent Witness; Disinterested Witness; Respectable Witness;* and *Witness.*

CREDIT, *common law, contracts.* The ability to borrow, on the opinion conceived by the lender that he will be repaid. This definition includes the effect and the immediate cause of credit. The debt due in consequence of such a contract is also called a credit; as, administrator of all the goods, chattels, effects and *credits*, &c.

2. The time extended for the payment of goods sold, is also called a credit; as, the goods were sold at six months' credit.

3. In commercial law, credit is understood as opposed to debit; credit is what is due to a merchant, debit, what is due by him.

4. According to M. Duvergier, credit also signifies that influence acquired by intrigue connected with certain social positions. 20 Toull. n. 19. This last species of credit is not of such value as to be the object of commerce. Vide, generally, 5 Taunt. R. 338.

CREDITOR, *persons, contracts.* A creditor is he who has a right to require the fulfilment of an obligation or contract.

2. Creditors may be divided into personal and real.

3. The former are so called, because their claims are mainly against the person, who can reach the property of their debtors only by virtue of the general rule by which he who has become personally obligated, is bound to fulfil his engagements, with all his property, acquired and to be acquired, which is a common guaranty for all his creditors.

4. The latter are called real, because they have mortgages or other securities binding on the real estates of their debtors.

5. It is proper to state that personal creditors may be divided into two classes: first, those who have a right on all the property of their debtors, without considering the origin, or the nature of their claims; secondly, those who, in consequence of some provision of law, are entitled to some special prerogative, either in the manner of recovery, or in the rank they are to hold among creditors; these are entitled to preference. As an example, may be mentioned the case of the United States; when they are creditors, they have always a preference in case of insolvent estates.

6. A creditor sometimes becomes so, unknown to his debtor, as is the case when the former receives an assignment of commercial paper, the title to recover which may be conveyed either by endorsement, or, in some cases, by mere delivery. But in general, it is essential there should be a privity of contract between the parties. Vide, generally, 7 Vin. Ab. 42; 3 Com Dig. 343; 8 Com. Dig. 388; 1 Supp. to Ves. Jr. 302; 2 Supp. to Ves. Jr. 305; Code, 7, 72, 6; Id. 8, 18; Dig. 42, 6, 17; Nov. 97, ch. 3; Bouv. Inst. Index, h. t.

CREEK, *mar. law.* Creeks are of two kinds, viz. creeks of the sea and creeks of ports. The former sort are such little inlets of the sea, whether within the precinct or extent of a port or without, which are narrow little passages, and have shore on either side of them. The latter, viz. creeks of ports, are by a kind of civil denomination such. They are such, that though possibly for their extent and situation they might be ports, yet they are either members of or dependent upon other ports. In England it began thus: the king could not conveniently have a customer and comptroller in every port or haven. But these custom officers were fixed at some eminent port; and the smaller adjacent ports became by that means creeks, or appendants of that where these custom officers were placed. 1 Chit. Com. Law, 726; Hale's Tract. de Portibus Maris, part 2, c. 1, vol. 1, p. 46; Com. Dig. Navigation, C; Callis, 34.

2. In a more popular sense, creek signifies a small stream, less than a river. 12 Pick. R. 184,

CRETION, *civil law*. The acceptance of a succession. Cretion was an act made before a magistrate, by which an instituted heir, who was required to accept of the succession within a certain time, declared within that time that he accepted the succession. Clef des Lois Rom. h. t.

2. Cretion is also used to signify the term during which the heir is allowed to make his election to take or not to take the inheritance. It is so called, because the heir is allowed to see, *cernere*, examine, and decide. Gaii, Inst. lib. 2, § 164.

CREW. Those persons who are employed in the navigation of a vessel.

2. A vessel to be seaworthy must have a sufficient crew. 1 Caines, R. 32; 1 John. R. 184.

3. In general, the master or captain (q. v.) has the selection of the crew. Vide *Muster roll; Seaman; Ship; Shipping articles.*

CRIB-BITING. A defect in horses, which consists in biting the crib while in the stable. This is not considered as a breach of a general warranty of soundness. Holt's Cas. 630.

CRIER. An inferior officer of a court, whose duty it is to open and adjourn the court, when ordered by the judges; to make proclamations and obey the directions of the court in anything which concerns the administration of justice.

CRIME. A crime is an offence against a public law. This word, in its most general signification, comprehends all offences; but, in its limited sense, it is confined to felony. 1 Chitty, Gen. Pr. 14.

2. The term *misdemeanor* includes every offence inferior to felony, but punishable by indictment, or by particular prescribed proceedings.

3. The term *offence*, also, may be considered as having the same meaning, but is usually, by itself, understood to be a crime not indictable but punishable, summarily, or by the forfeiture of a penalty. Burn's Just. Misdemeanor.

4. Crimes are defined and punished by statutes and by the common law. Most common law offences are as well known, and as precisely ascertained, as those which are defined by statutes; yet, from the difficulty of exactly defining and describing every act which ought to be punished, the vital and preserving principle has been adopted, that all immoral acts which tend to the prejudice of the community are punishable by courts of justice. 2 Swift's Dig. 257.

5. Crimes are *mala in se*, or bad in themselves; and these include all offences against the moral law; or they are *mala prohibita*, bad because prohibited, as being against sound policy; which, unless prohibited, would be innocent or indifferent. Crimes may be classed into such as affect—

6.—1. Religion and public worship: viz. blasphemy, disturbing public worship.

7.—2. The sovereign power: treason, misprision of treason.

8.—3. The current coin: as counterfeiting or impairing it.

9.—4. Public justice: 1. Bribery of judges or jurors, or receiving the bribe. 2. Perjury. 3. Prison breaking. 4. Rescue. 5. Barratry. 6. Maintenance. 7. Champerty. 8. Compounding felonies. 9. Misprision of felonies. 10. Oppression. 11. Extortion. 12. Suppressing evidence. 13. Negligence or misconduct in inferior officers. 14. Obstructing legal process. 15. Embracery.

10.—5. Public peace. 1. Challenges to fight a duel. 2. Riots, routs and unlawful assemblies. 3. Affrays. 4. Libels.

11.—6. Public trade. 1. Cheats. 2. Forestalling. 3. Regrating. 4. Engrossing. 5. Monopolies.

12.—7. Chastity. 1. Sodomy. 2. Adultery. 3. Incest. 4. Bigamy. 5. Fornication.

13.—8. Decency and morality. 1. Public indecency. 2. Drunkenness. 3. Violating the grave.

14.—9. Public police and economy. 1. Common nuisances. 2. Keeping disorderly houses and bawdy houses. 3. Idleness, vagrancy and beggary.

15.—10. Public policy. 1. Gambling. 2. Illegal lotteries.

16.—11. Individuals. 1. Homicide, which is justifiable, excusable or felonious. 2. Mayhem. 3. Rape. 4. Poisoning, with intent to murder. 5. Administering drugs to a woman quick with child to cause miscarriage. 6. Concealing death of bastard child. 7. Assault and battery, which is either simple or with intent to commit some other crime. 8. Kidnapping. 9. False imprisonment. 10. Abduction.

17.—12. Private property. 1. Burglary. 2. Arson. 3. Robbery. 4. Forgery. 5. Counterfeiting. 6. Larceny. 7. Receiving stolen goods, knowing them to have been stolen, or theft-bote. 8. Malicious mischief.

18.—13. The public, individuals, or their property, according to the intent of the criminal. 1. Conspiracy.

CRIME AGAINST NATURE. Sodomy. It is a crime not fit to be named; peccatum horribile, inter christianos non nominandum. 4 Bl. Com. 214. See *Sodomy*.

CRIMEN FALSI, *civil law, crime.* It is a fraudulent alteration, or forgery, to conceal or alter the truth, to the prejudice of another. This crime may be committed in three ways, namely: 1. By forgery. 2. By false declarations or false oath, perjury. 3. By acts; as, by dealing with false weights and measures, by altering the current coin, by making false keys, and the like. Vide Dig. 48, 10, 22; Dig. 34, 8, 2; Code, lib. 9, t. 22, l. 2, 5, 9. 11, 16, 17, 23, and 24; Merl. Rép. h. t.; 1 Bro. Civ. Law, 426; 1 Phil. Ev. 26; 2 Stark. Ev. 715.

2. What is understood by this term in the common law, is not very clearly defined. Peake's Ev. 133; 1 Phil. Ev. 24; 2 Stark. Ev. 715. It extends to forgery, perjury, subornation of perjury, suppression of testimony by bribery, and conspiracy to convict of perjury. See 12 Mod. 209; 2 S. & R. 552; 1 Greenl. Ev. § 373; and article *Faux*.

CRIMINAL. Relating to, or having the character of crime; as, criminal law, criminal conversation, &c. It also signifies a person convicted of a crime.

CRIMINAL CONVERSATION, *crim. law.* This phrase is usually employed to denote the crime of adultery. It is abbreviated *crim. con.* Bac. Ab. Marriage, E 2; 4 Blackf. R. 157.

2. The remedy for criminal conversation is, by an action on the case for damages. That the plaintiff connived, or assented to, his wife's infidelity, or that he prostituted her for gain, is a complete answer to the action. See *Connivance*. But the facts that the wife's character for chastity was bad before the plaintiff married her; that he lived with her after he knew of the criminal intimacy with the defendant; that he had connived at her intimacy with other men; or that the plaintiff had been false to his wife, only go in mitigation of damages. 4 N. Hamp. R. 501.

3. The wife cannot maintain an action for criminal conversation with her husband; and for this, among other reasons, because her husband, who is particeps criminis, must be joined with her as plaintiff.

CRIMINAL LETTERS. An instrument in Scotland, which contains the charges against a person accused of a crime. Criminal letters differ from an indictment, in that the former are not, like an indictment, the mere statement of the prosecutor, but sanctioned by a judge. Burt. Man. Pub. L. 301, 302.

CRIMINALITER. Criminally; opposed to *civiliter*, civilly.

2. When a person commits a wrong to the injury of another, he is answerable for it *civiliter*, whatever may have been his intent; but, unless his intent has been unlawful, he is not answerable *criminaliter*. 1 East, 104.

TO CRIMINATE. To accuse of a crime; to admit having committed a crime or misdemeanor.

2. It is a rule, that a witness cannot be compelled to answer any question which has a tendency to expose him to a penalty, or to any kind of punishment, or to a criminal charge. 3 Bouv. Inst. n. 3209–12; 4 St. Tr. 6; 10 How. St. Tr. 1090; 6 St. Tr. 649; 16 How. St. Tr. 1149; 2 Dougl. R. 593; 2 Ld. Raym. 1088; 24 How. St. Tr. 720; 16 Ves. jr. 242; 2 Swanst. Ch. R. 216; 1 Cranch. R. 144; 2 Yerg. R. 110; 5 Day, Rep. 260; 1 Carr. & Payne, 11; 2 Nott & M'C. 13; 6 Cowen, Rep. 254; 2 Peak. N. P. C. 105; 1 John. R. 498; 12 S. & R. 284; 8 Wend. 598.

3. An accomplice, admitted to give evidence against his associates in guilt, is bound to make a full and fair confession of the whole truth respecting the subject-matter of the prosecution; but he is not bound to answer with respect to his share in other offences, in which he was not concerned with the prisoner. 9 Cowen, R. 721, note (a); 2 Carr. & Payne, 411. Vide *Disgrace, Witness.*

CRIMINATION. The act by which a party accused is proved to be guilty.

2. It is a rule, founded in common sense, that no one is bound to criminate himself. A witness may refuse to answer a question, when the answer would criminate him, and subject him to punishment. And a party in equity is not bound to answer a bill, when the answer would form a step in the prosecution. Coop. Eq. Pl. 204; Mitf. Eq. Pl. by Jeremy, 194; Story, Eq. Pl. § 591; 14 Ves. 59.

CRITICISM. The art of judging skilfully of the merits or beauties, defects or faults of a literary or scientific performance, or of a production of art; when the criticism is reduced to writing, the writing itself is called a criticism.

2. Liberty of criticism must be allowed, or there would be neither purity of taste nor of morals. Fair discussion is essentially necessary to the truth of history and advancement of science. That publication, therefore, is not a libel, which has for its object, not to injure the reputation of an individual, but to correct misrepresentations of facts, to refute sophistical reasoning, to expose a vicious taste for literature, or to censure what is hostile to morality. 1 Campb. R. 351–2. As every man who publishes a book commits himself to the judgment of the public, any one may comment on his performance. If the commentator does not step aside from the work, or introduce fiction for the purpose of condemnation, he exercises a fair and legitimate right. And the critic does a good service to the public who writes down any vapid or useless publication, such as ought never to have appeared; and, although the author may suffer a loss from it, the law does not consider such loss an injury; because it is a loss which the party ought to sustain. It is the loss of fame and profit, to which he was never entitled. 1 Campb. R. 358, n. See 1 Esp. N. P. Cas. 28; 2 Stark. Cas. 73; 4 Bing. N. S. 92; S. C. 3 Scott, 340; 1 M. & M. 44; 1 M. & M. 187; Cooke on Def. 52.

CROFT, *obsolete*. A little close adjoining to a dwelling-house, and enclosed for pasture or arable, or any particular use. Jacob's Law Dict.

CROP. This word is nearly synonymous with emblements. (q. v.)

2. As between the landlord and tenant, the former has a lien, in some of the states, upon the crop for the rent, for a limited time, and if sold on an execution against the tenant, the purchaser succeeds to the liability of the tenant, for rent and good husbandry, and the crop is still liable to be distrained. Tenn. St. 1825, c. 21; Misso. St. 377; Del. St. 1829, 366; 1 N. J. R. C. 187; Aik. Dig. 357; 1 N. Y. R. S. 746; 1 Ky. R. L. 639; 5 Watts, R. 134; 4 Griff. Reg. 671, 404; 1 Hill. Ab. 148, 9; 5 Penn. St. R. 211.

3. A crop is not considered as a part of the real estate, so as to make a sale of it void, when the contract has not been reduced to writing, within the statute of frauds. 11 East, 362; 2 M. & S. 205; 5 B. & C. 829; 10 Ad. & El. 753; 9 B. & C. 561; but see 9 M. & W. 501.

4. If a husband sow land and die, and the land which was sown is assigned to the wife for her dower, she shall have the corn, and not the executors of the husband. 2 Inst. 81.

CROPPER, *contracts*. One who, having no interest in the land, works it in consideration of receiving a portion of the crop for his labor. 2 Rawle, R. 12.

CROSS, *contracts*. A mark made by persons who are unable to write, instead of their names.

2. When properly attested, and proved to have been made by the party whose name is written with the mark, it is generally admitted as evidence of the party's signature.

CROSS ACTION. An action by a defendant in an action, against the plaintiff in the same action, upon the same contract, or for the same tort; as, if Peter bring an action of trespass against Paul, and Paul bring another action of trespass against Peter, the subject of the dispute being an assault and battery, it is evident that Paul could not set off the assault committed upon him by Peter, in the action which Peter had brought against him; therefore the cross action became necessary.

CROSS BILLS, *practice*. When an individual prosecutes a bill of indictment against another, and the defendant procures another bill to be found against the first prosecutor, the bills so found by the grand jury are called cross bills. They most usually occur in cases of assault and battery.

2. In chancery practice it is not unusual for parties to file cross bills. Vide *Bill, cross*.

CROSS-EXAMINATION, *practice*. The examination of a witness, by the party who did not call him, upon matters to which he has been examined in chief.

2. Every party has a right to cross-examine a witness produced by his antagonist, in order to test whether the witness has the knowledge of the things he testifies; and if, upon examination, it is found that the witness had the means and ability to ascertain the facts about which he testifies, then his memory, his motives, every thing may be scrutinized by the cross-examination.

3. In cross-examinations a great latitude is allowed in the mode of putting questions, and the counsel may put *leading questions*. (q. v.) Vide further on this subject, and for some rules which limit the abuse of this right, 1 Stark. Ev. 96; 1 Phil. Ev. 210; 6 Watts & Serg. 75.

4. The object of a cross-examination is to sift the evidence, and try the credibility of a witness who has been called and given evidence in chief. It is one of the principal tests which the law has devised for the ascertainment of truth, and it is certainly one of the most efficacious. By this means the situation of the witness, with respect to the parties and the subject of litigation, his interest, his motives, his inclinations and his prejudices, his means of obtaining a correct and certain knowledge of the facts to which he testifies, the manner in which he has used those means, his powers of discerning the facts in the first instance, and of his capacity in retaining and describing them, are fully investigated and ascertained. The witness, however artful he may be, will seldom be able to elude the keen perception of an intelligent court or jury, unless indeed his story be founded on truth. When false, he will be liable to detection at every step. 1 Stark. Ev. 96; 1 Phil. Ev. 227; Fortesc. Rep. Pref. 2 to 4; Vaugh. R. 143.

5. In order to entitle a party to a cross-examination, the witness must have been sworn and examined; for, even if the witness be asked a question in chief, yet if he make no answer, the opponent has no right to cross-examine. 1 Cr. M. & Ros. 95; 16 S. & R. 77; Rosc. Cr. Ev. 128; 3 Car. & P. 16; S. C. 14 E. C. L. Rep. 189; 3 Bouv. Inst. n. 3217. Formerly, however, the rule seems to have been different. 1 Phil. Ev. 211.

6. A cross-examination of a witness is not always necessary or advisable. A witness tells the truth wholly or partially, or he tells a falsehood. If he tells the whole truth, a cross-examination may have the effect of rendering his testimony more circumstantial, and impressing the jury with a stronger opinion of its truth. If he tells only a part of the truth, and the part omitted is *favorable* to the client of the counsel cross-examining, he should direct the attention of the witness to the matters omitted. If the testimony of the witness be false, the whole force of the cross-examination should be directed to his credibility. This is done by questioning him as to his means of knowledge, his disinterestedness, and other matters calculated to show a want of integrity or veracity, if there is reason to believe the witness prejudiced, partial, or wilfully dishonest. Arch. Crim. Pl. 111. See *Credible Witness.*

CROWN. A covering for the head, commonly used by kings; figuratively, it signifies royal authority. By *pleas of the crown*, are understood criminal actions.

CRUELTY. This word has different meanings, as it is appplied to different things. Cruelty may be, 1. From husband towards the wife, or vice versa. 2. From superior towards inferior. 3. From master towards slave. 4. To animals. These will be separately considered.

2.—1. Between husband and wife, those acts which affect the life, the health, or even the comfort of the party aggrieved, and give a reasonable apprehension of bodily hurt, are called cruelty. What merely wounds the feelings is seldom admitted to be cruelty, unless the act be accompanied with bodily injury, either actual or menaced. Mere austerity of temper, petulance of manners, rudeness of language, a want of civil attention and accommodation, even occasional sallies of passion, will not amount to legal cruelty; 17 Conn. 189; a fortiori, the denial of little indulgences and particular accommodations, which the delicacy of the world is apt to number among its necessaries, is not cruelty. The negative descriptions of cruelty are perhaps the best, under the infinite variety of cases that may occur, by showing what is not cruelty. 1 Hagg. R. 35; S. C. 4 Eccles. R. 311, 312; 2 Hagg. Suppl. 1; S. C. 4 Eccles. R. 238, 1 McCord's Ch. R. 205; 2 J. J. Marsh. R. 324; 2 Chit. Pr. 461, 489; Poynt. on Mar. & Div. c. 15, p. 208; Shelf. on Mar & Div. 425; 1 Hagg. Cons. R. 37, 458, 2 Hagg. Cons. Rep. 154; 1 Phillim. 111, 132; 8 N. H. Rep. 307; 3 Mass. 321; 4 Mass. 487. It is to be remarked that exhibitions of passion and gusts of anger, which would be sufficient to create irreconcilable hatred between persons educated and trained to respect each other's feelings, would, with persons of coarse manners and habits, have but a momentary effect. An act which towards the latter would cause but a momentary difference, would with the former, be excessive cruelty. 1 Briand, Méd. Lég. 1ere part. c. 2, art. 3.

3.—2. Cruelty towards weak and helpless persons takes place where a party bound to provide for and protect them, either abuses them by whipping them unnecessarily, or by neglecting to provide for them those necessaries which their helpless condition requires. To expose a person of tender years, under a party's care, to the inclemency of the weather; 2 Campb. 650; or to keep such a child, unable to provide for himself, without adequate food; 1 Leach, 137; Russ. & Ry. 20; or an overseer neglecting to provide food and medical care to a pauper having urgent and immediate occasion for them; Russ. & Ry. 46, 47, 48; are examples of this species of cruelty.

4.—3. By the civil code of Louisiana, art. 192, it is enacted, that when the master shall be convicted of cruel treatment of his slave, the judge may pronounce, besides the penalty established for such cases, that the slave shall be sold at public auction, in order to place him out of the reach of the power which his master has abused.

5.—4. Cruelty to animals is an indictable offence. A defendant was convicted of a misdemeanor for tying the tongue of a calf so near the root as to prevent its sucking, in order to sell the cow at a greater price, by giving to her udder the appearance of being full of milk, while affording the calf all he needed. 6 Rogers, City Hall Rec. 62. A man may be indicted for cruelly beating his horse. 3 Rogers, City H. Rec. 191.

CRUISE, *mar. law.* A voyage or expedition in quest of vessels or fleets of the enemy which may be expected to sail through any particular track of the sea, at a certain season of the year; the region in which these cruises are performed is usually termed the rendezvous or cruising latitude.

2. When the ships employed for this purpose, which are accordingly called *cruisers*, have arrived at the destined station, they traverse the sea, backwards and forwards, under an easy sail, and within a limited space, conjectured to be in the track of their expected adversaries. Wesk Ins. h. t.; Lex Merc. Rediv. 271, 284; Dougl. R. 509; Park. Ins. 58; Marsh. Ins. 196, 199, 520; 2 Gallis. 268.

CRY DE PAYS, OR CRI DE PAÏS. Literally, cry of the country. In England, when a felony has been committed, *hue and cry* (q. v.) may be raised by the country, in the absence of the constable. It is then *cry de pays*. 2 Hale, P. C. 100.

CRYER, *practice.* An officer in a court, whose duty it is to make various proclamations ordered by the court.

CUEILLETTE. A term in French maritime law. Affreightment of a vessel *à cueillette*, is a contract by which the captain obligates himself to receive a partial cargo, only upon condition that he shall succeed in completing his cargo by other partial lading; that is, by gathering it (*en recueillant*) wherever he may be able to find it. If he fails to collect a cargo, such partial chartering is void. Code de Com. par M. Fournel, art. 286, n.

CUI ANTE DIVORTIUM. The name of an ancient writ, which was issued in favor of a woman divorced from her husband, to recover the lands and tenements which she had in fee simple, or in tail, or for life, from him to whom her husband alienated them during the marriage, when she could not gainsay it. F. N. B. 240. Vide *Sur cui ante divortium.*

CUI IN VITA. The name of a writ of entry for a widow against a person to whom the husband had, in his lifetime, aliened the lands of the wife. F. N. B. 193. This writ was founded sometimes on the stat. 13 Ed. I. c. 3, and sometimes on the common law. The object of this statute, was to enable the wife to avoid a judgment to recover her land which had been rendered on the default or confession of her husband. It is now of no use in England, because the stat. 32 H. VIII. c. 28, § 6, provides that no act of the husband, whether fine, feoffment, or other act of the husband during coverture, shall prejudice the wife. Both these statutes are reported as in force in Pennsylvania. 3 Bin. Appx. See Booth on Real Actions, 186; 6 Rep. 8, 9, Ferrers' Case. Still, that part of the stat. 13 Ed. I. c. 3, which relates to the pleadings and evidence in such cases is important if it can be enforced in the modern action of ejectment, viz: that which requires the tenant of the lands to show his right according to the form of the writ he sued out against the husband. See Report of the Commissioners to revise the Civil Code of Pennsylvania, Jan. 16, 1835, pp. 90, 91.

CUL DE SAC. This is a French phrase, which signifies, literally, the bottom of a bag, and, figuratively, a street not open at both ends. It seems not to be settled whether a *cul de sac* is to be considered a highway. See 1 Campb. R. 260; 11 East, R. 376, note; 5 Taunt. R. 137; 5 B. & Ald. 456; Hawk. P. C. b. 1, c. 76, s. 1; Dig. lib. 50, tit. 16, l. 43; Dig. lib. 43, t. 12, l. 1, § 13; Dig. lib. 47, tit. 10, l. 15, § 7.

CULPA. A fault committed without fraud, and this distinguishes it from *dolus*, which is a trick to deceive. See *Dolus*.

CULPRIT, *crim. law*. When a prisoner is arraigned, and he pleads not guilty, in the English practice, the clerk, who arraigns him on behalf of the crown, replies that the prisoner is guilty, and that he is ready to prove the accusation; this is done by two monosyllables, cul. prit. Vide *Abbreviations;* 4 Bl. Com. 339; 1 Chit. Cr. Law, 416.

CUM PERTINENTIS. With the appurtenances. See *Appurtenances*.

Cum onere. This term is usually employed to show that something is taken, *subject to a charge or burden.*

Cum testamento annexo. With the testament or will annexed. It often happens that the deceased, although he makes a will, appoints no executor, or else the appointment fails; in either of which events he is said to die *quasi intestatus*. 2 Inst. 397. The appointment of an executor fails, 1st. When the person appointed refuses to act. 2d. When the person appointed dies before the testator, or before he has proved the will, or when, from any other legal cause, he is incapable of acting. 3d. When the executor dies intestate, (and in some places, as in Pennsylvania, whether he die testate or intestate,) after having proved the will, but before he has administered all the personal estate of the deceased. In all these cases, as well as when no executor has been appointed, administration, with the will annexed, must be granted by the proper officer. In the case where the goods are not all administered before the death of the executor, the administration is also called an administration *de bonis non.*

2. The office of such an an administrator differs little from that of an executor. Vide Com. Dig. Administration; Will. Ex. p. 1, b. 5, c. 3, s. 1; 2 Bl. Com. 504–5· 11 Vin. Ab. 78; Toll. 92; Gord. Law of Deced. 98.

CUMULATIVE. Forming a heap; additional; as, cumulative evidence, or that which goes to prove the same point which has been established by other evidence. Cumulative legacy, or accumulative legacy, is a second bequest, given by the same testator to the same legatee. 2 Rop. Leg. 19. See 1 Saund. 134, n. 4; *Remedy*.

Cumulative legacy. Vide *Legacy accumulative;* and 8 Vin. Ab. 308; 1 Supp. to Ves. jr. 133, 282, 332.

CURATE, *eccl. law*. One who represents the incumbent of a church, person, or vicar, and takes care of the church, and performs divine service in his stead.

CURATOR, *persons, contracts*. One who has been legally appointed to take care of the interests of one who, on account of his youth, or defect of his understanding, or for some other cause, is unable to attend to them himself.

2. There are curators *ad bona*, of property, who administer the estate of a minor, take care of his person, and intervene in all his contracts; curators *ad litem*, of suits, who assist the minor in courts of justice, and act as curator *ad bona* in cases where the interests of the curator are opposed to the interests of the minor. Civ. Code of Louis. art. 357 to 366. There are also curators of insane persons; Id. art. 31; and of vacant successions and absent heirs. Id. art. 1105 to 1125.

3. The term curator is usually employed in the civil law, for that of guardian.

CURATORSHIP, *offices, contracts, in the civil law*. The power given by authority of law, to one or more persons, to administer the property of an individual, who is unable to take care of his own estate and affairs, either on account of his absence without an authorized agent, or in consequence of his prodigality, or want of mind. Poth. Tr. des Personnes, t. 6, s. 5. As to the laws of Louisiana, which authorize a curatorship, vide Civ. Code, art. 31, 50, et seq.; 357, et seq.; 382, 1105, et seq.

2. Curatorship differs from tutorship, (q. v.) in this, that the latter is instituted for the protection of property in the first place, and, secondly, of the person; while the former is intended to protect, first, the person, and, secondly, the property. 1 Leçons Elem. du Droit Civ. Rom. 241.

CURATRIX. A woman who has been appointed to the office of curator.

CURE. A restoration to health.

2. A person who had quitted the habit of drunkenness for the space of nine months, in consequence of medicines he had taken, and who had lost his appetite for ardent spirits, was held to have been cured. 7 Yerg. R. 146.

3. In a figurative sense, to cure is to remedy any defect; as, an *informal* statement of the plaintiff's cause of action in his declaration, is cured by verdict, provided it be substantially stated.

CURFEW. The name of a law, established during the reign of the English king, William, the conqueror, by which the people were commanded to dispense with fire and candle at eight o'clock at night.

2. It was abolished in the reign of Henry I., but afterwards it signified the time at which the *curfew* formerly took place. The word *curfew* is derived, probably, from *couvre feu*, or cover fire. 4 Bl. Com. 419, 420.

CURIA. A court of justice.

CURIA CLAUDENDA, WRIT DE, *Eng. law.* The name of a writ, used to compel a party to enclose his land. F. N. B. 297.

CURIA ADVISARE VULT, *practice.* The court will consider the matter. This entry is made on the record when the court wish to take time to consider of a case before they give a final judgment, which is made by an abbreviation, *cur. ad vult*, for the purpose of marking the continuance. In the technical sense, it is a continuance of the cause to another term.

CURIA REGIS. An English court, which assumed this name, during the reign of Henry II. It was *Curia* or *Aula Regis*, because it was held in the great hall of the king's palace; and where the king, for some time, administered justice in person. But afterwards, the judicial power was more properly entrusted to the king's judges. The judges who sat in this court were distinguished by the name of justices, or justiciaries. Besides these, the chief justiciary, the stewart of all England, the constable of all England, the chancellor, the chamberlain, and the treasurer, also took part in the judicial proceedings of this court.

CURIALITY, *Scotch law.* The same as courtesy. (q. v.) 1 Bell's Com. 61.

CURRENCY. The money which passes, at a fixed value, from hand to hand; money which is authorized by law.

2. By art. 1, s. 8, the Constitution of the United States authorizes congress "to coin money, and to regulate the value thereof." Changes in the currency ought not to be made but for the most urgent reasons, as they unsettle commerce, both at home and abroad. Suppose Peter contracts to pay Paul one thousand dollars in six months—the dollar of a certain fineness of silver, weighing one hundred and twelve and a half grains—and afterwards, before the money becomes due, the value of the dollar is changed, and it weighs now but fifty-six and a quarter grains; will one thousand of the new dollars pay the old debt? Different opinions may be entertained, but it seems that such payment would be complete; because, 1. The creditor is bound to receive the public currency; and, 2. He is bound to receive it at its legal value. 6 Duverg. n. 174.

CURRENT, *merc. law.* A term used to express present time; the current month; *i. e.* the present month. Price current, is the ordinary price at the time spoken of. A printed paper, containing such prices, is also called a price current.

2. Current, in another sense, signifies that which is readily received; as, current money.

CURSITOR BARON, *Eng. law.* An officer of the court of the exchequer, who is appointed by patent under the great seal, to be one of the barons of the exchequer.

CURTESY, or COURTESY, *Scotch law.* A life-rent, given by law to the surviving husband, of all his wife's heritage of which she died infeft, if there was a child of the marriage born alive. The child born of the marriage must be the mother's heir. If she had a child by a former marriage, who is to succeed to her estate, the husband has no right to the curtesy while such child is alive; so that the curtesy is due to the husband rather as father to the heir, than as husband to an heiress, conformable to the Roman law, which gives to the father the usufruct of what the child succeeds to by the mother. Ersk. Pr. L. Scot. B. 2, t. 9, s. 30. Vide *Estate by the curtesy.*

CURTILAGE, *estates.* The open space situated within a common enclosure belonging to a dwelling-house. Vide 2 Roll, Ab. 1, l. 30; Com. Dig. Grant, E 7, E 9; Russ. & Ry. 360; Id. 334, 357; Ry. & Mood. 13; 2 Leach, 913; 2 Bos. & Pull. 508; 2 East, P. C. 494; Russ. & Ry. 170, 289, 322; 22 Eng. Com. Law R. 330; 1 Ch. Pr. 175; Shep. Touchs. 94.

CUSTODY. The detainer of a person

by virtue of a lawful authority. To be in custody, is to be lawfully detained under arrest. Vide 14 Vin. Ab. 359; 3 Chit. Pr. 355. In another sense, custody signifies having the care and possession of a thing; as, the chancellor is entitled to the custody as the keeper of the seal.

CUSTOM. A usage which has acquired the force of law. It is, in fact, a lex loci, which regulates all local or real property within its limits. A repugnancy which destroys it, must be such as to show it never did exist. 5 T. R. 414. In Pennsylvania no customs have the force of law but those which prevail throughout the state. 6 Binn. 419, 20

2. A custom derives its force from the tacit consent of the legislature and the people, and supposes an original, actual deed or agreement. 2 Bl. Com. 30, 31; 1 Chit. Pr. 283. Therefore, custom is the best interpreter of laws: *optima est legum interpres consuetudo.* Dig. 1, 3, 37; 2 Inst. 18. It follows, therefore, there can be no custom in relation to a matter regulated by law. 8 M. R. 309. Law cannot be established or abrogated except by the sovereign will, but this will may be express or implied and presumed; and whether it manifests itself by words or by a series of facts, is of little importance. When a custom is public, peaceable, uniform, general, continued, reasonable and certain, and has lasted "time whereof the memory of man runneth not to the contrary," it acquires the force of law. And when any doubts arise as to the meaning of a statute, the custom which has prevailed on the subject ought to have weight in its construction, for the manner in which a law has always been executed is one of its modes of interpretation. 4 Penn. St. Rep. 13.

3. Customs are general or particular customs. 1. By general customs is meant the common law itself, by which proceedings and determinations in courts are guided. 2. Particular customs are those which affect the inhabitants of some particular districts only. 1 Bl. Com. 68, 74. Vide 1 Bouv. Inst. n. 121; Bac. Ab. h. t.; 1 Bl. Com. 76; 2 Bl. Com. 31; 1 Lill. Reg. 516; 7 Vin. Ab. 164; Com. Dig. h. t.; Nelson's Ab. h. t.; the various Amer. Digs. h. t.; Ayl. Pand. 15, 16; Ayl. Parerg. 194; Doct. Pl. 201; 3 W. C. C. R. 150; 1 Gilp. 486; Pet. C. C. R. 220; 1 Edw. Ch. R. 146; 1 Gall. R. 443; 3 Watts, R. 178; 1 Rep. Const. Ct. 303, 308; 1 Caines, R. 45; 15 Mass. R. 433; 1 Hill, R. 270; Wright, R. 573; 1 N. & M. 176; 5 Binn. R. 287; 5 Ham. R. 436; 3 Conn. R. 9; 2 Pet. R. 148; 6 Pet. R. 715; 6 Porter, R. 123; 2 N. H. Rep. 93; 1 Hall, R. 612; 1 Harr. & Gill, 239; 1 N. S. 192; 4 L. R. 160; 7 L. R. 529; Id. 215.

CUSTOM OF MERCHANTS, *lex mercatoria.* A system of customs acknowledged and taken notice of by all nations, and are, therefore, a part of the general law of the land. See *Law merchant*, and 1 Chit. Bl. 76, note 9.

CUSTOM-HOUSE. A place appointed by law, in ports of entry, where importers of goods, wares and merchandise are bound to enter the same, in order to pay or secure the duties or customs due to the government.

CUSTOMARY RIGHTS. Rights which are acquired by custom. They differ from *prescriptive rights* in this, that the former are local usages, belonging to all the inhabitants of a particular place or district; the latter are rights of individuals, independent of the place of their residence. Best on Pres. § 79; Cruise, Dig. t. 31, c. 1, § 7; 2 Greenl. Ev. § 542.

CUSTOMS. This term is usually applied to those taxes which are payable upon goods and merchandise imported or exported. Story, Const. § 949; Bac. Ab. Smuggling.

CUSTOS ROTULORUM, *Eng. law.* The principal justice of the peace of a county, who is the keeper of the records of the county. 1 Bl. Com. 349.

TO CUT, *crim. law.* To wound with an instrument having a sharp edge. 1 Russ. on Cr. 577. Vide *To Stab; Wound.*

CY PRES, *construction.* These are old French words, which signify *as near as.*

2. In cases where a perpetuity is attempted in a will, the courts do not, if they can avoid it, construe the devise to be utterly void, but expound the will in such a manner as to carry the testator's intentions into effect, as far as the rules respecting perpetuities will allow; this is called a construction *cy pres.* When the perpetuity is attempted in a deed, all the limitations are totally void. Cruise, Dig. t. 38, c. 9, s. 34; and vide 1 Vern. 250; 2 Ves. Jr. 380, 336, 357, 364; 3 Ves. Jr. 141, 220; 4 Ves. 13; Com. Dig. Condition, L 1; 1 Rop. Leg. 514; Swinb. pt. 4, s. 7, a. 4; Dane's Ab. Index, h. t.; Toull. Dr. Civ. Fr. liv. 3, t. 3, n. 586, 595, 611; Domat, Loix Civ.

liv. 6, t. 2, s. 1; 1 Supp. to Ves. Jr. 134, 259, 317; 2 Id. 316, 473; Boyle on Charities, Index, h. t.; Shelford on Mortmain, Index, h. t.; 3 Bro. C. C. 166; 2 Bro. C. C. 492; 4 Wheat. R. 1; S. C. 3 Peters, R. App. 481; 3 Peters, R. 99; 15 Ves. 232· 2 Sto. Eq. Jur. § 1169.

CZAR. A title of honor which is assumed by the emperor of all the Russias. See *Autocracy*.

CZARINA. The title of the empress of Russia.

CZAROWITZ. The title of the eldest son of the czar and czarina of Russia.

D.

DAM. A construction of wood, stone, or other materials, made across a stream of water for the purpose of confining it; a mole.

2. The owner of a stream not navigable, may erect a dam across it, and employ the water in any reasonable manner, either for his use or pleasure, so as not to destroy or render useless, materially diminish, or affect the application of the water by the proprietors below on the stream. He must not shut the gates of his dams and detain the water unreasonably, nor let it off in unusual quantities to the annoyance of his neighbors. 4 Dall. 211; 3 Caines, 207; 13 Mass. 420; 3 Pick, 268; 2 N. H. Rep. 532; 17 John. 306; 3 John. Ch. Rep. 282; 3 Rawle, 256; 2 Conn. Rep. 584; 5 Pick. 199; 20 John. 90; 1 Pick. 180; 4 Id. 460; 2 Binn. 475; 14 Serg. & Rawle, 71; Id. 9; 13 John. 212; 1 McCord, 580; 3 N. H. Rep. 321; 1 Halst. R. 1; 3 Kent, Com. 354.

3. When one side of the stream is owned by one person and the other by another, neither, without the consent of the other, can build a dam which extends beyond the *filum aquæ*, thread of the river, without committing a trespass. Cro. Eliz. 269; 12 Mass. 211; Ang. on W. C. 14, 104, 141; vide Lois des Bât. P. 1, c. 3, s. 1, a. 3; Poth. Traité du Contrat de Société, second app. 236; Hill. Ab. Index, h. t.; 7 Cowen, R. 266; 2 Watts, R. 327; 3 Rawle, R. 90; 17 Mass. R. 289; 5 Pick. R. 175; 4 Mass. R. 401. Vide *Inundation*.

DAMAGE, *torts*. The loss caused by one person to another, or to his property, either with the design of injuring him, or with negligence and carelessness, or by inevitable accident.

2. He who has caused the damage is bound to repair it; and, if he has done it maliciously, he may be compelled to pay beyond the actual loss. When damage occurs by accident, without blame to any one, the loss is borne by the owner of the thing injured; as, if a horse run away with his rider, without any fault of the latter, and injure the property of another person, the injury is the loss of the owner of the thing. When the damage happens by the act of God, or inevitable accident, as by tempest, earthquake or other natural cause, the loss must be borne by the owner. Vide Com. Dig. h. t.; Sayer on Damages.

3. Pothier defines damage (dommages et intérêts) to be the loss which some one has sustained, and the gain which he has failed of making. Obl. n. 159.

DAMAGE FEASANT, *torts*. This is a corruption of the French words *faisant dommage*, and signifies doing damage. This term is usually applied to the injury which animals belonging to one person do upon the land of another, by feeding there, treading down his grass, corn, or other production of the earth. 3 Bl. Com. 6; Co. Litt. 142, 161; Com. Dig. Pleader, 3 M 26. By the common law, a distress of animals or things damage feasant is allowed. Cow. Inst. 230; Gilb. on Distress and Replevin, 21. It was also allowed by the ancient customs of France. 11 Toull. 402, 3; Repértoire de Jurisprudence, Merlin, au mot Fourriere; 1 Fournel, Traité de Voisinage, au mot Abandon. Vide *Animals*.

DAMAGED GOODS. In the language of the customs, are goods subject to duties, which have received some injury either in the voyage home, or while bonded in warehouses. See *Abatement*, merc. law.

DAMAGES, *practice*. The indemnity given by law, to be recovered from a wrong doer by the person who has sustained an injury, either in his person, property, or relative rights, in consequence of the acts of another.

2. Damages are given either for breaches of contracts, or for tortious acts.

3. Damages for breach of contract may be given, for example, for the non-performance of a written or verbal agreement; or of a covenant to do or not to do a particular thing.

4. As to the measure of damages the general rule is, that the delinquent shall answer for all the injury which results from the immediate and direct breach of his agreement, but not from secondary and remote consequences.

5. In cases of an eviction, on a covenant of seisin and warranty, the rule seems to be to allow the consideration money, with interest and costs. 6 Watts & Serg. 527; 2 Dev. R. 30; 3 Brev. R. 458. See 7 Shepl. 260; 4 Dev. 46. But in Massachusetts, on the covenant of warranty, the measure of damages is the value of the land at the time of eviction. 4 Kent's Com. 462, 3, and the cases there cited; 3 Mass. 523; 4 Mass. 108; 1 Bay, 19, 265; 3 Desaus. Eq. R. 247; 4 Penn. St. R. 168.

6. In estimating the measure of damages sustained in consequence of the acts of a common carrier, it frequently becomes a question whether the value of the goods at the place of embarkation or the port of destination is the rule to establish the damages sustained. It has been ruled that the value at the port of destination is the proper criterion. 12 S. & R. 186; 8 John. R. 213; 10 John. R. 1; 14 John. R. 170; 15 John. R. 24. But contrary decisions have taken place. 3 Caines, R. 219; 4 Hayw. R. 112; and see 4 Mass. R. 115; 1 T. R. 31; 4 T. R. 582.

7. Damages for tortious acts are given for acts against the person, as an assault and battery; against the reputation, as libels and slander; against the property, as trespass, when force is used; or for the consequential acts of the tort-feasor, as, when a man, in consequence of building a dam on his own premises, overflows his neighbor's land; or against the relative rights of the party injured, as for criminal conversation with his wife.

8. No settled rule or line of distinction can be marked out when a possibility of damages shall be accounted too remote to entitle a party to claim a recompense: each case must be ruled by its own circumstances. Ham. N. P. 40; Kames on Eq. 73, 74. Vide 7 Vin. Ab. 247; Yelv. 45, a; Id. 176, a; Bac. Ab. h. t.; 1 Lilly's Reg. 525; Domat, liv. 3, t. 5, s. 2, n. 4; Toull. liv. 3, n. 286; 2 Saund. 107, note; 1 Rawle's Rep. 27; Coop. Just. 606; Com. Dig. h. t.; Bouv. Inst. Index, h. t. See *Cause; Remote.*

9. Damages for torts are either compensatory or vindictive. By compensatory damages is meant such as are given merely to recompense a party who has sustained a loss in consequence of the acts of the defendant, and where there are no circumstances to aggravate the act, for the purpose of compensating the plaintiff for his loss; as, for example, where the defendant had caused to be seized, property of A for the debt of B, when such property was out of A's possession, and there appeared reason to believe it was B's. Vindictive damages are such as are given against a defendant, who, in addition to the trespass, has been guilty of acts of outrage and wrong which cannot well be measured by a compensation in money; as, for example, where the defendant went to A's house, and with insult and outrage seized upon A's property, for a debt due by B, and carried it away, leaving A's family in distress. Sedgw. on Dam. 39; 2 Greenl. Ev. § 253; 1 Gallis. 483; 12 Conn. 580; 2 M. & S. 77; 4 S. & R. 19; 5 Watts, 375; 5 Watts & S. 524; 1 P. S. R. 190, 197.

10. In cases of loss of goods which have been insured from maritime dangers, when an adjustment is made, the damages are settled by valuing the property, not according to prime cost, but at the price at which it may be sold at the time of settling the average. Marsh. Inst. B. 1, c. 14, s. 2, p. 621. See *Adjustment; Price.*

DAMAGES, EXCESSIVE. Such damages as are unreasonably great, and not warranted by law.

2. The damages are excessive in the following cases: 1. When they are greater than is demanded by the writ and declaration. 6 Call, 85; 7 Wend. 330. 2. When they are greater than is authorized by the rules and principles of law; as in the case of actions upon contracts, or for torts done to property, the value of which may be ascertained by evidence. 4 Mass. 14; 5 Mass. 435; 6 Halst. 284.

3. But in actions for torts to the person or reputation of the plaintiff, the damages will not be considered excessive unless they are outrageous. 2 A. K. Marsh. 365; Hard. 586; 3 Dana, 464; 2 Pick. 113; 7 Pick. 82; 9 John. 45; 10 John. 443; 4 Mass. 1; 9 Pick. 11; 2 Penn. 578.

4. When the damages are excessive, a new trial will be granted on that ground.

DAMAGES INADEQUATE. Such as are unreasonably low, and less than is required by law.

2. Damages are inadequate, when the plaintiff sues for a breach of contract, and the damages given are less than the amount proved. 9 Pick. 11.

3. In actions for torts, the smallness of damages cannot be considered by the court. 3 Bibb, 34. See 11 Mass. 150.

4. In a proper case, a new trial will be granted on the ground of inadequate damages.

DAMAGES ON BILLS OF EXCHANGE, *contracts*. A penalty affixed by law to the non-payment of a bill of exchange when it is not paid at maturity, which the parties to it are obliged to pay to the holder.

2. The discordant and shifting regulations on this subject which have been enacted in the several states, render it almost impossible to give a correct view of this subject. The drawer of a bill of exchange may limit the amount of damages by making a memorandum in the bill, that they shall be a definite sum; as, for example, "In case of non-acceptance or non-payment, reëxchange and expenses not to exceed ——— dollars. 1 Bouv. Inst. n. 1133. The following abstract of the laws of several of the United States, will be acceptable to the commercial lawyer.

3.—*Alabama*. 1. When drawn on a person in the United States. By the Act of January 15, 1828, the damages on a protested bill of exchange drawn on a person, either in this or any other of the United States, are ten per cent. By the Act of December 21, 1832, the damages on such bills drawn on any person in this state, or upon any person payable in New Orleans, and purchased by the Bank of Alabama or its branches, are five per cent.

4.—2. Damages on protested bills drawn on persons out of the United States are twenty per cent.

5.—*Arkansas*. 1. It is provided by the Act of February 28, 1838, s. 7, Ark. Rev. Stat. 150, that "every bill of exchange expressed to be for value received, drawn or negotiated within this state, payable after date, to order or bearer, which shall be duly presented for acceptance or payment, and protested for non-acceptance or non-payment, shall be subject to damages in the following cases: *first*, if the bill have been drawn on any person at any place within this state, at the rate of two per centum on the principal sum specified in the bill: *second*, if the bill shall be drawn on any person, and payable in any of the states of Alabama, Louisiana, Mississippi, Tennessee, Kentucky, Ohio, Indiana, Illinois, and Missouri, or any point on the Ohio river, at the rate of four per centum on the principal sum in such bill specified: *third*, if the bill shall have been drawn on any person, and payable at any place within the limits of the United States, not hereinbefore expressed, at the rate of five per centum on the principal sum specified in the bill: *fourth*, if the bill shall have been drawn on any person, and payable at any port or place beyond the limits of the United States, at the rate of ten per centum on the sum specified in the bill.

6.—2. And, by the 8th section of the same act, if any bill of exchange, expressed to be for value received, and made payable to order or bearer, shall be drawn on any person at any place within this state, and accepted and protested for non-payment, there shall be allowed and paid to the holder, by the acceptor, damages in the following cases: *first*, if the bill be drawn by any person at any place within this state, at the rate of two per centum on the principal sum therein specified: *second*, if the bill be drawn at any place without this state, but within the limits of the United States, at the rate of six per centum on the sum therein specified: *third*, if the bill be drawn on any person at any place without the limits of the United States, at the rate of ten per centum on the sum therein specified. And, by sect. 9, in addition to the damages allowed in the two preceding sections to the holder of any bill of exchange protested for non-payment or non-acceptance, he shall be entitled to costs of protest, and interest at the rate of ten per centum per annum, on the amount specified in the bill, from the date of the protest until the amount of the bill shall be paid."

7.—*Connecticut*. 1. When drawn on another place in the United States. When drawn upon persons in the city of New York, two per cent. When in other parts of the state of New York, or the New England states (other than this,) New Jersey, Pennsylvania, Delaware, Maryland, Virginia, or the District of Columbia, three per cent. When on persons in North or South Carolina, Georgia, or Ohio, five per cent. On other states, territories or districts, in the United States, eight per cent. on the principal sum in each case, with interest on the amount of such sum, with the damage after notice and demand. Stat. tit. 71, Notes and Bills, 413, 414. When drawn on persons residing in Connecticut o damages are allowed.

8.—2. When the bill is drawn on persons out of the United States, twenty per cent. is said to be the amount which ought reasonably to be allowed. Swift's Ev. 336. There is no statutory provision on the subject.

9.—*Delaware.* If any person shall draw or endorse any bill of exchange upon any person in Europe, or beyond seas, and the same shall be returned back unpaid, with a legal protest, the drawer thereof and all others concerned shall pay and discharge the contents of the said bill, together with twenty per cent. advance for the damage thereof; and so proportionably for a greater or less sum, in the same specie as the same bill was drawn, or current money of this government equivalent to that which was first paid to the drawer or endorser.

10.—*Georgia.* 1. Bills on persons in the United States. First, in the state. No damages are allowed on protested bills of exchange drawn in the state, on a person in the state, except bank bills, on which the damages are ten per cent. for refusal to pay in specie. 4 Laws of Geo. 75. Secondly, upon bills drawn or negotiated in the state on persons out of the state, but within the United States, five per cent. and interest. Act of 1823, Prince's Dig. 454; 4 Laws of Geo. 212.

11.—2. When drawn upon a person out of the United States, ten per cent. damages and postage, protest and necessary expenses; also the premium, if any, on the face of the bill; but if at a discount, the discount must be deducted. Act of 1827, Prince's Dig. 462; 4 Laws of Geo. 221.

12.—*Indiana.* 1. When drawn by a person in the state on another person in Indiana, no damages are allowed.

13.—2. When drawn on a person in another state, territory, or district, five per cent. 3. When drawn on a person out of the United States, ten per cent. Rev. Code, c. 13, Feb. 17, 1838.

14.—*Kentucky.* 1. When drawn by a person in Kentucky on a person in the state, or in any other state, territory, or district of the United States, no damages are allowed. See Acts, Sessions of 182), p. 823.

15.—2. When on a person in a foreign country, damages are given at the rate of ten per cent. per ann. from the date of the bill until paid, but not more than eighteen months interest to be collected. 2 Litt. 101.

16.—*Louisiana.* The rate of damages to be allowed and paid upon the usual protest for non-acceptance, or for non-payment of bills of exchange, drawn or negotiated within this state, in the following cases, is as follows: on all bills of exchange drawn on or payable in foreign countries, ten dollars upon the hundred upon the principal sum specified in such bills; on all bills of exchange, drawn on and payable in other states in the United States, five dollars upon the hundred upon the principal sum specified in such bill. Act of March 7, 1838, s. 1.

17. By the second section of the same act it is provided that such damages shall be in lieu of interest, charge of protest, and all other charges, incurred previous to the time of giving notice of non-acceptance or non-payment; but the principal and damages shall bear interest thereafter.

18. By section 3, it is enacted, that if the contents of such bill be expressed in the money of account of the United States, the amount of the principal and of the damages herein allowed for the non-acceptance or non-payment shall be ascertained and determined, without any reference to the rate of exchange existing between this state and the place on which such bill shall have been drawn, at the time of the payment, on notice of non-acceptance or non-payment.

19.—*Maine.* 1. When drawn payable in the United States. The damages in addition to the interest are as follows: if for one hundred dollars or more, and drawn, accepted, or endorsed in the state, at a place, seventy-five miles distant from the place where drawn, one per cent.; if, for any sum, drawn, accepted, and endorsed in this state, and payable in New Hampshire, Vermont, Connecticut, Rhode Island, or New York, three per cent.; if payable in New Jersey, Pennsylvania, Delaware, Maryland, Virginia, South Carolina, Georgia, or the District of Columbia, six per cent.; if payable in any other state, nine per cent. Rev. St. tit. 10 c. 115, §§ 110, 111.

20.—2. Out of the United States, no

statutory provision. It is the usage to allow the holder of the bill the money for which it was drawn, reduced to the currency of the state, at par, and also the charges of protest with American interest upon those sums from the time when the bill should have been paid; and the further sum of one-tenth of the money for which the bill was drawn, with interest upon it from the time payment of the dishonored bill was demanded of the drawer. But nothing has been allowed for reëxchange, whether it is below or above par. Per Parsons, Ch. J. 6 Mass. 157, 161; see 6 Mass. 162.

21.—*Maryland.* 1. No damages are allowed when the bill is drawn in the state on another person in Maryland.

22.—2. When it is drawn on any "person, company, or society, or corporation in any other of the United States," eight per cent. damages on the amount of the bill are allowed, and an amount to purchase another bill, at the current exchange, and interest and losses of protest.

24.—3. If the bill be drawn on a "foreign country," fifteen per cent. damages are allowed, and the expense of purchasing a new bill as above, besides interest and costs of protest. See Act of 1785, c. 38.

25.—*Michigan.* 1. When a bill is drawn in the state on a person in the state, no damages are allowed.

26.—2. When drawn or endorsed within the state, and payable out of it, within the United States, the rule is as follows: in addition to the contents of the bill, with interest and costs, if payable within the states of Wisconsin, Illinois, Indiana, Ohio, and New York, three per cent. on the contents of the bill; if payable within the states of Missouri, Kentucky, Maine, New Hampshire, Vermont, Massachusetts, Rhode Island, Connecticut, New Jersey, Pennsylvania, Delaware, Maryland, Virginia, or the District of Columbia, five per centum; if payable elsewhere in the United States, out of Michigan, ten per cent. Rev. St. 156, s. 10.

27.—3. When the bill is drawn within this state, and payable out of the United States, the party liable must pay the same at the current rate of exchange at the time of demand of payment, and damages at the rate of five per cent. on the contents thereof, together with interest on the said oontents, which must be computed from the date of the protest, and are in full of all damages and charges and expenses. Rev. Stat. 156, s. 9.

28.—*Mississippi.* 1. When drawn on a person in the state, five per cent. damages are allowed. How. & Hutch. 376, ch. 35, s. 20, L. 1827; How. Rep. 3. 195.

29.—2. When drawn on a person in another state or territory, no damages are given. Id. 3. When drawn on a persou out of the United States, ten per cent. damages are given, and all charges incidental thereto, with lawful interest. How. & Hutch. 376, ch. 35, s. 19, L. 1837.

30.—*Missouri.* 1. When drawn on a person within the state, four per cent. damages on the sum specified in the bill are given. Rev. Code, 1835, § 8, cl. 1, p. 120.

31.—2. When on another state or territory, ten per cent. Rev. Code, 1835, § 8, cl. 2, p. 120. 3. When on a person out of the United States, twenty per cent. Rev. Code, 1835, § 8, cl. 3, p. 120.

32.—*New York.* By the Revised Statutes, Laws of N. Y. sess. 42, ch. 34, it is provided that upon bills drawn or negotiated within the state upon any person, at any place within the six states east of New York, or in New Jersey, Pennsylvania, Ohio, Delaware, Maryland, Virginia, or the District of Columbia, the damages to be allowed and paid upon the usual protest for non-acceptance or non-payment, to the holder of the bill, as purchaser thereof, or of some interest therein, for a valuable consideration, shall be three per cent. upon the principal sum specified in the bill; and upon any person at any place within the states of North Carolina, South Carolina, Georgia, Kentucky, and Tennessee, five per cent.; and upon any person in any other state or territory of the United States, or at any other place on, or adjacent to, this continent, and north of the equator, or in any British or foreign possessions in the West Indies, or elsewhere in the Western Atlantic Ocean, or in Europe, ten per cent. The damages are to be in lieu of interest, charges of protest, and all other charges incurred previous to, and at the time of, giving notice of non-acceptance or non-payment. But the holder will be entitled to demand and recover interest upon the aggregate amount of the principal sum specified in the bill, and the damages, from time of notice of the protest for non-acceptance, or notice of a demand and protest for non-payment. If the contents of the bill be expressed in the money of account of the United States, the amount due thereon, and the damages allowed for the non-payment, are to be ascertained and determined, without reference to the rate of exchange existing between New York and the place on which the bill is drawn. But if the contents of the bills be expressed in the money of account or currency of any foreign country, then the amount due, exclusive of the damages, is to be ascertained and determined by the rate of exchange, or the value of such foreign currency, at the time of the demand of payment.

33.—*Pennsylvania.* The Act of March 30, 1821, entitled an act concerning bills of exchange, enacts, that, § 1, "whenever any bill of exchange hereafter be drawn and endorsed within this commonwealth, upon any person or persons, or body corporate, of, or in any other state, territory, or place, shall be returned unpaid with a legal protest, the person or persons to whom the same shall or may be payable, shall be entitled to recover and receive of and from the drawer or drawers, or the endorser or endorsers of such bill of exchange, the damages hereinafter specified, over and above the principal sum for which such bill of exchange shall have been drawn, and the charges of protest, together with lawful interest on the amount of such principal sum, damages and charges of protest, from the time at which notice of said protest shall have been given, and the payment of said principal sum and damages, and charges of protest demanded; that is to say, if such bill shall have been drawn upon any person or persons, or body corporate, of, or in any of the United States or territories thereof, excepting the state of Louisiana, five per cent. upon such principal sum; if upon any person or persons, or body corporate, of, or in Louisiana, or of, or in any other state or place in North America, or the islands thereof, excepting the northwest coast of America and Mexico, or of, or in any of the West India or Bahama Islands, ten per cent. upon such principal sum; if upon any person or persons, or body corporate, of, or in the island of Madeira, the Canaries, the Azores, the Cape de Verd Islands, the Spanish Main, or Mexico, fifteen per cent. upon such principal sum; if upon any person or persons, or body corporate, of, or in any state or place in Europe, or any of the islands thereof, twenty per cent. upon such principal sum; if upon any person or persons, or body corporate, of, or in any other part of the world, twenty-five per cent. upon such principal sum.

34.—§ 2. "The damages, which, by this act, are to be recovered upon any bill of exchange, shall be in lieu of interest and all other charges, except the charges of protest, to the time when notice of the protest and demand of payment shall have been given and made aforesaid; and the amount of such bill and of the damages payable thereon, as specified in this act, shall be ascertained and determined by the rate of exchange, or value of the money or currency mentioned in such bill, at the time of notice of protest and demand of payment as before mentioned."

35.—*Tennessee.* 1. On a bill drawn or endorsed within the state upon any person or persons, or body corporate, of, or in, any other state, territory, or place, which shall be returned unpaid, with a legal protest, the holder shall be entitled to the damages hereinafter specified, over and above the principal sum for which such bill of exchange shall have been drawn, and the charges of protest, together with lawful interest on the amount of such principal sum, damages, and charges of protest, from the time at which notice of such protest shall have been given, and the payment of said principal sum, damages, and charges of protest demanded; that is to say, if such bill shall have been drawn on any person or persons, or body corporate, of, or in, any of these United States, or the territories thereof, three per cent. upon such principal sum: if upon any other person or persons, or body corporate, of, or in, any other state or place in North America, bordering upon the Gulf of Mexico, or of, or in, any of the West India Islands, fifteen per cent. upon such principal sum; if upon any person or persons, or body corporate, of, or in, any other part of the world, twenty per cent. upon such principal sum.

36.—2. The damages which, by this act, are to be recovered upon any bill of exchange, shall be in lieu of interest and all other charges, except charges of protest, to the time when notice of the protest and demand of payment shall have been given and made as aforesaid. Carr. & Nich. Comp. 125; Act of 1827, c. 14.

Damages, double or treble, *practice* In cases where a statute gives a party double or treble damages, the jury are to find single damages, and the court to enhance them, according to the statute Bro. Ab. Damages, pl. 70; 2 Inst. 416; 1 Wils. 126; 1 Mass. 155. In Sayer on Damages, p. 244, it is said, the jury may assess the statute damages; and it would seem from some of the modern cases, that either the jury or the court may assess. Say. R. 214; 1 Gallis, 29.

Damages, general, *torts*. General damages are such as the law implies to have accrued from the act of a tort-feasor. To call a man a thief, or to commit an assault and battery upon his person, are examples of this kind. In the first case the law presumes that calling a man a thief must be injurious to him, without showing that it is so; Sir W. Jones, 196; 1 Saund. 243, b. n. 5; and in the latter case, the law implies that his person has been more or less deteriorated, and that the injured party is not required to specify what injury he has sustained, nor to prove it. Ham. N. P. 40; 1 Chit. Pl. 386; 2 L. R. 76; 4 Bouv. Inst. n. 3584.

Damages, laying, *pleading*, In personal and mixed actions, (but not in penal actions, for obvious reasons,) the declaration must allege, in conclusion, that the injury is to the damage of the plaintiff; and must specify the amount of damages. Com. Dig. Pleader, C 84; 10 Rep. 116, b.

2. In personal actions there is a distinction between actions that sound in damages, and those that do not; but in either of those cases, it is equally the practice to lay damages. There is, however, this difference: that, in the former case, damages are the main object of the suit, and are, therefore, always laid high enough to cover the whole demand; but in the latter, the liquidated debt, or the chattel demanded, being the main object, damages are claimed in respect of the detention only, of such debt or chattel; and are, therefore, usually laid at a small sum. The plaintiff cannot recover greater damages than he has laid in the conclusion of his declaration. Com. Dig. Pleader, C 84; 10 Rep. 117, a, b; Vin. Ab. Damages, R.

3. In real actions, no damages are to be laid, because, in these, the demand is specially for the land withheld, and damages are in no degree the object of the suit. Steph. Pl. 426; 1 Chit. Pl. 397 to 400.

Damages, liquidated, *contracts*. When the parties to a contract stipulate for the payment of a certain sum, as a satisfaction fixed and agreed upon by them, for the doing or not doing of certain things particularly mentioned in the agreement; the sum so fixed upon is called *liquidated damages*. (q. v.) It differs from a penalty, because the latter is a forfeiture from which the defaulting party can be relieved. An agreement for liquidated damages can only be when there is an engagement for the performance of certain acts, the not doing of which would be an injury to one of the parties; or to guard against the performance of acts which, if done, would also be injurious. In such cases an estimate of the damages may be made by a jury, or by a previous agreement between the parties, who may foresee the consequences of a breach of the engagement, and stipulate accordingly. 1 H. Bl. 232; and vide 2 Bos. & Pul. 335, 350–355; 2 Bro. P. C. 431; 4 Burr, 2225; 2 T. R. 32. The civil law appears to agree with these principles. Inst. 3, 16, 7; Toull. liv. 3, n. 809; Civil Code of Louis. art. 1928, n. 5; Code Civil, 1152, 1153.

2. It is to be observed that the sum fixed upon will be considered as liquidated damages, or a penalty, according to the intent of the parties, and the mere use of the words; "penalty," "forfeiture," or "liquidated damages," will not be regarded as at all decisive of the question, if the instrument discloses, upon the whole, a different intent. 2 Story, Eq. § 1318; 6 B. & C. 224; 6 Bing. 141; 6 Iredell, 186; 3 Shepl. 273; 2 Ala. 425; 8 Misso. 467.

3. Rules have been adopted to ascertain whether such sum so agreed upon shall be considered a penalty or liquidated damages, which will be here enumerated by considering, first, those cases where it has been considered as a penalty; and, secondly, where it has been considered as liquidated damages.

4.—1. It has been treated as a penalty, 1st. Where the parties in the agreement have expressly declared the sum intended as a forfeiture or a penalty, and no other intent can be collected from the instrument. 2 B. & P. 340, 350, 630; 1 McMullan, 106; 2 Ala. 425; 5 Metc. 61; 1 H. Bl. 227; 1 Campb. 78; 7 Wheat. 14; 1 Pick. 451; 4 Pick. 179; 3 John. Cas. 297. 2d. Where it is doubtful whether it was intended as a penalty or not, and a certain debt or damages, less than the penalty, is made payable on the face of the instrument. 3 C. & P. 240; 6 Humph. 186. 3d. Where the agreement was made, evidently, for the attainment of another object, to which the sum specified is wholly collateral. 11 Mass. 76; 15 Mass. 488; 1 Bro. C. C. 418.

4th. Where the agreement contains several matters, of different degrees of importance, and yet the sum named is payable for the breach of any, even the least. 6 Bing. 141; 5 Bing. N. C. 390; 7 Scott, 364; sed vide, 7 John. 72; 15 John. 200. 5th. Where the contract is not under seal, and the damages are capable of being certainly known and estimated. 2 B. & Al. 704; 6 B. & C. 216; 1 M. & Malk. 41; 4 Dall. 150; 5 Cowen, 144.

5.—2. The sum agreed upon has been considered as liquidated damages, 1st. Where the damages are uncertain, and are not capable of being ascertained by any satisfactory and known rule. 2 T. R. 32; 1 Alc. & Nap. 389; 2 Burr, 2225; 10 Ves. 429; 3 M. & W. 545; 8 Mass. 223; 3 C. & P. 240; 7 Cowen, 307; 4 Wend. 468. 2d. Where, from the tenor of the agreement, or from the nature of the case, it appears that the parties have ascertained the amount of damages by fair calculation and adjustment. 2 Story, Eq. Juris. § 1318; 10 Mass. 459; 7 John. 72; 15 John. 200; 1 Bing. 302; 7 Conn. 291; 13 Wend. 507; 2 Greenl. Ev. § 259; 11 N. H. Rep. 234; 6 Blackf. 206; 26 Wend. 630; 17 Wend. 447; 22 Wend. 201; 7 Metc. 583; 2 Ala. 425; 2 Shepl. 250.

Vide, generally, 7 Vin. Ab. 247; 16 Vin. Ab. 58; 2 W. Bl. Rep. 1190; Coop. Just. 606; 1 Chit. Pr. 872; 2 Atk. 194; Finch. 117; Prec. in Ch. 102; 2 Bro. P. C. 436; Fonbl. 151, 2, note; Chit. Contr. 336; 11 N. Hamp. Rep. 234.

DAMAGES, SPECIAL, *torts*. Special damages are such as are in fact sustained, and are not implied by law; these are either superadded to general damages, arising from an act injurious in itself, as when some particular loss arises from the uttering of slanderous words, actionable in themselves, or are such as arise from an act indifferent and not actionable in itself, but injurious only in its consequences, as when the words become actionable only by reason of special damage ensuing. To constitute special damage the legal and natural consequence must arise from the tort, and not be a mere wrongful act of a third person, or a remote consequence. 1 Camp. 58; Ham. N. P. 40; 1 Chit. Pl. 385, 6.

DAMAGES, SPECIAL, *pleading*. As distinguished from the gist of the action, signify that special damage which is stated to result from the gist; as, if a plaintiff in an action of trespass for breaking his close, entering his house, and tossing his goods about, were to state that by means of the damage done to his house, he was obliged to seek lodging elsewhere.

2. Sometimes the special damage is said to constitute the gist of the action itself; for example, in an action wherein the plaintiff declares for slanderous words, which of themselves are not a sufficient ground or foundation for the suit, if any particular damage result to the plaintiff from the speaking of them, that damage is properly said to be the gist of the action.

3. But whether special damage be the gist of the action, or only collateral to it, it must be particularly stated in the declaration, as the plaintiff will not otherwise be permitted to go into evidence of it at the trial, because the defendant cannot also be prepared to answer it. Willes, 23. See *Gist*.

DAMAGES, UNLIQUIDATED. The unascertained amount which is due to a person by another for an injury to the person, property, or relative rights of the party injured. These damages, being unknown, cannot be set off against a claim which the tort feasor has against the party injured. 2 Dall. 237; S. C. 1 Yeates, 571; 10 Serg. & Rawle, 14; 5 Serg. & Rawle, 122.

DAMNIFICATION. That which causes a loss or damage to a society, or to one who has indemnified another. For example, when a society has entered into an obligation to pay the debt of the principal, and the principal has become bound in a bond to indemnify the surety, the latter has suffered a damnification the moment he becomes liable to be sued for the debt of the principal; and it has been held in an action brought by the surety upon a bond of indemnity, that the terror of suit, so that the surety dare not go about his business, is a damnification. Ow. 19; 2 Chit. R. 487; 1 Saund. 116; 8 East, 593; Cary, 26.

2. A judgment fairly obtained against a party for a cause against which another person is bound to indemnify him, with timely notice to that person of the bringing of the action, is admissible as evidence in an action brought against the guarantor on the indemnity. 7 Cranch, 300, 322. See F. N. B. Warrantia Chartæ; Lib. Int. Index, Warrantia Chartæ; 2 S. & R. 12, 13.

DAMNIFY. To cause damage, injury or loss.

DAMNOSA HÆREDITAS. A name

given by Lord Kenyon to that species of property of a bankrupt, which, so far from being valuable, would be a charge to the creditors; for example, a term of years, where the rent would exceed the revenue.

2. The assignees are not bound to take such property, but they must make their election, and, having once entered into possession, they cannot afterwards abandon the property. 7 East, R. 342; 3 Campb. 340.

DAMNUM ABSQUE INJURIA. A loss or damage without injury.

2. There are cases when the act of one man may cause a damage or loss to another, and for which the latter has no remedy; he is then said to have received damnum absque injuria; as, for example, if a man should set up a school in the neighborhood of another school, and, by that means, deprive the former of its patronage; or if a man should build a mill along side of another, and consequently reduce his custom. 9 Pick. 59, 528.

3. Another instance may be given of the case where a man using proper care and diligence, while excavating for a foundation, injures the adjoining house, owing to the unsuitable materials used in such house; here the injury is *damnum absque injuria.*

4. When a man slanders another by publishing the truth, the person slandered is said to have sustained loss without injury. Bac. Ab. Actions on the Case, C; Dane's Ab. Index, h. t.

DAMNUM FATALE, *civil law.* Damages caused by a fortuitous event, or inevitable accident; damages arising from the act of God. Among these were included losses by shipwreck, lightning, or other casualty; also losses by pirates or by vis major, by fire, robbery, and burglary; but theft was not numbered among these casualties.

2. In general, bailees are not liable for such damages. Story, Bailm. p. 471.

DANE-LAGE, *Eng. law.* That system of laws which was maintained in England while the Danes had possession of the country.

DANGERS OF THE SEA, *mar. law.* This phrase is sometimes put in bills of lading, the master of the ship agreeing to deliver the goods therein mentioned to the consignee, who is named, the dangers of the sea excepted. Sometimes the phrase is *Perils of the Sea.* (q. v.) See 1 Brock. R. 187.

DARREIN. A corruption of the French word *dernier*, the last. It is sometimes used, as, *darrein continuance*, the last continuance. When any matter has arisen in discharge of the defendant in action, he may take advantage of it, provided he pleads it *puis darrein continuance*; for if he neglect to do so, he waives his right. Vide article *Puis darrein continuance.*

DARREIN SEISIN. The name of a plea to a writ of entry or a writ of right. 3 Met. 175.

DATE. The designation or indication in an instrument of writing, of the time, and usually of the time and place, when and where it was made. When the place is mentioned in the date of a deed, the law intends, unless the contrary appears, that it was executed at the place of the date. Plowd. 7 b., 31 H. VI. This word is derived from the Latin *datum,* because when deeds and agreements were written in that language, immediately before the day, month and year in which they were made, was set down, it was usual to put the word *datum*, given.

2. All writings ought to bear a date, and in some it is indispensable, in order to make them valid, as in policies of insurance; but the date in these instruments is not inserted in the body of the writing, because as each subscription makes a separate contract, each underwriter sets down the day, month and year he makes his subscription. Marsh. Ins. 336.

3. Deeds, and other writings, when the date is an impossible one, take effect from the time of delivery; the presumption of law is, that the deed was dated on the day it bears date, unless, as just mentioned, the time is impossible; for example, the 32d day of January.

4. The proper way of dating, is to put the day, month, and year of our Lord; the hour need not be mentioned, unless specially required; an instance of which may be taken from the Pennsylvania Act of the 16th June, 1836, sect. 40, which requires the sheriff, on receiving a writ of *fieri facias,* or other writ of execution, to endorse thereon the day of the month, the year, and the *hour* of the day whereon he received the same.

5. In public documents, it is usual to give not only the day, the month, and the year of our Lord, but also the year of the United States, when issued by authority of the general government; or of the commonwealth, when issued under its authority. Vide, generally, Bac. Ab. Obligations, C; Com. Dig, Fait, B 3; Cruise, Dig. tit. 32, c. 20, s. 1–6; 1 Burr. 60; 2 Rol. Ab. 27, l. 22; 13 Vin. Ab. 34; Dane's Ab. Index, h. t. See *Almanac.*

DATION, *civil law, contracts.* The act of giving something. It differs from donation, which is a gift; dation, on the contrary, is giving something without any liberality; as, the giving of an office.

2. Dation in payment, *datio in solutionem*, which was the giving one thing in payment of another which was due, corresponds nearly to the *accord and satisfaction* of the common law.

DATION EN PAIEMENT, *civil law.* This term is used in Louisiana; it signifies that, when instead of paying a sum of money due on a preëxisting debt, the debtor gives and the creditor agrees to receive a movable or immovable.

2. It is somewhat like the accord and satisfaction of the common law. 16 Toull. n. 45; Poth. Vente, n. 601. Dation en paiement resembles in some respects the contract of sale; *dare in solutum, est quasi vendere.* There is, however, a very marked difference between a sale and a dation en paiement. 1st. The contract of sale is complete by the mere agreement of the parties; the dation en paiement requires a delivery of the thing given. 2d. When the debtor pays a certain sum which he supposed he was owing, and he discovers he did not owe so much, he may recover back the excess, not so when property other than money has been given in payment. 3d. He who has in good faith sold a thing of which he believed himself to be the owner, is not precisely required to transfer the property of it to the buyer; and, while he is not troubled in the possession of the thing, he cannot pretend that the seller has not fulfilled his obligations. On the contrary, the dation en paiement is good only when the debtor transfers to the creditor the property in the thing which he has agreed to take in payment; and if the thing thus delivered be the property of another, it will not operate as a payment. Poth. Vente, n. 602, 603, 604.

DATIVE. That which may be given or disposed of at will and pleasure. It sometimes means that which is not cast upon the party by the law, or by a testator, but which is given by the magistrate; in this sense it is, that tutorship is dative, when the tutor is appointed by the magistrate. Leç. Elem. § 239; Civ Code of L. art. 288, 1671.

DAUGHTER. An immediate female descendant. See *Son.*

DAUGHTER-IN-LAW. In Latin, *nurus*, is the wife of one's son.

DAY. A division of time. It is natural, and then it consists of twenty-four hours, or the space of time which elapses while the earth makes a complete revolution on its axis; or artificial, which contains the time, from the rising until the setting of the sun, and a short time before rising and after setting. Vide *Night;* and Co. Lit. 135, a.

2. Days are sometimes calculated exclusively, as when an act required that an appeal should be made within twenty days after a decision. 3 Penna. 200; 3 B. & A. 581; 15 Serg. & Rawle, 43. In general, if a thing is to be done within such a time after such a fact, the day of the fact shall be taken inclusively. Hob. 139; Doug. 463; 3 T. R. 623; Com. Dig. Temps, A; 3 East, 407.

3. The law, generally, rejects fractions of days, but in some cases it takes notice of such parts. 2 B. & A. 586. Vide *Date.*

4. By the custom of some places, the word *days* is understood to be working days, and not including Sundays. 3 Espin. N. P. C. 121. Vide, generally, 2 Chit. Bl. 141, note 3; 1 Chit. Pr. 774, 775; 3 Chit. Pr. 110; Lill. Reg. h. t.; 1 Rop. Leg. 518; 15 Vin. Ab. 554; Dig. 33, 1, 2; Dig. 50, 16, 2, 1; Id. 2, 12, 8; and articles *Hour; Month; Year.*

DAY BOOK, *mer. law.* An account book, in which merchants and others make entries of their daily transactions. This is generally a book of original entries, and as such may be given in evidence to prove the sale and delivery of merchandise or of work done.

DAY RULE, or DAY WRIT, *English practice.* A rule or order of the court, by which a prisoner on civil process, and not committed, is enabled, in term time, to go out of the prison, and its rule or bounds; a prisoner is enabled to quit the prison, for more or less time, by three kinds of rules, namely: 1. The day-rule. 2. The term-rule; and 3. The rules. See 9 East, R. 151.

DAYS IN BANK, *Eng. practice.* Days of appearance in the court of common pleas, usually called *bancum.* They are at the distance of about a week from each other, and are regulated by some festival of the church. 3 Bl. Com. 277.

DAYS OF GRACE. Certain days after the time limited by the bill or note, which the acceptor or drawer has a right to demand for payment of the bill or note; these days were so called because they were formerly gratuitously allowed, but now, by the custom of merchants, sanctioned by decisions of courts of justice, they are demandable of right. 6 Watts & Serg. 179. The number of these in the United States is generally three. Chitty on Bills, h. t. But where the established usage of the place where the instrument is payable, or of the bank at which it is payable, or deposited for collection, be to make the demand on the fourth or other day, the parties to the note will be bound by such usage. 5 How. U. S. Rep. 317; 1 Smith, Lead. Cas. 417. When the last day of grace happens on the 4th of July; 2 Caines' Cas. in Err. 195; or on Sunday; 2 Caines' R. 343; 7 Wend. 460; the demand must be made on the day previous. 13 John. 470; 7 Wend. 460; 12 Mass. 89; 6 Pick. 80; 2 Caines, 343; 2 McCord, 436. But see 2 Conn. 69. See 20 Wend. 205; 1 Metc. R. 43; 2 Cain. Cas. 195; 7 How. Miss. R. 129; 4 J. J. Marsh. 332.

2. In Louisiana, the days of grace are no obstacle to a set off, the bill being due, for this purpose, before the expiration of those days. Louis. Code, art. 2206.

3. In France all days of grace, of favor, of usage, or of local custom, for the payment of bills of exchange, are abolished. Code de Com. art. 135. See 8 Verm. 333; 2 Port. 286; 1 Conn. 329; 1 Pick. 401; 2 Pick. 125; 3 Pick. 414; 1 N. & M. 83.

Days of the week. These are Sunday, Monday, Tuesday, Wednesday, Thursday, Friday, Saturday. See *Week*.

2. The court will take judicial notice of the days of the week; for example, when a writ of inquiry was stated in the pleadings to have been executed on the fifteenth of June, and, upon an examination, it was found to be Sunday, the proceeding was held to be defective. Fortesc. 373; S. C. Str. 387.

DE. A preposition used in many Latin phrases; as, de bene esse, de bonis non.

De arbitratione facta, writ. In the ancient English law, when an action was brought for the same cause of action which had been before settled by arbitration, this writ was brought. Wats. on Arb. 256.

De bene esse, *practice*. A technical phrase applied to certain proceedings which are deemed to be well done for the present, or until an exception or other avoidance; that is, *conditionally*, and in that meaning the phrase is usually accepted. For example, a declaration is filed or delivered, special bail put in, witness examined, &c. de bene esse, or conditionally; good for the present.

2. When a judge has a doubt as to the propriety of finding a verdict, he may direct the jury to find one de bene esse; which verdict, if the court shall afterwards be of opinion it ought to have been found, shall stand. Bac. Ab. Verdict, A. Vide 11 S. & R. 84.

De bonis non. This phrase is used in cases where the goods of a deceased person have not all been administered. When an executor or administrator has been appointed, and the estate is not fully settled, and the executor or administrator is dead, has absconded, or from any cause has been removed, a second administrator is appointed to perform the duty remaining to be done, who is called an administrator *de bonis non*, an administrator of the goods not administered; and he becomes by the appointment the only representative of the deceased. 11 Vin. Ab. 111; 2 P. Wms. 340; Com. Dig. Administration, B 1; 1 Root's R. 425. And it seems that though the estate has been distributed, an administrator *de bonis non* may be appointed, if debts remain unsatisfied. 1 Root's R. 174.

De bonis propriis. Of his own goods When an executor or administrator has been guilty of a *devastavit*, (q. v.) he is responsible for the loss which the estate has sustained, *de bonis propriis*. He may also subject himself to the payment of a debt of the deceased, *de bonis propriis*, by his false plea, when sued in a representative capacity; as, if he plead *plene administravit*, and it be found against him, or a release to himself, when false. In this latter case the judgment is *de bonis testatoris si, et si non de bonis propriis*. 1 Saund. 336 b, n. 10; Bac. Ab. Executor, B 3.

De contumace capiendo. The name of a writ issued for the arrest of a defendant who is in contempt of the ecclesiastical court. 1 Nev. & Per. 680, 685, 689; 5 Dowl. 213, 646.

De domo reparanda. The name of an ancient common law writ, by which one tenant in common might compel his cotenant to concur in the expense of repairing the property held in common. 8 B. & C. 269; 1 Tho. Co. Litt. 216, note 17, and p. 787.

De donis, statute. The name of an English statute passed the 13 Edwd. I. c. 1, the real design of which was to introduce perpetuities, and to strengthen the power of the barons. 6 Co. 40 a; Co. Litt. 21; Bac. Ab. Estates in tail, *in prin.*

DE FACTO, *i. e.* in deed. A term used to denote a thing actually done; a president of the United States *de facto* is one in the exercise of the executive power, and is distinguished from one, who being legally entitled to such power is ejected from it; the latter would be a president *de jure*. An officer *de facto* is frequently considered as an officer *de jure*, and his official acts are of equal validity. 10 S. & R. 250; 4 Binn. R. 371; 11 S. & R. 411, 414; Coxe, 318; 9 Mass. 231; 10 Mass. 290; 15 Mass. 180; 5 Pick. 487.

DE HOMINE REPLEGIANDO. The name of a writ which is used to replevy a man out of prison, or out of the custody of a private person. See *Homine replegiando; Writ de homine replegiando.*

DE INJURIA, *pleading*. The name of a replication in an action for a tort, that the defendant committed the trespasses or grievances of his own wrong, without the cause by him in his plea alleged.

2. The import of this replication is to insist that the defendant committed the act complained of, from a motive and impulse altogether different from that insisted on by the plea. For example, if the defendant has justified a battery under a writ of *capias*, having averred, as he must do, that the arrest was made by virtue of the writ; the plaintiff may reply *de injuria sua propria absque tali causa*, that the defendant did the act of his own wrong, without the cause by him alleged. This replication, then, has the effect of denying the alleged motive contained in the plea, and to insist that the defendant acted from another, which was unlawful, and not in consequence of the one insisted upon in his plea. Steph. Pl. 186; 2 Chit. Pl. 523, 642; Hamm. N. P. 120, 121; Arch. Civ. Pl. 264; Com. Dig. Pleader, F 19.

3. The form of this replication is, "*precludi non*, because he says that the said defendant at the same time when, &c., of his own wrong, and without the cause by him in his said second plea alleged, committed the said trespass in the introductory part of that plea, in manner and form as the said plaintiff hath above in his said declaration complained against the said defendant, and this the said plaintiff prays may be inquired of by the country," &c. This is the uniform conclusion of such a replication. 1 Chit. Pl. 585.

4. The replication *de injuria* is only allowed when an excuse is offered for personal injuries. 1 B. & P. 76; 5 Johns. R. 112; 4 Johns. 150; 12 Johns. 491. Vide 7 Vin. Ab. 503; 3 Saund. 295, note; 1 Lilly's Reg. 587.

5. In England, where the extent of the general issues has been confined in actions on contracts, and special pleas have become common in assumpsit, it has become desirable, that the plaintiff, who has but one replication, should put in issue the several numerous allegations which the special pleas were found to contain; for, unless he could do this, he would labor under the hardship of being frequently compelled to admit the greater part of an entirely false story. It became, therefore, important to ascertain whether *de injuria* could not be replied to cases of this description; and, after numerous cases which were presented for adjudication, it was finally settled that *de injuria* may be replied in assumpsit, when the plea consits of matters of excuse. 3 C. M. & R. 65; 2 Bing. N. C. 579; 4 Dowl. 647.

6. The improper use of *de injuria* is ground of general demurrer. 2 Lev. 65; 4 Tyrw. 777. But if the defendant do not demur, the objection will not avail after verdict. Hob. 76: Sir T. Raym. 50.

7. *De injuria* puts in issue the whole of the defence contained in the plea. 5 B. & A. 420; 11 East, 451; 10 Bing. 157. But if the plea state some authority *in law*, which, *prima facie*, would be a justification of the act complained of, the plaintiff will not be allowed under the plea of *de injuria* to show an abuse of that authority so as to convert the defendant into a tort feasor *ab initio*. 1 Bing. 317; 1 Bing. N. S. 387. See 1 Smith's L. C. 53 to 61; 8 Co. 66.

DE JUDAISMO, STATUTUM. The name of a statute passed in the reign of Edw. I., which enacted severe and absurd penalties against the Jews. Barr. on Stat. 197.

2. The Jews were exceedingly oppressed during the middle ages throughout Christendom, and are so still in some countries. In France, a Jew was a serf, and his person and goods belonged to the baron on whose demesnes he lived. He could not change his domicil without permission of the baron, who could pursue him as a fugitive even on the domains of the king. Like an article of commerce, he might be lent or hired for a time, or mortgaged. If he became a Christian, his conversion was considered a larceny

of the lord, and his property and goods were confiscated. They were allowed to utter their prayers only in a low voice and without chanting. They were not allowed to appear in public without some badge or mark of distinction. Christians were forbidden to employ Jews of either sex as domestics, physicians or surgeons. Admission to the bar was forbidden to Jews. They were obliged to appear in court in person, when they demanded justice for a wrong done them, and it was deemed disgraceful to an advocate to undertake the cause of a Jew. If a Jew appeared in court against a Christian, he was obliged to swear by the ten names of God, and invoke a thousand imprecations against himself, if he spoke not the truth. Sexual intercourse between a Christian man and a Jewess was deemed a crime against nature, and was punishable with death by burning. *Quia est rem habere cum cane, rem habere à Christiano* cum Judaea quæ CANIS reputatur; sic comburi debet. 1 Fournel, Hist. des Avocats, 108, 110. See Merlin, Répert. au mot Juifs.

3. In the fifth book of the Decretals, it is provided, that if a Jew have a servant that desireth to be a Christian, the Jew shall be compelled to sell him to a Christian for twelve pence; that it shall not be lawful for them to take any Christian to be their servant; that they may repair their old synagogues, but not build new; that it shall not be lawful for them to open their doors or windows on good Friday; that their wives neither have Christian nurses, nor themselves be nurses to Christian women; that they wear different apparel from the Christians, whereby they may be known, &c. See Ridley's View of the Civ. and Eccl. Law, part 1, chap. 5, sect. 7; and Madox, Hist. of the Exchequer, Index, as to their condition in England.

DE JURE, by right. Vide *De facto*.

DE LUNATICO INQUIRENDO. The name of a writ directed to the sheriff, directing him to inquire by good and lawful men whether the party charged is a lunatic or not. See 4 Rawle, 234; 1 Whart. 52; 5 Halst. 217; 6 Wend. 497.

DE MEDIETATE LINGUÆ. Of half tongue. Vide *Medietas linguæ*.

DE MELIORIBUS DAMNIS. Of the better damages. When a plaintiff has sued several defendants, and the damages have been assessed severally against each, he has the choice of selecting the best, as he cannot recover the whole. This is done by making an election *de melioribus damnis*.

DE MERCATORIBUS. This is the name of a statute passed in the 11 Edw. I.; it is usually called the statute of Acton Burnell, De Mercatoribus. It was passed in consequence of the complaints of foreign merchants, who could not recover their claims, because the lands of the debtors could not be sold for their debts. It enacted that the chattels and devisable burgages of the debtor might be sold for the payment of their debts. Cruise, Dig. t. 14, s. 6.

DE NOVO. Anew; afresh. When a judgment upon an issue in part is reversed on error, for some mistake made by the court, in the course of the trial, a venire de novo is awarded in order that the case may again be submitted to a jury.

DE NOVI OPERIS NUNCIATIONE, *civil law*. Where a thing is intended to be done against another man's right, the party aggrieved may have in many cases, according to the civilians, an interdict or injunction, to hinder that which is intended to his prejudice: as where one buildeth an house contrary to the usual and received form of building, to the injury of his neighbor, there lieth an injunction *de novi operis nunciatione*, which being served, the offender is either to desist from his work or to put in sureties that he shall pull it down, if he do not in a short time avow, *i. e.* show, the lawfulness thereof Ridley's Civ. and Eccl. Law, part 1, chap 1, sect. 8.

DE ODIO ET ATIA. These words signify *from hatred and ill will*. When a person was committed on a charge of a crime, from such a motive, he could sue the writ *de otio et atia*, and procure his liberty on giving bail. The object is now obtained by a writ of *habeas corpus*. Vide *Writ de odio et atia*.

DE PARTITIONE FACIENDA. The name of a writ for making partition. Vide *Partition*.

DE PROPRIETATE PROBANDA, *Eng. practice*. The name of a writ which issues in a case of replevin, when the defendant claims property in the chattels replevied, and the sheriff makes a return accordingly. The writ directs the sheriff to summon an inquest to determine on the validity of the claim; and, if they find for the defendant, the sheriff merely returns their finding. The plaintiff is not concluded by such finding, he may come into the court above and traverse it. Hamm. N. P. 456.

DE QUOTA LITIS. The name of a part or

contract, in the civil law, by which one who has a claim difficult to recover, agrees with another to give a part, for the purpose of obtaining his services to recover the rest. 1 Duv. n., 201.

2. Whenever such an agreement amounts to champerty, it is void by law. 5 Monr. 416; 5 John. ch. 44.

3. Attorneys cannot lawfully make a bargain with their clients to receive for their compensation, a part of the thing sued for; in New York, 2 Caines, 147; Ohio, 1 Ham. 132; Alabama, 755; and some other states; but in some of the states such contracts are not unlawful.

DE REPARATIONE FACIENDA. The name of a writ, which lies by one tenant in common against the other, to cause him to aid in repairing the common property. 8 B. & C. 269.

DE RETORNO HABENDO. The name of a writ issued after a judgment has been given in replevin, that the defendant should have a return of the goods replevied. See 3 Bouv. Inst. n. 3376.

DE SON TORT. Of his own wrong. This term is usually applied to a person who, having no right to meddle with the affairs or estate of a deceased person, yet undertakes to do so, by acting as executor of the deceased. Vide *Executor de son tort.*

DE SON TORT DEMESNE, *of his own wrong, pleading.* The name of a replication in an action for a wrong or injury. When the defendant pleads a matter merely in excuse of an injury to the person or reputation of another, the plaintiff may reply *de son tort demesne sans tiel cause;* that it was the defendant's own wrong without such cause. Vide the articles, *De Injuria,* and *Without*, and also 8 Co. 69 a; Bro. h. t.; Com. Dig. Pleader, F 18.

DE UNA PARTE. A deed *de una parte*, is one where only one party grants, gives or binds himself to do a thing to another. It differs from a deed *inter partes.* (q. v.) 2 Bouv. Inst. n. 2001.

DE WARRANTIA DIEI, WRIT, *Eng. law.* Where a man is required to appear on a certain day in person, and before that day the king certifies that the party is in the king's service, he may sue this writ, commanding the justices not to record his default for that day for the cause before mentioned. F. N. B. 36.

DEACON, *Eccl. law.* A minister or servant in the church, whose office, in some churches, is to assist the priest in divine service, and the distribution of the sacrament.

DEAD. Something which has no life; figuratively, something of no value.

DEAD BODY, *crim. law.* A corpse.

2. To take up a dead body without lawful authority, even for the purposes of dissection, is a misdemeanor, for which the offender may be indicted at common law. 1 Russ. on Cr. 414; 1 Dowl. & R. 13; Russ. & Ry. 366, n. b; 2 Chit. Cr. Law, 35. This offence is punished by statute in New Hampshire, Laws of N. H. 339, 340 in Vermont, Laws of Vermont, 368, c. 361 in Massachusetts, stat. 1830, c. 51; 8 Pick. 370; 11 Pick. 350; in New York, 2 Rev. Stat. 688. Vide 1 Russ. 414, n. A.

3. The preventing a dead body from being buried, is also an indictable offence. 2 T. R. 734; 4 East, 460; 1 Russ. on Cr. 415 and 416, note A.

4. To inter a dead body found in a river, it seems, would render the offender liable to an indictment for a misdemeanor, unless he first sent for the coroner. 1 Kenyon's R. 250.

DEAD-BORN, *descent, persons.* Children dead-born are considered, in law, as if they had never been conceived, so that no one can claim a title, by descent, through such dead-born child. This is the doctrine of the civil law. Dig. 50, 16, 129. *Non nasci, et natum mori, pari sunt. Mortuus exitus, non est exitus.* Civil Code of Louis. art. 28. A child in ventre sa mere is considered in being, only when it is for its advantage, and not for the benefit of a third person. The rule in the common law is, probably, the same, that a dead-born child is to be considered as if he had never been conceived or born; in other words, it is presumed he never had life—it being a maxim of the common law, that mortuus exitus non est exitus. Co. Litt. 29 b. See 2 Paige, R. 35; Domat, liv. prél. t. 2, s. 1, n. 4, 6; 4 Ves. 334.

DEAD FREIGHT, *contracts.* When the charterer of a vessel has shipped part of the goods on board, and is not ready to ship the remainder, the master, unless restrained by his special contract, may take other goods on board, and the amount which is not supplied, required to complete the cargo, is called *dead freight.*

2. The dead freight is to be calculated according to the actual capacity of the vessel. 3 Chit. Com. Law, 399; 2 Stark. 450.

DEAD MAN'S PART, *English law.* By

the custom of London, when a deceased freeman of the city left a widow and children, after deducting what was called the widow's chamber, (q. v.) his personal property was divided into three parts; one of which belonged to the widow, another to the children, and the third to the administrator. When there was only a widow, or only children, in either case they respectively took one moiety, and the administrator the other; when there was neither widow nor child, the administrator took the whole for his own use; and this portion was called the *dead man's part*. By statute of 1 Jac. 2, c. 17, this was changed, and the dead man's part is declared to be subject to the statute of distribution. 2 Bl. Com. 518. See Bac. Ab. Customs of London, D 4.

DEAD LETTERS. Those which remain in the post-office, uncalled for.

2. By the Act of March 3, 1825, 3 Story. L. U. S. 1993, it is enacted, by § 26, "That the postmasters shall, respectively, publish, at the expiration of every three months, or oftener, when the postmaster general shall so direct, in one of the newspapers published at, or nearest, the place of his residence, for three successive weeks, a list of all the letters remaining in their respective offices; or, instead thereof, shall make out a number of such lists, and cause them to be posted at such public places, in their vicinity, as shall appear to them best adapted for the information of the parties concerned; and, at the expiration of the next three months, shall send such of the said letters as then remain on hand, as dead letters, to the general post-office, where the same shall be opened and inspected; and if any valuable papers, or matters of consequence, shall be found therein, it shall be the duty of the postmaster general to return such letter to the writer thereof, or cause a descriptive list thereof to be inserted in one of the newspapers published at the place most convenient to the supposed residence of the owner, if within the United States; and such letter, and the contents, shall be preserved, to be delivered to the person to whom the same shall be addressed, upon payment of the postage, and the expense of publication. And if such letter contain money, the postmaster general may appropriate it to the use of the department, keeping an account thereof, and the amount shall be paid by the department to the rightful claimant as soon as he shall be found."

3. And by the Act of July 2, 1836, 4 Sharsw. Cont. of Story, L. U. S. 2474, it is enacted by § 35, that advertisements of letters remaining in the post-offices, may, under the direction of the postmaster general, be made in more than one newspaper: provided, that the whole cost of advertising shall not exceed four cents for each letter.

DEAD-PLEDGE. A mortgage of lands or goods; mortuum vadium.

DEAF AND DUMB. No definition is requisite, as the words are sufficiently known. A person deaf and dumb is *doli capax* but with such persons who have not been educated, and who cannot communicate their ideas in writing, a difficulty sometimes arises on the trial.

2. A case occurred of a woman, deaf and dumb, who was charged with a crime. She was brought to the bar, and the indictment was then read to her, and the question, in the usual form, was put, guilty or not guilty? The counsel for the prisoner then rose, and stated that he could not allow his client to plead to the indictment, until it was explained to her that she was at liberty to plead guilty or not guilty. This was attempted to be done, but was found impossible, and she was discharged from the bar *simpliciter*.

3. A person, deaf and dumb, may be examined as a witness, provided he can be sworn, that is, if he is capable of understanding the terms of the oath, and assents to it; and if, after he is sworn, he can convey his ideas, with or without an interpreter, to the court and jury. Phil. Ev. 14.

DEAF, DUMB, AND BLIND. A man born deaf, dumb, and blind, is considered an idiot. (q. v.) 1 Bl. Com. 304; F. N. B. 233; 2 Bouv. Inst. n. 2111.

DEALINGS. Traffic, trade; the transaction of business between two or more persons.

2. The English statute 6 Geo. IV. c. 16, s. 81, declares all dealings with a bankrupt, within a certain time immediately before his bankruptcy, to be void. It has been held, under this statute, that payments were included under the term *dealings*. M. & M. 137; 3 Car. & P. 85; S. C. 14 Eng. C. L. R. 219.

DEAN, *eccl. law*. An ecclesiastical officer, who derives his name from the fact that he presides over ten canons, or, prebendaries, at least. There are several kinds of deans, namely: 1. Deans of chapters. 2. Deans of peculiars. 3. Rural deans. 4. Deans in the colleges. 5. Honorary deans. 6. Deans of provinces.

DEATH, *med. jur., crim. law, evidence.* The cessation of life.

2. It is either natural, as when it happens in the usual course, without any violence; or violent, when it is caused either by the acts of the deceased, or those of others. Natural death will not be here considered further than may be requisite to illustrate the manner in which violent death occurs. A violent death is either accidental or criminal; and the criminal act was committed by the deceased, or by another.

3. The subject will be considered, 1. As it relates to medical jurisprudence; and, 2. With regard to its effects upon the rights of persons.

4.—§ 1. It is the office of medical jurisprudence, by the light and information which it can bestow, to aid in the detection of crimes against the persons of others, in order to subject them to the punishment which is awarded by the criminal law. Medical men are very frequently called upon to make examinations of the bodies of persons who have been found dead, for the purpose of ascertaining the causes of their death. When it is recollected that the honor, the fortune, and even the life of the citizen, as well as the distribution of impartial justice, frequently depend on these examinations, one cannot but be struck at the responsibility which rests upon such medical men, particularly when the numerous qualities which are indispensably requisite to form a correct judgment, are considered. In order to form a correct opinion, the physician must be not only skilled in his art, but he must have made such examinations his special study. A man may be an enlightened physician, and yet he may find it exceedingly difficult to resolve, properly, the grave and almost always complicated questions which arise in cases of this kind. Judiciary annals, unfortunately, afford but too many examples of the fatal mistakes made by physicians, and others, when considering cases of violent deaths.

5. In the examination of bodies of persons who have come to a violent death, every precaution should be taken to ascertain the situation of the place where the body was found; as to whether the ground appears to have been disturbed from its natural condition; whether there are any marks of footsteps, their size, their number, the direction to which they lead, and whence they came; whether any traces of blood or hair can be found · and whether any, and what weapons or instruments, which could have caused death, are found in the vicinity; and these instruments should be carefully preserved so that they may be identified. A case or two may here be mentioned, to show the importance of examining the ground in order to ascertain the facts. Mr. Jeffries was murdered at Walthamstow, in England, in 1751, by his niece and servant. The perpetrators were suspected from the single circumstance that the dew on the ground surrounding the house had not been disturbed on the morning of the murder. Mr. Taylor, of Hornsey, was murdered in December, 1818, and his body thrown into the river. It was evident he had not gone into the river willingly, as the hands were found clenched and contained grass, which, in the struggle, he had torn from the bank. The marks of footsteps, particularly in the snow, have been found, not unfrequently, to correspond with the shoes or feet of suspected persons, and led to their detection. Paris, Med. Jur. vol. iii. p. 38, 41.

6. In the survey of the body the following rules should be observed: 1. It should be as thoroughly examined as possible without changing its position or that of any of the limbs; this is particularly desirable when, from appearances, the death has been caused by a wound, because by moving it, the altitude of the extremities may be altered, or the state of a fracture or luxation changed; for the internal parts vary in their position with one another, according to the general position of the body. When it is requisite to remove it, it should be done with great caution. 2. The clothes should be removed, as far as necessary, and it should be noted what compresses or bandages (if any) are applied to particular parts, and to what extent. 3. The color of the skin, the temperature of the body, the rigidity or flexibility of the extremities, the state of the eyes, and of the sphincter muscles, noting at the same time whatever swellings, ecchymosis, or livid, black, or yellow spots, wounds, ulcer, contusion, fracture, or luxation may be present. The fluids from the nose, mouth, ears, sexual organs, &c., should be examined; and, when the deceased is a female, it may be proper to examine the sexual organs with care, in order to ascertain whether before death she was ravished or not. 1 Briand, Méd. Lég. 2eme partie, ch. 1, art. 3, n. 5, p. 318. 4. The clothes of the deceased should be carefully examined, and if parts are torn or

defaced, this fact should be noted. A list should also be made of the articles found on the body, and of their state or condition, as whether the purse of the deceased had been opened; whether he had any money, &c. 5. The state of the body as to decomposition should be particularly stated, as by this it may sometimes be ascertained when the death took place; experience proves that in general after the expiration of fourteen days after death, decomposition has so far advanced, that identity cannot be ascertained, excepting in some strongly developed peculiarity; but in a drowned body, adipocire is not produced until five or six weeks after death; but this depends upon circumstances, and varies according to climate, season, &c. It is exceedingly important, however, to keep this fact in view in some judicial inquiries relative to the time of death. 1 Chit. Med. Jur. 443. A memorandum should be made of all the facts as they are ascertained; when possible, it should be made on the ground; but when this cannot be done, as when chemical experiments are to be made, or the body is to be dissected, they should be made in the place where these operations are performed. 1 Beck's Med. Jur. 5; Dr. Gordon Smith, 505; Ryan's Med. Jur. 145; Dr. Male's Elem. of Judicial and For. Med. 101; 3 Paris & Fonbl. Med. Jur. 23 to 25; Vilanova Y Mañes, Materia Criminal Forense, Obs. 11, cap. 7, n. 7; Trebuchet, Médécine Légale, 12, et seq.; 1 Briand, Méd. Lég. 2eme partie, ch. 1, art. 5. Vide article *Circumstances*.

7.—§ 2. In examining the law as to the effect which death has upon the rights of others, it will be proper to consider, 1. What is the presumption of life or death. 2. The effects of a man's death.

8.—1. It is a general rule, that persons who are proved to have been living, will be presumed to be alive till the contrary is proved; and when the issne is upon the death of a person, the proof of the fact lies upon the party who asserts the death. 2 East, 312; 2 Rolle's R. 461. But when a person has been absent for a long time, unheard from, the law will presume him to be dead. It has been adjudged, that after twenty-seven years; 3 Bro. C. C. 510; twenty years, in another ease; sixteen years; 5 Ves. 458; fourteen years; 3 Serg. & Rawle, 390; twelve years; 18 John. R. 141; seven years; 6 East, 80, 85; and even five years; Finck's R. 419; the presumption of death arises. It seems that even seven years has been agreed as the time when death may in general be presumed. 1 Phil. Ev. 159. See 24 Wend. R. 221; 4 Whart. R. 173. By the civil law, if any woman marry again without certain intelligence of the death of her husband, how longsoever otherwise her husband be absent from her, both she and he who married her shall be punished as adulterers. Authentics, 8th Coll.; Ridley's View of the Civ. and Ecc. Law, 82.

9. The survivorship of two or more is to be proved by facts, and not by any settled legal rule, or prescribed presumption. 5 B. & Adolp. 91; 27 E. C. L. R. 45; Cro. Eliz. 503; Bac. Ab. Execution, D; 2 Phillim. 261; 1 Mer. R. 308; 3 Hagg. Eccl. R. 748. But see 1 Yo. & Coll. N. C. 121; 1 Curt. R. 405, 406, 429. In the following cases, no presumption of survivorship was held to arise; where two men, the father and son, were hanged about the same time, and one was seen to struggle a little longer than the other; Cro. Eliz. 503; in the case of General Stanwix, who perished at sea in the same vessel with his daughter; 1 Bl. R. 610; and in the case of Taylor and his wife, who also perished by being wrecked at sea with her, to whom he had bequeathed the principal part of his fortune. 2 Phillim. R. 261; S. C. 1 Eng. Eccl. R. 250. Vide Fearne on Rem. iv.; Poth. Obl. by Evans, vol. ii., p. 345; 1 Beck's Med. Jur. 487 to 502. The Code Civil of Fance has provided for most, perhaps all possible cases, art. 720, 721 and 722. The provisions have been transcribed in the Civil Code of Louisiana, in these words:

10.—Art. 930. If several persons respectively entitled to inherit from one another, happen to perish in the same event, such as a wreck, a battle, or a conflagration, without any possibility of ascertaining who died first, the presumption of survivorship is determined by the circumstances of the fact.

11.—Art. 931. In defect of the circumstances of the fact, the determination must be guided by the probabilities resulting from the strength, age, and difference of sex, according to the following rules.

12.—Art. 932. If those who have perished together were under the age of fifteen years, the eldest shall be presumed to have survived. If both were of the age of sixty years, the youngest shall be presumed to have survived. If some were under fifteen years, and some above sixty, the first shall be presumed to have survived.

13.—Art. 933. If those who perished together, were above the age of fifteen years, and under sixty, the male must be presumed to have survived, where there was an equality of age, or a difference of less than one year. If they were of the same sex, the presumption of survivorship, by which the succession becomes open in the order of nature, must be admitted; thus the younger must be presumed to have survived the elder.

14.—2. The death of a man, as to its effects upon others, may be considered with regard, 1. To his contracts. 2. Torts committed by or against him. 3. The disposition of his estate; and, 4. To the liability or discharge of his bail.

15.—1st. The contracts of a deceased person are in general not affected by his death, and his executors or administrators are required to fulfil his engagements, and may enforce those in his favor. But to this general rule there are some exceptions; some contracts are either by the terms employed in making them, or by implication of law, to continue only during the life of the contracting party. Among these may be mentioned the following cases: 1. The contract of marriage. 2. The partnership of individuals. The contract of partnership is dissolved by death, unless otherwise provided for. Indeed the partnership will be dissolved by the death of one or more of the partners, and its effects upon the other partners or third persons will be the same, whether they have notice of the death or otherwise. 3 Mer. R. 593; Story, Partn. § 319, 336, 343; Colly. Partn. 71; 2 Bell's Com. 639, 5th ed.; 3 Kent, Com. 56, 4th ed.: Gow, Partn. 351; 1 Molloy, R. 465; 15 Ves. 218; S. C. 2 Russ. R. 325. 3. Contracts which are altogether personal; as, for example, where the deceased had agreed to accompany the other party to the contract, on a journey, or to serve another; Poth. Ob. P. 3, c. 7, a. 3, § 2 and 3; or to instruct an apprentice. Bac. Ab. Executor, P; 1 Burn's Just. 82, 3; Hamm. on Part. 157; 1 Rawle's R. 61.

16. The death of either a constituent or of an attorney puts an end to the power of attorney. To recall such power two things are necessary; 1st. The will or intention to recall; and, 2d. Special notice or general authority. Death is a sufficient recall of such power, answering both requisites. Either it is, according to one hypothesis, the intended termination of the authority; or, according to the other, the cessation of that will, the existence of which is requisite to the existence of the attorney's power; while on either supposition, the event is, or is supposed to be, notorious. But exceptions are admitted where the death is unknown, and the authority, in the meanwhile, is in action, and relied on. 3 T. R. 215; Poth. Ob. n. 448.

17.—2d. In general, when the tort feasor or the party who has received the injury dies, the action for the recovery of the damages dies with him; but when the deceased might have waived the tort, and maintained assumpsit against the defendant, his personal representative may do the same thing. See the article *Actio personalis moritur cum persona*, where this subject is more fully examined. When a person accused and guilty of crime dies before trial, no proceedings can be had against his representatives or his estate.

18.—3d. By the death of a person seised of real estate, or possessed of personal property at the time of his death; his property vests when he has made his will, as he has directed by that instrument; but when he dies intestate, his real estate vests in his heirs at law by descent, and his personal property, whether in possession or in action, belongs to his executors or administrators.

19.—4th. The death of a defendant discharges the special bail. Tidd, Pr. 243; but when he dies after the return of the *ca. sa.*, and before it is filed, the bail are fixed. 6 T. R. 284; 5 Binn. R. 332, 338; 2 Mass. R. 485; 1 N. H. Rep. 172; 12 Wheat. 604; 4 John. R. 407; 3 M'Cord, R. 49; 4 Pick. R. 120; 4 N. H. Rep. 29.

20. Death is also divided into natural and civil.

21. *Natural* death is the cessation of life.

22. *Civil* death is the state of a person who, though possessing natural life, has lost all his civil rights, and, as to them, is considered as dead. A person convicted and attainted of felony, and sentenced to the state prison for life, is, in the state of New York, in consequence of the act of 29th of March, 1799, and by virtue of the conviction and sentence of imprisonment for life, to be considered as civilly dead. 6 Johns. C. R. 118; 4 Johns. C. R. 228, 260; Laws of N. Y. Sess. 24, ch. 49, s. 29, 30, 31; 1 N. R. L. 157, 164; Co. Litt. 130, a;

3 Inst. 215; 1 Bl. Com. 132, 133; 4 Bl. Com. 332; 4 Vin. Ab. 152. See Code Civ. art. 22 a 25; 1 Toull. n. 280 and p. 254, 5, note; also, pp. 243–5, n. 272; 1 Malleville's Discussion of the Code Civil, 45, 49, 51, 57. Biret, Vocab. au mot Effigie.

23. Death *of a partner*. The following effects follow the death of a partner, namely: 1. The partnership is dissolved, unless otherwise provided for by the articles of partnership. Gow's Partn. 429. 2. The representatives of the deceased partner become tenants in common with the survivor in all partnership effects in possession. 3. Choses in action so far survive that the right to reduce them into possession vests exclusively in the survivor. 4. When recovered, the representatives of the deceased partner have, in equity, the same right of sharing and participating in them that their testator or intestate would have had had he been living. 5. It is the duty and the right of the surviving partner to settle the affairs of the firm, for which he is not allowed any compensation. 6. The surviving partner is alone to be sued at law for debts of the firm, yet recourse can be had in equity against the assets of the deceased debtor. Gow's Partn. 460. Vide *Capital Crime; Dissolution; Firm; Partners; Partnership; Punishment*. See, generally, Bouv. Inst. Index, h. t.

DEATH BED, *Scotch law*. The incapacity to exercise the power of disposing of one's property after being attacked with a mortal disease.

2. It commences with the beginning of such disease.

3. There are two exceptions to this general rule, namely: 1. If he survive for sixty days after the act; or, 2. If he go to kirk or market unattended. He is then said to be in legitima potestate, or in liege poustie. 1 Bell's Com. 84, 85.

DEATH BED OR DYING DECLARATIONS. In cases of homicide, those which are made *in extremis*, when the person making them is conscious of his danger and has given up all hopes of recovery, charging some other person or persons with the murder. See 1 Phil. Ev. 200; Stark. Ev. part 4, p. 458; 15 Johns. R. 288; 1 Hawk's R. 442; 2 Hawk's R. 31; M'Nally's Ev. 174; Swift's Ev. 124.

2. These declarations, contrary to the general rule that hearsay is not evidence, are constantly received. The principle of this exception is founded partly on the situation of the dying person, which is considered to be as powerful over his conscience as the obligation of an oath, and partly on the supposed absence of interest on the verge of the next world, which dispenses with a necessity of a cross-examination. But before such declarations can be admitted in evidence against a prisoner, it must be satisfactorily proved, that the deceased at the time of making them was conscious of his danger and had given up all hopes of recovery. 1 Phil. Ev. 215, 216; Stark. Ev. part 4, p. 460.

3. They are admissible, as such, only in cases of homicide, where the death of the deceased is the subject of the charge, and the circumstances of the death are the subject of the dying declarations. 2 B. & C. 605; 15 John. 286; 4 C. & P. 233. Vide. 2 M. & Rob. 53.

4. The declarant must not have been incapable of a religious sense of accountability to his Maker; for, if it appears that such religious sense was wanting, whether it arose from infidelity, imbecility or tender age, the declarations are alike inadmissible. 1 Greenl. Ev. § 157; 1. Phil. Ev. 289; Phil. & Am. Ev. 296; 2 Russ. on Cr. 688.

See, in general, Bac. Abr. Evidence, K; Addis. R. 332; East's P. C. 354, 356; 1 Stark. C. 522; 2 Hayw. R. 31; 1 Hawk's R. 442; Swift's Ev. 124; Pothier, by Evans, vol. 2, p. 293; Anth. N. P. 176, and note a; Str. 500.

DEATH'S PART, *English law*. That portion of the personal estate of a deceased man which remained after his wife and children had received their reasonable parts from his estate; which was, if he had both a wife and child or children, one-third part; if a wife and no child, or a child or children and no wife, one-half; if neither wife nor child, he had the whole to dispose of by his last will and testament; and if he made no will, the same was to go to his administrator. And within the city of London, and throughout the province of York, in case of intestacy, the wife and children were till lately entitled to their reasonable parts, and the residue only was distributable by the statute of distribution; but by the 11 G. I. c. 18, s. 17, 18, the power of devising was thrown generally open. Burn's L. Dict. See this Dict. tit. *Legitime*, and *Lex Falcidia*.

DEBATE, *legislation, practice*. A contestation between two or more persons, in which they take different sides of a ques tion, and maintain them, respectively, by facts and arguments; or it is a discussion, in writing, of some contested point.

2. The debate should be conducted with fairness, candor and decorum, and supported by facts and arguments founded in reason; when, in addition, it is ornamented y learning, and decorated by the powers of rhetoric, it becomes eloquent and persuasive. It is essential that the power of debate should be free, in order to an energetic discharge of his duty by the debator.

3. The Constitution of the United States, art. 1, s. 6, provides, that for any speech or debate, in either house, the senators and representatives shall not be questioned in any other place.

4. It is a rule of the common law, that counsel may, in the discharge of professional duty, use strong epithets, however derogatory to the character of the opponent, or his attorney, or other agent or witness, in commenting on the facts of the case, if pertinent to the cause, and stated in his instructions, without any liability to any action for the supposed slander, whether the thing stated were true or false. 1 B. & Ald. 232; 3 Dow's R. 273, 277, 279; 7 Bing. R. 459; S. C. 20 E. C. L. R. 198. Respectable and sensible counsel, however, will always refrain from the indulgence of any unjust severity, both on their own personal account, and because browbeating a witness, or other person, will injuriously affect their case in the eyes of a respectable court and jury. 3 Chit. Pr. 887, 8.

DEBENTURE. A certificate given, in pursuance of law, by the collector of a port of entry, for a certain sum, due by the United States, payable at a time therein mentioned, to an importer for drawback of duties on merchandise imported and exported by him, provided the duties arising on the importation of the said merchandise shall have been discharged prior to the time aforesaid. Vide Act of Congress of March 2, 1799, s. 80; Encyclopédie, h. t.; Dane's Ab. Index, h. t.

DEBET ET DETINET, *pleading*. He owes and detains. In an action of debt, the form of the writ is either in the *debet* and *detinet*,—that is, it states that the defendant owes and unjustly detains the debt or thing in question,—it is so brought between the original contracting parties; or, it is in the *detinet* only; that is, that the defendant unjustly detains from the plaintiff the debt or thing for which the action is brought; this is the form in an action by an executor, because the debt or duty is not due to him, but it is unjustly detained from him. 1 Saund. 1.

2. There is one case in which the writ must be in the *detinet* between the contracting parties. This is when the action is instituted for the recovery of goods, as a horse, a ship, and the like, the writ must be in the *detinet*, for it cannot be said a man owes another a horse, or a ship, but only that he detains them from him. 3 Bl. Com. 153, 4; 11 Vin. Ab. 321; Bac. Ab. Debt, F; 1 Lilly's Reg. 543; Dane's Ab. h. t.

DEBIT, *accounts, commerce*. A term used in book-keeping, to express the left-hand page of the ledger, to which are carried all the articles supplied or paid on the subject of an account, or that are charged to that account. It also signifies the balance of an account.

DEBITUM IN PRÆSENTI, SOLVENDUM IN FUTURO. A debt due at present, to be paid in future. There is a difference between a debt payable now and one payable at a future time. On the former an action may be brought, on the latter no action lies until it becomes due. See *Due; Owing;* and 13 Pet. 494; 11 Mass. 493.

DEBT, *contracts*. A sum of money due by certain and express agreement. 3 Bl. Com. 154. In a less technical sense, as in the " act to regulate arbitrations and proceedings in courts of justice" of Pennsylvania, passed the 21st of March, 1806, s. 5, it means any claim for money. In a still more enlarged sense, it denotes any kind of a just demand; as, the debts of a bankrupt. 4 S. & R. 506.

2. Debts arise or are proved by matter of record, as judgment debts; by bonds or specialties; and by simple contracts, where the quantity is fixed and specific, and does not depend upon any future valuation to settle it. 3 Bl. Com. 154; 2 Hill. R. 220.

3. According to the civilians, debts are divided into *active* and *passive*. By the former is meant what is due to us, by the latter, what we owe. By *liquid* debt, they understand one, the payment of which may be immediately enforced, and not one which is due at a future time, or is subject to a condition; by *hypothecary debt* is meant, one which is a lien over an estate; and a *doubtful debt*, is one the payment of which is uncertain. Clef des Lois Rom. h. t.

4. Debts are discharged in various ways, but principally by payment. See *Accord and Satisfaction; Bankruptcy; Confusion; Compensation; Delegation; Defeasance; Discharge of a contract; Extinction; Extinguishment; Former recovery; Lapse of time; Novation; Payment; Release; Rescission; Set off.*

5. In payment of debts, some are to be paid before others, in cases of insolvent estates; first, in consequence of the character of the creditor, as debts due to the United States are generally to be first paid; and secondly, in consequence of the nature of the debt, as funeral expenses and servants' wages, which are generally paid in preference to other debts. See *Preference; Privilege; Priority.*

DEBT, *remedies.* The name of an action used for the recovery of a debt *eo nomine* and in numero; though damages are generally awarded for the detention of the debt; these are, however, in most instances, merely nominal. 1 H. Bl. 550; Bull. N. P. 167; Cowp. 588.

2. The subject will be considered with reference, 1. To the kind of claim or obligation on which this action may be maintained. 2. The form of the declaration. 3. The plea. 4. The judgment.

3.—§ 1. Debt is a more extensive remedy for the recovery of money than assumpsit or covenant, for it lies to recover money due upon legal liabilities, as for money lent, paid, had and received, due on an account stated; Com. Dig. Dett, A; for work and labor, or for the price of goods, and a quantum valebant thereon; Com. Dig. Dett, B; Holt, 206; or upon simple contracts, express or implied, whether verbal or written, or upon contracts under seal, or of record, or by a common informer, whenever the demand for a sum is certain, or is capable of being reduced to certainty. Bull. N. P. 167. It also lies to recover money due on any specialty or contract under seal to pay money. Str. 1089; Com. Dig. Dett, A 4; 1 T. R. 40. This action lies on a record, or upon a judgment of a court of record; Gilb. Debt, 391; Salk. 109; 17 S. & R. 1; or upon a foreign judgment. 3 Shepl. 167; 3 Brev. 395. Debt is a frequent remedy on statutes, either at the suit of the party grieved, or of a common informer. Com. Dig. Action on Statute, E; Bac. Ab. Debt, A. See, generally, Bouv. Inst. Index, h. t.; Com. Dig. h. t.; Dane's Ab. h. t., Vin. Ab h. t.; Chit. Pl. 100 to 109; Selw. N. P. 553 to 682; Leigh's N. P. Index, h. t. Debt also lies in the *detinet*, for goods; which action differs from detinue, because it is not essential in this action, as in detinue, that the property in any specific goods should be vested in the plaintiff, at the time the action is brought; Dy. 24 b; and debt in the *debet* and *detinet* may be maintained on an instrument by which the defendant is bound to pay a sum of money lent, which might have been discharged, on or before the day of payment, in articles of merchandise. 4 Yerg. R. 171; see Com. Dig. Dett, A 5; Bac. Ab. Debt, F; 3 Woodd. 103, 4; 1 Dall. R. 458.

4.—§ 2. When the action is on a *simple* contract, the declaration must show the consideration of the contract, precisely as in assumpsit; and it should state either a legal liability or an express agreement, though not a promise to pay the debt. 2 T. R. 28, 30. When the action is founded on a *specialty* or *record*, no consideration need be shown, unless the performance of the consideration constitutes a condition precedent, when performance of such consideration must be averred. When the action is founded on a deed, it must be declared upon, except in the case of debt for rent. 1 New R. 104.

5.—§ 3. The *plea* to an action of debt is either general or special. 1. The plea of general issue to debt on simple contracts, or on statutes, or when the deed is only matter of inducement, is *nil debet*. See *Nil debet*. In general, when the action is on a specialty, the plea denying the existence of the contract is *non est factum;* 2 Ld. Raym. 1500; to debt on record, *nul tiel record.* 16 John. 55. Other matters must, in general, be pleaded specially.

6.—§ 4. For the form of the *judgment*, see *Judgment in debt.* Vide *Remedy.*

DEBTEE. One to whom a debt is due; a creditor; as, debtee executor. 3 Bl. Com. 18.

DEBTOR, *contracts.* One who owes a debt; he who may be constrained to pay what he owes.

2. A debtor is bound to pay his debt personally, and all the estate he possesses or may acquire, is also liable for his debt.

3. Debtors are joint or several; joint, when they all equally owe the debt in solido; in this case if a suit should be necessary to recover the debt, all the debtors must be sued together; or, when some are dead, the

survivors must be sued, but each is bound for the whole debt, having a right to contribution from the others; they are several, when each promises severally to pay the whole debt; and obligations are generally binding on both or all debtors jointly and severally. When they are severally bound each may be sued separately, and on the payment of debt by one, the others will be bound to contribution, where all had participated in the money or property, which was the cause of the debt.

4. Debtors are also principal and surety; the principal debtor is bound as between him and his surety to pay the whole debt; and if the surety pay it, he will be entitled to recover against the principal. Vide Bouv. Inst. Index, h. t.; Vin. Ab. Creditor and Debtor; Id. Debt; 8 Com. Dig. 288; Dig. 50, 16, 108; Id. 50, 16, 178, 3; Toull. liv. 2, n. 250.

DECAPITATION, *punishment*. The punishment of putting a person to death by taking off his head.

DECEDENT. In the acts of descent and distribution in Pennsylvania, this word is frequently used for a deceased person, testate or intestate.

DECEIT, *tort*. A fraudulent misrepresentation or contrivance, by which one man deceives another, who has no means of detecting the fraud, to the injury and damage of the latter.

2. Fraud, or the intention to deceive, is the very essence of this injury, for if the party misrepresenting was himself mistaken, no blame can attach to him. The representation must be made *malo animo*, but whether or not the party is himself to gain by it, is wholly immaterial.

3. Deceit may not only be by asserting a falsehood deliberately to the injury of another; as, that Paul is in flourishing circumstances, whereas he is in truth insolvent; that Peter is an honest man, when he knew him to be a rogue; that property, real or personal, possesses certain qualities, or belongs to the vendor, whereas he knew these things to be false; but by any act or demeanor which would naturally impress the mind of a careful man with a mistaken belief.

4. Therefore, if one whose manufactures are of a superior quality, distinguishes them by a particular mark, which facts are known to Peter, and Paul counterfeits this work, and affixes them to articles of the same description, but not made by such person, and sells them to Peter as goods of such manufacture, this is a deceit.

5. Again, the vendor having a knowledge of a defect in a commodity which cannot be obvious to the buyer, does not disclose it, or, if apparent, uses an artifice and conceals it, he has been guilty of a fraudulent misrepresentation; for there is an implied condition in every contract that the parties to it act upon equal terms, and the seller is presumed to have assured or represented to the vendee that he is not aware of any secret deficiencies by which the commodity is impaired, and that he has no advantage which himself does not possess.

6. But in all these cases the party injured must have no means of detecting the fraud, for if he has such means, his ignorance will not avail him; in that case he becomes the willing dupe of the other's artifice, and *volenti non fit injuria*. For example, if a horse is sold wanting an eye, and the defect is visible to a common observer, the purchaser cannot be said to be deceived, for by inspection he might discover it; but if the blindness is only discoverable by one experienced in such diseases, and the vendee is an inexperienced person, it is a deceit, provided the seller knew of the defect.

7. The remedy for a deceit, unless the right of action has been suspended or discharged, is by an action of trespass on the case. The old writ of deceit was brought for acknowledging a fine, or the like, in another name, and this being a perversion of law to an evil purpose, and a high contempt, the act was laid *contra pacem*, and a fine imposed upon the offender. See Bro. Abr. Disceit; Vin Abr. Disceit.

8. When two or more persons unite in a deceit upon another, they may be indicted for a conspiracy. (q. v.) Vide, generally, 2 Bouv. Inst. n. 2321–29; Skin. 119; Sid. 375; 3 T. R. 52–65; 1 Lev. 247; 1 Strange, 583; 1 Roll. Abr. 106; 7 Barr, Rep. 296; 11 Serg. & R. 309, 310; Com. Dig. Action upon the case for a deceit; Chancery, 3 F 1 and 2; 3 M 1; 3 N 1; 4 D 3; 4 H 4; 4 L 1; 4 O 2; Covin; Justices of the Peace, B 30; Pleader, 2 H; 1 Vin. Ab. 560; 8 Vin. Ab. 490; Doct. Pl. 51; Dane's Ab. Index, h. t.; 1 Chit. Pr. 832; Ham. N. P. c. 2, s. 4; Ayl. Pand. 99; 2 Day, 531; 12 Mass. 20; 3 Johns. 269; 6 Johns. 181; 2 Day, 205, 381; 4 Yeates, 522; 18 John. 395; 8

John. 23; 4 Bibb, 91; 1 N. & M. 197. Vide, also, articles *Equality; Fraud; Lie.*

TO DECEIVE. To induce another, either by words or actions, to take that for true which is not so. Wolff, Inst. Nat. § 356.

DECEM TALES, *practice.* In the English law this is a writ which gives to the sheriff *apponere decem tales;* i. e. to appoint ten such men for the supply of jurymen, when a sufficient number do not appear to make up a full jury.

DECENNARY, *Eng. law.* A town or tithing, consisting originally of ten families of freeholders. Ten tithings composed a hundred. 1 Bl. Com. 114.

DECIES TANTUM, *Eng. law.* The name of an obsolete writ which formerly lay against a juror who had taken money for giving his verdict; called so, because it was sued out to recover from him ten times as much as he took.

DECIMATION. The punishment of every tenth soldier by lot, was, among the Romans, called decimation.

DECIME. A French coin, of the value of a tenth part of a franc, or nearly two cents.

DECISION, *practice.* A judgment given by a competent tribunal. The French lawyers call the opinions which they give on questions propounded to them, decisions. Vide Inst. 1, 2, 8; Dig. 1, 2, 2.

DECLARANT. One who makes a declaration. Vide *Declarations.*

DECLARATION, *pleading.* A declaration is a specification, in a methodical and logical form, of the circumstances which constitute the plaintiff's cause of action. 1 Chit. Pl. 248; Co. Litt. 17, a, 303, a; Bac. Abr. Pleas, B; Com. Dig. Pleader, C 7; Lawes on Pl. 35; Steph. Pl. 36; 6 Serg. & Rawle, 28. In real actions, it is most properly called the *count;* in a personal one, the declaration. Steph. Pl. 36; Doct. Pl. 83; Lawes, Plead. 33; see F. N. B. 16, a, 60, d. The latter, however, is now the general term; being that commonly used when referring to real and personal actions without distinction. 3 Bouv. Inst. n. 2815.

2. The declaration in an action at law answers to the bill in chancery, the libel of the civilians, and the allegation of the ecclesiastical courts.

3. It may be considered with reference, 1st. To those general requisites or qualities which govern the whole declaration; and 2d. To its form, particular parts, and requisites.

4.—1. The general requisites or qualities of a declaration are, *first,* that it correspond with the process. But, according to the present practice of the courts, oyer of the writ cannot be craved; and a variance between the writ and declaration cannot be pleaded in abatement. 1 Saun. 318, a.

5.—*Secondly.* The second general requisite of a declaration is, that it contain a statement of all the facts necessary in point of law, to sustain the action, and no more. Co. Litt. 303, a; Plowd. 84, 122. See 2 Mass. 363; Cowp. 682; 6 East, R. 422; 5 T. R. 623; Vin. Ab. Declarations.

6.—*Thirdly.* These circumstances must be stated with certainty and truth. The certainty necessary in a declaration is, to a certain intent in general, which should pervade the whole declaration, and is particularly required in setting forth, 1st. The *parties;* it must be stated with certainty who are the parties to the suit, and therefore a declaration by or against "C D and Company," not being a corporation, is insufficient. See Com. Dig. Pleader, C 18; 1 Camp. R. 446; 1 T. R. 508; 3 Caines, R. 170. 2d. The *time;* in personal actions the declaration must, in general, state a time when every material or traversable fact happened; and when a venue is necessary, time must also be mentioned. 5 T. R. 620; Com. Dig. Plead. C 19; Plowd. 24; 14 East, R. 390. The precise time, however, is not material; 2 Dall. 346; 3 Johns. R. 43; 13 Johns. R. 253; unless it constitute a material part of the contract declared upon, or where the date, &c., of a written contract or record, is averred; 4 T. R. 590; 10 Mod. 313; 2 Camp. R. 307, 8, n.; or, in ejectment, in which the demise must be stated to have been made after the title of the lessor of the plaintiff, and his right of entry, accrued. 2 East, R. 257; 1 Johns. Cas. 283. 3d. The *place.* See *Venue.* 4th. Other circumstances necessary to maintain the action.

7.—2. The parts and particular requisites of a declaration are, *first,* the title of the court and term. See 1 Chit. Pl. 261, et seq.

8.—*Secondly.* The venue. Immediately after the title of the declaration follows the statement in the margin of the *venue,* or county in which the facts are alleged to have occurred, and in which the cause is tried. See *Venue.*

9.—*Thirdly.* The *commencement.* What is termed the commencement of the declaration follows the venue in the margin, and precedes the more circumstantial statement of the cause of action. It contains a statement, 1st. Of the names of the parties to the suit, and if they sue or be sued in another right, or in a political capacity, (as executors, assignees, *qui tam,* &c.) of the character or right in respect of which they are parties to the suit. 2d. Of the mode in which the defendant has been brought into court; and, 3d. A brief recital of the form of action to be proceeded in. 1 Saund. 318, n. 3; Id. 111, 112; 6 T. R. 130.

10.—*Fourthly.* The *statement of the cause of action,* in which all the requisites of certainty before mentioned must be observed, necessarily varies, according to the circumstances of each particular case, and the form of action, whether in assumpsit, debt, covenant, detinue, case, trover, replevin or trespass.

11.—*Fifthly.* The *several counts.* A declaration may consist of as many counts as the case requires, and the jury may assess entire or distinct damages on all the counts; 3 Wils. R. 185; 2 Bay, R. 206; and it is usual, particularly in actions of assumpsit, debt on simple contract, and actions on the case, to set forth the plaintiff's cause of action in various shapes in different counts, so that if the plaintiff fail in proof of one count, he may succeed in another. 3 Bl. Com. 295.

12.—*Sixthly.* The *conclusion.* In personal and mixed actions the declaration should conclude to the *damage* of the plaintiff; Com. Dig. Pleader, C 84; 10 Co. 116, b. 117, a.; unless in *scire facias* and in penal actions at the suit of a common informer.

13.—*Seventhly.* The *profert* and *pledges.* In an action at the suit of an executor or administrator, immediately after the conclusion to the damages, &c., and before the pledges, a profert of the letters testamentary or letters of administration should be made. Bac. Abr. Executor, C; Dougl. 5, in notes. At the end of the declaration, it is usual to add the plaintiff's common pledges to prosecute, John Doe and Richard Roe.

14. A declaration may be general or special; for example, in debt or bond, a declaration counting on the penal part only, is *general;* when it sets out both the penalty and the condition, and assigns the breach, it is *special.* Gould on Pl. c. 4, § 50.

See, generally, Bouv. Inst. Index, h. t.; 1 Chit. Pl. 248 to 402; Lawes, Pl. Index, h. t.; Arch. Civ. Pl. Index, h. t.; Steph. Pl. h. t.; Grah. Pr. h. t.; Com. Dig. Pleader, h. t.; Dane's Ab. h. t.; United States Dig. Pleadings ii.

Declaration of independence. This is a state paper issued by the congress of the United States of America, in the name and by the authority of the people, on the fourth day of July, 1776, wherein are set forth:

2.—1. Certain natural and unalienable rights of man; the uses and purposes of governments; the right of the people to institute or to abolish them; the sufferings of the colonies, and their right to withdraw from the tyranny of the king of Great Britain.

3.—2. The various acts of tyranny of the British king.

4.—3. The petitions for redress of these injuries, and the refusal to redress them; the recital of an appeal to the people of Great Britain, and of their being deaf to the voice of justice and consanguinity.

5.—4. An appeal to the Supreme Judge of the world for the rectitude of the intentions of the representatives.

6.—5. A declaration that the United Colonies are, and of right ought to be, free and independent states; that they are absolved from all allegiance to the British crown, and that all political connexion between them and the state of Great Britain, is and ought to be dissolved.

7.—6. A pledge by the representatives to each other of their lives, their fortunes, and their sacred honor.

8. The effect of this declaration was the establishment of the government of the United States as free and independent, and thenceforth the people of Great Britain have been held, as the rest of mankind, enemies in war, in peace friends.

Declaration of intention. The act of an alien, who goes before a court of record, and in a formal manner declares that it is, bona fide, his intention to become a citizen of the United States, and to renounce forever all allegiance and fidelity to any foreign prince, potentate, state, or sovereignty, whereof he may at the time be a citizen or subject. Act of Congress of April 14, 1802, s. 1.

2 This declaration must, in usual cases,

be made at least three years before his admission. Id. But there are numerous exceptions to this rule. See *Naturalization.*

DECLARATION OF TRUST. The act by which an individual acknowledges that a property, the title of which he holds, does in fact belong to another, for whose use he holds the same. The instrument in which the acknowledgment is made, is also called a declaration of trust; but such a declaration is not always in writing, though it is highly proper it should be so. Will. on Trust, 49, note y; Sudg. on Pow. 200. See Merl. Rép. Declaration au profit d'un tiers.

DECLARATION OF WAR. An act of the national legislature, in which a state of war is declared to exist between the United States and some other nation.

2. This power is vested in congress by the constitution, art. 1, s. 8. There is no form or ceremony necessary, except the passage of the act. A manifesto, stating the causes of the war, is usually published, but war exists as soon as the act takes effect. It was formerly usual to precede hostilities by a public declaration communicated to the enemy, and to send a herald to demand satisfaction. Potter, Antiquities of Greece, b. 3, c. 7; Dig. 49, 15, 24. But that is not the practice of modern times.

3. In some countries, as England, the power of declaring war is vested in the king, but he has no power to raise men or money to carry it on, which renders the right almost nugatory.

4. The public proclamation of the government of a state, by which it declares itself to be at war with a foreign power, which is named, and which forbids all and every one to aid or assist the common enemy, is also called a declaration of war.

DECLARATIONS, *evidence*. The statements made by the parties to a transaction, in relation to the same.

2. These declarations when proved are received in evidence, for the purpose of illustrating the peculiar character and circumstances of the transaction. Declarations are admitted to be proved in a variety of cases.

3.—1. In cases of rape, the fact that the woman made declarations in relation to it, soon after the assault took place, is evidence; but the particulars of what she said cannot be heard. 2 Stark. N. P. C, 242; S. C. 3 E. C. L. R. 344. But it is to be observed that these declarations can be used only to corroborate her testimony, and cannot be received as independent evidence; where, therefore, the prosecutrix died, these declarations could not be received. 9 C. & P. 420; S. C. 38 Eng. C. L. R. 173; 9 C. & P. 471; S. C. 38 E. C. L. R. 188.

4.—2. When more than one person is concerned in the commission of a crime, as in cases of riots, conspiracies, and the like, the declarations of either of the parties, made *while acting in the common design*, are evidence against the whole; but the declarations of one of the rioters or conspirators, made *after the accomplishment of their object*, and when they no longer acted together, are evidence only against the party making them. 2 Stark. Ev. 235; 2 Russ. on Cr. 572; Rosc. Cr. Ev. 324; 1 Breese, Rep. 269.

5. In civil cases the declarations of an agent, made while acting for his principal, are admitted in evidence as explanatory of his acts; but his confessions after he has ceased to act, are not evidence. 4. S. & R. 321.

6.—3. To prove a pedigree, the declarations of a deceased member of the family are admissible. Vide *Hearsay*, and the cases there cited.

7.—4. The dying declarations of a man who has received a mortal injury, as to the fact itself, and the party by whom it was committed, are good evidence; but the party making them must be under a full consciousness of approaching death. The declarations of a boy between ten and eleven years of age, made under a consciousness of approaching death, were received in evidence on the trial of a person for killing him, as being declarations in articulo mortis. 9 C. & P. 395; S. C. 38 E. C. L. R. 168. Evidence of such declarations is admissible only when the death of the deceased is the subject of the charge, and the circumstances of the death the subject of the dying declarations. 2 B. & C. 605; S. C 9 E. C. L. R. 196; 2 B. & C. 608; S. C 9 E. C. L. R. 198; 1 John. Rep. 159; 15 John. R. 286; 7 John. R. 95. But see contrà, 2 Car. Law Repos. 102. Vide *Death bed or Dying declarations;* 3 Bouv. Inst. n. 3071.

DECLARATORY. Something which explains, or ascertains what before was uncertain or doubtful; as a declaratory statute, which is one passed to put an end to a doubt as to what the law is, and which declares what it is, and what it has been. 1 Bl. Com. 86.

TO DECLARE. To make known or publish. By the constitution of the United States, congress have power to declare war. In this sense the word declare, signifies, not merely to make it known that war exists, but also to make war and to carry it on. 4 Dall. 37; 1 Story, Const. § 428; Rawle on the Const. 109. In pleading, to declare, is the act of filing a declaration.

DECOCTION, *med. jurisp.* The operation of boiling certain ingredients in a fluid, for the purpose of extracting the parts soluble at that temperature. *Decoction* also means the product of this operation.

2. In a case in which the indictment charged the prisoner with having administered to a woman a decoction of a certain shrub called savin, it appeared that the prisoner had administered an *infusion* (q. v.) and not a decoction; the prisoner's counsel insisted that he was entitled to an acquittal, on the ground that the medicine was misdescribed, but it was held that infusion and decoction are *ejusdem generis*, and that the variance was immaterial. 3 Camp. R. 74, 75.

DECONFES, *canon law in France.* Formerly those persons who died without confession were so called; whether they refused to confess or whether they were criminals to whom the sacrament was refused. Droit Canon, par M. L'Abbé André. Dupin, Gloss. to Loisel's Institutes, says, Le déconfês est celui qui meurt sans confession et sans testament car l'un n'alloit point sans l'autre. See *Intestate.*

DECORUM. Proper behaviour; good order.

2. Decorum is requisite in public places, in order to permit all persons to enjoy their rights; for example, decorum is indispensable in church, to enable those assembled, to worship. If, therefore, a person were to disturb the congregation, it would be lawful to put him out. The same might be done in case of a funeral. 1 Mod. 168; 1 Lev. 196; 2 Kebl. 124. But a request to desist should be first made, unless, indeed, when the necessity of the case would render such precaution impossible. In using force to restore order and decorum, care must be taken to use no more than is necessary; for any excess will render the party using it guilty of an assault and battery. Vide *Battery.*

DECOY. A pond used for the breeding and maintenance of water-fowl. 11 Mod. 74, 130; S. C. 3 Salk. 9; Holt, 14; 11 East, 571.

DECREE, *practice.* The judgment or sentence of a court of equity.

2. It is either interlocutory or final. The former is given on some plea or issue arising in the cause, which does not decide the main question; the latter settles the matter in dispute, and a final decree has the same effect as a judgment at law. 2 Madd. Ch. 462; 1 Chan. Cas. 27; 2 Vern. 89; 4 Bro. P. C. 287. Vide 7 Vin. Ab. 394; 7 Com. Dig. 445; 1 Supp. to Ves. Jr. 223; Bouv. Inst. Index, h. t.

DECREE, *legislation.* In some countries, as in France, some acts of the legislature, or of the sovereign, which have the force of law, are called *decrees;* as, the Berlin and Milan decrees.

DECREE ARBITRAL, *Scotch law.* A decree made by arbitrators chosen by the parties; an award. 1 Bell's Com. 643.

DECREE OF REGISTRATION, *Scotch law.* A proceeding by which the creditor has immediate execution; it is somewhat like a warrant of attorney to confess judgment. 1 Bell's Com. B. 1, c. 1, p. 4.

DECRETAL ORDER. *Chancery practice.* An order made by the court of chancery, upon a motion or petition, in the nature of a decree. 2 Dan. Ch. Pr. 637.

DECRETALS. *eccles. law.* The decretals are canononical epistles, written by the pope alone, or by the pope and cardinals, at the instance or suit of some one or more persons, for the ordering and determining some matter in controversy, and have the authority of a law in themselves.

2. The decretals were published in three volumes. The first volume was collected by Raymundus Barcinius, chaplain to Gregory IX., about the year 1231, and published by him to be read in schools, and used in the ecclesiastical courts. The second volume is the work of Boniface VIII. compiled about the year 1298, with additions to and alterations of the ordinances of his predecessors. The third volume is called the Clementines, because made by Clement V., and was published by him in the council of Vienna, about the year 1308. To these may be added the Extravagantes of John XXII. and other bishops of Rome, which, relatively to the others, are called Novellæ Constitutiones. Ridley's View, &c., 99, 100; 1 Fournel, Hist. des Avocats, 194–5.

3. The false decretals were forged in

the names of the early bishops of Rome, and first appeared about A. D. 845–850. The author of them is not known. They are mentioned in a letter written in the name of the council of Quiercy, by Charles the Bald, to the bishops and lords of France. See Van Espen Fleury, Droit de Canon, by André.

DEDI, *conveyancing*. I have given. This word amounts to a warranty in law, when it is in a deed; for example, if in a deed it be said, I have *given*, &c., to A B, this is a warranty to him and his heirs. Brooke, Abr. Guaranties, pl. 85. Yet the warranty wrought by this word is a special warranty, and extendeth to the heirs of the feoffee during the life of the donor only. Co. Litt. 384, b. Vide *Concessi*.

DEDICATION. Solemn appropriation. It may be expressed or implied.

2. An express dedication of property to public use is made by a direct appropriation of it to such use, and it will be enforced. 2 Peters, R. 566; 6 Hill, N. Y. Rep. 407.

3. But a dedication of property to public or pious uses may be implied from the acts of the owner. A permission to the public for the space of eight or even six years, to use a street without bar or impediment, is evidence from which a dedication to the public may be inferred. 2 Bouv. Inst. n. 1631; 11 East, R. 376; 12 Wheat. R. 585; 10 Pet. 662; 2 Watts, 23; 1 Whart. 469; 3 Verm, 279; 6 Verm. 365; 7 Ham. part 2, 135; 12 Wend. 172; 11 Ala. R. 63, 81; 1 Spencer, 86; 8 Miss. R. 448; 5 Watts & S. 141; Wright, 150; 6 Hill, 407; 24 Pick. 71; 6 Pet. 431, 498; 9 Port. 527; 3 Bing. 447; sed vide 5 Taunt. R. 125. Vide *Street*, and the following authorities: 3 Kent, Com. 450; 5 Taunt. 125; 5 Barn. & Ald. 454: 4 Barn. & Ald. 447; Math. Pres. 333. As to what shall amount to a dedication of an invention to public use, see 1 Gallis. 482; 1 Paine's C. C. R. 345; 2. Pet. R. 1; 7 Pet. R. 292; 4 Mason, R. 108. See *Destination.*

DEDIMUS, *practice*. The name of a writ to commission private persons to do some act in the place of a judge; as, to administer an oath of office to a justice of the peace, to examine witnesses, and the like. 4 Com. Dig. 319; 3 Com. Dig. 359; Dane's Ab. Index, h. t. Rey, in his Institutions Judiciaires, de l'Angleterre, tom. 2, p. 214, exposes the absurdity of the name given to this writ; he says it is appli cable to every writ which emanates from the same authority; *dedimus*, we have given.

DEDIMUS POTESTATEM DE ATTORNO FACIENDO. The name of a writ which was formerly issued by authority of the crown in England to authorize an attorney to appear for a defendant.

2. By statute of Westminster 2, 13 Edw. I., c. 10, all persons impleaded may make an attorney to sue for them in all pleas moved by or against them, in the superior courts there enumerated. 3 Mann. & Gran. 184, note.

DEED, *conveyancing*, *contracts*. A writing or instrument, under seal, containing some contract or agreement, and which has been delivered by the parties. Co. Litt. 171; 2 Bl. Com. 295; Shep. Touch. 50. This applies to all instruments in writing, under seal, whether they relate to the conveyance of lands, or to any other matter; a bond, a single bill, an agreement in writing, or any other contract whatever, when reduced to writing, which writing is sealed and delivered, is as much a deed as any conveyance of land. 2 Serg. & Rawle, 504; 1 Mood. Cr. Cas. 57; 5 Dana, 365; 1 How. Miss. R. 154; 1 McMullan, 373. Signing is not necessary at common law to make a deed. 2 Ev. Poth. 165; 11 Co. Rep. 27–8; 6 S. & R. 311.

2. Deed, in its more confined sense, signifies a writing, by which lands, tenements, and hereditaments are conveyed, which writing is sealed and delivered by the parties.

3. The formal parts of a deed for the conveyance of land are, 1st. The premises, which contains all that precedes the habendum, namely, the date, the names and descriptions of the parties, the recitals, the consideration, the receipt of the same, the grant, the full description of the thing granted, and the exceptions, if any.

4.—2d. The *habendum*, which states what estate or interest is granted by the deed; this is sometimes done in the premises.

5.—3d. The *tenendum*. This was formerly used to express the tenure by which the estate granted was to be held; but now that all freehold tenures have been converted into socage, the *tenendum* is of no use, and it is therefore joined to the *habendum*, under the formula *to have and to hold*.

6.—4th. The *redendum* is that part of

the deed by which the grantor reserves something to himself, out of the thing granted, as a rent, under the following formula, *Yielding and paying.*

7.—5th. The conditions upon which the grant is made. Vide *Conditions.*

8.—6th. The warranty, is that part by which the grantor warrants the title to the grantee. This is general when the warrant is against all persons, or special, when it is only against the grantor, his heirs, and those claiming under him. See *Warranty.*

9.—7th. The covenants, if any; these are inserted to oblige the parties or one of them, to do something beneficial to, or to abstain from something, which, if done, might be prejudicial to the other.

10.—8th. The conclusion, which mentions the execution and the date, either expressly, or by reference to the beginning.

11. The circumstances necessarily attendant upon a valid deed, are the following: 1. It must be written or printed on parchment or paper. Litt. 229, a; 2 Bl. Com. 297. 2. There must be sufficient parties. 3. A proper subject-matter, which is the object of the grant. 4. A sufficient consideration. 5. An agreement properly set forth. 6. It must be read, if desired. 7. It must be signed and sealed. 8. It must be delivered. 9. And attested by witnesses. 10. It should be properly acknowledged before a competent officer. 11. It ought to be recorded.

12. A deed may be avoided, 1. By alterations made in it subsequent to its execution, when made by the party himself, whether they be material or immaterial, and by any material alteration, made even by a stranger. Vide *Erasure; Interlineation.* 2. By the disagreement of those parties whose concurrence is necessary; for instance, in the case of a married woman by the disagreement of her husband. 3. By the judgment of a competent tribunal.

13. According to Sir William Blackstone, 2 Com. 313, deeds may be considered as (1), conveyances at common law, original and derivative. 1st. The original are, 1. Feoffment. 2. Gift. 3. Grant. 4. Lease. 5. Exchange; and 6. Partition. 2d. Derivative, which are, 7. Release. 8. Confirmation. 9. Surrender. 10. Assignment. 11. Defeasance. (2). Conveyances which derive their force by virtue of the statute of uses; namely, 12. Covenant to stand seised to uses. 13. Bargain and sale of lands. 14. Lease and release. 15. Deed to lead and declare uses. 16. Deed of revocation of uses.

14. The deed of bargain and sale, is the most usual in the United States. Vide *Bargain and Sale.* Chancellor Kent is of opinion that a deed would be perfectly competent in any part of the United States, to convey the fee, if it was to the following effect: "I, A B, in consideration of one dollar to me paid, by C D, do bargain and sell, (or in some of the states, grant) to C D, and his heirs, (in New York, Virginia, and some other states, the words, *and his heirs* may be omitted,) the lot of land, (describing it,) witness my hand and seal," &c. 4 Kent, Com. 452. Vide, generally, Bouv. Inst. Index, h. t.; Vin. Abr. Fait; Com. Dig. Fait; Shep. Touch. ch. 4; Dane's Ab. Index, h. t.; 4 Cruise's Dig. *passim.*

15. Title deeds are considered as part of the inheritance, and pass to the heir as real estate. A tenant in tail is, therefore, entitled to them, and chancery will enable him to get possession of them. 1 Bro. R. 206; 1 Ves. jr. 227; 11 Ves. 277; 15 Ves. 173. See Hill. Ab. c. 25; 1 Bibb, R. 333; 3 Mass. 487; 5 Mass. 472.

16. The cancellation, surrender, or destruction of a deed of conveyance, will not divest the estate which has passed by force of it. 1 Johns. Ch. Rep. 417; 2 Johns. Rep. 87. As to the effect of a redelivery of a deed, see 2 Bl. Com. 308; 2 H. Bl. 263, 264.

DEED POLL, *contracts.* A deed made by one party only is not indented, but polled or shaved quite even, and is, for this reason, called a *deed poll,* or single deed. Co. Litt. 299, a.

2. A deed poll is not, strictly speaking, an agreement between two persons; but a declaration of some one particular person, respecting an agreement made by him with some other person. For example, a feoffment from A to B by deed poll, is not an agreement between A and B, but rather a declaration by A addressed to all mankind, informing them that he thereby gives and enfeoffs B of certain land therein described.

3. It was formerly called *charta de una parte,* and usually began with these words, Sciant præsentes et futuri quod ego A, &c.; and now begins, "Know all men by these presents, that I, A B, have given, granted, and enfeoffed, and by these presents do give, grant and enfeoff," &c. Cruise, Real Prop. tit. 32, c. 1, s. 23.

DEFALCATION, *practice, contracts.*

The reduction of the claim of one of the contracting parties against the other, by deducting from it a smaller claim due from the former to the latter.

2. The law operates this reduction, in certain cases, for, if the parties die or are insolvent, the balance between them is the only claim; but if they are solvent and alive, the defendant may or may not defalcate at his choice. See *Set off*. For the etymology of this word, see Bracken. Law Misc. 186; 1 Rawle's R. 291; 3 Binn. R. 135.

3. Defalcation also signifies the act of a defaulter. The bankrupt act of August 19, 1841, (now repealed), declares that a person who owes debts which have been created in consequence of a defalcation as a public officer, or as executor, administrator, guardian or trustee, or while acting in any other fiduciary capacity, shall not have the benefit of that law.

DEFAMATION, *tort*. The speaking slanderous words of a person, so as, *de bonâ famâ aliquid detrahere*, to hurt his good fame. Vide *Slander*.

2. In the United States, the remedy for defamation is by an action on the case, where the words are slanderous.

3. In England, besides the remedy by action, proceedings may be instituted in the ecclesiastical court for redress of the injury. The punishment for defamation, in this court, is payment of costs and penance enjoined at the discretion of the judge. When the slander has been privately uttered, the penance may be ordered to be performed in a private place; when publicly uttered, the sentence must be public, as in the church of the parish of the defamed party, in time of divine service; and the defamer may be required publicly to pronounce that by such words, naming them, as set forth in the sentence, he had defamed the plaintiff, and, therefore, that he begs pardon, first, of God, and then of the party defamed, for uttering such words. Clerk's Assist. 225; 3 Burn's Eccl. Law, Defamation, pl. 14; 2 Chit. Pr. 471; Cooke on Def.

DEFAULT. The neglect to perform a legal obligation or duty; but in technical language by default is often understood the non-appearance of the defendant within the time prescribed by law, to defend himself; it also signifies the non-appearance of the plaintiff to prosecute his claim.

2. When the plaintiff makes default, he may be nonsuited; and when the defendant makes default, judgment by default is rendered against him. Com. Dig. Pleader, E 42; Id. B 11. Vide article *Judgment by Default*, and 7 Vin. Ab. 429; Doct. Pl. 208; Grah. Pr. 631. See, as to what will excuse or save a default, Cc. Litt. 259 b.

DEFAULT, *contracts, torts*. By the 4th section of the English statute of frauds, 29 Car. II., c. 3, it is enacted that "no action shall be brought to charge the defendant upon any special promise to answer for the debt, *default*, or miscarriage of another person, unless the agreement," &c., "shall be in writing," &c. By *default* under this statute is understood the non-performance of duty, though the same be not fonnded on a contract. 2 B. & A. 516.

DEFAULTER, *com. law*. One who is deficient in his accounts, or fails in making his accounts correct.

DEFEASANCE, *contracts, conveyancing*. An instrument which defeats the force or operation of some other deed or estate. That, which in the *same deed* is called a condition, in *another* deed is a defeasance.

2. Every defeasance must contain proper words, as that the thing shall be void. 2 Salk. 575; Willes, 108; and vide Carth. 64. A defeasance must be made *in eodem modo*, and by matter as high as the thing to be defeated; so that if one be by deed, the other must also be by deed. Touchs. 397.

3. It is a general rule, that the defeasance shall be a part of the same transaction with the conveyance; though the defeasance may be dated after the deed. 12 Mass. R. 456; 13 Pick. R. 413; 1 N. H. Rep. 41; but see 4 Yerg. 57, contra. Vide Bouv. Inst. Index, h. t.; Vin. Ab. h. t.; Com. Dig. h. t.; Id. Pleader, 2 W 35, 2 W 37; Lilly's Reg. h. t.; Nels. Ab. h. t.; 2 Saund. 47 n, note 1; Cruise, Dig. tit. 32, c. 7, s. 25; 18 John. R. 45; 9 Wend. R. 538; 2 Mass. R. 493.

DEFEASIBLE. What may be undone or annulled.

DEFECT. The want of something required by law.

2. It is a general rule that pleadings shall have these two requisites; 1. A matter sufficient in law. 2. That it be deduced and expressed according to the forms of law. The want of either of these is a defect.

3. Defects in matters of substance cannot be cured, because it does not appear that the plaintiff is entitled to recover; but

when the defects are in matter of form, they are cured by a verdict in favor of the party who committed them. 3 Bouv. Inst. n. 3292; 2 Wash. 1; 1 Hen. & Munf. 153; 16 Pick. 128, 541; 1 Day, 315; 4 Conn. 190; 5 Conn. 416; 6 Conn. 176; 12 Conn. 455; 1 P. C. C. R. 76; 2 Green, 133; 4 Blackf. 107; 2 M'Lean, 35; Bac. Ab. Verdict, X.

DEFENCE, *torts*. A forcible resistance of an attack by force.

2. A man is justified in defending his person, that of his wife, children, and servants, and for this purpose he may use as much force as may be necessary, even to killing the assailant, remembering that the means used must always be proportioned to the occasion, and an excess becomes, itself, an injury.

3. A man may also repel force by force in defence of his personal property, and even justify homicide against one who manifestly intends or endeavors by violence or surprise to commit a known felony, as robbery.

4. With respect to the defence or protection of the possession of real property, although it is justifiable even to kill a person in the act of attempting to commit a forcible felony, as burglary or arson, yet this justification can only take place when the party in possession is wholly without fault. 1 Hale, 440, 444; 1 East, P. C. 259, 277. When a forcible attack is made upon the dwelling-house of another, without any felonious intent, but barely to commit a trespass, it is in general lawful to oppose force by force, when the former was clearly illegal. 7 Bing. 305; S. C. 20 Eng. C. L. Rep. 139. Vide, generally, Ham. N. P. 136, 151; 1 Chit. Pr. 589, 616; Grot. lib. 2, c. 1; Rutherf. Inst. B. 1, c. 16.

DEFENCE, *pleading*, *practice*. It is defined to be the denial of the truth or validity of the complaint, and does not signify a justification. It is a general assertion that the plaintiff has no ground of action, which assertion is afterwards extended and maintained in the plea. 3 Bl. Com. 296; Co. Litt. 127. It is similar to the *contestatio litis* of the civilians.

2. Defence is of two descriptions; first, half defence, which is as follows, "*venit et defendit vim et injuriam, et dicit*," &c.; or secondly, full defence, "*venit et defendit vim et injuriam, quando*," &c. meaning "*quando et ubi curia consideravit*," (or when and where it shall behoove him,) "*et damna et quicquid quod ipse defendere debet et dicit*," &c. Co. Litt. 127, b; Bac. Abr. Pleas, D; Willis, 41.

3. In strictness, the words *quando*, &c. ought not to be added when only half defence is to be made; and after the words "*venit et defendit vim et injuriam*," the subject matter of the plea should immediately be stated. Gilb. C. P. 188; 8 T. R. 632; 3 B. & P. 9, n. a.

4. It has, however, now become the practice in all cases, whether half or full defence be intended, to state it as follows: "And the said C D, by M N, his attorney, comes and defends the *wrong*, (or in trespass, force) and injury, when, &c. and says," which will be considered only as half defence in cases where such defence should be made, and as full defence where the latter is necessary. 8 T. R. 633; Willis, 41; 3 B. & P. 9; 2 Saund. 209, c.

5. If full defence were made expressly by the words "when and where it shall behoove him," and "the damages and whatever else he ought to defend," the defendant would be precluded from pleading to the jurisdiction or in abatement, for by defending *when and where* it shall behoove him, the defendant acknowledges the jurisdiction of the court, and by defending the *damages* he waives all exception to the person of the plaintiff. 2 Saund. 209, c.; 3 Bl. Com. 297; Co. Litt. 127, b; Bac. Abr. Pleas, D.

6. Want of defence being only matter of form, the omission is aided by general demurrer. 3 Salk. 271. See further, 7 Vin. Abr. 497; 1 Chit. Pl. 410; Com. Dig. Abatement, I 16; Gould. on Pl. c. 2, s. 6–15; Steph. Pl. 430.

7. In another sense, defence signifies a justification; as, the defendant has made a successful defence to the charge laid in the indictment.

8. The Act of Congress of April 30, 1790, 1 Story, L. U. S. 89, acting upon the principles adopted in perhaps all the states, enacts, § 28, that every person accused and indicted of the crime of treason, or other capital offence, shall "be allowed and admitted to make his full defence by counsel learned in the law; and the court before whom such person shall be tried, or some judge thereof, shall, and they are hereby authorized and required, immediately upon his request, to assign to such person such counsel, not exceeding two, as such person shall desire, to whom such counsel shall have free access, at all seasonable hours; and every

such person or persons, accused or indicted of the crimes aforesaid, shall be allowed and admitted in his said defence, to make any proof that he or they can produce, by lawful witness or witnesses, and shall have the like process of the court where he or they shall be tried, to compel his or their witnesses to appear at his or their trial, as is usually granted to compel witnesses to appear on the prosecution against them."

9. Defences in equity may be classed in two divisions, namely, into *dilatory defences*, (q. v.) and into those which are peremptory. Matters of peremptory or permanent defences may be also divided into two sorts, first, those where the plaintiff never had any right to institute the suit; for example: 1. That the plaintiff had not a superior right to the defendant. 2. That the defendant has no interest. 3. That there is no privity between the plaintiff and defendant, or any right to sustain the suit. Secondly, those that insist that the original right, if any, is extinguished or determined; as, 1. When the right is determined by the act of the parties; or, 2. When it is determined by operation of law. 4 Bouv. Inst. n. 4199, et seq.; 1 Montag. Eq. Pl. 89. See *Dilatory Defence; Merits.*

TO DEFEND. To forbid. This word is used in some old English statutes in the sense it has in French, namely, to forbid. 5 Ric. 2, c. 7. Lord Coke uses the word in this sense: "it is defended by law to distrain on the highway." Co. Litt. 160, b. 161 a. In an old work, entitled, Legends, printed by Winkin de Worde, in 1527, fo. 96, we find examples of the use of the word in this sense, "He defended," (forbade) "to pay trewage," (tribute,) "for he said he was a king." "She wrote the obligation when she put her hand to the tree against the defence," (prohibition of God.)

2. In pleading, to defend is to deny; and the effect of the word "defends" is, that the defendant denies the right of the plaintiff, or the force and wrong charged. Steph. Pl. 432.

3. In contracts, *to defend* is to guaranty; to agree to indemnify. In most conveyances of land the grantor covenants to warrant and defend. It is his duty, then, to prevent all persons against whom he defends from doing any act which would evict him; when there is a mortgage upon the land, and the mortgagee demands possession or payment of the covenantee, and threatens suit, this is a breach of the covenant to defend, and for quiet enjoyment. 17 Mass. R. 586.

DEFENDANT. A party who is sued in a personal action. Vide *Demandant; Parties to Actions; Pursuer;* and Com. Dig. Abatement, F; Action upon the case upon assumpsit, E b; Bouv. Inst. Index, h. t.

2. At common law a defendant cannot have judgment to recover a sum of money of the plaintiff. But this rule is, in some cases, altered by the act of assembly in Pennsylvania, as by the Act of 1705, for defalcation, by which he may sue out a sci. fac. on the record of a verdict for a sum found in his favor. 6 Binn. Rep. 175. See Account 6.

DEFENDANT IN ERROR. A party against whom a writ of error is sued out.

DEFENDER, *canon law.* The name by which the defendant or respondent is known in the ecclesiastical courts.

DEFENSIVE ALLEGATION. The defence or mode of propounding a defence in the spiritual courts, is so called.

DEFICIT. This Latin term signifies that something is wanting. It is used to express the deficiency which is discovered in the accounts of an accountant, or in the money in which he has received.

DEFINITE NUMBER. An ascertained number; the term is usually applied in opposition to an indefinite number.

2. When there is a definite number of corporators, in order to do a lawful act, a majority of the whole must be present; but it is not necessary they should be unanimous; a majority of those present can, in general, perform the act. But when the corporators consist of an indefinite number, any number, consisting of a majority of those present, may do the act. 7 Cowen, R. 402; 9 B. & Cr. 648, 851; 7 S. & R. 517; Ang. & Am. on Corp. 281.

DEFINITION. An enumeration of the principal ideas of which a compound idea is formed, to ascertain and explain its nature and character; or it is that which denotes and points out the substance of a thing to us. Ayliffe's Pand. 59.

2. A definition ought to contain every idea which belongs to the thing defined, and exclude all others.

3. A definition should be, 1st. *Universal*, that is, such that it will apply equally to all individuals of the same kind. 2d. *Proper*, that is, such that it will not apply to any other individual of any other kind. 3d. *Clear*, that is, without any equivocal,

vague, or unknown word. 4th. *Short*, that is, without any useless word, or any foreign to the idea intended to be defined.

4. Definitions are always dangerous, because it is always difficult to prevent their being inaccurate, or their becoming so; *omnis definitio in jure civili periculosa est, parum est enim, ut non subverti possit.*

5. All ideas are not susceptible of definitions, and many words cannot be defined. This inability is frequently supplied, in a considerable degree, by descriptions. (q. v.)

DEFINITIVE. That which terminates a suit; a definitive sentence or judgment is put in opposition to an interlocutory judgment; final. (q. v.)

DEFLORATION. The act by which a woman is deprived of her virginity.

2. When this is done unlawfully, and against her will, it bears the name of rape; (q. v.) when she consents, it is fornication. (q. v.)

DEFORCIANT. One who wrongfully keeps the owner of lands and tenements out of the possession of them. 2 Bl. Com. 350.

DEFORCIARE. To withhold lands or tenements from the right owner. This is a word of art which cannot be supplied by any other word. Co. Litt. 331 b; 3 Tho. Co. Litt. 3; Bract. lib. 4, 238; Fleta, lib. 5, c. 11.

DEFORCEMENT, *tort*. In its most extensive sense it signifies the holding of any lands or tenements to which another person has a right; Co. Litt. 277; so that this includes, as well, an abatement, an intrusion, a disseisin, or a discontinuance, as any other species of wrong whatsoever, by which the owner of the freehold is kept out of possession. But, as contradistinguished from the former, it is only such a detainer of the freehold, from him who has the right of property, as falls within none of the injuries above mentioned. 3 Bl. Com. 173; Archb. Civ. Pl. 13; Dane's Ab. Index, h. t.

DEFORCEMENT, *Scotch law*. The opposition given, or resistance made, to messengers or other officers, while they are employed in executing the law.

2. This crime is punished by confiscation of movables, the one half to the king, and the other to the creditor at whose suit the diligence is used. Ersk. Pr. L. Scot. 4, 4, 32.

DEFUNCT. A term used for one that is deceased or dead. In some acts of assembly in Pennsylvania, such deceased person is called a decedent. (q. v.)

DEGRADATION, *punishment*, *ecclesiastical law*. A censure by which a clergyman is deprived of his holy orders, which he had as a priest or deacon.

TO DEGRADE, DEGRADING. To sink or lower a person in the estimation of the public.

2. As a man's character is of great importance to him, and it is his interest to retain the good opinion of all mankind, when he is a witness, he cannot be compelled to disclose any matter which would tend to disgrace or degrade him. 13 How. St. Tr. 17, 334; 16 How. St. Tr. 161. A question having that tendency, however, may be asked, and, in such case, when the witness chooses to answer it, the answer is conclusive. 1 Phil. Ev. 269; R. & M. 383.

DEGREE, *descents*. This word is derived from the French *degré*, which is itself taken from the Latin *gradus*, and signifies literally, a step in a stairway, or the round of a ladder.

2. Figuratively applied, and as it is understood in law, it is the distance between those who are allied by blood; it means the relations descending from a common ancestor, from generation to generation, as by so many steps. Hence, according to some Lexicographers, we obtain the word pedigree (q. v.) *par degrez*, by degree, the descent being reckoned *par degrez*. Minshew. Each generation lengthens the line of descent one degree, for the degrees are only the generations marked in a line by small circles or squares, in which the names of the persons forming it are written. Vide *Consanguinity; Line;* and also Ayliffe's Parergon, 209; Toull. Dr. Civ. Fran. liv. 3, t. 1, c. 3, n. 158; Aso & Man. Inst. B. 2, t. 4, c. 3, § 1.

DEGREE, *measures*. In angular measures, a degree is equal to sixty minutes, or the thirtieth part of a sine. Vide *Measure*.

DEGREE, *persons*. By degree, is understood the state or condition of a person. The ancient English statute of additions, for example, requires that in process, for the better description of a defendant, his *state*, *degree*, or *mystery*, shall be mentioned.

DEGREES, *academical*. Marks of distinction conferred on students, in testimony of their proficiency in arts and sciences. They are of pontifical origin. See 1 Schmidt's Thesaurus, 144; Vicat, ad voc. Doctores; Minshew, Dict. ad voc.Bacheler; Merl. Rép. ad voc.Université; Van Espen, p. 1, tit. 10, c. Giannone Istoria, di Napoli, lib. xi. c. 2, for a full account of this matter.

DEHORS. Out of; without. By this word is understood something out of the record, agreement, will, or other thing spoken of; something foreign to the matter in question.

DEI JUDICIUM. The judgment of God. This name was given to the barbarous and superstitious trial by ordeal.

DEL CREDERE, *contracts*. A *del credere* commission is one under which the agent, in consideration of an additional premium, engages to insure to his principal not only the solvency of the debtor, but the punctual discharge of the debt; and he is liable, in the first instance, without any demand from the debtor. 6 Bro. P. C. 287; Beawes, 429; 1 T. Rep. 112; Paley on Agency, 39.

2. If the agent receive the amount of sales, and remit the amount to the principal by a bill of exchange, he is not liable if it should be protested. 2 W. C. C. R. 378. See, also, Com. Dig. Merchant, B; 4 M. & S. 574.

DELAWARE. The name of one of the original states of the United States of America. For a time the counties of this state were connected with Pennsylvania, under the name of territories annexed to the latter. In 1703, a separation between them took place, and from that period down to the Revolution, the territories were governed by a separate legislature of their own, pursuant to the liberty reserved to them by a clause of their original charter. 1 Story, Constitution, § 127; 1 Votes of Assembly, 131, and part 2, p. 4, of Pennsylvania.

2. The constitution of this state was amended and adopted December 2, 1831. The powers of the government are divided into three branches, the legislative, the executive, and the judicial.

3.—1st. The *legislative* power of the state is vested in a general assembly, which consists of a senate and house of representatives.

4.—1. The *senate* is composed of three senators from each county; the number may be increased by the general assembly, two-thirds of each branch concurring, but the number of senators shall never be greater than one-half, nor less than two-thirds of the number of representatives. Art. 2, s. 3. The senators are chosen for four years by the citizens residing in the several counties.

5.—2. The *house of representatives* is composed of seven members from each county, but the general assembly, two-thirds of each branch concurring, may increase the number. The representatives are chosen for two years by the citizens residing in the several counties. Art. 2, s. 2.

6—2d. The supreme *executive* power of the state is vested in a governor, who is chosen by the citizens of the state. He holds his office during four years, from the third Tuesday in January next ensuing his election; and is not eligible a second time to the said office. Art. 3. Upon the happening of a vacancy, the speaker of the senate exercises the office, until a governor elected by the people shall be duly qualified. Art. 3, s. 14.

7.—3d. The judicial power is vested in a court of errors and appeals, a superior court, a court of chancery, an orphan's court, a court of oyer and terminer, a court of general sessions of the peace and jail delivery, a register's court, justices of the peace, and such other courts as the general assembly, with the concurrence of two-thirds of all the members of both houses shall, from time to time, establish. Art. 6.

DELAY, *civil law*. The time allowed either by law or by agreement of the parties to do something.

2. The law allows a delay, for a party who has been summoned to appear, to make defence, to appeal; it admits of a delay during which an action may be brought, certain rights exercised, and the like.

3. By the agreement of the parties there may be a delay in the payment of a debt, the fulfilment of a contract, &c. Vide Code, 3, 11, 4; Nov. 69, c. 2; Merl Rép. h. t.

DELECTUS PERSONÆ. This phrase, which literally signifies the choice of a person, is applied to show that partners have the right to select their copartners; and that no set of partners can take another person into the partnership, without the consent of each of the partners. Story on Partn. 6; Colly. on Partn. 4; 1 Swanst. 508; 2 Bouv. Inst. n. 1443.

DELEGATE. A person elected by the people of a territory of the United States, to congress, who has a seat in congress, and a right of debating, but not of voting. Ordinance of July, 13, 1787, 3 Story's L. U. S. 2076.

2. The delegates from the territories of

the United States are entitled to send and receive letters, free of postage, on the same terms and conditions as members of the senate and house of representatives of the United States; and also to the same compensation as is allowed to members of the senate and house of representatives. Act of February 18, 1802, 2 Story, L. U. S. 828.

3. A delegate is also a person elected to some deliberative assembly, usually one for the nomination of officers.

4. In contracts, a delegate is one who is authorized by another in the name of the latter; an attorney.

DELEGATION, *civil law.* It is a kind of novation, (q. v.) by which the original debtor, in order to be liberated from his creditor, gives him a third person, who becomes obliged in his stead to the creditor, or to the person appointed by him.

2. It results from this definition that a delegation is made by the concurrence of three parties, and that there may be a fourth. There must be a concurrence, 1. Of the party delegating, that is, the ancient debtor, who procures another debtor in his stead. 2. Of the party delegated, who enters into the obligation in the place of the ancient debtor, either to the creditor or to some other person appointed by him. 3. Of the creditor, who, in consequence of the obligation contracted by the party delegated, discharges the party delegating. Sometimes there intervenes a fourth party; namely, the person indicated by the creditor in whose favor the person delegated becomes obliged, upon the indication of the creditor, and by the order of the person delegating. Poth. Ob. part. 3, c. 2, art. 6. See Louis. Code, 2188, 2189; 3 Wend. 66; 5 N. H. Rep. 410; 20 John. R. 76; 1 Wend. 164; 14 Wend. 116; 11 Serg. & Rawle, 179.

3. Delegation is either perfect or imperfect. It is *perfect*, when the debtor who makes the delegation, is discharged by the creditor. It is *imperfect*, when the creditor retains his rights against the original debtor. 2 Duverg. n. 169. See *Novation.*

DELEGATION, *contracts.* The transfer of authority from one or more persons to one or more others.

2. In general, all persons *sui juris* may delegate to another authority to act for them, but to this rule there are exceptions; 1st. On account of the thing to be done; and 2d. Because the act is of a personal nature, and incapable of being delegated. 1. The thing to be done must be lawful; for an authority to do a thing unlawful, is absolutely void. 5 Co. 80. 2. Sometimes, when the thing to be done is lawful, it must be performed by the person obligated himself. Com. Dig. Attorney, C 3; Story, on Ag. § 12.

3. When a bare power or authority has been given to another, the latter cannot in general delegate that authority or any part of it to a third person, for the obvious reason that the principal relied upon the intelligence, skill and ability of his agent, and he cannot have the same confidence in a stranger. Bac. Ab. Authority, D; Com. Dig. Authority, C 3; 12 Mass. 241; 4 Mass. 597; 1 Roll. Ab. Authority, C 1, 15; 4 Camp. 183; 2 M. &. Selw. 298, 301; 6 Taunt. 146; 2 Inst. 507.

4. To this general rule that one appointed as agent, trustee, and the like, cannot delegate his authority, there are exceptions: 1. When the agent is expressly authorized to make a substitution. 1 Liverm. on Ag. 54. 2. When the authority is implied, as in the following cases: 1st. When by the laws such power is indispensable in order to accomplish the end proposed, as, for example, when goods are directed to be sold at auction, and the laws forbid such sales except by licensed auctioneers. 6 S. & R. 386. 2d. When the employment of such substitute is in the ordinary course of trade, as where it is the custom of trade to employ a ship broker or other agent for the purpose of procuring freight and the like. 2 M. & S. 301; 3 John. Ch. R. 167, 178; 6 S. & R. 386. 3d. When it is understood by the parties to be the mode in which the particular thing would be done. 9 Ves. 234; 3 Chit. Com Law, 206. 4th. When the powers thus delegated are merely mechanical in their nature. 1 Hill, (N. Y.) R. 501; Bunb. 166; Sugd. on Pow. 176.

5. As to the form of the delegation, it may be for general purposes, by a verbal or by a written declaration not under seal, or by acts and implications. 3 Chit. Com Law, 5, 194, 195; 7 T. R. 350. But when the act to be done must be under seal, the delegation must also be under seal. Co Litt. 48 b; 5 Binn. 613; 14 S. & R. 331; See *Authority.*

DELEGATION, *legislation.* It signifies the whole number of the persons who represent a district, a state, and the like, in a deliberative assembly; as, the delegation from Ohio, the delegation from the city of Philadelphia.

TO DELIBERATE. To examine, to consult, in order to form an opinion. Thus, a jury deliberate as to their verdict.

DELIBERATION, *contracts*, *crimes*. The act of the understanding, by which the party examines whether a thing proposed ought to be done or not to be done, or whether it ought to be done in one manner or another. The deliberation relates to the end proposed, to the means of accomplishing that end, or to both.

2. It is a presumption of law that all acts committed, are done with due deliberation, that the party intended to do what he has done. But he may show the contrary; in contracts, for example, he may show he has been taken by surprise; (q. v.) and when a criminal act is charged, he may prove that it was an accident, and not with deliberation, that in fact there was no intention or will. See *Intention; Will.*

DELIBERATION, *legislation*. The council which is held touching some business, in an assembly having the power to act in relation to it.

2. In deliberative assemblies, it is presumed that each member will listen to the opinions and arguments of the others before he arrives at a conclusion.

DELICT, *civil law*. The act by which one person, by fraud or malignity, causes some damage or tort to some other. In its most enlarged sense, this term includes all kinds of crimes and misdemeanors, and even the injury which has been caused by another, either voluntarily or accidentally without evil intention; but more commonly by delicts are understood those small offences which are punished by a small fine or a short imprisonment.

2. Delicts are either public or private; the public are those which affect the whole community by their hurtful consequences; the private is that which is directly injurious to a private individual Inst. 4, 18; Id. 4, 1; Dig. 47, 1; Id. 48, 1.

3. A *quasi-delict*, quasi delictum, is the act of a person, who without malignity, but by an inexcusable imprudence, causes an injury to another. Poth. Ob. n. 116; Ersk. Pr. Laws of Scotl. B. 4, t. 4, s. 1.

DELINQUENT, *civil law*. He who has been guilty of some crime, offence or failure of duty.

DELIRIUM, *med. jur*. A disease of the mind produced by inflammations, particularly in fevers, and other bodily diseases.

2. It is also occasioned by intoxicating agents.

3. Delirium manifests its first appearance "by a propensity of the patient to talk during sleep, and a momentary forgetfulness of his situation, and of things about him, on waking from it. And after being fully aroused, however, and his senses collected, the mind is comparatively clear and tranquil, till the next slumber, when the same scene is repeated. Gradually the mental disorder becomes more intense, and the intervals between its returns of shorter duration, until they are scarcely, or not at all perceptible. The patient lies on his back, his eyes, if open, presenting a dull and listless look, and is almost constantly talking to himself in a low, muttering tone. Regardless of persons or things around him, and scarcely capable of recognizing them when aroused by his attendants, his mind retires within itself to dwell upon the scenes and events of the past, which pass before it in wild and disorderly array, while the tongue feebly records the varying impressions, in the form of disjointed, incoherent discourse, or of senseless rhapsody. In the delirium which occurs towards the end of chronic diseases, the discourse is often more coherent and continuous, though the mind is no less absorbed in its own reveries. As the disorder advances, the voice becomes more indistinct, the fingers are constantly picking at the bed-clothes, the evacuations are passed insensibly, and the patient is incapable of being aroused to any further effort of attention. In some cases, delirium is attended with a greater degree of nervous and vascular excitement, which more or less modifies the above-mentioned symptoms. The eyes are open, dry, and bloodshot, intently gazing into vacancy, as if fixed on some object which is really present to the mind of the patient; the skin is hotter and dryer; and he is more restless and intractable. He talks more loudly, occasionally breaking out into cries and vociferation, and tosses about in bed, frequently endeavoring to get up, though without any particular object in view." Ray, Med. Jur. § 213.

4. "So closely does delirium resemble mania to the casual observer, and so important is it that they should be distinguished from each other, that it may be well to indicate some of the most common and prominent features of each. In mania, the

patient recognizes persons and things, and is perfectly conscious of, and remembers what is passing around him. In delirium, he can seldom distinguish one person or thing from another, and, as if fully occupied with the images that crowd upon his memory, gives no attention to those that are presented from without. In delirium, there is an entire abolition of the reasoning power; there is no attempt at reasoning at all; the ideas are all and equally insane; no single train of thought escapes the morbid influence, nor does a single operation of the mind reveal a glimpse of its natural vigor and acuteness. In mania, however false and absurd the ideas may be, we are never at a loss to discover patches of coherence, and some semblance of logical sequence in the discourse. The patient still reasons, but he reasons incorrectly. In mania, the muscular power is not perceptibly diminished, and the individual moves about with his ordinary ability. Delirium is invariably attended with great muscular debility; and the patient is confined to bed, and is capable of only a momentary effort of exertion. In mania, sensation is not necessarily impaired, and, in most instances, the maniac sees, hears, and feels with all his natural acuteness. In delirium, sensation is greatly impaired, and this avenue to the understanding seems to be entirely closed. In mania, many of the bodily functions are undisturbed, and the appearance of the patient might not, at first sight, convey the impression of disease. In delirium, every function suffers, and the whole aspect of the patient is indicative of disease. Mania exists alone and independent of any other disorder, while delirium is only a symptom or attendant of some other disease. Being a symptom only, the latter maintains certain relations with the disease on which it depends; it is relieved when that is relieved, and is aggravated when that increases in severity. Mania, though it undoubtedly tends to shorten life, is not immediately dangerous; whereas the disease on which delirium depends, speedily terminates in death, or restoration to health. Mania never occurs till after the age of puberty; delirium attacks all periods alike, from early childhood to extreme old age." Id. § 216.

5. In the inquiry as to the validity of testamentary dispositions, it is of great importance, in many cases, to ascertain whether the testator labored under delirium, or whether he was of sound mind. Vide *Sound mind; Unsound mind;* 2 Addams, R. 441; 1 Addams, Rep. 229, 383; 1 Hagg. R. 577; 2 Hagg. R. 142; 1 Lee, Eccl. R. 130; 2 Lee, Eccl. R. 229; 1 Hagg. Eccl. Rep. 256.

Delirium tremens, *med. jur.* A species of insanity which has obtained this name, in consequence of the tremor experienced by the delirious person, when under a fit of the disorder.

2. The disease called *delirium tremens* or *mania a potu*, is well described in the learned work on the Medical Jurisprudence of Insanity, by Dr. Ray, § 315, 316, of which the following is an extract: "It may be the immediate effect of an excess, or series of excesses, in those who are not habitually intemperate, as well as in those who are; but it most commonly occurs in habitual drinkers, after a few days of total abstinence from spirituous liquors. It is also very liable to occur in this latter class when laboring under other diseases, or severe external injuries that give rise to any degree of constitutional disturbance. The approach of the disease is generally indicated by a slight tremor and faltering of the hands and lower extremities, a tremulousness of the voice, a certain restlessness and sense of anxiety which the patient knows not how to describe or to account for, disturbed sleep, and impaired appetite. These symptoms having continued two or three days, at the end of which time they have obviously increased in severity, the patient ceases to sleep altogether, and soon becomes delirious. At first, the delirium is not constant, the mind wandering during the night, but during the day, when its attention is fixed, capable of rational discourse. It is not long, however, before it becomes constant, and constitutes the most prominent feature of the disease. This state of watchfulness and delirium continues three or four days, when, if the patient recover, it is succeeded by sleep, which, at first appears in uneasy and irregular naps, and lastly in long, sound, and refreshing slumbers. When sleep does not supervene about this period, the disease is fatal; and whether subjected to medical treatment, or left to itself, neither its symptoms nor duration are materially modified.

3. "The character of the delirium in this disease is peculiar, bearing a stronger resemblance to dreaming, than any other form of mental derangement. It would

seem as if the dreams which disturb and harass the mind during the imperfect sleep that precedes the explosion of the disease, continue to occupy it when awake, being then viewed as realities, instead of dreams. The patient imagines himself, for instance, to be in some particular situation, or engaged in certain occupations according to each individual's habits and profession, and his discourse and conduct will be conformed to this delusion, with this striking peculiarity, however, that he is thwarted at every step, and is constantly meeting with obstacles that defy his utmost efforts to remove. Almost invariably, the patient manifests, more or less, feelings of suspicion and fear, laboring under continual apprehension of being made the victim of sinister designs and practices. He imagines that certain people have conspired to rob or murder him, and insists that he can hear them in an adjoining apartment, arranging their plans and preparing to rush into his room; or that he is in a strange place where he is forcibly detained and prevented from going to his own home. One of the most common hallucinations is, to be constantly seeing devils, snakes, vermin, and all manner of unclean things around him and about him, and peopling every nook and corner of his apartment with these loathsome objects. The extreme terror which these delusions often inspire, produces in the countenance, an unutterable expression of anguish; and, in the hope of escaping from his fancied tormentors, the wretched patient endeavors to cut his throat, or jump from the window. Under the influence of these terrible apprehensions, he sometimes murders his wife or attendant, whom his disordered imagination identifies with his enemies, though he is generally tractable and not inclined to be mischievous. After perpetrating an act of this kind, he generally gives some illusive reason for his conduct, rejoices in his success, and expresses his regret at not having done it before. So complete and obvious is the mental derangement in this disease, so entirely are the thoughts and actions governed by the most unfounded and absurd delusions, that if any form of insanity absolves from criminal responsibility, this certainly must have that effect. 3 Am. Jur. 5—20.

DELIVERANCE, *practice*. A term used by the clerk in court to every prisoner who is arraigned and pleads *not guilty*, to whom he wishes a good *deliverance*. In modern practice this is seldom used.

DELIVERY, *conveyancing*. The transferring of a deed from the grantor to the grantee, in such a manner as to deprive him of the right to recall it; Dev. Eq. R. 14; or the delivery may be made and accepted by an attorney. This is indispensably necessary to the validity of a deed; 9 Shepl. 569; 2 Harring. 197; 16 Verm. 563; except it be the deed of a corporation, which, however, must be executed under their common seal. Watkin's Prin. Con. 300. But although, as a general rule, the delivery of a deed is essential to its perfection, it is never averred in pleading. 1 Wms. Saund. Rep 291, note; Arch. Dig. of Civ. Pl. 138.

2. As to the form, the delivery may be by words without acts; as, if the deed be lying upon a table, and the grantor says to the grantee, "take that as my deed," it will be a sufficient delivery; or it may be by acts without words, and therefore a dumb man may deliver a deed. Co. Litt. 36 a, note; 6 Sim. Rep. 31; Gresl. Eq. Ev. 120; Wood. B. 2, c. 3; 6 Miss. R. 326; 5 Shepl. 391; 11 Verm. 621; 6 Watts & S. 329; 23 Wend. 43; 3 Hill, 513; 2 Barr, 191, 193; 2 Ev. Poth. 165–6.

3. A delivery may be either *absolute*, as when it is delivered to the grantor himself; or it may be *conditional*, that is, to a third person to keep until some condition shall have been performed by the grantee, and then it is called an escrow. (q. v.) See 2 Bl. Com. 306; 4 Kent. Com. 446; 2 Bouv. Inst. n. 2018, et seq.; Cruise, Dig. tit. 32, c. 2, s. 87; 5 Serg. & Rawle, 523; 8 Watts, R. 1; and articles *Assent; Deed*.

4. The formula, "I deliver this as my act and deed," which means the actual delivery of the deed by the grantor into the hands or for the use of the grantee, is incongruous, not to say absurd, when applied to deeds which cannot in their nature be delivered to any person; as deeds of revocation, appointment, &c., under a power where uses to unborn children and the like, if in fact such instruments, though sealed, can be properly called deeds, *i. e.* writings sealed and delivered. Ritson's Practical Points, 146.

Delivery, *contracts*. The transmitting the possession of a thing from one person into the power and possession of another.

2. Originally, delivery was a clear and unequivocal act of giving possession, accomplished by placing the subject to be transferred in the hands of the buyer or his avowed agent, or in their respective

warehouses, vessels, carts, and the like. This delivery was properly considered as the true badge of transferred property, as importing full evidence of consent to transfer; preventing the appearance of possession in the transferrer from continuing the credit of property unduly; and avoiding uncertainty and risk in the title of the acquirer.

3. The complicated transactions of modern trade, however, render impossible a strict adherence to this simple rule. It often happens that the purchaser of a commodity cannot take immediate possession and receive the delivery. The bulk of the goods; their peculiar situation, as when they are deposited in public custody for duties, or in the hands of a manufacturer for the purpose of having some operation of his art performed upon them, to fit them for the market; the distance they are from the house; the frequency of bargains concluded by correspondence between distant countries, and many other obstructions, frequently render it impracticable to give or to receive actual delivery. In these and such like cases, something short of actual delivery has been considered sufficient to transfer the property.

4. In sales, gifts, and other contracts, where the party intends to transfer the property, the delivery must be made with the intent to enable the receiver to obtain dominion over it. 3 Serg. & Rawle, 20; 4 Rawle, 260; 5 Serg. & Rawle, 275; 9 John. 337. The delivery may be actual, by putting the thing sold in the hands or possession of the purchaser; or it may be symbolical, as where a man buys goods which are in a room, the receipt of the keys will be sufficient. 1 Yeates, 529; 5 Johns. R. 335; 1 East, R. 192; 3 Bos. & Pull. 233; 10 Mass. 308; 6 Watts & Serg. 94. As to what will amount to a delivery of goods and merchandise, vide 1 Holt, 18; 4 Mass. 661; 8 Mass. 287; 14 Johns. R. 167; 15 Johns. R. 349; 1 Taunt. R. 318; 2 H. Black. R. 316, 504; 1 New R. 69; 6 East, R. 614.

5. There is sometimes considerable difficulty in ascertaining the particular period when the property in the goods sold passes from the vendor to the vendee; and what facts amount to an actual delivery of the goods. Certain rules have been established, and the difficulty is to apply the facts of the case.

6.—1. Where goods are sold, if nothing remains to be done on the part of the seller. as between him and the buyer, before the article is to be delivered, the property has passed. East, R. 614; 4 Mass. 661; 8 Mass. 287; 14 Johns. 167; 15 Johns. 349; 1 Holt's R. 18; 3 Eng. C. L. R. 9.

7.—2. Where a chattel is made to order, the property therein is not vested in the *quasi* vendee, until finished and delivered, though he has paid for it. 1 Taunt. 318.

8.—3. The criterion to determine whether there has been a delivery on a sale, is to consider whether the vendor still retains, in that character, a right over the property. 2 H. Blackst. R. 316.

9.—4. Where a part of the goods sold by an entire contract, has been taken possession of by the vendee, that shall be deemed a taking possession of the whole. 2 H. Bl. R. 504; 1 New Rep. 69. Such partial delivery is not a delivery of the whole, so as to vest in the vendee the entire property in the whole, where some act, other than the payment of the price, is necessary to be performed in order to vest the property. 6 East, R. 614.

10.—5. Where goods are sent by order to a carrier, the carrier receives them as the vendee's agent. Cowp. 294; 3 Bos. & Pull. 582; 2 N. R. 119.

11.—6. A delivery may be made in a very slight manner; as where one buys goods which are in a room, the receipt of the key is sufficient. 1 Yeates, 529; 5 Johns. 335; 1 East, R. 192. See, also, 3 B. & P. 233; 7 East, Rep. 558; 1 Camp. 235.

12.—7. The vendor of bulky articles is not bound to deliver them, unless he stipulated to do so; he must give notice to the buyer that he is ready to deliver them. 5 Serg. & Rawle, 19; 12 Mass. 300; 4 Shepl. Rep. 49; and see 3 Johns. 399; 13 Johns. 294; 19 Johns. 218; 1 Dall. 171.

13.—8. A sale of bricks in a brick-yard, accompanied with a lease of the yard until the bricks should be sold and removed, was held to be valid against the creditors of the vendor, without an actual removal. 10 Mass. 308.

14.—9. Where goods were contracted to be sold upon condition that the vendee should give security for the price, and they are delivered without security being given, but with the declaration on the part of the vendor that the transaction should not be deemed a sale, until the security should be furnished; it was held that the goods remained the property of the vendor, notwithstanding the delivery. But it seems that in such cases the goods would be liable for the debts of the vendee's creditors, originating after the delivery; and that the vendee may, for a *bona fide* consideration, sell the goods while in his possession. 4 Mass. 405.

15.—10. Where goods are sold to be paid for on delivery, if, on delivery, the vendee refuses to pay for them, the property is not divested from the vendor. 13 Johns. 434; 1 Yeates, 529.

16.—11. If the vendor rely on the promises of the vendee to perform the conditions of the sale, and deliver the goods accordingly, the right of property is changed; but where performance and delivery are understood to be simultaneous, possession, obtained by artifice, will not vest a title in the vendee. 3 Serg. & Rawle, 20.

17.—12. Where, on the sale of a chattel, the purchase money is paid, the property is vested in the vendee, and if he permit it to remain in the custody of the vendor, he cannot call upon the latter for any subsequent loss or deterioration not arising from negligence. 2 Johns. 13; 2 Caines, R. 38; 3 Johns. 394.

18. In order to make a good *donatio mortis causâ*, it is requisite that there should be a delivery of the subject to or for the donee, where such delivery can be made. 3 Binn. R. 370; 1 Miles, Rep. 109, 110; 2 Ves. Jr. 120; 9 Ves. Jr. 1.

19. The delivery of the key of the place where bulky goods are deposited, is, however, a sufficient delivery of such goods. 2 Ves. Sen. 445. Vide 3 P. Wms. 357; 2 Bro. C. C. 612; 4 Barn. & A. 1; 3 Barn. & C. 45; Bouv. Inst. Index, h. t.

See *Sale; Stoppage in transitu; Tender;* and Domat, Lois Civiles, Liv. 1, tit. 2, s. 2; Harr. Dig. Sale, II. 3.

Delivery, *child-birth, med. jur.* The act of a woman giving birth to her offspring.

2. It is frequently of great importance to ascertain whether or not a delivery has taken place, and the time when it took place. Delivery may be considered with regard, 1. To pretended delivery. 2. To concealed delivery; and, 3. To the usual signs of delivery.

3.—1. In pretended delivery, the female declares herself to be a mother, without being so in reality; an act always prompted by folly or fraud.

4. Pretended delivery may present itself in three points of view. 1. When the female who feigns has never been pregnant. When thoroughly investigated, this may always be detected. There are signs which must be present, and cannot be feigned. An enlargement of the orifice of the uterus, and a tumefaction of the organs of generation, should always be present, and if absent, are conclusive against the fact. Annales d'Hygiène, tome ii. p. 227. 2. When the pretended pregnancy and delivery have been preceded by one or more deliveries. In this case, attention should be given to the following circumstances: the mystery, if any, which has been affected with regard to the situation of the female; her age; that of her husband; and particularly whether aged or decrepid. 3. When the woman has been actually delivered, and substitutes a living for a dead child. But little evidence can be obtained on this subject from a physical examination.

5.—2. Concealed delivery generally takes place when the woman either has destroyed her offspring, or it was born dead. In suspected cases, the following circumstances should be attended to: 1. The proofs of pregnancy which arise in consequence of the examination of the mother. When she has been pregnant, and has been delivered, the usual signs of delivery, mentioned below, will be present. A careful investigation as to the woman's appearance, before and since the delivery, will have some weight, though such evidence is not always to be relied upon, as such appearances are not unfrequently deceptive. 2. The proofs of recent delivery. 3. The connexion between the supposed state of parturition, and the state of the child that is found; for if the age of the child do not correspond to that time, it will be a strong circumstance in favor of the mother's innocence. A redness of the skin and an attachment of the umbilical cord to the navel, indicate a recent birth. Whether the child was living at its birth, belongs to the subject of infanticide. (q. v.)

6.—3. The usual signs of delivery are very well collected in Beck's excellent treatise on Medical Jurisprudence, and are here extracted:

If the female be examined within three or four days after the occurrence of delivery, the following circumstances will generally be observed: greater or less weakness, a slight paleness of the face, the eye a little sunken, and surrounded by a purplish or dark brown colored ring, and a whiteness of the skin, like a person convalescing from disease. The belly is soft, the skin of the abdomen is lax, lies in folds, and is traversed in various directions by shining reddish and whitish lines, which especially extend from the groins and pubis to the naval. These lines have sometimes been termed *lineæ albicantes*, and are particularly observed near the umbilical region, where the abdomen has experienced the greatest distention. The breasts become tumid and hard, and on pressure emit a fluid, which at first is serous, and afterwards gradually becomes whiter; and the presence of this secretion is generally accompanied with a full pulse and soft skin, covered with a moisture of a peculiar and somewhat acid odor. The areolæ round the nipples are dark colored. The external genital organs and vagina are dilated and tumefied throughout the whole of their extent, from the pressure of the fœtus. The uterus may be felt through the abdominal parietes, voluminous, firm, and globular, and rising nearly as high as the umbilicus. Its orifice is soft and tumid, and dilated so as to admit two or more fingers. The fourchette, or anterior margin of the perinæum, is sometimes torn, or it is lax, and appears to have suffered considerable distention. A discharge (termed the lochial) commences from the uterus, which is distinguished from the menses by its pale color, its peculiar and well-known smell, and its duration. The lochia are at first of a red color, and gradually become lighter until they cease.

7. These signs may generally be relied upon as indicating the state of pregnancy, yet it requires much experience in order not to be deceived by appearances.

8.—1. The lochial discharge might be mistaken for menstruation, or fluor albus, were it not for its peculiar smell; and this it has been found impossible, by any artifice, to destroy.

9.—2. Relaxation of the soft parts arises as frequently from menstruation as from delivery; but in these cases the os uteri and vagina are not so much tumefied, nor is there that tenderness and swelling. The parts are found pale and flabby, when all signs of contusion disappear, after delivery; and this circumstance does not follow menstruation.

10.—3. The presence of milk, though a usual sign of delivery, is not always to be relied upon, for this secretion may take place independent of pregnancy.

11.—4. The wrinkles and relaxations of the abdomen which follow delivery, may be the consequence of dropsy, or of lankness following great obesity. This state of the parts is also seldom striking after the birth of the first child, as they shortly resume their natural state.

Vide, generally, 1 Beck's Med. Jur. c 7, p. 206; 1 Chit. Med. Jur. 411; Ryan's Med. Jur. ch. 10, p. 133; 1 Briand, Méd. Lég. 1ere partie, c. 5.

DELUSION, *med. jurisp.* A diseased state of the mind, in which persons believe things to exist, which exist only, or in the degree they are conceived of only in their own imaginations, with a persuasion so fixed and firm, that neither evidence nor argument can convince them to the contrary.

2. The individual is, of course, insane. For example, should a parent unjustly persist without the least ground in attributing to his daughter a course of vice, and use her with uniform unkindness, there not being the slightest pretence or color of reason for the supposition, a just inference of insanity, or delusion, would arise in the minds of a jury: because a supposition long entertained and persisted in, after argument to the contrary, and against the natural affections of a parent, suggests that he must labor under some morbid mental delusion. 3 Addams' R. 90, 91; Id. 180; Hagg. R. 27; and see Dr. Connolly's Inquiry into Insanity, 384; Ray, Med. Jur. Prel. Views, § 20, p. 41, and § 22, p. 47; 3 Addams, R. 79; 1 Litt. R. 371; Annales d'Hygiène Publique, tom. 3, p. 370; 8 Watts, 70; 13 Ves 89; 1 Pow. Dev. by Jarman, 130, note; Shelf. on Lun. 296; 2 Bouv. Inst. n. 2104–10.

DEMAND, *contracts.* A claim; a legal obligation.

2. Lord Coke says, that *demand* is a word of art, and of an extent, in its signification, greater than any other word except claim. Litt. sect. 508; Co. Litt. 291; 2 Hill, R. 220; 9 S. & R. 124; 6 Watts and S. 226. Hence a release of all demands is, in general, a release of all covenants, real and personal, conditions, whether broken or not, annuities, recognizances, obligations, contracts, and the like. 3 Tho. Co. Litt. 427; 3 Penna. 120; 2 Hill, R. 228.

3. But a release of all demands does not discharge rent before it is due, if it be a rent incident to the reversion; for the rent

was not only not due, but the consideration —the future enjoyment of the lands—for which the rent was to be given, was not executed. 1 Sid. 141; 1 Lev. 99; 3 Lev. 274; Bac. Ab. Release, I.

DEMAND, *practice*. A requisition or a request by one individual to another to do a particular thing.

2. Demands are either express or implied. In many cases, an express demand must be made before the commencement of an action, some of which will be considered below; in other cases an implied demand is all that the law requires, and the bringing of an action is a sufficient demand in those cases. 1 Saund. 33, note 2.

3. A demand is frequently necessary to secure to a man all his rights, both in actions arising on contracts and those which are founded on some tort. It is requisite also, when it is intended to bring the party into contempt for not performing an order which has been made a rule of court.

4.—1. Whether a demand is requisite before the plaintiff can commence an action arising on contract, depends upon express or implied stipulations of the parties. In case of the sale of property, for example, to be paid for on delivery, a demand of it must be made before the commencement of an action for non-delivery, and proved on the trial, unless it can be shown that the seller has incapacitated himself by a resale and delivery of the property to another person, or otherwise. 1 East, R. 204; 5 T. R. 409; 10 East, R. 359; 5 B. & Ald. 712; 2 Bibb, 280; Hardin, 79; 1 Verm. 25; 5 Cowen, 516; 16 Mass. 453; 6 Mass. 61; 4 Mass. 474; 3 Bibb, 85; 3 Wend. 556; 5 Munf. R. 1; 2 Greenl. 308; 9 John. 361; 6 Hill, N. Y. Rep. 297.

5. On the same principles, a request on a general promise to marry is requisite, unless it be dispensed with by the party's marrying another person, which puts it out of his power to fulfil his contract, or that he refuses to marry at any time. 2 Dow. & Ry. 55; 1 Chit. Pr. 57, note (n), and 438, note (e).

6. A demand of rent must always be made before a reëntry for the non-payment of rent. Vide *Reëntry*.

7. When a note is given and no time of payment is mentioned, it is payable immediately. 8 John. R. 374; 5 Cowen, R. 516; 1 Conn. R. 404; 1 Bibb, R. 164; 1 Blackf. R. 233.

8. There are cases where a demand is not originally necessary, but becomes so by the act of the obligor. On a promissory note no express demand of payment is requisite before bringing an action, but if the debtor tenders the amount due to the creditor on the note, it becomes necessary before bringing an action, to make a demand of the debtor for payment; and this should be of the very sum tendered. 1 Campb. 181; Id. 474; 1 Stark. R. 323; 2 E. C. L. R. 409.

9. When a debt or obligation is payable, and no day of payment is fixed, it is payable on demand. In omnibus obligationibus in quibus dies non ponitur, presenti die debitur. Jac. Introd. 62; 7 T. R. 427; Barn. & Cr. 157. The demand must, however, be made in a reasonable time, for after the lapse of twenty years, a presumption will arise that the note has been paid; but, like some other presumptions, it may be rebutted, by showing the fact that the note remains unpaid. 5 Esp. R. 52; 1 D. & R. 16; Byles on Bills, 169.

10. When demand of the payment of a debt, secured by note or other instrument, is made, the party making it should be ready to deliver up such note or instrument, on payment. If it has been lost or destroyed, an indemnity should be offered. 2 Taunt. 61; 3 Taunt. 397; 5 Taunt. 30; 6 Mass. R. 524; 7 Mass. R. 483; 13 Mass. R. 557; 11 Wheat. R. 171; 4 Verm. R. 313; 7 Gill & Johns. 78; 3 Whart. R. 116; 12 Pick. R. 132; 17 Mass. 449.

11.—2. It is requisite in some cases arising *ex delicto*, to make a demand of restoration of the right before the commencement of an action.

12. The following are examples:— 1. When the wife, apprentice, or servant of one person, has been harbored by another, the proper course is to make a demand of restoration before an action brought, in order to constitute the party a wilful wrong doer, unless the plaintiff can prove an original illegal enticing away. 2 Lev. 63; Willes, 582; 1 Peake's C. N. P. 55; 5 East, 39; 6 T. R. 652; 4 Moore's R. 12; 16 E. C. L. R. 357.

13.—2. In cases where the taking of goods is lawful, but their subsequent detention becomes illegal, it is absolutely necessary, in order to secure sufficient evidence of a conversion on the trial, to give a formal notice of the owner's right to the property and possession, and to make a formal demand in writing of the delivery of such possession to the owner. The refusal to comply with such a demand, unless justified by some right which the possessor may have in the thing detained, will in general afford sufficient evidence of a conversion. 2 Saund. 47, note (e); 1 Chit. Pr. 566.

14.—3. When a nuisance has been erected or continued by a man on his own land, it is advisable, particularly in the case of a private nuisance, to give the party notice and request him to remove it, either before an entry is made for the purpose of abating it, or an action is commenced against the wrong doer; and a demand is always indispensable in cases of a continuance of a nuisance originally created by another person. 2 B. & C. 302; S. C. 9 E. C. L. R. 96; Cro. Jac. 555; 5 Co. 100, 101; 2 Phil. Ev. 8, 18, n. 119; 1 East, 111; 7 Vin. Ab. 506; 1 Ayl. Pand. 497; Bac. Ab. Rent, I. Vide articles *Abatement of Nuisance*, and *Nuisance*. For the allegation of a demand or request in a declaration, see article *Licet sæpius requisitus;* and Com. Dig. Pleader, C 70; 2 Chit. Pl. 84; 1 Saund. 33, note 2; 1 Chit. Pl. 322.

15.—4. When an order to pay money, or to do any other thing, has been made a rule of court, a demand for the payment of the money, or performance of the thing, must be made before an attachment will be issued for a contempt. 2 Dowl. P. C. 338, 448; 1 C. M. & R. 88, 459; 4 Tyr. 369; 2 Scott, 193; 4 Dowl. P. C. 114; 1 Hodges, 197; 1 Har. & Woll. 216; 1 Hodges, 157; Id. 337; 4 Dowl. P. C. 86.

Demand in reconvention. In Louisiana, this term is used to signify the demand which the defendant institutes in consequence of that which the plaintiff has brought against him. Code of Pr. art. 374. Vide *Cross action*.

DEMANDANT, *practice*. The plaintiff or party who brings a real action, is called the demandant. Co. Litt. 127; 1 Com. Dig. 85.

DEMENCY, *dementia, med. jur*. A defect, hebetude, or imbecility of the understanding, general or partial, but confined to individual faculties of the mind, particularly those concerned in associating and comparing ideas, whence proceeds great confusion and incapacity in arranging the thoughts. 1 Chit. Med. Jur. 351; Cyclop. Practical Med. tit. Insanity; Ray, Med. Jur. ch. 9; 1 Beck's Med. Jur. 547.

2. Demency is attended with a general enfeeblement of the moral and intellectual faculties, in consequence of age or disease, which were originally well developed and sound. It is characterised by forgetfulness of the past; indifference to the present and future, and a childish disposition. It differs from idiocy and imbecility. In these latter, the powers of the mind were never possessed, while in demency, they have been lost.

3. Demency may also be distinguished from mania, with which it is sometimes confounded. In the former, the mind has lost its strength, and thereby the reasoning faculty is impaired; while in the latter, the madness arises from an exaltation of vital power, or from a morbid excess of activity.

4. Demency is divided into acute and chronic. The former is a consequence of temporary errors of regimen, fevers, hemorrhages, &c., and is susceptible of cure; the latter, or chronic demency, may succeed mania, apoplexy, epilepsy, masturbation, and drunkenness, but is generally that incurable decay of the mind which occurs in old age.

5. When demency has been fully established in its last stages, the acts of the individual of a civil nature will be void, because the party had no consenting mind. Vide *Contracts; Wills;* 2 Phillim. R. 449. Having no legal will or intention, he cannot of course commit a crime. Vide *Insanity; Mania.*

DEMESNE, *Eng. law*. The name given to that portion of the lands of a manor which the lord retained in his own hands for the use of himself and family. These lands were called *terra dominicales* or *demesne lands*, because they were occupied by the lord, or dominus manerii, and his servants, &c. 2 Bl. Com. 90. Vide *Ancient Demesne; Demesne as of fee;* and *Son assault demesne.*

Demesne as of fee. A man is said to be seised *in his demesne as of fee* of a corporeal inheritance, because he has a property *dominicum* or *demesne* in the *thing* itself. 2 Bl. Com. 106. But when he has no dominion in the thing itself, as in the case of an incorporeal hereditament, he is said to be *seised* as of fee, and not in his *demesne* as of fee. Litt. s. 10; 17 S. & R. 196; Jones on Land Titles, 166.

2. Formerly it was the practice in an action on the case, *e. g.* for a nuisance to real estate, to aver in the declaration the seisin of the plaintiff in demesne as of fee; and this is still necessary, in order to estop the record with the land, so that it may run

with or attend the title. Arch. Civ. Pl. 104; Co. Ent. 9, pl. 8; Lill. Ent. 62; 1 Saund. Rep. 346; Willes, Rep. 508. But such an action may be maintained on the possession as well as on the seisin, although the effect of the record in this case upon the title would not be the same. Steph. on Pl. 322; Arch. Dig. 104; 1 Lutw. 120; 2 Mod. 71; 4 T. R. 718; 2 Saund. 113, b; Arch. Dig. 105; Cro. Car. 500. 575.

DEMIDIETAS. This word is used in ancient records for a moiety, or one half.

DEMIES. In some universities and colleges this term is synonymous with *scholars*. Boyle on Charities, 129.

DEMISE, *contracts*. In its most extended signification, it is a conveyance either in fee, for life, or for years. In its more technical meaning, it is a lease or conveyance for a term of years. Vide Com. L. & T. Index, h. t.; Ad. Eject. Index, h. t.; 2 Hill. Ab. 130; Com. Dig. h. t., and the heads there referred to. According to Chief Justice Gibson, the term demise strictly denotes a posthumous grant, and no more. 5 Whart. R. 278. See 4 Bing. N. C. 678; S. C. 33 Eng. C. L. R. 492; 2 Bouv. Inst. n. 1774, et seq.

DEMISE, *persons*. A term nearly synonymous with death. It is usually applied in England to the death of the king or queen.

DEMOCRACY, *government*. That form of government in which the sovereign power is exercised by the people in a body, as was the practice in some of the states of Ancient Greece; the term *representative democracy* has been given to a republican government like that of the United States.

DEMONSTRATION. Whatever is said or written to designate a thing or person. For example, a gift of so much money, with a fund particularly referred to for its payment, so that if the fund be not the testator's property at his death, the legacy will fail: this is called a demonstrative legacy. 4 Ves. 751; Lownd. Leg. 85; Swinb. 485.

2. A legacy given to James, who married my cousin, is demonstrative; these expressions present the idea of a demonstration, there are many James', but only one who married my cousin. Vide Ayl. Pand. 130; Dig. 12, 1, 6; Id. 35, 1, 34; Inst. 2, 20, 30.

3. By demonstration is also understood that proof which excludes all possibility of error; for example, mathematical deductions.

DEMURRAGE, *mar. law*. The freighter of a ship is bound not to detain it, beyond the stipulated or usual time, to load, or to deliver the cargo, or to sail. The extra days beyond the lay days (being the days allowed to load and unload the cargo), are called the days of *demurrage;* and that term is likewise applied to the payment for such delay, and it may become due, either by the ship's detention, for the purpose of loading or unloading the cargo, either before, or during, or after the voyage, or in waiting for convoy. 3 Kent, Com. 159; 2 Marsh, 721; Abbott on Ship. 192; 5 Com. Dig. 94, n., 505; 4 Taunt. 54, 55; 3 Chit. Comm. Law, 426; Harr. Dig. Ship and Shipping, VII.

DEMURRER. (From the Latin *demorari*, or old French *demorrer*, to wait or stay.) In pleading, imports, according to its etymology, that the objecting party *will not proceed* with the pleading, because no sufficient statement has been made on the other side; but will wait the judgment of the court whether he is bound to answer. 5 Mod. 232; Co. Litt. 71, b; Steph. Pl. 61.

2. A demurrer may be for insufficiency either in substance or in form; that is, it may be either on the ground that the case shown by the opposite party is essentially insufficient, or on the ground that it is stated in an inartificial manner; for the law requires in every pleading, two things; the one, that it be in matter sufficient; the other, that it be deduced and expressed according to the forms of law; and if either the one or the other of these be wanting, it is cause of demurrer. Hob. 164. A demurrer, as in its nature, so also in its form, is of two kinds; it is either general or special.

3. With respect to the effect of a demurrer, it is, first, a rule, that a demurrer admits all such matters of fact as are sufficiently pleaded. Bac. Abr. Pleas, N 3; Com. Dig. Pleader, Q 5. Again, it is a rule that, on a demurrer, the court will consider the whole record, and give judgment for the party who, on the whole, appears to be entitled to it. Com. Dig. Pleader, M 1, M 2; Bac. Abr. Pleas, N 3; 5 Rep. 29 a; Hob. 56; 2 Wils. 150; 4 East, 502; 1 Saund. 285, n. 5. For example, on a demurrer to the replication, if the court think the replication bad, but perceive a substantial fault in the plea, they will give judgment, not for the defendant, but for the plaintiff; 2 Wils. R. 150; provided the de-

claration be good; but if the declaration also be bad in substance, then upon the same principle, judgment would be given for the defendant. 5 Rep. 29 a. For when judgment is to be given, whether the issue be in law or fact, and whether the cause have proceeded to issue or not, the court is always to examine the whole record, and adjudge for the plaintiff or defendant, according to the legal right, as it may on the whole appear.

4. It is, however, subject to the following exceptions; first, if the plaintiff demur to a plea in abatement, and the court decide against the plea, they will give judgment of respondeat ouster, without regard to any defect in the declaration. Lutw. 1592, 1667; 1 Salk. 212; Carth. 172. Secondly, the court will not look back into the record, to adjudge in favor of an apparent right in the plaintiff, unless the plaintiff have himself put his action upon that ground. 5 Barn. & Ald. 507. Lastly, the court, in examining the whole record, to adjudge according to the apparent right, will consider the right in matter of substance, and not in respect of mere form, such as should have been the subject of a special demurrer. 2 Vent. 198–222.

5. There can be no demurrer to a demurrer; for a demurrer upon a demurrer, or pleading over when an issue in fact is offered, is a discontinuance. Salk. 219; Bac. Abr. Pleas, N 2.

6. Demurrers are general and special, and demurrers to evidence, and to interrogatories.

7.—1. A *general* demurrer is one which excepts to the sufficiency of a previous pleading in general terms, without showing specifically the nature of the objection; and such demurrer is sufficient, when the objection is on matter of substance. Steph. Pl. 159; 1 Chit. Pl. 639; Lawes, Civ. Pl. 167; Bac. Abr. Pleas, N 5; Co. Lit. 72 a.

8.—2. A *special demurrer* is one which excepts to the sufficiency of the pleadings on the opposite side, and shows specifically the nature of the objection and the particular ground of exception. Co. Litt. 72, a; Bac. Abr. Pleas, N 5.

9. A special demurrer is necessary, where it turns on matter of form only; that is, where, notwithstanding such objections, enough appears to entitle the opposite party to judgment, as far as relates to the merits of the cause. For, by two statutes, 27 Eliz. ch. 5, and 4 Ann. ch. 16, passed with a view to the discouragement of merely formal objections, it is provided in nearly the same terms, that the judges "shall give judgment according to the very right of the cause and matter in law as it shall appear unto them, without regarding any imperfection, omission, defect or want of form, except those only which the party demurring shall specifically and particularly set down and express, together with his demurrer, as the causes of the same." Since these statutes, therefore, no mere matter of form can be objected to on a general demurrer; but the demurrer must be in the special form, and the objection specifically stated. But, on the other hand, it is to be observed, that, under a special demurrer, the party may, on the argument, not only take advantage of the particular faults which his demurrer specifies, but also of all objections in substance, or regarding the very right of the cause, (as the statute expresses it,) as under those statutes, need not be particularly set down. It follows, therefore, that unless the objection be clearly of the substantial kind, it is the safer course, in all cases, to demur specially. Yet, where a general demurrer is plainly sufficient, it is more usually adopted in practice; because the effect of the special form being to apprise the opposite party more distinctly of the nature of the objection, it is attended with the inconvenience of enabling him to prepare to maintain his pleading by argument, or of leading him to apply the earlier to amend. With respect to the degree of particularity, with which, under these statutes, the special demurrer must assign the ground of objection, it may be observed, that it is not sufficient to object, in general terms, that the pleading is "uncertain, defective, and informal," or the like, but it is necessary to show in what respect, uncertain, defective, and informal. 1 Saund. 161, n. 1, 337 b, n. 3; Steph. Pl. 159, 161; 1 Chit. Pl. 642.

10.—3. A demurrer *to evidence* is analogous to a demurrer in pleading; the party from whom it comes declaring that he will not proceed, because the evidence offered on the other side, is not sufficient to maintain the issue. Upon joinder in demurrer, by the opposite party, the jury are, in general, discharged from giving any verdict; 1 Arch. Pr. 186; and the demurrer being entered on record, is afterwards argued and decided by the court in banc; and the judgment there given upon it, may ultimately be brought before a court of error. See 2 H. Bl. 187; 4 Chit. Pr. 15; Gould on Pl. c. 9, part 2, § 47; United States Dig. Pleading, VIII.

11.—4. Demurrer *to interrogatories*. By this phrase is understood the reasons which a witness tenders for not answering a particular question in interrogatories. 2 Swanst. R. 194. Strictly speaking, this is not a demurrer, which admits the facts stated, for the purpose of taking the opinion of the court; but by an abuse of the term, the witness' objection to answer is called a demurrer, in the popular sense. Gresl. Eq. Ev. 61.

12. The court are judicially to determine their validity. The witness must state his objection very carefully, for these demurrers are held to strict rules, and are readily overruled if they cover too much. 2 Atk. 524; 1 Y. & J. 32.

See, in general, as to demurrers, Bac. Abr. Pleas, N; Com. Dig. Pleader, Q; Saund. Rep. Index, tit. Demurrers; Lawes' Civ. Pl. ch. 8; 1 Chit. Pl. 639—649; Bouv. Inst. Index, h. t.

DEMURRER BOOK, *Eng. law.* When an issue in law is formed, a transcript is made upon paper of all the pleadings that have been filed or delivered between the parties, which transcript is called the demurrer book. Steph. Pl. 95. See *Paper book.*

DEMY SANKE or SANGUE. This is a barbarous corruption of demi sang, *half-blood.* (q. v.)

DENARII. An ancient general term for any sort of *pecunia numerata*, or ready money. The French use the word *denier* in the same sense: payer de ses propres deniers.

DENARIUS DEI. A term used in some countries to signify a certain sum of money which is given by one of the contracting parties to the other, as a sign of the completion of the contract.

2. It does not however bind the parties; he who received it may return it in a limited time, or the other may abandon it, and avoid the engagement.

3. It differs from *arrhæ* in this, that the latter is a part of the consideration, while the *denarius dei* is no part of it. 1 Duverg. n. 132; 3 Duverg. n. 49; Répert. de Jur. verbo Denier à Dieu.

DENIAL, *pleading.* To traverse the statement of the opposite party; a defence. See *Defence; Traverse.*

DENIER A DIEU, *French law.* It is a sum of money which the hirer of a thing gives to the other party as evidence, or for the consideration of the contract, which either party may annul, within twenty-four hours, the one who, giving the *denier à dieu*, by demanding, and the other by returning it. It differs from arrhæ. Vide *Arrhæ; Denarius Dei.*

DENIZATION, *Eng. law.* The act by which a foreigner becomes a subject of England; but he has not the rights either of a natural born subject, nor of one who has become naturalized. Bac. Ab. Aliens, B.

DENIZEN, *English law.* An alien born, who has obtained, *ex donatione legis*, letters patent to make him an English subject.

2. He is intermediate between a natural born subject and an alien. He may take lands by purchase or devise, which an alien cannot, but he is incapable of taking by inheritance. 1 Bl. Com. 374. In the United States there is no such civil condition

DENUNCIATION, *crim. law.* This term is used by the civilians to signify the act by which an individual informs a public officer, whose duty it is to prosecute offenders, that a crime has been committed. It differs from a complaint. (q. v.) Vide 1 Bro. C. L. 447; 2 Id. 389; Ayl. Parer. 210; Poth. Proc. Cr. sect. 2, § 2.

DEODAND, *English law.* This word is derived from *Deo dandum*, to be given to God; and is used to designate the instrument, whether it be an animal or inanimate thing, which has caused the death of a man. 3 Inst. 57; Hawk. bk. 1, c. 8.

2. The deodand is forfeited to the king, and was formerly applied to pious uses. But the presentment of a deodand by a grand jury, under their general charge from the judge of assize, is void. 1 Burr. Rep. 17.

DEPARTMENT. A portion of a country. In France, the country is divided into departments, which are somewhat similar to the counties in this country. The United States have been divided into military departments, including certain portions of the country. 1 Pet. 293.

2. By department is also meant the division of authority, as, the department of state, of the navy, &c.

DEPARTMENT OF THE NAVY, *government.* The Act of April 30, 1798, 1 Story's Laws, 498, establishes an executive department, under the denomination of the department of the navy, the chief officer of which shall be called the *secretary of the navy*. (q. v.)

2. A principal clerk, and such other clerks as he shall think necessary, shall be appointed by the secretary of the navy, who shall be employed in such manner as he shall deem most expedient. In case of vacancy in the office of the secretary, by removal or otherwise, it shall be the duty of the principal clerk to take charge and custody of all books, records, and documents of said office. Id. s. 2

DEPARTMENT OF STATE, *government*. The laws of the United States provide that there shall be an executive department, denominated the *department of state;* and a principal officer therein, called the *secretary of state.* (q. v.) Acts of July 27, 1789; September 15, 1789, s. 1. There shall be in such department an inferior officer, to be appointed by the secretary, and employed therein, as he shall deem proper, to be called the *chief clerk of the department of state.* (q. v.) Act of July 27, 1789, s. 2.

2. He may employ, besides, one chief clerk, whose compensation shall not exceed two thousand dollars per annum; two clerks, whose compensation shall not exceed one thousand six hundred dollars; four clerks, whose compensation shall not exceed one thousand four hundred dollars each; one clerk, whose compensation shall not exceed one thousand dollars; two clerks, whose compensation shall not exceed eight hundred dollars each; one messenger and assistant, at a compensation not exceeding one thousand and fifty dollars per annum; one superintendent of the patent office, whose compensation shall not exceed one thousand five hundred dollars; and, in the patent office, one clerk, whose compensation shall not exceed one thousand dollars; one machinist, at a compensation not exceeding seven hundred dollars; and one messenger, at a compensation not exceeding four hundred dollars per annum. Act of May 26, 1824; Act of April 20, 1818, s. 2.

3. By the Act of March 2, 1827, 3 Story's Laws, 2061, he is authorized to employ, in the state department, one additional clerk, whose compensation shall not exceed sixteen hundred dollars; two additional clerks, whose compensation shall not exceed one thousand dollars each; and one additional clerk for the patent office, whose compensation shall not exceed eight hundred dollars.

DEPARTMENT OF THE TREASURY OF THE UNITED STATES, *government*. The department of the treasury is constituted of the following officers, namely: the *secretary of the treasury*, (q. v.) the head of the department, two comptrollers, five auditors, a treasurer, a register, and a commissioner of the land office.

2. Each of these officers is required to perform certain appropriate duties, in which they are assisted by numerous clerks. They are prohibited from carrying on the business of trade or commerce, from being the owners or part owners of any sea vessel, from buying any public lands, from disposing or purchasing any securities of any state, or of the United States, from receiving or applying to their own use any emolument or gain in transacting business in this department, other than what shall be allowed by law, under the penalty of three thousand dollars, and of being removed from office, and of being thereafter incapable of holding any office under the United States. Gord. Dig. 228 to 248

DEPARTMENT OF WAR, *government*. The act of August 7, 1789, 1 Story's Laws, 31, creates an executive department, to be denominated the department of war; and there shall be a principal officer therein, to be called the *secretary for the department of war*. (q. v.)

2. There shall be in the said department, an inferior officer, to be appointed by the secretary, to be employed therein, and to be called the chief clerk in the department of war, and who, whenever the said principal officer shall be removed by the president, or in any other case of vacancy, shall, during such vacancy, have the charge and custody of all records, books, and papers, appertaining to the said department. Id.

DEPARTURE, *pleading*. Said to be when a party quits or departs from the case, or defence, which he has first made, and has recourse to another; it is when his replication or rejoinder contains matter not pursuant to the declaration, or plea, and which does not support and fortify it. Co. Litt. 304, a; 2 Saund. 84, a, n. (1); 2 Wils. 98; 1 Chit. Pl. 619. The following example will illustrate what is a departure: if to assumpsit, the defendant plead *infancy*, and to a replication of *necessaries*, rejoin, duress, payment, release, &c., the rejoinder is a departure, and a good cause of demurrer, because the defendant quits or departs from the case or defence which he first made, though either of these matters, newly pleaded, would have been a good bar, if first pleaded as such.

2. A departure in pleading is never allowed, for the record would, by such means, be spun out into endless prolixity; for he who has departed from and relinquished his first plea, might resort to a second, third, fourth, or even fortieth defence; pleading would, by such means, become infinite. He who had a bad cause, would never be brought to issue, and he who had a good one, would never obtain the end of his suit. Summary on Pleading, 92; 2 Saund. 84, a. n. (1); 16 East, R. 39; 1 M. & S. 395; Com. Dig. Pleader, F 7, 11; Bac. Abr. Pleas, L; Vin. Abr. Departure; 1 Archb. Civ. Pl. 247, 253; 1 Chit. Pl. 618.

3. A departure is cured by a verdict in favor of him who makes it, if the matter pleaded by way of departure is a sufficient answer, in substance, to what is before pleaded by the opposite party; that is, if it would have been sufficient, if pleaded in the first instance. 2 Saund. 84; 1 Lill. Ab. 444.

DEPARTURE, *maritime law*. A deviation from the course of the voyage insured.

2. A departure is justifiable or not justifiable; it is justifiable in consequence of the stress of weather, to make necessary repairs, to succor a ship in distress, to avoid capture, of inability to navigate the ship, mutiny of the crew, or other compulsion. 1 Bouv. Inst. n. 1189.

DEPENDENCY. A territory distinct from the country in which the supreme sovereign power resides, but belonging rightfully to it, and subject to the laws and regulations which the sovereign may think proper to prescribe. It differs from a *colony*, because it is not settled by the citizens of the sovereign or mother state; and from *possession*, because it is held by other title than that of mere conquest: for example, Malta was considered a dependency of Great Britain in the year 1813. 3 Wash. C. C. R. 286. Vide act of congress, March 1, 1809, commonly called the non-importation law.

DEPENDENT CONTRACT. One which it is not the duty of the contractor to perform, until some obligation contained in the same agreement has been performed by the other party. Ham. on Part. 17, 29, 30, 109.

DEPONENT, *witness*. One who gives information, on oath or affirmation, respecting some facts known to him, before a magistrate; he who makes a deposition.

DEPOPULATION. In its most proper signification, is the destruction of the people of a country or place. This word is, however, taken rather in a passive than an active one; we say depopulation, to designate a diminution of inhabitants, arising either from violent causes, or the want of multiplication. Vide 12 Co. 30.

DEPORTATION, *civil law*. Among the Romans a perpetual banishment, depriving the banished of his rights as a citizen; it differed from relegation (q. v.) and exile. (q. v.). 1 Bro. Civ. Law, 125 note; Inst. 1, 12, 1 and 2; Dig. 48, 22, 14, 1.

TO DEPOSE, *practice*. To make a deposition; to give testimony as a witness.

TO DEPOSE, *rights*. The act of depriving an individual of a public employment or office, against his will. Wolff, § 1063. The term is usually applied to the deprivation of all authority of a sovereign.

DEPOSIT, *contracts*. Usually defined to be a naked bailment of goods to be kept for the bailor, without reward, and to be returned when he shall require it. Jones' Bailm. 36, 117; 1 Bell's Com. 257. See also Dane's Abr. ch. 17, art. 1, § 3; Story on Bailm. c. 2, § 41. Pothier defines it to be a contract, by which one of the contracting parties gives a thing to another to keep, who is to do so gratuitously, and obliges himself to return it when he shall be requested. Traité du Depôt. See Code Civ. tit. 11, c. 1, art. 1915; Louisiana Code, tit. 13, c. 1, art. 2897.

2. Deposits, in the civil law, are divisible into two kinds; necessary and voluntary. A necessary deposit is such as arises from pressing necessity; as, for instance, in case of a fire, a shipwreck, or other overwhelming calamity; and thence it is called *miserabile depositum*. Louis. Code, 2935. A voluntary deposit is such as arises without any such calamity, from the mere consent or agreement of the parties. Dig. lib. 16, tit. 3, § 2.

3. This distinction was material in the civil law, in respect to the remedy, for in voluntary deposits the action was only *in simplum;* in the other *in duplum*, or twofold, whenever the depositary was guilty of any default. The common law has made no such distinction, and, therefore, in a necessary deposit, the remedy is limited to damages co-extensive with the wrong. Jones' Bailm. 48.

4. Deposits are again divided by the civil law into simple deposits, and seques-

trations; the former is when there is but one party depositor (of whatever number composed), having a common interest; the latter is where there are two or more depositors, having each a different and adverse interest. See *Sequestration*.

5. These distinctions give rise to very different considerations in point of responsibility and rights. Hitherto they do not seem to have been incorporated in the common law; though if cases should arise, the principles applicable to them would scarcely fail of receiving general approbation, at least, so far as they affect the rights and responsibilities of the parties. Cases of judicial sequestration and deposits, especially in courts of chancery and admiralty, may hereafter require the subject to be fully investigated. At present, there have been few cases in which it has been necessary to consider upon whom the loss should fall when the property has perished in the custody of the law. Story on Bailm. § 41–46.

6. There is another class of deposits noticed by Pothier, and called by him *irregular deposits*. This arises when a party having a sum of money which he does not think safe in his own hands, confides it to another, who is to return him, not the same money, but a like sum, when he shall demand it. Poth. Traité du Depôt, ch. 3, § 3. The usual deposit made by a person dealing with a bank is of this nature. The depositor, in such case, becomes merely a creditor of the depositary for the money or other thing which he binds himself to return.

7. This species of deposit is also called an *improper deposit*, to distinguish it from one that is *regular* and *proper*, and which latter is sometimes called a *special deposit*. 1 Bell's Com. 257–8. See 4 Blackf. R. 395.

8. There is a kind of deposit which may, for distinction's sake, be called a *quasi deposit*, which is governed by the same general rule as common deposits. It is when a party comes lawfully to the possession of another person's property by finding. Under such circumstances, the finder seems bound to the same reasonable care of it as any voluntary depositary *ex contractu*. Doct. & Stu. Dial. 2, ch. 38; Story on Bailm. § 85; and see Bac. Abr. Bailm. D.

See further, on the subject of deposits, Louis. Code, tit. 13; Bac. Abr. Bailment; Digest, *depositi vel contra;* Code, lib. 4, tit. 34; Inst. lib. 3, tit. 15, § 3; Nov. 73 and 78; Domat, liv. 1, tit. 7, et tom. 2, liv. 3, tit. 1, s. 5, n. 26; 1 Bouv. Inst. n 1053, et seq.

DEPOSITARY, *contracts*. He with whom a deposit is confided or made.

2. It is the essence of the contract of deposits that it should be gratuitous on the part of the depositary. 9 M. R. 470. Being a bailee without reward, the depositary is bound to slight diligence only, and he is not therefore answerable except for gross neglect. 1 Dane's Abr. c. 17, art. 2. But in every case good faith requires that he should take reasonable care; and what is reasonable care, must materially depend upon the nature and quality of the thing, the circumstances under which it is deposited, and sometimes upon the character and confidence, and particular dealing of the parties. See 14 Serg. & Rawle, 275. The degree of care and diligence is not altered by the fact, that the depositary is the joint owner of the goods with the depositor; for in such a case, if the possessor is guilty of gross negligence, he will still be responsible, in the same manner as a common depositary, having no interest in the thing. Jones' Bailm. 82, 83. As to the care which a depositary is bound to use, see 2 Ld. Raym. 909, 914; 1 Ld. Raym. 655; 2 Kent's Com. 438; 17 Mass. R. 479, 499; 4 Burr. 2298; 14 Serg. & Rawle, 275; Jones' Bailm. 8; Story on Bailm. § 63, 64.

3. The depositary is bound to return the deposit *in individuo*, and in the same state in which he received it; if it is lost, or injured, or spoiled, by his fraud or gross negligence, he is responsible to the extent of the loss or injury. Jones' Bailm. 36, 46, 120; 17 Mass. R. 479; 2 Hawk. N. Car. R. 145; 1 Dane's Abr. c. 17, art. 1 and 2. He is also bound to restore, not only the thing deposited, but any increase or profits which may have accrued from it; if an animal deposited bear young, the latter are to be delivered to the owner. Story on Bailm. § 99.

4. In general it may be laid down that a depositary has no right to use the thing deposited. Bac. Abr. Bailm. D; Jones' Bailm. 81, 82; 1 Dane's Abr. c. 17, art. 11, § 2. But this proposition must be received with many qualifications. There are certain cases, in which the use of the thing may be necessary for the due preservation of the deposit. There are others, again, where it would be mischievous; and others, again, where it would be, if not beneficial,

at least indifferent. Jones' Bailm. 81, 82; Owen's R. 123, 124; 2 Salk. 522; 2 Kent's Com. 450. The best general rule on the subject, is to consider whether there may or may not be an implied consent, on the part of the owner, to the use. If the use would be for the benefit of the deposit, the assent of the owner may well be presumed; if to his injury, or perilous, it ought not to be presumed; if the use would be indifferent, and other circumstances do not incline either way, the use may be deemed not allowable. Jones' Bailm. 80, 81; Story on Bailm. § 90; 1 Bouv. Inst. n. 1008, et seq.

DEPOSITION, *evidence*. The testimony of a witness reduced to writing, in due form of law, taken by virtue of a commission or other authority of a competent tribunal.

2. Before it is taken, the witness ought to be sworn or affirmed to declare the truth, the whole truth, and nothing but the truth. It should properly be written by the commissioner appointed to take it, or by the witness himself; 3 Penna. R. 41; or by one not interested in the matter in dispute, who is properly authorized by the commissioner. 8 Watts, R. 406, 524. It ought to answer all the interrogatories, and be signed by the witness, when he can write, and by the commissioner. When the witness cannot write, it ought to be so stated, and he should make his mark or cross.

3. Depositions in criminal cases cannot be taken without the consent of the defendant. Vide, generally, 1 Phil. Ev. 286; 1 Vern. 413, note; Ayl. Pand. 206; 2 Supp. to Ves. jr. 309; 7 Vin. Ab. 553; 12 Vin. Ab. 107; Dane's Ab. Index, h. t.; Com. Dig. Chancery, P 8, T 4, T 5; Com. Dig. Testmoigne, C 4.

4. The Act of September 24, 1789, s. 30, 1 Story's L. U. S. 64, directs that when the testimony of any person shall be necessary in any civil cause depending in any district, in any court of the United States, who shall live at a greater distance from the place of trial than one hundred miles, or is bound on a voyage to sea, or is about to go out of the United States, or out of such district, and to a greater distance from the place of trial than as aforesaid, before the time of trial, or is ancient, or very infirm, the deposition of such person may be taken, de bene esse, before any justice or judge of any of the courts of the United States, or before any chancellor, justice, or judge of a supreme or superior court, mayor, or chief magistrate of a city, or judge of a county court or court of common pleas of any of the United States, not being of counsel or attorney to either of the parties, or interested in the event of the cause; provided that a notification from the magistrate before whom the deposition is to be taken, to the adverse party, to be present at the taking of the same, and to put interrogatories, if he think fit, be first made out and served on the adverse party, or his attorney, as either may be nearest, if either is within one hundred miles of the place of such caption, allowing time for their attendance after being notified, not less than at the rate of one day, Sundays exclusive, for every twenty miles' travel. And in causes of admiralty and maritime jurisdiction, or other causes of seizure, when a libel shall be filed, in which an adverse party is not named, and depositions of persons, circumstanced as aforesaid, shall be taken before a claim be put in, the like notification, as aforesaid, shall be given to the person having the agency or possession of the property libelled at the time of the capture or seizure of the same, if known to the libellant. And every person deposing as aforesaid, shall be carefully examined and cautioned, and sworn or affirmed to testify *the whole truth*, and shall subscribe the testimony by him or her given, after the same shall be reduced to writing, which shall be done only by the magistrate taking the deposition, or by the deponent in his presence. And the deposition so taken shall be retained by such magistrate, until he deliver the same with his own hand into the court for which they are taken, or shall, together with a certificate of the reasons as aforesaid, of their being taken, and of the notice, if any given, to the adverse party, be by him, the said magistrate, sealed up and directed to such court, and remain under his seal until opened in court. And any person may be compelled to appear and depose as aforesaid, in the same manner as to appear and testify in court. And in the trial of any cause of admiralty or maritime jurisdiction in a district court, the decree in which may be appealed from, if either party shall suggest to and satisfy the court, that probably it will not be in his power to produce the witnesses, there testifying, before the circuit court, should an appeal be had, and shall move that their testimony shall be taken down in writing, it shall be so done

by the clerk of the court. And if an appeal be had, such testimony may be used on the trial of the same, if it shall appear to the satisfaction of the court, which shall try the appeal, that the witnesses are then dead, or gone out of the United States, or to a greater distance than as aforesaid, from the place where the court is sitting; or that, by reason of age, sickness, bodily infirmity, or imprisonment, they are unable to travel or appear at court, but not otherwise. And unless the same shall be made to appear on the trial of any cause, with respect to witnesses whose depositions may have been taken therein, such depositions shall not be admitted or used in the cause. *Provided*, That nothing herein shall be construed to prevent any court of the United States from granting a dedimus potestatem, to take depositions according to common usage, when it may be necessary to prevent a failure or delay of justice; which power they shall severally possess; nor to extend to depositions taken in perpetuam rei memoriam, which, if they relate to matters that may be cognizable in any court of the United States, a circuit court, on application thereto made as a court of equity, may, according to the usages in chancery, direct to be taken.

5. The Act of January 24, 1827, 3 Story's L. U. S. 2040, authorizes the clerk of any court of the United States within which a witness resides or where he is found, to issue a subpœna to compel the attendance of such witness, and a neglect of the witness to attend may be punished by the court whose clerk has issued the subpœna, as for a contempt. And when papers are wanted by the parties litigant, the judge of the court within which they are, may issue a subpœna duces tecum, and enforce obedience by punishment as for a contempt.

For the form and style of depositions, see Gresl. Eq. Ev. 77.

DEPOSITION, *eccl. law.* The act of depriving a clergyman, by a competent tribunal, of his clerical orders, to punish him for some offence, and to prevent his acting in future in his clerical character. Ayl. Par. 206.

DEPOSITOR, *contracts.* He who makes a deposit.

2. He is generally entitled to receive the deposit from the depositary, but to this rule there are exceptions; as when the depositor at the time of making the deposit had no title to the property deposited, and the owner claims it from the depositary, the depositor cannot recover it; and for this reason, that he can never be in a better situation than the owner. 1 Barn. & Ald. 450; 5 Taunt. 759. As to the place where the depositor is entitled to receive his deposit, see Story on Bailm. § 117–120; 1 Bouv. Inst. n. 1063.

DEPREDATION, *French law.* The pillage which is made of the goods of a decedent. Ferr. Mod. h. t.

DEPRIVATION, *ecclesiastical punishment.* A censure by which a clergyman is deprived of his parsonage, vicarage, or other ecclesiastical promotion or dignity. Vide Ayliffe's Parerg. 206; 1 Bl. Com. 393.

DEPUTY. One authorized by an officer to exercise the office or right which the officer possesses, for and in place of the latter.

2. In general, ministerial officers can appoint deputies; Com. Dig. Officer, D 1; unless the office is to be exercised by the ministerial officer in person; and where the office partakes of a judicial and ministerial character, although a deputy may be made for the performance of ministerial acts, one cannot be made for the performance of a judicial act; a sheriff cannot therefore make a deputy to hold an inquisition, under a writ of inquiry, though he may appoint a deputy to serve a writ.

3. In general, a deputy has power to do every act which his principal might do; but a deputy cannot make a deputy.

4. A deputy should always act in the name of his principal. The principal is liable for the deputy's acts performed by him as such, and for the neglect of the deputy; Dane's Ab. vol. 3, c. 76, a. 2; and the deputy is liable himself to the person injured for his own tortious acts. Dane's Ab. Index, h. t.; Com. Dig. Officer, D; Viscount, B. Vide 7 Vin. Ab. 556; Arch. Civ. Pl. 68; 16 John. R. 108.

DEPUTY OF THE ATTORNEY GENERAL. An officer appointed by the attorney general, who is to hold his office during the pleasure of the latter, and whose duty it is to perform, within a specified district, the duties of the attorney general. He must be a member of the bar. In Pennsylvania, by an act of assembly, passed May 3, 1850, district attorneys are elected by the people, who are required to perform the duties which, before that act, were performed by deputies of the attorney general.

Deputy district attorneys. The Act of Congress of March 3, 1815, 2 Story L. U. S. 1530, authorizes and directs the district attorneys of the United States to appoint by warrant, an attorney as their substitute or deputy in all cases when necessary to sue or prosecute for the United States, in any of the state or county courts, by that act invested with certain jurisdiction, within the sphere of whose jurisdiction the said district attorneys do not themselves reside or practice; and the said substitute or deputy shall be sworn or affirmed to the faithful execution of his duty.

DERELICT, *common law*. This term is applied in the common law in a different sense from what it bears in the civil law. In the former it is applied to lands left by the sea.

2. When so left by degrees the derelict land belongs to the owner of the soil adjoining, but when the sea retires suddenly, it belongs to the government. 2 Bl. Com. 262; 1 Bro. Civ. Law, 239; 1 Sumn. 328, 490; 1 Gallis. 133; Bee, R. 62, 178, 260; Ware, R. 332.

DERELICTO, *civil law*. Goods voluntarily abandoned by their owner; he must, however, leave them, not only *sine spe revertendi*, but also *sine animo revertendi;* his intention to abandon them may be inferred by the great length of time during which he may have been out of possession, without any attempt to regain them. 1 Bro. Civ. Law, 239; 2 Bro. Civ. Law, 51; Wood's Civ. Law, 156; 19 Amer. Jur. 219, 221, 222; Dane's Ab. Index, h. t.; 1 Ware's R. 41.

DERIVATIVE. Coming from another; taken from something preceding, secondary; as derivative title, which is that acquired from another person. There is considerable difference between an original and a derivative title. When the acquisition is original, the right thus acquired to the thing becomes property, which must be unqualified and unlimited, and since no one but the occupant has any right to the thing, he must have the whole right of disposing of it. But with regard to derivative acquisition, it may be otherwise, for the person from whom the thing is acquired may not have an unlimited right to it, or he may convey or transfer it with certain reservations of right. Derivative title must always be by contract.

2. Derivative conveyances are those which presuppose some other precedent conveyance, and serve only to enlarge, confirm, alter, restrain, restore, or transfer the interest granted by such original conveyance. 3 Bl. Com. 324.

Derivative power. An authority by which one person enables another to do an act for him. See *Powers*.

DEROGATION, *civil law*. The partial abrogation of a law; to derogate from a law is to enact something which is contrary to it; to abrogate a law is to abolish it entirely. Dig. lib. 50, t. 17, l. 102. See *Abrogation*.

DESCENDANTS. Those who have issued from an individual, and include his children, grandchildren, and their children to the remotest degree. Ambl. 327; 2 Bro. C. C. 30; Id. 230; 3 Bro. C. C. 367; 1 Rop. Leg. 115; 2 Bouv. n. 1956.

2. The descendants form what is called the direct descending line. Vide *Line*. The term is opposed to that of ascendants. (q. v.)

3. There is a difference between the number of ascendants and descendants which a man may have; every one has the same order of ascendants, though they may not be exactly alike as to numbers, because some may be descended from a common ancestor. In the line of descendants they fork differently, according to the number of children, and continue longer or shorter as generations continue or cease to exist. Many families become extinct, while others continue; the line of descendants is therefore diversified in each family.

DESCENDER. In the descent; as formedon in the descender. Bac. Ab. Formedon, A 1. Vide *Formedon*.

DESCENT. Hereditary succession. Descent is the title, whereby a person, upon the death of his ancestor, acquires the estate of the latter, as his heir at law. This manner of acquiring title is directly opposed to that of purchase. (q. v.) 2 Bouv. Inst. n. 1952, et seq.

2. It will be proper to consider, 1. What kind of property descends; and, 2. The general rules of descent.

3.—§ 1. All real estate, and all freehold of inheritance in land, descend to the heir. And, as being accessory to the land and making a part of the inheritance, fixtures, and emblements, and all things annexed to, or connected with the land, descend with it to the heir. Terms for years, and other estates less than freehold, pass to the executor, and are not subjects of descent. It is a rule at common law that no one can inherit real estate unless he was heir to the person *last seised.* This does not apply as a general rule in the United States. Vide article *Possessio fratris.*

4.—§ 2. The general rules of the law of descent.

1. It is a general rule in the law of inheritance, that if a person owning real estate, dies seised, or as owner, without devising the same, the estate shall descend to his descendants in the direct line of lineal descent, and if there be but one person, then to him or her alone; and if more than one person, and all of equal degree of consanguinity to the ancestor, then the inheritance shall descend to the several persons as tenants in common in equal parts, however remote from the intestate the common degree of consanguinity may be. This rule is in favor of the equal claims of the descending line, in the same degree, without distinction of sex, and to the exclusion of all other claimants. The following example will illustrate it; it consists of three distinct cases: 1. Suppose Paul shall die seised of real estate, leaving two sons and a daughter, in this case the estate would descend to them in equal parts; but suppose, 2. That instead of children, he should leave several grandchildren, two of them the children of his son Peter, and one the son of his son John, these will inherit the estate in equal proportions; or, 3. Instead of children and grandchildren, suppose Paul left ten great grandchildren, one the lineal descendant of his son John, and nine the descendants of his son Peter; these, like the others, would partake equally of the inheritance as tenants in common. According to Chancellor Kent, this rule prevails in all the United States, with this variation, that in Vermont the male descendants take double the share of females; and in South Carolina, the widow takes one-third of the estate in fee; and in Georgia, she takes a child's share in fee, if there be any children, and, if none, she then takes in each of those states, a moiety of the estate. In North and South Carolina, the claimant takes in all cases, *per stirpes*, though standing in the same degree. 4 Kent, Com. 371; Reeves' Law of Desc. *passim;* Griff. Law Reg., answers to the 6th interr. under the head of each state. In Louisiana the rule is, that in all cases in which representation is admitted, the partition is made by roots; if one root has produced several branches, the subdivision is also made by root in each branch, and the members of the branch take between them by heads. Civil Code, art. 895.

5.—2. It is also a rule, that if a person dying seised, or as owner of the land, leaves lawful issue of different degrees of consanguinity, the inheritance shall descend to the children and grandchildren of the ancestor, if any be living, and to the issue of such children and grandchildren as shall be dead, and so on to the remotest degree, as tenants in common; but such grandchildren and their descendants, shall inherit only such share as their parents respectively would have inherited if living. This rule may be illustrated by the following example: 1. Suppose Peter, the ancestor, had two children; John, dead, (represented in the following diagram by figure 1,) and Maria, living (fig. 2); John had two children, Joseph, living, (fig. 3,) and Charles, dead (fig. 4); Charles had two children, Robert, living, (fig. 5,) and James, dead (fig. 6); James had two children, both living, Ann, (fig. 7,) and William, (fig. 8.)

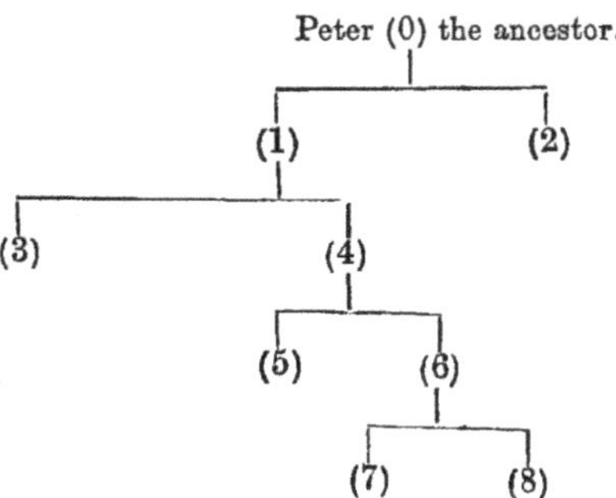

In this case Maria would inherit one-half; Joseph, the son of John, one-half of the half, or quarter of the whole; Robert, one-eighth of the whole; and Ann and William, each one-sixteenth of the whole, which they would hold as tenants in common in these proportions. This is called inheritance *per stirpes*, by roots, because the heirs take in such portions only as their immediate ancestors would have inherited if living.

6.—3. When the owner of land dies without lawful issue, leaving parents, it is the rule in some of the states, that the inheritance shall *ascend* to them, first to the father, and then to the mother, or jointly to both, under certain regulations prescribed by statute.

7.—4. When the intestate dies without issue or parents, the estate descends to his brothers and sisters and their representatives. When there are such relations, and all of equal degree of consanguinity to the intestate, the inheritance descends to them in equal parts, however remote from the intestate the common degree of consanguinity may be. When all the heirs are brothers and sisters, or all of them nephews and nieces, they take equally. When some are dead who leave issue, and some are living, then those who are living take the share they would have taken if all had been living, and the descendants of those who are dead inherit only the share which their immediate parents would have received if living. When the direct lineal descendants stand in equal degrees, they take *per capita*, by the head, each one full share; when, on the contrary, they stand in different degrees of consanguinity to the common ancestor, they take *per stirpes*, by roots, by right of representation. It is nearly a general rule, that the ascending line, after parents, is postponed to the collateral line of brothers and sisters. Considerable difference exists in the laws of the several states, when the next of kin are nephews and nieces, and uncles and aunts claim as standing in the same degree. In many of the states, all these relations take equally as being next of kin; this is the rule in the states of New Hampshire, Vermont, (subject to the claim of the males to a double portion as above stated,) Rhode Island, North Carolina, and Louisiana. In Alabama, Connecticut, Delaware, Georgia, Indiana, Illinois, Kentucky, Maine, Maryland, Massachusetts, Mississippi, Missouri, New Jersey, New York, Ohio, Pennsylvania, South Carolina, Tennessee, and Virginia, on the contrary, nephews and nieces take in exclusion of uncles and aunts, though they be of equal degree of consanguinity to the intestate. In Alabama, Connecticut, Georgia, Maryland, New Hampshire, Ohio, Rhode Island, and Vermont, there is no representation among collaterals after the children of brothers and sisters; in Delaware, none after the grandchildren of brothers and sisters. In Louisiana, the ascending line must be exhausted before the estate passes to collaterals. Code, art. 910. In North Carolina, claimants take *per stirpes* in every case, though they stand in equal degree of consanguinity to the common ancestor. As to the distinction between whole and half blood, vide *Half blood.*

8.—5. Chancellor Kent lays it down as a general rule in the American law of descent, that when the intestate has left no lineal descendants, nor parents, nor brothers, nor sisters, or their descendants, that the grandfather takes the estate, before uncles and aunts, as being nearest of kin to the intestate.

9.—6. When the intestate dies leaving no lineal descendants, nor parents, nor brothers, nor sisters, nor any of their descendants, nor grand parents, as a general rule, it is presumed, the inheritance descends to the brothers and sisters of both the intestate's parents, and to their descendants, equally. When they all stand in equal degree to the intestate, they take *per capita*, and when in unequal degree, *per stirpes.* To this general rule, however, there are slight variations in some of the states, as, in New York, grand parents do not take before collaterals.

10.—7. When the inheritance came to the intestate on the part of the father, then the brothers and sisters of the father and their descendants shall have the preference, and, in default of them, the estate shall descend to the brothers and sisters of the mother, and their descendants; and where the inheritance comes to the intestate on the part of his mother, then her brothers and sisters, and their descendants, have a preference, and in default of them, the brothers and sisters on the side of the father, and their descendants, inherit. This is the rule in Connecticut, New Jersey, New York, North Carolina, Ohio, Rhode Island, Tennessee, and Virginia. In Pennsylvania, it is provided by act of assembly, April 8, 1833, that no person who is not of the blood of the ancestors or other relations from whom any real estate descended, or by whom it was given or devised to the intestate, shall in any of the cases before mentioned, take any estate of inheritance therein, but such real estate subject to such life estate as may be in existence by virtue of this act, shall pass to and vest in such other persons as would be entitled by this act, if the persons not of the blood of such ancestor, or other relation, had never existed, or were dead at the decease of the intestate. In some of the states there is perhaps no distinction as to the descent, whether they have been acquired by purchase or by descent from an ancestor.

11.—8. When there is a failure of heirs under the preceding rules, the inheritance descends to the remaining next of kin of the intestate, according to the rules in the statute of distribution of the personal estate, subject to the doctrine in the preceding rules in the different states as to the half blood, to ancestral estates, and as to the equality of distribution. This rule prevails in several states, subject to some peculiarities in the local laws of descent, which extend to this rule.

12. It is proper before closing this article, to remind the reader, that in computing the degrees of consanguinity, the civil law is followed generally in this country, except in North Carolina, where the rules of the common law in their application to descents are adopted, to ascertain the degree of consanguinity. Vide the articles *Branch; Consanguinity; Degree; Line.*

DESCRIPTIO PERSONÆ. Description of the person. In wills, it frequently happens that the word heir is used as a *descriptio personæ;* it is then a sufficient designation of the person.

DESCRIPTION. A written account of the state and condition of personal property, titles, papers, and the like. It is a kind of inventory, (q. v.) but is more particular in ascertaining the exact condition of the property, and is without any appraisement of it.

2. When goods are found in the possession of a person accused of stealing them, a description ought to be made of them. Merl. Rép. h. t.

3. A description is less perfect than a definition. (q. v.) It gives some knowledge of the accidents and qualities of a thing; for example, plants, fruits, and animals, are described by their shape, bulk, color, and the like accidents. Ayl. Pand. 60.

4. Description may also be of a person, as description of a legatee. 1 Roper on Leg. chap. 2.

DESERTER. One who abandons his post; as, a soldier who abandons the public service without leave; or a sailor who abandons a ship when he has engaged to serve.

DESERTION, *crim. law.* An offence which consists in the abandonment of the public service, in the army or navy, without leave.

2. The Act of March 16, 1802, s. 19, enacts, that if any non-commissioned officer, musician, or private, shall desert the service of the United States, he shall, in addition to the penalties mentioned in the rules and articles of war, be liable to serve for and during such period as shall, with the time he may have served previous to his desertion, amount to the full term of his enlistment; and such soldier shall and may be tried by a court-martial, and punished, although the term of his enlistment may have elapsed previous to his being apprehended or tried.

3. By the articles of war, it is enacted, that "any non-commissioned officer or soldier who shall, without leave from his commanding officer, absent himself from his troop, company, or detachment, shall, upon being convicted thereof, be punished, according to the nature of his offence, at the discretion of a court-martial." Art. 21.

4. By the articles for the government of the navy, art. 16, it is enacted, that "if any person in the navy shall desert to an enemy, or rebel, he shall suffer death;" and by art. 17, "if any person in the navy shall desert, or shall entice others to desert, he shall suffer death, or such other punishment as a court-martial shall adjudge."

DESERTION, *torts.* The act by which a man abandons his wife and children, or either of them.

2. On proof of desertion, the courts possess the power to grant the wife, or such children as have been deserted, alimony (q. v.)

DESERTION, MALICIOUS. The act of a husband or wife, in leaving a consort, without just cause, for the purpose of causing a perpetual separation. Vide *Abandonment, malicious.*

DESERTION OF SEAMEN, *contracts.* The abandonment, by a sailor, of a ship or vessel, in which he engaged to perform a voyage, before the expiration of his time, and without leave.

2. Desertion, without just cause, renders the sailor liable, on his shipping articles, for damages, and will, besides, work a forfeiture of his wages previously earned. 3 Kent, Com. 155. It has been decided, in England, that leaving the ship before the completion of the voyage is not desertion, in the case, 1. Of the seaman's entering into the public service, either voluntarily or by impress; and 2. When he is compelled to leave it by the inhuman treatment of the

captain. 2 Esp. R. 269; 1 Bell's Com. 514, 5th ed.; 2 Rob. Adm. R. 232.

DESIGNATIO PERSONÆ. The persons described in a contract as being parties to it.

2. In all contracts, under seal, there must be some designatio personæ. In general, the names of the parties appear in the body of the deed, "between A B of, &c., of the one part, and C D of, &c., of the other part," being the common formula. But there is a sufficient designation and description of the party to be charged, if his name is written at the foot of the instrument.

3. A deed alleged to have been made between plaintiff and defendant began as follows: "'Tis agreed that a gray nag bought of A B by C D shall run twenty-five miles in two hours for £——, &c. In witness whereof, we have hereunto set our hands and seals." The plaintiff and defendant subscribed their names at the bottom of the writing, and afterwards sealed and delivered the document as their deed. Held, that the omission to state the names of the contracting parties in the body of the instrument, was supplied by the signatures at the bottom, and it sufficiently appeared whose deed it was. 1 Raym. 2; 1 Salk. 214; 2 B. & P. 339.

4. When a person is described in the body of the instrument by the name of James, and he signs the name of John, on being sued by the latter name he cannot deny it. 3 Taunt. 505; Cro. Eliz. 897, n. (a.) Vide 11 Ad. & Ell. 594; 3 P. & D. 271.

DESIGNATION, *wills*. The expression used by a testator, instead of the name of the person or the thing he is desirous to name; for example, a legacy to the eldest son of such a person, would be a designation of the legatee. Vide 1 Rop. Leg. ch. 2.

2. A bequest of the farm which the testator bought of such a person; or of the picture he owns, painted by such an artist, would be a designation of the thing devised or bequeathed.

DESPACHEURS. The name given, in some countries, to persons appointed to settle cases of average. Ord. Hamb. t. 21, art. 10.

DESPATCHES. Official communications of official persons, on the affairs of government.

2. In general, the bearer of despatches is entitled to all the facilities that can be given him, in his own country, or in a neutral state; but a neutral cannot, in general, be the bearer of despatches of one of the belligerent parties. 6 C. Rob. 465; see 2 Dodson, 54; Edw. 274.

DESPERATE. Of which there is no hope.

2. This term is used frequently, in making an inventory of a decedent's effects, when a debt is considered so bad that there is no hope of recovering it. It is then called a desperate debt, and, if it be so returned, it will be *prima facie*, considered as desperate. See Toll. Ex. 248; 2 Williams, Ex. 644; 1 Chit. Pr. 580. See *Sperate*.

DESPITUS. This word signifies, in our ancient law books, a contemptible person. Flet. lib. 4, c. 5, § 4. The English word despite is derived from it, which signifies spite or contempt; against one's will—defiance with contempt, or contempt of opposition.

DESPOT. This word, in its most simple and original acceptation, signifies *master and supreme lord;* it is synonymous with monarch; but, taken in bad part, as it is usually employed, it signifies a tyrant. In some states, despot is the title given to the sovereign, as king is given in others. Encyc. Lond.

DESPOTISM, *government*. That abuse of government, where the sovereign power is not divided, but united in the hands of a single man, whatever may be his official title. It is not, properly, a form of government. Toull. Dr. Civ. Fr. tit. prel. n. 32; Rutherf. Inst. b. 1, c. 20, § 1. Vide *Tyranny; Tyrant.*

DESRENABLE, *Law French.* Unreasonable. Britt. c. 121.

DESTINATION. The application which the testator directs shall be made of the legacy he gives; for example, when a testator gives to a hospital a sum of money, to be applied in erecting buildings, he is said to give a destination to the legacy. Destination also signifies the intended application of a thing. Mill stones, for example, taken out of a mill to be picked, and to be returned, have a destination, and are considered as real estate, although detached from the freehold. Heir looms, (q. v.) although personal chattels, are, by their destination, considered real estate; and money agreed or directed to be laid out in land, is treated as real property. Newl. on Contr.

ch. 3; Fonbl. Eq. B. 1, c. 6, § 9; 3 Wheat. R. 577; 2 Bell's Com. 2; Ersk. Inst. 2, 2, § 14. Vide *Mill.*

2. When the owner of two adjoining houses uses, during his life, the property in such a manner as to make one property subject to the other, and devises one property to one person, and the other to another, this is said not to be an easement or servitude, but a destination by the former owner. Lois des Bât. partie 1, c. 4, art. 3, § 3; 5 Har. & John. 82. See *Dedication.*

DESTINATION, *com. law.* The port at which a ship is to end her voyage is called her port of destination. Pard. n. 600.

DESUETUDE. This term is applied to laws which have become obsolete. (q. v.)

DETAINER. 1. The act of keeping a person against his will, or of keeping goods or property. All illegal detainers of the person amount to false imprisonment, and may be remedied by habeas corpus.

2.—2. A detainer or detention of goods is either lawful or unlawful; when lawful, the party having possession of them cannot be deprived of it. The detention may be unlawful, although the original taking was lawful; as when goods were distrained for rent and the rent was afterwards paid; or when they were pledged, and the money borrowed, and interest were afterwards paid; in these, and the like cases, the owner should make a demand, (q. v.) and if the possessor refuse to restore them, trover, detinue, or replevin, will lie, at the option of the plaintiff.

3.—3. There may also be a detainer of land; and this is either lawful and peaceable, or unlawful and forcible. 1. The detainer is lawful where the entry has been lawful, and the estate is held by virtue of some right. 2. It is unlawful and forcible, where the entry has been unlawful, and with force, and it is retained, by force, against right; or even when the entry has been peaceable and lawful, if the detainer be by force, and against right; as, if a tenant at will should detain with force, after the will has determined, he will be guilty of a forcible detainer. Hawk. P. C. ch. 64, s. 22; 2 Chit. Pr. 238; Com. Dig. B. 2; 8 Cowen, 216; 1 Hall, 240; 4 John. 198; 4 Bibb, 501. A forcible detainer is a distinct offence from a forcible entry. 8 Cowen, 216. See *Forcible entry and detainer.*

4.—4. A writ or instrument, issued or made by a competent officer, authorizing the keeper of a prison to keep in his custody a person therein named. A detainer may be lodged against one within the walls of a prison, on what account soever he is there. Com. Dig. Process, E 3 b.

DETENTION. The act of retaining a person or property, and preventing the removal of such person or property.

2. The detention may be occasioned by accidents, as, the detention of a ship by calms, or by ice; or it may be hostile, as the detention of persons or ships in a foreign country, by order of the government. In general, the detention of a ship does not change the nature of the contract, and therefore, sailors will be entitled to their wages during the time of the detention. 1 Bell's Com. 517, 519, 5th ed.; Mackel. Man. § 210.

3. A detention is legal when the party has a right to the property, and has come lawfully into possession. It is illegal when the taking was unlawful, as is the case of forcible entry and detainer, although the party may have a right of possession; but, in some cases, the detention may be lawful, although the taking may have been unlawful. 3 Penn. St. R. 20. When the taking was legal, the detention may be illegal; as, if one borrow a horse, to ride from A to B, and afterwards detain him from the owner, after demand, such detention is unlawful, and the owner may either retake his property, or have an action of replevin or detinue. 1 Chit. Pr. 135. In some cases, the detention becomes criminal, although the taking was lawful, as in embezzlement.

DETERMINABLE. What may come to an end, by the happening of a contingency; as a determinable fee. See 2 Bouv. Inst. n. 1695.

DETERMINABLE FEE. Also called a *qualified* or *base fee*, is one which has a quality subjoined to it, and which must be determined whenever the qualification annexed to it is at an end. A limitation to a man and his heirs on the part of his father, affords an example of this species of estate. Litt. § 254; Co. Litt. 27 a, 220; 1 Prest. on Estates, 449; 2 Bl. Com. 109; Cruise, tit 1, § 82; 2 Bouv. Inst. n. 1695.

DETERMINATE. That which is ascertained; what is particularly designated; as, if I sell you my horse Napoleon, the article sold is here determined. This is very different from a contract by which I would have sold you a horse, without a particular designation of any horse. 1 Bouv. Inst. n. 947, 950.

DETERMINATION. The end, the conclusion, of a right or authority; as, the determination of a lease. Com. Dig. Estates by Grant, G 10, 11, and 12. The determination of an authority is the end of the authority given; the end of the return day of a writ determines the authority of the sheriff; the death of the principal determines the authority of a mere attorney. By determination is also understood the decision or judgment of a court of justice.

DETINET. He detains. Vide *Debet et Detinet*, and *Detinuit*.

DETINUE, *remedies*. The name of an action for the recovery of a personal chattel in specie. 3 Bl. Com. 152; 3 Bouv. Inst. n. 3472; 1 J. J. Marsh. 500.

2. This action may be considered, 1. With reference to the nature of the thing to be recovered. 2. The plaintiff's interest therein. 3. The injury. 4. The pleadings. 5. The judgment.

3.—1. The goods which it is sought to recover, must be capable of being distinguished from all others, as a particular horse, a cow, &c., but not for a bushel of grain. Com. Dig. Detinue, B, C; 2 Bl. Com. 152; Co. Litt. 286 b; Bro. Det. 51. Detinue cannot be maintained where the property sued for had ceased to exist when the suit was commenced. 2 Dana, 332. See 5 Stew. & Port. 123; 1 Ala. R. 203.

4.—2. To support this action, the plaintiff must have a right to immediate possession, although he never had actual possession; a reversioner cannot, therefore, maintain it. A bailee, who has only a special property, may nevertheless support it when he delivered the goods to the defendant, or they were taken out of the bailee's custody. 2 Saund. 47, b, c, d; Bro. Ab. h. t.; 9 Leigh, R. 158; 1 How. Miss. R. 315; 5 How. Miss. R. 742; 4 B. Munr. 365.

5.—3. The gist of the action is the wrongful detainer, and not the original taking. The possession must have been acquired by the defendant by lawful means, as by delivery, bailment, or finding, and not tortiously. Bro. Abr. Det. 53, 36, 21; 1 Misso. R. 749. But a demand is not requisite, except for the purpose of entitling the plaintiff to damages for the detention between the time of the demand and that of the commencement of the action. 1 Bibb, 186; 4 Bibb, 340; 1 Misso. 9; 3 Litt. 46.

6.—4. The plaintiff may declare upon a bailment or a trover; but the practice, by the ancient common law, was to allege, simply, that the goods came to the hands, &c., of the defendant without more. Bro. Abr. Det. 10, per Littleton; 33 H. VI. 27. The trover or finding, when alleged, was not traversable, except when the defendant alleged delivery over of a chattel actually found to a third person, before action brought, in excuse of the detinue. Bro. Abr. Det. 1, 2. Nor is the bailment traversable, but the defendant must answer to the detinue. Bro. Abr. Det. 50–1. In describing the things demanded, much certainty is requisite, owing to the nature of the execution. A declaration for "a red cow with a white face," is not supported by proof that the cow was a yellow or sorrel cow. 1 Scam. R. 206. The general issue is *non detinet*, and under it special matter may be given in evidence. Co. Litt. 283.

7.—5. In this action the defendant frequently prayed garnishment of a third person, whom he alleged owned or had an interest in the thing demanded; but this he could not do without confessing the possession of the thing demanded, and made privity of bailment. Bro. Abr. Garnishment, 1; Interpleader, 3. If the prayer of garnishment was allowed, a sci. fac. issued against the person named as garnishee. If he made default, the plaintiff recovered against the defendant the chattel demanded, but no damages. If the garnishee appeared and the plaintiff made default, the garnishee recovered. If both appeared, and the plaintiff recovered; he had judgment against the defendant for the chattel demanded, and a distringas in execution; and against the garnishee a judgment for damages, and a fi. fa. in execution. The verdict and judgment must be such, that a special remedy may be had for the recovery of the goods detained, or a satisfaction in value for each parcel, in case they, or either of them, cannot be returned. Walker, R. 538; 7 Ala. R. 189; 4 Yerg. R. 570; 3 Monr. 59; 7 Ala. R. 807; 5 Miss. R. 489; 6 Monr. 52; 4 Dana, 58; 3 B. Munr. 313; 2 Humph. 59. The judgment is in the alternative, that the plaintiff recover the goods or the value thereof, if he cannot have the goods themselves, and his damages. Bro. Abr. Det. 48, 26, 3, 25; 4 Dana, R. 58; 2 Humph. 59; 3 B. Monr. 313, for the detention and full costs. Vide, generally, 1 Chit. Pl. 117; 3 Bl. Com. 152; 2 Reeve's Hist. C. L. 261, 333, 336; 3 Id. 66, 74; Bull. N. P. 50. This action has yielded to the more practical and less technical action of trover. 3 Bl. Com. 152.

DETINUIT, *practice*. He detained.

2. Where an action of replevin is instituted for goods which the defendant had taken, but which he afterwards restored, it is said to be brought in the *detinuit;* in such case the judgment is, that the plaintiff recover the damages assessed by the jury for the taking and unjust detention, or for the latter only, where the former was justifiable, and his costs. 4 Bouv. Inst. n. 3562.

3. When the replevin is in the *detinet*, that he detains the goods, the jury must find in addition to the above, the value of the chattels, (assuming they are still detained,) not in a gross sum, but each separate article must be separately valued, for perhaps the defendant may restore some of them, in which case the plaintiff is to recover the value of the remainder. Vide *Debet et Detinet*.

DEVASTAVIT. A devastavit is a mismanagement and waste by an executor, administrator, or other trustee, of the estate and effects trusted to him, as such, by which a loss occurs.

2. It takes place by direct abuse, by mal-administration, and by neglect.

3.—§ 1. *By direct abuse.* This takes place when the executor, administrator, or trustee, sells, embezzles, or converts to his own use, the goods entrusted to him; Com. Dig. Administration, I 1; releases a claim due to the estate; 3 Bac. Abr. 700; Hob. 266; Cro. Eliz. 43; 7 John. R. 404; 9 Mass. 352; or surrenders a lease below its value. 2 John. Cas. 376; 3 P. Wms. 330. These instances sufficiently show that any wilful waste of the property will be considered as a direct *devastavit*.

4.—§ 2. *By mal-administration.* Devastavit by mal-administration most frequently occurs by the payment of claims which were not due nor owing; or by paying others out of the order in which they ought to be paid; or by the payment of legacies before all the debts have been satisfied. 4 Serg. & Rawle, 394; 5 Rawle, 266.

5—§ 3. *By neglect.* Negligence on the part of an executor, administrator, or trustee, may equally tend to the waste of the estate, as the direct destruction or mal-administration of the assets, and render him guilty of a *devastavit*. The neglect to sell the goods at a fair price, within a reasonable time, or, if they are perishable goods, before they are wasted, will be a *devastavit*. And a neglect to collect a doubtful debt, which by proper exertion might have been collected, will be so considered. Bac. Ab. Executors, L.

6. The law requires from trustees, good faith and due diligence, the want of which is punished by making them responsible for the losses which may be sustained by the property entrusted to them; when, therefore, a party has been guilty of a *devastavit*, he is required to make up the loss out of his own estate. Vide Com. Dig. Administration, I; 11 Vin. Ab. 306; 1 Supp. to Ves. jr. 209; 1 Vern. 328; 7 East, R. 257; 1 Binn. 194; 1 Serg. & Rawle, 241; 1 John. R. 396; 1 Caines' Cas. 96; Bac. Ab. Executor, L; 11 Toull. 58, 59, n. 48.

DEVIATION, *insurance, contracts.* A voluntary departure, without necessity, or any reasonable cause, from the regular and usual course of the voyage insured.

2. From the moment this happens, the voyage is changed, the contract determined, and the insurer discharged from all subsequent responsibility. By the contract, the insurer only runs the risk of the contract agreed upon, and no other; and it is, therefore, a condition implied in the policy, that the ship shall proceed to her port of destination by the shortest and safest course, and on no account to deviate from that course, but in cases of necessity. 1 Mood. & Rob. 60; 17 Ves. 364; 3 Bing. 637; 12 East, 578.

3. The effect of a deviation is not to vitiate or avoid the policy, but only to determine the liability of the underwriters from the time of the deviation. If, therefore, the ship or goods, after the voyage has commenced, receive damage, then the ship deviates, and afterwards a loss happen, there, though the insurer is discharged from the time of the deviation, and is not answerable for the subsequent loss, yet he is bound to make good the damage sustained previous to the deviation. 2 Lord Raym. 842; 2 Salk. 444.

4. But though he is thus discharged from subsequent responsibility, he is entitled to retain the whole premium. Dougl. 271; 1 Marsh. Ins. 183; Park. Ins. 294. See 2 Phil. Ev. 60, n. (b) where the American cases are cited.

5. What amounts to a deviation is not easily defined, but a departure from the usual course of the voyage, or remaining at places where the ship is authorized to touch,

longer than necessary, or doing there what the insured is not authorized to do; as, if the ship have merely liberty to touch at a port, and the insured stay there to trade, or break bulk, it is a deviation. 4 Dall. 274; 1 Peters' C. C. R. 104; Marsh. Ins. B. 1, c. 6, s. 2. By the course of the voyage is not meant the shortest course the ship can take from her port of departure to her port of destination, but the regular and customary track, if such there be, which long usage has proved to be the safest and most convenient. 1 Marsh. Ins. 185. See 3 Johns. Cas. 352; 7 T. R. 162.

6. A deviation that will discharge the insurer, must be a voluntary departure from the usual course of the voyage insured, and not warranted by any necessity. If a deviation can be justified by necessity, it will not affect the contract; and necessity will justify a deviation, though it proceed from a cause not insured against. The cases of necessity which are most frequently adduced to justify a departure from the direct or usual course of the voyage, are, 1st. Stress of weather. 2d. The want of necessary repairs. 3d. Joining convoy. 4th. Succouring ships in distress. 5th. Avoiding capture or detention. 6th. Sickness of the master or mariner. 7th. Mutiny of the crew.

See Park, Ins. c. 17; 1 Bouv. Inst. n. 1187, et seq.; 2 John. Cas. 296; 11 Johns. R. 241; Pet. C. C. R. 98; 2 Johns. Rep. 89; 14 Johns. R. 315; 2 Johns. R. 138; 9 Johns. R. 192; 8 Johns. Rep. 491; 13 Mass. 68; 13 Mass. 539; Id. 118; 14 Mass. 12; 1 Johns. Cas. 313; 11 Johns. R. 241; 3 Johns. R. 352; 10 Johns. R. 83; 1 Johns. R. 301; 9 Mass. 436, 447; 3 Binn. 457; 7 Mass. 349; 5 Mass. 1; 8 Mass. 308; 6 Mass. 102, 121; 6 Mass. 122; 7 Cranch, 26; Id. 487; 3 Wheat. 159; 7 Mass. 365; 10 Mass. 21; Id. 347; 7 Johns. Rep. 364; 3 Johns. R. 352; 4 Dall. R. 274; 5 Binn. 403; 2 Serg. & Raw. 309; 2 Cranch, 240.

DEVIATION, *contracts*. When a plan has been adopted for a building, and in the progress of the work a change has been made from the original plan, the change is called a deviation.

2. When the contract is to build a house according to the original plan, and a deviation takes place, the contract shall be traced as far as possible, and the additions, if any have been made, shall be paid for according to the usual rate of charging. 3 Barn. & Ald. 47; and see 1 Ves. jr. 60; 10 Ves. jr. 306; 14 Ves. 413; 13 Ves. 73; Id. 81; 6 Johns. Ch. R. 38; 3 Cranch, 270; 5 Cranch, 262; 3 Ves. 693; 7 Ves. 274; Chit. Contr. 168; 9 Pick. 298.

3. The Civil Code of Louisiana, art. 2734, provides, that when an architect or other workman has undertaken the building of a house by the job, according to a plot agreed on between him and the owner of the ground, he cannot claim an increase of the price agreed on, on the plea of the original plot having been changed and extended, unless he can prove that such changes have been made in compliance with the wishes of the proprietor.

DEVISAVIT VEL NON, *practice*. The name of an issue sent out of a court of chancery, or one which exercises chancery jurisdiction, to a court of law, to try the validity of a paper asserted and denied to be a will, to ascertain whether or not the testator did devise, or whether or not that paper was his will. 7 Bro. P. C. 437; 2 Atk. 424; 5 Barr, 21.

DEVISE. A devise is a disposition of real property by a person's last will and testament, to take effect after the testator's death.

2. Its form is immaterial, provided the instrument is to take effect after the death of the party; and a paper in the form of an indenture, which is to have that effect, is considered as a devise. Finch. 195; 6 Watts, 522; 3 Rawle, 15; 4 Desaus. 617, 313; 1 Mod. 117; 1 Black. R. 345.

3. The term devise, properly and technically, applies only to real estate; the object of the devise must therefore be that kind of property. 1 Hill. Ab. ch. 36, n. 62 to 74. Devise is also sometimes improperly applied to a bequest or legacy. (q. v.) Vide 2 Bouv. Inst. n. 2095, et seq; 4 Kent, Com. 489; 8 Vin. Ab. 41; Com. Dig. Estates by Devise.

4. In the Year Book, 9 H. VI. 24, b A. D. 1430, Babington says, the nature of a devise, when lands are devisable, is, that one can devise that his lands shall be sold by executors; and this is good. And a devise in such form has always been in use. And so a man may have frank tenement of him who had nothing, in the same manner as one may have fire from a flint, and yet there is no fire in the flint. But it is to perform the last will of the devisor.

DEVISEE. A person to whom a devise has been made.

2. All persons who are in *rerum natura*,

and even embryos, may be devisees, unless excepted by some positive law. In general, he who can acquire property by his labor and industry, may receive a devise. C. & N. 353.

DEVISOR. A testator; one who devises his real estate.

2. As a general rule all persons who may sell an estate may devise it. The disabilities of devisors may be classed in three divisions. 1. Infancy. In some of the United States this disability is partially removed; in Illinois, Maryland, Mississippi and Ohio, an unmarried woman at the age of eighteen years may devise. 2. Coverture. In general, a married woman cannot devise; but in Connecticut and Ohio she may devise her lands; and in Illinois, her separate estate. In Louisiana, she may devise without the consent of her husband. Code, art. 132. 3. Idiocy and non sane memory. It is evident that a person non compos can make no devise, because he has no will.

3. The removal of the disability which existed at the time of the devise does not, of itself, render it valid. For example, when the husband dies, and the wife becomes a feme sole; when one non compos is restored to his sense; and when an infant becomes of age; these several acts do not make a will good, which at its making was void. 11 Mod. 123, 157; 2 Vern. 475; Comb, 84; 4 Rawle, R. 336. Vide *Testament or Will.*

DEVOIR. Duty. It is used in the statute of 2 Ric. II., c. 3, in the sense of duties or customs.

DEVOLUTION, *eccl. law.* The transfer, by forfeiture, of a right and power which a person has to another, on account of some act or negligence of the person who is vested with such right or power: for example, when a person has the right of presentation, and he does not present within the time prescribed, the right devolves on his next immediate superior. Ayl. Par. 331.

DI COLONNA, *mar. contracts.* This contract takes place between the owner of a ship, the captain and the mariners, who agree that the voyage shall be for the benefit of all. This is a term used in the Italian law. Targa, ch. 36, 37: Emerigon, Mar. Loans, s. 5.

2. The New England *whalers* are owned and navigated in this manner, and under this species of contract. The captain and his mariners are all interested in the profits of the voyage in certain proportion, in the same manner as the captain and crew of a privateer, according to the agreement between them. Such agreement, being very common in former times, all the mariners and the masters being interested in the voyage. It is necessary to know this, in order to understand many of the provisions of the laws of Oleron, Wisbuy, the Consolato del Mare, and other ancient codes of maritime and commercial law. Hall on Mar. Loans, 42.

TO DICTATE. To pronounce word for word what is destined to be at the same time written by another. Merlin. Rep. mot Suggestion, p. 500; Toull. Dr. Civ. Fr. liv. 3, t. 2, c. 5, n. 410.

DICTATOR, *civil law.* A Magistrate at Rome invested with absolute power. His authority over the lives and fortunes of the citizens was without bounds. His office continued but for six months. Hist. de la Jur. h. t.; Dig. 1, 2, 18; Id. 1, 1, 1.

DICTUM, *practice.* Dicta are judicial opinions expressed by the judges on points that do not necessarily arise in the case.

2. Dicta are regarded as of little authority, on account of the manner in which they are delivered; it frequently happening that they are given without much reflection, at the bar, without previous examination. "If," says Huston, J., in Frants *v.* Brown, 17 Serg. & Rawle, 292, "general dicta in cases turning on special circumstances are to be considered as establishing the law, nothing is yet settled, or can be long settled." "What I have said or written, out of the case trying," continues the learned judge, "or shall say or write, under such circumstances, may be taken as my opinion at the time, without argument or full consideration; but I will never consider myself bound by it, when the point is fairly trying and fully argued and considered. And I protest against any person considering such *obiter dicta* as my deliberate opinion." And it was considered by another learned judge. Mr. Baron Richards, to be a "great misfortune that dicta are taken down from judges, perhaps incorrectly, and then cited as absolute propositions." 1 Phillim. Rep. 406; S. C. 1 Eng. Ecc. R. 129; Ram. on Judgm. ch. 5, p. 36; Willes' Rep. 666; 1 H. Bl. 53–63; 2 Bos. & P. 375; 7 T. R. 287; 3 B. & A. 341; 2 Bing. 90. The doctrine of the courts of France on this subject is stated in 11 Toull. 177, n. 133.

3. In the French law, the report of a judgment made by one of the judges who

has given it, is called the *dictum*. Poth. Proc. Civ. partie 1, c. 5, art. 2.

DIES. A day. There are four sorts of days: 1. A natural day; as, the morning and the evening made the first day. 2. An artificial day; that is, from day-break until twilight in the evening. 3. An astrological day, *dies astrologicus*, from sun to sun. 4. A legal day, which is dies juridicus, and dies non juridicus. 1. Dies juridici, are all days given in term to the parties in court. Dies non juridici are those which are not appointed to do business in court, as Sundays, and the like. Dies in banco, days of appearance in the English court of common bench. 3 Bl. Com. 276. Vide *Day*, and 3 Com. Dig. 358.

DIES DATUS, *practice*. A day or time given to a defendant in a suit, which is in fact a continuance of the cause. It is so called when given before a declaration; when it is allowed afterwards it assumes the name of imparlance. (q. v.)

DIES NON OR DIES NON JURIDICI. Non-judicial days. Days during which courts do not transact any business, as Sunday. The entry of judgment upon such a day is void. W. Jones, 156.

DIET. An assembly held by persons having authority to manage the public affairs of the nation. In Germany, such assemblies are known by this name.

DIFFERENCE. A dispute, contest, disagreement, quarrel.

DIGEST, *civil law*. The name sometimes given to the Pandects of Justinian; it is so called because this compilation is reduced to order, *quasi digestiæ*.

2. It is an abridgment of the decisions of the prætors and the works of the learned and ancient writers on the law. It was made by order of the emperor Justinian, who, in 530, published an ordinance entitled *De Conceptione Digestorum*, which was addressed to Tribonian, and by which he was required to select some of the most distinguished lawyers to assist him in composing a collection of the best decisions of the ancient lawyers, and compile them in fifty books, without confusion or contradiction. The work was immediately commenced, and completed on the 16th of December, 533.

3. The Digest is divided in two different ways; the first, into fifty books, each book into several titles, and each title into several laws; at the head of each of them is the name of the lawyer from whose work it was taken.

4.—1. The first book contains twenty-two titles; the subject of the first is *De justicia et jure;* of the division of person and things; of magistrates, &c.

5.—2. The second, divided into fifteen titles, treats of the power of magistrates and their jurisdiction; the manner of commencing suits; of agreements and compromises.

6.—3. The third, composed of six titles, treats of those who can and those who cannot sue; of advocates and attorneys and syndics; and of calumny.

7.—4. The fourth, divided into nine titles, treats of causes of restitution; of submissions and arbitrations; of minors, carriers by water, inkeepers and those who have the care of the property of others.

8.—5. In the fifth there are six titles, which treat of jurisdiction and inofficious testaments.

9.—6. The subject of the sixth, in which there are three titles, is actions.

10.—7. The seventh, in nine titles, embraces whatever concerns usufructs, personal servitudes, habitations, the uses of real estate, and its appurtenances, and of the sureties required of the usufructuary.

11.—8. The eighth book, in six titles, regulates urban and rural servitudes.

12.—9. The ninth book, in four titles, explains certain personal actions.

13.—10. The tenth, in four titles, treats of mixed actions.

14.—11. The object of the eleventh book, containing eight titles, is to regulate interrogatories, the cases of which the judge was to take cognizance, fugitive slaves, of gamblers, of surveyors who made false reports, and of funerals and funeral expenses.

15.—12. The twelfth book, in seven titles, regulates personal actions in which the plaintiff claims the title of a thing.

16.—13. The thirteenth, treats of certain particular actions, in seven titles.

17.—14. This, like the last, regulates certain actions: it has six titles.

18.—15. The fifteenth, in four titles, treats of actions for which a father or master is liable, in consequence of the acts of his children or slaves, and those to which he is entitled; of the peculium of children and slaves, and of the actions on this right.

19.—16. The sixteenth, in three titles, contains the law relating to the senatus consultum velleianum, of compensation or set off, and of the action of deposit.

20.—17. The seventeenth, in two titles,

expounds the law of mandates and partnership.

21.—18. The eighteenth book, in seven titles, explains the contract of sale.

22.—19. The nineteenth, in five titles, treats of the actions which arise on a contract of sale.

23.—20. The law relating to pawns, hypothecation, the preference among creditors, and subrogation, occupy the twentieth book, which contains six titles.

24.—21. The twenty-first book, explains under three titles, the edict of the ediles relating to the sale of slaves and animals; then what relates to evictions and warranties.

25.—22. The twenty-second treats of interest, profits and accessories of things, proofs, presumptions, and of ignorance of law and fact. It is divided into six titles.

26.—23. The twenty-third, in five titles, contains the law of marriage, and its accompanying agreements.

27.—24. The twenty-fourth, in three titles, regulates donations between husband and wife, divorces, and their consequence.

28.—25. The twenty-fifth is a continuation of the subject of the preceding. It contains seven titles.

29.—26 and 27. These two books, each in two titles, contain the law relating to tutorship and curatorship.

30.—28. The twenty-eighth, in eight titles, contains the law on last wills and testaments.

31.—29. The twenty-ninth, in seven titles, is the continuation of the twenty-eighth book.

32.—30, 31, and 32. These three books, each divided into two titles, contain the law of trusts and specific legacies.

33.—33, 34, and 35. The first of these, divided into ten titles; the second, into nine titles; and the last into three titles, treat of various kinds of legacies.

34.—36. The thirty-sixth, containing four titles, explains the senatus consultum trebellianum, and the time when trusts become due.

35.—37. This book, containing fifteen titles, has two objects; first, to regulate successions; and, secondly, the respect which children owe their parents, and freedmen their patrons.

36.—38. The thirty-eighth book, in seventeen titles, treats of a variety of subjects; of successions, and of the degree of kindred in successions; of possession; and of heirs.

37.—39. The thirty-ninth explains the means which the law and the prætor take to prevent a threatened injury; and donations *inter vivos* and *mortis causâ.*

38.—40. The fortieth, in sixteen titles, treats of the state and condition of persons, and of what relates to freedmen and liberty.

39.—41. The different means of acquiring and losing title to property, are explained in the forty-first book, in ten titles.

40.—42. The forty-second, in eight titles, treats of the *res judicata*, and of the seizure and sale of the property of a debtor.

41.—43. Interdicts or possessory actions are the object of the forty-third book, in three titles.

42.—44. The forty-fourth contains an enumeration of defences which arise in consequence of the *res judicata*, from the lapse of time, prescription, and the like. This occupies six titles; the seventh treats of obligations and actions.

43.—45. This speaks of stipulations, by freedmen, or by slaves. It contains only three titles.

44.—46. This book, in eight titles, treats of securities, novations, and delegations, payments, releases, and acceptilations.

45.—47. In the forty-seventh book are explained the punishments inflicted for private crimes, *de privatis delictis*, among which are included larcenies, slander, libels, offences against religion, and public manners, removing boundaries, and other similar offences.

46.—48. This book treats of public crimes, among which are enumerated those of *læsæ majestatis*, adultery, murder, poisoning, parricide, extortion, and the like, with rules for procedure in such cases.

47.—49. The forty-ninth, in eighteen titles, treats of appeals, of the rights of the public treasury, of those who are in captivity, and of their repurchase.

48.—50. The last book, in seventeen titles, explains the rights of municipalities, and then treats of a variety of public officers.

49. Besides this division, Justinian made another, in which the fifty books were divided into seven parts: The first contains the first four books; the second, from the fifth to the eleventh book inclusive; the third, from the twelfth to the nineteenth inclusive; the fourth, from the twentieth to the twenty-seventh inclusive; the fifth, from the twenty-eighth to the thirty-sixth inclu-

sive; the sixth, commenced with the thirty-seventh, and ended with the forty-fourth book; and the seventh or last was composed of the last six books.

50. A third division, which, however, is said not to have been made by Justinian, is in three parts. The first, called *digestum vetus*, because it was the first printed. It commences with the first book, and includes the work to the end of the second title of the twenty-fourth book. The second, called *digestum infortiatum*, because it is supported or fortified by the other two, it being in the middle; it commences with the beginning of the third title of the twenty-fourth book and ends with the thirty-eighth. The third, which begins with the thirty-ninth book and ends with the work, is called *digestum novum*, because it was last printed.

51. The Digest, although compiled in Constantinople, was originally written in Latin, and afterwards translated into Greek.

52. This work was lost to all Europe during a considerable period, as indeed all the law works of Justinian were, except some fragments of the Code and Novels. During the pillage of Amalphi, in the war between the two soi-disant popes, Innocent II. and Anaclet II., a soldier discovered an old manuscript, which attracted his attention by its envelope of many colors. It was carried to the emperor, Clothaire II., and proved to be the Pandects of Justinian. The work was arranged in its present order by Warner, a German, whose name, Latinised, is Irnerius, who was appointed professor of Roman law at Bologna, by that emperor. 1 Fournel, Hist. des Avocats, 44, 46, 51.

53. The Pandects contain all whatsoever Justinian drew out of 150,000 verses of the old books of the Roman law. The style of the Digest is very grave and pure, and differs not much from "the eloquentist speech that ever the Romans used." The learning of the Digest stands rather in the discussing of subtle questions of law, and enumerations of the variety of opinions of ancient lawyers thereupon, than in practical matters of daily use. The Code of Justinian differs in these respects from the Digest. It is less methodical, but more practical; the style, however, is a barbarous Thracian phrase Latinised, such as never any mean Latinist spoke. The work is otherwise rude and unskilful. Ridley's View of the Civ. & Ecc. Law, pt. 1, ch. 2, § 1, and ch. 1, § 2.

54. Different opinions are entertained upon the merits of the Digest, or Pandects, Code, Authentics and Feuds, as a system of jurisprudence. By some it has been severely criticised, and even harshly censured, and by others as warmly defended—the one party discovering nothing but defects, and the other as obstinately determined to find nothing but what is good and valuable. See Felangieri della Legislazione, vol. 1, c. 7. It must be confessed that it is not without defects. It might have been comprehended in less extent, and in some parts arranged in better order. It must be confessed also that it is less congenial as a whole, with the principles of free government, than the common law of England. Yet, with all these defects, it is a rich fountain of learning and reason; and of this monument of the high culture and wisdom of the Roman jurists it may be said, as of all other works in which the good so much surpasses the bad,

> Ut plura nitent in carmine non ego paucis
> Offendar maculis, quas aut incuria fudit
> Aut humana parum cavit natura.
> HORAT. ART. POETIC, v. 351.

DIGNITIES, *English law.* Titles of honor.

2. They are considered as incorporeal hereditaments.

3. The genius of our government forbids their admission into the republic.

DILAPIDATION. Literally, this signifies the injury done to a building by taking stones from it; but in its figurative, which is also its technical sense, it means the waste committed or permitted upon a building.

DILATORY. That which is intended for delay. It is a maxim, that delays in law are odious, *dilationes in lege sunt odiosæ.* Plowd. 75.

DILATORY DEFENCE, *chancery practice.* A dilatory defence is one, the object of which is to dismiss, suspend, or obstruct the suit, without touching the merits, until the impediment or obstacle insisted on shall be removed.

2. These defences are of four kinds: 1. To the jurisdiction of the court. 2. To the person of the plaintiff or defendant. 3. To the form of proceedings, as that the suit is irregularly brought, or it is defective in its appropriate allegation of the parties; and, 4. To the propriety of maintaining the suit itself, because of the pendency of another suit for the same controversy. Montag. Eq. Pl. 88; Story Eq. Pl. § 434. Vide *Defence; Plea, dilatory.*

DILATORY PLEAS. Those which delay the plaintiff's remedy, by questioning, not the cause of action, but the propriety of the suit, or the mode in which the remedy is sought. Vide *Plea, dilatory*.

DILIGENCE, *contracts*. The doing things in proper time.

2. It may be divided into three degrees, namely: ordinary diligence, extraordinary diligence, and slight diligence. It is the reverse of negligence. (q. v.) Under that article is shown what degree of negligence, or want of diligence, will make a party to a contract responsible to the other. Vide Story, Bailm. Index h. t.; Ayl. Pand. 113; 1 Miles, Rep. 40.

DILIGENCE. In Scotland, there are certain forms of law, whereby a creditor endeavors to make good his payment, either by affecting the person of his debtor, or by securing the subjects belonging to him from alienation, or by carrying the property of these subjects to himself. They are either real or personal.

2. Real diligence is that which is proper to heritable or real rights, and of this kind there are two sorts: 1. Inhibitions. 2. Adjudication, which the law has substituted in the place of apprising.

3. Personal diligence is that by which the person of the debtor may be secured, or his personal estate affected. Ersk. Pr. L. Scotl. B. 2, t. 11, s. 1.

DIME, *money*. A silver coin of the United States, of the value of one-tenth part of a dollar or ten cents.

2. It weighs forty-one and a quarter grains. Of one thousand parts, nine hundred are of pure silver and one hundred of alloy. Act of January 18, 1837, s. 8 and 9, 4 Sharsw. cont. of Story's L. U. S. 2523-4.

DIMINUTION OF THE RECORD, *practice*. This phrase signifies that the record from an inferior court, sent up to a superior, is incomplete. When this is the case, the parties may suggest a diminution of the record, and pray a writ of *certiorari* to the justices of the court below to certify the whole record. Tidd's Pr. 1109; 1 S. & R. 472; Co. Ent. 232; 8 Vin. Ab. 552; 1 Lilly's Ab. 245; 1 Nels. Ab. 658; Cro. Jac. 597; Cro. Car. 91; Minor, R. 20; 4 Dev. R. 575; 1 Dev. & Bat. 382; 1 Munf. R. 119. Vide *Certiorari*.

DIOCESE, *eccl. law*. The district over which a bishop exercises his spiritual functions. 1 Bl. Com. 111.

DIPLOMA. An instrument of writing, executed by a corporation or society, certifying that a certain person therein named is entitled to a certain distinction therein mentioned.

2. It is usually granted by learned institutions to their members, or to persons who have studied in them.

3. Proof of the seal of a medical institution and of the signatures of its officers thereto affixed, by comparison with the seal and signatures attached to a diploma received by the witness from the same institution, has been held to be competent evidence of the genuineness of the instrument, although the witness never saw the officers write their names. 25 Wend. R. 469.

4. This word, which is also written duploma, in the civil law, signifies letters issued by a prince. They are so called, it is supposed, *a duplicatis tabellis*, to which Ovid is thought to allude, 1 Amor. 12, 2, 27, when he says, Tunc ego vos duplices rebus pro nomine sensi Sueton in Augustum, c. 26. Seals also were called Diplomata. Vicat ad verb.

DIPLOMACY. The science which treats of the relations and interests of nations with nations.

DIPLOMATIC AGENTS. This name has been given to public officers, who have been commissioned, according to law, to superintend and transact the affairs of the government which has employed them, in a foreign country. Vattel, liv. 4, c. 5.

2. These agents are of divers orders, and are known by different denominations. Those of the first order are almost the perfect representatives of the government by which they are commissioned; they are legates, nuncios, internuncios, ambassadors, ministers, plenipotentiaries. Those of the second order do not so fully represent their government; they are envoys, residents, ministers, chargés d'affaires, and consuls.

Vide these several words.

DIPLOMATICS. The art of judging of ancient charters, public documents or diplomas, and discriminating the true from the false. Encyc. Lond. h. t.

DIRECT. Straight forward; not collateral.

2. The direct line of descent, for example, is formed by a series of degrees between persons who descend one from another. Civ. Code of Lo. art. 886.

DIRECTION. The order and government of an institution; the persons who compose the board of directors are jointly called the direction. Direction, in another sense, is nearly synonymous with instruction. (q. v.)

DIRECTION, *practice*. That part of a bill in chancery which contains the address of the bill to the court; this must of course, contain the appropriate and technical description of the court.

DIRECTOR OF THE MINT. An officer whose duties are prescribed by the Act of Congress of January 18, 1837, 4 Sharsw. Cont. of Story L. U. S. 2524, as follows: The director shall have the control and management of the mint, the superintendence of the officers and persons employed therein, and the general regulation and supervision of the business of the several branches. And in the month of January of every year he shall make report to the president of the United States of the operation of the mint and its branches for the year preceding. And also to the secretary of the treasury, from time to time, as said secretary shall require, setting forth all the operations of the mint subsequent to the last report made upon the subject.

2. The director is required to appoint, with the approbation of the president, assistants to the assayer, melter and refiner, chief coiner and engraver, and clerks to the director and treasurer, whenever, on representation made by the director to the president, it shall be the opinion of the president that such assistants or clerks are necessary. And bonds may be required from such assistants and clerks in such sums as the director shall determine, with the approbation of the secretary of the treasury. The salary of the director of the mint, for his services, including travelling expenses incurred in visiting the different branches, and all other charges whatever, is three thousand five hundred dollars.

DIRECTORS. Persons appointed or elected according to law, authorized to manage and direct the affairs of a corporation or company. The whole of the directors collectively form the board of directors.

2. They are generally invested with certain powers by the acts of the legislature, to which they owe their existence.

3. In modern corporations, created by statutes, it is generally contemplated by the charter, that the business of the corporation shall be transacted exclusively by the directors. 2 Caines' R. 381. And the acts of such a board, evidenced by a legal vote, are as completely binding upon the corporation, and as complete authority to their agents, as the most solemn acts done under the corporate seal. 8 Wheat. R. 357, 8.

4. To make a legal board of directors, they must meet at a time when, and a place where, every other director has the opportunity of attending to consult and be consulted with; and there must be a sufficient number present to constitute a quorum. 3 L. R. 574; 13 L. R. 527; 6 L. R. 759. See 11 Mass. 288; 5 Litt. R. 45; 12 S. & R. 256; 1 Pet. S. C. R. 46. Vide Dane's Ab. h. t.

5. Directors of a corporation are trustees, and as such are required to use due diligence and attention to its concerns, and are bound to a faithful discharge of the duty which the situation imposes. They are liable to the stockholders whenever there has been gross negligence or fraud; but not for unintentional errors. 1 Edw. Ch. R. 513; 8 N. S. 80; 3. L. R. 575. See 4 Mann. & Gr. 552.

DIRECTORY. That which points out a thing or course of proceeding; for example, a directory law.

DIRIMANT IMPEDIMENTS, *canon law*. Those bars to a marriage, which, if consummated, render it null. They differ from prohibitive impediments. (q. v.)

DISABILITY. The want of legal capacity to do a thing.

2. Persons may be under disability, 1. To make contracts. 2. To bring actions.

3.—1. Those who want understanding, as idiots, lunatics, drunkards, and infants; or freedom to exercise their will, as married women, and persons in duress; or who, in consequence of their situation, are forbidden by the policy of the law to enter into contracts, as trustees, executors, administrators, or guardians, are under disabilities to make contracts. See *Parties; Contracts*.

4.—2. The disabilities to sue are, 1. Alienage, when the alien is an enemy. Bac. Ab. Abatement, B 3; Id. Alien, E; Com. Dig. Abatement, K; Co. Litt. 129. 2. Coverture; unless as co-plaintiff with her husband, a married woman cannot sue. 3. Infancy; unless he appears by guardian or prochein ami. Co. Litt. 135, b; 2 Saund. 117, f, n. 1; Bac. Ab. Infancy, K 2; 2

Conn. 357; 7 John. 373; Gould, Pl. c. 5, § 54. 4. That no such person as that named has any existence, is not, or never was, in *rerum naturâ*. Com. Dig. Abatement, E 16, 17; 1 Chit. Pl. 435; Gould on Pl. c. 5, § 58; Lawes' Pl. 104; 19 John. 308. By the law of England there are other disabilities; these are, 1. Outlawry. 2. Attainder. 3. Præmunire. 4. Popish recusancy. 5. Monachism.

5. In the acts of limitation it is provided that persons lying under certain disabilities, such as being *non compos*, an infant, in prison, or under coverture, shall have the right to bring actions after the disability shall have been removed.

6. In the construction of this saving in the acts, it has been decided that two disabilities shall not be joined when they occur in *different persons;* as, if a right of entry accrue to a feme covert, and during the coverture she die, and the right descends to her infant son. But the rule is otherwise when there are several disabilities in the *same person;* as, if the right accrues to an infant, and before he has attained his full age, he becomes *non compos mentis;* in this case he may establish his right after the removal of the last disability. 2 Prest. Abs. of Tit. 341; Shep. To. 31; 3 Tho. Co. Litt. pl. 18, note L; 2 H. Bl. 584; 5 Whart. R. 377. Vide *Incapacity*.

DISAFFIRMANCE. The act by which a person who has entered into a voidable contract; as, for example, an infant, does disagree to such contract, and declares he will not abide by it.

2. Disaffirmance is express or implied. The former, when the declaration is made in terms that the party will not abide by the contract. The latter, when he does an act which plainly manifests his determination not to abide by it; as, where an infant made a deed for his land, and, on coming of age, he made a deed for the same land to another. 2 Dev. & Bat. 320; 10 Pet. 58; 13 Mass. 371, 375.

TO DISAVOW. To deny the authority by which an agent pretends to have acted, as when he has exceeded the bounds of his authority.

2. It is the duty of the principal to fulfil the contracts which have been entered into by his authorized agent; and when an agent has exceeded his authority, he ought promptly to disavow such act, so that the other party may have his remedy against the agent. See *Agent; Principal.*

DISBURSEMENT. Literally, to take money out of a purse. Figuratively, to pay out money; to expend money; and sometimes it signifies to advance money.

2. A master of a ship makes disbursements, whether with his own money or that of the owner, when he defrays expenses for the ship.

3. An executor, guardian, trustee, or other accountant, is said to have made disbursements when he expended money on account of the estate which he holds. These, when properly made, are always allowed in the settlement of the accounts.

DISCHARGE, *practice*. The act by which a person in confinement, under some legal process, or held on an accusation of some crime or misdemeanor, is set at liberty; the writing containing the order for his being so set at liberty, is also called a discharge.

2. The discharge of a defendant, in prison under a ca. sa., when made by the plaintiff, has the operation of satisfying the debt, the plaintiff having no other remedy. 4 T. R. 526. But when the discharge is in consequence of the insolvent laws, or the defendant dies in prison, the debt is not satisfied. In the first place the plaintiff has a remedy against the property of the defendant, acquired after his discharge, and, in the last case, against the executors or administrators of the debtor. Bac. Ab. Execution, D; Bingh. on Execution, 266.

DISCHARGE OF A CONTRACT. The act of making a contract or agreement null.

2. Contracts may be discharged by, 1. Payment. 2. Accord and satisfaction. 8 Com. Dig. 917; 1 Nels. Abr. 18; 1 Lilly's Reg. 10, 16; Hall's Dig. 7; 1 Poth. Ob. 345. 3. Release. 8 Com. Dig. 906; 2 Nels. Ab. 69; 18 Vin. Ab. 294; 1 Vin. Abr. 192; 2 Saund. 48, a; Gow. on Partn. 225, 230; 15 Serg. & Rawle, 441; 1 Poth Ob. 397. 4. Set off. 8 Vin. Ab. 556, Discount; Hall's Dig. 226, 496; 7 Com. Dig. 335, Pleader, 2 G 17; 1 Poth. Ob. 408. 5. The rescission of the contracts. 1 Com. Dig. 289, note x; 8 Com. Dig. 349; Chit. on Contr. 275. 6. Extinguishment. 7 Vin. Abr. 367; 14 Serg. & Rawle, 209, 290; 8 Com. Dig. 394; 2 Nels. Abr. 818; 18 Vin. Abr. 493 to 515; 11 Vin. Abr. 461. 7. Confusion, where the duty to pay and the right to receive unite in the same person. 8 Serg. & Rawle, 24–30; 1 Poth. 425. 8. Extinction, or the loss of the

subject matter of the contract. Bac. Abr. 48; 8 Com. Dig. *349; 1 Poth. Ob. 429. 9. Defeasance. 2 Saund. 47, n. note 1. 10. The inability of one of the parties to fulfil his part. Hall's Dig. 40. 11. The death of the contractor, as where he undertook to teach an apprentice. 12. Bankruptcy. 13. By the act of limitations. 14. By lapse of time. Angell on Adv. Enjoym. *passim;* 15 Vin. Abr. 52, ‡99; 2 Saund. 63, n. b; Id. 66, n. 8; Id. 67, n. 10; Gow on Partn. 235; 1 Poth. 443, 449. 15. By neglecting to give notice to the person charged. Chit. on Bills, 245. 16. By releasing one of two partners. See *Receipt.* 17. By neglecting to sue the principal at the request of the surety, the latter is discharged. 8 Serg. & Rawle, 110. 18. By the discharge of a defendant, who has been arrested under a *capias ad satisfaciendum.* 8 Cowen, R. 171. 19. By a certificate and discharge under the bankrupt laws. Act of Congress of August, 1841.

Discharge of a jury, *practice.* The dismissal of a jury who had been charged with the trial of a cause.

2. Questions frequently arise, whether if the court discharge a jury before they render a verdict, in a criminal case, the prisoner can again be tried. In cases affecting life or members, the general rule is, that when a jury have been sworn and charged, they cannot be discharged by the court, or any other, but ought to give a verdict. But to this rule there are many exceptions; for example, when the jury are discharged at the request or with the consent of the prisoner and for his benefit, when ill practices have been used; when the prisoner becomes insane, or becomes suddenly ill, so that he cannot defend himself, or instruct others in his defence; when a juror or witness is taken suddenly ill; when a juror has absented himself, or, on account of his intoxication, is incapable to perform his duties as a juror. These and many similar cases, which may be readily imagined, render the discharge of the jury a matter of necessity, and, under such very extraordinary and striking circumstances, it is impossible to proceed with the trial, with justice to the prisoner or to the state.

3. The exception to the rule, then, is grounded on *necessity*, and not merely because the jury cannot agree. 6 Serg. & Rawle, 577; 3 Rawle's Rep. 501. In all these cases the court must exercise a just discretion in deciding what is and what is not a case of necessity. This is the law as to the exceptions in Pennsylvania. In other states, and some of the courts of the United States, it has been ruled that the authority of the court to discharge the jury rests in the *sound discretion of the court.* 4 Wash. C. C. R. 409; 18 Johns. 187; 2 Johns. Cas. 301; 2 Gall. 364; 9 Mass. 494; 1 Johns. Rep. 66; 2 Johns. Cas. 275; 2 Gallis. 364; 13 Wend. 55; Mart. & Yerg. 278; 3 Rawle, 498; 2 Dev. & Bat. 162; 6 S. & R. 577; 2 Misso. 166; 9 Leigh, 613; 10 Yerg. 535; 3 Humph. 70. Vide 4 Taunt. 309.

4. A distinction has been made between capital cases and other criminal cases, not capital. In cases of misdemeanors and in civil cases, the right to discharge rests in the sound discretion of the court, which is to be exercised with great caution. 9 Mass. 494; 3 Dev. & Batt. 115. In Pennsylvania this point seems not to be settled. 6 Serg. & Rawle, 599. The reader is referred to the word *Jeopardy*, and Story on the Const. § 1781; 9 Wheat. R. 579; Rawle on the Const. 132, 133; 1 Chit. Cr. Law, 629; 1 Dev. 491; 4 Ala. R. 173; 2 McLean, 114. See *Afforce.*

DISCHARGED. Released, or liberated from custody. It is not equivalent to acquitted in a declaration for a malicious prosecution. 2 Yeates, 475; 2 Term Rep. 231; 1 Strange, 114; Doug. 205; 3 Leon. 100.

DISCLAIMER. This word signifies to abandon, to renounce; also the act by which the renunciation is made. For example, a disclaimer is the act by which a patentee renounces a part of his title of invention.

2. In real actions, a disclaimer of the tenancy or title is frequently added to the plea of non tenure. Litt. § 391. If the action be one in which the demandant cannot recover damages, as formedon in the discender, the demandant or plaintiff was bound to pray judgment, &c., and enter, for thereby, he has the effect of his suit; et frustra fit per plura quod fieri potest per pauciora. But, if the demandant can recover damages and is unwilling to waive them, he should answer the disclaimer by averring that the defendant is tenant of the land, or claims to be such as the writ supposes, and proceed to try the question, otherwise he would lose his damages. The same course may be pursued in the action

of ejectment, although in Pennsylvania, the formality of such a replication to the disclaimer is dispensed with, and the fact is tried without it. 5 Watts, 70; 3 Barr, 367. Yet if the plaintiff is willing to waive his claim for damages, there is no reason why he may not ask for judgment upon the disclaimer without trial, for thereby he has the effect of his suit. Et frustra fit per plura, &c.

DISCLAIMER, *chancery pleading.* The renunciation of the defendant to all claims to the subject of the demand made by the plaintiff's bill.

2. A disclaimer is distinct in substance from an answer, though sometimes confounded with it, but it seldom can be put in without an answer; for if the defendant has been made a party by mistake, having had an interest which he has parted with, the plaintiff may require an answer sufficient to ascertain whether that is the fact or not. Mitf. Pl. 11, 14, 253; Coop. Eq. Pl. 309; Story, Eq. Pl. c. 17, § 838 to 844; 4 Bouv. Inst. n. 4211–14.

DISCLAIMER, *estates.* The act of a party by which he refuses to accept of an estate which has been conveyed to him. Vide *Assent; Dissent.*

2. It is said, that a disclaimer of a freehold estate must be in a court of record, because a freehold shall not be divested by bare words, *in pais.* Cruise, Dig. tit. 32, c. 26, s. 1, 2.

3. A disclaimer of tenancy is the act of a person in possession, who denies holding the estate from the person claiming to be the owner of it. 2 Nev. & M. 672. Vide 8 Vin. Ab. 501; Coote, L. & T. 348, 375; F. N. B. 179 k; Bull. N. P. 96; 16 East, R. 99; 1 Man. & Gran. 135; S. C. 39 Eng. C. L. Rep. 380, 385; 10 B. & Cr. 816; Gow, N. P. Cas. 180; 2 Nev. & Man. 673; 1 C. M. & R. 398; Co. Litt. 102, a.

DISCONTINUANCE, *pleading.* A chasm or interruption in the pleading.

2. It is a rule, that every pleading must be an answer to the whole of what is adversely alleged. Com. Dig. Pleader, E 1, F 4; 1 Saund. 28, n. 3; 4 Rep. 62, a. If, therefore, in an action of trespass for breaking a close, and cutting three hundred trees, the defendant pleads as to cutting all but two hundred trees, some matter of justification or title, and as to the two hundred trees says nothing, the plaintiff is entitled to sign judgment, as by nil dicit against him, in respect of the two hundred trees, and to demur, or reply to the plea, as to the remainder of the trespasses. On the other hand, if he demurs or replies to the plea, without signing judgment for the part not answered, the whole action is said to be discontinued. For the plea, if taken by the plaintiff as an answer to the whole action, it being, in fact, a partial answer only, is, in contemplation of law, a mere nullity, and a *discontinuance* takes place. And such discontinuance will amount to error on the record; such error is cured, however, after verdict, by the statute of Jeofails, 32 H. VIII. c. 80; and after judgment by *nil dicit,* confession, or *non sum informatus,* by stat. 4 Ann. c. 16. It is to be observed, that as to the plaintiff's course of proceeding, there is a distinction between a case like this, where the defendant does not profess to answer the whole, and a case where, by the commencement of his plea, he professes to do so, but, in fact, gives a defective and partial answer, applying to part only. The latter case amounts merely to insufficient pleading, and the plaintiff's course, therefore, is not to sign judgment for the part defectively answered, but to demur to the whole plea. 1 Saund. 28, n. 3. It is to be observed, also, that where the part of pleading to which no answer is given, is immaterial, or such as requires no separate or specific answer; for example, if it be mere matter of allegation, the rule does not in that case apply. Id. See Com. Dig. Pleader, W; Bac. Abr. Pleas, P.

DISCONTINUANCE, *estates.* An alienation made or suffered by the tenant in tail, or other tenant seised in *autre droit,* by which the issue in tail, or heir or successor, or those in reversion or remainder, are driven to their action, and cannot enter.

2. The term discontinuance is used to distinguish those cases where the party whose freehold is ousted, can restore it only by action, from those in which he may restore it by entry. Co. Litt. 325 a; 3 Bl. Com. 171; Ad. Ej. 35 to 41; Com. Dig. h. t.; Bac. Ab. h. t.; Vin. Ab. h. t.; Cruise's Dig. Index, h. t.; 2 Saund. Index, h. t.

DISCONTINUANCE, *practice.* This takes place when a plaintiff leaves a chasm in the proceedings of his cause, as by not continuing the process regularly from day to day, and time to time, as he ought. 3 Bl. Com. 296. See *Continuance.* A discontinuance, also, is an entry upon the record that the plaintiff discontinues his action.

2. The plaintiff cannot discontinue his action after a demurrer joined and entered, or after a verdict or a writ of inquiry, without leave of court. Cro. Jac. 35; 1 Lilly's Abr. 473; 6 Watts & Serg. 147. The plaintiff is, on discontinuance, generally liable for costs. But in some cases, he is not so liable. See 3 Johns. R. 249; 1 Caines' R. 116; 1 Johns. R. 143; 6 Johns. R. 333; 18 Johns. R. 252; 2 Caines' Rep. 380; Com. Dig. Pleader, W 5; Bac. Abr. Pleas, P.

DISCOUNT, *practice*. A set off, or defalcation in an action. Vin. Ab. h. t.

DISCOUNT, *contracts*. An allowance made upon prompt payment in the purchase of goods; it is also the interest allowed in advancing money upon bills of exchange, or other negotiable securities due at a future time And *to discount*, signifies the act of buying a bill of exchange, or promissory note, for a less sum than that which upon its face, is payable.

2. Among merchants, the term used when a bill of exchange is transferred, is, that the bill is *sold*, and not that it is *discounted*. See Poth. De l'Usure, n. 128; 3 Pet. R. 40.

DISCOVERT. Not covert, unmarried. The term is applied to a woman unmarried, or widow; one not within the bonds of matrimony.

DISCOVERY, *intern. law*. The act of finding an unknown country.

2. The nations of Europe adopted the principle, that the discovery of any part of America gave title to the government by whose subjects, or by whose authority it was made, against all European governments. This title was to be consummated by possession. 8 Wheat. 543.

DISCOVERY, *practice, pleading*. The act of disclosing or revealing by a defendant, in his answer to a bill filed against him in a court of equity. Vide *Bill of Discovery;* 8 Vin. Ab. 537; 8 Com. Dig. 515.

DISCOVERY, *rights*. The patent laws of the United States use this word as synonymous with invention or improvement. Act of July 4, 1836, s. 6.

TO DISCREDIT, *practice, evidence*. To deprive one of credit or confidence.

2. In general, a party may discredit a witness called by the opposite party, who testifies against him, by proving that his character is such as not to entitle him to credit or confidence, or any other fact which shows he is not entitled to belief. It is clearly settled, also, that the party voluntarily calling a witness, cannot afterwards impeach his character for truth and veracity. 1 Moo. & Rob. 414; 3 B. & Cress. 746; S. C. 10 Eng. Com. Law R. 220. But if a party calls a witness, who turns out unfavorable, he may call another to prove the same point. 2 Campb. R. 556; 2 Stark. R. 334; S. C. 3 E. C. L. R. 371; 1 Nev & Man. 34; 4 B. & Adolph. 193; S. C. 24 E. C. L. R. 47; 1 Phil. Ev. 229; Rosc. Civ. Ev. 96.

DISCREPANCY. A difference between one thing and another, between one writing and another; a variance. (q. v.)

2. Discrepancies are material and immaterial. A discrepancy is material when there is such a difference between a thing alleged, and a thing offered in evidence, as to show they are not substantially the same; as, when the plaintiff in his declaration for a malicious arrest averred, that "the plaintiff, in that action, did not prosecute his said suit, but therein made default," and the record was, that he obtained a rule to discontinue. 4 M. & M. 253. An immaterial discrepancy is one which does not materially affect the cause; as, where a declaration stated that a deed bore date in a certain year of our Lord, and the deed was simply dated "March 30, 1701." 2 Salk. 658; 19 John. 49; 5 Taunt. 707; 2 B. & A. 301; 8 Miss. R. 428; 2 M'Lean, 69; 1 Metc. 59; 21 Pick. 486.

DISCRETION, *practice*. When it is said that something is left to the discretion of a judge, it signifies that he ought to decide according to the rules of equity, and the nature of circumstances. Louis. Code, art. 3522, No. 13; 2 Inst. 50, 298; 4 Serg. & Rawle, 265; 3 Burr. 2539.

2. The discretion of a judge is said to be the law of tyrants; it is always unknown; it is different in different men; it is casual, and depends upon constitution, temper, and passion. In the best, it is oftentimes caprice; in the worst, it is every vice, folly, and passion, to which human nature is liable. Optima lex quæ minimum relinquit arbitrio judicis: optimus judex qui minimum sibi. Bac. Aph; 1 Day's Cas. 80, n.; 1 Pow. Mortg. 247, a; 2 Supp. to Ves. Jr. 391; Toull. liv. 3, n. 338; 1 Lill. Ab. 447.

3. There is a species of discretion which is authorized by express law, and, without

which, justice cannot be administered; for example, an old offender, a man of much intelligence and cunning, whose talents render him dangerous to the community, induces a young man of weak intellect to commit a larceny in company with himself; they are both liable to be punished for the offence. The law, foreseeing such a case, has provided that the punishment should be proportioned, so as to do justice, and it has left such apportionment to the discretion of the judge. It is evident that, without such discretion, justice could not be administered, for one of these parties assuredly deserves a much more severe punishment than the other.

DISCRETION, *crim. law.* The ability to know and distinguish between good and evil; between what is lawful and what is unlawful.

2. The age at which children are said to have discretion, is not very accurately ascertained. Under seven years, it seems that no circumstances of mischievous discretion can be admitted to overthrow the strong presumption of innocence, which is raised by an age so tender. 1 Hale, P. C. 27, 8; 4 Bl. Com. 23. Between the ages of seven and fourteen, the infant is, *prima facie*, destitute of criminal design, but this presumption diminishes as the age increases, and even during this interval of youth, may be repelled by positive evidence of vicious intention; for tenderness of years will not excuse a maturity in crime, the maxim in these cases being, *malitia supplet ætatem.* At fourteen, children are said to have acquired legal discretion. 1 Hale, P. C. 25.

DISCRETIONARY TRUSTS. Those which cannot be duly administered without the application of a certain degree of prudence and judgment; as when a fund is given to trustees to be distributed in certain charities to be selected by the trustees.

DISCUSSION, *civil law.* A proceeding, on the part of a surety, by which the property of the principal debtor is made liable before resort can be had to the sureties; this is called the *benefit of discussion.* This is the law in Louisiana. Civ. Code of Lo. art. 3014 to 3020. See Domat, 3, 4, 1 to 4; Burge on Sur. 329, 343, 348; 5 Toull. p. 544; 7 Toull. p. 93; 2 Bouv. Inst. n. 1414.

DISFRANCHISEMENT. The act of depriving a member of a corporation of his right as such, by expulsion. 1 Bouv. Inst. n. 192.

2. It differs from amotion, (q. v.) which is applicable to the removal of an officer from office, leaving him his rights as a member. Willc. on Corp. n. 708; Ang. & Ames on Corp. 237; and see *Expulsion.*

DISGRACE. Ignominy, shame, dishonor. No witness is required to disgrace himself. 13 How. St. Tr. 17, 334; 16 How. St. Tr. 161. Vide *Crimination; To Degrade.*

DISHERISON. Disinheritance; depriving one of an inheritance. Obsolete. Vide *Disinherison.*

DISHERITOR. One who disinherits, or puts another out of his freehold. Obsolete.

TO DISHONOR, *contr.* This term is applied to the nonfulfilment of commercial engagements. To dishonor a bill of exchange, or a promissory note, is to refuse or neglect to pay it at maturity.

2. The holder is bound to give notice to the parties to such instrument of its dishonor, and his laches will discharge the indorsers. Chit. on Bills, 394, 395, 256 to 278.

DISINHERISON, *civil law.* The act of depriving a forced heir of the inheritance which the law gives him.

2. In Louisiana, forced heirs may be deprived of their legitime, or legal portion, and of the seisin granted them by law, for just cause. The disinherison must be made in proper form, by name and expressly, and for a just cause, otherwise it is null.

3. The just causes for which parents may disinherit their children, are ten in number. 1. If the child has raised his or her hand to strike the parent, or if he or she has actually struck the parent; but a mere threat is not sufficient. 2. If the child has been guilty, towards a parent, of cruelty, of a crime, or grievous injury. 3. If the child has attempted to take away the life of either parent. 4. If the child has accused either parent of any capital crime, except, however, that of high treason. 5. If the child has refused sustenance to a parent, having the means to afford it. 6. If the child has neglected to take care of a parent, become insane. 7. If a child has refused to ransom them, when detained in captivity. 8. If the child used any act of violence or coercion to hinder a parent from making a will. 9. If the child has refused to become security for a parent, having the means, in order to take him out of prison. 10. If the son or daughter, being a minor, marries without the consent of his or her parents. Civil Code, art. 1609-1613.

4. The ascendants may disinherit their legitimate decendants, coming to their succession, for the first nine causes above expressed, when the acts of ingratitude, there mentioned, have been committed towards them, instead of towards their parents; but they cannot disinherit their descendants for the last cause. Art. 1614.

5. Legitimate children, dying without issue, and leaving a parent, cannot disinherit him or her, unless for the seven following causes, to wit: 1. If the parent has accused the child of a capital crime, except, however, the crime of high treason. 2. If the parent has attempted to take the child's life. 3. If the parent has, by any violence or force, hindered the child from making a will. 4. If the parent has refused sustenance to the child in necessity, having the means of affording it. 5. If the parent has neglected to take care of the child when in a state of insanity. 6. If the parent has neglected to ransom the child when in captivity. 7. If the father or mother have attempted the life the one of the other, in which case the child or descendant, making a will, may disinherit the one who has attempted the life of the other. Art. 1615.

6. The testator must express in the will for what reason he disinherited his forced heirs, or any of them, and the other heirs of the testator are moreover obliged to prove the facts on which the disinherison is founded, otherwise it is null. Art. 1616. Vide Nov 115; Ayl. Pand. B. 2, t. 29; Swinb. part 7, s. 22.

DISINHERITANCE. The act by which a person deprives his heir of an inheritance, who, without such act, would inherit.

2. By the common law, any one may give his estate to a stranger, and thereby disinherit his heir apparent. Coop. Justin. 495, 7 East, Rep. 106.

DISINTERESTED WITNESS. One who has no interest in the cause or matter in issue, and who is lawfully competent to testify.

2. In North Carolina and Tennessee, wills to pass lands must be attested by disinterested witnesses. See *Attesting Witness; Competent Witness; Credible Witness; Respectable Witness;* and *Witness.*

DISJUNCTIVE TERM. One which is placed between two contraries, by the affirming of one of which, the other is taken away: it is usually expressed by the word *or.* Vide 3 Ves. 450; 7 Ves. 454; 2 Rop. Leg. 290; 1 P. Wms. 433; 2 Cox, Rep. 213; 2 P. Wms. 283; 2 Atk. 643; 6 Ves. 341; 2 Ves. sr. 67; 2 Str. 1175; Cro. Eliz. 525, Pollexf. 645; 1 Bing. 500; 3 T. R. 470; 1 Ves. sr. 409; 3 Atk. 83, 85; Ayl. Pand. 56; 2 Miles, Rep. 49.

2. In the civil law, when a legacy is given to Caius *or* Titius, the word *or* is considered *and,* and both Caius and Titius are entitled to the legacy in equal parts. 6 Toull. n. 704. See *Copulative term; Construction,* subdivision, *And; Or.* Also, Bac Ab. Conditions, P 5.

DISMES. Another name for tithes. Dime, (q. v.) a piece of federal money, is sometimes improperly written disme.

TO DISMISS A CAUSE, *practice.* A term used in courts of chancery for removing a cause out of court without any further hearing.

DISOBEDIENCE. The want of submission to the orders of a superior.

2. In the army, disobedience is a misdemeanor.

3. For disobedience to parents, children may be punished; and apprentices may be imprisoned for disobedience to the lawful commands of their master. Vide *Correction.*

DISORDERLY HOUSE, *crim. law.* A house, the inmates of which behave so badly as to become a nuisance to the neighborhood.

2. The keeper of such house may be indicted for keeping a public nuisance. Hardr. 344; Hawk. b. 1, c. 78, s. 1 and 2; Bac. Ab. Inns, A; 1 Russ. on Cr. 298; 1 Wheel. C. C. 290; 1 Serg. & Rawle, 342; 2 Serg. & Rawle, 298; Bac. Ab. Nuisances, A; 4 Chit. Bl. Com. 167, 8, note. The husband must be joined with the wife in an indictment to suppress a disorderly house. Justice's Case, Law 16; 1 Shaw, 146. Vide *Bawdy house; Ill fame.*

DISPARAGEMENT. An injury by union or comparison with some person or thing of inferior rank or excellence; as, while the infant was in ward, by the English law, the guardian had the power of tendering him a suitable match without *disparagement.* 2 Bl. Com. 70.

TO DISPAUPER, *Eng. law.* To deprive a person of the privilege of suing in *forma pauperis.* (q. v.)

2. When a person has been admitted to sue in *forma pauperis,* and, before the suit is ended, it appears that the party has become the owner of a sufficient estate real or personal, or has been guilty of some wrong, he may be *dispaupered.*

DISPENSATION. A relaxation of law for the benefit or advantage of an individual. In the United States, no power exists, except in the legislature, to dispense with law, and then it is not so much a dispensation as a change of the law.

TO DISPONE, *Scotch law.* This is a technical word, which implies, it is said, a transfer of feudal property by a particular deed, and is not equivalent to the term *alienate;* but Lord Eldon says, "with respect to the word *dispone*, if I collect the opinions of a majority of the judges rightly, I am of opinion that the word dispone would have the same effect as the word *alienate.*" (q. v.) Sandford on Entails, 179, note.

DISPOSITION, *French law.* This word has several acceptations; sometimes it signifies the effective marks of the will of some person; and at others the instrument containing those marks.

2. The dispositions of man make the dispositions of the law to cease; for example, when a man bequeaths his estate, the disposition he makes of it, renders the legal disposition of it, if he had died intestate, to cease.

DISSEISED, *pleading.* This is a word with a technical meaning, which, when inserted in an indictment for forcible entry and detainer, has all the force of the words *expelled* or *unlawfully*, for the last is superfluous, and the first is implied in the word disseised. 8 T. R. 357; Cro. Jac. 32; vide 3 Yeates' R. 39; S. C. 4 Dall. Rep. 212.

DISSEISEE, *torts.* One who is wrongfully put out of possession of his lands.

DISSEISIN, *torts.* The privation of seisin. It takes the seisin or estate from one man and places it in another. It is an ouster of the rightful owner from the seisin or estate in the land, and the commencement of a new estate in the wrong doer. It may be by abatement, intrusion, discontinuance, or deforcement, as well as by disseisin, properly so called. Every dispossession is not a disseisin. A disseisin, properly so called, requires an ouster of the freehold. A disseisin at election is not a disseisin in fact; 2 Prest. Abs. tit. 279, et seq.; but by admission only of the injured party, for the purpose of trying his right in a real action. Co. Litt. 277; 3 Greenl. 316; 4 N. H. Rep. 371; 5 Cowen, 371; 6 John. 197; 2 Fairf. 309, 2 Greenl. 242; 5 Pet. 402; 6 Pick. 172.

2. Disseisin may be effected either in corporeal inheritances, or incorporeal. Disseisin of things corporeal, as of houses, lands, &c., must be by entry and actual dispossession of the freehold; as if a man enters, by force or fraud, into the house of another, and turns, or at least, keeps him or his servants out of possession. Disseisin of incorporeal hereditaments cannot be an actual dispossession, for the subject itself is neither capable of actual bodily possession nor dispossession. 3 Bl. Com. 169, 170. See 15 Mass. 495; 6 John. R. 197; 2 Watts, 23; 6 Pick. 172; 1 Verm. 155; 11 Pet. R. 41; 10 Pet. R. 414; 14 Pick. 374; 1 Dana's R. 279; 2 Fairf. 408; 11 Pick. 193; 8 Pick. 172; 8 Vin. Ab. 79; 1 Swift's Dig. 504; 1 Cruise, *65; Arch. Civ. Pl. 12; Bac. Ab. h. t.; 2 Supp. to Ves. Jr. 343; Dane's Ab. Index, h. t.; 1 Chit. Pr. 374, note (r.)

DISSEISOR, *torts.* One who puts another out of the possession of his lands wrongfully.

DISSENT, *contracts.* A disagreement to something which has been done. It is express or implied.

2. The law presumes that every person to whom a conveyance has been made has given his assent to it, because it is supposed to be for his benefit. To rebut the presumption, his dissent must be expressed. Vide 4 Mason, R. 206; 11 Wheat. R. 78; 1 Binn. R. 502; 2 Binn. R. 174; 6 Binn. R. 338; 12 Mass. R. 456; 17 Mass. R. 552; 3 John. Ch. R. 261; 4 John. Ch. R. 136, 529; and *Assent*, and the authorities there cited.

DISSOLUTION, *contracts.* The dissolution of a contract, is the annulling its effects between the contracting parties.

2. This dissolution of a partnership, is the putting an end to the partnership. Its dissolution does not affect contracts made between the partners and others; so that they are entitled to all their rights, and they are liable on their obligations, as if the partnership had not been dissolved. Vide article *Partnership*, and 3 Kent, Com. 27; Dane's Ab. h. t.; Gow on Partn. Index, h. t.; Wats. on Partn. h. t.; Bouv. Inst. Index, h. t.

DISSOLUTION, *practice.* The act of rendering a legal proceeding null, or changing its character; as, a foreign attachment in Pennsylvania is dissolved by entering bail to the action. Injunctions are dissolved by the court.

TO DISSUADE, *crim. law.* To induce a person not to do an act.

2. To dissuade a witness from giving evidence against a person indicted, is an indictable offence at common law. Hawk. B. 1, c. 21, s. 15. The mere attempt to stifle evidence, is also criminal, although the persuasion should not succeed, on the general principle that an incitement to commit a crime, is in itself criminal. 1 Russ. on Cr. 44; 6 East, R. 464; 2 East, R. 5, 21; 2 Str. 904; 2 Leach, 925. Vide *To Persuade*.

DISTRACTED PERSON. This term is used in the statutes of Illinois; Rev. Laws of Ill. 1833, p. 332; and New Hampshire; Dig. Laws of N. H. 1830, p. 339; to express a state of insanity.

TO DISTRAIN. To take and keep any personal chattel in custody, as a distress. (q. v.)

DISTRAINOR. One who makes a distress of goods and chattels to enforce some right.

DISTRESS, *remedies*. A distress is defined to be the taking of a personal chattel, without legal process, from the possession of the wrong doer, into the hands of the party grieved, as a pledge for the redress of an injury, the performance of a duty, or the satisfaction of a demand. 3 Bl. Com. 6. It is a general rule, that a man who has an entire duty, shall not split the entire sum and distrain for part of it at one time, and part of it at another time. But if a man seizes for the whole sum that is due him, but mistakes the value of the goods distrained, there is no reason why he should not afterwards complete his execution by making a further seizure. 1 Burr. 589. It is to be observed also, that there is an essential difference between distresses at common law and distresses prescribed by statute. The former are taken *nomine penæ*, (q. v.) as a means of compelling payment; the latter are similar to executions, and are taken as satisfaction for a duty. The former could not be sold; the latter might be. Their only similarity is, that both are replevisable. A consequence of this difference is, that *averia carucæ* are distrainable in the latter case, although there be other sufficient distress. 1 Burr. Rep. 588.

2. The remedy by distress to enforce the payment of arrears of rent is so frequently adopted by landlords, (Co. Lit. 162, b,) that a considerable space will be allotted to this article under the following heads: 1. The several kinds of rent for which a distress may be made. 2. The persons who may make it. 3. The goods which may be distrained. 4. The time when a distress may be made. 5. In what place it may be made. 6. The manner of making it, and disposing of the goods distrained. 7. When a distress will be a waiver of a forfeiture of the lease.

3.—§ 1. *Of the rents for which a distress may be made*. 1. A distress may generally be taken for any kind of rent in arrear, the detention of which, beyond the day of payment, is an injury to him who is entitled to receive it. 3 Bl. Com. 6. The rent must be reserved out of a corporeal hereditament, and must be certain in its quantity, extent, and time of payment, or at least be capable of being reduced to certainty. Co. Lit. 96, a.; 13 Serg. & Rawle, 64; 3 Penn. R. 30. An agreement that the lessee pay no rent, provided he make repairs, and the value of the repairs is uncertain, would not authorize the landlord to distrain. Addis. 347. Where the rent is a *certain* quantity of grain, the landlord may distrain for so many bushels in arrear, and name the value, in order that if the goods should not be replevied, or the arrears tendered, the officer may know what amount of money is to be raised by the sale, and in such case the tenant may tender the arrears in grain. 13 Serg. & Rawle, 52; See 3 Watts & S. 531. But where the tenant agreed, instead of rent, to render "one-half part of all the grain of every kind, and of all hemp, flax, potatoes, apples, fruit, and other produce of whatever kind that should be planted, raised, sown or produced, on or out of the demised premises, within and during the terms," the landlord cannot, perhaps, distrain at all; he cannot, certainly, distrain for a sum of money, although he and the tenant may afterwards have settled their accounts, and agreed that the half of the produce of the land should be fixed in money, for which the tenant gave his note, which was not paid. 13 Serg. & Rawle, 52. But in another case it was held, that on a demise of a grist mill, when the lessee is to render one-third of the toll, the lessor may distrain for rent. 2 Rawle, 11.

4.—2. With respect to the *amount* of the rent, for which a lessor may in different cases be entitled to make a distress, it may be laid down as a general rule, that whatever can properly be considered as a part of the rent, may be distrained for, whatever be the particular mode in which it is agreed to be paid. So that where a person entered into possession of certain premises, subject to the approbation of the landlord, which was afterwards obtained, by agreeing to pay in advance, rent from the time he came into possession, it was, in England, determined that the landlord might distrain for the whole sum accrued before and after the agreement. Cowp. 784. For on whatever day the tenant agrees that the rent shall be due, the law gives the landlord the power of distraining for it at that time. 2 T. R. 600. But see 13 S. & R. 60. In New York, it was determined, that an agreement that the rent should be paid in advance, is a personal covenant on which an action lies, but not distress. 1 Johns. R. 384. The supreme court of Pennsylvania declined deciding this point, as it was not necessarily before them. 13 Serg. & Rawle, 60. Interest due on rent cannot, in general, be distrained for; 2 Binn. 146; but may be recovered from the tenant by action, unless under particular circumstances. 6 Binn. 159.

5.—§ 2. *Of the persons entitled to make a distress.* 1. When the landlord is sole owner of the property out of which rent is payable to him, he may, of course, distrain in his own right.

6.—2. Joint tenants have each of them an estate in every part of the rent; each may, therefore, distrain alone for the whole, 3 Salk. 207, although he must afterwards account with his companions for their respective shares of the rent. 3 Salk. 17; 4 Bing. 562; 2 Brod. & B. 465; 5 Moore, 297; Y. B. 15 H. VII., 17, a; 1 Chit. Pr. 270; 1 Tho. Co. Litt. 783, note R; Bac. Ab. Account; 5 Taunt. 431; 2 Chit. R. 10; 3 Chit. Pl. 1297. But one joint tenant cannot avow solely, because the avowry is always upon the right, and the right of the rent is in all of them. Per Holt, 3 Salk. 207. They may all join in making the distress, which is the better way.

7.—3. Tenants in common do not, like joint tenants, hold by one title and by one right, but by different titles, and have several estates. Therefore they should distrain separately, each for his share, Co. Lit. s. 317, unless the rent be of an entire thing, as to render a horse, in which case, the thing being incapable of division, they must join. Co. Lit. 197, a. Each tenant in common is entitled to receive, from the lessee, his proportion of the rent; and therefore, when a person holding under two tenants in common, paid the whole rent to one of them, after having received a notice to the contrary from the other, it was held, that the party who gave the notice might afterwards distrain. 5 T. R. 246. As tenants in common have no original privity of estate between them, as to their respective shares, one may lease his part of the land to the other, rendering rent, for which a distress may be made, as if the land had been demised to a stranger. Bro. Ab. tit. Distress, pl. 65.

8.—4. It may be, perhaps, laid down as a general rule, that for rent due in right of the wife, the husband may distrain alone; 2 Saund. 195; even if it accrue to her in the character of executrix or administratrix. Ld. Raym. 369. With respect to the remedies for the recovery of the arrears of a rent accruing in right of his wife, a distinction is made between rent due for land, in which the wife has a chattel interest, and rent due in land, in which she has an estate of freehold and inheritance. And in some cases, a further distinction must be made between a rent accruing before and rent accruing after the coverture. See, on this subject, Co. Lit. 46, b, 300, a; 351, a; 1 Roll. Abr. 350; stat. 32 Hen. VIII. c. 37, s. 3.

9.—5. A tenant by the curtesy, has an estate of freehold in the lands of his wife, and in contemplation of law, a reversion on all land of the wife leased for years or lives, and may distrain at common law for all rents reserved thereon.

10.—6. A woman may be endowed of rent as well as of land; if a husband, therefore, tenant in fee, make a lease for years, reserving rent, and die, his widow shall be endowed of one-third part of the reversion by metes and bounds, together with a third part of the rent. Co. Litt. 32, a. The rent in this case is apportioned by the act of law, and therefore if a widow be endowed of a third part of a rent in fee, she may distrain for a third part thereof, and the heir shall distrain for the other part of the rent. Bro. Abr. tit. Avowry, pl. 139.

11.—7. A tenant for his own life or that of another, has an estate of freehold, and if he make a lease for years, reserving rent, he is entitled to distrain upon the lessee. It may here be proper to remark, that at common law, if a tenant for life made a lease for years, if he should so long live, at a certain rent, payable quarterly, and died before the quarter day, the tenant was discharged of that quarter's rent by the act of God. 10 Rep. 128. But the 11 Geo. II.

c. 19, s. 15, gives an action to the executors or administrators of such tenant for life.

12.—8. By the statute 32 Henry VIII. c. 37, s. 1, "the personal representatives of tenants in fee, tail, or for life, of rent-service, rent-charge, and rents-seck, and fee farms, may distrain for arrears upon the land charged with the payment, so long as the lands continue in seisin or possession of the tenant in demesne, who ought to have paid the rent or fee farm, or some person claiming under him by purchase, gift or descent." By the words of the statute, the distress must be made on the lands while in the possession of the "tenant in demesne," or some person claiming under him, by purchase, gift or descent; and therefore it extends to the possession of those persons only who claim under the tenant, and the statute does not comprise the tenant in dower or by the curtesy, for they come in, not under the party, but by act of law. 1 Leon. 302.

13.—9. The heir entitled to the reversion may distrain for rent in arrear which becomes due after the ancestor's death; the rent does not become due till the last minute of the natural day, and if the ancestor die between sunset and midnight, the heir, and not the executor, shall have the rent. 1 Saund, 287. And if rent be payable at either of two periods, at the choice of the lessee, and the lessor die between them, the rent being unpaid, it will go to the heir. 10 Rep. 128, b.

14.—10. Devisees, like heirs, may distrain in respect of their reversionary estate; for by a devise of the reversion the rent will pass with its incidents. 1 Ventr. 161.

15.—11. Trustees who have vested in them legal estates, as trustees of a married woman, or assignees of an insolvent, may of course distrain in respect of their legal estates, in the same manner as if they were beneficially interested therein.

16.—12. Guardians may make leases of their wards' lands in their own names, which will be good during the minority of the ward; and, consequently, in respect of such leases, they possess the same power of distress as other persons granting leases in their own rights. Cro. Jac. 55, 98.

17.—13. Corporations aggregate should generally make and accept leases or other conveyances of lands or rent, under their common seal. But if a lease be made by an agent of the corporation, not under their common seal, although it may be invalid as a lease, yet if the tenant hold under it, and pay rent to the bailiff or agent of the corporation, that is sufficient to constitute a tenancy at least from year to year, and to entitle the corporation to distrain for rent. 2 New Rep. 247. But see *Corporation*.

18.—§ 3. *Of the things which may or may not be distrained.* Goods found upon the premises demised to a tenant are generally liable to be distrained by a landlord for rent, whether such goods in fact belong to the tenant or other persons. Com. Dig. Distress, B 1. Thus it has been held, that a gentleman's chariot, which stood in a coach-house belonging to a common livery stable keeper, was distrainable by the landlord for the rent due him by the livery stable keeper for the coach-house. 3 Burr. 1498. So if cattle are put on the tenant's land by consent of the owners of the beasts, they are distrainable by the landlord immediately after for rent in arrear. 3 Bl. Com. 8. But goods are sometimes privileged from distress, either absolutely or conditionally.

19. First. Those of the first class are privileged, 1. In respect of the owner of them. 2. Because no one can have property in them. 3. Because they cannot be restored to the owner in the same plight as when taken. 4. Because they are fixed to the freehold. 5. Because it is against the policy of law that they should be distrained. 6. Because they are in the custody of the law. 7. Because they are protected by some special act of the legislature.

20.—1. The goods of a person who has some interest in the land jointly with the distrainer, as those of a joint tenant, although found upon the land, cannot be distrained. The goods of executors and administrators, or of the assignee of an insolvent regularly discharged according to law, cannot, in Pennsylvania, be distrained for more than one year's rent. The goods of a former tenant, rightfully on the land, cannot be distrained for another's rent. For example, a tenant at will, if quitting upon notice from his landlord, is entitled to the emblements or growing crops; and therefore even after they are reaped, if they remain on the land for the purpose of husbandry, they cannot be distrained for rent due by the second tenant. Willes, 131. And they are equally protected in the hands of a vendee. Ibid. They cannot be distrained, although the purchaser allow them to remain uncut an unreasonable time after they are ripe. 2 B. & B. 362; 5 Moore, 97, S. C.

21.—2. As every thing which is distrained is presumed to be the property of the tenant, it will follow that things wherein no man can have an absolute and valuable property, as cats, dogs, rabbits, and all animals feræ naturæ, cannot be distrained. Yet, if deer, which are of a wild nature, are kept in a private enclosure, for the purpose of sale or profit, this so far changes their nature, by reducing them to a kind of stock or merchandise, that they may be distrained for rent. 3 Bl. Com. 7.

22.—3. Such things as cannot be restored to the owner in the same plight as when they were taken, as milk, fruit, and the like, cannot be distrained. 3 Bl. Com. 9.

23.—4. Things affixed or annexed to the freehold, as furnaces, windows, doors, and the like, cannot be distrained, because they are not personal chattels, but belong to the realty. Co. Litt. 47, b. And this rule extends to such things as are essentially a part of the freehold, although for a time removed therefrom, as a millstone removed to be picked; for this is matter of necessity, and it still remains in contemplation of law, a part of the freehold. For the same reason an anvil fixed in a smith's shop cannot be distrained. Bro. Abr. Distress, pl. 23; 4 T. R. 567; Willis, Rep. 512; 6 Price's R. 3; 2 Chitty's R. 167.

24.—5. Goods are privileged in cases where the proprietor is either compelled from *necessity* to place his goods upon the land, or where he does so for *commercial* purposes. 17 S. & R. 139; 7 W. & S. 302; 8 W. & S. 302; 4 Halst. 110; 1 Bay, 102, 170; 2 McCord, 39; 3 B. & B. 75; 6 J. B. Moore, 243; 1 Bing. 283; 8 J. B. Moore, 254; 2 C. & P. 353; 1 Cr. & M. 380. In the first case, the goods are exempt, because the owner has no option; hence the goods of a traveller in an inn are exempt from distress. 7 H. 7, M. 1, p. 1; Hamm. N. P. 380, a.; 2 Keny. 439; Barnes, 472; 1 Bl. R. 483; 3 Burr. 1408. In the other, the interests of the community require that commerce should be encouraged, and adventurers will not engage in speculations, if the property embarked is to be made liable for the payment of debts they never contracted. Hence goods landed at a wharf, or deposited in a warehouse on storage, cannot be distrained. 17 Serg. & Rawle, 138; 5 Whart. R. 9, 14; 9 Shepl. 47; 23 Wend. 462. Valuable things in the way of trade are not liable to distress; as, a horse standing in a smith's shop to be shod, or in a common inn; or cloth at a tailor's house to be made into a coat; or corn sent to a mill to be ground, for these are privileged and protected for the benefit of trade. 3 Bl. Com. 8. On the same principle it has been decided, that the goods of a boarder are not liable to be distrained for rent due by the keeper of a boarding house; 5 Whart. R. 9; unless used by the tenant with the boarder's consent, and without that of the landlord. 1 Hill, 565.

25.—6. Goods taken in execution cannot be distrained. The law in some states gives the landlord the right to claim payment out of the proceeds of an execution for rent, not exceeding one year, and he is entitled to payment up to the day of seizure, though it be in the middle of a quarter; 2 Yeates, 274; 5 Binn. 505; but he is not entitled to the day of sale. 5 Binn. 505. See 18 Johns. R. 1. The usual practice is, to give notice to the sheriff that there is a certain sum due to the landlord as arrears of rent; which notice ought to be given to the sheriff, or person who takes the goods in execution upon the premises; for the sheriff is not bound to find out whether rent is due, nor is he liable to an action, unless there has been a demand of rent before the removal. 1 Str. 97, 214; 3 Taunt. 400, 2 Wils. 140; Com. Dig. Rent, D 8; 11 Johns. R. 185. This notice can be given by the immediate landlord only; a ground landlord is not entitled to his rent out of the goods of the under tenant taken in execution. 2 Str. 787. And where there are two executions, the landlord is not entitled to a year's rent on each. See Str. 1024. Goods distrained and replevied may be distrained by another landlord for subsequent rent. 2 Dall. 68.

26.—7. By some special acts of the legislature it is provided that tools of a man's trade, some designated household furniture, school books, and the like, shall be exempted from distress, execution, or sale. And by a recent Act of Assembly of Pennsylvania, April 9, 1849, property to the value of three hundred dollars, exclusive of all wearing apparel of the defendant and his family, and all bibles and school books in use in the family, are exempted from levy and sale on execution, or by distress for rent.

27.—Secondly. Besides the above mentioned goods and chattels, which are absolutely privileged from distress, there are others which are conditionally so, but which may be distrained under certain circumstances. These are, 1. Beasts of the plough, which are exempt if there be a sufficient distress besides on the land whence the rent issues. Co. Litt. 47, a; Bac. Abr. Distress, B. 2. Implements of trade; as, a loom in actual use; and there is a sufficient distress besides. 4 T. R. 565. 3. Other things in actual use; as, a horse whereon a person is riding, an axe in the hands of a person cutting wood, and the like. Co. Litt. 47, a.

28. -§ 4. *The time when a distress may be made.* 1. The distress cannot be made till the rent is due by the terms of the lease; as rent is not due until the last minute of the natural day on which it is reserved, it follows that a distress for rent cannot be maae on that day. 1 Saund. 287; Co. Litt. 47, b. n. 6. A previous demand is not generally necessary, although there be a clause in the lease, that the lessor may distrain for rent, "being lawfully demanded;" Bradb. 124; Bac. Abr. Rent, I; the making of the distress being a demand; though it is advisable to make such a demand. But where a lease provides for a special demand; as, if the clause were that if the rent should happen to be behind it should be demanded at a particular place *not on the land;* or be demanded *of the person of the tenant;* then such special demand is necessary to support the distress. Plowd. 69; Bac. Abr. Rent, I.

29.—2. A distress for rent can only be made during the day time. Co. Litt. 142, a.

30.—3. At common law a distress could not be made after the expiration of the lease; to remedy this evil the legislature of Pennsylvania passed an act making it "lawful for any person having any rent in arrear or due upon any lease for life or years or at will, ended or determined, to distrain for such arrears after the determination of the said respective leases, in the same manner as they might have done, if such lease had not been ended: provided, that such distress be made during the continuance of such lessor's title or interest." Act of March 21, 1772, s. 14, 1 Smith's Laws of Penna. 375. 4. In the city and county of Philadelphia, the landlord may, under certain circumstances, apportion his rent, and distrain before it becomes due. See act of March 25, 1825, s. 1, Pamph L. 114.

31.—§ 5. *In what place a distress may be made.* The distress may be made upon the land, or off the land. 1. Upon the land. A distress generally follows the rent, and is consequently confined to the land out of which it issues. If two pieces of land, therefore, are let by two separate demises, although both be contained in one lease, a joint distress cannot be made for them, for this would be to make the rent of one issue out of the other. Rep. Temp. Hardw. 245; S. C. Str. 1040. But where lands lying in different counties are let together by one demise, at one entire rent, and it does not appear that the lands are separate from each other, one distress may be made for the whole rent. Ld. Raym. 55; S. C. 12 Mod. 76. And where rent is charged upon land, which is afterwards held by several tenants, the grantee or landlord may distrain for the whole upon the land of any of them; because the whole rent is deemed to issue out of every part of the land. Roll. Abr. 671. If there be a house on the land, the distress may be made in the house; if the outer door or window be open, a distress may be taken out of it. Roll. Abr. 671. And if an outer door be open, an inner door may be broken open for the purpose of taking a distress. Comb. 47; Cas. Temp. Hard. 168. Barges on a river, attached to the leased premises (a wharf) by ropes, cannot be distrained. 6 Bingh. 150; 19 Eng. Com. Law R. 36.

32.—2. *Off the land.* By the 5th and 6th sections of the Pennsylvania act of assembly of March 21, 1772, copied from the 11 Geo. II. c. 19, it is enacted, that if any tenant for life, years, at will, or otherwise, shall fraudulently or clandestinely convey his goods off the premises to prevent the landlord from distraining the same, such person, or any person by him lawfully authorized, may, within thirty days after such conveyance, seize the same, wherever they shall be found, and dispose of them in such manner as if they had been distrained on the premises. Provided, that the landlord shall not distrain any goods which shall have been previously sold, *bona fide,* and for a valuable consideration, to one not privy to the fraud. To bring a case within the act, the removal must take place *after* the rent becomes due, and must be *secret,* not made in open day, for such removal cannot be said to be clandestine within the meaning of the act. 3 Esp. N. P. C. 15; 12 Serg. & Rawle, 217; 7 Bing. 423; 1 Moody & Malkin, 535. It has, however, been made a question, whether goods are protected that were fraudulently removed on the night before the rent had become due. 4 Camp. 135. The goods of a stranger cannot be pursued; they can be distrained only while they are on the premises. 1 Dall. 440.

33.—§ 6. *Of the manner of making a distress.* 1. A distress for rent may be made either by the person to whom it is due, or, which is the preferable mode, by a constable, or bailiff, or other officer properly authorized by him.

34.—2. If the distress be made by a constable, it is necessary that he should be properly authorized to make it; for which purpose the landlord should give him a written authority, or, as it is usually called, a warrant of distress; but a subsequent assent and recognition given by the party for whose use the distress has been made, is sufficient. Hamm. N. P. 382.

35.—3. When the constable is thus provided with the requisite authority to make a distress, he may distrain by seizing the tenant's goods, or some of them in the name of the whole, and declaring that he takes them as a distress for the sum expressed in the warrant to be due by the tenant to the landlord, and that he takes them by virtue of the said warrant; which warrant he ought, if required, to show. 1 Leon. 50.

36.—4. When making the distress it ought to be made for the whole rent; but if goods cannot be found at the time, sufficient to satisfy the rent, or the party mistake the value of the thing distrained, he may make a second distress. Bradb. 129, 30; 2 Tr. & H. Pr. 155; supra 1.

37.—5. As soon as a distress is made, an inventory of the goods distrained should be made, and a copy of it delivered to the tenant, together with a notice of taking such distress, with the cause for taking the same. This notice of taking a distress is not required by the statute to be in writing; and, therefore, parol or verbal notice may be given either to the tenant on the premises, or to the owner of the goods distrained. 12 Mod. 76. And although notice is directed by the act to specify the cause of taking, it is not material whether it accurately state the period of the rent's becoming due; Dougl. 279; or even whether the true cause of taking the goods be expressed therein. 7 T. R. 654. If the notice be not personally given, it should be left in writing at the tenant's house, or according to the directions of the act, at the mansion-house or other most notorious place on the premises charged with the rent distrained for.

38.—6. The distrainor may leave or impound the distress on the premises for the five days mentioned in the act, but becomes a trespasser after that time. 2 Dall. 69. As in many cases it is desirable for the sake of the tenant that the goods should not be sold as soon as the law permits, it is usual for him to sign an agreement or consent to their remaining on the premises for a longer time, in the custody of the distrainor, or of a person by him appointed for that purpose. While in his possession, the distrainor cannot use or work cattle distrained, unless it be for the owner's benefit, as to milk a cow, or the like. 5 Dane's Abr. 34.

39.—7. Before the goods are sold they must be appraised by two reputable freeholders, who shall take an oath or affirmation to be administered by the sheriff, undersheriff, or coroner, in the words mentioned in the act.

40.—8. The next requisite is to give six days' public notice of the time and place of sale of the things distrained; after which, if they have not been replevied, they may be sold by the proper officer, who may apply the proceeds to the payment and satisfaction of the rent, and the expenses of the distress, appraisement and sale. The overplus, if any, is to be paid to the tenant.

41.—§ 7. *When a distress will be a waiver of a forfeiture of the lease.* On this subject, see 1 B. & Adol. 428.

The right of distress, it seems, does not exist in the New England states. 4 Dane's Ab. 126; 7 Pick. R. 105; 3 Griff. Reg 404; 4 Griff. Reg. 1143; Aik. Dig. 357, nor in Alabama, Mississippi, North Carolina, nor Ohio; and in Kentucky, the right is limited to a distress for a pecuniary rent. 1 Hill. Ab. 156. Vide, generally, Bouv. Inst. Index, h. t.; Gilb. on Distr. by Hunt; Bradb. on Distr.; Com. Dig. h. t.; Bac. Ab. h. t.; Vin. Ab. h. t.; 2 Saund. Index, h. t.; Wilk. on Repl.; 3 Chit. Bl. Com. 6, note; Crabb on R. P. § 222 to 250.

DISTRESS INFINITE, *English practice.* A process commanding the sheriff to distrain a person from time to time, and continually afterwards, by taking his goods by way of pledge, to enforce the performance of something due from the party distrained upon.

In this case, no distress can be immoderate, because, whatever its value may be, it cannot be sold, but is to be immediately restored on satisfaction being made. 3 Bl. Com. 231. See *Distringas*.

DISTRIBUTION. By this term is understood the division of an intestate's estate ccording to law.

2. The English statute of 22 and 23 Car. II. c. 10, which was itself probably borrowed from the 118th Novel of Justinian, is the foundation of, perhaps, most acts of distribution in the several states. Vide 2 Kent, Com. 342, note; 8 Com. Dig. 522; 11 Vin. Ab. 189, 202; Com. Dig. Administration, H.

DISTRIBUTIVE JUSTICE. That virtue, whose object it is to distribute rewards and punishments to every one according to his merits or demerits. Tr. of Eq. 3; Lepage, El. du Dr. ch. 1, art. 3, § 2; 1 Toull. n. 7, note. See *Justice*.

DISTRICT. A certain portion of the country, separated from the rest for some special purposes.

2. The United States are divided into judicial districts, in each of which is established a district court; they are also divided into election districts; collection districts, &c.

DISTRICT ATTORNEYS OF THE UNITED STATES. There shall be appointed, in each judicial district, a meet person, learned in the law, to act as attorney of the United States in such district, who shall be sworn or affirmed to the faithful execution of his office. Act of September 24, 1789, s. 35, 1 Story's Laws, 67.

2. His duty is to prosecute, in such district, all delinquents, for crimes and offences cognizable under the authority of the United States, and all civil actions in which the United States shall be concerned, except in the supreme court, in the district in which that court shall be holden. Ib.

3. Their salaries vary in different districts. Vide Gordon's Dig. art. 403. By the Act of March 3, 1815, 2 Story's L. U. S. 1530, district attorneys are authorized to appoint deputies, in certain cases, to sue in the state courts. See *Deputy District Attorney*.

DISTRICT COURT. The name of one of the courts of the United States. It is held by a judge, called the district judge. Several courts under the same name have been established by state authority. Vide *Courts of the United States*.

DISTRICT OF COLUMBIA. The name of a district of country, ten miles square, situate between the states of Maryland and Virginia, over which the national government has exclusive jurisdiction. By the constitution, congress may "exercise exclusive jurisdiction in all cases whatsoever, over such district, not exceeding ten miles square, as may, by cession of particular states, and the acceptance of congress, become the seat of government of the United States." In pursuance of this authority, the states of Maryland and Virginia, ceded to the United States, a small territory on the banks of the Potomac, and congress, by the Act of July 16, 1790, accepted the same for the permanent seat of the government of the United States. The act provides for the removal of the seat of government from the city of Philadelphia to the District of Columbia, on the first Monday of December, 1800. It is also provided, that the laws of the state, within such district, shall not be affected by the acceptance, until the time fixed for the removal of the government thereto, and until congress shall otherwise by law provide.

2. It seems that the District of Columbia, and the territorial districts of the United States, are not states within the meaning of the constitution, and of the judiciary act, so as to enable a citizen thereof to sue a citizen of one of the states in the federal courts. 2 Cranch, 445; 1 Wheat, 91.

3. By the Act of July 11, 1846, congress retroceded the county of Alexandria, part of the District of Columbia, to the state of Virginia.

DISTRINGAS, *remedies*. A writ directed to the sheriff, commanding him to distrain one of his goods and chattels, to enforce his compliance of what is required of him, as for his appearance in a court on such a day, and the like. Com. Dig. Process, D 7; Chit. Pr. Index, h. t.; Sellon's Pr. Index, h. t.; Tidd's Pr. Index, h. t.; 11 East, 353. It is also a form of execution in the action of detinue, and assize of nuisance. Registrum Judiciale, 56; 1 Rawle, 44, 48; Bro. Abr. pl. 26; 22 H. VI. 41. This writ is likewise used to compel the appearance of a *corporation aggregate*. 4 Bouv. Inst. n. 4191.

DISTURBANCE, *torts*. A wrong done to an incorporeal hereditament, by hindering or disquieting the owner in the enjoyment of it. Finch. L. 187; 3 Bl. Com. 235; 1 Swift's Dig. 522; Com. Dig. Action upon the case for a disturbance, Pleader, 3 I 6; 1 Serg. & Rawle, 298.

DIVIDEND. A portion of the principal, or profits, divided among several owners of a thing.

2. The term is usually applied to the division of the profits arising out of bank or other stocks; or to the division, among the creditors, of the effects of an insolvent estate.

3. In another sense, according to some old authorities, it signifies one part of an indenture. T. L.

DIVISIBLE. The susceptibility of being divided.

2. A contract cannot, in general, be divided in such a manner that an action may be brought, or a right accrue, on a part of it. 2 Penna. R. 454. But some contracts are susceptible of division, as when a reversioner sells a part of the reversion to one man, and a part to another, each shall have an action for his share of the rent, which may accrue on a contract, to pay a particular rent to the reversioner. 3 Whart. 404; and see *Apportionment*. But when it is to do several things, at several times, an action will lie upon every default. 15 Pick. R. 409. See 1 Greenl. R. 316; 6 Mass. 344. See *Entire*.

DIVISION, *Eng. law*. A particular and ascertained part of a county. In Lincolnshire, division means what riding does in Yorkshire.

DIVISION OF OPINION. When, in a company or society, the parties having a right to vote are so divided that there is not a plurality of the whole in favor of any particular proposition, or when the voters are equally divided, it is said there is division of opinion.

2. In such a case, the Roman law, which seems founded in reason and common sense, directs, that when the division relates to the quantity of things included, as in the case of a judgment, if one of three judges votes for condemning a man to a fine of one hundred dollars, another, to one of fifty dollars, and the third to twenty-five, the opinion or vote of the last shall be the rule for the judgment; because the votes of all the others include that of the lowest; this is the case when unanimity is required. But when the division of opinions does not relate to the quantity of things, then it is always to be in favor of the defendant. It was a rule among the Romans that when the judges were equal in number, and they were divided into two opinions in cases of liberty, that opinion which favored it should prevail; and in other cases, it should be in favor of the defendant. Poth. Pand. liv. L. n. MDLXXIV.

3. When the judges of a court are divided into three classes, each holding a different opinion, that class which has the greatest number shall give the judgment; for example, on a habeas corpus, when a court is composed of four judges, and one is for remanding the prisoner, another is for discharging him on his own recognizance, and two others for discharging him absolutely, the judgment will be, that he be discharged. Rudyard's Case, Bac. Ab. Habeas Corpus, B 10, Court 5.

4. It is provided, by the Act of Congress of April 29, 1802, s. 6, that whenever any question shall occur before a circuit court, upon which the opinions of the judges shall be opposed, the point upon which the disagreement shall happen shall, during the same term, upon the request of either party, or their counsel, be stated, under the direction of the judges, and certified, under the seal of the court, to the supreme court, at their next session to be held thereafter, and shall, by the said court, be finally decided. And the decision of the supreme court, and their order in the premises, shall be remitted to the circuit court, and be there entered of record; and shall have effect according to the nature of the said judgment and order: *Provided*, That nothing herein contained shall prevent the cause from proceeding, if, in the opinion of the court, further proceedings can be had without prejudice to the merits: *And provided, also*, That imprisonment shall not be allowed, nor punishment in any case be inflicted, where the judges of the said court are divided in opinion upon the question touching the said imprisonment or punishment. See 5 N. S. 407.

DIVORCE. The dissolution of a marriage contracted between a man and a woman, by the judgment of a court of competent jurisdiction, or by an act of the legislature. It is so called from the diversity of the minds of those who are married; because such as are divorced go each a different way from the other. Ridley's Civ. & Eccl. Law, pp. 11, 112. Until a decree of divorce be actually made, neither party can treat the other as sole, even in cases where the marriage is utterly null and void for some preëxisting cause. Griffiths *v*

Smith, D. C. of Philadelphia, 3 Penn. Law Journal, 151, 153. A decree of divorce must also be made during the lifetime of both the parties. After the decease of either the marriage will be deemed as legal in all respects. Reeves' Dom. Rel. 204; 1 Bl. Com. 440. See Act of Pennsylvania, March 13, 1815, § 5.

2. Divorces are of two kinds; 1. *à vinculo matrimonii,* (q. v.) which dissolves and totally severs the marriage tie; and, 2. *à mensa et thoro,* (q. v.) which merely separates the parties.

3.—1. The divorce *à vinculo* was never granted by the ecclesiastical law, except for the most grave reasons. These, according to Lord Coke, (Co. Litt. 235, a,) are *causa præcontractus, causa metus, causa impotentiæ, seu frigiditatis, causa affinitatis, et causa consanguinitatis.* In England such a divorce bastardizes the issue, and generally speaking, is allowed only on the ground of some preëxisting cause. Reeves' Dom. Rel. 204–5; but sometimes by act of parliament for a supervenient cause. 1 Bl. Com. 440. When the marriage was dissolved for canonical causes of impediment, existing previous to its taking place, it was declared void *ab initio.*

4. In the United States, divorces *à vinculo* are granted by the state legislatures for such causes as may be sufficient to induce the members to vote in favor of granting them; and they are granted by the courts to which such jurisdiction is given, for certain causes particularly provided for by law.

5. In some states, the legislature never grants a divorce until after the courts have decreed one, and it is still requisite that the legislature shall act, to make the divorce valid. This is the case in Mississippi. In some states, as Wisconsin, the legislature cannot grant a divorce. Const. art. 4, s. 24.

6. The courts in nearly all the states have power to decree divorces *à vinculo,* for, first, causes which existed and which were a bar to a lawful marriage, as, precontract, or the existence of a marriage between one of the contracting parties and another person, at the time the marriage sought to be dissolved took place; consanguinity, or that degree of relationship forbidden by law; affinity in some states, as Vermont, Rev. Stat. tit. 16, c. 63, s. 1; impotence, (q. v.) idiocy, lunacy or other mental imbecility, which renders the party subject to it incapable of making a contract; when the contract was entered into in consequence of fraud. Secondly, the marriage may be dissolved by divorce for causes which have arisen since the formation of the contract, the principal of which are adultery; cruelty; wilful and malicious desertion for a period of time specified in the acts of the several states; to these are added, in some states, conviction of felony or other infamous crime; Ark. Rev. Stat. c. 50, s. 1, p. 333; being a fugitive from justice, when charged with an infamous crime. Laws of Lo. Act of April 2, 1832. In Tennessee the husband may obtain a divorce when the wife was pregnant at the time of marriage with a child of color; and also when the wife refuses for two years to follow her husband, who has gone *bona fide* to Tennessee to reside. Act of 1819, c. 20, and Act of 1835, c. 26; Carr. Nich. & Comp. 256, 257. In Kentucky and Maine, where one of the parties has formed a connexion with certain religionists, whose opinions and practices are inconsistent with the marriage duties. And, in some states, as Rhode Island and Vermont, for neglect and refusal on the part of the husband (he being of sufficient ability) to provide necessaries for the subsistence of his wife. In others, habitual drunkenness is a sufficient cause.

7. In some of the states divorces *a mensa et thoro* are granted for cruelty, desertion, and such like causes, while in others the divorce is *à vinculo.*

8. When the divorce is prayed for on the ground of adultery, in some and perhaps in most of the states, it is a good defence, 1st. That the other party has been guilty of the same offence. 2. That the husband has prostituted his wife, or connived at her amours. 3. That the offended party has been reconciled to the other by either express or implied condonation. (q. v.) 4. That there was no intention to commit adultery, as when the party, supposing his or her first husband or wife dead, married again. 5. That the wife was forced or ravished.

9. The effects of a divorce *à vinculo* on the property of the wife, are various in the several states. When the divorce is for the adultery or other criminal acts of the husband, in general the wife's lands are restored to her; when it is caused by the adultery or other criminal act of the wife, the husband has in general some qualified right of curtesy to her lands; when the

divorce is caused by some preëxisting cause, as consanguinity, affinity or impotence, in some states, as Maine and Rhode Island, the lands of the wife are restored to her. 1 Hill. Ab. 51, 2. See 2 Ashm. 455; 5 Blackf. 309. At common law, a divorce *à vinculo matrimonii* bars the wife of dower; Bract. lib. ii. cap. 39, § 4; but not a divorce *à mensa et thoro*, though for the crime of adultery. Yet by Stat. West. 1, 3 Ed. I. c. 34, elopement with an adulterer has this effect. Dyer, 195; Co. Litt. 32, a. n. 10; 3 P. Wms. 276, 277. If land be given to a man and his wife, and the heirs of their two bodies begotten, and they are divorced *à vinculo*, &c., they shall neither of them have this estate, but be barely tenants for life, notwithstanding the inheritance once vested in them. Co. Litt. 28. If a lease be made to husband and wife during coverture, and the husband sows the land, and afterwards they are divorced *à vinculo*, &c., the husband shall have the emblements in that case, for the divorce is the act of law. Mildmay's Case. As to personalty, the rule of the common law is, if one marry a woman who has goods, he may give them or sell them at his pleasure. If they are divorced, the woman shall have the goods back again, unless the husband has given them away or sold them; for in such case she is without remedy. If the husband aliened them by collusion, she may aver and prove the collusion, and thereupon recover the goods from the alienee. If one be bound in an obligation to a *feme sole*, and then marry her, and afterwards they are divorced, she may sue her former husband on the obligation, notwithstanding her action was in suspense during the marriage. And for such things as belonged to the wife before marriage, if they cannot be known, she could sue for, after divorce, only in the court Christian, for the action of account did not lie, because he was not her receiver to account. But for such things as remain in specie, and may be known, the common law gives her an action of detinue. 26 Hen. VIII. 1.

10. When a divorce *à vinculo* takes place, it is, in general, a bar to dower; but in Connecticut, Illinois, New York, and, it seems, in Michigan, dower is not barred by a divorce for the fault of the husband. In Kentucky, when a divorce takes place for the fault of the husband, the wife is entitled as if he were dead. 1 Hill. Ab. 61, 2.

11.—2. Divorces *à mensa et thoro*, are a mere separation of the parties for a time for causes arising since the marriage; they are pronounced by tribunals of competent jurisdiction. The effects of the sentence continue for the time it was pronounced, or until the parties are reconciled. A divorce *à mensa et thoro* deprives the husband of no marital right in respect to the property of the wife. Reeve's Dom. Rel. 204–5; Cro. Car. 462; but see 2 S. & R. 493. Children born after a divorce *à mensa et thoro* are not presumed to be the husband's, unless he afterwards cohabited with his wife. Bac. Ab. Marriage, &c. E.

12. By the civil law, the child of parents divorced, is to be brought up by the innocent party, at the expence of the guilty party. Ridley's View, part 1, ch. 3, sect. 9, cites 8th Collation.

Vide, generally, 1 Bl. Com. 440, 441; 3 Bl. Com. 94; 4 Vin. Ab. 205; 1 Bro. Civ. Law, 86; Ayl. Parerg. 225; Com. Dig. Baron and Feme, C; Coop. Justin. 434, et seq.; 6 Toullier, No. 294, pa. 308; 4 Yeates' Rep. 249; 5 Serg. & R. 375; 9 S. & R. 191, 3; Gospel of Luke, ch. xvi. v. 18; of Mark, ch. x. vs. 11, 12; of Matthew, ch. v. v. 32, ch. xix. v. 9; 1 Corinth. ch. vii. v. 15; Poynt. on Marr. and Divorce, Index, h. t.; Merl. Rép. h. t.; Clef des Lois Rom. h. t. As to the effect of the laws of a foreign state, where the divorce was decreed, see Story's Confl. of Laws, ch. 7, § 200. With regard to the ceremony of divorce among the Jews, see 1 Mann. & Gran. 228; S. C. 39 Eng. C. L. R. 425, 428. And as to divorces among the Romans, see Troplong, de l'Influence du Christianisme sur le Droit Civil des Romains, ch. 6. p. 205.

DOCKET, *practice*. A formal record of judicial proceedings.

2. The docket should contain the names of the parties, and a minute of every proceeding in the case. It is kept by the clerk or prothonotary of the court. A sheriff's docket is not a record. 9 Serg. & R. 91. Docket is also said to be a brief writing, on a small piece of paper or parchment, containing the substance of a larger writing.

DOCTORS COMMONS. A building in London used for a college of civilians. Here the judge of the court of arches, the judge of the admiralty, and the judge of the court of Canterbury, with other eminent civilians, reside. Commons signifies, in old English, pittance or allowance; because it is meant in common among societies, as Universities, Inns of Courts, Doctors Commons, &c. The Latin word is, demensum à demetiendo; dividing every one his part; Minsheu. It is called Doctors Commons, because the persons residing there live in a collegiate commoning together.

DOCUMENTS, *evidence.* The deeds, agreements, title papers, letters, receipts, and other written instruments used to prove a fact. Among the civilians, by documents is also understood evidence delivered in the forms established by law, of whatever nature such evidence may be, but applied principally to the testimony of witnesses. Savig. Dr. Rom. § 165.

2. Public documents are all such records, papers and acts, as are filed in the public offices of the United States or of the several states; as, for example, public statutes, public proclamations, resolutions of the legislature, the journals of either branch of the legislature, diplomatic correspondence communicated by the president to congress, and the like. These are in general evidence of the facts they contain or recite. 1 Greenl. § 491.

DOG. A well known domestic animal. In almost all languages this word is a term or name of contumely or reproach. See 3 Bulst. 226; 2 Mod. 260; 1 Leo. 148; and the title action on the case for defamation in the Digests; Minsheu's Dictionary.

2. A dog is said at common law to have no intrinsic value, and he cannot therefore be the subject of larceny. 4 Bl. Com. 236; 8 Serg. & Rawle, 571. But the owner has such property in him, that he may maintain trespass for an injury to his dog; "for a man may have property in some things which are of so base nature that no felony can be committed of them, as of a bloodhound or mastiff." 12 H. VIII. 3; 18 H. VIII. 2; 7 Co. 18 a; Com. Dig. Biens, F; 2 Bl. Com. 397; Bac. Ab. Trover, D; F. N. B. 86; Bro. Trespass, pl. 407; Hob. 283; Cro. Eliz. 125; Cro. Jac. 463; 2 Bl. Rep. 1117.

3. Dogs, if dangerous animals, may lawfully be killed, when their ferocity is known to their owner, or in self-defence; 13 John. R. 312; 10 John. R. 365; and when bitten by a rabid animal, a dog may be lawfully killed by any one. 13 John. R. 312.

4. When a dog, in consequence of his vicious habits, becomes a common nuisance, the owner may be indicted. And when he commits an injury, if the owner had a knowledge of his mischievous propensity, he is liable to an action on the case. Bull. N. P. 77; 2 Str. 1264; Lord Raym. 110; 1 B. & A. 620; 4 Camp. R. 198; 2 Esp. R. 482; 4 Cowen, 351; 6 S. & R. 36, Addis. R. 215; 1 Scam. 492; 23 Wend. 354; 17 Wend. 496; 4 Dev. & Batt. 146.

5. A man has a right to keep a dog to guard his premises, but not to put him at the entrance of his house, because a person coming there on lawful business may be injured by him, and this, though there may be another entrance to the house. 4 C. & P. 297; 6 C. & P. 1. But if a dog be chained, and a visitor so incautiously go near him that he is bitten, he has no right of action against the owner. 3 Chit. Bl. 154, n. 7. Vide *Animal; Knowledge; Scienter.*

DOGMA, *civil law.* This word is used in the first chapter, first section, of the second Novel, and signifies an ordinance of the senate. See also Dig. 27, 1, 6.

DOLI CAPAX. Capable of deceit, mischief, having knowledge of right and wrong. See *Discretion; Criminal law,* 2.

DOLLAR, *money.* A silver coin of the United States of the value of one hundred cents, or tenth part of an eagle.

2. It weighs four hundred and twelve and a half grains. Of one thousand parts, nine hundred are of pure silver and one hundred of alloy. Act of January 18, 1837, ss. 8 & 9, 4 Sharsw. Cont. of Story's L. U. S. 2523, 4; Wright, R. 162.

3. In all computations at the custom house, the specie dollar of Sweden and Norway shall be estimated at one hundred and six cents. The specie dollar of Denmark, at one hundred and five cents. Act of May 22, 1846.

DOLUS, *civil law.* A fraudulent address or trick used to deceive some one; a fraud. Dig. 4, 3, 1; Code, 2, 21.

2. Dolus differs from fault in this, that the latter proceeds from an error of the understanding; while to constitute the former, there must be a will or intention to do wrong. Wolff, Inst. § 17.

DOMAIN. It signifies sometimes, dominion, territory governed—sometimes, possession, estate—and sometimes, land about the mansion house of a lord. By *domain* is also understood the right to dispose at our pleasure of what belongs to us.

2. A distinction has been made between property and domain. The former is said to be that quality which is conceived to be in the thing itself, considered as belonging

to such or such person, exclusively of all others. By the latter is understood that right which the owner has of disposing of the thing. Hence domain and property are said to be correlative terms; the one is the active right to dispose, the other a passive quality which follows the thing, and places it at the disposition of the owner. 3 Toull. n. 83. But this distinction is too subtle for practical use. Puff. Droit de la Nature et des Gens, loi 4, c. 4, § 2. Vide 1 Bl. Com. 105, 106; 1 Bouv. Inst. n. 456; Clef des Lois Rom. h. t.; Domat, h. t.; 1 Hill. Ab. 24; 2 Hill. Ab. 237; and *Demesne as of fee; Property; Things.*

DOME-BOOK, DOOM-BOOK, or DOM-BEC. A book in which Alfred the Great, of England, after uniting the Saxon heptarchy, collected the various customs dispersed through the kingdom, and digested them into one uniform code. 4 Bl. Com. 411.

DOMESDAY, or DOMESDAY-BOOK. An ancient record made in the time of William the Conqueror, and now remaining in the English exchequer, consisting of two volumes of unequal sizes, containing surveys of the lands in England.

DOMESTICS. Those who reside in the same house with the master they serve: the term does not extend to workmen or laborers employed out of doors. 5 Binn. R. 167; Merl. Rép. h. t. The Act of Congress of April 30, 1790, s. 25, uses the word domestic in this sense.

2. Formerly, this word was used to designate those who resided in the house of another, however exalted their station, and who performed services for him. Voltaire, in writing to the French queen, in 1748, says, "Deign to consider, madam, that I am one of the domestics of the king, and consequently yours, my companions, the gentlemen of the king," &c.

3. Librarians, secretaries, and persons in such honorable employments, would not probably be considered domestics, although they might reside in the house of their respective employers.

4. Pothier, to point out the distinction between a domestic and a servant, gives the following example: A literary man who lives and lodges with you, solely to be your companion, that you may profit by his conversation and learning, is your domestic; for all who live in the same house and eat at the same table with the owner of the house, are his domestics, but they are not *servants.* On the contrary, your valet de chambre, to whom you pay wages, and who sleeps out of your house, is not, properly speaking, your domestic, but your servant. Poth. Proc. Cr. sect. 2, art. 5, § 5; Poth. Ob. 710, 828; 9 Toull. n. 314; H. De Pansey, Des Justices de Paix, c. 30, n. 1. Vide *Operative; Servant.*

DOMICIL. The place where a person has fixed his ordinary dwelling, without a present intention of removal. 10 Mass. 488; 8 Cranch, 278; Ersk. Pr. of Law of Scotl. B. 1, tit. 2, s. 9; Denisart, tit. Domicile, 1, 7, 18, 19; Voet, Pandect, lib. 5, tit. 1, 92, 97; 5 Madd. Ch. R. 379; Merl. Rép. tit. Domicile; 1 Binn. 349, n.; 4 Humph. 346. The law of domicil is of great importance in those countries where the maxim "actor sequitur forum rei" is applied to the full extent. Code Civil, art. 102, &c.; 1 Toullier, 318.

2. A man cannot be without a domicil, for he is not supposed to have abandoned his last domicil until he has acquired a new one. 5 Ves. 587; 3 Robins. 191; 1 Binn. 349, n.; 10 Pick. 77. Though by the Roman law a man might abandon his domicil, and, until he acquired a new one, he was without a domicil. By fixing his residence at two different places a man may have two domicils at one and the same time; as, for example, if a foreigner, coming to this country, should establish two houses, one in New York and the other in New Orleans, and pass one-half of the year in each; he would, for most purposes, have two domicils. But it is to be observed that circumstances which might be held sufficient to establish a commercial domicil in time of war, and a matrimonial, or forensic or political domicil in time of peace, might not be such as would establish a principal or testamentary domicil, for there is a wide difference in applying the law of domicil to contracts and to wills. Phill. on Dom. xx; 11 Pick. 410; 10 Mass. 488; 4 Wash. C. C. R. 514.

3. There are three kinds of domicils, namely: 1. The domicil of origin, *domicilium originis* vel *naturale.* 2. The domicil by operation of law, or necessary domicil. 3. Domicil of choice.

4.—§ 1. By domicil of origin is understood the home of a man's parents, not the place where, the parents being on a visit or journey, a child happens to be born. 2 B. & P. 231, note; 3 Ves. 198. Domicil of origin is to be distinguished from the accidental place of birth. 1 Binn. 349.

5.—§ 2. There are two classes of persons who acquire domicil by operation of law. 1st. Those who are under the control of another, and to whom the law gives the domicil of another. Among these are, 1. The wife. 2. The minor. 3. The lunatic, &c. 2d. Those on whom the state affixes a domicil. Among this class are found, 1. The officer. 2. The prisoner, &c.

6.—1st. Among those who, being under the control of another, acquire such person's domicil, are, 1. The wife. The wife takes the domicil of her husband, and the widow retains it, unless she voluntarily change it, or unless she marry a second time, when she takes the domicil of the second husband. A party may have two domicils, the one actual, the other legal; the husband's actual and the wife's legal domicil, are, prima facie, one. Addams' Ecc. R. 5, 19. 2. The domicil of the minor is that of the father, or in case of his death, of the mother. 5 Ves. 787; 2 W. & S. 568; 3 Ohio R. 101; 4 Greenl. R. 47. 3. The domicil of a lunatic is regulated by the same principles which operate in cases of minors; the domicil of such a person may be changed by the direction, or with the assent of the guardian, express or implied. 5 Pick. 20.

7.—2d. The law affixes a domicil. 1. Public officers, such as the president of the United States, the secretaries and such other officers whose public duties require a temporary residence at the capital, retain their domicils. Ambassadors preserve the domicils which they have in their respective countries, and this privilege extends to the ambassador's family. Officers, soldiers, and marines, in the service of the United States, do not lose their domicils while thus employed. 2. A prisoner does not acquire a domicil where the prison is, nor lose his old. 1 Milw. R. 191, 2.

8.—§ 3. The domicil of origin, which has already been explained, remains until another has been acquired. In order to change such domicil, there must be an actual removal with an intention to reside in the place to which the party removes. 3 Wash. C. C. R. 546. A mere intention to remove, unless such intention is carried into effect, is not sufficient. 5 Greenl. R. 143. When he changes it, he acquires a domicil in the place of his new residence, and loses his original domicil. But upon a return with an intention to reside, his original domicil is restored. 3 Rawle, 312; 1 Gallis. 274, 284; 5 Rob. Adm R. 99.

9. How far a settlement in a foreign country will impress a hostile character on a merchant, see Chitty's Law of Nations, 31 to 50; 1 Kent, Com. 74 to 80; 13 L. R. 296; 8 Cranch, 363; 7 Cranch, 506; 2 Cranch, 64; 9 Cranch, 191; 1 Wheat. 46; 2 Wheat. 76; 3 Wheat. 14; 2 Gall. R. 268; 2 Pet. Adm. Dec. 438; 1 Gall. R. 274. As to its effect in the administration of the assets of a deceased non-resident, see 3 Rawle's R. 312; 3 Pick. R. 128; 2 Kent, Com. 348; 10 Pick. R. 77. The law of Louisiana relating to the "domicil and the manner of changing the same" will be found in the Civil Code of Louisiana, tit. 2, art. 42 to 49. See, also, 8 M. R. 709; 4 N. S. 51; 6 N. S. 467; 2 L. R. 35; 4 L. R. 69; 5 N. S. 385; 5 L. R. 332; 8 L. R. 315; 13 L. R. 297; 11 L. R. 178; 12 L. R. 190.

See, on the subject generally, Bouv. Inst. Index, h. t.; 2 Bos. & Pul. 230, note; 1 Mason's Rep. 411; Toullier, Droit Civil Français, liv. 1, tit. 3, n. 362 à 378; Domat, tome 2, liv. 1, s. 3; Pothier, Introduction Générale aux Coutumes, n. 8 à 20; 1 Ashm. R. 126; Merl. Rép. tit. Domicile; 3 Meriv. R. 79; 5 Ves. 786; 1 Crompt. & J. 151; 1 Tyrwh. R. 91; 2 Tyrwh. R. 475; 2 Crompt. & J. 436; 3 Wheat. 14; 3 Rawle, 312; 7 Cranch, 506; 9 Cranch, 388; 5 Pick. 20; 1 Gallis, 274, 545; 10 Mass. 488; 11 Mass. 424; 13 Mass. 501; 2 Greenl. 411; 3 Greenl. 229, 354; 4 Greenl. 47; 8 Greenl. 203; 5 Greenl. 143, 4 Mason, 308; 3 Wash. C. C. R. 546; 4 Wash. C. C. R. 514; 4 Wend. 602; 8 Wend. 134; 5 Pick. 370; 10 Pick. 77; 11 Pick. 410; 1 Binn. 349, n.; Phil. on Dom. *passim*.

DOMINANT, *estates*. In the civil law, this term is used to signify the estate to which a servitude or easement is due from another estate; for example, where the owners of the estate, Blackacre, have a right of way or passage over the estate Whiteacre, the former is called the dominant, and the latter the servient estate. 2 Bouv. Inst. n. 1600.

DOMINION. The right of the owner of a thing to use it or dispose of it at his pleasure. See *Domain;* 1 White's New Coll. 85; Jacob's Intr. 39.

DOMINIUM, *empire, domain*. It is of three kinds: 1. *Directum dominium*, or usufructuary dominion; *dominium utile*, as between landlord and tenenant; or, 2. It is to full property and simple property. The former is such as belongs to the cultivator of his own estate; the other is the property of a tenant. 3. Dominion acquired by the law of nations, and dominion acquired by municipal law. By the law of nations, property may be acquired by occupation, by accession, by commixtion, by use or the pernancy of the usufruct, and by tradition or delivery. As to the *dominium eminens*, the right of the public, in cases of emergency, to seize upon the property of individuals, and convert it to public use, and the right of individuals, in similar cases, to commit a trespass on the persons and properties of others, see the opinion of chief justice McKean in Respublica *v.* Sparhawk, 1 Dallas, 362, and the case of Vanhorn *v.* Dorrance, 2 Dall. Rep. 304. See, further, as to dominium eminens, or the right of the community to take, at a fair price, the property of individuals for public use, the supplement of 1802 to the Pennsylvania compromising law, respecting the Wyoming controversy; also, Vattel, l. 1, c. 20, §§ 244–248; Bynkershoek, lib. 2, c. 15; Rousseau's Social Compact, c. 9; Domat, l. 1, tit. 8, § 1, p. 381, fol. ed.; the case of a Jew, whom the grand seignior was compelled by the mufti to purchase out, cited in Lindsay et al. *v.* The Commissioners, 2 Bay. S. Car. Rep. 41. See *Eminent domain.*

DOMITÆ. Subdued, tame, not wild; as, animals domitæ, which are tame or domestic animals.

DOMO REPARANDO. The name of an ancient writ in favor of a party who was in danger of being injured by the fall of his neighbor's house.

DONATIO MORTIS CAUSA, *contracts, legacies.* A gift in prospect of death. When a person in sickness, apprehending his dissolution near, delivers, or causes to be delivered to another, the possession of any personal goods, to keep as his own, in case of the donor's decease. 2 Bl. Com. 514; see Civ. Code of Lou. art. 1455.

2. The civil law defines it to be a gift under apprehension of death; as, when any thing is given upon condition that if the donor dies, the donee shall possess it absolutely, or return it if the donor should survive, or should repent of having made the gift, or if the donee should die before the donor. 1 Miles' Rep. 109–117.

3. Donations mortis causâ, are now reduced, as far as possible, to the similitude of legacies. Inst. t. 7, De Donationibus. See 2 Ves. jr. 119; Smith *v.* Casen, mentioned by the reporter at the end of Drury *v.* Smith, 1 P. Wms. 406; 2 Ves. sen. 434; 3 Binn. 366.

4. With respect to the nature of a donatio mortis causâ, this kind of gift so far resembles a legacy, that it is ambulatory and incomplete during the donor's life; it is, therefore, revocable by him; 7 Taunt. 231; 3 Binn. 366; and subject to his debts upon a deficiency of assets. 1 P. Wms. 405. But in the following particulars it differs from a legacy: it does not fall within an administration, nor require any act in the executors to perfect a title in the donee. Rop. Leg. 26.

5. The following circumstances are required to constitute a good donatio mortis causâ. 1st. That the thing given be personal property; 3 Binn. 370; a bond; 3 Binn. 370; 3 Madd. R. 184; bank notes; 2 Bro. C. C. 612; and a check offered for payment during the life of the donor, will be so considered. 4 Bro. C. C. 286.

6.—2d. That the gift be made by the donor in peril of death, and to take effect only in case the giver die. 3 Binn. 370; 4 Burn's Ecc. Law, 110.

7.—3d. That there be an actual delivery of the subject to, or for the donee, in cases where such delivery can be made. 3 Binn. 370; 2 Ves. jr. 120. See 9 Ves. 1, 7 Taunt. 224. But such delivery can be made to a third person for the use of the donee. 3 Binn. 370.

8. It is an unsettled question whether such kind of gift appearing in writing, without delivery of the subject, can be supported. 2 Ves. jr. 120. By the Roman and civil law, a gift mortis causâ, might be made in writing. Dig. lib. 39, t. 6, l. 28; 2 Ves. sen. 440; 1 Ves. sen. 314.

9. In Louisiana, no disposition mortis causâ, otherwise than by last will and testament, is allowed. Civ. Code, art. 1563.

See, in general, 1 Fonb. Tr. Eq. 288, n. (p); Coop. Just. 474, 492; Civ. Code of Lo. B. 3, 2, c. 1 and 6. Vin. Abr. Executors, Z 4; Bac. Abr. Legacies, A; Supp. to Ves. jr. vol. 1, p. 143, 170; vol. 2, 97, 215; Rop. Leg. ch. 1; Swinb. pt. 1, s. 7; 1 Miles, 109. &c.

DONATION, *contracts.* The act by which the owner of a thing, voluntarily transfers the title and possession of the same, from himself to another person, without any consideration; a gift. (q. v.)

2. A donation is never perfected until it is has been accepted, for the acceptance (q. v.) is requisite to make the donation complete. Vide *Assent*, and Ayl. Pand. tit. 9; Clef des Lois Rom. h. t.

DONATION INTER VIVOS, *contracts*. A contract which takes place by the mutual consent, of the giver, who divests himself of the thing given in order to transmit the title of it to the donee gratuitously, and the donee, who accepts the thing and acquires a legal title to it.

2. This donation takes place when the giver is not in any immediate apprehension of death, which distinguishes it from a *donatio mortis causâ*. (q. v.) 1 Bouv. Inst. n. 712. And see Civ. Code of Lo. art. 1453; Justin. Inst. lib. 2, tit. 7, § 2; Coop. Justin. notes 474–5; Johns. Dig. N. Y. Rep. tit. Gift.

DONEE. He to whom a gift is made, or a bequest given; one who is invested with a power to select an appointee, he is sometimes called an appointer.

DONIS, STATUTE DE. The stat. West. 2, namely, 13 Edw. I., c. 1, called the statute *de donis conditionalibus*. This statute revives, in some sort, the ancient feudal restraints, which were originally laid on alienations. 2 Bl. Com. 12.

DONOR. He who makes a gift. (q. v.)

DOOM. This word formerly signified a judgment. T. L.

DORMANT PARTNER. One who is a participant in the profits of a firm, but his name being concealed, his interest is not apparent. See *Partners*.

DOOR. The place of usual entrance in a house, or into a room in the house.

2. To authorize the breach of an outer door in order to serve process, the process must be of a criminal nature; and even then a demand of admittance must first have been refused. 5 Co. 93; 4 Leon. 41; T. Jones, 234; 1 N. H. Rep. 346; 10 John. 263; 1 Root, 83, 134; 21 Pick. R. 156. The outer door may also be broken open for the purpose of executing a writ of *habere facias*. 5 Co. 93; Bac. Ab. Sheriff, N. 3.

3. An outer door cannot in general be broken for the purpose of serving civil process; 13 Mass. 520; but after the defendant has been arrested, and he takes refuge in his own house, the officer may justify breaking an outer door to take him. Foster, 320; 1 Roll. R. 138, Cro. Jac. 555; 10 Wend. 300; 6 Hill, N. Y. Rep. 597. When once an officer is in the house, he may break open an inner door to make an arrest. Kirby, 386; 5 John. 352; 17 John. 127 See 1 Toull. n. 214, p. 88.

DOT. This French word is adopted in Louisiana. It signifies the fortune, portion, or dowry, which a woman brings to her husband by the marriage. 6 N. S. 460. See *Dote; Dowry*.

DOTAL PROPERTY. By the civil law, and in Louisiana, by this term is understood that property which the wife brings to the husband to assist him in bearing the expenses of the marriage establishment. Civil Code of Lo. art. 2315. Vide *Extra-dotal property*.

DOTATION, *French law*. The act by which the founder of a hospital, or other charity, endows it with property to fulfil its destination.

DOTE, *Span. law*. The property which the wife gives to the husband on account of marriage.

2. It is divided into *adventitia* and *profectitia;* the former is the dote which the father or grandfather, or other of the ascendants in the direct paternal line, give of their own property to the husband; the latter (*adventitia*) is that property which the wife gives to the husband, or that which is given to him for her by her mother, or her collateral relations, or a stranger. Aso & Man. Inst. B. 1, t. 7, c. 1, § 1.

DOTE ASSIGNANDO, *Eng. law*. The name of a writ which lay in favor of a widow, when it was found by office that the king's tenant was seised of tenements in fee or fee tail at the time of his death, and that he held of the king in chief.

DOTE UNDE NIHIL HABET. The name of a writ of dower which a widow sues against the tenant, who bought land of her husband in his lifetime, and in which her dower remains, of which he was seised solely in fee simple or fee tail. F. N. B. 147; Booth, Real Act. 166. See *Dower unde nihil habet*

DOUBLE. Twofold; as, double cost, double insurance; double plea.

DOUBLE COSTS, *practice*. According to the English law, when double costs are given by the statute, the term is not to be understood, according to its literal import, twice the amount of single costs, but in such case the costs are thus calculated. 1. the common costs; and, 2. *Half* of the common costs. Bac. Ab. Costs, E; 2 Str. 1048. This is not the rule in New York, nor in Pennsylvania. 2 Dunl. Pr. 731; 2 Rawle's R. 201.

2. In all cases where double or treble costs are claimed, the party must apply to the court for them before he can proceed to the taxation, otherwise the proceedings will be set aside as irregular. 4 Wend. R. 216. Vide *Costs;* and *Treble Costs*.

DOUBLE ENTRY. A term used among merchants to signify that books of account are kept in such a manner that they present the debit and credit of every thing. The term is used in contradistinction to *single entry*.

2. Keeping books by double entry is more exact, because, presenting all the active and all the passive property of the merchant, in their respective divisions, there cannot be placed an article to an account, which does not pass to some correspondent account elsewhere. It presents a perfect view of each operation, and, from the relation and comparison of the divers accounts, which always keep pace with each other, their correctness is proved; for every commercial operation is necessarily composed of two interests, which are connected together. The basis of this mode of keeping books, and the only condition required, is to write down every transaction and nothing else; and to make no entry without putting it down to the two agents of the operation. By this means a merchant whose transactions are extensive, comprising a great number of subjects, is able to know not only the general situation of his affairs, but also the situation of each particular operation. For example, when a merchant receives money, his cash account becomes debtor, and the person who has paid it, or the merchandise sold, is credited with it; when he pays money, the cash account is credited, and the merchandise bought, or the obligation paid, is debited with it. See *Single entry*.

DOUBLE INSURANCE, *contracts*. Where the insured makes two insurances on the same risk, and the same interest. 12 Mass. 214. It differs from re-insurance in this, that it is made by the insured, with a view of receiving a double satisfaction in case of loss; whereas a re-insurance is made by a former insurer, his executors or assigns, to protect himself and his estate from a risk to which they were liable by the first insurance. The two policies are considered as making but one insurance. They are good to the extent of the value of the effects put in risk; but the insured shall not be permitted to recover a double satisfaction. He can sue the underwriters on both the policies, but he can only recover the real amount of his loss, to which all the underwriters on both shall contribute in proportion to their several subscriptions. Marsh. Ins. B. 1, c. 4, s. 4; 5 S. & R. 473; 4 Dall. 348; 1 Yeates, 161; 9 S. & R. 103; 1 Wash. C. C. Rep. 419; 2 Wash. C. C. Rep. 186; 2 Mason, 475.

DOUBLE PLEA. The alleging, for one single purpose, two or more distinct grounds of defence, when one of them would be as effectual in law, as both or all. Vide *Duplicity*.

DOUBLE VOUCHER. A common recovery is sometimes suffered with double voucher, which occurs when the person first vouched to warranty, comes in and vouches over a third person. See a precedent, 2 Bl. Com. Appx. No. V. p. xvii.; also, *Voucher*.

2. The necessity for double voucher arises when the tenant in tail is not the tenant in the writ, but is tenant by warranty; that is, where he is vouched, and comes in and confesses the warranty. Generally speaking, to accomplish this result, a previous conveyance is necessary, by the tenant in tail, to a third person, in order to make such third person tenant to a writ of entry. Preston on Convey. 125–6.

DOUBLE WASTE. When a tenant, bound to repair, suffers a house to be wasted, and then unlawfully fells timber to repair it, he is said to commit double waste. Co. Litt. 53. See *Waste*.

DOUBT. The uncertainty which exists in relation to a fact, a proposition, or other thing; or it is an equipoise of the mind arising from an equality of contrary reasons. Ayl. Pand. 121.

2. The embarrassing position of a judge is that of being in doubt, and it is frequently the lot of the wisest and most enlightened to be in this condition; those who have little or no experience usually find no difficulty in deciding the most problematical questions.

3. Some rules, not always infallible, have been adopted in doubtful cases, in order to arrive at the truth. 1. In civil cases, the doubt ought to operate against him, who having it in his power to prove facts to remove the doubt, has neglected to do so. In cases of fraud when there is a doubt, the presumption of innocence (q. v.) ought to remove it. 2. In criminal cases, whenever a reasonable doubt exists as to the guilt of the accused, that doubt ought to operate in his favor. In such cases,

particularly, when the liberty, honor or life of an individual is at stake, the evidence to convict ought to be clear, and devoid of all reasonable doubt. See Best on Pres. § 195; Wils. on Cir. Ev. 26; Theory of Presumptive Proof, 64; 33 How. St. Tr. 506; Burnett, Cr. Law of Scotl. 522; 1 Greenl. Ev. § 1; D'Aguesseau, Œuvres, vol. xiii. p. 242; Domat, liv. 3, tit. 6.

4. No judge is presumed to have any doubt on a question of law, and he cannot therefore refuse to give a judgment on that account. 9 M. R. 355; Merlin, Répert. h. t.; Ayliffe's Pand. b. 2, t. 17; Dig. lib. 34, t. 5; Code, lib. 6, t. 38. Indeed, in some countries; in China, for example, ignorance of the law in a judge is punishable with blows. Penal Laws of China, B. 2, s. 61.

DOVE. The name of a well known bird.

2. Doves are animals *feræ naturæ*, and not the subject of larceny, unless they are in the owner's custody; as, for example, in a dove-house, or when in the nest before they can fly. 9 Pick. 15. See *Whelp*.

DOWAGER. A widow endowed; one who has a jointure.

2. In England, this is a title or addition given to the widows of princes, dukes, earls, and other noblemen.

DOWER. An estate for life, which the law gives the widow in the third part of the lands and tenements, or hereditaments of which the husband was solely seised, at any time during the coverture, of an estate in fee or in tail, in possession, and to which estate in the lands and tenements, the issue, if any, of such widow might, by possibility, have inherited. Watk. Prin. Con. 38; Litt. § 36; 7 Greenl. 383. Vide *Estate in Dower*. This is dower at common law.

2. Besides this, in England there are three other species of dower now subsisting; namely, dower by custom, which is, where a widow becomes entitled to a certain portion of her husband's lands in consequence of some local or particular custom; thus by the custom of gavelkind, the widow is entitled to a moiety of all the lands and tenements, which her husband held by that tenure.

3. Dower *ad ostium ecclesiæ*, is, when a man comes to the church door to be married, after troth plighted, endows his wife of a certain portion of his lands.

4. Dower *ex assensu patris*, was only a species of dower *ad ostium ecclesiæ*, made when the husband's father was alive, and the son, with his consent expressly given, endowed his wife, at the church door, of a certain part of his father's lands.

5. There was another kind, *de la plus belle*, to which the abolition of military tenures has put an end. Vide Cruise's Dig. t. 6, c. 1; 2 Bl. Com. 129; 15 Serg. & Rawle, 72; Poth. Du Douaire.

6. Dower is barred in various ways; 1. By the adultery of the wife, unless it has been condoned. 2. By a jointure settled upon the wife. 2 Paige, R. 511. 3. By the wife joining her husband in a conveyance of the estate. 4. By the husband and wife levying a fine, or suffering a common recovery. 10 Co. 49, b; Plowd. 504. 5. By a divorce *à vinculo matrimonii*. 6. By an acceptance, by the wife, of a collateral satisfaction, consisting of land, money, or other chattel interest, given instead of it by the husband's will, and accepted after the husband's death. In these cases she has a right to elect whether to take her dower or the bequest or devise. 4 Monr. R. 265; 5 Monr. R. 58; 4 Desaus. R. 146; 2 M'Cord, Ch. R. 280; 7 Cranch, R. 370; 5 Call, R. 481; 1 Edw. R. 435; 3 Russ. R. 192; 2 Dana, R. 342.

7. In some of the United States, the estate which the wife takes in the lands of her deceased husband, varies essentially from the right of dower at common law. In some of the states, she takes one-third of the profits, or in case of there being no children, one half. In others she takes the same right in fee, when there are no lineal descendants; and in one she takes two-thirds in fee, when there are no lineal ascendants or descendants, or brother or sister of the whole or half blood. 1 Hill. Ab. 57, 8; see Bouv. Inst. Index, h. t.

DOWER UNDE NIHIL HABET. This is a writ of right in its nature. It lies only against the tenant of the freehold. 12 Mass. 415; 2 Saund. 43, note 1; Hen. & Munf. 368; F. N. B. 148. It is a writ of entry, where the widow is deforced of the whole of her dower. Archb. Plead. 466, 7. A writ of right of dower lies for the whole or a part. 1 Rop. on Prop. 430; Steph. on Pl. 10. n; Booth, R. A. 166; Glanv. lib 4. c. 4, 5; 9 S. & R. 367. If the heir is fourteen years of age, the writ goes to him, if not, to his guardian. If the land be wholly aliened, it goes to the tenant, F. N. B. 7, or pernor of the profits, who may vouch the heir. If part only be aliened, the writ goes to the heir or guardian. The tenant cannot imparl; 2 Saund. 44, n; 1 Rop. on Prop. 430; the remedy being speedy. Fleta, lib. 5. c. 25, § 8, p. 427. He pleads without defence. Rast. Ent. 232, b. lib. Int. fo. 15; Steph. Pl. 431; Booth, 118; Jackson on Pl. 319.

DOWRESS. A woman entitled to dower.

2. In order to entitle a woman to the rights of a dowress at common law, she must have been lawfully married, her husband must be dead, he must have been seised, during the coverture, of an estate subject to dower. Although the marriage may be voidable, if it is not absolutely void at his death, it is sufficient to support the rights of the dowress. The husband and wife must have been of sufficient age to consent.

3. At common law an alien could not be endowed, but this rule has been changed in several states. 2 John. Cas. 29; 1 Harr. & Gill, 280; 1 Cowen, R. 89; 8 Cowen, R. 713.

4. The dowress' right may be defeated when her husband was not *of right* seised of an estate of inheritance; as, for example, dower will be defeated upon the restoration of the seisin under the prior title in the case of defeasible estates, as in case of reëntry for a condition broken, which abolishes the intermediate seisin. Perk. s. 311, 312, 317.

DOWRY. Formerly applied to mean that which a woman brings to her husband in marriage; this is now called a portion. This word is sometimes confounded with dower. Vide Co. Litt. 31; Civ. Code of Lo. art. 2317; Dig. 23, 3, 76; Code, 5, 12, 20.

DRAGOMAN. An interpreter employed in the east, and particularly at the Turkish court.

2. The Act of Congress of August 26, 1842, c. 201, s. 8, declares that it shall not be lawful for the president of the United States to allow a dragoman at Constantinople, a salary of more than two thousand five hundred dollars.

DRAIN. Conveying the water from one place to another, for the purpose of drying the former.

2. The right of draining water through another man's land. This is an easement or servitude acquired by grant or prescription. Vide 3 Kent, Com. 436; 7 Mann. & Gr. 354; *Jus aquæductus; Rain water; Stillicidium.*

DRAWBACK, *com. law.* An allowance made by the government to merchants on the reëxportation of certain imported goods liable to duties, which, in some cases, consists of the whole; in others, of a part of the duties which had been paid upon the importation. For the various acts of congress which regulate drawbacks, see Story, L. U. S. Index, h. t.

DRAWEE. A person to whom a bill of exchange is addressed, and who is requested to pay the amount of money therein mentioned.

2. The drawee may be only one person, or there may be several persons. The drawee may be a third person, or a man may draw a bill on himself. 18 Ves. jr. 69; Carth. 509; 1 Show. 163; 3 Burr. 1077.

3. The drawee should accept or refuse to accept the bill at furthest within twenty-four hours after presentment. 2 Smith's R. 243; 1 Ld. Raym. 281; Com. Dig. Merchant, F 6; Marius, 15; but it is said the holder is entitled to a definite answer if the mail go out in the meantime. Marius, 62. In case the bill has been left with the drawee for his acceptance, he will be considered as having accepted it, if he keep the bill a great length of time, or do any other act which gives credit to the bill, and induces the holder not to protest it; or is intended as a surprise upon him, and to induce him to consider the bill as accepted. Chit. on Bills, 227. When he accepts it, it is his duty to pay it at maturity.

DRAWER, *contracts.* The party who makes a bill of exchange.

2. The obligations of the drawer to the drawee and every subsequent holder lawfully entitled to the possession, are, that the person on whom he draws is capable of binding himself by his acceptance; that he is to be found at the place where he is described to reside, if a description be given in the bill; that if the bill be duly presented to him, he will accept in writing on the bill itself, according to its tenor, and that he will pay it when it becomes due, if presented in proper time for that purpose; and that if the drawee fail to do either, he, the drawer, will pay the amount, provided he have due notice of the dishonor.

3. The engagement of the drawer of a bill is in all its parts absolute and irrevocable. 2 H. Bl. 378; 3 B. & P. 291; Poth Contr. de Change, n. 58; Chit. Bills, 214 Dane's Ab. h. t.

DRAWING. A representation on paper, card, or other substance.

2. The Act of Congress of July 4, 1836, section 6, requires all persons who apply for letters patent for an invention, to accompany their petitions or specifications with a drawing or drawings of the whole, and written references, when the nature of the case admits of drawings.

DREIT. The same as *Droit*. (q. v.)

DRIFTWAY. A road or way over which cattle are driven. 1 Taunt. R. 279; Selw. N. P. 1037; Wool. on Ways, 1.

DRIP. The right of drip is an easement by which the water which falls on one house is allowed to fall upon the land of another.

2. Unless the owner has acquired the right by grant or prescription, he has no right so to construct his house as to let the water drip over his neighbor's land. 1 Roll. Ab. 107. Vide *Rain water; Stillicidium;* and 3 Kent, Com. 436; Dig. 43, 23, 4 et 6; 11 Ad. & Ell. 40; S. C. 39 E. C. L. R. 21.

DRIVER. One employed in conducting a coach, carriage, wagon, or other vehicle, with horses, mules, or other animals.

2. Frequent accidents occur in consequence of the neglect or want of skill of drivers of public stage coaches, for which the employers are responsible.

3. The law requires that a driver should possess reasonable skill and be of good habits for the journey; if, therefore, he is not acquainted with the road he undertakes to drive; 3 Bingh. Rep. 314, 321; drives with reins so loose that he cannot govern his horses; 2 Esp. R. 533; does not give notice of any serious danger on the road; 1 Camp. R. 67; takes the wrong side of the road; 4 Esp. R. 273; incautiously comes in collision with another carriage; 1 Stark. R. 423; 1 Campb. R. 167; or does not exercise a sound and reasonable discretion in travelling on the road, to avoid dangers and difficulties, and any accident happens by which any passenger is injured, both the driver and his employers will be responsible. 2 Stark. R. 37; 3 Engl. C. L. Rep. 233; 2 Esp. R. 533; 11 Mass. 57; 6 T. R. 659; 1 East, R. 106; 4 B. & A. 590; 6 Eng. C. L. R. 528; 2 McLean, R. 157. Vide *Common carriers; Negligence; Quasi Offence.*

DROIT. A French word, which, in that language, signifies the whole collection of laws, written and unwritten, and is synonymous to our word law. It also signifies a right, il n'existe point de droits sans devoirs, et *vice versâ*. 1 Toull. n. 96; Poth. h. t. With us it means right, *jus*. Co. Litt. 158. A person was said to have *droit droit, plurimum juris*, and *plurimum possessionis*, when he had the freehold, the fee, and the property in him. Id. 266; Crabb's H. Eng. L. 400.

Droit d'accession, *French civil law*. Specificatio. That property which is acquired by making a new species out of the material of another. Modus acquirendi quo quis ex alienâ materiâ suo nomine novam speciem faciens bona fide ejus speciei dominium cónsequitur. It is a rule of the civil law, that if the thing can be reduced to the former matter, it belongs to the owner of the matter, *e. g.* a statue made of gold, but if it cannot so be reduced, it belongs to the person who made it, *e. g.* a statue made of marble. This subject is treated of in the Code Civil de Napoleon, art. 565 to 577; Merlin Repértoire de Jurisp. *Accession;* Malleville's Discussion, art. 565. The Code Napoleon follows closely the Inst. of Just. lib. 2, tit. 1, §§ 25, 28.

2. Doddridge, in his English Lawyer, 125–6, states the common law thus: "If a man take, *wrongfully*, the material which was mine and is permanént, not adding anything thereunto than the form, only by alteration thereof, such thing, so newly formed by an exterior form, notwithstanding, still remaineth mine, and may be seized again by me, and I may take it out of his possession as mine own. But they say, if he add some other matter thereunto; as, of another man's leather doth make shoes or boots, or of my cloth, maketh garments, adding to the accomplishment thereof of his own, he hath thereby altered the property, so that the first owner cannot seize the thing so composed, but is driven to his action to recover his remedy: howbeit, he adds, in a case of that nature depending, the court had determined that the first owner might seize the same, notwithstanding such addition. But if the thing be transitory in its nature by the change, as if one take my corn or meal, and thereof make bread, I cannot, in that case, seize the bread, because, as the civil law speaketh, hæc species facta ex materia aliena, in pristinam formam reduci non potest, ergo ei à quo est facta cedit. So some have said, if a man take my barley, and thereof make malt, because it is changed into another nature, it cannot be seized by

me; but the rule is: That where the material *wrongfully* taken away, could not at first, before any alteration, be seized; for that it could not be distinguished from other things of that kind, as corn, money, and such like; there those things cannot be seized, because the property of those things cannot be distinguished: for, if my money be wrongfully taken away, and he that taketh it do make plate thereof, or do convert my plate into money, I cannot seize the same, for that money is undistinguishable from other money of that coin. But, if a butcher take wrongfully my ox and doth kill it, and bring it into the market to be sold, I may not seize upon the flesh, for it cannot be known from others of that kind; but if it be found hanging in the skin, where the mark may appear, I may seize the same, although when it was taken from me it had life, and now is dead. So, if a man cut down my tree, and square it into a beam of timber, I may seize the same, for he hath neither altered the nature thereof, nor added anything but exterior form thereunto; but if he lay the beam of timber into the building of a house, I may not seize the same, for being so set it is become parcel of the house, and so in supposition of law, after a sort, altered in its natnre. See Year Book 12 H. VIII. 9 b, 10 a; Bro. Ab. Property, 45; 5 H. VII. 15; Bro. Ab. Property, 23.

Droits of admiralty. Rights claimed by the government over the property of an enemy. In England, it has been usual, in maritime wars, for the government to seize and condemn, as droits of admiralty, the property of an enemy found in her ports at the breaking out of hostilities. 1 Rob. R. 196; 13 Ves. jr. 71; Edw. R. 60; 3 B. & P. 191.

Droit d'aubaine, *jus albinatus*. This was a rule by which all the property of a deceased foreigner, whether movable or immovable, was confiscated to the use of the state, to the exclusion of his heirs, whether claiming *ab intestato*, or under a will of the deceased. The word *aubain* signifies *hospes loci, peregrinus advena*, a stranger. It is derived, according to some, from *alibi*, elsewhere, *natus*, born, from which the word *albinus* is said to be formed. Others, as Cujas, derive the word directly from *advena*, by which word, aubains, or strangers, are designated in the capitularies of Charlemagne. See Du Cange and Dictionaire de Trevoux.

2. As the darkness of the middle ages wore away, and the light of civilization appeared, this barbarous and inhospitable usage was by degrees discontinued, and is now nearly abolished in the civilized world. It subsisted in France, however, in full force until 1791, and afterwards, in a modified form, until 1819, when it was formally abolished by law. For the gross abuses of this feudal exaction, see Dictionaire de l'Ancien Regime et des abus féodaux. *Aubain.* See *Albinatus jus.*

Droit-close. The name of an ancient writ directed to the lord of ancient demesne, and which lies for those tenants in ancient demesne who hold their lands and tenements by charter in fee simple, in fee tail, for life, or in dower. F. N. B. 23.

DROITURAL. What belongs of right; relating to right; as, real actions are either droitural or possessory; *droitural*, when the plaintiff seeks to recover the property. Finch's Law, 257.

DRUNKENNESS. Intoxication with strong liquor.

2. This is an offence generally punished by local regulations, more or less severely.

3. Although drunkenness reduces a man to a temporary insanity, it does not excuse him or palliate his offence, when he commits a crime during a fit of intoxication, and which is the immediate result of it. When the act is a remote consequence, superinduced by the antecedent drunkenness of the party, as in cases of *delirium tremens* or *mania a potu*, the insanity excuses the act. 5 Mason's R. 28; Amer. Jurist, vol. 3, p. 5—20; Martin and Yeager's R. 133, 147; Dane's Ab. Index, h. t.; 1 Russ. on Cr. 7; Ayliffe's Parerg. 231; 4 Bl. Com. 26.

4. As there must be a will and intentiou in order to make a contract, it follows, that a man who is in such a state of intoxication as not to know what he is doing, may avoid a contract entered into by him while in this state. 2 Aik. Rep. 167; 1 Green, R. 233; 2 Verm. 97; 1 Bibb, 168; 3 Hayw. R. 82; 1 Hill, R. 313; 1 South. R. 361; Bull. N. P. 172; 1 Ves. 19; 18 Ves. 15; 3 P. Wms. 130, n. a; Sugd. Vend. 154; 1 Stark. 126; 1 South. R. 361; 2 Hayw. 394; but see 1 Bibb, R. 406; Ray's Med. Jur. ch. 23, 24; Fonbl. Eq. B. 1, c. 2, § 3; 22 Am. Jur. 290; 1 Foderé, Méd. Lég. § 215. Vide *Ebriosity; Habitual drunkard.*

DRY. Used figuratively, it signifies that

which produces nothing; as, dry exchange; dry rent; rent seck.

DRY EXCHANGE, *contracts.* A term invented for disguising and covering usury; in which something was pretended to pass on both sides, when in truth nothing passed on one side, whence it was called *dry.* Stat. 3 Hen. VII. c. 5; Wolff, Ins. Nat. § 657.

DRY RENT, *contracts.* Rent-seck, was a rent reserved without a clause of distress.

DUCAT. The name of a foreign coin. The ducat of Naples shall be estimated in the computations of customs, at eighteen cents. Act of May 22, 1846.

DUCES TECUM, *practice, evidence.* Bring with thee. A writ commonly called a *subpœna duces tecum*, commanding the person to whom it is directed to bring with him some writings, papers, or other things therein specified and described, before the court. 1 Phil. Ev. 386.

2. In general all papers in the possession of the witness must be produced; but to this general rule there are exceptions, among which are the following: 1. That a party is not bound to exhibit his own title deeds. 1 Stark. Ev. 87; 3 C. & P. 591; 2 Stark. R. 203; 9 B. & Cr. 288. 2. One who has advanced money on a lease, and holds it as his security, is not bound to produce it. 6 C. & P. 728. 3. Attorneys and solicitors who hold the papers of their clients cannot be compelled to produce them, unless the client could have been so compelled. 6 Carr. & P. 728. See 5 Cowen, R. 153, 419; Esp. R. 405; 11 Price, R. 455; 1 Adol. & Ell. 31; 1 C. M. & R. 38; 1 Hud. & Brooke, 749. On the question how far this clause is obligatory on a witness, see 1 Dixon on Tit. Deeds, 98, 99, 102; 1 Esp. N. P. Cas. 405; 4 Esp. N. P. C. 43; 9 East, Rep. 473.

DUCKING-STOOL, *punishment.* An instrument used in dipping women in the water, as a punishment, on conviction of being common scolds. It is sometimes confounded with tumbrel. (q. v.)

2. This barbarous punishment was never in use in Pennsylvania. 12 Serg. & Rawle, 220.

DUCROIRE. This is a French word, which has the same meaning as the Italian phrase *del credere.* (q. v.) 2 Pard. Dr. Com. n. 564.

DUE. What ought to be paid; what may be demanded. It differs from owing in this, that, sometimes, what is owing is not due; a note, payable thirty days after date, is owing immediately after it is delivered to the payee, but it is not due until the thirty days have elapsed.

2. Bills of exchange, and promissory notes, are not due until the end of the three days of grace, (q. v.) unless the last of these days happen to fall on a Sunday, or other holyday, when it becomes due on the Saturday before, and not on the Monday following. Story, P. N. § 440; 1 Bell's Com. 410; Story on Bills, § 233; 2 Hill, N. Y. R. 587; 2 Applet. R. 264.

3. Due also signifies just or proper; as, a due presentment, and demand of payment, must be made. See 4 Rawle, 307; 3 Leigh, 389; 3 Cranch, 300.

DUE-BILL. An acknowledgment of a debt, in writing, is so called. This instrument differs from a promissory note in many particulars; it is not payable to order, nor is it assignable by mere endorsement. See *I O U; Promissory notes.*

DUELLING, *crim. law.* The fighting of two persons, one against the other, at an appointed time and place, upon a precedent quarrel. It differs from an affray in this, that the latter occurs on a sudden quarrel, while the former is always the result of design.

2. When one of the parties is killed, the survivor is guilty of murder. 1 Russ. on Cr. 443; 1 Yerger's R. 228. Fighting a duel, even where there is no fatal result, is, of itself, a misdemeanor. Vide 2 Com. Dig. 252; Roscoe's Cr. Ev. 610; 2 Chit. Cr. Law, 728; Id. 848; Com. Dig. Battel, B; 3 Inst. 157; 6 East, 464; Hawk. B. 1, c. 31, s. 21; 3 East, R. 581; 3 Bulst. 171, 4 Bl. Com. 199; Prin. Pen. Law, c. 19, p 245; Const. R. 107; 1 Stew. R. 506; 20 John. 457; 3 Cowen, 686. For cases of mutual combat, upon a sudden quarrel, Vide 1 Russ. on Cr. 495.

DUKE. The title given to those who are in the highest rank of nobility in England.

DUM FUIT INFRA ÆTATEM. The name of a writ which lies when an infant has made a feoffment in fee of his lands, or for life, or a gift in tail.

2. It may be sued out by him after he comes of full age, and not before; but, in the mean time, he may enter, and his entry remits him to his ancestor's rights. F. N. B. 192; Co. Litt. 247, 337.

DUM SOLA. While single or unmarried. This phrase is applied to single women, to denote that something has been done, or may be done, while the woman is or was unmarried. Example, when a judgment is rendered against a woman *dum sola*, and afterwards she marries, the *scire facias* to revive the judgment must be against both husband and wife.

DUM NON FUIT COMPOS MENTIS, *Eng. law*. The name of a writ, which the heirs of a person who was *non compos mentis*, and who aliened his lands, might have sued out, to restore him to his rights. T. L.

DUMB. One who cannot speak; a person who is mute. See *Deaf and dumb; Deaf, dumb, and blind; Mute, standing mute.*

DUMB-BIDDING, *contracts*. In sales at auction, when the amount which the owner of the thing sold is willing to take for the article, is written, and placed by the owner under a candlestick, or other thing, and it is agreed that no bidding shall avail unless equal to that; this is called dumb-bidding. Babingt. on Auct. 44.

DUNG. Manure. Sometimes it is real estate, and at other times personal property. When collected in a heap, it is personal estate; when spread out on the land, it becomes incorporated in it, and it is then real estate. Vide *Manure*.

DUNGEON. A cell under ground; a place in a prison built under ground, dark, or but indifferently lighted. In the prisons of the United States, there are few or no dungeons.

DUNNAGE, *mer. law*. Pieces of wood placed against the sides and bottom of the hold of a vessel, to preserve the cargo from the effect of leakage, according to its nature and quality. 2 Magens, 101, art. 125, 126; Abbott on Shipp. 227.

DUPEX QUERELA, *Eng. eccl. law*. A complaint in the nature of an appeal from the ordinary to his next immediate superior. 3 Bl. Com. 247.

DUPLICATA. It is the double of letters patent, letters of administration, or other instrument.

DUPLICATE. The double of any thing.

2. It is usually applied to agreements, letters, receipts, and the like, when two originals are made of either of them. Each copy has the same effect. The term duplicate means a document, which is essentially the same as some other instrument. 7 Mann. & Gr. 93. In the English law, it also signifies the certificate of discharge given to an insolvent debtor, who takes the benefit of the act for the relief of insolvent debtors

3. A duplicate writing has but one effect. Each duplicate is complete evidence of the intention of the parties. When a duplicate is destroyed, for example, in the case of a will, it is presumed both are intended to be destroyed; but this presumption possesses greater or less force, owing to circumstances. When only one of the duplicates is in the possession of the testator, the destruction of that is a strong presumption of an intent to revoke both; but if he possessed both, and destroys but one, it is weaker; when he alters one, and afterwards destroys it, retaining the other entire, it has been held that the intention was to revoke both. 1 P. Wms. 346; 13 Ves. 310; but that seems to be doubted. 3 Hagg. Eccl. R. 548.

DUPLICATUM JUS, *a twofold or double right*. These words, according to Bracton, lib. 4, c. 3, signify the same as *dreit dreit*, or *droit droit*, and are applied to a writ of right, patent, and such other writs of right as are of the same nature, and do, as it were, flow from it, as the writ of right. Booth on Real Actions, 87.

DUPLICITY, *pleading*. Duplicity of pleading consists in multiplicity of distinct matter to one and the same thing, whereunto several answers are required. Duplicity may occur in one and the same pleading. Double pleading consists in alleging, for one single purpose or object, two or more distinct grounds of defence, when one of them would be as effectual in law, as both or all.

2. This the common law does not allow, because it produces useless prolixity, and always tends to confusion, and to the multiplication of issues. Co. Litt. 304, a; Finch's Law, 393; 3 Bl. Com. 311; Bac. Ab. Pleas, K 1.

3. Duplicity may be in the declaration, or the subsequent proceedings. Duplicity in the declaration consists in joining, in one and the same count, different grounds of action, of different natures, Cro. Car. 20; or of the same nature, 2 Co. 4 a; 1 Saund. 58, n. 1; 2 Ventr. 198; Steph. Pl. 266; to enforce only a single right of recovery.

4. This is a fault in pleading, only because it tends to useless prolixity and confusion, and is, therefore, only a fault in form. The rule forbidding double pleading "extends," according to Lord Coke, "to pleas perpetual or peremptory, and not to pleas dilatory; for in their time and place a man may use divers of them." Co. Litt.

304, a. But by this is not meant that any dilatory plea may be double, or, in other words, that it may consist of different matters, or answers to one and the same thing; but merely that, as there are several kinds or classes of dilatory pleas, having distinct offices or effects, a defendant may use "divers of them" successively, (each being in itself single,) in their proper order. Steph. Pl. App. note 56.

5. The inconveniences which were felt in consequence of this strictness were remedied by the statute, 4 Ann. c. 16, s. 4, which provides, that "it shall be lawful for any defendant, or tenant, in any action or suit, or for any plaintiff in replevin, in any court of record, with leave of the court to plead as many several matters thereto as he shall think necessary for his defence."

6. This provision, or a similar one, is in force, probably, in most of the states of the American Union.

7. Under this statute, the defendant may, with leave of court, plead as many different pleas in bar, (each being in itself single,) as he may think proper; but although this statute allows the defendant to plead several distinct and substantive matters of defence, in several distinct pleas, to the whole, or one and the same part of the plaintiff's demand; yet, it does not authorize him to allege more than one ground of defence in one plea. Each plea must still be single, as by the rules of the common law. Lawes, Pl. 131; 1 Chit. Pl. 512.

8. This statute extends only to pleas to the declaration, and does not embrace replications, rejoinders, nor any of the subsequent pleadings. Lawes, Pl. 132; 2 Chit. Pl. 421; Com. Dig. Pleader, E 2; Story's Pl. 72, 76; 5 Am. Jur. 260–288. Vide, generally, 1 Chit. Pl. 230, 512; Steph. Pl. c. 2, s. 3, rule 1; Gould on Pl. c. 8, p. 1; Archb. Civ. Pl. 191; Doct. Pl. 222; 5 John. 240; 8 Vin. Ab. 183; U. S. Dig. Pleading, II. e and f.

DURANTE. A term equivalent to during, which is used in some law phrases, as *durante absentia*, during absence; *durante minor ætate*, during minority; *durante bene placito*, during our good pleasure.

DURANTE ABSENTIA. When the executor is out of the jurisdiction of the court or officer to whom belongs the probate of wills and granting letters of administration, letters of administration will be granted to another *during the absence* of the executor; and the person thus appointed is called the *administrator durante absentia*.

DURANTE MINORE ÆTATE. During the minority.

2. During his minority, an infant can enter into no contract, except those for his benefit. If he should be appointed an executor, administration of the estate will be granted, *durante minore ætate*, to another person. 2 Bouv. Inst. n. 1555.

DURESS. An actual or a threatened violence or restraint of a man's person, contrary to law, to compel him to enter into a contract, or to discharge one. 1 Fairf. 325.

2. Sir William Blackstone divides duress into two sorts: *First*. Duress of imprisonment, where a man actually loses his liberty. If a man be illegally deprived of his liberty until he sign and seal a bond, or the like, he may allege this duress, and avoid the bond. But, if a man be legally imprisoned, and either to procure his discharge, or on any other fair account, seal a bond or a deed, this is not by duress of imprisonment, and he is not at liberty to avoid it. 2 Inst. 482; 3 Caines' R. 168; 6 Mass. R. 511; 1 Lev. 69; 1 Hen. & Munf. 350; 5 Shepl. R. 338. Where the proceedings at law are a mere pretext, the instrument may be avoided. Aleyn, 92; 1 Bl. Com. 136.

3. *Second*. Duress per minas, which is either for fear of loss of life, or else for fear of mayhem, or loss of limb; and this must be upon a sufficient reason. 1 Bl. Com. 131. In this case, a man may avoid his own act. Id. Lord Coke enumerates four instances in which a man may avoid his own act by reason of menaces: 1st. For fear of loss of life. 2d. Of member. 3d. Of mayhem. 4th. Of imprisonment. 2 Inst. 483; 2 Roll. Abr. 124; Bac. Ab. Duress; Id. Murder, A; 2 Str. R. 856; Fost. Cr. Law, 322; 2 St. R. 884; 2 Ld. Raym. 1578; Sav. Dr. Rom. § 114.

4. In South Carolina, duress of goods, under circumstances of great hardship, will avoid a contract. 2 Bay, R. 211; 1 Bay, R. 470. But see Hardin, R. 605; 2 Gallis. R. 337.

5. In Louisiana consent to a contract is void if it be produced by violence or threats, and the contract is invalid. Civ. Code of Louis. art. 1844.

6. It is not every degree of violence or any kind of threats, that will invalidate a contract; they must be such as would naturally operate on a person of ordinary

firmness, and inspire a just fear of great injury to person, reputation or fortune. The age, sex, state of health, temper and disposition of the party, and other circumstances calculated to give greater or less effect to the violence or threats, must be taken into consideration. Id. art. 1845. The author of Fleta states the rule of the ancient common law thus: "Est autem metus præsentis vel futuri periculi causâ mentis trepidatio; est præsertim viri constantis et non cujuslibet vani hominis vel meticulosi et talis debet esse metus qui in se contineat mortis periculum, vel corporis cruciatura."

7. A contract by violence or threats, is void, although the party in whose favor the contract is made, did not exercise the violence or make the threats, and although he were ignorant of them. Id. 1846.

8. Violence or threats are cause of nullity, not only where they are exercised on the contracting party, but when the wife, the husband, the descendants or ascendants of the party are the object of them. Id. 1847. Fleta adds on this subject: "et exceptionem habet si sibi ipsi inferatur vis et metus verumetiam si vis ut filio vel filiæ, patri vel fratri, vel sorori et aliis domesticis et propinquis."

9. If the violence used be only a legal constraint, or the threats only of doing that which the party using them had a right to do, they shall not invalidate the contract. A just and legal imprisonment, or threats of any measure authorized by law, and the circumstances of the case, are of this description. Id. 1850. See Norris Peake's Evid. 440, and the cases cited; also, 6 Mass. Rep. 506, for the general rule at common law.

10. But the mere forms of law to cover coercive proceedings for an unjust and illegal cause, if used or threatened in order to procure the assent to a contract, will invalidate it; an arrest without cause of action, or a demand of bail in an unreasonable sum, or threat of such proceeding, by this rule invalidate a contract made under their pressure. Id. 1851.

11. All the above articles relate to cases where there may be some other motive besides the violence or threats for making the contract. When, however, there is no other cause for making the contract, any threats, even of slight injury, will invalidate it. Id. 1853.

Vide, generally, 2 Watts, 167; 1 Bailey, 84, 6 Mass. 511; 6 N. H. Rep. 508; 2 Gallis. R. 337.

DUTIES. In its most enlarged sense, this word is nearly equivalent to taxes, embracing all impositions or charges levied on persons or things; in its more restrained sense, it is often used as equivalent to *customs*, (q. v.) or *imposts*. (q. v.) Story. Const. § 949. Vide, for the rate of duties payable on goods and merchandise, Gord. Dig. B. 7, t. 1, c. 1; Story's L. U. S. Index, h. t.

DUTY, *natural law*. A human action which is exactly conformable to the laws which require us to obey them.

2. It differs from a legal obligation, because a duty cannot always be enforced by the law; it is our duty, for example, to be temperate in eating, but we are under no legal obligation to be so; we ought to love our neighbors, but no law obliges us to love them.

3. Duties may be considered in the relation of man towards God, towards himself, and towards mankind. 1. We are bound to obey the will of God as far as we are able to discover it, because he is the sovereign Lord of the universe who made and governs all things by his almighty power, and infinite wisdom. The general name of this duty is piety: which consists in entertaining just opinions concerning him, and partly in such affections towards him, and such worship of him, as is suitable to these opinions.

4.—2. A man has a duty to perform towards himself; he is bound by the law of nature to protect his life and his limbs; it is his duty, too, to avoid all intemperance in eating and drinking, and in the unlawful gratification of all his other appetites.

5.—3. He has duties to perform towards others. He is bound to do to others the same justice which he would have a right to expect them to do to him.

DWELLING HOUSE. A building inhabited by man. A mansion. (q. v.)

2. A part of a house is, in one sense, a dwelling house; for example, where two or more persons rent of the owner different parts of a house, so as to have among them the whole house, and the owner does not reserve or occupy any part, the separate portion of each will, in cases of burglary, be considered the dwelling house of each. 1 Mood. Cr. Cas. 23.

3. At common law, in cases of burglary, under the term dwelling house are included

the out-houses within the curtilage or common fence with the dwelling house. 3 Inst. 64; 4 Bl. Com. 225; and vide Russ & Ry. Cr. Cas. 170; Id. 186; 16 Mass. 105; 16 John. 203; 18 John. 115; 4 Call, 109; 1 Moody, Cr. Cas. 274; *Burglary; Door; House; Jail; Mansion.*

DYING DECLARATIONS. When a man has received a mortal wound or other injury, by which he is in imminent danger of dying, and believes that he must die, and afterwards does die, the statements he makes as to the manner in which he received such injury, and the person who committed it, are called his dying declarations.

2. These declarations are received in evidence against the person thus accused, on the ground that the party making them can have no motive but to tell the truth. The following lines have been put into the mouth of such a man:

Have I not hideous Death before my view,
Retaining but a quantity of life,
Which bleeds away, even as a form of wax
Resolveth from his figure 'gainst the fire?
What in the world should make me now deceive,
Since I must lose the use of all deceit?
Why then should I be false, since it is true
That I must die here, and live hence by truth.

See *Death; Deathbed or dying declarations; Declarations.*

DYNASTY. A succession of kings in the same line or family; government; sovereignty.

DYSNOMY. Bad legislation; the enactment of bad laws.

DYSPEPSIA, *med. jur., contracts.* A state of the stomach in which its functions are disturbed, without the presence of other diseases; or when, if other diseases are present, they are of minor importance. Dunglison's Med. Dict. h. t.

2. Dyspepsia is not, in general, considered as a disease which tends to shorten life, so as to make a life uninsurable; unless the complaint has become organic dyspepsia, or was of such a degree at the time of the insurance, as, by its excess, to tend to shorten life. 4 Taunt. 763.

DYVOUR, *Scotch law.* A bankrupt.

DYVOUR'S HABIT. *Scotch law.* A habit which debtors, who are set free on a *cessio bonorum*, are obliged to wear, unless in the summons and process of *cessio*, it be libelled, sustained, and proved that the bankruptcy proceeds from misfortune. And bankrupts are condemned to submit to the habit, even where no suspicion of fraud lies against them, if they have been dealers in an illicit trade. Ersk. Pr. L. Scot. 4, 3, 13. This practice was bottomed on that of the Roman civil law, which Filangieri says is better fitted to excite laughter than compassion. He adds: "Si conduce il debitore vicino ad una colonna a quest' officio destinata, egli l'abbraccia nel mentre, che uno araldo grida Cedo bonis ed un al tro gli abza le vesti, e palesa agli spettatori le sue natiche. Finita questa ceremonia il debitore è messo in libertà." Filangieri della legislazione, cap. iv.

E.

E CONVERSO. On the other side or hand; on the contrary.

E PLURIBUS UNUM. One from more. The motto of the arms of the United States.

EAGLE, *money.* A gold coin of the United States, of the value of ten dollars. It weighs two hundred and fifty-eight grains. Of one thousand parts, nine hundred are of pure gold, and one hundred of alloy. Act of January 18, 1837, 4 Sharsw. Cont. of Story's L. U. S. 2523, 4. Vide *Money.*

EAR-WITNESS. One who attests to things he has heard himself.

EARL, *Eng. law.* A title of nobility next below a marquis and above a viscount.

2. Earls were anciently called *comites*, because they were wont *comitari regem*, to wait upon the king for counsel and advice. He was also called *shireman*, because each earl had the civil government of a shire.

3. After the Norman conquest they were called *counts*, whence the shires obtained the names of counties. They have now nothing to do with the government of counties, which has entirely devolved on the sheriff, the earl's deputy, or *vice comes.*

EARLDOM. The seigniory of an earl; the title and dignity of an earl.

EARNEST, *contracts*. The payment of a part of the price of goods sold, or the delivery of part of such goods, for the purpose of binding the contract.

2. The effect of earnest is to bind the goods sold, and upon their being paid for without default, the buyer is entitled to them. But notwithstanding the earnest, the money must be paid upon taking away the goods, because no other time for payment is appointed; earnest only binds the bargain, and gives the buyer a right to demand, but a demand without payment of the money is void; after earnest given the vendor cannot sell the goods to another, without a default in the vendee, and therefore if the latter does not come and pay, and take the goods, the vendor ought to go and request him, and then if he does not come, pay for the goods and take them away in convenient time, the agreement is dissolved, and he is at liberty to sell them to any other person. 1 Salk. 113: 2 Bl. Com. 447; 2 Kent, Com. 389; Ayl. Pand. 450; 3 Campb. R. 426.

EASEMENTS, *estates*. An easement is defined to be a liberty, privilege or advantage, which one man may have in the lands of another, without profit; it may arise by deed or prescription. Vide 1 Serg. & Rawle, 298; 5 Barn. & Cr. 221; 3 Barn. & Cr. 339; 3 Bing. R. 118; 3 McCord, R. 131, 194; 2 McCord, R. 451; 14 Mass. R. 49; 3 Pick. R. 408.

2. This is an incorporeal hereditament, and corresponds nearly to the servitudes or services of the civil law. Vide Lilly's Reg. h. t.; 2 Bouv. Inst. n. 1600, et seq.; 3 Kent, Com. 344: Cruise, Dig. t. 31, c. 1, s. 17; 2 Hill. Ab. c. 5; 9 Pick. R. 51; 1 Bail. R. 56; 5 Mass. R. 129; 4 McCord's R. 102; Whatl. on Eas. *passim;* and the article *Servitude.*

EASTER TERM, *Eng. law*. One of the four terms of the courts. It is now a fixed term beginning on the 15th of April and ending the 8th of May in every year. It was formerly a movable term.

EAT INDE SINE DIE. Words used on an acquittal, or when a prisoner is to be discharged, *that he may go without day*, that is, that he be dismissed. Dane's Ab. Index, h. t.

EAVES-DROPPERS, *crim. law*. Such persons as wait under walls or windows or the eaves of a house, to listen to discourses, and thereupon to frame mischievous tales.

2. The common law punishment for this offence is fine, and finding sureties for good behaviour. 4 Bl. Com. 167; Burn's Just h. t.; Dane's Ab. Index, h. t.; 1 Russ. Cr. 302.

3. In Tennessee, an indictment will not lie for eaves-dropping. 2 Tenn. R. 108.

ECCHYMOSIS, *med. jur.* Blackness. It is an extravasation of blood by rupture of capillary vessels, and hence it follows contusion; but it may exist, as in cases of scurvy, and other morbid conditions, without the latter. Ryan's Med. Jur. 172.

ECCLESIA. In classical Greek this word signifies any assembly, and in this sense it is used in Acts xix. 39. But ordinarily, in the New Testament, the word denotes a Christian assembly, and is rendered into English by the word *church*. It occurs thrice only in the Gospels, viz. in Matt. xvi. 18, and xviii. 17; but very frequently in the other parts of the New Testament, beginning with Acts ii. 47. In Acts xix. 37, the word *churches*, in the common English version, seems to be improperly used to denote heathen temples. Figuratively, the word *church* is employed to signify the building set apart for the Christian assemblies; but the word ecclesia is not used in the New Testament in that sense.

ECCLESIASTIC. A clergyman; one destined to the divine ministry, as, a bishop, a priest, a deacon. Dom. Lois Civ. liv. prél. t. 2, s. 2, n. 14.

ECCLESIASTICAL. Belonging to, or set apart for the church; as, distinguished from civil or secular. Vide *Church.*

ECCLESIASTICAL COURTS, *English law*. Courts held by the king's authority as supreme governor of the church, for matters which chiefly concern religion.

2. There are ten courts which may be ranged under this class. 1. The Archdeacon's Court. 2. The Consistory Court. 3. The Court of Arches. 4. The Court of Peculiars. 5. The Prerogative Court. 6. The Court of Delegates, which is the great court of appeals in all ecclesiastical causes. 7. The Court of Convocation. 8. The Court of Audience. 9. The Court of Faculties. 10. The Court of Commissioners of Review.

ECCLESIASTICAL LAW. By this phrase it is intended to include all those rules which govern ecclesiastical tribunals. Vide *Law Canon.*

ECCLESIASTICS, *canon law.* Those persons who compose the hierarchial state of the church. They are regular and secular. Aso & Man. Inst. B. 2, t. 5, c. 4, § 1.

ECLAMPSIA PARTURIENTIUM, *med. jur.* The name of a disease accompanied by apoplectic convulsions, and which produces aberration of mind at childbirth. The word Eclampsia is of Greek origin—Significat splendorem fulgorem *effulgentiam,* et emicationem quales ex oculis aliquando prodeunt. Metaphorice sumitur de emicatione flammæ vitalis in pubertate et ætatis vigore. Castelli, Lex. Medic.

2. An ordinary person, it is said, would scarcely observe it, and it requires the practised and skilled eye of a physician to discover that the patient is acting in total unconsciousness of the nature and effect of her acts. There can be but little doubt that many of the tragical cases of infanticide proceed from this cause. The criminal judge and lawyer cannot inquire with too much care into the symptoms of this disease, in order to discover the guilt of the mother, where it exists, and to ascertain her innocence, where it does not. See two well reported cases of this kind in the Boston Medical Journal, vol. 27, No. 10, p. 161.

EDICT. A law ordained by the sovereign, by which he forbids or commands something; it extends either to the whole country, or only to some particular provinces.

2. Edicts are somewhat similar to public proclamations. Their difference consists in this, that the former have authority and form of law in themselves, whereas the latter are at most, declarations of a law, before enacted by congress, or the legislature.

3. Among the Romans this word sometimes signified a *citation* to appear before a judge. The edict of the emperors, also called *constitutiones principum,* were new laws which they made of their own motion, either to decide cases which they had foreseen, or to abolish or change some ancient laws. They were different from their rescripts or decrees. These edicts were the sources which contributed to the formation of the Gregorian, Hermogenian, Theodosian, and Justinian Codes. Vide Dig. 1, 4, 1, 1; Inst. 1, 2, 7; Code, 1, 1; Nov. 139.

EDICT PERPETUAL. The title of a compilation of all the edicts. This collection was made by Salvius Julianus, a jurist who was selected by the emperor Adrian for the purpose, and who performed his task with credit to himself.

EDICTS OF JUSTINIAN. These are thirteen constitutions or laws of that prince, found in most editions of the *corpus juris civilis,* after the Novels. Being confined to matters of police in the provinces of the empire, they are of little use.

EFFECT. The operation of a law, of an agreement, or an act, is called its effect.

2. By the laws of the United States, a patent cannot be granted for an effect only, but it may be for a new mode or application of machinery to produce effects. 1 Gallis. 478; see 4 Mason, 1; Pet. C. C. R. 394; 2 N. H. R. 61.

EFFECTS. This word used *simpliciter* is equivalent to *property* or *worldly substance,* and may carry the whole personal estate, when used in a will. 5 Madd. Ch. Rep. 72; Cowp. 299; 15 Ves. 507; 6 Madd. Ch. R. 119. But when it is preceded and connected with words of a narrower import, and the bequest is not residuary, it will be confined to species of property *ejusdem generis* with those previously described. 13 Ves. 39; 15 Ves. 326; Roper on Leg. 210.

EFFIGY, *crim. law.* The figure or representation of a person.

2. To make the effigy of a person with an intent to make him the object of ridicule, is a libel. (q. v.) Hawk. b. 1, c. 73, s. 2; 14 East, 227; 2 Chit. Cr. Law, 866.

3. In France an execution by effigy or in effigy is adopted in the case of a criminal who has fled from justice. By the public exposure or exhibition of a picture or representation of him on a scaffold, on which his name and the decree condemning him are written, he is deemed to undergo the punishment to which he has been sentenced. Since the adoption of the Code Civil, the practice has been to affix the names, qualities or addition, and the residence of the condemned person, together with an extract from the sentence of condemnation, to a post set upright in the ground, instead of exhibiting a portrait of him on the scaffold. Répertoire de Villargues; Biret, Vocab.

EFFRACTION. A breach, made by the use of force.

EFFRACTOR. One who breaks through, one who commits a burglary.

EGO. I, myself. This term is used in forming genealogical tables, to represent the person who is the object of inquiry.

EIGNE, *persons.* This is a corruption of the French word *ainé*, eldest or first born.

2. It is frequently used in our old law books; *bastard eigne* signifies an elder bastard when spoken of two children, one of whom was born before the marriage of his parents, and the other after; the latter is called *mulier puisne.* Litt. sect. 399.

EIRE, or EYRE, *English law.* A journey. Justices in eyre, were itinerant judges, who were sent once in seven years with a general commission in divers counties, to hear and determine such causes as were called pleas of the crown. Vide *Justices in eyre.*

EJECTMENT, *remedies.* The name of an action which lies for the recovery of the possession of real property, and of damages for the unlawful detention. In its nature it is entirely different from a real action. 2 Term Rep. 696, 700. See 17 S. & R. 187, and authorities cited.

2. This subject may be considered with reference, 1st. To the form of the proceedings. 2d. To the nature of the property or thing to be recovered. 3d. To the right to such property. 4th. To the nature of the ouster or injury. 5th. To the judgment.

3.—1. In the English practice, which is still adhered to in some states, in order to lay the foundation of this action, the party claiming title enters upon the land, and then gives a lease of it to a third person, who, being ejected by the other claimant, or some one else for him, brings a suit against the ejector in his own name; to sustain the action the lessee must prove a good title in the lessor, and, in this collateral way, the title is tried. To obviate the difficulty of proving these forms, this action has been made, substantially, a fictitious process. The defendant agrees, and is required to confess that a lease was made to the plaintiff, that he entered under it, and has been ousted by the defendant; or, in other words, to admit lease, entry, and ouster, and that he will rely only upon his title. An actual entry, however, is still supposed, and therefore, an ejectment will not lie, if the right of entry is gone. 3 Bl. Com. 199 to 206. In Pennsylvania, New York, Arkansas, and perhaps other states, these fictions have all been abolished, and the writ of ejectment sets forth the possession of the plaintiff, and an unlawful entry on the part of the defendant.

4.—2. This action is in general sustainable only for the recovery of the possession of property upon which an entry might in point of fact be made, and of which the sheriff could deliver actual possession: it cannot, therefore, in general, be sustained for the recovery of property which, in legal consideration, is not tangible; as, for a rent, or other incorporeal heriditaments, a water-course, or for a mere privilege of a landing held in common with other citizens of a town. 2 Yeates, 331; 3 Bl. Com. 206; Yelv. 143; Run. Eject. 121 to 136; Ad. Eject. c. 2; 9 John. 298; 16 John. 284.

5.—3. The title of the party having a right of entry may be in fee-simple, fee-tail, or for life or years; and if it be the *best* title to the property the plaintiff will succeed. The plaintiff must recover on the strength of his title, and not on the weakness or deficiency of that of the defendant. Addis. Rep. 390; 2 Serg. & Rawle, 65; 3 Serg. & Rawle, 288; 4 Burr. 2487; 1 East, R. 246; Run. Eject. 15; 5 T. R. 110.

6.—4. The injury sustained must in fact or in point of law have amounted to an ouster or dispossession of the lessor of the plaintiff, or of the plaintiff himself, where the fictions have been abolished; for if there be no ouster, or the defendant be not in possession at the time of bringing the action, the plaintiff must fail. 7 T. R. 327; 1 B. & P. 573; 2 Caines' R. 335.

7.—5. The judgment is, that the plaintiff do recover his term, of and in the tenements, and, unless the damages be remitted, the damages assessed by the jury with the costs of increase. In Pennsylvania, however, and, it is presumable, in all those states where the fictitious form of this action has been abolished, the plaintiff recovers possession of the land generally, and not simply a term of years in the land. See 2 Scam. 251; 4 B. Monr. 210; 3 Harr. 73; 1 McLean, 87.

Vide, generally, Adams on Ej.; 4 Bouv. Inst. n. 3651, et seq.; Run. Ej.; Com. Dig. h. t.; Dane's Ab. h. t.; 1 Chit. Pl. 188 to 193; 18 E. C. L. R. 158; Woodf. L. & T. 354 to 417; 2 Phil. Ev. 169; 8 Vin. Ab. 323; Arch. Civ. Pl. 503; 2 Sell. Pr. 85; Chit. Pr. Index, h. t.; Bac. Ab. h. t.; Doct. Pl. 227; Am. Dig. h. t.; Report of the

Commissioners to Revise the Civil Code of Pennsylvania, January 16, 1835, pp. 80, 81, 83; Coop. Justinian, 448.

EJUSDEM GENERIS. Of the same kind.

2. In the construction of laws, wills and other instruments, when certain things are enumerated, and then a phrase is used which might be construed to include other things, it is generally confined to things *ejusdem generis;* as, where an act (9 Ann. c. 20) provided that a writ of quo warranto might issue against persons who should usurp "the offices of mayors, bailiffs, port reeves, and *other offices*, within the cities, towns, corporate boroughs, and *places*, within Great Britain," &c.; it was held that "other offices" meant offices *ejusdem generis;* and that the word "places" signified places of the same kind; that is, that the offices must be *corporate offices*, and the places must be *corporate places.* 5 T. R. 375, 379; 5 B. & C. 640; 8 D. & Ry. 393; 1 B. & C. 237.

3. So, in the construction of wills, when certain articles are enumerated, the term *goods* is to be restricted to those *ejusdem generis.* Bac. Ab. Legacies, B; 3 Rand. 191; 3 Atk. 61; Abr. Eq. 201; 2 Atk. 113.

ELDEST. He or she who has the greatest age.

2. The laws of primogeniture are not in force in the United States; the eldest child of a family cannot, therefore, claim any right in consequence of being the eldest.

ELECTION. This term, in its most usual acceptation, signifies the choice which several persons collectively make of a person to fill an office or place. In another sense, it means the choice which is made by a person having the right, of selecting one of two alternative contracts or rights. Elections, then, are of men or things.

2.—§ 1. Of men. These are either public elections, or elections by companies or corporations.

3.—1. Public elections. These should be free and uninfluenced either by hope or fear. They are, therefore, generally made by ballot, except those by persons in their representative capacities, which are *viva voce.* And to render this freedom as perfect as possible, electors are generally exempted from arrest in all cases, except treason, felony, or breach of the peace, during their attendance on election, and in going to and returning from them. And provisions are made by law, in several states, to prevent the interference or appearance of the military on the election ground.

4. One of the cardinal principles on the subject of elections is, that the person who receives a majority or plurality of votes is the person elected. Generally a plurality of the votes of the electors present is sufficient; but in some states a majority of *all* the votes is required. Each elector has one vote.

5.—2. Elections by corporations or companies are made by the members, in such a way as their respective constitutions or charters direct. It is usual in these cases to vote a greater or lesser number of votes in proportion as the voter has a greater or less amount of the stock of the company or corporation, if such corporation or company be a pecuniary institution. And the members are frequently permitted to vote by proxy. See 7 John. 287; 9 John. 147; 5 Cowen, 426; 7 Cowen, 153; 8 Cowen, 387; 6 Wend. 509; 1 Wend. 98.

6.—§ 2. The election of things. 1. In contracts, when a debtor is obliged, in an alternative obligation, to do one of two things, as to pay one hundred dollars or deliver one hundred bushels of wheat, he has the choice to do the one or the other, until the time of payment; he has not the choice, however, to pay a part in each. Poth. Obl. part 2, c. 3, art. 6, No. 247; 11 John. 59. Or, if a man sell or agree to deliver one of two articles, as a horse or an ox, he has the election till the time of delivery; it being a rule that "in case an election be given of two several things, always he, which is the first agent, and which ought to do the first act, shall have the election." Co. Litt. 145, a; 7 John. 465; 2 Bibb, R. 171. On the failure of the person who has the right to make his election in proper time, the right passes to the opposite party. Co. Litt. 145, a; Viner, Abr. Election, B, C; Poth. Obl. No. 247; Bac. Ab. h. t. B; 1 Desaus. 460; Hopk. R. 337. It is a maxim of law, that an election once made and pleaded, the party is concluded, *electio semel facta, et placitum testatum, non patitur regressum.* Co. Litt. 146; 11 John. 241.

7.—2. Courts of equity have adopted the principle, that a person shall not be permitted to claim under any instrument, whether it be a deed or will, without giving full effect to it, in every respect, so far as such person is concerned. This doctrine is called into exercise when a testator gives what does not belong to him, but to some other person, and gives to that person some estate of his own; by virtue of which gift a condition is implied, either that he shall part with his own estate or shall not take the bounty. 9 Ves. 515; 10 Ves. 609; 13 Ves. 220. In such a case, equity will not allow the first legatee to insist upon that by which he would deprive another legatee under the same will of the benefit to which he would be entitled, if the first legatee permitted the whole will to operate, and therefore compels him to make his election between his right independent of the will, and the benefit under it. This principle of equity does not give the disappointed legatee the right to detain the thing itself, but gives a right to compensation out of something else. 2 Rop. Leg. 378, c. 23, s. 1. In order to impose upon a party, claiming under a will, the obligation of making an election, the intention of the testator must be expressed, or clearly implied in the will itself, in two respects; first, to dispose of that which is not his own; and, secondly, that the person taking the benefit under the will should take under the condition of giving effect thereto. 6 Dow. P. C. 179; 13 Ves. 174; 15 Ves. 390; 1 Bro. C. C. 492; 3 Bro. C. C. 255; 3 P. Wms. 315; 1 Ves. jr. 172, 335; S. C. 2 Ves. jr. 367, 371; 3 Ves. jr. 65; Amb. 433; 3 Bro. P. C. by Toml. 277; 1 B. & Beat. 1; 1 McClel. R. 424, 439, 541. See, generally, on this doctrine, Roper's Legacies, c. 23; and the learned notes of Mr. Swanston to the case Dillon *v.* Parker, 1 Swanst. R. 394, 408; Com. Dig. Appendix, tit. Election; 3 Desaus. R. 504; 3 Leigh, R. 389; Jacob, R. 505; 1 Clark & Fin. 303; 1 Sim. R. 105; 13 Price, R. 607; 1 McClel. R. 439; 1 Y. & C. 66; 2 Story, Eq. Jur. § 1075 to 1135; Domat, Lois Civ. liv. 4, tit. 2, § 3, art. 3, 4, 5; Poth. Pand. lib. 30, t. 1, n. 125; Inst. 2, 20, 4; Dig. 30, 1, 39, 7.

8. There are many other cases where a party may be compelled to make an election, which it does not fall within the plan of this work to consider. The reader will easily inform himself by examining the works above referred to.

9.—3. The law frequently gives several forms of action to the injured party, to enable him to recover his rights. To make a proper election of the proper remedy is of great importance. To enable the practitioner to make the best election, Mr. Chitty, in his valuable Treatise on Pleadings, p. 207, et seq., has very ably examined the subject, and given rules for forming a correct judgment; as his work is in the hands of every member of the profession, a reference to it here is all that is deemed necessary to say on this subject. See also, Hammond on Parties to Actions; Brown's Practical Treatise on Actions at Law, in the 45th vol. of the Law Library; U. S. Dig. Actions IV.

Election of actions, *practice.* It is frequently at the choice of the plaintiff what kind of an action to bring; a skilful practitioner would naturally select that in which his client can most easily prove what is his interest in the matter affected; may recover all his several demands against the defendant; may preclude the defendant from availing himself of a defence, which he might otherwise establish; may most easily introduce his own evidence; may not be embarrassed by making too many or too few persons parties to the suit; may try it in the county most convenient to himself; may demand bail where it is for the plaintiff's interest; may obtain a judgment with the least expense and delay; may entitle himself to costs; and may demand bail in error. 1 Chit. Pl. 207 to 214.

2. It may be laid down as a general rule, that when a statute prescribes a new remedy, the plaintiff has his election either to adopt such remedy, or proceed at common law. Such statutory remedy is cumulative, unless the statute expressly, or by necessary implication, takes away the common law remedy. 1 S. & R. 32; 6 S. & R. 20; 5 John. 175; 10 John. 389; 16 John. 220; 1 Call, 243; 2 Greenl. 404; 5 Greenl. 38; 6 Harr. & John. 383; 4 Halst. 384; 3 Chit. Pr. 130.

Election of a devise or legacy. It is an admitted principle, that a person shall not be permitted to claim under any instrument, whether it be a deed or a will, without giving full effect to it in every respect, so far as such person is concerned. When a testator, therefore, gives what belongs to another and not to him, and gives to the owner some estate of his own; this gift is under an implied condition, either that he shall part with his own estate, or not take the bounty. 9 Ves. 515; 10 Ves. 609; 13 Ves. 220; 2 Ves. 697; 1 Suppl. to Ves jr. 222; Id. 55; Id. 340. If, for example, a testator undertakes to dispose of an estate belonging to B, and devise to B other lands, or bequeath to him a legacy by the same will, B will not be permitted to keep his own estate, and enjoy at the same time the benefit of the devise or bequest made in his favor, but must elect whether he will part with his own estate, and accept the provisions in the will, or continue in possession of the former and reject the latter. See 2 Vern. 581; Forr. 176; 1 Swanst. 436, 447; 1 Bro. C. C. 480; 2 Rawle, 168: 17 S. & R. 16; 2 Gill, R. 182, 201; 1 Dev. Eq. R. 283; 3 Desaus. 346; 6 John. Ch. R. 33; Riley, Ch. R. 205; 1 Whart. 490; 5 Dana, 345; White's L. C. in Eq. *233.

2. The foundation of the equitable doctrine of election, is the intention, explicit or presumed, of the author of the instrument to which it is applied, and such is the import of the expression by which it is described as proceeding, sometimes on a tacit, implied, or constructive condition, sometimes on equity. See Cas. temp. Talb. 183; 2 Vern. 582; 2 Ves. 14; 1 Eden, R. 536; 1 Ves. 306. See, generally, 1 Swan. 380 to 408, 414, 425, 432, several very full notes.

3. As to what acts of acceptance or acquiescence will constitute an implied election, see 1 Swan. R. 381, n. a; and the cases there cited.

ELECTOR, *government*. One who has the right to make choice of public officers; one who has a right to vote.

2. The qualifications of electors are generally the same as those required in the person to be elected; to this, however, there is one exception; a naturalized citizen may be an elector of president of the United States, although he could not constitutionally be elected to that office.

ELECTORS OF PRESIDENT. Persons elected by the people, whose sole duty is to elect a president and vice-president of the U. S.

2. The Constitution provides, Am. art. 12, that "the electors shall meet in their respective states, and vote by ballot for president and vice-president, one of whom at least shall not be an inhabitant of the same state with themselves; they shall name in their ballots the person voted for as president, and in distinct ballots the person voted for as vice-president; and they shall make distinct lists of all persons voted for as president, and of all persons voted for as vice-president, and of the number of votes for each; which list they shall sign and certify, and transmit, sealed, to the seat of the government of the United States, directed to the president of the senate; the president of the senate shall, in the presence of the senate and the house of representatives, open all the certificates, and the votes shall then be counted; the person having the greatest number of votes for president, shall be the president, if such number be the majority of the whole number of electors appointed; and if no person have such majority, then from the persons having the highest numbers, not exceeding three, on the list of those voted for as president, the house of representatives shall choose immediately, by ballot, the president. But in choosing the president, the votes shall be taken by states, the representation from each state having one vote; a quorum, for this purpose, shall consist of a member or members from two-thirds of the states, and a majority of all the states shall be necessary to a choice. And if the house of representatives shall not choose a president whenever the right of choice shall devolve upon them, before the fourth day of March next following, then the vice-president shall act as president, as in the case of the death or other constitutional disability of the president.

3.—2. "The person having the greatest number of votes as vice-president shall be vice-president, if such number be a majority of the whole number of electors appointed; and if no person have a majority, then from the two highest numbers on the list, the senate shall choose the vice-president; a quorum for the purpose shall consist of two-thirds of the whole number of senators, and a majority of the whole number shall be necessary to a choice. But no person constitutionally ineligible to the office of president, shall be eligible to that of vice-president of the United States." Vide 3 Story, Const. § 1448 to 1470.

ELEEMOSYNARY. Charitable; almsgiving.

2. Eleemosynary corporations are colleges, schools, and hospitals. 1 Wood. Lect. 474; Skinn. 447; 1 Lord Raym. 5; 2 T. R. 346.

ELEGIT, *Eng. practice, remedies*. A writ of execution directed to the sheriff, commanding him to make delivery of a moiety of the party's land, and all his goods, beasts of the plough only excepted.

2. The sheriff, on the receipt of the writ, holds an inquest to ascertain the value of the lands and goods he has seized, and

then they are delivered to the plaintiff, who retains them until the whole debt and damages have been paid and satisfied; during that term he is called tenant by elegit. Co. Litt. 289. Vide Pow. Mortg. Index, h. t.; Wats. Sher. 206. As to the law of the several states on the subject of seizing land and extending it, see 1 Hill. Ab. 555-6.

ELIGIBILITY. Capacity to be elected.

2. Citizens are in general eligible to all offices; the exceptions arise from the want of those qualifications which the constitution requires; these are such as regard his person, his property, or relations to the state.

3.—1. In general, no person is eligible to *any* office, until he has attained the full age of twenty-one years; no one can be elected a senator of the United States, who shall not have attained the age of thirty years, been a citizen of the United States nine years, and who shall not be an inhabitant of the state for which he shall be chosen. Const. art. 1, s. 3. No person, except a natural born citizen, or a citizen of the United States at the time of the adoption of this constitution, is eligible to the office of president, and no person shall be eligible to that office, who shall not have attained the age of thirty-five years, and been fourteen years a resident within the United States. Const. art. 2, s. 1.

4.—2. A citizen may be ineligible in consequence of his relations to the state; for example, holding an office incompatible with the office sought. Vide *Ineligibility*. Because he has not paid the taxes the law requires; because he has not resided a sufficient length of time in the state.

5.—3. He may be ineligible for want of certain property qualifications required by some law.

ELISORS, *practice*. Two persons appointed by the court to return a jury, when the sheriff and the coroner have been challenged as incompetent; in this case the elisors return the writ of venire directed to them, with a panel of the juror's names, and their return is final, no challenge being allowed to their array. 3 Bl. Com. 355; 3 Cowen, 296; 1 Cowen, 32.

ELL. A measure of length. In old English the word signifies *arm*, which sense it still retains in the word *elbow*. Nature has no standard of measure. The cubit, the ell, the span, palm, hand, finger, (being taken from the individual who uses them,) varies. So of the foot, pace, mile, or mille passuum. See Report on Weights and Measures, by the Secretary of State of the United States, Feb. 22, 1821; *Fathom*.

ELOIGNE, *practice*. This word signifies, literally, to remove to a distance; to remove afar off. It is used as a return to a writ of replevin, when the chattels have been removed out of the way of the sheriff. Vide *Elongata*.

ELONGATA, *practice*. The return made by the sheriff to a writ of replevin, when the goods have been removed to places unknown to him. See, for the form of this return, Wats. Sher. Appx. c. 18, s. 3, p. 454; 3 Bl. Com. 148.

2. On this return the plaintiff is entitled to a capias in withernam. Vide *Withernam*, and Wats. Sher. 300, 301. The word *eloigné*, (q. v.) is sometimes used as synonymous with elongata.

ELOPEMENT. This term is used to denote the departure of a married woman from her husband, and dwelling with an adulterer.

2. While the wife resides with her husband, and cohabits with him, however exceptionable her conduct may be, yet he is bound to provide her with necessaries, and to pay for them; but when she elopes, the husband is no longer liable for her alimony, and is not bound to pay debts of her contracting, when the separation is notorious; and whoever gives her credit under these circumstances, does so at his peril. Chit. Contr. 49; 4 Esp. R. 42; 3 Pick. R. 289; 1 Str. R. 647, 706; 6 T. R. 603; 11 John. R. 281; 12 John. R. 293; Bull. N. P. 135; Stark. Ev. part 4, p. 699.

ELOQUENCE OR ORATORY. The act or art of speaking well upon any subject with a view to persuade. It comprehends a good elocution, correct and appropriate expressions uttered with fluency, animation and suitable action. The principal rules of the art, which must be sought for in other works, are summarily expressed in the following lines:

"Be brief, be pointed; let your matter stand
Lucid in order, solid, and at hand;
Spend not your words on trifles, but condense;
Strike with the mass of thoughts, not drops of sense;
Press to the close with vigor once begun,
And leave, (how hard the task!) leave off when done;
Who draws a labor'd length of reasoning out,
Put straws in lines for winds to whirl about;
Who draws a tedious tale of learning o'er,
Counts but the sands on ocean's boundless shore;
Victory in law is gain'd as battles fought,
Not by the numbers, but the forces brought;

What boots success in skirmishes or in fray,
If rout and ruin following close the day?
What worth a hundred posts maintain'd with skill,
If these all held, the foe is victor still?
He who would win his cause, with power must
frame
Points of support, and look with steady aim:
Attack the weak, defend the strong with art,
Strike but few blows, but strike them to the heart;
All scatter'd fires but end in smoke and noise,
The scorn of men, the idle play of boys.
Keep, then, this first great precept ever near,
Short be your speech, your matter strong and clear,
Earnest your manner, warm and rich your style,
Severe in taste, yet full of grace the while;
So may you reach the loftiest heights of fame,
And leave, when life is past, a deathless name."

ELSEWHERE. In another place.

2. Where one devises all his land in A, B and C, three distinct towns, and *elsewhere*, and had lands of much greater value than those in A, B and C, in another county, the lands in the other county were decreed to pass by the word elsewhere; and by Lord Chancellor King, assisted by Raymond, Ch. J., and other judges, the word elsewhere, was adjudged to be the same as if the testator had said he devised all his lands in the three towns particularly mentioned, or in any other place whatever. 3 P. Wms. 56. See also Prec. Chan. 202; 2 Vern. 461; 2 Vern. 560; 3 Atk. 492; Cowp. 360; Id. 808; 2 Barr. 912; 5 Bro. P. C. 496; S. C. 1 East, 456; 1 Vern. 4 n.

3.—2. As to the effect of the word elsewhere, in the case of lands not purchased at the time of making the will, see 3 Atk. 254; 2 Vent. 351. Vide *Alibi.*

EMANCIPATION. An act by which a person, who was once in the power of another, is rendered free. By the laws of Louisiana, minors may be emancipated. Emancipation is express or implied.

2. Express emancipation. The minor may be emancipated by his father, or, if he has no father, by his mother, under certain restrictions. This emancipation takes place by the declaration, to that effect, of the father or mother, before a notary public, in the presence of two witnesses. The orphan minor may, likewise, be emancipated by the judge, but not before he has arrived at the full age of eighteen years, if the family meeting, called to that effect, be of opinion that he is able to administer his property. The minor may be emancipated against the will of his father and mother, when they ill treat him excessively, refuse him support, or give him corrupt example.

3. The marriage of the minor is an implied emancipation.

4. The minor who is emancipated has the full administration of his estate, and may pass all acts which may be confined to such administration; grant leases, receive his revenues and moneys which may be due him, and give receipts for the same. He cannot bind himself legally, by promise or obligation, for any sum exceeding the amount of one year of his revenue. When he is engaged in trade, he is considered as having arrived to the age of majority, for all acts which have any relation to such trade.

5. The emancipation, whatever be the manner in which it may have been effected, may be revoked, whenever the minor contracts engagements which exceed the limits prescribed by law.

6. By the English law, filial emancipation is recognized, chiefly, in relation to the parochial settlement of paupers. See 3 T. R. 355; 6 T. R. 247; 8 T. R. 479; 2 East, 276; 10 East, 88; 11 Verm. R. 258, 477. See *Manumission.*

See Coop. Justin. 441, 480; 2 Dall. Rep. 57, 58; Civil Code of Louisiana, B. 1, tit. 8, c. 3; Code Civ. B. 1, tit. 10, c. 2; Dict. de Droit, par Ferrière; Dict. de Jurisp. art. Emancipation.

EMBARGO, *maritime law.* A proclamation, or order of state, usually issued in time of war, or threatened hostilities, prohibiting the departure of ships or goods from some, or all the ports of such state, until further order. 2 Wheat. 148.

2. The detention of ships by an embargo is such an injury to the owner as to entitle him to recover on a policy of insurance against "arrests or detainments." And whether the embargo be legally or illegally laid, the injury to the owner is the same; and the insurer is equally liable for the loss occasioned by it. Marsh. Ins. B. 1, c. 12, s. 5; 1 Kent, Com. 60; 1 Bell's Com. 517, 5th ed.

3. An embargo detaining a vessel at the port of departure, or in the course of the voyage, does not, of itself, work a dissolution of a charter party, or the contract with the seamen. It is only a temporary restraint imposed by authority for legitimate political purposes, which suspends, for a time, the performance of such contracts, and leaves the rights of parties untouched. 1 Bell's Com. 517; 8 T. R. 259; 5 Johns. R. 308; 7 Mass. R. 325, 3 B. & P. 405–434; 4 East, R. 546–566.

EMBEZZLEMENT, *crim. law.* The fraudulently removing and secreting of personal property, with which the party has been entrusted, for the purpose of applying it to his own use.

2. The Act of April 30, 1790, s. 16, 1 Story, L. U. S. 86, provides, that if any person, within any of the places under the sole and exclusive jurisdiction of the United States, or upon the high seas, shall take and carry away, with an intent to steal or purloin, the personal goods of another; or if any person or persons, having, at any time hereafter, the charge or custody of any arms, ordnance, munition, shot, powder, or habiliments of war, belonging to the United States, or of any victuals provided for the victualling of any soldiers, gunners, marines, or pioneers, shall, for any lucre or gain, or wittingly, advisedly, and of purpose to hinder or impede the service of the United States, embezzle, purloin, or convey away, any of the said arms, ordnance, munition, shot or powder, habiliments of war, or victuals, that then, and in every of the cases aforesaid, the persons so offending, their counsellors, aiders and abettors, (knowing of, and privy to the offences aforesaid,) shall, on conviction, be fined, not exceeding the fourfold value of the property so stolen, embezzled or purloined; the one moiety to be paid to the owner of the goods, or the United States, as the case may be, and the other moiety to the informer and prosecutor, and be publicly whipped, not exceeding thirty-nine stripes.

3. The Act of April 20, 1818, 3 Story, 1715, directs that wines and distilled spirits shall, in certain cases, be deposited in the public warehouses of the United States, and then it is enacted, s. 5, that if any wines, or other spirits, deposited under the provisions of this act, shall be embezzled, or fraudulently hid or removed, from any store or place wherein they shall have been deposited, they shall be forfeited, and the person or persons so embezzling, hiding, or removing the same, or aiding or assisting therein, shall be liable to the same pains and penalties as if such wines or spirits had been fraudulently unshipped or landed without payment of duty.

4. By the 21st section of the act to reduce into one the several acts establishing and regulating the post-office, passed March 3, 1825, 3 Story, 1991, the offence of embezzling letters is punished with fine and imprisonment. Vide *Letter*.

5. The act more effectually to provide for the punishment of certain crimes against the United States, and for other purposes, passed March 3, 1825, s. 24, 3 Story, 2006, enacts, that if any of the gold or silver coins which shall be struck or coined at the mint of the United States, shall be debased, or made worse, as to the proportion of fine gold or fine silver therein contained, or shall be of less weight or value than the same ought to be, pursuant to the several acts relative thereto, through the default or with the connivance of any of the officers or persons who shall be employed at the said mint, for the purpose of profit or gain, or otherwise, with a fraudulent intent; and if any of the said officers or persons shall embezzle any of the metals which shall, at any time, be committed to their charge for the purpose of being coined; or any of the coins which shall be struck or coined, at the said mint; every such officer, or person who shall commit any, or either, of the said offences, shall be deemed guilty of felony, and shall be sentenced to imprisonment and hard labor for a term not less than one year, nor more than ten years, and shall be fined in a sum not exceeding ten thousand dollars.

6. When an embezzlement of a part of the cargo takes place on board of a ship, either from the fault, fraud, connivance or negligence of any of the crew, they are bound to contribute to the reparation of the loss, in proportion to their wages. When the embezzlement is fixed on any individual, he is solely responsible; when it is made by the crew, or some of the crew, but the particular offender is unknown, and from the circumstances of the case, strong presumptions of guilt apply to the whole crew, all must contribute. The presumption of innocence is always in favor of the crew, and the guilt of the parties must be established, beyond all reasonable doubt, before they can be required to contribute. 1 Mason's R. 104; 4 B. & P. 347; 3 Johns. Rep. 17; 1 Marsh. Ins. 241; Dane's Ab. Index, h. t.; Wesk. Ins. 194; 3 Kent, Com. 151; Hardin, 529.

EMBLEMENTS, *rights.* By this term is understood the crops growing upon the land. By crops is here meant the products of the earth which grow yearly and are raised by annual expense and labor, or "great manurance and industry," such as grain; but not fruits which grow on trees which are not to be planted yearly, or grass, and the like, though they are annual. Co. Litt. 55, b; Com. Dig. Biens, G; Ham. Part. 183, 184.

2. It is a general rule, that when the estate is terminated by the act of God in any other way than by the death of the tenant for life, or by act of the law, the tenant is entitled to the emblements; and when he dies before harvest time, his executors shall have the emblements, as a return for the labor and expense of the deceased in tilling the ground. 9 Johns. R. 112; 1 Chit. P. 91; 8 Vin. Ab. 364; Woodf. L. & T. 237; Toll. Ex. book 2, c. 4; Bac. Ab. Executors, H 3; Co. Litt. 55; Com. Dig. Biens, G; Dane's Ab. Index, h. t.; 1 Penna. R. 471; 3 Penna. 496; Ang. Wat. Co. 1; Bouv. Inst. Index, h. t.

EMBRACEOR, *criminal law.* He who, when a matter is on trial between party and party, comes to the bar with one of the parties, and having received some reward so to do, speaks in the case or privily labors the jury, or stands there to survey or overlook them, thereby to put them in fear and doubt of the matter. But persons learned in the law may speak in a case for their clients. Co. Litt. 369; Terms de la Ley. A person who is guilty of embracery. (q. v.)

EMBRACERY, *crim. law.* An attempt to corrupt or influence a jury, or any way incline them to be more favorable to the one side than to the other, by money, promises, threats, or persuasions; whether the juror on whom such attempt is made give any verdict or not, or whether the verdict be true or false. Hawk. 259; Bac. Ab. Juries, M 3; Co. Litt. 157, b, 369, a; Hob. 294; Dy. 84, a, pl. 19; Noy, 102; 1 Str. 643; 11 Mod. 111, 118; Com. 601; 5 Cowen, 503.

EMENDALS, *Eng. law.* This ancient word is said to be used in the accounts of the inner temple, where so much in emendals at the foot of an account signifies so much in bank, in stock, for the supply of emergencies. Cunn. Law Dict.

EMIGRANT. One who quits his country for any lawful reason, with a design to settle elsewhere, and who takes his family and property, if he has any, with him. Vatt. b. 1, c. 19, § 224.

EMIGRATION. The act of removing from one place to another. It is sometimes used in the same sense as expatriation, (q. v.) but there is some difference in the signification. Expatriation is the act of abandoning one's country, while emigration is, perhaps not strictly, applied to the act of removing from one part of the country to another. Vide 2 Kent, Com. 36.

EMINENCE. A title of honor given to cardinals.

EMINENT DOMAIN. The right which the people or government retain over the estates of individuals, to resume the same for public use.

2. It belongs to the legislature to decide what improvements are of sufficient importance to justify the exercise of the right of eminent domain. See 2 Hill. Ab. 568; 1 U. S. Dig. 560; 1 Am. Eq. Dig. 312; 3 Toull. n. 30, p. 23; Ersk. Inst. B. 2, tit. 1, s. 2; Grotius, h. t. See Dominium.

EMISSARY. One who is sent from one power or government into another nation for the purpose of spreading false rumors and to cause alarm. He differs from a spy (q. v.)

EMISSION, *med. jur.* The act by which any matter whatever is thrown from the body; thus it is usual to say, emission of urine, emission of semen, &c.

2. In cases of rape, when the fact of penetration is proved, it may be left to the jury whether emission did or did not take place. Proof of emission would perhaps be held to be evidence of penetration. Addis. R. 143; 2 So. Car. Const. R. 351; 2 Chitty, Crim. Law, 810; 1 Beck's Med. Jur. 140; 1 Russ. C. & M. 560; 1 East, P. C. 437.

TO EMIT. To put out; to send forth.

2. The tenth section of the first article of the constitution, contains various prohibitions, among which is the following: No state shall emit bills of credit. To emit bills of credit is to issue paper intended to circulate through the community for its ordinary purposes, as money, which paper is redeemable at a future day. 4 Pet. R. 410, 432; Story on Const. § 1358. Vide *Bills of credit.*

EMMENAGOGUES, *med. jur.* The name of a class of medicines which are believed to have the power of favoring the discharge of the menses. These are *black hellebore*, *savine*, (vide *Juneperius Sabina*,) *madder*, *mercury*, *polygala*, *senega*, and *pennyroyal* They are sometimes used for the criminal purpose of producing abortion. (q. v.) They always endanger the life of the woman. 1 Beck's Medical Jur. 316; Dungl. Med. Dict. h. t.; Parr's Med. Dict. h. t.; 3 Paris and Fonbl. Med. Jur. 88.

EMOLUMENT. The lawful gain or profit which arises from an office.

EMPALEMENT. A punishment in which a sharp pole was forced up the fundament. Encyc. Lond. h. t.

TO EMPANEL, *practice*. To make a list or roll, by the sheriff or other authorized officer, of the names of jurors who are summoned to appear for the performance of such service as jurors are required to perform.

EMPEROR, *an officer*. This word is synonymous with the Latin *imperator;* they are both derived from the verb *imperare*. Literally, it signifies *he who commands*.

2. Under the Roman republic, the title emperor was the generic name given to the commanders-in-chief in the armies. But even then the application of the word was restrained to the successful commander, who was declared emperor by the acclamations of the army, and was afterwards honored with the title by a decree of the senate.

3. It is now used to designate some sovereign prince who bears this title. Ayl. Pand. tit. 23.

EMPHYTEOSIS, *civil law*. The name of a contract by which the owner of an uncultivated piece of land granted it to another either in perpetuity, or for a long time, on condition that he should improve it, by building, planting or cultivating it, and should pay for it an annual rent; with a right to the grantee to alienate it, or transmit it by descent to his heirs, and under a condition that the grantor should never reënter as long as the rent should be paid to him by the grantee or his assigns. Inst. 3, 25, 3; 18 Toull. n. 144.

2. This has a striking resemblance to a ground-rent. (q. v.) See Nouveau Denisart, mot Emphytéose; Merl. Réper. mot Emphytéose; Faber, De jure emphyt. Definit. 36; Code, 4, 66, 1.

EMPIRE. This word signifies, first, authority or command; it is the power to command or govern those actions of men which would otherwise be free; secondly, the country under the government of an emperor; but sometimes it is used to designate a country subject to kingly power, as the British empire. Wolff, Inst. § 833.

EMPLOYED. One who is in the service of another. Such a person is entitled to rights and liable to perform certain duties.

2. He is entitled to a just compensation for his services; when there has been a special contract, to what has been agreed upon; when not, to such just recompense as he deserves.

3. He is bound to perform the services for which he has engaged himself; and for a violation of his engagement he may be sued, but he is not liable to corporal correction. An exception to this rule may be mentioned; on the ground of necessity, a sailor may be punished by reasonable correction, when it is necessary for the safety of the vessel, and to maintain discipline. 1 Bouv. Inst. n. 1001; 2 Id. n. 2296.

EMPLOYEE. One who is authorized to act for another; a mandatory.

EMPLOYMENT. An employment is an office; as, the secretary of the treasury has a laborious and responsible employment; an agency, as, the employment of an auctioneer; it signifies also the act by which one is engaged to do something. 2 Mart. N. S. 672; 2 Harr. Cond. Lo. R. 778.

2. The employment of a printer to publish the laws of the United States, is not an office. 17 S. & R. 219, 223. See *Appointment*.

EMPLOYER. One who has engaged or hired the services of another. He is entitled to rights and bound to perform duties.

2.—1. His rights are, to be served according to the terms of the contract. 2. He has a right against third persons for an injury to the person employed, or for harboring him, so as to deprive the employer of his services. 2 Bouv. Inst. n. 2295.

3. His duties are to pay the workman the compensation agreed upon, or if there be no special agreement, such just recompense as he deserves. Vide *Hire; Hirer*.

EMPTION. The act of buying.

EMPTOR. A buyer; a purchaser.

EN DEMEURE. In default. This term is used in Louisiana. 3 N. S. 574 See *Mora, in*.

ENABLING POWERS. A term used in equity. When the donor of a power, who is the owner of the estate, confers upon persons not seised of the fee, the right of creating interests to take effect out of it, which could not be done by the donee of the power, unless by such authority; this is called an *enabling power*. 2 Bouv. Inst. n. 1928.

TO ENACT. To establish by law; to perform or effect; to decree. The usual formula in making laws is, *Be it enacted*.

ENCEINTE, *med. jur*. A French word, which signifies pregnant.

2. When a woman is pregnant, and is convicted of a capital crime, she cannot lawfully be punished till after her delivery.

3. In the English law, where a widow is suspected to feign herself with child, in order to produce a supposititious heir to the estate, the presumptive heir may have a writ *de ventre inspiciendo*, to examine whether she be with child or not. Cro. Eliz. 566; 4 Bro. C. C. 90. As to the signs of pregnancy, see 1 Beck's Med. Jur. 157. See, generally, 4 Bl. Com. 394; 2 P. Wms. 591; 1 Cox, C. C. 297; and *Pregnancy; Privement enceinte.*

ENCLOSURE. An artificial fence put around one's estate. Vide *Close.*

ENCROACHMENT. An unlawful gaining upon the right or possession of another; as, when a man sets his fence beyond his line; in this case the proper remedy for the party injured is an action of ejectment, or an action of trespass.

ENCUMBRANCE. A burden or charge upon an estate or property, so that it cannot be disposed of without being subject to it. A mortgage, a lien for taxes, are examples of encumbrances.

2. These do not affect the possession of the grantee, and may be removed or extinguished by a definite pecuniary value. See 2 Greenl. R. 22; 5 Greenl. R. 94.

3. There are encumbrances of another kind which cannot be so removed, such as easements; for example, a highway, or a preëxisting right to take water from the land. Strictly speaking, however, these are not encumbrances, but appurtenances to estates in other lands, or in the language of the civil law, servitudes. (q. v.) 5 Conn. R. 497; 10 Conn. R. 422; 15 John. R. 483; and see 8 Pick. R. 349; 2 Wheat. R. 45. See 15 Verm. R. 683; 1 Metc. 480; 9 Metc. 462; 1 App. R. 313; 4 Ala. 21; 4 Humph. 99; 18 Pick. 403; 1 Ala. 645; 22 Pick. 447; 11 Gill & John. 472.

ENDEAVOR, *crim. law.* An attempt. (q. v.) Vide *Revolt.*

ENDORSEMENT. Vide *Indorsement.*

ENDOWMENT. The bestowing or assuring of a dower to a woman. It is sometimes used metaphorically for the setting a provision for a charitable institution, as the endowment of a hospital.

ENEMY, *international law.* By this term is understood the whole body of a nation at war with another. It also signifies a citizen or subject of such a nation, as when we say an alien enemy. In a still more extended sense, the word includes any of the subjects or citizens of a state in amity with the United States, who have commenced, or have made preparations for commencing hostilities against the United States; and also the citizens or subjects of a state in amity with the United States, who are in the service of a state at war with them. Salk. 635; Bac. Ab. Treason, G.

2. An enemy cannot, as a general rule, enter into any contract which can be enforced in the courts of law; but the rule is not without exceptions; as, for example, when a state permits expressly its own citizens to trade with the enemy; and perhaps a contract for necessaries, or for money to enable the individual to get home, might be enforced. 7 Pet. R. 586.

3. An alien enemy cannot, in general, sue during the war, a citizen of the United States, either in the courts of the United States, or those of the several states. 1 Kent, Com. 68; 15 John. R. 57; S. C. 16 John. R. 438. Vide Marsh. Ins. c. 2, s. 1; Park. Ins. Index. h. t.; Wesk. Ins. 197; Phil. Ins. Index. h. t.; Chit. Comm. Law, Index, h. t.; Chit. Law of Nations, Index, h. t.

4. By the term enemy is also understood, a person who is desirous of doing injury to another. The Latins had two terms to signify these two classes of persons; the first, or the public enemy, they called *hostis*, and the latter, or the private enemy, *inimicus.*

TO ENFEOFF. To make a gift of any corporeal hereditaments to another. Vide *Feoffment.*

TO ENFRANCHISE. To make free; to incorporate a man in a society or body politic. Cunn. L. D. h. t. Vide *Disfranchise.*

ENGAGEMENT. This word is frequently used in the French law to signify not only a contract, but the obligations arising from a *quasi contract.* The terms *obligations* (q. v.) and *engagements*, are said to be synonymous; 17 Toull. n. 1; but the Code seems specially to apply the term engagement to those obligations which the law imposes on a man without the intervention of any contract, either on the part of the obligor or the obligee. Art. 1370.

ENGLESHIRE. A law was made by Canutus, for the preservation of his Danes, that when a man was killed, the hundred or town should be liable to be amerced, unless it could be proved that the person killed was an Englishman. This proof was called *Engleshire*. It consisted, generally, of the testimony of two males on the part of the father of him that had been killed, and two females on the part of his mother. Hal. Hist. P. C. 447; 4 Bl. Com. 195; Spelman, Gloss. See *Francigena*.

TO ENGROSS, *practice, conveyancing*. To copy the rude draught of an instrument in a fair and large hand. See 3 Bouv. Inst. n. 2421, note.

ENGROSSER. One who purchases large quantities of any commodities in order to have the command of the market, and to sell them again at high prices.

TO ENJOIN. To command; to require; as, private individuals are not only permitted, but enjoined by law to arrest an offender when present at the time a felony is committed or dangerous wound given, on pain of fine and imprisonment if the wrong doer escape through their negligence. 1 Hale, 587; 1 East, P. C. 298, 304; Hawk. B. 2, c. 12, s. 13; R. & M. C. C. 93.

2. In a more technical sense, to enjoin, is to command or order a defendant in equity to do or not to do a particular thing by writ of injunction. Vide *Injunction*.

TO ENLARGE. To extend; as, to enlarge a rule to plead, is to extend the time during which a defendant may plead. To enlarge, means also to set at liberty; as, the prisoner was enlarged on giving bail.

ENLARGING. Extending or making more comprehensive; as, an enlarging statute, which is one extending the common law.

ENITIA PARS. The part of the eldest. Co. Litt. 166; Bac. Ab. Coparceners, C.

2. When partition is voluntarily made among coparceners in England, the eldest has the first choice, or *primer election*, (q. v.) and the part which she takes is called *enitia pars*. This right is purely personal, and descends; it is also said that even her assignee shall enjoy it; but this has also been doubted. The word *enitia* is said to be derived from the old French, *eisne*, the eldest. Bac. Ab. Coparceners, C; Keilw. 1 a, 49 a; 2 And. 21; Cro. Eliz. 18.

ENJOYMENT. The right which a man possesses of receiving all the product of a thing for his necessity, his use, or his pleasure.

ENLISTMENT. The act of making a contract to serve the government in a subordinate capacity, either in the army or navy. The contract so made, is also called an enlistment. See, as to the power of infants to enlist, 4 Binn. 487; 5 Binn. 423; 6 Binn. 255; 1 S. & R. 87; 11 S. & R. 93.

ENORMIA. Wrongful acts. See *Alia Enormia*.

TO ENROLL. To register; to enter on the rolls of chancery, or other courts; to make a record.

ENROLLMENT, *Eng. law*. The registering or entering in the rolls of chancery, king's bench, common pleas, or exchequer, or by the clerk of the peace in the records of the quarter sessions, of any lawful act; as a recognizance, a deed of bargain and sale, and the like. Jacob, L. D.

TO ENTAIL. To create an estate tail. Vide *Tail*.

ENTIRE. That which is not divided; that which is whole.

2. When a contract is entire, it must in general be fully performed, before the party can claim the compensation which was to have been paid to him; for example, when a man hires to serve another for one year, he will not be entitled to leave him at any time before the end of the year, and claim compensation for the time, unless it be done by the consent or default of the party hiring. 6 Verm. R. 35; 2 Pick. R. 267; 4 Pick. R. 103; 10 Pick. R. 209; 4 McCord's R. 26, 246; 4 Greenl. R. 454; 2 Penna. R. 454; 15 John. R. 224; 4 Pick. R. 114; 9 Pick. R. 298; 19 John. R. 337; 4 McCord, 249; 6 Harr. & John. 38. See *Divisible*.

ENTIRETY, or ENTIERTIE. This word denotes the whole, in contradistinction to moiety, which denotes the half part. A husband and wife, when jointly seized of land, are seized by entierties and not *pur mie* as joint tenants are. Jacob's Law Dict.; 4 Kent, 362; 2 Kent, 132; Hart *v.* Johnson, 3 Penna. Law Journ. 350, 357.

ENTREPOT. A warehouse; a magazine where goods are deposited, and which are again to be removed.

ENTRY, *criminal law*. The unlawful breaking into a house, in order to commit a crime. In cases of burglary, the least entry with the whole or any part of the body, hand, or foot, or with any instrument or weapon, introduced for the purpose of committing a felony, is sufficient to complete the offence. 3 Inst. 64.

ENTRY, *estates, rights*. The taking possession of lands by the legal owner.

2. A person having a right of possession

may assert it by a *peaceable* entry, and *being in possession may retain it*, and plead that it is his soil and freehold; and this will not break in upon any rule of law respecting the mode of obtaining the possession of lands. 3 Term Rep. B. R. 295. When another person has taken possession of lands or tenements, and the owner peaceably makes an entry thereon, and declares that he thereby takes possession of the same, he shall, by this notorious act of ownership, which is equal to a feodal investiture, be restored to his original right. 3 Bl. Com. 174.

3. A right of entry is not assignable at common law. Co. Litt. 214 a. As to the law on this subject in the United States, vide *Buying of titles;* 4 Kent, Com. 439; 2 Hill. Ab. c. 33, § 42 to 52; also, article *Reëntry;* Bac. Ab. Descent, G; 8 Vin. Ab. 441.

4. In another sense, entry signifies the going upon another man's lands or his tenements. An entry in this sense may be justifiably made on another's land or house, first, when the law confers an authority; and secondly, when the party has authority in fact.

5.—First, 1. An officer may enter the close of one against whose person or property he is charged with the execution of a writ. In a civil case, the officer cannot open (even by unlatching) the outer inlet to a house, as a door or window opening into the street; 18 Edw. IV., Easter, 19, pl. 4; Moore, pl. 917, p. 668; Cooke's case, Wm. Jones, 429; although it has been closed for the purpose of excluding him. Cowp. 1. But in a criminal case, a constable may break open an outer door to arrest one within suspected of felony. 13 Edw. IV., Easter, 4, p. 9. If the outer door or window be open, he may enter through it to execute a civil writ; Palm. 52; 5 Rep. 91; and, having entered, he may, in every case, if necessary, break open an inner door. 1 Brownl. 50.

6.—2. The lord may enter to distrain, and go into the house for that purpose, the outer door being open. 5 Rep. 91.

7.—3. The proprietors of goods or chattels may enter the land of another upon which they are placed, and remove them, provided they are there without his default; as where his tree has blown down into the adjoining close by the wind, or his fruit has fallen from a branch which overhung it. 20 Vin. Abr. 418.

8.—4. If one man is bound to repair a bridge, he has a right of entry given him by law for that purpose. Moore, 889.

9.—5. A creditor has a right to enter the close of his debtor, to demand the duty owing, though it is not to be rendered there. Cro. Eliz. 876.

10.—6. If trees are excepted out of a demise, the lessor has the right of entering, to prune or fell them. Cro. Eliz. 17; 11 Rep. 53.

11.—7. Every traveller has, by law, the privilege of entering a common inn, at all seasonable times, provided the host has sufficient accommodation, which, if he has not, it is for him to declare.

12.—8. Every man may throw down a public nuisance, and a private one may be thrown down by the party grieved, and this before any prejudice happens, but only from the probability that it may happen. 5 Rep. 102; and see 1 Brownl. 212; 12 Mod. 510; Wm. Jones, 221; 1 Str. 683. To this end, the abator has authority to enter the close in which it stands. See *Nuisance*.

13.—9. An entry may be made on the land of another, to exercise or enjoy therein an incorporeal right or hereditament to which he is entitled. Hamm. N. P. 172. See, generally, Bouv. Inst. Index, h. t.; 2 Greenl. Ev. § 627; *License*.

ENTRY, *commercial law.* The act of setting down the particulars of a sale, or other transaction, in a merchant's or tradesman's account books; such entries are, in general, *prima facie* evidence of the sale and delivery, and of work done; but unless the entry be the original one, it is not evidence. Vide *Original entry*.

ENTRY AD COMMUNEM LEGEM, *Eng. law.* The name of a writ which lies in favor of the reversioner, when the tenant for term of life, tenant for term of another's life, tenant by the curtesy, or tenant in dower, aliens and dies. T. L.

ENTRY OF GOODS, *commercial law.* An entry of goods at the custom-house is the submitting to the officers appointed by law, who have the collection of the customs, goods imported into the United States, together with a statement or description of such goods, and the original invoices of the same.

The act of March 2, 1799, s. 36, 1 Story, L. U. S. 606, and the act of March 1, 1823, 3 Story, L. U. S. 1881, regulate the manner of making entries of goods.

ENTRY, WRIT OF. The name of a writ issued for the purpose of obtaining possession of land from one who has entered unlawfully, and continues in possession. This is a mere possessory action, and does not decide the right of property.

2. The writs of entry were commonly brought, where the tenant or possessor of the land entered lawfully; that is, without fraud or force; 13 Edw. I. c. 25; although sometimes they were founded upon an entry made by wrong. The forms of these writs are very various, and are adapted to the title and estate of the demandant. Booth enumerates and particularly discusses twelve varieties. Real Actions, pp. 175–200. In general they contain an averment of the manner in which the defendant entered. At the common law these actions could be brought only *in the degrees*, but the Statute of Marlbridge, c. 30; Rob. Dig. 147, cited as c. 29; gave a writ adapted to cases beyond the degrees, called a writ of entry *in the post*. Booth, 172, 173. The denomination of these writs by degrees, is derived from the circumstance that estates are supposed by the law to pass *by degrees* from one person to another, either by descent or purchase. Similar to this idea, or rather corresponding with it, are the gradations of consanguinity, indicated by the very common term *pedigree*. But in reference to the writs of entry, the degrees recognized were only two, and the writs were quaintly termed writs in the *per*, and writs in the *per* and *cui*. Examples of these writs are given in Booth on R. A. pp. 173, 174. The writ in the *per* runs thus: "Command A, that he render unto B, one messuage, &c., into which he has not entry except (*per*) by C," &c. The writ in the *per* and *cui* contains another gradation in the transmission of the estate, and read thus: "Command A, that he render, &c., one messuage, into which he hath not entry but (*per*) by C, (*cui*) to whom the aforesaid B demised it for a term of years, now expired," &c. 2 Institute, 153; Co. Litt. b, 239, a. Booth, however, makes three degrees, by accounting the estate in the *per*, the second degree. The difference is not substantial. If the estate had passed further, either by descent or conveyance, it was said to be out of the degrees, and to such cases the writ of entry on the statute of Marlbridge, only, was applicable. 3 Bl. Com. 181, 182; Report of Com. to Revise Civil Code of Penna. January 15, 1835, p. 85. Vide *Writ of entry*.

TO ENURE. To take or have effect; or serve to the use, benefit, or advantage of a person. The word is often written *inure*. A release to the tenant for life, *enures* to him in reversion; that is, it has the same effect for him as for the tenant for life. A discharge of the principal enures to the benefit of the surety.

ENVOY, *international law*. In diplomatic language, an envoy is a minister of the second rank, on whom his sovereign or government has conferred a degree of dignity and respectability, which, without being on a level with an ambassador, immediately follows, and among ministers, yields the preëminence to him alone.

2. Envoys are either ordinary or extraordinary; by custom the latter is held in greater consideration. Vattel, liv. 4, c. 6, § 72.

EPILEPSY, *med. jur.* A disease of the brain, which occurs in paroxysms, with uncertain intervals between them.

2. These paroxysms are characterized by the loss of sensation, and convulsive motions of the muscles. When long continued and violent, this disease is very apt to end in dementia. (q. v.) It gradually destroys the memory, and impairs the intellect, and is one of the causes of an unsound mind. 8 Ves. 87. Vide Dig. 50, 16, 123; Id. 21, 1, 4, 5.

EPISCOPACY, *eccl. law*. A form of government by diocesan bishops; the office or condition of a bishop.

EPISTLES, *civil law*. The name given to a species of rescript. Epistles were the answers given by the prince, when magistrates submitted to him a question of law. Vide *Rescripts*.

EQUALITY. Possessing the same rights, and being liable to the same duties. See 1 Toull. No. 170, 193, Int.

2. Persons are all equal before the law, whatever adventitious advantages some may possess over others. All persons are protected by the law, and obedience to it is required from all.

3. Judges in court, while exercising their functions, are all upon an equality, it being a rule that *inter pares non est potestas;* a judge cannot, therefore, punish another judge of the same court for using any expression in court, although the words used might have been a contempt in any other person. Bac. Ab., Of the court of sessions, of justices of the peace.

4. In contracts the law presumes the parties act upon a perfect equality; when,

therefore, one party uses any fraud or deceit to destroy this equality, the party grieved may avoid the contract. In case of a grant to two or more persons jointly, without designating what each takes, they are presumed to take in equal proportions. 4 Day, 395.

5. It is a maxim, that when the equity of the parties is equal, the law must prevail. 3 Call, R. 259. And that, as between different creditors, equality is equity. 4 Bouv. Inst. n. 3725; 1 Page, R. 181. See Kames on Eq. 75. Vide *Deceit; Fraud.*

EQUINOX. The name given to two periods of the year when the days and nights are equal; that is, when the space of time between the rising and setting of the sun is one half of a natural day. Dig. 43, 13, 1, 8. Vide *Day.*

EQUITABLE. That which is in conformity to the natural law. Wolff, Inst. § 83.

EQUITABLE ESTATE. An equitable estate is a right or interest in land, which, not having the properties of a legal estate, but being merely a right of which courts of equity will take notice, requires the aid of such court to make it available.

2. These estates consist of uses, trusts, and powers. See 2 Bouv. Inst. n. 1884. Vide *Cestui que trust; Cestui que use.*

EQUITABLE MORTGAGE, *Eng. law.* The deposit of title-deeds, by the owner of an estate, with a person from whom he has borrowed money, with an accompanying agreement to execute a regular mortgage, or by the mere deposit, without even any verbal agreement respecting a regular security. 2 Pow. on Mort. 49 to 61; 1 Mad. Ch. Pr. 537; 4 Madd. R. 249; 1 Bro. C. C. 269; 12 Ves. 197; 3 Younge & J. 150; 1 Rus. R. 141.

2. In Pennsylvania, there is no such thing as an equitable mortgage. 3 P. S. R. 233; 3 Penna. R. 239; 17 S. & R. 70; 1 Penna. R. 447.

EQUITY. In the early history of the law, the sense affixed to this word was exceedingly vague and uncertain. This was owing, in part, to the fact, that the chancellors of those days were either statesmen or ecclesiastics, perhaps not very scrupulous in the exercise of power. It was then asserted that equity was bounded by no certain limits or rules, and that it was alone controlled by conscience and natural justice. 3 Bl. Com. 433, 440, 441.

2. In a moral sense, that is called equity which is founded, *ex æquo et bono*, in natural justice, in honesty, and in right. In an enlarged legal view, "equity, in its true and genuine meaning, is the soul and spirit of the law; positive law is construed, and rational law is made by it. In this, equity is made synonymous with justice; in that, to the true and sound interpretation of the rule." 3 Bl. Com. 429. This equity is justly said to be a supplement to the laws; but it must be directed by science. The Roman law will furnish him with sure guides, and safe rules. In that code will be found, fully developed, the first principles and the most important consequences of natural right. "From the moment when principles of decision came to be acted upon in chancery," says Mr. Justice Story, "the Roman law furnished abundant materials to erect a superstructure, at once solid, convenient and lofty, adapted to human wants, and enriched by the aid of human wisdom, experience and learning." Com. on Eq. Jur. § 23; Digest, 54.

3. But equity has a more restrained and qualified meaning. The remedies for the redress of wrongs, and for the enforcement of rights, are distinguished into two classes; first, those which are administered in courts of common law; and, secondly, those which are administered in courts of equity. Rights which are recognized and protected, and wrongs which are redressed by the former courts, are called legal rights and legal injuries. Rights which are recognized and protected, and wrongs which are redressed by the latter courts only, are called equitable rights and equitable injuries. The former are said to be rights and wrongs at common law, and the remedies, therefore, are remedies at common law; the latter are said to be rights and wrongs in equity, and the remedies, therefore, are remedies in equity. Equity jurisprudence may, therefore, properly be said to be that portion of remedial justice which is exclusively administered by a court of equity, as contradistinguished from that remedial justice, which is exclusively administered by a court of law. Story, Eq. § 25. Vide *Chancery*, and the authorities there cited; and 3 Chit. Bl. Com. 425 n. 1; Dane's Ab. h. t.; Ayl. Pand. 37; Fonbl. Eq. b. 1, c. 1; Wooddes. Lect. 114; Bouv. Inst. Index, h. t.

EQUITY, COURT OF. A court of equity is one which administers justice, where there are no legal rights, or legal rights, but courts of law do not afford a complete remedy, and where the complainant has also an equitable right. Vide *Chancery*.

EQUITY OF REDEMPTION. A right which the mortgagee of an estate has of redeeming it, after it has been forfeited at law by the non-payment at the time appointed of the money secured by the mortgage to be paid, by paying the amount of the debt, interest and costs.

2. An equity of redemption is a mere creature of a court of equity, founded on this principle, that as a mortgage is a pledge for securing the repayment of a sum of money to the mortgagee, it is but natural justice to consider the ownership of the land as still vested in the mortgagor, subject only to the legal title of the mortgagee, so far as such legal title is necessary to his security.

3. In Pennsylvania, however, redemption is a legal right. 11 Serg. & Rawle, 223.

4. The phrase equity of redemption is indiscriminately, though perhaps not correctly applied, to the right of the mortgagor to regain his estate, both *before* and *after* breach of condition. In North Carolina by statute the former is called a *legal right of redemption;* and the latter the *equity of redemption*, thereby keeping a just distinction between these estates. 1 N. C. Rev. St. 266; 4 McCord, 340.

5. Once a mortgage always a mortgage, is a universal rule in equity. The right of redemption is said to be as inseparable from a mortgage, as that of replevying from a distress, and every attempt to limit this right must fail. 2 Chan. Cas. 22; 1 Vern. 33, 190; 2 John. Ch. R. 30; 7 John. Ch. R. 40; 7 Cranch, R. 218; 2 Cowen, 324; 1 Yeates, R. 584; 2 Chan. R. 221; 2 Sumner, R. 487.

6. The right of redemption exists, not only in the mortgagor himself, but in his heirs, and personal representatives, and assignee, and in every other person who has an interest in, or a legal or equitable lien upon the lands; and therefore a tenant in dower, a jointress, a tenant by the curtesy, a remainder-man and a reversioner, a judgment creditor, and every other incumbrancer, unless he be an incumbrancer *pendente lite*, may redeem. 4 Kent, Com. 156; 5 Pick. R. 149; 9 John. R. 591, 611; 9 Mass. R. 422; 2 Litt. R. 334; 1 Pick. R. 485; 14 Wend. R. 233; 5 John. Ch. R. 482; 6 N. H. Rep. 25; 7 Vin. Ab. 52. Vide, generally, Cruise, Dig. tit. 15, c. 3; 4 Kent, Com. 148; Pow. on Mortg. ch. 10 and 11; 2 Black. Com. 158; 13 Vin. Ab. 458; 2 Supp. to Ves. Jr. 368; 2 Jac. & Walk. 194, n.; 1 Hill. Ab. c. 31; and article *Stellionate*.

EQUIVALENT. Of the same value. Sometimes a condition must be literally accomplished in formâ specificâ; but some may be fulfilled by an equivalent, *per æquipolens*, when such appears to be the intention of the parties; as, I promise to pay you one hundred dollars, and then die, my executor may fulfil my engagement; for it is equivalent to you whether the money be paid to you by me or by him. Roll. Ab. 451; 1 Bouv. Inst. n. 760.

EQUIVOCAL. What has a double sense.

2. In the construction of contracts, it is a general rule that when an expression may be taken in two senses, that shall be preferred which gives it effect. Vide *Ambiguity; Construction; Interpretation;* and Dig. 22, 1, 4; Id. 45, 1, 80; Id. 50, 17, 67.

EQUULEUS. The name of a kind of rack for extorting confessions. Encyc. Lond.

ERASURE, *contracts, evidence*. The obliteration of a writing; it will render it void or not under the same circumstances as an interlineation. (q. v.) Vide 5 Pet. S. C. R. 560; 11 Co. 88; 4 Cruise, Dig. 368; 13 Vin. Ab. 41; Fitzg. 207; 5 Bing. R. 183; 3 C. & P. 55; 2 Wend. R. 555; 11 Conn. R. 531; 5 M. R. 190; 2 L. R. 291; 3 L. R. 56; 4 L. R. 270.

2. Erasures and interlineations are presumed to have been made after the execution of a deed, unless the contrary be proved. 1 Dall. 67; 1 Pet. 169; 4 Bin. 1; 10 Serg. & R. 64, 170, 419; 16 Serg. & R. 44.

EREGIMUS. We have erected. In England, whenever the right of creating or granting a new office is vested in the king, he must use proper words for the purpose, as *eregimus*, constituimus, and the like. Bac. Ab. Offices, &c., E.

EROTIC MANIA, *med. jur.* A name given to a morbid activity of the sexual propensity. It is a disease or morbid affection of the mind, which fills it with a crowd of voluptuous images, and hurries its victim to acts of the grossest licentiousness, in the absence of any lesion of the intellectual powers. Vide *Mania*.

ERROR. A mistake in judgment or deviation from the truth, in matters of fact, and from the law in matters of judgment.

2.—1. *Error of fact.* The law has wisely provided that a person shall be excused, if, intending to do a lawful act, and pursuing lawful means to accomplish his object, he commit an act which would be criminal or unlawful, if it were done with a criminal design or in an unlawful manner; for example, thieves break into my house, in the night time, to commit a burglary; I rise out of my bed, and seeing a person with a drawn sword running towards my wife, I take him for one of the burglars, and shoot him down, and afterwards find he was one of my friends, whom, owing to the dimness of the light, I could not recognize, who had lodged with me, rose on the first alarm, and was in fact running towards my wife, to rescue her from the hands of an assassin; still I am innocent, because I committed an error as to a fact, which I could not know, and had no time to inquire about.

3. Again, a contract made under a clear error is not binding; as, if the seller and purchaser of a house situated in New York, happen to be in Philadelphia, and, at the time of the sale, it was unknown to both parties that the house was burned down, there will be no valid contract; or if I sell you my horse Napoleon, which we both suppose to be in my stable, and at the time of the contract he is dead, the sale is void. 7 How. Miss. R. 371; 3 Shepl. 45; 20 Wend. 174; 9 Shepl. 363; 2 Brown, 27; 5 Conn. 71; 6 Mass. 84; 12 Mass. 36. See *Sale*.

4. Courts of equity will in general correct and rectify all errors in fact committed in making deeds and contracts founded on good considerations. See *Mistake*.

5.—2. *Error in law.* As the law is, or which is the same thing, is presumed to be certain and definite, every man is bound to understand it, and an error of law will not, in general, excuse a man, for its violation.

6. A contract made under an error in law, is in general binding, for were it not so, error would be urged in almost every case. 2 East, 469; see 6 John. Ch. R. 166; 8 Cowen, 195; 2 Jac. & Walk. 249; 1 Story, Eq. Jur. 156; 1 Younge & Coll. 232; 6 B. & C. 671; Bowy. Com. 135; 3 Sav. Dr. Rom. App. viii. But a foreign law will for this purpose be considered as a fact. 3 Shepl. 45; 9 Pick. 112; 2 Ev. Pothier, 369, &c. See, also, *Ignorance; Marriage; Mistake*.

7. By error, is also understood a mistake made in the trial of a cause, to correct which a writ of error may be sued out of a superior court.

Error, writ of. A writ of error is one issued from a superior to an inferior court, for the purpose of bringing up the record and correcting an alleged error committed in the trial in the court below. But it cannot deliver the body from prison. Bro. Abr. Acc. pl. 45. The judges to whom the writ is directed have no power to return the record *nisi judicium inde redditum sit*. Nor can it be brought except on the final judgment. See Metcalf's Case, 11 Co. Rep. 38, which is eminently instructive on this subject. Vide *Writ of Error*.

ESCAPE. An escape is the deliverance of a person who is lawfully imprisoned, out of prison, before such a person is entitled to such deliverance by law. 5 Mass. 310.

2. It will be proper to consider, first, what is a lawful imprisonment; and, secondly, the different kinds of escapes.

3. When a man is imprisoned in a proper place under the process of a court having jurisdiction in the case, he is lawfully imprisoned, notwithstanding the proceedings may be irregular; but if the court has not jurisdiction the imprisonment is unlawful, whether the process be regular or otherwise. Bac. Ab. Escape in civil cases, A 1; 13 John. 378; 5 John. 89; 1 Cowen, 309; 8 Cowen, 192; 1 Root, R. 288.

4. Escapes are divided into voluntary and negligent; actual or constructive; civil and criminal; and escapes on mesne process and execution.

5.—1. A voluntary escape is the giving to a prisoner, voluntarily, any liberty not authorized by law. 5 Mass. 310; 2 Chipm. 11. Letting a prisoner confined under final process, out of prison for any, even the shortest time, is an escape, although he afterwards return; 2 Bl. Rep. 1048; 1 Roll. Ab. 806; and this may be, (as in the case of imprisonment under a *ca. sa.*) although an officer may accompany him. 3 Co. 44 a; Plowd. 37; Hob. 202; 1 Bos. & Pull. 24; 2 Bl. Rep. 1048.

6. The effect of a voluntary escape in a civil case, when the prisoner is confined under final process, is to discharge the debtor, so that he cannot be retaken by the sheriff; but he may be again arrested if he was confined only on mesne process. 2 T. R. 172; 2 Barn. & A. 56. And the plaintiff may retake the prisoner in either case.

In a criminal case, on the contrary, the officer not only has a right to recapture his prisoner, but it is his duty to do so. 6 Hill, 344; Bac. Ab. Escape in civil cases, C.

7.—2. A negligent escape takes place when the prisoner goes at large, unlawfully, either because the building or prison in which he is confined is too weak to hold him, or because the keeper by carelessness lets him go out of prison.

8. The consequences of a negligent escape are not so favorable to the prisoner confined under final process, as they are when the escape is voluntary, because in this case, the prisoner is to blame. He may therefore be retaken.

9.—3. The escape is actual, when the prisoner in fact gets out of prison and unlawfully regains his liberty.

10.—4. A constructive escape takes place when the prisoner obtains more liberty than the law allows, although he still remains in confinement. The following cases are examples of such escapes: When a man marries his prisoner. Plowd. 17; Bac. Ab. Escape, B 3. If an underkeeper be taken in execution, and delivered at the prison, and neither the sheriff nor any authorized person be there to receive him. 5 Mass. 310. And when the keeper of a prison made one of the prisoners confined for a debt a turnkey, and trusted him with the keys, it was held that this was a constructive escape. 2 Mason, 486.

11. Escapes in civil cases are, when the prisoner is charged in execution or on mesne process for a debt or duty, and not for a criminal offence, and he unlawfully gains his liberty. In this case, we have seen, the prisoner may be retaken, if the escape have not been voluntary; and that he may be retaken by the plaintiff when the escape has taken place without his fault, whether the defendant be confined in execution or not; and that the sheriff may retake the prisoner, who has been liberated by him, when he was not confined on final process.

12. Escapes in criminal cases take place when a person lawfully in prison, charged with a crime or under sentence, regains his liberty unlawfully. The prisoner being to blame for not submitting to the law, and in effecting his escape, may be retaken whether the escape was voluntary or not. And he may be indicted, fined and imprisoned for so escaping. See *Prison*.

13. Escape on mesne process is where the prisoner is not confined on final process, but on some other process issued in the course of the proceedings, and unlawfully obtains his liberty; such escape does not make the officer liable, provided that on the return day of the writ, the prisoner is forthcoming.

14. Escape on final process is when the prisoner obtains his liberty unlawfully while lawfully confined, and under an execution or other final decree. The officer is then, in general, liable to the plaintiff for the amount of the debt.

ESCAPE WARRANT. A warrant issued in England against a person who being charged in custody in the king's bench or Fleet prison, in execution or mesne process, escapes and goes at large. Jacob's L. D. h. t.

ESCHEAT, *title to lands*. According to the English law, escheat denotes an obstruction of the course of descent, and a consequent determination of the tenure, by some unforeseen contingency; in which case the land naturally results back, by a kind of reversion, to the original grantor, or lord of the fee. 2 Bl. Com. 244.

2. All escheats, under the English law, are declared to be strictly feudal, and to import the extinction of tenure. Wright on Ten. 115 to 117; 1 Wm. Bl. R. 123.

3. But as the feudal tenures do not exist in this country, there are no private persons who succeed to the inheritance by escheat. The state steps in, in the place of the feudal lord, by virtue of its sovereignty, as the original and ultimate proprietor of all the lands within its jurisdiction. 4 Kent, Com. 420. It seems to be the universal rule of civilized society, that when the deceased owner has left no heirs, it should vest in the public, and be at the disposal of the government. Code, 10, 10, 1; Domat, Droit Pub. liv. 1, t. 6, s. 3, n. 1. Vide 10 Vin. Ab. 139; 1 Bro. Civ. Law, 250; 1 Swift's Dig. 156; 2 Tuck. Blacks. 244, 245, n.; 5 Binn. R. 375; 3 Dane's Ab. 140, sect. 24; Jones on Land Office Titles in Penna. 5, 6, 93. For the rules of the Roman Civil Law, see Code Justinian, book 10.

ESCHEATOR. The name of an officer whose duties are generally to ascertain what escheats have taken place, and to prosecute the claim of the commonwealth for the purpose of recovering the escheated property. Vide 10 Vin. Ab. 158.

ESCROW, *conveyancing, contracts*. A conditional delivery of a deed to a stranger and not to the grautee himself, until certain conditions shall be performed, and then it is to be delivered to the grantee. Until the condition be performed and the deed delivered over, the estate does not pass, but remains in the grantor. 2 Johns. R. 248; Perk. 137, 138.

2. Generally, an escrow takes effect from the second delivery, and is to be considered as the deed of the party from that time; but this general rule does not apply when justice requires a resort to fiction. The relation back to the first delivery, so as to give the deed effect from that time, is allowed in cases of necessity, to avoid injury to the operation of the deed, from events happening between the first and second delivery. For example, when a feme sole makes a deed and delivers it as an escrow, and then marries before the second delivery, the relation back to the time when she was sole, is necessary to render the deed valid. Vide 2 Bl. Com. 307; 2 Bouv. Inst. n. 2024; 4 Kent, Com. 446; Cruise, Dig. t. 32, c. 2, s. 87 to 91; Com. Dig. Fait, A 3; 13 Vin. Ab. 29; 5 Mass. R. 60; 2 Root, R. 81; 5 Conn. R. 113; 1 Conn. R. 375; 6 Paige's R. 314; 2 Mass. R. 452; 10 Wend. R. 310; 4 Greenl. R. 20; 2 N. H. Rep. 71; 2 Watts, R. 359; 13 John. R. 285; 4 Day's R. 66; 9 Mass. R. 310; 1 John. Cas. 81; 6 Wend. R. 666; 2 Wash. R. 58; 8 Mass. R. 238; 4 Watts, R. 180; 9 Mass. Rep. 310; 2 Johns. Rep. 258–9; 13 Johns. Rep. 285; Cox, Dig. tit. Escrow; Prest. Shep. Touch. 56, 57, 58; Shep. Prec. 54, 56; 1 Prest. Abst. 275; 3 Prest. Ab. 65; 3 Rep. 35; 5 Rep. 84.

ESCUAGE, *old Eng. law*. Service of the shield. Tenants who hold their land by escuage, hold by knight's service. 1 Tho. Co. Litt. 272; Littl. s. 95, 86 b.

ESNECY. Eldership. In the English law, this word signifies the right which the eldest coparcener of lands has to choose one of the parts of the estate after it has been divided.

ESPLEES. The products which the land or ground yields; as the hay of the meadows, the herbage of the pasture, corn or other produce of the arable, rents and services. Termes de la Ley; see 11 Serg. & R. 275; Dane's Ab. Index, h. t.

ESPOUSALS, *contracts*. A mutual promise between a man and a woman to marry each other, at some other time: it differs from a marriage because then the contract is completed. Wood's Inst. 57; vide Dig. 23, 1, 1; Code, 5, 1, 4; Novel 115, c. 3, s. 11; Ayliffe's Parerg. 245; Aso & Man. Inst. B. 1, t. 6, c. 1, § 1.

ESQUIRE. A title applied by courtesy to officers of almost every description, to members of the bar, and others. No one is entitled to it by law, and, therefore, it confers no distinction in law.

2. In England, it is a title next above that of a gentleman, and below a knight. Camden reckons up four kinds of esquires, particularly regarded by the heralds: 1. The eldest sons of knights and their eldest sons, in perpetual succession. 2. The eldest sons of the younger sons of peers, and their eldest sons in like perpetual succession. 3. Esquires created by the king's letters patent, or other investiture, and their eldest sons. 4. Esquires by virtue of their office, as justices of the peace, and others who bear any office of trust under the crown.

ESSOIN, *practice*. An excuse which a party bound to be in court on a particular day, offers for not being there. 1 Sell. Pr. 4; Lee's Dict. h. t.

2. Essoin day is the day on which the writ is returnable. It is considered for many purposes as the first day of the term 1 T. R. 183. See 2 T. R. 16 n.; 4 Moore's R. 425. Vide *Exoine*.

ESTABLISH. This word occurs frequently in the Constitution of the United States, and it is there used in different meanings. 1. To settle firmly, to fix unalterably; as, to establish justice, which is the avowed object of the constitution. 2. To make or form; as, to establish an uniform rule of naturalization, and uniform laws on the subject of bankruptcies, which evidently does not mean that these laws shall be unalterably established as justice. 3. To found, to create, to regulate; as, congress shall have power to establish post roads and post offices. 4. To found, recognize, confirm or admit; as, congress shall make no law respecting an establishment of religion. 5. To create, to ratify, or confirm; as, we, the people, &c., do ordain and establish this constitution. 1 Story, Const. § 454.

ESTADAL, *Spanish law*. In Spanish America, this was a measure of land of sixteen square varas or yards. 2 White's Coll. 139.

ESTATE. This word has several meanings: 1. In its most extensive sense, it is applied to signify every thing of which riches or fortune may consist, and includes personal and real property; hence we say per sonal estate, real estate. 8 Ves. 504. 2. In its more limited sense, the word estate is applied to lands. It is so applied in two senses. The first describes or points out the land itself, without ascertaining the extent or nature of the interest therein; as, "my estate at A." The second, which is the proper and technical meaning of estate, is the degree, quantity, nature and extent of interest which one has in real property; as, an estate in fee, whether the same be a fee simple or fee tail; or an estate for life or for years, &c. Lord Coke says: Estate signifies such inheritance, freehold, term of years, tenancy by statute merchant, staple, eligit, or the like, as any man hath in lands or tenements, &c. Co. Lit. § 650, 345 a. See Jones on Land Office Titles in Penna. 165—170.

2. In Latin, it is called *status*, because it signifies the condition or circumstances in which the owner stands with regard to his property.

3. Estates in land may be considered in a fourfold view—with regard, 1. To the quantity of interest which the tenant has in the tenement. 2. To the time during which that quantity of interest is to be enjoyed. 3. To the number and connexion of the tenants. 4. To what conditions may be annexed to the estate.

4.—I. The quantity of interest which the tenant has in his tenement is measured by its duration and extent. An estate, considered in this point of view, is said to be an *estate of freehold*, and an *estate less than freehold.*

5.—§ 1. Freehold estates are of inheritance and not of inheritance. An estate in fee, (q. v.) which is the estate most common in this country, is a freehold estate of inheritance. Estates of freehold not of inheritance, are the following:

6.—1st. *Estates for life.* An estate for life is a freehold interest in lands, the duration of which is confined to the life or lives of some particular person or persons, or to the happening or not happening of some uncertain event.

7. Estates for life are divided into conventional or legal estates. The first created by the act of the parties, and the second by operation of law.

8.—1. Life estates may be created by express words; as, if A conveys land to B, for the term of his natural life; or they may arise by construction of law, as, if A conveys land to B, without specifying the term or duration, and without words of limitation. In the last case, B cannot have an estate in fee, according to the English law, and according to the law of those parts of the United States which have adopted and not altered the common law in this particular, but he will take the largest estate which can possibly arise from the grant, and that is an estate for life. Co. Litt. 42, a. So a conveyance "to I M, and his generation, to endure as long as the waters of the Delaware should run," passes no more than a life estate. 3 Wash. C. C. Rep. 498. The life estate may be either for a man's own life, or for the life of another person, and in this last case it is termed an estate *per autre vie.* There are some estates for life, which may depend upon future contingencies, before the death of the person to whom they are granted; for example, an estate given to a woman *dum sola fuerit*, or *durante viduitate*, or to a man and woman during coverture, or as long as the granteo shall dwell in a particular house, is determinable upon the happening of the event. In the same manner, a house usually worth one hundred dollars a year, may be granted to a person till he shall have received one thousand dollars; this will be an estate for life, for as the profits are uncertain, and may rise or fall, no precise time can be fixed for the determination of the estate. On the contrary, where the time is fixed, although it may extend far beyond any life, as a term for five hundred years, this does not create a life estate.

9.—2. The estates for life created by operation of law, are, 1st. Estates tail after possibility of issue extinct. 2d. Estates by the curtesy. 3d. Dower. 4th. Jointure. Vide Cruise, Dig. tit. 3; 4 Kent, Com. 23; 1 Brown's Civ. Law, 191; 2 Bl. Com. 103 The estate for life is somewhat similar to the usufruct (q. v.) of the civil law.

10. The incidents to an estate for life, are principally the following: 1. Every tenant for life, unless restrained by covenant or agreement, may of common right take upon the land demised to him reasonable estovers or botes. Co. Litt. 41.

11.—2. The tenant for life, or his representatives, shall not be prejudiced by any sudden determination of his estate, because such determination is contingent or uncertain. Co. Litt. 55.

12.—3. Under tenants or lessees of an estate for life, have the same, and even greater indulgences than the lessors, the original tenants for life; for when the tenant for life shall not have the emblements, because the estate determines by his own act, the exception shall not reach his lessee, who is a third person. 1 Roll. Ab. 727; 2 Bl. Com. 122.

13.—2d. *Estates by the curtesy.* An estate by the curtesy is an estate for life, created by act of law, which is defined as follows: When a man marries a woman, seised at any time during the coverture of an estate of inheritance, in severalty, in coparcenary, or in common, and has issue by her born alive, and which might by possibility inherit the same estate as heir to the wife, and the wife dies in the lifetime of the husband, he holds the lands during his life by the curtesy of England, and it is immaterial whether the issue be living at the time of the seisin, or at the death of the wife, or whether it was born before or after the seisin. Litt. s. 35; Co. Litt. 29, b; 8 Co. 34. By Act of Assembly of Pennsylvania, the birth of issue is not necessary, in all cases where the issue, if any, would have inherited.

14. There are four requisites indispensably necessary to the existence of this estate: 1. Marriage. 2. Seisin of the wife, which must have been seisin in deed, and not merely seisin in law; it seems, however, that the rigid rules of the common law, have been relaxed, in this respect, as to what is sometimes called waste or wild lands. 1 Pet. 505. 3. Issue. 4. Death of the wife.

15.—1. The marriage must be a lawful marriage; for a void marriage does not entitle the husband to the curtesy; as if a married man were to marry a second wife, the first being alive, he would not be entitled to the curtesy in such second wife's estate. But if the marriage had been merely voidable, he would be entitled, because no marriage, merely voidable, can be annulled after the death of the parties. Cruise, Dig. tit. 5, c. 1, s. 6.

16.—2. The seisin of the wife must, according to the English law, be a seisin in deed; but this strict rule has been somewhat qualified by circumstances in this country. Where the wife is owner of wild uncultivated land, not held adversely, she is considered as seised in fact, and the husband is entitled to his curtesy. 8 John. 262; 8 Cranch, 249; 1 Pet. 503; 1 Munf. 162; 1 Stew. 590. When the wife's estate is in reversion or remainder, the husband is not, in general, entitled to the curtesy, unless the particular estate is ended during coverture. Perk. s. 457, 464; Co. Litt. 20, a; 3 Dev. R. 270; 1 Sumn. 263; but see 3 Atk. 469; 7 Viner, Ab. 149, pl. 11. The wife's seisin must have been such as to enable her to inherit. 5 Cowen, 74.

17.—3. The issue of the marriage, to entitle the husband to the curtesy, must possess the following qualifications: 1. Be born alive. 2. In the lifetime of the mother. 3. Be capable of inheriting the estate.

18.—1st. The issue must be born alive. As to what will be considered life, see *Birth; Death; Life.*

19.—2d. The issue must be born in the lifetime of the mother; and if the child be born after the death of the mother, by the performance of the Cæsarian operation, the husband will not be entitled to the curtesy; as there was no issue born at the instant of the wife's death, the estate vests immediately on the wife's death to the child, *in ventre sa mere*, and the estate being once vested, it cannot be taken from him. Co. Litt. 29, b.; 8 Co. Rep. 35, a. It is immaterial whether the issue be born before or after the seisin of the wife. 8 Co. Rep. 35, b.

20.—3d. The issue must be capable of inheriting the estate; when, for example, lands are given to a woman and the heirs male of her body, and she has a daughter, this issue will not enable her husband to take his curtesy. Co. Litt. 29, a.

21.—4th. The death of the wife is requisite to make the estate by the curtesy complete.

22. This estate is generally prevalent in the United States; in some of them it has received a modification. In Pennsylvania the right of the husband takes place although there be no issue of the marriage, in all cases where the issue, if any, would have inherited. In Vermont, the title by curtesy has been laid under the equitable restriction of existing only in the event that the children of the wife entitled to inherit, died within age and without children. In South Carolina, tenancy by the curtesy, *eo nomine*, has ceased by the provisions of an act passed in 1791, relative to the distribution of intestates' estates, which gives to the husband surviving his wife, the same share of her real estate, as she would have taken out of his, if left a widow, and that is one moiety, or one-third of it in fee, ac-

cording to circumstances. In Georgia, tenancy by the curtesy does not exist, because, since 1785, all marriages vest the real, equally with the personal estate, in the husband. 4 Kent, Com. 29. In Louisiana, where the common law has not been adopted in this respect, this estate is unknown.

23. This estate is not peculiar to the English law, as Littleton erroneously supposes; Litt. s. 35; for it is to be found, with some modifications, in the ancient laws of Scotland, Ireland, Normandy and Germany. In France there were several customs, which gave a somewhat similar estate to the surviving husband, out of the wife's inheritances. Merlin, Répert. mots Linotte, et Quarte de Conjoint pauvre.

24.—3d. *Estate in dower.* Dower is an estate for life which the law gives the widow in the third part of the lands and tenements, or hereditaments of which the husband was solely seised, at any time during the coverture, of an estate in fee or in tail, in possession, and to which estate in the lands and tenements the issue, if any of such widow, might, by possibility, have inherited. In Pennsylvania, the sole seisin of the husband is not necessary. Watk. Prin. Con. 38; Lit. § 36; Act of Penna. March 31, 1812.

25. To create a title to the dower, three things are indispensably requisite: 1. Marriage. This must be a marriage not absolutely void, and existing at the death of the husband; a wife *de facto*, whose marriage is voidable by decree, as well as a wife *de jure*, is entitled to it; and the wife shall be endowed, though the marriage be within the age of consent, and the husband dies within that age. Co. Litt. 33, a; 7 Co. 42; Doct. & Stud. 22; Cruise, Dig. t. 6, c. 2, s, 2, et seq.

26.—2. Seisin. The husband must have been seised, some time during the coverture, of the estate of which the wife is dowable. Co. Litt. 31, a. An actual seisin is not indispensable, a seisin in law is sufficient. As to the effect of a transitory seisin, see 4 Kent, Com. 38; 2 Bl. Com. 132; Co. Litt. 31, a.

27.—3. Death of the husband. This must be a natural death; though there are authorities which declare that a civil death shall have the same effect. Cruise, Dig. tit. 6, ch. 2, § 22. Vide, generally, 8 Vin. Ab. 210; Bac. Ab. Dower; Com. Dig. Dower; Id. App. tit. Dower; 1 Supp. to Ves. jr. 173, 189; 2 Id. 49; 1 Vern. R. by Raithby, 218, n. 358, n.; 1 Salk. R. 291; 2 Ves. jr. 572; 5 Ves. 130; Arch. Civ. Pl. 469; 2 Sell. Pr. 200; 4 Kent, Com. 35; Amer. Dig. h. t.; Pothier, Traité du Douaire; 1 Swift's Dig. 85; Perk. 300, et seq.

28.—4th. *Estate tail after possibility of issue extinct.* By this awkward, but perhaps necessary periphrasis, justified by Sir William Blackstone, 2 Com. 124, is meant the estate which is thus described by Littleton, § 32; "when tenements are given to a man and his wife in special tail, if one of them die without issue, the survivor is tenant in tail after possibility of issue extinct."

29. This estate, though, strictly speaking, not more than an estate for life, partakes in some circumstances of the nature of an estate tail. For a tenant in tail after possibility of issue extinct, has eight qualities or privileges in common with a tenant in tail. 1. He is dispunishable for waste. 2. He is not compellable to attorn. 3. He shall not have aid of the person in reversion. 4. Upon his alienation no writ of entry *in consimili casu* lies. 5. After his death, no writ of intrusion lies. 6. He may join the mise in a writ of right in a special manner. 7. In a præcipe brought by him he shall not name himself tenant for life. 8. In a præcipe brought against him, he shall not be named barely tenant for life.

30. There are, however, four qualities annexed to this estate, which prove it to be, in fact, only an estate for life. 1. If this tenant makes a feoffment in fee, it is a forfeiture. 2. If an estate tail or in fee descends upon him, the estate tail after possibility of issue extinct is merged. 3. If he is impleaded and makes default, the person in reversion shall be received, as upon default of any other tenant for life. 4. An exchange between this tenant and a bare tenant for life, is good; for, with respect to duration, their estates are equal. Cruise, Dig. tit. 4; Tho. Co. Litt. B. 2, c. 17; Co. Lit. 28, a.

31. Nothing but absolute impossibility of having issue, can give rise to this estate. Thus, if a person gives lands to a man and *his* wife, and to the heirs of their two bodies, and they live to a hundred years, without having issue, yet they are tenants in tail; for the law sees no impossibility of their having issue, until the death of one of them. Co. Litt. 28, a. See *Tenant in tail after possibility of issue extinct.*

32.—§ 2. An estate less than freehold is an estate which is not in fee, nor for life; for although a man has a lease for a thousand years, which is much longer than any life, yet it is not a freehold, but a mere estate for years, which is a chattel interest. Estates less than freehold are estates for years, estates at will, and estates at sufferance.

33.—1. *An estate for years*, is one which is created by a lease for years, which is a contract for the possession and profits of land for a determinate period, with the recompense of rent; and it is deemed an estate for years, though the number of years should exceed the ordinary limits of human life; and it is deemed an estate for years though it be limited to less than a single year. It is denominated a *term*, because its duration is absolutely defined.

34. An estate for life is higher than an estate for years, though the latter should be for a thousand years. Co. Litt. 46, a; 2 Kent, Com. 278; 1 Brown's Civ. Law, 191; 4 Kent, Com. 85; Cruise's Dig. tit. 8; 4 Rawle's R. 126; 8 Serg. & Rawle, 459; 13 Id. 60; 10 Vin.. Ab. 295, 318 to 325.

35.—3. *An estate at will* is not bounded by any definite limits with respect to time; but as it originated in mutual agreement, so it depends upon the concurrence of both parties. As it depends upon the will of both, the dissent of either may determine it. Such an estate or interest cannot, consequently, be the subject of conveyance to a stranger, or of transmission to representatives. Watk. Prin. Con. 1; Co. Litt. § 68.

36. Estates at will have become infrequent under the operation of judicial decisions. Where no certain term is agreed on, they are now construed to be tenancies from year to year, and each party is bound to give reasonable notice of an intention to terminate the estate. When the tenant holds over by consent given, either expressly or by implication, after the determination of a lease for years, it is held evidence of a new contract, without any definite period, and is construed to be a tenancy from year to year. 4 Kent, Com. 210; Cruise, Dig. tit. 9, c. 1.

37.—3. *An estate at sufferance.* The estate of a tenant who comes into possession of land by lawful title, but holds over by wrong after the determination of his interest. Co. Litt. 57, b. He has a bare naked possession, but no estate which he can transfer or transmit, or which is capable of enlargement by release, for he stands in no privity to his landlord.

38. There is a material distinction between the case of a person coming to an estate by act of the party, and afterwards holding over, and by act of the law and then holding over. In the first case, he is regarded as a tenant at sufferance; and in the other, as an intruder, abator, and trespasser. Co. Litt. 57, b; 2 Inst. 134; Cruise, Dig. t. 9, c. 2; 4 Kent, Com. 115; 13 Serg. & Rawle, 60, 8 Serg. & Rawle, 459; 4 Rawle, 459; 4 Rawle's R. 126.

39.—II. As to the time of their enjoyment, estates are considered either in possession, (q. v.) or expectancy. (q. v.) The latter are either remainders, (q. v.) which are created by the act of the parties, and these are vested or contingent; or reversions, (q. v.) created by act of law.

40.—III. An estate may be holden in a variety of ways, the most common of which are, 1. In severalty. 2. In joint tenancy. 3. In common. 4. In coparcenary. These will be separately considered.

41.—1. *An estate in severalty*, is where only one tenant holds the estate in his own right, without any other person being joined or connected with him, in point of interest, during the continuance of his estate.

42.—2. *An estate in joint tenancy*, is where lands or tenements are granted to two or more persons, to hold in fee simple, fee tail, for life, for years, or at will. 2 Bl. Com. 179. Joint tenants always take by purchase, and necessarily have equal shares; while tenants in common, also coparceners, claiming under ancestors in different degrees, may have unequal shares; and the proper and best mode of creating an estate in joint tenancy, is to limit to A B and C D, and their assigns, if it be an estate for life; or to A B and C D, and their heirs, if in fee. Watk. Prin. Con. 86.

43. The creation of the estate depends upon the expression in the deed or devise, by which the tenants hold, for it must be created by the acts of the parties, and does not result from the operation of law. Thus, an estate given to a number of persons, without any restriction or explanation, will be construed a joint tenancy; for every part of the grant can take effect only, by considering the estate equal in all, and the union of their names gives them a name in every respect.

44. The properties of this estate arise

from its unities; these are, 1. Unity of title; the estate must have been created and derived from one and the same conveyance. 2. There must be a unity of time; the estate must be created and vested at the same period. 3. There must be a unity of interest; the estate must be for the same duration, and for the same quantity of interest. 4. There must be a unity of possession; all the tenants must possess and enjoy at the same time, for each must have an entire possession of every parcel, as of the whole. One has not possession of one-half, and another of the other half, but each has an undivided moiety of the whole, and not the whole of an undivided moiety.

45. The distinguishing incident of this estate, is the right of survivorship, or *jus accrescendi;* at common law, the entire tenancy or estate, upon the death of any of the joint tenants, went to the survivors, and so on to the last survivor, who took an estate of inheritance. The right of survivorship, except, perhaps, in estates held in trust, is abolished in Pennsylvania, New York, Virginia, Kentucky, Indiana, Missouri, Tennessee, North and South Carolina, Georgia, and Alabama. Griffith's Register, h. t. In Connecticut it never was recognized. 1 Root, Rep. 48; 1 Swift's Digest, 102. Joint tenancy may be destroyed by destroying any of its constituent unities, except that of time. 4 Kent, Com. 359. Vide Cruise, Dig. tit. 18; 1 Swift's Dig. 102; 14 Vin. Ab. 470; Bac. Ab. Joint Tenants, &c.; 3 Saund. 319, n. 4; 1 Vern. 353; Com. Dig. Estates by Grant, K 1; 4 Kent, Com. 353; 2 Bl. Com. 181; 1 Litt. sec. 304; 2 Woodd. Lect. 127; 2 Preston on Abst. 67; 5 Binn. Rep. 18; *Joint tenant, Survivor; Entirety.*

46.—3. *An estate in common,* is one which is held by two or more persons by unity of possession.

47. They may acquire their estate by purchase, and hold by several and distinct titles, or by title derived at the same time, by the same deed or will; or by descent. In this respect the American law differs from the English common law.

48. This tenancy, according to the common law, is created by deed or will, or by change of title from joint tenancy or coparcenary; or it arises, in many cases, by construction of law. Litt. sec. 292, 294, 298, 302; 2 Bl. Com. 192; 2 Prest. on Abstr. 75.

49. In this country it may be created by descent, as well as by deed or will. 4 Kent, Com. 363. Vide Cruise, Dig. tit. 20; Com. Dig. Estates by Grant, K 8.

50. Estates in common can be dissolved in two ways only; first, by uniting all the titles and interests in one tenant; secondly, by making partition.

51.—4. *An estate in coparcenary,* is an estate of inheritance in lands which descend from the ancestor to two or more persons who are called coparceners or parceners.

52. This is usually applied, in England, to cases where lands descend to females, when there are no male heirs.

53. As in the several states, estates generally descend to all the children equally, there is no substantial difference between coparceners and tenants in common. The title inherited by more persons than one, is, in some of the states, expressly declared to be a tenancy in common, as in New York and New Jersey, and where it is not so declared the effect is the same; the technical distinction between coparcenary and estates in common may be considered as essentially extinguished in the United States. 4 Kent, Com. 363. Vide *Estates.*

54.—IV. *An estate upon condition* is one which has a qualification annexed to it by which it may, upon the happening or not happening of a particular event, be created, or enlarged, or destroyed. Conditions may be annexed to estates in fee, for life, or for years. These estates are divided into estates upon condition express, or in deed; and upon conditions implied, or in law.

55. Estates upon *express* conditions are particularly mentioned in the contract between the parties. Litt. s. 225; 4 Kent, Com. 117; Cruise, Dig. tit. 13.

56. Estates upon condition in law are such as have a condition *impliedly* annexed to them, without any condition being specified in the deed or will. Litt. s. 378, 380; Co. Litt. 215, b; 233, b; 234, b.

57. Considered as to the title which may be had in them, estates are legal and equitable. 1. A *legal* estate is one, the right to which can be enforced in a court of law. 2. An *equitable,* is a right or interest in land, which not having the properties of a legal estate, but being merely a right of which courts of equity will take notice, require the aid of such a court to make it available. See, generally, Bouv. Inst. Index, h. t.

ESTER EN JUGEMENT, *French law.* *Stare in judicio.* To appear before a tribunal either as plaintiff or defendant.

ESTIMATION OF VALUES. As the value of most things is variable, according to circumstances, the law in many cases determines the time at which the value of a thing should be taken; thus, the value of an advancement, is to be taken at the time of the gift. 1 Serg. & R. 425. Of a gift in frank-marriage, at the time of partition between the parceners, and the bringing of the gift in frank-marriage into hotchpot. But this is a case *sui generis*. Co. Lit. § 273; 1 Serg. & R. 426. Of the yearly value of properties; at the time of partition. 1 Tho. Co. Lit. 820. Of a bequest of so many pieces of coin; at the time of the will made. Godolph, O. L. 273, part 3, chap. 1. § 3. Of assets to make lineal warranty a bar; at the time of the descent. Co. Lit. 374, b. Of lands warranted; at the time of the warranty. Beames' Glanv. 75 n.; 2 Serg. & Rawle, 444, *see Eviction* 2. Of a ship lost at sea; her value is to be taken at the port from which she sailed, deducting one-fifth; 2 Serg. & Rawle, 258; 1 Caines, 572; 2 Condy. Marshall, 545; but different rules prevail on this subject in different nations. 2 Serg. & R. 259. Of goods lost at sea; their value is to be taken at the port of delivery. 2 Serg. & R. 257. The comparative value of a life estate, and the remainder in fee, is one-third for the life and two-thirds for the remainder in fee; and moneys due upon a mortgage of lands devised to one for life, and the remainder in fee to another, are to be apportioned by the same rule. 1 Vern. 70; 1 Chit. Cas. 223, 224, 271; Francis' Max. 3, § 12, and note. See *Exchange*, 3–2.

ESTOPPEL, *pleading*. An estoppel is a preclusion, in law, which prevents a man from alleging or denying a fact, in consequence of his own previous act, allegation or denial of a contrary tenor. Steph. Pl. 239. Lord Coke says, "an estoppel is, when a man is concluded by his own act or acceptance, to say the truth." Co. Litt. 352, a. And Blackstone defines "an estoppel to be a special plea in bar, which happens where a man has done some act, or executed some deed, which estops or precludes him from averring any thing to the contrary. 3 Com. 308. Estoppels are odious in law; 1 Serg. & R. 444; they are not admitted in equity against the truth. Id. 442. Nor can jurors be estopped from saying the truth, because they are sworn to do so, although they are estopped from finding against the admission of the parties in their pleadings. 2 Rep. 4; Salk. 276; B. N. P. 298, 2 Barn. & Ald. 662; Angel on Water Courses, 228–9. See Co. Litt. 352, a, b, 351, a. notes.

2. An estoppel may arise either from matter of *record;* from the *deed* of the party; or from matter *in pays;* that is, matter of *fact*.

3. Thus, any confession or admission made in pleading, in a court of record, whether it be express, or implied from pleading over without a traverse, will forever preclude the party from afterwards contesting the same fact in any subsequent suit with his adversary. Com. Dig. Estoppel, A 1. This is an estoppel by matter of record.

4. As an instance of an estoppel by *deed*, may be mentioned the case of a bond reciting a certain fact. The party executing that bond, will be precluded from afterwards denying in any action brought upon that instrument, the fact so recited. 5 Barn. & Ald. 682.

5. An example of an estoppel by matter *in pays* occurs when one man has accepted rent of another. He will be estopped from afterwards denying, in any action with that person, that he was, at the time of such acceptance, his tenant. Com. Dig. Estoppel, A 3; Co. Litt. 352, a.

6. This doctrine of law gives rise to a kind of pleading that is neither by way of traverse, nor confession and avoidance: viz. a pleading, that, waiving any question of fact, relies merely on the estoppel, and, after stating the previous act, allegation, or denial, of the opposite party, prays judgment, if he shall be received or admitted to aver contrary to what he before did or said. This pleading is called a pleading by way of estoppel. Steph. 240.

7. Every estoppel ought to be reciprocal, that is, to bind both parties: and this is the reason that regularly a stranger shall neither take advantage or be bound by an estoppel. It should be directly affirmative, and not by inference nor against an estoppel. Co. Lit. 352, a, b; 1 Serg. & R. 442–3; 9 Serg. & R. 371, 430; 4 Yeates, 38; 1 Serg. & R. 444; Com. Dig. Estoppel, C; 3 Johns. Cas. 101; 2 Johns. R. 382; 8 W. & S. 135; 2 Murph. 67; 4 Monr. 370. Privies in blood, privies in estate, and privies in law, are bound by, and may take advantage of

estoppels. Co. Litt. 352; 2 Serg. & Rawle, 508; 5 Day, R. 88.

See the following cases relating to estoppels by—

Matter of record: 4 Mass. R. 625; 10 Mass. R. 155; Munf. R. 466; 3 East, R. 354; 2 Barn. & Ald. 362, 971; 17 Mass. R. 365; Gilm. R. 235; 5 Esp. R. 58; 1 Show. 47; 3 East, R. 346.

Matter of writing: 12 Johns. R. 347; 5 Mass. R. 395; Id. 286; 6 Mass. R. 421; 3 John. Cas. 174; 5 John. R. 489; 2 Caines' R. 320; 3 Johns. R. 331; 14 Johns. R. 193; Id. 224; 17 Johns. R. 161; Willes, R. 9, 25; 6 Binn. R. 59; 1 Call, R. 429; 6 Munf. R. 120; 1 Esp. R. 89; Id. 159; Id. 217; 1 Mass. R. 219.

Matter in pays: 4 Mass. R. 181; Id. 273; 15 Mass. R. 18; 2 Bl. R. 1259; 1 T. R. 760, n.; 3 T. R. 14; 6 T. R. 62; 4 Munf. 124; 6 Esp. R. 20; 2 Ves. 236; 2 Camp. R. 344; 1 Stark. R. 192.

And see, in general, 10 Vin. Abr. 420, tit. Estoppel; Bac. Abr. Pleas, I 11; Com. Dig. Estoppel; Id. Pleader, S 5; Arch. Civ. Pl. 218; Doct. Pl. 255; Stark. Ev. pt. 2, p. 206, 302; pt. 4, p. 30; 2 Smith's Lead. Cas. 417–460. Vide *Term*.

ESTOVERS, *estates*. The right of taking necessary wood for the use or furniture of a house or farm, from off another's estate. The word *bote* is used synonymously with the word estovers. 2 Bl. Com. 35; Dane's Ab. Index, h. t.; Woodf. L. & T. 232; 10 Wend. 639; 2 Bouv. Inst. n. 1652–57.

ESTRAYS. Cattle whose owner is unknown.

2. In the United States, generally, it is presumed by local regulations, they are subject to being sold for the benefit of the poor, or some other public use, of the place where found.

ESTREAT. This term is used to signify a true copy or note of some original writing or record, and specially of fines and amercements imposed by a court, and *extracted* from the record, and certified to a proper officer or officers authorized and required to collect them. Vide F. N. B. 57, 76.

ESTREPE. This word is derived from the French, *estropier*, to cripple. It signifies an injury to lands, to the damage of another, as a reversioner. This is prevented by a writ of estrepement.

ESTREPEMENT. The name of a writ which lay at common law to prevent a party in possession from committing waste on an estate, the title to which is disputed, after judgment obtained in any real action, and before possession was delivered by the sheriff.

2. But as waste might be committed in some cases, pending the suit, the statute of Gloucester gave another writ of estrepement pendente placito, commanding the sheriff firmly to inhibit the tenant "ne faciat vastum vel strepementum pendente placito dicto indiscusso." By virtue of either of these writs, the sheriff may resist those who commit waste or offer to do so; and he may use sufficient force for the purpose. 3 Bl. Com. 225, 226.

3. This writ is sometimes directed to the sheriff and the party in possession of the lands, in order to make him amenable to the court as for a contempt in case of his disobedience to the injunction of the writ. At common law the process proper to bring the tenant into court is a venire facias, and thereon an attachment. Upon the defendant's coming in, the plaintiff declares against him. The defendant usually pleads "that he has done no waste contrary to the prohibition of the writ." The issue on this plea is tried by a jury, and in case they find against the defendant, they assess damages which the plaintiff recovers. But as this verdict convicts the defendant of a contempt, the court proceed against him for that cause as in other cases. 2 Co. Inst. 329; Rast. Ent. 317; Brev. Judic. 88; More's Rep. 100; 1 Bos. & Pull. 121; 2 Lilly's Reg. tit. Estrepement; 5 Rep. 119; Reg. Brev. 76, 77.

4. In Pennsylvania, by legislative enactment, the remedy by estrepement is extended for the benefit of any owner of lands leased for years or at will, at any time during the continuance or after the expiration of such demise, and due notice given to the tenant to leave the same, agreeably to law, or for any purchaser at sheriff or coroner's sale of lands. &c., after he has been declared the highest bidder by the sheriff or coroner; or for any mortgagee or judgment creditor, after the lands bound by such judgment or mortgage, shall have been condemned by inquisition, or which may be subject to be sold by a writ of venditioni exponas or levari facias. Vide 10 Vin. Ab. 497; Woodf. Landl. & Ten, 447; Archb. Civ. Pl. 17; 7 Com. Dig. 659.

ET CÆTERA. A Latin phrase, which has been adopted into English; it signifies, *and the others, and so of the rest;* it is commonly abbreviated, &c.

2. Formerly the pleader was required to be very particular in making his defence. (q. v.) By making full defence, he impliedly admitted the jurisdiction of the court, and the competency of the plaintiff to sue; and half defence was used when the defendant intended to plead to the jurisdiction, or disability. To prevent the inconveniences which might arise by pleading full or half defence, it became the practice to plead in the following form: "And the said C D, by E F, his attorney, comes and defends the wrong and injury, when, &c., and says," which was either full or half defence. 2 Saund. 209, c.; Steph. Pl. 432; 2 Chit. Pl. 455.

3. In practice, the &c. is used to supply the place of words which have been omitted. In taking recognizance, for example, it is usual to make an entry on the docket of the clerk of the court, as follows: A B, tent, &c., in the sum of $1000, to answer, &c. 6 S. & R. 427.

ET NON. And not. These words are sometimes employed in pleading to convey a pointed denial. They have the same effect as *without this*, absque hoc. 3 Bouv. Inst. n. 2981, note.

EUNDO MORANDO, ET REDEUNDO. This Latin phrase signifies going, remaining, and returning. It is employed in cases where a person either as a party, a witness, or one acting in some other capacity, as an elector, is privileged from arrest, in order to give him that freedom necessary to the performance of his respective obligations, to signify that he is protected from arrest *eundo, morando et redeundo*. See 3 Bouv. Inst. n. 3380.

EUNOMY. Equal laws, and a well adjusted constitution of government.

EUNUCH. A male whose organs of generation have been so far removed or disorganized, that he is rendered incapable of reproducing his species. Domat, Lois Civ. liv. prel. tit. 2, s. 1, n. 10.

EVASION. A subtle device to set aside the truth, or escape the punishment of the law; as if a man should tempt another to strike him first, in order that he might have an opportunity of returning the blow with impunity. He is nevertheless punishable, because he becomes himself the aggressor in such a case. Wishard, 1 H. P. C. 81; Hawk. P. C. c. 31, § 24, 25; Bac. Ab. Fraud, A.

2. An escape from custody.

EVICTION. The loss or deprivation which the possessor of a thing suffers, either in whole or in part, of his right of property in such a thing, in consequence of the right of a third person established before a competent tribunal. 10 Rep. 128; 4 Kent, Com. 475–7; 3 Id. 464–5.

2. The eviction may be total or partial. It is total, when the possessor is wholly deprived of his rights in the whole thing; partial, when he is deprived of only a portion of the thing; as, if he had fifty acres of land, and a third person recovers by a better title twenty-five; or, of some right in relation to the thing; as, if a stranger should claim and establish a right to some easement over the same. When the grantee suffers a total eviction, and he has a covenant of seisin, he recovers from the seller, the consideration money, with interest and costs, and no more. The grantor has no concern with the future rise or fall of the property, nor with the improvements made by the purchaser. This seems to be the general rule in the United States. 3 Caines' R. 111; 4 John. R. 1; 13 Johns. R. 50; 4 Dall. R. 441; Cooke's Tenn. R. 447; 1 Harr. & Munf. 202; 5 Munf. R. 415; 4 Halst. R. 139; 2 Bibb, R. 272. In Massachusetts, the measure of damages on a covenant of warranty, is the value of the land at the time of eviction. 3 Mass R. 523; 4 Mass. R. 108. See, as to other states, 1 Bay, R. 19, 265; 3 Des. Eq. R. 245; 2 Const. R. 584; 2 McCord's R. 413; 3 Call's R. 326.

3. When the eviction is only *partial*, the damages to be recovered under the covenant of seisin, are a rateable part of the original price, and they are to bear the same ratio to the whole consideration, that the value of land to which the title has failed, bears to the value of the whole tract. The contract is not rescinded, so as to entitle the vendee to the whole consideration money, but only to the amount of the relative value of the part lost. 5 Johns. R. 49; 12 Johns. R. 126; Civ. Code of Lo. 2490; 4 Kent's Com. 462. Vide 6 Bac. Ab. 44; 1 Saund. R. 204; note 2, and 322 a, note 2; 1 Bouv. Inst. n. 656.

EVIDENCE. That which demonstrates, makes clear, or ascertains the truth of the very fact or point in issue; 3 Bl. Com. 367; or it is whatever is exhibited to a court or jury, whether it be by matter of record, or writing, or by the testimony of witnesses, in order to enable them to pronounce with certainty, concerning the truth of any matter in dispute; Bac. Ab. Evidence, *in pr.;* or it is that which is legally submitted to a jury, to enable them to decide upon the questions in dispute or issue, as pointed out by the pleadings and distinguished from all comment or argument. 1 Stark. Ev. 8.

2. Evidence may be considered with reference to, 1. The *nature* of the evidence. 2. The *object* of the evidence. 3. The *instruments* of evidence. 4. The *effect* of evidence.

3.—§ 1. As to its *nature*, evidence may be considered with reference to its being, 1. Primary evidence. 2. Secondary evidence. 3. Positive. 4. Presumptive. 5. Hearsay. 6. Admissions.

4.—1. *Primary evidence.* The law generally requires that the best evidence the case admits of should be given; B. N. P. 293; 1 Stark. Ev. 102, 390; for example, when a written contract has been entered into, and the object is to prove what it was, it is requisite to produce the original writing if it is to be attained, and in that case no copy or other inferior evidence will be received.

5. To this general rule there are several exceptions. 1. As it refers to the *quality* rather than to the *quantity* of evidence, it is evident that the fullest proof that every case admits of, is not requisite; if, therefore, there are several eye-witnesses to a fact, it may be sufficiently proved by one only. 2. It is not always requisite, when the matter to be proved has been reduced to writing, that the writing should be produced; as, if the narrative of a fact to be proved has been committed to writing, it may yet be proved by parol evidence. A receipt for the payment of money, for example, will not exclude parol evidence of payment. 4 Esp. R. 213; and see 7 B. & C. 611; S. C. 14 E. C. L. R. 101; 1 Campb. R. 439; 3 B. & A. 566; 5 E. C. L. R. 377.

6.—2. *Secondary evidence.* That species of proof which is admissible on the loss of primary evidence, and which becomes by that event the best evidence. 3 Yeates, Rep. 530.

7. It is a rule that the best evidence, or that proof which most certainly exhibits the true state of facts to which it relates, shall be required, and the law rejects secondary or inferior evidence, when it is attempted to be substituted for evidence of a higher or superior nature. This is a rule of policy, grounded upon a reasonable suspicion, that the substitution of inferior for better evidence arises from sinister motives; and an apprehension that the best evidence, if produced, would alter the case to the prejudice of the party. This rule relates not to the measure and quantity of evidence, but to its quality when compared with some other evidence of superior degree. It is not necessary in point of law, to give the fullest proof that every case may admit of. If, for example, there be several eye witnesses to a fact, it may be proved by the testimony of one only.

8. When primary evidence cannot be had, then secondary evidence will be admitted, because then it is the best. But before such evidence can be allowed, it must be clearly made to appear that the superior evidence is not to be had. The person who possesses it must be applied to, whether he be a stranger or the opposite party; in the case of a stranger, a subpœna and attachment, when proper, must be taken out and served; and, in the case of a party, notice to produce such primary evidence must be proved before the secondary evidence will be admitted. 7 Serg. & Rawle, 116; 6 Binn. 228; 4 Binn. R. 295, note; 6 Binn. R. 478; 7 East, R. 66; 8 East, R. 278; 3 B. & A. 296; S. C. 5 E. C. L. R. 291.

9. After proof of the due execution of the original, the contents should be proved by a counterpart, if there be one, for this is the next best evidence; and it seems that no evidence of a mere copy is admissible until proof has been given that the counterpart cannot be produced. 6 T. R. 236. If there be no counterpart, a copy may be proved in evidence by any witness who knows that it is a copy, from having compared it with the original. Bull. N. P. 254; 1 Keb. 117; 6 Binn. R. 234; 2 Taunt. R. 52; 1 Campb. R. 469; 8 Mass. R. 273. If there be no copy, the party may produce an abstract, or even give parol evidence of the contents of a deed. 10 Mod. 8; 6 T. R. 556.

10. But it has been decided that there are no degrees in secondary evidence: and when a party has laid the foundation for such evidence, he may prove the contents of a deed by parol, although it appear that an attested copy is in existence. 6 C. & P. 206; 8 Id. 389.

11.—3. *Positive or direct* evidence is that which, if believed, establishes the truth of a fact in issue, and does not arise from any presumption. Evidence is direct and positive, when the very facts in dispute are communicated by those who have the actual knowledge of them by means of their senses. 1 Phil. Ev. 116; 1 Stark. 19. In one sense, there is but little direct or positive proof, or such proof as is acquired by means of one's own sense, all other evidence is presumptive; but, in common acceptation, direct and positive evidence is that which is communicated by one who has actual knowledge of the fact.

12.—4. *Presumptive* evidence is that which is not direct, but where, on the contrary, a fact which is not positively known, is presumed or inferred from one or more other facts or circumstances which are known. Vide article *Presumption*, and Rosc. Civ. Ev. 13; 1 Stark. Ev. 18.

13.—5. *Hearsay*, is the evidence of those who relate, not what they know themselves, but what they have heard from others.

14. Such mere recitals or assertions cannot be received in evidence, for many reasons, but principally for the following: first, that the party making such declarations is not on oath; and, secondly, because the party against whom it operates, has no opportunity of cross-examination. 1 Phil. Ev. 185. See, for other reasons, 1 Stark. Ev. pt. 1, p. 44. The general rule excluding hearsay evidence, does not apply to those declarations to which the party is privy, or to admissions which he himself has made. See *Admissions.*

15. Many facts, from their very nature, either absolutely, or usually exclude direct evidence to prove them, being such as are either necessarily or usually, imperceptible by the senses, and therefore incapable of the ordinary means of proof. These are questions of pedigree or relationship, character, prescription, custom, boundary, and the like; as also questions which depend upon the exercise of particular skill and judgment. Such facts, some from their nature, and others from their antiquity, do not admit of the ordinary and direct means of proof by living witnesses; and, consequently, resort must be had to the best means of proof which the nature of the cases afford. See *Boundary; Custom; Opinion; Pedigree; Prescription.*

16.—6. *Admissions* are the declarations which a party by himself, or those who act under his authority, make of the existence of certain facts. Vide *Admissions.*

17.—§ 2. The *object* of evidence is next to be considered. It is to ascertain the truth between the parties. It has been discovered by experience that this is done most certainly by the adoption of the following rules, which are now binding as law: 1. The evidence must be confined to the point in issue. 2. The substance of the issue must be proved, but only the substance is required to be proved. 3. The affirmative of the issue must be proved.

18.—1. It is a general rule, both in civil and criminal cases, that the evidence shall be confined to the point in issue. Justice and convenience require the observance of this rule, particularly in criminal cases, for when a prisoner is charged with an offence, it is of the utmost importance to him that the facts laid before the jury should consist exclusively of the transaction, which forms the subject of the indictment, and, which alone, he has come prepared to answer. 2 Russ. on Cr. 694; 1 Phil. Ev. 166.

19. To this general rule, there are several exceptions, and a variety of cases which do not fall within the rule. 1. In general, evidence of collateral facts is not admissible; but when such a fact is material to the issue joined between the parties, it may be given in evidence; as, for example, in order to prove that the acceptor of a bill knew the payee to be a fictitious person; or that the drawer had general authority from him to fill up bills with the name of a fictitious payee, evidence may be given to show that he had accepted similar bills before they could, from their date, have arrived from the place of date. 2 H. Bl. 288.

20.—2. When special damage sustained by the plaintiff is not stated in the declaration, it is not one of the points in issue, and therefore, evidence of it cannot be received, yet a damage which is the necessary result of the defendant's breach of contract, may be proved, notwithstanding it is not in the declaration. 11 Price's Reports, 19.

21.—3. In general, evidence of the character of either party to a suit is inadmissible, yet in some cases such evidence may be given. Vide article *Character.*

22.—4. When evidence incidentally applies to another person or thing not included in the transaction in question, and with regard to whom or to which it is inadmissible; yet if it bear upon the point in issue, it will be received. 8 Bingh. Rep. 376; S. C. 21 Eng. C. L. R. 325; and see 1 Phil. Ev. 158; 2 East, P. C. 1035; 2 Leach, 985;

S. C. 1 New Rep. 92; Russ. & Ry. C. C. 376; 2 Yeates, 114; 9 Conn. Rep. 47.

23.—5. The *acts* of others, as in the case of conspirators, may be given in evidence against the prisoner, when referable to the issue; but *confessions* made by one of several conspirators after the offence has been completed, and when the conspirators no longer act in concert, cannot be received. Vide article *Confession*, and 10 Pick. 497; 2 Pet. Rep. 364; 2 Brec. R. 269; 3 Serg. & Rawle, 9; 1 Rawle, 362, 458; 2 Leigh's R. 745; 2 Day's Cas. 205; 3 Serg. & Rawle, 220; 3 Pick. 33; 4 Cranch, 75; 2 B. & A. 573-4; S. C. 5 E. C. L. R. 381.

24.—6. In criminal cases, when the offence is a cumulative one, consisting itself in the commission of a number of acts, evidence of those acts is not only admissible, but essential to support the charge. On an indictment against a defendant for a conspiracy, to cause himself to be believed a man of large property, for the purpose of defrauding tradesmen; after proof of a representation to one tradesman, evidence may therefore be given of a representation to another tradesman at a different time. 1 Camph. Rep. 399; 2 Day's Cas. 205; 1 John. R. 99; 4 Rogers' Rec. 143; 2 Johns. Cas. 193.

25.—7. To prove the guilty knowledge of a prisoner, with regard to the transaction in question, evidence of other offences of the same kind, committed by the prisoner, though not charged in the indictment, is admissible against him. As in the case where a prisoner had passed a counterfeit dollar, evidence that he had other counterfeit dollars in his possession is evidence to prove the guilty knowledge. 2 Const. R. 758; Id. 776; 1 Bailey, R. 300; 2 Leigh's R. 745; 1 Wheeler's Cr. Cas. 415; 3 Rogers' Rec. 148; Russ. & Ry. 132; 1 Campb. Rep. 324; 5 Randolph's R. 701.

26.—2. The substance of the issue joined between the parties must be proved. 1 Phil. Ev. 190. Under this rule will be considered the *quantity* of evidence required to support particular averments in the declaration or indictment.

27. And, *first*, of civil cases. 1. It is a fatal variance in a contract, if it appear that a party who ought to have been joined as plaintiff has been omitted. 1 Saund. 291 h, n.; 2 T. R. 282. But it is no variance to omit a person who might have been joined as defendant, because the non-joinder ought to have been pleaded in abatement. 1 Saund. 291 d, n. 2. The consideration of the contract must be proved; but it is not necessary for the plaintiff to set out in his declaration, or prove on the trial, the several parts of a contract consisting of distinct and collateral provisions; it is sufficient to state so much of the contract as contains the entire consideration of the act, and the entire act to be done in virtue of such consideration, including the time, manner, and other circumstances of its performance. 6 East, R. 568; 4 B. & A. 387; 6 E. C. L. R. 455.

28.—*Secondly*. In criminal cases, it may be laid down, 1. That it is, in general, sufficient to prove what constitutes an offence. It is enough to prove so much of the indictment as shows that the defendant has committed a substantive crime therein specified. 2 Camph. R. 585; 1 Harr & John. 427. If a man be indicted for robbery, he may be found guilty of larceny, and not guilty of the robbery. 2 Hale, P. C. 302. The offence of which the party is convicted, must, however, be of the same class with that of which he is charged. 1 Leach, 14; 2 Stra. 1133.

29.—2. When the intent of the prisoner furnishes one of the ingredients in the offence, and several intents are laid in the indictment, each of which, together with the act done, constitutes an offence, it is sufficient to prove one intent only. 3 Stark. R. 35; 14 E. C. L. R. 154, 163.

30.—3. When a person or thing, necessary to be mentioned in an indictment, is described with circumstances of greater particularity than is requisite, yet those circumstances must be proved. 3 Rogers' Rec. 77; 3 Day's Cas. 283. For example, if a party be charged with stealing a *black* horse, the evidence must correspond with the averment, although it was unnecessary to make it. Roscoe's Cr. Ev. 77; 4 Ohio, 350.

31.—4. The name of the prosecutor, or party injured, must be proved as laid, and the rule is the same with reference to the name of a third person introduced into the indictment, as descriptive of some person or thing.

32.—5. The affirmative of the issue must be proved. The general rule with regard to the burthen of proving the issue, requires that the party who asserts the affirmative should prove it. But this rule ceases to operate the moment the presumption of law is thrown into the other scale. When the issue is on the legitimacy of a child, therefore, it is incumbent on the party asserting the illegitimacy to prove it. 2 Selw. N. P. 709. Vide *Onus Probandi; Presumption;* 2 Gall. R. 485; and 1 McCord, 573.

33.—§ 3. The consideration of the *instruments* of evidence will be the subject of this head. These consist of records, private writings, or witnesses.

34.—1. Records are to be proved by an exemplification, duly authenticated, (Vide *Authentication*,) in all cases where the issue is *nul tiel record*. In other cases, an examined copy, duly proved, will, in general, be evidence. Foreign laws as proved in the mode pointed out under the article *Foreign laws*.

35.—2. Private writings are proved by producing the attesting witness; or in case of his death, absence, or other legal inability to testify, as if, after attesting the paper, he becomes infamous, his handwriting may be proved. When there is no witness to the instrument, it may be proved by the evidence of the handwriting of the party, by a person who has seen him write, or in a course of correspondence has become acquainted with his hand. See *Comparison of handwriting*, and 5 Binn. R. 349; 10 Serg. & Rawle, 110; 11 Serg. & Rawle, 333; 3 W. C. C. R. 31; 11 Serg. & Rawle, 347; 6 Serg. & Rawle, 12, 312; 1 Rawle, R. 223; 3 Rawle, R. 312; 1 Ashm. R. 8; 3 Penn. R. 136.

36. Books of original entry, when duly proved, are *prima facie* evidence of goods sold and delivered, and of work and labor done. Vide *Original entry*.

37.—3. Proof by witnesses. The testimony of witnesses is called parol evidence, or that which is given *viva voce*, as contradistinguished from that which is written or documentary. It is a general rule, that oral evidence shall in no case be received as equivalent to, or as a substitute for, a written instrument, where the latter is required by law; or to give effect to a written instrument which is defective in any particular which by law is essential to its validity; or to contradict, alter or vary a written instrument, either appointed by law, or by the contract of the parties, to be the appropriate and authentic memorial of the particular facts it recites; for by doing so, oral testimony would be admitted to usurp the place of evidence decidedly superior in degree. 1 Serg. & Rawle, 464; Id. 27; Addis. R. 361; 2 Dall. 172; 1 Yeates, 140; 1 Binn. 616; 3 Marsh. Ken. R. 333; 4 Bibb, R. 473; 1 Bibb, R. 271; 11 Mass. R. 30; 13 Mass. R. 443; 3 Conn. 9; 20 Johns. 49; 12 Johns. R. 77; 3 Camp. 57; 1 Esp. C. 53; 1 M. & S. 21; Bunb. 175.

38. But parol evidence is admissible to defeat a written instrument, on the ground of fraud, mistake, &c., or to apply it to its proper subject matter; or, in some instances, as ancillary to such application, to explain the meaning of doubtful terms, or to rebut presumptions arising extrinsically. In these cases, the parol evidence does not usurp the place, or arrogate the authority of, written evidence, but either shows that the instrument ought not to be allowed to operate at all, or is essential in order to give to the instrument its legal effect. 1 Murph. R. 426; 4 Desaus. R. 211; 1 Desaus. R. 345; 1 Bay, R. 247; 1 Bibb, R. 271; 11 Mass. R. 30; see 1 Pet. C. C. R. 85; 1 Binn. R. 610; 3 Binn R. 587: 3 Serg. & Rawle, 340; Poth. Obl. Pl. 4, c. 2.

39.—§ 4. The *effect* of evidence. Under this head will be considered, 1st. The effect of judgments rendered in the United States, and of records lawfully made in this country; and, 2d. The effect of foreign judgments and laws.

40.—1. As a general rule, a judgment rendered by a court of competent jurisdiction, directly upon the point in issue, is a bar between the same parties: 1 Phil. Ev. 242; and privies in blood, as an heir; 3 Mod. 141; or privies in estate; 1 Ld. Raym. 730; B. N. P. 232; stand in the same situation as those they represent; the verdict and judgment may be used for or against them, and is conclusive. Vide *Res Judicata*.

41. The Constitution of the United States, art. 4, s. 1, declares, that "Full faith and credit shall be given, in each state, to the public acts, records, and judicial proceedings of every other state. And congress may, by general laws, prescribe the manner in which such acts, records, and proceedings, shall be proved, and the effect thereof." Vide article *Authentication*, and 7 Cranch, 481; 3 Wheat. R. 234; 10 Wheat. R. 469; 17 Mass. R. 546; 9 Cranch, 192; 2 Yeates, 532; 7 Cranch, 408; 3 Bibb's R. 369; 5 Day's R. 563; 2 Marsh. Kty. R. 293.

42.—2. As to the effect of foreign laws, see article *Foreign Laws*. For the force and effect of foreign judgments, see article *Foreign Judgments*.

Vide, generally, the Treatises on Evidence, of Gilbert, Phillips, Starkie, Roscoe, Swift, Bentham, Macnally, Peake, Greenleaf, and Bouv. Inst. Index, h. t.; the various Digests, h. t.

EVIDENCE, CIRCUMSTANTIAL. The proof of facts which usually attend other facts sought to be proved; that which is not direct evidence. For example, when a witness testifies that a man was stabbed with a knife, and that a piece of the blade was found in the wound, and it is found to fit exactly with another part of the blade found in the possession of the prisoner; the facts are directly attested, but they only prove circumstances, and hence this is called circumstantial evidence.

2. Circumstantial evidence is of two kinds, namely, certain and uncertain. It is *certain* when the conclusion in question necessarily follows; as, where a man had received a mortal wound, and it was found that the impression of a bloody *left* hand had been made on the *left* arm of the deceased, it was certain some other person than the deceased must have made such mark. 14 How. St. Tr. 1324. But it is *uncertain* whether the death was caused by suicide or by murder, and whether the mark of the bloody hand was made by the assassin, or by a friendly hand that came too late to the relief of the deceased. Id. Vide *Circumstances.*

EVIDENCE, CONCLUSIVE. That which, while uncontradicted, satisfies the judge and jury; it is also that which cannot be contradicted.

2. The record of a court of common law jurisdiction is conclusive as to the facts therein stated. 2 Wash. 64; 2 H. & M. 55; 6 Conn. 508. But the judgment and record of a prize court is not conclusive evidence in the state courts, unless it had jurisdiction of the subject-matter; and whether it had or not, the state courts may decide. 1 Conn. 429. See, as to the conclusiveness of the judgments of foreign courts of admiralty, 4 Cranch, 421, 434; 3 Cranch, 458; Gilmer, 16; Const. R. 381; 1 N. & M. 537.

EVIDENCE, DIRECT. That which applies immediately to the *factum probandum*, without any intervening process; as, if A testifies he saw B inflict a mortal wound on C, of which he instantly died. 1 Greenl. Ev. § 13.

EVIDENCE, EXTRINSIC. External evidence, or that which is not contained in the body of an agreement, contract, and the like.

2. It is a general rule that extrinsic evidence cannot be admitted to contradict, explain, vary or change the terms of a contract or of a will, except in a latent ambiguity, or to rebut a resulting trust. 14 John. 1; 1 Day, R. 8; 6 Conn. 270.

EVOCATION, *French law.* The act by which a judge is deprived of the cognizance of a suit over which he had jurisdiction, for the purpose of conferring on other judges the power of deciding it. This is done with us by writ of *certiorari.*

EWAGE. A toll paid for water passage. Cowell. The same as *aquagium.* (q. v.)

EX CONTRACTU. This term is applied to such things as arise *from a contract;* as an action which arises *ex contractu.* Vide *Action.*

EX DELICTO. Those actions which arise in consequence of a crime, misdemeanor, fault or tort; actions arising *ex delicto* are case, replevin, trespass, trover. See *Action.*

EX DOLO MALO. Out of fraud or deceit. When a cause of action arises from fraud or deceit, it cannot be supported: *Ex dolo malo, non oritur actio.*

EX ÆQUO ET BONO. In equity and good conscience. A man is bound to pay money which *ex æquo et bono* he holds for the use of another.

EX MERO MOTU. Mere motion of a party's own free will. To prevent injustice, the courts will, *ex mero motu,* make rules and orders which the parties would not strictly be entitled to ask for.

EX MORA. From the delay; from the default. All persons are bound to make amends for damages which arise from their own default.

EX NECESSITATE LEGIS. From the necessity of law.

EX NECESSITATE REI. From the necessity of the thing. Many acts may be done *ex necessitate rei,* which would not be justifiable without it; and sometimes property is protected, *ex necessitate rei,* which, under other circumstances, would not be so. For example, property put upon the land of another from necessity, cannot be distrained for rent. See *Distress; Necessity.*

EX OFFICIO. By virtue of his office.

2. Many powers are granted and exercised by public officers which are not ex-

pressly delegated. A judge, for example may, ex officio, be a conservator of the peace, and a justice of the peace.

EX PARTE. Of the one part. Many things may be done *ex parte*, when the opposite party has had notice; an affidavit or deposition is said to be taken *ex parte* when only one of the parties attends to taking the same. *Ex parte* paterna, on the side of the father, or property descended to a person from his father; *ex parte* materna, on the part of the mother.

EX POST FACTO, *contracts, crim. law.* This is a technical expression, which signifies, that something has been done after another thing, in relation to the latter.

2. An estate granted, may be made good or avoided by matter ex post facto, when an election is given to the party to accept or not to accept. 1 Co. 146.

3. The Constitution of the United States, art. 1, sec. 10, forbids the states to pass any *ex post facto law;* which has been defined to be one which renders the act punishable in a manner in which it was not punishable when it was committed. 6 Cranch, 138. This definition extends to laws passed after the act, and affecting a person by way of punishment of that act, either in his person or estate. 3 Dall. 386; 1 Blackf. Ind. R. 193; 2 Pet. U. S. Rep. 413; 1 Kent, Com. 408; Dane's Ab. Index, h. t.

4. This prohibition in the constitution against passing *ex post facto* laws, applies exclusively to criminal or penal cases, and not to civil cases. Serg. Const. Law, 356. Vide 2 Pick. R. 172; 11 Pick. R. 28; 2 Root, R. 350; 5 Monr. 133; 9 Mass. R. 363; 3 N. H. Rep. 475; 7 John. R. 488; 6 Binn. R. 271; 1 J. J. Marsh, 563; 2 Pet. R. 681; and the article *Retrospective*.

EX VI TERMINI. By force of the term; as a bond *ex vi termini* imports a sealed instrument.

EX VISITATIONE DEI. By or from the visitation of God. This phrase is frequently employed in inquisitions by the coroner, where it signifies that the death of the deceased is a natural one.

EX TEMPORE. From the time; without premeditation.

EXACTION, *torts.* A wilful wrong done by an officer, or by one who, under color of his office, takes more fee or pay for his services than what the law allows. Between *extortion* and *exaction* there is this difference; that in the former case the officer extorts more than his due, when something is due to him; in the latter, he exacts what is not his due, when there is nothing due to him. Wishard; Co. Litt. 368.

EXAMINATION, *crim. law.* By the common law no one is bound to accuse himself. *Nemo tenetur prodere seipsum.* In England, by the statutes of Philip and Mary, (1 & 2 P. & M. c. 13; 2 & 3 P. & M. c. 10,) the principles of which have been adopted in several of the United States, the justices before whom any person shall be brought, charged with any of the crimes therein mentioned, shall take the examination of the prisoner, as well as that of the witnesses, in writing, which the magistrates shall subscribe, and deliver to the officers of the court where the trial is to be had. The signature of the prisoner, when not specially required by statute, is not indispensable, though it is proper to obtain it, when it can be obtained. 1 Chit. Cr. Law, 87; 2 Leach, Cr. Cas. 625.

2. It will be proper to consider, 1. The requisites of such examination. 2. How it is to be proved. 3. Its effects.

3.—1. It is required that it should, 1st. Be voluntarily made, without any compulsion of any kind; and, 2d. It must be reduced to writing. 1st. The law is particularly solicitous to let the prisoner be free in making declarations in his examination; and if the prisoner has not been left entirely free, or did not consider himself to be so, or if he did not feel at liberty wholly to decline any explanation or declaration whatever, the examination is not considered voluntary, and the writing cannot be read in evidence against him, nor can parol evidence be received of what the prisoner said on the occasion. 5 C. & P. 312; 7 C. & P. 177; 1 Stark. R. 242; 6 Penn. Law Journ. 120. The prisoner, of course, cannot be sworn, and make his statement under oath. Bull. N. P. 242; 4 Hawk. P. C. book 2, c. 46, § 37; 4 C. & P. 564. 2*a*. The statute requires that the examination shall be reduced to writing, or so much as may be material, and the law presumes the magistrate did his duty and took down all that was material. Joy on Conf. 89–92; 1 Greenl. Ev. § 227. The prisoner need not sign the examination so reduced to writing, to give it validity; but, if being asked to sign it, he absolutely refuse, it will be considered incomplete. 2 Stark. R. 483; 2 Leach, Cr. Cas. 627, n.

4.—2. The certificate of the magistrate is conclusive evidence of the manner in which the examination was conducted. 7 C. & P. 177; 9 C. & P. 124; 1 Stark. R. 242. Before it can be given in evidence, its identity must be proved, as well as the identity of the prisoner. When the prisoner has signed the examination, proof of his handwriting is sufficient evidence that he has read it; but if he has merely made his mark, or not signed it at all, the magistrate or clerk must identify the prisoner, and prove that the writing was duly read to him, and that he assented to it. 1 Greenl. Ev. § 520; 1 M. & Rob. 395.

5.—3. The effect of such an examination, when properly taken and proved, is sufficient to found a conviction. 1 Greenl. Ev. § 216.

EXAMINATION, *practice.* The interrogation of a witness, in order to ascertain his knowledge as to the facts in dispute between parties. When the examination is made by the party who called the witness, it is called an *examination in chief.* When it is made by the other party, it is known by the name of *cross-examination.* (q. v.)

2 The examination is to be made in open court, when practicable; but when, on account of age, sickness, or other cause, the witness cannot be so examined, then it may be made before authorized commissioners. In the examination in chief the counsel cannot ask leading questions, except in particular cases. Vide *Cross-examination; Leading question.*

3. The laws of the several states require the private examination of a feme covert before a competent officer, in order to pass her title to her own real estate or the interest she has in that of her husband: as to the mode in which this is to be done, see *Acknowledgment.* See, also, 3 Call, R. 394; 5 Mason's R. 59; 1 Hill, R. 110; 4 Leigh, R. 498; 2 Gill & John. 1; 3 Rand. R. 468; 1 Monr. R. 49; 3 Monr. R. 397; 1 Edw. R. 572; 3 Yerg. R. 548; 1 Yerg. R. 413; 3 J. J. Marsh. R. 241; 2 A. K. Marsh. R. 67; 6 Wend. R. 9; 1 Dall. 11, 17; 3 Yeates, R. 471; 8 S. & R. 299; 4 S. & R. 273.

EXAMINED COPY. This phrase is applied to designate a paper which is a copy of a record, public book, or register, and which has been compared with the original. 1 Campb. 469.

2. Such examined copy is admitted in evidence, because of the public inconvenience which would arise, if such record, public book, or register, were removed from place to place, and because any fraud or mistake made in the examined copy would be so easily detected. 1 Greenl. Ev. § 91; 1 Stark. Ev. 189–191. But an answer in chancery, on which the defendant was indicted for perjury, or where the original must be produced in order to identify the party by proof of handwriting, an examined copy would not be evidence. 1 M. & Rob. 189. Vide *Copy.*

EXAMINERS, *practice.* Persons appointed to question students of law, in order to ascertain their qualifications before they are admitted to practice. Officers in the courts of chancery whose duty it is to examine witnesses, are also called examiners. Com. Dig. Chancery, P 1. For rules as to the mode of taking examinations, see Gresl. Eq. Ev. pt. 1, c. 3, s. 2.

EXAMPLE. An example is a case put to illustrate a principle. Examples illustrate, but do not restrain or change the laws: *illustrant non restringunt legem.* Co. Litt. 24, a.

EXCAMBIATOR. The name of an exchanger of lands; a broker. This term is now obsolete.

EXCAMBIUM. Exchange. (q. v.)

EXCEPTIO REI JUDICATÆ, *civil law.* The name of a plea by which the defendant alleges that the matter in dispute between the parties has been before adjudged. See *Res judicata.*

EXCEPTION, *Eng. Eq. practice.* Re-interrogation. 2 Benth. Ev. 208, n.

EXCEPTION, *legislation, construction.* Exceptions are rules which limit the extent of other more general rules, and render that just and proper, which would be, on account of its generality, unjust and improper. For example, it is a general rule that parties competent may make contracts; the rule that they shall not make any contrary to equity, or *contra bonos mores,* is the exception.

EXCEPTION, *contracts.* An exception is a clause in a deed, by which the lessor excepts something out of that which he granted before by the deed.

2. To make a valid exception, these things must concur: 1. The exception must be by apt words; as, saving and excepting, &c. 2. It must be of part of the thing previously described, and not of some other

thing. 3. It must be part of the thing only, and not of all, the greater part, or the effect of the thing granted; an exception, therefore, in a lease, which extends to the whole thing demised, is void. 4. It must be of such thing as is severable from the demised premises, and not of an inseparable incident. 5. It must be of such a thing as he that accepts may have, and which properly belongs to him. 6. It must be of a particular thing out of a general, and not of a particular thing out of a particular thing. 7. It must be particularly described and set forth; a lease of a tract of land, except one acre, would be void, because that acre was not particularly described. Woodf. Landl. and Ten. 10; Co. Litt. 47 a; Touchs. 77; 1 Shepl. R. 337; Wright's R. 711; 3 John. R. 375; 8 Conn. R. 369; 6 Pick. R. 499; 6 N. H. Rep. 421. Exceptions against common right and general rules are construed as strictly as possible. 1 Barton's Elem. Conv. 68.

3. An exception differs from a *reservation;* the former is always part of the thing granted; the latter is of a thing not in esse but newly created or reserved. An exception differs also from an explanation, which by the use of a *videlicet*, *proviso*, &c., is allowed only to explain doubtful clauses precedent, or to separate and distribute generals, into particulars. 3 Pick. R. 272.

EXCEPTION, *practice*, *pleading*. This term is used in the civil, nearly in the same sense that the word *plea* has in the common law. Merl. Rèpert. h. t.; Ayl. Parerg. 251.

2. In chancery practice, it is the allegation of a party in writing, that some pleading or proceeding in a cause is insufficient. 1 Harr. Ch. Pr. 228.

3. Exceptions are dilatory or peremptory. Bract. lib. 5, tr. 5; Britton, cap. 91, 92; 1 Lilly's Ab. 559. Dilatory exceptions are such as do not tend to defeat the action, but only to retard its progress. Poth. Proc. civ. partie 1, c. 2, s. 2, art. 1; Code of Pract. of Lo. art. 332. Declinatory exceptions have this effect, as well as the exception of discussion opposed by a third possessor, or by a surety in an hypothecary action, or the exception taken in order to call in the warrantor. Id.; 7 N. S. 282; 1 L. R. 38, 420. These exceptions must, in general, be pleaded *in limine litis* before issue joined. Civ. Code of Lo. 2260; 1 N. S. 703; 2 N. S. 389; 4 L. R. 104; 10 L. R. 546. A declinatory exception is a species of dilatory exception, which merely declines the jurisdiction of the judge before whom the action is brought. Code of Pr of L. 334.

4. Peremptory exceptions are those which tend to the dismissal of the action. Some relate to forms, others arise from the law. Those which relate to forms tend to have the cause dismissed, owing to some nullities in the proceedings. These must be pleaded *in limine litis*. Peremptory exceptions founded on law, are those which, without going into the merits of the cause, show that the plaintiff cannot maintain his action, either because it is prescribed, or because the cause of action has been destroyed or extinguished. These may be pleaded at any time previous to definitive judgment. Id. art. 343, 346; Poth. Proc. Civ. partie 1, c. 2, s. 1, 2, 3. These, in the French law, are called *Fins de non recevoir*. (q. v.)

5. By exception is also meant the objection which is made to the decision of a judge in the course of a trial. See *Bill of Exception.*

EXCHANGE, *com. law.* This word has several significations.

2.—1. Exchange is a negotiation by which one person transfers to another, funds which he has in a certain place, either at a price agreed upon, or which is fixed by commercial usage. This transfer is made by means of an instrument which represents such funds, and is well known by the name of a bill of exchange.

3.—2. The price which is paid in order to obtain such transfer, is also known among merchants by the name of exchange; as, exchange on England is five per cent. See 4 Wash. C. C. R. 307. Exchange on foreign money is to be calculated according to the usual rate at the time of trial. 5 S. & R. 48.

4.—3. Barter, (q. v.) or the transfer of goods and chattels for other goods and chattels, is also known by the name of exchange, though the term barter is more commonly used.

5.—4. The French writers on commercial law, denominate the profit which arises from a maritime loan, exchange, when such profit is a per centage on the money lent, considering it in the light of money lent in one place to be returned in another, with a difference in amount in the sum borrowed and that paid, arising from the difference of time and place. Hall on Mar. Loans, 56, n.; and the articles *Interest; Maritime; Premium.*

6.—5. By exchange is also meant, the place where merchants, captains of vessels, exchange agents and brokers, assemble to transact their business. Code de Comm. art. 71.

7.—6. According to the Civil Code of Louisiana, art. 1758, exchange imports a reciprocal contract, by which the parties enter into mutual agreement. 14 Pet. 133.

Vide the articles *Bills of Exchange; Damages on Bills of Exchange*, and *Reëxchange*. Also Civ. Code of Lo. art. 2630.

EXCHANGE, *conveyancing*. An exchange is a mutual grant of equal interests in land, the one in consideration of the other. 2 Bl. Com. 323; Litt. s. 62; Touchs. 289; Watk. Prin. Con. It is said that exchange, in the United States, does not differ from bargain and sale. 2 Bouv. Inst. n. 2055.

2. There are five circumstances necessary to an exchange. 1. That the estates given be equal. 2. That the word *escambium* or exchange be used, which cannot be supplied by any other word, or described by circumlocution. 3. That there be an execution by entry or claim in the life of the parties. 4. That if it be of things which lie in grant, it be by deed. 5. That if the lands lie in several counties, it be by deed indented; or if the thing lie in grant, though they be in one county. In practice this mode of conveyancing is nearly obsolete. Vide Cruise, Dig. tit. 32; Perk. ch. 4; 10 Vin. Ab. 125; Com. Dig. h. t.; Nels. Ab. h. t.; Co. Litt. 51; Hardin's R. 593; 1 N. H. Rep. 65; 3 Har. & John. 361; 1 Rolle's Ab. 813; 3 Wils. R. 489. Vide Watk. Prin. Con. b. 2, c. 5; Horsman, 362; and 3 Wood, 243, for forms.

EXCHEQUER, *Eng. law*. An ancient court of record set up by William the Conqueror. It is called exchequer from the chequered cloth, resembling a chessboard, which covers the table there. 3 Bl. Com. 45. It consists of two divisions; the receipt of the exchequer, which manages the royal revenue; and the court, or judicial part of it, which is again divided into a court of equity, and a court of common law. Id. 44.

2. In this court all personal actions may be brought, and suits in equity commenced, the plaintiff in both (fictitiously for the most part) alleging himself to be the king's debtor, in order to give the court jurisdiction of the cause. Wooddes. Lect. 69. But by stat. 2 Will. IV. c. 39, s. 1, a change has been made in this respect.

EXCHEQUER CHAMBER, *Eng. law*. A court erected by statute 31 Ed. III. c. 12, to determine causes upon writs of error from the common law side of the court of exchequer. 3 Bl. Com. 55. Another court of exchequer chamber was created by the stat. 27 El. c. 8, consisting of the justices of the common bench, and the barons of the exchequer. It has authority to examine by writ of error the proceedings of the king's bench, not so generally as that erected by the statute of Edw. III., but in certain enumerated actions.

EXCISES. This word is used to signify an inland imposition, paid sometimes upon the consumption of the commodity, and frequently upon the retail sale. 1 Bl. Com. 318; 1 Tuck. Bl. Com. Appx. 341; Story, Const. § 950.

EXCLUSIVE, *rights*. Debarring one from participating in a thing. An exclusive right or privilege, is one granted to a person to do a thing, and forbidding all others to do the same. A patent right or copyright, are of this kind.

EXCLUSIVE, *computation of time*. Shut out; not included. As when an act is to be done within a certain time, as ten days from a particular time, one day is to be included and the other excluded. Vide Hob. 139; Cowp. 714; Lofft, 276; Dougl. 463; 2 Mod. 280; Sav. 124; 3 Penna. Rep. 200; 1 Serg. & Rawle, 43; 3 B. & A. 581; Com. Dig. Temps, A; 3 East, 407; Com. Dig. Estates, G 8; 2 Chit. Pr. 69, 147.

EXCOMMUNICATION, *eccl. law*. An ecclesiastical sentence, pronounced by a spiritual judge against a Christian man, by which he is excluded from the body of the church, and disabled to bring any action, or sue any person in the common law courts. Bac. Ab. h. t.; Co. Litt. 133–4. In early times it was the most frequent and most severe method of executing ecclesiastical censure, although proper to be used, said Justinian, (Nov. 123,) only upon grave occasions. The effect of it was to remove the excommunicated person not only from the sacred rites but from the society of men. In a certain sense it interdicted the use of fire and water, like the punishment spoken of by Cæsar, (lib. 6 de Bell. Gall.) as inflicted by the Druids. Innocent IV. called it the nerve of ecclesiastical discipline. On repentance, the excommunicated person was absolved and received again to communion These are said to be the powers of binding and loosing—the keys of the kingdom of heaven. This kind of punishment seems to have been adopted from the Roman usage of interdicting the use of fire and water. Fr. Duaren, De Sacris Eccles. Ministeriis, lib. 1, cap. 3. See Ridley's View of the Civil and Ecclesiastical Law, 245, 246, 249.

EXCOMMUNICATIO CAPIENDO, WRIT OF, *Eng. eccl. law.* A writ issuing out of chancery, founded on a bishop's certificate that the defendant had been excommunicated, which writ is returnable in the king's bench. F. N. B. 62, 64, 65; Bac. Ab. Excommunication, E. See Statutes 3 Ed. I. c. 15; 9 Ed. II. c. 12; 2 & 3 Ed. VI. c. 13; 5 & 6 Ed. VI. c. 4; 5 Eliz. c. 23; 1 H. V. c. 5; also Cro. Eliz. 224, 680; Cro. Car. 421; Cro. Jac. 567; 1 Vent. 146; 1 Salk. 293, 294, 295.

EXCUSABLE HOMICIDE, *crim. law.* The killing of a human being, when the party killing is not altogether free from blame, but the necessity which renders it excusable, may be said to be partly induced by his own act. 1 East, P. C. 220.

EXCUSE. A reason alleged for the doing or not doing a thing.

2. This word presents two ideas differing essentially from each other. In one case an excuse may be made in order to show that the party accused is not guilty; in another, by showing that though guilty, he is less so, than he appears to be. Take, for example, the case of a sheriff who has an execution against an individual, and who in performance of his duty, arrests him; in an action by the defendant against the sheriff, the latter may prove the facts, and this shall be a sufficient excuse for him: this is an excuse of the first kind, or a complete justification; the sheriff was guilty of no offence. But suppose, secondly, that the sheriff has an execution against Paul, and by mistake, and without any malicious design, he arrests Peter instead of Paul; the fact of his having the execution against Paul and the mistake being made, will not justify the sheriff, but it will extenuate and excuse his conduct, and this will be an excuse of the second kind.

3. Persons are sometimes excused for the commission of acts, which ordinarily are crimes, either because they had no intention of doing wrong, or because they had no power of judging, and therefore had no criminal will (q. v.); or having power of judging they had no choice, and were compelled by necessity. Among the first class may be placed infants under the age of discretion, lunatics, and married women committing an offence in the presence of their husbands, not *malum in se,* as treason or murder; 1 Hale's P. C. 44, 45; or in offences relating to the domestic concern or management of the house, as the keeping of a bawdy house. Hawk. b. 1, c. 1, s. 12. Among acts of the second kind may be classed, the beating or killing another in self-defence; the destruction of property in order to prevent a more serious calamity, as the tearing down of a house on fire, to prevent its spreading to the neighboring property, and the like. See Dalloz, Dict. h. t.

EXEAT, *eccl. law.* This is a Latin term, which is used to express the written permission which a bishop gives to an ecclesiastic to exercise the functions of his ministry in another diocese.

TO EXECUTE. To make, to perform, to do, to follow out. This term is frequently used in the law; as, to execute a deed is to make a deed.

2. It also signifies to perform, as to execute a contract; hence some contracts are called executed contracts, and others are called executory contracts.

3. To execute also means to put to death by virtue of a lawful sentence; as, the sheriff executed the convict.

EXECUTED. Something done; something completed. This word is frequently used in connexion with others to designate a quality of such other words; as an executed contract; an executed estate; an executed trust, &c. It is opposed to executory.

2. An executed contract is one which has been fulfilled; as, where the buyer has paid the price of the thing purchased by him. See *Agreement.*

3. An executed estate is when there is vested in the grantee a present and immediate right of present or future enjoyment; and, in another sense, the term applies to the time of enjoyment; and in that sense, an estate is said to be executed, when it confers a present right of present enjoyment. When the right of enjoyment in possession is to arise at a future period, only the estate is executed; that is, it is merely vested in point of interest: when the right of immediate enjoyment is annexed to the estate, then only is the estate vested in possession. 1 Prest. on Est. 62.

4. Trusts executed are, when by deed

or will, lands are conveyed, or devised, in terms or in effect, to and for the use of one person or several persons, in trust for others, without any direction that the trustees shall make any farther conveyance; so that it does not appear that the author of the trusts had a view to a future instrument for accomplishing his intention. Prest. on Est. 188.

EXECUTIO NON. These words occur in the stat. 13 Ed. I. cap. 45, in the following connexion: Et . . . precipiatur vicecomiti quod scire faciat parti . . . quod sit ad certum diem ostensura si quid sciat dicere quare hujusmodi irrotulata vel in fine contenta *executionem habere non debeant*. This statute is the origin of the scire facias post annum et diem quare executionem non, etc. To a plea in bar to such a writ, the defendant should conclude that the plaintiff ought not to have or maintain his aforesaid execution thereof against him, which is called the *executio non*, as in other cases by *actio non*. (q. v.) 10 Mod. 112; Yelv. 218.

EXECUTION, *contracts*. The accomplishment of a thing; as the execution of a bond and warrant of attorney, which is the signing, sealing, and delivery of the same.

EXECUTION, *crim. law*. The putting a convict to death, agreeably to law, in pursuance of his sentence.

EXECUTION, *practice*. The act of carrying into effect the final judgment of a court, or other jurisdiction. The writ which authorizes the officer so to carry into effect such judgment is also called an execution.

2. A distinction has been made between an execution which is used to make the money due on a judgment out of the property of the defendant, and which is called a *final* execution; and one which tends to an end but is not absolutely final, as a *capias ad satisfaciendum*, by virtue of which the body of the defendant is taken, to the intent that the plaintiff shall be satisfied his debt, &c., the imprisonment not being absolute, but until he shall satisfy the same; this is called an execution *quousque*. 6 Co. 87.

3. Executions are either to recover specific things, or money. 1. Of the first class are the writs of *habere facias seisinam;* (q. v.) *habere facias possessionem;* (q. v.) *retorno habendo;* (q. v.) *distringas*. (q. v.) 2. Executions for the recovery of money are those which issue against the body of the defendant, as the *capias ad satisfaciendum*, (q. v.); an attachment, (q. v.); those which issue against his goods and chattels; namely, the *fieri facias*, (q. v.); the *venditioni exponas*, (q. v.); those which issue against his lands, the *levari facias;* (q. v.) the *liberari facias;* the *elegit*. (q. v.) Vide 10 Vin. Ab. 541; 1 Ves. jr. 430; 1 Sell. Pr. 512; Bac. Ab. h. t.: Com. Dig. h. t.; the various Digests, h. t.: Tidd's Pr. Index, h. t.; 3 Bouv. Inst. n. 3365, et seq. Courts will at any time grant leave to amend an execution so as to make it conformable to the judgment on which it was issued. 1 Serg. & R. 98. A writ of error lies on an award of execution. 5 Rep. 32, a; 1 Rawle, Rep. 47, 48; *Writ of Execution*.

EXE'CUTION PARE'E. By the term *exécution parée*, which is used in Louisiana, is meant a right founded on an authentic act; that is, an act passed before a notary, by which the creditor may immediately, without citation or summons, seize and cause to be sold, the property of his debtor, out of the proceeds of which to receive his payment. It imports a confession of judgment, and is not unlike a warrant of attorney. Code of Pr. of Lo. art. 732; 6 Toull. n 208; 7 Toull. 99.

EXECUTIONER. The name given to him who puts criminals to death, according to their sentence; a hangman.

2. In the United States, executions are so rare that there are no executioners by profession. It is the duty of the sheriff or marshal to perform this office, or to procure a deputy to do it for him.

EXECUTIVE, *government*. That power in the government which causes the laws to be executed and obeyed: it is usually confided to the hands of the chief magistrate; the president of the United States is invested with this authority under the national government; and the governor of each state has the executive power in his hands.

2. The officer in whom is vested the executive power is also called the executive.

3. The Constitution of the United States directs that "the executive power shall be vested in a president of the United States of America." Art. 2, s. 1. Vide Story, Const. B. 3, c. 36.

EXECUTOR, *trusts*. The word executor, taken in its largest sense, has several acceptations. 1. Executor dativus, who is one called an administrator to an intestate. 2. Executor testamentarius, or one appointed to the office by the last will of a testator, and this is what is usually meant by the term.

2. In the civil law, the person who is appointed to perform the duties of an executor as to goods, is called hæres testamentarius; the term executor, it is said, is a barbarism unknown to that law. 3 Atk. 304.

3. An executor, as the term is at present accepted, is the person to whom the execution of a last will and testament of personal estate is, by the testator's appointment, confided, and who has accepted of the same. 2 Bl. Com. 503; 2 P. Wms. 548; Toller, 30; 1 Will. on Ex. 112; Swinb. pt. 4, s. 2, pl. 2.

4. Generally speaking, all persons who are capable of making wills may be executors, and some others beside, as infants and married women. 2 Bl. Com. 503.

5. An executor is absolute or qualified; his appointment is absolute when he is constituted certainly, immediately, and without restriction in regard to the testator's effects, or limitation in point of time. It may be qualified by limitation as to the time or place wherein, or the subject matters whereon, the office is to be exercised; or the creation of the office may be conditional. It may be qualified. 1st. By limitations in point of time, for the time may be limited when the person appointed shall begin, or when he shall cease to be executor; as, if a man be appointed executor upon the marriage of testator's daughter. Swinb. p. 4, s. 17, pl. 4. 2. The appointment may be limited to a place; as, if one be appointed executor of all the testator's goods in the state of Pennsylvania. 3. The power of the executor may be limited as to the subject matter upon which it is to be exercised; as, when a testator appoints A the executor of his goods and chattels in possession; B, of his choses in action. One may be appointed executor of one thing, only, as of a particular claim or debt due by bond, and the like. Off. Ex. 29; 3 Phillim. 424. But although a testator may thus appoint separate executors of distinct parts of his property, and may divide their authority, yet *quoad* the creditors of the testator they are all executors, and act as one executor, and may be sued as one executor. Cro. Car. 293. 4. The appointment may be conditional, and the condition may be either precedent or subsequent. Godolph. Orph. Leg. pt. 2, c. 2, s. 1; Off. Ex. 23.

6. An executor derives his interest in the estate of the deceased entirely from the will, and it vests in him from the moment of the testator's death. 1 Will. Ex. 159; Com. Dig. Administration, B 10; 5 B. & A. 745; 2 W. Bl. Rep. 692. He acquires an absolute legal title to the personalty by appointment, but nothing in the lands of the testator, except by devise. He can touch nothing which was not personal at the testator's decease, except by express direction. 9 Serg. & Rawle, 431; Gord. Law Dec. 93. Still his interest in the goods of the deceased is not that absolute, proper and ordinary interest, which every one has in his own proper goods. He is a mere trustee to apply the goods for such purposes as are sanctioned by law. 4 T. R. 645; 9 Co. 88; 2 Inst. 236; Off. Ex. 192. He represents the testator, and therefore may sue and recover all the claims he had at the time of his death; and may be sued for all debts due by him. 1 Will. Ex. 508, et seq. By the common law, however, such debts as were not due by some writing could not be recovered against the executors of a deceased debtor. The remedy was only in conscience or by a quo minus in the exchequer. Afterwards an action on the case in banco regis was given. Crompt. Jurisdic. 66, b; Plowd. Com. 183; 11 H. VII. 26.

7. The following are the principal duties of an executor: 1. Within a convenient time after the testator's death, to collect the goods of the deceased, provided he can do so peaceably; when he is resisted, he must apply to the law for redress.

8.—2. To bury the deceased in a manner suitable to the estate he leaves behind him; and when there is just reason to believe he died insolvent, he is not warranted in expending more in funeral expenses (q.v.) than is absolutely necessary. 2 Will. Ex. 636; 1 Salk. 296; 11 Serg. & Rawle, 204; 14 Serg. & Rawle, 64.

9.—3. The executor should prove the will in the proper office.

10.—4. He should make an inventory (q. v.) of the goods of the intestate, which should be filed in the office.

11.—5. He should ascertain the debts and credits of the estate, and endeavor to collect all claims with as little delay as possible, consistently with the interest of the estate.

12.—6. He should advertise for debts and credits: *see forms of advertisements*, 1 Chit. Pr. 521.

13.—7. He should reduce the whole of the goods, not specifically bequeathed, into money, with all due expedition.

14.—8. Keep the money of the estate safely, but not mixed with his own, or he may be charged interest on it.

15.—9. Be at all times ready to account, and actually file an account within a year.

16.—10. Pay the debts and legacies in the order required by law.

17. Co-executors, however numerous, are considered, in law, as an individual person, and, consequently, the acts of any one of them, in respect of the administration of the assets, are deemed, generally, the acts of all. Bac. Ab. Executor, D; Touch. 484; for they have all a joint and entire authority over the whole property. Off. Ex. 213; 1 Rolle's Ab. 924; Com. Dig. Administration, B 12. On the death of one or more of several joint executors, their rights and powers survive to the survivors.

18. When there are several executors and all die, the power is in common transferred to the executor of the last surviving executor, so that he is executor of the first testator; and the law is the same when a sole executor dies leaving an executor, the rights are vested in the latter. This rule has been changed, in Pennsylvania, and, perhaps, some other states, by legislative provision; there, in such case, administration cum testamento annexo must be obtained, the right does not survive to the executor of the executor. Act of Pennsylvania, of March 15, 1832, s. 19. In general, executors are not responsible for each other, and they have a right to settle separate accounts. See *Joint Executors*.

19. Executors may be classed into general and special; instituted and substituted; rightful and executor de son tort; and executor to the tenor.

20. A *general* executor is one who is appointed to administer the whole estate, without any limit of time or place, or of the subject-matter.

21. A *special* executor is one who is appointed or constituted to administer either a part of the estate, or the whole for a limited time, or only in a particular place.

22. An *instituted* executor is one who is appointed by the testator without any condition, and who has the first right of acting when there are substituted executors. An example will show the difference between an instituted and substituted executor: suppose a man makes his son his executor, but if he will not act, he appoints his brother, and if neither will act, his cousin; here the son is the instituted executor, in the first degree, the brother is said to be substituted in the second degree, and the cousin in the third degree, and so on. See *Heir, instituted*, and Swinb. pt. 4, s. 19, pl. 1.

23. A *substituted* executor is a person appointed executor, if another person who has been appointed refuses to act.

24. A *rightful* executor is one lawfully appointed by the testator, by his will. Deriving his authority from the will, he may do most acts, before he obtains letters testamentary, but he must be possessed of them before he can declare in action brought by him, as such. 1 P. Wms. 768; Will. on Ex. 173.

25. An executor *de son tort*, or of his own wrong, is one, who, without lawful authority, undertakes to act as executor of a person deceased. To make an executor *de son tort*, the act of the party must be, 1. Unlawful. 2. By asserting ownership, as taking goods or cancelling a bond, and not committing a mere trespass. Dyer, 105, 166; Cro. Eliz. 114. 3. An act done before probate of will, or granting letters of administration. 1 Salk. 313. One may be executor *de son tort* when acting under a forged will, which has been set aside. 3 T. R. 125. An executor *de son tort*. The law on this head seems to have been borrowed from the civil law doctrine of *pro hærede gestio*. See Heinnec. Antiq. Syntagma, lib. 2, tit. 17, § 16, p. 468. He is, in general, held responsible for all his acts, when he does anything which might prejudice the estate, and receives no advantage whatever in consequence of his assuming the office. He cannot sue a debtor of the estate, but may be sued generally as executor. See a good reading on the liabilities of executors *de son tort*, in Godolph. Orph. Legacy, 91, 93, and 10 Wentw. Pl. 378, for forms of declaring; also, 5 Co. Rep. 50 b, 31 a; Yelv. 137; 1 Brownlow, 103; Salk. 28; Ham. Parties, 273; Imp. Mod. Pl. 94. As to what acts will make a person liable as executor *de son tort*, see Godolph. O. ubi sup.; Gord. Law of Dec. 87, 89; Off. Ex. 181; Bac. Ab. Executor, &c., B 3; 11 Vin. Ab. 215; 1 Dane's Ab. 561; Bull. N. P. 48; Com. Dig. Administration, C 3; Ham. on Part. 146 to 156; 8 John. R

426; 7 John. R. 161; 4 Mass. 654; 3 Penna. R. 129; 15 Serg. & Rawle, 39.

26.—2. The usurpation of an office or character cannot confer the rights and privileges of it, although it may charge the usurper with the duties and obligations annexed to it. On this principle, an executor *de son tort* is an executor only for the purpose of being sued, not for the purpose of suing. In point of form, he is sued as if he were a rightful executor. He is not denominated in the declaration executor (*de son tort*) of his own wrong. It would be improper to allege that the deceased person with whose estate he has intermeddled died intestate. Nor can he be made a co-defendant with a rightful executor. Ham. Part. 146, 272, 273; Lawes on Plead. 190, note; Com. Dig. Abatement, F 10. If he take out letters of administration, he is still liable to be sued as executor, and in general, it is better to sue him as executor than as administrator. Godolph. O. Leg. 93, 94, 95, §§ 2, 3.

27. An executor *to the tenor*. This phrase is used in the ecclesiastical law, to denote a person who is not directly appointed by the will an executor, but who is charged with the duties which appertain to one; as, "I appoint A B to discharge all lawful demands against my will." 3 Phill. 116; 1 Eccl. Rep. 374; Swinb. 247; Wentw. Ex. part 4, s. 4, p. 230.

Vide, generally, Bouv. Inst. Index, h. t.; 11 Vin. Ab. h. t.; Bac. Ab. h. t.; Rolle, Ab. h. t.; Nelson's Ab. h. t.; Dane's Ab. Index, h. t.; Com. Dig. Administration; 1 Supp. to Ves. jr. 8, 90, 356, 438; 2 Id. 69; 1 Vern. 302–3; Yelv. 84 a; 1 Salk. 318; 18 Engl. C. L. Rep. 185; 10 East, 295; 2 Phil. Ev. 289; 1 Rop. Leg. 114; American Digests, h. t.; Swinburne, Williams, Lovelass, and Roberts' several treatises on the law of Executors; Off. Ex. per totum; Chit. Pr. Index, h. t. For the various pleas that may be pleaded by executors, see 7 Wentw. Plead. 596, 602; 10 Id. 378; Cowp. 292. For the origin and progress of the law in relation to executors, the reader is referred to 5 Toull. n. 576, note; Glossaire du Droit Français, par Delaurière, verbo Exécuteurs Testamentaires, and the same author on art. 297, of the Custom of Paris; Poth. Des Donations Testamentaires.

EXECUTORY. Whatever may be executed; as an executory sentence or judgment, an executory contract.

EXECUTORY DEVISE, *estates*. An executory devise is a limitation by will of a future contingent interest in lands, contrary to the rules of limitation of contingent estates in conveyances at law. When the limitation by will does not depart from those rules prescribed for the government of contingent remainders, it is, in that case, a contingent remainder, and not an executory devise. 4 Kent, Com. 257; 1 Eden's R. 27; 3 T. R. 763.

2. An executory devise differs from a contingent remainder in three material points. 1. It needs no particular estate to precede and support it; for example, a devise to A B, upon his marriage. 2. A fee may be limited after a fee, as in the case of a devise of land to C D, in fee, and if he dies without issue, or before the age of twenty-one, then to E F, in fee. 3. A term for years may be limited over after a life estate created in the same. 2 Bl. Com. 172, 173.

3. To prevent perpetuities, a rule has been adopted that the contingency must happen during the time of a life or lives in being and twenty-one years after, and the months allowed for gestation in order to reach beyond the minority of a person not in esse at the time of making the executory devise. 3 P. Wms. 258; 7 T. R. 100; 2 Bl. Com. 174; 7 Cranch, 456; 1 Gilm 194; 2 Hayw. 375.

4. There are several kinds of executory devises; two relative to real estate, and one in relation to personal estate.

5.—1. When the devisor parts with his whole estate, but upon some contingency, qualifies the disposition of it, and limits an estate on that contingency. For example, when the testator devises to Peter for life, remainder to Paul, in fee, provided that if James should within three months after the death of Peter pay one hundred dollars to Paul, then to James in fee; this is an executory devise to James, and if he dies during the life of Peter, his heir may perform the condition. 10 Mod. 419; Prec. in Ch. 486; 2 Binn. 532; 5 Binn. 252; 7 Cranch, 456; 6 Munf. 187; 1 Desaus. 137, 183; 4 Id. 340, 459; 5 Day, 517.

6.—2. When the testator gives a future interest to arise upon a contingency, but does not part with the fee in the meantime, as in the case of a devise of the estate to the heirs of John after the death of John; or a devise to John in fee, to take effect six months after the testator's death; or a devise to the daughter of John, who shall marry Robert within fifteen years. T. Raym. 82; 1 Salk. 226; 1 Lutw. 798.

7.—3. The executory bequest of a chattel interest is good, even though the ulterior legatee be not at the time *in esse*, and chattels so limited are protected from the demands of creditors beyond the life of the first taker, who cannot pledge them, nor dispose of them beyond his own life interest in them. 2 Kent, Com. 285; 2 Serg. & Rawle, 59; 1 Desaus. 271; 4 Desaus. 340; 1 Bay, 78. But such a bequest, after an indefinite failure of issue, is bad. See 2 Serg. & R. 62; Watk. Prin. Con. 112, 116; Harg. note, 1 Tho. Co. Litt. 595–6, 515–16.

Vide, Com. Dig. Estates by Devise, N 16; Fearne on Rem. 381; Cruise's Dig. Index, h. t.; 4 Kent, Com. 357 to 381; 2 Hill. Ab. c. 43, p. 533.

Executory process, *via executoria.* In Louisiana, this is a process which can be resorted to only in two cases, namely: 1. When the creditor's right arises from an act importing a confession of judgment, and which contains a privilege or mortgage in his favor. 2. When the creditor demands the execution of a judgment which has been rendered by a tribunal different from that within whose jurisdiction the execution is sought. Code of Practice, art. 732.

Executory trust. A trust is said to be *executory* where some further act is requisite to be done by the author of the trust himself or by the trustees, to give it its full effect; as, in the case of marriage articles; or, as in the case of a will, where property is vested in trustees in trust to settle or convey; for, it is apparent in both of these cases, a further act, namely, a settlement or a conveyance, is contemplated.

2. The difference between an executed and an executory trust, is this, that courts of equity in cases of *executed* trusts will construe the limitations in the same manner as similar legal limitations. White's L. C. in Eq. 18. But, in cases of *executory* trusts, a court of equity is not, as in the case of executed trusts, bound to construe technical expressions with legal strictness, but will mould the trusts according to the intent of the creator of such trusts. White's L. C. Eq. 18.

3. When a voluntary trust is executory, and not executed, if it could not be enforced at law, because it is a defective conveyance, it is not helped in equity, in favor of a volunteer. 4 John. Ch. 498, 500; 4 Paige, 305; 1 Dev. Eq. R. 93.

4. But where the trust, though voluntary, has been executed in part, it will be sustained or enforced in equity. 1 John. Ch. R. 329; 7 Penn. St. R. 175, 178; White's L. C. in Eq. *176; 18 Ves. 140; 1 Keen's R. 551; 6 Ves. 656; 3 Beav. 238.

EXECUTRIX. A woman who has been appointed by will to execute such will or testament. See *Executor*.

EXEMPLIFICATION, *evidence.* A perfect copy of a record, or office book lawfully kept, so far as relates to the matter in question. 3 Bouv. Inst. n. 3107. Vide, generally, 1 Stark. Ev. 151; 1 Phil. Ev. 307; 7 Cranch, 481; 3 Wheat. 234; 10 Wheat. 469; 9 Cranch, 122; 2 Yeates, 532; 1 Hayw. 359; 1 John. Cas. 238. As to the mode of authenticating records of other states, see articles *Authentication*, and *Evidence*.

EXEMPTION. A privilege which dispenses with the general rule; for example, in Pennsylvania, and perhaps in all the other states, clergymen are exempt from serving on juries. Exemptions are generally allowed, not for the benefit of the individual, but for some public advantage.

EXEMPTS. Persons who are not bound by law, but excused from the performance of duties imposed upon others.

2. By the Act of Congress of May 8, 1792, 1 Story, L. U. S. 252, it is provided, § 2. That the vice-president of the United States; the officers, judicial and executive, of the government of the United States; the members of both houses of congress, and their respective officers; all custom-house officers, with their clerks; all post officers, and stage drivers, who are employed in the care and conveyance of the mail of the post office of the United States; all ferrymen employed at any ferry on the post road; all inspectors of exports; all pilots; all mariners, actnally employed in the sea service of any citizen or merchant within the United States; and all persons who now are, or may hereafter be, exempted by the laws of the respective states, shall be, and are hereby, exempted from militia dnty, notwithstanding their being above the age of eighteen, and under the age of forty-five years.

EXEQUATUR, *French law.* This Latin word was, in the ancient practice, placed at the bottom of a judgment emanating from another tribunal, and was a permission and authority to the officer to execute it within the jurisdiction of the judge who put it below the judgment.

2. We have something of the same kind in our practice. When a warrant for the arrest of a criminal is issued by a justice of the peace of one county, and he flies into another, a justice of the latter county may endorse the warrant and then the ministerial officer may execute it in such county. This is called *backing* a warrant.

EXEQUATUR, *internat. law.* A declaration made by the executive of a government near to which a consul has been nominated and appointed, after such nomination and appointment has been notified, addressed to the people, in which is recited the appointment of the foreign state, and that the executive having approved of the consul as such, commands all the citizens to receive, countenance, and, as there may be occasion, favorably assist the consul in the exercise of his place, giving and allowing him all the privileges, immunities, and advantages, thereto belonging. 3 Chit. Com. Law, 56; 3 Maule & Selw. 290; 5 Pardes. n. 1445.

EXERCITOR. A term in the *civil law,* to denote the person who fits out and equips a vessel, whether he be the absolute or qualified owner, or even a mere agent. Emer. on Mar. Loans, c. 1, s. 1.

2. In English, we generally use the word "ship's husband," but exercitor is generally used to designate and distinguish from among several part owners of a ship, the one who has the immediate care and management of her. Hall on Mar. Loans, 142, n. See Dig. 19, 2, 19, 7; Id. 14, 1, 1, 15; Vicat, Vocab.; *Ship's husband.*

EXHEREDATION, *civil law.* The act by which a forced heir is deprived of his legitimate or legal portion which the law gives him; disinherison. (q. v.)

EXHIBIT, *practice.* Where a paper or other writing is on motion, or on other occasion, proved; or if an affidavit to which the paper writing is annexed, refer to it, it is usual to mark the same with a capital letter, and to add, "This paper writing, marked with the letter A, was shown to the deponent at the time of his being sworn by me, and is the writing by him referred to in the affidavit annexed hereto." Such paper or other writing, with this attestation, signed by the judge or other person before whom the affidavit shall have been sworn, is called an *exhibit.* Vide Stra. 674; 2 P. Wms. 410; Gresl. Eq. Ev. 98.

TO EXHIBIT. To produce a thing publicly, so that it may be taken possession of, or seized. Dig. 10, 4, 2. To exhibit means also to file of record; as, it is the practice in England in personal actions, when an officer or prisoner of the king's bench is defendant, to proceed against such defendant in the court in which he is an officer, by *exhibiting,* that is, *filing* a bill against him. Steph. Pl. 52, n. (*l*); 2 Sell. Pr. 74. In medical language, to exhibit signifies to administer, to cause a thing to be taken by a patient. Chit. Med. Jur. 9.

EXHIBITANT. One who exhibits any thing; one who is complainant in articles of the peace. 12 Adol. & Ellis, 599; 40 E. C. L. R. 124.

EXHIBITION, *Scotch law.* An action for compelling the production of writings. In Pennsylvania, a party possessing writings is compelled to produce them on proper notice being given, in default of which judgment is rendered against him.

EXIGENT, or EXIGI FACIAS, *practice.* A writ issued in the course of proceedings to outlawry, deriving its name and application from the mandatory words found therein, signifying, "that you cause to be exacted or required; and it is that proceeding in an outlawry which, with the writ of proclamation, issued at the same time, immediately precedes the writ of *capias utlagatum.* 2 Virg. Cas. 244.

EXIGIBLE. That which may be exacted; demandable; requirable.

EXILE, *civil law.* The interdiction of all places except one in which the party is forced to make his residence.

2. This punishment did not deprive the sufferer of his right of citizenship, or of his property, unless the exile were perpetual, in which case confiscation not unfrequently was a part of the sentence. Exile was temporary or perpetual. Dig. 48, 22, 4; Code, 10, 59, 2. Exile differs from deportation, (q. v.) and relegation. (q. v.) Vide 2 Lev. 191; Co. Litt. 133, a.

EXILIUM. By this term is understood that kind of waste which either drove away the inhabitants into a species of exile, or had a tendency to do so; as the prostrating or extirpating of trees in an orchard or avenue, or about any house. Bac. Ab. Waste, A; Bract. lib. 4, c. 18, s. 13; 1 Reeves' Hist. Law, 386.

EXITUS. Issue, child, or offspring; rents or profits of land. Cowell, h. v. In pleading, it is the issue, or the end, termination, or conclusion of the pleadings, and is so called, because an issue brings the pleadings to a close. 3 Bl. Com. 314.

EXIGENDARY, *Eng. law.* An officer who makes out exigents.

EXOINE, *French law.* An act or instrument in writing, which contains the reasons why a party in a civil suit, or a person accused, who has been summoned, agreeably to the requisitions of a decree, does not appear. Poth. Procéd. Crim. s. 3, art. 3. Vide *Essoin.*

EXONERATION. The taking off a burden or duty.

2. It is a rule in the distribution of an intestate's estate that the debts which he himself contracted, and for which he mortgaged his land as security, shall be paid out of the personal estate in exoneration of the real.

3. But when the real estate is charged with the payment of a mortgage at the time the intestate buys it, and the purchase is made subject to it, the personal is not in that case to be applied in exoneration of the real estate. 2 Pow. Mortg. 780; 5 Hayw 57; 3 Johns. Ch. R. 229.

4. But the rule for exonerating the real estate out of the personal, does not apply against specific or pecuniary legatees, nor the widow's right to paraphernalia, and with reason not against the interest of creditors. 2 Ves. jr. 64; 1 P. Wms. 693; Id. 729; 2 Id. 120, 335 3 Id. 367. Vide Pow. Mortg. Index, h. t.

EXONERATUR, *practice.* A short note entered on a bail piece, that the bail is exonerated or discharged in consequence of having fulfilled the condition of his obligation, made by order of the court or of a judge upon a proper cause being shown.

2. A surrender is the most usual cause; but an exoneratur may be entered in other cases, as in case of death of the defendant, or his bankruptcy. 1 Arch. Pr. 280, 281, 282; Tidd's Pr. 240.

EXPATRIATION. The voluntary act of abandoning one's country and becoming the citizen or subject of another.

2. Citizens of the United States have the right to expatriate themselves until restrained by congress; but it seems that a citizen cannot renounce his allegiance to the United States without the permission of government, to be declared by law. To be legal, the expatriation must be for a purpose which is not unlawful, nor in fraud of the duties of the emigrant at home.

3. A citizen may acquire in a foreign country commercial privileges attached to his domicil, and be exempted from the operation of commercial acts embracing only persons resident in the United States or under its protection. 2 Cranch, 120. Vide Serg. Const. Law, 318, 2d ed; 2 Kent, Com. 36; Grotius, B. 2, c. 5, s. 24; Puffend. B. 8, c. 11, s. 2, 3; Vattel, B. 1, c. 19, s. 218, 223, 224, 225; Wyckf. tom. i. 117, 119; 3 Dall. 133; 7 Wheat. 342; 1 Pet. C. C. R. 161; 4 Hall's Law Journ. 461; Bracken. Law Misc. 409; 9 Mass. R. 461. For the doctrine of the English courts on this subject, see 1 Barton's Elem. Conveyancing, 31, note: Vaugh, Rep. 227, 281, 282, 291; 7 Co. Rep. 16; Dyer, 2, 224, 298 b, 300 b; 2 P. Wms. 124; 1 Hale, P. C. 68; 1 Wood. 382.

EXPECTANCY, *estates.* Having a relation to or dependence upon something future.

2. Estates are of two sorts, either in *possession*, sometimes called estates executed; or in *expectancy*, which are executory. Expectancies are, first, created by the parties, called a *remainder;* or by act of law, called a *reversion.*

3. A bargain in relation to an expectancy is, in general, considered invalid. 2 Ves. 157; Sel. Cas. in Ch. 8; 1 Bro. C. C. 10; Jer. Eq. Jur. 397.

EXPECTANT. Having relation to, or depending upon something; this word is frequently used in connexion with *fee*, as *fee expectant.*

EXPECTATION. That which may be expected, although contingent. In the doctrine of life annuities, that share or number of the years of human life which a person of a given age may expect to live, upon an equality of chances.

2. In general, the heir apparent will be relieved from a contract made in relation to his expectancy. See *Post Obit.*

EXPENSÆ LITIS. Expenses of the suit; the costs which are generally allowed to the successful party.

EXPERTS. From the Latin *experti*, which signifies, instructed by experience. Persons who are selected by the courts or the parties in a cause on account of their knowledge or skill, to examine, estimate, and ascertain things, and make a report of their opinions. Merl. Répert. mot Expert; 2 Lois des Bâtimens, 253; 2 N. S. 1; 5 N. S. 557; 3 L. R. 350; 11 L. R. 314; 11 S. & R. 336; Ray. Med. Jur. Prel. Views, § 29; 3 Bouv. Inst. n. 3208.

EXPILATION, *civil law.* The crime of abstracting the goods of a succession.

2. This is said not to be a theft, because the property no longer belongs to the deceased, nor to the heir before he has taken possession. In the common law, the grant of letters testamentary, or letters of administration, relate back to the time of the death of the testator or intestate, so that the property of the estate is vested in the executor or administrator from that period.

EXPIRATION. Cessation; end. As, the expiration of a lease, of a contract, or statute.

2. In general, the expiration of a contract puts an end to all the engagements of the parties, except to those which arise from the non-fulfilment of obligations created during its existence. For example, the expiration of a partnership so dissolves it, that the parties cannot in general create any new liability, but it still subsists, to enable the parties to fulfil engagements in which the partners have engaged, or to compel others to perform their obligations towards them. See *Dissolution; Contracts.*

3. When a statute is limited as to time, it expires by mere lapse of time, and then it has no force whatever; and, if such a statute repealed or supplied a former statute, the first statute is, *ipso facto*, revived by the expiration of the repealing statute; 6 Whart. 294; 1 Bland, R. 664; unless it appear that such was not the intention of the legislature. 3 East, 212; Bac. Ab. Statute, D.

EXPORTATION, *commercial law.* The act of sending goods and merchandise from one country to another. 2 Mann. & Gran. 155; 3 Mann. & Gran. 959.

2. In order to preserve equality among the states, in their commercial relations, the constitution provides that "no tax or duty shall be laid on articles exported from any state." Art. 1, s. 9. And to prevent a pernicious interference with the commerce of the nation, the 10th section of the 1st article of the constitution contains the following prohibition · "No state shall, without the consent of congress, lay any imposts or duties on imports or exports, except what may be absolutely necessary for executing its inspection laws; and the net produce of all duties and imposts, laid by any state on imports or exports, shall be for the use of the treasury of the United States; and all such laws shall be subject to the revision and control of the congress." Vide 12 Wheat. 419; and the article *Importation.*

EXPOSÉ. A French word, sometimes applied to a written document, containing the reasons or motives for doing a thing. The word occurs in diplomacy.

EXPOSITION DE PART, *French law.* The abandonment of a child, unable to take care of itself, either in a public or private place.

2. If the child thus exposed should be killed in consequence of such exposure; as, if it should be devoured by animals, the person thus exposing it would be guilty of murder. Rosc. Cr. Ev. 591.

EXPRESS. That which is made known, and not left to implication. The opposite of implied. It is a rule, that when a matter or thing is expressed, it ceases to be implied by law: *expressum facit cessare tacitum.* Co. Litt. 183; 1 Bouv. Inst. n. 97.

EXPRESSION. The term or use of language employed to explain a thing.

2. It is a general rule, that expressions shall be construed, when they are capable of several significations, so as to give operation to the agreement, act, or will, if it can be done; and an expression is always to be understood in the sense most agreeable to the nature of the contract. Vide *Clause; Construction; Equivocal; Interpretation; Words.*

EXPROMISSION, *civil law.* The act by which a creditor accepts a new debtor, who becomes bound instead of the old, the latter being released. It is a species of novation. (q. v.) 1 Bouv. Inst. n. 802. Vide *Delegation.*

EXPROMMISSOR, *civil law.* By this term is understood the person who alone becomes bound for the debt of another, whether the latter were obligated or not. He differs from a surety, who is bound together with his principal. Dig. 12, 4, 4; Dig. 16, 1, 13; Id. 24, 3, 64, 4; Id. 38, 1, 37, 8.

EXPULSION. The act of depriving a member of a body politic, corporate, or of a society, of his right of membership therein by the vote of such body or society, for some violation of his duties as such, or for some offence which renders him unworthy of longer remaining a member of the same.

2. By the Constitution of the United States, art. 1, s. 5, § 2, each house may determine the rules of its proceedings, punish its members for disorderly behaviour, and, with the concurrence of two-thirds, expel a member. In the case of John Smith, a senator from Ohio, who was expelled from the senate in 1807, the committee made a report which embraces the following points:

3.—1. That the senate may expel a member for a high misdemeanor, such as a conspiracy to commit treason. Its authority is not confined to an act done in its presence.

4.—2. That a previous conviction is not requisite, in order to authorize the senate to expel a member from their body, for a high offence against the United States.

5.—3. That although a bill of indictment against a party for treason and misdemeanor has been abandoned, because a previous indictment against the principal party had terminated in an acquittal, owing to the inadmissibility of the evidence upon that indictment, yet the senate may examine the evidence for themselves, and if it be sufficient to satisfy their minds that the party is guilty of a high misdemeanor, it is a sufficient ground of expulsion.

6.—4. That the 5th and 6th articles of the amendments of the Constitution of the United States, containing the general rights and privileges of the citizen, as to criminal prosecutions, refer only to prosecutions at law, and do not affect the jurisdiction of the senate as to expulsion.

7.—5. That before a committee of the senate, appointed to report an opinion relative to the honor and privileges of the senate, and the facts respecting the conduct of the member implicated, such member is not entitled to be heard in his defence by counsel, to have compulsory process for witnesses, and to be confronted with his accusers. It is before the senate that the member charged is entitled to be heard.

8.—6. In determining on expulsion, the senate is not bound by the forms of judicial proceedings, or the rules of judicial evidence; nor, it seems, is the same degree of proof essential which is required to convict of a crime. The power of expulsion must, in its nature, be discretionary, and its exercise of a more summary character. 1 Hall's Law Journ. 459, 465.

9. Corporations have the right of expulsion in certain cases, as such power is necessary to the good order and government of corporate bodies; and the cases in which the inherent power may be exercised are of three kinds. 1. When an offence is committed which has no immediate relation to a member's corporate duty, but is of so infamous a nature as renders him unfit for the society of honest men; such as the offences of perjury, forgery, and the like. But before an expulsion is made for a cause of this kind, it is necessary that there should be a previous conviction by a jury, according to the law of the land. 2. When the offence is against his duty as a corporator, in which case he may be expelled on trial and conviction before the corporation. 3. The third is of a mixed nature, against the member's duty as a corporator, and also indictable by the law of the land. 2 Binn. 448. See, also, 2 Burr. 536.

10. Members of what are called joint stock incorporated companies, or indeed members of any corporation owning property, cannot, without express authority in the charter, be expelled, and thus deprived of their interest in the general fund. Ang. & Ames on Corp. 238.

See, generally, Ang. & Ames on Corp. ch. 11; Willcock on Mun. Corp. 270; 11 Co. 99; 2 Bing. 293; 5 Day, 329; Sty. 478; 6 Conn. R. 532; 6 Serg. & Rawle, 469; 5 Binn. 486.

EXTENSION, *comm. law.* This term is applied among merchants to signify an agreement made between a debtor and his creditors, by which the latter, in order to enable the former, embarrassed in his circumstances, to retrieve his standing, agree to wait for a definite length of time after their several claims should become due and payable, before they will demand payment.

2. Among the French, a similar agreement is known by the name of atermoiement. Merl. Rép. mot Atermoiement.

EXTENT IN AID, *English practice.* An exchequer process, formerly much used, and now liable to be abused; it is regulated by 57 Geo. III. c. 117.

EXTENT IN CHIEF, *English practice.* An execution issuing out of the exchequer at the suit of the crown. It is a mere fiscal writ. See West on Extents; 2 Tidd. Index.

2. When land was extended at a valua-

tion too low, there was no remedy at common law but to pay the money. 15 H. VII. Nor yet in chancery, unless there was fraud, because the extent was made by the oath of a jury, and deemed reasonable according to the writ of extent for that cause: otherwise every verdict might be examined in a court of chancery. Crompt. on Jurisdic. 55 a.

EXTENUATION. That which renders a crime or tort less heinous than it would be without it: it is opposed to aggravation. (q. v.)

2. In general, extenuating circumstances go in mitigation of punishment in criminal cases, or of damages in those of a civil nature. See *Aggravation; Mitigation.*

EXTERRITORIALITY. This term is used by French jurists to signify the immunity of certain persons, who, although in the state, are not amenable to its laws; foreign sovereigns, ambassadors, ministers plenipotentiary, and ministers from a foreign power, are of this class. Fœlix, Droit Intern. Privé, liv. 2, tit. 2, c. 2, s. 4. See *Ambassador; Conflict of Laws; Minister.*

EXTINCTION OF A THING. When a thing which is the subject of a contract has been destroyed, the contract is of course rescinded; as, for example, if Paul sell his horse Napoleon to Peter, and promises to deliver him to the buyer in ten days, and in the mean time the horse dies, the contract is rescinded, as it is impossible to deliver a thing which is not *in esse;* but if Paul engage to deliver a horse to Peter in ten days, and, for the purpose of fulfilling his contract, he buys a horse, and it dies, this is no cause for rescinding the contract, because he can buy another and complete it afterwards. When the subject of the contract is an individual, and not generally one of a species, the contract may be rescinded; when it is one of a species which has been destroyed, then it may still be completed, and it will be enforced. Leç. El. Dr. Rom. § 1009.

EXTINGUISHMENT, *contracts.* The destruction of a right or contract—the act by which a contract is made void.

2. An extinguishment may be by matter of fact and by matter of law. 1. It is by matter of fact either express, as when one receives satisfaction and full payment of a debt, and the creditor releases the debtor; 11 John. 513; or implied, as when a person hath a yearly rent out of lands and becomes owner either by descent or purchase, of the estate subject to the payment of the rent, the latter is extinguished; 3 Stew. 60; but the person must have as high an estate in the land as in the rent, or the rent will not be extinct. Co. Litt. 147. See *Merger.*

3. There are numerous cases where the claim is extinguished by operation of law; for example, where two persons are jointly, but not severally liable, for a simple contract debt, a judgment obtained against one is at common law an extinguishment of the claim on the other debtor. Pet. C. C. 301; see 2 John. 213. Vide, generally, Bouv. Inst. Index, h. t.; 2 Root, 492; 3 Conn. 62; 1 Hamm. 187; 11 John. 513; 4 Conn. 428; 6 Conn. 373; 1 Halst. 190; 4 N. H. Rep. 251; Co. Litt. 147 b; 1 Roll. Ab. 933; 7 Vin. Ab. 367; 11 Vin. Ab. 461; 18 Vin. Ab. 493 to 515; 3 Nels. Ab. 818; 14 Serg. & Rawle, 209; Bac. Ab. h. t.; 5 Whart. R. 541. Vide *Discharge of a Debt.*

EXTORSIVELY. A technical word used in indictments for extortion. In North Carolina, it seems, the crime of extortion may be charged without using this word. 1 Hayw. R. 406.

EXTORTION, *crimes.* In a large sense it signifies any oppression, under color of right: but in a more strict sense it means the unlawful taking by any officer, by color of his office, of any money or thing of value that is not due to him, or more than is due, or before it is due. 4 Bl. Com. 141; 1 Hawk. P. C. c. 68, s. 1; 1 Russ. Cr. *144. To constitute extortion, there must be the receipt of money or something of value; the taking a promissory note, which is void, is not sufficient to make an extortion. 2 Mass. R. 523; see Bac. Ab. h. t.; Co. Litt. 168. It is extortion and oppression for an officer to take money for the performance of his duty, even though it be in the exercise of a discretionary power. 2 Burr. 927. It differs from exaction. (q. v.) See 6 Cowen, R. 661; 1 Caines, R. 130; 13 S. & R. 426; 1 Yeates, 71; 1 South. 324; 3 Penna. R. 183; 7 Pick. 279; 1 Pick. 171.

EXTRA-DOTAL PROPERTY. In Louisiana this term is used to designate that property which forms no part of the dowry of a woman, and which is also called paraphernal property. Civ. Co. Lo. art. 2315. Vide *Dotal Property.*

EXTRA VIAM. Out of the way. When, in an action of trespass, the defendant pleads a right of way, the defendant may reply *extra viam*, that the trespass was committed beyond the way, or make a new assignment. 16 East, 343, 349.

EXTRACT. A part of a writing. In general this is not evidence, because the *whole* of the writing may explain the part extracted, so as to give it a different sense; but sometimes extracts from public books are evidence, as the extracts from the registers of births, marriages and burials, kept according to law, when the whole of the matter has been extracted which relates to the cause or matter in issue.

EXTRADITION, *civil law*. The act of sending, by authority of law, a person accused of a crime to a foreign jurisdiction where it was committed, in order that he may be tried there. Merl. Rép. h. t.

2. By the constitution and laws of the United States, fugitives from justice (q. v.) may be demanded by the executive of the one state where the crime has been committed from that of another where the accused is. Const. United States, art. 4, s. 2, 2; 3 Story, Com. Const. U. S. § 1801, et seq.

3. The government of the United States is bound by some treaty stipulations to surrender criminals who take refuge within the country, but independently of such conventions, it is questionable whether criminals can be surrendered. 1 Kent. Com. 36; 4 John. C. R. 106; 1 Amer. Jurist, 297; 10 Serg. & Rawle, 125; 22 Amer. Jur. 330; Story's Confl. of Laws, p. 520; Wheat. Intern. Law, 111.

4. As to when the extradition or delivery of the supposed criminal is complete is not very certain. A case occurred in France of a Mr. Cassado, a Spaniard, who had taken refuge in Bayonne. Upon an application made to the French government, he was delivered to the Spanish consul who had authority to take him to Spain, and while in the act of removing him with the assistance of French officers, a creditor obtained an execution against his person, and made an attempt to execute it and retain Cassado in France, but the council of state, (conseil d'état) on appeal, decided that the courts could not interfere, and directed Cassado to be delivered to the Spanish authorities. Morrin, Dict. du Dr. Crim. h. v.

EXTRAJUDICIAL. That which does not belong to the judge or his jurisdiction, notwithstanding which he takes cognizance of it. Extrajudicial judgments and acts are absolutely void. Vide *Coram non judice*, and Merl. Répert. mots Excés de Pouvoir.

EXTRAVAGANTES, *canon law*. This is the name given to the constitutions of the popes posterior to the Clementines; they are thus called *quasi vagantes extra corpus juris*, to express that they were out of the canonical law, which at first contained only the decrees of Gratian; afterwards the decretals of Gregory IX., the sexte of Boniface VIII., the Clementines, and at last the extravagantes were added to it. There are the extravagantes of John XXII., and the common extravagantes. The first contain twenty epistles, decretals or constitutions of that pope, divided under fifteen titles, without any subdivision into books. The others are epistles, decretals or constitutions of the popes who occupied the holy see, either before or after John XXII.; they are divided into books like the decretals.

EXTREMIS. When a person is sick beyond the hope of recovery, and near death, he is said to be in extremis.

2. A will made in this condition, if made without undue influence, by a person of sound mind, is valid.

3. The declarations of persons in extremis, when made with a full consciousness of approaching death, are admissible in evidence when the death of the person making them is the subject of the charge, and the circumstances of the death the subject of such declarations. 2 B. & C. 605; S. C. 9 Eng. C. L. Rep. 196; and see 15 John. 286; 1 John. Rep. 159; 2 John. R. 31; 7 John. 95; 2 Car. Law. Repos. 102; 5 Whart. R. 396–7.

EY. A watery place; water. Co. Litt. 6.

EYE-WITNESS. One who saw the act or fact to which he testifies. When an eye-witness testifies, and is a man of intelligence and integrity, much reliance must be placed on his testimony, for he has the means of making known the truth.

EYOTT. A small island arising in a river. Fleta, lib. 3, c. 2, s. b; Bract. lib. 2, c. 2. See *Island*.

EYRE. Vide *Eire Justiciarii Itinerantes*.

F.

F, *punishment*, *English law*. Formerly felons were branded and marked with a hot iron, with this letter, on being admitted to the benefit of clergy.

FACIO UT DES. A species of contract in the civil law, which occurs when a man agrees to perform anything for a price, either specifically mentioned or left to the determination of the law to set a value on it. As when a servant hires himself to his master for certain wages or an agreed sum of money. 2 Bl. Com. 445.

FACIO UT FACIAS. A species of contract in the civil law, which occurs when I agree with a man to do his work for him if he will do mine for me. Or if two persons agree to marry together, or to do any other positive acts on both sides. Or it may be to forbear on one side in consideration of something done on the other. 2 Bl. Com. 444.

FACT. An action; a thing done. It is either simple or compound.

2. A fact is simple when it expresses a purely material act unconnected with any moral qualification; for example, to say Peter went into his house, is to express a simple fact. A compound fact contains the materiality of the act, and the qualification which that act has in its connexion with morals and the law. To say, then, that Peter has stolen a horse, is to express a compound fact; for the fact of stealing, expresses at the same time, the material fact of taking the horse, and of taking him with the guilty intention of depriving the owner of his property and appropriating it to his own use; which is a violation of the law of property.

3. Fact is also put in opposition to law; in every case which has to be tried there are facts to be established, and the law which bears on those facts.

4. Facts are also to be considered as material or immaterial. Material facts are those which are essential to the right of action or defence, and therefore of the substance of the one or the other—these must always be proved; or immaterial, which are those not essential to the cause of action—these need not be proved. 3 Bouv. Inst. n. 3150–53.

5. Facts are generally determined by a jury; but there are many facts, which, not being the principal matters in issue, may be decided by the court; such, for example, whether a subpœna has or has not been served; whether a party has or has not been summoned, &c. As to pleading material facts, see Gould. Pl. c. 3, s. 28. As to quality of facts proved, see 3 Bouv. Inst. n. 3150. Vide Eng. Ecc. R. 401–2, and the article *Circumstances*.

FACTO. In fact, in contradistinction to the lawfulness of the thing; it is applied to anything actually done. Vide *Ex post facto*.

FACTOR, *contracts*. An agent employed to sell goods or merchandise consigned or delivered to him, by, or for his principal, for a compensation commonly called factorage or commission. Paley on Ag. 13; 1 Liverm. on Ag. 68; Story on Ag. § 33; Com. Dig. Merchant, B; Mal. Lex Merc. 81; Beawes, Lex Merc. 44; 3 Chit. Com. Law, 193; 2 Kent, Com. 622, note d, 3d. ed.; 1 Bell's Com. 385, § 408, 409; 2 B. & Ald. 143. He is also called a commission merchant, or consignee.

2. When he resides in the same state or country with his principal, he is called a home factor; and a foreign factor when he resides in a different state or country. 3 Chit. Com. Law, 193; 1 T. R. 112; 4 M. & S. 576; 1 Bell's Com. 289, § 313.

3. When the agent accompanies the ship, taking a cargo aboard, and it is consigned to him for sale, and he is to purchase a return cargo out of the proceeds, such agent is properly called a factor; he is, however, usually known by the name of a supercargo. Beawes, Lex Merc. 44, 47; Liverm. on Ag. 69, 70; 1 Domat, b. 1, t. 16, § 3, art. 2.

4. A factor differs from a broker, in some important particulars, namely; he may buy and sell for his principal in his own name, as well as in the name of his principal; on the contrary, a broker acting as such should buy and sell in the name of his principal. 3 Chit. Com. Law, 193, 210, 541; 2 B. & Ald. 143, 148; 3 Kent, Com. 622, note d, 3d. ed. Again, a factor is entrusted with the possession, management,

disposal, and control of the goods to be bought and sold, and has a special property and a lien on them; the broker, on the contrary, has usually no such possession, management, control, or disposal of the goods, nor any such special property nor lien. Paley on Ag. 13, Lloyd's ed.; 1 Bell's Com. 385.

5. Before proceeding further, it will be proper to consider the difference which exists in the liability of a home or domestic factor and a foreign factor.

6. By the usages of trade, or intendment of law, when *domestic* factors are employed in the ordinary business of buying and selling goods, it is presumed that a reciprocal credit between the principal and the agent and third persons has been given. When a purchase has been made by such a factor, he, as well as his principal, is deemed liable for the debt; and in case of a sale, the buyer is responsible both to the factor and principal for the purchase money; but this presumption may be rebutted by proof of exclusive credit. Story, Ag. §§ 267, 291, 293; Paley, Ag. 243, 371; 9 B. & C. 78; 15 East, R. 62.

7. *Foreign* factors, or those acting for principals residing in a foreign country, are held personally liable upon all contracts made by them for their employers, whether they describe themselves in the contract as agents or not. In such cases, the presumption is, that the credit is given exclusively to the factor. But this presumption may be rebutted by a proof of a contrary agreement. Story, Ag. § 268; Paley, Ag. 248, 373; Bull. N. P. 130; Smith, Merc. Law, 66; 2 Liverm. Ag. 249; 1 B. & P. 398; 15 East, R. 62; 9 B. & C. 78.

8. A factor is liable to duties, which will be first considered; and, afterwards, a statement of his rights will be made.

9.—1. *His duties.* He is required to use reasonable skill and ordinary diligence in his vocation; in general, he has a right to sell the goods, but he cannot pawn them. The latter branch of this rule, however, is altered by statute in some of the states. See Act of Penna. April 14, 1834, §§ 3, 4, 6, postea, 20. He is bound to obey his instructions, but when he has none, he may and ought to act according to the general usages of trade; sell for cash, when that is usual, or give credit on sales, when that is customary. He is bound to render a just account to his principal, and to pay him the moneys he may receive for him.

10.—2. *His rights.* He has the right to sell the goods in his own name; and, when untrammeled by instructions, he may sell them at such times and for such prices, as, in the exercise of a just discretion, he may think best for his employer. 3 Man. Gran. & Scott, 380. He is, for many purposes, between himself and third persons, to be considered as the owner of the goods. He may, therefore, recover the price of goods sold by him, in his own name, and, consequently, he may receive payment and give receipts, and discharge the debtor, unless, indeed, notice has been given by the principal to the debtor not to pay. He has a lien on the goods for advances made by him, and for his commissions.

11. Mr. Bell, in his Commentaries, vol. 1, page 265, 5th ed., lays down the following rules with regard to the rights of the principal, in those cases in which the goods in the factor's hands have been changed in the course of his transactions.

12.—1. When the factor has sold the goods of his principal, and failed before the price of the goods has been paid, the principal is the creditor, and entitled to a preference over the creditors of the factor. Cook's B. L. 4th ed. p. 400.

13.—2. When bills have been taken for the price, and are still in the factor's hands, undiscounted at his failure; or where goods have been taken in return for those sold; the principal is entitled to them, as forming no part of the divisible fund. Willes, R. 400.

14.—3. When the price has been paid in money, coin, bank notes, &c., it remains the property of the principal, if kept distinct as his. 5 T. R. 277; 2 Burr. 1369; 5 Ves. Jr. 169; 2 Mont. B. L. 233, notes.

15.—4. When a bill received for goods, or placed with the factor, has been discounted, or when money coming into his hands has been paid away, the endorsee of the bill, or the person receiving the money, will be free from all claim at the instance of the principal. Vide 1 B. & P. 539, 648.

16.—5. When the factor sinks the name of the principal entirely; as, where he is employed to sell goods, and receives a del credere commission, for which he engages to guarantee the payment to the principal, it is not the practice to communicate the names of the purchasers to the principal, except where the factor fails. Under these circumstances, the following points have been settled. 1. When the factor fails, the principal is the creditor of the buyer, and has a direct action against him for the price. Cook's B. L. 400; and vide Bull. N. P. 42; 2 Stra. 1182. But persons contracting with the factor in his own name, and bona fide, are entitled to set off the factor's debt to them. 7 T. R. 360. 2. Where the factor is entrusted with the money or property of his principal to buy stock, bills, and the like, and misapplies it, the produce will be the principal's, if clearly distinguishable. 3 M. & S. 562.

17.—6. When the factor purchases goods for the behoof of his principal, but on his own general current account, without mention of the principal, the goods vest in the factor, and the principal has only an obligation against the factor's estate. But when the factor, after purchasing the goods, writes to his principal that he has bought such a quantity of goods in consequence of his order, and that they are lying in his warehouse, or elsewhere, the property would seem to be vested in the principal.

18. It may, therefore, be laid down as a general rule, that when the property remitted by the principal, or acquired for him by his order, is found distinguishable in the hands of the factor, capable of being traced by a clear and connected chain of identity, in no one link of it degenerating from a specific trust into a general debt, the creditors of the factor, who has become bankrupt, have no right to the specific property. Much discrimination is requisite in the application of this doctrine, as may be seen by the case of Ex parte Sayers, 5 Ves. Jr. 169.

19. A factor has no right to barter the goods of his principal, nor to pledge them for the purpose of raising money for himself, or to secure a debt he may owe. See ante, 9.—1. But he may pledge them for advances made to his principal, or for the purpose of raising money for him, or in order to reimburse himself to the amount of his own lien. 2 Kent, Com. 3d. ed., 625 to 628; 4 John. R. 103; Story on Bailm. § 325, 326, 327. Another exception to the general rule that a factor cannot pledge the goods of his principal, is, that he may raise money by pledging the goods, for the payment of duties, or any other charge or purpose allowed or justified by the usages of trade. 2 Gall. 13; 6 Serg. & Rawle, 386; Paley on Ag. 217; 3 Esp. R. 182.

20. The legislature of Pennsylvania, by an act entitled "An act for the amendment of the law relating to factors," passed April 14, 1834, have made the following provisions. This act was prepared by the persons appointed to revise the civil code of that state, and was adopted without alteration by the legislature. It is here inserted, with a belief that it will be found useful to the commercial lawyer of the other states.

21.—§ 1. Whenever any person entrusted with merchandise, and having authority to sell or consign the same, shall ship, or otherwise transmit the same to any other person, such other person shall have a lien thereon—

22.—I. For any money advanced, or negotiable security given by him on the faith of such consignment, to or for the use of the person in whose name such merchandise was shipped or transmitted.

23.—II. For any money or negotiable security, received for the use of such consignee, by the person in whose name such merchandise was shipped or transmitted.

24.—§ 2. But such lien shall not exist for any of the purposes aforesaid, if such consignee shall have notice by the bill of lading, or otherwise, before the time of such advance or receipt, that the person in whose name such merchandise was shipped or transmitted, is not the actual owner thereof.

25.—§ 3. Whenever any consignee or factor, having possession of merchandise, with authority to sell the same, or having possession of any bill of lading, permit, certificate, receipt, or order, for the delivery of merchandise, with the like authority, shall deposit or pledge such merchandise, or any part thereof, with any other person, as a security for any money advanced, or negotiable instrument given by him on the faith thereof; such other person shall acquire, by virtue of such contract, the same interest in, and authority over, the said merchandise, as he would have acquired thereby if such consignee or factor had been the actual owner thereof. *Provided*, That such person shall not have notice by such document or otherwise, before the time of such advance or receipt, that the holder of such merchandise or document is not the actual owner of such merchandise.

26.—§ 4. If any person shall accept or take such merchandise or document from any such consignee or factor, in deposit or pledge for any debt or demand previously due by, or existing against, such consignee or factor, and without notice as aforesaid, and if any person shall accept or take such merchandise or document from any such consignee or factor, in deposit or pledge, without notice or knowledge that the person making such deposit or pledge, is a consignee or factor only, in every such case the person accepting or taking such merchandise or document in deposit or pledge, shall acquire the same right and interest in such merchandise as was possessed, or could have been enforced, by such consignee or factor against his principal at the time of making such deposit or pledge, and further or other right or interest.

27.—§ 5. Nothing in this act contained shall be construed or taken—

I. To affect any lien which a consignee or factor may possess at law, for the expenses and charges attending the shipment, or transmission and care of merchandise consigned, or otherwise intrusted to him.

28.—II. Nor to prevent the actual owner of merchandise from recovering the same from such consignee or factor, before the same shall have been deposited or pledged as aforesaid, or from the assignees or trustees of such consignee or factor, in the event of his insolvency.

29.—III. Nor to prevent such owner from recovering any merchandise, so as aforesaid deposited or pledged, upon tender of the money, or of restoration of any negotiable instrument so advanced, or given to such consignee or factor, and upon tender of such further sum of money, or of restoration of such other negotiable instrument, if any, as may have been advanced or given by such consignee or factor to such owner, or on tender of a sum of money equal to the amount of such instrument.

30.—IV. Nor to prevent such owner from recovering, from the person accepting or taking such merchandise in deposit or pledge, any balance or sum of money remaining in his hands as the produce of the sale of such merchandise, after deducting the amount of money or the negotiable instrument so advanced or given upon the security thereof as aforesaid.

31.—§ 6. If any consignee or factor shall deposite or pledge any merchandise or document as aforesaid, consigned or intrusted to him as a security for any money borrowed, or negotiable instrument received by such consignee or factor, and shall apply and dispose of the same to his own use, in violation of good faith, and with intent to defraud the owner of such merchandise, and if any consignee or factor shall, with the like fraudulent intent, apply or dispose of, to his own use, any money or negotiable instrument, raised or acquired by the sale or other disposition of such merchandise, such consignee or factor shall, in every such case, be deemed guilty of a misdemeanor, and shall be punished by a fine, not exceeding two thousand dollars, and by imprisonment, for a term not exceeding five years.

FACTORAGE. The wages or allowances paid to a factor for his services; it is more usual to call this commissions. 1 Bouv. Inst. n. 1013; 2 Id. n. 1288.

FACTORY, *Scotch law.* A contract which partakes of a mandate and locatio ad operandum, and which is in the English and American law books discussed under the title of Principal and Agent. 1 Bell's Com. 259.

FACTUM. A deed; a man's own act and deed.

2. When a man denies by his plea that he made a deed on which he is sued, he pleads *non est factum.* (q. v.) Vide *Deed; Fait.*

FACTUM, *French law.* A memoir which contains summarily the fact on which a contest has happened, the means on which a party founds his pretensions, with the refutation of the means of the adverse party. Vide *Brief.*

FACULTY, *canon law.* A license; an authority. For example, the ordinary having the disposal of all seats in the nave of a church, may grant this power, which, when it is delegated, is called a faculty, to another.

2. Faculties are of two kinds; first, when the grant is to a man and his heirs in gross; second, when it is to a person and his heirs, as appurtenant to a house which he holds in the parish. 1 T. R. 429, 432; 12 Co. R. 106.

FACULTY, *Scotch law.* Equivalent to ability or power. The term faculty is more properly applied to a power founded on the consent of the party from whom it springs, and not founded on property. Kames on Eq. 504.

FAILURE. A total defect; an omission; a non-performance. Failure also signifies a stoppage of payment; as, there has been a failure to-day, some one has stopped payment.

2. According to the French code of commerce, art. 437, every merchant or trader who suspends payment is in a state of failure. Vide *Bankruptcy; Insolvency.*

FAILURE OF ISSUE. When there is a want of issue to take an estate limited over by an executory devise.

2. Failure of issue is definite or indefinite. When the precise time for the failure of issue is fixed by the will, as in the case of a devise to Peter, but if he dies without issue living *at the time of his death*, then to another, this is a failure of issue *definite*. An *indefinite* failure of issue is the very converse or opposite of this, and it signifies a general failure of issue, whenever it may happen, without fixing any time, or a certain or definite period, within which it must happen. 2 Bouv. Inst. n. 1849.

FAILURE OF RECORD. The neglect to produce the record after having pleaded it. When a defendant pleads a matter, and offers to prove it by the record, and then pleads *nul tiel record*, a day is given to the defendant to bring in the record; if he fails to do so, he is said to fail, and there being a *failure of record*, the plaintiff is entitled to judgment. Termes de lay Ley. See the form of entering it; 1 Saund. 92, n. 3.

FAINT PLEADER. A false, fraudulent, or collusory manner of pleading, to the deception of a third person. 3 E. I., c. 19.

FAIR. A privileged market.

2. In England, fairs are granted by the king's patent.

3. In the United States, fairs are almost unknown. They are recognized in Alabama; Aik. Dig. 409, note; and in North Carolina, where they are regulated by statute. 1 N. C. Rev. St. 282. See Domat, Dr. Public, liv. 1, t. 7, s. 3, n. 1.

FAIR-PLAY MEN. About the year 1769, there was a tract of country in Pennsylvania, situate between Lycoming creek and Pine creek, in which the proprietaries prohibited the making of surveys, as it was doubtful whether it had or had not been ceded by the Indians. Although settlements were forbidden, yet adventurers settled themselves there; being without the pale of ordinary authorities, the inhabitants annually elected a tribunal, in rotation, of three of their number, whom they denominated *fair-play men*, who had authority to decide all disputes as to boundaries. Their decisions were final, and enforced by the whole community en masse. Their decisions are said to have been just and equitable. 2 Smith's Laws of Pennsylvania 195; Serg. Land Laws, 77.

FAIR PLEADER. This is the name of a writ given by the statute of Marlebridge, 52 H. III., c. 11. Vide *Beau Pleader.*

FAIT, *conveyancing*. A deed lawfully executed. Com. Dig. h. t.; Cunn. Dict. h. t.

FAITH. Probity; good faith is the very soul of contracts. Faith also signifies confidence, belief; as, full faith and credit ought to be given to the acts of a magistrate while acting within his jurisdiction. Vide *Bona fide.*

FALCIDIAN LAW, *civil law, plebisscitum.* A statute or law enacted by the people, made during the reign of Augustus, on the proposition of Falcidius, who was a tribune in the year of Rome 714.

2. Its principal provision gave power to fathers of families to bequeath three-fourths of their property, but deprived them of the power to give away the other fourth, which was to descend to the heir.

3. The same rule, somewhat modified, has been adopted in Louisiana; "donations *inter vivos* or *mortis causa*," says the Civil Code, art. 1480, "cannot exceed two-thirds of the property of the disposer, if he leaves at his decease a legitimate child; one-half, if he leaves two children; and one-third, if he leaves three, or a greater number."

4. By the common law, the power of the father to give his property is unlimited. He may bequeath it to his children equally, to one in preference to another, or to a stranger, in exclusion of the whole of them. Over his real estate, his wife has a right of dower, or a similar right given to her by act of assembly, in, perhaps, all the states.

FALSE. Not true; as, false pretences; unjust, unlawful, as, false imprisonment. This word is frequently used in composition.

FALSE IMPRISONMENT, *torts.* Any intentional detention of the person of another not authorized by law, is false imprisonment. 1 Bald. 571; 9 N. H. Rep. 491; 2 Brev. R. 157. It is any illegal imprisonment, without any process whatever, or under color of process wholly illegal, without regard to the question whether any crime has been committed, or a debt due. 1 Chit. Pr. 48; 5 Verm. 588; 3 Blackf. 46; 3 Wend. 350; 5 Wend. 298; 9 John. 117; 1 A. K. Marsh. 345; Kirby, 65; Hardin 249.

2. The remedy is, in order to be restored to liberty, by writ of *habeas corpus*, and to recover damages for the injury, by action of trespass vi et armis. To punish

the wrong done to the public, by the false imprisonment of an individual, the offender may be indicted. 4 Bl. Com. 218, 219; 2 Burr. 993. Vide Bac. Ab. Trespass, D 3; Dane's Ab. Index, h. t. Vide 9 N. H. Rep. 491; 2 Brev. R. 157; *Malicious Prosecution; Regular and Irregular Process.*

FALSE JUDGMENT, *Eng. law.* The name of a writ which lies when a false judgment has been given in the county court, court baron, or other courts not of record. F. N. B. 17, 18; 3 Bouv. Inst. n. 3364.

FALSE PRETENCES, *criminal law.* False representations and statements, made with a fraudulent design, to obtain "money, goods, wares, and merchandise," with intent to cheat. 2 Bouv. Inst. n. 2308.

2. This subject may be considered under the following heads: 1. The nature of the false pretence. 2. What must be obtained. 3. The intent.

3.—1. When the false pretence is such as to impose upon a person of ordinary caution, it will doubtless be sufficient. 11 Wend. R. 557. But although it may be difficult to restrain false pretences to such as an ordinarily prudent man may avoid, yet it is not every absurd or irrational pretence which will be sufficient. 2 East, P. C. 828. It is not necessary that all the pretences should be false, if one of them, *per se*, is sufficient to constitute the offence. 14 Wend. 547. And although other circumstances may have induced the credit, or the delivery of the property, yet it will be sufficient if the false pretences had such an influence that, without them, the credit would not have been given, or the property delivered. 11 Wend. R. 557; 14 Wend. R. 547; 13 Wend. Rep. 87. The false pretences must have been used before the contract was completed. 14 Wend. Rep. 546; 13 Wend. Rep. 311. In North Carolina, the cheat must be effected by means of some token or contrivance adapted to impose on an ordinary mind. 3 Hawks, R. 620; 4 Pick. R. 178.

4.—2. The wording of the statutes of the several states on this subject is not the same, as to the acts which are indictable. In Pennsylvania, the words of the act are, "every person who, with intent to cheat or defraud another, shall designedly, by color of any false token or writing, or by any false pretence whatever, obtain from any person any money, personal property or other valuable things," &c. In Massachusetts, the intent must be to obtain "money, goods, wares, merchandise, or other things." Stat. of 1815, c. 136. In New York, the words are "money, goods, or chattels, or other effects." Under this statute it has been holden that obtaining a signature to a note; 13 Wend. R. 87; or an endorsement on a promissory note; 9 Wend. Rep. 190; fell within the spirit of the statute; and that where credit was obtained by false pretence, it was also within the statute. 12 John. R. 292.

5.—3. There must be an intent to cheat or defraud some person. Russ. & Ry. 317; 1 Stark. Rep. 396. This may be inferred from a false representation. 13 Wend. R. 87. The intent is all that is requisite; it is not necessary that the party defrauded should sustain any loss. 11 Wend. R. 18; 1 Carr. & Marsh. 516, 537.

FALSE RETURN. A return made by the sheriff, or other ministerial officer, to a writ, in which is stated a fact contrary to the truth, and injurious to one of the parties or some one having an interest in it.

2. In this case the officer is liable for damages to the party injured. 2 Esp. Cas. 475. See *Falso retorno brevium.*

FALSE TOKEN. A false document or sign of the existence of a fact, in general used for the purpose of fraud. Vide *Token*, and 2 Stark Ev. 563.

FALSEHOOD. A wilful act or declaration contrary to truth. It is committed either by the wilful act of the party, or by dissimulation, or by words. It is wilful, for example, when the owner of a thing sells it twice, by different contracts to different individuals, unknown to them; for in this the seller must wilfully declare the thing is his own, when he knows that it is not so. It is committed by dissimulation when a creditor, having an understanding with his former debtor, sells the land of the latter, although he has been paid the debt which was due to him.

2. Falsehood by word is committed when a witness swears to what he knows not to be true. Falsehood is usually attendant on crime. Roscoe, Cr. Ev. 362.

3. A slander must be false to entitle the plaintiff to recover damages. But whether a libel be true or false the writer or publisher may be indicted for it. Bul. N. P. 9; Selw. N. P. 1047, note 6; 5 Co. 125; Hawk. B, 1, c. 73, s. 6. Vide Dig. 48, 10, 31; Id. 22, 6, 2; Code, 9, 22, 20

4. It is a general rule, that if a witness testifies falsely as to any one material fact,

the whole of his testimony must be rejected; but still the jury may consider whether the wrong statement be of such character, as to entitle the witness to be believed in other respects. 5 Shepl. R. 267. See *Lie*.

TO FALSIFY, *crim. law*. To prove a thing to be false; as, "to falsify a record." Tech. Dict.; Co. Litt. 104 b. To alter or make false a record. This is punishable at common law. Vide *Forgery*.

2. By the Act of Congress of April 30, 1790, s. 15, 1 Story's L. U. S. 86, it is enacted, that if any person shall feloniously steal, take away, alter, falsify, or otherwise avoid, any record, writ, process, or other proceedings in any of the courts of the United States, by means whereof any judgment shall be reversed, made void, or not take effect; or if any person shall acknowledge, or procure to be acknowledged, in any of the courts aforesaid, any recognizance, bail, or judgment, in the name or names of any other person or persons not privy or consenting to the same, every such person, or persons, on conviction thereof, shall be fined not exceeding five thousand dollars, or be imprisoned not exceeding seven years, and be whipped not exceeding thirty-nine stripes. *Provided nevertheless*, that this act shall not extend to the acknowledgment of any judgment or judgments by any attorney or attorneys, duly admitted, for any person or persons against whom any such judgment or judgments shall be had or given.

TO FALSIFY, *chancery practice*. When a bill to open an account has been filed, the plaintiff is sometimes allowed to surcharge and falsify such account; and if any thing has been inserted that is a wrong charge, he is at liberty to show it, and that is a *falsification*. 2 Ves. 565; 11 Wheat. 237. See *Account stated; Surcharge*.

FALSO RETORNO BREVIUM, *old English law*. The name of a writ which might have been sued out against a sheriff, for falsely returning writs. Cunn. Dict.

FAMILY, *domestic relations*. In a limited sense it signifies the father, mother, and children. In a more extensive sense it comprehends all the individuals who live under the authority of another, and includes the servants of the family. It is also employed to signify all the relations who descend from a common ancestor, or who spring from a common root. Louis. Code, art. 3522, No. 16; 9 Ves. 323.

2. In the construction of wills, the word family, when applied to personal property, is synonymous with *kindred*, or *relations*. It may, nevertheless, be confined to particular relations by the context of the will, or may be enlarged by it, so that the expression may in some cases mean children, or next of kin, and in others, may even include relations by marriage. 1 Rop. on Leg. 115; 1 Hov. Supp. 365, notes, 6 and 7; Brown *v.* Higgs; 4 Ves. 708; 2 Ves. jr. 110; 3 East, Rep. 172; 5 Ves. 156; 17 Ves. 255; 5 M. & S. 126. Vide article *Legatee*. See Dig. lib. 50, t. 16, l. 195, s. 2.

FAMILY ARRANGEMENTS. This term has been used to signify an agreement made between a father and his son, or children; or between brothers, to dispose of property in a different manner to that which would otherwise take place.

2. In these cases frequently the mere relation of the parties will give effect to bargains otherwise without adequate consideration. 1 Chit. Pr. 67; 1 Turn. & Russ. 13.

FAMILY BIBLE. A Bible containing an account of the births, marriages, and deaths of the members of a family.

2. An entry by a father, made in a Bible, stating that Peter, his eldest son, was born in lawful wedlock of Maria, his wife, at a time specified, is evidence to prove the legitimacy of Peter. 4 Campb. 401. But the entry, in order to be evidence, must be an original entry, and, when it is not so, the loss of the original must be proved before the copy can be received. 6 Serg. & Rawle, 135. See 10 Watts, R. 82.

FAMILY EXPENSES. The sum which it costs a man to maintain a family.

2. Merchants and traders who desire to exhibit the true state of their affairs in their books, keep an exact account of family expenses, which, in case of failure, is very important, and at all times proper.

FAMILY MEETINGS. Family councils, or family meetings in Louisiana, are meetings of at least five relations, or in default of relations of minors or other persons on whose interest they are called upon to deliberate, then of the friends of such minors or other persons.

2. The appointment of the members of the family meeting is made by the judge. The relations or friends must be selected from among those domiciliated in the parish in which the meeting is held; the relations are selected according to their proximity, beginning with the nearest. The relation is

preferred to the connexion in the same degree, and among relations of the same degree, the eldest is preferred. The under tutor must also be present. 6 N. S. 455.

3. The family meeting is held before a justice of the peace, or notary public, appointed by the judge for the purpose. It is called for a fixed day and hour, by citations delivered at least three days before the day appointed for the purpose.

4. The members of the family meeting, before commencing their deliberations, take an oath before the officer before whom the meeting is held, to give their advice according to the best of their knowledge, touching the interests of the person on whom they are called upon to deliberate. The officer before whom the family meeting is held, must make a particular proces-verbal of the deliberations, cause the members of the family meeting to sign it, if they know how to sign, he must sign it himself, and deliver a copy to the parties that they may have it homologated. Civil Code of Louis. B. 1, tit. 8, c. 1, s. 6, art. 305 to 311; Code Civ. B. 1, tit. 10, c. 2, s. 4.

FAMOSUS LIBELLUS. Among the civilians these words signified that species of *injuria* which corresponds nearly to libel or slander.

FANEGA, *Spanish law*. A measure of land, which is not the same in every province. Diccionario de la Acad.; 2 White's Coll. 49. In Spanish America, the fanega consisted of six thousand and four hundred square varas or yards. 2 White's Coll. 138.

FARE. It signifies a voyage or passage; in its modern application, it is the money paid for a passage. 1 Bouv. Inst. n. 1036.

FARM, *estates*. A portion or tract of land, some of which is cultivated. 2 Binn. 238. In parlance, and for the purpose of description in a deed, a farm means a messuage with out-buildings, gardens, orchard, yard, and land usually occupied with the same for agricultural purposes; Plowd. 195; Touch. 93; 1 Tho. Co. Litt. 208, 209, n. N; but in the English law, and particularly in a description in a declaration in ejectment, it denotes a leasehold interest for years in any real property, and means anything which is held by a person who stands in the relation of tenant to a landlord. 6 T. R. 532; 2 Chit. Pl. 879, n. *e*.

2. By the conveyance of a farm, will pass a messuage, arable land, meadow, pasture, wood, &c., belonging to or used with it. 1 Inst. 5, a; Touch. 93; 4 Cruise, 321; Bro. Grants, 155; Plowd. 167.

3. In a will, the word farm may pass a freehold, if it appear that such was the intention of the testator. 6 T. R. 345; 9 East, 448. See 6 East, 604, n; 8 East, 339.

To FARM LET. These words in a lease have the effect of creating a lease for years. Co. Litt. 45 b; 2 Mod. 250.

FARMER. One who is lessee of a farm. It is said that every lessee for life or years, although it be but of a small house and land, is called *farmer*. This word implies no mystery except it be that of husbandman. Cunn. Dict. h. t. In common parlance, a farmer is one who cultivates a farm, whether he be the owner of it or not.

FARO, *crim. law*. There is a species of game called faro-table, or faro-bank, which is forbidden by law in many states; and the persons who keep it for the purpose of playing for money or other valuable thing, may generally be indicted at common law for a nuisance. 1 Roger's Rec. 66. It is played with cards in this manner: a pack of cards is displayed on the table so that the face of each card may be seen by the spectators. The man who keeps the bank, as it is termed, and who is called the banker, sits by the table with another pack of cards, and a bag containing money, some of which is displayed, or sometimes instead of money, *chips*, or small pieces of ivory or other substance are used. The parties who play with the banker, are called punters or pointeurs. Suppose the banker and A, a punter, wish to play for five dollars, the banker shuffles the pack which he holds in his hand, while A lays his money intended to be bet, say five dollars, on any card he may choose as aforesaid. The banker then runs the cards alternately into two piles, one on the right the other on the left, until he reaches, in the pack, the card corresponding to that on which A has laid his money. If, in this alternative, the card chosen comes on the right hand, the banker takes up the money; if on the other, A is entitled to five dollars from the banker. Several persons are usually engaged at the same table with the banker. 1 Rog. Rec. 66, note; Encycl Amer. h. t.

FARRIER. One who takes upon himself the public employment of shoeing horses.

2. Like an innkeeper, a common carrier, and other persons who assume a *public* employment, a farrier is bound to serve the

public as far as his employment goes, and an action lies against him for refusing, when a horse is brought to him at a reasonable time for such purpose, if he refuse; Oliph. on Horses, 131; and he is liable for the unskilfulness of himself or servant in performing such work; 1 Bl. Com. 431; but not for the malicious act of the servant in purposely driving a nail into the foot of the horse, with the intention of laming him. 2 Salk. 440.

FATHER, *domestic relations*. He by whom a child is begotten.

2. A father is the natural guardian of his children, and his duty by the natural law consists in maintaining them and educating them during their infancy, and making a necessary provision for their happiness in life. This latter, however, is a duty which the law does not enforce.

3. By law, the father is bound to support his children, if of sufficient ability, even though they have property of their own. 1 Bro. C. C. 387; 4 Mass. R. 97; 2 Mass. R. 415; 5 Rawle, 323. But he is not bound, without some agreement, to pay another for maintaining them; 9 C. & P. 497; nor is he bound to pay their debts, unless he has authorized them to be contracted. 38 E. C. L. R. 195, n. See 8 Watts, R. 366; 1 Craig. & Phil. 317; *Bind; Mother; Parent*. This obligation ceases as soon as the child becomes of age, unless he becomes chargeable to the public. 1 Ld. Ray. 699.

4. The rights of the father are to have authority over his children, to enforce all his lawful commands, and to correct with moderation his children for disobedience. A father may delegate his power over the person of his child to a tutor or instructor, the better to accomplish the purposes of his education. This power ceases on the arrival of the child at the age of twenty-one years. Generally, the father is entitled to the services of his children during their minority. 4 S. & R. 207; Bouv. Inst. Index, h. t.

FATHER-IN-LAW. In latin, *socer*, is the father of one's wife, or of one's husband.

FATHER PUTATIVE. A reputed father. Vide *Putative father*.

FATHOM. A measure of length, equal to six feet. The word is probably derived from the Teutonic word *fad*, which signifies the thread or yarn drawn out in spinning to the length of the arm, before it is run upon the spindle. Webster; Minsheu. See *Ell*. Vide *Measure*.

FATUOUS PERSON. One entirely destitute of reason; *is qui omnino desipit*. Ersk. Inst. B. 1, tit. 7, s. 48.

FAUBOURG. A district or part of a town adjoining the principal city; as, a faubourg of New Orleans. 18 Lo. R. 286.

FAULT, *contracts, civil law*. An improper act or omission, which arises from ignorance, carelessness, or negligence. The act or omission must not have been meditated, and must have caused some injury to another. Leç. Elem. § 783. See *Dolus, Negligence*. 1 Miles' Rep. 40.

2.—1. Faults or negligence are usually divided into, gross, ordinary, and slight: 1. Gross fault or neglect, consists in not observing that care towards others, which a man the least attentive, usually takes of his own affairs. Such fault may, in some cases, afford a presumption of fraud, and in very gross cases it approaches so near, as to be almost undistinguishable from it, especially when the facts seem hardly consistent with an honest intention. But there may be a gross fault without fraud. 2 Str. 1099; Story, Bailm. § 18–22; Toullier, 1. 3, t. 3, § 231. 2. Ordinary faults consist in the omission of that care which mankind generally pay to their own concerns; that is, the want of ordinary diligence. 3. A slight fault consists in the want of that care which very attentive persons take of their own affairs. This fault assimilates itself, and, in some cases, is scarcely distinguishable, from mere accident, or want of foresight. This division has been adopted by common lawyers from the civil law. Although the civilians generally agree in this division, yet they are not without a difference of opinion. See Pothier, Observation générale, sur le précédent Traité, et sur les suivants; printed at the end of his Traité des Obligations, where he cites Accurse, Alciat, Cujas, Duaren, D'Avezan, Vinnius, and Heineccius, in support of this division. On the other side the reader is referred to Thomasius, tom. 2, Dissertationem, page 1006; Le Brun, cited by Jones, Bailm. 27; and Toullier, Droit Civil Français, liv. 3, tit. 3, § 231.

3.—2. These principles established, different rules have been made as to the responsibilities of parties for their faults in relation to their contracts. They are reduced by Pothier to three.

4.—1. In those contracts where the party derives no benefit from his undertaking, he is answerable only for his gross faults.

5.—2. In those contracts where the parties have a reciprocal interest, as in the contract of sale, they are responsible for ordinary neglect.

6.—3. In those contracts where the party receives the only advantage, as in the case of loan for use, he is answerable for his slight fault. Poth. Observ. Générale; Traité des Oblig. § 142; Jones, Bailm. 119; Story, Bailm. 12. See also Ayliffe, Pand. 108; Civ. C. Lou. 3522; 1 Com. Dig. 413; 5 Id. 184; Wesk. on Ins. 370.

FAUX, *French law.* A falsification or fraudulent alteration or suppression of a thing by words, by writings, or by acts without either. Biret, Vocabulaire des Six Codes.

2. The crimen falsi of the civil law. Toullier says, "Le faux s'entend de trois manières: dans le sens le plus étendre, c'est l'alteration de la vérité, avec ou sans mauvaises intentions; il est à peu prés synonyme de mensonge; dans un sens moins étendu, c'est l'alteration de la vérité, accompagnée de dol, *mutatio veritatis cum dolo facta;* enfin, dans le sens étroit, ou plutôt legal du mot, quand il s'agit de savoir si le faux est un crime, le faux est l'alteration frauduleuse de la vérité, dans les determinés et punis par la loi." Tom. 9, n. 188. "*Faux* may be understood in three ways: in its most extended sense, it is the alteration of truth, with or without intention; it is nearly synonymous with lying; in a less extended sense, it is the alteration of truth, accompanied with fraud, *mutatio veritatis cum dolo facta;* and lastly, in a narrow, or rather the legal sense of the word, when it is a question to know if the *faux* be a crime, it is the fraudulent alteration of the truth, in those cases ascertained and punished by the law." See *Crimen Falsi.*

FAVOR. Bias; partiality; lenity; prejudice.

2. The grand jury are sworn to inquire into all offences which have been committed, and of all violations of law, without fear, *favor*, or affection. Vide *Grand Jury.* When a juror is influenced by bias or prejudice, so that there is not sufficient ground for a principal challenge, he may nevertheless be challenged for favor. Vide *Challenge*, and Bac. Ab. Juries, E; Dig. 50, 17, 156, 4; 7 Pet. R. 160.

FEAL. Faithful. This word is not used.

FEALTY. Fidelity, allegiance.

2. Under the feudal system, every owner of lands held them of some superior lord, from whom or from whose ancestors, the tenant had received them. By this connexion the lord became bound to protect the tenant in the enjoyment of the land granted to him; and, on the other hand, the tenant was bound to be faithful to his lord, and defend him against all his enemies. This obligation was called *fidelitas*, or fealty. 1 Bl. Com. 366; 2 Bl. Com. 86; Co. Litt. 67, b; 2 Bouv. Inst. n. 1566.

FEAR, *crim. law.* Dread, consciousness of approaching danger.

2. Fear in the person robbed is one of the ingredients required to constitute a robbery from the person, and without this the felonious taking of the property is a larceny. It is not necessary that the owner of the property should be in fear of his own person, but fear of violence to the person of his child; 2 East, P. C. 718; or of his property; Id. 731; 2 Russ. 72; is sufficient. 2 Russ. 71 to 90. Vide *Putting in fear*, and Ayl. Pand. tit. 12, p. 106; Dig. 4, 2, 3 and 6.

FEASTS. Certain established periods in the Christian church. Formerly the days of the feasts of saints were used to indicate the dates of instruments, and memorable events. 8 Toull. n. 81. These are yet used in England; there they have Easter term, Hilary term, &c.

FEDERAL, *government.* This term is commonly used to express a league or compact between two or more states.

2. In the United States the central government of the Union is federal. The constitution was adopted "to form a more perfect union" among the states, for the purpose of self-protection and for the promotion of their mutual happiness.

FEE, FEODUM or FEUDUM, *estates* From the French, fief. A fee is an estate which may continue forever. The word fee is explained to signify that the land, or other subject of property, belongs to its owner, and is transmissible, in the case of an individual, to those whom the law appoints to succeed him, under the appellation of heirs; and in the case of corporate bodies, to those who are to take on themselves the corporate function; and from the manner in which the body is to be continued, are denominated successors. 1 Co. Litt. 1, 271, b; Wright's Ten. 147, 150; 2 Bl. Com. 104. 106; Bouv. Inst. Index h. t.

2. Estates in fee are of several sorts, and have different denominations, according to their several natures and respective qualities. They may with propriety be divided into, 1. Fees simple. 2. Fees determinable. 3. Fees qualified. 4. Fees conditional; and 5. Fees tail.

3.—1. A fee simple is an estate in lands or tenements which, in reference to the ownership of individuals, is not restrained to any heirs in particular, nor subject to any condition or collateral determination, except the laws of escheat and the canons of descent, by which it may be qualified, abridged or defeated. In other words, an estate in fee simple absolute, is an estate limited to a person and his heirs general or indefinite. Watk. Prin. Con. 76. And the omission of the word *his* will not vitiate the estate, nor are the words "and assigns forever" necessary to create it, although usually added. Co. Litt. 7, b; 9, b; 237, b; Plowd. 28, b; 29, a; Bro. Abr. Estates, 4. 1 Co. Litt. 1, b; Plowd. 557; 2 Bl. Com. 104, 106; Hale's Analysis, 74. The word *fee-simple* is sometimes used by the best writers on the law as contrasted with estates tail. 1 Co. Litt. 19. In this sense, the term comprehends all other fees as well as the estate, properly, and in strict propriety of technical language, peculiarly distinguished by this appellation.

4.—2. A *determinable fee* is an estate which may continue forever. Plowd. 557; Shep. Touch. 97. It is a quality of this estate while it falls under this denomination, that it is liable to be determined by some act or event, expressed on its limitation, to circumscribe its continuance, or inferred by the law as bounding its extent. 2 Bl. Com. 109. Limitations to a man and his heirs, till the marriage of such a person shall take place; Cro. Jac. 593; 10 Vin. Abr. 133; till debts shall be paid; Fearne, 187; until a minor shall attain the age of twenty-one years; 3 Atk. 74; Ambler, 204; 9 Mod. 28; 10 Vin. Abr. 203; Fearne, 342; are instances of such a determinable fee.

5.—3. *Qualified fee*, is an interest given on its first limitation, to a man and to certain of his heirs, and not to extend to all of them generally, nor confined to the issue of his body. A limitation to a man and *his heirs on the part of his father*, affords an example of this species of estate. Litt. § 254; 1 Inst. 27, a 220; 1 Prest. on Estates, 449.

6.—4. A *conditional fee*, in the more general acceptation of the term, is when, to the limitation of an estate a condition is annexed, which renders the estate liable to be defeated. 10 Rep. 95, b. In this application of the term, either a determinable or a qualified fee may at the same time be a conditional fee. An estate limited to a man and his heirs, to commence on the performance of a condition, is also frequently described by this appellation. Prest. on Est. 476; Fearne, 9.

7.—5. As to *fee-tail*, see *Tail*.

FEE FARM, *Eng. law*. A perpetual farm or rent. 1 Tho. Co. Litt. 446, n. 5.

FEE FARM RENT, *contracts, Eng. law*. When the lord, upon the creation of a tenancy, reserves to himself and his heirs, either the rent for which it was before let to farm, or at least one-fourth part of that farm rent, it is called a fee farm rent, because a *farm rent* is reserved upon a grant in fee. 2 Inst. 44.

FEES, *compensation*. Certain perquisites allowed by law to officers concerned in the administration of justice, or in the performance of duties required by law, as a recompense for their labor and trouble. Bac. Ab. h. t.; Latch, 18.

2. The term fees differs from costs in this, that the former are, as above mentioned, a recompense to the officer for his services, and the latter, an indemnification to the party for money laid out and expended in his suit. 11 S. & R. 248; 9 Wheat. 262; See 4 Binn. 267. Vide *Costs; Color of office; Exaction; Extortion*.

FEIGNED ACTION, *practice*. An action brought on a pretended right, when the plaintiff has no true cause of action, for some illegal purpose. In a feigned action the words of the writ are true; it differs from *false action*, in which case the words of the writ are false. Co. Litt. 361, sect. 689. Vide *Fictitious action*.

FEIGNED ISSUE, *pract*. An issue brought by consent of the parties, or the direction of a court of equity, or such courts as possess equitable powers, to determine before a jury some disputed matter of fact, which the court has not the power or is unwilling to decide. 3 Bl. Com. 452; Bouv. Inst. Index, h. t.

FELO DE SE, *criminal law*. A felon of himself; a self-murderer.

2. To be guilty of this offence, the deceased must have had the will and intention of committing it, or else he committed no crime. As he is beyond the reach of human

laws, he cannot be punished; the English law, indeed, attempts to inflict a punishment by a barbarous burial of his body, and by forfeiting to the king the property which he owned, and which would belong to his relations. Hawk. P. C. c. 9; 4 Bl. Com. 189. The charter of privileges granted by William Penn to the inhabitants of Pennsylvania, contains the following clause: "If any person, through temptation or melancholy, shall destroy himself, his estate, real and personal, shall, notwithstanding, descend to his wife and children, or relations, as if he had died a natural death."

FELON, *crimes.* One convicted and sentenced for a felony.

2. A felon is infamous, and cannot fill any office, or become a witness in any case, unless pardoned, except in cases of absolute necessity, for his own preservation and defence; as, for example, an affidavit in relation to the irregularity of a judgment in a cause in which he is a party. 2 Salk. R. 461; 2 Str. 1148; Martin's R. 25; Stark. Ev. part 2, tit. Infamy. As to the effect of a conviction in one state, where the witness is offered in another, see 17 Mass. R. 515; 2 Harr. & McHen. R. 120, 378; 1 Harr. & Johns. R. 572. As to the effect upon a copartnership by one of the partners becoming a felon, see 2 Bouv. Inst. n. 1493.

FELONIOUSLY, *pleadings.* This is a technical word which must be introduced into every indictment for a felony, charging the offence to have been committed feloniously; no other word, nor any circumlocution, will supply its place. Com. Dig. Indictment, G 6; Bac. Ab. Indictment, G 1; 2 Hale, 172, 184; Hawk. B. 2, c. 25, s. 55; Cro. C. C. 37; Burn's Just. Indict. ix.; Williams' Just. Indict. iv.; Cro. Eliz. 193; 5 Co. 121; 1 Chit. Cr. Law, 242.

FELONY, *crimes.* An offence which occasions a total forfeiture of either lands or goods, or both, at common law, to which capital or other punishment may be superadded, according to the degree of guilt. 4 Bl. Com, 94, 5; 1 Russ. Cr. *42; 1 Chit. Pract. 14; Co. Litt. 391; 1 Hawk. P. C. c. 37; 5 Wheat. R. 153, 159.

FEMALE. This term denotes the sex which bears young.

2. It is a general rule, that the young of female animals which belong to us, are ours, *nam fœtus ventrem sequitur.* Inst. 2, 1, 19; Dig. 6, 1, 5, 2. The rule is, in general, the same with regard to slaves; but when a female slave comes into a free state, even without the consent of her master, and is there delivered of a child, the latter is free. Vide *Feminine; Gender; Masculine.*

FEME, or, more properly, FEMME. Woman.

2. This word is frequently used in law. *Baron and feme*, husband and wife; *feme covert*, a married woman; *feme sole*, a single woman.

3. A feme *covert*, is a married woman. A feme covert may sue and be sued at law, and will be treated as a feme sole, when the husband is *civiliter mortuus.* Bac. Ab. Baron and Feme, M; see article, *Parties to Actions*, part 1, section 1, § 7, n. 3; or where, as it has been decided in England, he is an alien and has left the country, or has never been in it. 2 Esp. R. 554; 1 B. & P. 357. And courts of equity will treat a married woman as a feme sole, so as to enable her to sue or be sued, whenever her husband has abjured the realm, been transported for felony, or is civilly dead. And when she has a separate property, she may sue her husband in respect of such property, with the assistance of a next friend of her own selection. Story, Eq. Pl. § 61; Story, Eq. Jur. § 1368; and see article, *Parties to a suit in equity*, § 1, n. 2; Bouv. Inst. Index, h. t.

4. Coverture subjects a woman to some duties and disabilities, and gives her some rights and immunities, to which she would not be entitled as a feme sole. These are considered under the articles, *Marriage*, (q. v.) and *Wife.* (q. v.)

5. A feme sole trader, is a married woman who trades and deals on her own account, independently of her husband. By the custom of London, a feme covert, being a *sole trader*, may sue and be sued in the city courts, as a feme sole, with reference to her transactions in London. Bac. Ab. Baron and Feme, M.

6. In Pennsylvania, where any mariners or others go abroad, leaving their wives at shop-keeping, or to work for their livelihood at any other trade, all such wives are declared to be feme sole traders, with ability to sue and be sued, without naming the husbands. Act of February 22, 1718. See Poth. De la Puissance du Mari, n. 20.

7. By a more recent act, April 11, 1848, of the same state, it is provided, that in all cases where debts may be contracted for necessaries for the support and maintenance of the family of any married

woman, it shall be lawful for the creditor, in such case, to institute suit against the husband and wife for the price of such necessaries, and after obtaining a judgment, have an execution against the husband alone; and if no property of the said husband be found, the officer executing the said writ shall so return, and thereupon an alias execution may be issued, which may be levied upon and satisfied out of the separate property of the wife, secured to her under the provisions of the first section of this act. *Provided*, That judgment shall not be rendered against the wife, in such joint action, unless it shall have been proved that the debt sued for in such action, was contracted by the wife, or incurred for articles necessary for the support of the family of the said husband and wife.

FEMININE. What belongs to the female sex.

2. When the feminine is used, it is generally confined to females; as, if a man bequeathed all his mares to his son, his horses would not pass. Vide 3 Brev. R. 9; *Gender; Man; Masculine.*

FENCE. A building or erection between two contiguous estates, so as to divide them; or on the same estate, so as to divide one part from another.

2. Fences are regulated by the local laws. In general, fences on boundaries are to be built on the line, and the expense, when made no more expensively than is required by the law, is borne equally between the parties. See the following cases on the subject. 2 Miles, 337, 395; 2 Greenl. 72; 11 Mass. 294; 3 Wend. 142; 2 Metc. 180; 15 Conn. 526; 2 Miles, 447; Bouv. Inst. Index, h. t.

3. A partition fence is presumed to be the common property of both owners of the land. 8 B. & C. 257, 259, note a. When built upon the land of one of them, it is his; but if it were built equally upon the land of both, at their joint expense, each would be the owner in severalty of the part standing on his own land. 5 Taunt. 20; 2 Greenl. Ev. § 617.

FEOD. The same as fief. Vide *Fief* or *Feud.*

FEOFFMENT, *conveyancing.* A gift of any corporeal hereditaments to another. It operates by transmutation of possession, and it is essential to its completion that the seisin be passed. Watk. Prin. Conv. 183. This term also signifies the instrument or deed by which such hereditament is conveyed.

2. This instrument was used as one of the earliest modes of conveyance of the common law. It signified, originally, the grant of a feud or fee; but it came, in time, to signify the grant of a free inheritance in fee, respect being had to the perpetuity of the estate granted, rather than to the feudal tenure. The feoffment was, likewise, accompanied by livery of seisin. The conveyance by feoffment, with livery of seisin, has become infrequent, if not obsolete, in England; and in this country it has not been used in practice. Cruise, Dig. t. 32, c. 4. s. 3; Touchs. c. 9; 2 Bl. Com. 20; Co. Litt. 9; 4 Kent, Com. 467; Perk. c. 3; Com. Dig. h. t.; 12 Vin. Ab. 167; Bac. Ab. h. t. *in pr.;* Doct. Plac. 271; Dane's Ab. c. 104, a. 3, s. 4. He who gives or enfeoffs is called the *feoffor;* and the person enfeoffed is denominated the *feoffee.* 2 Bl. Com. 20. See 2 Bouv. Inst. n. 2045, note.

FERÆ. Wild, savage, not tame.

FERÆ BESTIÆ. Wild beasts. See *Animals; Feræ naturæ.*

FERÆ NATURÆ. Of a wild nature.

2. This term is used to designate animals which are not usually tamed. Such animals belong to the person who has captured them only while they are in his power; for if they regain their liberty his property in them instantly ceases, unless they have *animum revertendi,* which is to be known only by their habit of returning. 2 Bl. Com. 386; 3 Binn. 546; Bro. Ab. Propertie, 37; Com. Dig. Biens, F; 7 Co. 17, b; 1 Chit. Pr. 87; Inst. 2, 1, 15; 13 Vin. Ab. 207.

3. Property in animals *feræ naturæ* is not acquired by hunting them and pursuing them; if, therefore, another person kill such animal in the sight of the pursuer, he has a right to appropriate it to his own use. 3 Caines, 175. But if the pursuer brings the animal within his own control, as by entrapping it, or wounding it mortally, so as to render escape impossible, it then belongs to him. Id. Though if he abandons it, another person may afterwards acquire property in the animal. 20 John. 75. The owner of land has a qualified property in animals feræ naturæ, when, in consequence of their inability and youth, they cannot go away. See Y. B. 12 H. VIII., 9 B, 10 A; 2 Bl. Com. 394; Bac. Ab. Game. Vide *Whelp.*

FERM or FEARM. By this ancient word is meant land, fundus; (q. v.) and, it is said, houses and tenements may pass by it. Co. Litt. 5 a.

FERRY. A place where persons and things are taken across a river or other stream in boats or other vessels, for hire. 4 N. S. 426; S. C. 3 Harr. Lo. R. 341.

2. In England a ferry is considered a franchise which cannot be set up without the king's license. In most, perhaps all of the United States, ferries are regulated by statute.

3. The termini of a ferry are at the water's edge. 15 Pick. R. 254; and see 8 Greenl. R. 367; 4 John. Ch. R. 161; 2 Porter, R. 296; 7 Pick. R. 448; 2 Car. Law Repos. 69; 2 Dev. R. 403; 1 Murph. 279; 1 Hayw. R. 457; Vin. Ab. h. t.; Com. Dig. Piscary B; 6 B. & Cr. 703; 12 East, R. 333; 1 Bail. R. 469; 3 Watts, R. 219; 1 Yeates, R. 167; 9 S. & R. 26.

FERRYMAN. One employed in taking persons across a river or other stream, in boats or other contrivances at a ferry. The owner of a ferry is not considered a ferryman, when it is rented and in the possession of a tenant. Minor, R. 366.

2. Ferrymen are considered as common carriers, and are therefore the legal judges to decide when it is proper to pass over or not. 1 M'Cord, R. 444; Id. 157; 1 N. & M. 19; 2 N. & M. 17. They are to regulate how the property to be taken across shall be put in their boats or flats; 1 M'Cord, 157; and as soon as the carriage is fairly on the drop or slip of a flat, although driven by the owner's servant, it is in possession of the ferryman, and he is answerable. 1 M'Cord's R. 439.

FESTINUM REMEDIUM. A speedy remedy.

2. This is said of those cases where the remedy for the redress of an injury is given without any unnecessary delay. Bac. Ab. Assise, A. The action of Dower is festinum remedium, and so is Assise.

FETTERS. A sort of iron put on the legs of malefactors, or persons accused of crimes.

2. When a prisoner is brought into court to plead he shall not be put in fetters. 2 Inst. 315; 3 Inst. 34; 2 Hale, 119; Hawk. b. 2, c. 28, s. 1; Kel. 10; 1 Chitty's Cr. Law, 417. An officer having arrested a defendant on a civil suit, or a person accused of a crime, has no right to handcuff him unless it is necessary, or he has attempted to make his escape. 4 B. & C. 596; 10 Engl. C. L. Rep. 412, S. C.

FEUD. This word, in Scotland, signifies a combination of kindred to revenge injuries or affronts done to any of their blood. Vide *Fief.*

FEUDA. In the early feudal times grants were made, in the first place, only during the pleasure of the grantor, and called *munera;* (q. v.) afterwards for life, called *beneficia;* (q. v.) and, finally, they were extended to the vassal and his sons, and then they acquired the name of *feudal.* Dalr. Feud. Pr. 199.

FEUDAL. A term applied to whatever concerned a feud; as *feudal law; feudal rights.*

FEUDAL LAW. By this phrase is understood a political system which placed men and estates under hierarchical and multiplied distinctions of lords and vassals. The principal features of this system were the following.

2. The right to all lands was vested in the sovereign. These were parcelled out among the great men of the nation by its chief, to be held of him, so that the king had the *Dominum directum*, and the grantee or vassal, had what was called *Dominum utile.* It was a maxim *nùlle terre sans seigneur.* These tenants were bound to perform services to the king, generally of a military character. These great lords again granted parts of the lands they thus acquired, to other inferior vassals, who held under them, and were bound to perform services to the lord.

3. The principles of the feudal law will be found in Littleton's Tenures; Wright's Tenures; 2 Blackstone's Com. c. 5; Dalrymple's History of Feudal Property; Sullivan's Lectures; Book of Fiefs; Spellman, Treatise of Feuds and Tenures; Le Grand Coutumier; the Salic Laws; The Capitularies; Les Establissements de St. Louis; Assizes de Jerusalem; Poth. Des Fiefs. Merl. Rép. Feodalité; Dalloz, Dict. Feodalité; Guizot, Essais sur l'Histoire de France, Essai 5eme.

4. In the United States the feudal law never was in its full vigor, though some of its principles are still retained. "Those principles are so interwoven with every part of our jurisprudence," says Ch. J. Tilghman, 3 S. & R. 447, "that to attempt to eradicate them would be to destroy the whole. They are massy stones worked into the foundation of our legal edifice. Most

of the inconveniences attending them have been removed, and the few that remain can be easily removed, by acts of the legislature." See 3 Kent, Com. 509, 4th ed.

FIAR, *Scotch law.* He whose property is burdened with a life rent. Ersk. Pr. of L. Scot. B. 2, t. 9, s. 23.

FIAT, *practice.* An order of a judge, or of an officer, whose authority, to be signified by his signature, is necessary to authenticate the particular acts.

FICTION OF LAW. The assumption that a certain thing is true, and which gives to a person or thing, a quality which is not natural to it, and establishes, consequently, a certain disposition, which, without the fiction, would be repugnant to reason and to truth. It is an order of things which does not exist, but which the law prescribes or authorizes; it differs from presumption, because it establishes as true, something which is false; whereas presumption supplies the proof of something true. Dalloz, Dict. h. t. See 1 Toull. 171, n. 203; 2 Toull. 217, n. 203; 11 Toull. 11, n. 10, note 2; Ferguson, Moral Philosophy, part 5, c. 10, s. 3; Burgess on Insolvency, 139, 140; Report of the Revisers of the Civil Code of Pennsylvania, March 1, 1832, p. 8.

2. The law never feigns what is impossible; *fictum est id quod factum non est sed fieri potuit.* Fiction is like art; it imitates nature, but never disfigures it; it aids truth, but it ought never to destroy it. It may well suppose that what was possible, but which is not, exists; but it will never feign that what was impossible, actually is. D'Aguesseau, Œuvres, tome iv. page 427, 47e Plaidoyer.

3. Fictions were invented by the Roman prætors, who, not possessing the power to abrogate the law, were nevertheless willing to derogate from it, under the pretence of doing equity. Fiction is the resource of weakness, which, in order to obtain its object, assumes as a fact, what is known to be contrary to truth: when the legislator desires to accomplish his object, he need not feign, he commands. Fictions of law owe their origin to the legislative usurpations of the bench. 4 Benth. Ev. 300.

4. It is said that every fiction must be framed according to the rules of law, and that every legal fiction must have equity for its object. 10 Co. 42; 10 Price's R. 154; Cowp. 177. To prevent their evil effects, they are not allowed to be carried further than the reasons which introduced them necessarily require. 1 Lill. Ab. 610; 2 Hawk. 320; Best on Pres. § 20.

5. The law abounds in fictions. That an estate is in *abeyance;* the doctrine of *remitter,* by which a party who has been disseised of his freehold, and afterwards acquires a defective title, is remitted to his former good title; that one thing done today, is considered as done at a preceding time by the doctrine of *relation;* that, because one thing is proved, another shall be presumed to be true, which is the case in all *presumptions;* that the heir, executor, and administrator stand by *representation,* in the place of the deceased; are all fictions of law. "Our various introduction of John Doe and Richard Roe," says Mr. Evans, (Poth. on Ob. by Evans, vol. ii. p. 43,) "our solemn process upon disseisin by Hugh Hunt; our casually losing and finding a ship (which never was in Europe) in the parish of St. Mary Le Bow, in the ward of Cheap; our trying the validity of a will by an imaginary wager of five pounds; our imagining and compassing the king's death, by giving information which may defeat an attack upon an enemy's settlement in the antipodes; our charge of picking a pocket, or forging a bill with force and arms; of neglecting to repair a bridge, against the peace of our lord the king, his crown and dignity; are circumstances, which, looked at by themselves, would convey an impression of no very favorable nature, with respect to the wisdom of our jurisprudence." Vide 13 Vin. Ab. 209; Merl. Rép. h. t.; Dane's Ab. Index, h. t.; and Rey, des Inst. de l'Angl. tome 2, p. 219, where he severely cesures these fictions as absurd and useless.

FICTITIOUS. Pretended; supposed; as, fictitious actions; fictitious payee.

FICTITIOUS ACTIONS, *practice.* Suits brought on pretended rights.

2. They are sometimes brought, usually on a pretended wager, for the purpose of obtaining the opinion of the court on a point of law. Courts of justice were constituted for the purpose of deciding really existing questions of right between parties, and they are not bound to answer impertinent questions which persons think proper to ask them in the form of an action on a wager. 12 East, 248. Such an attempt has been held to be a contempt of court; and Lord Hardwicke in such a case committed the parties and their attorneys. Rep. temp. Hardw. 237. See also Comb. 425; 1 Co.

83; 6 Cranch, 147-8. Vide *Feigned actions.*

3. The court of the king's bench fined an attorney forty pounds for stating a special case for the opinion of the court, the greater part of which statement was fictitious. 3 Barn. & Cr. 597; S. C. 10 E. C. L. R. 193.

FICTITIOUS PAYEE, *contracts.* A supposed person; a payee, who has no existence.

2. When the name of a fictitious payee has been used, in making a bill of exchange, and it has been endorsed in such name, it is considered as having the effect of a bill payble to bearer, and a bona fide holder, ignorant of that fact, may recover on it, against all prior parties who were privy to the transaction. 2 H. Bl. 178, 288; 3 T. R. 174, 182, 481; 3 Bro. C. C. 238. Vide *Bills of Exchange*, § 1.

FIDEI-COMMISSARY, *civil law.* One who has a beneficial interest in an estate, which, for a time, is committed to the faith or trust of another. This term has nearly the same meaning as *cestui que trust* has in our law. 2 Bouv. Inst. n. 1895, note.

FIDEI-COMMISSUM, *civil law.* A gift which a man makes to another, through the agency of a third person, who is requested to perform the desire of the giver. For example, when a testator writes, "I institute for my heir, Lucius Titius," he may add, "I pray my heir, Lucius Titius, to deliver, as soon as he shall be able, my succession to Caius Seius: *cùm igitur aliquis scripserit Lucius Titius heres esto;* potest ajicere, *rogo te Luci Titi, ut cùm poteris hereditatem meam adire, eam Caio Sceio reddas, restituas.* Inst. 2, 23, 2; vide Code 6, 42.

2. Fidei-commissa were abolished in Louisiana by the code. 5 N. S. 302.

3. The *uses* of the common law, it is said, were borrowed from the Roman *fideicommissum.* 1 Cru. Dig. 388; Bac. Read. 19; 1 Madd. Ch. 446-7.

4. The fidei-commissa of the civil law, have been supposed to resemble entails, though some writers have declared that the Roman law was a stranger to entails. 2 Bouv. Inst. n. 1708.

FIDE-JUSSIO, *civil law.* The contract of suretyship.

FIDE-JUSSOR, *civil law.* One who becomes security for the debt of another, promising to pay it in case the principal does not do so.

2. He differs from co-obligor in this, that the latter is equally bound to a debtor with his principal, while the former is not liable till the principal has failed to fulfil his engagement. Dig. 12, 4, 4; Id. 16, 1, 13; Id. 24, 3, 64; Id. 38, 1, 37; Id. 50, 17, 110, and 14, 6, 20; Hall's Pr. 33; Dunl. Ad. Pr. 300; Clerke's Prax. tit. 63, 4, 5.

3. The obligation of the fide-jussor was an accessory contract, for, if the principal obligation was not previously contracted, his engagement then took the name of mandate. Leç. Elem. § 872; Code Nap. 2012.

FIDUCIA, *civil law.* A contract by which we sell a thing to some one, that is, transmit to him the property of the thing, with the solemn forms of emancipation, on condition that he will sell it back to us. This species of contract took place in the emancipation of children, in testaments, and in pledges. Poth. Pand. h. t.

FIDUCIARY. This term is borrowed from the civil law. The Roman laws called a fiduciary heir, the person who was instituted heir, and who was charged to deliver the succession to a person designated by the testament. Merl. Répert. h. t. But Pothier, Pand. vol. 22, h. t., says that *fiduciarius heres* properly signifies the person to whom a testator has sold his inheritance, under the condition that he should sell it to another. Fiduciary may be defined to be, in trust, in confidence.

2. A fiduciary contract is defined to be, an agreement by which a person delivers a thing to another, on the condition that he will restore it to him. The following formula was employed: *Ut inter bonos agere opportet, ne propter te fidemque tuam frauder.* Cicer. de Offic. lib. 3, cap. 13; Leç. du Dr. Civ. Rom. § 237, 238. See 2 How. S. C. Rep. 202, 208; 6 Watts & Serg. 18; 7 Watts, 415.

FIEF or FEUD. In its origin, a fief was a district of country, allotted to one of the chiefs who invaded the Roman empire, as a stipend or reward; with a condition annexed that the possessor should do service faithfully both at home and in the wars, to him by whom it was given. The law of fiefs supposed that originally all lands belonged to lords, who had had the generosity to abandon them to others, from whom the actual possessors derived their rights upon the sole reservation of certain services more or less onerous as a sign of superiority. To this superiority was added that which gives the right of dispensing justice, a right which was originally attached to all fiefs, and conferred upon those who possessed it, the most eminent part of public power. Henrion de Pansey, Pouvoir Municipal; 2 Bl. Com. 45; Encyclopédie, h. t.; Merl. Rép. h. t.

FIELD. A part of a farm separately enclosed; a close. 1 Chit. Pr. 160. The Digest defines a field to be a piece of land without a house; ager est locus, que sine villa est. Dig. 50, 16, 27.

FIERI FACIAS, *practice*. The name of a writ of execution. It is so called because, when writs were in Latin, the words directed to the sheriff were, *quod fieri facias de bonis et catallis*, &c., that you cause to be made of the goods and chattels, &c. Co. Litt. 290 b.

2. The foundation of this writ is a judgment for debt or damages, and the party who has recovered such a judgment is generally entitled to it, unless he is delayed by the stay of execution which the law allows in certain cases after the rendition of the judgment, or by proceedings in error.

3. This subject will be considered with regard to, 1. The form of the writ. 2. Its effects. 3. The manner of executing it.

4.—1. The writ is issued in the name of the commonwealth or of the government, as required by the constitution, and directed to the sheriff, commanding him that of the goods and chattels, and (where lands are liable for the payment of debts, as in Pennsylvania,) of the lands and tenements of the defendant, therein named, in his bailiwick, he cause to be levied as well a certain debt of —— dollars, which the plaintiff, (naming him,) in the court of —— (naming it,) recovered against him, as —— dollars, like money which to the said plaintiff were adjudged for his damages, which he had by the detention of that debt, and that he, (the sheriff,) have that money before the judges of the said court, on a day certain, (being the return day therein mentioned,) to render to the said plaintiff his debt and damages aforesaid, whereof the said defendant is convict. It must be tested in the name of the officer, as directed by the constitution or laws; as, "Witness the honorable John B. Gibson, our chief justice, at Philadelphia, the tenth day of October, in the year of our Lord one thousand eight hundred and forty-eight." It must be signed by the prothonotary, or clerk of the court, and sealed with its seal. The signature of the prothonotary, it has been decided, in Pennsylvania, is not indispensable. The amount of the debt, interest, and costs, must also be endorsed on the writ. This form varies as it is issued on a judgment in debt, and one obtained for damages merely. The execution being founded on the judgment, must, of course, follow, and be warranted by it. 2 Saund. 72 h, k; Bing. on Ex. 186. Hence, where there is more than one plaintiff or defendant, it must be in the name of all the plaintiffs, against all the defendants. 6 T. R. 525. It is either for the plaintiff or the defendant. When it is against an executor or administrator, for a liability of the testator or intestate, it is conformable to the judgment, and must be only against the goods of the deceased, unless the defendant has made himself personally liable by his false pleading, in which case the judgment is *de bonis testatoris si, et si non, de bonis propriis*, and the fieri facias must conform to it. 4 Serg. & Rawle, 394; 18 John. 502; 1 Serg. & Rawle, 453; 1 Dall. 481; and see Tidd's Pr. 933; Com. Dig. Pleader, 2 D. 15; 1 Hayw. 298; 2 Hayw. 112.

5.—2. At common law, the writ bound the goods of the defendant or party against whom it was issued, from the teste day; by which must be understood that the writ bound the property against the party himself, and all claiming by assignment from, or by representation under him; 4 East, R. 538; so that a sale by the defendant, of his goods to a *bona fide* purchaser, did not protect them from a *fieri facias* tested before, although not issued or delivered to the sheriff till after the sale. Cro. Eliz. 174; Cro. Jac. 451; 1 Sid. 271. To remedy this manifest injustice, the statute of frauds, 29 Car. II. c. 3, s. 16, was passed. The principles of this statute have been adopted in most of the states. Griff. Law Reg. Answers to No. 38, under No. III. The statute enacts "that no writ of *fieri facias*, or other writ of execution, shall bind the property of the goods of the party, against whom such writ of execution is sued forth, but from the time that such writ shall be delivered to the sheriff, under-sheriff, or coroners, to be executed; and for the better manifestation of the said time, the sheriffs, &c., their deputies or agents, shall, upon the receipt of any such writ, (without fee for doing the same,) endorse upon the back thereof, the day of the month and year whereon he or they received the same." Vide 2 Binn. R. 174; 2 Serg. & Rawle,

157; 2 Yeates, 177; 8 Johns. R. 446; 12 Johns. R. 320; 1 Hopk. R. 368; 3 Penna. R. 247; 3 Rawle, 401; 1 Whart. R. 377.

6.—3. The execution of the writ is made by levying upon the goods and chattels of the defendant, or party against whom it is issued; and, in general, seizing a part of the goods in the name of the whole on the premises, is a good seizure of the whole. Ld. Raym. 725; 2 Serg. & Rawle, 142; 4 Wash. C. C. R. 29; but see 1 Whart. Rep. 377. The sheriff cannot break the outer door of a house for the purpose of executing a *fieri facias*; 5 Co. 92; nor can a window be broken for this purpose. W. Jones, 429. See articles *Door; House.* He may, however, enter the house, if it be open, and, being once lawfully entered, he may break open an inner door or chest to seize the goods of the defendant, even without any request to open them. 4 Taunt. 619; 3 B. & P. 223; Cowp. 1. Although the sheriff is authorized to enter the house of the party to search for goods, he cannot enter that of a stranger, for that purpose, without being guilty of a trespass, unless the defendant's goods are actually in the house. Com. Dig. Execution, C 5: 1 Marsh. R. 565. The sheriff may break the outer door of a barn; 1 Sid. 186; S. C. 1 Keb. 689; or of a store disconnected with the dwelling-house, and forming no part of the curtilage. 16 Johns. R. 287. The *fi. fa.* may be executed at any time before, and on the return day, but not on Sunday, where it is forbidden by statute. Wats. on Sheriffs, 173; 5 Co. 92; Com. Dig. Execution, c. 5.

Vide 3 Bouv. Inst. n. 3383, et seq.; Wats. on Sher. ch. 10; Bing. Ex. c. 1, s. 4; Gilb. on Exec. Index, h. t.; Grah. Pr. 321; Troub. & Hal. Pr. Index, h. t.; Com. Dig. Execution, C 4; Process, F 5, 7; Caines' Pr. Index, h. t.; Tidd's Pr. Index, h. t.; Sell. Pr. Index, h. t.

FIERI FECI, *practice.* The return which the sheriff, or other proper officer, makes to certain writs, signifying, "I have caused to be made."

2. When the officer has made this return, a rule may be obtained upon him, after the return day, to pay the money into court, and if he withholds payment, an action of debt may be had on the return, or assumpsit for money had and received may be sustained against him. 3 Johns. R. 183.

FIFTEENTH, *Eng. law.* The name of a tax levied by authority of parliament for the use of the king, which consisted of one-fifteenth part of the goods of those who were subject to it. T. L.

FIGURES, *Numerals.* They are either Roman, made with letters of the Alphabet, for example, MDCCLXXVI; or they are Arabic, as follows, 1776.

2. Roman figures may be used in contracts and law proceedings, and they will be held valid; but Arabic figures, probably owing to the ease with which they may be counterfeited, or altered, have been holden not to be sufficient to express the sum due on a contract; but, it seems, that if the amount payable and due on a promissory note be expressed in figures or ciphers, it will be valid. Story on Bills, § 42, note; Story, Prom. Notes, § 21. Indictments have been set aside because the day or year was expressed in figures. 13 Vin Ab. 210; 1 Ch. Rep. 319; S. C. 18 Eng. Com. Law Rep. 95.

3. Bills of exchange, promissory notes, checks and agreements of every description, are usually dated with Arabic figures; it is, however, better to date deeds and other formal instruments, by writing the words at length. Vide 1 Ch. Cr. L. 176; 1 Verm. R. 336; 5 Toull. n. 336; 4 Yeates, R. 278; 2 John. R. 233; 1 How. Mis. 256; 6 Blackf. 533.

FIGURES OF SPEECH. By figures of speech is meant that manner of speaking or writing, which has for its object to give to our sentiments and thoughts a greater force, more vivacity and agreeableness.

2. This subject belongs more particularly to grammar and rhetoric, but the law has its figures also. Sometimes fictions come in aid of language, when found insufficient by the law; language, in its turn, by means of tropes and figures, sometimes lends to fictions a veil behind which they are hidden; sometimes the same denominations are preserved to things which have ceased to be the same, and which have been changed; at other times they lend to things denominations which supposed them to have been modified.

3. In this immense subject, it will not be expected that examples should be here given of every kind of figures; the principal only will be noticed. The law is loaded with abstract ideas; abstract in itself, it has often recourse to metaphors, which, as it were, touch our senses. The inventory is *faithful*, a defect is *covered*, an account

is *liquidated*, a right is *open* or *closed*, an obligation is *extinguished*, &c. But the law has metaphors which are properly its own; as civil fruits, &c. The state or condition of a man who has been deprived by the law of almost all his social prerogatives or rights, has received the metaphorical name of *civil death*. Churches being called the *houses of God*, formerly were considered an asylum, because to seize a person in the house of another was considered a wrong. *Mother country*, is applied to the country from which people emigrate to a colony; though this pretended analogy is very different in many points, yet this external ornament of the idea soon became an integral part of the idea; and on the faith of this metaphor, this pretended filiation became the source whence flowed the duties which bound the colonies to the metropolis or mother country.

4. In public speaking, the use of figures, when natural and properly selected, is of great force; such ornaments impress upon the mind of the hearers the ideas which the speaker desires to convey, fix their attention and disposes them to consider favorably the subject of inquiry. See 3 Bouv. Inst. n. 3243.

FILACER, FILAZIER, or FILZER, *English law*. An officer of the court of common pleas, so called because he files those writs on which he makes out process.

FILE, *practice*. A thread, string, or wire, upon which writs and other exhibits in courts and offices are fastened or filed, for the more safe keeping and ready turning to the same. The papers put together in order, and tied in bundles, are also called a file.

2. A paper is said to be filed, when it is delivered to the proper officer, and by him received to be kept on file. 13 Vin. Ab. 211.

FILIATION, *civil law*. The descent of son or daughter, with regard to his or her father, mother, and their ancestors.

2. Nature always points out the mother by evident signs, and whether married or not, she is always certain: *mater semper certa est, etiamsi vulgô conceperit*. There is not the same certainty with regard to the father, and the relation may not know or feign ignorance as to the paternity, the law has therefore established a legal presumption to serve as a foundation for paternity and filiation.

3. When the mother is or has been married, her husband is presumed to be the father of the children born during the coverture, or within a competent time afterwards, whether they were conceived during the coverture or not: *pater is est quem nuptiæ demonstrant*.

4. This rule is founded on two presumptions; one on the cohabitation before the birth of the child; and the other that the mother has faithfully observed the vow she made to her husband.

5. This presumption may, however, be rebutted by showing either that there has been no cohabitation, or some physical or other impossibility that the husband could be the father. See *Access; Bastard; Gestation; Natural children; Paternity; Putative father*. 1 Bouv. Inst. n. 302, et seq.

FILIUS. The son, the immediate male descendant. This term is used in making genealogical tables.

FILIUS MULIERATUS. The eldest legitimate son of parents, who, before their marriage, had illegitimate children. Vide *Mulier*.

FILIUS POPULI. The son of the people; a bastard.

FILLEY. A mare not more than one year old. Russ. & Ry. 416; Id. 494.

FILUM. The middle; the thread of anything; as filum aquæ; filum viæ.

FILUM AQUÆ. The thread or middle of a water course. (q. v.)

2. It is a general rule, that in grants of lands bounded on rivers and streams above tide water, unless otherwise expressed, the grant extends usque ad filum aquæ, and that not only the banks, but the bed of the river, and the islands therein, together with exclusive right of fishing, pass to the grantee 5 Wend. 423.

FILUM VIÆ. The thread or middle of the road.

2. Where a law requires travellers meeting each other on a road to drive their carriages to the right of the middle of the road, the parties are bound to keep on their side of the worked part of the road, although the whole of the smooth or most travelled path may be upon one side of the filum viæ. 7 Wend. 185; 5 Conn. 305.

FIN DE NON RECEVOIR, *French law*. An exception or plea founded on law, which, without entering into the merit of the action, shows that the plaintiff has no right to bring it, either because the time during which it ought to have been brought has elapsed, which is called *prescription*, or that there has been a compromise, accord and satisfaction, or any other cause which has destroyed the right of action which once subsisted. Poth. Proc. Civ. partie 1, c. 2, s. 2, art. 2; Story, Confl. of Laws, § 580.

FINAL. That which puts an end to anything.

2. It is used in opposition to interlocutory; as, a final judgment, is a judgment which ends the controversy between the parties litigant. 1 Wheat. 355; 2 Pet. 449. See 12 Wheat. 135; 4 Dall. 22; 9 Pet. 1; 6 Wheat. 448; 3 Cranch, 179; 6 Cranch, 51; Bouv. Inst. Index, h. t.

FINANCIER. A person employed in the economical management and application of public money or finances; one who is employed in the management of money.

FINANCES. By this word is understood the revenue or public resources of money of the state.

FINDER. One who lawfully comes to the possession of another's personal property, which was then lost.

2. The finder is entitled to certain rights and liable to duties which he is obliged to perform. This is a species of deposit, which, as it does not arise *ex contractu*, may be called a *quasi* deposit, and it is governed by the same general rules as common deposits. The finder is required to take the same reasonable care of the property found, as any voluntary depositary *ex contractu*. Doct. & St. Dial. 2, c. 38; 2 Bulst. 306, 312; S. C. 1 Rolle's R. 125.

3. The finder is not bound to take the goods he finds; yet, when he does undertake the custody, he is required to exercise reasonable diligence in preserving the property; and he will be responsible for gross negligence. Some of the old authorities laid down that "if a man find butter, and by his negligent keeping, it putrify; or, if a man find garments, and by his negligent keeping, they be moth eaten, no action lies." So it is if a man find goods and lose them again; Bac. Ab. Bailment, D; and in support of this position; Leon. 123, 223; Owen, 141; and 2 Bulstr. 21, are cited. But these cases, if carefully examined, will not, perhaps, be found to decide the point as broadly as it is stated in Bacon. A finder would doubtless be held responsible for gross negligence.

4. On the other hand, the finder of an article is entitled to recover all expenses which have necessarily occurred in preserving the thing found; as, if a man were to find an animal, he would be entitled to be reimbursed for his keeping, for advertising in a reasonable manner that he had found it, and to any reward which may have been offered by the owner for the recovery of such lost thing. Domat, l. 2, t. 9, s. 2, n. 2. Vide Story, Bailm. § 35.

5. And when the owner does not reclaim the goods lost, they belong to the finder. 1 Bl. Com. 296; 2 Kent's Com. 290. The acquisition of treasure by the finder, is evidently founded on the rule that what belongs to none naturally, becomes the property of the first occupant: *res nullius naturaliter fit primi occupantis*. How far the finder is responsible criminally, see 1 Hill, N. Y. Rep. 94; 2 Russ. on Cr. 102; Rosc. Cr. Ev. 474. See *Taking*.

FINDING, *practice*. That which has been ascertained; as, the finding of the jury is conclusive as to matters of fact when confirmed by a judgment of the court. 1 Day, 238; 2 Day, 12.

FINDING A VERDICT. The act of the jury in agreeing upon a verdict.

FINE. This word has various significations. It is employed, 1. To mean a sum of money, which, by judgment of a competent jurisdiction, is required to be paid for the punishment of an offence. 2. To designate the amount paid by the tenant, on his entrance, to the lord. 3. To signify a special kind of conveyance.

FINE, *conveyance, practice*. An amicable composition or agreement of a suit, either actual or fictitious, by leave of the court, by which the lands in question become, or are acknowledged to be, the right of one of the parties. Co. Litt. 120; 2 Bl. Com. 349; Bac. Abr. Fines and Recoveries. A fine is so called, because it puts an *end*, not only to the suit thus commenced, but also to all other suits and controversies concerning the same matter. Such concords, says Doddridge, (Eng. Lawyer, 84, 85,) have been in use in the civil law, and are called transactions (q. v.) whereof they say thus: Transactiones sunt de eis quæ in controversia sunt, à lite futura aut pendente ad certam compositionem reducuntur, dando aliquid vel accipiendo. Or shorter, thus: Transactio est de re dubia et lite ancipite ne dum ad finem ducta, non gratuita pactio. It is commonly defined an assurance by matter of record, and is founded upon a supposed previously existing right, and upon a writ requiring the party to perform his covenant; although a fine may be levied upon any writ by which lands may be demanded, charged, or bound. It has also been defined an acknowledgment on record of a previous gift or feoffment, and prima facie carries a fee, although it may be limited to an estate for life or in fee tail. Prest. on Convey. 200, 202, 268, 269; 2 Bl. Com. 348-9.

2. The stat. 18 E. I., called *modus levandi fines*, declares and regulates the manner in which they should be levied and carried on; and that is as follows: 1. The party to whom the land is conveyed or assured, commences an action at law against the other, generally an action of covenant, by suing out of a writ of *præcipe*, called a writ of covenant, that the one shall convey the lands to the other, on the breach of which agreement the action is brought. The suit being thus commenced, then follows, 2. The *licentia concordandi*, or leave to compromise the suit. 3. The *concord* or agreement itself, after leave obtained by the court; this is usually an acknowledgment from the deforciants, that the lands in question are the lands of the complainants. 4. The *note* of the fine, which is only an abstract of the writ of covenant, and the concord; naming the parties, the parcels of land, and the agreement. 5. The foot of the fine or the conclusion of it, which includes the whole matter, reciting the parties, day, year, and place, and before whom it was acknowledged or levied.

3. Fines thus levied, are of four kinds. 1. What in law French is called a fine *sur cognizance de droit, come ceo que il ad de son done;* or a fine upon the acknowledgment of the right of the cognizee, as that which he has of the gift of the cognizor. This fine is called a feoffment of record. 2. A fine *sur cognizance de droit tantum*, or acknowledgment of the right merely. 3. A fine *sur concessit*, is where the cognizor, in order to make an end of disputes, though he acknowledges no precedent right, yet grants to the consignee an estate *de novo*, usually for life or years, by way of a supposed composition. 4. A fine *sur done grant et render*, which is a double fine, comprehending the fine *sur cognizance de droit come ceo*, &c., and the fine *sur concessit;* and may be used to convey particular limitations of estate, and to persons who are strangers, or not named in the writ of the covenant, whereas the fine *sur cognizance de droit come ceo*, &c., conveys nothing but an absolute estate, either of inheritance, or at least of freehold. Salk. 340. In this last species of fines, the cognizee, after the right is acknowledged to be in him, grants back again, or renders to the cognizor, or perhaps to a stranger, some other estate in the premises. 2 Bl. Com. 348 to 358. See Cruise on Fines; Vin. Abr. Fine; Sheph. Touch. c. 2; Bac. Ab. Fines and Recoveries; Com. Dig. Fine.

FINE, *criminal law.* Pecuniary punishment imposed by a lawful tribunal, upon a person convicted of crime or misdemeanor. See Shep. Touchs. 2; Bac. Abr. Fines and Amercements.

2. The amount of the fine is frequently left to the discretion of the court, who ought to proportion the fine to the offence. To prevent the abuse of excessive fines, the Constitution of the United States directs that "excessive bail shall not be required, nor excessive fines imposed, nor cruel and unusual punishments inflicted." Amendm. to the Constitution, art. 8. See *Division of opinion.*

FINE FOR ALIENATION. During the vigor of the feudal law, a fine for alienation was a sum of money which a tenant by knight's service paid to his lord for permission to alienate his right in the estate he held, to another, and by that means to substitute a new tenant for himself. 2 Bl. Com. 71. But when the tenant held land of the king, *in capite*, by socage tenure, he was bound to pay such a fine, as well as in the case of knight service. 2 Bl. Com. 89. These fines are now abolished. In France, a similar demand from the tenant, made by the lord when the former alienated his estate, was called *lods et vente.* This imposition was abolished, with nearly every feudal right, by the French revolution.

FIRE, ACCIDENTAL. One which arises in consequence of some human agency, without any intention, or which happens by some natural cause, without human agency.

2. Whether a fire arises purely by accident, or from any other cause, when it becomes uncontrollable and dangerous to the public, a man may, in general, justify the destruction of a house on fire for the protection of the neighborhood, for the maxim *salus populi est suprema lex*, applies in such case. 11 Co. 13; Jac. Inter. 122, max. 115. Vide *Accident; Act of God*, and 3 Saund. 422 a, note 2; 3 Co. Litt. 57 a, n. 1; Ham. N. P. 171; 1 Cruise's Dig. 151, 2; 1 Vin. Ab. 215; 1 Rolle's Ab. 1; Bac. Ab. Action on the case, F; 2 Lois des Bâtim. 124; Newl. on

Contr. 323; 1 T. R. 310, 708; Amb. 619; 6 T. R. 489.

3. When real estate is let, and the tenant covenants to pay the rent during the term, unless there are proper exceptions to such covenants, and the premises are afterwards destroyed by fire, during the term, the rent must be paid, although there be no enjoyment; for the common rule prevails, *res perit domino*. The tenant, by the accident, loses his term, the landlord, the residence. Story, Eq. Jur. § 102.

FIREBOTE. Fuel for necessary use; a privilege allowed to tenants to take necessary wood for fuel.

FIRKIN. A measure of capacity equal to nine gallons. The word firkin is also used to designate a weight, used for butter and cheese, of fifty-six pounds avoirdupois.

FIRM. The persons composing a partnership, taken collectively, are called the firm. Sometimes this word is used synonymously with partnership.

2. The name of a firm should be distinct from the names of all other firms. When there is a confusion in this respect, the partners composing one firm may, in some cases, be made responsible for the debts of another. For example, where three persons carried on a trade under the firm of King and Company, and two of those persons, with another, under the same firm, carried on another partnership; a bill under the firm, and which was drawn on account of the one partnership, was made the ground of an action of assumpsit against the other. Lord Kenyon was of opinion that this company was liable; that the partner not connected with the company that drew the bill, having traded along with the other partner under that firm, persons taking bills under it, though without his knowledge, had a right to look to him for payment. Peake's N. P. Cas. 80; and see 7 East, R. 210; 2 Bell's Com. 670, 5th ed.; 3 Mart. N. S. 39. But it would seem, 1st. That any act distinctly indicating credit to be given to one of the partnerships, will fix the election of the creditor to that company; and 2d. That making a claim on either of the firms, or, when they are insolvent, on either of the estates, will have the same effect.

3. When the style of the firm has been agreed upon, for example, John Doe and Company, the partners who sign the name of the firm are required to use such name in the style adopted, and a departure from it may have the double effect of rendering the individual partner who signs it, personally liable not only to third persons, but to his co-partners; Story, Partn. § 102, 202; and it will be a breach of the agreement, if the partner sign his own name, and add, "for himself and partners." Colly. Partn. B. 2, c. 2, § 2; 2 Jac. & Walk. 266.

4. As a general rule a firm will be bound by the acts of one of the partners in the course of their trade and business, and will be discharged by transactions with a single partner. For example, the payment or satisfaction of a debt by a partner, is a satisfaction and payment by them all; and a release to one partner, is a release to them all. Co. Litt. 232 n; 6 T. R. 525. Vide *Partner; Partnership.*

5. It not unfrequently happens that the name of the firm is the name of only one of the partners, and that such partner does business in his own name on his private or separate account. In such case, if the contract be entered into for the firm, and there is express or implied proof of that fact, the partnership will be bound by it; but when there is no such proof, the presumption will be that the debt was contracted by the partner on his own separate account, and the firm will not be responsible. Story on Part. § 139; Colly. on Partn. Book 3, c. 1, § 2, 17 Serg. & Rawle, 165; 5 Mason, 176; 5 Peters, 529; 9 Pick. 274; 2 Bouv. Inst. n. 1442, et seq.

FIRMAN. A passport granted by the Great Mogul, to captains of foreign vessels, to trade within the territories over which he has jurisdiction; a permit.

FIRST PURCHASER. In the English law of descent, the first purchaser was he who first acquired an estate in a family, which still owns it. A purchase of this kind signifies any mode of acquiring an estate, except by descent. 2 Bl. Com. 220.

FISC, *civil law.* The treasury of a prince. The public treasury. Hence *to confiscate* a thing, is to appropriate it to the *fisc.* Paillet, Droit Public, 21, n, says that *fiscus,* in the Roman law, signified the treasure of the prince, and *ærarium,* the treasure of the state. But this distinction was not observed in France. See Law 10, ff. De jure Fisci.

FISCAL. Belonging to the fisc, or public treasury.

FISH An animal which inhabits the water, breathes by the means of gills, and swims by the aid of fins, and is oviparous.

2. Fishes in rivers and in the sea, are considered as animals *feræ naturæ,* and con-

sequently no one has any property in them until they have been captured; and, like other wild animals, if having been taken, they escape and regain their liberty, the captor loses his property in them. Vide *Feræ Naturæ*. The owner of a fishery in the lower part of a stream cannot construct any contrivance by which to obstruct the passage of fish up the stream. 5 Pick. R. 199.

FISHERY, *estates*. A place prepared for catching fish with nets or hooks. This term is commonly applied to the place of drawing a seine, or net. 1 Whart. R. 131, 2.

2. The right of fishery is to be considered as to tide or navigable waters, and to rivers not navigable. A river where the tide ebbs and flows is considered an arm of the sea. By the common law of England every navigable river within the realm as far as the sea ebbs and flows is deemed a royal river, and the fisheries therein as belonging to the crown by prerogative, yet capable of being granted to a subject to be held or disposed of as private property. The profit of such fisheries, however, when retained by the crown, is not commonly taken and appropriated by the king, unless of extraordinary value, but left free to all the people. Dav. Rep. 155; 7 Co. 16, a; Plowd, 154, a. Within the tide waters of navigable rivers in some of the United States, private or several fisheries were established, during the colonial state, and are still held and enjoyed as such, as in the Delaware. 1 Whart. 145, 5; 1 Baldw. Rep. 76. On the high seas the right of fishing *jure gentium* is common to all persons, as a general rule. In rivers not navigable, that is, where there is no flux or reflux of the tide, the right of fishing is incident to the owner of the soil over which the water passes, and to the riparian proprietors, when a stream is owned by two or more. 6 Cowen's R. 369; 5 Mason's R. 191; 4 Pick. R. 145; 5 Pick. R. 199. The rule, that the right of fishery, within his territorial limits, belongs exclusively to the riparian owner, extends alike to great and small streams. The owners of farms adjoining the Connecticut river, above the flowing of the tide, have the exclusive right of fishing opposite their farms, to the middle of the river; although the public have an easement in the river as a public highway, for passing and repassing with every kind of water craft. 2 Conn. R. 481. The right of fishery may exist, not only in the owner of the soil or the riparian proprietor, but also in another who has acquired it by grant or otherwise. Co. Litt. 122 a, n. 7; Schul. Aq. R. 40, 41; Ang. W. C. 184; sed vide 2 Salk. 637.

3. Fisheries have been divided into—

1. *Several fisheries*. A several fishery is one to which the party claiming it has the right of fishing, independently of all others, as that no person can have a coëxtensive right with him in the object claimed, but a partial and independent right in another, or a limited liberty, does not derogate from the right of the owner. 5 Burr. 2814. A several fishery, as its name imports, is an exclusive property; this, however, is not to be understood as depriving the territorial owner of his right to a several fishery, when he grants to another person permission to fish; for he would continue to be the several proprietor, although he should suffer a stranger to hold a coëxtensive right with himself. Woolr. on Wat. 96.

4.—2. *Free fisheries*. A free fishery is said to be a franchise in the hands of a subject, existing by grant or prescription, distinct from an ownership in the soil. It is an exclusive right, and applies to a public navigable river, without any right in the soil. 3 Kent, Com. 329. Mr. Woolrych says, that sometimes a free fishery is confounded with a several, sometimes it is said to be synonymous with common, and again treated as distinct from either. Law of Waters, &c. 97.

5.—3. *Common of Fishery*. A common of fishery is not an exclusive right, but one enjoyed in common with certain other persons. 3 Kent, Com. 329. A distinction has been made between a common fishery, (*commune piscarium*,) which may mean for all mankind, as in the sea, and a common of fishery, (*communium piscariæ*,) which is a right, in common with certain other persons, in a particular stream. 8 Taunt. R. 183. Mr. Angell seems to think that *common of fishery* and *free fishery*, are convertible terms. Law of Water Courses, c. 6, s. 3, 4.

6. These distinctions in relation to several, free, and common of fishery, are not strongly marked, and the lines are sometimes scarcely perceptible. "Instead of going into the black letter books, to learn what was a fishery, and a free fishery, and a several fishery," says Huston, J., "I am disposed to regard our own acts, even though differing from old

feudal times." 1 Whart. R. 132. See 14 Mass. R. 488; 2 Bl. Com. 39, 40; 7 Pick. R. 79. Vide, generally, Ang. Wat. Co. Index, h. t; Woolr. on Wat. Index, h. t; Schul. Aq. R. Index, h. t; 2 Hill. Ab. ch. 18, p. 163; Dane's Ab. h. t; Bac. Ab. Prerogative, B 3; 12 John. R. 425; 14 John. R. 255; 14 Wend. R. 42; 10 Mass. R. 212; 13 Mass. R. 477; 20 John. R. 98; 2 John. R. 170; 6 Cowen, R. 369; 1 Wend. R. 237; 3 Greenl. R. 269; 3 N. H. Rep. 321; 1 Pick. R. 180; 2 Conn. R. 481; 1 Halst. 1; 5 Harr. and Johns. 195; 4 Mass. R. 527; and the articles *Arm of the sea; Creek; Navigable River; Tide.*

TO FIX. To render liable.

2. This term is applied to the condition of special bail; when the plaintiff has issued a *ca. sa.* which has been returned by the sheriff, *non est*, the bail are said to be fixed, unless the defendant be surrendered within the time allowed *ex gratia*, by the practice of the court. 5 Binn. R. 332; Coxe, R. 110; 12 Wheat. R. 604; 4 John. R. 407; 1 Caines, R. 588. The defendant's death after the return is no excuse for not surrendering him during the time allowed *ex gratia*. See *Act of God; Death.* In New Hampshire, 1 N. H. Rep. 472, and Massachusetts, 2 Mass. R. 485, the bail are not fixed until judgment is obtained against them on a *scire facias*, or unless the defendant die after the return of *non est* on the execution against him. In North Carolina, the bail are not fixed till judgment against them. 3 Dev. R. 155. When the bail are fixed, they are absolutely responsible.

FIXTURES, *property*. Personal chattels annexed to land, and which may be afterwards severed and removed by the party who has annexed them, or his personal representative, against the will of the owner of the freehold.

2. Questions frequently arise as to whether fixtures are to be considered real estate, or a part of the freehold; or whether they are to be treated as personal property. To decide these, it is proper to consider the mode of annexation, the object and customary use of the thing, and the character of the contending parties.

3.—1. The annexation may be actual or constructive; 1st. By actual connexation or annexation is understood every mode by which a chattel can be joined or united to the freehold. The article must not however be laid upon the ground; it must be fastened, fixed or set into the land, or into some such erection as is unquestionably a part of the realty. Bull. N. P. 34; 3 East, R. 38; 9 East, R. 215; 1 Taunt. 21; Pothier, Traité des Choses, § 1. Locks, iron stoves set in brick-work, posts, and window blinds, afford examples of actual annexation. See 5 Hayw. 109; 20 John. 29; 1 Harr. and John. 289; 3 M'Cord, 553; 9 Conn. 63; 1 Miss. 508, 620; 7 Mass. 432; 15 Mass. 159; 3 Stew. 314. 2d. Some things have been held to be parcel of the realty, which are not in a real sense annexed, fixed, or fastened to the freehold; for example, deeds or chattels which relate to the title of the inheritance, go to the heir; Shep. Touch. 469; but loose, movable machinery, not attached nor affixed, which is used in prosecuting any business to which the freehold is adapted, is not considered as part of the real estate, nor as an appurtenance to it. 12 New H. Rep. 205. See, however, 2 Watts & S. 116, 390. It is also laid down that deer in a park, fish in a pond, and doves in a dove-house, go to the heir and not to the executor, being, with keys and heir-looms, constructively annexed to the inheritance. Sheph. Touchs. 90; Pothier, Traité des Choses, § 1.

4.—2. The general rule is, that fixtures once annexed to the freehold, become a part of the realty. But to this rule there are exceptions. These are, 1st. Where there is a manifest intention to use the fixtures in some employment distinct from that of the occupier of the real estate. 2d. Where it has been annexed for the purpose of carrying on a trade; 3 East, 88; 4 Watts, 330; but the distinction between fixtures for trade and those for agriculture does not in the United States, seem to have been generally admitted to prevail. 8 Mass. R. 411; 16 Mass. R. 449; 4 Pick. R. 311; and see 2 Peter's Rep. 137. The fact that it was put up for the purposes of trade indicates an intention that the thing should not become a part of the freehold. See 1 H. Bl. 260. But if there be a clear intention that the thing should be annexed to the realty, its being used for the purposes of trade would not perhaps bring the case within one of the exceptions. 1 H. Bl. 260.

5.—3. There is a difference as to what fixtures may or may not be removed, as the parties claiming them stand in one relation or another. These classes of persons will be separately considered.

6.—1st. When the question as to fixtures arises between the executor and the heir

The rule as between these persons has retained much of its original strictness, that the fixtures belong to the real estate, or the heir; but if the ancestor manifested an intention, which is to be inferred from circumstances, that the things affixed should be considered as personalty, they must be so considered, and will belong to the executor. See Bac. Abr. Executors and Administrators; 2 Str. 1141; 1 P. Wms. 94; Bull. N. P. 34.

7.—2d. As between vendor and vendee. The rule is as strict between these persons as between the executor, and the heir; and fixtures erected by the vendor for the purpose of trade and manufactures, as pot-ash kettles for manufacturing ashes, pass to the vendee of the land. 6 Cowen, R. 663; 20 Johns. R. 29. Between mortgagor and mortgagee, the rule seems to be the same as that between vendor and vendee. Amos & F. on Fixt. 188; 15 Mass. R. 159; 1 Atk. 477; 16 Verm. 124; 12 N. H. Rep. 205.

8.—3d. Between devisee and executor. On a devise of real estate, things permanently annexed to the realty, at the time of the testator's death, will pass to the devisee. His right to fixtures will be similar to that of the vendee. 2 Barn. & Cresw. 80.

9.—4th. Between landlord and tenant for years. The ancient rule is relaxed, aud the right of removal of fixtures by the tenant is said to be very extensive. 3 East, 38. But his right of removal is held to depend rather upon the question whether the estate will be left in the condition in which he took it. 4 Pick. R. 311.

10.—5th. In cases between tenants for life or their executors and the remaindermen or reversioners, the right to sever fixtures seems to be the same as that of the tenant for years. It has been held that the steam engines erected in a colliery, by a tenant for life, should belong to the executor and not go to the remainder-man. 3 Atk. R. 13.

11.—6th. In a case between the landlord and a tenant at will, there seems to be no reason why the same privilege of removing fixtures should not be allowed. 4 Pick. R. 511; 5 Pick. R. 487.

12. The time for exercising the right of removal of fixtures is a matter of importance; a tenant for years may remove them at any time before he gives up the possession of the premises, although it should be after his term has expired, and he is holding over. 1 Barn. & Cres. 79, 2 East, 88. Tenants for life or at will, having uncertain interests in the land, may, after the determination of their estates, not occasioned by their own faults, have a reasonable time within which to remove their fixtures. Hence their right to bring an action for them. 3 Atk. 13. In case of their death the right passes to their representatives.

See, generally, Vin. Abr. Landlord and Tenant, A; Bac. Abr. Executors, &c. H 3; Com. Dig. Biens, B and C; 2 Chitty's Bl. 281, n. 23; Pothier, Traité des Choses; 4 Co. 63, 64; Co. Litt. 53, a, and note 5, by Hargr.; Moore, 177; Hob. 234; 3 Salk. 368; 1 P. Wms. 94; 1 Atk. 553; 2 Vern. 508; 3 Atk. 13; 1 H. Bl. 259, n; Ambl. 113; 2 Str. 1141; 3 Esp. 11; 2 East, 88; 3 East, 38; 9 East, 215; 3 Johns. R. 468; 7 Mass. 432; 6 Cowen, 665; 2 Kent, Com. 280; Ham. Part. 182; Jurist, No. 19, p. 53; Arch. L. & T. 359; Bouv. Inst. Index, h. t.

FLAG OF THE UNITED STATES. By the act entitled, "An act to establish the flag of the United States," passed April 4, 1818, 3 Story's L. U. S., 1667, it is enacted—

2.—§ 1. That from and after the fourth day of July next, the flag of the United States be thirteen horizontal stripes, alternate red and white: that the union bo twenty stars, white in a blue field.

3.—§ 2. That, on the admission of every new state into the Union, one star be added to the union of the flag; and that such addition shall take effect on the fourth day of July then next succeeding such admission.

FLAGRANS CRIMEN. This, among the Romans, signified that a crime was then or had just been committed; for example, when a crime has just been committed and the *corpus delictum* is publicly exposed; or if a mob take place; or if a house be feloniously burned, these are severally *flagrans crimen.*

2. The term used in France is *flagrant délit.* The code of criminal instruction gives the following concise definition of it, art. 41: "Le délit qui se commet actuellement ou qui vient de se commettre, est un flagrant délit."

FLAGRANTE DELICTO. The act of committing a crime; when a person is arrested *flagrante delicto*, the only evidence required to convict him, is to prove that fact.

FLEET, *punishment, Eng. law, Saxon fleot*. A place of running water, where the tide or float comes up. A prison in London, so called from a river or ditch which was formerly there, on the side of which it stood.

FLETA. The title of an ancient law book, supposed to have been written by a judge who was confined in the Fleet prison. It is written in Latin, and is divided into six books. The author lived in the reigns of Ed. II. and Ed. III. See lib. 2, cap. 66, § Item quod nullus; lib. 1, cap. 20, § qui cœperunt, pref. to 10th Rep. Edward II. was crowned, A. D. 1306. Edward III. was crowned 1326, and reigned till A. D. 1377. During this period the English law was greatly improved, and the lawyers and judges were very learned. Hale's Hist. C. L. 173. Blackstone, 4 Com. 427, says, of this work, "that it was for the most part law, until the alteration of tenures took place." The same remark he applies to Britton and Hingham.

FLIGHT, *crim. law*. The evading the course of justice, by a man's voluntarily withdrawing himself. 4 Bl. Com. 387. Vide *Fugitive from justice*.

FLORIDA. The name of one of the new states of the United States of America. It was admitted into the Union by virtue of the act of congress, entitled An Act for the admission of the states of Iowa and Florida into the Union, approved March 3, 1845.

2. The constitution was adopted on the eleventh day of January, eighteen hundred and thirty-nine. The powers of the government are divided into three distinct branches, namely, the legislative, the executive, and the judicial,

3.—§ 1. Of the *legislative* power. 1. The legislative power of this state shall be vested in two distinct branches, the one to be styled the senate, the other the house of representatives, and both together, "The General Assembly of the State of Florida," and the style of the laws shall be, "Be it enacted by the Senate and House of Representatives of the State of Florida in General Assembly convened."

4.—2. A majority of each house shall constitute a quorum to do business, but a smaller number may adjourn from day to day. and may compel the attendance of absent members in such manner, and under such penalties, as each house may prescribe.

5.—3. Each house may determine the rules of its own proceedings, punish its members for disorderly behaviour, and, with the consent of two-thirds, expel a member; but not a second time for the same cause.

6.—4. Each house, during the session, may punish, by imprisonment, any person not a member, for disrespectful or disorderly behaviour in its presence, or for obstructing any of its proceedings, provided such imprisonment shall not extend beyond the end of the session.

7.—5. Each house shall keep a journal of its proceedings, and cause the same to be published immediately after its adjournment, and the yeas and nays of the members of each house shall be taken, and entered upon the journals, upon the final passage of every bill, and may, by any two members, be required upon any other question, and any member of either house shall have liberty to dissent from, or protest against, any act or resolution which he may think injurious to the public, or an individual, and have the reasons of his dissent entered on the journal.

8.—6. Senators and representatives shall in all cases, except treason, felony or breach of the peace, be privileged from arrest during the session of the general assembly, and in going to, or returning from the same, allowing one day for every twenty miles such member may reside from the place at which the general assembly is convened; and for any speech or debate, in either house, they shall not be questioned in any other place.

9.—7. The general assembly shall make provision, by law, for filling vacancies that may occur in either house, by the death, resignation, (or otherwise,) of any of its members.

10.—8. The doors of each house shall be open, except on such occasions as, in the opinion of the house, the public safety may imperiously require secrecy.

11.—9. Neither house shall, without the consent of the other, adjourn for more than three days, nor to any other place than that in which they may be sitting.

12.—10. Bills may originate in either house of the general assembly, and all bills passed by one house may be discussed, amended or rejected by the other; but no bill shall have the force of law until, on three several days, it be read in each house, and free discussion be allowed thereon, unless in cases of urgency, four-fifths of the house in which the same shall be depending, may deem it expedient to dispense with the rule; and every bill, having passed both houses, shall be signed by the speaker and president of their respective houses.

13.—11. Each member of the general assembly shall receive from the public treasury such compensation for his services, as may be fixed by law, but no increase of compensation shall take effect during the term for which the representatives were elected when such law passed.

14.—12. The sessions of the general assembly shall be annual, and commence on the fourth Monday in November in each year, or at such other time as may be prescribed by law.

15. The *senators* will be considered with regard, 1. To the qualification of the electors. 2. The qualification of the members. 3. The number of members. 4. The time of their election. 5. The length of service.

16.—1st. The senators shall be elected by the qualified voters. Const. art. 4, s. 5.

17.—2d. No man shall be a senator unless he be a white man, a citizen of the United States, and shall have been an inhabitant of Florida two years next preceding his election, and the last year thereof a resident of the district or county for which he shall be chosen, and shall have attained the age of twenty-five years. Const. art. 4, s. 5. And to this there are the following exceptions:

All banking officers of any bank in the state are ineligible until after twelve months after they shall go out of such office. Art. 6, 3.

All persons who shall fight, or send, or accept a duel, the probable issue of which may be death, whether committed in or out of the state. Art. 6, s. 5.

All collectors or holders of public money. Art. 6, s. 6.

All ministers of the Gospel. Art. 6, s. 10.

All persons who shall have procured their elections by bribery.

All members of congress, or persons holding or exercising any office of profit under the United States, or under a foreign power. Art. 6, s. 18.

18.—3d. The number of senators may be varied by the general assembly, but it shall never be less than one-fourth, nor more than one-half of the whole number of the house of representatives. Art. 9, s. 2.

19.—4th. The time and place of their election is the same as those for the house of representatives. Art. 4, s. 5.

20.—5th. They are elected for the term of two years. Art. 4, s. 5.

21. The *house of representatives* will be considered under the same heads.

22.—1st. Members of the house of representatives shall be chosen by the qualified voters.

23.—2d. No person shall be a representative unless he be a white man, a citizen of the United States, and shall have been an inhabitant of the state two years next preceding his election, and the last year thereof a resident of the county for which he shall be chosen, and have attained the age of twenty-one years. Art. 4, s. 4. And the same persons are disqualified, who are disqualified as senators.

24.—3d. The number of members shall never exceed sixty. Art. 4, s. 18.

25.—4th. The time of holding the election is the first Monday of October annually.

26.—5th. Members of the house of representatives are elected for one year from the day of the commencement of the general election, and no longer. Art. 4, s. 2.

27.—§ 2. Of the *executive*. The supreme executive power is vested in a chief magistrate, who is styled the governor of Florida. Art. 3.

28. No person shall be eligible to the office of governor, unless he shall have attained the age of thirty years, shall have been a citizen of the United States ten years, or an inhabitant of Florida at the time of the adoption of the constitution, (being a citizen of the United States,) and shall have resided in Florida at least five years preceding the day of election.

29. The governor shall be elected for four years, by the qualified electors, at the time and place where they shall vote for representatives; and shall remain in office until a successor shall be chosen and qualified, and shall not be eligible to reëlection until the expiration of four years thereafter.

30. His general powers are as follows: 1. He is commander-in-chief of the army, navy, and militia of the state. 2. He shall take care that the laws be faithfully executed. 3. He may require information from the officers of the executive department. 4. He may convene the general assembly by proclamation upon particular occasions. 5. He shall, from time to time, give information to the general assembly.

6. He may grant pardons, after conviction, in all cases except treason and impeachment, and in these cases, with the consent of the senate; and he may respite the sentence in these cases until the end of the next session of the senate. 7. He may approve or veto bills.

31. In case of vacancy in the office of governor, the president of the senate shall act in his place, and in case of his default, the speaker of the house of representatives shall fill the office of governor. Art. 3, s. 21.

32.—§ 3. Of the *judicial* department. 1. The judicial power of this state, both as to matters of law and equity, shall be vested in a supreme court, courts of chancery, circuit courts, and justices of the peace: Provided, the general assembly may also vest such criminal jurisdiction as may be deemed necessary in corporation courts; but such jurisdiction shall not extend to capital offences. Art. 5, s. 1.

33.—2. Justices of the supreme court, chancellors, and judges of the circuit courts, shall be elected by the concurrent vote of a majority of both houses of the general assembly. Art. 5, s. 11.

34.—3. The judges of the circuit courts shall, at the first session of the general assembly to be holden under the constitution, be elected for the term of five years, and shall hold their office for that term, unless sooner removed, under the provisions in the constitution; and at the expiration of five years, the justices of the supreme courts, and the judges of the circuit courts, shall be elected for the term of, and during their good behaviour.

35. Of the *supreme* court. 1. The powers of the supreme court are vested in, and its duties performed by, the judges of the several circuit courts, and they, or a majority of them, shall hold such session of the supreme court, and at such time and place as may be directed by law. Art. 5, s. 3. But no justice of the supreme court shall sit as judge, or take any part in the appellate court, on the trial or hearing of any case which shall have been decided by him in the court below. Art. 5, s. 18.

36.—2. The supreme court, except in cases otherwise directed in this constitution, shall have appellate jurisdiction only. Provided, that the said court shall always have power to issue writs of injunction, mandamus, *quo warranto*, *habeas corpus*, and such other remedial and original writs, as may be necessary to give it a general superintendance and control of all other courts. Art. 5, s. 2.

37.—3. The supreme court shall exercise appellate jurisdiction in all cases brought by appeal or writ of error from the several circuit courts, when the matter in controversy exceeds in amount or value fifty dollars.

38. Of the *circuit* courts. 1. The state is to be divided into circuits, and the circuit courts, held within such circuits, shall have original jurisdiction in all matters, civil and criminal, within the state, not otherwise excepted in this constitution. Art. 5, s. 6.

FLORIN. The name of a foreign coin. In all computations of customs, the florin of the southern states of Germany, shall be estimated at forty cents; the florin of the Austrian empire, and of the city of Augsburg, at forty-eight and one-half cents. Act March 22, 1846. The florin of the United Netherlands is computed at the rate of forty cents. Act of March 2, 1799, § 61. Vide *Foreign Coins.*

FLOTSAM, or FLOTSAN. A name for the goods which float upon the sea when a ship is sunk, in distinction from *Jetsam*, (q. v.) and *Legan*. (q. v.) Bract. lib. 2, c. 5; 5 Co. 106; Com. Dig. Wreck, A; Bac. Ab. Court of Admiralty, B.

FLUMEN, *civ. law.* The name of a servitude which consists in the right of turning the rain water, gathered in a spout, on another's land. Ersk. Inst. B. 2, t. 9, n. 9. Vicat, ad vocem. See *Stillicidium.*

FŒDUS. A league; a compact.

FŒNUS NAUTICUS. The name given to marine interest. (q. v.)

2. The amount of such interest is not limited by law, because the lender runs the risk of losing his principal. Ersk. Inst. B. 4, t. 4, n. 76. See *Marine Interest.*

FŒTICIDE, *med. jur.* Recently, this term has been applied to designate the act by which criminal abortion is produced. 1 Beck's Med. Jur. 288; Guy, Med. Jur. 133. See *Infanticide; Prolicide.*

FŒTURA, *civil law.* The produce of animals, and the fruit of other property, which are acquired to the owner of such animals and property, by virtue of his right. Bowy. Mod. C. L. c. 14, p. 81.

FŒTUS, *med. jur.* The unborn child. The name of embryo is sometimes given to it; but, although the terms are occasionally used indiscriminately, the latter is more frequently employed to designate the state of an unborn child during the first three months after conception, and by some until quickening. A fœtus is sometimes described by the uncouth phrase of *infant in ventre sa mere*.

2. It is sometimes of great importance, particularly in criminal law, to ascertain the age of the fœtus, or how far it has progressed towards maturity. There are certain signs which furnish evidence on this subject, the principal of which are, the size and weight, and the formation of certain parts; as the cartilages, bones, &c. These are not always the same, much of course must depend upon the constitution and health of the mother, and other circumstances which have an influence on the fœtus. The average length and weight of the fœtus at different periods of gestation, as deduced by Doctor Beck, from various observers, and as found by Maygrier, is here given.

	Beck.	Maygrier.	Maygrier.	Beck.
	Length.		Weight.	
At 30 days	3 to 5 lines.	10 to 12 lines.		9 to 10 grains.
2 months	2 inches.	4 inches.	2 ounces.	5 drachms.
3 do.	3½ inches.	6 inches.	2 to 3 ounces.	2½ ounces.
4 do.	5 to 6 inches.	8 inches.	4 to 5 ounces.	7 to 8 ounces.
5 do.	7 to 9 inches.	10 inches.	9 to 10 ounces.	16 ounces.
6 do.	9 to 12 inches.	12 inches.	1 to 2 pounds.	2 pounds.
7 do.	12 to 14 inches.	14 inches.	2 to 3 pounds.	3 pounds.
8 do.	16 inches.	16 inches.	3 to 4 pounds.	4 pounds.

3. The discordance apparent between them proves that the observations which have been made, are only an approximation to truth.

4. It is proper to remark that the Paris pound *poids de marc*, which was the weight used by Maygrier, differs from *avoirdupois* weight used by Dr. Beck. The pound *poids de marc*, of sixteen ounces, contains 9216 Paris grains, whilst the *avoirdupois* contains only 8532.5 Paris grains. The Paris inch is 1.065977 English inch.

Vide, generally, 1 Beck's Med. Jur. 239; 2 Dunglison's Human Physiology, 391; Ryan's Med. Jur. 137; 1 Chit. Med. Jur. 403; 1 Briand, Méd. Lég. prém. partie, c. 4, art. 2; and the articles *Birth; Dead Born; Fœticide; In ventre sa mere; Infanticide; Life;* and *Quick with child*.

FOLCMOTE. The name of a court among the Saxons. It was literally an assembly of the people or inhabitants of the tithing or town; its jurisdiction extended over disputes between neighbors, as to matters of trespass in meadows, corn, and the like.

FOLD-COURSE, *Eng. law*. By this phrase is understood land used as a sheep-walk; it also signifies land to which the sole right of folding the cattle of others is appurtenant; sometimes it means merely such right of folding. It is also used to denote the right of folding on another's land, which is called common foldage. Co. Litt. 6 a, note 1; W. Jo. 375; Cro. Car. 432; 2 Vent. 139.

FOLK-LAND, *Eng. law*. Land formerly held at the pleasure of the lord, and resumed at his discretion. It was held in villenage. 2 Bl. Com. 90.

FOOT. A measure of length, containing one-third of a yard, or twelve inches. See *Ell*. Figuratively, it signifies the conclusion, the end; as, the foot of the fine, the foot of the account.

FOOT OF THE FINE, *estates, conveyancing*. The fifth part of the conclusion of a fine. It includes the whole matter, reciting the names of the parties, day, year, and place, and before whom it was acknowledged or levied. 2 Bl. Com. 351.

FOR THAT, *pleading*. It is a maxim in law, regulating alike every form of action, that the plaintiff shall state his complaint in positive and direct terms, and not by way of recital. "For that," is a positive allegation; "For that whereas," in Latin "quod cum," (q. v.) is a recital. Hamm. N. P. 9.

FORBEARANCE, *contracts*. The act

by which a creditor waits for the payment of the debt due him by the debtor, after it has become due.

2. When the creditor agrees to forbear with his debtor, this is a sufficient consideration to support an assumpsit made by the debtor. 4 John. R. 237; 2 Nott & McCord, 133; 2 Binn. R. 510; Com. Dig. Action upon the case upon assumpsit, B 1; Dane's Ab. Index, h. t.; 1 Leigh's N. P. 31; 1 Penna. R. 385; 4 Wash. C. C. R. 148; 5 Rawle's R. 69.

3. The forbearance must be of some right which can be enforced with effect against the party forborne; if it cannot be so enforced by the party forbearing, he has sustained no detriment, and the party forborne has derived no benefit. 4 East, 455; 5 B. & Ald. 123. See 1 B. & A. 605; Burge on Sur. 12, 13. Vide *Giving time.*

FORCE. A power put in motion. It is, 1. Actual; or 2. Implied.

2.—§ 1. If a person with force break a door or gate for an illegal purpose, it is lawful to oppose force to force; and if one enter the close of another, *vi et armis*, he may be expelled immediately, without a previous request; for there is no time to make a request. 2 Salk. 641; 8 T. R. 78, 357. And see tit. *Battery*, § 2. When it is necessary to rely upon actual force in pleading, as in the case of a forcible entry, the words "*manu forti*," or "with a strong hand," should be adopted. 8 T. R. 357, 358. But in other cases, the words "*vi et armis*," or "with force and arms," is sufficient. Id.

3.—§ 2. The entry into the ground of another, without his consent, is breaking his close, for force is implied in every trespass *quare clausum fregit*. 1 Salk. 641; Co. Litt. 257, b; 161, b; 162, a; 1 Saund. 81, 140, n. 4; 8 T. R. 78, 358; Bac. Ab. Trespass; this Dict. tit. *Close*. In the case of false imprisonment, force is implied. 1 N. R. 255. And the same rule prevails where a wife, a daughter or servant, have been enticed away or debauched, though in fact they consented, the law considering them incapable of consenting. See 3 Wils. 18; Fitz. N. B. 89, O; 5 T. R. 361; 6 East, 387; 2 N. R. 365, 454.

4. In general, a mere nonfeasance cannot be considered as forcible; for where there has been no act, there cannot be force, as in the case of the mere detention of goods, without an unlawful taking. 2 Saund. 47, k 1. In general, by force is understood unlawful violence. Co. Litt. 161, b.; Bouv. Inst. Index, h. t. Vide *Arms*.

FORCE AND ARMS. The same as *vi et armis*. (q. v.)

FORCED HEIRS. In Louisiana they are those persons whom the testator or donor cannot deprive of the portion of his estate reserved for them by law, except in cases where he has a just cause to disinherit them. Civ. Code of Lo. art. 1482. As to the portion of the estate they are entitled to, see the article *Legitime*. As to the causes for which forced heirs may be deprived of this right, see *Disinherison*.

FORCIBLE ENTRY or DETAINER, *crim. law*. An offence committed by unlawfully and violently taking or keeping possession of lands and tenements, with menaces, force and arms, and without the authority of law. Com. Dig. h. t.

2. The proceedings in case of forcible entry or detainer, are regulated by statute in the several states. (q. v.) The offence is generally punished by indictment. 4 Bl. Com. 148; 1 Russ. on Cr. 283. A forcible entry and a forcible detainer, are distinct offences. 1 Serg. & Rawle, 124; 8 Cowen, 226.

3. In the civil and French law, a similar remedy is given for this offence. The party injured has two actions, a criminal or a civil. The action is called *actio interdictum undèvie*. In French, *l'action reintegrande*. Poth. Proc. Civ. Partie 2, c. 3 art. 3; 11 Toull. Nos. 123, 134, 135, 137 pp. 179, 180, 182, and, generally, from p 163. Vide, generally, 3 Pick. 31; 3 Halst R. 48; 2 Tyler's R. 64; 2 Root's R. 411 Id. 472; 4 Johns. R. 150; 8 Johns. R 44; 10 Johns. R. 304; 1 Caines' R. 125 2 Caines' R. 98; 9 Johns. R. 147; 2 Johns. Cas. 400; 6 Johns. R. 334; 2 Johns. R. 27; 3 Caines' R. 104; 11 John. R. 504; 12 John. R. 31; 13 Johns. R. 158; Id. 340; 16 Johns. R. 141; 8 Cowen, 226; 1 Coxe's R. 258; Id. 260; 1 South. R. 125; 1 Halst. R. 396; 3 Id. 48; 4 Id. 37; 6 Id. 84; 1 Yeates, 501; Addis. R. 14, 17, 43, 316, 355; 3 Serg. & Rawle, 418; 3 Yeates, 49; 4 Dall. 212; 4 Yeates, 326; 3 Harr. & McHen. 428, 2 Bay, R. 355; 2 Nott & McCord, 121; 1 Const. R. 325; Cam. & Norw. 337, 340; Com. Dig. h. t.; Vin. Ab. h. t.; Bac. Ab. h. t.; 2 Chit. Pr. 231 to 241.

4. The civil law punished even the owner of an estate, in proportion to the

violence used, when he forcibly took possession of it, *a fortiori*, a stranger. Domat, Supp. au Dr. Pub. l. 3, t. 4, s. 3.

FORECLOSURE, *practice*. A proceeding in chancery, by which the mortgagor's right of redemption of the mortgaged premises is barred or foreclosed forever.

2. This takes place when the mortgagor has forfeited his estate by non-payment of the money due on the mortgage at the time appointed, but still retains the equity of redemption; in such case the mortgagee may file a bill, calling on the mortgagor, in a court of equity, to redeem his estate presently, or in default thereof, to be forever closed or barred from any right of redemption.

3. In some cases, however, the mortgagee obtains a decree for a sale of the land, under the direction of an officer of the court, in which case the proceeds are applied to the discharge of encumbrances, according to their priority. This practice has been adopted in Indiana, Kentucky, Maryland, South Carolina, Tennessee, and Virginia. 4 Kent, Com. 180. When it is the practice to foreclose without a sale, its severity is mitigated by enlarging the time of redemption from six months to six months, or for shorter periods, according to the equity arising from the circumstances. Id. Vide 2 John. Ch. R. 100; 5 Pick. R. 418; 1 Sumn. R. 401; 7 Conn. R. 152; 5 N. H. Rep. 30; 1 Hayw. R. 482; 5 Han. R. 554; 5 Yerg. 240; 2 Pick. R. 540; 4 Pick. R. 6; 2 Gallis. 154; 9 Cowen's R. 346; 4 Greenl. R. 495; Bouv. Inst. Index, h. t.

FOREHAND RENT, *Eng. law*. A species of rent which is a premium given by the tenant at the time of taking the lease, as on the renewal of leases by ecclesiastical corporations, which is considered in the nature of an improved rent. 1 T. R. 486; 3 T. R. 461; 3 Atk. 473; Crabb. on R. P. § 155.

FOREIGN. That which belongs to another country; that which is strange. 1 Peters, R. 343.

2. Every nation is foreign to all the rest, and the several states of the American Union are foreign to each other, with respect to their municipal laws. 2 Wash. R. 282; 4 Conn. 517; 6 Conn. 480; 2 Wend. 411; 1 Dall. 458, 463; 6 Binn. 321; 12 S. & R. 203; 2 Hill R. 319; 1 D. Chipm. 303; 7 Monroe, 585; 5 Leigh, 471; 3 Pick. 293.

3. But the reciprocal relations between the national government and the several states composing the United States are not considered as foreign, but domestic. 9 Pet. 607; 5 Pet. 398; 6 Pet. 317; 4 Cranch, 384; 4 Gill & John. 1, 63. Vide *Attachment*, for foreign attachment; *Bill of exchange*, for foreign bills of exchange; *Foriegn Coins; Foreign Judgment; Foreign Laws; Foreigners.*

FOREIGN ATTACHMENT. The name of a writ. By virtue of a foreign attachment, the property of an absent debtor is seised for the purpose of compelling an appearance, and, in default of that, to pay the claim of the plaintiff. Vide *Attachment.*

FOREIGN COINS, *com. law*. The money of foreign nations.

2. Congress have, from time to time, regulated the rates at which certain foreign coins should pass. The acts now in force are the following.

3. The act of June 25, 1834, 4 Sharsw. Cont. of Story's L. U. S. 2373, enacts, sec. 1. That from and after the passage of this act, the following silver coins shall be of the legal value and shall pass current as money within the United States, by tale, for the payment of all debts and demands, at the rate of one hundred cents the dollar, that is to say, the dollars of Mexico, Peru, Chili, and Central America, of not less weight than four hundred and fifteen grains each, and those re-stamped in Brazil of the like weight, of not less fineness than ten ounces, fifteen pennyweights of pure silver, in the troy pound of twelve ounces of standard silver; and five franc pieces of France, when of not less fineness than ten ounces and sixteen pennyweights in twelve ounces troy weight of standard silver, and weighing not less than three hundred and eighty-four grains each, at the rate of ninety-three cents each.

4. The act of June 28, 1834, 4 Sharsw. Cont. of Story's L. U. S, 2377, enacts, sect. 1. That from and after the thirty-first day of July next, the following gold coins shall pass current as money within the United States, and be receivable in all payments, by weight, for the payment of all debts and demands, at the rates following, that is to say: the gold coins of Great Britain and Portugal and Brazil, of not less than twenty-two carats fine, at the rate of ninety-four cents and eight-tenths of a cent per pennyweight; the gold coins of France nine-tenths fine, at the rate of ninety-three

cents and one-tenth of a cent per pennyweight; and the gold coins of Spain, Mexico, and Colombia, of the fineness of twenty carats three grains and seven-sixteenths of a grain, at the rates of eighty-nine cents and nine-tenths of a cent per pennyweight.

5. By the act of March 3, 1823, 3 Story's L. U. S. 1923, it is enacted, sect. 1. That from and after the passage of this act, the following gold coins shall be received in all payments on account of public lands, at the several and respective rates following, and not otherwise, viz.: the gold coins of Great Britain and Portugal, and of their present standard, at the rate of one hundred cents for every twenty-seven grains, or eighty-eight cents and eight-ninths per pennyweight; the gold coins of France of their present standard, at the rate of one hundred cents for every twenty-seven and a half grains, or eighty-seven and a quarter cents per pennyweight; and the gold coins of Spain of their present standard, at the rate of one hundred cents for every twenty-eight and a half grains or eighty-four cents per pennyweight.

6. The act of March 2, 1799, 1 Story's L. U. S. 573, to regulate the collection of duties on imports and tonnage, sect. 61, p. 626, enacts, That the ad valorem rates of duty upon goods, wares, and merchandise, at the place of importation, shall be estimated by adding twenty per cent. to the actual costs thereof, if imported from the Cape of Good Hope, or from any place beyond the same; and ten per cent. on the actual cost thereof, if imported from any other place or country, including all charges; commissions, outside packages, and insurance, only excepted. That all foreign coins and currencies shall be estimated at the following rates; each pound sterling of Great Britain, at four dollars and forty-four cents; each livre tournois of France, at eighteen and a half cents; each florin, or guilder of the United Netherlands, at forty cents; each marc-banco of Hamburg, at thirty-three and one-third cents; each rix dollar of Denmark, at one hundred cents: each rial of plate, and each rial of vellon, of Spain, the former at ten cents, the latter at five cents, each; each milree of Portugal, at one dollar and twenty-four cents; each pound sterling of Ireland, at four dollars and ten cents; each tale of China, at one dollar and forty-eight cents; each pagoda of India, at one dollar and ninety four cents; each rupee of Bengal, at fifty-five cents and one half; and all other denominations of money, in value as nearly as may be to the said rates, or the intrinsic value thereof, compared with money of the United States: *Provided*, That it shall be lawful for the president of the United States to cause to be established fit and proper regulations for estimating the duties on goods, wares, and merchandise, imported into the United States, in respect to which the original cost shall be exhibited in a depreciated currency, issued and circulated under authority of any foreign government.

7. By the act of July 14, 1832, s 16, 4 Sharsw. Cont. of Story's L. U. S. 2326, the law is changed as to the value of the pound sterling, in calculating the rates of duties. It is thereby enacted, that from and after the said third day of March, one thousand eight hundred and thirty-three, in calculating the rate of duties, the pound sterling shall be considered and taken as of the value of four dollars and eighty cents.

8. The act of March 3, 1843, provides, That in all computations of the value of foreign moneys of account at the custom houses of the United States, the thaler of Prussia shall be deemed and taken to be of the value of sixty-eight and one-half cents; the mil-reis of Portugal shall be deemed and taken to be of the value of one hundred and twelve cents; the rix dollar of Bremen shall be deemed and taken to be of the value of seventy-eight and three quarter cents; the thaler of Bremen, of seventy-two grotes, shall be deemed and taken to be of the value of seventy-one cents; that the mil-reis of Madeira shall be deemed and taken to be of the value of one hundred cents; the mil-reis of the Azores shall be deemed and taken to be of the value of eighty-three and one-third cents; the marc-banco of Hamburg shall be deemed and taken to be of the value of thirty-five cents; the rouble of Russia shall be deemed and taken to be of the value of seventy-five cents; the rupee of British India shall be deemed and taken to be of the value of forty-four and one half cents; and all former laws inconsistent herewith are hereby repealed.

9. And the act of May 22, 1846, further directs, That in all computations at the custom-house, the foreign coins and money of account herein specified shall be estimated as follows, to wit: The specie dollar

of Sweden and Norway, at one hundred and six cents. The specie dollar of Denmark, at one hundred and five cents. The thaler of Prussia and of the Northern States of Germany, at sixty-nine cents. The florin of the Southern States of Germany, at forty cents. The florin of the Austrian empire, and of the city of Augsburg, at forty-eight and one half cents. The lira of the Lombardo-Venetian Kingdom, and the lira of Tuscany, at sixteen cents. The franc of France, and of Belgium, and the lira of Sardinia, at eighteen cents six mills. The ducat of Naples, at eighteen cents. The ounce of Sicily, at two dollars and forty cents. The pound of the British provinces of Nova Scotia, New Brunswick, Newfoundland, and Canada, at four dollars. And all laws inconsistent with this act are hereby repealed.

FOREIGN JUDGMENT, *evidence*, *remedies*. A judgment rendered in a foreign state.

2. In Louisiana it has been decided that a judgment rendered by a Spanish tribunal, under the former government of the country, is not a foreign judgment. 4 M. R. 301; Id. 310.

3. The subject will be considered with regard, 1st. To the manner of proving such judgment; and 2d. Its efficacy.

4.—1. Foreign judgments are authenticated in various ways; 1. By an exemplification, certified under the great seal of the state or country where it was rendered. 2. By a copy proved to be a true copy. 3. By the certificate of an officer authorized by law, which certificate must, itself, be properly authenticated. 2 Cranch, 238; 2 Caines' R. 155; 5 Cranch, 335; 7 Johns. R. 514; 8 Mass. R. 273; 2 Munf. R. 43; 4 Camp. R. 28; 2 Russ. on Cr. 723. There is a difference between the judgments of courts of common law jurisdiction and courts of admiralty, as to the mode of proof of judgments rendered by them. Courts of admiralty are under the law of nations; certificates of such judgments with their seals affixed, will therefore be admitted in evidence without further proof. 5 Cranch, 335; 3 Conn. R. 171.

5.—2. A judgment rendered in a foreign country by a court *de jure*, or even a court *de facto*, 4 Binn. 371, in a matter within its jurisdiction, when the parties litigant had been notified and have had an opportunity of being heard, either establishing a demand against the defendant or discharging him from it, is of binding force. 1 Dall. R. 191; 9 Serg. & Rawle, 260; 10 Serg. & Rawle, 240; 1 Pet. C. C. R. 155; 1 Spears, Eq. Cas. 229; 7 Branch, 481. As to the plea of the act of limitation to a suit on a foreign judgment, see Bac. Ab. h. t.; 2 Vern. 540; 5 John. R. 132; 13 Serg. & Rawle, 395; 1 Speers, Eq. Cas. 219, 229.

6. For the manner of proving a judgment obtained in a sister state, see the article *Authentication*. For the French law in relation to the force of foreign judgments, see Dalloz, Dict. mot Etranger, art. 6.

FOREIGN LAWS, *evidence*. The laws of a foreign country. They will be considered with regard to, 1. The manner in which they are to be proved. 2. Their effect when proved.

2.—1. The courts do not judicially take notice of foreign laws, and they must therefore be proved as facts. Cowp. 144; 3 Esp. C. 163; 3 Campb. R. 166; 2 Dow & Clark's R. 171; 1 Cranch, 38; 2 Cranch, 187, 236, 237; 6 Cranch, 274; 2 Harr. & John. R. 193; 3 Gill & John. R. 234; 4 Conn. R. 517; 4 Cowen, R. 515, 516, note; Pet. C. C. R. 229; 8 Mass. R. 99; 1 Paige's R. 220: 10 Watts, R. 158. The manner of proof varies according to circumstances. As a general rule the best testimony or proof is required, for no proof will be received which pre-supposes better testimony attainable by the party who offers it. When the best testimony cannot be obtained, secondary evidence will be received. 2 Cranch, 237.

3. Authenticated copies of written laws and other public documents must be produced when they can be procured; but should they be refused by the competent authorities, then inferior proof may be admissible. Id.

4. When our own government has promulgated a foreign law or ordinance of a public nature as authentic, that is held sufficient evidence of its existence. 1 Cranch, 38; 1 Dall. 462; 6 Binn. 321; 12 Serg. & Rawle, 203.

5. When foreign laws cannot be proved by some mode which the law respects as being of equal authority to an oath, they must be verified by the sanction of an oath.

6. The usual modes of authenticating them are by an exemplification under the great seal of a state; or by a copy proved by oath to be a true copy; or by a certificate of an officer authorized by law, which must, itself, be duly authenticated. 2 Cranch, 238· 2 Wend. 411; 6 Wend

475; 5 Serg. & Rawle, 523; 15 Serg. & Rawle, 84; 2 Wash. C. C. R. 175.

7. Foreign unwritten laws, customs and usages, may be proved, and are ordinarily proved by parol evidence; and when such evidence is objected to on the ground that the law in question is a written law, the party objecting must show that fact. 15 Serg. & R. 87; 2 L. R. 154. Proof of such unwritten law is usually made by the testimony of witnesses learned in the law, and competent to state it correctly under oath. 2 Cranch, 237; 1 Pet. C. C. R. 225; 2 Wash. C. C. R. 175; 15 Serg. & R. 84; 4 John. Ch. R. 520; Cowp. 174; 2 Hagg. R. App. 15 to 144.

8. In England certificates of persons in high authority have been allowed as evidence in such cases. 3 Hagg. Eccl. R. 767, 769.

9. The public seal of a foreign sovereign or state affixed to a writing purporting to be a written edict, or law, or judgment, is, of itself, the highest evidence, and no further proof is required of such public seal. 2 Cranch, 238; 2 Conn. R. 85; 1 Wash. C. C. R. 363; 4 Dall. 413, 416, 6 Wend. 475; 9 Mod. 66.

10. But the seal of a foreign court is not, in general, evidence, without further proof, and it must therefore be established by competent testimony. 3 John. R. 310; 2 Harr. & John. 193; 4 Cowen, 526, n.; 3 East, 221.

11. As courts of admiralty are courts under the laws of nations, their seals will be admitted as evidence without further proofs. 5 Cranch, 335; 3 Conn. 171. This is an exception to the general rule.

12. The mode of authenticating the laws and records of the several states of the American Union, is peculiar, and will be found under the article *Authentication*. It may hereby be observed that the rules prescribed by acts of congress do not exclude every other mode of authentication, and that the courts may admit proof of the acts of the legislatures of the several states, although not authenticated under the acts of congress. Accordingly a printed volume, purporting on its face to contain the laws of a sister state, is admissible, as *primâ facie* evidence, to prove the statute law of that state. 4 Cranch, 384; 12 S. & R. 203; 6 Binn. 321; 5 Leigh, 571.

13.—2. The effect of such foreign laws, when proved, is properly referable to the court; the object of the proof of foreign laws, is to enable the court to instruct the jury what is, in point of law, the result from foreign laws, to be applied to the matters in controversy before them. The court are therefore to decide what is the proper evidence of the laws of a foreign country; and when evidence is given of those laws, the court are to judge of their applicability to the matter in issue. Story, Confl. of L. § 638; 2 Harr. & John. 193. 219; 4 Conn. R. 517; 3 Harr. & John. 234, 242; Cowp. 174. Vide *Opinion*.

Foreign nation or state. A nation totally independent of the United States of America

2. The constitution authorizes congress to regulate commerce with "foreign nations." This phrase does not include an Indian tribe, situated within the boundaries of a state, and exercising the powers of government and sovereignty. 5 Pet. R. 1. Vide *Nation*.

Foreign plea. One which, if true, carries the cause out of the court where it is brought, by showing that the matter alleged is not within its jurisdiction. 2 Lill. Pr. Reg. 374; Carth. 402; Lill. Ent. 475. It must be on oath and before imparlance. Bac. Ab. Abatement, R.

FOREIGNERS. Aliens; persons born in another country than the United States, who have not been naturalized. 1 Pet. R. 349. Vide 8 Com. Dig. 615, and the articles *Alien; Citizens*.

FOREJUDGED THE COURT. An officer of the court who is expelled the same, is, in the English law, said to be forejudged the court. Cunn. Dict. h. t.

FOREMAN. The title of the presiding member of a grand jury.

FOREST. By the English law, a forest is a circuit of ground properly under the king's protection, for the peaceable living and abiding of beasts of hunting and the chase, and distinguished not only by having bounds and privileges, but also by having courts and offices. 12 Co. 22. The signification of forest in the United States is the popular one of an extensive piece of woodland. Vide *Purlieu*.

FORESTALLING, *crim. law*. Every practice or device, by act, conspiracy, words, or news, to enhance the price of victuals or other provisions. 3 Inst. 196; Bac. Ab. h. t.; 1 Russ. Cr. 169; 4 Bl. Com. 158.

2. All endeavors whatever to enhance the common price of any merchandise, and all kinds of practices which have that ten-

dency, whether by spreading false rumors, or by buying things in a market before the accustomed hour, are offences at common law, and come under the notion of forestalling, which includes all kind of offences of this nature. Hawk. P. C. b. 1, c. 80, s. 1. Vide 13 Vin. Ab. 430; Dane's Ab. Index, h. t.; 4 Com. Dig. 391; 1 East, Rep. 132.

FORFEITURE, *punishment*, *torts*. Forfeiture is a punishment annexed by law to some illegal act, or negligence, in the owner of lands, tenements, or hereditaments, whereby he loses all his interest therein, and they become vested in the party injured, as a recompense for the wrong which he alone, or the public together with himself, hath sustained. 2 Bl. Com. 267.

2. Lands, tenements and hereditaments, may be forfeited by various means: 1. By the commission of crimes and misdemeanors. 2. By alienation contrary to law. 3. By the non-performance of conditions. 4. By waste.

3.—1. *Forfeiture for crimes*. By the Constitution of the United States, art. 3, s. 3, it is declared that no attainder of treason shall work corruption of blood, or forfeiture, except during the life of the person attainted. And by the Act of April 30, 1790, s. 24, 1 Story's Laws U. S. 88, it is enacted, that no conviction or judgment for any of the offences aforesaid, shall work corruption of blood, or any forfeiture of estate. As the offences punished by this act are of the blackest dye, including cases of treason, the punishment of forfeiture may be considered as being abolished. The forfeiture of the estate for crime is very much reduced in practice in this country, and when it occurs, the state takes the title the party had, and no more. 4 Mason's R. 174; Dalrymple on Feudal Property, c. 4, p. 145–154; Fost. C. L. 95.

4.—2. *Forfeiture by alienation*. By the English law, estates less than a fee may be forfeited to the party entitled to the residuary interest by a breach of duty in the owner of the particular estate. When a tenant for life or years, therefore, by feoffment, fine, or recovery, conveys a greater estate than he is by law entitled to do, he forfeits his estate to the person next entitled in remainder or reversion. 2 Bl. Com. 274. In this country, such forfeitures are almost unknown, and the more just principle prevails, that the conveyance by the tenant operates only on the interest which he possessed, and does not affect the remainder-man or reversioner. 4 Kent, Com. 81, 82, 424; 1 Hill. Ab. c. 4, s. 25 to 34; 3 Dall. Rep. 486; 5 Ohio, R. 30.

5.—3. *Forfeiture by non-performance of conditions*. An estate may be forfeited by a breach or non-performance of a condition annexed to the estate, either expressed in the deed at its original creation, or impliedly by law, from a principle of natural reason. 2 Bl. Com. 281; and see Ad Eject. 140 to 173. Vide article *Re-entry;* 12 Serg. & Rawle, 190.

6.—4. *Forfeiture by waste*. Waste is also a cause of forfeiture. 2 Bl. Com. 283. Vide article *Waste*.

7. By forfeiture is also understood the neglect of an obligor to fulfil his obligation in proper time; as, when one has entered into a bond for a penal sum, upon condition to pay a smaller at a particular day, and he fails to do it, there is then said to be a forfeiture. Again, when a party becomes bound in a certain sum by a recognizance to pay a certain sum, with a condition that he will appear at court to answer or prosecute a crime, and he fails to do it, there is a forfeiture of the recognizance. Courts of equity, and now courts of law, will relieve from the forfeiture of a bond; and, upon a proper case shown, criminal courts will in general relieve from the forfeiture of a recognizance to appear. See 3 Yeates, 93; 2 Wash. C. C. 442; 2 Blackf. 104, 200; Breeze, 257.

Vide, generally, 2 Bl. Com. ch. 18; Bouv. Inst. Index, h. t.; 2 Kent's Com. 318; 4 Id. 422; 10 Vin. Ab. 371, 394; 13 Vin. Ab. 436; Bac. Ab. Forfeiture; Com. Dig. h. t.; Dane's Ab. h. t.; 1 Bro. Civ. L. 252; 4 Bl. Com. 382; and Considerations on the Law of Forfeiture for High Treason, London ed. 1746.

FORFEITURE OF MARRIAGE, *old Eng. law*. The name of a penalty formerly incurred by a ward in chivalry, when he or she married contrary to the wishes of his or her guardian in chivalry. The latter, who was the ward's lord, had an interest in controlling the marriage of his female wards, and he could exact a price for his consent; and, at length, it became customary to sell the marriage of wards of both sexes. 2 Bl. Com. 70.

2. When a male ward refused an equal match provided by his guardian, he was obliged, on coming of age, to pay him the value of the marrriage; that is, as much as

he had been bona fide offered for it; or, if the guardian chose, as much as a jury would assess, taking into consideration all the real and personal property of the ward; and the guardian could claim this value, although he might have made no tender of the marriage. Co. Litt. 82 a; 2 Inst. 92; 5 Co. 126 b; 6 Co. 70 b.

3. When a male ward between his age of fourteen and twenty-one years, refused to accept an offer of an equal match, and during that period formed an alliance elsewhere, without his permission, he incurred *forfeiture of marriage;* that is, he became liable to pay double the value of the marriage. Co. Litt. 78 b, 82 b.

FORGERY, *crim. law.* Forgery at common law has been held to be "the fraudulent making and alteration of a writing to the prejudice of another man's right." 4 Bl. Com. 247. By a more modern writer, it is defined, as "a false making; a making malo animo, of any written instrument, for the purpose of fraud and deceit." 2 East, P. C. 852.

2. This offence at common law is of the degree of a misdemeanor. 2 Russel, 1437. There are many kinds of forgery, especially subjected to punishment by statutes enacted by the national and state legislatures.

3. The subject will be considered, with reference, 1. To the making or alteration requisite to constitute forgery. 2. The written instruments in respect of which forgery may be committed. 3. The fraud and deceit to the prejudice of another man's right. 4. The statutory provisions under the laws of the United States, on the subject of forgery.

4.—1. The making of a whole written instrument in the name of another with a fraudulent intent is undoubtedly a sufficient making; but a fraudulent insertion, alteration, or erasure, even of a letter, in any material part of the instrument, whereby a new operation is given to it, will amount to a forgery; and this, although it be afterwards executed by a person ignorant of the deceit. 2 East, P. C. 855.

5. The fraudulent application of a true signature to a false instrument for which it was not intended, or *vice versa,* will also be a forgery. For example, it is forgery in an individual who is requested to draw a will for a sick person in a particular way, instead of doing so, to insert legacies of his own head, and then procuring the signature of such sick person to be affixed to the paper without revealing to him the legacies thus fraudulently inserted. Noy, 101; Moor, 759, 760; 3 Inst. 170; 1 Hawk. c. 70, s. 2; 2 Russ. on Cr. 318; Bac. Ab. h. t. A.

6. It has even been intimated by Lord Ellenborough, that a party who makes a copy of a receipt, and adds to such copy material words not in the original, and then offers it in evidence on the ground that the original has been lost, may be prosecuted for forgery. 5 Esp. R. 100.

7. It is a sufficient making where, in the writing, the party assumes the name and character of a person in existence. 2 Russ. 327. But the adoption of a false *description* and *addition,* where a false name is not assumed, and there is no person answering the description, is not a forgery. Russ. & Ry. 405.

8. Making an instrument in a fictitious name, or the name of a non-existing person, is equally a forgery, as making it in the name of an existing person; 2 East, P. C. 957; 2 Russ. on Cr. 328; and although a man may make the instrument in his own name, if he represent it as the instrument of another of the same name, when in fact there is no such person, it will be a forgery in the name of a non-existing person; 2 Leach, 775; 2 East, P. C. 963; but the correctness of this decision has been doubted. Rosc. Cr. Ev. 384.

9. Though, in general, a party cannot be guilty of forgery by a mere *non-feasance,* yet, if in drawing a will, he should fraudulently omit a legacy, which he had been directed to insert, and by the omission of such bequest, it would cause a material alteration in the limitation of a bequest to another; as, where the omission of a devise of an estate for life to one, causes a devise of the same lands to another to pass a present estate which would otherwise have passed a remainder only, it would be a forgery. Moor, 760; Noy, 101; 1 Hawk. c. 70, s. 6; 2 East, P. C. 856; 2 Russ. on Cr. 320.

10. It may be observed, that the offence of forgery may be complete without a publication of the forged instrument. 2 East, P. C. 855; 3 Chit. Cr. L. 1038.

11.—2. With regard to the thing forged, it may be observed, that it has been holden to be forgery at common law fraudulently to falsify, or falsely make records and other matters of a public nature; 1 Rolle's Ab. 65, 68; a parish register; 1 Hawk. c. 70; a letter in the name of a magistrate, the governor of a gaol, directing the discharge of a prisoner. 6 Car. & P. 129; S. C. 25 Eng. C. L. R. 315.

12. With regard to private writings, it is forgery fraudulently to falsify or falsely to make a deed or will; 1 Hawk. b. 1, c. 70, s. 10; or any private document, whereby another person may be prejudiced. 2 Greenl. Rep. 365; Addis. R. 33; 2 Binn. R. 322; 2 Russ. on Cr. b. 4, c. 32, s. 2; 2 East, P. C. 861; 3 Chit. Cr. Law, 1022 to 1038.

13.—3. The intent must be to defraud another, but it is not requisite that any one should have been injured; it is sufficient that the instrument forged might have proved prejudicial. 3 Gill & John. 220; 4 W. C. C. R. 726. It has been holden that the jury ought to infer an intent to defraud the person who would have to pay the instrument, if it were genuine, although from the manner of executing the forgery, or from the person's ordinary caution, it would not be likely to impose upon him; and although the object was general to defraud whoever might take the instrument, and the intention of the defrauding in particular, the person who would have to pay the instrument, if genuine, did not enter into the contemplation of the prisoner. Russ. & Ry. 291; vide Russ. on Cr. b. 4, c. 32, s. 3; 2 East, P. C. 853; 1 Leach, 367; 2 Leach, 775; Rosc. Cr. Ev. 400.

14.—4. Most, and perhaps all the states in the Union, have passed laws making certain acts to be forgery, and the national legislature has also enacted several on this subject, which are here referred to. Act of March 2, 1803, 2 Story's L. U. S. 888; Act of March 3, 1813, 2 Story's L. U. S. 1304; Act of March 1, 1823, 3 Story's L. U. S. 1889; Act of March 3, 1825, 3 Story's L. U. S. 2003; Act of October 12, 1837, 9 Laws U. S. 696.

15. The term forgery, is also applied to the making of false or counterfeit coin. 2 Virg. Cas. 356. See 10 Pet. 613; 4 Wash. C. C. 733. For the law respecting the forgery of coin, see article *Money*. And for the act of congress punishing forgery in the District of Columbia, see 4 Sharsw. Cont. of Story's Laws U. S. 2234.

Vide, generally, Hawk. b. 1, c. 51 and 70; 3 Chit. Cr. Law, 1022 to 1048; 4 Bl. Com. 247 to 250; 2 East, P. C. 840 to 1003; 2 Russ. on Cr. b. 4, c. 32; 13 Vin. Ab. 459; Com. Dig. h. t.; Dane's Ab. h. t.; Williams' Just. h. t.; Burn's Just. h. t.; Rosc. Cr. Ev. h. t.; Stark. Ev. h. t. Vide article *Frank*.

FORISFAMILIATION, *law of Scotl.* By this is understood the act by which a father gives to a child his share of his legitime, and the latter renounces all further claim. From this time, the child who has so received his share, is no longer accounted a child in the division of the estate. Ersk. Inst. 655, n. 23; Burt. Man. P. R. part 1, c. 2, s. 3, page 35.

FORM, *practice.* The model of an instrument or legal proceeding, containing the substance and the principal terms, to be used in accordance with the laws; or, it is the act of pursuing, in legal proceedings, and in the construction of legal instruments, the order required by law. Form is usually put in contradistinction to substance. For example, by the operation of the statute of 27 Eliz. c. 5, s. 1, all merely formal defects in pleading, except in dilatory pleas, are aided on general demurrer.

2. The difference between matter of form, and matter of substance, in general, under this statute, as laid down by Lord Hobart, is, that "*that* without which *the right* doth sufficiently appear to the court, is *form;*" but that any defect "by reason whereof the *right appears not,*" is a defect in substance. Hob. 233.

3. A distinction somewhat more definite, is, that if the *matter* pleaded be in itself insufficient, without reference to the manner of pleading it, the defect is substantial; but that if the fault is in the manner of alleging it, the defect is formal. Dougl. 683. For example, the omission of a consideration in a declaration in assumpsit; or of the performance of a condition precedent, when such condition exists; of a conversion of property of the plaintiff, in trover; of knowledge in the defendant, in an action for mischief done by his dog; of malice, in action for malicious prosecution, and the like, are all defects in *substance.* On the other hand, duplicity; a negative pregnant; argumentative pleading; a special plea, amounting to the general issue; omission of a day, when time is immaterial; of a place, in transitory actions, and the like, are only faults in form. Bac. Ab. Pleas, &c. N 5, 6; Com. Dig. Pleader, Q 7; 10 Co. 95 a; 2 Str. 694; Gould, Pl. c. 9, § 17, 18; 1 Bl. Com. 142.

4. At the same time that fastidious objections against trifling errors of form, arising from mere clerical mistakes, are not

encouraged or sanctioned by the courts, it has been justly observed, that "infinite mischief has been produced by the facility of the courts in overlooking matters of form; it encourages carelessness, and places ignorance too much upon a footing with knowledge amongst those who practice the drawing of pleadings." 1 B. & P. 59; 2 Binn. Rep. 434. See, generally, Bouv. Inst. Index, h. t.

FORMA PAUPERIS, *English law*. When a person is so poor that he cannot bear the charges of suing at law or in equity, upon making oath that he is not worth five pounds, and bringing a certificate from a counsellor at law, that he believes him to have a just cause, he is permitted to sue *in forma pauperis*, in the manner of a pauper; that is, he is allowed to have original writs and subpœnas gratis, and counsel assigned him without fee. 3 Bl. Com. 400. See 3 John. Ch. R. 65; 1 Paige, R. 588; 3 Paige, R. 273; 5 Paige, R. 58; 2 Moll. R. 475; 1 Beat. R. 54.

FORMALITY. The conditions which must be observed in making contracts, and the words which the law gives to be used in order to render them valid; it also signifies the conditions which the law requires to make regular proceedings.

FORMEDON, *old Eng. law*. The writ of formedon is nearly obsolete, it having been superseded by the writ of ejectment. Upon an alienation of the tenant in tail, by which the estate in tail is discontinued, and the remainder or reversion is by the failure of the particular estate, displaced and turned into a mere right, the remedy is by action of formedon, (*secundum formam doni*,) because the writ comprehends the *form* of the *gift*. This writ is in the nature of a writ of right, and the action of formedon is the highest a tenant in tail can have. This writ is distinguished into three species; a *formedon* in the *descender*, in the *remainder*, and in the *reverter*. 3 Bl. Com. 191; Bac. Ab. h. t.; 4 Mass. 64.

FORMER RECOVERY. A recovery in a former action.

2. It is a general rule, that in a real or personal action, a judgment unreversed, whether it be by confession, verdict or demurrer, is a perpetual bar, and may be pleaded to any new action of the same or a like nature, for the same cause. Bac. Ab. Pleas, I 12, n. 2; 6 Co. 7; Hob. 4, 5; Ventr. 170.

3. There are two exceptions to this general rule. 1. The case of mutual dealings between the parties, when the defendant omits to set off his counter demand; in that case he may recover in a cross action. 2. When the defendant in ejectment neglects to bring forward his title, he may avail himself of a new suit. 1 John. Cas. 492, 502, 510. It is evident that in these cases the cause of the second action is not the same as that of the first, and, therefore, a former recovery cannot be pleaded. In real actions, one is not a bar to an action of a higher nature. 6 Co. 7. Vide 12 Mass. 337; *Res Judicata; Thing Adjudged*.

FORMULARY. A book of forms or precedents for matters of law; the form.

FORNICATION, *crim. law*. The unlawful carnal knowledge of an unmarried person with another, whether the latter be married or unmarried. When the party is married, the offence, as to him or her, is known by the name of adultery. (q. v.) Fornication is, however, included in every case of adultery, as a larceny is included in robbery. 2 Hale's P. C. 302.

FORPRISE. Taken beforehand. This word is sometimes, though but seldom, used in leases and conveyances, implying an exception or reservation. Forprise, in another sense, is taken for any exaction. Cunn. Dict. h. t.

TO FORSWEAR, *crim. law, torts*. To swear to a falsehood.

2. This word has not the same meaning as perjury. It does not, *ex vi termini*, signify a false swearing before an officer or court having authority to administer an oath, on an issue. A man may be forsworn by making a false oath before an incompetent tribunal, as well as before a lawful court. Hence, to say that a man is forsworn, will or will not be slander, as the circumstances show that the oath was or was not taken before a lawful authority. Cro. Car. 378; Lut. 1292; 1 Rolle, Ab. 39, pl. 7; Bac. Ab. Slander, B 3; Cro. Eliz. 609; 13 Johns. R. 80; Id. 48; 12 Mass. 496; 1 Johns. R. 505; 2 Johns. R. 10; 1 Hayw. R. 116.

FORTHWITH. When a thing is to be done forthwith, it seems that it must be performed as soon as by reasonable exertion, confined to that object, it may be done. This is the import of the term; it varies, of course, with every particular case. 4 Tyr. 837; Styles' Register, 452, 3.

FORTIORI or A FORTIORI. An epi

thet for any conclusion or inference, which is much stronger than another. "If it be so, in a feoffment passing a new right, *à fortiori*, *much more* is it for the restitution of an ancient right." Co. Litt. 253, 260.

FORTUITOUS EVENT. A term in the civil law to denote that which happens by a cause which cannot be resisted. Louis. Code, art. 2522, No. 7. Or it is that which neither of the parties has occasioned or could prevent. Lois des Bât. Pt. 2, c. 2, § 1. It is also defined to be an unforeseen event which cannot be prevented. Dict. de Jurisp. Cas fortuit.

2. There is a difference between a fortuitous event or inevitable accident, and irresistible force. By the former, commonly called the act of God, is meant any accident produced by physical causes, which are irresistible; such as a loss by lightning or storms, by the perils of the seas, by inundations and earthquakes, or by sudden death or illness. By the latter is meant such an interposition of human agency, as is, from its nature and power, absolutely uncontrollable. Of this nature are losses occasioned by the inroads of a hostile army, or by public enemies. Story on Bailm. § 25; Lois des Bât. Pt. 2, c. 2, § 1.

3. Fortuitous events are fortunate or unfortunate. The accident of finding a treasure is a fortuitous event of the first class. Lois des Bât. Pt. 2, c. 2, § 2.

4. Involuntary obligations may arise in consequence of fortuitous events. For example, when, to save a vessel from shipwreck, it is necessary to throw goods overboard, the loss must be borne in common; there arises, in this case, between the owners of the vessel and of the goods remaining on board, an obligation to bear proportionably the loss which has been sustained. Lois des Bât. Pt. 2, c. 2, § 2.

See, in general, Dig. 50, 17, 23; Id. 16, 3, 1; Id. 19, 2, 11; Id. 44, 7, 1; Id. 18, 6, 10; Id. 13, 6, 18; Id. 26, 7, 50; *Act of God; Accident; Perils of the Sea.*

FORUM. This term signifies jurisdiction, a court of justice, a tribunal.

2. The French divide it into *for extérieur*, which is the authority which human justice exercises on persons and property, to a greater or lesser extent, according to the quality of those to whom it is entrusted; and *for intérieur*, which is the moral sense of justice which a correct conscience dictates. Merlin, Répert. mot For.

3. By forum res sitæ is meant the tribunal which has authority to decide respecting something in dispute, located within its jurisdiction; therefore, if the matter in controversy is land, or other immovable property, the judgment pronounced in the *forum res sitæ* is held to be of universal obligation, as to all matters of right and title on which it professes to decide, in relation to such property. And the same principle applies to all other cases of proceedings *in rem*, where the subject is movable property, within the jurisdiction of the court pronouncing the judgment. Story, Confl. Laws, §§ 532, 545, 551, 591, 592; Kaims on Eq. B. 3, c. 8, s. 4; 1 Greenl. Ev. § 541.

FORWARDING MERCHANT, *contracts*. A person who receives and forwards goods, taking upon himself the expenses of transportation, for which he receives a compensation from the owners, but who has no concern in the vessels or wagons by which they are transported, and no interest in the freight. Such an one is not deemed a common carrier, but a mere warehouseman or agent. 12 Johns. 232; 7 Cowen's R. 497. He is required to use only ordinary diligence in sending the property by responsible persons. 2 Cowen's R. 593.

FOSSA, *Eng. law.* A ditch full of water, where formerly women who had committed a felony were drowned; the grave. Cowel, Int.

FOUNDATION. This word, in the English law, is taken in two senses, *fundatio incipiens*, and *fundatio perficiens*. As to its political capacity, an act of incorporation is metaphorically called its foundation; but as to its dotation, the first gift of revenues is called the foundation. 10 Co. 23, a.

FOUNDLING. A new-born child, abandoned by its parents, who are unknown. The settlement of such a child is in the place where found.

FOURCHER, *English law.* A French word, which means to fork. Formerly, when an action was brought against two, who, being jointly concerned, were not bound to answer till both appeared, and they agreed not to appear both in one day; the appearance of one excused the other's default, who had a day given him to appear with the other: the defaulter, on the day appointed, appeared; but the first then made default; in this manner they forked each other, and practiced this for delay. Vide 2 Inst. 250; Booth, R. A. 16.

FRACTION. A part of any thing broken. A combination of numbers, in arithmetic and algebra, representing one or more parts of a unit or integer. Thus, four-fifths is a fraction, formed by dividing a unit into five equal parts, and taking one part four times. In law, the term fraction is usually applied to the division of a day.

2. In general, there are no fractions in days. Co. Litt. 225; 2 Salk. 625; 2 P. A. Browne, 18; 11 Mass. 204. But in some cases a fraction will be taken into the account, in order to secure a party his rights; 3 Chit. Pr. 111; 8 Ves. 80; 4 Campb. R. 197; 2 B. & Ald. 586; Savig. Dr. Rom. § 182; Rob. Dig. of Engl. Statutes in force in Pennsylvania, 431-2; and when it is required by a special law. Vide article *Date*.

FRANC, *com. law*. The name of a French coin. Five franc pieces, when not of less fineness than ten ounces and sixteen pennyweights in twelve ounces troy weight of standard silver, and weighing not less than three hundred and eighty-four grains each, are made a legal tender, at the rate of ninety-three cents each. Act of June 25, 1834, s. 1, 4 Sharsw. cont. of Story's L. U. S. 2373.

2. In all computations at the custom-house, the franc of France and of Belgium shall be estimated at eighteen cents six mills. Act of May 22, 1846. See *Foreign coins*.

FRANCHISE. This word has several significations: 1. It is a right reserved to the people by the constitution; hence we say, the elective franchise, to designate the right of the people to elect their officers. 2. It is a certain privilege, conferred by grant from the government, and vested in individuals.

2. Corporations, or bodies politic, are the most usual franchises known to our law. They have been classed among incorporeal hereditaments, perhaps improperly, as they have no inheritable quality.

3. In England, franchises are very numerous; they are said to be royal privileges in the hands of a subject. Vide 3 Kent, Com. 366; 2 Bouv. Inst. n. 1686; Cruise, Dig. tit. 27; 2 Bl. Com. 37; 15 Serg. & Rawle, 130; Finch, 164.

FRANCIGENA. Formerly, in England, every alien was known by this name, as Franks is the generic name of foreigners in the Turkish dominions.

FRANK. The privilege of sending and receiving letters, through the mails, free of postage.

2. This privilege is granted to various officers, not for their own special benefit, but with a view to promote the public good.

3. The Act of the 3d of March, 1845, s. 1, enacts, That members of congress, and delegates from the territories, may receive letters, not exceeding two ounces in weight, free of postage, during the recess of congress; and the same privilege is extended to the vice-president of the United States.

4. It is enacted, by 3d section, That all printed or lithographed circulars and handbills, or advertisements, printed or lithographed, on quarto post or single cap paper, or paper not larger than single cap, folded, directed, and unsealed, shall be charged with postage, at the rate of two cents for each sheet, and no more, whatever be the distance the same may be sent; and all pamphlets, magazines, periodicals, and every other kind and description of printed or other matter, (except newspapers,) which shall be unconnected with any manuscript communication whatever, and which it is or may be lawful to transmit by the mail of the United States, shall be charged with postage, at the rate of two and a half cents for each copy sent, of no greater weight than one ounce, and one cent additional shall be charged for each additional ounce of the weight of every such pamphlet, magazine, matter, or thing, which may be transmitted through the mail, whatever be the distance the same may be transported; and any fractional excess, of not less than one-half of an ounce, in the weight of any such matter or thing, above one or more ounces, shall be charged for as if said excess amounted to a full ounce.

5. And, by the 8th section, That each member of the senate, each member of the house of representatives, and each delegate from a territory of the United States, the secretary of the senate, and the clerk of the house of representatives, may, during each session of congress, and for a period of thirty days before the commencement, and thirty days after the end of each and every session of congress, send and receive through the mail, free of postage, any letter, newspaper, or packet, not exceeding two ounces in weight; and all postage charged upon any letters, packages, petitions, memorials, or other matters or things, received during any session of congress, by any senator, member, or delegate of the

house of representatives, touching his official or legislative duties, by reason of any excess of weight, above two ounces, on the matter or thing so received, shall be paid out of the contingent fund of the house of which the person receiving the same may be a member. And they shall have the right to frank written letters from themselves during the whole year, as now authorized by law.

6. The 5th section repeals all acts, and parts of acts, granting or conferring upon any person whatsoever the franking privilege.

7. The 23d section enacts, That nothing in this act contained shall be construed to repeal the laws granting the franking privilege to the president of the United States when in office, and to all ex-presidents, and the widows of the former presidents, Madison and Harrison.

8. The Act of March 1, 1847, enacts as follows:

§ 3. That all members of congress, delegates from territories, the vice-president of the United States, the secretary of the senate, and the clerk of the house of representatives, shall have the power to send and receive public documents free of postage during their term of office; and that the said members and delegates shall have the power to send and receive public documents, free of postage, up to the first Monday of December following the expiration of their term of office.

§ 4. That the secretary of the senate and clerk of the house of representatives shall have the power to receive, as well as to send, all letters and packages, not weighing over two ounces, free of postage, during their term of office.

§ 5. That members of congress shall have the power to receive, as well as to send, all letters and packages, not weighing over two ounces, free of postage, up to the first Monday in December following the expiration of their term of office.

FRANK, FREE. This word is used in composition, as frank-almoign, frank-marriage, frank-tenement, &c.

FRANK-ALMOIGN, *old English law.* This is a French law word, signifying free-alms.

2. Formerly religious corporations, aggregate or sole, held lands of the donor, to them and their successors forever, in frank-almoign. The service which they were bound to render for these lands was not certainly defined; they were, in general, to pray for the souls of the donor, his ancestors, and successors. 2 Bl. Com. 101.

FRANK-MARRIAGE, *English law.* It takes place, according to Blackstone, when lands are given by one man to another, together with a wife who is daughter or kinswoman of the donor, to hold in *frank-marriage.* By this gift, though nothing but the word frank-marriage is expressed, the donees shall have the tenements to them and the heirs of their two bodies begotten; that is, they are tenants in special tail. It is called *frank* or *free* marriage, because the donees are liable to no service but fealty. This is now obsolete, even in England. 2 Bl. Com. 115.

FRANK-TENEMENT, *estates.* The same as freehold, (q. v.) or *liberum tenementum.*

FRATER. A brother. Vide *Brother.*

FRATRICIDE, *criminal law.* He who kills his brother or sister. The crime of such a person is also called fratricide.

FRAUD, TO DEFRAUD, *torts.* Unlawfully, designedly, and knowingly, to appropriate the property of another, without a criminal intent.

2. *Illustrations.* 1. Every appropriation of the right of property of another is not fraud. It must be unlawful; that is to say, such an appropriation as is not permitted by law. Property loaned may, during the time of the loan, be appropriated to the use of the borrower. This is not fraud, because it is permitted by law. 2. The appropriation must be not only unlawful, but it must be made with a knowledge that the property belongs to another, and with a design to deprive him of the same. It is unlawful to take the property of another; but if it be done with a design of preserving it for the owners, or if it be taken by mistake, it is not done designedly or knowingly, and, therefore, does not come within the definition of fraud. 3. Every species of unlawful appropriation, not made with a criminal intent, enters into this definition, when designedly made, with a knowledge that the property is another's; therefore, such an appropriation, intended either for the use of another, or for the benefit of the offender himself, is comprehended by the term. 4. Fraud, however immoral or illegal, is not in itself a crime or offence, for want of a criminal intent. It only becomes such in the cases provided by law. Liv. System of Penal Law, 739.

FRAUD, *contracts, torts.* Any trick or artifice employed by one person to induce another to fall into an error, or to detain him in it, so that he may make an agreement contrary to his interest. The fraud may consist either, first, in the misrepresentation, or, secondly, in the concealment of a material fact. Fraud, force and vexation, are odious in law. Booth, Real Actions, 250. Fraud gives no action, however, without damage; 3 T. R. 56; and in matters of contract it is merely a defence; it cannot in any case constitute a new contract. 7 Vez. 211; 2 Miles' Rep. 229. It is essentially ad hominem. 4 T. R. 337-8.

2. Fraud avoids a contract, *ab initio*, both at law and in equity, whether the object be to deceive the public, or third persons, or one party endeavor thereby to cheat the other. 1 Fonb. Tr. Equity, 3d ed. 66, note; 6th ed. 122, and notes; Newl. Cont. 352; 1 Bl. R. 465; Dougl. Rep. 450; 3 Burr. Rep. 1909; 3 V. & B. Rep. 42; 3 Chit. Com. Law, 155, 306, 698; 1 Sch. & Lef. 209; Verpl. Contracts, *passim;* Domat, Lois Civ. p. 1, l. 4, t. 6, s. 3, n. 2.

3. The following enumeration of frauds, for which equity will grant relief, is given by Lord Hardwicke, 2 Ves. 155. 1. Fraud, *dolus malus*, may be actual, arising from facts and circumstances of imposition, which is the plainest case. 2. It may be apparent from the intrinsic nature and subject of the bargain itself; such as no man in his senses, and not under delusion, would make on the one hand, and such as no honest and fair man would accept on the other, which are inequitable and unconscientious bargains. 1 Lev. R. 111. 3. Fraud, which may be presumed from the circumstances and condition of the parties contracting. 4. Fraud, which may be collected and inferred in the consideration of a court of equity, from the nature and circumstances of the transaction, as being an imposition and deceit on other persons, not parties to the fraudulent agreement. 5. Fraud, in what are called catching bargains, (q. v.) with heirs, reversioners, or expectants on the life of the parents. This last seems to fall, naturally, under one or more of the preceding divisions.

4. Frauds may be also divided into actual or positive and constructive frauds.

5. An *actual or positive fraud* is the intentional and successful employment of any cunning, deception, or artifice, used to circumvent, cheat, or deceive another. 1 Story, Eq. Jur. § 186; Dig. 4, 3, 1, 2; Id. 2, 14, 7, 9.

6. By *constructive fraud* is meant such a contract or act, which, though not originating in any actual evil design or contrivance to perpetrate a positive fraud or injury upon other persons, yet, by its tendency to deceive or mislead them, or to violate private or public confidence, or to impair or injure the public interests, is deemed equally reprehensible with positive fraud, and, therefore, is prohibited by law, as within the same reason and mischief as contracts and acts done *malo animo*. Constructive frauds are such as are either against public policy, in violation of some special confidence or trust, or operate substantially as a fraud upon private rights, interests, duties, or intentions of third persons; or unconscientiously compromit, or injuriously affect, the private interests, rights or duties of the parties themselves. 1 Story, Eq. ch. 7, § 258 to 440.

7. The civilians divide frauds into *positive*, which consists in doing one's self, or causing another to do, such things as induce a belief of the truth of what does not exist; or *negative*, which consists in doing or dissimulating certain things, in order to induce the opposite party into error, or to retain him there. The intention to deceive, which is the characteristic of fraud, is here present. Fraud is also divided into that which has induced the contract, *dolus dans causum contractui*, and incidental or accidental fraud. The former is that which has been the cause or determining motive of the contract, that without which the party defrauded would not have contracted, when the artifices practised by one of the parties have been such that it is evident, without them, the other would not have contracted. Incidental or accidental fraud is that by which a person, otherwise determined to contract, is deceived on some accessories or incidents of the contract; for example, as to the quality of the object of the contract, or its price, so that he has made a bad bargain. Accidental fraud does not, according to the civilians, avoid the contract, but simply subjects the party to damages. It is otherwise where the fraud has been the determining cause of the contract, *qui causam dedit contractui;* in that case the contract is void. Toull. Dr. Civ. Fr. Liv. 3, t. 3, c. 2, n. § 5, n. 86, et seq. See also 1 Malleville, Analyse de la Discussion de Code Civil, pp. 15, 16; Bouv. Inst. Index, h. t. Vide *Catching bargain; Lesion; Voluntary Conveyance.*

FRAUDS, STATUTE OF. The name commonly given to the statute 29 Car. II., c. 3, entitled "An act for prevention of frauds and perjuries." This statute has been re-enacted in most of the states of the Union, generally with omissions, amendments, or alterations. When the *words* of the statute have been used, the construction put upon them has also been adopted. Most of the acts of the different states will be found in Anthon's Appendix to Shep. Touchst. See also the Appendix to the second edition of Roberts on Frauds.

FRAUDULENT CONVEYANCE. A conveyance of property without any consideration of value, for the purpose of delaying or hindering creditors. These are declared void by the statutes 13 Eliz. c. 6, and 27 Eliz. c. 4, the principles of which have been adopted in perhaps all the states of the American Union. See *Voluntary Conveyance.*

2. But although such conveyance is void as regards purchasers and creditors, it is valid as between the parties. 6 Watts, 429, 453; 5 Binn. 109; 1 Yeates, 291; 3 W. & S. 255; 4 Iredell, 102; 9 Pick. 93; 20 Pick. 247; 3 Mass. 573, 580; 4 Mass. 354; 1 Hamm. 469; 2 South. 738; 2 Hill, S. C. Rep. 488; 7 John. 161; 1 Bl. 262.

FREE. Not bound to servitude; at liberty to act as one pleases. This word is put in opposition to slave.

2. Representatives and direct taxes shall be apportioned among the several states, which may be included within this Union, according to their respective numbers, which shall be determined by adding to the whole number of *free* persons, including those bound to service for a term of years, and excluding Indians not taxed, three-fifths of all other persons. Const. U. S. art. 1, s. 2.

3. It is also put in contradistinction to being bound as an apprentice; as, an apprentice becomes *free* on attaining the age of twenty-one years.

4. The Declaration of Independence asserts that all men are born *free*, and in that sense, the term includes all mankind.

FREE COURSE, *mar. law.* Having the wind from a favorable quarter.

2. To prevent collision of vessels, it is the duty of the vessel having a free course to give way to a vessel beating up to windward and tacking. 3 Hagg. Adm. R. 215, 326. And at sea, it is the duty of such vessel, in meeting another, to go to leeward. 3 Car. & P. 528. See 9 Car. & P. 528; 2 W. Rob. 225; 2 Dodson, 87.

FREE SHIPS. By this is understood neutral vessels. Free ships are sometimes considered as making free goods.

FREE WARREN, *Eng. law.* A franchise erected for the preservation and custody of beasts and fowls of warren. 2 Bl. Com. 39; Co. Litt. 233.

FREEDMEN. The name formerly given by the Romans to those persons who had been released from a state of servitude. Vide *Liberti libertini.*

FREEDOM. Liberty; the right to do what is not forbidden by law. Freedom does not preclude the idea of subjection to law; indeed, it presupposes the existence of some legislative provision, the observance of which insures freedom to us, by securing the like observance from others. 2 Har. Cond. L. R. 208.

FREEHOLD, *estates.* An estate of freehold is an estate in lands or other real property, held by a free tenure, for the life of the tenant or that of some other person; or for some uncertain period. It is called liberum tenementum, frank tenement or freehold; it was formerly described to be such an estate as could only be created by livery of seisin, a ceremony similar to the investiture of the feudal law. But since the introduction of certain modern conveyances, by which an estate of freehold may be created without livery of seisin, this description is not sufficient.

2. There are two qualities essentially requisite to the existence of a freehold estate. 1. Immobility; that is, the subject-matter must either be land, or some interest issuing out of or annexed to land. 2. A sufficient legal indeterminate duration; for if the utmost period of time to which an estate can last, is fixed and determined, it is not an estate of freehold. For example, if lands are conveyed to a man and his heirs, or for his life, or for the life of another, or until he shall be married, or go to Europe, he has an estate of freehold; but if such lands are limited to a man for one hundred or five hundred years, if he shall so long live, he has not an estate of freehold. Cruise on Real Property, t. 1, s. 13, 14 and 15; Litt. § 59; 1 Inst. 42, a; 5 Mass. R. 419; 4 Kent, Com. 23; 2 Bouv. Inst. 1690, et seq. Freehold estates are of inheritance or not of inheritance. Cruise, t. 1, s. 42.

FREEHOLDER. A person who is the owner of a freehold estate.

FREEMAN. One who is in the enjoyment of the right to do whatever he pleases, not forbidden by law. One in the possession of the civil rights enjoyed by the people generally. 1 Bouv. Inst. n. 164. See 6 Watts, 556.

FREIGHT, *mar. law, contracts.* The sum agreed on for the hire of a ship, entirely or in part, for the carriage of goods from one port to another; 13 East, 300, note; but in its more extensive sense it is applied to all rewards or compensation paid for the use of ships. 1 Pet. Adm. R. 206; 2 Boulay-Paty, t. 8, s. 1; 2 B. & P. 321; 4 Dall. R. 459; 3 Johns. R. 335; 2 Johns. R. 346; 3 Pardess, n. 705.

2. It will be proper to consider 1. How the amount of freight is to be fixed. 2. What acts must be done in order to be entitled to freight. 3. Of the lien of the master or owner.

3.—1. The amount of freight is usually fixed by the agreement of the parties, and if there be no agreement, the amount is to be ascertained by the usage of the trade, and the circumstances and reason of the case. 3. Kent, Com. 173. Pothier is of opinion that when the parties agree as to the conveyance of the goods, without fixing a price, the master is entitled to freight at the price usually paid for merchandise of a like quality at the time and place of shipment, and if the prices vary he is to pay the mean price. Charte-part, n. 8. But there is a case which authorizes the master to require the highest price, namely, when goods are put on board without his knowledge. Id. n. 9. When the merchant hires the whole ship for the entire voyage, he must pay the freight though he does not fully lade the ship; he is of course only bound to pay in proportion to the goods he puts on board, when he does not agree to provide a full cargo. If the merchant agrees to furnish a return cargo, and he furnishes none, and lets the ship return in ballast, he must make compensation to the amount of the freight; this is called *dead freight*, (q. v.) in contradistinction to freight due for the actual carriage of goods. Roccus, note 72–75; 1 Pet. Adm. R. 207; 10 East, 530; 2 Vern. R. 210.

4.—2. The general rule is, that the delivery of the goods at the place of destination, in fulfilment of the agreement of the charter party, is required, to entitle the master or owner of the vessel to freight. But to this rule there are several exceptions:

5.—1. When a cargo consists of live stock, and some of the animals die in the course of the voyage, without any fault or negligence of the master or crew, and there is no express agreement respecting the payment of freight, it is in general to be paid for all that were put on board; but when the contract is to pay for the transportation of them, then no freight is due for those which die on the voyage. Molloy, b. 2, c. 4, s. 8; Dig. 14, 2, 10; Abb. Ship. 272.

6.—2. An interruption of the regular course of the voyage, happening without the fault of the owner, does not deprive him of his freight if the ship afterwards proceed with the cargo to the place of destination, as in the case of capture and recapture. 3 Rob. Adm. R. 101.

7.—3. When the ship is forced into a port short of her destination, and cannot finish the voyage, if the owner of the goods will not allow the master a reasonable time to repair, or to proceed in another ship, the master will be entitled to the whole freight; and, if after giving his consent the master refuse to go on, he is not entitled to freight.

8.—4. When the merchant accepts of the goods at an intermediate port, it is the general rule of marine law, that freight is to be paid according to the proportion of the voyage performed, and the law will imply such contract. The acceptance must be voluntary, and not one forced upon the owner by any illegal or violent proceedings, as, from it, the law implies a contract that freight *pro rata parte itineris* shall be accepted and paid. 2 Burr. 883; 7 T. R. 381; Abb. Shipp. part 3, c. 7, s. 13; 3 Binn. 445; 5 Binn. 525; 2 Serg. & Rawle, 229; 1 W. C. C. R. 530; 2 Johns. R. 323; 7 Cranch, R. 358; 6 Cowen, R. 504; Marsh. Ins. 281, 691; 3 Kent, Com. 182; Com. Dig. Merchant, E 3 a note, pl. 43, and the cases there cited.

9.—5. When the ship has performed the whole voyage, and has brought only a part of her cargo to the place of destination; in this case there is a difference between a general ship, and a ship chartered for a specific sum for the whole voyage. In the former case, the freight is to be paid for the goods which may be delivered at their place of destination; in the latter it has been questioned whether the freight could be apportioned, and it seems, that in such case a partial performance is not sufficient, and that a special payment cannot be claimed except in special cases. 1 Johns. R. 24;

1 Bulstr. 167; 7 T. R. 381; 2 Campb. N. P. R. 466. These are some of the exceptions to the general rule, called for by principles of equity, that a partial performance is not sufficient, and that a partial payment or rateable freight cannot be claimed.

10.—6. In general, the master has a lien on the goods, and need not part with them until the freight is paid; and when the regulations of the revenue require them to be landed in a public warehouse, the master may enter them in his own name and preserve the lien. His right to retain the goods may, however, be waived either by an express agreement at the time of making the original contract, or by his subsequent agreement or consent. Vide 18 Johns. R. 157; 4 Cowen, R. 470; 1 Paine's R. 358; 5 Binn. R. 392.

Vide, generally, 13 Vin. Ab. 501; Com. Dig. Merchant, E 3, a; Bac. Ab. Merchant, D; Marsh. Ins. 91; 10 East, 394; 13 East, 300, n.; 3 Kent, Com. 173; 2 Bro. Civ. & Adm. L. 190; Merl. Rép. h. t.; Poth. Charte-Partie, h. t.; Boulay-Paty, h. t.; Pardess. Index, Affrétement.

FREIGHTER, *contracts*. He to whom a ship or vessel has been hired. 3 Kent, Com. 173; 3 Pardess. n. 704.

2. The freighter is entitled to the enjoyment of the vessel according to contract, and the vessel hired is the only one that he is bound to take; there can, therefore, be no substitution without his consent. When the vessel has been chartered only in part, the freighter is only entitled to the space he has contracted for; and in case of his occupying more room, or putting on board a greater weight, he must pay freight on the principles mentioned under the article of freight.

3. The freighter is required to use the vessel agreeably to the provisions of the charter party, or, in the absence of any such provisions, according to the usages of trade; he cannot load the vessel with merchandise which would render it liable to condemnation for violating the laws of a foreign state. 3 John. R. 105. The freighter is also required to return the vessel as soon as the time for which he chartered her has expired, and to pay the freight.

FRESH PURSUIT. The act of pursuing cattle which have escaped, or are being driven away from land, when they were liable to be distrained, into other places. 3 Bouv. Inst. n. 2470.

FRESH SUIT, *Eng. law*. An earnest pursuit of the offender, when a robbery has been committed, without ceasing, until he has been arrested or discovered. Toml. Law Dict. h. t.

FRIBUSCULUM, *civil law*. A slight dissension between husband and wife, which produced a momentary separation, without any intention to dissolve the marriage, in which it differed from a divorce. Poth. Pand. lib. 50, s. 106. Vicat, Vocab. This amounted to a separation, (q. v.) in our law.

FRIENDLESS MAN. This name was sometimes anciently given to an outlaw.

FRIGIDITY, *med. juris*. The same as impotence. (q. v.)

FRUCTUS INDUSTRIALES. The fruits or produce of the earth which are obtained by the industry of man, as growing corn.

FRUIT, *property*. The produce of tree or plant containing the seed or used for food. Fruit is considered real estate, before it is separated from the plant or tree on which it grows; after its separation it acquires the character of personalty, and may be the subject of larceny; it then has all the qualities of personal property.

2. The term fruit, among the civilians, signifies not only the production of trees and other plants, but all sorts of revenue of whatever kind they may be. Fruits may be distinguished into two kinds; the first called natural fruits, are those which the earth produces without culture, as hay, the production of trees, minerals, and the like; or with culture, as grain and the like. Secondly, the other kind of fruits, known by the name of civil fruits, are the revenue which is not produced by the earth, but by the industry of man, or from animals, from some estate, or by virtue of some rule of law. Thus, the rent of a house, a right of fishing, the freight of a ship, the toll of a mill, are called, by a metaphorical expression, fruits. Domat, Lois Civ. liv. 3, tit. 5, s. 3, n. 3. See Poth. De la Communauté, n. 45.

FUERO JURGO. A Spanish code of laws, said to be the most ancient in Europe. Barr. on the Stat. 8, note.

FUGAM FECIT, *Eng. law*. He fled. This phrase, in an inquisition, signifies that a person fled for treason or felony. The effect of this is to make the party forfeit his goods absolutely, and the profits of his lands until he has been pardoned or acquitted.

FUGITIVE. A runaway; one who is at

liberty, and endeavors, by going away, to escape.

FUGITIVE SLAVE. One who has escaped from the service of his master.

2. The Constitution of the United States, art. 4, s. 2, 3, directs that "no person held to service or labor in one state, under the laws thereof, escaping into another, shall, in consequence of any laws or regulation therein, be discharged from such service or labor, but shall be delivered up, on claim of the party to whom such service or labor may be due." In practice summary ministerial proceedings are adopted, and not the ordinary course of judicial investigations, to ascertain whether the claim of ownership be established beyond all legal controversy. Vide, generally, 3 Story, Com. on Const. § 1804–1806; Serg. on Const. ch. 31, p. 387; 9 John. R. 62; 5 Serg. & Rawle, 62; 2 Pick. R. 11; 2 Serg. & Rawle, 306; 3 Id. 4; 1 Wash. C. C. R. 500; 14 Wend. R. 507, 539; 18 Wend. R. 678; 22 Amer. Jur. 344.

FUGITIVE FROM JUSTICE, *crim. law*. One who, having committed a crime within one jurisdiction, goes into another in order to evade the law, and avoid its punishment.

2. By the Constitution of the United States, art. 4, s. 2, it is provided, that "a person charged in any state with treason, felony or other crime, who shall flee from justice, and be found in another state, shall, on demand of the executive authority of the same state from which he fled, be delivered up, to be removed to the state having jurisdiction of the crime." The act of thus delivering up a prisoner, is, by the law of nations, called *extradition*. (q. v.)

3. Different opinions are entertained in relation to the duty of a nation, by the law of nations, independently of any treaty stipulations, to surrender fugitives from justice when properly demanded. Vide 1 Kent, Com. 36; 4 John. C. R. 106; 1 Amer. Jurist, 297; 10 Serg. & Rawle, 125; 3 Story, Com. Const. United States, § 1801; 9 Wend. R. 218; 2 John. R. 479; 5 Binn. R. 617; 4 Johns. Ch. R. 113; 22 Am. Jur. 351; 24 Am. Jur. 226; 14 Pet. R. 540; 2 Caines, R. 213.

4. Before the executive of the state can be called upon to deliver an individual, it must appear, first, that a proper and formal requisition of another governor has been made; secondly, that the requisition was founded upon an affidavit that the crime was committed by the person charged, or such other evidence of that fact as may be sufficient; thirdly, that the person against whom it is directed, is a fugitive from justice. 6 Law Report, 57.

FULL AGE. A person is said to have full age at twenty-one years, whether the person be a man or woman. See *Age*.

FULL COURT. When all the judges are present and properly organized, it is said there is a full court; a court in banc.

FULL DEFENCE, *pleading*. A denial of all wrong or injury. It is expressed in the following formula: "And the said C D, (the defendant,) by E F, his attorney, comes, and defends the wrong or injury, (or force and injury,) when and where it shall behoove him, and the damages and whatsoever else he ought to defend." Bac. Ab. Pleas, &c. D; Co. Litt. 127 b; Lawes on Pl. 89; 2 Chit. Pl. 409; 2 Saund. 209 c; Gould on Pl. c. 2, § 6. See *Defence; Et Cetera; Half Defence*.

FUNCTION, *office*. Properly, the occupation of an office; by the performance of its duties, the officer is said to fill his function. Dig. lib. 32, l. 65, § 1.

FUNCTIONARY. One who is in office or in some public employment.

FUNCTUS OFFICIO. This term is applied to something which once had life and power, but which now has no virtue whatsoever; as, for example, a warrant of attorney on which a judgment has been entered, is *functus officio*, and a second judgment, cannot be entered by virtue of its authority. When arbitrators cannot agree and choose an umpire, they are said to be *functi officio*. Watts. on Arb. 94. If a bill of exchange be sent to the drawee, and he passes it to the credit of the holder, it is *functus officio*, and cannot be further negotiated. 5 Pick. 85. When an agent has completed the business with which he was entrusted, his agency is *functus officio*. 2 Bouv. Inst. n. 1382.

FUNDAMENTAL. This word is applied to those laws which are the foundation of society. Those laws by which the exercise of power is restrained and regulated, are fundamental. The Constitution of the United States is the fundamental law of the land. See Wolff, Inst. Nat. § 984.

FUNDED DEBT. That part of the national debt for which certain funds are appropriated towards the payment of the interest.

FUNDING SYSTEM, *Eng. law*. The name given to a plan which provides that on the creation of a public loan, funds shall immediately be formed, and secured by law, for the payment of the interest, until the state shall redeem the whole, and also for the gradual redemption of the capital itself. This gradual redemption of the capital is called the *sinking* of the debt, and the fund so appropriated is called the *sinking fund*.

FUNDS. Cash on hands; as, A B is in funds to pay my bill on him; stocks, as, A B has $1000 in the funds. By public funds is understood, the taxes, customs, &c. appropriated by the government for the discharge of its obligations.

FUNDUS, *civil law*. Any portion of land whatever, without considering the use or employ to which it is applied.

FUNERAL EXPENSES. Money expended in procuring the interment of a corpse.

2. The person who orders the funeral is responsible personally for the expenses, and if the estate of the deceased should be insolvent, he must lose the amount. But if there are assets sufficient to pay these expenses, the executor or administrator is bound, upon an implied assumpsit, to pay them. 1 Campb. N. P. R. 298; Holt, 309; Com. on Contr. 529; 1 Hawke's R. 394; 13 Vin. Ab. 563.

3. Frequent questions arise as to the amount which is to be allowed to the executor or administrator for such expenses. It is exceedingly difficult to gather from the numerous cases which have been decided upon this subject, any certain rule. Courts of equity have taken into consideration the circumstances of each case, and when the executors have acted with common prudence and in obedience to the will, their expenses have been allowed. In a case where the testator directed that his remains should be buried at a church thirty miles distant from the place of his death, the sum of sixty pounds sterling was allowed. 3 Atk. 119. In another case, under peculiar circumstances, six hundred pounds were allowed. Preced. in Ch. 29. In a case in Pennsylvania, where the intestate left a considerable estate, and no children, the sum of two hundred and fifty-eight dollars and seventy-five cents was allowed, the greater part of which had been expended in erecting a tombstone over a vault in which the body was interred. 14 Serg. & Rawle, 64.

4. It seems doubtful whether the husband can call upon the separate personal estate of his wife, to pay her funeral expenses. 6 Madd. R. 90.

Vide 2 Bl. Com. 508; Godolph. p. 2; 3 Atk. 249; Off. Ex. 174; Bac. Ab. Executors, &c., L 4; Vin. Ab. h. t.

FUNGIBLE. A term used in the civil, French, and Scotch law, it signifies anything whatever, which consists in quantity, and is regulated by number, weight, or measure; such as corn, wine, or money. Hein. Elem. Pand. Lib. 12, t. 1, § 2; 1 Bell's Com. 225 n. 2; Ersk. Pr. Scot. Law, B. 3, t. 1, § 7; Poth. Prêt de Consomption, No. 25; Dict. de Jurisprudence, mot Fongible; Story, Bailm. § 284; 1 Bouv. Inst. n. 987, 1098.

FURCA. The gallows. 3 Inst. 58.

FURIOSUS. An insane man; a madman; a lunatic.

2. In general, such a man can make no contract, because he has no capacity or will: *Furiosus nullum negotium genere potest, quia non intelligit quod agit*. Inst. 3, 20, 8. Indeed, he is considered so incapable of exercising a will, that the law treats him as if he were absent: *Furiosi nulla voluntas est. Furiosus absentis loco est*. Dig. lib. 1, tit. ult. l. 40, l. 124, § 1. See *Insane; Non compos mentis*.

FURLINGUS. A furlong, or a furrow one-eighth part of a mile long. Co. Litt. 5. b.

FURLONG. A measure of length, being forty poles, or one-eighth of a mile. Vide *Measures*.

FURLOUGH. A permission given in the army and navy to an officer or private to absent himself for a limited time.

FURNITURE. Personal chattels in the use of a family. By the term household furniture in a will, all personal chattels will pass which may contribute to the use or convenience of the householder, or the ornament of the house; as, plate, linen, china, both useful and ornamental, and pictures. Amb. 610; 1 John. Ch. R. 329, 388; 1 Sim. & Stu. 189; S. C. 3 Russ. Ch. Cas. 301; 2 Williams on Ex. 752; 1 Rop. on Leg. 203-4; 3 Ves. 312, 313.

FURTHER ASSURANCE. This phrase is frequently used in covenants, when a covenantor has granted an estate, and it is supposed some further conveyance may be required. He then enters into a covenant for further assurance, that is, to make any other conveyance which may be lawfully required.

FURTHER HEARING, *crim. law, practice*. Hearing at another time.

2. Prisoners are frequently committed

for further hearing, either when there is not sufficient evidence for a final commitment, or because the magistrate has not time, at the moment, to hear the whole of the evidence. The magistrate is required by law, and by every principle of humanity, to hear the prisoner as soon as possible after a commitment for further hearing; and if he neglect to do so within a reasonable time, he becomes a trespasser. 10 Barn. & Cresw. 28; S. C. 5 Man. & Ry. 53. Fifteen days were held an unreasonable time, unless under special circumstances. 4 Carr. & P. 134; 4 Day, 98; 6 S. & R. 427.

3. In Massachusetts, magistrates may, by statute, adjourn the case for ten days. Rev. Laws, 135, s. 9.

4. It is the practice in England to commit for three days, and then from three days to three days. 1 Chitty's Criminal Law, 74.

FUTURE DEBT. In Scotland this term is applied to a debt which though created is not due, but is to become so at a future day. 1 Bell's Com. 315, 5th ed.

FUTURE STATE, *evidence*. A state of existence after this life.

2. A witness who does not believe in any future state of existence was formerly inadmissible as a witness. The true test of a witnesses' competency, on the ground of his religious principles, is, whether he believes in the existence of a God, who will punish him if he swears falsely; and within this rule are comprehended those who believe future punishments will not be eternal. 2 Watts & Serg. 263. See the authorities cited under the article *Infidel*. But it seems now to be settled, that when the witness believes in a God who will reward or punish him, even in this world, he is competent. Willes, 550. Vide *Atheist*.

G.

GABEL. A tax, imposition, or duty. This word is said to have the same signification that *gabelle* formerly had in France. Cunn. Dict. h. t. But this seems to be an error; for gabelle signified in that country, previously to its revolution, a duty upon salt. Merl. Rép. h. t. Lord Coke says, that *gabel* or *gavel*, *gablum*, *gabellum*, *gabelletum*, *galbelletum*, and *gavillettum* signify a rent, duty, or service, yielded or done to the king or any other lord. Co. Litt. 142, a.

GAGE, *contracts*. Personal property placed by a debtor in possession of his creditor, as a security for his debt; a pawn. (q. v.) Hence *mortgage* is a dead pledge.

GAGER DEL LEY. *Wager of law*. (q. v.)

GAIN. The word is used as synonymous with profits. (q. v.) See *Fruit*.

GAINAGE, *old Eng. law*. It signifies the draft oxen, horses, wain, plough, and furniture for carrying on the work of tillage by the baser sort of soke men and villeins, and sometimes the land itself, or the profits raised by cultivating it. Bract. lib. 1, c. 9.

GALLON, *measures*. A gallon is a liquid measure, containing two hundred and thirty-one cubic inches, or four quarts.

GALLOWS. An erection on which to hang criminals condemned to death.

GAME. Birds and beasts of a wild nature, obtained by fowling and hunting. Bac. Ab. h. t.; *Animals; Feræ naturæ*.

GAMING. A contract between two or more persons by which they agree to play by certain rules at cards, dice, or other contrivance, and that one shall be the loser, and the other the winner. When considered in itself, and without regard to the end proposed by the players, there is nothing in it contrary to natural equity, and the contract will be considered as a reciprocal gift, which the parties make of the thing played for, under certain conditions.

2. There are some games which depend altogether upon skill, others, upon chance, and some others are of a mixed nature. Billiards is an example of the first; lottery of the second; and backgammon of the last.

3. In general, at common law all games

are lawful, unless some fraud has been practiced, or such games are contrary to public policy. Each of the parties to the contract must, 1. Have a right to the money or thing played for. 2. He must have given his full and free consent, and not been entrapped by fraud. 3. There must be equality in the play. 4. The play must be conducted fairly. But even when all these rules have been observed, the courts will not countenance gaming by giving too easy a remedy for the recovery of money won at play. Bac. Ab. h. t. A.

4. But when fraud has been practiced, as in all other cases, the contract is void; and in some cases, when the party has been guilty of cheating, by playing with false dice, cards and the like, he may be indicted at common law, and fined and imprisoned, according to the heinousness of the offence. 1 Russ. on Cr, 406.

5. Statutes have been passed in perhaps all the states forbidding gaming for money, at certain games, and prohibiting the recovery of money lost at such games. Vide Bac. Ab. h. t.; Dane's Ab. Index, h. t.; Poth. Traité du Jeu; Merlin, Repértoire, mot Jeu; Barbeyrac, Traité du Jeu, tome 1, p. 104, note 4; 1 P. A. Browne's Rep. 171: 1 Overt. R. 360; 3 Pick. 446; 7 Cowen, 496; 1 Bibb, 614; 1 Miss. 635; Mart. & Yerg. 262; 1 Bailey, 315; 6 Rand. 694; 8 Cowen, 139; 2 Blackf. 251; 3 Blackf. 294; and *Stakeholder; Wagers.*

GAMING HOUSES, *crim. law.* Houses kept for the purpose of permitting persons to gamble for money or other valuable thing. They are nuisances in the eye of the law, being detrimental to the public, as they promote cheating and other corrupt practices. 1 Russ. on Cr. 299; Roscoe's Cr. Ev. 663; Hawk. B. 1, ch. 75, s. 6; 3 Denio's R. 101; 8 Cowen, 139. This offence is punished in Pennsylvania, and perhaps in most of the states, by statutory provisions.

GANANCIAL, *Spanish law.* A term which in Spanish signifies nearly the same as acquets. *Bienes gananciales* are thus defined: "Aquellos que el marido y la muger ó cualquiera de los dos adquieren ó aumentan durante el matrimonio por compra ó otro contrato, ó mediante su trabajo é industria, como tambien los frutos de los bienos proprios que cada uno elevó al matrimonio, et de los que subsistiendo este adquieran para si por cualquier titulo." 1 Febr. Nov. lib. 1, tit. 2, c. 8, s. 1. This is a species of community; the property of which it is formed belongs in common to the two consorts, and, on the dissolution of the marriage, is divisible between them in equal shares. It is confined to their future acquisition *durante el matrimonio,* and the *frutos* or rents and profits of the other property. 1 Burge on Confl. of Laws, 418, 419; Aso & Man. Inst. B. 1, t. 7, c. 5, § 1.

GAOL. A prison or building designated by law or used by the sheriff, for the confinement or detention of those, whose persons are judicially ordered to be kept in custody. This word, sometimes written *jail,* is said to be derived from the Spanish *jaula,* a cage, (derived from *caula,*) in French gêole, gaol. 1 Mann. & Gran. 222, note *a.* Vide 6 John. R. 22; 14 Vin. Ab. 9; Bac. Ab. h. t.; Dane's Ab. Index, h. t.; 4 Com. Dig. 619; and the articles *Gaoler; Prison; Prisoner.*

GAOL-DELIVERY, *Eng. law.* To insure the trial, within a certain time, of all prisoners, a patent in the nature of a letter is issued from the king to certain persons, appointing them his justices, and authorizing them to deliver his goals. Cromp. Jurisd. 125; 4 Inst. 168; 4 Bl. Com. 269; 2 Hale, P. C. 22, 32; 2 Hawk. P. C. 14, 28. In the United States, the judges of the criminal courts are required to cause the accused to be tried within the times prescribed by the local statutes, and the constitutions require a speedy trial.

GAOLER. The keeper of a gaol or prison, one who has the legal custody of the place where prisoners are kept.

2. It is his duty to keep the prisoners in safe custody, and for this purpose he may use all necessary force. 1 Hale, P. C. 601. But any oppression of a prisoner under a pretended necessity will be punished; for the prisoner, whether he be a debtor or a criminal, is entitled to the protection of the laws from oppression.

GARDEN. A piece of ground appropriated to raising plants and flowers.

2. A garden is a parcel of a house and passes with it. Br. Feoffm. de terre, 53; 2 Co. 32; Plowd. 171; Co. Litt. 5 b, 56 a, b. But see Moore, 24; Bac. Ab. Grants, I.

GARNISH, *Eng. law.* Money paid by a prisoner to his fellow prisoners on his entrance into prison.

To GARNISH. To warn; to garnish the heir, is to warn the heir. Obsolete.

GARNISHEE, *practice.* A person who has money or property in his possession, belonging to a defendant, which money or property has been attached in his hands, and he has had notice of such attachment; he is so called because he has had warning or notice of the attachment.

2. From the time of the notice of the attachment, the garnishee is bound to keep the property in his hands to answer the plaintiff's claim, until the attachment is dissolved, or he is otherwise discharged. Vide Serg. on Att. 88 to 110; Com. Dig. Attachment, E.

3. There are garnishees also in the action of detinue. They are persons against whom process is awarded, at the prayer of the defendant, to warn them to come in and interplead with the plaintiff. Bro. Abr. Detinue, *passim*.

GARNISHMENT. A warning to any one for his appearance, in a cause in which he is not a party, for the information of the court, and explaining a cause. For example, in the practice of Pennsylvania, when an attachment issues against a debtor, in order to secure to the plaintiff a claim due by a third person to such debtor, notice is given to such third person, which notice is a garnishment, and he is called the garnishee.

2. In detinue, the defendant cannot have a sci. fac. to garnish a third person unless he confess the possession of the chattel or thing demanded. Bro. Abr. Garnishment, 1, 5. And when the garnishee comes in, he cannot vary or depart from the allegation of the defendant in his prayer of garnishment. The plaintiff does not declare *de novo* against the garnishee; but the garnishee, if he appears in due time, may have oyer of the original declaration to which he pleads. See Bro. Abr. Garnishee and Garnishment, pl. 8, and this title, *passim*.

GAUGER. An officer appointed to examine all tuns, pipes, hogsheads, barrels, and tierces of wine, oil, and other liquids, and to give them a mark of allowance, as containing lawful measure.

GAVEL. A tax, imposition or tribute; the same as *gabel*. (q. v.)

GAVELKIND. Given to all the kindred, or the *hold* or *tenure of a family*, not the *kind* of tenure. *Eng. law*. A tenure or custom annexed or belonging to land in Kent, by which the lands of the father are equally divided among all his sons, or the land of the brother among all his brothers, if he have no issue of his own. Litt. s. 210.

GELD, *old Eng. law*. It signifies a fine or compensation for an offence, also, rent, money or tribute.

GEMOTE. An assembly. Wittena gemote, during the time of the Saxons in England, signified an assembly of wise men. The parliament.

GENDER. That which designates the sexes.

2. As a general rule, when the masculine is used it includes the feminine, as, man (q. v.) sometimes includes women. This is the general rule, unless a contrary intention appears. But in penal statutes, which must be construed strictly, when the masculine is used and not the feminine, the latter is not in general included. 3 C. & P. 225. An instance to the contrary, however, may be found in the construction, 25 Ed. III, st. 5, c. 2, § 1, which declares it to be high treason, "When a man doth compass or imagine the death of *our lord the king*," &c. These words, "our lord the king," have been construed to include a *queen* regnant. 2 Inst. 7, 8, 9; H. P. C. 12; 1 Hawk. P. C. c. 17; Bac. Ab. Treason, D.

3. Pothier says that the masculine often includes the feminine, but the feminine never includes the masculine; that according to this rule if a man were to bequeath to another all his horses, his mares would pass by the legacy; but if he were to give all his mares, the horses would not be included. Poth. Introd. au titre 16, des Testaments et Donations Testamentaires, n. 170; 3 Brev. R. 9. In the Louisiana code in the French language, it is provided that the word *fils*, sons, comprehends *filles*, daughters. Art. 3522, n. 1. Vide Ayl. Pand. 57; 4 Car. & Payne, 216; S. C. 19 Engl. Com. Law R. 351; Barr. on the Stat. 216, note; *Feme; Feme covert; Feminine; Male; Man; Sex; Women; Worthiest of blood.*

GENEALOGY. The summary history or table of a house or family, showing how the persons there named are connected together.

2. It is founded on the idea of a lineage or family. Persons descended from the common father constitute a family. Under the idea of degrees is noted the nearness or remoteness of relationship, in which one person stands with respect to another. A series of several persons, descended from a common progenitor, is called a *line*. (q. v.) Children stand to each other in the relation either of full blood or half blood, according as they are descended from the same parents, or have only one parent in common

For illustrating descent and relationship, genealogical tables are constructed, the order of which depends on the end in view. In tables, the object of which is to show all the individuals embraced in a family, it is usual to begin with the oldest progenitor, and to put all the persons of the male or female sex in descending, and then in collateral lines. Other tables exhibit the ancestors of a particular person in ascending lines both on the father's and mother's side. In this way 4, 8, 16, 32, &c. ancestors are exhibited, doubling at every degree. Some tables are constructed in the form of a tree, after the model of canonical law, (*arbor consanguinitatis*,) in which the progenitor is placed beneath, as if for the root or stem. Vide *Branch; Line.*

GENER. A son-in-law. Dig. 50, 16, 156.

GENERAL. This word has several meanings, namely: 1. A principal officer, particularly in the army. 2. Something opposed to special; as, a general verdict, the general issue, which expressions are used in contradistinction to special verdict, special issue. 3. Principal, as the general post office. 4. Not select, as a general ship. (q. v.) 5. Not particular, as a general custom. 6. Not limited, as general jurisdiction. 7. This word is sometimes annexed or prefixed to other words to express or limit the extent of their signification; as *Attorney General*, *Solicitor General*, the *General Assembly*, &c.

GENERAL ASSEMBLY. This name is given in some of the states to the senate and house of representatives, which compose the legislative body.

GENERAL IMPARLANCE, *pleading*. One granted upon a prayer, in which the defendant reserves to himself no exceptions, and is always from one term to another. Gould on Pl. c. 2, § 17.

2. After such imparlance, the defendant cannot plead to the jurisdiction nor in abatement, but only to the action or merits. See *Imparlance.*

GENERAL ISSUE, *pleading*. A plea which traverses or denies at once the whole indictment or declaration, without offering any special matter, to evade it. It is called the general issue, because, by importing an absolute and general denial of what is alleged in the indictment or declaration, it amounts at once to an issue. 2 Bl. Com. 305.

2. The general issue in criminal cases, is, *not guilty*. In civil cases, the general issues are almost as various as the forms of action; in assumpsit, the general issue is *non-assumpsit;* in debt, *nil debet;* in detinue, *non detinet;* in trespass, *non cul.* or *not guilty;* in replevin, *non cepit*, &c.

3. Any matter going to show that a deed or contract, or other instrument is void, may be given in evidence under the general issue; 10 Mass. 267, 274; 14 Pick. 303, 305; such as usury. 2 Mass. 540; 12 Mass. 26; 15 Mass. 48, 54. See 4 N. Hamp. R. 40; 2 Wend. 246; 6 Mass. 460; 10 Mass. 281. But a right to give evidence under the general issue, any matter which would avail under a special plea, does not extend to matters in abatement. 9 Mass. 366; 14 Mass. 273; Gould on Pl. c. 4, pt. 1, § 9, et seq.; *Special Issue.*

GENERAL LAND OFFICE. One of the departments of government of the United States.

2. It was established by the Act of April 25, 1812, 2 Story's Laws U. S. 1238; another act was passed March 24, 1824, 3 Story, 1938, which authorized the employment of additional officers. And it was reörganized by the following act, entitled "An act to reörganize the General Land Office," approved July 4, 1836.

3.—§ 1. *Be it enacted, &c.* That from and after the passage of this act, the executive duties now prescribed, or which may hereafter be prescribed by law, appertaining to the surveying and sale of the public lands of the United States, or in anywise respecting such public lands, and, also, such as relate to private claims of land, and the issuing of patents for all grants of land under the authority of the government of the United States, shall be subject to the supervision and control of the commissioner of the general land office, under the direction of the president of the United States.

4.—§ 2. That there shall be appointed in said office, by the president, by and with the advice and consent of the senate, two subordinate officers, one of whom shall be called principal clerk of the public lands, and the other principal clerk on private land claims, who shall perform such duties as may be assigned to them by the commissioners of the general land office; and in case of vacancy in the office of the commissioner of the general land office, or of the absence or sickness of the commissioner, the duties of said office shall devolve upon and be performed, ad interim, by the principal clerk of the public lands.

5.—§ 3. That there shall be appointed by the president, by and with the advice and consent of the senate, an officer to be styled the principal clerk of the surveys, whose duty it shall be to direct and superintend the making of surveys, the returns thereof, and all matters relating thereto, which are done through the officers of the surveyor general; and he shall perform such other duties as may be assigned to him by the commissioner of the general land office.

6.—§ 4. That there shall be appointed by the president, by and with the consent of the senate, a recorder of the general land office, whose duty it shall be, in pursuance of instructions from the commissioner, to certify and affix the seal of the general land office to all patents for public lands, and he shall attend to the correct engrossing and recording and transmission of such patents. He shall prepare alphabetical indexes of the names of patentees, and of persons entitled to patents; and he shall prepare such copies and exemplifications of matters on file, or recorded in the general land office, as the commissioner may from time to time direct.

7.—§ 5. That there shall be appointed by the president, by and with the advice and consent of the senate, an officer to be called the solicitor of the general land office, with an annual salary of two thousand dollars, whose duty it shall be to examine and present a report to the commissioner, of the state of facts in all cases referred by the commissioner to his attention which shall involve questions of law, or where the facts are in controversy between the agents of government and individuals, or there are conflicting claims of parties before the department, with his opinion thereon; and, also, to advise the commissioner, when required thereto, on all questions growing out of the management of the public lands, or the title thereto, private land claims, Virginia military scrip, bounty lands, and preemption claims; and to render such further professional services in the business of the department as may be required, and shall be connected with the discharge of the duties thereof.

8.—§ 6. That it shall be lawful for the president of the United States, by and with the advice and consent of the senate, to appoint a secretary, with a salary of fifteen hundred dollars per annum, whose duty it shall be, under the direction of the president, to sign in his name, and for him, all patents for land sold or granted under the authority of the United States.

9.—§ 7. That it shall be the duty of the commissioner, to cause to be prepared, and to certify, under the seal of the general land office, such copies of records, books, and papers on file in his office, as may be applied for, to be used in evidence in courts of justice.

10.—§ 8. That whenever the office of recorder shall become vacant, or in case of the sickness or absence of the recorder, the duties of his office shall be performed, ad interim, by the principal clerk on private land claims.

11.—§ 9. That the receivers of the land offices shall make to the secretary of the treasury monthly returns of the moneys received in their several offices, and pay over such money pursuant to his instructions. And they shall also make to the commissioner of the general land office, like monthly returns, and transmit to him quarterly accounts current of the debits and credits of their several offices with the United States.

12.—§ 10. That the commissioner of the general land office shall be entitled to receive an annual salary of three thousand dollars; the recorder of the general land office an annual salary of fifteen hundred dollars; the principal clerk of the surveys, an annual salary of eighteen hundred dollars; and each of the said principal clerks an annual salary of eighteen hundred dollars—from and after the date of their respective commissions; and that the said commissioner be authorized to employ, for the service of the general land office, one clerk, whose annual salary shall not exceed fifteen hundred dollars; four clerks, whose annual salary shall not exceed fourteen hundred dollars each; sixteen clerks, whose annual salary shall not exceed thirteen hundred dollars each; twenty clerks, whose annual salary shall not exceed twelve hundred dollars each; five clerks, whose annual salary shall not exceed eleven hundred dollars each; thirty-five clerks, whose annual salary shall not exceed one thousand dollars each; one principal draughtsman, whose annual salary shall not exceed fifteen hundred dollars; one assistant draughtsman, whose annual salary shall not exceed twelve hundred dollars; two messengers, whose annual salary shall not exceed seven hundred dollars each; three assistant messengers, whose annual salary shall not exceed three hundred and fifty dollars each; and two packers, to make up packages of patents, blank forms, and other things necessary to be transmitted to the district land offices, at a salary of four hundred and fifty dollars each.

13.—§ 11. That such provisions of the Act of the 25th of April, in the year one thousand eight hundred and twelve, entitled An act for the establishment of a general land office in the department of the treasury, and of all acts amendatory thereof, as are inconsistent with the provisions of this act, be, and the same are hereby repealed.

14.—§ 12. That from the first day of the month of October, until the first day of the month of April, in each and every year, the general land office and all the bureaus and offices therein, as well as those in the departments of the treasury, war, navy, state, and general post-office, shall be open for the transaction of the public business at least eight hours in each and every day, except Sundays and the twenty-fifth day of December; and from the first day of April until the first day of October, in each year, all the aforesaid offices and bureaus shall be kept open for the transaction of the public business at least ten hours, in each and every day, except Sundays and the fourth day of July.

15.—§ 13. That if any person shall apply to any register of any land office to enter any land whatever, and the said register shall knowingly and falsely inform the person so applying that the same has already been entered, and refuse to permit the person so applying to enter the same, such register shall be liable therefor, to the person so applying, for five dollars for each acre of land which the person so applying offered to enter, to be recovered by action of debt, in any court of record having jurisdiction of the amount.

16.—§ 14. That all and every of the officers whose salaries are hereinbefore provided for, are hereby prohibited from directly or indirectly purchasing, or in any way becoming interested in the purchase of, any of the public land; and in case of a violation of this section by such officer, and on proof thereof being made to the president of the United States, such officer, so offending, shall be, forthwith, removed from office.

General ship. One which is employed by the master or owners, on a particular voyage, and is hired by a number of persons, unconnected with each other, to convey their respective goods to the place of destination.

2. This contract, although usually made with the master, and not with the owners, is considered in law to be made with them also, and that both he and they are separately bound to the performance of it. Abbott on Ship. 112, 215, 216.

General special imparlance, *pleading*. One in which the defendant reserves to himself "all advantages and exceptions whatsoever." 2 Chit. Pl. 408.

2. This kind of imparlance allows the defendant not only to plead in abatement and to the action, but also to the jurisdiction of the court. Gould on Pl. c. 2, § 19. See *Imparlance*.

General traverse, *pleading*. One preceded by a general inducement, and denying, in general terms, all that is last before alleged on the opposite side, instead of pursuing the words of the allegations, which it denies. Gould on Pl. vii. 5, 6.

2. Of this sort of traverse, the replication *de injuriâ suâ propria, absque tali causa*, in answer to a justification, is a familiar example. Bac. Ab. Pleas, H 1; Steph. Pl. 171; Gould, Pl. c. 7, § 5; Archb. Civ. Pl. 194. Vide *Traverse; Special Traverse.*

GENS. A word used by the Romans to represent race and nation. 1 Tho. Co. Litt. 259, n. 13. In the French law, it is used to signify people or nations, as Droit des Gens, the law of nations.

GENTLEMAN. In the English law, according to Sir Edward Coke, is one who bears a coat of armor. 2 Inst. 667. In the United States, this word is unknown to the law, but in many places it is applied, by courtesy, to all men. See Poth. Proc. Crim. sect. 1, App. § 3.

GENTLEWOMAN. This word is unknown to the law in the United States, and is but little used. In England it was, formerly, a good addition of the state or degree of a woman. 2 Inst. 667.

GENUS. It denotes the number of beings, or objects, which agree in certain general properties, common to them all, so that genus is, in fact, only an abstract idea, expressed by some general name or term; or rather a name or term, to signify what is called an abstract idea. Thus, goods is the generic name, and includes, generally, all personal property; but this word may be restrained, particularly in bequests to such goods as are of the same kind as those previously enumerated. Vide 3 Ves 311; 11 Ves. 657; 1 Eq. Cas. Ab. 201, pl. 14; 2 Ves. sen. 278, 280; Dig. 50, 17, 80; Id. 12, 1, 2, 3.

GEORGIA. The name of one of the original states of the United States of America. George the Second granted a charter to Lord Percival, and twenty others, for the government of the province of Georgia. It was governed under this charter till the year 1751, when it was surrendered to the crown. From that period to the time of the American revolution, the colony was governed as other royal provinces.

2. The constitution of the state, as revised, amended, and compiled by the convention of the state, was adopted at Louisville, on the 30th day of May, 1798. It directs, art. 1, s. 1, that the legislative, executive, and judiciary departments of government shall be distinct, and each department shall be confided to a separate body of magistracy.

3.—1. The legislative power is vested in two separate and distinct branches, to wit, a senate and house of representatives, styled "the General Assembly." 1st. The senate is elected annually, and is composed of one member from each county, chosen by the electors thereof. The senate elect, by ballot, a president out of their own body. 2d. The house of representatives is composed of members from all the counties, according to their respective numbers of free white persons, and including three-fifths of all the people of color. The enumeration is made once in seven years, and any county containing three thousand persons, according to the foregoing plan of enumeration, is entitled to two members; seven thousand to three members; and twelve thousand to four members; but each county shall have at least one, and not more than four members. The representatives are chosen annually. The house of representatives choose their speaker and other officers.

4.—2. The executive power is vested in a governor, elected by the general assembly, who holds his office for the term of two years. In case of vacancy in his office, the president of the senate acts as governor, until the disability is removed, or until the next meeting of the general assembly.

5.—3. The judicial powers of the state are, by the 3d article of the constitution, distributed as follows:

§ 1. The judicial powers of this state shall be vested in a superior court, and in such inferior jurisdictions as the legislature shall, from time to time, ordain and establish. The judges of the superior courts shall be elected for the term of three years, removable by the governor, on the address of two-thirds of both houses for that purpose, or by impeachment and conviction thereon. The superior court shall have exclusive and final jurisdiction in all criminal cases which shall be tried in the county wherein the crime was committed; and in all cases respecting titles to land, which shall be tried in the county where the land lies; and shall have power to correct errors in inferior judicatories by writs of *certiorari*, as well as errors in the superior courts, and to order new trials on proper and legal grounds: Provided, That such new trials shall be determined, and such errors corrected, in the superior court of the county in which such action originated. And the said court shall also have appellative jurisdiction in such other cases as the legislature may by law direct, which shall in no case tend to remove the cause from the county in which the action originated; and the judges thereof, in all cases of application for new trials, or correction of error, shall enter their opinions on the minutes of the court. The inferior courts shall have cognizance of all civil cases, which shall be tried in the county wherein the defendant resides, except in cases of joint obligors, residing in different counties, which may be commenced in either county; and a copy of the petition and process served on the party or parties residing out of the county in which the suit may be commenced, shall be deemed sufficient service, under such rules and regulations as the legislature may direct; but the legislature may, by law, to which two-thirds of each branch shall concur, give concurrent jurisdiction to the superior courts. The superior and inferior courts shall sit in each county twice in every year, at such stated times as the legislature shall appoint.

6.—§ 2. The judges shall have salaries adequate to their services, established by law, which shall not be increased or diminished during their continuance in office; but shall not receive any other perquisites or emoluments whatever, from parties or others, on account of any duty required of them.

7.—§ 3. There shall be a state's attorney and solicitors appointed by the legislature, and commissioned by the governor, who shall hold their offices for the term of three years, unless removed by sentence on impeachment, or by the governor, on the address of each branch of the general assembly. They shall have salaries adequate to their services, established by law, which shall not be increased or diminished during their continuance in office.

8.—§ 4. Justices of the inferior courts shall be appointed by the general assembly, and be commissioned by the governor, and shall hold their commissions during good behaviour, or as long as they respectively reside in the county for which they shall be appointed, unless removed by sentence on impeachment, or by the governor, on the address of two-thirds of each branch of the general assembly. They may be compensated for their services in such manner as the legislature may by law direct.

9.—§ 5. The justices of the peace shall be nominated by the inferior courts of the several counties, and commissioned by the governor; and there shall be two justices of the peace in each captain's district, either or both of whom shall have power to try all cases of a civil nature within their district, where the debt or litigated demand does not exceed thirty dollars, in such manner as the legislature may by law direct. They shall hold their appointments during good behaviour, or until they shall be removed by conviction, on indictment in the superior court, for mal-practice in office, or for any felonious or infamous crime, or by the governor, on the address of two-thirds of each branch of the legislature.

10.—§ 6. The powers of a court of ordinary or register of probates, shall be invested in the inferior courts of each county; from whose decision there may be an appeal to the superior court, under such restrictions and regulations as the general assembly may by law direct; but the inferior court shall have power to vest the care of the records, and other proceedings therein, in the clerk, or such other person as they may appoint; and any one or more justices of the said court, with such clerk or other person, may issue citations and grant temporary letters in time of vacation, to hold until the next meeting of the said court; and such clerk or other person may grant marriage licenses.

11.—§ 7. The judges of the superior courts, or any one of them, shall have power to issue writs of mandamus, prohibition, scire facias, and all other writs which may be necessary for carrying their powers fully into effect.

GERMAN, *relations*, *germanus*. Whole or entire, as respects genealogy or descent; thus, "brother-german," denotes one who is brother both by the father and mother's side; "cousins-german," those in the first and nearest degree, *i. e.* children of brothers or sisters. Tech. Dict.; 4 M. & C. 56.

GERONTOCOMI, *civil law*. Officers appointed to manage hospitals for poor old persons. Clef des Lois Rom. mot Administrateurs.

GESTATION, *med. jur.* The time during which a female, who has conceived, carries the embryo or fœtus in her uterus. By the common consent of mankind, the term of gestation is considered to be ten *lunar* months, or forty weeks, equal to nine *calendar* months and a week. This period has been adopted, because general observation, when it could be correctly made, has proved its correctness. Cyclop. of Pract. Med. vol. 4, p. 87, art. Succession of inheritance. But this may vary one, two, or three weeks. Co. Litt. 123 b, Harg. & Butler's, note 190*; Ryan's Med. Jurisp. 121; Coop. Med. Jur. 18; Civ. Code of Louis. art. 203–211; 1 Beck's Med. Jur. 478. See *Pregnancy*.

GIFT, *conveyancing*. A voluntary conveyance; that is, a conveyance not founded on the consideration of money or blood. The word denotes rather the motive of the conveyance; so that a feoffment or grant may be called a gift when gratuitous. A gift is of the same nature as a settlement; neither denotes a form of assurance, but the nature of the transaction. Watk. Prin. 199, by Preston. The operative words of this conveyance are *do* or *dedi*. The maker of this instrument is called the donor, and he to whom it is made, the donee. 2 Bl. Com. 316; Litt. 59; Touchs. ch. 11.

GIFT, *contracts*. The act by which the owner of a thing, voluntarily transfers the title and possession of the same, from himself to another person who accepts it, without any consideration. It differs from a grant, sale, or barter in this, that in each of these cases there must be a consideration, and a gift, as the definition states, must be without consideration.

2. The manner of making the gift may be in writing, or verbally, and, as far as personal chattels are concerned, they are

equally binding. Perk. § 57; 2 Bl. Com. 441. But real estate must be transferred by deed.

3. There must be a transfer made with an intention of passing the title, and delivering the possession of the thing given, and it must be accepted by the donee. 1 Madd. Ch. R. 176, Am. ed. p. 104; sed vide 2 Barn. & Ald. 551; Noy's Rep. 67.

4. The transfer must be without consideration, for if there be the least consideration, it will change the contract into a sale or barter, if possession be delivered; or if not, into an executory contract. 2 Bl. Com. 440.

5. Gifts are divided into gifts *inter vivos*, and gifts *causa mortis;* and also into simple or proper gifts; that is, such as are to take immediate effect, without any condition; and qualified or improper gifts, or such as derive their force upon the happening of some condition or contingency; as, for example, a *donatio causa mortis.* Vide *Donatio causa mortis; Gifts inter vivos;* and Vin. Ab. h. t.; Com. Dig. Biens, D 2, and Grant; Bac. Ab. Grant; 14 Vin. Ab. 19; 3 M. & S. 7; 5 Taunt. 212; 1 Miles, R. 109.

GIFT INTER VIVOS. A gift made from one or more persons, without any prospect of immediate death, to one or more others.

2. These gifts are so called to distinguish them from gifts causa mortis, (vide *Donatio causa mortis,*) from which they differ essentially. 1. A gift inter vivos, when completed by delivery, passes the title to the thing so that it cannot be recovered back by the giver; the gift *causa mortis* is always given upon the implied condition that the giver may, at any time during his life, revoke it. 7 Taunt. 231; 3 Binn. 366. 2. A gift *inter vivos* may be made by the giver at any time; the donatio causa mortis must be made by the donor while in peril of death. In both cases there must be a delivery. 2 Kent's Com. 354; 1 Beav. R. 605; 1 Miles, R. 109.

GIFTOMAN, *Swedish law.* He who has a right to dispose of a woman in marriage.

2. This right is vested in the father, if living; if dead, in the mother. They may nominate a person in their place: but for want of such nomination, the brothers german; and for want of them, the consanguine brothers; and in default of the latter, uterine brothers have the right, but they are bound to consult the paternal or maternal grandfather. Swed. Code, tit. of Marriage, c. 1.

GILL. A measure of capacity, equal to one-fourth of a pint. Vide *Measure.*

GIRANTEM, *mer. law.* An Italian word, which signifies the drawer. It is derived from *girare*, to draw, in the same manner as the English verb to murder, is transformed into *murdrare* in our old indictments. Hall, Mar. Loans, 183, n.

GIRTH. A girth or yard is a measure of length. The word is of Saxon origin, taken from the circumference of the human body. Girth is contracted from *girdeth*, and signifies as much as girdle. See *Ell.*

GIST, *pleading.* Gist of the action is the essential ground or object of it, in point of law, and without which there is no cause of action. Gould on Pl. c. 4, § 12. But it is observable that the substance or gist of the action is not always the principal cause of the plaintiff's complaint in point of fact, nor that on which he recovers all or the greatest part of his damages.

2. It frequently happens that upon that part of his declaration which contains the substance or gist of the action, he only recovers nominal damages, and he gets his principal satisfaction on account of matter altogether collateral thereto. A familiar instance of this is the case where a father sues the defendant for a trespass for the seduction of his daughter. The gist of the action is the trespass, and the loss of his daughter's services, but the collateral cause is the injury done to his feelings, for which the principal damages are given. In stating the substance or gist of the action, every thing must be averred which is necessary to be proved at the trial. Vide 1 Vin. Ab. 598; 2 Phil. Ev. 1, note. See Bac. Abr. Pleas, B; Doct. Pl. 85. See *Damages, special, in pleading;* 1 Vin. Ab. 598; 2 Phil. Ev. 1, n.

GIVER, *contracts.* He who makes a gift. (q. v.) By his gift, the giver always impliedly agrees with the donee that he will not revoke the gift.

GIVING IN PAYMENT. This term is used in Louisiana; it signifies that a debtor, instead of paying a debt he owes in money, satisfies his creditor by giving in payment a movable or immovable. Vide *Dation en paiement.*

GIVING TIME, *contracts.* Any agreement by which a creditor gives his debtor a delay or time in paying his debt, beyond that contained in the original agreement. When other persons are responsible to him, either as drawer, endorser, or surety, if such time be given without the consent of the latter, it discharges them from responsibility to him. 1 Gall. Rep. 32; 7 John. R. 332; 10 John. Rep. 180; Id. 587; Kirby, R. 397; 3 Binn. R. 523; 2 John. Ch. R. 554; 3 Desaus. Ch. Rep. 604; 2 Desaus. Ch. R. 230, 389; 2 Ves. jr. 504; 6 Ves. jr. 805; 3 Atk. 91; 2 Bos. & Pull. 62; 4 M. & S. 232; Bac. Ab. Obligations, D; 6 Dow. P. C. 238; 3 Meriv. R. 272: 5 Barn. & A. 187. Vide 1 Leigh's N. P. 31; 1 B. & P. 652; 2 B. & P. 61; 3 B. & P. 363; 8 East, R. 570; 3 Price, R. 521; 2 Campb. R. 178; 12 East, R. 38; 5 Taunt. R. 319; S. C. 1 E. C. L. R. 119; Rosc. Civ. Ev. 171; 8 Watts, R. 448; 4 Penn. St. R. 73; 10 Paige, 76; and the article *Forbearance*.

2. But mere delay in suing, without fraud or any agreement with the principal, is not such giving time as will discharge the surety. 1 Gallis. 32; 2 Pick. 581; 3 Blackf. 93; 7 John. 332. See *Surety*.

GLADIUS. In our old Latin authors, and in the Norman laws, this word was used to signify supreme jurisdiction, *jus gladii*.

GLEANING. The act of gathering such grain in a field where it grew, as may have been left by the reapers after the sheaves were gathered.

2. There is a custom in England, it is said, by which the poor are allowed to enter and glean upon another's land after harvest without being guilty of a trespass. 3 Bl. Com. 212. But it has been decided that the community are not entitled to claim this privilege as a right. 1 Hen. Bl. 51. In the United States, it is believed, no such right exists. This right seems to have existed in some parts of France. Merl. Rép. mot Glanage. As to whether gleaning would or would not amount to larceny, vide Woodf. Landl. & Ten. 242; 2 Russ. on Cr. 99. The Jewish law may be found in the 19th chapter of Leviticus, verses 9 and 10. See Ruth, ii. 2, 3; Isaiah, xvii. 6.

GLEBE, *eccl. law*. The land which belongs to a church. It is the dowry of the church. Gleba est terra qua consistit dos ecclesiæ. Lind. 254; 9 Cranch, Rep. 329. In the civil law it signified the soil of an inheritance; there were serfs of the glebe, called *glebæ addicti*. Code, 11, 47, 7 et 21; Nov. 54, c. 1.

GLOSS. Interpretation, comment, explanation, or remark, intended to illustrate the text of an author.

GLOSSATOR. A commentator or annotator of the Roman law. One of the authors of the Gloss.

GLOUCESTER, STATUTE OF. An English statute, passed 6 Edw. I., A. D., 1278; so called, because it was passed at Gloucester. There were other statutes made at Gloucester, which do not bear this name. See stat. 2 Rich. II.

GO WITHOUT DAY. These words have a technical sense. When a party is dismissed the court, he is said to go without day; that is, there is no day appointed for him to appear again.

GOD. From the Saxon *god*, good. The source of all good; the supreme being.

1. Every man is presumed to believe in God, and he who opposes a witness on the ground of his unbelief is bound to prove it. 3 Bouv. Inst. n. 3180.

2. *Blasphemy* against the Almighty, by denying his being or providence, was an offence punishable at common law by fine and imprisonment, or other infamous corporal punishment. 4 Bl. Com. 60; 1 East, P. C. 3; 1 Russ. on Crimes, 217. This offence has been enlarged in Pennsylvania, and perhaps most of the states, by statutory provision. Vide *Christianity; Blasphemy;* 11 Serg. & Rawle, 394.

3. By article 1, of amendments to the Constitution of the United States, it is provided that "Congress shall make no laws respecting an establishment of religion, or prohibiting the free exercise thereof." In the United States, therefore, every one is allowed to worship God according to the dictates of his own conscience.

GOD AND MY COUNTRY. When a prisoner is arraigned, he is asked, How will you be tried? he answers, *By God and my country*. This practice arose when the prisoner had the right to choose the mode of trial, namely, by ordeal or by jury, and then he elected by *God* or by *his country*, that is, by jury. It is probable that originally it was *By God* or *my country;* for the question asked supposes an option in the prisoner, and the answer is meant to assert his innocence by declining neither sort of trial. 1 Chit. Cr. Law, 416; Barr. on the Stat. 73, note.

GOD BOTE, *eccl. law*. An ecclesiastical or church fine imposed upon an offender for crimes and offences committed against God.

GOING WITNESS. One who is going out of the jurisdiction of the court, although only into a state or country under the general sovereignty; as, for example, if he is going from one to another of the United States; or, in Great Britain, from England to Scotland. 2 Dick. 454.

GOLD. A metal used in making money, or coin. It is pure when the metal is unmixed with any other. Standard gold, is gold mixed with some other metal, called alloy. Vide *Money*.

GOOD BEHAVIOUR. Conduct authorized by law. Surety of good behaviour may be demanded from any person who is justly suspected, upon sufficient grounds, of intending to commit a crime or misdemeanor. Surety for good behaviour is somewhat similar to surety of the peace, but the recognizance is more easily forfeited, and it ought to be demanded with greater caution. 1 Binn. 98, n.; 2 Yeates, 437; 14 Vin. Ab. 21; Dane's Ab. Index, h. t. As to what is a breach of good behaviour, see 2 Mart. N. S. 683; Hawk. b. 1, c. 61, s. 6; 1 Chit. Pr. 676. Vide *Surety of the peace*.

GOOD AND LAWFUL MEN, *probi et legales homines*. The law requires that those who serve on juries shall be good and lawful men; by which is understood those qualified to serve on juries; that is, that they be of full age, citizens, not infamous nor *non compos mentis*, and they must be resident in the county where the venue is laid. Bac. Ab. Juries, A; Cro. Eliz. 654; 3 Inst. 30; 2 Rolle's R. 82; Cam. & Norw. 38.

GOOD CONSIDERATION, *contracts*. A good consideration is one which flows from kindred or natural love and affection alone, and is not of a pecuniary nature. Vin. Ab. Consideration, B; 1 Bouv. Inst. n. 613. Vide *Consideration*.

GOOD WILL. By this term is meant the benefit which arises from the establishment of particular trades or occupations. Mr. Justice Story describes a good will to be the advantage or benefit which is acquired by an establishment, beyond the mere value of the capital, stocks, funds, or property employed therein, in consequence of the general public patronage and encouragement, which it receives from constant or habitual customers, on account of its local position, or common celebrity, or reputation for skill or affluence, or punctuality, or from other accidental circumstances or necessities, or even from ancient partialities, or prejudices. Story, Partn. § 99; see 17 Ves. 336; 1 Hoffm. R. 68; 16 Am. Jur. 87.

2. As between partners, it has been held that the good-will of a partnership trade survives; 5 Ves. 539; but this appears to be doubtful; 15 Ves. 227; and a distinction, in this respect, has been suggested between commercial and professional partnerships; the advantages of established connexions in the latter being held to survive, unless the benefit is excluded by positive stipulation. 3 Madd. 79. As to the sale of the good-will of a trade or business, see 3 Meriv. 452; 1 Jac. & Walk. 589; 2 Swanst. 332; 1 Ves. & Beames, 505; 17 Ves. 346; 2 Madd. 220; Gow on Partn. 428; Collyer on Partn. 172, note; 2 B. & Adolph. 341; 4 Id. 592, 596; 1 Rose, 123; 5 Russ. 29; 2 Watts, 111; 1 Chit. Pr. 858; 1 Sim. & Stu. 74; 2 Russ. R. 170; 1 Jac. & W. 380; 1 Russ. R. 376; 1 P. & W. 184; 2 Mad. R. 198; 1 T. R. 118. Vide 5 Bos. & Pull. 67; 1 Bro. C. C. 160, as to the effect of a bankrupt's assignment on a good-will; and 16 Amer. Jur. 87.

GOODS, *property*. For some purposes this term includes money, valuable securities, and other mere personal effects. The term *goods and chattels*, includes not only personal property in possession, but also choses in action. 12 Co. 1; 1 Atk. 182. The term *chattels* is more comprehensive than that of *goods*, and will include all animate as well as inanimate property, and also a *chattel real*, as a lease for years of house or land. Co. Litt. 118; 1 Russ. Rep. 376. The word *goods* simply and without qualification, will pass the whole personal estate when used in a will, including even stocks in the funds. But in general it will be limited by the context of the will. Vide 2 Supp. to Ves. jr. 289; 1 Chit. Pr. 89, 90; 1 Ves. jr. 63; Hamm. on Parties, 182; 3 Ves. 212; 1 Yeates, 101; 2 Dall. 142; Ayl. Pand. 296; Wesk. Ins. 260; 1 Rop. on Leg. 189; 1 Bro. C. C. 128; Sugd. Vend. 493, 497; and the articles *Biens; Chattels; Furniture*.

2. Goods are said to be of different kinds, as *adventitious*, such as are given or arise otherwise than by succession; *dotal goods*, or those which accrue from a dowry, or marriage portion; *vacant goods*, those which are abandoned or left at large.

GOODS SOLD AND DELIVERED. This phrase is frequently used in actions of assumpsit, and the sale and delivery of goods are the foundation of the action. When a plaintiff declares for goods sold and delivered, he is required to prove, first, the contract of sale; secondly, the delivery of the goods, or such disposition of them as will be equivalent to it; and, thirdly, their value. 11 Shepl. 505. These will be separately considered.

2.—1. The contract of *sale* may be express, as where the purchaser actually bought the goods on credit, and promised to pay for them at a future time; or implied, where from his acts the defendant manifested an intention to buy them; as, for example, when one takes goods by virtue of a sale made by a person who has no authority to sell, and the owner afterwards affirms the contract, he may maintain an action for goods sold and delivered. 12 Pick. 120. Again, if the goods come to the hands of the defendant tortiously, and are converted by him to his own use, the plaintiff may waive the tort, and recover as for goods sold and delivered. 3 N. H. Rep. 384; 1 Miss. R. 430, 643; 3 Watts, 277; 5 Pick. 285; 4 Binn. 374; 2 Gill & John. 326; 3 Dana, 552; 5 Greenl. 323.

3.—2. The *delivery* must be made in accordance with the terms of the sale, for if there has not been such delivery no action can be maintained. 2 Ired. R. 12; 15 Pick. 171; 3 John. 534.

4.—3. The plaintiff must prove the *value* of the goods; where there is an express agreement as to their value, that must be established by evidence, but where there is no such express agreement, the value of the goods at the time of sale must be proved. Coxe, 261. And the purchaser of goods cannot defend, against an action for the purchase money, by showing that the property was of no value. 8 Port. 133.

5. To support an action for goods sold and delivered, it is indispensable that the goods should have been sold for money, and that the credit on which they were sold should have expired. But where the goods have been sold on a credit to be paid for by giving a note or bill, and the purchaser does not give it according to contract, although the seller cannot recover in assumpsit for goods sold and delivered till the credit has expired, yet he may proceed immediately for a breach of the agreement. 21 Wend. 175.

6. When goods have been sold to be paid for partly in money, and partly in goods to be delivered to the vendor, the plaintiff must declare specially, and he can not recover on the common count for goods sold and delivered. 1 Chit. Pl. 339; 1 Leigh's N. P. 88; 1 H. Bl. 287; Holt, 179.

GOUT, *med. jur., contracts.* An inflammation of the fibrous and ligamentous parts of the joints.

2. In cases of insurance on lives, when there is warranty of health, it seems that a man subject to the gout, is a life capable of being insured, if he has no sickness at the time to make it an unequal contract. 2 Park, Ins. 583.

GOVERNMENT, *natural and political law.* The manner in which sovereignty is exercised in each state.

2. There are three simple forms of government, the democratic, the aristocratic, and monarchical. But these three simple forms may be varied to infinity by the mixture and divisions of their different powers. Sometimes by the word government is understood the body of men, or the individual in the state, to whom is entrusted the executive power. It is taken in this sense when the government is spoken of in opposition to other bodies in the state.

3. Governments are also divided into monarchical and republican; among the monarchical states may be classed empires, kingdoms, and others; in these the sovereignty resides in a single individual. There are some monarchical states under the name of duchies, counties, and the like. Republican states are those where the sovereignty is in several persons. These are subdivided into aristocracies, where the power is exercised by a few persons of the first rank in the state; and democracies, which are those governments where the common people may exercise the highest powers. 1 Bouv. Inst. n. 20. See *Aristocracy; Democracy; Despotism; Monarchy; Theocracy.*

4. It should be remembered, however, that governments, for the most part, have not been framed on models. Their parts and their powers grew out of occasional acts, prompted by some urgent expediency, or some private interest, which, in the course of time, coalesced and hardened into usages. These usages became the object of respect and the guide of conduct long before they were embodied in written laws. This subject is philosophically treated by Sir James McIntosh, in his History of England. See vol. 1, p. 71, et seq.

GOVERNOR. The title of the execu

tive magistrate in each state and territory of the United States. Under the names of the particular states, the reader will find some of the duties of the governor of such state.

GRACE. That which a person is not entitled to by law, but which is extended to him as a favor; a pardon, for example, is an act of grace. There are certain days allowed to a payer of a promissory note or bill of exchange, beyond the time which appears on its face, which are called *days of grace*. (q. v.)

GRADUS. This is a Latin word, literally signifying a step; figuratively it is used to designate a person in the ascending or descending line, in genealogy; a degree.

GRAFFER. This word is a corruption of the French word *greffier*, a clerk, or prothonotary. It signifies a notary or scrivener; vide stat. 5 Hen. VIII. c. 1.

GRAFT. A figurative term in chancery practice, to designate the right of a mortgagee in premises, to which the mortgagor at the time of making the mortgage had an imperfect title, but who afterwards obtained a good title. In this case the new mortgage is considered a *graft* into the old stock, and, as arising in consideration of the former title. 1 Ball & Beat. 46; Id. 40; Id. 57; 1 Pow. on Mortg. 190. See 9 Mass. 34. The same principle has obtained by legislative enactment in Louisiana. If a person contracting an obligation towards another, says the Civil Code, art. 2371, grants a mortgage on property of which he is not then the owner, this mortgage shall be valid, if the debtor should ever acquire the ownership of the property, by whatever right.

GRAIN, *weight*. The twenty-fourth part of a pennyweight.

2. For scientific purposes the grain only is used, and sets of weights are constructed in decimal progression, from 10,000 grains downward to one hundredth of a grain.

GRAIN, *corn*. It signifies wheat, rye, barley, or other corn sown in the ground. In Pennsylvania, a tenant for a certain term is entitled to the way-going crop. 5 Binn. 289, 258; 2 Binn. 487; 2 Serg. & Rawle, 14.

GRAINAGE, *Eng. law*. The name of an ancient duty collected in London, consisting of one-twentieth part of the salt imported into that city.

GRAMME. A French weight. The gramme is the weight of a cubic centimetre of distilled water, at the temperature of zero. It is equal to 15.4441 grains troy, or 5.6481 drachms avoirdupois. Vide *Measure*.

GRAND. An epithet frequently used to denote that the thing to which it is joined is of more importance and dignity, than other things of the same name; as, *grand assize*, a writ in a real action to determine the right of property in land; *grand cape*, a writ used in England, on a plea of land, when the tenant makes default in appearance at the day given for the king to take the land into his hands; *grand days*, among the English lawyers, are those days in term which are solemnly kept in the inns of court and chancery, namely, Candlemas day, in Hilary term; Ascension day, in Easter term; and All Saint's day, in Michaelmas term; which days are *dies non juridici*. *Grand distress* is the name of a writ so called because of its extent, namely, to all the goods and chattels of the party distrained within the county; this writ is believed to be peculiar to England. *Grand Jury*. (q. v.) *Grand serjeantry*, the name of an ancient English military tenure.

GRAND BILL OF SALE, *Eng. law*. The name of an instrument used for the transfer of a ship, while she is at sea; it differs from a common bill of sale. (q. v.) See 7 Mart. Lo. R. 318; 1 Harr. Cond. Lo. R. 567.

GRAND COUTUMIER. Two collections of laws bore this title. The one, also called the Coutumier of France, is a collection of the customs, usages, and forms of practice, which had been used from time immemorial in France: the other, called the Coutumier de Normandie, which indeed made a part of the former, with some alterations, was composed about the fourteenth of Henry II., in 1229, and is a collection of the Norman laws not as they stood at the Conquest of England, by William the Conqueror, but some time afterwards, and contains many provisions, probably borrowed from the old English or Saxon laws. Hale's Hist. C. L. c. 6.

GRAND JURY, *practice*. A body of men, consisting of not less than twelve nor more than twenty-four, respectively returned by the sheriff of every county to every session of the peace, oyer and terminer and general gaol delivery, to whom indictments are preferred. 4 Bl. Com. 302; 1 Chit. C. L. 310, 1.

2. There is just reason to believe that this institution existed among the Saxons. Crabb's C. L. 35. By the constitutions of Clarendon, enacted 10 H. II. A. D. 1164, it is provided, that "if such men were sus-

pected, whom none wished or dared to accuse, the sheriff, being thereto required by the bishop, should swear twelve men of the neighborhood, or village, to declare the truth" respecting such supposed crime; the jurors being summoned as witnesses or accusers, rather than judges. If this institution did not exist before, it seems to be pretty certain that this statute established grand juries, or recognized them, if they existed before.

3. A view of the important duties of grand juries will be taken, by considering, 1. The organization of the grand jury. 2. The extent of its jurisdiction. 3. The mode of doing business. 4. The evidence to be received. 5. Their duty to make presentments. 6. The secrecy to be observed by the grand jury.

4.—1. *Of the organization of the grand jury.* The law requires that twenty-four citizens shall be summoned to attend on the grand jury; but in practice, not more than twenty-three are sworn, because of the inconvenience which else might arise, of having twelve, who are sufficient to find a true bill, opposed to other twelve who might be against it. 6 Adolph. & Ell. 236; S. C. 33 E. C. L. R. 66; 2 Caines, R. 98. Upon being called, all who present themselves are sworn, as it scarcely ever happens that all who are summoned are in attendance. The grand jury cannot consist of less than twelve, and from fifteen to twenty are usually sworn. 2 Hale, P. C. 161; 7 Sm. & Marsh. 58. Being called into the jury-box, they are usually permitted to select a foreman whom the court appoints, but the court may exercise the right to nominate one for them. The foreman then takes the following oath or affirmation, namely: "You, A B, as foreman of this inquest for the body of the —— of ——, do swear, (or affirm) that you will diligently inquire, and true presentments make, of all such articles, matters and things as shall be given you in charge, or otherwise come to your knowledge touching the present service; the commonwealth's counsel, your fellows and your own, you shall keep secret; you shall present no one for envy, hatred or malice; nor shall you leave any one unpresented for fear, favor, affection, hope of reward or gain; but shall present all things truly, as they come to your knowledge, according to the best of your understanding, (so help you God.") It will be perceived that this oath contains the substance of the duties of the grand jury. The foreman having been sworn or affirmed, the other grand jurors are sworn or affirmed according to this formula: "You and each of you do swear (or affirm) that the same oath (or affirmation) which your foreman has taken on his part, you and every one of you shall well and truly observe on your part." Being so sworn or affirmed, and having received the charge of the court, the grand jury are organized, and may proceed to the room provided for them to transact the business which may be laid before them. 2 Burr. 1088; Bac. Ab. Juries, A. The grand jury constitute a regular body until discharged by the court, or by operation of law, as where they cannot continue by virtue of an act of assembly beyond a certain day. But although they have been formally discharged by the court, if they have not separated, they may be called back, and fresh bills submitted to them. 9 C. & P. 43; S. C. 38 E. C. L. R. 28.

5.—2. *The extent of the grand jury's jurisdiction.* Their jurisdiction is co-extensive with that of the court for which they inquire, both as to the offences triable there, and the territory over which such court has jurisdiction.

6.—3. *The mode of doing business.* The foreman acts as president, and the jury usually appoint one of their number to perform the duties of secretary. No records are to be kept of the acts of the grand jury, except for their own use, because, as will be seen hereafter, their proceedings are to be secret. Being thus prepared to enter upon their duties, the grand jury are supplied with bills of indictment by the attorney-general or other officer representing the state or commonwealth against offenders. On these bills are endorsed the names of the witnesses by whose testimony they are supported. The witnesses are in attendance in another room, and must be called when wanted. Before they are examined as to their knowledge of the matters mentioned in the indictment, care must be taken that they have been sworn or affirmed. For the sake of convenience, they are generally sworn or affirmed in open court before they are sent to be examined, and when so qualified, a mark to that effect is made opposite their names.

7. In order to save time, the best practice is to find a true bill, as soon as the jury are satisfied that the defendant ought to be put upon his trial. It is a waste of

time to examine any other witness after they have arrived at that conclusion. Twelve at least must agree, in order to find a true bill; but it is not required that they should be unanimous. Unless that number consent, the bill must be ignored. When a defendant is to be put upon his trial, the foreman must write on the back of the indictment "a true bill," sign his name as foreman, and date the time of finding. On the contrary, where there is not sufficient evidence to authorize the finding of the bill, the jury return that they are ignorant whether the person accused committed the offence charged in the bill, which is expressed by the foreman endorsing on the bill "ignoramus," signing his name as before, and dating the time.

8.—4. *Of the evidence to be received.* In order to ascertain the facts which the jury have not themselves witnessed, they must depend upon the statement of those who know them, and who will testify to them. When the witness, from his position and ability, has been in a condition to know the facts about which he testifies, he is deserving of implicit confidence; if, with such knowledge, he has no motive for telling a false or exaggerated story, has intelligence enough to tell what he knows, and give a probable account of the transaction. If, on the other hand, from his position he could not know the facts, or if knowing them, he distorts them, he is undeserving of credit. The jury are the sole judges of the credit and confidence to which a witness is entitled.

9. Should any member of the jury be acquainted with any fact on which the grand jury are to act, he must, before he testifies, be sworn or affirmed, as any other witness, for the law requires this sanction in all cases.

10. As the jury are not competent to try the accused, but merely to investigate the case so far as to ascertain whether he ought to be put on his trial, they cannot hear evidence in his favor; theirs is a mere preliminary inquiry; it is when he comes to be tried in court that he may defend himself by examining witnesses in his favor, and showing the facts of the case.

11.—5. *Of presentments.* The jury are required to make true presentments of all such matters which may be given to them in charge, or which have otherwise come to their knowledge. A presentment, properly speaking, is the notice taken by the grand jury of any offence from their own knowledge, as of a nuisance, a libel, or the like. In these cases, the authors of the offence should be named, so that they may be indicted.

12.—6. *Of the secrecy to be observed by the grand jury.* The oath which they have taken obliges them to keep secret the commonwealth's counsel, their fellows and their own. Although contrary to the general spirit of our institutions, which do not shun daylight, this secrecy is required by law for wise purposes. It extends to the votes given in any case, to the evidence delivered by witnesses, and the communications of the jurors to each other; the disclosure of these facts, unless under the sanction of law, would render the imprudent juror who should make them public, liable to punishment. Giving intelligence to a defendant that a bill has been found against him, to enable him to escape, is so obviously wrong, that no one can for a moment doubt its being criminal. The grand juror who should be guilty of this offence might, upon conviction, be fined and imprisoned. The duration of the secrecy appears not to be definitely settled, but it seems this injunction is to remain as long as the particular circumstances of each case require. In a case, for example, where a witness swears to a fact in open court, on the trial, directly in opposition to what he swore before the grand jury, there can be no doubt the injunction of secrecy, as far as regards this evidence, would be at an end, and the grand juror might be sworn to testify what this witness swore to in the grand jury's room, in order that the witness might be prosecuted for perjury. 2 Russ. Cr. 616; 4 Greenl. Rep. 439; but see contra, 2 Halst. R. 347; 1 Car. & K. 519.

Vide, generally, 1 Chit. Cr. Law, 162, 1 Russ. Cr. 291; 2 Russ. Cr. 616; 2 Stark. Ev. 232, n. 1; 1 Hawk. 65, 506; 2 Hawk. ch. 25; 3 Story, Const. § 1778; 2 Swift's Dig. 370; 4 Bl. Com. 402; Archb. Cr. Pl. 63; 7 Sm. Laws Penna. 685.

GRANDCHILDREN, *domestic relations.* The children of one's children. Sometimes these may claim bequests given in a will to children, though in general they can make no such claim. 6 Co. 16.

GRANDFATHER, *domestic relations.* The father of one's father or mother. The father's father is called the paternal grandfather; the mother's father is the maternal grandfather.

GRANDMOTHER, *domestic relations.* The mother of one's father or mother. The father's mother is called the paternal grandmother; the mother's mother is the maternal grandmother.

GRANT, *conveyancing, concessio.* Technically speaking, grants are applicable to the conveyance of incorporeal rights, though in the largest sense, the term comprehends everything that is granted or passed from one to another, and is applied to every species of property. Grant is one of the usual words in a feoffment, and differs but little except in the subject-matter; for the operative words used in grants are *dedi et concessi*, "have given and granted."

2. Incorporeal rights are said to lie in grant and not in livery, for existing only in idea, in contemplation of law, they cannot be transferred by livery of possession; of course at common law, a conveyance in writing was necessary, hence they are said to be in grant, and to pass by the delivery of the deed.

3. To render the grant effectual, the common law required the consent of the tenant of the land out of which the rent, or other incorporeal interest proceeded; and this was called *attornment.* (q. v.) It arose from the intimate alliance between the lord and vassal existing under the feudal tenures. The tenant could not alien the feud without the consent of the lord, nor the lord part with his seigniory without the consent of the tenant. The necessity of attornment has been abolished in the United States. 4 Kent, Com. 479. He who makes the grant is called the grantor, and he to whom it is made, the grantee. Vide Com. Dig. h. t.; 14 Vin. Ab. 27; Bac. Ab. h. t.; 4 Kent, Com. 477; 2 Bl. Com. 317, 440; Perk. ch. 1; Touchs. c. 12; 8 Cowen's R. 36.

4. By the word *grant*, in a treaty, is meant not only a formal grant, but any concession, warrant, order, or permission to survey, possess or settle; whether written or parol, express, or presumed from possession. Such a grant may be made by law, as well as by a patent pursuant to a law. 12 Pet. R. 410. See, generally, 9 A. & E. 532; 5 Mass. 472; 9 Pick. 80.

GRANT, BARGAIN, AND SELL. By the laws of the states of Pennsylvania, Delaware, Missouri, and Alabama, it is declared that the words *grant, bargain, and sell,* shall amount to a covenant that the grantor was seised of an estate in fee, freed from encumbrances done or suffered by him, and for quiet enjoyment as against all his acts These words do not amount to a general warranty, but merely to a covenant that the grantor has not done any acts, nor created any encumbrance, by which the estate may be defeated. 2 Binn. R. 95; 3 Penna. R. 313; 3 Penna. R. 317, note; 1 Rawle, 377; 1 Misso. 576. Vide 2 Caines' R. 188; 1 Murph. R. 343; Id. 348; Ark. Rev. Stat. ch. 31, s. 1; 11 S. & R. 109.

GRANTEE. He to whom a grant is made.

GRANTOR. He by whom a grant is made.

GRASSHEARTH, *old Engl. law.* The name of an ancient customary service of tenants' doing one day's work for their landlord.

GRATIFICATION. A reward given voluntarily for some service or benefit rendered, without being requested so to do, either expressly or by implication.

GRATIS. Without reward or consideration.

2. When a bailee undertakes to perform some act or work *gratis*, he is answerable for his gross negligence, if any loss should be sustained in consequence of it; but a distinction exists between non-feasance and misfeasance; between a total omission to do an act which one gratuitously promises to do, and a culpable negligence in the execution of it; in the latter case he is responsible, while in the former he would not, in general, be bound to perform his contract. 4 Johns. R. 84; 5 T. 143; 2 Ld. Raym. 913.

GRATIS DICTUM. A saying not required; a statement voluntarily made without necessity.

GRATUITOUS CONTRACT, *civ. law.* One, the object of which is for the benefit of the person with whom it is made, without any profit, received or promised, as a consideration for it; as, for example, a gift. 1 Bouv. Inst. n. 709.

GRAVAMEN. The grievance complained of; the substantial cause of the action. See Greenl. Ev. § 66.

GRAVE. A place where a dead body is interred.

2. The violation of the grave, by taking up the dead body, or stealing the coffin or grave clothes, is a misdemeanor at common law. 1 Russ. on Cr. 414. A singular case, illustrative of this subject, occurred in Louisiana. A son, who inherited a large estate from his mother, buried her with all her

jewels, worth $2000; he then made a sale of all he inherited from his mother, for $30,000. After this, a thief broke the grave and stole the jewels, which, after his conviction, were left with the clerk of the court, to be delivered to the owner. The son claimed them, and so did the purchaser of the inheritance; it was held that the jewels, although buried with the mother, belonged to the son, and that they passed to the purchaser by a sale of the whole inheritance. 6 Robins. L. R. 488. See *Dead Body*.

3. In New York, by statutory enactment, it is provided, that every person who shall open a grave, or other place of interment, with intent, 1. To remove the dead body of any human being, for the purpose of selling the same, or for the purpose of dissection; or, 2. To steal the coffin, or any part thereof, or the vestments or other articles interred with any dead body, shall, upon conviction, be punished by imprisonment, in a state prison, not exceeding two years, or in a county gaol, not exceeding six months, or by fine not exceeding two hundred and fifty dollars, or by both such fine and imprisonment. Rev. Stat. part 4, tit. 5, art. 3, § 15.

GREAT CATTLE. By this term, in the English law, is meant all manner of beasts except sheep and yearlings. 2 Rolle's Rep. 173.

GREAT CHARTER. The name of the charter granted by the English King John, securing to the English people their principal liberties; *magna charta*. (q. v.)

GREAT LAW. The name of an act of the legislature of Pennsylvania, passed at Chester, immediately after the arrival of William Penn, December 7th, 1682. Serg. Land Laws of Penn. 24, 230.

GREE, *obsolete*. It signified satisfaction; as, to make gree to the parties, is, to agree with, or satisfy them for, an offence done.

GREEN WAX, *Eng. law*. The name of the estreats of fines, issues, and amercements in the exchequer, delivered to the sheriff under the seal of that court, which is made with green wax.

GROS BOIS, or GROSSE BOIS. Such wood as, by the common law or custom, is reputed timber. 2 Inst. 642.

GROSS. Absolute, entire, not depending on another. Vide *Common*.

GROSS ADVENTURE. By this term the French law writers signify a maritime loan, or bottomry. (q. v.) It is so called because the lender exposes his money to the perils of the sea; and contributes to the gross or general average. Poth. h. t.; Pard. Dr. Com. h. t.

GROSS AVERAGE, *mar. law*. That kind of average which falls on the ship, cargo, and freight, and is distinguished from particular average. See *Average*.

GROSS NEGLIGENCE. *Lata culpa*, or, as the Roman lawyers most accurately call it, *dolo proxima*, is, in practice, considered as equivalent to *dolus* or fraud itself, and consists, according to the best interpreters, in the omission of that care which even inattentive and thoughtless men never fail to take of their own property. Jones on Bailments, 20. It must not be confounded, however, with fraud, for it may exist consistently with good faith and honesty of intention, according to common law authorities.

GROSS WEIGHT. The total weight of goods or merchandise, with the chests, bags, and the like, from which are to be deducted tare and tret.

GROUND RENT, *estates*. In Pennsylvania, this term is used to signify a perpetual rent issuing out of some real estate. This rent is redeemable where there is a covenant in the deed that, before the expiration of a period therein named, it may be redeemed by the payment of a certain sum of money; or it is irredeemable, when there is no such agreement; and, in the latter case, it cannot be redeemed without the consent of both parties. See 1 Whart. R. 337; 4 Watts, R. 98; Cro. Jac. 510; 6 Halst. 262; 7 Wend. 463; 7 Pet. 596; 2 Bouv. Inst. n. 1659, and note, and *Emphyteosis*.

GROUNDAGE, *mar. law*. The consideration paid for standing a ship in a port. Jacobs, Dict. h. t. Vide *Demurrage*.

GUARANTEE, *contracts*. He to whom a guaranty is made.

2. The guarantee is entitled to receive payment, in the first place, from the debtor, and, secondly, from the guarantor. He must be careful not to give time beyond that stipulated in the original agreement, to the debtor, without the consent of the guarantor; the guarantee should, at the instance of the guarantor, bring an action against the principal for the recovery of the debt. 2 Johns. Ch. R. 554; 17 Johns. R. 384; 8 Serg. & Rawle, 116; 10 Serg. & Rawle, 33; 2 Bro. C. C. 579, 582; 2 Ves.

jr. 542. But the mere omission of the guarantee to sue the principal debtor will not, in general, discharge the guarantor. 8 Serg. & Rawle, 112; 3 Yeates, R. 157; 6 Binn. R. 292, 300.

GUARANTOR, *contracts*. He who makes a guaranty.

2. The guarantor is bound to fulfil the engagement he has entered into, provided the principal debtor does not. He is bound only to the extent that the debtor is, and any payment made by the latter, or release of him by the creditor, will operate as a release of the guarantor; 3 Penna. R. 19; or even if the guarantee should give time to the debtor beyond that contained in the agreement, or substitute a new agreement, or do any other act by which the guarantor's situation would be worse, the obligation of the latter would be discharged. Smith on Mer. Law, 285.

3. A guarantor differs from a surety in this, that the former cannot be sued until a failure on the part of the principal, when sued; while the latter may be sued at the same time with the principal. 10 Watts, 258.

GUARANTY, *contracts*. A promise made upon a good consideration, to answer for the payment of some debt, or the performance of some duty, in case of the failure of another person, who is, in the first instance, liable to such payment or performance. 1 Miles' Rep. 277.

2. The English statute of frauds, 29 Car. II. c. 3, which, with modification, has been adopted in most of the states; 3 Kent's Com. 86; requires, that "upon any special promise to answer for the debt, default, or miscarriage of another person, the agreement, or some memorandum, or note thereof, must be in writing, and signed by the party to be charged therewith, or some other thereunto by him lawfully authorized." This clause of the statute is not in force in Pennsylvania. To render this statute valid, under the statute, its form must be in writing; it must be made upon a sufficient consideration; and it must be to fulfil the engagement of another.

3.—1. The agreement must be in writing, and signed by the party to be bound, or some one authorized by him. It should substantially contain the names of the party promising, and of the person on whose behalf the promise is made; the promise itself, and the consideration for it.

4.—2. The word *agreement* in the statute includes the consideration for the promise, as well as the promise itself; if, therefore, the guaranty be for a subsisting debt, or engagement of another person, not only the engagement, but the consideration for it, must appear in the writing. 5 East, R. 10. This has been the construction which has been given in England, and which has been followed in New York and South Carolina, though it has been rejected in several other states. 3 John. R. 210; 8 John. R. 29; 2 Nott & McCord, 372, note; 4 Greenl. R. 180, 387; 6 Conn. R. 81; 17 Mass. R. 122. The decisions have all turned upon the force of the word *agreement;* and where by statute the word *promise* has been introduced, by requiring the *promise or agreement* to be in writing, as in Virginia, the construction has not been so strict. 5 Cranch's R. 151, 2.

5.—3. The guaranty must be to answer for the debt or default of another. The term debt implies, that the liability of the principal debtor had been previously incurred; but a default may arise upon an executory contract, and a promise to pay for goods to be furnished to another, is a collateral promise to pay on the other's default, provided the credit was given, in the first instance, solely to the other. It is a general rule, that when a promise is made by a third person, previous to the sale of goods, or other credit given, or other liability incurred, it comes within the statute, when it is conditional upon the default of another, who is solely liable in the first instance, otherwise not; the only inquiry to ascertain this, is, to whom was it agreed that the vendor or creditor should look in the first instance? Many nice distinctions have been made on this subject. 1st. When a party actually purchases goods himself, which are to be delivered to a third person, for his sole use, and the latter was not to be responsible, this is not a case of guaranty, because the person to whom the goods were furnished, never was liable. 8 T. R. 80. 2d. Where a person buys goods, or incurs any other liability, jointly with another, but for the use of that other, and this fact is known to the creditor, the guaranty must be in writing. 8 John. R. 89. 3d. A person may make himself liable, in the third place, by adding his credit to that of another, but conditionally only, in case of the other's default. This species of promise comes immediately within the meaning of the statute, and in the cases is sometimes termed a *collateral promise*.

6. Guaranties are either special or for a particular transaction, or they are continuing guaranties; that is, they are to be valid for other transactions, though not particularly mentioned. 2 How. U. S. 426; 1 Metc. 24; 7 Pet. 113; 12 East, 227; 6 M. & W. 612; 6 Sc. N. S. 549; 2 Campb. 413; 3 Campb. 220; 3 M. & P. 573; S. C. 6 Bing. 244; 2 M. & Sc. 768; S. C. 9 Bing. 618; 3 B. & Ald. 593; 1 C. & M. 48; S. C. 1 Tyr. 164.

Vide, generally, Fell on Mercantile Guaranties; Bouv. Inst. Index, h. t.; 3 Kent's Com. 86; Theob. P. & S. c. 2 & 3; Smith on Mer. Law, c. 10; 3 Saund. 414, n. 5; Wheat. Dig. 182; 14 Wend. 231. The following authorities refer to cases of *special* guaranties of notes. 6 Conn. 81; 20 John. 367; 1 Mason, 368; 8 Pick. 423; 2 Dev. & Bat. 470; 14 Wend. 231. Of *absolute* guaranties. 2 Har. & J. 186; 3 Fairf. 193; 1 Mason, 323; 12 Pick. 123. *Conditional* guaranties. 12 Conn. 438. To *promises* to guaranty. 8 Greenl. 234; 16 John. 67.

GUARDIANS, *domestic relations*. Guardians are divided into, guardians of the person, in the civil law called tutors; and guardians of the estate, in the same law known by the name of curators. For the distinction between them, vide article *Curatorship;* 2 Kent, Com. 186; 1 Bouv. Inst. n. 336, et. seq.

2.—1. A guardian of the person is one who has been lawfully invested with the care of the person of an infant, whose father is dead.

3. The guardian must be properly appointed; he must be capable of serving; he must be appointed guardian of an infant; and after his appointment he must perform the duties imposed on him by his office.

4.—1st. In England, and in some of the states where the English law has been adopted in this respect, as in Pennsylvania; Rob. Dig. 312, by stat. 12 Car. II. c. 24; power is given to the father to appoint a testamentary guardian for his children, whether born or unborn. According to Chancellor Kent, this statute has been adopted in the state of New York, and probably throughout this country. 2 Kent, Com. 184. The statute of Connecticut, however, is an exception; there the father cannot appoint a testamentary guardian. 1 Swift's Dig. 48.

5. All other kinds of guardians, to be hereafter noticed, have been superseded in practice by guardians appointed by courts having jurisdiction of such matters. Courts of chancery, orphans' courts, and courts of a similar character having jurisdiction of testamentary matters in the several states, are, generally speaking, invested with the power of appointing guardians.

6.—2d. The person appointed must be capable of performing the duties; an idiot, therefore, cannot be appointed guardian.

7.—3d. The person over whom a guardian is appointed, must be an infant; for after the party has attained his full age, he is entitled to all his rights, if of sound mind, and, if not, the person appointed to take care of him is called a committee. (q. v.) No guardian of the person can be appointed over an infant whose father is alive, unless the latter be non compos mentis, in which case one may be appointed, as if the latter were dead.

8.—4th. After his appointment, the guardian of the person is considered as standing in the place of the father, and of course the relative powers and duties of guardian and ward correspond, in a great measure, to those of parent and child; in one prominent matter they are different. The father is entitled to the services of his child, and is bound to support him; the guardian is not entitled to the ward's services, and is not bound to maintain him out of his own estate.

9.—2. A guardian of the estate is one who has been lawfully invested with the power of taking care and managing the estate of an infant. 1 John. R. 561; 7 John. Ch. R. 150. His appointment is made in the same manner as that of a guardian of a person. It is the duty of the guardian to take reasonable and prudent care of the estate of the ward, and manage it in the most advantageous manner; and when the guardianship shall expire, to account with the ward for the administration of the estate.

10. Guardians have also been divided into guardians by nature; guardians by nurture; guardians in socage; testamentary guardians; statutory guardians; and guardians ad litem.

11.—1. Guardian by *nature*, is the father, and, on his death, the mother; this guardianship extends only to the custody of the person; 3 Bro. C. C. 186; 1 John. Ch. R. 3; 3 Pick. R. 213; and continues till the child shall acquire the age of twenty one years. Co. Litt. 84 a.

12.—2. Guardian by *nurture*, occurs only when the infant is without any other guardian, and the right belongs exclusively to the parents, first to the father, and then to the mother. It extends only to the person, and determines, in males and females, at the age of fourteen. This species of guardianship has become obsolete.

13.—3. Guardian in *socage*, has the custody of the infant's lands as well as his person. The common law gave this guardianship to the next of blood to the child to whom the inheritance could not possibly descend. This species of guardianship has become obsolete, and does not perhaps exist in this country; for the guardian must be a relation by blood who cannot possibly inherit, and such a case can rarely exist. 2 Wend. 153; 15 Wend. 631; 6 Paige, 390; 7 Cowen, 36; 5 John. 66.

14.—4. *Testamentary* guardians; these are appointed under the stat. 12 Car. II., above mentioned; they supersede the claims of any other guardian, and extend to the person, and real and personal estate of the child, and continue till the ward arrives at full age.

15.—5. Guardians *appointed by the courts*, by virtue of statutory authority. The distinction of guardians by nature, and by socage, appear to have become obsolete, and have been essentially superseded in practice by the appointment of guardians by courts of chancery, orphans' courts, probate courts, and such other courts as have jurisdiction to make such appointments. Testamentary guardians might, as well as those of this class, be considered as statutory guardians, inasmuch as their appointment is authorized by a statute.

16.—6. Guardian *ad litem*, is one appointed for the infant to defend him in an action brought against him. Every court, when an infant is sued in a civil action, has power to appoint a guardian *ad litem* when he has no guardian, for as the infant cannot appoint an attorney, he would be without assistance if such a guardian were not appointed. The powers and duties of a guardian *ad litem* are confined to the defence of the suit. F. N. B. 27; Co. Litt. 88 b, note 16; Id. 135 b, note 1; see generally Bouv. Inst. Index, h. t.; Coop. Inst. 445 to 455.

GUARDIANS OF THE POOR. The name given to officers whose duties are very similar to those of overseers of the poor, (q. v.) that is, generally to relieve the distresses of such poor persons who are unable to take care of themselves.

GUARDIANSHIP, *persons*. The power or protective authority given by law, and imposed on an individual who is free and in the enjoyment of his rights, over one whose weakness on account of his age, renders him unable to protect himself. Vide *Tutor*.

GUBERNATOR, *civil law*. A pilot or steersman of a ship. 2 Pet. Adm. Dec. Appx. lxxxiii.

GUEST. A traveller who stays at an inn or tavern with the consent of the keeper. Bac. Ab. Inns, C 5; 8 Co. 32. And if, after having taken lodgings at an inn, he leaves his horse there, and goes elsewhere to lodge, he is still to be considered a guest. But not if he merely leaves goods for which the landlord receives no compensation. 1 Salk. 388; 2 Lord Raym. 866; Cro. Jac. 188. The length of time a man is at an inn makes no difference, whether he stays a day, or a week, or a month, or longer, so always, that, though not strictly *transiens*, he retains his character as a traveller. But if a person comes upon a special contract to board and sojourn at an inn, he is not in the sense of the law a guest, but a boarder. Bac. Ab. Inns, C. 5; Story, Bailm. § 477.

2. Inkeepers are generally liable for all goods belonging to the guest, brought within the inn. It is not necessary that the goods should have been in the special keeping of the innkeeper to make him liable. This rule is founded on principles of public utility, to which all private considerations ought to yield. 2 Kent, Com. 459; 1 Hayw. N. C. Rep. 40; 14 John. R. 175; Dig. 4, 9, 1. Vide 3 Barn. & Ald. 283; 4 Maule & Selw. 306; 1 Holt's N. P. 209; 1 Salk. 387; S. C. Carth. 417; 1 Bell's Com. 469; Dane's Ab. Index, h. t.; Yelv. 67, a; Smith's Leading Cases, 47; 8 Co. 32.

GUIDON DE LA MER, (LE). The name of a treatise on maritime law, written in Rouen, then Normandy, in 1671, as is supposed. It was received on the continent of Europe almost as equal in authority to one of the ancient codes of maritime law. The author of this work is unknown. This tract or treatise is contained in the "Collection de Lois Maritimes," by J. M. Pardessus, vol. 2, p. 371, et seq.

GUILD. A fraternity or company. Guildhall, the place of meeting of guilds. Beame's Glanville, 108 (n).

GUILT, *crim. law*. That quality which renders criminal and liable to punishment or it is that disposition to violate the law, which has manifested itself by some act already done. The opposite of innocence. Vide Rutherf. Inst. B. 1, c. 18, s. 10.

2. In general every one is presumed innocent until guilt has been proved; but in some cases the presumption of guilt overthrows that of innocence; as, for example, where a party destroys evidence to which the opposite party is entitled. The spoliation of papers, material to show the neutral character of a vessel, furnishes strong presumption against the neutrality of the ship. 2 Wheat. 227. Vide *Spoliation.*

GUILTY. The state or condition of a person who has committed a crime, misdemeanor or offence.

2. This word implies a malicious intent, and must be applied to something universally allowed to be a crime. Cowp. 275.

3. In pleading, it is a plea by which a defendant who is charged with a crime, misdemeanor or tort, admits or confesses it. In criminal proceedings, when the accused is arraigned, the clerk asks him, "How say you, A B, are you guilty or not guilty?" His answer, which is given *ore tenus*, is called his plea; and when he admits the charge in the indictment he answers or pleads *guilty*.

H.

HABEAS CORPORA, *English practice.* A writ issued out of the C. P. commanding the sheriff to compel the appearance of a jury in the cause between the parties. It answers the same purpose in that court as the *Distringas juratores* answers in the K. B. For a form, see Boote's Suit at Law, 151.

HABEAS CORPUS, *remedies.* A writ of habeas corpus is an order in writing, signed by the judge who grants the same, and sealed with the seal of the court of which he is a judge, issued in the name of the sovereign power where it is granted, by such a court or a judge thereof, having lawful authority to issue the same, directed to any one having a person in his custody or under his restraint, commanding him to produce such person at a certain time and place, and to state the reasons why he is held in custody, or under restraint.

2. This writ was at common law considered as a remedy to remove the illegal restraint on a freeman. But anterior to the 31 Charles II. its benefit was, in a great degree, eluded by time-serving judges, who awarded it only in term time, and who assumed a discretionary power of awarding or refusing it. 3 Bulstr. 23. Three or four years before that statute was passed there had been two very great cases much agitated in Westminster Hall, upon writs of habeas corpus for private custody, viz: the cases of Lord Leigh; 2 Lev. 128; and Sir Robert Viner, Lord Mayor of London. 3 Keble, 434, 447, 470, 504; 2 Lev. 128; Freem. 389. But the courts wisely drew the line of distinction between civil constitutional liberty, as opposed to the power of the crown, and liberty as opposed to the violence and power of private persons. Wilmot's Opinions, 85, 86.

3. To secure the full benefit of it to the subject, the statute 31 Car. II. c. 2, commonly called the *habeas corpus* act, was passed. This gave to the writ the vigor, life, and efficacy requisite for the due protection of the liberty of the subject. In England this is considered as a high prerogative writ, issuing out of the court of king's bench, in term time or vacation, and running into every part of the king's dominions. It is also grantable as a matter of right, *ex debito justitæ*, upon the application of any person.

4. The interdict *De homine libero exhibendo* of the Roman law, was a remedy very similar to the writ of *habeas corpus.* When a freeman was restrained by another, contrary to good faith, the prætor ordered that such person should be brought before him that he might be liberated. Dig. 43, 29, 1.

5. The *habeas corpus* act has been substantially incorporated into the jurisprudence of every state in the Union, and the right to the writ has been secured by most

of the constitutions of the states, and of the United States. The statute of 31 Car. II. c. 2, provides that the person imprisoned, if he be not a prisoner convict, or in execution of legal process, or committed for treason or felony, plainly expressed in the warrant, or has not neglected wilfully, by the space of two whole terms after his imprisonment, to pray a *habeas corpus* for his enlargement, may apply by any one in his behalf, in vacation time, to a judicial officer for the writ of *habeas corpus*, and the officer, upon view of the copy of the warrant of commitment, or upon proof of denial of it after due demand, must allow the writ to be directed to the person in whose custody the party is detained, and made returnable immediately before him. And, in term time, any of the said prisoners may obtain his writ of *habeas corpus*, by applying to the proper court.

6. By the habeas corpus law of Pennsylvania, (the Act of February 18, 1785,) the benefit of the writ of habeas corpus is given in "all cases where any person, not being committed or detained for any criminal, or supposed criminal matter," who "shall be confined or restrained of his or her liberty, under any color or pretence whatsoever." A similar provision is contained in the habeas corpus act of New York. Act of April 21, 1818, sect. 41, ch. 277.

7. The Constitution of the United States, art. 1, s. 9, n. 2, provides, that "the privilege of the writ of habeas corpus shall not be suspended, unless when, in cases of rebellion or invasion, the public safety may require it;" and the same principle is contained in many of the state constitutions. In order still more to secure the citizen the benefit of this great writ, a heavy penalty is inflicted upon the judges who are bound to grant it, in case of refusal.

8. It is proper to consider, 1. When it is to be granted. 2. How it is to be served. 3. What return is to be made to it. 4. The hearing. 5. The effect of the judgment upon it.

9.—1. The writ is to be granted whenever a person is in actual confinement, committed or detained as aforesaid, either for a criminal charge, or, as in Pennsylvania and New York, in all cases where he is confined or restrained of his liberty, under any color or pretence whatsoever. But persons discharged on bail will not be considered as restrained of their liberty so as to be entitled to a writ of habeas corpus, directed to their bail. 3 Yeates, R. 263; 1 Serg & Rawle, 356.

10.—2. The writ may be served by any free person, by leaving it with the person to whom it is directed, or left at the gaol or prison with any of the under officers, under keepers, or deputy of the said officers or keepers. In Louisiana, it is provided that if the person to whom it is addressed shall refuse to receive the writ, he who is charged to serve it, shall inform him of its contents; if he to whom the writ is addressed conceal himself, or refuse admittance to the person charged to serve it on him, the latlat shall affix the order on the exterior of the place where the person resides, or in which the petitioner is confined. Lo. Code of Pract. art. 803. The service is proved by the oath of the party making it.

11.—3. The person to whom the writ is addressed or directed, is required to make a return to it, within the time prescribed; he either complies, or he does not. If he *complies*, he must positively answer, 1. Whether he has or has not in his power or custody the person to be set at liberty, or whether that person is confined by him; if he return that he has not, and has not had him in his power or custody, and the return is true, it is evident that a mistake was made in issuing the writ; if the return is false, he is liable to a penalty, and other punishment, for making such a false return. If he return that he has such person in his custody, then he must show by his return, further, by what authority, and for what cause, he arrested or detained him. If he *does not comply*, he is to be considered in contempt of the court under whose seal the writ has been issued, and liable to a severe penalty, to be recovered by the party aggrieved.

12.—4. When the prisoner is brought before the judge, his judicial discretion commences, and he acts under no other responsibility than that which belongs to the exercise of ordinary judicial power. The judge or court before whom the prisoner is brought on a habeas corpus, examines the return and papers, if any, referred to in it, and if no legal cause be shown for the imprisonment or restraint; or if it appear, although legally committed, he has not been prosecuted or tried within the periods required by law, or that, for any other cause, the imprisonment cannot be legally continued, the prisoner is discharged from custody. In the case of wives, children, and wards, all the court does, is to see that they are under no illegal restraint. 1 Strange, 445; 2 Strange, 982; Wilmot's Opinions, 120.

13. For those offences which are bailable, when the prisoner offers sufficient bail, he is to be bailed.

14. He is to be remanded in the following cases: 1. When it appears he is detained upon legal process, out of some court having jurisdiction of criminal matters. 2. When he is detained by warrant, under the hand and seal of a magistrate, for some offence for which, by law, the prisoner is not bailable. 3. When he is a convict in execution, or detained in execution by legal civil process. 4. When he is detained for a contempt, specially and plainly charged in the commitment, by some existing court having authority to commit for contempt. 5. When he refuses or neglects to give the requisite bail in a case bailable of right. The judge is not confined to the return, but he is to examine into the causes of the imprisonment, and then he is to discharge, bail, or remand, as justice shall require. 2 Kent, Com. 26; Lo. Code of Prac. art. 819.

15.—5. It is provided by the habeas corpus act, that a person set at liberty by the writ, shall not again be imprisoned for the same offence, by any person whomsoever, other than by the legal order and process of such court wherein he shall be bound by recognizance to appear, or other court having jurisdiction of the cause. 4 Johns. R. 318; 1 Binn. 374; 5 John. R. 282.

16. The *habeas corpus* can be suspended only by authority of the legislature. The constitution of the United States provides, that the privilege of the writ of *habeas corpus* shall not be suspended unless when, in cases of invasion and rebellion, the public safety may require it. Whether this writ ought to be suspended depends on political considerations, of which the legislature is to decide. 4 Cranch, 101. The proclamation of a military chief, declaring martial law, cannot, therefore, suspend the operation of the law. 1 Harr. Cond. Rep. Lo. 157, 159; 3 Mart. Lo. R. 531.

17. There are various kinds of this writ; the principal of which are explained below.

18. *Habeas corpus ad deliberandum et recipiendum*, is a writ which lies to remove a prisoner to take his trial in the county where the offence was committed. Bac. Ab. Habeas Corpus, A.

19. *Habeas corpus ad faciendum et recipiendum*, is a writ which issues out of a court of competent jurisdiction, when a person is sued in an inferior court, commanding the inferior judges to produce the body of the defendant, together with the day and cause of his caption and detainer, (whence this writ is frequently denominated *habeas corpus cum causâ*) to *do and receive* whatever the court or the judge issuing the writ shall consider in that behalf. This writ may also be issued by the bail of a prisoner, who has been taken upon a criminal accusation, in order to surrender him in his own discharge; upon the return of this writ, the court will cause an exoneretur to be entered on the bail piece, and remand the prisoner to his former custody. Tidd's Pr. 405; 1 Chit. Cr. Law, 132.

20. *Habeas corpus ad prosequendum*, is a writ which issues for the purpose of removing a prisoner in order to prosecute. 3 Bl. Com. 130.

21. *Habeas corpus ad respondendum*, is a writ which issues at the instance of a creditor, or one who has a cause of action against a person who is confined by the process of some inferior court, in order to remove the prisoner and charge him with this new action in the court above. 2 Mod. 198; 3 Bl. Com. 107.

22. *Habeas corpus ad satisfaciendum*, is a writ issued at the instance of a plaintiff for the purpose of bringing up a prisoner, against whom a judgment has been rendered, in a superior court to charge him with the process of execution. 2 Lill. Pr. Reg. 4, 3 Bl. Com. 129, 130.

23. *Habeas corpus ad subjiciendum*, by way of eminence called the writ of *habeas corpus*, (q. v.) is a writ directed to the person detaining another, and commanding him to produce the body of the prisoner, with the day and cause of his caption and detention, *ad faciendum, subjiciendum, et recipiendum*, to do, submit to, and receive, whatsoever the judge or court awarding such writ shall consider in that behalf. 3 Bl. Com. 131; 3 Story, Const. § 1333.

24. *Habeas corpus ad testificandum*, a writ issued for the purpose of bringing a prisoner, in order that he may testify, before the court. 3 Bl. Com. 130.

25. *Habeas corpus cum causâ*, is a writ which may be issued by the bail of a prisoner, who has been taken upon a criminal accusation, in order to render him in their own discharge. Tidd's Pr. 405. Upon the

return of this writ the court will cause an exoneretur to be entered on the bail piece, and remand the defendant to his former custody. Id. ibid.; 1 Chit. Cr. Law, 132. Vide, generally, Bac. Ab. h. t.; Vin. Ab. h. t.; Com. Dig. h. t.; Nels. Ab. h. t.; the various American Digests, h. t.; Lo. Code of Prac. art. 791 to 827; Dane's Ab. Index, h. t.; Bouv. Inst. Index, h. t.

HABENDUM, *conveyancing*. This is a Latin word, which signifies to have.

2. In conveyancing, it is that part of a deed which usually declares what estate or interest is granted by it, its certainty, duration, and to what use. It sometimes qualifies the estate, so that the general implication of the estate, which, by construction of law, passes in the premises, may by the habendum be controlled; in which case the habendum may enlarge the estate, but not totally contradict, or be repugnant to it. It may abridge the premises. Perk. § 170, 176; Br. Estate, 36 Cont. Co. Litt. 299. It may explain the premises. More, 43; 2 Jones, 4. It may enlarge the premises. Co. Lit. 299; 2 Jones, 4. It may be frustrated by the premises, when they are general; Skin. 544; but it cannot frustrate the premises, though it may restrain them. Skin. 543. Its proper office is not to give anything, but to limit or define the certainty of the estate to the feoffee or grantee, who should be previously named in the premises of the deed, or it is void. Cro. Eliz. 903. In deeds and devises it is sometimes construed distributively, reddendo singula singulis. 1 Saund. 183-4, notes 3 and 4; Yelv. 183, and note 1.

3. The habendum commences in our common deeds, with the words "to have and to hold." 2 Bl. Com. 298; 14 Vin. Ab. 143; Com. Dig. Fait, E 9; 2 Co. 55 a; 8 Mass. R. 175; 1 Litt. R. 220; Cruise, Dig. tit. 32, c. 20, s. 69 to 93; 5 Serg. & Rawle, 375; 2 Rolle, Ab. 65; Plowd. 153; Co. Litt. 183; Martin's N. C. Rep. 28; 4 Kent, Com. 456; 3 Prest. on Abstr. 206 to 210; 5 Barnw. & Cres. 709; 7 Greenl. R. 455; 6 Conn. R. 289; 6 Har. & J. 132; 3 Wend. 99.

HABERDASHER. A dealer in miscellaneous goods and merchandise.

HABERE. To have. This word is used in composition.

HABERE FACIAS POSSESSIONEM, *practice, remedies*. The name of a writ of execution in the action of ejectment.

2. The sheriff is commanded by this writ that, without delay, he cause the plaintiff to have possession of the land in dispute which is therein described; a *fi. fa.* or *ca. sa.* for costs may be included in the writ. The duty of the sheriff in the execution and return of that part of the writ, is the same as on a common *fi. fa.* or *ca. sa.* The sheriff is to execute this writ by delivering a full and actual possession of the premises to the plaintiff. For this purpose he may break an outer or inner door of the house and, should be be violently opposed, he may raise the *posse comitatus*. Wats. on Sher. 60, 215; 5 Co. 91 b.; 1 Leon. 145; 3 Bouv. Inst. n. 3375.

3. The name of this writ is abbreviated *hab. fa. poss.* Vide 10 Vin. Ab. 14; Tidd's Pr. 1081, 8th Engl. edit.; 2 Arch. Pr. 58; 3 Bl. Com. 412; Bing. on Execut. 115, 252; Bac. Ab. h. t.

HABERE FACIAS SEISINAM, *practice, remedies*. The name of a writ of execution, used in most real actions, by which the sheriff is directed that he cause the demandant to have seisin of the lands which he has recovered. 3 Bouv. Inst. n. 3374.

2. This writ may be taken out at any time within a year and day after judgment. It is to be executed nearly in the same manner as the writ of *habere facias possessionem*, and, for this purpose, the officer may break open the outer door of a house to deliver seisin to the demandant. 5 Co. 91 b; Com. Dig. Execution, E; Wats. Off. of Sheriff, 238. The name of this writ is abbreviated *hab. fac. seis.* Vide Bingh. on Exec. 115, 252; Bac. Ab. h. t.

HABERE FACIAS VISUM, *practice*. The name of a writ which lies when a view is to be taken of lands and tenements. F. N. B. Index, verbo View.

HABIT. A disposition or condition of the body or mind acquired by custom or a frequent repetition of the same act. See 2 Mart. Lo. Rep. N. S. 622.

2. The *habit of dealing* has always an important bearing upon the construction of commercial contracts. A ratification will be inferred from the *mere habit of dealing* between the parties; as, if a broker has been accustomed to settle losses on policies in a particular manner, without any objection being made, or with the silent approbation of his principal, and he should afterward settle other policies in the same manner, to which no objection should be made within a reasonable time, a just presumption would arise of an implied ratifica-

tion; for if the principal did not agree to such settlement he should have declared his dissent. 2 Bouv. Inst. 1313–14.

HABITATION, *civil law.* It was the right of a person to live in the house of another without prejudice to the property.

2. It differed from a usufruct in this, that the usufructuary might have applied the house to any purpose, as, a store or manufactory; whereas the party having the right of habitation could only use it for the residence of himself and family. 1 Bro. Civ. Law, 184; Domat. l. 1, t. 11, s. 2, n. 7.

HABITATION, *estates.* A dwelling-house, a home-stall. 2 Bl. Com. 4; 4 Bl. Com. 220. Vide *House.*

HABITUAL DRUNKARD. A person given to ebriety or the excessive use of intoxicating drink, who has lost the power or the will, by frequent indulgence, to control his appetite for it.

2. By the laws of Pennsylvania an habitual drunkard is put nearly upon the same footing with a lunatic; he is deprived of his property, and a committee is appointed by the court to take care of his person and estate Act of June 13, 1836, Pamph. p. 589. Vide 6 Watts' Rep. 139; 1 Ashm. R. 71.

3. *Habitual drunkenness*, by statutory provisions in some of the states, is a sufficient cause for divorce. 1 Bouv. Inst. n. 296.

HABITUALLY. Customarily, by habit, or frequent use or practice, or so frequently as to show a design of repeating the same act. 2 N. S. 622: 1 Mart. Lo. R. 149.

2. In order to found proceedings in lunacy, it is requisite that the insanity should be *habitual*, yet it is not necessary that it should be continued. 1 Bouv. Inst. n. 379.

HAD BOTE, *Engl. law.* A recompense or amends made for violence offered to a person in holy orders.

HÆREDES PROXIMI. The children or descendants of the deceased. Dalr. Feud. Pr. 110; Spellm. Remains.

HÆREDES REMOTIORES. The kinsmen other than children or descendants. Dalr. Feud. Pr. 110; Spellm. Remains.

HÆREDITAS. An inheritance, or an estate which descends to one by succession. At common law an inheritance never ascends, *hæreditas nunquam ascendit.* But in many of the states of the Union provision is made by statute in favor of ascendants.

HÆREDITAS JACENS. This is said of an inheritance which is not taken by the heirs, but remains in abeyance.

HÆRES, *civil law.* An heir, one who succeeds to the whole inheritance.

2. These are of various kinds. 1. *Hæres natus*, an heir born; the heir at law: he is distinguished from, 2. *Hæres factus*, or an heir created by will, a testamentary heir, to whom the whole estate of the testator is given. 3. *Hæres fiduciarius*, an heir to whom the estate is given in trust for another. Just. 2, 23, 1, 2. *Hæres legitimus*, a lawful heir; this is one who is manifested by the marriage of his parents; *hæres legitimus est quem nuptiæ demonstrant; hæres suus*, one's own heir, a proper heir; descendants. Just. 3, 1, 4, 5.

HALF. One equal part of a thing divided into two parts, either in fact or in contemplation. A moiety. This word is used in composition; as, half cent, half dime, &c.

HALF-BLOOD, *parentage, kindred.* When persons have only one parent in common, they are of the half-blood. For example, if John marry Sarah and has a son by that marriage, and after Sarah's death he marry Maria, and has by her another son, these children are of the half-blood; whereas two of the children of John and Sarah would be of the whole blood.

2. By the English common law, one related to an intestate of the half-blood only, could never inherit, upon the presumption that he is not of the blood of the original purchaser; but this rule has been greatly modified by the 3 and 4 Wm. IV. c. 106.

3. In this country the common law principle on this subject may be considered as not in force, though in some states some distinction is still preserved between the whole and the half-blood. 4 Kent, Com. 403, n.; 2 Yerg. 115; 1 M'Cord, 456; Dane's Ab. Index, h. t.; Reeves on Descents, *passim.* Vide *Descents.*

HALF-BROTHER AND HALF-SISTER. Persons who have the same father but different mothers; or the same mother but different fathers.

HALF CENT, *money.* A copper coin of the United States, of the value of one two-hundredth part of a dollar, or five mills. It weighs eighty-four grains. Act of January

18, 1837, s. 12, 4 Sharswood's cont. of Story's L. U. S. 2523, 4. Vide *Money*.

Half defence, *pleading*. It is the peculiar form of a defence, which is as follows, "venit et defendit vim et injuriam, et dicit," &c. It differs from full defence. Vide *Defence; Et cetera*.

Half dime, *money*. A silver coin of the United States, of the value of one-twentieth part of a dollar, or five cents. It weighs twenty grains and five-eighths of a grain. Of one thousand parts, nine hundred are of pure silver, and one hundred are of alloy. Act of January 18, 1837, s. 8 and 9, 4 Sharswood's cont. of Story's L. U. S. 2523, 4. Vide *Money*.

Half dollar, *money*. A silver coin of the United States of the value of fifty cents. It weighs two hundred and six and one-fourth grains. Of one thousand parts, nine hundred are of pure silver, and one hundred of alloy. Act of January 18, 1837, s. 8 and 9, 4 Sharsw. cont. of Story's L. U. S. 2523, 4. Vide *Money*.

Half eagle, *money*. A gold coin of the United States, of the value of five dollars. It weighs one hundred and twenty-nine grains. Of one thousand parts, nine hundred are of pure gold, and one hundred of alloy. Act of January 18, 1837, 4 Sharsw. cont. of Story's L. U. S. 2523, 4. Vide *Money*.

Half proof, *semiplena probatio, civil law*. Full proof is that which is sufficient to end the controversy, while half proof is that which is insufficient, as the foundation of a sentence or decree, although in itself entitled to some credit. Vicat, voc. *Probatio*.

Half seal. A seal used in the English chancery for the sealing of commissions to delegates appointed upon any appeal, either in ecclesiastical or marine causes.

Half year. In the computation of time, a half year consists of one hundred and eighty-two days. Co. Litt. 135 b; Rev. Stat. of N. Y. part 1, c. 19, t. 1, § 3.

HALL. A public building used either for the meetings of corporations, courts, or employed to some public uses; as the city hall, the town hall. Formerly this word denoted the chief mansion or habitation.

HALLUCINATION, *med. jur.* It is a species of mania, by which "an idea reproduced by the memory is associated and embodied by the imagination." This state of mind is sometimes called delusion or waking dreams.

2. An attempt has been made to distinguish *hallucinations* from illusions; the former are said to be dependent on the state of the intellectual organs; and, the latter, on that of those of sense. Ray, Med. Jur. § 99; 1 Beck, Med. Jur. 538, note. An instance is given of a temporary hallucination in the celebrated Ben Johnson, the poet. He told a friend of his that he had spent many a night in looking at his great toe, about which he had seen Turks and Tartars, Romans and Carthagenians, fight, in his imagination. 1 Coll. on Lun. 34. If, instead of being temporary, this affection of his mind had been permanent, he would doubtless have been considered insane. See, on the subject of spectral illusions, Hibbert, Alderson and Farrar's Essays; Scott on Demonology, &c.; Bostock's Physiology, vol. 3, p. 91, 161; 1 Esquirol, Maladies Mentales, 159.

HALMOTE. The name of a court among the Saxons. It had civil and criminal jurisdiction.

HAMESUCKEN, *Scotch law*. The crime of hamesucken consists in "the felonious seeking and invasion of a person in his dwelling house." 1 Hume, 312; Burnett, 86; Alison's Princ. of the Cr. Law of Scotl. 199.

2. The mere breaking into a house, without personal violence, does not constitute the offence, nor does the violence without an entry with intent to commit an assault. It is the combination of both which completes the crime. 1. It is necessary that the invasion of the house should have proceeded from forethought malice; but it is sufficient, if, from any illegal motive, the violence has been meditated, although it may not have proceeded from the desire of wreaking personal revenge, properly so called. 2. The place where the assault was committed must have been the proper dwelling house of the party injured, and not a place of business, visit, or occasional residence. 3. The offence may be committed equally in the day as in the night, and not only by effraction of the building by actual force, but by an entry obtained by fraud, with the intention of inflicting personal violence, followed by its perpetration. 4. But unless the injury to the person be of a grievous and material character, it is not hamesucken, though the other requisites to the crime have occurred. When this is the case, it is immaterial whether the violence be done *lucri causâ*, or from personal spite. 5. The punishment

of hamesucken in aggravated cases of injury, is death; in cases of inferior atrocity, an arbitrary punishment. Alison's Pr. of Cr. Law of Scotl. ch. 6; Ersk. Pr. L. Scotl. 4, 9, 23. This term was formerly used in England instead of the now modern term *burglary*. 4 Bl. Com. 223.

HAMLET, *Eng. law*. A small village; a part or member of a vill.

HANAPER OFFICE, *Eng. law*. This is the name of one of the offices belonging to the English court of chancery. 3 Bl. Com. 49.

HAND. That part of the human body at the end of the arm.

2. Formerly the hand was considered as the symbol of good faith, and some contracts derive their names from the fact that the hand was used in making them; as handsale, (q. v.) mandatum, (q. v.) which comes from *à manu datâ*. The hand is still used for various legal or forensic purposes. When a person is accused of a crime and he is arraigned, and he is asked to hold up his right hand: and when one is sworn as a witness, he is required to lay his right hand on the Bible, or to hold it up.

3. Hand is also the name of a measure of length used in ascertaining the height of horses. It is four inches long. See *Measure: Ell*.

4. In a figurative sense, by hand is understood a particular form of writing; as if B writes a good hand. Various kinds of hand have been used, as, the secretary hand, the Roman hand, the court hand, &c. Wills and contracts may be written in any of these, or any other which is intelligible.

HANDBILL. A printed or written notice put up on walls, &c., in order to inform those concerned of something to be done.

HANDSALE, *contracts*. Anciently, among all the northern nations, shaking of hands was held necessary to bind a bargain; a custom still retained in verbal contracts; a sale thus made was called *handsale, venditio per mutuam manum complexionem*. In process of time the same word was used to signify the price or earnest which was given immediately after the shaking of hands, or instead thereof. In some parts of the country it is usual to speak of hand money, as the part of the consideration paid or to be paid at the execution of a contract of sale. 2 Bl. Com. 448. Heineccius, *de Antique* Jure Germanico, lib. 2, § 335; Toull. Dr. Civ. Fr. liv. 3, t. 3, c. 2, n. 33.

HANDWRITING, *evidence*. Almost every person's handwriting has something whereby it may be distinguished from the writing of others, and this difference is sometimes intended by the term.

2. It is sometimes necessary to prove that a certain instrument or name is in the handwriting of a particular person; that is done either by the testimony of a witness, who saw the paper or signature actually written, or by one who has by sufficient means, acquired such a knowledge of the general character of the handwriting of the party, as will enable him to swear to his belief, that the handwriting of the person is the handwriting in question. 1 Phil. Ev. 422; Stark. Ev. h. t.; 2 John. Cas. 211; 5 John. R. 144; 1 Dall. 14; 2 Greenl. R. 33; 6 Serg. & Rawle, 568; 1 Nott & M'Cord, 554; 19 Johns. R. 134; Anthon's N. P. 77; 1 Ruffin's R. 6; 2 Nott & M'Cord, 400; 7 Com. Dig. 447; Bac. Ab. Evidence, M; Dane's Ab. Index, h. t.

HANGING, *punishment*. Death by the halter, or the suspending of a criminal, condemned to suffer death, by the neck, until life is extinct. A mode of capital punishment.

HANGMAN. The name usually given to a man employed by the sheriff to put a man to death, according to law, in pursuance of a judgment of a competent court, and lawful warrant. The same as executioner. (q. v.)

HAP. An old word which signifies to catch; as, "to hap the rent," "to hap the deed poll." Techn. Dict. h. t.

HARBOR. A place where ships may ride with safety; any navigable water protected by the surrounding country; a haven. (q. v.) It is public property. 1 Bouv. Inst. n. 435.

To HARBOR, *torts*. To receive clandestinely or without lawful authority a person for the purpose of so concealing him that another having a right to the lawful custody of such person, shall be deprived of the same; for example, the harboring of a wife or an apprentice, in order to deprive the husband or the master of them; or in a less technical sense, it is the reception of persons improperly. 10 N. H. Rep. 247; 4 Scam. 498.

2. The harboring of such persons will subject the harborer to an action for the injury; but in order to put him completely in the wrong, a demand should be made for their restoration, for in cases where the

harborer has not committed any other wrong than merely receiving the plaintiff's wife, child, or apprentice, he may be under no obligation to return them without a demand. 1 Chit. Pr. 564; Dane's Ab. Index, h. t.; 2 N. Car. Law Repos. 249; 5 How. U. S. Rep. 215, 227.

HARD LABOR, *punishment*. In those states where the penitentiary system has been adopted, convicts who are to be imprisoned, as part of their punishment, are sentenced to perform *hard labor*. This labor is not greater than many freemen perform voluntarily, and the quantity required to be performed is not at all unreasonable. In the penitentiaries of Pennsylvania it consists in being employed in weaving, shoemaking, and such like employments.

HART. A stag or male deer of the forest five years old complete.

HAT MONEY, *mar. law*. The name of a small duty paid to the captain and mariners of a ship, usually called primage. (q. v.)

TO HAVE. These words are used in deeds for the conveyance of land, in that clause which usually declared for what estate the land is granted. The same as Habendum. (q. v.) Vide *Habendum; Tenendum*.

HAVEN. A place calculated for the reception of ships, and so situated, in regard to the surrounding land, that the vessel may ride at anchor in it in safety. Hale, de Port. Mar. c. 2; 2 Chit. Com. Law, 2; 15 East, R. 304, 5. Vide *Creek; Port; Road*.

HAWKERS. Persons going from place to place with goods and merchandise for sale. To prevent impositions they are generally required to take out licenses, under regulations established by the local laws of the states.

HAZARDOUS CONTRACT, *civil law*. When the performance of that which is one of its objects, depends on an uncertain event, the contract is said to be hazardous. Civ. Co. of Lo. art. 1769; 1 Bouv. Inst. n. 707.

2. When a contract is hazardous, and the lender may lose all or some part of his principal, it is lawful for him to charge more than lawful interest for the use of his money. Bac. Ab. Usury, D; 1 J. J. Marsh, 596; 3 J. J. Marsh, 84.

HEAD BOROUGH, *English law*. Formerly he was a chief officer of a borough, but now he is an officer subordinate to constable. St. Armand, Hist. Essay on the Legisl. Power of Eng. 88.

HEALTH. Freedom from pain or sickness; the most perfect state of animal life. It may be defined, the natural agreement and concordant dispositions of the parts of the living body.

2. Public health is an object of the utmost importance, and has attracted the attention of the national and state legislatures.

3. By the act of Congress of the 25th of February, 1799, 1 Story's L. U. S. 564, it is enacted: 1. That the quarantines and other restraints, which shall be established by the laws of any state, respecting any vessels arriving in or bound to any port or district thereof, whether coming from a foreign port or some other part of the United States, shall be observed and enforced by all officers of the United States, in such place. Sect. 1. 2. In times of contagion the collectors of the revenue may remove, under the provisions of the act, into another district. Sect. 4. 3. The judge of any district court may, when a contagious disorder prevails in his district, cause the removal of persons confined in prison under the laws of the United States, into another district. Sect. 5. 4. In case of the prevalence of a contagious disease at the seat of government, the president of the United States may direct the removal of any or all public offices to a place of safety. Sect. 6. 5. In case of such contagious disease, at the seat of government, the chief justice, or in case of his death or inability, the senior associate justice of the supreme court of the United States, may issue his warrant to the marshal of the district court within which the supreme court is by law to be holden, directing him to adjourn the said session of the said court to such other place within the same or adjoining district as he may deem convenient. And the district judges may, under the same circumstances, have the same power to adjourn to some other part of their several districts. Sect. 7.

3. Offences against the provisions of the health laws are generally punished by fine and imprisonment. These are offences against public health, punishable by the common law by fine and imprisonment, such for example, as selling unwholesome provisions. 4 Bl. Com. 162; 2 East's P. C. 822; 6 East, R. 133 to 141; 3 M. & S. 10; 4 Campb. R. 10.

4. Private injuries affecting a man's

health arise upon a breach of contract, express or implied; or in consequence of some tortious act unconnected with a contract.

5.—1. Those injuries to health which arise upon contract are, 1st. The misconduct of medical men, when, through neglect, ignorance, or wanton experiments, they injure their patients. 1 Saund. 312, n. 2. 2d. By the sale of unwholesome food; though the law does not consider a sale to be a warranty as to the goodness or quality of a personal chattel, it is otherwise with regard to food and liquors. 1 Rolle's Ab. 90, pl. 1, 2.

6.—2. Those injuries which affect a man's health, and which arise from tortious acts unconnected with contracts, are, 1st. Private nuisances. 2d. Public nuisances. 3d. Breaking quarantine. 4th. By sudden alarms, and frightening; as by raising a pretended ghost. 4 Bl. Com. 197, 201, note 25; 1 Hale, 429; Smith's Forens. Med. 37 to 39; 1 Paris & Fonbl. 351, 352. For private injuries affecting his health a man may generally have an action on the case.

HEALTH OFFICER. The name of an officer invested with power to enforce the health laws. The powers and duties of health officers are regulated by local laws.

HEARING, *chancery practice*. The term hearing is given to the trial of a chancery suit.

2. The hearing is conducted as follows. When the cause is called on in court, the pleadings on each side are opened in a brief manner to the court by the junior counsel for the plaintiff; after which the plaintiff's leading counsel states the plaintiff's, case, and the points in issue, and submits to the court his arguments upon them. Then the depositions (if any) of the plaintiff's witnesses, and such parts of the defendant's answer as support the plaintiff's case are read by the plaintiff's solicitor; after which the rest of the plaintiff's counsel address the court; then the same course of proceedings is observed on the other side, excepting that no part of the defendant's answer can be read in his favor, if it be replied to; the leading counsel for the plaintiff is then heard in reply; after which the court pronounces the decree. Newl. Pr. 153, 4; 14 Vin. Ab. 233; Com. Dig. Chancery, T. 1, 2, 3.

HEARING, *crim. law*. The examination of a prisoner charged with a crime or misdemeanor, and of the witnesses for the accuser.

2. The magistrate should examine with care all the witnesses for the prosecution, or so many of them as will satisfy his mind that there is sufficient ground to believe the prisoner guilty, and that the case ought to be examined in court and the prisoner ought to be tried. If, after the hearing of all such witnesses, the offence charged is not made out, or, if made out, the matter charged is not criminal, the magistrate is bound to discharge the prisoner.

3. When the magistrate cannot for want of time, or on account of the absence of a witness, close the hearing at one sitting, he may adjourn the case to another day, and, in bailable offences, either take bail from the prisoner for his appearance on that day, or commit him for a further hearing. See *Further hearing*.

4. After a final hearing, unless the magistrate discharge the prisoner, it is his duty to take bail in bailable offences, and he is the sole judge of the amount of bail to be demanded; this, however, must not be excessive. He is the sole judge, also, whether the offence be bailable or not. When the defendant can give the bail required, he must be discharged; when not, he must be committed to the county prison, to take his trial, or to be otherwise disposed of according to law. See 1 Chit. Cr. Law, 72, ch. 2.

HEARSAY EVIDENCE. The evidence of those who relate, not what they know themselves, but what they have heard from others.

2. As a general rule, hearsay evidence of a fact is not admissible. If any fact is to be substantiated against a person, it ought to be proved in his presence by the testimony of a witness sworn or affirmed to speak the truth.

3. There are, however, exceptions to the rule. 1. Hearsay is admissible when it is introduced, not as a medium of proof in order to establish a distinct fact, but as being in itself a part of the transaction in question, when it is a part of the *res gestæ*. 1 Phil. Ev. 218; 4 Wash. C. C. R. 729; 14 Serg. & Rawle, 275; 21 How. St. Tr. 535; 6 East, 193.

4.—2. What a witness swore on a former trial, between the same parties, and where the same point was in issue as in the second action, and he is since dead, what he swore to is in general, evidence. 2 Show. 47; 11

John. R. 446; 2 Hen. & Munf. 193; 17 John. R. 176. But see 14 Mass. 234; 2 Russ. on Cr. 683, and the notes.

5.—3. The dying declarations of a person who has received a mortal injury, as to the fact itself, and the party by whom it was committed, are good evidence under certain circumstances. Vide *Declarations*, and 15 John. R. 286; 1 Phil. Ev. 215; 2 Russ. on Cr. 683.

6.—4. In questions concerning public rights, common reputation is admitted to be evidence.

7.—5. The declarations of deceased persons in cases where they appear to have been made against their interest, have been admitted.

8.—6. Declarations in cases of birth and pedigree are also to be received in evidence.

9.—7. Boundaries may be proved by hearsay evidence, but, it seems, it must amount to common tradition or repute. 6 Litt. 7; 6 Pet. 341; Cooke, R. 142; 4 Dev. 342; 1 Hawks, 45; 4 Hawks, 116; 4 Day, 265. See 3 Ham. 283; 3 Bouv. Inst. n. 3065, et seq.

10. There are perhaps a few more exceptions which will be fonnd in the books referred to below. 2 Russ. on Cr. B. 6, c. 3; Phil. Ev. ch. 7, s. 7; 1 Stark. Ev. 40; Rosc. Cr. Ev. 20; Rosc. Civ. Ev. 19 to 24; Bac. Ab. Evidence, K; Dane's Ab. Index, h. t. Vide also, Dig. 39, 3, 2, 8; Id. 22, 3, 28. See Gresl. Eq. Ev. pt. 2, c. 3, s. 3, p. 218, for the rules in courts of equity, as to receiving hearsay evidence; 20 Am. Jur. 68.

HEDGE-BOTE. Wood used for repairing hedges or fences. 2 Bl. Com. 35; 16 John. 15.

HEIFER. A young cow, which has not had a calf. A beast of this kind two years and a half old, was held to be improperly described in the indictment as a cow. 2 East, P. C. 616; 1 Leach, 105.

HEIR. One born in lawful matrimony, who succeeds by descent, and right of blood, to lands, tenements or hereditaments, being an estate of inheritance. It is an established rule of law, that God alone can make an heir. Beame's Glanville, 146; 1 Thomas, Co. Lit. 931; and Butler's note, p. 938. Under the word heirs are comprehended the heirs of heirs in infinitum. 1 Co. Litt. 7 b, 9 a, 237 b; Wood's Inst. 69. According to many authorities, heir may be *nomen collectivum*, as well in a deed as in a will, and operate in both in the same manner, as heirs in the plural number. 1 Roll Abr. 253; Ambl. 453; Godb. 105; T. Jones, 111; Cro. Eliz. 313; 1 Burr. 38; 10 Vin. Abr. 233, pl. 1; 8 Vin. Abr. 233; sed vide 2 Prest. on Est. 9, 10. In wills, in order to effectuate the intention of the testator, the word *heirs* is sometimes construed to mean next of kin; 1 Jac. & Walk. 388; and children. Ambl. 273. See further, as to the force and import of this word, 2 Vent. 311; 1 P. Wms. 229; 3 Bro. P. C. 60, 454; 2 P. Wms. 1, 369; 2 Black. R. 1010; 4 Ves. 26, 766, 794; 2 Atk. 89, 580; 5 East, Rep. 533; 5 Burr. 2615; 11 Mod. 189; 8 Vin. Abr. 317; 1 T. R. 630; Bac. Abr. Estates in fee simple, B.

2. There are several kinds of heirs specified below.

3. By the civil law, heirs are divided into testamentary or instituted heirs; legal heirs, or heirs of the blood; to which the Civil Code of Louisiana has added irregular heirs. They are also divided into unconditional and beneficiary heirs.

4. It is proper here to notice a difference in the meaning of the word heir, as it is understood by the common and by the civil law. By the civil law, the term *heirs* was applied to all persons who were called to the succession, whether by the act of the party or by operation of law. The person who was created universal successor by a will, was called the testamentary heir; and the next of kin by blood was, in cases of intestacy, called the heir at law, or heir by intestacy. The executor of the common law is, in many respects, not unlike the testamentary heir of the civil law. Again, the administrator in many respects corresponds with the heir by intestacy. By the common law, executors—unless expressly authorized by the will—and administrators, have no right, except to the personal estate of the deceased; whereas, the heir by the civil law was authorized to administer both the personal and real estate. 1 Brown's Civ. Law, 344; Story, Confl. of Laws, § 508.

5. All free persons, even minors, lunatics, persons of insane mind or the like, may transmit their estates as intestate ab intestato, and inherit from others. Civ. Code of Lo. 945; Accord, Co. Lit. 8 a.

6. The child in its mother's womb, is considered as born for all purposes of its own interest; it takes all successions opened in its favor, after its conception, provided it be capable of succeeding at the moment of

its birth. Civ. Code of Lo. 948. Nevertheless, if the child conceived is reputed born, it is only in the hope of its birth; it is necessary then that the child be born alive, for it cannot be said that those who are born dead ever inherited. Id. 949. See *In ventre sa mere.*

HEIR APPARENT. One who has an indefeasible right to the inheritance, provided he outlive the ancestor. 2 Bl. Com. 208.

HEIR, BENEFICIARY. A term used in the civil law. Beneficiary heirs are those who have accepted the succession, under the benefit of an inventory regularly made. Civ. Code of Lo. art. 879. If the heir apprehend that the succession will be burdened with debts beyond its value, he accepts with benefit of inventory, and in that case he is responsible only for the value of the succession. See *Inventory, benefit of.*

HEIR, COLLATERAL. A collateral heir is one who is not of the direct line of the deceased, but comes from a collateral line; as, a brother, sister, an uncle and aunt, a nephew, niece, or cousin of the deceased.

HEIR, CONVENTIONAL, *civil law.* A conventional heir is one who takes a succession by virtue of a contract; for example, a marriage contract, which entitles the heir to the succession.

HEIR, FORCED. Forced heirs are those who cannot be disinherited. This term is used among the civilians. Vide *Forced heirs.*

HEIR, GENERAL. Heir at common law, in the English law. The heir at common law is he who, after his father or ancestor's death has a right to, and is introduced into all his lands, tenements and hereditaments. He must be of the whole blood, not a bastard, alien, &c. Bac. Abr. Heir, B 2; *Coparceners; Descent.*

HEIR, IRREGULAR. In Louisiana, irregular heirs are those who are neither testamentary nor legal, and who have been established by law to take the succession. See Civ. Code of Lo. art. 874. When the deceased has left neither lawful descendants nor ascendants, nor collateral relations, the law calls to his inheritance either the surviving husband or wife, or his or her natural children, or the state. Id. art. 911. This is called an irregular succession.

HEIR AT LAW. He who, after his ancestor's death intestate, has a right to all lands, tenements, and hereditaments, which belonged to him, or of which he was seised. The same as heir general. (q. v.)

HEIR, LEGAL, *civil law.* A legal heir is one who is of the same blood of the deceased, and who takes the succession by force of law; this is different from a testamentary or conventional heir, who takes the succession in virtue of the disposition of man. See Civil Code of Louis. art. 873, 875; Dict. de Jurisp., Heritier legitime. There are three classes of legal heirs, to wit: the children and other lawful descendants; the fathers and mothers and other lawful ascendants; and the collateral kindred. Civ. Code of Lo. art. 883.

HEIR LOOM, *estates.* This word seems to be compounded of heir and loom, that is, a frame, *viz.* to weave in. Some derive the word loom from the Saxon *loma*, or *geloma*, which signifies utensils or vessels generally. However this may be, the word *loom*, by time, is drawn to a more general significa tion, than it, at the first, did bear, compre hending all implements of household; as, tables, presses, cupboards, bedsteads, wainscots, and which, by the custom of some countries, having belonged to a house, are never inventoried after the decease of the owner, as chattels, but accrue to the heir, with the house itself. *Minsheu.* The term *heir looms* is applied to those chattels which are considered as annexed and necessary to the enjoyment of an inheritance.

2. They are chattels which, contrary to the nature of chattels, descend to the heir, along with the inheritance, and do not pass to the executor of the last proprietor. Charters, deeds, and other evidences of the title of the land, together with the box or chest in which they are contained; the keys of a house, and fish in a fish pond, are all heir looms. 1 Inst. 3 a; Id. 185 b; 7 Rep. 17 b; Cro. Eliz. 372; Bro. Ab. Charters, pl. 13; 2 Bl. Com. 28; 14 Vin. Ab. 291.

HEIR PRESUMPTIVE. A presumptive heir is one who, in the present circumstances, would be entitled to the inheritance, but whose rights may be defeated by the contingency of some nearer heir being born. 2 Bl. Com. 208. In Louisiana, the presumptive heir is he who is the nearest relation of the deceased, capable of inheriting. This quality is given to him before the decease of the person from whom he is to inherit, as well as after the opening of the succession, until he has accepted or renounced it. Civ. Code of Lo. art. 876.

HEIR, TESTAMENTARY, *civil law.* A testamentary heir is one who is constituted heir by testament executed in the form prescribed by law. He is so called to distinguish him from the legal heirs, who are called to the succession by the law; and from conventional heirs, who are so constituted by a contract *inter vivos*. See *Hæres factus; Devisee.*

HEIR, UNCONDITIONAL. A term used in the civil law, adopted by the Civil Code of Louisiana. Unconditional heirs are those who inherit without any reservation, or without making an inventory, whether their acceptance be express or tacit. Civ. Code of Lo. art. 878.

HEIRESS. A female heir to a person having an estate of inheritance. When there is more than one, they are called *co-heiresses*, or *co-heirs*.

HEPTARCHY, *Eng. law*. The name of the kingdom or government established by the Saxons, on their establishment in Britain; so called because it was composed of *seven* kingdoms, namely, Kent, Essex, Sussex, Wessex, East Anglia, Mercia, and Northumberland.

HERALDRY, *civil and canon law*. The art or office of a herald. It is the art, practice, or science of recording genealogies, and blazoning arms or ensigns armorial. It also teaches whatever relates to the marshaling of cavalcades, processions, and other public ceremonies. Encyc.; Ridley's View of the Civil and Canon Law, pt. 2, c. 1, § 6.

HERBAGE, *English law*. A species of easement, which consists in the right to feed one's cattle on another man's ground.

HEREDITAMENTS, *estates*. Anything capable of being inherited, be it corporeal or incorporeal, real, personal, or mixed, and including not only lands and everything thereon, but also heir looms, and certain furniture which, by custom, may descend to the heir, together with the land. Co. Litt. 5 b; 1 Tho. Co. Litt. 219; 2 Bl. Com. 17. By this term such things are denoted, as may be the subject-matter of inheritance, but not the inheritance itself; it cannot, therefore, by its own intrinsic force, enlarge an estate, *prima facie* a life estate, into a fee. 2 B. & P. 251; 8 T. R. 503; 1 Tho. Co. Litt. 219, note T.

2. Hereditaments are divided into corporeal and incorporeal. Corporeal hereditaments are confined to lands. (q. v.) Vide *Incorporeal hereditaments*, and Shep. To. 91; Cruise's Dig. tit. 1, s. 1; Wood's Inst. 221; 3 Kent, Com. 321; Dane's Ab. Index, h. t.; 1 Chit. Pr. 203–229; 2 Bouv. Inst n. 1595, et seq.

HEREDITARY. That which is inherited.

HERESY, *Eng. law*. The adoption of any erroneous religious tenet, not warranted by the established church.

2. This is punished by the deprivation of certain civil rights, and by fine and imprisonment. 1 East, P. C. 4.

3. In other countries than England, by heresy is meant the profession, by Christians, of religious opinions contrary to the dogmas approved by the established church of the respective countries. For an acconnt of the origin and progress of the laws against heresy, see Giannoni's Istoria di Napoli, vol. 3, pp. 250, 251, &c.

4. In the United States, happily, we have no established religion; there can, therefore, be no legal heresy. Vide *Apostacy; Christianity*.

HERISCHILD. A species of English military service, or knight's fee.

HERIOTS, *Eng. law*. A render of the best beast or other goods, as the custom may be, to the lord, on the death of the tenant. 2 Bl. Com. 97.

2 They are usually divided into two sorts, heriot service, and heriot custom; the former are such as are due upon a special reservation in the grant or lease of lands, and therefore amount to little more than a mere rent; the latter arise upon no special reservation whatsoever, but depend merely upon immemorial usage and custom. These are defined to be a customary tribute of goods and chattels, payable to the lord of the fee, on the decease of the owner of the land. 2 Bl. Com. 422. Vide Com. Dig. Copyhold, K 18; Bac. Ab. h. t.; 2 Saund. Index, h. t.; 1 Vern. 441.

HERITAGE. By this word is understood, among the civilians, every species of immovable which can be the subject of property, such as lands, houses, orchards, woods, marshes, ponds, &c., in whatever mode they may have been acquired, either by descent or purchase. 3 Toull. 472. It is something that can be inherited. Co. Litt. s. 731.

HERMAPHRODITES. Persons who have in the sexual organs the appearance of both sexes. They are adjudged to belong to that which prevails in them. Co. Litt. 2, 7; Domat, Lois Civ. liv. 1, t. 2, s 1, n. 9.

2. The sexual characteristics in the hu

man species are widely separated, and the two sexes are never, perhaps, united in the same individual. 2 Dunglison's Hum. Physiol. 304; 1 Beck's Med. Jur. 94 to 110.

3. Dr. William Harris, in a lecture delivered to the Philadelphia Medical Institute, gives an interesting account of a supposed hermaphrodite who came under his own observation in Chester county, Pennsylvania. The individual was called Elizabeth, and till the age of eighteen, wore the female dress, when she threw it off, and assumed the name of Rees, with the dress and habits of a man; at twenty-five, she married a woman, but had no children. Her clitoris was five or six inches long, and in coition, which she greatly enjoyed, she used this instead of the male organ. She lived till she was sixty years of age, and died in possession of a large estate, which she had acquired by her industry and enterprise. Medical Examiner, vol. ii. p. 314. Vide 1 Briand, Méd. Lég. c. 2, art. 2, § 2, n. 2; Dict. des Sciences Méd. art. Hypospadias, et art. Impuissance; Guy, Med. Jur. 42, 47.

HIDE, *measures.* In England, a hide of land, according to some ancient manuscripts, contained one hundred and twenty acres. Co. Litt. 5; Plowd. 167; Touchst. 93.

HIERARCHY, *eccl. law.* A hierarchy signified, originally, *power of the priest;* for in the beginning of societies, the priests were entrusted with all the power; but, among the priests themselves, there were different degrees of power and authority, at the summit of which was the sovereign pontiff, and this was called the hierarchy. Now it signifies, not so much the *power of the priests* as the *order of power.*

HIGH. This word has various significations: 1. Principal or chief, as high constable, high sheriff. 2. Prominent, in a bad sense, as high treason. 3. Open, not confined, as high seas.

HIGH CONSTABLE. An officer appointed in some cities bears this name. His powers are generally limited to matters of police, and are not more extensive in these respects than those of *constables.* (q. v.)

HIGH COURT OF DELEGATES, *English law.* The name of a court established by stat. 25 Hen. VIII. c. 19, s. 4. No permanent judges are appointed, but in every case of appeal to this court, there issues a special commission, under the great seal of Great Britain, directed to such persons as the lord chancellor, lord keeper, or lords commissioners of the great seal, for the time being, shall think fit to appoint to hear and determine the same. The persons usually appointed, are three puisne judges, one from each court of common law, and three or more civilians; but in special cases, a fuller commission is sometimes issued, consisting of spiritual and temporal peers, judges of the common law, and civilians, three of each description. In case of the court being equally divided, or no common law judge forming part of the majority, a commission of adjuncts issues, appointing additional judges of the same description. 1 Hagg. Eccl. R. 384; 2 Hagg. Eccl. R. 84; 3 Hagg. Eccl. R. 471; 4 Burr. 2251.

HIGH SEAS. This term, which is frequently used in the laws of the United States, signifies the unenclosed waters of the ocean, and also those waters on the sea coast which are without the boundaries of low water mark. 1 Gall. R. 624; 5 Mason's R. 290; 1 Bl. Com. 110; 2 Hagg. Adm. R. 398; Dunl. Adm. Pr. 32, 33.

2. The Act of Congress of April 30, 1790, s. 8, 1 Story's L. U. S. 84, enacts, that if any person shall commit upon the *high seas,* or in any river, haven, basin, or bay, out of the jurisdiction of any particular state, murder, &c., which, if committed within the body of a county, would, by the laws of the United States, be punishable with death, every such offender, being thereof convicted, shall suffer death; and the trial of crimes committed on the high seas, or in any place out of the jurisdiction of any particular state, shall be in the district where the offender is apprehended, or into which he may first be brought. See 4 Dall. R. 426; 3 Wheat. R. 336; 5 Wheat. 184, 412; 3 W. C. C. R. 515; Serg. Const. Law, 334; 13 Am. Jur. 279, 1 Mason, 147, 152; 1 Gallis. 624.

HIGH TREASON, *English law.* Treason against the king, in contradistinction with petit treason, which is the treason of a servant towards his master; a wife towards her husband; a secular or religious man against his prelate. See *Petit treason; Treason.*

HIGH WATER MARK. That part of the shore of the sea to which the waves ordinarily reach when the tide is at its highest. 6 Mass. R. 435; 1 Pick. R. 180; 1 Halst. R. 1; 1 Russ. on Cr. 107; 2 East, P. C. 803. Vide *Sea shore; Tide.*

HIGHEST BIDDER, *contracts.* He who, at an auction, offers the greatest price for the property sold.

2. The highest bidder is entitled to have

the article sold at his bid, provided there has been no unfairness on his part. A distinction has been made between the *highest* and the *best* bidder. In judicial sales, where the highest bidder is unable to pay, it is said the sheriff may offer the property to the next highest, who will pay, and he is considered the highest best bidder. 1 Dall. R. 419.

HIGHWAY. A passage or road through the country, or some parts of it, for the use of the people. 1 Bouv. Inst. n. 442. The term *highway* is said to be a generic name for all kinds of pubiio ways. 6 Mod. R. 255.

2. Highways are universally laid out by public authority, and repaired at the public expense, by direction of law. 4 Burr. Rep. 2511.

3. The public have an easement over a highway, of which the owner of the land cannot deprive them; but the soil and freehold still remain in the owner, and he may use the land above and below consistently with the easement. He may, therefore, work a mine, sink a drain or water course, under the highway, if the easement remains unimpaired. Vide *Road; Street; Way;* and 4 Vin. Ab. 502; Bac. Ab. h. t.; Com. Dig. Chemin; Dane's Ab. Index, h. t.; Egremont on Highways; Wellbeloved on Highways; Woolrych on Ways; 1 N. H. Rep. 16; 1 Conn. R. 103; 1 Pick. R. 122; 1 M'Cord's R. 67; 2 Mass. R. 127; 1 Pick. R. 122; 3 Rawle, R. 495; 15 John. R. 483; 16 Mass. R. 33; 1 Shepl. R. 250; 4 Day, R. 330; 2 Bail. R. 271; 1 Yeates, Rep. 167.

4. The owners of lots on opposite sides of a highway, are prima facie owners, each of one half of the highway; 9 Serg. & Rawle, 33; Ham. Parties, 275; Bro. Abr. Nuisance, pl. 18; and the owner may recover the possession in ejectment, and have it delivered to him, subject to the public easement. Adams on Eject. 19, 18; 2 Johns. Rep. 357; 15 Johns. Rep. 447; 6 Mass. 454; 2 Mass. 125.

5. If the highway is impassable, the public have the right to pass over the adjacent soil; but this rule does not extend to private ways, without an express grant. Morg. Vad. Mec. 456-7; 1 Tho. Co. Lit. 275, note; 1 Barton, Elem. Conv. 271; Yelv. 142, note 1.

HIGHWAYMAN. A robber on the highway.

HILARY TERM, *Eng. law.* One of the four terms of the courts, beginning the 11th and ending the 31st day of January in each year.

HIGLER, *Eng. law.* A person who carries from door to door, and sells by retail, small articles of provisions, and the like.

HIRE, *contracts.* A bailment, where a compensation is to be given for the use of a thing, or for labor or services about it. 2 Kent's Com. 456; 1 Bell's Com. 451; Story on Bailm. § 369; see 1 Bouv. Inst. n. 980, et seq; Pothier, Contrat de Louage, ch. 1, n. 1; Domat, B. 1, tit. 4, § 1, n. 1; Code Civ. art. 1709, 1710; Civ. Code of Lo. art. 2644, 2645. See this Dict. *Hirer; Letter.*

2. The contract of letting and hiring is usually divided into two kinds; first, *Locatio*, or *Locatio conductio rei*, the bailment of a thing to be used by the hirer, for a compensation to be paid by him.

3. Secondly, *Locatio operis*, or the hire of the labor and services of the hirer, for a compensation to be paid by the letter.

4. And this last kind is again subdivided into two classes: 1. *Locatio operis faciendi*, or the hire of labor and work to be done, or care and attention to be bestowed on the goods let by the hirer, for a compensation; or,

5.—2. *Locatio operis mercium vehendarum*, or the hire and carriage of goods from one place to another, for a compensation. Jones' Bailm. 85, 86, 90, 103, 118; 2 Kent's Com. 456; Code Civ. art. 1709, 1710, 1711.

6. This contract arises from the principles of natural law; it is voluntary, and founded in consent; it involves mutual and reciprocal obligations; and it is for mutual benefit. In some respects it bears a strong resemblance to the contract of sale; the principal difference between them being, that in cases of sale, the owner parts with the whole proprietary interest in the thing; and in cases of hire, the owner parts with it only for a temporary use and purpose. In a sale, the thing itself is the object of the contract; in hiring, the use of the thing is its object. Vinnius, lib. 3, tit. 25, in pr.; Pothier, Louage, n. 2, 3, 4; Jones' Bailm. 86; Story on Bailm. § 371.

7. Three things are of the essence of the contract: 1. That there should be a thing to be let. 2. A price for the hire. 3. A contract possessing a legal obligation. Pothier, Louage, n. 6; Civ. Code of Lo. art. 2640.

8. There is a species of contract in which, though no price in money be paid, and which, strictly speaking, is not the contract of hiring, yet partakes of its nature. According to Pothier, it is an agreement which must be classed with contracts *do ut des*. (q. v.) It frequently takes place among poor people in the country. He gives the following example: two poor neighbors, each owning a horse, and desirous to plough their respective fields, to do which two horses are required, one agrees that he will let the other have his horse for a particular time, on condition that the latter will let the former have his horse for the same length of time. Du Louage, n. 458. This contract is not a hiring, strictly speaking, for want of a price; nor is it a loan for use, because there is to be a recompense. It has been supposed to be a partnership; but it is different from that contract, because there is no community of profits. This contract is, in general, ruled by the same principles which govern the contract of hiring. 19 Toull. n. 247.

9. Hire also means the price given for the use of the thing hired; as, the hirer is bound to pay the hire or recompense.

Vide Domat. liv. 1, tit. 4; Poth. Contrat de Louage; Toull. tomes 18, 19, 20; Merl. Répert. mot Louage; Dalloz, Dict. mot Louage; Argou, Inst. liv. 3, c. 27.

HIRER, *contracts*. Called, in the civil law, *conductor*, and, in the French law, *conducteur*, *procureur*, *locataire*, is he who takes a thing from another, to use it, and pays a compensation therefor. Wood's Inst. B. 3, c. 5, p. 236; Pothier, Louage, n. 1; Domat, B. 1, tit. 4, § 1, n. 2; Jones' Bailm. 70; see this Dict. *Letter*.

2. There is, on the part of the hirer, an implied obligation, not only to use the thing with due care and moderation, but not to apply it to any other use than that for which it is hired; for example, if a horse is hired as a saddle horse, the hirer has no right to use the horse in a cart, or to carry loads, or as a beast of burden. Pothier, Louage, n. 189; Domat, B. 1, tit. 4, § 2, art. 2, 3; Jones' Bailm. 68, 88; 2 Saund. 47 g, and note; 1 Bell's Com. 454; 1 Cowen's R. 322; 1 Meigs, R. 459. If a carriage and horses are hired to go from Philadelphia to New York, the hirer has no right to go with them on a journey to Boston. Jones' Bailm. 68; 2 Ld. Raym. 915. So, if they are hired for a week, he has no right to use them for a month. Jones' Bailm. 68; 2 Ld. Raym. 915; 5 Mass. 104. And if the thing be used for a different purpose from that which was intended by the parties, or in a different manner, or for a longer period, the hirer is not only responsible for all damages, but if a loss occur, although by inevitable casualty, he will be responsible therefor. 1 Rep. Const. C. So. Car. 121; Jones' Bailm. 68, 121; 2 Ld. Raym. 909, 917. In short, such a misuser is deemed a conversion of the property, for which the hirer is deemed responsible. Bac. Abr. Bailment, C; Id. Trover, C, D, E; 2 Saund. 47 g; 2 Bulst. 306, 309.

3. The above rules apply to cases where the hirer has the possession as well as the use of the thing hired; when the owner or his agents retain the possession, the hirer is not in general responsible for an injury done to it. For example, when the letter of a carriage and a pair of horses sent his driver with them, and an injury occurred, the hirer was held not to be responsible. 9 Watts, R. 556, 562; 5 Esp. R. 263; Poth. Louage, n. 196; Jones, Bailm. 88; Story, Bailm. § 403. But see 1 Bos. & P. 404, 409; 5 Esp. N. P. c 35; 10 Am. Jur. 256.

4. Another implied obligation of the hirer is to restore the thing hired, when the bailment is determined. 4 T. R. 260; 3 Camp. 5, n.; 13 Johns. R. 211.

5. The time, the place, and the mode of restitution of the thing hired, are governed by the circumstances of each case, and depend upon rules of presumption of the intention of the parties, like those in other cases of bailment. Story on Bailm. § 415.

6. There is also an implied obligation on the part of the hirer, to pay the hire or recompense. Pothier, Louage, n. 134; Domat, B. 2, tit. 2, § 2, n. 11; Code Civ. art. 1728.

See, generally, Bouv. Inst. Index, h. t., *Employer; Hire; Letter*.

HIS EXCELLENCY. A title given by the constitution of Massachusetts to the governor of that commonwealth. Const. part 2, c. 2, s. 1, art. 1. This title is customarily given to the governors of the other states, whether it be the official designation in their constitutions and laws or not.

HIS HONOR. A title given by the constitution of Massachusetts to the lieutenant governor of that commonwealth.

Const. part 2, c. 2, s. 2, art. 1. It is also customarily given to some inferior magistrates, as the mayor of a city.

HISTORY, *evidence.* The recital of facts written and given out for true.

2. Facts stated in histories may be read in evidence, on the ground of their notoriety. Skin. R. 14; 1 Ventr. R. 149. But these facts must be of a public nature, and the general usages and customs of the country. Bull. N. P. 248; 7 Pet. R. 554; 1 Phil. & Am. Ev. 606; 30 Howell's St. Tr. 492. Histories are not admissible in relation to matters not of a public nature, such as the custom of a particular town, a descent, the boundaries of a county, and the like. 1 Salk. 281; S. C. Skin. 623; T. Jones, 164; 6 C. & P. 586, note. See 9 Ves. 347; 10 Ves. 354; 3 John. 385; 1 Binn. 399; and *Notoriety.*

HODGE-PODGE ACT. A name given to a legislative act which embraces many subjects. Such acts, besides being evident proofs of the ignorance of the makers of them, or of their want of good faith, are calculated to create a confusion which is highly prejudicial to the interests of justice. Instances of this wretched legislation are everywhere to be found. See Barring. on the Stat. 449. Vide *Title; Legislation.*

HŒRES FACTUS, *civil law.* An heir instituted by testament; one made an heir by the testator. Vide *Heir.*

HŒRES NATUS, *civil law.* An heir by intestacy; he on whom an estate descends by operation of law. Vide *Heir.*

HOGSHEAD. A measure of wine, oil, and the like, containing half a pipe; the fourth part of a tun, or sixty-three gallons.

TO HOLD. These words are now used in a deed to express by what tenure the grantee is to have the land. The clause which commences with these words is called the tenendum. Vide *Habendum; Tenendum.*

2. To hold, also means to decide, to adjudge, to decree; as, the court in that case *held* that the husband was not liable for the contract of the wife, made without his express or implied authority.

3. It also signifies to bind under a contract, as the obligor is *held* and firmly bound. In the constitution of the United States, it is provided, that no person *held* to service or labor in one state under the laws thereof, escaping into another, shall, in consequence of any law or regulation therein, be discharged from such service or labor, but shall be delivered up on the claim of the party to whom such service or labor may be due. Art. 4, sec. 3, § 3; 2 Serg. & R. 306; 3 Id. 4; 5 Id. 52; 1 Wash. C. C. R. 500; 2 Pick. 11; 16 Pet. 539, 674.

HOLDER. The holder of a bill of exchange is the person who is legally in the possession of it, either by endorsement or delivery, or both, and entitled to receive payment either from the drawee or acceptor, and is considered as an assignee. 4 Dall. 53. And one who endorses a promissory note for collection, as an agent, will be considered the holder for the purpose of transmitting notices. 2 Hall, R. 112; 6 How. U. S. 248; 20 John. 372. Vide *Bill of Exchange.*

HOLDING OVER. The act of keeping possession by the tenant, without the consent of the landlord, of premises which the latter, or those under whom he claims, had leased to the former, after the term has expired.

2. When a proper notice has been given, this injury is remedied by ejectment, or, under local regulations, by summary proceedings. Vide 2 Yeates' R. 523; 2 Serg. & Rawle, 486; 5 Binn. 228; 8 Serg. & Rawle, 459; 1 Binn. 334, n.; 5 Serg. & Rawle, 174; 2 Serg. & Rawle, *50; 4 Rawle, 123.

HOLOGRAPH. What is written by one's own hand. The same as Olograph. Vide *Olograph.*

HOMAGE, *Eng. law.* An acknowledgment made by the vassal in the presence of his lord, that he is his man, that is, his subject or vassal. The form in law French was, *Jeo deveigne vostre home.*

2. Homage was liege and feudal. The former was paid to the king, the latter to the lord. Liege, was borrowed from the French, as Thaumas informs us, and seems to have meant a service that was personal and inevitable. Houard, Cout. Anglo Norman, tom. 1, p. 511; Beames; Glanville, 215, 216, 218, notes.

HOME PORT. The port where the owner of a ship resides; this is a relative term.

HOMESTALL. The mansion-house.

HOMESTEAD. The place of the house or home place. Homestead farm does not necessarily include all the parcels of land owned by the grantor, though lying and occupied together. This depends upon the intention of the parties when the term is mentioned in a deed, and is to be gathered from the context. 7 N. H. Rep. 241; 15 John. R. 471. See *Manor; Mansion.*

HOMICIDE, *crim. law.* According to Blackstone, it is the killing of any human creature. 4 Com. 177. This is the most extensive sense of this word, in which the intention is not considered. But in a more limited sense, it is always understood that the killing is by human agency, and Hawkins defines it to be the killing of a man by a man. 1 Hawk. c. 8, s. 2. See Dalloz, Dict. h. t. Homicide may perhaps be described to be the destruction of the life of one human being, either by himself, or by the act, procurement, or culpable omission of another. When the death has been intentionally caused by the deceased himself, the offender is called *felo de se;* when it is caused by another, it is justifiable, excusable, or felonious.

2. The person killed must have been born; the killing before birth is called fœticide. (q. v.)

3. The destruction of human life at any period after birth, is homicide, however near it may be to extinction, from any other cause.

4.—1. Justifiable homicide is such as arises, 1st. From unavoidable necessity, without any will, intention or desire, and without any inadvertence in the party killing, and therefore without blame; as, for instance, the execution, according to law, of a criminal who has been lawfully sentenced to be hanged; or, 2d. It is committed for the advancement of public justice; as, if an officer, in the lawful execution of his office, either in a civil or criminal case, should kill a person who assaults and resists him. 4 Bl. Com. 178–180. See *Justifiable homicide.*

5.—2. Excusable homicide is of two kinds: 1st. Homicide *per infortunium.* (q. v.); or, 2d. *Se defendendo,* or self defence. (q. v.) 4 Bl. Com. 182, 3.

6.—3. Felonious homicide, which includes, 1. Self-murder, or suicide; 2. Manslaughter, (q. v.); and, 3. Murder. (q. v.)

Vide, generally, 3 Inst. 47 to 57; 1 Hale, P. C. 411 to 502; 1 Hawk. c. 8; Fost. 255 to 337; 1 East, P. C. 214 to 391; Com. Dig. Justices, L. M.; Bac. Ab. Murder and Homicide: Burn's Just. h. t.; Williams' Just. h. t.; 2 Chit. Cr. Law, ch. 9; Cro. C. C. 285 to 300; 4 Bl. Com. 176 to 204; 1 Russ. Cr. 421 to 553; 2 Swift's Dig. 267 to 292.

HOMINE CAPTO IN WITHERNAM, *Engl. law.* The name of a writ directed to the sheriff, and commanding him to take one who has taken any bondsman, and conveyed him out of the country, so that he cannot be replevied. Vide *Withernam;* Thesaurus, Brev. 63.

HOMINE ELIGENDO, *English law.* The name of a writ directed to a corporation, requiring the members to make choice of a new man, to keep the one part of a seal appointed for statutes merchant. Techn. Dict. h. t.

HOMINE REPLEGIANDO. When a man is unlawfully in custody, he may be restored to his liberty by writ *de homine replegiando,* upon giving bail; or by a writ of *habeas corpus,* which is the more usual remedy. Vide *Writ de homine replegiando.*

HOMO. This Latin word, in its most enlarged sense, includes both man and woman. 2 Inst. 45. Vide *Man.*

HOMOLOGATION, *civil law.* Approbation, confirmation by a court of justice, a judgment which orders the execution of some act; as, the approbation of an award, and ordering execution on the same. Merl. Repért. h. t.; Civil Code of Louis. Index, h. t.; Dig. 4, 8; 7 Toull. n. 224. To homologate, is to say the like, *similiter dicere.* 9 Mart. L. R. 324.

HONESTY. That principle which requires us to give every one his due. *Nul ne doit s'enrichir aux depens du droit d'autrui.*

2. The very object of social order is to promote honesty, and to restrain dishonesty; to do justice and to prevent injustice. It is no less a maxim of law than of religion, *do unto others as you wish to be done by.*

HONOR. High estimation. A testimony of high estimation. Dignity. Reputation. Dignified respect of character springing from probity, principle, or moral rectitude. A duel is not justified by any insult to our honor. Honor is also employed to signify integrity in a judge, courage in a soldier, and chastity in a woman. To deprive a woman of her honor is, in some cases, punished as a public wrong, and by an action for the recovery of damages done to the relative rights of a husband or a father. Vide *Criminal conversation.*

2. In England, when a peer of parliament is sitting judicially in that body, his pledge of honor is received instead of an oath; and in courts of equity, peers, peeresses, and lords of parliament, answer on their honor only. But the courts of com-

mon law know no such distinction. It is needless to add, that as we are not encumbered by a nobility, there is no such distinction in the United States, all persons being equal in the eye of the law.

HONOR, *Eng. law.* The seigniory of a lord paramount. 2 Bl. Com. 91.

To HONOR, *contr.* To accept a bill of exchange; to pay a bill accepted, or a promissory note, on the day it becomes due. 7 Taunt. 164; 1 T. R. 172. Vide *To Dishonor.*

HONORARIUM. A recompense for services rendered. It is usually applied only to the recompense given to persons whose business is connected with science; as the fee paid to counsel.

2. It is said this *honorarium* is purely voluntary, and differs from a fee, which may be recovered by action. 5 Serg. & Rawle, 412; 3 Bl. Com. 28; 1 Chit. Rep. 38; 2 Atk. 332; but see 2 Penna. R. 75; 4 Watts' R. 334; Vide Dalloz, Dict. h. t., and *Salary.* See *Counsellor at law.*

HORS DE SON FEE, *pleading in the ancient English law.* These words signify *out of his fee.* A plea which was pleaded, when a person who pretended to be the lord, brought an action for rent services, as issuing out of his land: because if the defendant could prove the land was out of his fee, the action failed. Vide 9 Rep. 30; 2 Mod. 104; 1 Danvers' Ab. 655; Vin. Ab. h. t.

HORSE. Until a horse has attained the age of four years, he is called a colt. (q. v.) Russ. & Ry. 416. This word is sometimes used as a generic name for all animals of the horse kind. 3 Brev. 9. Vide *Colt; Gender;* and Yelv. 67, a.

HOSTAGE. A person delivered into the possession of a public enemy in the time of war, as a security for the performance of a contract entered into between the belligerents.

2. Hostages are frequently given as a security for the payment of a ransom bill, and if they should die, their death would not discharge the contract. 3 Burr. 1734; 1 Kent, Com. 106; Dane's Ab. Index, h. t.

HOSTELLAGIUM, *Engl. law.* A right reserved to the lords to be lodged and entertained in the houses of their tenants.

HOSTILITY: A state of open enmity; open war. Wolff, Dr. de la Nat. § 1191. Hostility, as it regards individuals, may be permanent or temporary; it is permanent when the individual is a citizen or subject of the government at war, and temporary when he happens to be domiciliated or resident in the country of one of the belligerents; in this latter case the individual may throw off the national character he has thus acquired by residence, when he puts himself in motion, *bona fide,* to quit the country *sine animo revertendi.* 3 Rob. Adm. Rep. 12; 3 Wheat. R. 14.

2. There may be a hostile character merely as to commercial purposes, and hostility may attach only to the person as a temporary enemy, or it may attach only to the property of a particular description. This hostile character in a commercial view, or one limited to certain intents and purposes only, will attach in consequence of having possessions in the territory of the enemy, or by maintaining a commercial establishment there, or by a personal residence, or by particular modes of traffic, as by sailing under the enemy's flag or passport. 9 Cranch, 191; 5 Rob. Adm. Rep. 21, 161; 1 Kent, Com. 73; Wesk. on Ins. h. t.; Chit. Law of Nat. Index, h. t.

HOTCHPOT, *estates.* This homely term is used figuratively to signify the blending and mixing property belonging to different persons, in order to divide it equally among those entitled to it. For example, if a man seised of thirty acres of land, and having two children, should, on the marriage of one of them, give him ten acres of it, and then die intestate seised of the remaining twenty; now, in order to obtain his portion of the latter, the married child must bring back the ten acres he received, and add it to his father's estate, when an equal division of the whole will take place, and each be entitled to fifteen acres. 2 Bl. Com. 190. The term hotchpot is also applied to bringing together all the personal estate of the deceased, with the advancements he has made to his children, in order that the same may be divided agreeably to the provisions of the statute for the distribution of intestate's estates. In bringing an advancement into hotchpot, the donee is not required to account for the profits of the thing given; for example, he is not required to bring into hotchpot the produce of negroes, nor the interest of money. The property must be accounted for at its value when given. 1 Wash. R. 224; 17 Mass. 358; 2 Desaus. 127; 3 Rand. R. 117; 3 Pick. R. 450; 3 Rand. 559; Coop. Justin. 575.

2. In Louisiana the term collation is used instead of hotchpot. The collation of

goods is the supposed or real return to the mass of the succession, which an heir makes of property which he received in advance of his share or otherwise, in order that such property may be divided together with the other effects of the succession. Civ. Code of Lo. art. 1305; and vide from that article to article 1367.

Vide, generally, Bac. Ab. Coparceners, E; Bac. Ab. Executors, &c., K; Com. Dig. Guardian, G 2, Parcener, C 4; 8 Com. Dig. App. tit. Distribution, Statute of, III. For the French law, see Merl. Repért. mots Rapport à succession.

HOUR, *measure of time*. The space of sixty minutes, or the twenty-fourth part of a natural day. Vide *Date; Fraction;* and Co. Litt. 135; 3 Chit. Pr. 110.

HOUSE, *estates*. A place for the habitation and dwelling of man. This word has several significations, as it is applied to different things. In a grant or demise of a house, the curtilage and garden will pass, even without the words "with the appurtenances," being added. Cro. Eliz. 89; S. C. 3 Leon. 214; 1 Plowd. 171; 2 Saund. 401, note 2, 4 Penn. St. R. 93.

2. In a grant or demise of a house with the appurtenances, no more will pass, although other lands have been occupied with the house. 1 P. Wms. 603; Cro. Jac. 526; 2 Co. 32; Co. Litt. 5 d.; Id. 36 a. b.; 2 Saund. 401, note 2.

3. If a house, originally entire, be divided into several apartments, with an outer door to each apartment, and no communication with each other subsists, in such case the several apartments are considered as distinct houses. 6 Mod. 214; Woodf. Land. & Ten. 178.

4. In cases of burglary, the mansion or dwelling-house in which the burglary might be committed, at common law includes the outhouses, though not under the same roof or adjoining to the dwelling-house, provided they were within the curtilage, or common fence, as the dwelling or mansion house. 3 Inst. 64; 1 Hale, 558; 4 Bl. Com. 225; 2 East, P. C. 493; 1 Hayw. N. C. Rep. 102, 142; 2 Russ. on Cr. 14.

5. The term house, in case of arson, includes not only the dwelling but all the outhouses, as in the case of burglary. It is a maxim in law that every man's house is his castle, and there he is entitled to perfect security; this asylum cannot therefore be legally invaded, unless by an officer duly authorized by legal process; and this process must be of a criminal nature to authorize the breaking of an outer door; and even with it, this cannot be done until after demand of admittance and refusal. 5 Co. 93; 4 Leon. 41; T. Jones, 234. The house may be also broken for the purpose of executing a writ of *habere facias*. 5 Co. 93; Bac. Ab. Sheriff, N 3.

6. The house protects the owner from the service of all civil process in the first instance, but not if he is once lawfully arrested and he takes refuge in his own house; in that case, the officer may pursue him and break open any door for the purpose. Foster, 320; 1 Rolle, R. 138; Cro. Jac. 555, Bac. Ab. *ubi sup.* In the civil law the rule was nemo de domo sua extrahi debet. Dig. 50, 17, 103. Vide, generally, 14 Vin. Ab. 315; Yelv. 29 a, n. 1; 4 Rawle, R. 342; Arch. Cr. Pl. 251; and *Burglary*.

7. House is used figuratively to signify a collection of persons, as the house of representatives; or an institution, as the house of refuge; or a commercial firm, as the house of A B & Co. of New Orleans; or a family, as, the house of Lancaster, the house of York.

HOUSE OF COMMONS, *Eng. law*. The representatives of the people, in contradistinction to the nobles, taken collectively are called the house of commons.

2. This house must give its consent to all bills before they acquire the authority of law, and all laws for raising revenue must originate there.

HOUSE OF CORRECTION. A prison where offenders of a particular class are confined. The term is more common in England than in the United States.

HOUSE OF LORDS, *Eng. law*. The English lords, temporal and spiritual, when taken collectively and forming a branch of the parliament, are called the House of Lords.

2. Its assent is required to all laws. As a court of justice, it tries all impeachments.

HOUSE OF REFUGE, *punishment*. The name given to a prison for juvenile delinquents. These houses are regulated in the United States on the most humane principles, by special local laws.

HOUSE OF REPRESENTATIVES, *government*. The popular branch of the legislature.

2. The Constitution of the United States, art. 1, s. 2, 1, provides, that "the house of

representatives shall be composed of members chosen every second year by the people of the several states; and the electors of each state, shall have the qualifications requisite for electors of the most numerous branch of the state legislature."

3. The general qualifications of electors of the assembly, or most numerous branch of the legislature, in the several state governments, are, that they be of the age of twenty-one years and upwards, and free resident citizens of the state in which they vote, and have paid taxes: several of the state constitutions have prescribed the same or higher qualifications, as to property, in the elected, than in the electors.

4. The constitution of the United States, however, requires no evidence of property in the representatives, nor any declarations as to his religious belief. He must be free from undue bias or dependence, by not holding any office under the United States. Art. 1, s. 6, 2.

5. By the constitutions of the several states, the most numerous branch of the legislature generally bears the name of the house of representatives. Vide Story on Constitution of the United States, chap. 9; 1 Kent's Com. 228.

6. By the Act of June 22, 1842, c. 47, it is provided,

§ 1. That from and after the third day of March, one thousand eight hundred and forty-three, the house of representatives shall be composed of members elected agreeably to a ratio of one representative for every seventy thousand six hundred and eighty persons in each state, and of one additional representative for each state having a fraction greater than one moiety of the said ratio, computed according to the rule prescribed by the constitution of the United States; that is to say: Within the state of Maine, seven; within the state of New Hampshire, four; within the state of Massachusetts, ten; within the state of Rhode Island, two; within the state of Connecticut, four; within the state of Vermont, four; within the state of New York, thirty-four; within the state of New Jersey, five; within the state of Pennsylvania, twenty-four; within the state of Delaware, one; within the state of Maryland, six; within the state of Virginia, fifteen; within the state of North Carolina, nine; within the state of South Carolina, seven; within the state of Georgia, eight; within the state of Alabama, seven; within the state of Louisiana, four; within the state of Mississippi, four; within the state of Tennessee, eleven; within the state of Kentucky, ten; within the state of Ohio, twenty-one; within the state of Indiana, ten; within the state of Illinois, seven; within the state of Missouri, five; within the state of Arkansas, one; within the state of Michigan, three.

7.—§ 2. That in every case where a state is entitled to more than one representative, the number to which each state shall be entitled under this apportionment shall be elected by districts composed of contiguous territory, equal in number to the number of representatives to which said state may be entitled, no one district electing more than one representative.

8. For the constitutions of the houses of representatives in the several states, the reader is referred to the names of the states in this work. Vide *Congress.*

HOUSE-BOTE. An allowance of necessary timber out of the landlord's woods, for the repairing and support of a house or tenement. This belongs of common right to any lessee for years or for life. House-bote is said to be of two kinds, *estoveriam ædificandi et ardendi.* Co. Litt. 41.

HOUSEKEEPER. One who occupies a house.

2. A person who occupies every room in the house, under a lease, except one, which is reserved for his landlord, who pays all the taxes, is not a housekeeper. 1 Chit. Rep. 502. Nor is a person a housekeeper, who takes a house, which he afterwards underlets to another, whom the landlord refuses to accept as his tenant; in this case, the under-tenant paid the taxes, and let to the tenant the first floor of the house, and the rent was paid for the whole house to the tenant, who paid it to the landlord. Id. note.

3. In order to make the party a housekeeper, he must be in actual possession of the house; 1 Chit. Rep. 288; and must occupy a whole house. 1 Chit. Rep. 316. See 1 Barn. & Cresw. 178; 2 T. R. 406; 1 Bott, 5; 3 Petersd. Ab. 103, note; 2 Mart. Lo. R. 313.

HOVEL. A place used by husbandmen to set their ploughs, carts, and other farming utensils, out of the rain and sun. Law Latin Dict. A shed; a cottage; a mean house.

HOYMAN. The master or captain of a hoy.

2. Hoymen are liable as common carriers. Story, Bailm. § 496.

HUE AND CRY, *Eng. law.* A mode of pursuing felons, or such as have dangerously wounded any person, or assaulted any one with intent to rob him, by the constable, for the purpose of arresting the offender. 2 Hale, P. C. 100.

HUEBRA, *Spanish law.* An acre of land; or as much as can be ploughed in a day by two oxen. Sp. Dict.; 2 White's Coll. 49.

HUISSIER. An usher of a court. In France, an officer of this name performs many of the duties which in this country devolve on the sheriff or constable. Dalloz, Dict. h. t. See 3 Wend. 173.

HUNDRED, *Eng. law.* A district of country originally comprehending one hundred families. In many cases, when an offence is committed within the hundred, the inhabitants are civilly responsible to the party injured.

2. This rule was probably borrowed from the nations of German origin, where it was known. Montesq. Esp. des Lois, liv. 30, c. 17. It was established by Clotaire, among the Franks. 11 Toull. n. 237.

3. To make the innocent pay for the guilty, seems to be contrary to the first principles of justice, and can be justified only by necessity. In some of the United States laws have been passed making cities or counties responsible for the destruction of property by a mob. This can be justified only on the ground that it is the interest of every one that property should be protected, and that it is for the general good such laws should exist.

HUNDRED GEMOTE. The name of a court among the Saxons. It was holden every month, for the benefit of the inhabitants of the hundred.

HUNDREDORS. In England they are inhabitants of a local division of a county, who, by several statutes, are held to be liable in the cases therein specified, to make good the loss sustained by persons within the hundred, by robbery or other violence, therein also specified. The principal of these statutes are, 13 Edw. I. st. 2, c. 1, s. 4; 28 Edw. III. c. 11; 27 Eliz. c. 13; 29 Car. II. c. 7; 8 Geo. II. c. 16; 22 Geo. II. c. 24.

HUNGER. The desire for taking food. Hunger is no excuse for larceny. 1 Hale, P. C. 54; 4 Bl. Com. 31. But it is a matter which applies itself strongly to the consciences of the judges in mitigation of the punishment.

2. When a person has died, and it is suspected he has been starved to death, an examination of his body ought to be made, to ascertain whether or not he died of hunger. The signs which usually attend death from hunger are the following: The body is much emaciated, and a fœtid, acrid odor exhales from it, although death may have been very recent. The eyes are red and open, which is not usual in other causes of death. The tongue and throat are dry, even to aridity, and the stomach and intestines are contracted and empty. The gall bladder is pressed with bile, and this fluid is found scattered over the stomach and intestines, so as to tinge them very extensively. The lungs are withered, but all the other organs are generally in a healthy state. The blood vessels are usually empty. Foderé, tom. ii. p. 276, tom. iii. p. 231; 2 Beck's Med. Jur. 52; see Eunom. Dial. 2, § 47, p. 142, and the note at p. 384.

HUNTING. The act of pursuing and taking wild animals; the chase.

2. The chase gives a kind of title by occupancy, by which the hunter acquires a right or property in the game which he captures. In the United States, the right of hunting is universal, and limited only so far as to exclude hunters from committing injuries to private property or to the public; as, by shooting on public roads. Vide *Feræ naturæ; Occupancy.*

HURDLE, *Eng. law.* A species of sledge, used to draw traitors to execution.

HUSBAND, *domestic relations.* A man who has a wife.

2. The husband, as such, is liable to certain obligations, and entitled to certain rights, which will be here briefly considered.

3. First, of his obligations. He is bound to receive his wife at his home, and should furnish her with all the necessaries and conveniences which his fortune enables him to do, and which her situation requires; but this does not include such luxuries as, according to her fancy, she deems necessaries; vide article *Cruelty*, where this matter is considered. He is bound to love his wife, and to bear with her faults, and, if possible, by mild means to correct them; and he is required to fulfil towards her his marital promise of fidelity, and can, therefore, have no carnal connexion with any other woman,

without a violation of his obligations. As he is bound to govern his house properly, he is liable for its misgovernment, and he may be punished for keeping a disorderly house, even where his wife had the principal agency, and he is liable for her torts, as for her slander or trespass. He is also liable for the wife's debts, incurred before coverture, provided they are recovered from him during their joint lives; and generally for such as are contracted by her, after coverture, for necessaries, or by his authority, express or implied. See 5 Whart. 395; 5 Binn. 235; 1 Mod. 138; 5 Taunt. 356; 7 T. R. 166; 3 Camp. 27; 3 B. & Cr. 631; 5 W. & S. 164.

4. Secondly, of his rights. Being the head of the family, the husband has a right to establish himself wherever he may please, and in this he cannot be controlled by his wife; he may manage his affairs his own way; buy and sell all kinds of personal property, without any control, and he may buy any real estate he may deem proper, but, as the wife acquires a right in the latter, he cannot sell it, discharged of her dower, except by her consent, expressed in the manner prescribed by the laws of the state where such lands lie. At common law, all her *personal* property, in possession, is vested in him, and he may dispose of it as if he had acquired it by his own contract; this arises from the principle that they are considered one person in law; 2 Bl. Com. 433; and he is entitled to all her property in action, provided he reduces it to possession during her life. Id. 434. He is also entitled to her *chattels real*, but these vest in him not absolutely, but *sub modo;* as, in the case of a lease for years, the husband is entitled to receive the rents and profits of it, and may, if he pleases, sell, surrender, or dispose of it during the coverture, and it is liable to be taken in execution for his debts; and, if he survives her, it is, to all intents and purposes, his own. In case his wife survives him, it is considered as if it had never been transferred from her, and it belongs to her alone. In his wife's freehold estate, he has a life estate, during the joint lives of himself and wife; and, at common law, when he has a child by her who could inherit, he has an estate by the curtesy. But the rights of a husband over the wife's property, are very much abridged in some of the United States, by statutes. See Act of Pennsylvania, passed April 11, 1848.

5. The laws of Louisiana differ essentially from those of the other states, as to the rights and duties of husband and wife, particularly as it regards their property. Those readers, desirous of knowing the legislative regulations on this subject, in that state, are referred to the Civil Code of Louis. B. 1, tit. 4; B. 3, tit. 6.

Vide, generally, articles *Divorce; Marriage; Wife;* and Bac. Ab. Baron and Feme; Rop. H. & W.; Prater on H. & W., Clancy on the Rights, Duties and Liabilities of Husband and Wife; Canning on the Interest of Husband and Wife, &c.; 1 Phil. Ev. 63; Woodf. L. & T. 75; 2 Kent, Com. 109; 1 Salk. 113 to 119‡; Yelv. 106 a, 156 a, 166 a; Vern. by Raithby, 7, 17, 48, 261; Chit. Pr. Index, h. t.; Poth. du Contr. de Mar. n. 379; Bouv. Inst. Index, h. t.

HUSBAND, *mar. law.* The name of an agent who is authorized to make the necessary repairs to a ship, and to act in relation to the ship, generally, for the owner. He is usually called ship's husband. Vide *Ship's Husband.*

HUSBRECE, *old Eng. law.* The ancient name of the offence now called burglary.

HUSTINGS, *Engl. law.* The name of a court held before the lord mayor and aldermen of London; it is the principal and supreme court of the city. See 2 Inst. 327; St. Armand, Hist. Essay on the Legisl. Power of England, 75.

HYDROMETER. An instrument for measuring the density of fluids; being immersed in fluids, as in water, brine, beer, brandy, &c., it determines the proportion of their densities, or their specific gravities, and thence their qualities.

2. By the Act of Congress of January 12, 1825, 3 Story's Laws U. S. 1976, the secretary of the treasury is authorized, under the direction of the president of the United States, to adopt and substitute such hydrometer as he may deem best calculated to promote the public interest, in lieu of that now prescribed by law, for the purpose of ascertaining the proof of liquors; and that after such adoption and substitution, the duties imposed by law upon distilled spirits shall be levied, collected and paid, according to the proof ascertained by any hydrometer so substituted and adopted.

HYPOBOLUM, *civ. law.* The name of the bequest or legacy given by the husband to his wife, at his death, above her dowry. Techn. Dict. h. t.

HYPOTHECATION, *civil law.* This term is used principally in the civil law; it is defined to be a right which a creditor has over a thing belonging to another, and which consists in the power to cause it to be sold, in order to be paid his claim out of the proceeds

2. There are two species of hypothecation, one called pledge, *pignus*, and the other properly denominated hypothecation. Pledge is that species of hypothecation which is contracted by the delivery of the debtor to the creditor, of the thing hypothecated. Hypothecation, properly so called, is that which is contracted without delivery of the thing hypothecated. 2 Bell's Com. 25, 5th ed.

3. Hypothecation is further divided into general and special. When the debtor hypothecates to his creditor all his estate and property, which he has, or may have, the hypothecation is general; when the hypothecation is confined to a particular estate, it is special.

4. Hypothecations are also distinguished into conventional, legal and tacit. 1. Conventional hypothecations are those which arise by the agreement of the parties. Dig. 20, 1, 5.

5.—2. Legal hypothecation is that which has not been agreed upon by any contract, express or implied; such as arises from the effect of judgments and executions.

6.—3. A tacit, which is also a legal hypothecation, is that which the law gives in certain cases, without the consent of the parties, to secure the creditor; such as, 1st. The lien which the public treasury has over the property of public debtors. Code, 8, 15, 1. 2d. The landlord has a lien on the goods in the house leased, for the payment of his rent. Dig. 20, 2, 2; Code, 8, 15, 7. 3d. The builder has a lien, for his bill, on the house he has built. Dig. 20, 1. 4th. The pupil has a lien on the property of the guardian for the balance of his account. Dig. 46, 6, 22; Code, 5, 37, 20. 5th. There is hypothecation of the goods of a testator for the security of a legacy he has given. Code, 6, 43, 1.

7. In the common law, cases of hypothecation, in the strict sense of the civil law, that is, of a pledge of a chattel, without possession by the pledgee, are scarcely to be found; cases of bottomry bonds and claims for seamen's wages against ships are the nearest approach to it; but these are liens and privileges rather than hypothecations. Story, Bailm. § 288. It seems that chattels not in existence, though they cannot be pledged, can be hypothecated, so that the lien will attach, as soon as the chattel has been produced. 14 Pick. R. 497.

Vide, generally, Poth. de l' Hypothèque; Poth. Mar. Contr. translated by Cushing, note 26, p. 145; Commercial Code of France, translated by Rodman, note 52, p. 351; Merl. Répertoire, mot Hypothèque, where the subject is fully considered; 2 Bro. Civ. Law, 195; Ayl. Pand. 524; 1 Law Tracts, 224; Dane's Ab. h. t.; Abbott on Ship. Index, h. t.; 13 Ves. 599; Bac. Ab. Merchant, &c. G; Civil Code of Louis. tit. 22, where this sort of security bears the name of mortgage. (q. v.)

HYPOTHEQUE, *French law.* Properly, the right acquired by the creditor over the immovable property which has been assigned to him by his debtor, as security for his debt, although he be not placed in possession of it. The hypothèque might arise in two ways. 1. By the express agreement of the debtor, which was the conventional hypothèque. 2. By disposition of law, which was the implied or legal hypothèque. This was nothing but a lien or privilege which the creditor enjoyed of being first paid out of the land subjected to this incumbrance. For example, the landlord had hypothèque on the goods of his tenant or others, while on the premises let. A mason had the same on the house he built. A pupil or a minor on the land of his tutor or curator, who had received his money. Domat, Loix Civiles, l. 3, & 1; 2 Bouv. Inst. n. 1817.

I.

IBIDEM. This word is used in references, when it is intended to say that a thing is to be found in the same place, or that the reference has for its object the same thing, case, or other matter.

I O U, *contracts.* The memorandum I O U, (I owe you), given by merchants to each other, is a mere evidence of the debt, and does not amount to a promissory note. Esp. Cas. N. A. 426; 4 Carr. & Payne, 324; 19 Eng. Com. L. Rep. 405; 1 Man. & Gran. 46; 39 E. C. L. R. 346; 1 Campb. 499; 1 Esp. R. 426; 1 Man. Gr. & Sc. 543; Dowl. & R. N. P. Cas. 8.

ICTUS ORBIS, *med. jurisp.* A maim, a bruise, or swelling; any hurt without cutting the skin. When the skin is cut, the injury is called a wound. (q. v.) Bract. lib. 2, tr. 2, c. 5 and 24.

2. *Ictus* is often used by medical authors in the sense of *percussus.* It is applied to the pulsation of the arteries, to any external lesion of the body produced by violence; also to the wound inflicted by a scorpion or venomous reptile. Orbis is used in the sense of circle, circuit, rotundity. It is applied also to the eye balls. *Oculi dicuntur orbes. Castelli Lexicon Medicum.*

IDEM SONANS. Sounding the same.

2. In pleadings, when a name which it is material to state, is wrongly spelled, yet if it be idem sonans with that proved, it is sufficient, as *Segrave* for *Seagrave,* 2 Str. R. 889; *Keen* for *Keene,* Thach. Cr. Cas. 67; *Deadema* for *Diadema,* 2 Ired. 346; *Hutson* for *Hudson,* 7 Miss. R. 142; *Coonrad* for *Conrad,* 8 Miss. R. 291. See 5 Pike, 72; 6 Ala. R. 679; vide also Russ. & Ry. 412; 2 Taunt. R. 401. In the following cases the variances there mentioned were declared to be fatal. Russ. & Ry. 351; 10 East, R. 83; 5 Taunt. R. 14; 1 Baldw. R. 83; 2 Crom. & M. 189; 6 Price, R. 2; 1 Chit. R. 659; 13 E. C. L. R. 194. See, generally, 3 Chit. Pr. 231, 2; 4 T. R. 611; 3 B. & P. 559; 1 Stark. R. 47; 2 Stark. R. 29; 3 Camp. R. 29; 6 M. & S. 45; 2 N. H. Rep. 557; 7 S. & R. 479; 3 Caines, 219; 1 Wash. C. C. R. 285; 4 Cowen, 148; and the article *Name.*

IDENTITATE NOMINIS, *Engl. law.* The name of a writ which lies for a person taken upon a capias or exigent and committed to prison, for another man of the same name; this writ directs the sheriff to inquire whether he be the same person against whom the action was brought, and if not, then to discharge him. F. N. B. 267. In practice, a party in this condition would be relieved by *habeas corpus.*

IDENTITY, *evidence.* Sameness.

2. It is frequently necessary to identify persons and things. In criminal prosecutions, and in actions for torts and on contracts, it is required to be proved that the defendants have in criminal actions, and for injuries, been guilty of the crime or injury charged; and in an action on a contract, that the defendant was a party to it. Sometimes, too, a party who has been absent, and who appears to claim an inheritance, must prove his identity; and, not unfrequently, the body of a person which has been found dead must be identified: cases occur when the body is much disfigured, and, at other times, there is nothing left but the skeleton. Cases of considerable difficulty arise, in consequence of the omission to take particular notice; 2 Stark. Car. 239; Ryan's Med. Jur. 301; and in consequence of the great resemblance of two persons. 1 Hall's Am. Law Journ. 70; 1 Beck's Med. Jur. 509; 1 Paris, Med. Jur. 222; 3 Id. 143; Trail. Med. Jur. 33; Foderé, Méd. Lég. ch. 2, tome 1, p. 78—139.

3. In cases of larceny, trover, replevin, and the like, the things in dispute must always be identified. Vide 4 Bl. Com. 396.

4. M. Briand, in his Manuel Complet de Médicine Légale, 4eme partie, ch. 1, gives rules for the discovery of particular marks, which an individual may have had, and also the true color of the hair, although it may have been artificially colored. He also gives some rules for the purpose of discovering, from the appearance of a skeleton, the sex, the age, and the height of the person when living, which he illustrates by various examples. See, generally, 6 C. & P 677; 1 C. & M. 730; 3 Tyr. 806; Shelf. on Mar. & Div. 226; 1 Hagg. Cons. R. 189; Best on Pres. Appx. case 4; Wills on Circums. Ev. 143, et seq.

IDES, NONES and CALENDS, *civil law.* This mode of computing time, formerly in use among the Romans, is yet used in several chanceries in Europe, particularly in that of the pope. Many ancient instruments bear these dates; it is therefore proper to notice them here. These three words designate all the days of the month.

2. The calends were the first day of every month, and were known by adding the names of the months; as *calendis januarii, calendis februarii*, for the first days of the months of January and February. They designated the following days by those before the *nones*. The fifth day of each month, except those of March, May, July, and October; in those four months the *nones* indicated the seventh day; *nonis* martii, was therefore the seventh day of March, and so of the rest. In those months in which the nones indicated the fifth day, the second was called *quarto nonas* or 4 *nonas*, that is to say, *quarto die ante nonas*, the fourth day before the *nones*. The words *die* and *ante*, being understood, were usually suppressed. The third day of each of those eight months was called *tertio*, or 3 *nonas*. The fourth, was *pridie* or 2 *nonas;* and the fifth was *nonas*. In the months of March, May, July and October, the second day of the months was called *sexto* or 6 *nonas;* the third, *quinto*, or 5 *nonas;* the fourth, *quarto*, or 4 *nonas;* the fifth, *tertio*, or 3 *nonas;* the sixth, *pridie*, usually abridged *prid.* or *pr.* or 2 *nonas;* and the seventh, *nones*. The word *nonæ* is so applied, it is said, because it indicates the ninth day before the ides of each month.

3. In the months of March, May, July and October, the fifteenth day of the months was the *Ides*. These are the four months, as above mentioned, in which the nones were on the seventh day. In the other eight months of the year the *nones* were the fifth of the month, and the *ides* the thirteenth; in each of them the *ides* indicated the ninth day after the *nones*. The seven days between the *nones* and the *ides*, which we count 8, 9, 10, 11, 12, 13, and 14, in March, May, July and October, the Romans counted *octavo*, or 8 *idus; septimo*, or 7 *idus; sexto*, or 6 *idus; quinto*, or 5 *idus; quarto*, or 4 *idus; tertio*, or 3 *idus; pridie*, or 2 *idus;* the word *ante* being understood as mentioned above. As to the other eight months of the year, in which the nones indicated the fifth day of the month, instead of our 6, 7, 8, 9, 10, 11, and 12, the Romans counted *octavo idus, septimo*, &c. The word is said to be derived from the Tuscan, iduare, in Latin *dividere*, to divide, because the day of ides divided the month into equal parts. The days from the ides to the end of the month were computed as follows; for example, the fourteenth day of January, which was the next day after the ides, was called *decimo nono*, or 19 *kalendas*, or ante *kalendas febrarii;* the fifteenth, *decimo octavo*, or 18 *kalendas februarii*, and so of the rest, counting in a retrograde manner to *pridie* or 2 *kalendas februarii*, which was the thirty-first day of January.

4. As in some months the ides indicate the thirteenth, and in some the fifteenth of the month, and as the months have not an equal number of days, it follows that the *decimo nono* or 19 *kalendas* did not always happen to be the next day after the *Ides;* this was the case only in the months of January, August and December. *Decimo sexto* or the 16th in February; *decimo septimo* or 17, March, May, July and October; *decimo octavo* or 18, in April, June, September, and November. Merlin, Répertoire de Jurisprudence, mots Ides, Nones et Calendes.

A Table of the Calends of the Nones and the Ides.

	Jan., Aug., Dec. 31 days.	March, May. July, Oct. 31 days.	April, June, Sept., Nov. 30 days.	Febru'y 28, bissextile; 29 days.
1	Calendis.	Calendis	Calendis	Calendis
2	4 Nonas.	6 Nonas	4 Nonas	4 Nonas
3	3 Nonas.	5 Nonas	3 Nonas	3 Nonas
4	Prid. Non.	4 Nonas	Prid. Non.	Prid. Non.
5	Nonis	3 Nonas	Nonis	Nonis
6	8 Idus	Prid. Non.	8 Idus	8 Idus
7	7 Idus	Nonis	7 Idus	7 Idus
8	6 Idus	8 Idus	6 Idus	6 Idus
9	5 Idus	7 Idus	5 Idus	5 Idus
10	4 Idus	6 Idus	4 Idus	4 Idus
11	3 Idus	5 Idus	3 Idus	3 Idus
12	Prid. Idus	4 Idus	Prid. Idus	Prid. Idus
13	Idibus	3 Idus	Idibus	Idibus
14	19 Cal.	Prid. Idus	18 Cal.	16 Cal.
15	18 Cal.	Idibus	17 Cal.	15 Cal.
16	17 Cal.	17 Cal.	16 Cal.	14 Cal.
17	16 Cal.	16 Cal.	15 Cal.	13 Cal.
18	15 Cal.	15 Cal.	14 Cal.	12 Cal.
19	14 Cal.	14 Cal.	13 Cal.	11 Cal.
20	13 Cal.	13 Cal.	12 Cal.	10 Cal.
21	12 Cal.	12 Cal.	11 Cal.	9 Cal.
22	11 Cal.	11 Cal.	10 Cal.	8 Cal.
23	10 Cal.	10 Cal.	9 Cal.	7 Cal.
24	9 Cal.	9 Cal.	8 Cal.	6 Cal.*
25	8 Cal.	8 Cal.	7 Cal.	5 Cal.
26	7 Cal.	7 Cal.	6 Cal.	4 Cal.
27	6 Cal.	6 Cal.	5 Cal.	3 Cal.
28	5 Cal.	5 Cal.	4 Cal.	Prid. Cal.
29	4 Cal.	4 Cal.	3 Cal.	
30	3 Cal.	3 Cal.	Prid. Cal.	
31	Prid. Cal.	Prid. Cal.		

* If February is bissextile. *Sexto Calencas* (6 Cal.) is counted twice, viz: for the 24th and 25th of the month. Hence the word *bis-sextils*.

IDIOCY, *med. jur.* That condition of mind, in which the reflective, or all or a part of the affective powers, are either entirely wanting, or are manifested to the least possible extent.

2. Idiocy generally depends upon organic defects. The most striking physical trait, and one seldom wanting, is the diminutive size of the head, particularly of the anterior superior portions, indicating a deficiency of the anterior lobes of the brain. According to Gall, whose observations on this subject are entitled to great consideration, its circumference, measured immediately over the orbitar arch, and the most prominent part of the occipital bone, is between 11½ and 14½ inches. Gall, sur les Fonctions, p. 329. In the intelligent adult, it usually measures from 21 to 22 inches. Chit. Med. Jur. 248. See, on this subject, the learned work of Dr. Morton, of Philadelphia, entitled Crania Americana. The brain of an idiot equals that of a new born infant; that is, about one-fourth, one-fifth, or one-sixth of the cerebral mass of an adult's in the enjoyment of his faculties. The above is the only constant character observed in the heads of idiots. In other respects their forms are as various as those of other persons. When idiocy supervenes in early infancy, the head is sometimes remarkable for immense size. This unnatural enlargement arises from some kind of morbid action preventing the development of the cerebral mass, and producing serous cysts, dropsical effusions, and the like.

3. In idiocy the features are irregular; the forehead low, retreating, and narrowed to a point; the eyes are unsteady, and often squint; the lips are thick, and the mouth is generally open; the gums are spongy, and the teeth are defective; the limbs are crooked and feeble. The senses are usually entirely wanting; many are deaf and dumb, or blind; and others are incapable of perceiving odors, and show little or no discrimination in their food for want of taste. Their movements are constrained and awkward, they walk badly, and easily fall, and are not less awkward with their hands, dropping generally what is given to them. They are seldom able to articulate beyond a few sounds. They are generally affected with rickets, epilepsy, scrofula, or paralysis. Its subjects seldom live beyond the twenty-fifth year, and are incurable, as there is a natural deformity which cannot be remedied. Vide Chit. Med. Jur. 345; Ray's Med. Jur. c. 2; 1 Beck's Med. Jur. 571, Shelf. on Lun. Index, h. t.; and *Idiot*.

IDIOT, *persons*. A person who has been without understanding from his nativity, and whom the law, therefore, presumes never likely to attain any. Shelf. on Lun. 2.

2. It is an imbecility or sterility of mind, and not a perversion of the understanding. Chit. Med. Jur. 345, 327, note *s;* 1 Russ. on Cr. 6; Bac. Ab. h. t. A; Bro. Ab. h. t.; Co. Litt. 246, 247; 3 Mod. 44; 1 Vern. 16; 4 Rep. 126; 1 Bl. Com. 302. When a man cannot count or number twenty, nor tell his father's or mother's name, nor how old he is, having been frequently told of it, it is a fair presumption that he is devoid of understanding. F. N. B. 233. Vide 1 Dow, P. C. new series, 392; S. C. 3 Bligh, R. new series, 1. Persons born deaf, dumb, and blind, are presumed to be idiots, for the senses being the only inlets of knowledge, and these, the most important of them, being closed, all ideas and associations belonging to them are totally excluded from their minds. Co. Litt. 42; Shelf. on Lun. 3. But this is a mere presumption, which, like most others, may be rebutted; and doubtless a person born deaf, dumb, and blind, who could be taught to read and write, would not be considered an idiot. A remarkable instance of such an one may be found in the person of Laura Bridgman, who has been taught how to converse and even to write. This young woman was, in the year 1848, at school at South Boston. Vide Locke on Human Understanding, B. 2, c. 11, §§ 12, 13; Ayliffe's Pand. 234; 4 Com. Dig. 610; 8 Com. Dig. 644.

3. Idiots are incapable of committing crimes, or entering into contracts. They cannot of course make a will; but they may acquire property by descent.

Vide, generally, 1 Dow's Parl. Cas. new series, 392; 3 Bligh's R. 1; 19 Ves. 286 352, 353; Stock on the Law of Non Compotes Mentis; Bouv. Inst. Index, h. t.

IDIOTA INQUIRENDO, WRIT DE. This is the name of an old writ which directs the sheriff to inquire whether a man be an idiot or not. The inquisition is to be made by a jury of twelve men. Fitz. N. B. 232.

IDLENESS. The refusal or neglect to engage in any lawful employment, in order to gain a livelihood.

2. The vagrant act of 17 G. II. c. 5, which, with some modifications, has been

adopted, in perhaps most of the states, describes idle persons to be those who, not having wherewith to maintain themselves, live idle, without employment, and refuse to work for the usual and common wages. These are punishable according to the different police regulations, with fine and imprisonment. In Pennsylvania, vagrancy is punished, on a conviction before a magistrate, with imprisonment for one month.

IGNIS JUDICIUM, *Eng. law.* The name of the old judicial trial by fire.

IGNOMINY. Public disgrace, infamy, reproach, dishonor. Ignominy is the opposite of esteem. Wolff, § 145. See *Infamy.*

IGNORAMUS, *practice.* We are ignorant. This word, which in law means we are uninformed, is written on a bill by a grand jury, when they find that there is not sufficient evidence to authorize their finding it a true bill. Sometimes, instead of using this word, the grand jury endorse on the bill, *Not found.* 4 Bl. Com. 305. Vide *Grand Jury.*

IGNORANCE. The want of knowledge.

2. Ignorance is distinguishable from error. Ignorance is want of knowledge; error is the non-conformity or opposition of our ideas to the truth. Considered as a motive of our actions, ignorance differs but little from error. They are generally found together, and what is said of one is said of both.

3. Ignorance and error, are of several kinds. 1. When considered as to their object, they are of law and of fact. 2. When examined as to their origin, they are voluntary or involuntary. 3. When viewed with regard to their influence on the affairs of men, they are essential or non-essential.

4.—§ 1. Ignorance of law and fact. 1. *Ignorance of law,* consists in the want of knowledge of those laws which it is our duty to understand, and which every man is presumed to know. The law forbids any one to marry a woman whose husband is living. If any man, then, imagined he could marry such a woman, he would be ignorant of the law; and, if he married her, he would commit an error as to a matter of law. How far a party is bound to fulfil a promise to pay, upon a supposed liability, and in ignorance of the law, see 12 East, R. 38; 2 Jac. & Walk. 263; 5 Taunt. R. 143; 3 B. & Cresw. R. 280; 1 John. Ch. R. 512, 516; 6 John. Ch. R. 166; 9 Cowen's R. 674; 4 Mass. R. 342; 7 Mass. R. 452; 7 Mass R. 488; 9 Pick. R. 112; 1 Binn. R. 27. And whether he can be relieved from a contract entered into in ignorance or mistake of the law; 1 Atk. 591; 1 Ves. & Bea. 23, 30; 1 Chan. Cas. 84; 2 Vern. 243; 1 John. Ch. R. 512; 2 John. Ch. R. 51; 1 Pet. S. C. R. 1; 6 John. Ch. R. 169, 170; 8 Wheat. R. 174; 2 Mason, R. 244, 342.

5.—2. *Ignorance of fact,* is the want of knowledge as to the fact in question. It would be an error resulting from ignorance of a fact, if a man believed a certain woman to be unmarried and free, when, in fact, she was a married woman; and were he to marry her under that belief, he would not be criminally responsible. Ignorance of the laws of a foreign government, or of another state, is ignorance of a fact. 9 Pick. 112. Vide, for the difference between ignorance of law and ignorance of fact, 9 Pick. R. 112; Clef. des Lois Rom. mot Fait; Dig. 22, 6, 7.

6.—§ 2. Ignorance is either voluntary or involuntary. 1. It is voluntary when a party might, by taking reasonable pains, have acquired the necessary knowledge. For example, every man might acquire a knowledge of the laws which have been promulgated, a neglect to become acquainted with them is therefore voluntary ignorance. Doct. & St. 1, 46; Plowd. 343.

7.—2. Involuntary ignorance is that which does not proceed from choice, and which cannot be overcome by the use of any means of knowledge known to him and within his power; as, the ignorance of a law which has not yet been promulgated.

8.—§ 3. Ignorance is either essential or non-essential. 1. By *essential* ignorance is understood that which has for its object some essential circumstance so intimately connected with the matter in question, and which so influences the parties that it induces them to act in the business. For example, if A should sell his horse to B, and at the time of the sale the horse was dead, unknown to the parties, the fact of the death would render the sale void. Poth. Vente, n. 3 and 4; 2 Kent, Com. 367.

9.—2. *Non-essential* or accidental ignorance is that which has not of itself any necessary connexion with the business in question, and which is not the true consideration for entering into the contract; as if a man should marry a woman whom he believed to be rich, and she proved to be poor, this fact would not be essential, and the marriage would therefore be good. Vide, generally, Ed. Inj. 7; 1 Johns. Ch. R. 512; 2 Johns. Ch. R. 41; S. C. 14 Johns. R 501; Dougl. 467; 2 East, R. 469; 1 Campb. 134; 5 Taunt. 379; 3 M. & S. 378; 12 East, R. 38; 1 Vern. 243; 3 P. Wms. 127, n.; 1 Bro. C. C. 92; 10 Ves. 406; 2 Madd. R. 163; 1 V. & B. 30; 2 Atk. 112, 591; 3 P. Wms. 315; Mos. 364; Doct. & Stud. Dial. 1, c. 26, p. 92; Id. Dial. 2, ch. 46, p. 303; 2 East, R. 469; 12 East, R. 38; 1 Fonbl. Eq. B. 1, ch. 2, § 7, note *v*; 8 Wheat. R. 174; S. C. 1 Pet. S. C. R. 1; 1 Chan. Cas. 84; 1 Story, Eq. Jur. § 137, note 1; Dig. 22, 6; Code, 1, 16; Clef des Lois Rom. h. t.; Merl. Répert. h. t.; 3 Sav. Dr. Rom. Appendice viii., pp. 337 to 444.

ILL FAME. This is a technical expression, that which means not only bad character as generally understood, but every person, whatever may be his conduct and character in life, who visits bawdy houses, gaming houses, and other places which are of ill fame, is a person of ill fame. 1 Rogers' Recorder, 67; Ayl. Par. 276; 2 Hill, 558; 17 Pick. 80; 1 Hagg. Eccl. R. 720; 2 Hagg. Cons. R. 24; 1 Hagg. Cons. R. 302, 303; 1 Hagg. Eccl. R. 767; 2 Greenl. Ev. § 44.

ILLEGAL. Contrary to law; unlawful.

2. It is a general rule, that the law will never give its aid to a party who has entered into an illegal contract, whether the same be in direct violation of a statute, against public policy, or opposed to public morals. Nor to a contract which is fraudulent, which affects the defendant or a third person.

3. A contract in violation of a statute is absolutely void, and, however disguised, it will be set aside, for no form of expression can remove the substantial defect inherent in the nature of the transaction; the courts will investigate the real object of the contracting parties, and if that be repugnant to the law, it will vitiate the transaction.

4. Contracts against the *public policy* of the law, are equally void as if they were in violation of a public statute; a contract not to marry *any one*, is therefore illegal and void. See *Void.*

5. A contract against the purity of manners is also illegal; as, for example, an agreement to cohabit unlawfully with another, is therefore void; but a bond given for past cohabitation, being considered as a remuneration for past injury, is binding. 4 Bouv. Inst. n. 3853.

6. All contracts which have for their object, or which may in their consequences, be injurious to third persons, altogether unconnected with them, are in general illegal and void. Of the first, an example may be found in the case where a sheriff's officer received a sum of money from a defendant for admitting to bail, and agreed to pay the bail, part of the money which was so exacted. 2 Burr. 924. The case of a wager between two persons, as to the character of a third, is an example of the second class. Cowp. 729; 4 Camp. 152; 1 Rawle, 42; 1 B. & A. 683. Vide *Illicit; Unlawful.*

ILLEGITIMATE. That which is contrary to law; it is usually applied to children born out of lawful wedlock. A bastard is sometimes called an illegitimate child.

ILLEVIABLE. A debt or duty that cannot or ought not to be levied. *Nihil* set upon a debt is a mark for *illeviable.*

ILLICIT. What is unlawful; what is forbidden by the law. Vide *Unlawful.*

2. This word is frequently used in policies of insurance, where the assured warrants against illicit trade. By illicit trade is understood that "which is made unlawful by the laws of the country to which the object is bound." The assured having entered into this warranty, is required to do no act which will expose the vessel to be legally condemned. 2 L. R. 337, 338. Vide *Insurance; Trade; Warranty.*

ILLICITE. Unlawfully.

2. This word has a technical meaning, and is requisite in an indictment where the act charged is unlawful; as, in the case of a riot. 2 Hawk. P. C. 25, § 96.

ILLINOIS. The name of one of the United States of America. This state was admitted into the Union by virtue of a "Resolution declaring the admission of the state of Illinois into the Union," passed December 3, 1818, in the following words: *Resolved,* &c. That, whereas, in pursuance of an Act of Congress, passed on the eighteenth day of April, one thousand eight hundred and eighteen, entitled "An act to enable the people of the Illinois territory to form a constitution and state government, and for the admission of such state into the Union, on an equal footing with the original states," the people of said territory did, on the twenty-sixth day of August, in the present year, by a convention called for that purpose, form for themselves a constitution and state government, which constitution and state government, so formed, is republican, and in conformity to the principles of the articles of compact between the original states and the people and states in the territory northwest of the river Ohio, passed on the thirteenth day of July, one thousand seven hundred and eighty-seven: *Resolved*, &c. That the state of Illinois shall be one, and is hereby declared to be one, of the United States of America, and admitted into the Union on an equal footing with the original states, in all respects whatever.

2. A constitution for this state was adopted in convention held at Kaskaskia, on the 26th day of August, 1818, which continued in force until the first day of April, 1848. A convention to revise the constitution assembled at Springfield, June 7, 1847, in pursuance of an act of the general assembly of the state of Illinois, entitled "An act to provide for the call of a convention." On the first day of August, 1848, this convention adopted a constitution of the state of Illinois, and by the 13th section of the schedule thereof it provided that this constitution shall be the supreme law of the land from and after the first day of April, A. D. 1848.

3. It will be proper to consider, 1. The rights of citizens to vote at elections. 2. The distribution of the powers of government.

4.—1. The sixth article directs that,

§ 1. In all elections, every white male citizen above the age of twenty-one years, having resided in the state one year next preceding any election, shall be entitled to vote at such election; and every white male inhabitant of the age aforesaid, who may be a resident of the state at the time of the adoption of this constitution, shall have the right of voting as aforesaid; but no such citizen or inhabitant shall be entitled to vote, except in the district or county in which he shall actually reside at the time of such election.

§ 2. All votes shall be given by ballot.

§ 5. No elector loses his residence in the state by reason of his absence on business of the United States, or this state.

§ 6. No soldier, seaman or mariner of the United States, is deemed a resident of the state, in consequence of being stationed within the state.

5. The second article distributes the powers of the government as follows:

§ 1. The powers of the government of the state of Illinois shall be divided into three distinct departments, and each of them be confided to a separate body of magistracy, to wit: Those which are legislative, to one; those which are executive, to another; and those which are judicial, to another.

§ 2. No person, or collection of persons, being one of these departments, shall exercise any power properly belonging to either of the others, except as hereinafter expressly directed or permitted; and all acts in contravention of this section shall be void.

These will be separately considered.

6. The *legislative department* will be considered by taking a view, 1. Of those parts of the constitution which relate to the *general assembly*. 2. Of the senate. 3. Of the house of representatives.

7.—1st. Of the *general assembly*. The third article of the constitution provides as follows:

§ 1. The legislative authority of this state shall be vested in a general assembly; which shall consist of a senate and house of representatives, both to be elected by the people.

§ 2. The first election for senators and representatives shall be held on the Tuesday after the first Monday in November, one thousand eight hundred and forty-eight; and thereafter, elections for members of the general assembly shall be held once in two years, on the Tuesday next after the first Monday in November, in each and every county, at such places therein as may be provided by law.

§ 7. No person elected to the general assembly shall receive any civil appointment within this state, or to the senate of the United States, from the governor, the governor and senate, or from the general assembly, during the term for which he shall have been elected; and all such appointments, and all votes given for any such member for any such office or appointment, shall be void; nor shall any member of the general assembly be interested, either directly or indirectly, in any contract with the state, or any county thereof, authorized by any law passed during the time for which he shall have been elected, or during one year after the expiration thereof.

§ 12. The senate and house of representatives, when assembled, shall each choose a speaker and other officers, (the speaker of the senate excepted.) Each house shall judge of the qualifications and election of its own members, and sit upon its own adjournments. Two-thirds of each house shall constitute a quorum; but a smaller number may adjourn from day to day, and compel the attendance of absent members.

§ 13. Each house shall keep a journal of its proceedings, and publish them. The yeas and nays of the members on any question shall, at the desire of any two of them, be entered on the journals.

§ 14. Any two members of either house shall have liberty to dissent and protest against any act or resolution, which they may think injurious to the public, or to any individual, and have the reasons of their dissent entered on the journals.

§ 15. Each house may determine the rules of its proceedings, punish its members for disorderly behaviour, and, with the concurrence of two-thirds of all the members elected, expel a member, but not a second time for the same cause; and the reason for such expulsion shall be entered upon the journal, with the names of the members voting on the question.

§ 16. When vacancies shall happen in either house, the governor, or the person exercising the powers of governor, shall issue writs of election to fill such vacancies.

§ 17. Senators and representatives shall, in all cases, except treason, felony, or breach of the peace, be privileged from arrest during the session of the general assembly, and in going to and returning from the same; and for any speech or debate in either house, they shall not be questioned in any other place.

§ 18. Each house may punish, by imprisonment during its session, any person, not a member, who shall be guilty of disrespect to the house, by any disorderly or contemptuous behaviour in their presence: *Provided*, such imprisonment shall not, at any one time, exceed twenty-four hours.

§ 19. The doors of each house, and of committees of the whole, shall be kept open, except in such cases as in the opinion of the house require secrecy. Neither house shall, without the consent of the other, adjourn for more than two days, nor to any other place than that in which the two houses shall be sitting.

8.—2d. Of the *senate*. The senate will be considered by taking a view of, 1. The qualification of senators. 2. Their election. 3. By whom elected. 4. When elected. 5. Number of senators. 6. The duration of their office.

9. First. Art. 3, s. 4, of the Constitution, directs that "No person shall be a senator who shall not have attained the age of thirty years; who shall not be a citizen of the United States, five years an inhabitant of this state, and one year in the county or district in which he shall be chosen, immediately preceding his election, if such county or district shall have been so long erected; but if not, then within the limits of the county or counties, district or districts, out of which the same shall have been taken, unless he shall have been absent on the public business of the United States, or of this state, and shall not, moreover, have paid a state or county tax."

10. Secondly. The senators at their first session herein provided for, shall be divided by lot, as near as can be, into two classes. The seats of the first class shall be vacated at the expiration of the second year, and those of the second class at the expiration of the fourth year; so that one-half thereof, as near as possible, may be biennially chosen forever thereafter. Art. 3, s. 5.

11. Thirdly. The senators are elected by the people.

12. Fourthly. The first election shall be held on the Tuesday after the first Monday in November, 1848; and thereafter the elections shall be on the Tuesday after the first Monday in November, once in two years. Art. 3, s. 2.

13. Fifthly. The senate shall consist of twenty-five members, and the house of representatives shall consist of seventy-five members, until the population of the state shall amount to one million of souls, when five members may be added to the house, and five additional members for every five hundred thousand inhabitants thereafter, until the whole number of representatives shall amount to one hundred; after which, the number shall neither be increased nor diminished; to be apportioned among the several counties according to the number of white inhabitants. In all future apportionments, where more than one county shall be thrown into a representative district, all the representatives to which said counties may be entitled shall be elected by the entire district. Art. 3, s. 6.

14. Sixthly. The senators at their first session herein provided for shall be divided by lot, as near as can be, into two classes. The seats of the first class shall be vacated at the expiration of the second year, and those of the second class at the expiration of the fourth year, so that one-half thereof,

as near as possible, may be biennially chosen forever thereafter. Art. 3, s. 5.

15.—3. The *house of representatives.* This will be considered in the same order which has been observed in relation to the senate.

16. First. No person shall be a representative who shall not have attained the age of twenty-five years; who shall not be a citizen of the United States, and three years an inhabitant of this state; who shall not have resided within the limits of the county or district in which he shall be chosen twelve months next preceding his election, if such county or district shall have been so long erected; but if not, then within the limits of the county or counties, district or districts, out of which the same shall have been taken, unless he shall have been absent on the public business of the United States, or of this state; and who, moreover, shall not have paid a state or county tax. Art. 3, s. 3.

17. Secondly. They are elected biennially.

18. Thirdly. Representatives are elected by the people.

19. Fourthly. Representatives are elected at the same time that senators are elected.

20. Fifthly. The house of representatives shall consist of seventy-five members. See ante, No. 16.

21. Sixthly. Their office continues for two years.

22.—2. The *executive department.* The executive power is vested in a governor. Art. 4, s. 1. It will be proper to consider, 1. His qualifications. 2. His election. 3. The duration of his office. 4. His authority and duty.

23. First. No person except a citizen of the United States shall be eligible to the office of governor; nor shall any person be eligible to that office who shall not have attained the age of thirty-five years, and been ten years a resident of this state, and fourteen years a citizen of the United States. Art. 4, s. 4.

24. Secondly. His election is to be on the Tuesday next after the first Monday in November. The first election in 1848, and every fourth year afterwards.

25. Thirdly. He remains in office for four years. The first governor is to be installed on the first Monday of January, 1849, and the others every fourth year thereafter.

26. Fourthly. His authority and duty. He may give information and recommend measures to the legislature—grant reprieves, commutations and pardons, except in cases of treason and impeachment, but in these cases he may suspend execution of the sentence until the meeting of the legislature—require information from the officers of the executive department, and take care that the laws be faithfully executed—on extraordinary occasions, convene the general assembly by proclamation—be commander-in-chief of the army and navy of the state, except when they shall be called into the service of the United States—nominate, and, by and with the consent and advice of the senate, appoint all officers whose offices are established by the constitution, or which may be created by law, and whose appointments are not otherwise provided for—in case of disagreement between the two houses with respect to the time of adjournment, adjourn the general assembly to such time as he thinks proper, provided it be not to a period beyond a constitutional meeting of the same. Art. 4. He has also the *veto* power.

27. A *lieutenant governor* shall be chosen at every election of governor, in the same manner, continue in office for the same time, and possess the same qualifications. In voting for governor and lieutenant governor, the electors shall distinguish whom they vote for as governor, and whom as lieutenant-governor. Art. 4, s. 14. The following are his principal powers and duties:

§ 15. The lieutenant governor shall, by virtue of his office, be speaker of the senate, have a right, when in committee of the whole, to debate and vote on all subjects, and, whenever the senate are equally divided, to give the casting vote.

§ 16. Whenever the government shall be administered by the lieutenant governor, or he shall be unable to attend as speaker of the senate, the senators shall elect one of their own number as speaker for that occasion; and if, during the vacancy of the office of governor, the lieutenant governor shall be impeached, removed from his office, refuse to qualify, or resign, or die, or be absent from the state, the speaker of the senate shall, in like manner, administer the government.

§ 17. The lieutenant governor, while he acts as speaker of the senate, shall receive for his services the same compensation which shall, for the same period, be allowed to the speaker of the house of representatives, and no more.

§ 18. If the lieutenant governor shall be called upon to administer the government, and shall, while in such administration, resign, die, or be absent from the state, during the recess of the general assembly, it shall be the duty of the secretary of state, for the time being, to convene the senate for the purpose of choosing a speaker.

§ 19. In case of the impeachment of the governor, his absence from the state, or inability to discharge the duties of his office, the powers, duties, and emoluments of the office shall devolve upon the lieutenant governor; and in case of his death, resignation, or removal, then upon the speaker of the senate for the time being, until the governor, absent or impeached, shall return or be acquitted; or until the disqualification or inability shall cease; or until a new governor shall be elected and qualified.

§ 20. In case of a vacancy in the office of governor, for any other cause than those herein enumerated, or in case of the death of the governor elect before he is qualified, the powers, duties, and emoluments of the office devolve upon the lieutenant governor, or speaker of the senate, as above provided, until a new governor be elected and qualified.

28.—3. The *judiciary department.* The judicial power is vested in one supreme court, in circuit courts, in county courts, and in justices of the peace; but inferior local courts, of civil and criminal jurisdiction, may be established by the general assembly in the cities of the state, but such courts shall have a uniform organization and jurisdiction in such cities. Art. 5, s. 1. These will be separately considered.

29.—1st. Of the *supreme court,* its organization and jurisdiction. 1. Of its *organization.* 1st. The judges must be citizens of the United States; have resided in the state five years previous to their respective elections; and two years next preceding their election in the division, circuit, or county in which they shall respectively be elected; and not be less than thirty-five years of age at the time of their election. 2d. The judges are elected each one in a particular district, by the people. But the legislature may change the mode of election. 3d. The supreme court consists of a chief justice and three associates, any two of whom form a quorum; and a concurrence of two of said judges is necessary to a decision. 4th. They hold their office for nine years. After the first election, the judges are to draw by lot, and one is to go out of office in three, one in six, and the other in nine years. And one judge is to be elected every third year. 2. Of the *jurisdiction* of the supreme court. This court has original jurisdiction in cases relative to the revenue, in cases of *mandamus, habeas corpus,* and in such cases of impeachment as may be by law directed to be tried before it, and it has appellate jurisdiction in all other cases.

30.—2d. Of the *circuit courts,* their organization and jurisdiction. 1st. Of their *organization.* The state is divided into nine judicial districts, in each of which a circuit judge, having the same qualifications as the supreme judges, except that he may be appointed at the age of thirty years, is elected by the qualified electors, who holds his office for six years and until his successor shall be commissioned and qualified; but the legislature may increase the number of circuits. 2d. Of their *jurisdiction.* The circuit courts have jurisdiction in all cases at law and equity, and in all cases of appeals from all inferior courts.

31.—3d. Of the *county courts.* There is in each county a court to be called a county court. It is composed of one judge, elected by the people, who holds his office for four years. Its jurisdiction extends to all probate and such other jurisdiction as the general assembly may confer in civil cases, and in such criminal cases as may be prescribed by law, when the punishment is by fine only, not exceeding one hundred dollars. The county judge, with such justices of the peace in each county as may be designated by law, shall hold terms for the transaction of county business, and shall perform such other duties as the general assembly shall prescribe; *Provided,* the general assembly may require that two justices, to be chosen by the qualified electors of each county, shall sit with the county judge in all cases; and there shall be elected, quadrennially, in each county, a clerk of the county court, who shall be *ex officio* recorder, whose compensation shall be fees; *Provided,* the general assembly may, by law, make the clerk of the circuit court *ex officio* recorder, in lieu of the county clerk.

32.—4th. Of *justices of the peace.* There shall be elected in each county in this state, in such districts as the general assembly may direct, by the qualified electors thereof, a competent number of justices of the peace, who shall hold their offices for the term of four years, and until their successors shall have been elected and qualified, and who shall perform such duties, receive such compensation, and exercise such jurisdiction as may be prescribed by law.

ILLITERATE. This term is applied to one unacquainted with letters.

2. When an ignorant man, unable to read, signs a deed or agreement, or makes his mark instead of a signature, and he alleges, and can prove, that it was falsely read to him, he is not bound by it, in consequence of the fraud. And the same effect would result, if the deed or agreement were falsely read to a blind man, who could have read before he lost his sight, or to a foreigner who did not understand the language. For a plea of "laymen and unlettered," see Bauer *v.* Roth, 4 Rawle, Rep. 85 and pp. 94, 95.

3. To induce an illiterate man, by false representations and false reading, to sign a note for a greater amount than that agreed on, is indictable as a cheat. 1 Yerg. 76. Vide, generally, 2 Nels. Ab. 946; 2 Co. 3; 11 Co. 28; Moor, 148.

ILLUSION. A species of mania in which the sensibility of the nervous system is altered, excited, weakened or perverted. The patient is deceived by the false appearance of things, and his reason is not sufficiently active and powerful to correct the error, and this last particular is what distinguishes the sane from the insane. Illusions are not unfrequent in a state of health, but reason corrects the errors and dissipates them. A square tower seen from a distance may appear round, but on approaching it, the error is corrected. A distant mountain may be taken for a cloud, but as we approach, we discover the truth. To a person in the cabin of a vessel under sail, the shore appears to move; but reflection and a closer examination soon destroy this illusion. An insane individual is mistaken on the qualities, connexions, and causes of the impressions he actually receives, and he forms wrong judgments as to his internal and external sensations; and his reason does not correct the error. 1 Beck's Med. Jur. 538; Esquirol, Maladies Mentales, prém. partie, III., tome 1, p. 202. Dict. des Sciences Médicales, Hallucination, tome 20, p. 64. See *Hallucination.*

ILLUSORY APPOINTMENT, *chancery practice.* Such an appointment or disposition of property under a power as is merely nominal and not substantial.

2. Illusory appointments are void in equity. Sugd. Pow. 489; 1 Vern. 67; 1 T. R. 438, note; 4 Ves. 785; 16 Ves. 26; 1 Taunt. 289; and the article *Appointment.*

TO IMAGINE, *Eng. law.* In cases of treason the law makes it a crime to imagine the death of the king. In order to complete the offence there must, however, be an overt act; the terms *compassing* and *imagining* being synonymous. It has been justly remarked that the words to compass and imagine are too vague for a statute whose penalty affects the life of a subject. Barr. on the Stat. 243, 4. Vide *Fiction.*

IMBECILITY, *med. jur.* A weakness of the mind, caused by the absence or obliteration of natural or acquired ideas; or it is described to be an abnormal deficiency either in those faculties which acquaint us with the qualities and ordinary relations of things, or in those which furnish us with the moral motives that regulate our relations and conduct towards our fellow men. It is frequently attended with excessive activity of one or more of the animal propensities.

2. Imbecility differs from idiocy in this, that the subjects of the former possess some intellectual capacity, though inferior in degree to that possessed by the great mass of mankind; while those of the latter are utterly destitute of reason. Imbecility differs also from stupidity. (q. v.) The former consists in a defect of the mind, which renders it unable to examine the data presented to it by the senses, and therefrom to deduce the correct judgment; that is, a defect of intensity, or reflective power. The latter is occasioned by a want of intensity, or perceptive power.

3. There are various degrees of this disease. It has been attempted to classify the degrees of imbecility, but the careful observer of nature will perhaps be soon satisfied that the shades of difference between one species and another, are almost imperceptible. Ray, Med. Jur. ch. 3; 1 Beck, Med. Jur. 550, 542; 1 Hagg. Ecc. R. 384; 2 Philm. R. 449; 1 Litt. R. 252. 5 John. Ch. R. 161; 1 Litt. R. 101; Des Maladies mentales, considérées dans leurs rapports avec la legislation civille et criminelle, 8; Georget, Discussion medico-légale sur la folie, 140.

IMMATERIAL. What is not essential

unimportant; what is not requisite; what is informal; as, an immaterial averment, an immaterial issue.

2. When a witness deposes to something immaterial, which is false, although he is guilty of perjury in *foro conscientiæ*, he cannot be punished for perjury. 2 Russ. on Cr. 521; 1 Hawk. b. 1, c. 69, s. 8; Bac. Ab. Perjury, A.

IMMATERIAL AVERMENT. One alleging with needless particularity or unnecessary circumstances, what is material and requisite, and which, properly, might have been stated more generally, or without such circumstances or particulars; or, in other words, it is a statement of unnecessary particulars, in connexion with, and as descriptive of, what is material. Gould on Pl. c. 3, § 186.

2. It is highly improper to introduce immaterial averments, because, when they are made, they must be proved; as, if a plaintiff declare for rent on a demise which is described as reserving a certain annual rent, payable "by four even and equal quarterly payments," &c.; and on the trial it appears that there was no stipulation with regard to the time or times of payment of the rents, the plaintiff cannot recover. The averment as to the time, though it need not have been made, yet it must be proved, and the plaintiff having failed in this, he cannot recover; as there is a variance between the contract declared upon and the contract proved. Dougl. 665.

3. But when the immaterial averment is such that it may be struck out of the declaration, without striking out at the same time the cause of action, and when there is no variance between the contract as laid in the declaration and that proved, immaterial averments then need not be proved. Gould on Pl. c. 3, § 188.

IMMATERIAL ISSUE. One taken on a point not proper to decide the action; for example, if in an action of debt on bond, conditioned for the payment of ten dollars and fifty cents at a certain day, the defendant pleads the payment of ten dollars according to the form of the condition, and the plaintiff, instead of demurring, tenders issue upon the payment, it is manifest that, whether this issue be found for the plaintiff or the defendant, it will remain equally uncertain whether the plaintiff is entitled to maintain his action, or not; for, in an action for the penalty of a bond, conditioned to pay a certain sum, the only material question is, whether the exact sum were paid or not, and the question of payment of a part is a question quite beside the legal merits. Hob. 113; 5 Taunt. 386.

IMMEDIATE. That which is produced directly by the act to which it is ascribed, without the intervention or agency of any distinct intermediate cause.

2. For *immediate* injuries the remedy is trespass; for those which are *consequential*, an action on the case. 11 Mass. R. 59, 137, 525; 1 & 2 Ohio R. 342; 6 S. & R. 348; 18 John. 257; 19 John. 381; 2 H. & M. 423; 1 Yeates, R. 586; 12 S. & R. 210; Coxe, R. 339; Harper's R. 113; 6 Call's R. 44; 1 Marsh. R. 194.

3. When an immediate injury is caused by negligence, the injured party may elect to regard the negligence as the immediate cause of action, and declare in case; or to consider the act itself as the immediate injury, and sue in trespass. 14 John. 432; 6 Cowen, 342; 3 N. H. Rep. 465; sed vide 3 Conn. 64; 2 Bos. & Pull. New Rep. by Day, 448, note. See *Cause*.

IMMEMORIAL. That which commences beyond the time of memory. Vide *Memory, time of*.

IMMEMORIAL POSSESSION. In Louisiana, by this term is understood that of which no man living has seen the beginning, and the existence of which he has learned from his elders. Civ. Code of Lo. art. 762; 2 M. R. 214; 7 L. R. 46; 3 Toull. p. 410; Poth. Contr. de Societé, n. 244; 3 Bouv. Inst. n. 3069, note.

IMMIGRATION. The removing into one place from another. It differs from emigration, which is the moving from one place into another. Vide *Emigration*.

IMMORAL CONSIDERATION. One contrary to good morals, and therefore invalid. See *Moral obligation*.

IMMORALITY. That which is *contra bonos mores*. In England, it is not punishable in some cases, at the common law, on account of the ecclesiastical jurisdictions: *e. g.* adultery. But except in cases belonging to the ecclesiastical courts, the court of king's bench is the *custos morum*, and may punish *delicto contra bonos mores*. 3 Burr. Rep. 1438; 1 Bl. Rep. 94; 2 Strange, 788. In Pennsylvania, and most, if not all the United States, all such cases come under one and the same jurisdiction.

2. Immoral contracts are generally void; an agreement in consideration of future illicit cohabitation between the parties; 3

Burr. 1568; S. C. 1 Bl. Rep. 517; 1 Esp. R. 13; 1 B. & P. 340, 341; an agreement for the value of libelous and immoral pictures, 4 Esp. R. 97; or for printing a libel, 2 Stark. R. 107; or for an immoral wager, Chit. Contr. 156, cannot, therefore, be enforced. For whatever arises from an immoral or illegal consideration, is void: *quid turpi ex causa promissum est non valet.* Inst. 3, 20, 24.

3. It is a general rule, that whenever an agreement appears to be illegal, immoral, or against public policy, a court of justice leaves the parties where it finds them; when the agreement has been executed, the court will not rescind it; when executory, the count will not help the execution. 4 Ohio R. 419; 4 John. R. 419; 11 John. R. 388; 12 John. R. 306; 19 John. R. 341; 3 Cowen's R. 213; 2 Wils. R. 341.

IMMOVABLES, *civil law.* Things are movable or immovable. Immovables, *res immobiles,* are things in general, such as cannot move themselves or be removed from one place to another. But this definition, strictly speaking, is applicable only to such things as are immovable by their own nature, and not to such as are so only by the destination of the law.

2. There are things immovable by their nature, others by their destination, and others by the objects to which they are applied.

3.—1. Lands and buildings or other constructions, whether they have their foundations in the soil or not, are immovable by their nature. By the common law, buildings erected on the land are not considered real estate, unless they have been let into, or united to the land, or to substances previously connected therewith. Ferard on Fixt. 2.

4.—2. Things, which the owner of the land has placed upon it for its service and improvement, are immovables by destination, as seeds, plants, fodder, manure, pigeons in a pigeon-house, bee-hives, and the like. By the common law, erections with or without a foundation, when made for the purpose of trade, are considered personal estate. 2 Pet. S. C. Rep. 137; 3 Atk 13; Ambl. 113.

5 –3. A servitude established on real estate, is an instance of an immovable, which is so considered in consequence of the object to which it is applied. Vide Civil Code of Louis. B. 2, t. 1, c. 2, art. 453–463; Poth. Des Choses, § 1; Poth. de la Communauté, n. 25, et seq; Clef des Lois Romaines, mot Immeubles.

IMMUNITY. An exemption from serving in an office, or performing duties which the law generally requires other citizens to perform. Vide Dig. lib. 50, t. 6; 1 Chit. Cr. L. 821; 4 Har. & M'Hen. 341.

IMMUTABLE. What cannot be removed, what is unchangeable. The laws of God being perfect, are immutable, but no human law can be so considered.

IMPAIRING THE OBLIGATION OF CONTRACTS. The Constitution of the United States, art. 1, s. 9, cl. 1, declares that no state shall "pass any bill of attainder, *ex post facto* law, or law impairing the obligation of contracts."

2. Contracts, when considered in relation to their effects, are executed, that is, by transfer of the *possession* of the thing contracted for; or they are executory, which gives only a right of *action* for the subject of the contract. Contracts are also express or implied. The constitution makes no distinction between one class of contracts and the other. 6 Cranch, 135; 7 Cranch, 164.

3. The *obligation* of a contract here spoken of is a legal, not a mere moral obligation; it is the law which binds the party to perform his undertaking. The obligation does not inhere or subsist in the contract itself, *proprio vigore,* but in the law applicable to the contract. 4 Wheat. R. 197; 12 Wheat. R. 318; and this law is not the universal law of nations, but it is the law of the state where the contract is made. 12 Wheat. R. 213. Any law which enlarges, abridges, or in any manner changes the intention of the parties, resulting from the stipulations in the contract, necessarily impairs it. 12 Wheat. 256; Id. 327; 3 Wash. C. C. Rep. 319; 8 Wheat. 84; 4 Wheat. 197.

4. The constitution forbids the *states* to pass any law impairing the obligation of contracts, but there is nothing in that instrument which prohibits *Congress* from passing such a law. Pet. C. C. R. 322. Vide, generally, Story on the Const. § 1368 to 1391; Serg. Const. Law, 356; Rawle on the Const. h. t.; Dane's Ab. Index, h. t., 10 Am. Jur. 273–297.

TO IMPANEL, *practice.* The writing the names of a jury on a schedule, by the sheriff or other officer lawfully authorized.

IMPARLANCE, *pleading and practice.* Imparlance, from the French, *parler,* to speak, or licentia loquendi, in its most general signification, means time given by the court to either party to answer the pleading of his opponent, as either to plead, reply, rejoin, &c., and is said to be nothing else but the continuance of the cause till a further day. Bac. Abr. Pleas, C. But the more common signification of the term is time to plead. 2 Saund. 1, n. 2; 2 Show. 310; Barnes, 346; Lawes, Civ. Pl. 93, 94.

2. Imparlances are of three descriptions: First. A common or general imparlance. Secondly. A special imparlance. Thirdly. A general special imparlance.

3.—1. A general imparlance is the entry of a general prayer and allowance of time to plead till the next term, without reserving to the defendant the benefit of any exception; so that, after such an imparlance, the defendant cannot object to the jurisdiction of the court, or plead any matter in abatement. This kind of imparlance is always from one term to another.

4.—2. A special imparlance reserves to the defendant all exception to the writ, bill, or count; and, therefore, after it, the defendant may plead in abatement, though not to the jurisdiction of the court.

5.—3. A general special imparlance contains a saving of all exceptions whatsoever, so that the defendant, after this, may plead, not only in abatement, but he may also plead a plea which affects the jurisdiction of the court, as privilege. He cannot, however, plead a tender, and that he was always ready to pay, because, by craving time, he admits he is not ready, and so falsifies his plea. Tidd's Pr. 418, 419. The last two kinds of imparlances are, it seems, sometimes from one day to another in the same term. See, in general, Com. Dig. Abatement, I 19, 20, 21; 1 Chit. Pl. 420; Bac. Abr. Pleas, C; 14 Vin. Abr. 335; Com. Dig. Pleader, D; 1 Sell. Pr. 265; Doct. Pl. 291; Encycl. de M. D'Alembert, art. Delai (Jurisp.)

IMPEACHMENT, *const. law, punishments*. Under the constitution and laws of the United States, an impeachment may be described to be a written accusation, by the house of representatives of the United States, to the senate of the United States, against an officer. The presentment, or written accusation, is called articles of impeachment.

2. The constitution declares that the house of representatives shall have the sole power of impeachment; art. 1, s. 2, cl. 5; and that the senate shall have the sole power to try all impeachments. Art. 1, s. 3, cl. 6.

3. The persons liable to impeachment are the president, vice-president, and all civil officers of the United States. Art. 2, s. 4. A question arose upon an impeachment before the senate, in 1799, whether a senator was a civil officer of the United States, within the purview of this section of the constitution, and it was decided by the senate, by a vote of fourteen against eleven, that he was not. Senate Journ., January 10th, 1799; Story on Const. § 791; Rawle on Const. 213, 214; Serg. Const. Law, 376.

4. The offences for which a guilty officer may be impeached are, treason, bribery, and other high crimes and misdemeanors. Art. 2, s. 4. The constitution defines the crime of treason. Art. 3, s. 3. Recourse must be had to the common law for a definition of bribery. Not having particularly mentioned what is to be understood by "other high crimes and misdemeanors," resort, it is presumed, must be had to parliamentary practice, and the common law, in order to ascertain what they are. Story, § 795.

5. The mode of proceeding, in the institution and trial of impeachments, is as follows: When a person who may be legally impeached has been guilty, or is supposed to have been guilty, of some malversation in office, a resolution is generally brought forward by a member of the house of representatives, either to accuse the party, or for a committee of inquiry. If the committee report adversely to the party accused, they give a statement of the charges, and recommend that he be impeached; when the resolution is adopted by the house, a committee is appointed to impeach the party at the bar of the senate, and to state that the articles of impeachment against him will be exhibited in due time, and made good before the senate, and to demand that the senate take order for the appearance of the party to answer to the impeachment. The house then agree upon the articles of impeachment, and they are presented to the senate by a committee appointed by the house to prosecute the impeachment; the senate then issues process, summoning the party to appear at a given day before them, to answer to the articles. The process is served by the sergeant-at-arms of the senate, and a return is made of it to the senate, under oath. On the return-day of the process, the senate resolves itself into a court

of impeachment, and the senators are sworn to do justice, according to the constitution and laws. The person impeached is called to answer, and either appears or does not appear. If he does not appear, his default is recorded, and the senate may proceed *ex parte*. If he does appear, either by himself or attorney, the parties are required to form an issue, and a time is then assigned for the trial. The proceedings on the trial are conducted substantially as they are upon common judicial trials. If any debates arise among the senators, they are conducted in secret, and the final decision is given by yeas and nays; but no person can be convicted without the concurrence of two-thirds of the members present. Const. art. 1, s. 2, cl. 6.

6. When the president is tried, the chief justice shall preside. The judgment, in cases of impeachment shall not extend further than to removal from office, and disqualification to hold and enjoy any office of honor, trust, or profit under the United States. Proceedings on impeachments under the state constitutions are somewhat similar. Vide *Courts of the United States*.

IMPEACHMENT, *evidence*. An allegation, supported by proof, that a witness who has been examined is unworthy of credit.

2. Every witness is liable to be impeached as to his character for truth; and, if his general character is good, he is presumed, at all times, to be ready to support it. 3 Bouv. Inst. n. 3224, et seq.

IMPEACHMENT OF WASTE. It signifies a restraint from committing waste upon lands or tenements; or a demand of compensation for waste done by a tenant who has but a particular estate in the land granted, and, therefore, no right to commit waste.

2. All tenants for life, or any less estate, are liable to be impeached for waste, unless they hold *without impeachment of waste;* in the latter case, they may commit waste without being questioned, or any demand for compensation for the waste done. 11 Co. 82.

IMPEDIMENTS, *contracts*. Legal objections to the making of a contract. Impediments which relate to the person are those of minority, want of reason, coverture, and the like; they are sometimes called disabilities. Vide *Incapacity*.

2. In the civil law, this term is used to signify bars to a marriage. These impediments are classed, as they are applied to particular persons, into absolute and relative; as they relate to the contract and its validity, they are dirimant, (q. v.) and prohibitive. (q. v.) 1. The *absolute* impediments are those which prevent the person subject to them from marrying at all, without either the nullity of marriage, or its being punishable. 2. The *relative* impediments are those which regard only certain persons with regard to each other; as, the marriage of a brother to a sister. 3. The *dirimant* impediments are those which render a marriage void; as, where one of the contracting parties is already married to another person. 4. *Prohibitive* impediments are those which do not render the marriage null, but subject the parties to a punishment. Bowy. Mod. Civ. Law, 44, 45.

IMPERFECT. That which is incomplete.

2. This term is applied to rights and obligations. A man has a right to be relieved by his fellow-creatures, when in distress; but this right he cannot enforce by law; hence it is called an imperfect right. On the other hand, we are bound to be grateful for favors received, but we cannot be compelled to perform such imperfect obligations. Vide Poth. Ob. art. Préliminaire; Vattel, Dr. des Gens, Prel. notes, § 17; and *Obligations*.

IMPERIUM. The right to command, which includes the right to employ the force of the state to enforce the laws; this is one of the principal attributes of the power of the executive. 1 Toull. n. 58.

IMPERTINENT, *practice, pleading*. What does not appertain, or belong to; *id est, qui ad rem non pertinet*.

2. Evidence of facts which do not belong to the matter in question, is impertinent and inadmissible. In general, what is immaterial is impertinent, and what is material is, in general, not impertinent. 1 McC. & Y. 337. See Gresl. Ev. Ch. 3, s. 1, p. 229. Impertinent matter, in a declaration or other pleading, is that which does not belong to the subject; in such case it is considered as mere surplusage, (q. v.) and is rejected. Ham. N. P. 25. Vide 2 Ves. 24; 5 Madd. R. 450; Newl. Pr. 38; 2 Ves. 631; 5 Ves. 656; 18 Eng. Com. Law R. 201; Eden on Inj. 71.

3. There is a difference between matter merely impertinent and that which is scandalous; matter may be impertinent, without being scandalous; but if it is scandalous, it must be impertinent.

4. In equity a bill cannot, according to

the general practice, be referred for impertinence after the defendant has answered or submitted to answer, but it may be referred for scandal at any time, and even upon the application of a stranger to the suit. Coop. Eq. Pl. 19; 2 Ves. 631; 6 Ves. 514; Story, Eq. Pl. § 270. Vide Gresl. Eq. Ev. p. 2, c. 3, s. 1; 1 John. Ch. R. 103; 1 Paige's R. 555; 1 Edw. R. 350; 11 Price, R. 111; 5 Paige's R. 522; 1 Russ. & My. 28; Bouv. Inst. Index, h. t.; *Scandal.*

IMPETRATION. The obtaining any thing by prayer or petition. In the ancient English statutes, it signifies a pre-obtaining of church benefices in England from the church of Rome, which belonged to the gift of the king, or other lay patrons.

TO IMPLEAD, *practice.* To sue or prosecute by due course of law. 9 Watts, 47.

IMPLEMENTS. Such things as are used or *employed* for a trade, or furniture of a house.

IMPLICATA, *mar. law.* In order to avoid the risk of making fruitless voyages, merchants have been in the habit of receiving small adventures on freight at so much per cent., to which they are entitled at all events, even if the adventure be lost. This is what the Italians call *implicata.* Targa, chap. 34; Emer. Mar. Loans, s. 5.

IMPLICATION. An inference of something not directly declared, but arising from what is admitted or expressed.

2. It is a rule that when the law gives anything to a man, it gives him by implication all that is necessary for its enjoyment. It is also a rule that when a man accepts an office, he undertakes by implication to use it according to law, and by non-user he may forfeit it. 2 Bl. Com. 152.

3. An estate in fee simple will pass by implication; 6 John. R. 185; 18 John. R. 31; 2 Binn. R. 464, 532; such implication must not only be a possible or probable one, but it must be plain and necessary; that is, so strong a probability of intention, that an intention contrary to that imputed to the testator cannot be supposed. 1 Ves. & B. 466; Willes, 141; 1 Ves. jr. 564; 14 John. R. 198. Vide, generally, Com. Dig. Estates by Devise, N 12, 13; 2 Rop. Leg. 342; 14 Vin. Ab. 341; 5 Ves. 805; 5 Ves. 582; 3 Ves. 676.

IMPORTATION, *comm. law.* The act of bringing goods and merchandise into the United States from a foreign country. 9 Cranch, 104, 120; 5 Cranch, 368; 2 Mann. & Gr. 155, note *a.*

2. To prevent the mischievous interference of the several states with the national commerce, the constitution of the United States, art. 1, s. 10, provides as follows: "No state shall, without the consent of the congress, lay any imposts or duties on imports or exports, except what may be absolutely necessary for executing its inspection laws; and the net produce of all duties and imposts, laid by any state on imports or exports, shall be for the use of the treasury of the United States; and all such laws shall be subject to the revision and control of the congress."

3. This apparently plain provision has received a judicial construction. In the year 1821, the legislature of Maryland passed an act requiring that all importers of foreign articles, commodities, &c., by the bale or package, of wine, rum, &c., and other persons selling the same by wholesale, bale or package, hogshead, barrel or tierce, should, before they were authorized to sell, take out a license for which they were to pay fifty dollars, under certain penalties. A question arose whether this act was or was not a violation of the constitution of the United States, and particularly of the above clause, and the supreme court decided against the constitutionality of the law. 12 Wheat. 419.

4. The act of congress of March 1, 1817, 3 Story, L. U. S. 1622, provides:

5.—§ 1. That, after the 30th day of September next, no goods, wares, or merchandise, shall be imported into the United States from any foreign port or place, except in vessels of the United States, or in such foreign vessels as truly or wholly belong to the citizens or subjects of that country of which the goods are the growth, production or manufacture; or from which such goods, wares or merchandise, can only be or most usually are, first shipped for transportation: Provided, nevertheless, That this regulation shall not extend to the vessels of any foreign nation which has not adopted, and which shall not adopt a similar regulation.

6.—§ 2. That all goods, wares or merchandise, imported into the United States contrary to the true intent and meaning of this act, and the ship or vessel wherein the same shall be imported, together with her cargo, tackle, apparel, and furniture, shall be forfeited to the United States; and such goods, wares, or merchandise, ship, or vessel, and cargo, shall be liable to be seized, prosecuted, and condemned, in like manner, and under the same regulations, restrictions, and provisions, as have been heretofore established for the recovery, collection, distribution, and remission, of forfeitures to the United States by the several revenue laws.

7.—§ 4. That no goods, wares, or merchandise, shall be imported, under penalty of forfeiture thereof, from one port of the United States to another port of the United States, in a vessel belonging wholly or in part to a subject of any foreign power; but this clause shall not be construed to prohibit the sailing of any foreign vessel from one to another port of the United States, provided no goods, wares, or merchandise, other than those imported in such vessel from some foreign port, and which shall not have been unladen, shall be carried from one port or place to another in the United States.

8.—§ 6. That after the 30th day of September next, there shall be paid upon every ship or vessel of the United States, which shall be entered in the United States from any foreign port or place, unless the officers, and at least two-thirds of the crew thereof, shall be proved citizens of the United States, or persons not the subjects of any foreign prince or state, to the satisfaction of the collector, fifty cents per ton: And provided also, that this section shall not extend to ships or vessels of the United States, which are now on foreign voyages, or which may depart from the United States prior to the first day of May next, until after their return to some port of the United States.

9.—§ 7. That the several bounties and remissions, or abatements of duty, allowed by this act, in the case of vessels having a certain proportion of seamen who are American citizens, or persons not the subjects of any foreign power, shall be allowed only in the case of vessels having such proportion of American seamen during their whole voyage, unless in case of sickness, death or desertion, or where the whole or part of the crew shall have been taken prisoners in the voyage. Vide article *Entry of goods at the Custom-house.*

IMPORTS. Importations; as no state shall lay any duties on imports or exports. Const. U. S. Art. 1, s. 10; 7 How. U. S. Rep. 477.

IMPORTUNITY. Urgent solicitation, with troublesome frequency and pertinacity.

2. Wills and devises are sometimes set aside in consequence of the importunity of those who have procured them. Whenever the importunity is such as to deprive the devisor of the freedom of his will, the devise becomes fraudulent and void. Dane's Ab. ch. 127, a. 14, s. 5, 6, 7; 2 Phillim. R. 551, 2.

IMPOSITIONS. Imposts, taxes, or contributions.

IMPOSSIBILITY. The character of that which cannot be done agreeably to the accustomed order of nature.

2. It is a maxim that no one is bound to perform an impossibility. A l'impossible nul n'est tenu. 1 Swift's Dig. 93; 6 Toull. n. 121, 481.

3. As to impossible conditions in contracts, see Bac. Ab. Conditions, M; Co. Litt. 206; Roll. Ab. 420; 6 Toull. n. 486, 686; Dig. 2, 14, 39; Id. 44, 7, 31; Id. 50, 17, 185; Id. 45, 1, 69. On the subject of impossible conditions in wills, vide 1 Rop. Leg. 505; Swinb. pt. 4, s. 6; 6 Toull. 614. Vide, generally, Dane's Ab. Index, h. t.; Clef des Lois Rom. par Fieffé Lacroix, h. t.; Com. Dig. Conditions, D 1 & 2; Vin. Ab. Conditions, C a, D a, E a.

IMPOSTS. This word is sometimes used to signify taxes, or duties, or impositions; and, sometimes, in the more restrained sense of a duty on imported goods and merchandise. The Federalist, No. 30; 3 Elliott's Debates, 289; Story, Const. § 949.

2. The Constitution of the United States, art. 1, s. 8, n. 1, gives power to congress "to lay and collect taxes, duties, imposts and excises." And art. 1, s. 10, n. 2, directs that "no state shall, without the consent of congress, lay any imposts, or duties on imports or exports, except what may be absolutely necessary for executing its inspection laws." See Bac. Ab. Smuggling, B; 2 Inst. 62; Dy. 165 n.; Sir John Davis on Imposition.

IMPOTENCE, *med. jur.* The incapacity for copulation or propagating the species. It has also been used synonymously with *sterility.*

2. Impotence may be considered as incurable, curable, accidental or temporary. Absolute or incurable impotence, is that for which there is no known relief, principally originating in some malformation or defect of the genital organs. Where this defect existed at the time of the marriage, and was incurable, by the ecclesiastical law and the law of several of the American states,

the marriage may be declared void *ab initio.* Com. Dig. Baron and Feme, C 3; Bac. Ab. Marriage, &c., E 3; 1 Bl. Com. 440; Beck's Med. Jur. 67; Code, lib. 5, t. 17, l. 10; Poynt. on Marr. and Div. ch. 8; 5 Paige, 554; Merl. Rép. mot Impuissance. But it seems the party naturally impotent cannot allege that fact for the purpose of obtaining a divorce. 3 Phillim. R. 147; S. C. 1 Eng. Eccl. R. 384. See 3 Phillim. R. 325; S. C. 1 Eng. Eccl. R. 408; 1 Chit. Med. Jur. 377; 1 Par. & Fonbl. 172, 173, note *d*; Ryan's Med. Jur. 95 to 111; 1 Bl. Com. 440; 2 Phillm. R. 10; 1 Hagg. R. 725. See, as to the signs of impotence, 1 Briand, Méd. Lég. c. 2, art. 2, § 2, n. 1; Dictionnaire des Sciences Médicales, art. Impuissance; and, generally, Trebuchet, Jur. de la Méd. 100, 101, 102; 1 State Tr. 315; 8 State Tr. App. No. 1, p. 23; 3 Phillm. R. 147; 1 Hagg. Eccl. R. 523; Foderé, Méd. Lég. § 237.

IMPRESCRIPTIBILITY. The state of being incapable of prescription.

2. A property which is held in trust is imprescriptible; that is, the trustee cannot acquire a title to it by prescription; nor can the borrower of a thing get a right to it by any lapse of time, unless he claims an adverse right to it during the time required by law.

IMPRIMATUR. A license or allowance to one to print.

2. At one time, before a book could be printed in England, it was requisite that a permission should be obtained; that permission was called an *imprimatur*. In some countries where the press is liable to censure, an imprimatur is required.

IMPRIMERY. In some of the ancient English statutes this word is used to signify a printing-office, the art of printing, a print or impression.

IMPRIMIS. In the first place; as, imprimis, I direct my just debts to be paid. See *Item*.

IMPRISONMENT. The restraint of a person contrary to his will. 2 Inst. 589; Baldw. Rep. 239, 600. Imprisonment is either lawful or unlawful; lawful imprisonment is used either for crimes or for the appearance of a party in a civil suit, or on arrest in execution.

2. Imprisonment for crimes is either for the appearance of a person accused, as when he cannot give bail; or it is the effect of a sentence, and then it is a part of the punishment.

3. Imprisonment in civil cases takes place when a defendant on being sued on bailable process refuses or cannot give the bail legally demanded, or is under a *capias ad satisfaciendum*, when he is taken in execution under a judgment. An unlawful imprisonment, commonly called *false imprisonment*, (q. v.) means any illegal imprisonment whatever, either with or without process, or under color of process wholly illegal, without regard to any question whether any crime has been committed or a debt due.

4. As to what will amount to an imprisonment, the most obvious modes are confinement in a prison or a private house, but a forcible detention in the street, or the touching of a person by a peace officer by way of arrest, are also imprisonments. Bac. Ab. Trespass, D 3; 1 Esp. R. 431, 526. It has been decided that lifting up a person in his chair, and carrying him out of the room in which he was sittting with others, and excluding him from the room, was not an imprisonment; 1 Chit. Pr. 48; and the merely giving charge of a person to a peace officer, not followed by any actual apprehension of the person, does not amount to an imprisonment, though the party to avoid it, next day attend at a police; 1 Esp. R. 431; New Rep. 211; 1 Carr. & Payn. 153; S. C. 11 Eng. Com. Law, R. 351; and if, in consequence of a message from a sheriff's officer holding a writ, the defendant execute and send him a bail bond, such submission to the process will not constitute an arrest. 6 Bar. & Cres. 528; S. C. 13 Eng. Com. Law Rep. 245; Dowl. & R. 233. Vide, generally, 14 Vin. Ab. 342; 4 Com. Dig. 618; 1 Chit. Pr. 47; Merl. Répert. mot Emprisonment; 17 Eng. Com. L. R. 246, n.

IMPROBATION. The act by which perjury or falsehood is proved. Techn. Dict. h. t.

IMPROPRIATION, *eccl. law.* The act of employing the revenues of a church living to one's own use; it is also a parsonage or ecclesiastical living in the hands of a layman, or which descends by inheritance. Techn. Dict. h. t.

IMPROVEMENT, *estates.* This term is of doubtful meaning. It would seem to apply principally to buildings, though generally it extends to amelioration of every description of property, whether real or personal; it is generally explained by other words.

2. Where, by the terms of a lease, the

covenant was to leave at the end of the term a water-mill with all the fixtures, fastenings, and *improvements*, during the demise fixed, fastened, or set up on or upon the premises, in good plight and condition, it was held to include a pair of new mill-stones set up by the lessee during the term, although the custom of the country in general authorized the tenant to remove them. 9 Bing. 24; 3 Sim. 450; 2 Ves. & Bea. 349. Vide 3 Yeates, 71; Addis. R. 335; 4 Binn. R. 418; 5 Binn. R. 77; 5 S. & R. 266; 1 Binn. R. 495; 1 John. Ch. R. 450; 15 Pick. R. 471. Vide *Profits*. 2 Man. & Gra. 729, 757; S. C. 40 Eng. C. L. R. 598, 612.

3. Tenants in common are not bound to pay for *permanent improvements*, made on the common property, by one of the tenants in common without their consent. 2 Bouv. Inst. n. 1881.

IMPROVEMENT, *rights*. An addition of some useful thing to a machine, manufacture or composition of matter.

2. The patent law of July 4, 1836, authorizes the granting of a patent for any new and useful improvement on any art, machine, manufacture or composition of matter. Sect. 6. It is often very difficult to say what is a new and useful improvement, the cases often approach very near to each other. In the present improved state of machinery, it is almost impracticable not to employ the same elements of motion, and in some particulars, the same manner of operation, to produce any new effect. 1 Gallis. 478; 2 Gallis. 51. See 4 B. & Ald. 540; 2 Kent, Com. 370.

IMPUBER, *civil law*. One who is more than seven years old, or out of infancy, and who has not attained the age of an adult, (q. v.) and who is not yet in his puberty; that is, if a boy, till he has attained his full age of fourteen years, and, if a girl, her full age of twelve years. Domat, Liv. Prel. t. 2, s. 2, n. 8.

IMPUNITY. Not being punished for a crime or misdemeanor committed. The impunity of crimes is one of the most prolific sources whence they arise. *Impunitas continuum affectum tribuit delinquenti*. 4 Co. 45, a; 5 Co. 109, a.

IMPUTATION. The judgment by which we declare that an agent is the cause of his free action, or of the result of it, whether good or ill. Wolff, § 3.

IMPUTATION OF PAYMENT. This term is used in Louisiana to signify the appropriation which is made of a payment, when the debtor owes two debts to the creditor. Civ. Code of Lo. art. 2159 to 2262. See 3 N. S. 483; 6 N. S. 28; Id. 113; Poth. Ob. n. 539, 565, 570; Durant. Des Contr. Liv. 3, t. 3, § 3, n. 191; 10 L. R. 232, 352; 7 Toull. n. 173, p. 246.

IN ALIO LOCO. In another place. Vide *Cepit in alio loco*.

IN ARTICULO MORTIS. In the article of death; at the point of death. As to the effect of this condition on wills, see *Nuncupative;* as to the testimony of such person, see *Dying declarations*.

IN AUTRE DROIT. In another's right. An executor, administrator or trustee, is said to have the property confided to him in such character, *in autre droit*.

IN BLANK. This is generally applied to indorsements, as indorsements in blank, which is one not restricted, made by the indorser simply writing his name. See *Indorsement*.

IN CHIEF. Evidence is said to be *in chief* when it is given in support of the case opened by the leading counsel. Vide *To Open—Opening*. The term is used to distinguish evidence of this nature from evidence obtained on a *cross-examination*. (q. v.) 3 Chit. 890. By evidence *in chief* is sometimes meant that evidence, which is given, in contradistinction to evidence which is obtained on the witness' *voir dire*.

2. Evidence in chief should be confined to such matters as the pleadings and the opening warrant, and a departure from this rule, will be sometimes highly inconvenient, if not fatal. Suppose, for example, that two assaults have been committed, one in January and the other in February, and the plaintiff prove his cause of action to have been the assault in January, he cannot abandon that, and afterwards prove another committed in February, unless the pleadings and openings extend to both. 1 Campb R. 473. See also, 6 Carr. & P. 73; S. C. 25 E. C. L. R. 288; 1 Mood. & R. 282.

IN COMMENDAM. The state or condition of a church living, which is void or vacant, and it is commended to the care of some one. In Louisiana, there is a species of partnership called a partnership in commendam. Vide *Commendam*.

IN CUSTODIA LEGIS. In the custody of the law. In general, when things are in custodia legis, they cannot be distrained, nor otherwise interfered with by a private person.

IN ESSE. In being. A thing in existence. It is used in opposition to *in posse.* A child in *ventre sa mere* is a thing *in posse;* after he is born, he is *in esse.* Vide 1 Supp. to Ves. jr. 466; 2 Suppl. to Ves. jr. 155, 191. Vide *Posse.*

IN EXTREMIS. This phrase is used to denote the end of life; as, a marriage *in extremis,* is one made at the end of life. Vide *Extremis.*

IN FACIENDO. In doing, or in feasance. 2 Story, Eq. Jurisp. § 1308.

IN FAVOREM LIBERTATIS. In favor of liberty.

IN FAVOREM VITÆ. In favor of life.

IN FIERI. In the course of execution; a thing commenced but not completed. A record is said to be *in fieri* during the term of the court, and, during that time, it may be amended or altered at the sound discretion of the court. See 2 B. & Adol. 971.

IN FORMA PAUPERIS. In the character or form of a pauper. In England, in some cases, when a poor person cannot afford to pay the costs of a suit as it proceeds, he is exempted from such payment, having obtained leave to sue in forma pauperis.

IN FORO CONSCIENTIÆ. Before the tribunal of conscience; conscientiously. This term is applied in opposition to the obligations which the law enforces.

2. In the sale of property, for example, the concealment of facts by the vendee which may enhance the price, is wrong *in foro conscientiæ,* but there is no legal obligation on the part of the vendee to disclose them, and the contract will be good if not vitiated by fraud. Poth. Vent. part 2, c. 2, n. 233; 2 Wheat. 185, note *c.*

IN FRAUDEM LEGIS. In fraud of the law. Every thing done in fraudem legis is void in law. 2 Ves. sen. 155, 156; Bouv. Inst. n. 585, 3834.

IN GREMIO LEGIS. In the bosom of the law. This is a figurative expression, by which is meant that the subject is under the protection of the law; as, where land is in abeyance.

IN GROSS. At large; not appurtenant or appendant, but annexed to a man's person: *e. g.* Common granted to a man and his heirs by deed, is common in gross; or common in gross may be claimed by prescriptive right. 2 Bl. Com. 34.

IN INVITUM. Against an unwilling party; against one who has not given his consent See *Invito domino.*

IN JUDICIO. In the course of trial, a course of legal proceedings.

IN JURE. In law; according to law, rightfully. Bract. fol. 169, b.

IN LIMINE. In or at the beginning. This phrase is frequently used; as, the courts are anxious to check crimes *in limine.*

IN LITEM, *ad litem.* For a suit; to the suit. Greenl. Ev. § 348.

IN LOCO PARENTIS. In the place of a parent; as, the master stands towards his apprentice *in loco parentis.*

IN MITIORI SENSU, *construction.* Formerly in actions of slander it was a rule to take the expression used *in mitiori sensu,* in the mildest acceptation; and ingenuity was, upon these occasions, continually exercised to devise or discover a meaning which by some remote possibility the speaker might have intended; and some ludicrous examples of this ingenuity may be found. To say of a man who was making his livelihood by buying and selling merchandise, he is a base, broken rascal, he has broken twice, and I'll make him break a third time, was gravely asserted not to be actionable—"ne poet dar porter action, car poet estre intend de *burstness de belly,*" Latch, 114. And to call a man a thief was declared to be no slander for this reason, "perhaps the speaker might mean he had stolen a lady's heart."

2. The rule now is to construe words agreeably to the meaning usually attached to them. 1 Nott & McCord, 217; 2 Nott & McCord, 511; 8 Mass. R. 248; 1 Wash. R. 152; Kirby, R. 12; 7 Serg. & Rawle, 451; 2 Binn. 34; 3 Binn. 515.

IN MORA. In default. Vide *mora, in.*

IN NUBIBUS. In the clouds. This is a figurative expression to signify a state of suspension or abeyance. 1 Co. 137.

IN NULLO EST ERRATUM, *pleading.* A plea to errors assigned on proceedings in error, by which the defendant in error affirms there is no error in the record. As to the effect of such plea, see 1 Vent. 252; 1 Str. 684; 9 Mass. R. 532; 1 Burr. 410; T. Ray. 231. It is a general rule that the plea *in nullo est erratum* confesses the fact assigned for error; Yelv. 57; Dane's Ab. Index, h. t.; but not a matter assigned contrary to the record. 7 Wend. 55; Bac. Ab. Error, G.

IN ODIUM SPOLIATORIS. In hatred of a despoiler. All things are presumed against a despoiler or wrong doer: *in odio spoliatoris omnia præsumuntur.*

IN PARI CAUSA. In an equal cause. It is a rule that when two persons have equal rights in relation to a particular thing, the party in possession is considered as having the better right: *in pari causa possessor potior est.* Dig. 50, 17, 128; 1 Bouv. Inst. n. 952.

IN PARI DELICTO. In equal fault; equal in guilt. Neither courts of law nor equity will interpose to grant relief to the parties, when an illegal agreement has been made, and both parties stand *in pari delicto.* The law leaves them where it finds them, according to the maxim, *in pari delicto potior est conditio defendentis et possidendis.* 1 Bouv. Inst. n. 769.

IN PARI MATERIA. Upon the same matter or subject. Statutes in pari materia are to be construed together.

IN PERPETUAM REI MEMORIAM. For the perpetual memory or remembrance of a thing. Gilb. For. Rom. 118.

IN PERSONAM, *remedies.* A remedy *in personam,* is one where the proceedings are against the person, in contradistinction to those which are against specific things, or *in rem.* (q. v.) 3 Bouv. Inst. n. 2646.

IN POSSE. In possibility; not in actual existence; used in contradistinction to *in esse.*

IN PRÆSENTI. At the present time; used in opposition to *in futuro.* A marriage contracted in words *de præsenti* is good; as, I take Paul to be my husband, is a good marriage, but words *de futuro* would not be sufficient, unless the ceremony was followed by consummation. 1 Bouv. Inst. n. 258.

IN PRINCIPIO. At the beginning. This is frequently used in citations; as Bac. Ab. Legacies, *in pr.*

IN PROPRIA PERSONA. In his own person; himself; as the defendant appeared *in propriâ personâ;* the plaintiff argued the cause in propriâ personâ.

IN RE. In the matter; as in re A B, in the matter of A B.

IN REBUS. In things, cases or matters.

IN REM, *remedies.* This technical term is used to designate proceedings or actions instituted *against the thing,* in contradistinction to personal actions which are said to be *in personam.* Proceedings in rem include not only judgments of property as forfeited, or as prize in the admiralty, or the English exchequer, but also the decisions of other courts upon the personal *status,* or relations of the party, such as marriage, divorce, bastardy, settlement, or the like. 1 Greenl. Ev. §§ 525, 541.

2. Courts of admiralty enforce the performance of a contract by seizing into their custody the very subject of hypothecation; for in these cases the parties are not personally bound, and the proceedings are confined to the thing in specie. Bro. Civ. and Adm. Law, 98; and see 2 Gall. R. 200; 3 T. R. 269, 270.

3. There are cases, however, where the remedy is either *in personam* or *in rem.* Seamen, for example, may proceed against the ship or cargo for their wages, and this is the most expeditious mode; or they may proceed against the master or owners. 4 Burr. 1944; 2 Bro. C. & A. Law, 396. Vide, generally, 1 Phil. Ev. 254; 1 Stark. Ev. 228; Dane's Ab. h. t.; Serg. Const. Law, 202, 203, 212.

IN RERUM NATURA. In the nature of things; in existence.

IN SOLIDO. A term used in the civil law, to signify that a contract is joint.

2. Obligations are *in solido,* first, between several creditors; secondly, between several debters. 1. When a person contracts the obligation of one and the same thing, in favor of several others, each of these is only creditor for his own share, but he may contract with each of them for the whole when such is the intention of the parties, so that each of the persons in whose favor the obligation is contracted, is creditor for the whole, but that a payment made to any one liberates the debtor against them all. This is called solidity of obligation. Poth. Obl. pt. 2, c. 3, art. 7. The common law is exactly the reverse of this, for a general obligation in favor of several persons, is a joint obligation to them all, unless the nature of the subject, or the particularity of the expression, lead to a different conclu sion. Evans' Poth. vol. 2, p. 56. See tit *Joint and Several; Parties to action.*

3.—2. An obligation is contracted *in solido* on the part of the debtors, when each of them is obliged for the whole, but so that a payment made by one liberates them all. Poth. Obli. pt. 2, c. 3, art. 7, s 1. See 9 M. R. 322; 5 L. R. 287; 2 N. S. 140; 3 L. R. 352; 4 N. S. 317; 5 L. R. 122; 12 M. R. 216; Burge on Sur. 398–420.

IN STATU QUO. In the same situation; in the same place; as, between the time of the submission and the time when the award was rendered, things remained *in statu quo*.

IN TERROREM. By way of threat, terror, or warning. For example, when a legacy is given to a person upon condition not to dispute the validity or the dispositions in wills and testaments, the conditions are not in general obligatory, but only *in terrorem;* if, therefore, there exist *probabilis causa litigandi*, the non-observance of the conditions will not be a forfeiture. 2 Vern. 90; 1 Hill. Ab. 253; 3 P. Wms. 344; 1 Atk. 404. But when the acquiescence of the legatee appears to be a material ingredient in the gift, the bequest is only *quousque* the legatee shall refrain from disturbing the will. 2 P. Wms. 52; 2 Ventr. 352. For cases of legacies given to a wife while she shall continue unmarried, see 1 Madd. R. 590; 1 Rop. Leg. 558.

IN TERROREM POPULI. To the terror of the people. An indictment for a riot is bad, unless it conclude in terrorem populi. 4 Carr. & Payne, 373.

IN TOTIDEM VERBIS. In just so many words; as, the legislature has declared this to be a crime *in totidem verbis.*

IN TOTO. In the whole; wholly; completely; as, the award is void in toto. In the whole the part is contained: *in toto et pars continetur*. Dig. 50, 17, 123.

IN TRANSITU. During the transit, or removal from one place to another.

2. The transit continues until the goods have arrived at their place of destination, and nothing remains to be done to complete the delivery; or until the goods have been delivered, before reaching their place of destination, and the person entitled takes an actual or symbolical possession. Vide *Stoppage in transitu; Transitus.*

IN VADIO. In pledge; in gage.

IN VENTRE SA MERE. In his mother's womb.

2.—1. In law a child is for all beneficial purposes considered as born while in ventre sa mere. 5 T. R. 49; Co. Litt. 36; 1 P. Wms. 329; Civ. Code of Lo. art. 948. But a stranger can acquire no title by descent through a child *in ventre sa mere*, who is not subsequently born alive. See *Birth; Dead Born.*

3.—2. Such a child is enabled to have an estate limited to his use. 1. Bl. Com. 130.

4.—3. May have a distributive share of intestate property. 1 Ves. 81.

5.—4. Is capable of taking a devise of lands. 2 Atk. 117; 1 Freem. 224, 293.

6.—5. Takes under a marriage settlement a provision made for children living at the death of the father. 1 Ves. 85.

7.—6. Is capable of taking a legacy, and is entitled to a share in a fund bequeathed to children under a general description of "children," or of "children living at the testator's death." 2 H. Bl. 399; 2 Bro. C. C. 320; S. C. 2 Ves. jr 673; 1 Sim. & Stu. 181; 1 B. & P. 243; 5 T. R. 49. See, also, 1 Ves. sr. 85; Id. 111; 1 P. Wms. 244, 341; 2 Bro. C. C. 63; Amb. 708, 711; 1 Salk. 229; 2 P. Wms. 446; 2 Atk. 114; Pre. Ch. 50; 2 Vern. 710; 3 Ves. 486; 7 T. R. 100; 4 Ves. 322; Bac. Ab. Legacies, &c., A; 1 Rop. Leg. 52, 3; 5 Serg. & Rawle, 40.

8.—7. May be appointed executor. Bac. Ab. Infancy, B.

9.—8. A bill may be brought in its behalf, and the court will grant an injunction to stay waste. 2 Vern. 710; Pr. Ch. 50.

10.—9. The mother of a child *in ventre sa mere* may detain writings on its behalf. 2 Vern. 710.

11.—10. May have a guardian assigned to it. 1 Bl. Com. 130.

12.—11. The destruction of such a child is a high misdemeanor. 1 Bl. Com. 129, 130.

13.—12. And the birth of a posthumous child amounts, in Pennsylvania, to the revocation of a will previously executed, so far as regards such child. 3 Binn. 498. See Coop. Just. 496. See, as to the law of Virginia on this subject, 3 Munf. 20. Vide *Fœtus.*

IN WITNESS WHEREOF. These words, which, when conveyancing was in the Latin language, were *in cujus rei testimonium*, are the initial words of the concluding clause in deeds. "In witness whereof the said parties have hereunto set their hands," &c.

INADEQUATE PRICE. This term is applied to indicate the want of a sufficient consideration for a thing sold, or such a price as, under ordinary circumstances, would be considered insufficient.

2. Inadequacy of price is frequently connected with fraud, gross misrepresentations, or an intentional concealment of the defects in the thing sold. In these cases it is clear the vendor cannot compel the buyer to fulfil the contract. 1 Lev. 111; 1 Bro. P. C. 187; 6 John. R. 110; 3 Cranch,

270; 4 Dall. R. 250; 3 Atk. 283; 1 Bro. C. C. 440.

3. In general, however, inadequacy of price is not sufficient ground to avoid a contract, particularly when the property has been sold by auction. 7 Ves. jr. 30; 3 Bro. C. C. 228; 7 Ves. jr. 35, note. But if an uncertain consideration, as a life annuity, be given for an estate, and the contract be executory, equity, it seems, will enter into the adequacy of the consideration. 7 Bro. P. C. 184; 1 Bro. C. C. 156. Vide 1 Yeates, R. 312; Sugd. Vend. 189 to 199; 1 B. & B. 165; 1 M'Cord's Ch. R. 383, 389, 390; 4 Desaus. R. 651. Vide *Price*.

INADMISSIBLE. What cannot be received. Parol evidence, for example, is inadmissible to contradict a written agreement.

INALIENABLE. This word is applied to those things, the property of which cannot be lawfully transferred from one person to another. Public highways and rivers are of this kind; there are also many rights which are inalienable, as the rights of liberty, or of speech.

INAUGURATION. This word was applied by the Romans to the ceremony of dedicating some temple, or raising some man to the priesthood, after the *augurs* had been consulted. It was afterwards applied to the *installation* (q. v.) of the emperors, kings, and prelates, in imitation of the ceremonies of the Romans when they entered into the temple of the augurs. It is applied in the United States to the installation of the chief magistrate of the republic, and of the governors of the several states.

INCAPACITY. The want of a quality legally to do, give, transmit, or receive something.

2. It arises from nature, from the law, or from both. From nature, when the party has not his senses, as, in the case of an idiot; from the law, as, in the case of a bastard who cannot inherit; from nature and the law, as, in the case of a married woman, who cannot make contracts or a will.

3. In general, the incapacity ceases with the cause which produces it. If the idiot should obtain his senses, or the married woman's husband die, their incapacity would be at an end.

4. When a cause of action arises during the incapacity of a person having the right to sue, the act of limitation does not, in general, commence to run till the incapacity has been removed. But two incapacities cannot be joined in order to come within the statute.

INCENDIARY, *crim. law*. One who maliciously and wilfully sets another person's house on fire; one guilty of the crime of arson.

2. This offence is punished by the statute laws of the different states according to their several provisions. The civil law punished it with death, Dig. 47, 9, 12, 1, by the offender being cast into the fire. Id. 48, 19, 28, 12; Code, 9, 1, 11. Vide Dane's Ab. Index, h. t.

INCEPTION. The commencement; the beginning. In making a will, for example, the writing is its inception. 3 Co. 31 b; Plowd. 343. Vide *Consummation; Progression.*

INCEST. The carnal copulation of a man and a woman related to each other in any of the degrees within which marriage is prohibited by law. Vide *Marriage.* It is punished by fine and imprisonment, under the laws of the respective states. Vide 1 Smith's Laws of Pennsylv. 26; Dane's Ab. Index, h. t.; Dig. 23, 2, 68; 6 Conn. R. 446; Penal Laws of China, B. 1, s. 2, § 10; Sw. part 2, § 17, p. 103.

INCH. From the Latin *uncia*. A measure of length, containing one-twelfth part of a foot.

INCHOATE. That which is not yet completed or finished. Contracts are considered inchoate until they are executed by all the parties who ought to have executed them. For example, a covenant which purports to be tripartite, and is executed by only two of the parties, is incomplete, and no one is bound by it. 2 Halst. 142. Vide *Locus pœnitentiæ.*

INCIDENT. A thing depending upon, appertaining to, or following another, called the princinal.

2. The power of punishing for contempt is incident to a court of record; rent is incident to a reversion; distress to rent; estovers of woods to a tenancy for a life or years. 1 Inst. 151; Noy's Max. n. 13, Vin. Ab. h. t.; Dane's Ab. h. t.; Com. Dig. h. t., and the references there; Bro Ab. h. t.; Roll's Ab. 75.

INCIPITUR, *practice*. This word, which means "it is begun," signifies the commencement of the entry on the roll on signing judgment, &c.

INCLUSIVE. Comprehended in computation. In computing time, as ten days from a particular time, one day is generally to be included and one excluded. Vide article *Exclusive*, and the authorities there cited.

INCOME. The gain which proceeds from property, labor, or business; it is applied particularly to individuals; the income of the government is usually called revenue.

2. It has been holden that a devise of the income of land, is in effect the same as a devise of the land itself. 9 Mass. 372; 1 Ashm. 136.

INCOMPATIBILITY, *offices, rights.* This term is used to show that two or more things ought not to exist at the same time in the same person; for example, a man cannot at the same time be landlord and tenant of the same land; heir and devise of the same thing; trustee and cestui que trust of the same property.

2. There are offices which are incompatible with each other by constitutional provision; the vice-president of the United States cannot act as such when filling the office of president; Const. art. 1, s. 3, n. 5; and by the same instrument, art. 1, s. 6, n. 2, it is directed that "no senator or representative shall, during the time for which he was elected, be appointed to any civil office under the authority of the United States, which shall have been created or the emoluments whereof shall have been increased, during such time; and no person holding any office under the United States, shall be a member of either house, during his continuance in office."

3. Provisions rendering offices incompatible are to be found in most of the constitutions of the states, and in some of their laws. In Pennsylvania, the acts of the 12th of February, 1802, 3 Smith's Laws of Pa. 485; and 6th of March, 1812, 5 Sm. L. Pa. 309, contain various provisions, making certain offices incompatible with each other. At common law, offices subordinate and interfering with each other have been considered incompatible; for example, a man cannot be at once a judge and prothonotary or clerk of the same court. 4 Inst. 100. Vide 4 S. & R. 277; 17 S. & R. 219; and the article *Office*.

INCOMPETENCY, *French law.* The state of a judge who cannot take cognizance of a dispute brought before him; it implies a want of jurisdiction.

2. Incompetency is material, *ratione materiæ*, or personal, *ratione personæ*. The first takes place when a judge takes cognizance of a matter over which another judge has the sole jurisdiction, and this cannot be cured by the appearance or agreement of the parties.

3. The second is, when the matter in dispute is within the jurisdiction of the judge, but the parties in the case are not; in which case they make the judge competent, unless they make their objection before they take defence. See Peck, 374; 17 John. 13; 12 Conn. 88; 3 Cowen, Rep. 724; 1 Penn. 195; 4 Yeates, 446. When a party has a privilege which exempts him from the jurisdiction, he may waive the privilege. 4 McCord, 79; Wright, 484; 4 Mass. 593; Pet. C. C. R. 489; 5 Cranch, 288; 1 Pet. R. 449; 4 W. C. C. R. 84; 8 Wheat. 699; Merl. Rép. mot Incompétence.

4. It is a maxim in the common law, *aliquis non debet esse judex in propriâ causâ.* Co. Litt. 141, a; see 14 Vin. Abr. 573; 4 Com. Dig. 6. The greatest delicacy is constantly observed on the part of judges, so that they never act when there could be the possibility of doubt whether they could be free from bias, and even a distant degree of relationship has induced a judge to decline interfering. 1 Knapp's Rep. 376. The slightest degree of pecuniary interest is considered as an insuperable objection. But at common law, interest forms the only ground for challenging a judge. It is not a ground of challenge that he has given his opinion before. 4 Bin. 349; 2 Bin. 454. See 4 Mod. 226; Comb. 218; Hard. 44; Hob. 87; 2 Binn. R. 454; 13 Mass. R. 340; 5 Mass. R. 92; 6 Pick. 109; Peck, R. 374; Coxe, Rep. 190; 3 Ham. R. 289; 17 John. Rep. 133; 12 Conn. R. 88; 1 Penning. R. 185; 4 Yeates, R. 466; 3 Cowen, R. 725; Salk. 396; Bac. Ab. Courts, B; and the articles *Competency; Credibility; Interest; Judge; Witness.*

INCOMPETENCY, *evidence.* The want of legal fitness or ability in a witness to be heard as such on the trial of a cause.

2. The objections to the competency (q. v.) of a witness are four-fold. The first ground is the want of understanding; a second is defect of religious principles; a third arises from the conviction of certain crimes, or infamy of character; the fourth is on account of interest. (q. v.) 1 Phil. Ev. 15.

INCONCLUSIVE. What does not put an end to a thing. Inconclusive presumptions are those which may be overcome by opposing proof; for example, the law presumes that he who possesses personal property is the owner of it, but evidence is allowed to contradict this presumption, and show who is the true owner. 3 Bouv. Inst. n. 3063.

INCONTINENCE. Impudicity, the indulgence in unlawful carnal connexions. Wolff, Dr. de la Nat. § 862.

INCORPORATION. This term is frequently confounded, particularly in the old books, with corporation. The distinction between them is this, that by incorporation is understood the act by which a corporation is created; by corporation is meant the body thus created. Vide *Corporation.*

INCORPORATION, *civil law.* The union of one domain to another.

INCORPOREAL. Not consisting of matter.

2 Things incorporeal are those which are not the object of sense, which cannot be seen or felt, but which we can easily conceive in the understanding, as rights, actions, successions, easements, and the like. Dig. lib. 6, t. 1; Id. lib. 41, t. 1, l. 43, § 1; Poth. Traité des Choses, § 2.

INCORPOREAL HEREDITAMENT, *title, estates.* A right issuing out of, or annexed unto a thing corporeal.

2. Their existence is merely in idea and abstracted contemplation, though their effects and profits may be frequently the objects of our bodily senses. Co. Litt. 9 a; Poth. Traité des Choses, § 2. According to Sir William Blackstone, there are ten kinds of incorporeal hereditaments; namely, 1. Advowsons. 2. Tithes. 3. Commons. 4. Ways. 5. Offices. 6. Dignities. 7. Franchises. 8. Corodies. 9. Annuities. 10. Rents. 2 Bl. Com. 20.

3. But, in the United States, there are no advowsons, tithes, dignities, nor corodies. The others have no necessary connexion with real estate, and are not hereditary, and, with the exception of annuities, in some cases, cannot be transferred, and do not descend.

INCORPOREAL PROPERTY, *civil law.* That which consists in legal right merely; or, as the term is, in the common law, of choses in actions. Vide *Corporeal property.*

TO INCULPATE. To accuse one of a crime or misdemeanor.

INCUMBENT, *eccles. law.* A clerk resident on his benefice with cure; he is so called because he does, or ought to, bend the whole of his studies to his duties. In common parlance, it signifies one who is in the possession of an office, as, the present incumbent.

INCUMBRANCE. Whatever is a lien upon an estate.

2. The right of a third person in the land in question to the diminution of the value of the land, though consistent with the passing of the fee by the deed of conveyance, is an incumbrance; as, a public highway over the land. 1 Appl. R. 313; 2 Mass. 97; 10 Conn. 431. A private right of way. 15 Pick. 68; 5 Conn. 497. A claim of dower. 22 Pick. 477; 2 Greenl. 22. A lien by judgment or mortgage. 5 Greenl. 94; 15 Verm. 683. Or any outstanding, elder, and better title, will be considered as incumbrances, although in strictness some of them are rather estates than incumbrances. 4 Mass. 630; 2 Greenl. 22; 22 Pick. 447; 5 Conn. 497; 8 Pick. 346; 15 Pick. 68; 13 John. 105; 5 Greenl. 94; 2 N. H. Rep. 458; 11 S. & R. 109; 4 Halst. 139; 7 Halst. 261; Verm. 676, 2 Greenl. Ev. § 242.

3. In cases of sales of real estate, the vendor is required to disclose the incumbrances, and to deliver to the purchaser the instruments by which they were created, or on which the defects arise; and the neglect of this will be considered as a fraud. Sugd. Vend. 6; 1 Ves. 96; and see 6 Ves. jr. 193; 10 Ves. jr. 470; 1 Sch. & Lef. 227; 7 Serg. & Rawle, 73.

4. Whether the tenant for life, or the remainder-man, is to keep down the interest on incumbrances, see Turn. R. 174; 3 Mer. R. 566; 5 Ves. 99; 4 Ves. 24. See, generally, 14 Vin. Ab. 352; Com. Dig. Chancery, 4 A 10, 4 I. 3; 9 Watts, R. 152.

INDEBITATUS ASSUMPSIT, *remedies, pleadings.* That species of action of assumpsit, in which the plaintiff alleges in his declaration, first a debt, and then a promise in consideration of the debt, that the defendant, *being indebted, he promised* the plaintiff to pay him. The promise so laid is, generally, an implied one only. Vide 1 Chit. Pl. 334; Steph. Pl. 318; Yelv. 21; 4 Co. 92 b. For the history of this form of action, see 3 Reeves' Hist. Com. Law; 2 Comyn on Contr. 549 to 556; 1 H. Bl. 550, 551; 3 Black. Com. 154; Yelv. 70. Vide *Pactum Constitutæ Pecuniæ.*

INDEBITI SOLUTIO, *civil law.* The

payment to one of what is not due to him. If the payment was made by mistake, the civilians recovered it back by an action called *condictio indebiti;* with us, such money may be recovered by an action of *assumpsit*.

INDEBTEDNESS. The state of being in debt, without regard to the ability or inability of the party to pay the same. See 1 Story, Eq. 343; 2 Hill. Ab. 421.

2. But in order to create an indebtedness, there must be an actual liability at the time, either to pay then or at a future time. If, for example, a person were to enter and become surety for another, who enters into a rule of reference, he does not thereby become a debtor to the opposite party until the rendition of the judgment on the award. 1 Mass. 134. See *Creditor; Debt; Debtor.*

INDECENCY. An act against good behaviour and a just delicacy. 2 Serg. & R. 91.

2. The law, in general, will repress indecency as being contrary to good morals, but, when the public good requires it, the mere indecency of disclosures does not suffice to exclude them from being given in evidence. 3 Bouv. Inst. n. 3216.

3. The following are examples of indecency: the exposure by a man of his naked person on a balcony, to public view, or bathing in public; 2 Campb. 89; or the exhibition of bawdy pictures. 2 Chit. Cr. Law, 42; 2 Serg. & Rawle, 91. This indecency is punishable by indictment. Vide 1 Sid. 168; S. C. 1 Keb. 620; 2 Yerg. R. 482, 589; 1 Mass. Rep. 8; 2 Chan. Cas. 110; 1 Russ. Cr. 302; 1 Hawk. P. C. c. 5, s. 4; 4 Bl. Com. 65, n.; 1 East, P. C. c. 1, s. 1; Burn's Just. Lewdness.

INDEFEASIBLE. That which cannot be defeated or undone. This epithet is usually applied to an estate or right which cannot be defeated.

INDEFENSUS. One sued or impleaded, who refuses or has nothing to answer.

INDEFINITE. That which is undefined; uncertain.

INDEFINITE FAILURE OF ISSUE, *executory devise.* A general failure of issue, whenever it may happen, without fixing a time, or certain or definite period, within which it must take place. The issue of the first taker must be extinct, and the issue of the issue *ad infinitum*, without regard to the time or any particular event. 2. Bouv. Inst. n. 1849.

INDEFINITE NUMBER. A number which may be increased or diminished at pleasure.

2. When a corporation is composed of an indefinite number of persons, any number of them consisting of a majority of those present may do any act unless it be otherwise regulated by the charter or by-laws. See *Definite number.*

INDEFINITE PAYMENT, *contracts.* That which a debtor who owes several debts to a creditor, makes without making an *appropriation*; (q. v.) in that case the creditor has a right to make such appropriation.

INDEMNITY. That which is given to a person to prevent his suffering damage. 2 McCord, 279. Sometimes it signifies diminution; a tenant who has been interrupted in the enjoyment of his lease may require an indemnity from the lessor, that is, a reduction of his rent.

2. It is a rule established in all just governments that when private property is required for public use, indemnity shall be given by the public to the owner. This is the case in the United States. See Code Civil, art. 545. See *Damnification.*

3. Contracts made for the purpose of indemnifying a person for doing an act for which he could be indicted, or an agreement to compensate a public officer for doing an act which is forbidden by law, or omitting to do one which the law commands, are absolutely void. But when the agreement with an officer was not to induce him to neglect his duty, but to test a legal right, as to indemnify him for not executing an execution, it was held to be good. 1 Bouv. Inst. n. 780.

INDENTURE, *conveyancing.* An instrument of writing containing a conveyance or contract between two or more persons, usually indented or cut unevenly, or in and out, on the top or side.

2. Formerly it was common to make two instruments exactly alike, and it was then usual to write both on the same parchment, with some words or letters written between them, through which the parchment was cut, either in a straight or indented line, in such a manner as to leave one-half of the word on one part, and half on the other. The instrument usually commences with these words, "This indenture," which were not formerly sufficient unless the parchment or paper was actually indented to make an indenture; 5 Co. 20; but now, if the form of indenting the parchment be wanting, it may be supplied by

being done in court, this being mere form. Besides, it would be exceedingly difficult, with even the most perfect instruments, to cut parchment or paper without indenting it. Vide Bac. Ab. Leases, &c. E 2; Com. Dig. Fait, C, and note d; Litt. sec. 370; Co. Litt. 143 b, 229 a; Cruise, Dig. t. 32, c. 1, s. 24; 2 Bl. Com. 294; 1 Sess. Cas. 222.

INDEPENDENCE. A state of perfect irresponsibility to any superior; the United States are free and independent of all earthly power.

2. Independence may be divided into *political* and *natural* independence. By the former is to be understood that we have contracted no tie except those which flow from the three great natural rights of safety, liberty and property. The latter consists in the power of being able to enjoy a permanent well-being, whatever may be the disposition of those from whom we call ourselves independent. In that sense a nation may be independent with regard to most people, but not independent of the whole world. Vide *Declaration of Independence.*

INDEPENDENT CONTRACT. One in which the mutual acts or promises have no relation to each other, either as equivalents or considerations. Civil Code of Lo. art. 1762; 1 Bouv. Inst. n. 699.

INDETERMINATE. That which is uncertain or not particularly designated; as, if I sell you one hundred bushels of wheat, without stating what wheat. 1 Bouv. Inst. n. 950.

INDIAN TRIBE. A separate and distinct community or body of the aboriginal Indian race of men found in the United States.

2. Such a tribe, situated within the boundaries of a state, and exercising the powers of government and sovereignty, under the national government, is deemed politically a state; that is, a distinct political society, capable of self-government; but it is not deemed a foreign state, in the sense of the constitution. It is rather a domestic dependent nation. Such a tribe may properly be deemed in a state of pupilage; and its relation to the United States resembles that of a ward to a guardian. 5 Pet. R. 1, 16, 17; 20 John. R. 193; 3 Kent, Com. 308 to 318; Story on Const. § 1096; 4 How. U. S. 567; 1 McLean, 254; 6 Hill, 546; 8 Ala. R. 48.

INDIANS. The aborigines of this country are so called.

2. In general, Indians have no political rights in the United States; they cannot vote at the general elections for officers, nor hold office. In New York they are considered as citizens and not as aliens, owing allegiance to the government and entitled to its protection. 20 John. 188, 633. But it was ruled that the Cherokee nation in Georgia was a distinct community. 6 Pet. 515. See 8 Cowen, 189; 9 Wheat. 673; 14 John. 181, 332; 18 John. 506.

INDIANA. The name of one of the new states of the United States. This state was admitted into the Union by virtue of the "Resolution for admitting the state of Indiana into the Union," approved December 11, 1816, in the following words: Whereas, in pursuance of an act of congress, passed on the nineteenth day of April, one thousand eight hundred and sixteen, entitled "An act to enable the people of the Indiana territory to from a constitution and state government, and for the admission of that state into the Union," the people of the said territory did, on the twenty-ninth day of June, in the present year, by a convention called for that purpose, form for themselves a constitution and state government, which constitution and state government, so formed, is republican, and in conformity with the principles of the articles of compact between the original states and the people and states in the territory north-west of the river Ohio, passed on the thirteenth day of July, one thousand seven hundred and eighty-seven.

2. Resolved, That the state of Indiana shall be one, and is hereby declared to be one of the United States of America, and admitted into the Union on an equal footing with the original states, in all respects whatever.

3. The first constitution of the state was adopted in the year eighteen hundred and sixteen, and has since been superseded by the present constitution, which was adopted in the year eighteen hundred and fifty-one. The powers of the government are divided into three distinct departments, and each of them is confided to a separate body of magistracy, to wit: those which are legislative, to one; those which are executive, including the administrative, to another; and those which are judicial to a third. Art. III.

4.—1st. The legislative authority of the state is vested in a general assembly, which consists of a senate and house of representatives, both elected by the people.

5.—1. The senate is composed of a number of persons, who shall not exceed fifty. Art. IV. s. 2. The number shall be fixed by law. Art. IV. s. 5. A senator shall, 1. Have attained the age of twenty-five years. 2. Be a citizen of the United States. 3. Have resided, next preceding his election, two years in this state, the last twelve months of which must have been in the county or district in which he may be elected. Senators shall be elected for the term of four years, and one-half as nearly as possible shall be elected every two years.

6.—2. The number of representatives is to be fixed by law. It shall never exceed one hundred members. Art. IV. s. 2, 5.

7. To be qualified for a representative, a person must, 1. Have attained the age of twenty-one years. 2. Be a citizen of the United States. 3. Have been for two years next preceding his election an inhabitant of this state, and for one year next preceding his election an inhabitant of the county or district whence he may be chosen. Art. IV. s. 7. Representatives are elected for the term of two years from the day next after their general election. Art. IV. s. 3. And they shall be chosen by the respective electors of the counties. Art. IV. s. 2.

8.—2d. The *executive* power of this state is vested in a governor. And, under certain circumstances, this power is exercised by the lieutenant-governor.

9.—1. The *governor* is elected at the time and place of choosing members of the general assembly. Art. V. s. 3. The person having the highest number of votes for governor shall be elected; but, in case two or more persons shall have an equal and the highest number of votes for the office, the general assembly shall, by joint vote, forthwith proceed to elect one of the said persons governor. He shall hold his office during four years, and is not eligible more than four years in any period of eight years. The official term of the governor shall commence on the second Monday of January, in the year one thousand eight hundred and fifty-three, and on the same day every fourth year thereafter. His requisite qualifications are, that he shall, 1. Have been a citizen of the United States for five years. 2. Be at least thirty years of age. 3. Have resided in the state five years next preceding his election. 4. Not hold any office under the United States, or this state. He is commander-in-chief of the army and navy of the state, when not in the service of the United States, and may call out such forces, to execute the laws, to suppress insurrection, or to repel invasion. He shall have the power to remit fines and forfeitures; grant reprieves and pardons, except treason and cases of impeachments; and to require information from executive officers. When, during a recess of the general assembly, a vacancy shall happen in any office, the appointment of which is vested in the general assembly, or when at any time a vacancy shall have happened in any other state office, or in the office of judge of any court, the governor shall fill such vacancy by appointment, which shall expire when a successor shall have been elected and qualified. He shall take care that the laws be faithfully executed. Should the seat of government become dangerous, from disease or a common enemy, he may convene the general assembly at any other place. He is also invested with the veto power. Art. V.

10.—2. The *lieutenant-governor* shall be chosen at every election for a governor, in the same manner, continue in office for the same time, and possess the same qualifications. In voting for governor and lieutenant-governor, the electors shall distinguish whom they vote for as governor, and whom as lieutenant-governor. He shall, by virtue of his office, be president of the senate; have a right, when in committee of the whole, to debate and vote on all subjects, and when the senate are equally divided, to give the casting vote. In case of the removal of the governor from office, death, resignation, or inability to discharge the duties of the office, the lieutenant-governor shall exercise all the powers and authority appertaining to the office of governor. Whenever the government shall be administered by the lieutenant-governor, or he shall be unable to attend as president of the senate, the senate shall elect one of their own members as president for that occasion. And the general assembly shall, by law, provide for the case of removal from office, death, resignation, or inability, both of the governor and lientenant-governor, declaring what officer shall then act as governor; and such officer shall act accordingly, until the disability be removed, or a governor be elected. The lieutenant-governor, while he acts as president of the senate, shall receive for his services the same compensation as the speaker of the house of representatives. The lieutenant-governor shall not be eligible to any other office during the term for which he shall have been elected.

11.—3. The *judicial* power of the state is vested by article VII. of the Constitution as follows:

§ 1. The judicial power of this state shall be vested in a supreme court, in circuit courts, and in such other inferior courts as the general assembly may direct and establish.

12.—§ 2. The supreme court shall consist of not less than three nor more than five judges, a majority of whom form a quorum, which shall have jurisdiction coëxtensive with the limits of the state, in appeals and writs of error, under such regulations and restrictions as may be prescribed by law. It shall also have such original jurisdiction as the general assembly may confer. And upon the decision of every case, shall give a statement, in writing, of each question arising in the record of such case, and the decision of the court thereon.

13.—§ 3. The circuit courts shall each consist of one judge. The state shall, from time to time, be divided into judicial circuits. They shall have such civil and criminal jurisdiction as may be prescribed by law. The general assembly may provide by law, that the judge of one circuit may hold the court of another circuit in case of necessity or convenience; and in case of temporary inability of any judge, from sickness or other cause, to hold the courts in his circuit, provision shall be made by law for holding such courts.

14.—§ 4. Tribunals of conciliation may be established with such powers and duties as shall be prescribed by law; or the powers and duties of the same may be conferred on other courts of justice; but such tribunals or other courts when sitting as such, shall have no power to render judgment to be obligatory on the parties, unless they voluntarily submit their matters of difference, and agree to abide the judgment of such tribunal or court.

15.—§ 5. The judges of the supreme court, the circuit and other inferior courts, shall hold their offices during the term of six years, if they shall so long behave well, and shall, at stated times, receive for their services a compensation, which shall not be diminished during their continuance in office.

16.—§ 6. All judicial officers shall be conservators of the peace in their respective jurisdiction.

17.—§ 7. The state shall be divided into as many districts as there are judges of the supreme court; and such districts shall be formed of contiguous territory, as nearly equal in population, as without dividing a county the same can be made. One of said judges shall be elected from each district, and reside therein; but said judges shall be elected by the electors of the state at large.

18.—§ 8. There shall be elected by the voters of the state, a clerk of the supreme court, who shall hold his office four years, and whose duties shall be prescribed by law.

19.—§ 9. There shall be elected in each judicial circuit by the voters thereof, a prosecuting attorney, who shall hold his office for two years.

20.—§ 10. A competent number of justices of the peace shall be elected by the qualified electors in each township in the several counties, and shall continue in office four years, and their powers and duties shall be prescribed by law.

21.—§ 11. Every person of good moral character, being a voter, shall be entitled to admission to practice law in all courts of justice.

INDICIA, *civil law*. Signs, marks. Example: in replevin, the chattel must possess *indicia*, or earmarks, by which it can be distinguished from all others of the same description. 4 Bouv. Inst. n. 3556. This term is very nearly synonymous with the common law phrase, "circumstantial evidence." It was used to designate the facts giving rise to the indirect inference, rather than the inference itself; as, for example, the possession of goods recently stolen, vicinity to the scene of the crime, sudden change in circumstances or conduct, &c. Mascardus, de Prob. lib. 1, quæst. 15; Dall. Dict. Compétence Criminelle, 92, 415; Morin, Dict. du Droit Criminel, mots Accusation, Chambre du Conseil.

2. Indicia may be defined to be conjectures which result from circumstances not absolutely necessary and certain, but merely probable, and which may turn out not to be true, though they have the ap-

pearance of truth. Denisart, mot Indices. See Best on Pres. 13, note *f*.

3. However numerous indicia may be, they only show that a thing may be, not that it has been. An indicium can have effect only when a connexion is essentially necessary with the principal. Effects are known by their causes, but only when the effects can arise only from the causes to which they are attributed. When several causes may have produced one and the same effect, it is, therefore, unreasonable to attribute it to any one of such causes. A combination of circumstances sometimes conspire against an innocent person, and, like mute witnesses, depose against him. There is danger in such cases, that a jury may be misled; their minds prejudiced; their indignation unduly excited, or their zeal seduced. Under impressions thus produced, they may forget their true relation to the accused, and condemn a man whom they would have acquitted had they required that proof and certainty which the law demands. See D'Aguesseau, Œuvres, vol. xiii. p. 243. See *Circumstances*.

INDICTED, *practice*. When a man is accused by a bill of indictment preferred by a grand jury, he is said to be indicted.

INDICTION, *computation of time*. An indiction contained a space of fifteen years.

2. It was used in dating at Rome and in England. It began at the dismission of the Nicene council, A. D. 312. The first year was reckoned the first of the first indiction, the second, the third, &c., till fifteen years afterwards. The sixteenth year was the first year of the second indiction, the thirty-first year was the first year of the third indiction, &c.

INDICTMENT, *crim. law, practice*. A written accusation of one or more persons of a crime or misdemeanor, presented to, and preferred upon oath or affirmation, by a grand jury legally convoked. 4 Bl. Com. 299; Co. Litt. 126; 2 Hale, 152; Bac. Ab. h. t.; Com. Dig. h. t. A; 1 Chit. Cr. L. 168.

2. This word, indictment, is said to be derived from the old French word *inditer*, which signifies *to indicate; to show*, or *point out*. Its object is to indicate the offence charged against the accused. Rey, des Inst. l'Angl. tome 2, p. 347.

3. To render an indictment valid, there are certain essential and formal requisites. The essential requisites are, 1st. That the indictment be presented to some court having jurisdiction of the offence stated therein. 2d. That it appear to have been found by the grand jury of the proper county or district. 3d. That the indictment be found a true bill, and signed by the foreman of the grand jury. 4th. That it be framed with sufficient certainty; for this purpose the charge must contain a certain description of the crime or misdemeanor, of which the defendant is accused, and a statement of the facts by which it is constituted, so as to identify the accusation. Cowp. 682, 3; 2 Hale, 167; 1 Binn. R. 201; 3 Binn. R. 533; 1 P. A. Bro. R. 360; 6 S. & R. 398; 4 Serg. & Rawle, 194; 4 Bl. Com. 301; 3 Yeates, R. 407; 4 Cranch, R. 167. 5th. The indictment must be in the English language. But if any document in a foreign language, as a libel, be necessarily introduced, it should be set out in the original tongue, and then translated, showing its application. 6 T. R. 162.

4. Secondly, the formal requisites are, 1st. The *venue*, which at common law should always be laid in the county where the offence has been committed, although the charge is in its nature transitory, as a battery. Hawk. B. 2, c. 25, s. 35. The venue is stated in the margin thus, "City and county of ——, to wit." 2d. The *presentment*, which must be in the present tense, and is usually expressed by the following formula, "the grand inquest of the commonwealth of ——, inquiring for the city and county aforesaid, upon their oaths and affirmations present." See, as to the venue, 1 Pike, R. 171; 9 Yerg. 357. 3d. The *name and addition of the defendant;* but in case an error has been made in this respect, it is cured by the plea of the defendant. Bac. Ab. Misnomer, B; Indictment, G 2; 2 Hale, 175; 1 Chit. Pr. 202. 4th. The *names of third persons*, when they must be necessarily mentioned in the indictment, should be stated with certainty to a common intent, so as sufficiently to inform the defendant who are his accusers. When, however, the names of third persons cannot be ascertained, it is sufficient, in some cases, to state "a certain person or persons to the jurors aforesaid unknown." Hawk. B. 2, c. 25, s. 71; 2 East, P. C. 651, 781; 2 Hale, 181; Plowd. 85; Dyer, 97, 286; 8 C. & P. 773. See *Unknown*. 5th. The *time* when the offence was committed, should in general be stated to be on a specific year and day. In some offences, as in perjury, the day must be pre

cisely stated; 2 Wash. C. C. Rep. 328; but although it is necessary that a day certain should be laid in the indictment, yet, in general, the prosecutor may give evidence of an offence committed on any other day previous to the finding of the indictment. 5 Serg. & Rawle, 316. Vide 11 Serg. & Rawle, 177; 1 Chit. Cr. Law, 217, 224; 1 Ch. Pl. Index, tit. Time. See 17 Wend. 475; 2 Dev. 567; 5 How. Mis. 14; 4 Dana, 496; C. & N. 369; 1 Hawks, 460. 6th. The *offence should be properly described.* This is done by stating the substantial circumstances necessary to show the nature of the crime; and, next, the formal allegations and terms of art required by law. 1. As to the substantial circumstances. The whole of the facts of the case necessary to make it appear judicially to the court that the indictors have gone upon sufficient premises, should be set forth; but there should be no unnecessary matter or any thing which on its face makes the indictment repugnant, inconsistent, or absurd. 2 Hale, 183; Haw. b 2, c. 25, s. 57; Bac. Ab. h. t. G 1; Com. Dig. h. t. G 3; 2 Leach, 660; 2 Str. 1226. All indictments ought to charge a man with a particular offence, and not with being an offender in general: to this rule there are some exceptions, as indictments against a common barrator, a common scold, and the keeper of a common bawdy house; such persons may be indicted by these general words. 1 Chit. Cr. Law, 230, and the authorities there cited. The offence must not be stated in the disjunctive, so as to leave it uncertain on what it is intended to rely as an accusation; as, that the defendant erected *or* caused to be erected a nuisance. 2 Str. 900; 1 Chit. Cr. Law, 236. 2. There are certain terms of art used, so appropriated by the law to express the precise idea which it entertains of the offence, that no other terms, however synonymous they may seem, are capable of filling the same office: such, for example, as traitorously, (q. v.) in treason; feloniously, (q. v.) in felony; burglariously, (q. v.) in burglary; maim, (q. v.) in mayhem, &c. 7th. The conclusion of the indictment should conform to the provision of the constitution of the state on the subject, where there is such provision; as in Pennsylvania, Const. art. V., s. 11, which provides, that "all prosecutions shall be carried on in the name and by the authority of the commonwealth of Pennsylvania, *and conclude against the peace and dignity of the same.*" As to the necessity and propriety of having several counts in an indictment, vide 1 Chit. Cr. Law, 248; as to joinder of several offences in the same indictment, vide 1 Chit. Cr. Law, 253; Arch. Cr. Pl. 60; several defendants may in some cases be joined in the same indictment. Id. 255; Arch. Cr. Pl. 59. When an indictment may be amended, see Id. 297 Stark. Cr. Pl. 286; or quashed, Id. 298, Stark. Cr. Pl. 331; Arch. Cr. 66. Vide, generally, Arch. Cr. Pl. B. 1, part 1, c. 1, p. 1 to 68; Stark. Cr. Pl. 1 to 336; 1 Chit. Cr. Law, 168 to 304; Com. Dig. h. t.; Vin. Ab. h. t.; Bac. Ab. h. t.; Dane's Ab. h. t.; Nels. Ab. h. t.; Burn's Just. h. t.; Russ. on Cr. Index, h. t.

5. By the Constitution of the United States, Amendm. art. 5, no person shall be held to answer for a capital, or otherwise infamous crime, unless on a presentment or indictment of a grand jury, except in cases arising in the land or naval forces, or in the militia, when in actual service in time of war, or public danger.

INDICTOR. He who causes another to be indicted. The latter is sometimes called the indictee.

INDIFFERENT. To have no bias nor partiality. 7 Conn. 229. A juror, an arbitrator, and a witness, ought to be indifferent, and when they are not so, they may be challenged. See 9 Conn. 42.

INDIRECT EVIDENCE. That proof which does not prove the fact in question, but proves another, the certainty of which may lead to the discovery of the truth of the one sought.

INDIVISIBLE. That which cannot be separated.

2. It is important to ascertain when a consideration or a contract, is or is not indivisible. When a consideration is entire and indivisible, and it is against law, the contract is void in toto. 11 Verm. 592; 2 W. & S. 235. When the consideration is divisible, and part of it is illegal, the contract is void only *pro tanto.*

3. To ascertain whether a contract is divisible or indivisible, is to ascertain whether it may or may not be *enforced in part,* or *paid in part,* without the consent of the other party. See 1 Bouv. Inst. n. 694, and articles *Divisible; Entire.*

INDIVISUM. That which two or more persons hold in common without partition; undivided. (q. v.)

TO INDORSE. To write on the back. Bills of exchange and promissory notes are indorsed by the party writing his name on the back; writing one's name on the back of a writ, is to indorse such writ. 7 Pick. 117. See 13 Mass. 396.

INDORSEE, *contracts*. The person in whose favor an indorsement is made.

2. He is entitled to all the rights of the indorser, and, if the bill or note have been indorsed over to him before it became due, he may be entitled to greater rights than the payee and indorser would have had, had he retained it till it became due, as none of the parties can make a set-off, or inquire into the consideration of the bill which he then holds. If he continues to be the holder (q. v.) when the bill becomes due, he ought to make a legal demand, and give notice in case of non-acceptance or non-payment. Chitty on Bills, *passim*.

INDORSEMENT, *crim. law, practice*. When a warrant for the arrest of a person charged with a crime has been issued by a justice of the peace of one county, which is to be executed in another county, it is necessary in some states, as in Pennsylvania, that it should be indorsed by a justice of the county where it is to be executed; this indorsement is called backing. (q. v.)

INDORSEMENT, *contracts*. In its most general acceptation, it is what is written on the back of an instrument of writing, and which has relation to it;. as, for example, a receipt or acquittance on a bond; an assignment on a promissory note.

2. Writing one's name on the back of a bill of exchange, or a promissory note payable to order, is what is usually called an indorsement. It will be convenient to consider, 1. The form of an indorsement; and, 2. Its effect.

3.—1. An indorsement is in full, or in blank. In full, when mention is made of the name of the indorsee; and in blank, when the name of the indorsee is not mentioned. Chitty on Bills, 170; 13 Serg. & Rawle, 315. A blank indorsement is made by writing the name of the indorser on the back; a writing or assignment on the face of the note or bill would, however, be considered to have the force and effect of an indorsement. 16 East, R. 12. When an indorsement has been made in blank, any after attempt to restrain the negotiability of the bill will be unavailing. 1 E. N. P. C. 180; 1 Bl. Rep. 295; Ham. on Parties, 104.

4. Indorsements may also be restrictive, conditional, or qualified. A restrictive indorsement may restrain the negotiability of a bill, by using express words to that effect, as by indorsing it "payable to J. S. only," or by using other words clearly demonstrating his intention to do so. Dougl. 637. The indorser may also make his indorsement conditional, and if the condition be not performed, it will be invalid. 4 Taunt. Rep. 30. A qualified indorsement is one which passes the property in the bill to the indorsee, but is made without responsibility to the indorser; 7 Taunt. R. 160; the words commonly used are, *sans recours*, without recourse. Chit. on Bills, 179; 3 Mass. 225; 12 Mass. 14, 15.

5.—2. The effects of a regular indorsement may be considered, 1. As between the indorser and the indorsee. 2. Between the indorser and the acceptor. And, 3. Between the indorser and future parties to the bill.

6.—1. An indorsement is sometimes an original engagement; as, when a man draws a bill payable to his own order, and indorses it; mostly, however, it operates as an assignment, as when the bill is perfect, and the payee indorses it over to a third person. As an assignment, it carries with it all the rights which the indorsee had, with a guaranty of the solvency of the debtor. This guaranty is, nevertheless, upon condition that the holder will use due diligence in making a demand of payment from the acceptor, and give notice of non-acceptance or non-payment. 13 Serg. & Rawle, 311.

7.—2. As between the indorsee and the acceptor, the indorsement has the effect of giving to the former all the rights which the indorser had against the acceptor, and all other parties liable on the bill, and it is unnecessary that the acceptor or other party should signify his consent or knowledge of the indorsement; and if made before the bill is paid, it conveys all these rights without any set-off, as between the antecedent parties. Being thus fully invested with all the rights in the bill, the indorsee may himself indorse it to another when he becomes responsible to all future parties as an indorser, as the others were to him.

8.—3. The indorser becomes responsible by that act to all persons who may afterwards become party to the bill.

Vide Chitty on Bills, ch. 4; 3 Kent, Com. 58; Vin. Abr. Indorsement; Com. Dig. Fait, E 2; 13 Serg. & Rawle, 311; Merl. Répert. mot Endossement; Pard. Droit

Com. 344–357; 7 Verm. 356; 2 Dana, R. 90; 3 Dana, R. 407; 8 Wend 600; 4 Verm. 11; 5 Harr. & John. 115; Bouv. Inst. Index, h. t.

INDORSER, *contracts*. The person who makes an indorsement.

2. The indorser of a bill of exchange, or other negotiable paper, by his indorsement undertakes to be responsible to the holder for the amount of the bill or note, if the latter shall make a legal demand from the payer, and, in default of payment, give proper notice thereof to the indorser. But the indorser may make his indorsement conditional, which will operate as a transfer of the bill, if the condition be performed; or he may make it qualified, so that he shall not be responsible on non-payment by the payer. Chitty on Bills, 179, 180.

3. To make an indorser liable on his indorsement, the instrument must be commercial paper, for the indorsement of a bond or single bill will not, per se, create a responsibility. 13 Serg. & Rawle, 311. But see Treval *v.* Fitch, 5 Whart. 325; Hopkins *v.* Cumberland Valley R. R. Co., 3 Watts & Serg. 410.

4. When there are several indorsers, the first in point of time is generally, but not always, first responsible; there may be circumstances which may cast the responsibility, in the first place, as between them, on a subsequent indorsee. 5 Munf. R. 252.

INDUCEMENT, *pleading*. The statement of matter which is introductory to the principal subject of the declaration or plea, &c., but which is necessary to explain and elucidate it; such matter as is not introductory to or necessary to elucidate the substance or gist of the declaration or plea, &c. nor is collaterally applicable to it, not being inducement but surplusage. Inducement or conveyance, which are synonymous terms, is in the nature of a preamble to an act of assembly, and leads to the principal subject of the declaration or plea, &c. the same as that does to the purview or providing clause of the act. For instance, in an action for a nuisance to property in the possession of the plaintiff, the circumstance of his being possessed of the property should be stated as inducement, or by way of introduction to the mention of the nuisance. Lawes, Pl. 66, 67; 1 Chit. Pl. 292; Steph. Pl. 257; 14 Vin. Ab. 405; 20 Id. 345; Bac. Ab. Pleas. &c. I 2.

INDUCEMENT, *contracts, evidence*. The moving cause of an action.

2. In contracts, the benefit which the obligor is to receive is the inducement to making them. Vide *Cause; Consideration.*

3. When a person is charged with a crime, he is sometimes induced to make confessions by the flattery of hope, or the torture of fear. When such confessions are made in consequence of promises or threats by a person in authority, they cannot be received in evidence. In England a distinction has been made between *temporal* and *spiritual* inducements; confessions made under the former are not receivable in evidence, while the latter may be admitted. Joy on Conf. ss. 1 and 4.

INDUCLÆ LEGALES, *Scotch law*. The days between the citation of the defendant, and the day of appearance. Bell's Scotch Law Dict. h. t. The days between the test and the return day of the writ.

INDUCTION, *eccles. law*. The giving a clerk, instituted to a benefice, the actual possession of its temporalties, in the nature of livery of seisin. Ayl. Parerg. 299.

INDULGENCE. A favor granted.

2. It is a general rule that where a creditor gives indulgence, by entering into a binding contract with a principal debtor, by which the surety is or may be damnified, such surety is discharged, because the creditor has put it out of his power to enforce immediate payment, when the surety would have a right to require him to do so. 6 Dow, P. C. 238; 3 Meriv. 272; Bac. Ab. Oblig. D; and see *Giving Time*.

3. But mere inaction by the creditor, if he do not deprive himself of the right to sue the principal, does not in general discharge the surety. See *Forbearance*.

INELIGIBILITY. The incapacity to be lawfully elected.

2. This incapacity arises from various causes, and a person may be incapable of being elected to one office who may be elected to another; the incapacity may also be perpetual or temporary.

3.—1. Among perpetual inabilities may be reckoned, 1. The inability of women to be elected to a public office. 2. Of citizens born in a foreign country to be elected president of the United States.

4.—2. Among the temporary inabilities may be mentioned, 1. The holding of an office declared by law to be incompatible with the one sought. 2. The non-payment of the taxes required by law. 3. The want of certain property qualifications required by the constitution. 4. The want of age, or being over the age required. Vide *Eligibility; Incompatibility.*

INEVITABLE ACCIDENT. A term used in the civil law, nearly synonymous with *fortuitous event.* (q. v.) 2 Sm. & Marsh. 572. In the common law commonly called the *act of God.* (q. v.) 2 Smed. & Marsh. Err. & App. 572.

INFAMIS. Among the Romans was one who, in consequence of the application of a general rule, and not by virtue of an arbitrary decision of the censors, lost his political rights, but preserved his civil rights. Sav. Dr. Rom. § 79.

INFAMY, *crim. law, evidence.* That state which is produced by the conviction of crime and the loss of honor, which renders the infamous person incompetent as a witness.

2. It is to be considered, 1st. What crimes or punishment incapacitate a witness. 2d. How the guilt is to be proved. 3d. How the objection is answered. 4th. The effect of infamy.

3.—1. When a man is convicted of an offence which is inconsistent with the common principles of honesty and humanity, the law considers his oath to be of no weight, and excludes his testimony as of too doubtful and suspicious a nature to be admitted in a court of justice to deprive another of life, liberty or property. Gilb. L. E. 256; 2 Bulst. 154; 1 Phil. 23; Bull. N. P. 291. The crimes which render a person incompetent, are treason; 5 Mod. 16, 74; felony; 2 Bulst. 154; Co. Litt. 6; T. Raym. 369; all offences founded in fraud, and which come within the general notion of the crimen falsi of the Roman law; Leach, 496; as perjury and forgery; Co. Litt. 6; Fort. 209; piracy; 2 Roll. Ab. 886; swindling, cheating; Fort. 209; barratry; 2 Salk. 690; and the bribing a witness to absent himself from a trial, in order to get rid of his evidence. Fort. 208. It is the crime and not the punishment which renders the offender unworthy of belief. 1 Phill. Ev. 25.

4.—2. In order to incapacitate the party, the judgment must be proved as pronounced by a court possessing competent jurisdiction. 1 Sid. 51; 2 Stark. C. 183; Stark. Ev. part 2, p. 144, note 1; Id. part 4, p. 716. But it has been held that a conviction of an infamous crime in another country, or another of the United States, does not render the witness incompetent on the ground of infamy. 17 Mass. 515. Though this doctrine appears to be at variance with the opinions entertained by foreign jurists, who maintain that the state or condition of a person in the place of his domicil accompanies him everywhere. Story, Confl. § 620, and the authorities there cited; Fœlix, Traité De Droit Intern. Privé, § 31; Merl. Répert, mot Loi, § 6, n. 6.

5.—3. The objection to competency may be answered, 1st. By proof of pardon. See *Pardon.* And, 2d. By proof of a reversal by writ of error, which must be proved by the production of the record.

6.—4. The judgment for an infamous crime, even for perjury, does not preclude the party from making an affidavit with a view to his own defence. 2 Salk. 461; 2 Str. 1148; Martin's Rep. 45. He may, for instance, make an affidavit in relation to the irregularity of a judgment in a cause in which he is a party, for otherwise he would be without a remedy. But the rule is confined to defence, and he cannot be heard upon oath as complainant. 2 Salk. 461; 2 Str. 1148. When the witness becomes incompetent from infamy of character, the effect is the same as if he were dead; and if he has attested any instrument as a witness, previous to his conviction, evidence may be given of his handwriting. 2 Str 833; Stark. Ev. part 2, sect. 193; Id. part 4, p. 723.

7. By infamy is also understood the expressed opinion of men generally as to the vices of another. Wolff, Dr. de la Nat. et des Gens, § 148.

INFANCY. The state or condition of a person under the age of twenty-one years. Vide *Infant.*

INFANT, *persons.* One under the age of twenty-one years. Co. Litt. 171.

2. But he is reputed to be twenty-one years old, or of full age, the first instant of the last day of the twenty-first year next before the anniversary of his birth; because, according to the civil computation of time, which differs from the natural computation, the last day having commenced, it is considered as ended. Savig. Dr. Rom. § 182. If, for example, a person were born at any hour of the first day of January, 1810, (even a few minutes before twelve o'clock of the night of that day,) he would be of full age at the first instant of the thirty-first of December, 1831, although nearly forty-eight hours before he had actually attained the full age of twenty-one years, according to years, days, hours and minutes, because there is, in this case, no fraction of a day

1 Sid. 162; S. C. 1 Keb. 589; 1 Salk. 44; Raym. 84; 1 Bl. Com. 463, 464, note 13, by Chitty; 1 Lilly's Reg. 57; Com. Dig. Enfant, A; Savig. Dr. Rom. §§ 383, 384.

3. A curious case occurred in England of a young lady who was born after the house clock had struck, while the parish clock was striking, and before St. Paul's had begun to strike twelve on the night of the fourth and fifth of January, 1805, and the question was whether she was born on the fourth or fifth of January. Mr. Coventry gives it as his opinion that she was born on the fourth, because the house clock does not regulate anything but domestic affairs, that the parochial clock is much better evidence, and that a metropolitan clock ought to be received with "implicit acquiescence." Cov. on Conv. Ev. 182–3. It is conceived that this can only be prima facie, because, if the fact were otherwise, and the parochial and metropolitan clocks should both have been wrong, they would undoubtedly have had no effect in ascertaining the age of the child.

4. The sex makes no difference, a woman is therefore an infant until she has attained her age of twenty-one years. Co. Litt. 171. Before arriving at full age, an infant may do many acts. A *male* at fourteen is of discretion, and may consent to marry; and at that age he may disagree to and annul a marriage he may before that time have contracted; he may then choose a guardian; and, if his discretion be proved, may, at common law, make a will of his personal estate; and may act as executor at the age of seventeen years. A *female* at seven may be betrothed or given in marriage; at nine she is entitled to dower; at twelve may consent or disagree to marriage; and, at common law, at seventeen may act as executrix.

5. Considerable changes of the common law have probably taken place in many of the states. In Pennsylvania, to act as an executor, the party must be of full age. In general, an infant is not bound by his contracts, unless to supply him for necessaries. Selw. N. P. 137; Chit. Contr. 31; Bac. Ab. Infancy, &c. I 3; 9 Vin. Ab. 391; 1 Com. Contr. 150, 151; 3 Rawle's R. 351; 8 T. R. 335; 1 Keb. 905, 913; S. C. 1 Sid. 258; 1 Lev. 168; 1 Sid. 129; 1 Southard's R. 87. Sed vide 6 Cranch, 226; 3 Pick. 492; 1 Nott & M'Cord, 197. Or, unless he is empowered to enter into a contract, by some legislative provision; as, with the consent of his parent or guardian to put himself apprentice, or to enlist in the service of the United States. 4 Binn. 487; 5 Binn. 423.

6. Contracts made with him, may be enforced or avoided by him on his coming of age. See *Parties to contracts; Voidable.* But to this general rule there is an exception; he cannot avoid contracts for necessaries, because these are for his benefit. See *Necessaries.* The privilege of avoiding a contract on account of infancy, is strictly personal to the infant, and no one can take advantage of it but himself. 3 Green, 343; 2 Brev. 438. When the contract has been performed, and it is such as he would be compellable by law to perform, it will be good and bind him. Co. Litt. 172 a. And all the acts of an infant, which do not touch his interest, but take effect from an authority which he has been trusted to execute, are binding. 3 Burr. 1794; Fonbl. Eq. b. 1, c. 2, § 5, note c.

7. The protection which the law gives an infant is to operate as a shield to him, to protect him from improvident contracts, but not as a sword to do injury to others. An infant is therefore responsible for his torts, as, for slander, trespass, and the like; but he cannot be made responsible in an action ex delicto, where the cause arose on a contract. 3 Rawle's R. 351; 6 Watts' R. 9; 25 Wend. 399; 3 Shep. 233; 9 N. H. Rep. 441; 10 Verm. 71; 5 Hill, 391. But see contra, 6 Cranch, 226; 15 Mass. 359; 4 M'Cord, 387.

8. He is also punishable for a crime, if of sufficient discretion, or *doli capax.* 1 Russ. on Cr. 2, 3. Vide, generally, Bouv. Inst. Index, h. t.; Bingh. on Infancy; 1 Hare & Wall. Sel. Dec. 103, 122; the various Abridgments and Digests, tit. Enfant, Infancy; and articles *Age; Birth; Capax Doli; Dead born; Fœtus; In ventre sa mere.*

INFANTICIDE, *med. juris.* The murder of a new born infant. Dalloz, Dict. Homicide, § 4; Code Pénal, 300. There is a difference between this offence and those known by the name of *prolicide,* (q. v.) and *fœticide.* (q. v.)

2. To commit infanticide the child must be wholly born; it is not sufficient that it was born so far as the head and breathed, if it died before it was wholly born. 5 Carr. & Payn. 329; 24 Eng. C. L. Rep. 344; S. C. 6 Carr. & Payn. 349; S. C. 25 Eng. C. L. Rep. 433.

3. When this crime is to be proved from

circumstances, it is proper to consider whether the child had attained that size and maturity by which it would have been enabled to maintain an independent existence; whether it was born alive; and, if born alive, by what means it came to its death. 1 Beck's Med. Jur. 331 to 428, where these several questions are learnedly considered. See also 1 Briand, Méd Lég. prém. part. c. 8; Cooper's Med. Jur. h. t. Vide Ryan's Med. Jur. 137; Med. Jur. 145, 194; Dr. Cummin's Proof of Infanticide considered; Lécieux, Considerations Médico-légales sur l'Infanticide; Duvergie, Médicine Légale, *art.* Infanticide.

INFEOFFMENT, *estates.* The act or instrument of feoffment. (q. v.) In Scotland it is synonymous with *saisine,* meaning the instrument of possession; formerly it was synonymous with investiture. Bell's Sc. L. Dict. h. t.

INFERENCE. A conclusion drawn by reason from premises established by proof.

2. It is the province of the judge who is to decide upon the facts to draw the inference. When the facts are submitted to the court, the judges draw the inference; when they are to be ascertained by a jury, it is their duty to do so. The witness is not permitted as a general rule to draw an inference, and testify that to the court or jury. It is his duty to state the facts simply as they occurred. Inferences differ from presumptions. (q. v.)

INFERIOR. One who in relation to another has less power and is below him; one who is bound to obey another. He who makes the law is the superior; he who is bound to obey it, the inferior. 1 Bouv. Inst. n. 8.

INFERIOR COURTS. By this term are understood all courts except the supreme courts. An inferior court is a court of limited jurisdiction, and it must appear on the face of its proceedings that it has jurisdiction, or its proceedings will be void. 3 Bouv. Inst. n. 2529.

INFIDEL, *persons, evidence.* One who does not believe in the existence of a God, who will reward or punish in this world or that which is to come. Willes' R. 550. This term has been very indefinitely applied. Under the name of infidel, Lord Coke comprises Jews and heathens; 2 Inst. 506; 3 Inst. 165; and Hawkins includes among infidels, such as do not believe either in the Old or New Testament. Hawk. P. C. b 2, c. 46, s. 148.

2. It is now settled that when the witness believes in a God who will reward or punish him even in this world he is competent. See Willes, R. 550. His belief may be proved from his previous declarations and avowed opinions; and when he has avowed himself to be an infidel, he may show a reform of his conduct, and change of his opinion since the declarations proved; when the declarations have been made for a very considerable space of time, slight proof will suffice to show he has changed his opinion. There is some conflict in the cases on this subject, some of them are here referred to: 18 John. R. 98; 1 Harper, R. 62; 4 N. Hamp. R. 444; 4 Day's Cas. 51; 2 Cowen, R. 431, 433 n., 572; 7 Conn. R. 66; 2 Tenn. R. 96; 4 Law Report, 268; Alis. Pr. Cr. Law, 438; 5 Mason, 16; 15 Mass. 184; 1 Wright, 345; So. Car. Law Journ. 202. Vide *Atheist; Future state.*

INFIRM. Weak, feeble.

2. When a witness is infirm to an extent likely to destroy his life, or to prevent his attendance at the trial, his testimony *de bene esse* may be taken at any age. 1 P. Will. 117; see *Aged witness; Going witness.*

INFLUENCE. Authority, credit, ascendance.

2. Influence is proper or improper Proper influence is that which one person gains over another by acts of kindness and attention, and by correct conduct. 3 Serg. & Rawle, 269. Improper influence is that dominion acquired by any person over a mind of sanity for general purposes, and of sufficient soundness and discretion to regulate his affairs in general, which prevents the exercise of his discretion, and destroys his free will. 1 Cox's Cas. 355. When the former is used to induce a testator to make a will, it will not vitiate it; but when the latter is the moving cause, the will cannot stand. 1 Hagg. R. 581; 2 Hagg. 142; 5 Serg. & Rawle, 207; 13 Serg. & Rawle, 323; 4 Greenl. R. 220; 1 Paige, R. 171; 1 Dow. & Cl. 440; 1 Speers, 93.

3. A contract to use a party's influence to induce a person in authority to exercise his power in a particular way, is void, as being against public policy. 5 Watts & Serg. 315; 5 Penn. St. Rep. 452; 7 Watts, 152.

INFORMALITY. The want of those forms required by law. Informality is a good ground for a plea in abatement. Com. Dig. Abatement, H 1, 6; Lawes, Pl. 106; Gould, Pl. c. 5, part 1, § 132.

INFORMATION. An accusation or complaint made in writing to a court of competent jurisdiction, charging some person with a specific violation of some public law. It differs in nothing from an indictment in its form and substance, except that it is filed at the discretion of the proper law officer of the government, *ex officio*, without the intervention or approval of a grand jury. 4 Bl. Com. 308, 9.

2. In the French law, the term information is used to signify the act or instrument which contains the depositions of witnesses against the accused. Poth. Proc. Cr. sect. 2, art. 5.

3. Informations have for their object either to punish a crime or misdemeanor, and these have, perhaps, never been resorted to in the United States; or to recover penalties or forfeitures, which are quite common. For the form and requisites of an information for a penalty, see 2 Chit. Pr. 155 to 171. Vide Blake's Ch. 49; 14 Vin. Ab. 407; 3 Story, Constitution, § 1780; 3 Bl. Com. 261.

4. In summary proceedings before justices of the peace, the complaint or accusation, at least when the proceedings relate to a penalty, is called an information, and it is then taken down in writing and sworn to. As the object is to limit the informer to a certain charge, in order that the defendant may know what he has to defend, and the justice may limit the evidence and his subsequent adjudication to the allegations in the information, it follows that the substance of the particular complaint must be stated, and it must be sufficiently formal to contain all material averments. 8 T. R. 286; 5 Barn. & Cres. 251; 11 E. C. L. R. 217; 2 Chit. Pr. 156. See 1 Wheat. R. 9.

INFORMATION IN THE NATURE OF A WRIT OF QUO WARRANTO, *remedies*. The name of a proceeding against any one who usurps a franchise or office.

2. Informations of this kind are filed in the highest courts of ordinary jurisdiction in the several states, either by the attorney-general, of his own authority, or by the prosecutor, who is entitled, pro forma, to use his name, as the case may be. 6 Cowen, R. 102, n.; 10 Mass. 290; 2 Dall. 112; 2 Halst. R. 101; 1 Rep. Const. Ct. So. Car. 36; 3 Serg. & Rawle, 52; 15 Serg. & Rawle, 127. Though, in form, these informations are criminal, they are, in their nature, but civil proceedings. 3 T. R. 484; Kyd on Corp. 439. They are used to try a civil right, or to oust a wrongful possessor of an office. 3 Dall. 490; 1 Serg. & Rawle. 385. For a full and satisfactory statement of the law on this subject, the reader is referred to Angell on Corp. ch. 20. p. 469. And see *Quo Warranto*.

INFORMATUS NON SUM, *pleading, practice*. I am not informed; a formal answer made in court, or put upon record by an attorney when he has nothing to say in defence of his client. Styles' Reg. 372.

INFORMER. A person who informs or prefers an accusation against another, whom he suspects of the violation of some penal statute.

2. When the informer is entitled to the penalty or part of the penalty, upon the conviction of an offender, he is, or is not a competent witness, accordingly as the statute creating the penalty has or has not made him so. 1 Phil. Ev. 97; Rosc. Cr. Ev. 107; 5 Mass. R. 57; 1 Dall. 68; 1 Saund. 262, c. Vide articles *Prosecutor; Rewards*.

INFORTIATUM, *civil law*. The second part of the Digest or Pandects of Justinian, is called *infortiatum;* see *Digest*. This part, which commences with the third title of the twenty-fourth book, and ends with the thirty-eighth book, was thus called because it was the middle part, which, it was said, was supported and fortified by the two others. Some have supposed that this name was given to it, because it treats of successions, substitutions, and other important matters, and being more used than the others, produced greater fees to the lawyers.

INFRA, *Latin*. Below, under, beneath, underneath. The opposite of *supra*, above. Thus we say *primo gradu est* supra, pater, mater; infra, filius, filia. In the first degree of kindred in the ascending line; above, is the father and the mother; below, in the descending line, the son and daughter. Inst. 3, 6, 1.

2. In another sense, this word signifies *within;* as, *infra corpus comitatûs*, within the body of the county; *infra præsidia*, within the guards.

3. It also signifies *during;* as *infra furorem*, during the madness.

INFRA ÆTATEM. Under age; that is,

during infancy, or before arriving at the full age of twenty-one years.

INFRA CORPUS COMITATUS. Within the body of the county.

2. The common law courts have jurisdiction infra corpus comitatûs; the admiralty, on the contrary, has no such jurisdiction, unless, indeed, the tide water may extend within such county. 5 Howard's U. S. Rep. 441, 451.

INFRA DIGNITATEM CURIÆ. Below the dignity of the court. Example, in equity a demurrer will lie to a bill on the ground of the triviality of the matter in dispute, as being below the dignity of the court. See 4 John. Ch. 183; 4 Paige, 364; 4 Bouv. Inst. n. 4237.

INFRA HOSPITIUM. Within the inn; when once a traveller's baggage comes infra hospitium, that is, in the care and under the charge of the innkeeper, it is at his risk. See *Guest; Innkeeper*.

INFRA PRÆSIDIA. This term is used in relation to prizes, to signify that they have been brought completely in the power of the captors, that is, within the towns, camps, ports or fleet of the captors. Formerly, the rule was, and perhaps still in some countries is, that the act of bringing a prize *infra præsidia*, changed the property; but the rule now established is, that there must be a sentence of condemnation to effect this purpose. 1 Rob. Adm. R. 134; 1 Kent's Com. 104; Chit. Law of Nat. 98; Abb. Sh. 14; Hugo, Droit Romain, § 90.

INFRACTION. The breach of a law or agreement; the violation of a compact. In the French law this is the generic expression to designate all actions which are punishable by the code of France.

INFUSION, *med. jur.* A pharmaceutical operation, which consists in pouring a hot or cold fluid upon a substance, whose medical properties it is desired to extract. *Infusion* is also used for the product of this operation. Although *infusion* differs from *decoction*, (q. v.) they are said to be *ejusdem generis;* and in the case of an indictment which charged the prisoner with giving a decoction, and the evidence was that he had given an infusion, the difference was held to be immaterial. 3 Camp. R. 74.

INGENUI, *civ. law.* Those freemen who were born free. Vicat, vocab.

2. They were a class of freemen, distinguished from those who, born slaves, had afterwards legally obtained their freedom; the latter were called at various periods, sometimes *liberti*, sometimes *libertini*. An unjust or illegal servitude did not prevent a man from being *ingenuus*.

INGRATITUDE. The forgetfulness of a kindness or benefit.

2. In the civil law, ingratitude on the part of a legatee, was sufficient to defeat a legacy in his favour. In Louisiana, donations *inter vivos* are liable to be revoked or dissolved on account of the ingratitude of the donee; but the revocation on this account can take place only in the three following cases: 1. if the donee has attempted to take the life of the donor. 2. If he has been guilty towards him of cruel treatment, crimes or grievous injuries. 3. If he has refused him food when in distress. Civ. Code of Lo. art. 1546, 1547; Poth. Donations Entrevifs, s. 3, art. 1, § 1. There are no such rules in the common law. Ingratitude is not punishable by law.

INGRESS, EGRESS AND REGRESS. These words are frequently used in leases to express the right of the lessee to enter, go upon, and return from the lands in question.

INGRESSU. An ancient writ of entry, by which the plaintiff or complainant sought an entry into his lands. Techn. Dict. h. t.

INGROSSING, *practice.* The act of copying from a rough draft a writing in order that it may be executed; as, ingrossing a deed.

INHABITANT. One who has his domicil in a place is an inhabitant of that place; one who has an actual fixed residence in a place.

2. A mere intention to remove to a place will not make a man an inhabitant of such place, although as a sign of such intention he may have sent his wife and children to reside there. 1 Ashm. R. 126. Nor will his intention to quit his residence, unless consummated, deprive him of his right as an inhabitant. 1 Dall. 480. Vide 10 Ves. 339; 14 Vin. Ab. 420; 1 Phil. Ev. Index, h. t.; Const. of Mass., part 2, c. 1, s. 2, a. 1; Kyd on Corp. 321; Anal. des Pand. de Poth. mot Habitans; Poth. Pand. lib. 50, t. 1, s. 2; 6 Adolph. & Ell. 153; 33 Eng. Common Law Rep. 31.

3. The inhabitants of the United States may be classed into, 1. Those born within the country; and, 2. Those born out of it.

4.—1. The *natives* consist, 1st. Of white persons, and these are all citizens of the United States, unless they have lost that right. 2d. Of the aborigines, and these are not in general citizens of the United States, nor do they possess any political power. 3d. Of negroes, or descendants of the African race, and these generally possess no political authority whatever, not being able to vote, nor to hold any office. 4th. Of the children of foreign ambassadors, who are citizens or subjects as their fathers are or were at the time of their birth.

5.—2. Persons *born out of the jurisdiction of the United States*, are, 1st. Children of citizens of the United States, or of persons who have been such; they are citizens of the United States, provided the father of such children shall have resided within the same. Act of Congress of April 14, 1802, § 4. 2d. Persons who were in the country at the time of the adoption of the constitution; these have all the rights of citizens. 3d. Persons who have become naturalized under the laws of any state before the passage of any law on the subject of naturalization by Congress, or who have become naturalized under the acts of congress, are citizens of the United States, and entitled to vote for all officers who are elected by citizens, and to hold any office except those of president and vice-president of the United States. 4th. Children of naturalized citizens, who were under the age of twenty-one years, at the time of their parent's being so naturalized or admitted to the rights of citizenship, are, if then dwelling in the United States, considered as citizens of the United States, and entitled to the same rights as their respective fathers. 5th. Persons who resided in a territory which was annexed to the United States by treaty, and the territory became a state; as, for example, a person who, born in France, moved to Louisiana in 1806, and settled there, and remained in the territory until it was admitted as a state, it was held, that although not naturalized under the acts of congress, he was a citizen of the United States. Desbois' Case, 2 Mart. Lo. R. 185. 6th. Aliens or foreigners, who have never been naturalized, and these are not citizens of the United States, nor entitled to any political rights whatever. See *Alien; Body politic; Citizen; Domicil; Naturalization.*

INHERENT POWER. An authority possessed without its being derived from another. It is a right, ability or faculty of doing a thing, without receiving that right, ability or faculty from another.

INHERITANCE, *estates.* A perpetuity in lands to a man and his heirs; or it is the right to succeed to the estate of a person who died intestate. Dig. 50, 16, 24. The term is applied to lands.

2. The property which is inherited is called an inheritance.

3. The term inheritance includes not only lands and tenements which have been acquired by descent, but also every fee simple or fee tail, which a person has acquired by purchase, may be said to be an inheritance, because the purchaser's heirs may inherit it. Litt. s. 9.

4. Estates of inheritance are divided into inheritance absolute, or fee simple; and inheritance limited, one species of which is called fee tail. They are also divided into corporeal, as houses and lands; and incorporeal, commonly called incorporeal hereditaments. (q. v.) 1 Cruise, Dig. 68; Sw. 163; Poth. des Retraits, n. 28.

5. Among the civilians, by inheritance is understood the succession to all the rights of the deceased. It is of two kinds, 1. That which arises by testament, when the testator gives his succession to a particular person; and, 2. That which arises by operation of law, which is called succession *ab intestat.* Hein. Leç. El. § 484, 485.

INHIBITION, *Scotch law.* A personal prohibition which passes by letters under the signet, prohibiting the party inhibited to contract any debt, or do any deed, by which any part of the lands may be aliened or carried off, in prejudice of the creditor inhibiting. Ersk. Pr. L. Scot. B. 2, t. 11, s. 2. See *Diligences.*

2. In the civil law, the prohibition which the law makes, or a judge ordains to an individual, is called inhibition.

INHIBITION, *Eng. law.* The name of a writ which forbids a judge from further proceeding in a cause depending before him; it is in the nature of a prohibition. T. de la Ley; F. N. B. 39.

INIQUITY. Vice; contrary to equity; injustice.

2. Where, in a doubtful matter, the judge is required to pronounce, it is his duty to decide in such a manner as is the least against equity.

INITIAL. Placed at the beginning. The initials of a man's name are the first letters of his name; as, G. W. for George Washington. When in a will the legatee is described by the initials of his name only, parol evidence may be given to prove his identity. 3 Ves. 148. And a signature made simply with initials is binding. 1 Denio, R. 471. But see Ersk. Inst. B. 3, t. 2, n. 8.

INITIALIA TESTIMONII, *Scotch law.* Before a witness can be examined in chief, he may be examined with regard to his disposition, whether he bear good or ill will towards either of the parties; whether he has been prompted what to say; whether he has received a bribe, and the like. This previous examination, which somewhat resembles our *voir dire*, is called *initialia testimonii.*

INITIATE. A right which is incomplete. By the birth of a child, the husband becomes tenant by the curtesy *initiate*, but his estate is not *consummate* until the death of the wife. 2 Bouv. Inst. n. 1725.

INITIATIVE, *French law.* The name given to the important prerogative given by the *charte constitutionelle*, art. 16, to the late king to propose through his ministers projects of laws. 1 Toull. n. 39. See *Veto.*

INJUNCTION, *remedies, chancery, practice.* An injunction is a prohibitory writ, specially prayed for by a bill, in which the plaintiff's title is set forth, restraining a person from committing or doing an act (other than criminal acts) which appear to be against equity and conscience. Mitf. Pl. 124; 1 Madd. Ch. Pr. 126.

2. Injunctions are of two kinds, the one called the writ remedial, and the other the judicial writ.

3.—1st. The former kind of injunction, or remedial writ, is in the nature of a prohibition, directed to, and controlling, not the inferior court, but the party. It is granted, when a party is doing or is about to do an act against equity or good conscience, or litigious or vexatious; in these cases, the court will not leave the party to feel the mischief or inconvenience of the wrong, and look to the courts of common law for redress, but will interpose its authority to restrain such unjustifiable proceedings.

4. Remedial injunctions are of two kinds; common or special. 1. It is common when it prays to stay proceedings at law, and will be granted, of course; as, upon an attachment for want of an appearance, or of an answer; or upon a *dedimus* obtained by the defendant to take his answer in the country; or upon his praying for time to answer, &c. Newl. Pr. 92; 13 Ves, 323. 2. A special injunction is obtained only on motion or petition, with notice to the other party, and is applied for, sometimes on affidavit before answer, but more frequently upon the merits disclosed in the defendant's answer. Injunctions before answer are granted in cases of waste and other injuries of so urgent a nature, that mischief would ensue if the plaintiff were to wait until the answer were put in; but the court will not grant an injunction during the pendency of a plea or demurrer to the bill, for, until that be argued, it does not appear whether or not the court has jurisdiction of the cause. The injunction granted in this stage of the suit, is to continue till answer or further order; the injunction obtained upon the merits confessed in the answer, continues generally till the hearing of the cause.

5. An injunction is generally granted for the purpose of preventing a wrong, or preserving property in dispute pending a suit. Its effect, in general, is only *in personam*, that is, to attach and punish the party if disobedient in violating the injunction. Ed. Inj. 363; Harr. Ch. Pr. 552.

6. The principal injuries which may be prevented by injunction, relate to the *person*, to *personal property*, or to *real property*. These will be separately considered.

7.—1. With respect to the *person*, the chancellor may prevent a breach of the peace, by requiring sureties of the peace. A court of chancery has also summary and extensive jurisdiction for the protection of the *relative rights of persons*, as between husband and wife, parent and child, and guardian and ward; and in these cases, on a proper state of facts, an injunction will be granted. For example, an injunction may be obtained by a parent to prevent the marriage of his infant son. 1 Madd. Ch. Pr. 348; Ed. Inj. 297; 14 Ves. 206; 19 Ves. 282; 1 Chitt. Pr. 702.

8.—2. Injunctions respecting *personal property*, are usually granted, 1st. To restrain a partner or agent from making or negotiating bills, notes or contracts, or doing other acts injurious to the partner or principal. 3 Ves. jr. 74; 3 Bro. C. C. 15; 2 Campb. 619; 1 Price, R. 503; 1 Mont on Part. 93; 1 Madd. Ch. Pr. 160; Chit Bills, 58, 61; 1 Hov. Supp. to Ves. jr *335; Woodd. Lect. 416.

9.—2d. To restrain the negotiation of bills or notes obtained by fraud, or without consideration. 8 Price, R. 631; Chit. Bills, 31 to 41; Ed. Inj. 210; Blake's Ch. Pr. 338; 2 Anst. 519; 3 Anst. 851; 2 Ves. jr. 493; 1 Fonb. Eq. 43; 1 Madd

Ch. Pr. 154. 3d. To deliver up void or satisfied deeds. 1 V. & B. 244; 11 Ves. 535; 17 Ves. 111. 4th. To enter into and deliver a proper security. 1 Anst. 49. 5th. To prevent breaches of covenant or contract, and enjoin the performance of others. Ed. Inj. 308. 6th. To prevent a breach of confidence or good faith, or to prevent other loss; as, for example, to restrain the *disclosure of secrets*, which came to the defendant's knowledge in the course of any confidential employment. 1 Sim. R. 483; and see 1 Jac. & W. 394. An injunction will be granted to prevent the publication of private letters without the author's consent. Curt. on Copyr. 90; 2 Atk. 342; Ambl. 737; 2 Swanst. 402, 427; 1 Ball & Beat. 207; 2 Ves. & B. 19; 1 Mart. Lo. R. 297; Bac. Ab. Injunction A. But the publication will be allowed when necessary to the defence of the character of the party who received them. 2 Ves. & B. 19. 7th. To prevent improper sales, payments, or conveyances. Chit. Eq. Dig. tit. Practice, xlvii. 8th. To prevent loss or inconvenience; this can be obtained on filing a bill *quia timet*. (q. v.) 1 Madd. Ch. Pr. 218 to 225. 9th. To prevent waste of property by an executor or administrator. Ed. Inj. 300; 1 Madd. Ch. Pr. 160, 224. 10th. To restrain the infringement of patents; Ed. Inj. ch. 12; 14 Ves. 130; 1 Madd. Ch. Pr. 137; or of copyrights; Ed. Inj. c. 13; 8 Ves. 225; 17 Ves. 424. 11th. To stay proceedings in a court of law. These proceedings will be stayed when justice cannot be done in consequence of accident; 1 John. Cas. 417; 4 John. Ch. R. 287, 194; Latch, 24, 146, 148; 1 Vern. 180, 247; 1 Ch. C. 77, 120; 1 Eq. Cas. Ab. 92; or mistake; 1 John. Ch. R. 119, 607; 2 John. Ch. R. 585; 4 John. Ch. R. 85; Id. 144; 2 Munf. 187; 1 Day's Cas. Err. 139; 3 Ch. R. 55; Finch, 413; 2 Freem. 16; Fitzg. 118; or fraud. 1 John. Ch. R. 402; 2 John. Ch. R. 512; 4 John. Ch. R. 65. But no injunction will be granted to stay proceedings in a criminal case. 2 John. Ch. R. 387; 6 Mod. 12; 2 Ves. 396.

9.—3. Injunctions respecting real property, may be obtained, 1st. To prevent wasteful trespasses or irreparable damages, although the owner may be entitled to retake possession, if he can do so, without a breach of the peace. 1 Chit. Pr. 722. 2d. To compel the performance of lawful works in the least injurious manner. 1 Turn. & Myl. 181. 3d. To prevent waste. 3 Tho. Co. Litt. 241, M; 1 Madd. Ch. Pr. 138; Ed. Inj. ch. 8, 9, and 10; 1 John. Ch. R. 11; 2 Atk. 183. 4th. To prevent the creation of a nuisance, either private or public. 1. Private nuisance; for example, to restrain the owner of a house from making any erections or improvements, so as materially to darken or obstruct the ancient lights and windows of an adjoining house. 2 Russ. R. 121. 2. Public nuisances. Though usual to prosecute the parties who create nuisances, by indictment, yet, in some cases, an injunction may be had to prevent the creating of such nuisance. 5 Ves. 129; 1 Mad. Ch. 156; Ed. Inj. ch. 11.

10.—2d. An injunction of the second kind, called the *judicial writ*, issues subsequently to a decree. It is a direction to yield up, to quit, or to continue possession of lands, and is properly described as being in the nature of an execution. Ed. Inj. 2.

11. Injunctions are also divided into temporary and perpetual. 1. A temporary injunction is one which is granted until some stage of the suit shall be reached; as, until the defendant shall file his answer; until the hearing; and the like. 2. A perpetual injunction is one which is issued when, in the opinion of the court, at the hearing, the plaintiff has established a case, which entitles him to an injunction; or when a bill, praying for an injunction, is taken pro confesso; in such cases a perpetual injunction will be decreed. Ed. Inj. 253.

12. The interdict (q. v.) of the Roman law resembles, in many respects, our injunction. It was used in three distinct, but cognate senses. 1. It was applied to signify the edicts made by the prætor, declaratory of his intention to give a remedy in certain cases, chiefly to preserve or to restore possession; this interdict was called edictal; edictale, quod prætoriis edictis proponitur, ut sciant omnes eâ formâ posse implorari. 2. It was used to signify his order or decree, applying the remedy in the given case before him, and then was called decretal; decretale, quod prætor re natâ implorantibus decrevit. It is this which bears a strong resemblance to the injunction of a court of equity. 3. It was used, in the last place, to signify the very remedy sought in the suit commenced under the prætor's edict; and thus it became the denomination of the action itself. Livingston on the Batture case, 5 Am. Law Jour. 271; 2 Story,

Eq. Jur. § 865; Analyse des Pandectes de Pothier, h. t.; Dict. du Dig. h. t.; Clef des Lois Rom. h. t.; Heineccii, Elem. Pand. Ps. 6, § 285, 286.

Vide, generally, Eden on Injunctions; 1 Madd. Ch. Pr. 125 to 165; Blake's Ch. Pr. 330 to 344; 1 Chit. Pr. 701 to 731; Coop. Eq. Pl. Index, h. t.; Redesd. Pl. Index, h. t.; Smith's Ch. Pr. h. t.; 14 Vin. Ab. 442; 2 Hov. Supp. to Ves. jr. 173, 434, 442; Com. Dig. Chancery, D 8; Newl. Pr. c. 4, s. 7; Bouv. Inst. Index, h. t.

INJURIA ABSQUE DAMNO. Injury without damage. Injury without damage or loss will not bear an action. The following cases illustrate this principle. 6 Mod. Rep. 46, 47, 49; 1 Shower, 64; Willes, Rep. 74, note; 1 Lord Ray. 940, 948; 2 Bos. & Pull. 86; 9 Rep. 113; 5 Rep. 72; B. N. P. 120.

INJURIOUS WORDS. This phrase is used, in Louisiana, to signify slander, or libelous words. Code, art. 3501.

INJURY. A wrong or tort.

2. Injuries are divided into public and private; and they affect the person, personal property, or real property.

3.—1. They affect the *person* absolutely or relatively. The *absolute* injuries are, threats and menaces, assaults, batteries, wounding, mayhems; injuries to health, by nuisances or medical malpractices. Those affecting reputation are, verbal slander, libels, and malicious prosecutions; and those affecting personal liberty are, false imprisonment and malicious prosecutions. The *relative* injuries are those which affect the rights of a husband; these are, abduction of the wife, or harboring her, adultery and battery; those which affect the rights of a parent, as, abduction, seduction, or battery of a child; and of a master, seduction, harboring and battery of his apprentice or servant. Those which conflict with the rights of the inferior relation, namely, the wife, child, apprentice, or servant, are, withholding conjugal rights, maintenance, wages, &c.

4.—2. Injuries to *personal property*, are, the unlawful taking and detention thereof from the owner; and other injuries are, some damage affecting the same while in the claimant's possession, or that of a third person, or injuries to his reversionary interests.

5.—3. Injuries to *real property* are, ousters, trespasses, nuisances, waste, subtraction of rent, disturbance of right of way, and the like.

6. Injuries arise in three ways. 1. By nonfeasance, or the not doing what was a legal obligation, or duty, or contract, to perform. 2. Misfeasance, or the performance, in an improper manner, of an act which it was either the party's duty, or his contract, to perform. 3. Malfeasance, or the unjust performance of some act which the party had no right, or which he had contracted not to do.

7. The remedies are different, as the injury affects private individuals, or the public. 1. When the injuries affect a private right and a private individual, although often also affecting the public, there are three descriptions of remedies: 1st. The preventive, such as defence, resistance, recaption, abatement of nuisance, surety of the peace, injunction, &c. 2d. Remedies for compensation, which may be by arbitration, suit, action, or summary proceedings before a justice of the peace. 3d. Proceedings for punishment, as by indictment, or summary proceedings before a justice. 2. When the injury is such as to affect the public, it becomes a crime, misdemeanor, or offence, and the party may be punished by indictment or summary conviction, for the public injury; and by civil action at the suit of the party, for the private wrong. But in cases of felony, the remedy by action for the private injury is generally *suspendid* until the party particularly injured has fulfilled his duty to the public by prosecuting the offender for the public crime; and in cases of homicide the remedy is *merged* in the felony. 1 Chit. Pr. 10; Ayl. Pand. 592. See 1 Miles' Rep. 316, 17; and article *Civil Remedy*.

8. There are many injuries for which the law affords no remedy. In general, it interferes only when there has been a visible bodily injury inflicted by force or poison, while it leaves almost totally unprotected the whole class of the most malignant mental injuries and sufferings, unless in a few cases, where, by descending to a fiction, it sordidly supposes some pecuniary loss, and sometimes—under a mask, and contrary to its own legal principles—affords compensation to wounded feelings. A parent, for example, cannot sue, in that character, for an injury inflicted on his child; and when his own domestic happiness has been destroyed, unless the fact will sustain the allegation that the daughter was the ser-

vant of her father, and that, by reason of such seduction, he lost the benefit of her services. Another instance may be mentioned :—A party cannot recover damages for *verbal* slander in many cases; as, when the facts published are true, for the defendant would justify and the party injured must fail. A case of this kind, remarkably hard, occurred in England. A young nobleman had seduced a young woman, who, after living with him some time, became sensible of the impropriety of her conduct. She left him secretly, and removed to an obscure place in the kingdom, where she obtained a situation, and became highly respected in consequence of her good conduct—she was even promoted to a better and more public employment—when she was unfortunately discovered by her seducer. He made proposals to her to renew their illicit intercourse, which were rejected; in order to force her to accept them, he published the history of her early life, and she was discharged from her employment, and lost the good opinion of those on whom she depended for her livelihood. For this outrage the culprit could not be made answerable, civilly or criminally. Nor will the law punish *criminally* the author of *verbal* slander, imputing even the most infamous crimes, unless done with intent to extort a chattel, money, or valuable thing. The law presumes, perhaps unnaturally enough, that a man is incapable of being alarmed or affected by such injuries to his feelings. Vide 1 Chit. Med. Jur. 320. See, generally, Bouv. Inst. Index, h. t.

INJURY, *civil law.* In the technical sense of the term it is a delict committed in contempt, or outrage of any one, whereby his body, his dignity, or his reputation, is maliciously injured. Voet, Com. ad Pand. lib. 47, t. 10, n. 1.

2. Injuries may be divided into two classes, with reference to the means used by the wrong doer, namely, by words and by acts. The first are called verbal injuries, the latter real.

3. A *verbal* injury, when directed against a private person, consists in the uttering contumelious words, which tend to expose his character, by making him little or ridiculous. Where the offensive words are uttered in the heat of a dispute, and spoken to the person's face, the law does not presume any malicious intention in the utterer, whose resentment generally subsides with his passion; and yet, even in that case, the truth of the injurious words seldom absolves entirely from punishment. Where the injurious expressions have a tendency to blacken one's moral character, or fix some particular guilt upon him, and are deliberately repeated in different companies, or handed about in whispers to confidants, it then grows up to the crime of slander, agreeably to the distinction of the Roman law, l. 15, § 12, *de injur.*

4. A *real* injury is inflicted by any fact by which a person's honor or dignity is affected; as striking one with a cane, or even aiming a blow without striking; spitting in one's face; assuming a coat of arms, or any other mark of distinction proper to another, &c. The composing and publishing defamatory libels may be reckoned of this kind. Ersk. Pr. L. Scot. 4, 4, 45.

INJUSTICE. That which is opposed to justice.

2. It is either natural or civil. 1. Natural injustice is the act of doing harm to mankind, by violating natural rights. 2. Civil injustice, is the unlawful violation of civil rights.

INLAGARE. To admit or restore to the benefit of law.

INLAGATION. The restitution of one outlawed to the protection of the law. Bract. lib. 2, c. 14.

INLAND. Within the same country.

2. It seems not to be agreed whether the term inland applies to all the United States or only to one state. It has been holden in New York that a bill of exchange by one person in one state, on another person in another, is an inland bill of exchange; 5 John. Rep. 375; but a contrary opinion seems to have been held in the circuit court of the United States for Pennsylvania. Whart. Dig. tit. Bills of Exchange, E, pl. 78. Vide 2 Phil. Ev. 36, and *Bills of Exchange.*

INMATE. One who dwells in a part of another's house, the latter dwelling, at the same time, in the said house. Kitch. 45, b; Com. Dig. Justices of the Peace, B 85; 1 B. & Cr. 578; 8 E. C. L. R. 153; 2 Dowl. & Ryl. 743; 8 B. & Cr. 71; 15 E. C. L. R. 154; 2 Mann. & Ryl. 227; 9 B. & Cr. 176; 17 E. C. L. R. 335; 4 Mann. & Ryl. 151; 2 Russ. on Cr. 937; 1 Deac. Cr. L. 185; 2 East, P. Cr. 499, 505; 1 Leach's Cr. L. 90, 237, 427; Alcock's Registration Cases, 21; 1 Mann. & Gran. 83; 39 E. C. L. R. 365. Vide *Lodger.*

INN. A house where a traveller is furnished with every thing he has occasion for while on his way. Bac. Ab. Inns. B; 12 Mod. 255; 3 B. & A. 283; 4 Campb. 77; 2 Chit. Rep. 484; 3 Chit. Com. Law, 365, n. 6.

2. All travellers have a lawful right to enter an inn for the purpose of being accommodated. It has been held that an innkeeper in a town through which lines of stages pass, has no right to exclude the driver of one of these lines from his yard and the common public rooms, where travellers are usually placed, who comes there at proper hours, and in a proper manner, to solicit passengers for his coach, and without doing any injury to the innkeeper. 8 N. H. R. 523; Hamm. N. P. 170. Vide *Entry; Guest.*

INNAVIGABLE. Not capable of being navigated.

INNINGS, *estates.* Lands gained from the sea by draining. Cunn. L. Dict. h. t.; Law of Sewers, 31.

INNKEEPER. He is defined to be the keeper of a common inn for the lodging and entertainment of travellers and passengers, their horses and attendants, for a reasonable compensation. Bac. Ab. Inns, &c.; Story, Bailm. § 475. But one who entertains strangers occasionally, although he may receive compensation for it, is not an innkeeper. 2 Dev. & Bat. 424.

2. His duties will be first considered; and, secondly, his rights.

3.—1. He is bound to take in and receive all travellers and wayfaring persons, and to entertain them, if he can accommodate them, for a reasonable compensation; and he must guard their goods with proper diligence. He is liable only for the goods which are brought within the inn. 8 Co. 32; Jones' Bailm. 91. A delivery of the goods into the custody of the innkeeper is not, however, necessary, in order to make him responsible; for although he may not know anything of such goods, he is bound to pay for them if they are stolen or carried away, even by an unknown person; 8 Co. 32; Hayw. N. C. R. 41; 14 John. R. 175; 1 Bell's Com. 469; and if he receive the guest, the custody of the goods may be considered as an accessory to the principal contract; and the money paid for the apartments as extending to the care of the box and portmanteau. Jones' Bailm. 94; Story, Bailm. § 470; 1 Bl. Com. 430; 2 Kent, Com. 458 to 463. The degree of care which the innkeeper is bound to take is uncommon care, and he will be liable for a slight negligence. He is responsible for the acts of his domestics and servants, as well as for the acts of his other guests, if the goods are stolen or lost; but he is not responsible for any tort or injury done by his servants or others, to the person of his guest, without his own coöperation or consent. 8 Co. 32. The innkeeper will be excused whenever the loss has occurred through the fault of the guest. Story, Bailm. § 483; 4 M. & S. 306; S. C. 1 Stark. R. 251, note; 2 Kent, Com. 461, 1 Yeates' R. 34.

4.—2. The innkeeper is entitled to a just compensation for his care and trouble in taking care of his guest and his property; and to enable him to obtain this, the law invests him with some peculiar privileges, giving him a lien upon the goods, of the guest, brought into the inn, and, it is said, upon the person of his guest, for his compensation. 3 B. & Ald. 287; 8 Mod. 172; 1 Shower, Rep. 270; Bac. Ab. Inns, &c., D. But the horse of the guest can be detained only for his own keeping, and not for the boarding and personal expenses of the guest. Bac. Ab. h. t. The landlord may also bring an action for the recovery of his compensation.

Vide, generally, 1 Vin. Ab. 224; 14 Vin. Ab. 436; Bac. Ab. h. t.; Yelv. 67, a, 162, a; 2 Kent, Com. 458; Ayl. Pand. 266; 9 Pick. 280; 21 Wend. 285; 1 Yeates, 35: Oliph. on the Law of Horses, 125; Bouv. Inst. Index, h. t.

INNOCENCE. The absence of guilt.

2. The law presumes in favor of innocence, even against another presumption of law: for example, when a woman marries a second husband within the space of twelve months after her husband had left the country, the presumption of innocence preponderates over the presumption of the continuance of life. 2 B. & A. 386; 3 Stark. Ev. 1249. An exception to this rule respecting the presumption of innocence has been made in the case of the publication of a libel, the principal being presumed to have authorized the sale, when a libel is sold by his agent in his usual place of doing business. 1 Russ. on Cr. 341; 10 Johns. R. 443; Bull. N. P. 6; Greenl. Ev. § 36. See 4 Nev. & M. 341; 2 Ad. & Ell. 540; 5 Barn. & Ad. 86; 1 Stark. N. P. C. 21; 2 Nev. & M. 219.

INNOCENT CONVEYANCES. **This** term is used in England, technically, **to** signify those conveyances made by a tenant of his leasehold, which do not occasion a forfeiture; these are conveyances by lease and release, bargain and sale, and a covenant to stand seised by a tenant for life. 1 Chit. Pr. 243, 244.

2. In this country forfeitures for alienation of a greater right than the tenant possesses, are almost unknown. The more just principle prevails that the conveyance by the tenant, whatever be its form, operates only on his interest. Vide *Forfeiture*.

INNOMINATE CONTRACTS, *civil law*. Contracts which have no particular names, as permutation and transaction, are so called. Inst. 2, 10, 13. There are many innominate contracts, but the Roman lawyers reduced them to four classes, namely, *do ut des*, *do ut facias*, *facio ut des*, and *facio ut facias*. (q. v.) Dig. 2, 14, 7, 2.

INNOTESCIMUS, *English law*. An epithet used for *letters-patent*, which are always of a charter of feoffment, or some other instrument not of record, concluding with the words *Innotescimus per præsentes*, &c. Tech. Dict. h. t.

INNOVATION. Change of a thing established for something new.

2. Innovations are said to be dangerous, as likely to unsettle the common law. Co. Litt. 370, b; Id. 282, b. Certainly no innovations ought to be made by the courts, but as every thing human is mutable, no legislation can be, or ought to be immutable; changes are required by the alteration of circumstances; amendments, by the imperfections of all human institutions; but laws ought never to be changed without great deliberation, and a due consideration of the reasons on which they were founded, as of the circumstances under which they were enacted. Many innovations have been made in the common law, which philosophy, philanthropy and common sense approve. The destruction of the *benefit of clergy;* of *appeal*, in felony; of *trial by battle and ordeal;* of the right of *sanctuary;* of the privilege to *abjure the realm,* of *approvement*, by which any criminal who could, in a judicial combat, by skill, force or fraud kill his accomplice, secured his own pardon; of *corruption of blood;* of *constructive treason;* will be sanctioned by all wise men, and none will desire a return to these barbarisms. The reader is referred to the case of James *v.* the Commonwealth, 12 Serg. & R. 220, and 225 to 236, where Duncan, J., exposes the absurdity of some ancient laws, with much sarcasm.

INNOVATION, *Scotch law*. The exchange of one obligation for another, so that the second shall come in the place of the first. Bell's Scotch Law Dict. h. t. The same as *Novation*. (q. v.)

INNS OF COURT, *Engl. law*. The name given to the colleges of the English professors and students of the common law.

2. The four principal Inns of Court are the Inner Temple and Middle Temple, (formerly belonging to the Knights Templars) Lincoln's Inn, and Gray's Inn, (anciently belonging to the earls of Lincoln and Gray.) The other inns are the two Sergeants' Inns. The Inns of Chancery were probably so called because they were once inhabited by such clerks, as chiefly studied the forming of writs, which regularly belonged to the cursitors, who are officers of chancery. These are Thavie's Inn, the New Inn, Symond's Inn, Clement's Inn, Clifford's Inn, Staple's Inn, Lion's Inn, Furnival's Inn and Barnard's Inn. Before being called to the bar, it is necessary to be admitted to one of the Inns of Court

INNUENDO, *pleading*. An averment which explains the defendant's meaning by reference to antecedent matter. Salk. 513, 1 Ld. Raym. 256; 12 Mod. 139; 1 Saund. 243. The innuendo is mostly used in actions for slander.

An innuendo, as, "he the said plaintiff meaning," is only explanatory of some matter expressed; it serves to apply the slander to the precedent matter, but cannot add or enlarge, extend, or change the sense of the previous words, and the matter to which it alludes must always appear from the antecedent parts of the declaration or indictment. 1 Chit. Pl. 383; 3 Caines' Rep. 76; 7 Johns. R. 271; 5 Johns. R. 211; 8 Johns. R. 109; 8 N. H. Rep. 256.

3. It is necessary only when the intent may be mistaken, or when it cannot be collected from the libel or slander itself. Cowp. 679; 5 East, 463.

4. If the innuendo materially enlarge the sense of the words it will vitiate the declaration or indictment. 6 T. R. 691; 5 Binn. 218; 5 Johns. R. 220; 6 Johns. R. 83; 7 Johns. Rep. 271. But when the new matter stated in an innuendo is not necessary to support the action, it may be rejected as surplusage. 9 East, R. 95; 7 Johns. R. 272. Vide, generally, Stark. on

Slan. 293; 1 Chit. Pl. 383; 3 Chit. Cr. Law, 873; Bac. Ab. Slander, R; 1 Saund. 243, n. 4; 4 Com. Dig. 712; 14 Vin. Ab. 442; Dane's Ab. Index, h. t.; 4 Co. 17.

INOFFICIOUS, *civil law*. This word is frequently used with others; as, inofficious testament, *inofficiosum testamentum;* inofficious gift, *donatio inofficiosa*. An inofficious testament is one not made according to the rules of piety; that is, one made by which the testator has unlawfully omitted or disinherited one of his heirs. Such a disposition is void by the Roman civil law. Dig. 5, 2, 5; see Code, 3, 29; Nov. 115; Ayl. Pand. 405; Civil Code of Lo. art. 3522, n. 21.

INOPS CONSILII. Destitute or without counsel. In the construction of wills a greater latitude is given, because the testator is supposed to have been inops consilii.

INQUEST. A body of men appointed by law to inquire into certain matters; as, the inquest examined into the facts connected with the alleged murder; the grand jury is sometimes called the *grand inquest*. The judicial inquiry itself is also called an inquest. The finding of such men, upon an investigation, is also called an inquest or an inquisition.

2. An inquest of office was bound to find for the king upon the direction of the court. The reason given is that the inquest concluded no man of his right, but only gave the king an opportunity to enter so that he could have his right tried. Moore, 730; Vaughan, 135; 3 H. VII. 10; 2 H. IV. 5; 3 Leon. 196.

INQUIRY, WRIT OF. A writ of inquiry is one issued where a judgment has been entered in a case sounding in damages, without any particular amount being ascertained; this writ is for the purpose of ascertaining the amount to which the plaintiff is entitled. Vide *Writ of Inquiry*.

INQUISITION, *practice*. An examination of certain facts by a jury impannelled by the sheriff for the purpose; the instrument of writing on which their decision is made is also called an inquisition. The sheriff or coroner and the jury who make the inquisition, are called the inquest.

2. An inquisition on an untimely death, if omitted by the coroner, may be taken by justices of gaol delivery and oyer and terminer, or of the peace, but it must be done publicly and openly, otherwise it will be quashed. Inquisitions either of the coroner, or of the other jurisdictions, are traversable. 1 Burr. 18, 19.

INQUISITOR. A designation of sheriffs, coroners, *super visum corporis*, and the like, who have power to inquire into certain matters.

2. The name of an officer among ecclesiastics, who is authorized to inquire into heresies, and the like, and to punish them. An ecclesiastical judge.

INROLLMENT. The act of putting upon a roll. Formerly, the record of a suit was kept on skins of parchment, which, best to preserve them, were kept upon a roll, or in the form of a roll; what was written upon them was called the inrollment. After, when such records came to be kept in books, the making up of the record retained the old name of inrollment.

INSANE. One deprived of the use of reason, after he has arrived at the age when he ought to have it, either by a natural defect or by accident. Domat, Lois Civ. Lib. prél. tit. 2, s. 1, n. 11.

INSANITY, *med. jur*. A continued impetuosity of thought, which, for the time being, *totally* unfits a man for judging and acting in relation to the matter in question, with the composure requisite for the maintenance of the social relations of life. Various other definitions of this state have been given, but perhaps the subject is not susceptible of any satisfactory definition, which shall, with precision, include all cases of insanity, and exclude all others. Ray, Med. Jur. § 24, p. 50.

2. It may be considered in a threefold point of view: 1. A chronic disease, manifested by deviations from the healthy and natural state of the mind, such deviations consisting in a morbid perversion of the feelings, affections and habits. 2. Disturbances of the intellectual faculties, under the influence of which the understanding becomes susceptible of hallucinations or erroneous impressions of a particular kind. 3. A state of mental incoherence or constant hurry and confusion of thought. Cyclo. Practical Medicine, h. t.; Brewster's Encyclopædia, h. t.; Observations on the Deranged Manifestations of the Mind, or Insanity, 71, 72; Merl. Répert. mots Démence, Folie, Imbécilité; 6 Watts & Serg. 451.

3. The diseases included under the name of insanity have been arranged under two divisions, founded on two very different

conditions of the brain. Ray, Med. Jur. ch. 1, § 33.

4.—1. The want of, or a defective development of the faculties. 1st. Idiocy, resulting from, 1. Congenital defect. 2. An obstacle to the development of the faculties, supervening in infancy. 2d. Imbecility, resulting from, 1. Congenital defects. 2. An obstacle to the development of the faculties, supervening in infancy.

5.—2. The lesion of the faculties subsequent to their development. In this division may be classed, 1st. Mania, which is, 1. Intellectual, and is general or partial. 2. Affective, and is general or partial. 2d. Dementia, which is, 1. Consecutive to mania, or injuries of the brain. 2. Senile, or peculiar to old age.

6. There is also a disease which has acquired the name of *Moral insanity.* (q. v.)

7. Insanity is an excuse for the commission of acts which in others would be crimes, because the insane man has no intention; it deprives a man also from entering into any valid contract. Vide *Lunacy; Non compos mentis*, and Stock on the Law of Non Compotes Mentis; 1 Hagg. Cons. R. 417; 3 Addams, R. 90, 91, 180, 181; 3 Hagg. Eccl. R. 545, 598, 600; 2 Greenl. Ev. §§ 369, 374; Bouv. Inst. Index, h. t.

INSCRIPTION, *civil law.* An engagement which a person, who makes a solemn accusation of a crime against another, enters into, that he will suffer the same punishment, if he has accused the other falsely, which would have been inflicted upon him had he been guilty. Code, 9, 1, 10; Id. 9, 2, 16 and 17.

INSCRIPTION, *evidence.* Something written or engraved.

2. Inscriptions upon tombstones and other proper places, as rings, and the like, are held to be evidence of pedigree. Bull. N. P. 233; Cowp. 591; 10 East, R. 120; 13 Ves. 145; Vin. Ab. Ev. T. b. 87: 3 Stark. Ev. 1116.

INSCRIPTIONES. The name given by the old English law to any written instrument by which anything was granted. Blount.

INSENSIBLE. In the language of pleading, that which is unintelligible is said to be insensible. Steph. Pl. 378.

INSIDIATORES VIARUM. Persons who lie in wait, in order to commit some felony or other misdemeanor.

INSIMUL. Together; jointly. This word is used in composition; as, *insimul computassent; non tenent insimul.*

INSIMUL COMPUTASSENT, *practice, actions.* They accounted together.

2. When an account has been stated, and a balance ascertained between the parties, they are said to have computed together, and the amount due may be recovered in an action of assumpsit, which could not have been done, if the defendant had been the mere bailiff or partner of the plaintiff, and there had been no settlement made; for in that case, the remedy would be an action of account render, or a bill in chancery. It is usual in actions of assumpsit, to add a count commonly called *insimul computassent*, or an *account stated.* (q. v.) Lawes on Pl. in Ass. 488.

INSINUATION, *civil law.* The transcription of an act on the public registers, like our recording of deeds. It was not necessary in any other alienation, but that appropriated to the purpose of donation. Inst. 2, 7, 2; Poth. Traité des Donations, entre vifs, sect. 2, art. 3, § 3; Encyclopédie; 8 Toull. n. 198.

INSOLVENCY. The state or condition of a person who is insolvent. (q. v.)

2. Insolvency may be simple or notorious. Simple insolvency is the debtor's inability to pay his debts, and is attended by no legal badge of notoriety or promulgation. Notorious insolvency is that which is designated by some public act, by which it becomes notorious and irretrievable, as applying for the benefit of the insolvent laws, and being discharged under the same.

3. Insolvency is a term of more extensive signification than bankruptcy, and includes all kinds of inability to pay a just debt. 2 Bell's Commentaries, 162, 5th ed.

INSOLVENT. This word has several meanings. It signifies a person whose estate is not sufficient to pay his debts. Civ. Code of Louisiana, art. 1980. A person is also said to be insolvent, who is under a present inability to answer, in the ordinary course of business, the responsibility which his creditors may enforce, by recourse to legal measures, without reference to his estate proving sufficient to pay all his debts, when ultimately wound up. 3 Dowl. & Ryl. Rep. 218; 1 Maule & Selw. 338; 1 Campb. R. 492, n.; Sugd. Vend. 487, 488. It signifies the situation of a person who has done some notorious act to divest himself of all his property, as a general assignment, or an application for relief, under bankrupt or insolvent laws. 1 Peters' R. 195; 2 Wheat. R. 396; 7 Toull. n. 45; Domat, liv. 4, t. 5, n. 1 et 2; 2 Bell's Com. 162, 5th ed.

2. When an insolvent delivers or offers to deliver up all his property for the benefit of his creditors, he is entitled to be discharged under the laws of the several states from all liability to be arrested. Vide 2 Kent, Com. 321; Ingrah. on Insolv. 9; 9 Mass. R. 431; 16 Mass. R. 53.

3. The reader will find the provisions made by the national legislature on this subject, by a reference to the following acts of congress, namely: Act of March 3, 1797, 1 Story, L. U. S. 465; Act of March 2, 1799, 1 Story, L. U. S. 630; Act of March 2, 1831, 4 Sharsw. Cont. of Story, L. U. S. 2236; Act of June 7, 1834, 4 Sharsw. Cont. of Story, L. U. S. 2358; Act of March 2, 1837, 4 Sharsw. Cont. of Story, L. U. S. 2536. See *Bankrupt*.

INSPECTION, *comm. law*. The examination of certain articles made by law subject to such examination, so that they may be declared fit for commerce. The decision of the inspectors is not final; the object of the law is to protect the community from fraud, and to preserve the character of the merchandise abroad. 8 Cowen, R. 45. See 1 John. 205; 13 John. R. 331; 2 Caines, R. 312; 3 Caines, R. 207.

INSPECTION, *practice*. Examination.

2. The inspection of all public records is free to all persons who have an interest in them, upon payment of the usual fees. 7 Mod. 129; 1 Str. 304; 2 Str. 260, 954, 1005. But it seems a mere stranger who has no such interest, has no right at common law. 8 T. R. 390. Vide *Trial by inspection*.

INSPECTOR. The name given to certain officers whose duties are to examine and inspect things over which they have jurisdiction; as, inspector of bark, one who is by law authorized to examine bark for exportation, and to approve or disapprove of its quality. Inspectors of customs are officers appointed by the general government: as to their duties, see Story's L. U. S. vol. 1, 590, 605, 609, 610, 612, 619, 621, 623, 650; ii. 1490, 1516; iii. 1650, 1790.

INSPEXIMUS. We have seen. A word sometimes used in letters-patent, reciting a grant, *inspeximus* such former grant, and so reciting it verbatim; it then grants such further privileges as are thought convenient. 5 Co. 54.

INSTALLATION or INSTALMENT. The act by which an officer is put in public possession of the place he is to fill. The president of the United States, or a governor, is installed into office, by being sworn agreeably to the requisition of the constitution and laws. Vide *Inauguration*.

INSTALMENT, *contracts*. A part of a debt due by contract, and agreed to be paid at a time different from that fixed for the payment of the other part. For example, if I engage to pay you one thousand dollars, in two payments, one on the first day of January, and the other on the first day of July, each of these payments or obligations to pay will be an instalment.

2. In such case each instalment is a separate debt so far that it may be tendered at any time, or the first may be sued for although the other shall not be due. Dane's Ab. vol. iii. ch. 93, art. 3, s. 11, page 493, 4; 1 Esp. R. 129; Id. 226; 3 Salk. 6, 18; 2 Esp. R. 235; 1 Maule & Selw. 706.

3. A debtor who by failing to pay three instalments of rent due on a lease would forfeit his estate, may, in order to save it, tender one instalment to prevent the forfeiture, although there may be two due at the time, and he is not bound to tender both. 6 Toull. n. 688.

INSTANCE, *civil* and *French law*. It signifies, generally, all sorts of actions and judicial demands. Dig. 44, 7, 58.

INSTANCE COURT, *Eng. law*. The English court of admiralty is divided into two distinct tribunals; the one having, generally, all the jurisdiction of the admiralty, except in prize cases, is called the *instance court;* the other, acting under a special commission, distinct from the usual commission given to judges of the admiralty, to enable the judge in time of war to assume the jurisdiction of prizes, and called *prize court*.

2. In the United States, the district courts of the U. S. possess all the powers of courts of admiralty, whether considered as instance or prize courts. 3 Dall. R. 6. Vide 1 Gall. R. 563; Bro. Civ. & Adm. Law, ch. 4 & 5; 1 Kent, Com. 355, 378. Vide *Courts of the United States; Prize Court*.

INSTANT. An indivisible space of time.

2. Although it cannot be actually divided, yet by intendment of law, it may be applied to several purposes; for example, he who lays violent hands upon him-

self, commits no felony till he is dead, and when he is dead he is not in being so as to be termed a felon; but he is so adjudged in law, *eo instante*, at the very instant this fact is done. Vin. Ab. Instant, A, pl. 2; Plowd. 258; Co. Litt. 18; Show. 415.

INSTANTER. Immediately; presently. This term, it is said, means that the act to which it applies, shall be done within twenty-four hours; but a doubt has been suggested by whom is the account of the hours to be kept, and whether the term instanter as applied to the subject-matter may not be more properly taken to mean "before the rising of the court," when the act is to be done in court; or, "before the shutting of the office the same night," when the act is to be done there. 1 Taunt. R. 343; 6 East, R. 587, n. e; Tidd's Pr. 3d ed. 508, n.; 3 Chit. Pr. 112. Vide, 3 Burr. 1809; Co. Litt. 157; Styles' Register, 452.

INSTAR. Likeness; resemblance; equivalent; as, *instar dentium*, like teeth; instar omnium, equivalent to all.

INSTIGATION. The act by which one incites another to do something, as to injure a third person, or to commit some crime or misdemeanor, to commence a suit or to prosecute a criminal. Vide *Accomplice*.

INSTITOR, *civ. law*. A clerk in a store; an agent.

2. He was so called because he watched over the business with which he was charged; and it is immaterial whether he was employed in making a sale in a store, or whether charged with any other business. Institor appellatus est ex eo, quòd negotio gerendo instet; nec multum facit tabernæ sit præpositus, an cuilibet alii negotiationi. Dig. lib. 14, tit. 3, l. 3. Mr. Bell says, that the charge given to a clerk to manage a store or shop, is called institorial power. 1 Bell's Com. 479, 5th ed.; Ersk. Inst. B. 3, t. 3, § 46; 1 Stair's Inst. by Brodie, B. 1, tit. 11, §§ 12, 18, 19; Story on Ag. § 8.

INSTITUTE, *Scotch law*. The person first called in the tailzie; the rest, or the heirs of tailzie, are called substitutes. Ersk. Pr. L. Scot. 3, 8, 8. See *Tailzie, Heir of; Substitutes*.

2. In the civil law, an institute is one who is appointed heir by testament, and is required to give the estate devised to another person, who is called the substitute.

TO INSTITUTE. To name or to make an heir by testament. Dig. 28, 5, 65. To make an accusation; to commence an action.

INSTITUTES. The principles or first elements of jurisprudence.

2. Many books have borne the title of Institutes. Among the most celebrated in the common law, are the Institutes of Lord Coke, which, however, on account of the want of arrangement and the diffusion with which his books are written, bear but little the character of Institutes; in the civil law the most generally known are those of Caius, Justinian, and Theophilus.

3. The Institutes of Caius are an abridgment of the Roman law, composed by the celebrated lawyer Caius or Gaius, who lived during the reign of Marcus Aurelius.

4. The Institutes of Justinian, so called, because they are, as it were, masters and instructors to the ignorant, and show an easy way to the obtaining of the knowledge of the law, are an abridgment of the Code and of the Digest, composed by order of that emperor: his intention in this composition was to give a summary knowledge of the law to those persons not versed in it, and particularly to merchants. The lawyers employed to make this book, were Trihonian, Theophilus, and Dorotheus. The work was first published in the year 533, and received the sanction of statute law, by order of the emperor. The Institutes of Justinian are divided into four books: each book is divided into two titles, and each title into parts. The first part is called *principium*, because it is the commencement of the title; those which follow are numbered and called paragraphs. The work treats of the rights of persons, of things, and of actions. The first book treats of persons: the second, third, and the first five titles of the fourth book, of things; and the remainder of the fourth book, of actions. This work has been much admired on account of its order and scientific arrangement, which presents, at a single glance, the whole jurisprudence of the Romans. It is too little known and studied. The late Judge Cooper, of Pennsylvania, published an edition with valuable notes.

5. The Institutes of Theophilus are a paraphrase of those of Justinian, composed in Greek, by a lawyer of that name, by order of the emperor Phocas. Vide 1 Kent, Com. 538; Profession d'Avocat, tom. ii. n. 536, page 95; Introd. à l'Etude du Droit Romain, p. 124; Dict. de Jurisp. h. t.; Merl. Répert. h. t.; Encyclopédie de d'Alembert, h. t.

INSTITUTION, *eccl. law*. The act by

which the ordinary commits the cure of souls to a person presented to a benefice.

INSTITUTION, *political law.* That which has been established and settled by law for the public good; as, the American institutions guaranty to the citizens all privileges and immunities essential to freedom.

INSTITUTION, *practice.* The commencement of an action; as, A B has instituted a suit against C D, to recover damages for a trespass.

INSTITUTION OF HEIR, *civil law.* The act by which a testator nominates one or more persons to succeed him in all his rights, active and passive. Poth. Tr. des Donations Testamentaires, c. 2, s. 1, § 1; Civ. Code of Lo. art. 1598; Dig. lib. 28, tit. 5, l. 1; and lib. 28, tit. 6, l. 2, § 4.

INSTRUCTION, *French law.* This word signifies the means used and formality employed to prepare a case for trial. It is generally applied to criminal cases, and is then called criminal instruction; it is then defined the acts and proceedings which tend to prove positively a crime or delict, in order to inflict on the guilty person the punishment which he deserves.

INSTRUCTIONS, *com. law, contracts.* Orders given by a principal to his agent, in relation to the business of his agency.

2. The agent is bound to obey the instructions he has received, and when he neglects so to do, he is responsible for the consequences, unless he is justified by matter of necessity. 4 Binn. R. 361; 1 Liverm. Agency, 368.

3. Instructions differ materially from authority, as regards third persons. When a written authority is known to exist, or, by the nature of the transaction, it is presupposed, it is the duty of persons dealing with an agent to ascertain the nature and extent of his authority; but they are not required to make inquiry of the agent as to any private instructions from his principal, for the obvious reason that they may be presumed to be secret and of a confidential nature, and therefore not to be communicated to third persons. 5 Bing. R. 442.

4. Instructions are given as applicable to the usual course of things, and are subject to two qualifications which are naturally, and perhaps necessarily implied in every mercantile agency. 1. As instructions are applicable only to the ordinary course of affairs, the agent will be justified, in cases of extreme necessity and unforeseen emergency, in deviating from them; as, for example, when goods on hand are perishable and perishing, or when they are accidentally injured and must be sold to prevent further loss; or if they are in imminent danger of being lost by the capture of the port where they are, they may be transferred to another port. Story on Ag. § 85, 118, 193; 3 Chit. Com. Law, 218; 4 Binn. 361; 1 Liverm. on Ag. 368. 2. Instructions must be lawful; if they are given to perform an unlawful act, the agent is not bound by them. 4 Campb. 183; Story on Ag. § 195. But the lawfulness of such instruction does not relate to the laws of foreign countries. Story, Confl. of Laws, § 245; 1 Liverm. on Ag. 15–19. As to the construction of letters of instruction, see 3 Wash. C. C. R. 151; 4 Wash. C. C. R. 551; 1 Liv. on Ag. 403; Story on Ag. § 74; 2 Wash. C. C. R. 132; 2 Crompt. & J. 244; 1 Knapp, R. 381.

INSTRUCTIONS, *practice.* The statements of a cause of action, given by a client to his attorney, and which, where such is the practice, are sent to his pleader to put into legal form of a declaration. Warr. Stud. 284.

2. Instructions to counsel are their indemnity for any aspersions they may make on the opposite party; but attorneys who have a just regard to their own reputation will be cautious, even under instructions, not to make any unnecessary attack upon a party or witness. For such unjustifiable conduct the counsel will be held responsible. Eunom. Dial. 2, § 43, p. 132. For a form of instructions, see 3 Chit. Pr. 117, and 120 n.

INSTRUMENT, *contracts.* The writing which contains some agreement, and is so called because it has been *prepared* as a memorial of what has taken place or been agreed upon. The agreement and the instrument in which it is contained are very different things, the latter being only evidence of the existence of the former. The instrument or form of the contract may be valid, but the contract itself may be void on account of fraud. Vide Ayl. Parerg. 305; Dunl. Ad. Pr. 220.

INSTRUMENTA. This word is properly applied to designate that kind of evidence which consists of writings not under seal, as court rolls, accounts, and the like. 3 Tho. Co. Litt. 487.

INSULA, *Latin.* An island. In the Roman law the word is applied to a house not connected with other houses, but separated by a surrounding space of ground. Calvini Lex; Vicat, Vocab. ad voc.

INSUFFICIENCY. What is not competent; not enough.

INSUPER, *Eng. law.* The balance due by an accountant in the exchequer, as apparent by his account. The auditors in settling his account say there remains so much *insuper* to such accountant.

INSURABLE INTEREST. That right of property which may be the subject of an insurance.

2. The policy of commerce, and the various complicated rights which different persons may have in the same thing, require that not only those who have an *absolute* property in ships or goods, but those also who have a *qualified* property in them, may be at liberty to insure them. For example, when a ship is mortgaged, and the mortgage has become absolute, the owner of the *legal* estate has an insurable interest, and the mortgagor, on account of his *equity*, has also an insurable interest. 1 Burr. 489. See 20 Pick. 259; 1 Pet. 163.

INSURANCE, *contracts.* It is defined to be a contract of indemnity from loss or damage arising upon an uncertain event. 1 Marsh. Ins. 104. It is more fully defined to be a contract by which one of the parties, called the *insurer*, binds himself to the other, called the *insured*, to pay him a sum of money, or otherwise indemnify him, in case of the happening of a fortuitous event, provided for in a general or special manner in the contract, in consideration of a premium which the latter pays, or binds himself to pay him. Pardess. part 3, t. 8, n. 588; 1 Bouv. Inst. n. 1174.

2. The instrument by which the contract is made is denominated a *policy;* the events or causes to be insured against, *risks* or *perils;* and the thing insured, the *subject* or *insurable interest.*

3. *Marine* insurance relates to property and risks at sea; insurance of property on shore against fire, is called *fire* insurance; and the various contracts in such cases, are *fire* policies. Insurance of the lives of individuals are called insurances on *lives.* Vide *Double Insurance; Re-Insurance.*

INSURANCE AGAINST FIRE. A contract by which the insurer, in consequence of a certain premium received by him, either in a gross sum or by annual payments, undertakes to indemnify the insured against all loss or damage which he may sustain to a certain amount, in his house or other buildings, stock, goods, or merchandise, mentioned in the policy, by fire, during the time agreed upon. 2 Marsh. Ins. B. 4, p. 784; 1 Stuart's L. C. R. 174; Park. Ins. c. 23, p. 441.

2. The risks and losses insured against, are "all losses or damage by fire," during the time of the policy, to the houses or things insured.

3.—1. There must be an actual fire or ignition to entitle the insured to recover; it is not sufficient that there has been a great and injurious increase of heat, while nothing has taken fire, which ought not to be on fire. 4 Campb. R. 360.

4.—2. The loss must be within the policy, that is, within the time insured. 5 T. R. 695; 1 Bos. & P. 470· 6 East, R 571.

5.—3. The insurers are liable not only for loss by burning, but for all damages and injuries, and reasonable charges attending the removal of articles though never touched by the fire. 1 Bell's Com. 626, 7, 5th ed.

6. Generally there is an exception in the policy, as to fire occasioned "by invasion, foreign enemy, or any military, or usurped power whatsoever," and in some there is a further exception of riot, tumult, or civil commotion. For the construction of these provisoes, see the articles *Civil Commotion* and *Usurped Power.*

INSURANCE, MARINE, *contracts.* Marine insurance is a contract whereby one party, for a stipulated premium, undertakes to indemnify the other against certain perils or sea risks, to which his ship, freight, or cargo, or some of them may be exposed, during a certain voyage, or a fixed period of time. 3 Kent, Com. 203; Boulay-Paty, Dr. Commercial, t. 10.

2. This contract is usually reduced to writing; the instrument is called a policy of insurance. (q. v.)

3. All persons, whether natives, citizens, or aliens, may be insured, with the exception of alien enemies.

4. The insurance may be of goods on a certain ship, or without naming any, as upon goods on board any *ship* or *ships.* The subject insured must be an insurable legal interest.

5. The contract requires the most perfect good faith; if the insured make false representations to the insurer, in order to procure his insurance upon better terms, it

will avoid the contract, though the loss arose from a cause unconnected with the misrepresentation, or the concealment happened through mistake, neglect, or accident, without any fraudulent intention. Vide Kent, Com. Lecture, 48; Marsh. Ins. c. 4; Pardessus, Dr. Com. part 4, t. 5, n. 756, et seq.; Boulay-Paty, Dr. Com. t. 10.

INSURANCE ON LIVES, *contracts.* The insurance of a life is a contract whereby the insurer, in consideration of a certain premium, either in a gross sum or periodical payments, undertakes to pay the person for whose benefit the insurance is made, a stipulated sum, or an annuity equivalent thereto, upon the death of the person whose life is insured, whenever this shall happen, if the insurance be for the whole life, or in case this shall happen within a certain period, if the insurance be for a limited time. 2 Marsh. Ins. 766; Park on Insurance, 429.

2. The insured is required to make a representation or declaration, previous to the policy being issued, of the age and state of health of the person whose life is insured; and the party making it is bound to the truth of it. Park, Ins. 650; Marsh. Ins. 771; 4 Taunt. R. 763.

3. In almost every life policy there are several exceptions, some of them applicable to all cases, others to the case of insurance of one's life. The exceptions are, 1. Death abroad, or at sea. 2. Entering into the naval or military service without the previous consent of the insurers. 3. Death by suicide. 4. Death by duelling. 5. Death by the hand of justice. The last three are not understood to be excepted when the insurance is on another's life. 1 Bell's Com. 631, 5th ed. See 1 Beck's Med. Jur. 518.

INSURED, *contracts.* The person who procures an insurance on his property.

2. It is the duty of the insured to pay the premium, and to represent fully and fairly all the circumstances relating to the subject-matter of the insurance, which may influence the determination of the underwriters in undertaking the risk, or estimating the premium. A concealment of such facts amounts to a fraud, which avoids the contract. 1 Marsh. Ins. 464; Park, Ins. h. t.

INSURER, *contracts.* One who has obliged himself to insure the safety of another's property, in consideration of a premium paid, or secured to be paid, to him. It is his duty to pay any loss which has arisen on the property insured. Vide Marsh. Ins. Index, h. t.; Park. Ins. Index, h. t.; Phill. Ins. h. t.; Wesk. Ins. h. t.; Pardess. Index, art. Assureur.

INSURGENT. One who is concerned in an insurrection. He differs from a rebel in this, that rebel is always understood in a bad sense, or one who unjustly opposes the constituted authorities; insurgent may be one who justly opposes the tyranny of constituted authorities. The colonists who opposed the tyranny of the English government were insurgents, not rebels.

INSURRECTION. A rebellion of citizens or subjects of a country against its government.

2. The Constitution of the United States, art. 1, s. 8, gives power to congress "to provide for calling forth the militia to execute the laws of the Union, suppress insurrections, and repel invasions."

3. By the act of Congress of the 28th of February, 1795, 1 Story's L. U. S. 389, it is provided:—

§ 1. That whenever the United States shall be invaded, or be in imminent danger of invasion, from any foreign nation or Indian tribe, it shall be lawful for the president of the United States to call forth such number of the militia of the state, or states, most convenient to the place of danger, or scene of action, as he may judge necessary to repel such invasion, and to issue his orders, for that purpose, to such officer or officers of the militia as he shall think proper. And in case of an insurrection in any state, against the government thereof, it shall be lawful for the president of the United States, on application of the legislature of such state, or of the executive, (when the legislature cannot be convened,) to call forth such number of the militia of any other state or states, as may be applied for, as he may judge sufficient to suppress such insurrection.

4.—§ 2. That, whenever the laws of the United States shall be opposed, or the execution thereof obstructed, in any state, by combinations too powerful to be suppressed by the ordinary course of judicial proceedings, or by the powers vested in the marshals by this act, it shall be lawful for the president of the United States to call forth the militia of such state, or of any other state or states, as may be necessary to suppress such combinations, and to cause the laws to be duly executed; and the use of militia so to be called forth may be continued, if necessary, until the expiration of thirty days after the commencement of the then next session of congress.

5.—§ 3. That whenever it may be necessary, in the judgment of the president, to use the military force hereby directed to be called forth, the president shall forthwith, by proclamation, command such insurgents to disperse, and retire peaceably to their respective abodes, within a limited time.

INTAKERS, *Eng. law.* The name given to receivers of goods stolen in Scotland, who take them to England. 9 H. V., c. 27.

INTEGER. Whole, untouched. Res integra means a question which is new and undecided. 2 Kent, Com. 177.

INTENDED TO BE RECORDED. This phrase is frequently used in conveyancing, in deeds which recite other deeds which have not been recorded. In Pennsylvania, it has been construed to be a covenant, on the part of the grantor, to procure the deed to be recorded in a reasonable time. 2 Rawle's Rep. 14.

INTENDANT. One who has the charge, management, or direction of some office, department, or public business.

INTENDMENT OF LAW. The true meaning, the correct understanding, or intention of the law; a presumption or inference made by the courts. Co. Litt. 78.

2. It is an intendment of law that every man is innocent until proved guilty, vide *Innocence;* that every one will act for his own advantage, vide *Assent;* Fin. Law, 10, Max. 54, that every officer acts in his office with fidelity: that the children of a married woman, born during the coverture, are the children of the husband, vide *Bastardy;* many things are intended after verdict, in order to support a judgment, but intendment cannot supply the want of certainty in a charge in an indictment for a crime. 5 Co. 121; vide Com. Dig. Pleader, C 25, and S 31; Dane's Ab. Index, h. t.; 14 Vin. Ab. 449; 1 Halst. 132; 1 Harris. 133.

INTENTION. A design, resolve, or determination of the mind.

2. Intention is required in the commission of crimes and injuries, in making contracts, and wills.

3.—1. Every crime must have necessarily two constituent parts, namely, an act forbidden by law, and an intention. The act is innocent or guilty just as there was or was not an intention to commit a crime; for example, a man embarks on board of a ship, at New York, for the purpose of going to New Orleans; if he went with an intention to perform a lawful act, he is perfectly innocent; but if his intention was to levy war against the United States, he is guilty of an overt act of treason. Cro. Car. 332; Fost. 202, 203; Hale, P. C. 116. The same rule prevails in numerous civil cases; in actions founded on malicious injuries, for instance, it is necessary to prove that the act was accompanied by a wrongful and malicious intention. 2 Stark. Ev. 739.

4. The intention is to be proved, or it is inferred by the law. The existence of the intention is usually matter of inference; and proof of external and visible acts and conduct serves to indicate, more or less forcibly, the particular intention. But, in some cases, the inference of intention necessarily arises from the facts. *Exteriora acta indicant interiora animi secreta.* 8 Co. 146. It is a universal rule, that a man shall be taken to intend that which he does, or which is the necessary and immediate consequence of his act; 3 M. & S. 15; Hale, P. C. 229; in cases of homicide, therefore, malice will generally be inferred by the law. Vide *Malice*, and Jacob's Intr. to the Civ. Law, Reg. 70; Dig. 24, 18.

5. But a bare intention to commit a crime, without any overt act towards its commission, although punishable in foro conscientiæ, is not a crime or offence for which the party can be indicted; as, for example, an intention to pass counterfeit bank notes, knowing them to be counterfeit. 1 Car. Law Rep. 517.

6.—2. In order to make a contract, there must be an intention to make it; a person non compos mentis, who has no contracting mind, cannot, therefore, enter into any engagement which requires an intention; for to make a contract the law requires a fair and serious exercise of the reasoning faculty. Vide *Gift; Occupancy.*

7.—3. In wills and testaments, the intention of the testator must be gathered from the whole instrument; 3 Ves. 105; and a codicil ought to be taken as a part of the will; 4 Ves. 610; and when such intention is ascertained, it must prevail, unless it be in opposition to some unbending rule of law. 6 Cruise's Dig. 295; Rand. on Perp. 121; Cro. Jac. 415. "It is written," says Swinb. p. 10, "that the will or meaning of the testator is the queen or empress of the testament; because the will doth rule the testament, enlarge and restrain it, and in every respect moderate and direct the same, and is, indeed, the very efficient cause thereof. The will, therefore, and meaning of the testator ought, before all things, to be sought for diligently, and, being found, ought to be observed faithfully." 6 Pet. R. 68.

Vide, generally, Bl. Com. Index, h. t.; 2 Stark. Ev. h. t.; Ayl. Pand. 95; Dane's Ab. Index, h. t.; Rob. Fr. Conv. 30. As to intention in changing a residence, see article *Inhabitant.*

INTER. Between, among; as, inter vivos, between living persons; inter alia, among others.

INTER ALIA. Among other things; as, "the said premises, which inter alia, Titius granted to Caius."

INTER ALIOS. Between other parties, who are strangers to the proceeding in question.

INTERCOMMONING, *Eng. law.* Where the commons of two manors lie together, and the inhabitants, or those having a right of common of both, have time out of mind depastured their cattle, without any distinction, this is called intercommoning.

INTER CANEM ET LUPUM. Literally, between the dog and the wolf. Metaphorically, the twilight; because then the dog seeks his rest, and the wolf his prey. 3 Inst. 63.

INTER PARTES. This, in a technical sense, signifies an agreement professing in the outset, and before any stipulations are introduced, to be made between such and such persons; as, for example, "This Indenture, made the —— day of ——, 1848, between A B of the one part, and C D of the other." It is true that every contract is in one sense *inter partes,* because to be valid there must be two parties at least; but the technical sense of this expression is as above mentioned. Addis. on Contr. 9.

2. This being a solemn declaration, the effect of such introduction is to make all the covenants, comprised in a deed to be covenants between the parties and none others; so that should a stipulation be found in the body of a deed by which "the said A B covenants with E F to pay him one hundred dollars," the words "with E F" are inoperative, unless they have been used to denote for whose benefit the stipulation may have been made, being in direct contradiction with what was previously declared, and C D alone can sue for the nonpayment; it being a maxim that where two opposite intentions are expressed in a contract, the first in order shall prevail. 8 Mod. 116; 1 Show. 58; 3 Lev. 138; Carth. 76; Roll. R. 196; 7 M. & W. 63. But this rule does not apply to simple contracts *inter partes.* 2 D. & R. 277; 3 D. & R. 273, Addis. on Contr. 244, 256.

3. When there are more than two sides to a contract *inter partes,* for example, a deed; as when it is made between A B, of the first part; C D, of the second; and E F, of the third, there is no objection to on covenanting with another in exclusion of the third. See 5 Co. 182; 8 Taunt. 245; 4 Ad. & Ell. N. S. 207; Addis. on Contr. 267.

INTER SE, INTER SESE. Among themselves. Story on Part § 405.

INTER VIVOS. Between living persons; as, a gift *inter vivos,* which is a gift made by one living person to another; see *Gifts inter vivos.* It is a rule that a fee cannot pass by grant or transfer, *inter vivos,* without appropriate words of inheritance. 2 Prest. on Est. 64.

INTERCOURSE. Communication; commerce; connexion by reciprocal dealings between persons or nations, as by interchange of commodities, treaties, contracts, or letters.

INTERCHANGEABLY. Formerly when deeds of land were made, where there were covenants to be performed on both sides, it was usual to make two deeds exactly similar to each other, and to exchange them; in the attesting clause, the words, "In witness whereof the parties have hereunto *interchangeably* set their hands," &c., were constantly inserted, and the practice has continued, although the deed is, in most cases, signed by the grantor only. 7 Penn. St. Rep. 329.

INTERDICT, *civil law.* Among the Romans it was an ordinance of the prætor, which forbade or enjoined the parties in a suit to do something particularly specified, until it should be decided definitely who had the right in relation to it. Like an injunction, the interdict was merely personal in its effects, and it had also another similarity to it, by being temporary or perpetual. Dig. 43, 1, 1, 3, and 4. See Story, Eq. Jur. § 865; Halif. Civ. Law, ch. 6; Vicat, Vocab. h. v.; Hein. Elem. Pand. Ps. 6, § 285. Vide *Injunction.*

INTERDICT, OR INTERDICTION, *eccles. law.* An ecclesiastical censure, by which divine services are prohibited either to particular persons or particular places. These tyrannical edicts, issued by ecclesiastical powers, have never been in force in the United States.

INTERDICTED OF FIRE AND WATER. Formerly those persons who were banished for some crime, were interdicted of fire and water; that is, by the judgment order was given that no man should receive them into his house, but should deny them fire and water, the two necessary elements of life.

INTERDICTION, *civil law*. A legal restraint upon a person incapable of managing his estate, because of mental incapacity, from signing any deed or doing any act to his own prejudice, without the consent of his curator or interdictor.

2. Interdictions are of two kinds, voluntary or judicial. The first is usually executed in the form of an obligation by which the obligor binds himself to do no act which may affect his estate without the consent of certain friends or other persons therein mentioned. The latter, or judicial interdiction, is imposed by a sentence of a competent tribunal, which disqualifies the party on account of imbecility, madness, or prodigality, and deprives the person interdicted of the right to manage his affairs and receive the rents and profits of his estate.

3. The Civil Code of Louisiana makes the following provisions on this subject:

Art. 382. No person above the age of majority, who is subject to an habitual state of madness or insanity, shall be allowed to take charge of his own person or to administer his estate, although such person shall, at times, appear to have the possession of his reason.

4.—383. Every relation has a right to petition for the interdiction of a relation; and so has every husband a right to petition for the interdiction of his wife, and every wife of her husband.

5.—384. If the insane person has no relations and is not married, or if his relations or consort do not act, the interdiction may be solicited by any stranger, or pronounced *ex officio* by the judge, after having heard the counsel of the person whose interdiction is prayed for, whom it shall be the duty of the judge to name, if one be not already named by the party.

385. Every interdiction shall be pronounced by the judge of the parish of the domicil or residence of the person to be interdicted.

386. The acts of madness, insanity or fury, must be proved to the satisfaction of the judge, that he may be enabled to pronounce the interdiction, and this proof may be established, as well by written as by parol evidence; and the judge may moreover interrogate or cause to be interrogated by any other person commissioned by him for that purpose, the person whose interdiction is petitioned for, or cause such person to be examined by physicians, or other skilful persons, in order to obtain their report upon oath on the real situation of him who is stated to be of unsound mind.

387. Pending the issue of the petition for interdiction, the judge may, if he deems it proper, appoint for the preservation of the movable, and for the administration of the immovable estate of the defendant, an administrator *pro tempore*.

388. Every judgment, by which an interdiction is pronounced, shall be provisionally executed, notwithstanding the appeal.

389. In case of appeal, the appellate court may, if they deem it necessary, proceed to the hearing of new proofs, and question or cause to be questioned, as above provided, the person whose interdiction is petitioned for, in order to ascertain the state of his mind.

390. On every petition for interdiction, the cost shall be paid out of the estate of the defendant, if he shall be interdicted, and by the petitioner, if the interdiction prayed for shall not be pronounced.

391. Every sentence of interdiction shall be published three times, in at least two of the newspapers printed in New Orleans, or made known by advertisements at the door of the court-house of the parish of the domicil of the person interdicted, both in the French and English languages; and this duty is imposed upon him who shall be appointed curator of the person interdicted, and shall be performed within a month after the date of the interdiction, under the penalty of being answerable for all damages to such persons as may, through ignorance, have contracted with the person interdicted.

392. No petition for interdiction, if the same shall have once been rejected, shall be acted upon again, unless new facts, happening posterior to the sentence, shall be alleged.

393. The interdiction takes place from the day of presenting the petition for the same.

394. All acts done by the person interdicted, from the date of the filing the petition for interdiction until the day when the same is pronounced, are null.

395. No act anterior to the petition for the interdiction, shall be annulled, except where it shall be proved that the cause of such interdiction notoriously existed at the time when the deeds, the validity of which is contested, were made, or that the party who contracted with the lunatic or insane person, could not have been deceived as to the situation of his mind.

Notoriously, in this article, means that the insanity was generally known by the persons who saw and conversed with the party.

396. After the death of a person, the validity of acts done by him cannot be contested for cause of insanity, unless his interdiction was pronounced or petitioned for, previous to the death of such person, except in cases in which mental alienation manifested itself within ten days previous to the decease, or in which the proof of the want of reason results from the act itself which is contested.

397. Within a month, to reckon from the date of the judgment of interdiction, if there has been no appeal from the same, or if there has been an appeal, then within a month from the confirmative sentence, it shall be the duty of the judge of the parish of the domicil or residence of the person interdicted, to appoint a curator to his person and estate.

398. This appointment is made according to the same forms as the appointment to the tutorship of minors.

After the appointment of the curator to the person interdicted, the duties of the administrator, pro tempore, if he shall not have been appointed curator, are at an end; and he shall give an account of his administration to the curator.

399. The married woman, who is interdicted, is of course under the curatorship of her husband. Nevertheless, it is the duty of the husband, in such case, to cause to be appointed by the judge, a curator *ad litem*; who may appear for the wife in every case when she may have an interest in opposition to the interest of her husband, or one of a nature to be pursued or defended jointly with his.

400. The wife may be appointed curatrix to her husband, if she has, in other respects, the necessary qualifications.

She is not bound to give security.

401. No one, except the husband, with respect to his wife, or wife with respect to her husband, the relations in the ascending line with respect to the relations in the descending line, and vice versa, the relations in the descending line with respect to the relations in the ascending line, can be compelled to act as curator to a person interdicted more than ten years, after which time the curator may petition for his discharge.

402. The person interdicted is, in every respect, like the minor who has not arrived at the age of puberty, both as it respects his person and estate; and the rules respecting the guardianship of the minor, concerning the oath, the inventory and the security, the mode of administering the sale of the estate, the commission on the revenues, the excuses, the exclusion or deprivation of the guardianship, mode of rendering the accounts, and the other obligations, apply with respect to the person interdicted.

403. When any of the children of the person interdicted is to be married, the dowry or advance of money to be drawn from his estate is to be regulated by the judge, with the advice of a family meeting.

404. According to the symptoms of the disease, under which the person interdicted labors, and according to the amount of his estate, the judge may order that the interdicted person be attended in his own house, or that he be placed in a bettering-house, or indeed, if he be so deranged as to be dangerous, he may order him to be confined in safe custody.

405. The income of the person interdicted shall be employed in mitigating his sufferings, and in accelerating his cure, under the penalty against the curator of being removed in case of neglect.

406. He who petitions for the interdiction of any person, and fails in obtaining such interdiction, may be prosecuted for and sentenced to pay damages, if he shall have acted from motives of interest or passion.

407. Interdiction ends with the cause which gave rise to it. Nevertheless, the person interdicted cannot resume the exercise of his rights, until after the definite judgment by which a repeal of the interdiction is pronounced.

408. Interdiction can only be revoked by the same solemnities which were observed in pronouncing it.

6.—409. Not only lunatics and idiots are liable to be interdicted, but likewise all persons who, owing to certain infirmities, are incapable of taking care of their persons and administering their estates.

7. Such persons shall be placed under the care of a curator, who shall be appointed and shall administer in conformity with the rules contained in the present chapter.

8.—410. The person interdicted cannot be taken out of the state without a judicial order, given on the recommendation of a family meeting, and on the opinion delivered under oath of at least two physicians, that they believe the departure necessary to the health of the person interdicted.

9.—411. There shall be appointed by the judge a superintendent to the person interdicted; whose duty it shall be to inform the judge, at least once in three months, of the state of the health of the person interdicted, and of the manner in which he is treated.

10. To this end, the superintendent shall have free access to the person interdicted, whenever he wishes to see him.

11.—412. It is the duty of the judge to visit the person interdicted, whenever, from the information he receives, he shall deem it expedient.

12. This visit shall be made at times when the curator is not present.

13.—413. Interdiction is not allowed on account of profligacy or prodigality.

Vide Ray's Med. Jur. chap. 25; 1 Hagg. Eccl. Rep. 401; *Committee; Habitual Drunkard.*

INTERESSE TERMINI, *estates.* An interest in the term. The demise of a term in land does not vest any estate in the lessee, but gives him a mere right of entry on the land, which right is called his interest in the term, or *interesse termini.* Vide Co. Litt. 46; 2 Bl. Com. 144; 10 Vin. Ab. 348; Dane's Ab. Index, h. t.; Watk. Prin. Con. 15.

INTEREST, *estates.* The right which a man has in a chattel real, and more particularly in a future term. It is a word of less efficacy and extent than estates, though, in legal understanding, an interest extends to estates, rights and titles which a man has in or out of lands, so that by a grant of his whole interest in land, a reversion as well as the fee simple shall pass. Co. Litt. 345.

INTEREST, *contracts.* The right of property which a man has in a thing, commonly called *insurable interest.* It is not easy to give an accurate definition of insurable interest. 1 Burr. 480; 1 Pet. R. 163; 12 Wend 507; 16 Wend. 385; 16 Pick. 397; 13 Mass. 61, 96; 3 Day, 108; 1 Wash. C. C. Rep. 409.

2. The policy of commerce and the various complicated rights which different persons may have in the same thing, require that not only those who have an absolute property in ships and goods, but those also who have a qualified property therein, may be at liberty to insure them. For example, when a ship is mortgaged, after the mortgage becomes absolute, the owner of the *legal* estate has an insurable interest, and the mortgagor, on account of his *equity*, has also an insurable interest. 2 T. R. 188; 1 Burr. 489; 13 Mass. 96; 10 Pick. 40; and see 1 T. R. 745; Marsh. Ins. h. t.; 6 Meeson & Welsby, 224.

3. A man may not only insure his own life for the benefit of his heirs or creditors, and assign the benefit of this insurance to others having thus or otherwise an interest in his life, but he may insure the life of another in which he may be interested. Marsh. Ins. Index, h. t.; Park, Ins. Index, h. t.; 1 Bell's Com. 629, 5th ed.; 9 East, R. 72. Vide *Insurance.*

INTEREST, *evidence.* The benefit which a person has in the matter about to be decided and which is in issue between the parties. By the term benefit is here understood some pecuniary or other advantage, which if obtained, would increase the witness' estate, or some loss, which would decrease it.

2. It is a general rule that a party who has an interest in the cause cannot be a witness. It will be proper to consider this matter by taking a brief view of the *thing* or subject in dispute, which is the object of the interest; the *quantity* of interest; the *quality* of interest; when an interested witness can be examined; when the interest must exist; how an interested witness can be rendered competent.

3.—1. To be disqualified on the ground of interest, the witness must gain or lose by the *event* of the cause, or the verdict must be lawful evidence *for or against him* in another suit, or the record must be an instrument of evidence for or against him. 3 John. Cas. 83; 1 Phil. Ev. 36; Stark. Ev. pt. 4, p. 744. But an interest in the *question* does not disqualify the witness. 1 Caines, 171; 4 John. 302; 5 John. 255; 1 Serg. & R. 32, 36; 6 Binn. 266; 1 H. & M. 165, 168.

4.—2. The *magnitude* of the interest is altogether immaterial, even a liability for the most trifling costs will be sufficient.

5 T. R. 174; 2 Vern. 317; 2 Greenl. 194; 11 John. 57.

5.—3. With regard to the quality, the interest must be *legal*, as contradistinguished from mere prejudice or bias, arising from relationship, friendship, or any of the numerous motives by which a witness may be supposed to be influenced. Leach, 154; 2 St. Tr. 334, 891; 2 Hawk. ch. 46, s. 25. It must be a *present*, *certain*, *vested* interest, and not uncertain and contingent. Dougl. 134; 2 P. Wms. 287; 3 S. & R. 132; 4 Binn. 83; 2 Yeates, 200; 5 John. 256; 7 Mass. 25. And it must have been acquired without fraud. 3 Camp. 380; 1 M. & S. 9; 1 T. R. 37.

6.—4. To the general rule that interest renders a witness incompetent, there are some exceptions. *First*. Although the witness may have an interest, yet if his interest is equally strong on the other side, and no more, the witness is reduced to a state of neutrality by an equipoise of interest, and the objection to his testimony ceases. 7 T. R. 480, 481, n.; 1 Bibb, R. 298; 2 Mass. R. 108; 2 S. & R. 119; 6 Penn. St. Rep. 322.

7. *Secondly*. In some instances the law admits the testimony of one interested, from the extreme necessity of the case; upon this ground the servant of a tradesman is admitted to prove the delivery of goods and the payment of money, without any release from the master. 4 T. R. 490; 2 Litt. R. 27.

8.—5. The interest, to render the witness disqualified, must exist at the time of his examination. A deposition made at a time when the witness had no interest, may be read in evidence, although he has afterwards acquired an interest. 1 Hoff. R. 21.

9.—6. The objection to incompetency on the ground of interest may be removed by an extinguishment of that interest by means of a release, executed either by the witness, when he would receive an advantage by his testimony, or by those who have a claim upon him when his testimony would be evidence of his liability. The objection may also be removed by payment. Stark. Ev. pt. 4, p. 757. See Benth. Rationale of Jud. Ev. 628–692, where he combats the established doctrines of the law, as to the exclusion on the ground of interest; and *Balance*.

INTEREST FOR MONEY, *contracts*. The compensation which is paid by the borrower to the lender or by the debtor to the creditor for its use.

2. It is proposed to consider, 1. Who is bound to pay interest. 2. Who is entitled to receive it. 3. On what claim it is allowed. 4. What interest is allowed. 5. How it is computed. 6. When it will be barred. 7. Rate of interest in the different states.

3—§ 1. *Who is bound to pay interest?* 1. The contractor himself, who has agreed, either expressly or by implication, to pay interest, is of course bound to do so.

4.—2. Executors, administrators, assignees of bankrupts or of insolvents, and trustees, who have kept money an unreasonable length of time, and have made or who might have made it productive, are chargeable with interest. 2 Ves. 85; 1 Bro. C. C. 359; Id. 375; 2 Ch. Co. 235, Chan. Rep. 389; 1 Vern. 197; 2 Vern. 548; 3 Bro. C. C. 73; Id. 433; 4 Ves. 620; 1 Johns. Ch. R. 508; Id. 527, 535, 6; Id. 620; 1 Desaus. Ch. R. 193, n; Id 208; 1 Wash. 2; 1 Binn. R. 194; 3 Munf. 198, pl. 3; Id. 289, pl. 16; 1 Serg. & Rawle, 241; 4 Desaus. Ch. Rep. 463; 5 Munf. 223, pl. 7, 8; 1 Ves. jr. 236; Id. 452; Id. 89; 1 Atk. 90; see 1 Supp. to Ves. jr. 30; 11 Ves. 61; 15 Ves. 470; 1 Ball & Beat. 230; 1 Supp. to Ves. jr. 127, n. 3; 1 Jac. & Walk. 140; 3 Meriv. 43; 2 Bro. C. C. 156; 5 Ves. 839; 7 Ves. 152; 1 Jac. & Walk. 122; 1 Pick. 530; 13 Mass. R. 232; 3 Call, 538; 4 Hen. & Munf. 415; 2 Esp. N. P. C. 702; 2 Atk. 106; 2 Dall. 182; 4 Serg. & Rawle, 116; 1 Dall. 349; 3 Binn. 121. As to the distinction between executors and trustees, see Mr. Coxe's note to Fellows *v.* Mitchell, 1 P. Wms. 241; 1 Eden, 357, and the cases there collected.

5.—3. Tenant for life must pay interest on encumbrances on the estate. 4 Ves. 33; 1 Vern. 404, n. by Raithby. In Pennsylvania the heir at law is not bound to pay interest on a mortgage given by his ancestor.

6.—4. In Massachusetts a bank is liable, independently of the statute of 1809, c. 37, to pay interest on their bills, if not paid when presented for payment. 8 Mass. 445.

7.—5. Revenue officers must pay interest to the United States from the time of receiving the money. 6 Binney's Rep. 266.

8.—§ 1 *Who are entitled to receive interest*. 1. The lender upon an express or implied contract.

9.—2. An executor was not allowed interest in a case where money due to his testatrix was out at interest, and before money came to his hands, he advanced his own in payment of debts of the testatrix. Vin. Ab. tit. Interest, C. pl. 13.

10. In Massachusetts a trustee of property placed in his hands for security, who was obliged to advance money to protect it, was allowed interest at the compound rate. 16 Mass. 228.

11.—§ 3. *On what claims allowed.* First. On express contracts. Secondly. On implied contracts. And, thirdly. On legacies.

12. First. *On express contracts.* 1. When the debtor expressly undertakes to pay interest, he or his personal representatives having assets are bound to pay it. But if a party has accepted the principal, it has been determined that he cannot recover interest in a separate action. 1 Esp. N. P. C. 110; 3 Johns. 220. See 1 Camp. 50; 1 Dall. 315; Stark. Ev. pt. iv. 787; 1 Hare & Wall. Sel. Dec. 345.

13. Secondly. *On implied contracts.* 1. On money lent, or laid out for another's use. Bunb. 119; 2 Bl. Rep. 761; S. C. 3 Wils. 205; 2 Burr. 1077; 5 Bro. Parl. Ca 71; 1 Ves. jr. 63; 1 Dall. 349; 1 Binn. 488; 2 Call, 102; 2 Hen. & Munf. 381; 1 Hayw. 4; 3 Caines' Rep. 226, 234, 238, 245; see 3 Johns. Cas. 303; 9 Johns. 71; 3 Caines' Rep. 266; 1 Conn. Rep. 32; 7 Mass. 14; 1 Dall. 349; 6 Binn. R. 163; Stark. Ev. pt. iv. 789, n. (y), and (z); 11 Mass. 504; 1 Hare & Wall. Sel. Dec. 346.

14.—2. For goods sold and delivered, after the customary or stipulated term of credit has expired. Doug. 376; 2 B. & P. 337; 4 Dall. 289; 2 Dall. 193; 6 Binn. 162; 1 Dall. 265, 349.

15.—3. On bills and notes. If payable at a future day certain, after due; if payable on demand, after a demand made. Bunb. 119; 6 Mod. 138; 1 Str. 649; 2 Ld. Raym. 733; 2 Burr. 1081; 5 Ves. jr. 133; 15 Serg. & R. 264. Where the terms of a promissory note are, that it shall be payable by instalments, and on the failure of any instalment, the whole is to become due, interest on the whole becomes payable from the first default. 4 Esp. 147. Where, by the terms of a bond, or a promissory note, interest is to be paid annually, and the principal at a distant day, the interest may be recovered before the principal is due. 1 Binn. 165; 2 Mass. 568; 3 Mass. 221.

16.—4. On an account stated, or other liquidated sum, whenever the debtor knows precisely what he is to pay, and when he is to pay it. 2 Black. Rep. 761, S. C. Wils. 205; 2 Ves. 365; 8 Bro. Parl. C. 561; 2 Burr. 1085; 5 Esp. N. P. C. 114; 2 Com. Contr. 207; Treat. Eq. lib. 5, c. 1, s. 4; 2 Fonb. 438; 1 Hayw. 173; 2 Cox, 219; 1 V. & B. 345; 1 Supp. to Ves. jr. 194; Stark. Ev. pt. iv. 789, n. (a). But interest is not due for unliquidated damages, or on a running account where the items are all on one side, unless otherwise agreed upon. 1 Dall. 265; 4 Cowen, 496; 6 Cowen, 193; 5 Verm. 177; 2 Wend. 501; 1 Spears, 209; Rice, 21; 2 Blackf. 313; 1 Bibb, 443.

17.—5. On the arrears of an annuity secured by a specialty. 14 Vin. Ab. 458, pl. 8; 3 Atk. 579; 9 Watts, R. 530.

18.—6. On a deposit by a purchaser, which he is entitled to recover back, paid either to a principal, or an auctioneer. Sugd. Vend. 327; 3 Campb. 258; 5 Taunt. 625. Sed vide 4 Taunt. 334, 341.

19.—7. On purchase money, which has lain dead, where the vendor cannot make a title. Sugd. Vend. 327.

20.—8. On purchase money remaining in purchaser's hands to pay off encumbrances. 1 Sch. & Lef. 134. See 1 Wash. 125; 5 Munf. 342; 6 Binn. 435.

21.—9. On judgment debts. 14 Vin. Abr. 458, pl. 15; 4 Dall. 251; 2 Ves. 162; 5 Binn. R. 61; Id. 220; 1 Harr. & John. 754; 3 Wend. 496; 4 Metc. 317; 1 Hare & Wall. Sel. Dec. 350. In Massachusetts the principal of a judgment is recovered by execution; for the interest the plaintiff must bring an action. 14 Mass. 239.

22.—10. On judgments affirmed in a higher court. 2 Burr. 1097; 2 Str. 931; 4 Burr. 2128; Dougl. 752, n. 3; 2 H. Bl. 267; Id. 284; 2 Camp. 428, n.; 3 Taunt. 503; 4 Taunt. 30.

23.—11. On money obtained by fraud, or where it has been wrongfully detained. 9 Mass. 504; 1 Camp. 129; 3 Cowen, 426.

24.—12. On money paid by mistake, or recovered on a *void* execution. 1 Pick. 212; 9 Serg. & Rawle, 409.

25.—13. Rent in arrear due by covenant bears interest, unless under special circumstances, which may be recovered in action; 1 Yeates, 72; 6 Binn. 159; 4 Yeates, 264; but no distress can be made for such interest. 2 Binn. 246. Interest cannot, however, be recovered for arrears of rent payable in wheat. 1 Johns. 276. See 2 Call, 249; Id. 253; 3 Hen. & Munf. 463; 4 Hen. & Munf. 470; 5 Munf. 21.

26.—14. Where, from the course of dealing between the parties, a promise to pay interest is implied. 1 Campb. 50; Id. 52; 3 Bro. C. C. 436; Kirby, 207.

27. Thirdly, *Of interest on legacies*. 1. *On specific legacies*. Interest on specific legacies is to be calculated from the date of the death of testator. 2 Ves. sen. 563; 6 Ves. 345; 5 Binn. 475; 3 Munf. 10.

28.—2. A *general* legacy, when the time of payment is *not* named by the testator, is not payable till the end of one year after testator's death, at which time the interest commences to run. 1 Ves. jr. 366; 1 Sch. & Lef. 10; 5 Binn. 475; 13 Ves. 333; 1 Ves. 308; 3 Ves. & Bea. 183. But where only the interest is given, no payment will be due till the end of the second year, when the interest will begin to run. 7 Ves. 89.

29.—3. Where a general legacy is given, and the time of payment is named by the testator, interest is not allowed before the arrival of the appointed period of payment, and that notwithstanding the legacies are vested. Prec. in Chan. 337. But when that period arrives, the legatee will be entitled, although the legacy be charged upon a dry reversion. 2 Atk. 108. See also Daniel's Rep. in Exch. 84; 3 Atk. 101; 3 Ves. 10; 4 Ves. 1; 4 Bro. C. C. 149, n.; S. C. 1 Cox, 133. Where a legacy is given payable at a future day with interest, and the legatee dies before it becomes payable, the arrears of the interest up to the time of his death must be paid to his personal representatives. McClel. Exch. Rep. 141. And a bequest of a sum to be paid annually for life bears interest from the death of testator. 5 Binn. 475.

30.—4. Where the legatee is a child of the testator, or one towards whom he has placed himself in *loco parentis*, the legacy bears interest from the testator's death, whether it be particular or residuary; vested, but payable at a future time, or contingent, if the child have no maintenance. In that case the court will do what, in common presumption, the father would have done, provide necessaries for the child. 2 P. Wms. 31; 3 Ves. 287; Id. 13; Bac. Abr. Legacies, K 3; Fonb. Eq. 431, n. j.; 1 Eq. Cas. Ab. 301, pl. 3; 3 Atk. 432; 1 Dick. Rep. 310; 2 Bro. C. C. 59; 2 Rand. Rep. 409. In case of a child *in ventre sa mère*, at the time of the father's decease, interest is allowed only from its *birth*. 2 Cox, 425. Where maintenance or interest is given by the will, and the rate specified, the legatee will not, in general, be entitled to claim more than the maintenance or rate specified. 3 Atk. 697, 716; 3 Ves. 286, n.; and see further, as to interest in cases of legacies to children, 15 Ves. 363; 1 Bro. C. C. 267; 4 Madd. R. 275; 1 Swanst. 553; 1 P. Wms. 783; 1 Vern. 251; 3 Vesey & Beames, 183.

31.—5. Interest is not allowed by way of maintenance to any other person than the legitimate children of the testator; 3 Ves. 10; 4 Ves. 1; unless the testator has put himself in loco parentis. 1 Sch. & Lef 5, 6. A wife; 15 Ves. 301; a niece; 3 Ves. 10; a grandchild; 15 Ves. 301; 6 Ves. 546; 12 Ves. 3; 1 Cox, 133; are therefore not entitled to interest by way of maintenance. Nor is a legitimate child entitled to such interest if he have a maintenance; although it may be less than the amount of the interest of the legacy. 1 Scho. & Lef. 5; 3 Ves. 17. Sed vide 4 John. Ch. Rep. 103; 2 Rop. Leg. 202.

32.—6. Where an intention though not expressed is fairly inferable from the will, interest will be allowed. 1 Swanst. 561, note; Coop. 143.

33.—7. Interest is not allowed for maintenance, although given by immediate bequest for maintenance, if the parent of the legatee, who is under moral obligation to provide for him, be of sufficient ability, so that the interest will accumulate for the child's benefit, until the principal becomes payable. 3 Atk. 399; 3 Bro. C. C. 416; 1 Bro. C. C. 386; 3 Bro. C. C. 60. But to this rule there are some exceptions. 3 Ves. 730; 4 Bro. C. C. 223; 4 Madd. 275, 289; 4 Ves. 498.

34.—8. Where a fund, particular or residuary, is given upon a contingency, the intermediate interest undisposed of, that is to say, the intermediate interest between the testator's death, if there be no previous legatee for life, or, if there be, between the death of the previous taker and the happening of the contingency, will sink into the residue for the benefit of the next of kin or executor of the testator, if not bequeathed by him; but if not disposed of, for the benefit of his residuary legatee. 1 Bro. C. C. 57; 4 Bro. C. C. 114; Meriv. 384; 2 Atk. 329; Forr. 145; 2 Rop. Leg. 224.

35.—9. Where a legacy is given by immediate bequest whether such legacy be particular or residuary, and there is a condition to divest it upon the death of the legatee under twenty-one, or upon the happening of some other event, with a limitation over, and the legatee dies before twenty-one, or before such other event happens, which nevertheless does take place, yet as the legacy was payable at the end of a year after the testator's death, the legatee's representatives, and not the legatee over, will be entitled to the interest which accrued during the legatee's life, until the happening of the event which was to divest the legacy. 1 P. Wms. 500; 2 P. Wms. 504; Ambl. 448; 5 Ves. 335; Id. 522.

36.—10. Where a residue is given, so as to be vested but not payable at the end of the year from the testator's death, but upon the legatee's attaining twenty-one, or upon any other contingency, and with a bequest over divesting the legacy, upon the legatee's dying under age, or upon the happening of the contingency, then the legatee's representatives in the former case, and the legatee himself in the latter, shall be entitled to the interest that became due, during the legatee's life, or until the happening of the contingency. 2 P. Wms. 419; 1 Bro. C. C. 81; Id. 335; 3 Meriv. 335.

37.—11. Where a residue of personal estate is given, generally, to one for life with remainder over, and no mention is made by the testator respecting the interest, nor any intention to the contrary to be collected from the will, the rule appears to be now settled that the person taking for life is entitled to interest from the death of the testator, on such part of the residue, bearing interest, as is not necessary for the payment of debts. And it is immaterial whether the residue is only given generally, or directed to be laid out, with all convenient speed, in funds or securities, or to be laid out in lands. See 6 Ves. 520; 9 Ves. 549, 553; 2 Rop. Leg. 234; 9 Ves. 89.

38.—12. But where a residue is directed to be laid out in land, to be settled on one for life, with remainder over, and the testator directs the interest to accumulate in the meantime, until the money is laid out in lands, or otherwise invested on security, the accumulation shall cease at the end of one year from the testator's death, and from that period the tenant for life shall be entitled to the interest. 6 Ves. 520; 7 Ves. 95; 6 Ves. 528, Id. 529; 2 Sim. & Stu. 396.

39.—13. Where no time of payment is mentioned by the testator, annuities are considered as commencing from the death of the testator; and consequently the first payment will be due at the end of the year from that event; if, therefore, it be not made then, interest, in those cases wherein it is allowed at all, must be computed from that period. 2 Rop. Leg. 249; 5 Binn. 475. See 6 Mass. 37; 1 Hare & Wall. Sel. Dec. 356.

40.—§ 4. As to the *quantum* or *amount* of interest allowed. 1. During what time. 2. Simple interest. 3. Compound interest. 4. In what cases given beyond the penalty of a bond. 5. When foreign interest is allowed.

41. First. *During what time.* 1. In actions for money had and received, interest is allowed, in Massachusetts, from the time of serving the writ. 1 Mass. 436. On debts payable on demand, interest is payable only from the demand. Addis. 137. See 12 Mass. 4. The words "with interest for the same," bear interest from date. Addis. 323-4; 1 Stark. N. P. C. 452; Id. 507.

42.—2. The mere circumstance of war existing between two nations, is not a sufficient reason for abating interest on debts due by the subjects of one belligerent to another. 1 Peters' C. C. R. 524. But a prohibition of all intercourse with an enemy, during war, furnishes a sound reason for the abatement of interest until the return of peace. Id. See, on this subject, 2 Dall. 132; 2 Dall. 102; 4 Dall. 286; 1 Wash. 172; 1 Call, 194; 3 Wash. C. C. R. 396; 8 Serg. & Rawle, 103; Post. § 7.

43. Secondly. *Simple interest.* 1. Interest upon interest is not allowed except in special cases; 1 Eq. Cas. Ab. 287; Fonbl. Eq. b. 1, c. 2, § 4, note a; U. S. Dig. tit. Accounts, IV.; and the uniform current of decisions is against it, as being a hard, oppressive exaction, and tending to usury. 1 Johns. Ch. R. 14; Cam. & Norw. Rep. 361. By the civil law, interest could not be demanded beyond the principal sum, and payments exceeding that amount, were applied to the extinguishment of the principal. Ridley's View of the Civil, &c. Law, 84, Authentics, 9th Coll.

44. Thirdly. *Compound interest.* 1. Where a partner has overdrawn the partnership funds, and refuses, when called upon to account, to disclose the profits, recourse would be had to compound interest as a substitute for the profits he might reasonably be supposed to have made. 2 Johns. Ch. R. 213.

45.—2. When executors, administrators, or trustees, convert the trust money to their own use, or employ it in business or trade, they are chargeable with compound interest. 1 Johns. Ch. R. 620.

46.—3. In an action to recover the annual interest due on a promissory note, interest will be allowed on each year's interest until paid. 2 Mass. 568; 8 Mass. 455. See, as to charging compound interest, the following cases: 1 Johns. Ch. Rep. 550; Cam. & Norw. 361; 1 Binn. 165; 4 Yeates, 220; 1 Hen. & Munf. 4; 1 Vin. Abr. 457, tit. Interest, C; Com. Dig. Chancery, 3 S 3; 3 Hen. & Munf. 89; 1 Hare & Wall. Sel. Dec. 371. An infant's contract to pay interest on interest, after it has accrued, will be binding upon him, when it is for his benefit. 1 Eq. Cas. Ab. 286; 1 Atk. 489; 3 Atk. 613. Newl. Contr. 2.

47. Fourthly. *When given beyond the penalty of a bond.* 1. It is a general rule that the penalty of a bond limits the amount of the recovery. 2 T. R. 388. But, in some cases, the interest is recoverable beyond the amount of the penalty. The recovery depends on principles of law, and not on the arbitrary discretion of a jury. 3 Caines' Rep. 49.

48.—2. The exceptions are, where the bond is to account for moneys to be received; 2 T. R. 388; where the plaintiff is kept out of his money by writs of error; 2 Burr. 1094; 2 Evans' Poth. 101-2; or delayed by injunction; 1 Vern. 349; 16 Vin. Abr. 303; if the recovery of the debt be delayed by the obligor; 6 Ves. 92; 1 Vern. 349; Show. P. C. 15; if extraordinary emoluments are derived from holding the money; 2 Bro. P. C. 251; or the bond is taken only as a collateral security; 2 Bro. P. C. 333; or the action be on a judgment recovered on a bond. 1 East, R. 436. See, also, 4 Day's Cas. 30; 3 Caines' R. 49; 1 Taunt. 218; 1 Mass. 308; Com. Dig. Chancery, 3 S 2; Vin. Abr. Interest, E.

49.—3. But these exceptions do not obtain in the administration of the debtor's assets, where his other creditors might be injured by allowing the bond to be rated beyond the penalty. 5 Ves. 329; see Vin. Abr. Interest, C, pl. 5.

50. Fifthly. *When foreign interest is allowed.* 1. The rate of interest allowed by law where the contract is made, may, in general, be recovered; hence, where a note was given in China, payable eighteen months after date, without any stipulation respecting interest, the court allowed the Chinese interest of one per cent. per month from the expiration of the eighteen months. 1 Wash C. C. R. 253.

51.—2. If a citizen of another state advance money there, for the benefit of a citizen of the state of Massachusetts, which the latter is liable to reimburse, the former shall recover interest, at the rate established by the laws of the place where he lives. 12 Mass. 4. See, further, 1 Eq. Cas. Ab. 289; 1 P. Wms. 395; 2 Bro. C. C. 3; 14 Vin. Abr. 460, tit. Interest, F.

52.—§ 5. *How computed.* 1. In casting interest on notes, bonds, &c., upon which partial payments have been made, every payment is to be first applied to keep down the interest, but the interest is never allowed to form a part of the principal so as to carry interest. 17 Mass. R. 417; 1 Dall. 378.

53.—2. When a partial payment exceeds the amount of interest due when it is made, it is correct to compute the interest to the time of the first payment, add it to the principal, subtract the payment, cast interest on the remainder to the time of the second payment, add it to the remainder, and subtract the second payment, and in like manner from one payment to another, until the time of judgment, 1 Pick. 194; 4 Hen. & Munf. 431; 8 Serg. & Rawle, 458; 2 Wash. C. C. R. 167. See 3 Wash. C. C. R. 350; Id. 396.

54.—3. Where a partial payment is made *before* the debt is due, it cannot be apportioned, part to the debt and part to the interest. As, if there be a bond for one hundred dollars, payable in one year, and, at the expiration of six months, fifty dollars be paid in. This payment shall not be apportioned part to the principal and part to the interest, but at the end of the year, interest shall be charged on the whole sum, and the obligor shall receive credit for the interest of fifty dollars for six months. 1 Dall. 124.

55.—§ 6. *When interest will be barred.* 1. When the money due is tendered to the person entitled to it, and he refuses to receive it, the interest ceases. 3 Campb. 296. Vide 8 East, 168; 3 Binn. 295.

56.—2. Where the plaintiff was absent in foreign parts, beyond seas, evidence of that fact may be given in evidence to the jury on the plea of payment, in order to extinguish the interest during such absence 1 Call, 133. But see 9 Serg. & Rawle, 263.

57.—3. Whenever the law prohibits the

payment of the principal, interest, during the prohibition, is not demandable. 2 Dall. 102; 1 Peters' C. C. R. 524. See, also, 2 Dall. 132; 4 Dall. 286.

58.—4. If the plaintiff has accepted the principal, he cannot recover the interest in a separate action. 1 Esp. N. P. C. 110; 3 Johns. 229. See 14 Wend. 116.

59.—§ 7. *Rate of interest allowed by law in the different states.*

Alabama. Eight per centum per annum is allowed. Notes not exceeding one dollar bear interest at the rate of one hundred per centum per annum. Some of the bank charters prohibit certain banks from charging more than six per cent. upon bills of exchange, and notes negotiable at the bank, not having more than six months to run; and over six and under nine, not more than seven per cent.; and over nine months, to charge not more than eight per cent. Aikin's Dig. 236.

60. *Arkansas.* Six per centum per annum is the legal rate of interest; but the parties may agree in writing for the payment of interest not exceeding ten per centum per annum, on money due and to become due on any contract, whether under seal or not. Rev. St. c. 80, s. 1, 2. Contracts where a greater amount is reserved are declared to be void. Id. s. 7. But this provision will not affect an innocent endorsee for a valuable consideration. Id. s. 8.

61. *Connecticut.* Six per centum is the amount allowed by law.

62. *Delaware.* The legal amount of interest allowed in this state is at the rate of six per centum per annum. Laws of Del. 314.

63. *Georgia.* Eight per centum per annum interest is allowed on all liquidated demands. 1 Laws of Geo. 270; 4 Id. 488; Prince's Dig. 294, 295.

64. *Illinois.* Six per centum per annum is the legal interest allowed when there is no contract, but by agreement the parties may fix a greater rate. 3 Griff. L. Reg. 423.

65. *Indiana.* Six per centum per annum is the rate fixed by law, except in Union county. On the following funds loaned out by the state, namely, Sinking, Surplus, Revenue, Saline, and College funds, seven per cent.; on the Common School Fund, eight per cent. Act of January 31, 1842.

66. *Kentucky.* Six per centum per annum is allowed by law. There is no provision in favor of any kind of loan. See Sessions Acts, 1818, p. 707.

67. *Louisiana.* The Civil Code provides, art. 2895, as follows: Interest is either legal or conventional. Legal interest is fixed at the following rates, to wit: at five per cent. on all sums which are the object of a judicial demand, whence this is called judicial interest; and sums discounted by banks, at the rate established by their charters. The amount of conventional interest cannot exceed ten per cent. The same must be fixed in writing, and the testimonial proof of it is not admitted. See, also, art. 1930 to 1939.

68. *Maine.* Six per centum per annum is the legal interest, and any contract for more is voidable as to the excess, except in case of letting cattle, and other usages of a like nature, in practice among farmers, or maritime contracts among merchants, as bottomry, insurance, or course of exchange, as has been heretofore practiced. Rev. St. 4, c. 69, §§ 1, 4.

69. *Maryland.* Six per centum per annum, is the amount limited by law, in all cases.

70. *Massachusetts.* The interest of money shall continue to be at the rate of six dollars, and no more, upon one hundred dollars for a year; and at the same rate for a greater or less sum, and for a longer or shorter time. Rev. Stat. c. 35, s. 1.

71. *Michigan.* Seven per centum is the legal rate of interest; but on stipulation in writing, interest is allowed to any amount not exceeding ten per cent. on loans of money, but only on such loans. Rev. St. 160, 161.

72. *Mississippi.* The legal interest is six per centum; but on all bonds, notes, or contracts in writing, signed by the debtor for the *bona fide* loan of money, expressing therein the rate of interest fairly agreed on between the parties for the use of money so loaned, eight per cent. interest is allowed. Laws of 1842.

73. *Missouri.* When no contract is made as to interest, six per centum per annum is allowed. But the parties may agree to pay any higher rate, not exceeding ten per cent. Rev. Code, § 1, p. 333.

74. *New Hampshire.* No person shall take interest for the loan of money, wares, or merchandise, or any other personal estate whatsoever, above the value of six pounds for the use or forbearance of one hundred pounds for a year, and after that rate for a

greater or lesser sum, or for a longer or shorter time. Act of February 12, 1791, s. 1. Provided, that nothing in this act shall extend to the letting of cattle, or other usages of a like nature, in practice among farmers, or to maritime contracts among merchants, as bottomry, insurance, or course of exchange, as hath been heretofore used. Id. s. 2.

75. *New Jersey.* Six per centum per annum is the interest allowed by law for the loan of money, without any exception. Statute of December 5, 1823, Harr. Comp. 45.

76. *New York.* The rate is fixed at seven per centum per annum. Rev. Stat. part 2, c. 4, t. 3, s. 1. Moneyed institutions, subject to the safety-fund act, are entitled to receive the legal interest established, or which may thereafter be established by the laws of this state, on all loans made by them, or notes, or bills, by them severally discounted or received in the ordinary course of business; but on all notes or bills by them discounted or received in the ordinary course of business, which shall be matured in sixty-three days from the time of such discount, the said moneyed corporations shall not take or receive more than at the rate of six per centum per annum in advance. 2 Rev. Stat. p. 612.

77. *North Carolina.* Six per centum per annum is the interest allowed by law. The banks are allowed to take the interest off at the time of making a discount.

78. *Ohio.* The legal rate of interest on all contracts, judgments or decrees in chancery, is six per centum per annum, and no more. 29 Ohio Stat. 451; Swan's Coll. Laws, 465. A contract to pay a higher rate is good for principal and interest, and void for the excess. Banks are bound to pay twelve per cent. interest on all their notes during a suspension of specie payment. 37 Acts 30, Act of February 25, 1839, Swan's Coll. 129.

79. *Pennsylvania.* Interest is allowed at the rate of six per centum per annum for the loan or use of money or other commodities. Act of March 2, 1723. And lawful interest is allowed on judgments. Act of 1700, 1 Smith's L. of Penn. 12. See 6 Watts, 53; 12 S. & R. 47; 13 S. & R. 221; 4 Whart. 221; 6 Binn. 435; 1 Dall. 378; 1 Dall. 407; 2 Dall. 92; 1 S. & R. 176; 1 Binn. 488; 2 Pet. 538; 8 Wheat. 355.

80. *Rhode Island.* Six per centum is allowed for interest on loans of money. 3 Griff. Law Reg. 116.

81. *South Carolina.* Seven per centum per annum, or at that rate, is allowed for interest. 4 Cooper's Stat. of S. C. 364. When more is reserved, the amount lent and interest may be recovered. 6 Id. 409.

82. *Tennessee.* The interest allowed by law is six per centum per annum. When more is charged it is not recoverable, but the principal and legal interest may be recovered. Act of 1835, c. 50, Car. & Nich. Comp. 406, 407.

83. *Vermont.* Six per centum per annum is the legal interest. If more be charged and paid, it may be recovered back in an action of assumpsit. But these provisions do not extend "to the letting of cattle and other usages of a like nature among farmers, or maritime contracts, bottomry or course of exchange, as has been customary." Rev. St. c. 72, ss. 3, 4, 5.

84. *Virginia.* Interest is allowed at the rate of six per centum per annum. Act of Nov. 22 1796, 1 Rev. Code ch. 209. Vide 1 Hare & Wall. Sel. Dec. 344, 373.

INTEREST, MARITIME. By maritime interest is understood the profit of money lent on bottomry or respondentia, which is allowed to be greater than simple interest because the capital of the lender is put in jeopardy. There is no limit by law as to the amount which may be charged for maritime interest. It is fixed generally by the agreement of the parties.

2. The French writers employ a variety of terms in order to distinguish it according to the nature of the case. They call it *interest*, when it is stipulated to be paid by the month, or at other stated periods. It is a *premium*, when a gross sum is to be paid at the end of the voyage, and here the risk is the principal object they have in view. When the sum is a per centage on the money lent, they call it *exchange*, considering it in the light of money lent at one place to be returned in another, with a difference in amount between the sum borrowed and that which is paid, arising from the difference of time and place. When they intend to combine these various shades into one general denomination, they make use of the term *maritime profit*, to convey their meaning. Hall on Mar. Loans, 56, n.

INTERIM. In the mean time; in the meanwhile. For example, one appointed between the time that a person is made bankrupt, to act in the place of the assignee, until the assignee shall be appointed, is an assignee ad interim. 2 Bell's Com. 355.

INTERLINEATION, *contracts, evidence.* Writing between two lines.

2. Interlineations are made either *before* or *after* the execution of an instrument. Those made before should be noted previously to its execution; those made after are made either by the party in whose favor they are, or by strangers.

3. When made by the party himself, whether the interlineation be material or immaterial, they render the deed void; 1 Gall. Rep. 71; unless made with the consent of the opposite party. Vide 11 Co. 27 a; 9 Mass. Rep. 307; 15 Johns. R. 293; 1 Dall. R. 57; 1 Halst. R. 215; but see 1 Pet. C. C. R. 364; 5 Har. & John. 41; 2 L. R. 290; 2 Ch. R. 410; 4 Bing. R. 123; Fitzg. 207, 223; Cov. on Conv. Ev. 22; 2 Barr. 191.

4. When the interlineation is made by a stranger, if it be immaterial, it will not vitiate the instrument, but if it be material, it will in general avoid it. Vide Cruise, Dig. tit. 32, c. 26, s. 8; Com. Dig. Fait, F 1.

5. The ancient rule, which is still said to be in force, is, that an alteration shall be presumed to have been made *before* the execution of the instrument. Vin. Ab. Evidence, Q, a 2; Id. Faits, U; 1 Swift's Syst. 310; 6 Wheat. R. 481; 1 Halst. 215. But other cases hold the presumption to be that a material interlineation was made *after* the execution of an instrument, unless the contrary be proved. 1 Dall. 67. This doctrine corresponds nearly with the rules of the canon law on this subject. The canonists have examined it with care. Vide 18 Pick. R. 172; Toull. Dr. Civ. Fr. liv. 3, t. 3, c. 4, n. 115, and article *Erasure.*

INTERLOCUTORY. This word is applied to signify something which is done between the commencement and the end of a suit or action which decides some point or matter, which however is not a final decision of the matter in issue; as, interlocutory judgments, or decrees or orders. Vide *Judgment, interlocutory.*

INTERLOPERS. Persons who interrupt the trade of a company of merchants, by pursuing the same business with them in the same place, without lawful authority.

INTERNATIONAL. That which pertains to intercourse between nations. International law is that which regulates the intercourse between, or the relative rights of nations.

INTERNUNCIO. A minister of a second order, charged with the affairs of the court of Rome, where that court has no nuncio under that title.

INTERPELATION, *civil law.* The act by which, in consequence of an agreement, the party bound declares that he will not be bound beyond a certain time. Wolff, Inst. Nat. § 752.

2. In the case of a lease from year to year, or to continue as long as both parties please, a notice given by one of them to the other of a determination to put an end to the contract, would bear the name of interpelation.

INTERPLEADER, *practice.* Interpleaders may be had at law and in equity.

2. An interpleader at law is a proceeding in the action of detinue, by which the defendant states the fact that the thing sued for is in his hands, and that it is claimed by a third person, and that whether such person or the plaintiff is entitled to it, is unknown to the defendant, and thereupon the defendant prays, that a process of garnishment may be issued to compel such third person, so claiming, to become defendant in his stead. 3 Reeves, Hist. of the Eng. Law, ch. 23; Mitford, Eq. Pl. by Jeremy, 141; Story, Eq. Jur. §§ 800, 801, 802. Interpleader is allowed to avoid inconvenience; for two parties claiming adversely to each other, cannot be entitled to the same thing. Bro. Abr. Interpleader, 4 Hence the rule which requires the defendant to allege that different parties demand the same thing. Id. pl. 22.

3. If two persons sue the same person in detinue for the thing, and both actions are depending in the same court at the same time, the defendant may plead that fact, produce the thing (*e. g.* a deed or charter) in court, and aver his readiness to deliver it to either as the court shall adjudge; and thereupon pray that they may interplead. In such a case it has been settled that the plaintiff whose writ bears the earliest teste has the right to begin the interpleading, and the other will be compelled to answer. Bro. Abr. Interpl. 2.

4. In equity, interpleaders are common Vide *Bill of Interpleader*, and 8 Vin. Ab. 419; Doct. Pl. 247; 3 Bl. Com. 448; Com. Dig. Chancery, 3 T; 2 Story, Eq. Jur. § 800.

INTERPRETATION. The explication

of a law, agreement, will, or other instrument, which appears obscure or ambiguous.

2. The object of interpretation is to find out or collect the intention of the maker of the instrument, either from his own words, or from other conjectures, or both. It may then be divided into three sorts, according to the different means it makes use of for obtaining its end.

3. These three sorts of interpretations are either literal, rational, or mixed. When we collect the intention of the writer from his words only, as they lie before us, this is a *literal* interpretation. When his words do not express his intention perfectly, but either exceed it, or fall short of it, so that we are to collect it from probable or rational conjectures only, this is *rational* interpretation; and when his words, though they do express his intention, when rightly understood, are in themselves of doubtful meaning, and we are forced to have recourse to like conjectures to find out in what sense he used them; this sort of interpretation is *mixed;* it is partly literal, and partly rational.

4. According to the civilians there are three sorts of interpretations, the authentic, the usual, and the doctrinal.

5.—1. The *authentic* interpretation is that which refers to the legislator himself, in order to fix the sense of the law.

6.—2. When the judge interprets the law so as to accord with prior decisions, the interpretation is called *usual.*

7.—3. It is *doctrinal* when it is made agreeably to rules of science. The commentaries of learned lawyers in this case furnish the greatest assistance. This last kind of interpretation is itself divided into three distinct classes. Doctrinal interpretation is extensive, restrictive, or declaratory. 1st. It is *extensive* whenever the reason of the law has a more enlarged sense than its terms, and it is consequently applied to a case which had not been explained. 2d. On the contrary, it is *restrictive* when the expressions of the law have a greater latitude than its reasons, so that by a restricted interpretation, an exception is made in a case which the law does not seem to have embraced. 3d. When the reason of the law and the terms in which it is conceived agree, and it is only necessary to explain them to have the sense complete, the interpretation is *declaratory.*

8. The term interpretation is used by foreign jurists in nearly the same sense that we use the word construction. (q. v.)

9. Pothier, in his excellent treatise on Obligations, lays down the following rules for the interpretation of contracts:

10.—1. We ought to examine what was the common intention of the contracting parties rather than the grammatical sense of the terms.

11.—2. When a clause is capable of two significations, it should be understood in that which will have some operation rather than that in which it will have none.

12.—3. Where the terms of a contract are capable of two significations, we ought to understand them in the sense which is most agreeable to the nature of the contract.

13.—4. Any thing, which may appear ambiguous in the terms of a contract, may be explained by the common use of those terms in the country where it is made.

14.—5. Usage is of so much authority in the interpretation of agreements, that a contract is understood to contain the customary clauses although they are not expressed; in contractibus tacite veniunt ea quæ sunt moris et consuetudinis.

15.—6. We ought to interpret one clause by the others contained in the same act, whether they precede or follow it.

16.—7. In case of doubt, a clause ought to be interpreted against the person who stipulates anything, and in discharge of the person who contracts the obligation.

17.—8. However general the terms may be in which an agreement is conceived, it only comprises those things respecting which it appears that the contracting parties proposed to contract, and not others which they never thought of.

18.—9. When the object of the agreement is to include universally everything of a given nature, (une universalité de choses) the general description will comprise all particular articles, although they may not have been in the knowledge of the parties. We may state, as an example of this rule, an engagement which I make with you to abandon my share in a succession for a certain sum. This agreement includes everything which makes part of the succession, whether known or not; our intention was to contract for the whole. Therefore it is decided that I cannot object to the agreement, under pretence that considerable property has been found to belong to the succession of which we had not any knowledge.

19.—10. When a case is expressed in a contract on account of any doubt which there may be whether the engagement resulting from the contract would extend to such case, the parties are not thereby understood to restrain the extent which the engagement has of right, in respect to all cases not expressed.

20.—11. In contracts as well as in testaments, a clause conceived in the plural may be frequently distributed into several particular classes.

21.—12. That which is at the end of a phrase commonly refers to the whole phrase, and not only to that which immediately precedes it, provided it agrees in gender and number with the whole phrase.

22. For instance, if in the contract for sale of a farm, it is said to be sold with all the corn, small grain, fruits and wine that have been *got this year*, the terms, that have been *got this year*, refer to the whole phrase, and not to the wine only, and consequently the old corn is not less excepted than the old wine; it would be otherwise if it had been said, all the wine that has been got this year, for the expression is in the singular, and only refers to the wine and not to the rest of the phrase, with which it does not agree in number. Vide 1 Bouv. Inst. n. 86, et seq.

INTERPRETER. One employed to make a translation. (q. v.)

2. An interpreter should be sworn before he translates the testimony of a witness. 4 Mass. 81; 5 Mass. 219; 2 Caines' Rep. 155.

3. A person employed between an attorney and client to act as interpreter, is considered merely as the organ between them, and is not bound to testify as to what he has acquired in those confidential communications. 1 Pet. C. C. R. 356; 4 Munf. R. 273; 3 Wend. R. 337. Vide *Confidential Communications.*

INTERREGNUM, *polit. law.* In an established government, the period which elapses between the death of a sovereign and the election of another is called interregnum. It is also understood for the vacancy created in the executive power, and for any vacancy which occurs when there is no government.

INTERROGATOIRE, *French law.* An act, or instrument, which contains the interrogatories made by the judge to the person accused, on the facts which are the object of the accusation, and the answers of the accused. Poth. Proc. Crim. s. 4, art. 2, § 1. Vide *Information.*

INTERROGATORIES. Material and pertinent questions, in writing, to necessary points, not confessed, exhibited for the examination of witnesses or persons who are to give testimony in the cause.

2. They are either original and direct on the part of him who produces the witnesses, or cross and counter, on behalf of the adverse party, to examine witnesses produced on the other side. Either party, plaintiff or defendant, may exhibit original or cross interrogatories.

3. The form which interrogatories assume, is as various as the minds of the persons who propound them. They should be as distinct as possible, and capable of a definite answer; and they should leave no loop-holes for evasion to an unwilling witness. Care must be observed to put no leading questions in original interrogatories, for these always lead to inconvenience; and for scandal or impertinence, interrogatories will, under certain circumstances, be suppressed. Vide Will. on Interrogatories, *passim;* Gresl. Eq. Ev. pt. 1, c. 3, s. 1; Vin. Ab. h. t.; Hind's Pr. 317; 4 Bouv. Inst. n. 4419, et seq.

INTERRUPTION. The effect of some act or circumstance which stops the course of a prescription or act of limitations.

2. Interruption of the use of a thing is natural or civil. *Natural* interruption is an interruption in fact, which takes place whenever by some act we cease truly to possess what we formerly possessed. Vide 4 Mason's Rep. 404; 2 Y. & Jarv. 285. A right is not interrupted by mere trespassers, if the trespassers were unknown; but if they were known, and the trespasses frequent, and no legal proceeding instituted in consequence of them, they then become *legitimæ interruptiones*, of which Bracton speaks, and are converted into adverse assertions of right, and if not promptly and effectually litigated, they defeat the claim of rightful prescription; and mere threats of action for the trespasses, without following them up, will have no effect to preserve the right. Knapp, R. 70, 71; 3 Bar. & Ad. 863; 2 Saund. 175, n. e; 1 Camp. 260; 4 Camp. 16; 5 Taunt. 125; 11 East, 376.

3. *Civil* interruption is that which takes place by some judicial act, as the commencement of a suit to recover the thing in dispute, which gives notice to the possessor

that the thing which he possesses does not belong to him. When the title has once been gained by prescription, it will not be lost by interruption of it for ten or twenty years. 1 Inst. 113 b. A simple acknowledgment of a debt by the debtor, is a sufficient interruption to prevent the statute from running. Indeed, whenever an agreement, express or implied, takes place between the creditor and the debtor, between the possessor and the owner, which admits the indebtedness or the right to the thing in dispute, it is considered a civil conventional interruption which prevents the statute or the right of prescription from running. Vide 3 Burge on the Confl. of Laws, 63.

INTERVAL. A space of time between two periods.

2. When a person is unable to perform an act at any two given periods, but in the interval he has performed such act, as when a man is found to be insane in the months of January and March, and he enters into a contract or makes a will in the interval, in February, he will be presumed to have been insane at that time; and the onus will lie to show his sanity, on the person who affirms such act. See *Lucid interval*.

INTERVENTION, *civil law*. The act by which a third party becomes a party in a suit pending between other persons.

2. The intervention is made either to be joined to the plaintiff, and to claim the same thing he does, or some other thing connected with it; or, to join the defendant, and with him to oppose the claim of the plaintiff, which it is his interest to defeat. Poth. Procéd. Civ. 1ere part. ch. 2, s. 6, § 3. In the English ecclesiastical courts, the same term is used in the same sense.

3. When a third person, not originally a party to the suit or proceeding, but claiming an interest in the subject-matter in dispute, may, in order the better to protect such interest, interpose his claim, which proceeding is termed intervention. 2 Chit. Pr. 492; 3 Chit. Com. Law, 633; 2 Hagg. Cons. R. 137; 3 Phillim. R. 586; 1 Addams, R. 5; Ought. tit. 14; 4 Hagg. Eccl. R. 67; Dunl. Ad. Pr. 74. The intervener may come in at any stage of the cause, and even after judgment, if an appeal can be allowed on such judgment. 2 Hagg. Cons. R. 137; 1 Eng. Eccl. R. 480; 2 Eng. Eccl. R. 13.

INTESTACY. The state or condition of dying without a will.

INTESTABLE. One who cannot lawfully make a testament.

2. An infant, an insane person, or one civilly dead, cannot make a will, for want of capacity or understanding; a married woman cannot make such a will without some special authority, because she is under the power of her husband. They are all intestable.

INTESTATE. One who, having lawful power to make a will, has made none, or one which is defective in form. In that case, he is said to die intestate, and his estate descends to his heir at law. See *Testate*.

2. This term comes from the Latin *intestatus*. Formerly, it was used in France indiscriminately with *de-confess;* that is, without confession. It was regarded as a crime, on account of the omission of the deceased person to give something to the church, and was punished by privation of burial in consecrated ground. This omission, according to Fournel, Hist. des Avocats, vol. 1, p. 116, could be repaired by making an ampliative testament in the name of the deceased. See Vely, tom. 6, page 145; Henrion De Pansey, Authorité Judiciare, 129 and note. Also, 3 Mod. Rep. 59, 60, for the Law of Intestacy in England.

INTIMATION, *civil law*. The name of any judicial act by which a notice of a legal proceeding is given to some one; but it is more usually understood to mean the notice or summons which an appellant causes to be given to the opposite party, that the sentence will be reviewed by the superior judge.

2. In the Scotch law, it is an instrument of writing, made under the hand of a notary, and notified to a party, to inform him of a right which a third person had acquired; for example, when a creditor assigns a claim against his debtor, the assignee or cedent must give an intimation of this to the debtor, who, till then, is justified in making payment to the original creditor. Kames' Eq. B. 1, p. 1, s. 1.

INTRODUCTION. That part of a writing in which are detailed those facts which elucidate the subject. In chancery pleading, the *introduction* is that part of a bill which contains the names and description of the persons exhibiting the bill. In this part of the bill are also given the places of abode, title, or office, or business, and the character in which they sue, if it is in *autre droit*, and such other description as is required to show the jurisdiction of the court. 4 Bouv. Inst. n. 4156.

INTROMISSION, *Scotch law.* The assuming possession of property belonging to another, either on legal grounds, or without any authority; in the latter case, it is called *vicious* intromission. Bell's S. L. Dict. h. t.

INTRONISATION, *French eccl. law.* The installation of a bishop in his episcopal see. Clef des Lois Rom. h. t.; André.

INTRUDER. One who, on the death of the ancestor, enters on the land, unlawfully, before the heir can enter.

INTRUSION, *estates, torts.* When an ancestor dies seised of an estate of inheritance expectant upon an estate for life, and then the tenant dies, and between his death and the entry of the heir, a stranger unlawfully enters upon the estate, this is called an intrusion. It differs from an abatement, for the latter is an entry into lands void by the death of a tenant in fee, and an intrusion, as already stated, is an entry into land void by the death of a tenant for years. F. N. B. 203; 3 Bl. Com. 169; Archb. Civ. Pl. 12; Dane's Ab. Index, h. t.

INTRUSION, *remedies.* The name of a writ, brought by the owner of a fee simple, &c., against an intruder. New Nat. Br. 453.

INUNDATION. The overflow of waters by coming out of their bed.

2. Inundations may arise from three causes; from public necessity, as in defence of a place it may be necessary to dam the current of a stream, which will cause an inundation to the upper lands; they may be occasioned by an invincible force, as by the accidental fall of a rock in the stream; or they may result from the erections of works on the stream. In the first case, the injury caused by the inundation is to be compensated as other injuries done in war; in the second, as there was no fault of any one, the loss is to be borne by the unfortunate owner of the estate; in the last, when the riparian proprietor is injured by such works as alter the level of the water where it enters or where it leaves the property on which they are erected, the person injured may recover damages for the injury thus caused to his property by the inundation. 9 Co. 59; 4 Day's R. 244; 17 Serg. & Rawle, 383; 3 Mason's R. 172; 7 Pick. R. 198; 7 Cowen, R. 266; 1 B. & Ald. 258; 1 Rawle's R. 218; 5 N. H. Rep. 232; 9 Mass. R. 316; 4 Mason's R. 400; 1 Sim. & Stu. 203; 1 Coxe's R. 460. Vide Schult. Aq. R. 122; Ang. W. C. 101; 5 Ohio, R. 322, 421; and art. *Dam.*

TO INURE. To take effect; as, the pardon inures.

INVALID. In a physical sense, it is that which is wanting force; in a figurative sense, it signifies that which has no effect.

INVASION. The entry of a country by a public enemy, making war.

2. The Constitution of the United States, art. 1, s. 8, gives power to congress "to provide for calling the militia to execute the laws of the Union, suppress insurrections, and repel invasions." Vide *Insurrection.*

INVENTION. A contrivance; a discovery. It is in this sense this word is used in the patent laws of the United States. 17 Pet. 228; S. C. 1 How. U. S. 202. It signifies not something which has been found ready made, but something which, in consequence of art or accident, has been formed; for the invention must relate to some new or useful art, machine, manufacture, or composition of matter, or some new and useful improvement on any art, machine, manufacture or composition of matter, not before known or used by others. Act of July 4, 1836, 4 Sharsw. continuation of Story's L. U. S. 2506; 1 Mason, R. 302; 4 Wash. C. C. R. 9. Vide *Patent.* By invention, the civilians understand the finding of some things which had not been lost; they must either have been abandoned, or they must never have belonged to any one, as a pearl found on the sea shore. Leç. Elem. § 350.

INVENTIONES. This word is used in some ancient English charters to signify *treasure-trove.*

INVENTOR. One who invents or finds out something.

2. The patent laws of the United States authorize a patent to be issued to the original inventor; if the invention is suggested by another, he is not the inventor within the meaning of those laws; but in that case the suggestion must be of the specific process or machine; for a general theoretical suggestion, as that steam might be applied to the navigation of the air or water, without pointing out by what specific process or machine that could be accomplished, would not be such a suggestion as to deprive the person to whom it had been made from being considered as the inventor. Dav. Pat. Cas. 429; 1 C. & P. 558; 1 Russ. & M. 187; 4 Taunt. 770. But see 1 M. G. & S. 551; 3 Man. Gr. & Sc. 97.

3. The applicant for a patent must be both the *first* and *original* inventor. 4 Law Report. 342.

INVENTORY. A list, schedule, or enumeration in writing, containing, article by article, the goods and chattels, rights and credits, and, in some cases, the lands and tenements, of a person or persons. In its most common acceptation, an inventory is a conservatory act, which is made to ascertain the situation of an intestate's estate, the estate of an insolvent, and the like, for the purpose of securing it to those entitled to it.

2. When the inventory is made of goods and estates assigned or conveyed in trust, it must include all the property conveyed.

3. In case of intestate estates, it is required to contain only the personal property, or that to which the administrator is entitled. The claims due to the estate ought to be separated; those which are desperate or bad ought to be so returned. The articles ought to be set down separately, as already mentioned, and separately valued.

4. The inventory is to be made in the presence of at least two of the creditors of the deceased, or legatees or next of kin, and, in their default and absence, of two honest persons. The appraisers must sign it, and make oath or affirmation that the appraisement is just to the best of their knowledge. Vide, generally, 14 Vin. Ab. 465; Bac. Ab. Executors, &c., E 11; 4 Com. Dig. 714; Ayliffe's Pand. 414; Ayliffe's Parerg. 305; Com. Dig. Administration, B 7; 3 Burr. 1922; 2 Addams' Rep. 319; S. C. 2 Eccles. R. 322; Lovel. on Wills, 38; 2 Bl. Com. 514; 8 Serg. & Rawle, 128; Godolph. 150, and the article *Benefit of Inventory*.

TO INVEST, *contracts*. To lay out money in such a manner that it may bring a revenue; as, to invest money in houses or stocks; to give possession.

2. This word, which occurs frequently in the canon law, comes from the Latin word *investire*, which signifies to clothe or adorn; and is used, in that system of jurisprudence, synonymously with enfeoff. Both words signify to put one into the possession of, or to invest with a fief, upon his taking the oath of fealty or fidelity to the prince or superior lord.

INVESTITURE, *estates*. The act of giving possession of lands by actual seisin. When livery of seisin was made to a person, by the common law he was invested with the whole fee; this, the foreign feudists and sometimes our own law writers call investiture, but generally speaking, it is termed by the common law writers, the seisin of the fee. 2 Bl. Com. 209, 313; Fearne on Rem. 223, n. (z).

2. By the canon law investiture was made *per baculum et annulum*, by the ring and crosier, which were regarded as symbols of the episcopal jurisdiction. Ecclesiastical and secular fiefs were governed by the same rule in this respect that previously to investiture, neither a bishop, abbey or lay lord could take possession of a fief conferred upon them previously to investiture by the prince.

3. Pope Gregory VI. first disputed the right of sovereigns to give investiture of ecclesiastical fiefs, A. D. 1045, but Pope Gregory VII. carried on the dispute with much more vigor, A. D. 1073. He excommunicated the emperor, Henry IV. The Popes Victor III., Urban II. and Paul II., continued the contest. This dispute, it is said, cost Christendom sixty-three battles, and the lives of many millions of men. De Pradt.

INVIOLABILITY. That which is not to be violated. The persons of ambassadors are inviolable. See *Ambassador*.

INVITO DOMINO, *crim. law*. Without the consent of the owner.

2. In order to constitute larceny, the property stolen must be taken *invito domino;* this is the very essence of the crime. Cases of considerable difficulty arise when the owner has, for the purpose of detecting thieves, by himself or his agents, delivered the property taken, as to whether they are larcenies or not; the distinction seems to be this, that when the owner procures the property to be taken, it is not larceny; and when he merely leaves it in the power of the defendant to execute his original purpose of taking it, in the latter case it will be considered as taken *invito domino*. 2 Bailey's Rep. 569; Fost. 123; 2 Russ. on Cr. 66, 105; 2 Leach, 913; 2 East, P. C. 666; Bac. Ab. Felony, C; Alis. Prin. 273 2 Bos. & Pull. 508; 1 Carr. & Marsh. 217 article *Taking*.

INVOICE, *commerce*. An account of goods or merchandise sent by merchants to their correspondents at home or abroad, in which the marks of each package, with other particulars, are set forth. Marsh. Ins. 408; Dane's Ab. Index, h. An invoice ought to contain a detailed statement, which should indicate the nature, quantity, quality, and price of the things sold, deposited, &c. 1 Pardess. Dr. Com. n. 248. Vide *Bill of Lading;* and 2 Wash. C. C. R. 113; Id. 155.

INVOICE BOOK, *commerce, accounts.* One in which invoices are copied.

INVOLUNTARY. An involuntary act is that which is performed with constraint, (q. v.) or with repugnance, or without the will to do it. An action is involuntary then, which is performed under duress. Wolff, § 5. Vide *Duress.*

IOWA. The name of one of the new states of the United States of America.

2. This state was admitted into the Union by the act of congress, approved the 3d day of March, 1845.

3. The powers of the government are divided into three separate departments, the legislative, the executive, and judicial; and no person charged with the exercise of power properly belonging to one of these departments, shall exercise any function appertaining to either of the others, except in cases provided for in the constitution.

4.—I. The legislative authority of this state is vested in a senate and house of representatives, which are designated the general assembly of the state of Iowa.

5.—§ 1. Of the *senate.* This will be considered with reference, 1. To the qualifications of the electors. 2. The qualifications of the members. 3. The length of time for which they are elected. 4. The time of their election. 5. The number of senators.

6.—1. Every white male citizen of the United States, of the age of twenty-one years, who shall have been a resident of the state six months next preceding the election, and the county in which he claims his vote twenty days, shall be entitled to vote at all elections which are now or hereafter may be authorized by law. But with this exception, that no person in the military, naval, or marine service of the United States, shall be considered a resident of this state, by being stationed in any garrison, barrack, military or naval place or station within this state. And no idiot or insane person, or person convicted of any infamous crime, shall be entitled to the privilege of an elector. Art. 3.

7.—2. Senators must be twenty-five years of age, be free white male citizens of the United States, and have been inhabitants of the state or territory one year next preceding their election; and at the time of their elections have an actual residence of thirty days in the county or district they may be chosen to represent. Art. 4, s. 5.

8.—3. The senators are elected for four years. They are so classed that one-half are renewed every two years. Art. 4, s. 5.

9.—4. They are chosen every second year, on the first Monday in August. Art. 4, s. 3.

10.—5. The number of senators is not less than one-third, nor more than one-half the representative body. Art. 4, s. 6.

11.—§ 2. Of the *house of representatives.* This will be considered in the same order which has been observed with regard to the senate.

12.—1. The electors qualified to vote for senators are electors of members of the house of representatives.

13.—2. No person shall be a member of the house of representatives who shall not have attained the age of twenty-one years; be a free male white citizen of the United States, and have been an inhabitant of the state or territory one year next preceding his election; and at the time of his election have an actual residence of thirty days in the county or district he may be chosen to represent. Art. 4, s. 4.

14.—3. Members of the house of representatives are chosen for two years. Art 4, s. 3.

15.—4. They are elected at the same time that senators are elected.

16.—5. The number of representatives is not limited.

17. The two houses have respectively the following powers. Each house has power—

To choose its own officers, and judge of the qualification of its members.

To sit upon its adjournments; keep a journal of its proceedings and publish the same; punish members for disorderly behaviour, and, with the consent of two-thirds, expel a member, but not a second time for the same offence; and shall have all other power necessary for a branch of the general assembly of a free and independent state.

18. The house of representatives has the power of impeachment, and the senate is a court for the trial of persons impeached.

19.—II. The supreme executive power

is vested in a chief magistrate, who is called the governor of the state of Iowa. Art. 5, s. 1.

20. The governor shall be elected by the qualified electors, at the time and place of voting for members of the general assembly, and hold his office for four years from the time of his installation, and until his successor shall be duly qualified. Art. 5, s. 2.

21. No person shall be eligible to the office of governor, who is not a citizen of the United States, a resident of the state two years next preceding his election, and attained the age of thirty-five years at the time of holding said election. Art. 5, s. 3.

22. Various powers are conferred on the governor; among others, he shall be commander-in-chief of the militia, army, and navy of the state; transact executive business with the officers of the government; see that the laws are faithfully executed; fill vacancies by granting temporary commissions; on extraordinary occasions convene the general assembly by proclamation; communicate by message with the general assembly at every session; adjourn the two houses when they cannot agree upon the time of an adjournment; may grant reprieves and pardons, and commute punishments after conviction, except in cases of impeachment; shall be keeper of the great seal; and sign all commissions. He is also invested with the veto power.

23. When there is a vacancy in the office of governor, or in case of his impeachment, the duties of his office shall devolve on the secretary of state; on his default, on the president of the senate; and if the president cannot act, on the speaker of the house of representatives.

24.—III. The judicial power shall be vested in a supreme court, district courts, and such inferior courts as the general assembly may, from time to time, establish. Art. 6, s. 1.

25.—§ 1. The supreme court shall consist of a chief justice and two associates, two of whom shall be a quorum to hold court. Art. 6, s. 2.

26. The judges of the supreme court shall be elected by joint ballot of both branches of the general assembly, and shall hold their courts at such time and place as the general assembly may direct, and hold their office for six years, and until their successors are elected and qualified, and shall be ineligible to any other office during the term for which they may be elected Art. 6, s. 3.

27. The supreme court shall have appellate jurisdiction only in all cases in chancery, and shall constitute a court for the correction of errors at law, under such restrictions as the general assembly may by law prescribe. It shall have power to issue all writs and process necessary to do justice to parties, and exercise a supervisory control over all inferior judicial tribunals, and the judges of the supreme court shall be conservators of the peace throughout the state. Art. 6, s. 3.

28.—§ 2. The district court shall consist of a judge who shall be elected by the qualified electors of the district in which he resides, at the township election, and hold his office for the term of five years, and until his successor is duly elected and qualified, and shall be ineligible to any other office during the term for which he may be elected.

29. The district court shall be a court of law and equity, and have jurisdiction in all civil and criminal matters arising in their respective districts, in such manner as shall be prescribed by law. The judges of the district courts shall be conservators of the peace in their respective districts. The first general assembly shall divide the state into four districts, which may be increased as the exigencies require. Art. 6, s. 4.

IPSE. He, himself; the very man.

IPSO FACTO. By the fact itself.

2. This phrase is frequently employed to convey the idea that something which has been done contrary to law is void. For example, if a married man, during the life of his wife, of which he had knowledge, should marry another woman, the latter marriage would be void *ipso facto;* that is, on that fact being proved, the second marriage would be declared void *ab initio*.

IPSO JURE. By the act of the law itself, or by mere operation of law.

IRE AD LARGUM. To go at large; to escape, or be set at liberty. Vide *Ad largum*.

IRONY, *rhetoric*. A term derived from the Greek, which signifies dissimulation. It is a refined species of ridicule, which, under the mask of honest simplicity or ignorance, exposes the faults and errors of others, by seeming to adopt or defend them.

2. In libels irony may convey imputations more effectually than direct assertion, and render the publication libelous. Hob

215; Hawk. B. 1, c. 73, s. 4; 3 Chit. Cr. Law, 869; Bac. Ab. Libel, A 3.

IRREGULAR. That which is done contrary to the common rules of law; as, irregular process, which is that issued contrary to law and the common practice of the court. Vide *Regular and Irregular Process.*

IRREGULAR DEPOSIT. This name is given to that kind of deposit, where the thing deposited need not be returned; as, where a man deposits, in the usual way, money in bank for safe keeping, for in this case the title to the identical money becomes vested in the bank, and he receives in its place other money.

IRREGULARITY, *practice.* The doing or not doing that in the conduct of a suit at law, which, conformably with the practice of the court, ought or ought not to be done.

2. A party entitled to complain of irregularity, should except to it previously to taking any step by him in the cause; Lofft. 323, 333; because the taking of any such step is a waiver of any irregularity. 1 Bos. & Phil. 342; 2 Smith's R. 391; 1 Taunt. R. 58; 2 Taunt. R. 243; 3 East, R. 547; 2 New R. 509; 2 Wils. R. 380.

3. The court will, on motion, set aside proceedings for irregularity. On setting aside a judgment and execution for irregularity, they have power to impose terms on the defendant, and will restrain him from bringing an action of trespass, unless a strong case of damage appears. 1 Chit. R. 133, n.; and see Baldw. R. 246. Vide 3 Chit. Pr. 509; and *Regular and Irregular Process.*

4. In the canon law, this term is used to signify any impediment which prevents a man from taking holy orders.

IRRELEVANT EVIDENCE. That which does not support the issue, and which, of course, must be excluded. See *Relevant.*

IRREPLEVISABLE, *practice.* This term is applied to those things which cannot legally be replevied. For example, in Pennsylvania no goods seized in execution or for taxes, can be replevied.

IRRESISTIBLE FORCE. This term is applied to such an interposition of human agency, as is, from its nature and power, absolutely uncontrollable; as the inroads of a hostile army. Story on Bailm. § 25; Lois des Bâtim. pt. 2. c. 2, § 1. It differs from *inevitable accident*; (q. v.) the latter being the effect of physical causes, as, lightning, storms, and the like.

IRREVOCABLE. That which cannot be revoked.

2. A will may at all times be revoked by the same person who made it, he having a disposing mind; but the moment the testator is rendered incapable to make a will he can no longer revoke a former will, because he wants a disposing mind. Letters of attorney are generally revocable; but when made for a valuable consideration they become irrevocable. 7 Ves. jr. 28; 1 Caines' Cas. in Er. 16; Bac. Ab. Authority, E. Vide *Authority; License; Revocation.*

IRRIGATION. The act of wetting or moistening the ground by artificial means.

2. The owner of land over which there is a current stream, is, as such, the proprietor of the current. 4 Mason's R. 400. It seems the riparian proprietor may avail himself of the river for irrigation, provided the river be not thereby materially lessened, and the water absorbed be imperceptible or trifling. Ang. W. C. 34; and vide 1 Root's R. 535; 8 Greenl. R. 266; 2 Conn. R. 584; 2 Swift's Syst. 87; 7 Mass. R. 136; 13 Mass. R. 420; 1 Swift's Dig. 111; 5 Pick. R. 175; 9 Pick. 59; 6 Bing. R. 379; 5 Esp. R. 56; 2 Conn. R. 584; Ham. N. P. 199; 2 Chit. Bl. Com. 403, n. 7; 22 Vin. Ab. 525; 1 Vin. Ab. 557; Bac. Ab. Action on the case, F. The French law coincides with our own. 1 Lois des Bâtimens, sect. 1, art. 3, page 21.

IRRITANCY. In Scotland, it is the happening of a condition or event by which a charter, contract or other deed, to which a clause irritant is annexed, becomes void. Ersk. Inst. B. 2, t. 5, n. 25. Irritancy is a kind of forfeiture. It is legal or conventional. Burt. Man. P. R. 298.

ISLAND. A piece of land surrounded by water.

2. Islands are in the sea or in rivers. Those in the sea are either in the open sea, or within the boundary of some country.

3. When new islands arise in the open sea, they belong to the first occupant: but when they are newly formed so near the shore as to be within the boundary of some state, they belong to that state.

4. Islands which arise in rivers when in the middle of the stream, belong in equal parts to the riparian proprietors when they arise mostly on one side, they will belong to the riparian owners up to the middle of the

stream. Bract. lib. 2, c. 2; Fleta, lib. 3, c. 2, s. 6; 2 Bl. 261; 1 Swift's Dig. 111; Schult. Aq. R. 117; Woolr. on Waters, 38; 4 Pick. R. 268; Dougl. R. 441; 10 Wend. 260; 14 S. & R. 1. For the law of Louisiana, see Civil Code, art. 505, 507.

5. The doctrine of the common law on this subject, founded on reason, seems to have been borrowed from the civil law. Vide Inst. 2, 1, 22; Dig. 41, 1, 7; Code, 7, 41, 1.

ISSINT. This is a Norman French word which signifies *thus, so*. It has given the name to a part of a plea, because when pleas were in that language this word was used. In actions founded on deeds, the defendant may, instead of pleading *non est factum* in the common form, allege any special matter which admits the execution of the writing in question, but which, nevertheless, shows that it is not in law his deed; and may conclude with and so it is not his deed; as that the writing was delivered to A B as an escrow, to be delivered over on certain conditions, which have not been complied with, "and *so* it is not his act;" or that at the time of making the writing, the defendant was a feme covert, "and *so* it is not her act." Bac. Ab. Pleas, H 3, I 2; Gould on Pl. c. 6, part 1, § 64.

2. An example of this form of plea, which is sometimes called the special general issue, occurs in 4 Rawle, Rep. 83, 84.

ISSUABLE, *practice*. Leading or tending to an issue. An issuable plea is one upon which the plaintiff can take issue and proceed to trial.

ISSUE, *kindred*. This term is of very extensive import, in its most enlarged signification, and includes all persons who have descended from a common ancestor. 17 Ves. 481; 19 Ves. 547; 3 Ves. 257; 1 Rop. Leg. 88; and see Wilmot's Notes, 314, 321. But when this word is used in a will, in order to give effect to the testator's intention it will be construed in a more restricted sense than its legal import conveys. 7 Ves. 522; 19 Ves. 73; 1 Rop. Leg. 90. Vide Bac. Ab. Curtesy of England, D; 8 Com. Dig. 473; and article *Legatee*, II. § 4.

ISSUE, *pleading*. An issue, in pleading, is defined to be a single, certain and material point issuing out of the allegations of the parties, and consisting, regularly, of an affirmative and negative. In common parlance, issue also signifies the entry of the pleadings. 1 Chit. Pl. 630.

2. Issues are *material* when properly formed on some material point, which will decide the question in dispute between the parties; and *immaterial*, when formed on some immaterial fact, which though found by the verdict will not determine the merits of the cause, and would leave the court at a loss how to give judgment. 2 Saund. 319, n. 6.

3. Issues are also divided into issues in *law* and issues in *fact*. 1. An *issue in law* admits all the facts and rests simply upon a question of law. It is said to consist of a single point, but by this it must be understood that such issue involves, necessarily, only a single rule or principle of law, or that it brings into question the legal sufficiency of a single fact only. It is meant that such an issue reduces the whole controversy to the single question, whether the facts confessed by the issue are sufficient in law to maintain the action or defence of the party who alleged them. 2. An *issue in fact*, is one in which the parties disagree as to their existence, one affirming they exist, and the other denying it. By the common law, every issue in fact, subject to some exceptions, which are noticed below, must consist of a direct affirmative allegation on the one side, and of a direct negative on the other. Co. Litt. 126, a; Bac. Ab. Pleas, &c. G 1; 5 Pet. 149; 2 Black. R. 1312; 8 T. R. 278. But it has been holden that when the defendant pleaded that he was born in France, and the plaintiff replied that he was born in England, it was sufficient to form a good issue. 1 Wils. 6; 2 Str. 1177. In this case, it will be observed, there were two *affirmatives*, and the ground upon which the issue was holden to be good is that the second affirmative is so contrary to the first, that the first cannot in any degree be true. The exceptions above mentioned to the rule that a direct affirmative and a direct negative are required, are the following: 1st. The general issue upon a writ of right is formed by two affirmatives: the demandant, on one side, avers that he has greater right than the tenant; and, on the other, that the tenant has a greater right than the demandant. This issue is called the mise. (q. v.) Lawes, Pl. 232; 3 Chit. Pl. 652; 3 Bl. Com. 195, 305. 2d. In an action of dower, the court merely demands the third part of acres of land, &c., as the dower of the demandant of the endowment of A B, heretofore the husband, &c., and the general issue is, that A B was

not seised of such estate, &c., and that he could not endow the demandant thereof, &c. 2 Saund. 329, 330. This mode of negation, instead of being direct, is merely argumentative, and argumentativeness is not generally allowed in pleading.

4. Issues in fact are divided into general issues, special issues, and common issues.

5. The *general issue* denies in direct terms the whole declaration; as in personal actions, where the defendant pleads *nil debet*—that he owes the plaintiff nothing; or *non culpabilis*—that he is not guilty of the facts alleged in the declaration; or in real actions, where the defendant pleads *nul tort*, no wrong done—or *nul disseisin*, no disseisin committed. These pleas, and the like, are called general issues, because, by importing an absolute and general denial of all the matters alleged in the declaration, they at once put them all in issue.

6. Formerly the general issue was seldom pleaded, except where the defendant meant wholly to deny the charge alleged against him; for when he meant to avoid and justify the charge, it was usual for him to set forth the particular ground of his defence as a special plea, which appears to have been necessary to apprize the court and the plaintiff of the particular nature and circumstances of the defendant's case, and was originally intended to keep the law and the fact distinct. And even now it is an invariable rule, that every defence which cannot be specially pleaded, may be given in evidence at the trial upon the general issue, so the defendant is in many cases obliged to plead the particular circumstances of his defence specially, and cannot give them in evidence on that general plea. But the science of special pleading having been frequently perverted to the purposes of chicane and delay, the courts have in some instances, and the legislature in others, permitted the general issue to be pleaded, and special matter to be given in evidence under it at the trial, which at once includes the facts, the equity, and the law of the case. 3 Bl. Com. 305, 6; 3 Green. Ev. § 9.

7. The *special issue* is when the defendant takes issue upon any one substantial part of the declaration, and rests the weight of his case upon it; he is then said to take a special issue, in contradistinction to the general issue, which denies and puts in issue the whole of the declaration. Com. Dig. Pleader, R 1, 2.

8. *Common issue* is the name given to that which is formed on the single plea of *non est factum*, when pleaded to an action of covenant broken. This is so called, because to an action of covenant broken there can properly be no general issue, since the plea of *non est factum*, which denies the deed only, and not the breach, does not put the whole declaration in issue. 1 Chit. Pl. 482; Lawes on Pl. 113; Gould, Pl. c. 6, part 1, § 7 and § 10, 2.

9. Issues are formal and informal.

10. A *formal* issue is one which is formed according to the rules required by law, in a proper and artificial manner.

11. An *informal* issue is one which arises when a material allegation is traversed in an improper or inartificial manner. Bac. Ab. Pleas, &c., G 2, N 5; 2 Saund. 319, a, n. 6. The defect is cured by verdict, by the statute of 32 H. VIII. c. 30.

12. Issues are also divided into actual and feigned issues.

13. An *actual issue* is one formed in an action brought in the regular manner, for the purpose of trying a question of right between the parties.

14. A *feigned issue* is one directed by a court, generally by a court exercising equitable powers, for the purpose of trying before a jury a matter in dispute between the parties. When in a court of equity any matter of fact is strongly contested, the court usually directs the matter to be tried by a jury, especially such important facts as the validity of a will, or whether A is the heir at law of B.

15. But as no jury is summoned to attend this court, the fact is usually directed to be tried in a court of law upon a *feigned issue*. For this purpose an action is brought in which the plaintiff by a fiction declares that he laid a wager for a sum of money with the defendant, for example, that a certain paper is the last will and testament of A; then avers it is his will, and therefore demands the money; the defendant admits the wager but avers that it is not the will of A, and thereupon that issue is joined, which is directed out of chancery to be tried; and thus the verdict of the jurors at law determines the fact in the court of equity.

16. These feigned issues are frequently used in the courts of law, by consent of the parties, to determine some disputed rights without the formality of pleading, and by this practice much time and expense are saved in the decision of a cause. 3 Bl.

Com. 452. The consent of the court must also be previously obtained; for the trial of a feigned issue without such consent is a contempt, which will authorize the court to order the proceeding to be stayed, and punish the parties engaged. 4 T. R. 402. See *Fictitious action*. See, generally, Bouv. Inst. Index, h. t.

ISSUE ROLL, *Eng. law*. The name of a record which contains an entry of the term of which the demurrer book, issue or paper book is entitled, and the warrants of attorney supposed to have been given by the parties at the commencement of the cause, and then proceeds with the transcript of the declaration and subsequent pleadings, continuances, and award of the mode of the decision as contained in the demurrer, issue or paper book. Steph. Pl. 98, 99. After final judgment, the issue roll is no longer called by that name, but assumes that of *judgment roll*. 2 Arch. Pr. 206.

ISSUES, *Eng. law*. The goods and profits of the lands of a defendant against whom a writ of *distringas* or *distress infinite* has been issued, taken by virtue of such writ, are called *issues*. 3 Bl. Com. 280; 1 Chit. Cr. Law, 351.

ISTHMUS. A tongue or strip of land between two seas. Glos. on Law, 37, book 2, tit. 3, of the Dig.

ITA EST. These words signify *so it is*. Among the civilians when a notary dies, leaving his register, an officer who is authorized to make official copies of his notarial acts, writes instead of the deceased notary's name, which is required, when he is living, *ita est*.

ITA QUOD. The name or condition in a submission which is usually introduced by these words "so as the award be made of and upon the premises," which from the first word is called the *ita quod*.

2. When the submission is with an *ita quod*, the arbitrator must make an award of all matters submitted to him of which he had notice, or the award will be entirely void. 7 East, 81; Cro. Jac. 200; 2 Vern. 109; 1 Ca. Chan. 86; Roll. Ab. Arbitr. L. 9.

ITEM. Also; likewise; in like manner; again; a second time. These are the various meanings of this Latin adverb. Vide *Construction*.

2. In law it is to be construed conjunctively, in the sense of *and*, or *also*, in such a manner as to connect sentences. If therefore a testator bequeath a legacy to Peter payable out of a particular fund, or charged upon a particular estate, *item* a legacy to James, James' legacy as well as Peter's will be a charge upon the same property. 1 Atk. 436; 3 Atk. 256; 1 Bro. C. C. 482; 1 Rolle's Ab. 844; 1 Mod. 100; Cro. Car. 368; Vaugh. 262; 2 Rop. on Leg. 349; 1 Salk. 234. Vide *Disjunctive*.

ITER. A foot way. Vide *Way*.

ITINERANT. Travelling or taking a journey. In England there were formerly judges called *Justices itinerant*, who were sent with commissions into certain counties to try causes.

J.

JACTITATION OF MARRIAGE, *Eng. eccl. law*. The boasting by an individual that he or she has married another, from which it may happen that they will acquire the reputation of being married to each other.

2. The ecclesiastical courts may in such cases entertain a libel by the party injured; and, on proof of the facts, enjoin the wrongdoer to perpetual silence; and, as a punishment, make him pay the costs. 3 Bl. Com. 93; 2 Hagg. Cons. R. 423; Id. 285; 2 Chit. Pr. 459.

JACTURA. The same as jettison. (q v.) 1 Bell's Com. 586, 5th ed.

JAIL. A prison; a place appointed by law for the detention of prisoners. A jail is an inhabited dwelling-house within the statute of New York, which makes the malicious burning of an inhabited dwelling-house to be arson. 8 John. 115; see 4 Call, 109. Vide *Gaol; Prison*.

JEOFAILE. This is a law French phrase, which signifies, "I am in an error; I have failed." There are certain statutes called statutes of *amendment* and *jeofails* because, where a pleader perceives any slip in the form of his proceedings, and acknowledges the error, (jeofaile,) he is at liberty by those statutes to amend it. The amendment, however, is seldom made, but the benefit is attained by the court's overlooking the exception. 3 Bl. Com. 407; 1 Saund. 228, n. 1; Doct. Pl. 287; Dane's Ab. h. t.

JEOPARDY. Peril, danger.

2. This is the meaning attached to this word used in the act establishing and regulating the post office department. The words of the act are, "or if, in effecting such robbery of the mail the first time, the offender shall wound the person having the custody thereof, or put his life in jeopardy by the use of dangerous weapons, such offender shall suffer death." 3 Story's L. U. S. 1992. Vide Baldw. R. 93–95.

3. The constitution declares that no person shall "for the same offence, be twice put in jeopardy of life and limb." The meaning of this is, that the party shall not be tried a second time for the same offence after he has once been convicted or acquitted of the offence charged, by the verdict of a jury, and judgment has passed thereon for or against him; but it does not mean that he shall not be tried for the offence, if the jury have been discharged from necessity or by consent, without giving any verdict; or, if having given a verdict, judgment has been arrested upon it, or a new trial has been granted in his favor; for, in such a case, his life and limb cannot judicially be said to have been put in jeopardy. 4 Wash. C. C. R. 410; 9 Wheat. R. 579; 6 Serg. & Rawle, 577; 3 Rawle, R. 498; 3 Story on the Const. § 1781. Vide 2 Sumn. R. 19. This great privilege is secured by the common law. Hawk. P. C., B. 2, 35; 4 Bl. Com. 335.

4. This was the Roman law, from which it has been probably engrafted upon the common law. Vide Merl. Rép. art. *Non bis in idem*. Qui de crimine publico accusationem deductus est, says the Code, 9, 2, 9, ab alio super eodem crimine deferri non potest. Vide article *Non bis in idem*.

JERGUER, *Engl. law.* An officer of the custom-house, who oversees the waiters. Techn. Dict. h. t.

JETTISON, or JETSAM. The casting out of a vessel, from necessity, a part of the lading; the thing cast out also bears the same name; it differs from flotsam in this, that in the latter the goods float, while in the former they sink, and remain under water; it differs also from ligan. (q. v.)

2. The jettison must be made for sufficient cause, and not from groundless timidity. In must be made in a case of extremity, when the ship is in danger of perishing by the fury of a storm, or is laboring upon rocks or shallows, or is closely pursued by pirates or enemies.

3. If the residue of the cargo be saved by such sacrifice, the property saved is bound to pay a proportion of the loss. In ascertaining such average loss, the goods lost and saved are both to be valued at the price they would have brought at the place of delivery, on the ship's arrival there, freight, duties and other charges being deducted. Marsh. Ins. 246; 3 Kent, Com. 185 to 187; Park. Ins. 123; Poth. Charte-partie, n. 108, et suiv; Boulay-Paty, Dr. Com. tit. 13; Pardessus, Dr. Com. n. 734; 1 Ware's R. 9.

JEUX DE BOURSE, *French law.* This is a kind of gambling or speculation, which consists of sales and purchases, which bind neither of the parties to deliver the things which are the object of the sale, and which are settled by paying the difference in the value of the things sold between the day of the sale, and that appointed for delivery of such things. 1 Pard. Dr. Com. n. 162.

JEWS. See De Judaismo Statutum.

JOB. By this term is understood among workmen, the whole of a thing which is to be done. In this sense it is employed in the Civil Code of Louisiana, art. 2727; "to build by plot, or to work by the job," says that article, "is to undertake a building for a certain stipulated price." See Durant. du Contr. de Louage, liv. 3, t. 8, n. 248, 263; Poth. Contr. de Louage, n. 392, 394; and *Deviation*.

JOBBER, *commerce.* One who buys and sells articles for others. Stock-jobbers are those who buy and sell stocks for others; this term is also applied to those who speculate in stocks on their own account.

JOCALIA. Jewels; this term was formerly more properly applied to those ornaments which women, although married, call their own. When these *jocalia* are not suitable to her degree, they are assets for the payment of debts. 1 Roll. Ab. 911. Vide *Paraphernalia*.

JOINDER OF ACTIONS, *practice.* The putting two or more causes of action in the same declaration.

2. It is a general rule, that in real ac

tions there can never be but one count. 8 Co. 86, 87; Bac. Ab. Action, C; Com. Dig. Action, G. A count in a real, and a count in a mixed action, cannot be joined in the same declaration; nor a count in a mixed action, and a count in a personal action; nor a count in a mixed action with a count in another, as ejectment and trespass.

3. In mixed actions, there may be two counts in the same declaration; for example, waste lies upon several leases, and ejectment upon several demises and ousters. 8 Co. 87 b; Poph. 24; Cro. Eliz. 290; Ow. 11. Strictly, however, ejectment at common law, is a personal action, and a count in trespass for an assault and battery, may be joined with it; for both sound in trespass, and the same judgment is applicable to both.

4. In personal actions, the use of several counts in the same declaration is quite common. Sometimes they are applied to distinct causes of actions, as upon several promissory notes; but it more frequently happens that the various counts introduced, do not really relate to different claims, but are adopted merely as so many different forms of propounding the same demand. The joinder in action depends on the *form* of action, rather than on the subject-matter of it; in an action against a carrier, for example, if the plaintiff declare in assumpsit, he cannot join a count in trover, as he may if he declare against him in case. 1 T. R. 277; but see 2 Caines' R. 216; 3 East, R. 70. The rule as to joinder is, that when the same plea may be pleaded, and the same judgment given on all the counts of the declaration, or when the counts are all of the same nature, and the same judgment is to be given upon them all, though the pleas be different, as in the case of debt upon bond and simple contract, they may be joined. 2 Saund. 117, c. When the same form of action may be adopted, the plaintiff may join as many causes of action as he may choose, though he acquired the rights affected by different titles; but the rights of the plaintiffs, and the liabilities of the defendant, must be in his own character, or in his representative capacity, exclusively. A plaintiff cannot sue, therefore, for a cause of action in his own *right*, and another cause in his character as *executor*, and join them; nor can he sue the defendant for a debt due by himself, and another due by him as executor.

5. In criminal cases, different offences may be joined in the same indictment, if of the same nature, but an indictment may be quashed, at the discretion of the court, when the counts are joined in such a manner as will confound the evidence. 1 Chit. Cr. Law, 253–255. In Pennsylvania, it has been decided that when a defendant was indicted at one session of the court for a conspiracy to cheat a third person, and at another session of the same court he was indicted for another conspiracy to cheat another person, the two bills might be tried by the same jury, against the will of the defendant, provided he was not thereby deprived of any material right, as the right to challenge; whether he should be so tried or not seems to be a matter of discretion with the court. 5 S. & R. 59; 12 S. & R. 69. Vide *Separate Trial.*

Vide, generally, 2 Saund. 117, b. to 117, c.; Com. Dig. Action, G; 2 Vin. Ab. 38; Bac. Ab. Actions in General, C; 13 John. R. 462; 10 John. R. 240; 11 John. R. 479; 1 John. R. 503; 3 Binn. 555; 1 Chit. Pl. 196 to 205; Arch. Civ. Pl. 172 to 176; Steph. Pl. Index, h. t.; Dane's Ab. h. t.

JOINDER IN DEMURRER. When a demurrer is offered by one party, the adverse party joins with him in demurrer, and the answer which he makes is called a joinder in demurrer. Co. Litt. 71 b. But this is a mere formality.

JOINDER OF ISSUE, *pleadings.* The act by which the parties to a cause arrive at that stage of it in their pleadings, that one asserts a fact to be so, and the other denies it. For example, when one party denies the fact pleaded by his antagonist, who has tendered the issue thus, "And this he prays may be inquired of by the country," or, "And of this he puts himself upon the country," the party denying the fact may immediately subjoin, "And the said A B does the like;" when the issue is said to be joined.

JOINDER OF PARTIES TO ACTIONS. It is a rule in actions *ex contractu* that all who have a legal interest in the contract, and no others, must join in action founded on a breach of such contract; whether the parties are too many or too few, it is equally fatal. 8 S. & R. 308; 4 Watts, 456; 1 Breese, 286; 6 Pick. 359; 6 Mass. 460; 2 Conn. 697; 6 Wend. 629; 2 N. & M. 70; 1 Bailey, 13; 5 Verm. 116; 3 J. J. Marsh. 165; 16 John. 34; 19 John. 213; 2 Greenl. 117; 2 Penn. 817.

2. In actions *ex contractu* all obligors,

jointly and not severally liable, and no others, must be made defendants. 1 Saund. 153, note 1; 1 Breese, 128; 11 John. 101; 2 J. J. Marsh. 38; 2 John. 213.

3. In actions *ex delicto*, when an injury is done to the property of two or more joint owners, they must join in the action. 1 Saund. 291, g; 11 Pick. 269; 12 Pick. 120; 7 Mass. 135; 13 John. 286.

4. When a tort is of such a nature that it may be committed by several, they may all be joined in an action *ex delicto*, or they may be sued severally. But when the tort cannot be committed jointly, as, for example, slander, two or more persons cannot be sued jointly, although they may have uttered the same words. 6 John. 32. See, generally, 3 Bouv. Inst. n. 2648, et seq.

JOINT. United, not separate; as, joint action, or one which is brought by several persons acting together; joint bond, a bond given by two or more obligors.

JOINT CONTRACT. One in which the contractors are jointly bound to perform the promise or obligation therein contained, or entitled to receive the benefit of such promise or obligation.

2. It is a general rule that a joint contract survives, whatever may be the beneficial interests of the parties under it; where a partner, covenantor, or other person entitled, having a joiut interest in a contract not running with the land, dies, the right to sue survives in the other partner, &c. 1 Dall. 65, 248; Addis. on Contr. 285. And when the obligation or promise is to perform something jointly by the obligors or promissors, and one dies, the action must be brought against the survivor. Ham. on Part. 156.

3. When all the parties interested in a joint contract die, the action must be brought by the executors or administrators of the last surviving obligee, against the executors or administrators of the last surviving obligor. Addis. on Contr. 285. See *Contracts; Parties to Actions; Coobligor.*

JOINT EXECUTORS. It is proposed to consider, 1. The interest which they have in the estate of the deceased. 2. How far they are liable for each other's acts. 3. The rights of the survivor.

2.—§ 1. Joint executors are considered in law as but one person, representing the testator, and, therefore, the acts of any one of them, which relate either to the delivery, gift, sale, payment, possession or release of the testator's goods, are deemed, as regards the persons with whom they contract, the acts of all. Bac. Abr. h. t.; 11 Vin. Abr. 358; Com. Dig. Administration, B 12; 1 Dane's Abr. 583; 2 Litt. (Kentucky) R. 315; Godolph. 314; Dyer, 23, in marg.; 16 Serg. & Rawle, 337. But an executor cannot, without the knowledge of his coexecutor, confess a judgment for a claim, part of which was barred by the act of limitations, so as to bind the estate of the testator. 6 Penn. St. Rep. 267.

3.—§ 2. As a general rule, it may be laid down that each executor is liable for his own wrong, or *devastavit* only, and not for that of his colleague. He may be rendered liable, however, for the misplaced confidence which he may have reposed in his coëxecutor. As, if he signs a receipt for money, in conjunction with another executor, and he receives no part of the money, but agrees that the other executor shall retain it, and apply it to his own use, this is his own misapplication, for which he is responsible. 1 P. Wms. 241, n. 1; 1 Sch. & Lef. 341; 2 Sch. & Lef. 231; 7 East, R. 256; 11 John. R. 16; 11 Serg. & Rawle, 71; Hardr. 314; 5 Johns. Ch. R. 283; and see 2 Bro. C. C. 116; 3 Bro C. C. 112; 2 Penn. R. 421; Fonb. Eq. B. 2, c. 7, s. 5, n. k.

4.—§ 3. Upon the death of one of several joint executors, the right of administering the estate of the testator devolves upon the survivor. 3 Atk. 509, Com. Dig. Administration, B 12; Hamm. on Parties, 148.

5. In Pennsylvania, by legislative enactment, it is provided, "that where testators may devise their estates to their executors to be sold, or direct such executors to sell and convey such estates, or direct such real estate to be sold, without naming or declaring who shall sell the same, if one or more of the executors die, it shall or may be lawful for the surviving executor to bring actions for the recovery of the possession thereof, and against trespassers thereon; to sell and convey such real estate, or manage the same for the benefit of the persons interested therein." Act of March 12, 1800, 3 Sm. L. 433.

JOINT STOCK BANKS. In England they are a species of *quasi corporations*, or companies regulated by deeds of settlement, and, in this respect, they stand in the same situation as other unincorporated bodies. But they differ from the latter in this, that they are invested by certain statutes with powers and privileges usually incident to corporations. These enactments provide for the continuance of the partnership, notwithstanding a change of partners. The death, bankruptcy, or the sale by a partner of his share, does not affect the identity of the partnership; it continues the same body, under the same name, by virtue of the act of parliament, notwithstanding these changes. 7 Geo. IV., c. 46, s. 9.

JOINT TENANTS, *estates.* Two or more persons to whom are granted lands or tenements to hold in fee simple, fee tail, for life, for years, or at will. 2 Black. Com. 179. The estate which they thus hold is called an estate in joiut tenancy. Vide *Estate in joint tenancy; Jus accrescendi; Survivor.*

JOINT TRUSTEES. Two or more persons who are entrusted with property for the benefit of one or more others.

2. Unlike joint executors, joint trustees cannot act separately, but must join both in conveyances and receipts, for one cannot sell without the others, or receive more of the consideration-money, or be more a trustee than his partner. The trust having been given to the whole, it requires their joint act to do anything under it. They are not responsible for money received by their co-trustees, if the receipt be given for the mere purposes of form. But if receipts be given under circumstances purporting that the money, though not received by both, was under the control of both, such a receipt shall charge, and the consent that the other shall misapply the money, particularly where he has it in his power to secure it, renders him responsible. 11 Serg. & Rawle, 71. See 1 Sch. & Lef. 341; 5 Johns. Ch. R. 283; Fonbl. Eq. B. 2, c. 7, s. 5; Bac. Abr. Uses and Trusts, K; 2 Bro. Ch. R. 116; 3 Bro. Ch. R. 112. In the case of the Attorney General *v.* Randall, a different doctrine was held. Id. pl. 9.

JOINTRESS or JOINTURESS. A woman who has an estate settled on her by her husband, to hold during her life, if she survive him. Co. Litt. 46.

JOINTURE, *estates.* A competent livelihood of freehold for the wife, of lands and tenements; to take effect in profit or possession, presently after the death of the husband, for the life of the wife at least.

2. Jointures are regulated by the statute of 27 Hen. VIII. c. 10, commonly called the statute of *uses.*

3. To make a good jointure, the following circumstances must concur, namely. 1. It must take effect, in possession or profit, immediately from the death of the husband. 2. It must be for the wife's life, or for some greater estate. 3. It must be limited to the wife herself, and not to any other person in trust for her. 4. It must be made in satisfaction for the wife's whole dower, and not of part of it only. 5. The estate limited to the wife must be expressed or averred to be, in satisfaction of her whole dower. 6. It must be made before marriage. A jointure attended with all these circumstances is binding on the widow, and is a complete bar to the claim of dower; or rather it prevents its ever arising. But there are other modes of limiting an estate to a wife, which, Lord Coke says, are good jointures within the statute, provided the wife accepts of them after the death of the husband. She may, however, reject them, and claim her dower. Cruise, Dig. tit. 7: 2 Bl. Com. 137; Perk. h. t. In its more enlarged sense, a jointure signifies a joint estate, limited to both husband and wife. 2 Bl. Com. 137. Vide 14 Vin. Ab. 540; Bac. Ab. h. t.; 2 Bouv. Inst. n. 1761, et seq.

JOUR. A French word, signifying day. It is used in our old law books, as, *tout jours*, for ever. It is also frequently employed in the composition of words, as, *journal*, a day book; *journeyman*, a man who works by the day; *journeys account.* (q. v.)

JOURNAL, *mar. law.* The book kept on board of a ship or other vessel, which contains an account of the ship's course, with a short history of every occurrence during the voyage. Another name for log-book. (q. v.) Chit. Law of Nat. 199.

JOURNAL, *common law.* A book used among merchants, in which the contents of the waste-book are separated every month, and entered on the debtor and creditor side, for more convenient posting in the ledger.

JOURNAL, *legislation.* An account of the proceedings of a legislative body.

2. The Constitution of the United States, art. 1, s. 5, directs that "each house shall keep a journal of its proceedings; and from time to time publish the same, excepting such parts as may, in their judgment, require secrecy." Vide 2 Story, Const. 301.

3. The constitutions of the several states contain similar provisions.

4. The journal of either house is evidence of the action of that house upon all

matters before it. 7 Cowen, R. 613; Cowp. 17.

JOURNEYS ACCOUNT, *Eng. practice*. When a writ abated without any fault of the plaintiff, he was permitted to sue out a new writ, within as little time as he possibly could after abatement of the first writ, which was *quasi* a continuance of the first writ, and placed him in a situation in which he would have been, supposing he had still proceeded on that writ. This was called *journeys account*.

2. This mode of proceeding has fallen into disuse, the practice now being to permit that writ to be quashed, and to sue out another. Vide Termes de la Ley, h. t.; Bac. Ab. Abatement, Q; 14 Vin. Ab. 558; 4 Com. Dig. 714; 7 Mann. & Gr. 762.

JUDEX. This word has several significations: 1. The judge, one who declares the law, *qui jus dicit;* one who administers justice between the parties to a cause, when lawfully submitted to him. 2. The judicial power, or the court. 3. Anciently, by judex was also understood a juror. Vide *Judge*.

JUDEX A QUO. A judge from whom an appeal may be taken; a judge of a court below. See A quo; 6 Mart. Lo. Rep. 520.

JUDEX AD QUEM. A judge to whom an appeal may be taken; a superior judge.

JUDGE. A public officer, lawfully appointed to decide litigated questions according to law. This, in its most extensive sense, includes all officers who are appointed to decide such questions, and not only judges properly so called, but also justices of the peace, and jurors, who are judges of the facts in issue. See 4 Dall. 229; 3 Yeates, R. 300. In a more limited sense, the term judge signifies an officer who is so named in his commission, and who presides in some court.

2. Judges are appointed or elected, in a variety of ways, in the United States; they are appointed by the president, by and with the consent of the senate; in some of the states they are appointed by the governor, the governor and senate, or by the legislature. In the United States, and some of the states, they hold their offices during good behaviour; in others, as in New York, during good behaviour, or until they shall attain a certain age; and in others for a limited term of years.

3. Impartiality is the first duty of a judge; before he gives an opinion, or sits in judgment in a cause, he ought to be certain that he has no bias for or against either of the parties; and if he has any (the slightest) interest in the cause, he is disqualified from sitting as judge; *aliquis non debet esse judex in propriâ causâ;* 8 Co. 118, 21 Pick. Rep. 101; 5 Mass. 92; 13 Mass. 340; 6 Pick. R. 109; 14 S. & R. 157-8; and when he is aware of such interest, he ought himself to refuse to sit on the case. It seems it is discretionary with him whether he will sit in a cause in which he has been of counsel. 2 Marsh. 517; Coxe, 164; see 2 Binn. 454. But the delicacy which characterizes the judges in this country, generally, forbids their sitting in such a cause.

4. He must not only be impartial, but he must follow and enforce the law, whether good or bad. He is bound to declare what the law is, and not to make it; he is not an arbitrator, but an interpreter of the law. It is his duty to be patient in the investigation of the case, careful in considering it, and firm in his judgment. He ought, according to Cicero, "never to lose sight that he is a man, and that he cannot exceed the power given him by his commission; that not only power, but public confidence has been given to him; that he ought always seriously to attend not to his wishes but to the requisitions of law, of justice and religion." Cic. pro. Cluentius. A curious case of judicial casuistry is stated by Aulus Gellius Att. Noct. lib. 14, cap. 2, which may be interesting to the reader.

5. While acting within the bounds of his jurisdiction, the judge is not responsible for any error of judgment, nor mistake he may commit as a judge. Co. Litt. 294; 2 Inst. 422; 2 Dall. R. 160; 1 Yeates, R. 443; 2 N. & M'C. 168; 1 Day, R. 315; 1 Root, R. 211; 3 Caines, R. 170; 5 John. R. 282; 9 John. R. 395; 11 John. R. 150; 3 Marsh. R. 76; 1 South. R. 74; 1 N. H. Rep. 374; 2 Bay, 1, 69; 8 Wend. 468; 3 Marsh. R. 76. When he acts corruptly, he may be impeached. 5 John. R. 282; 8 Cowen, R. 178; 4 Dall. R. 225.

6. A judge is not competent as a witness in a cause trying before him, for this, among other reasons, that he can hardly be deemed capable of impartially deciding on the admissibility of his own testimony, or of weighing it against that of another. 2 Martin's R. N. S. 312.

Vide Com. Dig. Courts, B 4, C 2, E 1, P 16—Justices, I 1, 2, and 3; 14 Vin. Ab. 573; Bac. Ab. Courts, &c., B; 1 Kent, Com. 291; Ayl. Parerg. 309; Story, Const.

Index, h. t. See U. S. Dig. Courts, I, where will be found an abstract of various decisions relating to the appointment and powers of judges in different states. Vide *Equality; Incompetency.*

JUDGE ADVOCATE. An officer who is a member of a court martial.

2. His duties are to prosecute in the name of the United States, but he shall so far consider himself as counsel for the prisoner, after the prisoner shall have made his plea, as to object to leading questions to any of the witnesses, or any question to the prisoner, the answer to which might tend to criminate himself. He is further to swear the members of the court before they proceed upon any trial. Rules and Articles of War, art. 69, 2 Story, L. U. S. 1001; Lid. Jud. Adv. *passim.*

JUDGE'S NOTES. They are short statements, made by a judge on the trial of a cause, of what transpires in the course of such trial. They usually contain a statement of the testimony of witnesses; of documents offered or admitted in evidence; of offers of evidence and whether it has been received or rejected, and the like matters.

2. In general judge's notes are not evidence of what transpired at a former trial, nor can they be read to prove what a deceased witness swore to on such former trial, for they are no part of the record, and he is not officially bound to make them. But in chancery, when a new trial is ordered of an issue sent out of chancery to a court of law, and it is suggested that some of the witnesses in the former trial are of an advanced age, an order may be made that, in the event of death or inability to attend, their testimony may be read from the judge's notes. 1 Greenl. Ev. § 166.

JUDGMENT, *practice.* The decision or sentence of the law, given by a court of justice or other competent tribunal, as the result of proceedings instituted therein. for the redress of an injury.

2. The language of judgments, therefore, is not that "it is decreed," or "resolved," by the court; but "it is considered," (consideratum est per curiam) that the plaintiff recover his debt, damages, or possession, as the case may require, or that the defendant do go without day. This implies that the judgment is not so much the decision of the court, as the sentence of the law pronounced and decreed by the court, after due deliberation and inquiry.

3. To be valid, a judicial judgment must be given by a competent judge or court, at a time and place appointed by law, and in the form it requires. A judgment would be null, if the judge had not jurisdiction of the matter; or, having such jurisdiction, he exercised it when there was no court held, or out of his district; or if he rendered a judgment before the cause was prepared for a hearing.

4. The judgment must confine itself to the question raised before the court, and cannot extend beyond it. For example, where the plaintiff sued for an injury committed on his lands by animals owned and kept carelessly by defendant, the judgment may be for damages, but it cannot command the defendant for the future to keep his cattle out of the plaintiff's land. That would be to usurp the power of the legislature. A judgment declares the rights which belong to the citizen, the law alone rules future actions. The law commands all men, it is the same for all, because it is general; judgments are particular decisions, which apply only to particular persons, and bind no others; they vary like the circumstances on which they are founded.

5. Litigious contests present to the courts facts to appreciate, agreements to be construed, and points of law to be resolved. The judgment is the result of the full examination of all these.

6. There are four kinds of judgments in civil cases, namely: 1. When the facts are admitted by the parties, but the law is disputed; as in case of judgment upon demurrer. 2. When the law is admitted, but the facts are disputed; as in case of judgment upon a verdict. 3. When both the law and the facts are admitted by confession; as in the case of cognovit actionem, on the part of the defendant; or nolle prosequi, on the part of the plaintiff. 4. By default of either party in the course of legal proceedings, as in the case of judgment by nihil dicit, or non sum informatus, when the defendant has omitted to plead or instruct his attorney to do so, after a proper notice; or in cases of judgment by non pros; or, as in case of nonsuit, when the plaintiff omits to follow up his proceedings.

7. These four species of judgments, again, are either interlocutory or final. Vide 3 Black. Com. 396; Bingh. on Judgm. 1 For the lien of judgments in the several states, vide *Lien.*

8. A list of the various judgments is here given.

9. Judgment in *assumpsit* is either in favor of the plaintiff or defendant; when in favor of the plaintiff, it is that he recover a specified sum, assessed by a jury, or on reference to the prothonotary, or other proper officer, for the damages which he has sustained, by reason of the defendant's nonperformance of his promises and undertakings, and for full costs of suit. 1 Chit. Pl. 100. When the judgment is for the defendant, it is that he recover his costs.

10. Judgment in *actions on the case* for torts, when for the plaintiff, is that he recover a sum of money ascertained by a jury, for his damages occasioned by the committing of the grievances complained of, and the costs of suit. 1 Ch. Pl. 147. When for the defendant, it is for costs.

11. Judgment of *cassetur breve*, or *billa*, is in cases of pleas in abatement where the plaintiff prays that his "writ" or "bill" "may be quashed, that he may sue or exhibit a better one." Steph. Pl. 130, 131, 128; Lawes, Civ. Pl.

12. Judgment by *confession*. When instead of entering a plea, the defendant chooses to confess the action; or, after pleading, he does, at any time before trial, both confess the action and withdraw his plea or other allegations; the judgment against him, in these two cases, is called a judgment by *confession* or *by confession relictâ verificatione*. Steph. Pl. 130.

13. *Contradictory* judgment. By this term is understood, in the state of Louisiana, a judgment which has been given after the parties have been heard, either in support of their claims, or in their defence. Code of Pract. art. 535; 11 L. R. 366, 569. A judgment is called contradictory to distinguish it from one which is rendered by default.

14. Judgment in *covenant;* when for the plaintiff, is that he recover an ascertained sum for his damages, which he has sustained by reason of the breach or breaches of the defendant's covenant, together with costs of suit. 1 Chitty's Plead. 116, 117. When for the defendant, the judgment is for costs.

15. Judgment in the *action of debt;* when for the plaintiff, is that he recover his debt, and, in general, nominal damages for the detention thereof; and in cases under the 8 and 9 Wm. III. c. 11, it is also awarded, that the plaintiff have execution for the damages sustained by the breach of a bond, conditioned for the performance of covenants; and that plaintiff recover full costs of suit. 1 Chitty's Pl. 108, 9.

16. In some penal and other particular actions the plaintiff does not, however, always recover costs. Espinasse on Pen. Act. 154; Hull. on Costs, 200; Bull. N. P. 333; 5 Johns. R. 251.

17. When the judgment is for the defendant, it is generally for costs. In some penal actions, however, neither party can recover costs, 5 Johns. R. 251.

18. Judgment by *default*, is a judgment rendered in consequence of the non-appearance of the defendant, and is either by *nil dicit;* vide *Judgment by nil dicit*, or by *non sum informatus;* vide *Judgment by non sum informatus*.

19. This judgment is interlocutory in assumpsit, covenant, trespass, case, and replevin, where the sole object of the action is damages; but in debt, damages not being the principal object of the action, the plaintiff usually signs final judgment in the first instance. Vide Com. Dig. Pleader, B 11 and 12, E 42; 7 Vin. Ab. 429; Doct. Pl. 208; Grah. Pr. 631; Dane's Ab. Index, h. t.; 3 Chit. Pr. 671 to 680; Tidd's Pr. 563; 1 Lilly's Reg. 585; and article *Default*.

20. Judgment in the *action of detinue;* when for the plaintiff, is in the alternative, that he recover the goods, or the value thereof, if he cannot have the goods themselves, and his damage for the detention and costs. 1 Ch. Pl. 121, 2; 1 Dall. R. 458.

21. Judgment *in error*, is a judgment rendered by a court of error, on a record sent up from an inferior court. These judgments are of two kinds, of affirmance and reversal. When the judgment is for the defendant in error, whether the errors assigned be in law or in fact, it is "that the former judgment be affirmed, and stand in full force and effect, the said causes and matters assigned for error notwithstanding, and that the defendant in error recover $— for his damages, charges and costs which he hath sustained," &c. 2 Tidd's Pr. 1126; Arch. Forms, 221. When it is for the plaintiff in error, the judgment is that it be reversed or recalled. It is to be *reversed* for error in law, in this form, that it "be reversed, annulled and altogether holden for nought." Arch. Forms, 224. For error in fact the judgment is *recalled*, *revocatur*. 2 Tidd, Pr. 1126.

22. A *final* judgment is one which puts an end to the suit.

23. When the issue is one in *fact*, and is tried by a jury, the jury at the time that they try the issue, assess the damages, and the judgment is final in the first instance, and is that *the plaintiff do recover the damages assessed.*

24. When an interlocutory judgment has been rendered, and a writ of inquiry has issued to ascertain the damages, on the return of the inquisition the plaintiff is entitled to a final judgment, namely, *that he recover the amount of damages so assessed.* Steph. Pl. 127, 128.

25. An *interlocutory* judgment, is one given in the course of a cause, before final judgment. When the action sounds in damages, and the issue is an issue in law, or when any issue in fact not tried by a jury is decided in favor of the plaintiff, then the judgment is that the plaintiff ought to recover his damages without specifying their amount; for, as there has been no trial by jury in the case, the amount of damages is not yet ascertained. The judgment is then said to be interlocutory.

26. To ascertain such damages it is the practice to issue a writ of inquiry. Steph. Pl. 127. When the action is founded on a promissory note, bond, or other writing, or any other contract by which the amount due may be readily computed, the practice is, in some courts, to refer it to the prothonotary or clerk to assess the damages.

27. There is one species of interlocutory judgment which establishes nothing but the inadequacy of the defence set up; this is the judgment for the plaintiff on demurrer to a plea in abatement, by which it appears that the defendant has mistaken the law on a point which does not affect the merits of his case; and it being but reasonable that he should offer, if he can, a further defence, that judgment is that he do answer over, in technical language, judgment of respondeat ouster. (q. v.) Steph. Plead, 126; Bac. Ab. Pleas, N. 4; 2 Arch. Pr. 3.

28. Judgment of *nil capiat per breve* or *per billam.* When an issue arises upon a declaration or peremptory plea, and it is decided in favor of the defendant, the judgment is, in general, *that the plaintiff take nothing by his writ,* (*or bill,*) *and that the defendant go thereof without day,* &c. This is called a judgment of *nil capiat per breve,* or *per billam.* Steph. Pl. 128.

29. Judgment by *nil dicit,* is one rendered against a defendant for want of a plea. The plaintiff obtains a rule on the defendant to plead within a time specified, of which he serves a notice on the defendant or his attorney; if the defendant neglect to enter a plea within the time specified, the plaintiff may sign judgment against him.

30. Judgment of *nolle prosequi,* is a judgment entered against the plaintiff, where, after appearance and before judgment, he says, "he will not further prosecute his suit." Steph. Pl. 130; Lawes' Civ. Pl. 166.

31. Judgment of *non obstante veredicto,* is a judgment rendered in favor of the plaintiff, *without regard to the verdict* obtained by the defendant.

32. The motion for such judgment is made where after a pleading by the defendant in confession and avoidance, as, for example, a plea in bar, and issue joined thereon, and verdict found for the defendant, the plaintiff on retrospective examination of the record, conceives that such plea was bad in substance, and might have been made the subject of demurrer on that ground. If the plea was itself substantially bad in law, of course the verdict, which merely shows it to be true in point of fact, cannot avail to entitle the defendant to judgment; while on the other hand the plea being in confession and avoidance, involves a confession of the plaintiff's declaration, and shows that he was entitled to maintain his action. In such case, therefore, the court will give judgment for the plaintiff, *without regard to the verdict;* and this, for the reasons above explained, is called a judgment *upon confession.* Sometimes it may be expedient for the plaintiff to move for judgment non obstante, &c., even though the verdict be in his own favor; for, if in such case as above described, he takes judgment as *upon the verdict,* it seems that such judgment would be erroneous, and that the only safe course is to take it *as upon confession.* 1 Wils 63; Cro. Eliz. 778; 2 Roll. Ab. 99. See also, Cro. Eliz. 214; 6 Mod. 10; Str. 394; 1 Ld. Raym. 641; 8 Taunt. 413; Rast. Ent. 622; 1 Wend. 307; 2 Wend. 624; 5 Wend. 513; 4 Wend. 468; 6 Cowen, R. 225. See this Dict. *Repleader,* for the difference between a repleader and a judgment non obstante veredicto.

33. Judgment by *non sum informatus,* is one which is rendered, when instead of entering a plea, the defendant's attorney says he is not informed of any answer to be given to the action. Steph. Pl. 130.

34. Judgment of *non pros.,* (from non

prosequitur,) is one given against the plaintiff, in any class of actions, for not declaring, or replying, or surrejoining, &c., or for not entering the issue.

35. Judgment of *nonsuit*, *practice*, is one against the plaintiff, which happens when, on trial by jury, the plaintiff, on being called or demanded, at the instance of the defendant, to be present while the jury give their verdict, fails to make his appearance.

36. In this case, no verdict is given, but the judgment of *nonsuit* passes against the plaintiff. So if, after issue be joined, the plaintiff neglect to bring such issue on to be tried in due time, as limited by the practice of the court, in the particular case, judgment will be also given against him for this default; and it is called judgment *as in case of nonsuit*. Steph. Pl. 131.

37. After suffering a nonsuit, the plaintiff may commence another action for the same cause for which the first had been instituted.

38. In some cases, plaintiffs having obtained information in what manner the jury had agreed upon their verdict before it was delivered in court, have, when the jury were ready to give in such verdict against them, suffered a nonsuit for the purpose of commencing another action and obtaining another trial. To prevent this abuse, the legislature of Pennsylvania have provided, by the Act of March 28, 1814, 6 Reed's L. 208, that "whenever on the trial of any cause, the jury shall be ready to give in their verdict, the plaintiff shall not be called, nor shall he then be permitted to suffer a nonsuit."

39. Judgment *quod computet*. The name of an interlocutory judgment in an action of account render that the defendant *do account*, quod *computet*. Vide 4 Wash. C. C. R. 84; 2 Watts, R. 95; 1 Penn. R. 138.

40. Judgment *quod recuperet*. When an issue in *law*, other than one arising on a dilatory plea, or an issue in *fact*, is decided in favor of the plaintiff, the judgment is, *that the plaintiff do recover*, which is called a judgment *quod recuperet*. Steph. Pl. 126; Com. Dig. Abatement, I 14, I 15; 2 Arch. Pr. 3. This judgment is of two kinds, namely, interlocutory or final.

41. Judgment *in replevin*, is either for the plaintiff or defendant.

42.—§ 1. For the plaintiff. 1. When the declaration is in the *detinuit*, that is, where the plaintiff declares, that the chattels "were detained until replevied by the sheriff," the judgment is that he recover the damages assessed by the jury for the taking and unjust detention, or for the latter only, where the former was justifiable, as also his costs. 5 Serg. & Rawle, 133; Ham. N. P. 488.

43.—2. If the replevin is in the *detinet*, that is, where the plaintiff declares that the chattels taken are "yet detained," the jury must find, in addition to the above, the value of the chattels, (assuming that they are still detained,) not in a gross sum, but each separate article; for the defendant, perhaps, will restore some, in which case the plaintiff is to recover the value of the remainder. Ham. N. P. 489; Fitz. N. B. 159, b; 5 Serg. & Rawle, 130.

44.—§ 2. For the defendant. 1. If the replevin be *abated*, the judgment is, that the writ or plaint abate, and that the defendant (having avowed) have a return of the chattels.

45.—2. When the plaintiff is *nonsuited*, the judgment for the defendant, at common law, is, that the chattels be restored to him, and this without his first assigning the purpose for which they were taken, because, by abandoning his suit, the plaintiff admits that he had no right to dispossess the defendant by prosecuting the replevin. The form of this judgment is simply "to have a return," without adding the words "to hold irreplevisable." Ham. N. P. 490.

46. As to the form of judgments in cases of nonsuit, under the 21 Hen. VIII. c. 19, and 17 Car. II. c. 7, see Ham. N. P. 490, 491; 2 Ch. Plead. 161; 8 Wentw. Pl. 116; 5 Serg. & Rawle, 132; 1 Saund 195, n. 3; 2 Saund. 286, n. 5. It is still in the defendant's option, in these cases, to take his judgment *pro retorno habendo* at common law. 5 Serg. & Rawle, 132; 1 Lev. 255; 3 T. R. 349.

47.—3. When the avowant succeeds upon the merits of his case, the common law judgment is, that he "have return irreplevisable," for it is apparent that he is by law entitled to keep possession of the goods. 5 Serg. & Rawle, 135; Ham. N. P. 493; 1 Chit. Pl. 162. For the form of judgments in favor of the avowant, under the last mentioned statutes, see Ham. N. P. 494–5.

48. Judgment of *respondeat ouster*. When there is an issue in law, arising on a *dilatory plea*, and it is decided in favor of the plaintiff, the judgment is only that the

defendant answer over, which is called a judgment of *respondeat ouster*. The pleading is accordingly resumed, and the action proceeds. Steph. Pl. 126; see Bac. Abr. Pleas, N 4; 2 Arch. Pr. 3.

49. Judgment of *retraxit*, is one where, after appearance and before judgment, the plaintiff enters upon the record that he "withdraws his suit;" in such case judgment is given against him. Steph. Pl. 130.

50. Judgment in an *action of trespass*, when for the plaintiff, is, that he recover the damages assessed by the jury, and the costs. For the defendant, that he recover the costs.

51. Judgment in *action on the case for trover*, when for the plaintiff, is, that he recover damages and costs. 1 Ch. Pl. 157. For the defendant, the judgment is, that he recover his costs.

52. Judgment of *capiatur*. At common law, on conviction, in a civil action, of a forcible wrong, alleged to have been committed *vi et armis*, &c., the defendant was obliged to pay a fine to the king, for the breach of the peace implied in the act, and a judgment of *capiatur pro fine* was rendered against him, under which he was liable to be arrested, and imprisoned till the fine was paid. But by the 5 W. & M. c. 12, the judgment of *capiatur pro fine* was abolished. Gould on Pl. § 38, 82; Bac. Ab. Fines and Amercements, C 1; 1 Ld. Raym. 273, 4; Style, 346. See *Judgment of misericordiâ*.

53. Judgment of *misericordiâ*. At common law, the party to a suit who did not prevail was punished for his unjust vexation, and therefore judgment was given against him, *quod sit in misericordiâ pro falso clamore*. Hence, when the plaintiff sued out a writ, the sheriff was obliged to take pledges of prosecution before he returned it, which, when fines and amercements were considerable, were real and responsible persons, and answerable for those amercements; but now they are never levied, and the pledges are merely formal, namely, John Doe and Richard Roe. Bac. Ab. Fines, &c., C 1; 1 Lord Ray. 273, 4.

54. In actions where the judgment was against the defendant, it was entered at common law, with a *misericordiâ* or a *capiatur*. With a misericordiâ in actions on contracts, with a capiatur in actions of trespass, or other forcible wrong, alleged to have been committed *vi et armis*. See *Judgment of capiatur;* Gould on Pl. c. 4, §§ 38, 82, 83.

55. Judgment *quod partitio fiat*, is a judgment, in a writ of partition, that partition be made; this is not a final judgment The final judgment is, *quod partitio facta firma et stabilis in perpetuum teneatur*. Co. Litt. 169; 2 Bl. Rep. 1159.

56. Judgment *quod partes replacitent*. The name of a judgment given when the court award a repleader.

57. When issue is joined on an immaterial point, or a point on which the court cannot give a judgment determining the right, they award a repleader or judgment *quod partes replacitent*. See Bac. Ab. Pleas, &c., M; 3 Hayw. 159; Peck's R. 325. See, generally, Bouv. Inst. Index, h. t.

JUDGMENT, ARREST OF, *practice*. This takes place when the court withhold judgment from the plaintiff on the ground that there is some error appearing on the face of the record, which vitiates the proceedings. In consequence of such error, on whatever part of the record it may arise, from the commencement of the suit to the time when the motion in arrest of judgment is made, the court are bound to arrest the judgment.

2. It is, however, only with respect to objections apparent on the record, that such motions can be made. They cannot, in general, be made in respect to formal objections. This was formerly otherwise, and judgments were constantly arrested for matters of mere form; 3 Bl. Com. 407; 2 Reeves, 448; but this abuse has been long remedied by certain statutes passed at different periods, called the statutes of amendment and jeofails, by the effect of which, judgments, cannot, in general, now be arrested for any objection of form. Steph. Pl. 117; see 3 Bl. Com. 393; 21 Vin. Ab. 457; 1 Sell. Pr. 496.

JUDGMENT ROLL, *Eng. law*. A record made of the issue roll, (q. v.) which, after final judgment has been given in the cause, assumes this name. Steph. Pl. 133. Vide *Issue Roll*.

JUDICATURE. The state of those employed in the administration of justice, and in this sense it is nearly synonymous with judiciary. This term is also used to signify a tribunal; and sometimes it is employed to show the extent of jurisdiction, as, the judicature is upon writs of error, &c. Com. Dig. Parliament, L 1; and see Com. Dig. Courts, A.

JUDICES PEDANEOS. Among the Romans, the prætors, and other great magistrates, did not themselves decide the actions which arose between private individuals; these were submitted to judges chosen by the parties, and these judges were called *judices pedaneos*. In choosing them, the plaintiff had the right to nominate, and the defendant to accept or reject those nominated. Heinnec. Antiq. lib. 4, tit. b, n. 40; 7 Toull. n. 353.

JUDICIAL. Belonging, or emanating from a judge, as such.

2. Judicial sales, are such as are ordered by virtue of the process of courts. 1 Supp. to Ves. jr., 129, 160; 2 Ves. jr., 50.

3. A judicial writ is one issued in the progress of the cause, in contradistinction to an original writ. 3 Bl. Com. 282.

4. Judicial decisions, are the opinions or determinations of the judges in causes before them. Hale, H. C. L. 68; Willes' R. 666; 3 Barn. & Ald. 122; 4 Barn. & Adol. 207; 1 H. Bl. 63; 5 M. & S. 185.

5. Judicial power, the authority vested in the judges. The constitution of the United States declares, that "the judicial power of the United States shall be vested in one supreme court, and in such inferior courts as the congress may, from time to time, ordain and establish." Art. 3, s. 1.

6. By the constitutions of the several states, the judicial power is vested in such courts as are enumerated in each respectively. *See the names of the several states.* There is nothing in the constitution of the United States to forbid or prevent the legislature of a state from exercising judicial functions; 2 Pet. R. 413; and judicial acts have occasionally been performed by the legislatures. 2 Root, R. 350; 3 Greenl. R. 334; 3 Dall. R. 386; 2 Pet. R. 660; 16 Mass. R. 328; Walk. R. 258; 1 New H. Rep. 199; 10 Yerg. R. 59; 4 Greenl. R. 140; 2 Chip. R. 77; 1 Aik. R. 314. But a state legislature cannot annul the judgments, nor determine the jurisdiction of the courts of the United States; 5 Cranch, R. 115; 2 Dall. R. 410; nor authoritatively declare what the law is, or has been, but what it shall be. 2 Cranch, R. 272; 4 Pick. R. 23. Vide Ayl. Parerg. 27; 3 M. R. 248; 4 M. R. 451; 9 M. R. 325; 6 M. R. 668; 12 M. R. 349; 3 N. S. 551; 5 N. S. 519; 1 L. R. 438; 7 M. R. 325; 9 M. R. 204; 10 M. R. 1.

JUDICIAL ADMISSIONS. Those which are generally made in writing in court by the attorney of the party; they appear upon the record, as in the pleadings and the like.

JUDICIAL CONFESSIONS, *criminal law.* Those voluntarily made before a magistrate, or in a court, in the due course of legal proceedings. A preliminary examination, taken in writing, by a magistrate lawfully authorized, pursuant to a statute, or the plea of guilty, made in open court to an indictment, are sufficient to found a conviction upon them.

JUDICIAL CONVENTIONS. Agreements entered into in consequence of an order of court; as, for example, entering into a bond on taking out a writ of sequestration. 6 N. S. 494.

JUDICIAL MORTGAGE. In Louisiana, it is the lien resulting from judgments, whether these be rendered on contested cases, or by default, whether they be final or provisional, in favor of the person obtaining them. Civ. Code of Lo. art. 3289.

JUDICIAL SALE. A sale by authority of some competent tribunal, by an officer authorized by law for the purpose.

2. The officer who makes the sale, conveys all the rights of the defendant, or other person against whom the process has been issued, in the property sold. Under such a sale there is no warranty, either express or implied, of the thing sold. 9 Wheat. 616. When real estate is sold by the sheriff or marshal, the sale is subject to the confirmation of the court, or it may be set aside. See 4 Wash. C. C. R. 45; Wallace, 128; 4 Wash. C. C. R. 322.

JUDICIAL WRITS, *Eng. practice.* The capias and all other writs subsequent to the original writ not issuing out of chancery, but from the court into which the original was returnable, and being grounded on what had passed in that court in consequence of the sheriff's return, were called *judicial* writs, in contradistinction to the writs issued out of chancery, which were called *original* writs. 3 Bl. Com. 282.

JUDICIARY. That which is done while administering justice; the judges taken collectively; as, the liberties of the people are secured by a wise and independent judiciary. See *Courts;* and 3 Story, Const. B. 3, c. 38.

JUDICIUM DEI. The judgment of God. The English law formerly impiously called the judgments on trials by ordeal, by battle, and the like, the judgments of God.

JUICIO DE CONCURSO. This term is Spanish, and is used in Louisiana. It is the name of an action brought for the purpose of making a distribution of an insolvent's estate. It differs from all other actions in this important particular, that all the parties to it except the insolvent, are at once plaintiffs and defendants. Each creditor is plaintiff against the failing debtor, to recover the amount due by him, and against the co-creditors, to diminish the amount they demand from his estate, and each is, of necessity, defendant against the opposition made by the other creditors against his demand. From the peculiar situation in which the parties are thus placed, many distinct and separate suits arise, and are decided during the pendency of the main one, by the insolvent in which they originate. 4 N. S. 601; 3 Harr. Cond. Lo. R. 409.

JUNIOR. Younger.

2. This has been held to be no part of a man's name, but an addition by use, and a convenient distinction between a father and son of the same name. 10 Mass. R. 203; 10 Paige, 170; 1 Pick. R. 388; 7 John. R. 549; 2 Caines, 164; 1 Pick. 388; 15 Pick. 7; 17 Pick. 200; 3 Metc. 330.

3. Any matter that distinguishes persons renders the addition of *junior* or *senior* unnecessary. 1 Mod. Ent. 35; Salk. 7. But if father and son have both the same name, the father shall be, *prima facie*, intended, if *junior* be not added, or some other matter of distinction. Salk. 7; 6 Rep. 20; 11 Rep. 39; Hob. 330. If father and son have the same name and addition, and the former sue the latter, the writ is abateable unless the son have the further addition of junior, or the younger. But if the father be the defendant and the son the plaintiff, there is no need of the further addition of *senior*, or the elder, to the name of the father. 2 Hawk. 187; Laws of Women, 380.

JUNIPERUS SABINA, *med. jur.* This plant is commonly called savine.

2. It is used for lawful purposes in medicine, but too frequently for the criminal intent of producing abortion, generally endangering the life of the woman. It is usually administered in powder or oil. The dose of oil for lawful purposes, for a grown person, is from two to four drops. Parr's Med. Dictionary, article Sabina. Foderé mentions a case where a large dose of powdered savine had been administered to an ignorant girl, in the seventh month of her pregnancy, which had no effect on the fœtus. It was, however, near taking the life of the girl. Foderé, tome iv. p. 431. Given in sufficiently large doses, four or six grains in the form of powder, kills a dog in a few hours, and even its insertion into a wound has the same effect. Orfila, Traité des Poisons, tome iii. p. 42. For a form of indictment for administering savine to a woman quick with child, see 3 Chit. Cr. Law, 798. Vide 1 Beck's Med. Jur. 316.

JURA PERSONARUM. The rights and duties of persons are so called.

JURA RERUM. The rights which a man may acquire in and to such external *things* as are unconnected with his person, are called *jura rerum.* 2 Bl. Com. 1.

JURA SUMMA IMPERII. Rights of sovereignty or supreme dominion.

JURAMENTÆ CORPORALIA. Corporal oaths. These oaths are so called, because the party making oath must touch the Bible, or other thing by which he swears.

JURAMENTUM JUDICIALE. A term in the civil law. The oath called *juramentum judiciale* is that which the judge, of his own accord, defers to either of the parties.

2. It is of two kinds. 1st. That which the judge defers for the decision of the cause, and which is understood by the general name *juramentum judiciale*, and is sometimes called suppletory oath, *juramentum suppletorium.*

3.—2d. That which the judge defers in order to fix and determine the amount of the condemnation which he ought to pronounce, and which is called *juramentum in litem.* Poth. on Oblig. P. 4, c. 3, s. 3, art. 3.

JURAT, *practice.* That part of an affidavit where the officer certifies that the same was "sworn" before him.

2. The jurat is usually in the following form, namely: "Sworn and subscribed before me, on the —— day of ——, 1842, J. P. justice of the peace."

3. In some cases it has been holden that it was essential that the officer should sign the jurat, and that it should contain his addition and official description. 3 Caines, 128. But see 6 Wend. 543; 12 Wend. 223; 2 Cowen. 552; 2 Wend. 283; 2 John. 479; Harr. Dig. h. t.; Am. Eq. Dig. h. t.

JURATA. A certificate placed at the bottom of an affidavit, declaring that the witness has been sworn or affirmed to the truth of the facts therein alleged. Its usual form is, "Sworn (or affirmed) before me, the —— day of ——, 18—." The *Jurat.* (q. v.)

JURATS, *officers.* In some English corporations, jurats are officers who have much the same power as aldermen in others. Stat. 1 Ed. IV.; Stat. 2 & 3 Ed. VI., c. 30; 13 Ed. I., c. 26.

JURE. By law; by right; in right; as, *jure civilis*, by the civil law; *jure gentium*, by the law of nations; *jure representationis*, by right of representation; *jure uxoris*, in right of a wife.

JURIDICAL. Signifies used in courts of law; done in conformity to the laws of the country, and the practice which is there observed.

JURIDICAL DAYS. Dies juridici. Days in court on which the law is administered.

JURIS ET DE JURE. A phrase employed to denote conclusive presumptions of law, which cannot be rebutted by evidence. The words signify of law and from law. Best on Presumption, § 17.

JURISCONSULT. One well versed in jurisprudence; a jurist; one whose profession it is to give counsel on questions of law.

JURISDICTION, *practice.* A power constitutionally conferred upon a judge or magistrate, to take cognizance of, and decide causes according to law, and to carry his sentence into execution. 6 Pet. 591; 9 John. 239. The tract of land or district within which a judge or magistrate has jurisdiction, is called his territory, and his power in relation to his territory is called his territorial jurisdiction.

2. Every act of jurisdiction exercised by a judge without his territory, either by pronouncing sentence or carrying it into execution, is null. An inferior court has no jurisdiction beyond what is expressly delegated. 1 Salk. 404, n.; Gilb. C. P. 188; 1 Saund. 73; 2 Lord Raym. 1311; and see Bac. Ab. Courts, &c., C, et seq.; Bac. Ab. Pleas, E 2.

3. Jurisdiction is original, when it is conferred on the court in the first instance, which is called *original jurisdiction;* (q. v.) or it is *appellate*, which is when an appeal is given from the judgment of another court. Jurisdiction is also *civil*, where the subject-matter to be tried is not of a criminal nature; or *criminal*, where the court is to punish crimes. Some courts and magistrates have both civil and criminal jurisdiction. Jurisdiction is also concurrent, exclusive, or assistant. *Concurrent jurisdiction* is that which may be entertained by several courts. It is a rule that in cases of concurrent jurisdictions, that which is first seized of the case shall try it to the exclusion of the other. *Exclusive jurisdiction* is that which has alone the power to try or determine the suit, action, or matter in dispute. *Assistant jurisdiction* is that which is afforded by a court of chancery, in aid of a court of law; as, for example, by a bill of discovery, by the examination of witnesses *de bene esse*, or out of the jurisdiction of the court; by the perpetuation of the testimony of witnesses, and the like.

4. It is the law which gives jurisdiction; the consent of parties, cannot, therefore, confer it, in a matter which the law excludes. 1 N. & M. 192; 3 M'Cord, 280; 1 Call. 55; 1 J. J. Marsh. 476; 1 Bibb, 263; Cooke, 27; Minor, 65; 3 Litt. 332; 6 Litt. 303; Kirby, 111; 1 Breese, 32; 2 Yerg. 441; 1 Const. R. 478. But where the court has jurisdiction of the matter, and the defendant has some privilege which exempts him from the jurisdiction, he may waive the privilege. 5 Cranch, 288; 1 Pet. 449; 8 Wheat. 699; 4 W. C. C. R. 84; 4 M'Cord, 79; 4 Mass. 593; Wright, 484. See Hardin, 448; 2 Wash. 213.

5. Courts of inferior jurisdiction must act within their jurisdiction, and so it must appear upon the record. 5 Cranch, 172; Pet. C. C. R. 36; 4 Dall. 11; 2 Mass. 213; 4 Mass. 122; 8 Mass. 86; 11 Mass. 513; Pr. Dec. 380; 2 Verm. 329; 3 Verm. 114; 10 Conn. 514; 4 John. 292; 3 Yerg. 355; Walker, 75; 9 Cowen, 227; 5 Har. & John. 36; 1 Bailey, 459; 2 Bailey, 267. But the legislature may, by a general or special law, provide otherwise. Pet. C. C. R. 36. Vide 1 Salk. 414; Bac. Ab. Courts, &c., C, D; Id. Prerogative, E 5; Merlin, Rép. h. t.; Ayl. Par. 317, and the art. *Competency.* As to the force of municipal laws beyond the territorial jurisdiction of the state, see Wheat. Intern. Law, part 2, c. 2, § 7, et seq.; Story, Confl. of Laws, c. 2; Huberus, lib. 1, t. 3; 13 Mass. R. 4; Pard. Dr. Com. part. 6, t. 7, c. 2, § 1; and the articles *Conflict of Laws; Courts of the United States.* See, generally, Bouv. Inst. Index, h. t.

JURISDICTION CLAUSE. That part of a bill in chancery which is intended to give jurisdiction of the suit to the court, by a general averment that the acts complained of are contrary to equity, and tend to the injury of the plaintiff, and that he has no remedy, or not a complete remedy, without the assistance of a court of equity, is called the *jurisdiction clause.* Mitf. Eq. Pl. by Jeremy, 43.

2. This clause is unnecessary, for if the court appear from the bill, to have jurisdiction, the bill will be sustained without this clause; and if the court have not jurisdiction, the bill will be dismissed though the clause may be inserted. Story, Eq. Pl. § 34.

JURISPRUDENCE. The science of the law. By science here, is understood that connexion of truths which is founded on principles either evident in themselves, or capable of demonstration; a collection of truths of the same kind, arranged in methodical order. In a more confined sense, jurisprudence is the practical science of giving a wise interpretation to the laws, and making a just application of them to all cases as they arise. In this sense, it is the habit of judging the same questions in the same manner, and by this course of judgments forming precedents. 1 Ayl. Pand. 3; Toull. Dr. Civ. Fr. tit. prel. s. 1, n. 1, 12, 99; Merl. Rép. h. t.; 19 Amer. Jurist, 3.

JURIST. One well versed in the science of the law. The term is usually applied to students and practitioners of law.

JUROR, *practice.* From *juro*, to swear; a man who is sworn or affirmed to serve on a jury.

2. Jurors are selected from citizens, and may be compelled to serve by fine; they generally receive a compensation for their services; while attending court they are privileged from arrest in civil cases.

JURY. A body of men selected according to law, for the purpose of deciding some controversy.

2. This mode of trial by jury was adopted soon after the conquest of England, by William, and was fully established for the trial of civil suits in the reign of Henry II. Crabb's C. L. 50, 51. In the old French law they are called *inquests* or *tourbes* of ten men. 2 Loisel's Instit. 238, 246, 248.

3. Juries are either grand juries, (q. v.) or petit juries. The former having been treated of elsewhere, it will only be necessary to consider the latter. A petit jury consists of twelve citizens duly qualified to serve on juries, impanneled and sworn to try one or more issues of facts submitted to them, and to give a judgment respecting the same, which is called a verdict.

4. Each one of the citizens so impanneled and sworn is called a juror. Vide *Trial.*

5. The constitution of the United States directs, that "the trial of all crimes, except in cases of impeachment, shall be by jury;" and this invaluable institution is also secured by the several state constitutions. The constitution of the United States also provides that in suits at common law, where the value in controversy shall exceed twenty dollars, the right of trial by jury shall be preserved. Amendm. VII.

6. It is scarcely practicable to give the rules established in the different states to secure impartial juries; it may, however, be stated that in all, the selection of persons who are to serve on the jury is made by disinterested officers, and that out of the lists thus made out, the jurors are selected by lot.

JURY BOX. A place set apart for the jury to sit in during the trial of a cause.

JURY LIST. A paper containing the names of jurors impanneled to try a cause, or it contains the names of all the jurors summoned to attend court.

JUS. Law or right. This term is applied in many modern phrases. It is also used to signify equity. Story, Eq. Jur. § 1; Bract. lib. 1, c. 4, p. 3; Tayl. Civ. Law, 147; Dig. 1, 1, 1.

2. The English law, like the Roman, has its *jus antiquum, jus novum* and *jus novissimum.* The *jus novum* may be supposed to have taken its origin about the end of the reign of Henry VII. A. D. 1509. It assumed a regular form towards the end of the reign of Charles II. A. D. 1685, and from that period the *jus novissimum* may be dated. Lord Coke, who was born 40 years after the death of Henry VII. is most advantageously considered as the connecting link of the jus antiquum and jus novissimum of English law. *Butler's Remin.*

JUS ABUTENDI. The right to abuse. By this phrase is understood the right to abuse property, or having full dominion over property. 3 Toull. n. 86.

JUS ACCRESCENDI. The right of survivorship.

2. At common law, when one of several

joint tenants died, the entire tenancy or estate went to the survivors, and so on to the last survivor, who took an estate of inheritance. This right, except in estates held in trust, has been abolished by statute in Alabama, Delaware, Georgia, Illinois, Indiana, Kentucky, Michigan, Missouri, Mississippi, New York, North Carolina, Pennsylvania, South Carolina, Tennessee, and Virginia. Griff. Reg. h. t.; 1 Hill. Ab. 439, 440. In Connecticut, 1 Root, Rep. 48; 1 Swift's Dig. 102. In Louisiana, this right was never recognized. See 11 Serg. & R. 192; 2 Caines, Cas. Err. 326; 3 Verm. 543; 6 Monr. R. 15; *Estate in common; Estate in joint tenancy.*

JUS AD REM, *property, title.* This phrase is applied to designate the right a man has in relation to a thing; it is not the right in the thing itself, but only against the person who has contracted to deliver it. It is a mere imperfect or inchoate right. 2 Bl. Com. 312; Poth. Dr. de Dom. de Proprieté, ch. prél. n. 1. This phrase is nearly equivalent to *chose in action.* 2 Wooddes. Lect. 235. See 2 P. Wms. 491; 1 Mason, 221; 1 Story, Eq. Jur. 506; 2 Story, Eq. Jur. § 1215; Story, Ag. § 352; and *Jus in re.*

JUS AQUÆDUCTUS, *civ. law.* The name of a servitude which gives to the owner of land the right to bring down water through or from the land of another, either from its source or from any other place.

2. Its privilege may be limited as to the time when it may be exercised. If the source fails, the servitude ceases, but revives when the water returns. If the water rises in, or naturally flows through the land, its proprietor cannot by any grant divert it so as to prevent it flowing to the land below. 2 Roll. Ab. 140, l. 25; Lois des Bât. part. 1, c. 3, s. 1, art. 1. But if it had been brought into his land by artificial means, it seems it would be strictly his property, and that it would be in his power to grant it. Dig. 8, 3, 1 & 10; 3 Burge on the Confl. of Laws, 417. Vide *Rain water; River; Water-course.*

JUS CIVILE. Among the Romans by *jus civile* was understood the civil law, in contradistinction to the public law, or *jus gentium.* 1 Savigny, Dr. Rom. c. 1, § 1.

JUS CIVITATIS. Among the Romans the collection of laws which are to be observed among all the members of a nation, were so called. It is opposed to *jus gentium,* which is the law which regulates the affairs of nations among themselves. 2 Lepage, El. du Dr. ch. 5, page 1.

JUS CLOACÆ, *civil law.* The name of a servitude which requires the party who is subject to it, to permit his neighbor to conduct the waters which fall on his grounds over those of the servient estate.

JUS DARE. To give or to make the law. *Jus dare* belongs to the legislature; *jus dicere* to the judge.

JUS DICERE. To declare the law. This word is used to explain the power which the court has to expound the law; and not to make it, *jus dare.*

JUS DELIBERANDI. The right of deliberating, which in some countries, where the heir may have *benefit of inventory,* (q. v.) is given to him to consider whether he will accept or renounce the succession.

2. In Louisiana he is allowed ten days before he is required to make his election. Civ. Code, art. 1028.

JUS DISPONENDI. The right to dispose of a thing.

JUS DUPLICATUM, *property, title.* When a man has the possession as well as the property of anything, he is said to have a double right, *jus duplicatum.* Bract. l. 4, tr. 4, c. 4; 2 Bl. Com. 199.

JUS FECIALE. Among the Romans it was that species of international law which had its foundation in the religious belief of different nations, such as the international law which now exists among the Christian people of Europe. Sav. Dr. Rom. ch. 2, § 11.

JUS FIDUCIARUM, *civil law.* A right to something held in trust; for this there was a remedy in conscience. 2 Bl. Com. 328.

JUS GENTIUM. The *law of nations.* (q. v.) Although the Romans used these words in the sense we attach to *law of nations,* yet among them the sense was much more extended. Falck, Encyc. Jur. 102, n. 42.

2. Some modern writers have made a distinction between the laws of nations which have for their object the conflict between the laws of different nations, which they call *jus gentium privatum,* or private international law; and those laws of nations which regulate those matters which nations, as such, have with each other, which is denominated *jus gentium publicum,* or public international law. Fœlix, Droit Interm. Privé, n. 14.

JUS GLADII. Supreme jurisdiction. The right to absolve from, or condemn a man to death.

JUS HABENDI. The right to have and enjoy a thing.

JUS INCOGNITUM. An unknown law. This term is applied by the civilians to obsolete laws, which, as Bacon truly observes, are unjust, for the law to be just must give warning before it strikes. Bac. Aphor. 8, s. 1; Bowy. Mod. Civ. Law, 33. But until it has become obsolete no custom can prevail against it. Vide *Obsolete*.

JUS LEGITIMUM, *civil law*. A legal right which might have been enforced by due course of law. 2 Bl. Com. 328.

JUS MARITI, *Scotch law*. The right of the husband to administer, during the marriage, his wife's goods and the rents of her heritage.

2. In the common law, by *jus mariti* is understood the rights of the husband; as, *jus mariti* cannot attach upon a bequest to the wife, although given during coverture, until the executor has assented to the legacy. 1 Bail. Eq. R. 214.

JUS MERUM. A simple or bare right; a right to property in land, without possession, or the right of possession.

JUS PATRONATUS, *eccl. law*. A commission from the bishop, directed usually to his chancellor and others of competent learning, who are required to summon a jury composed of six clergymen and six laymen, to inquire into and examine who is the rightful patron. 3 Bl. Com. 246.

JUS PERSONARUM. The right of persons.

2. A branch of the law which embraces the theory of the different classes of men who exist in a state which has been formed by nature or by society; it includes particularly the theory of the ties of families, and the legal form and juridical effects of the relations subsisting between them. The Danes, the English, and the learned in this country, class under this head the relations which exist between men in a political point of view. Blackstone, among others, has adopted this classification. There seems a confusion of ideas when such matters are placed under this head. Vide Bl. Com. Book 1.

JUS PRECARIUM, *civil law*. A right to a thing held for another, for which there was no remedy. 2 Bl. Com. 328.

JUS POSTLIMINII, *property, title*. The right to claim property after re-capture. Vide *Postliminy;* Marsh. Ins. 573; 1 Kent, Com. 108; Dane's Ab. Index, h. t.

JUS PROJICIENDI, *civil law*. The name of a servitude; it is the right which the owner of a building has of projecting a part of his building towards the adjoining house, without resting on the latter. It is extended merely over the ground. Dig. 50, 16, 242, 1; Dig. 8, 2, 25; Dig. 8, 5, 8, 5.

JUS PROTEGENDI, *civil law*. The name of a servitude; it is a right by which a part of the roof or tiling of one house is made to extend over the adjoining house. Dig. 50, 16, 242, 1; Dig. 8, 2, 25; Dig. 8, 5, 8, 5.

JUS QUÆSITUM. A right to ask or recover; for example, in an obligation there is a binding of the obligor, and a *jus quæsitum* in the obligee. 1 Bell's Com. 323, 5th ed.

JUS IN RE, *property, title*. The right which a man has in a thing, by which it belongs to him. It is a complete and full right. Poth. Dr. de Dom. de Prop. n. 1.

2. This phrase of the civil law conveys the same idea as *thing in possession* does with us. 4 Wooddes. Lect. 235; vide 2 P. Wms. 491; 1 Mason, 221; 1 Story, Eq. Jur. § 506; 2 Story, Eq. Jur. §. 1215; Story, Ag. § 352; and *Jus ad rem*.

JUS RELICTA, *Scotch law*. The right of a wife, after her husband's death, to a third of movables, if there be children; and to one-half, if there be none.

JUS RERUM. The right of things. Its principal object is to ascertain how far a person can have a permanent dominion over things, and how that dominion is acquired. Vide Bl. Com. Book 2.

JUS STRICTUM. A Latin phrase, which signifies law interpreted without any modification, and in its utmost rigor.

JUS UTENDI. The right to use property, without destroying its substance. It is employed in contradistinction to the *jus abutendi*. (q. v.) 3 Toull. n. 86.

JUST. This epithet is applied to that which agrees with a given law which is the test of right and wrong. 1 Toull. prel. n. 5; Aust. Jur. 276, n. It is that which accords with the perfect rights of others Wolff, Inst. § 83; Swinb. part 1, s. 2, n. 5, and part 1, § 4, n. 3. By just is also understood full and perfect, as a just weight Swinb. part 1, s. 3, n. 5.

JUSTICE. The constant and perpetual disposition to render every man his due. Just. Inst. B. 1, tit. 1. Toullier defines it to be the conformity of our actions and our will to the law. Dr. Civ. Fr. tit. prel. n. 5. In the most extensive sense of the word, it differs little from virtue, for it includes within itself the whole circle of virtues. Yet the common distinction between them is that that which considered positively and in itself, is called virtue, when considered relatively and with respect to others, has the name of justice. But justice being in itself a part of virtue, is confined to things simply good or evil, and consists in a man's taking such a proportion of them as he ought.

2. Justice is either distributive or commutative. Distributive justice is that virtue whose object is to distribute rewards and punishments to each one according to his merits, observing a just proportion by comparing one person or fact with another, so that neither equal persons have unequal things, nor unequal persons things equal. Tr. of Eq. 3, and Toullier's learned note, Dr. Civ. Fr. tit. prel. n. 7, note.

3. Commutative justice is that virtue whose object it is to render to every one what belongs to him, as nearly as may be, or that which governs contracts. To render commutative justice, the judge must make an equality between the parties, that no one may be a gainer by another's loss. Tr. Eq. 3.

4. Toullier exposes the want of utility and exactness in this division of distributive and commutative justice, adopted in the *compendium* or abridgments of the ancient doctors, and prefers the division of *internal* and *external* justice; the first being a conformity of our *will*, and the latter a conformity of our *actions* to the law: their union making perfect justice. Exterior justice is the object of jurisprudence; interior justice is the object of morality. Dr. Civ. Fr. tit. prel. n. 6 et 7.

5. According to the Frederician code, part 1, book 1, tit. 2, s. 27, justice consists simply in letting every one enjoy the rights which he has acquired in virtue of the laws. And as this definition includes all the other rules of right, there is properly but one single general rule of right, namely, *Give every one his own*.

See, generally, Puffend. Law of Nature and Nations, B. 1, c. 7, s. 89; Elementorum Jurisprudentiæ Universalis, lib. 1, definito, 17, 3, 1; Gro. lib. 2, c. 11, s. 3; Ld. Bac. Read. Stat. Uses, 306; Treatise of Equity, B. 1, c. 1, s. 1.

JUSTICES. Judges. Officers appointed by a competent authority to administer justice. They are so called, because, in ancient times the Latin word for judge was *justicia*. This term is in common parlance used to designate justices of the peace.

JUSTICES IN EYRE. They were certain judges established if not first appointed, A. D. 1176, 22 Hen. II. England was divided into certain circuits, and three justices in eyre, or justices itinerant, as they were sometimes called, were appointed to each district, and made the circuit of the kingdom once in seven years for the purpose of trying causes. They were afterwards directed by Magna Charta, c. 12, to be sent into every county once a year. The itinerant justices were sometimes mere justices of assize or dower, or of general gaol delivery, and the like. 3 Bl. Com. 58–9; Crabb's Eng. Law, 103–4. Vide *Eire*.

JUSTICES OF THE PEACE. Public officers invested with judicial powers for the purpose of preventing breaches of the peace, and bringing to punishment those who have violated the law.

2. These officers, under the Constitution of the United States and some of the states, are appointed by the executive; in others, they are elected by the people, and commissioned by the executive. In some states they hold their office during good behaviour, in others for a limited period.

3. At common law, justices of the peace have a double power in relation to the arrest of wrong doers; when a felony or breach of the peace has been committed in their presence, they may personally arrest the offender, or command others to do so; and in order to prevent the riotous consequences of a tumultuous assembly, they may command others to arrest affrayers, when the affray has been committed in their presence. If a magistrate be not present when a crime is committed, before he can take a step to arrest the offender, an oath or affirmation must be made by some person cognizant of the fact, that the offence has been committed, and that the person charged is the offender, or there is probable cause to believe that he has committed the offence.

4. The Constitution of the United States directs, that "no warrants shall issue, but upon probable cause, supported by oath or affirmation." Amendm. IV. After his arrest, the person charged is brought before the justice of the peace, and after hearing he is discharged, held to bail to answer to the complaint, or, for want of bail, committed to prison.

5. In some, perhaps all the United States, justices of the peace have jurisdiction

in civil cases, given to them by local regulations. In Pennsylvania, their jurisdiction in cases of contracts, express or implied, extends to one hundred dollars.

Vide, generally, Burn's Justice; Graydon's Justice; Bache's Manual of a Justice of the Peace; Com. Dig. h. t.; 15 Vin. Ab. 3; Bac. Ab. h. t.; 2 Sell. Pr. 70; 2 Phil. Ev. 239; Chit. Pr. h. t.; Amer. Dig. h. t.

JUSTICIAR, or JUSTICIER. A judge, or justice; the same as justiciary. (q. v.)

JUSTICIARII ITINERANTES, *Eng. law.* They were formerly justices, who were so called because they went from county to county to administer justice. They were usually called justices in eyre, (q. v.) to distinguish them from justices residing at Westminster, who were called *justicii residentes.* Co. Litt. 293. Vide *Itinerant.*

JUSTICIARII RESIDENTES, *Eng. law.* They were justices or judges, who usually resided in Westminster; they were so called to distinguish them from justices in eyre. Co. Litt. 293. Vide *Justiciarii Itinerantes.*

JUSTICIARY, *officer.* Another name for a judge. In Latin, he was called *justiciciarius*, and in French, *justicier.* Not used. Bac. Ab. Courts and their Jurisdiction, A.

JUSTICIES, *Eng. law.* The name of a writ which acquires its name from the mandatory words which it contains, "that you do A B justice."

2. The county court has jurisdiction in cases where damages are claimed, only to a certain amount; but sometimes suits are brought there when greater damages are claimed. In such cases, an original writ, by this name, issues out of chancery, in order to give the court jurisdiction. See 1 Saund. 74, n. 1.

JUSTIFIABLE HOMICIDE. That which is committed with the intention to kill, or to do a grievous bodily injury, under circumstances which the law holds sufficient to exculpate the person who commits it.

2. It is justifiable, 1. When a judge or other magistrate acts in obedience to the law. 2. When a ministerial officer acts in obedience to a lawful warrant, issued by a competent tribunal. 3. When a subaltern officer, or soldier, kills in obedience to the lawful commands of his superior. 4. When the party kills in lawful self-defence.

3.—§ 1. A judge who, in pursuance of his duty, pronounces sentence of death, is not guilty of homicide; for it is evident, that as the law prescribes the punishment of death for certain offences, it must protect those who are entrusted with its execution. A judge, therefore, who pronounces sentence of death, in a legal manner, on a legal indictment, legally brought before him, for a capital offence committed within his jurisdiction, after a lawful trial and conviction of the defendant, is guilty of no offence.

4.—2. Magistrates, or other officers entrusted with the preservation of the public peace, are justified in committing homicide, or giving orders which lead to it, if the excesses of a riotous assembly cannot be otherwise repressed.

5.—§ 2. An officer entrusted with a legal warrant, criminal or civil, and lawfully commanded by a competent tribunal to execute it, will be justified in committing homicide, if, in the course of advancing to discharge his duty, he be brought into such perils that, without doing so, he cannot either save his life, or discharge the duty which he is commanded by the warrant to perform. And when the warrant commands him to put a criminal to death, he is justified in obeying it.

6.—§ 3. A soldier on duty is justified in committing homicide, in obedience to the command of his officer, unless the command was something plainly unlawful.

7.—§ 4. A private individual will, in many cases, be justified in committing homicide, while acting in self-defence. See *Self-defence.*

Vide, generally, 1 East, P. C. 219; Hawk. B. 1, c. 28, s. 1, n. 22; Allis. Prin. 126–139; 1 Russ. on Cr. 538; Bac. Ab. Murder, &c., E; 2 Wash. C. C. 515; 4 Mass. 391; 1 Hawkes, 210; 1 Coxe's R. 424; 5 Yerg. 459; 9 C. & P. 22; S. C. 38 Eng. C. L. R. 20.

JUSTIFICATION. The act by which a party accused shows and maintains a good and legal reason in court, why he did the thing he is called upon to answer.

2. The subject will be considered by examining, 1. What acts are justifiable. 2. The manner of making the justification. 3. Its effects.

3.—§ 1. The acts to be justified are those committed with a warrant, and those committed without a warrant. 1. It is a general rule, that a warrant or execution, issued by a court having jurisdiction, whether the same be right or wrong, justifies the officer to whom it is directed, and who is by law required to execute it, and is a complete justification to the officer for obeying its command. But when the warrant is not merely voidable, but is absolutely void, as, for want of jurisdiction in the court which issued it, or by reason of the privilege of the defendant, as in the case of the arrest of an ambassador, who cannot waive his privilege and immunities by submitting to be arrested on such warrant, the officer is no longer justified. 1 Baldw. 240; see 4 Mass. 232; 13 Mass. 286, 334; 14 Mass. 210. 2. A person may justify many acts, while acting without any authority from a court or magistrate. He may justifiably, even, take the life of an aggressor, while acting in the defence of himself, his wife, children, and servant, or for the protection of his house, when attacked with a felonious intent, or even for the protection of his personal property. See *Self-defence.* A man may justify what would, otherwise, have been a trespass, an entry on the land of another for various purposes; as, for example, to demand a debt due to him by the owner of the land; to remove chattels which belong to him, but this entry must be peaceable; to exercise an incorporeal right; ask for lodgings at an inn. See 15 East, 615, note e; 2 Lill. Ab. 134; 15 Vin. Ab. 31; Ham. N. P. 48 to 66; Dane's Ab. Index, h. t.; *Entry.* It is an ancient principle of the common law, that a trespass may be justified in many cases. Thus: a man may enter on the land of another, to kill a fox or otter, which are beasts against the common profit. 11 H. VIII. 10. So, a house may be pulled down if the adjoining one be on fire, to prevent a greater destruction. 13 H. VIII. 16, b. Tua res agitur paries cum proximus ardet. So, the suburbs of a city may be demolished in time of war, for the good of the commonwealth. 8 Ed. IV. 35, b. So, a man may enter on his neighbor to make a bulwark in defence of the realm. 21 H. VII. b. So, a house may be broken to arrest a felon. 13 Ed. IV. 9, a; Dodd. Eng. Lawy. 219, 220. In a civil action, a man may justify a libel, or slanderous words, by proving their truth, or because the defendant had a right, upon the particular occasion, either to write and publish the writing, or to utter the words; as, when slanderous words are found in a report of a committee of congress, or in an indictment, or words of a slanderous nature are uttered in the course of debate in the legislature by a member, or at the bar, by counsel, when properly instructed by his client on the subject. See *Debate; Slander;* Com. Dig. Pleader, 2 L 3 to 2 L 7.

4.—§ 2. In general, justification must be specially pleaded, and it cannot be given in evidence under the plea of the general issue.

5.—§ 3. When the plea of justification is supported by the evidence, it is a complete bar to the action. Vide *Excuse.*

JUSTIFICATORS. A kind of compurgators, or those who, by oath, justified the innocence or oaths of others, as in the case of wagers of law.

JUSTIFYING BAIL, *practice.* The production of bail in court, who there justify themselves against the exception of the plaintiff.

K.

KENTUCKY. The name of one of the new states of the United States of America.

2. This state was formerly a part of Virginia, and the latter state, by an act of the legislature, passed December 18, 1789, "consented that the district of Kentucky, within the jurisdiction of the said commonwealth, and according to its actual boundaries at the time of passing the act aforesaid, should be formed into a new state." By the act of congress of February 4, 1791, 1 Story's L. U. S. 168, congress consented that, after the first day of June, 1792, the district of Kentucky should be formed into a new state, separate from and independent of the commonwealth of Virginia. And by the second section it is enacted, that upon the aforesaid first day of June, 1792, the said new state, by the name and style of the state of Kentucky, shall be received and admitted into the Union, as a new and entire member of the United States of America.

3. The constitution of this state was adopted August 17, 1799. The powers of the government are divided into three distinct departments, and each of them is confided to a separate body of magistracy, to wit: those which are legislative, to one; those which are executive, to another; and those which are judicial, to another.

4.—1. The legislative power is vested in two distinct branches; the one styled the house of representatives, and the other the senate; and both together, the general assembly of the commonwealth of Kentucky. 1. The house of representatives is elected yearly, and consists of not less than fifty-eight, nor more than one hundred members. 2. The members of the senate are elected for four years. The senate consists of twenty-four members, at least, and for every three members above fifty-eight which shall be added to the house of representatives, one member shall be added to the senate.

5.—2. The executive power is vested in a chief magistrate, who is styled the governor of the commonwealth of Kentucky. The governor is elected for four years. He is commander-in-chief of the army and navy of the commonwealth, except when called into actual service of the United States. He nominates, and, with the consent of the senate, appoints all officers, except those whose appointment is otherwise provided for. He is invested with the pardoning power, except in certain cases, as impeachment and treason. A lieutenant-governor is chosen at every election of governor, in the same manner, and to continue in office for the same time as the governor. He is, ex officio, speaker of the senate, and acts as governor when the latter is impeached, or removed from office, or dead, or refuses to qualify, resigns, or is absent from the state.

6.—3. The judicial power, both as to matters of law and equity, is vested in one supreme court, styled the court of appeals, and in such inferior courts as the general assembly may, from time to time, erect and establish. The judges hold their office during good behaviour.

KEY. An instrument made for shutting and opening a lock.

2. The keys of a house are considered as real estate, and descend to the heir with the inheritance. But see 5 Blackf. 417.

3. When the keys of a warehouse are delivered to a purchaser of goods locked up there, with a view of effecting a delivery of such goods, the delivery is complete. The doctrine of the civil law is the same. Dig. lib. 41, t. 1, l. 9, § 6; and lib. 18, t. 1, l. 74.

KEY, *estates*. A wharf at which to land goods from, or to load them in a vessel. This word is now generally spelled *Quay*, from the French, *quai*.

KEYAGE. A toll paid for loading and unloading merchandise at a key or wharf.

KEELAGE. The right of demanding money for the bottom of ships resting in a port or harbor. The money so paid is also called *keelage*.

KEELS. This word is applied, in England, to vessels employed in the carriage of coals. Jacob, L. D.

KIDNAPPING. The forcible and unlawful abduction and conveying away of a man, woman, or child, from his or her home, without his or her will or consent, and sending such person away, with an intent to deprive him or her of some right. This is an offence at common law.

KILDERKIN. A measure of capacity equal to eighteen gallons. See *Measure*.

KINDRED. Relations by blood.

2. Nature has divided the kindred of every one into three principal classes. 1. His children, and their descendants. 2. His father, mother, and other ascendants. 3. His collateral relations; which include, in the first place, his brothers and sisters, and their descendants; and, secondly, his uncles, cousins, and other relations of either sex, who have not descended from a brother or sister of the deceased. All kindred then are descendants, ascendants, or collaterals. A husband or wife of the deceased, therefore, is not his or her kindred. 14 Ves. 372. Vide Wood's Inst. 50; Ayl. Parerg. 325; Dane's Ab. h. t.; Toll. Ex. 382, 3; 2 Chit. Bl. Com. 516, n. 59; Poth. Des Successions, c. 1, art. 3.

KING. The chief magistrate of a kingdom, vested usually with the executive power.

2. The following table of the reigns of English and British kings and queens, commencing with the Reports, is added, to assist the student in many points of chronology.

	Accession.
Henry III.,	1216
Edward I.,	1272
Edward II.,	1307
Edward III.,	1327
Richard II.,	1377
Henry IV.,	1399
Henry V.,	1413
Henry VI.,	1422
Edward IV.,	1461
Edward V.,	1483
Richard III.,	1483
Henry VII.,	1485
Henry VIII.,	1509
Edward VI.,	1547
Mary,	1553
Elizabeth,	1558
James I.,	1603
Charles I.,	1625
Charles II.,	1660
James II.,	1685
William III.,	1689
Anne,	1702
George I.,	1714
George II.,	1727
George III.,	1760
George IV.,	1820
William IV.,	1830
Victoria,	1837

Vide article *Reports*.

KING'S BENCH. The name of the supreme court of law in England. It is so called because formerly the king used to sit there in person, the style of the court being still *coram ipso rege*, before the king himself. During the reign of a queen, it is called the Queen's Bench, and during the protectorate of Cromwell, it was called the Upper Bench. It consists of a chief justice, and three other judges, who are, by their office, the principal coroners and conservators of the peace. 3 Bl. Com. 41.

2. This court has jurisdiction in criminal matters, in civil causes, and is a supervisory tribunal to keep other jurisdictions within their proper bounds.

3.—1. Its *criminal* jurisdiction extends over all offenders, and not only over all capital offences but also over all other misdemeanors of a public nature; it being considered the *custos morum* of the realm. Its jurisdiction is so universal that an act of parliament appointing that all crimes of a certain denomination shall be tried before certain judges, does not exclude the jurisdiction of this court, without negative words. It may also proceed on indictments removed into that court out of the inferior courts by certiorari.

4.—2. Its *civil* jurisdiction is against the officers or ministers of the court entitled to its privilege. 2 Inst. 23; 4 Inst. 71; 2 Bulstr. 123. And against prisoners for trespasses. In these last cases a declaration may be filed against them in debt, covenant or account: and this is done also upon the notion of a privilege, because the common pleas could not obtain or procure the prisoners of the king's bench to appear in their court.

5.—3. Its supervisory powers extend, 1. To issuing writs of error to inferior jurisdictions, and affirming or reversing their judgments. 2. To issuing writs of mandamus to compel inferior officers and courts to perform the duties required of them by law. Bac. Ab. Court of King's Bench.

KINGDOM. A country where an officer called a king exercises the powers of government, whether the same be absolute or limited. Wolff, Inst. Nat. § 994. In some kingdoms the executive officer may be a woman, who is called a queen.

KINTLIDGE, *merc. law.* This term is used by merchants and seafaring men to signify a ship's ballast. Merc. Dict.

KIRBY'S QUEST. An ancient record remaining with the remembrancer of the English Exchequer, so called from being the inquest of John De Kirby, treasurer to Edward I.

KISSING. Kissing the bible is a ceremony used in taking the corporal oath, the object being, as the canonists say, to denote the assent of the witness to the oath in the form it is imposed. The witness kisses either the whole bible, or some portion of it; or a cross in some countries. See the ceremony explained in Oughton's Ordo. Tit. lxxx. Consitt. on Courts, part 3, sect. 1, § 3; Junkin on the Oath, 173, 180; 2 Evan's Pothier, 234.

KNAVE. A false, dishonest, or deceitful person. This signification of the word has arisen by a long perversion of its original meaning.

2. To call a man a knave has been held to be actionable. 1 Rolle's Ab. 52; 1 Freem. 277.

KNIGHT'S FEE, *old Eng. law.* An uncertain measure of land, but, according to some opinions it is said to contain six hundred and eighty acres. Co. Litt. 69, a.

KNIGHT'S SERVICE, *Eng. law.* It was, formerly, a tenure of lands. Those who held by knight's service were called "milites qui per loricas terras suas defendunt;" soldiers who defend the country by their armor. The incidents of knight's service were homage, fealty, warranty, wardship, marriage, reliefs, heriots, aids, escheats, and forfeiture. Vide *Socage.*

KNOWINGLY, *pleadings.* The word "knowingly," or "well knowing," will supply the place of a positive averment in an indictment or declaration, that the defendant knew the facts subsequently stated; if notice or knowledge be unnecessarily stated, the allegation may be rejected as surplusage. Vide Com. Dig. Indictment, G 6; 2 Stra. 904; 2 East, 452; 1 Chit. Pl. *367. Vide *Scienter.*

KNOWLEDGE. Information as to a fact.

2. Many acts are perfectly innocent when the party performing them is not aware of certain circumstances attending them; for example, a man may pass a counterfeit note and be guiltless, if he did not know it was so; he may receive stolen goods if he were not aware of the fact that they were stolen. In these and the like cases it is the guilty knowledge which makes the crime. See, as to the manner of proving guilty knowledge, Archb. Cr. Pl. 110, 111. Vide *Animal; Dog; Evidence Ignorance; Scienter.*

END OF VOLUME I.

CPSIA information can be obtained
at www.ICGtesting.com
Printed in the USA
LVHW041313310522
720087LV00003B/319

9 783375 030704